Julia Quinn started writing her first book one month after finishing college and has been tapping away at her keyboard ever since. She is the author of award-winning historical romance novels, including the *New York Times* bestselling Bridgerton series which begins with *The Duke and I*. Other titles in this series are: *The Viscount Who Loved Me*, *An Offer from a Gentleman*, *Romancing Mr Bridgerton, To Sir Phillip, With Love*, *When He Was Wicked, It's in His Kiss* and *On the Way to the Wedding*. She is a graduate of Harvard and Radcliffe colleges and lives with her family in Colorado.

Visit Julia Quinn online at juliaquinn.com

ALSO BY JULIA QUINN

***Bridgerton Series*:**

The Duke and I
The Viscount Who Loved Me
An Offer from a Gentleman
Romancing Mr Bridgerton
To Sir Phillip, With Love
When He Was Wicked
It's in His Kiss
On the Way to the Wedding

Rokesby Series:

Because of Miss Bridgerton
The Girl with the Make-Believe Husband
The Other Miss Bridgerton
First Comes Scandal

Bevelstoke:

The Secret Diaries of Miss Miranda Cheever
What Happens in London
Ten Things I Love About You

Two Dukes of Wyndham:

The Lost Duke of Wyndham
Mr Cavendish, I Presume

Splendid Trilogy:

Splendid
Dancing at Midnight
Minx
Where's My Hero?

Agents of the Crown:

To Catch an Heiress
How to Marry a Marquis

Lyndon Sisters:

Everything and the Moon
Brighter than the Sun

Julia Quinn

The Duke and I

PIATKUS

PIATKUS

First published in the US in 2000 by Avon Books,
An imprint of HarperCollins, New York
First published in Great Britain in 2006 by Piatkus Books
This paperback edition published in 2020 by Piatkus by arrangement with Avon

26

A CIP catalogue record for this book
is available from the British Library.

ISBN 978-0-349-42921-2

Printed and bound in Great Britain by Clays Ltd, Elcograf S.p.A.

Papers used by Piatkus are from well-managed forests
and other responsible sources.

FSC www.fsc.org MIX Paper from responsible sources FSC® C104740

Piatkus
An imprint of
Little, Brown Book Group
Carmelite House
50 Victoria Embankment
London EC4Y 0DZ

Hachette Ireland
8 Castlecourt Centre
Castleknock
Dublin 15

An Hachette UK Company
www.hachette.co.uk

www.littlebrown.co.uk

For Danelle Harmon and Sabrina Jeffries,
without whom I never would have
turned this book in on time.

And for Martha
of The Romance Journal electronic bulletin board,
for suggesting I call it Daphne's Bad Heir Day.

And also for Paul,
even though his idea of dancing
is standing still while he
holds my hand and watches me twirl.

The Duke and I

Prologue

The birth of Simon Arthur Henry Fitzranulph Basset, Earl Clyvedon, was met with great celebration. Church bells rang for hours, champagne flowed freely through the gargantuan castle that the newborn would call home, and the entire village of Clyvedon quit work to partake of the feast and holiday ordered by the young earl's father.

'This,' the baker said to the blacksmith, 'is no ordinary baby.'

For Simon Arthur Henry Fitzranulph Basset would not spend his life as Earl Clyvedon. That was a mere courtesy title. Simon Arthur Henry Fitzranulph Basset – the baby who possessed more names than any baby could possibly need – was the heir to one of England's oldest and richest dukedoms. And his father, the ninth Duke of Hastings, had waited years for this moment.

As he stood in the hall outside his wife's confinement room, cradling the squalling infant, the duke's heart near burst with pride. Already several years past forty, he had watched his cronies – dukes and earls, all – beget heir after heir. Some had had to suffer through a few daughters before siring a precious son, but in the end, they'd all been assured that their lines would continue, that their blood would pass forward into the next generation of England's elite.

But not the Duke of Hastings. Though his wife had managed to conceive five times in the fifteen years of their marriage, only twice had she carried to full term, and both of those infants had been stillborn. After the fifth pregnancy, which had ended with a bloody miscarriage in the fifth month, surgeons and physicians alike had warned their graces that they absolutely must not make another attempt to have a child. The duchess's very life was in danger. She was too frail, too weak, and perhaps, they said gently, too old. The duke was simply going to have to reconcile himself to the fact that the dukedom would pass out of the Basset family.

But the duchess, God bless her, knew her role in life, and after a six-month recuperative period, she opened the connecting door between their bedrooms, and the duke once again commenced his quest for a son.

Five months later, the duchess informed the duke that she had conceived. The duke's immediate elation was tempered by his grim determination that nothing – absolutely nothing – would cause this pregnancy to go awry. The duchess was confined to her bed the minute it was realized that she'd missed her monthly courses. A physician was brought in to visit her every day, and halfway through the pregnancy, the duke located the most respected doctor in London and paid him a king's ransom to abandon his practice and take up residence at Clyvedon Castle temporarily.

The duke was taking no chances this time. He would have a son, and the dukedom would remain in Basset hands.

The duchess experienced pains a month early, and pillows were tucked under her hips. Gravity might keep the babe inside, Dr. Stubbs explained. The duke thought that a sound argument, and, once the doctor had retired for the evening, placed yet another pillow under his wife, raising her to a twenty-degree angle. She remained that way for a month.

And then finally, the moment of truth arrived. The household prayed for the duke, who so wanted an heir, and a few remembered to pray for the duchess, who had grown thin and frail even as her belly had grown round and wide. They tried not to be too hopeful – after all, the duchess had already delivered and buried two babes. And even if she did manage to safely deliver a child, it could be, well, a girl.

As the duchess's screams grew louder and more frequent, the duke shoved his way into her chamber, ignoring the protests of the doctor, the midwife, and her grace's maid. It was a bloody mess, but the duke was determined to be present when the babe's sex was revealed.

The head appeared, then the shoulders. All leaned forward to watch as the duchess strained and pushed, and then . . .

And then the duke knew that there was a God, and He still smiled on the Bassets. He allowed the midwife one minute to clean the babe, then took the little boy into his arms and marched into the great hall to show him off.

'I have a son!' he boomed. 'A perfect little son!'

And while the servants cheered and wept with relief, the duke looked down upon the tiny little earl, and said, 'You are perfect. You are a Basset. You are mine.'

The duke wanted to take the boy outside to prove to everyone that he had finally sired a healthy male child, but there was a slight chill in the early April air, so he allowed the midwife to take the babe back to his mother. The duke mounted one of his prized geldings and rode off to celebrate, shouting his good fortune to all who would listen.

Meanwhile, the duchess, who had been bleeding steadily since the birth, slipped into unconsciousness, and then finally just slipped away.

The duke mourned his wife. He truly did. He hadn't loved her, of course, and she hadn't loved him, but they'd been friends in an oddly distant sort of way. The duke hadn't expected anything more from marriage than a son and an heir, and in that regard, his wife had proven herself an exemplary spouse. He arranged for fresh flowers to be laid at the base of her funereal monument every week, no matter the season, and her portrait was moved from the sitting room to the hall, in a position of great honor over the staircase.

And then the duke got on with the business of raising his son.

There wasn't much he could do in the first year, of course. The babe was too young for lectures on land management and responsibility, so the duke left Simon in the care of his nurse and went to London, where his life continued much as it had before he'd been blessed by parenthood, except that he forced everyone – even the king – to gaze upon the miniature he'd had painted of his son shortly after his birth.

The duke visited Clyvedon from time to time, then returned for good on Simon's second birthday, ready to take the young lad's education in hand. A pony had been purchased, a small gun had been selected for future use at the fox hunt, and tutors were engaged in every subject known to man.

'He's too young for all that!' Nurse Hopkins exclaimed.

'Nonsense,' Hastings replied condescendingly. 'Clearly, I don't expect him to master any of this anytime soon, but it is never too early to begin a duke's education.'

'He's not a duke,' Nurse muttered.

'He will be.' Hastings turned his back on her and crouched beside his son, who was building an asymmetrical castle with a set of blocks on the floor. The duke hadn't been down to Clyvedon in several months, and was pleased with Simon's growth. He was a sturdy, healthy young boy, with glossy brown hair and clear blue eyes.

'What are you building there, son?'

Simon smiled and pointed.

Hastings looked up at Nurse Hopkins. 'Doesn't he speak?'

She shook her head. 'Not yet, your grace.'

The duke frowned. 'He's two. Shouldn't he be speaking?'

'Some children take longer than others, your grace. He's clearly a bright young boy.'

'Of course he's bright. He's a Basset.'

Nurse nodded. She always nodded when the duke talked about the superiority of the Basset blood. 'Maybe,' she suggested, 'he just doesn't have anything he wants to say.'

The duke didn't look convinced, but he handed Simon a toy soldier, patted him on the head, and left the house to go exercise the new mare he'd purchased from Lord Worth.

Two years later, however, he wasn't so sanguine.

'*Why isn't he talking?*' he boomed.

'I don't know,' Nurse answered, wringing her hands.

'What have you done to him?'

'I haven't done anything!'

'If you'd been doing your job correctly, *he*' – the duke jabbed an angry finger in Simon's direction – 'would be speaking.'

Simon, who was practicing his letters at his miniature desk, watched the exchange with interest.

'He's four years old, God damn it,' the duke roared. 'He should be able to speak.'

'He can write,' Nurse said quickly. 'Five children I've raised, and not a one of them took to letters the way Master Simon has.'

'A fat lot of good writing is going to do him if he can't talk.' Hastings turned to Simon, rage burning in his eyes. 'Talk to me, damn you!'

Simon shrank back, his lower lip quivering.

'Your grace!' Nurse exclaimed. 'You're scaring the child.'

Hastings whipped around to face her. 'Maybe he needs scaring. Maybe what he needs is a good dose of discipline. A good paddling might help him find his voice.'

The duke grabbed the silver-backed brush Nurse used on Simon's hair and advanced on his son. 'I'll make you talk, you stupid little—'

'No!'

Nurse gasped. The duke dropped the brush. It was the first time they'd ever heard Simon's voice.

'What did you say?' the duke whispered, tears forming in his eyes.

Simon's fists balled at his sides, and his little chin jutted out as he said, 'Don't you h-h-h-h-h-h-h—'

The duke's face turned deathly pale. 'What is he saying?'

Simon attempted the sentence again. 'D-d-d-d-d-d-d—'

'My God,' the duke breathed, horrified. 'He's a moron.'

'He's not a moron!' Nurse cried out, throwing her arms around the boy.

'D-d-d-d-d-d-d-don't you h-h-h-h-h-h-hit' – Simon took a deep breath – '*me*.'

Hastings sank onto the window seat, his head dropping into his hands. 'What have I done to deserve this? What could I have possibly done . . . '

'You should be giving the boy praise!' Nurse Hopkins admonished. 'Four years you've been waiting for him to speak, and—'

'And he's an idiot!' Hastings roared. 'A goddamned, bloody little idiot!'

Simon began to cry.

'Hastings is going to go to a half-wit,' the duke moaned. 'All those years of praying for an heir, and now it's all for ruin. I should have let the title go to my cousin.' He turned back to his son, who was sniffling and wiping his eyes, trying to appear strong for his father. 'I can't even look at him,' he gasped. 'I can't even bear to look at him.'

And with that, the duke stalked out of the room.

Nurse Hopkins hugged the boy close. 'You're not an idiot,' she whispered fiercely. 'You're the smartest little boy I know. And if anyone can learn to talk properly, I know it's you.'

Simon turned into her warm embrace and sobbed.

'We'll show him,' Nurse vowed. 'He'll eat his words if it's the last thing I do.'

Nurse Hopkins proved true to her word. While the Duke of Hastings removed himself to London and tried to pretend he had no son, she spent every waking minute with

Simon, sounding out words and syllables, praising him lavishly when he got something right, and giving him encouraging words when he didn't.

The progress was slow, but Simon's speech did improve. By the time he was six, 'd-d-d-d-d-d-d-don't' had turned into 'd-d-don't,' and by the time he was eight, he was managing entire sentences without faltering. He still ran into trouble when he was upset, and Nurse had to remind him often that he needed to remain calm and collected if he wanted to get the words out in one piece.

But Simon was determined, and Simon was smart, and perhaps most importantly, he was damned stubborn. He learned to take breaths before each sentence, and to think about his words before he attempted to say them. He studied the feel of his mouth when he spoke correctly, and tried to analyze what went wrong when he didn't.

And finally, at the age of eleven, he turned to Nurse Hopkins, paused to collect his thoughts, and said, 'I think it is time we went to see my father.'

Nurse looked up sharply. The duke had not laid eyes on the boy in seven years. And he had not answered a single one of the letters Simon had sent him.

Simon had sent nearly a hundred.

'Are you certain?' she asked.

Simon nodded.

'Very well, then. I'll order the carriage. We'll leave for London on the morrow.'

The trip took a day and a half, and it was late afternoon by the time their carriage rolled up to Basset House. Simon gazed at the busy London streetscape with wonder as Nurse Hopkins led him up the steps. Neither had ever visited Basset House before, and so Nurse didn't know what to do when she reached the front door other than knock.

The door swung open within seconds, and they found themselves being looked down upon by a rather imposing butler.

'Deliveries,' he intoned, reaching to close the door, 'are made in the rear.'

'Hold there!' Nurse said quickly, jamming her foot in the door. 'We are not servants.'

The butler looked disdainfully at her garments.

'Well, I am, but he's not.' She grabbed Simon's arm and yanked him forward. 'This is Earl Clyvedon, and you'd do well to treat him with respect.'

The butler's mouth actually dropped open, and he blinked several times before saying, 'It is my understanding that Earl Clyvedon is dead.'

'What?' Nurse screeched.

'I most certainly am not!' Simon exclaimed, with all the righteous indignation of an eleven-year-old.

The butler examined Simon, recognized immediately that he had the look of the Bassets, and ushered them in.

'Why did you think I was d-dead?' Simon asked, cursing himself for misspeaking, but not surprised. He was always most likely to stutter when he was angry.

'It is not for me to say,' the butler replied.

'It most certainly is,' Nurse shot back. 'You can't say something like that to a boy of his years and not explain it.'

The butler was silent for a moment, then finally said, 'His grace has not mentioned you in years. The last I heard, he said he had no son. He looked quite pained as he said it, so no one pursued the conversation. We – the servants, that is – assumed you'd passed on.'

Simon felt his jaw clench, felt his throat working wildly.

'Wouldn't he have gone into mourning?' Nurse demanded. 'Did you think about that? How could you have assumed the boy was dead if his father was not in mourning?'

The butler shrugged. 'His grace frequently wears black. Mourning wouldn't have altered his costume.'

'This is an outrage,' Nurse Hopkins said. 'I demand you summon his grace at once.'

Simon said nothing. He was trying too hard to get his emotions under control. He had to. There was no way he'd be able to talk with his father while his blood was racing so.

The butler nodded. 'He is upstairs. I'll alert him immediately to your arrival.'

Nurse started pacing wildly, muttering under her breath and referring to his grace with every vile word in her surprisingly extensive vocabulary. Simon remained in the center of the room, his arms angry sticks at his sides as he took deep breaths.

You can do this, he shouted in his mind. *You can do this*.

Nurse turned to him, saw him trying to control his temper, and immediately gasped. 'Yes, that's it,' she said quickly, dropping to her knees and taking his hands in hers. She knew better than anyone what would happen if Simon tried to face his father before he calmed down. 'Take deep breaths. And make sure to think about your words before you speak. If you can control—'

'I see you're still mollycoddling the boy,' came an imperious voice from the doorway.

Nurse Hopkins straightened and turned slowly around. She tried to think of something respectful to say. She tried to think of anything that would smooth over this awful situation. But when she looked at the duke, she saw Simon in him, and her rage began anew. The duke might look just like his son, but he was certainly no father to him.

'You, sir,' she spat out, 'are despicable.'

'And you, madam, are fired.'

Nurse lurched back.

'No one speaks to the Duke of Hastings that way,' he roared. 'No one!'

'Not even the king?' Simon taunted.

Hastings whirled around, not even noticing that his son had spoken clearly. 'You,' he said in a low voice.

Simon nodded curtly. He'd managed one sentence properly, but it had been a short one, and he didn't want to push his luck. Not when he was this upset. Normally, he could go days without a stutter, but now . . .

The way his father stared at him made him feel like an infant. An idiot infant.

And his tongue suddenly felt awkward and thick.

The duke smiled cruelly. 'What do you have to say for yourself, boy? Eh? What do you have to *say?*'

'It's all right, Simon,' Nurse Hopkins whispered, throwing a furious glance at the duke. 'Don't let him upset you. You can do it, sweetling.'

And somehow her encouraging tone made it all the worse. Simon had come here to prove himself to his father, and now his nurse was treating him like a baby.

'What's the matter?' the duke taunted. 'Cat got your tongue?'

Simon's muscles clenched so hard he started to shake.

Father and son stared at each other for what felt like an eternity, until finally the duke swore and stalked toward the door. 'You are my worst failure,' he hissed at his son. 'I don't know what I did to deserve you, but God help me if I ever lay eyes on you again.'

'Your grace!' Nurse Hopkins said indignantly. This was no way to speak to a child.

'Get him out of my sight,' he spat at her. 'You can keep your job just so long as you keep him away from me.'

'Wait!'

The duke turned slowly around at the sound of Simon's voice. 'Did you say something?' he drawled.

Simon took three long breaths in through his nose, his mouth still clamped together in anger. He forced his jaw to relax and rubbed his tongue against the roof of his mouth, trying to remind himself of how it felt to speak properly. Finally, just as the duke was about to dismiss him again, he opened his mouth and said, 'I am your son.'

Simon heard Nurse Hopkins breathe a sigh of relief, and something he'd never seen before blossomed in his father's eyes. Pride. Not much of it, but there was something there, lurking in the depths; something that gave Simon a whisper of hope.

'I am your son,' he said again, this time a little louder, 'and I am not d—'

Suddenly his throat closed up. And Simon panicked.

You can do this. You can do this.

But his throat felt tight, and his tongue felt thick, and his father's eyes started to narrow . . .

'I am not d-d-d—'

'Go home,' the duke said in a low voice. 'There is no place for you here.'

Simon felt the duke's rejection in his very bones, felt a peculiar kind of pain enter his body and creep around his heart. And, as hatred flooded his body and poured from his eyes, he made a solemn vow.

If he couldn't be the son his father wanted, then by God, he'd be the *exact opposite* . . .

1

The Bridgertons are by far the most prolific family in the upper echelons of society. Such industriousness on the part of the viscountess and the late viscount is commendable, although one can find only banality in their choice of names for their children. Anthony, Benedict, Colin, Daphne, Eloise, Francesca, Gregory, and Hyacinth – orderliness is, of course, beneficial in all things, but one would think that intelligent parents would be able to keep their children straight without needing to alphabetize their names.

Furthermore, the sight of the viscountess and all eight of her children in one room is enough to make one fear one is seeing double – or triple – or worse. Never has This Author seen a collection of siblings so ludicrously alike in their physical regard. Although This Author has never taken the time to record eye color, all eight possess similar bone structure and the same thick, chestnut hair. One must pity the viscountess as she seeks advantageous marriages for her brood that she did not produce a single child of more fashionable coloring. Still, there are advantages to a family of such consistent looks – there can be no doubt that all eight are of legitimate parentage.

Ah, Gentle Reader, your devoted Author wishes that that were the case amid all large families . . .

LADY WHISTLEDOWN'S SOCIETY PAPERS,
26 APRIL 1813

'Oooooooooohhhhhhhhhh!' Violet Bridgerton crumpled the single-page newspaper into a ball and hurled it across the elegant drawing room.

Her daughter Daphne wisely made no comment and pretended to be engrossed in her embroidery.

'Did you read what she said?' Violet demanded. 'Did you?'

Daphne eyed the ball of paper, which now rested under a mahogany end table. 'I didn't have the opportunity before you, er, finished with it.'

'Read it, then,' Violet wailed, her arm slicing dramatically through the air. 'Read how that woman has maligned us.'

Daphne calmly set down her embroidery and reached under the end table. She smoothed the sheet of paper out on her lap and read the paragraph about her family. Blinking, she looked up. 'This isn't so bad, Mother. In fact, it's a veritable benediction compared to what she wrote about the Featheringtons last week.'

'How am I supposed to find you a husband while *that woman* is slandering your name?'

Daphne forced herself to exhale. After nearly two seasons in London, the mere mention of the word husband was enough to set her temples pounding. She wanted to marry, truly she did, and she wasn't even holding out for a true love match. But was it really too much to hope for a husband for whom one had at least some affection?

Thus far, four men had asked for her hand, but when Daphne had thought about living the rest of her days in the company of any of them, she just couldn't do it. There were a number of men she thought might make reasonably good husbands, but the problem was – none of them was interested. Oh, they all *liked her*. Everyone liked her. Everyone thought she was funny and kind and a quick wit, and no one thought her the least bit unattractive, but at the same time, no one was dazzled by her beauty, stunned into speechlessness by her presence, or moved to write poetry in her honor.

Men, she thought with disgust, were interested only in those women who terrified them. No one seemed inclined to court someone like her. They all adored her, or so they said, because she was so easy to talk to, and she always seemed to understand how a man felt. As one of the men Daphne had thought might make a reasonably good husband had said, 'Deuce take it, Daff, you're just not like regular females. You're positively normal.'

Which she might have managed to consider a compliment if he hadn't proceeded to wander off in search of the latest blond beauty.

Daphne looked down and noticed that her hand was clenched into a fist. Then she looked up and realized her mother was staring at her, clearly waiting for her to say something. Since she had already exhaled, Daphne cleared her throat, and said, 'I'm sure Lady Whistledown's little column is not going to hurt my chances for a husband.'

'Daphne, it's been two years!'

'And Lady Whistledown has only been publishing for three months, so I hardly see how we can lay the blame at her door.'

'I'll lay the blame wherever I choose,' Violet muttered.

Daphne's fingernails bit her palms as she willed herself not to make a retort. She knew her mother had only her best interests at heart, she knew her mother loved her. And she loved her mother, too. In fact, until Daphne had reached marriageable age, Violet had been positively the best of mothers. She still was, when she wasn't despairing over the fact that after Daphne she had three more daughters to marry off.

Violet pressed a delicate hand to her chest. 'She cast aspersions on your parentage.'

'No,' Daphne said slowly. It was always wise to proceed with caution when contradicting her mother. 'Actually, what she said was that there could be no doubt that we are all legitimate. Which is more than one can say for most large families of the ton.'

'She shouldn't have even brought it up,' Violet sniffed.

'Mother, she's the author of a scandal sheet. It's her job to bring such things up.'

'She isn't even a real person,' Violet added angrily. She planted her hands on her slim hips, then changed her mind and shook her finger in the air. 'Whistledown, ha! I've never heard of any Whistledowns. Whoever this depraved woman is, I doubt she's one of us. As if anyone of breeding would write such wicked lies.'

'Of course she's one of us,' Daphne said, her brown eyes filling with amusement. 'If she weren't a member of the ton, there is no way she'd be privy to the sort of news she reports. Did you think she was some sort of impostor, peeking in windows and listening at doors?'

'I don't like your tone, Daphne Bridgerton,' Violet said, her eyes narrowing.

Daphne bit back another smile. 'I don't like your tone,' was Violet's standard answer when one of her children was winning an argument.

But it was too much fun to tease her mother. 'I wouldn't be surprised,' she said, cocking her head to the side, 'if Lady Whistledown was one of your friends.'

'Bite your tongue, Daphne. No friend of mine would ever stoop so low.'

'Very well,' Daphne allowed, 'it's probably not one of your friends. But I'm certain it's someone we know. No interloper could ever obtain the information she reports.'

Violet crossed her arms. 'I should like to put her out of business once and for all.'

'If you wish to put her out of business,' Daphne could not resist pointing out, 'you shouldn't support her by buying her newspaper.'

'And what good would that do?' Violet demanded. 'Everyone else is reading it. My puny little embargo would do nothing except make me look ignorant when everyone else is chuckling over her latest gossip.'

That much was true, Daphne silently agreed. Fashionable London was positively addicted to *Lady Whistledown's Society Papers*. The mysterious newspaper had arrived on the doorstep of every member of the ton three months earlier. For two weeks it was delivered unbidden every Monday, Wednesday, and Friday. And then, on the third Monday, butlers across London waited in vain for the pack of paperboys who normally delivered *Whistledown*, only to discover that instead of free delivery, they were selling the gossip sheet for the outrageous price of five pennies a paper.

Daphne had to admire the fictitious Lady Whistledown's savvy. By the time she started forcing people to pay for their gossip, all the *ton* was addicted. Everyone forked over their pennies, and somewhere some meddlesome woman was getting very rich.

While Violet paced the room and huffed about this 'hideous slight' against her family, Daphne looked up to make certain her mother wasn't paying her any attention, then let her eyes drop to peruse the rest of the scandal sheet. *Whistledown* – as it was now called – was a curious mix of commentary, social news, scathing insult, and the occasional compliment. What set it apart from any previous society news sheets was that the author actually listed her subjects' names in full. There was no hiding behind abbreviations such as Lord S—— and Lady G——. If Lady Whistledown wanted to write about someone, she used his full name. The *ton* declared themselves scandalized, but they were secretly fascinated.

This most recent edition was typical *Whistledown*. Aside

from the short piece on the Bridgertons – which was really no more than a description of the family—

Lady Whistledown had recounted the events at the previous night's ball. Daphne hadn't attended, as it had been her younger sister's birthday, and the Bridgertons always made a big fuss about birthdays. And with eight children, there were a lot of birthdays to celebrate.

'You're reading that rubbish,' Violet accused.

Daphne looked up, refusing to feel the least bit guilty. 'It's a rather good column today. Apparently Cecil Tumbley knocked over an entire tower of champagne glasses last night.'

'Really?' Violet asked, trying not to look interested.

'Mmm-hmm,' Daphne replied. 'She gives quite a good account of the Middlethorpe ball. Mentions who was talking to whom, what everyone was wearing—'

'And I suppose she felt the need to offer her opinions on that point,' Violet cut in.

Daphne smiled wickedly. 'Oh, come now, Mother. You know that Mrs. Featherington has always looked dreadful in purple.'

Violet tried not to smile. Daphne could see the corners of her mouth twitching as she tried to maintain the composure she deemed appropriate for a viscountess and mother. But within two seconds, she was grinning and sitting next to her daughter on the sofa. 'Let me see that,' she said, snatching up the paper. 'What else happened? Did we miss anything important?'

Daphne said, 'Really, Mother, with Lady Whistledown as a reporter, one needn't actually *attend* any events.' She waved toward the paper. 'This is almost as good as actually being there. Better, probably. I'm certain we had better food last night than they did at the ball. And give that back.' She yanked the paper back, leaving a torn corner in Violet's hands.

'Daphne!'

Daphne affected mock righteousness. 'I was reading it.'

'Well!'

'Listen to this.'

Violet leaned in.

Daphne read: '"The rake formerly known as Earl Clyvedon has finally seen fit to grace London with his presence. Although he has not yet deigned to make an appearance at a respectable evening function, the new Duke of Hastings has been spotted several times at White's and once at Tattersall's.' She paused to take a breath. '"His grace has resided abroad for six years. Can it be any coincidence that he has returned only now that the old duke is dead?"'

Daphne looked up. 'My goodness, she *is* blunt, isn't she? Isn't Clyvedon one of Anthony's friends?'

'He's Hastings now,' Violet said automatically, 'and yes, I do believe he and Anthony were friendly at Oxford. And Eton as well, I think.' Her brow scrunched and her blue eyes narrowed with thought. 'He was something of a hellion, if my memory serves. Always at odds with his father. But reputed to be quite brilliant. I'm fairly sure that Anthony said he took a first in mathematics. Which,' she added with a maternal roll of her eyes, 'is more than I can say for any of my children.'

'Now, now, Mother,' Daphne teased. 'I'm sure I would take a first if Oxford would only see fit to admit women.'

Violet snorted. 'I corrected your arithmetic papers when your governess was ill, Daphne.'

'Well, maybe in history, then,' Daphne said with a grin. She looked back down at the paper in her hands, her eyes straying to the new duke's name. 'He sounds quite interesting,' she murmured.

Violet looked at her sharply. 'He's quite unsuitable for a young lady of your years is what he is.'

'Funny how my "years," as you put it, volley back and forth between being so young that I cannot even meet Anthony's friends and being so old that you despair of my ever contracting a good marriage.'

'Daphne Bridgerton, I don't—'

'—like my tone, I know.' Daphne grinned. 'But you love me.'

Violet smiled warmly and wrapped an arm around Daphne's shoulder. 'Heaven help me, I do.'

Daphne gave her mother a quick peck on the cheek. 'It's the curse of motherhood. You're required to love us even when we vex you.'

Violet just sighed. 'I hope that someday you have children—'

'—just like me, I know.' Daphne smiled nostalgically and rested her head on her mother's shoulder. Her mother could be overly inquisitive, and her father had been more interested in hounds and hunting than he'd been in society affairs, but theirs had been a warm marriage, filled with love, laughter, and children. 'I could do a great deal worse than follow your example, Mother,' she murmured.

'Why, Daphne,' Violet said, her eyes growing watery, 'what a lovely thing to say.'

Daphne twirled a lock of her chestnut hair around her finger, and grinned, letting the sentimental moment melt into a more teasing one. 'I'm happy to follow in your footsteps when it comes to marriage and children, Mother, just so long as I don't have to have *eight*.'

At that exact moment, Simon Basset, the new Duke of Hastings and the erstwhile topic of the Bridgerton ladies' conversation, was sitting at White's. His companion was none other than Anthony Bridgerton, Daphne's eldest brother. The two cut a striking pair, both tall and athletic, with thick dark hair. But where Anthony's eyes were the same deep chocolate brown as his sister's, Simon's were icy blue, with an oddly penetrating gaze.

It was those eyes as much as anything that had earned him his reputation as a man to be reckoned with. When he stared at a person, clear and unwavering, men grew uncomfortable. Women positively shivered.

But not Anthony. The two men had known each other for years, and Anthony just laughed when Simon raised a brow and turned his icy gaze upon him. 'You forget, I've seen you with your head being lowered into a chamber pot,' Anthony had once told him. 'It's been difficult to take you seriously ever since.'

To which Simon had replied, 'Yes, but if I recall, you were the one holding me over that fragrant receptacle.'

'One of my proudest moments, to be sure. But you had your revenge the next night in the form of a dozen eels in my bed.'

Simon allowed himself a smile as he remembered both the incident and their subsequent conversation about it. Anthony was a good friend, just the sort a man would want by his side in a pinch. He'd been the first person Simon had looked up upon returning to England.

'It's damned fine to have you back, Clyvedon,' Anthony said, once they'd settled in at their table at White's. 'Oh, but I suppose you'll insist I call you Hastings now.'

'No,' Simon said rather emphatically. 'Hastings will always be my father. He never answered to anything else.' He paused. 'I'll assume his title if I must, but I won't be called by his name.'

'If you must?' Anthony's eyes widened slightly. 'Most men would not sound quite so resigned about the prospect of a dukedom.'

Simon raked a hand through his dark hair. He knew he was supposed to cherish his birthright and display unwavering pride in the Basset family's illustrious history, but the truth was it all made him sick inside. He'd spent his entire life not living up to his father's expectations; it seemed ridiculous now to try to live up to his name. 'It's a damned burden is what it is,' he finally grumbled.

'You'd best get used to it,' Anthony said pragmatically, 'because that's what everyone will call you.'

Simon knew it was true, but he doubted if the title would ever sit well upon his shoulders.

'Well, whatever the case,' Anthony added, respecting his

friend's privacy by not delving further into what was obviously an uncomfortable topic, 'I'm glad to have you back. I might finally get some peace next time I escort my sister to a ball.'

Simon leaned back, crossing his long, muscular legs at the ankles. 'An intriguing remark.'

Anthony raised a brow. 'One that you're certain I'll explain?'

'But of course.'

'I ought to let you learn for yourself, but then, I've never been a cruel man.'

Simon chuckled. 'This coming from the man who dunked my head in a chamber pot?'

Anthony waved his hand dismissively. 'I was young.'

'And now you're a model of mature decorum and respectability?'

Anthony grinned. 'Absolutely.'

'So tell me,' Simon drawled, 'how, exactly, am I meant to make your existence that much more peaceful?'

'I assume you plan to take your place in society?'

'You assume incorrectly.'

'But you *are* planning to attend Lady Danbury's ball this week,' Anthony said.

'Only because I am inexplicably fond of the old woman. She says what she means, and – ' Simon's eyes grew somewhat shuttered.

'And?' Anthony prompted.

Simon gave his head a little shake. 'It's nothing. Just that she was rather kind to me as a child. I spent a few school holidays at her house with Riverdale. Her nephew, you know.'

Anthony nodded once. 'I see. So you have no intention of entering society. I'm impressed by your resolve. But allow me to warn you – even if you do not choose to attend the *ton*'s events, *they* will find you.'

Simon, who had chosen that moment to take a sip of his

brandy, choked on the spirit at the look on Anthony's face when he said, 'they.' After a few moments of coughing and sputtering, he finally managed to say, 'Who, pray tell, are "they"?'

Anthony shuddered. 'Mothers.'

'Not having had one myself, I can't say I grasp your point.'

'Society mothers, you dolt. Those fire-breathing dragons with daughters of – God help us – marriageable age. You can run, but you'll never manage to hide from them. And I should warn you, my own is the worst of the lot.'

'Good God. And here I thought Africa was dangerous.'

Anthony shot his friend a faintly pitying look. 'They will hunt you down. And when they find you, you will find yourself trapped in conversation with a pale young lady all dressed in white who cannot converse on topics other than the weather, who received vouchers to Almack's, and hair ribbons.'

A look of amusement crossed Simon's features. 'I take it, then, that during my time abroad you have become something of an eligible gentleman?'

'Not out of any aspirations to the role on my part, I assure you. If it were up to me, I'd avoid society functions like the plague. But my sister made her bow last year, and I'm forced to escort her from time to time.'

'Daphne, you mean?'

Anthony looked up in surprise. 'Did the two of you ever meet?'

'No,' Simon admitted, 'but I remember her letters to you at school, and I recalled that she was fourth in the family, so she had to start with D, and—'

'Ah, yes,' Anthony said with a slight roll of his eyes, 'the Bridgerton method of naming children. Guaranteed to make certain no one forgets who you are.'

Simon laughed. 'It worked, didn't it?'

'Say, Simon,' Anthony suddenly said, leaning forward, 'I've promised my mother I'll have dinner at Bridgerton House later this week with the family. Why don't you join me?'

Simon raised a dark brow. 'Didn't you just warn me about society mothers and debutante daughters?'

Anthony laughed. 'I'll put my mother on her best behavior, and don't worry about Daff. She's the exception that proves the rule. You'll like her immensely.'

Simon narrowed his eyes. Was Anthony playing matchmaker? He couldn't tell.

As if Anthony were reading his thoughts, he laughed. 'Good God, you don't think I'm trying to pair you off with Daphne, do you?'

Simon said nothing.

'You would never suit. You're a bit too brooding for her tastes.'

Simon thought that an odd comment, but instead chose to ask, 'Has she had any offers, then?'

'A few.' Anthony kicked back the rest of his brandy, then let out a satisfied exhale. 'I've allowed her to refuse them all.'

'That's rather indulgent of you.'

Anthony shrugged. 'Love is probably too much to hope for in a marriage these days, but I don't see why she shouldn't be happy with her husband. We've had offers from one man old enough to be her father, another old enough to be her father's younger brother, one who was rather too high in the instep for our often boisterous clan, and then this week, dear God, that was the worst!'

'What happened?' Simon asked curiously.

Anthony gave his temples a weary rub. 'This last one was perfectly amiable, but a rather bit dim in the head. You'd think, after our rakish days, I'd be completely without feelings—'

'Really?' Simon asked with a devilish grin. 'You'd think that?'

Anthony scowled at him. 'I didn't particularly enjoy breaking this poor fool's heart.'

'Er, wasn't Daphne the one to do that?'

'Yes, but I had to *tell* him.'

'Not many brothers would allow their sister such latitude with their marriage proposals,' Simon said quietly.

Anthony just shrugged again, as if he couldn't imagine treating his sister in any other way. 'She's been a good sister to me. It's the least I can do.'

'Even if it means escorting her to Almack's?' Simon said wickedly.

Anthony groaned. 'Even then.'

'I'd console you by pointing out that this will all be over soon, but you've what, three other sisters waiting in the wings?'

Anthony positively slumped in his seat. 'Eloise is due out in two years, and Francesca the year after that, but then I've a bit of a reprieve before Hyacinth comes of age.'

Simon chuckled. 'I don't envy you your responsibilities in that quarter.' But even as he said the words, he felt a strange longing, and he wondered what it would be like to be not quite so alone in this world. He had no plans to start a family of his own, but maybe if he'd had one to begin with, his life would have turned out a bit differently.

'So you'll come for supper, then?' Anthony stood. 'Informal, of course. We never take meals formally when it's just family.'

Simon had a dozen things to do in the next few days, but before he could remind himself that he needed to get his affairs in order, he heard himself saying, 'I'd be delighted.'

'Excellent. And I'll see you at the Danbury bash first?'

Simon shuddered. 'Not if I can help it. My aim is to be in and out in under thirty minutes.'

'You really think,' Anthony said, raising a doubtful brow, 'that you're going to be able to go to the party, pay your respects to Lady Danbury, and leave?'

Simon's nod was forceful and direct.

But Anthony's snort of laughter was not terribly reassuring.

2

The new Duke of Hastings is a most interesting character. While it is common knowledge that he was not on favorable terms with his father, even This Author is unable to learn the reason for the estrangement.

LADY WHISTLEDOWN'S SOCIETY PAPERS,
26 APRIL 1813

Later that week, Daphne found herself standing on the fringes of Lady Danbury's ballroom, far away from the fashionable crowd. She was quite content with her position.

Normally she would have enjoyed the festivities; she liked a good party as well as the next young lady, but earlier that evening, Anthony had informed her that Nigel Berbrooke had sought him out two days earlier and asked for her hand. Again. Anthony had, of course, refused (again!), but Daphne had the sinking feeling that Nigel was going to prove uncomfortably persistent. After all, two marriage proposals in two weeks did not paint a picture of a man who accepted defeat easily.

Across the ballroom she could see him looking this way and that, and she shrank further into the shadows.

She had no idea how to deal with the poor man. He wasn't very bright, but he also wasn't unkind, and though she knew she had to somehow put an end to his infatuation, she was finding it far easier to take the coward's way out and simply avoid him.

She was considering slinking into the ladies' retiring

room when a familiar voice stopped her in her tracks.

'I say, Daphne, what are you doing all the way over here?'

Daphne looked up to see her eldest brother making his way toward her. 'Anthony,' she said, trying to decide if she was pleased to see him or annoyed that he might be coming over to meddle in her affairs. 'I hadn't realized you would be in attendance.'

'Mother,' he said grimly. No other words were necessary.

'Ah,' Daphne said with a sympathetic nod. 'Say no more. I understand completely.'

'She made a list of potential brides.' He shot his sister a beleaguered look. 'We do love her, don't we?'

Daphne choked on a laugh. 'Yes, Anthony, we do.'

'It's temporary insanity,' he grumbled. 'It has to be. There is no other explanation. She was a perfectly reasonable mother until you reached marriageable age.'

'Me?' Daphne squeaked. 'Then this is all my fault? You're a full eight years older than I am!'

'Yes, but she wasn't gripped by this matrimonial fervor until you came along.'

Daphne snorted. 'Forgive me if I lack sympathy. I received a list last year.'

'Did you?'

'Of course. And lately she's been threatening to deliver them to me on a weekly basis. She badgers me on the issue of marriage far more than you could ever imagine. After all, bachelors are a challenge. Spinsters are merely pathetic. And in case you hadn't noticed, I'm female.'

Anthony let out a low chuckle. 'I'm your brother. I don't notice those things.' He gave her a sly, sideways look. 'Did you bring it?'

'My list? Heavens, no. What can you be thinking?'

His smile widened. 'I brought mine.'

Daphne gasped. 'You didn't!'

'I did. Just to torture Mother. I'm going peruse it right in front of her, pull out my quizzing glass—'

'You don't have a quizzing glass.'

He grinned – the slow, devastatingly wicked smile that all Bridgerton males seemed to possess. 'I bought one just for this occasion.'

'Anthony, you absolutely cannot. She will *kill* you. And then, somehow, she'll find a way to blame me.'

'I'm counting on it.'

Daphne swatted him in the shoulder, eliciting a loud enough grunt to cause a half dozen partygoers to send curious looks in their direction.

'A solid punch,' Anthony said, rubbing his arm.

'A girl can't live long with four brothers without learning how to throw one.' She crossed her arms. 'Let me see your list.'

'After you just assaulted me?'

Daphne rolled her brown eyes and cocked her head in a decidedly impatient gesture.

'Oh, very well.' He reached into his waistcoat, pulled out a folded slip of paper, and handed it to her. 'Tell me what you think. I'm sure you'll have no end of cutting remarks.'

Daphne unfolded the paper and stared down at her mother's neat, elegant handwriting. The Viscountess Bridgerton had listed the names of eight women. Eight very eligible, very wealthy young women.

'Precisely what I expected,' Daphne murmured.

'Is it as dreadful as I think?'

'Worse. Philipa Featherington is as dumb as a post.'

'And the rest of them?'

Daphne looked up at him under raised brows. 'You didn't really want to get married this year, anyway, did you?'

Anthony winced. 'And how was your list?'

'Blessedly out-of-date, now. Three of the five married last season. Mother is still berating me for letting them slip through my fingers.'

The two Bridgertons let out identical sighs as they slumped against the wall. Violet Bridgerton was undeterred in her mission to marry off her children. Anthony, her eldest son, and Daphne, her eldest daughter, had borne the brunt of the pressure, although Daphne suspected that the viscountess might have cheerfully married off ten-year-old Hyacinth if she'd received a suitable offer.

'Good God, you look a pair of sad sorts. What are you doing so far off in the corner?'

Another instantly recognizable voice. 'Benedict,' Daphne said, glancing sideways at him without moving her head. 'Don't tell me Mother managed to get you to attend tonight's festivities.'

He nodded grimly. 'She has completely bypassed cajoling and moved on to guilt. Three times this week she has reminded me I may have to provide the next viscount, if Anthony here doesn't get busy.'

Anthony groaned.

'I assume that explains your flight as well to the darkest corners of the ballroom?' Benedict continued. 'Avoiding Mother?'

'Actually,' Anthony replied, 'I saw Daff skulking in the corner and—'

'Skulking?' Benedict said with mock horror.

She shot them both an irritated scowl. 'I came over to hide from Nigel Berbrooke,' she explained. 'I left Mother in the company of Lady Jersey, so she's not likely to pester me anytime soon, but Nigel—'

'Is more monkey than man,' Benedict quipped.

'Well, I wouldn't have put it *that* way precisely,' Daphne said, trying to be kind, 'but he isn't terribly bright, and it's so much easier to stay out of his way than to hurt his feelings. Of course now that you lot have found me, I shan't be able to avoid him for long.'

Anthony voiced a simple, 'Oh?'

Daphne looked at her two older brothers, both an inch above six feet with broad shoulders and melting brown eyes. They each sported thick chestnut hair – much the same color as her own – and more to the point, they could not go anywhere in polite society without a small gaggle of twittering young ladies following them about.

And where a gaggle of twittering young ladies went, Nigel Berbrooke was sure to follow.

Already Daphne could see heads turning in their direction. Ambitious mamas were nudging their daughters and pointing to the two Bridgerton brothers, off by themselves with no company save for their sister.

'I knew I should have made for the retiring room,' Daphne muttered.

'I say, what's that piece of paper in your hand, Daff?' Benedict inquired.

Somewhat absentmindedly, she handed him the list of Anthony's supposed brides.

At Benedict's loud chortle, Anthony crossed his arms, and said, 'Try not to have too much fun at my expense. I predict you'll be receiving a similar list next week.'

'No doubt,' Benedict agreed. 'It's a wonder Colin – ' His eyes snapped up. 'Colin!'

Yet another Bridgerton brother joined the crowd.

'Oh, Colin!' Daphne exclaimed, throwing her arms around him. 'It's so *good* to see you.'

'Note that we didn't receive similarly enthusiastic greetings,' Anthony said to Benedict.

'You I see all the time,' Daphne retorted. 'Colin's been away a full year.' After giving him one last squeeze, she stepped back, and scolded, 'We didn't expect you until next week.'

Colin's one-shoulder shrug matched his lopsided smile to perfection. 'Edinburgh grew dull.'

'Ah,' Daphne said with a shrewd look in her eye. 'Then you ran out of money.'

Colin laughed and held up his hands in surrender. 'Guilty as charged.'

Anthony hugged his brother, and said gruffly, 'It's damned

fine to have you home, brother. Although the funds I sent you should have lasted you at least until—'

'Stop,' Colin said helplessly, laughter still tinging his voice. 'I promise you may scold me all you want tomorrow. Tonight I merely wish to enjoy the company of my beloved family.'

Benedict let out a snort. 'You must be completely broke if you're calling us "beloved." But he leaned forward to give his brother a hearty hug all the same. 'Welcome home.'

Colin, always the most devil-may-care of the family, grinned, his green eyes twinkling. 'Good to be back. Although I must say the weather is not nearly so fine as on the Continent, and as for the women, well, England would be hard pressed to compete with the signorina I—'

Daphne punched him in the arm. 'Kindly recall that there is a lady present, churl.' But there was little ire in her voice. Of all her siblings, Colin was the closest to her in age – only eighteen months her elder. As children, they had been inseparable – and always in trouble. Colin was a natural prankster, and Daphne had never needed much convincing to go along with his schemes. 'Does Mother know you're home?' she asked.

Colin shook his head. 'I arrived to an empty house, and—'

'Yes, Mother put the younger ones to bed early tonight,' Daphne interrupted.

'I didn't want to wait about and twiddle my thumbs, so Humboldt gave me your direction and I came here.'

Daphne beamed, her wide smile lending warmth to her dark eyes. 'I'm glad you did.'

'Where is Mother?' Colin asked, craning his neck to peer over the crowd. Like all Bridgerton males, he was tall, so he didn't have to stretch very far.

'Over in the corner with Lady Jersey,' Daphne replied.

Colin shuddered. 'I'll wait until she's extricated herself. I have no wish to be flayed alive by that dragon.'

'Speaking of dragons,' Benedict said pointedly. His head didn't move, but his eyes flicked off to the left.

Daphne followed his line of vision to see Lady Danbury marching slowly toward them. She carried a cane, but Daphne swallowed nervously and steeled her shoulders. Lady Danbury's often cutting wit was legendary among the ton. Daphne had always suspected that a sentimental heart beat under her acerbic exterior, but still, it was always terrifying when Lady Danbury pressed one into conversation.

'No escape,' Daphne heard one of her brothers groan.

Daphne shushed him and offered the old lady a hesitant smile.

Lady Danbury's brows rose, and when she was but four feet away from the group of Bridgertons, she stopped, and barked, 'Don't pretend you don't see me!'

This was followed by a thump of the cane so loud that Daphne jumped back just enough to trample Benedict's toe.

'Euf,' said Benedict.

Since her brothers appeared to have gone temporarily mute (except for Benedict, of course, but Daphne didn't think that grunts of pain counted as intelligible speech) Daphne swallowed, and said, 'I hope I did not give that impression, Lady Danbury, for—'

'Not you,' Lady Danbury said imperiously. She jabbed her cane into the air, making a perfectly horizontal line that ended perilously close to Colin's stomach. 'Them.'

A chorus of mumbled greetings emerged as a response.

Lady Danbury flicked the men the briefest of glances before turning back to Daphne, and saying, 'Mr. Berbrooke was asking after you.'

Daphne actually felt her skin turn green. 'He was?'

Lady Danbury gave her a curt nod. 'I'd nip that one in the bud, were I you, Miss Bridgerton.'

'Did you tell him where I was?'

Lady Danbury's mouth slid into a sly, conspiratorial smile.

'I always knew I liked you. And no, I did not tell him where you were.'

'Thank you,' Daphne said gratefully.

'It'd be a waste of a good mind if you were shackled to that nitwit,' Lady Danbury said, 'and the good Lord knows that the *ton* can't afford to waste the few good minds we've got.'

'Er, thank you,' Daphne said.

'As for you lot' – Lady Danbury waved her cane at Daphne's brothers – 'I still reserve judgment. You'—

she pointed the cane at Anthony – 'I'm inclined to be favorable toward, since you refused Berbrooke's suit on your sister's behalf, but the rest of you . . . Hmmph.'

And with that she walked away.

'"Hmmph?"' Benedict echoed. '"Hmmph?" She purports to quantify my intelligence and all she comes up with is "Hmmph?"'

Daphne smirked. 'She *likes* me.'

'You're welcome to her,' Benedict grumbled.

'Rather sporting of her to warn you about Berbrooke,' Anthony admitted.

Daphne nodded. 'I believe that was my cue to take my leave.' She turned to Anthony with a beseeching look. 'If he comes looking for me—'

'I'll take care of it,' he said gently. 'Don't worry.'

'Thank you.' And then, with a smile to her brothers, she slipped out of the ballroom.

As Simon walked quietly through the halls of Lady Danbury's London home, it occurred to him that he was in a singularly good mood. This, he thought with a chuckle, was truly remarkable, considering the fact that he was about to attend a society ball and thus subject himself to all the horrors Anthony Bridgerton had laid out before him earlier that afternoon.

But he could console himself with the knowledge that after today, he needn't bother with such functions again; as he had told Anthony earlier that afternoon, he was only attending this particular ball out of loyalty to Lady Danbury, who, despite her curmudgeonly ways, had always been quite nice to him as a child.

His good mood, he was coming to realize, derived from the simple fact that he was pleased to be back in England.

Not that he hadn't enjoyed his journeys across the globe. He'd traveled the length and breadth of Europe, sailed the exquisitely blue seas of the Mediterranean, and delved into the mysteries of North Africa. From there he'd gone on to the Holy Land, and then, when inquiries revealed that it was not yet time to return home, he crossed the Atlantic and explored the West Indies. At that point he considered moving on to the United States of America, but the new nation had seen fit to enter into conflict with Britain, so Simon had stayed away.

Besides, that was when he'd learned that his father, ill for several years, had finally died.

It was ironic, really. Simon wouldn't have traded his years of exploration for anything. Six years gave a man a lot of time to think, a lot of time to learn what it meant to be a man. And yet the only reason the then-twenty-two-year-old Simon had left England was because his father had suddenly decided that he was finally willing to accept his son.

Simon hadn't been willing to accept his father, though, and so he'd simply packed his bags and left the country, preferring exile to the old duke's hypocritical overtures of affection.

It had all started when Simon had finished at Oxford. The duke hadn't originally wanted to pay for his son's schooling; Simon had once seen a letter written to a tutor stating that he refused to let his idiot son make a fool of the family at Eton. But Simon had had a hungry mind as well as a stubborn heart, and so he'd ordered a carriage to take him to Eton, knocked on the headmaster's door, and announced his presence.

It had been the most terrifying thing he'd ever done, but he'd somehow managed to convince the headmaster that the mix-up was the school's fault, that somehow Eton must have lost his enrollment papers and fees. He'd copied all of his father's mannerisms, raising an arrogant brow, lifting his chin, and looking down his nose, and generally appearing as if he thought he owned the world.

And the entire time, he'd been quaking in his shoes, terrified that at any moment his words would grow garbled and land on top of each other, that 'I am Earl Clyvedon, and I am here to begin classes,' would instead come out as, 'I am Earl Clyvedon, and I am h-h-h-h-h-h—'

But it hadn't, and the headmaster, who'd spent enough years educating England's elite to immediately recognize Simon as a member of the Basset family, had enrolled him posthaste and without question. It had taken several months for the duke (who was always quite busy with his own pursuits) to learn of his son's new status and change in residence. By that point, Simon was well ensconced at Eton, and it would have looked very bad if the duke had pulled the boy out of school for no reason.

And the duke didn't like to look bad.

Simon had often wondered why his father hadn't chosen to make an overture at that time. Clearly Simon wasn't tripping over his every word at Eton; the duke would have heard from the headmaster if his son weren't able to keep up with his studies. Simon's speech still occasionally slipped, but by then he'd grown remarkably proficient in covering up his mistakes with a cough or, if he was lucky enough to be taking a meal at the time, a well-timed sip of tea or milk.

But the duke never even wrote him a letter. Simon supposed his father had grown so used to ignoring his son that it didn't even matter that he wasn't proving to be an embarrassment to the Basset name.

After Eton, Simon followed the natural progression to

Oxford, where he earned the reputations of both scholar and rake. Truth be told, he hadn't deserved the label of rake any more than most of the young bucks at university, but Simon's somewhat aloof demeanor somehow fed the persona.

Simon wasn't exactly certain how it had happened, but gradually he became aware that his peers craved his approval. He was intelligent and athletic, but it seemed his elevated status had more to do with his manner than anything else. Because Simon didn't speak when words were not necessary, people judged him to be arrogant, just as a future duke should be. Because he preferred to surround himself with only those friends with whom he truly felt comfortable, people decided he was exceptionally discriminating in his choice of companions, just as a future duke should be.

He wasn't very talkative, but when he did say something, he had a quick and often ironic wit – just the sort of humor that guaranteed that people would hang on his every word. And again, because he didn't constantly run off at the mouth, as did so many of the *ton*, people were even *more* obsessed with what he had to say.

He was called 'supremely confident,' 'heartstoppingly handsome,' and 'the perfect specimen of English manhood.' Men wanted his opinion on any number of topics.

The women swooned at his feet.

Simon never could quite believe it all, but he enjoyed his status nonetheless, taking what was offered him, running wild with his friends, and enjoying the company of all the young widows and opera singers who sought his attention – and every escapade was all the more delicious for knowing that his father must disapprove.

But, as it turned out, his father didn't *entirely* disapprove. Unbeknownst to Simon, the Duke of Hastings had already begun to grow interested in the progress of his only son. He requested academic reports from the university and hired a Bow Street Runner to keep him apprised of Simon's extracurricular activities. And eventually, the duke stopped expecting every missive to contain tales of his son's idiocy.

It would have been impossible to pinpoint exactly when his change of heart occurred, but one day the duke realized that his son had turned out rather nicely, after all.

The duke puffed out with pride. As always, good breeding had proven true in the end. He should have known that Basset blood could not produce an imbecile.

Upon finishing Oxford with a first in mathematics, Simon came to London with his friends. He had, of course, taken bachelor's lodgings, having no wish to reside with his father. And as Simon went out in society, more and more people misinterpreted his pregnant pauses for arrogance and his small circle of friends for exclusivity.

His reputation was sealed when Beau Brummel – the then recognized leader of society – had asked a rather involved question about some trivial new fashion. Brummel's tone had been condescending and he had clearly hoped to embarrass the young lord. As all London knew, Brummel loved nothing better than to reduce England's elite into blithering idiots. And so he had pretended to care about Simon's opinion, ending his question with a drawled, 'Don't you think?'

As an audience of gossips watched with baited breath, Simon, who couldn't have cared less about the specific arrangement of the Prince's cravat, simply turned his icy blue eyes on Brummel, and answered, 'No.'

No explanation, no elaboration, just, 'No.'

And then he walked away.

By the next afternoon, Simon might as well have been the king of society. The irony was unnerving. Simon didn't care for Brummel or his tone, and he would probably have delivered a more loquacious set-down if he'd been sure he could do so without stumbling over his words. And yet in this particular instance, less had most definitely proven to be more, and Simon's terse sentence had turned out to be far more deadly than any long-winded speech he might have uttered.

Word of the brilliant and devastatingly handsome Hastings heir naturally reached the duke's ears. And although he did not immediately seek Simon out, Simon began to hear bits and pieces of gossip that warned him that his relationship with his father might soon see a change. The duke had laughed when he'd heard of the Brummel incident, and said, 'Naturally. He's a Basset.' An acquaintance mentioned that the duke had been heard crowing about Simon's first at Oxford.

And then the two came face-to-face at a London ball.

The duke would not allow Simon to give him the cut direct.

Simon tried. Oh, how he tried. But no one had the ability to crush his confidence like his father, and as he stared at the duke, who might as well have been a mirror image, albeit slightly older version, of himself, he couldn't move, couldn't even try to speak.

His tongue felt thick, his mouth felt odd, and it almost seemed as if his stutters had spread from his mouth to his body, for he suddenly didn't even feel right in his own skin.

The duke had taken advantage of Simon's momentary lapse of reason by embracing him with a heartfelt, 'Son.'

Simon had left the country the very next day.

He'd known that it would be impossible to avoid his father completely if he remained in England. And he refused to act the part of his son after having been denied a father for so many years.

Besides, lately he'd been growing bored of London's wild life. Rake's reputation aside, Simon didn't really have the temperament of a true debauche. He had enjoyed his nights on the town as much as any of his dissolute cronies, but after three years in Oxford and one in London, the endless round of parties and prostitutes was growing, well, old.

And so he left.

Now, however, he was glad to be back. There was something soothing about being home, something peaceful and serene about an English springtime. And after six years of solitary travel, it was damned good to find his friends again.

He moved silently through the halls, making his way to the ballroom. He hadn't wanted to be announced; the last thing he desired was a declaration of his presence. The afternoon's conversation with Anthony Bridgerton had reaffirmed his decision not to take an active role in London society.

He had no plans to marry. Ever. And there wasn't much point in attending *ton* parties if one wasn't looking for a wife.

Still, he felt he owed some loyalty to Lady Danbury after her many kindnesses during his childhood, and truth be told, he held a great deal of affection for the forthright old lady. It would have been the height of rudeness to spurn her invitation, especially since it had come accompanied by a personal note welcoming him back to the country.

Since Simon knew his way around this house, he'd entered through a side door. If all went well, he could slip unobtrusively into the ballroom, give his regards to Lady Danbury, and leave.

But as he turned a corner, he heard voices, and he froze.

Simon suppressed a groan. He'd interrupted a lovers' tryst. Bloody hell. How to extricate himself without notice? If his presence was discovered, the ensuing scene was sure to be replete with histrionics, embarrassment, and no end of tedious emotion. Better just to melt into the shadows and let the lovers go on their merry way.

But as Simon started backing quietly up, he heard something that caught his attention.

'No.'

No? Had some young lady been forced into the deserted hallway against her will? Simon had no great desire to be anyone's hero, but even he could not let such an insult pass. He craned his neck slightly, pressing his ear forward so that he might hear better. After all, he might have heard incorrectly. If no one needed saving, he certainly wasn't going to charge forward like some bullish fool.

'Nigel,' the girl was saying, 'you really shouldn't have followed me out here.'

'But I love you!' the young man cried out in a passionate voice. 'All I want is to make you my wife.'

Simon nearly groaned. Poor besotted fool. It was painful to listen to.

'Nigel,' she said again, her voice surprisingly kind and patient, 'my brother has already told you that I cannot marry you. I hope that we may continue on as friends.'

'But your brother doesn't understand!'

'Yes,' she said firmly, 'he does.'

'Dash it all! If you don't marry me, who will?'

Simon blinked in surprise. As proposals went, this one was decidedly *un*romantic.

The girl apparently thought so, too. 'Well,' she said, sounding a bit disgruntled, 'it's not as if there aren't dozens of other young ladies in Lady Danbury's ballroom right now. I'm sure one of them would be thrilled to marry you.'

Simon leaned forward slightly so that he could get a glimpse of the scene. The girl was in shadows, but he could see the man quite clearly. His face held a hangdog expression, and his shoulders were slumped forward in defeat. Slowly, he shook his head. 'No,' he said forlornly, 'they don't. Don't you see? They . . . they . . . '

Simon winced as the man fought for words. He didn't appear to be stuttering so much as emotionally overcome, but it was never pleasant when one couldn't get a sentence out.

'No one's as nice as you,' the man finally said. 'You're the only one who ever smiles at me.'

'Oh, Nigel,' the girl said, sighing deeply. 'I'm sure that's not true.'

But Simon could tell she was just trying to be kind. And

as she sighed again, it became apparent to him that she would not need any rescuing. She seemed to have the situation well in hand, and while Simon felt vague pangs of sympathy for the hapless Nigel, there wasn't anything he could do to help.

Besides, he was beginning to feel like the worst sort of voyeur.

He started inching backward, keeping his eye focused on a door that he knew led to the library. There was another door on the other side of that room, one that led to the conservatory. From there he could enter the main hall and make his way to the ballroom. It wouldn't be as discreet as cutting through the back corridors, but at least poor Nigel wouldn't know that his humiliation had had a witness.

But then, just a footstep away from a clean getaway, he heard the girl squeal.

'You have to marry me!' Nigel cried out. 'You have to! I'll never find anyone else—'

'Nigel, stop!'

Simon turned around, groaning. It looked like he was going to have to rescue the chit, after all. He strode back into the hall, putting his sternest, most dukish expression on his face. The words, 'I believe the lady asked you to stop,' rested on the tip of his tongue, but it seemed that he wasn't fated to play the hero tonight, after all, because before he could make a sound, the young lady pulled back her right arm and landed a surprisingly effective punch squarely on Nigel's jaw.

Nigel went down, his arms comically flailing in the air as his legs slid out from under him. Simon just stood there, watching in disbelief as the girl dropped to her knees.

'Oh dear,' she said, her voice squeaking slightly. 'Nigel, are you all right? I didn't mean to hit you so hard.'

Simon laughed. He couldn't help it.

The girl looked up, startled.

Simon caught his breath. She had been in shadows until

now, and all he'd been able to discern of her appearance was a wealth of thick, dark hair. But now, as she lifted her head to face him, he saw that she had large, equally dark eyes, and the widest, lushest mouth he'd ever seen. Her heart-shaped face wasn't beautiful by society standards, but something about her quite simply sucked the breath from his body.

Her brows, thick but delicately winged, drew together. 'Who,' she asked, not sounding at all pleased to see him, 'are you?'

3

It has been whispered to This Author that Nigel Berbrooke was seen at Moreton's Jewelry Shop purchasing a diamond solitaire ring. Can a new Mrs. Berbrooke be very far behind?

LADY WHISTLEDOWN'S SOCIETY PAPERS,
28 APRIL 1813

The night, Daphne decided, couldn't possibly get much worse. First she'd been forced to spend the evening in the darkest corner of ballroom (which wasn't such an easy task, since Lady Danbury clearly appreciated both the aesthetic and illuminating qualities of candles), then she'd managed to trip over Philipa Featherington's foot as she tried to make her escape, which had led Philipa, never the quietest girl in the room, to squeal, 'Daphne Bridgerton! Are you hurt?' Which must have captured Nigel's attention, for his head had snapped up like startled bird, and he'd immediately started hurrying across the ballroom. Daphne had hoped, no prayed that she could outrun him and make it to the ladies' retiring room before he caught up with her, but no, Nigel had cornered her in the hall and started wailing out his love for her.

It was all embarrassing enough, but now it appeared this man – this shockingly handsome and almost disturbingly poised stranger – had witnessed the entire thing. And worse, he was laughing!

Daphne glared at him as he chuckled at her expense.

She'd never seen him before, so he had to be new to London. Her mother had made certain that Daphne had been introduced to, or at least been made aware of, all eligible gentlemen. Of course, this man could be married and therefore not on Violet's list of potential victims, but Daphne instinctively knew that he could not have been long in London without all the world whispering about it.

His face was quite simply perfection. It took only a moment to realize that he put all of Michelangelo's statues to shame. His eyes were oddly intense – so blue they practically glowed. His hair was thick and dark, and he was tall – as tall as her brothers, which was a rare thing.

This was a man, Daphne thought wryly, who could quite possibly steal the gaggle of twittering young ladies away from the Bridgerton men for good.

Why that annoyed her so much, she didn't know. Maybe it was because she knew a man like him would never be interested in a woman like her. Maybe it was because she felt like the veriest frump sitting there on the floor in his splendid presence. Maybe it was simply because he was standing there laughing as if she were some sort of circus amusement.

But whatever the case, an uncharacteristic peevishness rose within her, and her brows drew together as she asked, 'Who are you?'

Simon didn't know why he didn't answer her question in a straightforward manner, but some devil within caused him to reply, 'My intention had been to be your rescuer, but you clearly had no need of my services.'

'Oh,' the girl said, sounding slightly mollified. She clamped her lips together, twisting them slightly as she considered his words. 'Well, thank you, then, I suppose. Pity you didn't reveal yourself ten seconds earlier. I'd rather not have had to hit him.'

Simon looked down at the man on the ground. A bruise was already darkening on his chin, and he was moaning, 'Laffy, oh Laffy. I love you, Laffy.'

'You're Laffy, I presume?' Simon murmured, sliding his gaze up to her face. Really, she was quite an attractive little thing, and from this angle the bodice of her gown seemed almost decadently low.

She scowled at him, clearly not appreciating his attempt at subtle humor – and also clearly not realizing that his heavy-lidded gaze had rested on portions of her anatomy that were not her face. 'What are we to do with him?' she asked.

'"We?"' Simon echoed.

Her scowl deepened. 'You did say you aspired to be my rescuer, didn't you?'

'So I did.' Simon planted his hands on his hips and assessed the situation. 'Shall I drag him out into the street?'

'Of course not!' she exclaimed. 'For goodness sake, isn't it still raining outside?'

'My dear Miss Laffy,' Simon said, not particularly concerned about the condescending tone of his voice, 'don't you think your concern is slightly misplaced? This man tried to attack you.'

'He didn't try to attack me,' she replied. 'He just . . .

He just . . . Oh, very well, he tried to attack me. But he would never have done me any real harm.'

Simon raised a brow. Truly, women were the most contrary creatures. 'And you can be sure of that?'

He watched as she carefully chose her words. 'Nigel isn't capable of malice,' she said slowly. 'All he is guilty of is misjudgment.'

'You're a more generous soul than I, then,' Simon said quietly.

The girl let out another sigh, a soft, breathy sound that Simon somehow felt across his entire body. 'Nigel's not a bad person,' she said with quiet dignity. 'It's just that he isn't always terribly bright, and perhaps he mistook kindness on my part for something more.'

Simon felt a strange sort of admiration for this girl. Most women of his acquaintance would have been in hysterics at this point, but she – whoever she was – had taken the situation firmly in hand, and was now displaying a generosity of spirit that was astounding. That she could even think to defend this Nigel person was quite beyond him.

She rose to her feet, dusting her hands off on the sage green silk of her skirts. Her hair had been styled so that one thick lock fell over her shoulder, curling seductively at the top of her breast. Simon knew he should be listening to her – she was prattling on about something, as women were wont to do – but he couldn't seem to take his eyes off that single dark lock of hair. It fell like a silky ribbon across her swanlike neck, and Simon had the most appalling urge to close the distance between them and trace the line of her hair with his lips.

He'd never dallied with an innocent before, but all the world had already painted him a rake. What could be the harm? It wasn't as if he were going to ravish her. Just a kiss. Just one little kiss.

It was tempting, so deliciously, maddeningly tempting.

'Sir! Sir!'

With great reluctance, he dragged his eyes up to her face. Which was, of course, delightful in and of itself, but it was difficult to picture her seduction when she was scowling at him.

'Were you listening to me?'

'Of course,' he lied.

'You weren't.'

'No,' he admitted.

A sound came from the back of her throat that sounded suspiciously like a growl. 'Then why,' she ground out, 'did you say you were?'

He shrugged. 'I thought it was what you wanted to hear.'

Simon watched with fascinated interest as she took a deep breath and muttered something to herself. He couldn't hear her words, but he doubted any of them could be construed as complimentary. Finally, her voice almost comically even, she said, 'If you don't wish to aid me, I'd prefer it if you would just leave.'

Simon decided it was time to stop acting like such a boor, so he said, 'My apologies. Of course I'll help you.'

She exhaled, and then looked back to Nigel, who was still lying on the floor, moaning incoherently. Simon looked down, too, and for several seconds they just stood there, staring at the unconscious man, until the girl said, 'I really didn't hit him very hard.'

'Maybe he's drunk.'

She looked dubious. 'Do you think? I smelled spirits on his breath, but I've never seen him drunk before.'

Simon had nothing to add to that line of thought, so he just asked, 'Well, what do you want to do?'

'I suppose we could just leave him here,' she said, the expression in her dark eyes hesitant.

Simon thought that was an excellent idea, but it was obvious she wanted the idiot cared for in a more tender manner. And heaven help him, but he felt the strangest compulsion to make her happy. 'Here is what we're going to do,' he said crisply, glad that his tone belied any of the odd tenderness he was feeling. 'I am going to summon my carriage—'

'Oh, good,' she interrupted. 'I really didn't want to leave him here. It seemed rather cruel.'

Simon thought it seemed rather generous considering the big oaf had nearly attacked her, but he kept that opinion to himself and instead continued on with his plan. 'You will wait in the library while I'm gone.'

'In the library? But—'

'In the library,' he repeated firmly. 'With the door shut. Do you really want to be discovered with Nigel's body should anyone happen to wander down this hallway?'

'His body? Good gracious, sir, you needn't make it sound as if he were dead.'

'As I was saying,' he continued, ignoring her comment

completely, 'you will remain in the library. When I return, we will relocate Nigel here to my carriage.'

'And how will we do that?'

He gave her a disarmingly lopsided grin. 'I haven't the faintest idea.'

For a moment Daphne forgot to breathe. Just when she'd decided that her would-be rescuer was irredeemingly arrogant, he had to go and smile at her like that. It was one of those boyish grins, the kind that melted female hearts within a ten-mile radius.

And, much to Daphne's dismay, it was awfully hard to remain thoroughly irritated with a man under the influence of such a smile. After growing up with four brothers, all of whom had seemed to know how to charm ladies from birth, Daphne had thought she was immune.

But apparently not. Her chest was tingling, her stomach was turning cartwheels, and her knees felt like melted butter.

'Nigel,' she muttered, desperately trying to force her attention away from the nameless man standing across from her, 'I must see to Nigel.' She crouched down and shook him none too gently by the shoulder. 'Nigel? Nigel? You have to wake up now, Nigel.'

'Daphne,' Nigel moaned. 'Oh, Daphne.'

The dark-haired stranger's head snapped around. 'Daphne? Did he say Daphne?'

She drew back, unnerved by his direct question and the rather intense look in his eyes. 'Yes.'

'Your name is Daphne?'

Now she was beginning to wonder if he was an idiot. 'Yes.'

He groaned. 'Not Daphne Bridgerton.'

Her face slid into a puzzled frown. 'The very one.'

Simon staggered back a step. He suddenly felt physically ill, as his brain finally processed the fact that she had thick, chestnut hair. The famous Bridgerton hair. Not to mention the Bridgerton nose, and cheekbones, and – Bugger it all, this was Anthony's *sister!*

Bloody hell.

There were rules among friends, commandments, really, and the most important one was Thou Shalt Not Lust After Thy Friend's Sister.

While he stood there, probably staring at her like a complete idiot, she planted her hands on her hips, and demanded, 'And who are *you?*'

'Simon Basset,' he muttered.

'The duke?' she squeaked.

He nodded grimly.

'Oh, dear.'

Simon watched with growing horror as the blood drained from her face. 'Good God, woman, you're not going to swoon, are you?' He couldn't imagine why she would, but Anthony – her brother, he reminded himself – had spent half the afternoon warning him about the effects of a young, unmarried duke on the young, unmarried female population. Anthony had specifically singled out Daphne as the exception to the rule, but still, she looked deucedly pale. 'Are you?' he demanded, when she said nothing. 'Going to swoon?'

She looked offended that he'd even considered the notion. 'Of course not!'

'Good.'

'It's just that—'

'What?' Simon asked suspiciously.

'Well,' she said with a rather dainty shrug of her shoulders, 'I've been warned about you.'

This was really too much. 'By whom?' he demanded.

She stared at him as if he were an imbecile. 'By everyone.'

'That, my d—' He felt something suspiciously like a stammer coming on, and so he took a deep breath to steady his tongue. He'd become a master at this kind of control. All she would see was a man who looked as if he were trying to keep his temper in check. And considering the direction of their conversation, that image could not seem terribly far-fetched.

'My dear Miss Bridgerton,' Simon said, starting anew in a more even and controlled tone, 'I find that difficult to believe.'

She shrugged again, and he had the most irritating sensation that she was enjoying his distress. 'Believe what you will,' she said blithely, 'but it was in the paper today.'

'*What?*'

'In *Whistledown,*' she replied, as if that explained anything.

'Whistle-which?'

Daphne stared at him blankly for a moment until she remembered that he was newly returned to London. 'Oh, you must not know about it,' she said softly, a wicked little smile crossing her lips. 'Fancy that.'

The duke took a step forward, his stance positively menacing. 'Miss Bridgerton, I feel I should warn you that I am within an inch of strangling the information out of you.'

'It's a gossip sheet,' she said, hastily backing up a step. 'That's all. It's rather silly, actually, but everyone reads it.'

He said nothing, just arched one arrogant brow.

Daphne quickly added, 'There was a report of your return in Monday's edition.'

'And what' – his eyes narrowed dangerously – 'precisely' – now they turned to ice – 'did it say?'

'Not very much, ah, precisely,' Daphne hedged. She tried to back up a step, but her heels were already pressing against the wall. Any further and she'd be up on her tiptoes. The duke looked beyond furious, and she was beginning to think that she should try for a quick escape and just leave him here with Nigel. The two were perfect for each other – madmen, the both of them!

'Miss Bridgerton.' There was a wealth of warning in his voice.

Daphne decided to take pity on him since, after all, he

was new to town and hadn't had time to adjust to the new world according to *Whistledown*. She supposed she couldn't really blame him for being so upset that he'd been written about in the paper. It had been rather startling for Daphne the first time as well, and she'd at least had the warning of a month's previous *Whistledown* columns. By the time Lady Whistledown got around to writing about Daphne, it had been almost anticlimactic.

'You needn't upset yourself over it,' Daphne said, attempting to lend a little compassion to her voice but probably not succeeding. 'She merely wrote that you were a terrible rake, a fact which I'm sure you won't deny, since I have long since learned that men positively *yearn* to be considered rakes.'

She paused and gave him the opportunity to prove her wrong and deny it. He didn't.

She continued, 'And then my mother, whose acquaintance I gather you must have made at some point or another before you left to travel the world, confirmed it all.'

'Did she?'

Daphne nodded. 'She then forbade me ever to be seen in your company.'

'Really?' he drawled.

Something about the tone of his voice – and the way his eyes seemed to have grown almost smoky as they focused on her face – made her extremely uneasy, and it was all she could do not to shut her eyes.

She refused – absolutely refused – to let him see how he'd affected her.

His lips curved into a slow smile. 'Let me make certain I have this correctly. Your mother told you I am a very bad man and that you are under no circumstances to be seen with me.'

Confused, she nodded.

'Then what,' he asked, pausing for dramatic effect, 'do you think your mother would say about *this* little scenario?'

She blinked. 'I beg your pardon?'

'Well, unless you count Nigel here' – he waved his hand toward the unconscious man on the floor – 'no one has actually *seen* you in my presence. And yet . . . ' He let his words trail off, having far too much fun watching the play of emotions on her face to do anything but drag this moment out to its lengthiest extreme.

Of course most of the emotions on her face were varying shades of irritation and dismay, but that made the moment all the sweeter.

'And yet?' she ground out.

He leaned forward, narrowing the distance between them to only a few inches. 'And yet,' he said softly, knowing that she'd feel his breath on her face, 'here we are, completely alone.'

'Except for Nigel,' she retorted.

Simon spared the man on the floor the briefest of glances before returning his wolfish gaze to Miss Bridgerton. 'I'm not terribly concerned about Nigel,' he murmured. 'Are you?'

Simon watched as she looked down at Nigel in dismay. It had to be clear to her that her spurned suitor wasn't going to save her should Simon decide to make an amorous advance. Not that he would, of course. After all, this was Anthony's younger sister. He might have to remind himself of this at frequent intervals, but it wasn't a fact that was likely to slip his mind on a permanent basis.

Simon knew that it was past time to end this little game. Not that he thought she would report the interlude to Anthony; somehow he knew that she would prefer to keep this to herself, stewing over it in privately righteous fury, and, dare he hope it – just a touch of excitement?

But even as he knew it was time to stop this flirtation and get back to the business of hauling Daphne's idiotic suitor out of the building, he couldn't resist one last comment. Maybe it was the way her lips pursed when she was annoyed. Or maybe it was the way they parted when she was shocked. All he knew was that he was helpless against his own devilish nature when it came to this girl.

And so he leaned forward, his eyes heavy-lidded and seductive as he said, 'I think I know what your mother would say.'

She looked a little befuddled by his onslaught, but still she managed a rather defiant, 'Oh?'

Simon nodded slowly, and he touched one finger to her chin. 'She'd tell you to be very, very afraid.'

There was a moment of utter silence, and then Daphne's eyes grew very wide. Her lips tightened, as if she were keeping something inside, and then her shoulders rose slightly, and then . . .

And then she laughed. Right in his face.

'Oh, my goodness,' she gasped. 'Oh, that was funny.'

Simon was not amused.

'I'm sorry.' This was said between laughs. 'Oh, I'm sorry, but really, you shouldn't be so melodramatic. It doesn't suit you.'

Simon paused, rather irritated that this slip of a girl had shown such disrespect for his authority. There were advantages to being considered a dangerous man, and being able to cow young maidens was supposed to be one of them.

'Well, actually, it does suit you, I ought to admit,' she added, still grinning at his expense. 'You looked quite dangerous. And very handsome, of course.' When he made no comment, her face took on a bemused expression, and she asked, 'That was your intention, was it not?'

He still said nothing, so she said, 'Of course it was. And I would be remiss if I did not tell you that you would have been successful with any other woman besides me.'

A comment he couldn't resist. 'And why is that?'

'Four brothers.' She shrugged as if that should explain everything. 'I'm quite immune to your games.'

'Oh?'

She gave his arm a reassuring pat. 'But yours was a most

admirable attempt. And truly, I'm quite flattered you thought me worthy of such a magnificent display of dukish rakishness.' She grinned, her smile wide and unfeigned. 'Or do you prefer rakish dukishness?'

Simon stroked his jaw thoughtfully, trying to regain his mood of menacing predator. 'You're a most annoying little chit, did you know that, Miss Bridgerton?'

She gave him her sickliest of smiles. 'Most people find me the soul of kindness and amiability.'

'Most people,' Simon said bluntly, 'are fools.'

Daphne cocked her head to the side, obviously pondering his words. Then she looked over at Nigel and sighed. 'I'm afraid I have to agree with you, much as it pains me.'

Simon bit back a smile. 'It pains you to agree with me, or that most people are fools?'

'Both.' She grinned again – a wide, enchanting smile that did odd things to his brain. 'But mostly the former.'

Simon let out a loud laugh, then was startled to realize how foreign the sound was to his ears. He was a man who frequently smiled, occasionally chuckled, but it had been a very long time since he'd felt such a spontaneous burst of joy. 'My dear Miss Bridgerton,' he said, wiping his eyes, 'if you are the soul of kindness and amiability, then the world must be a very dangerous place.'

'Oh, for certain,' she replied. 'At least to hear my mother tell it.'

'I can't imagine why I do not recall your mother,' Simon murmured, 'because she certainly sounds a memorable character.'

Daphne raised a brow. 'You don't remember her?'

He shook his head.

'Then you don't know her.'

'Does she look like you?'

'That's an odd question.'

'Not so very odd,' Simon replied, thinking that Daphne was exactly right. It was an odd question, and he had no idea why he'd voiced it. But since he had, and since she had questioned it, he added, 'After all, I'm told that all of you Bridgertons look alike.'

A tiny, and to Simon mysterious, frown touched her face. 'We do. Look alike, that is. Except for my mother. She's rather fair, actually, with blue eyes. We all get our dark hair from our father. I'm told I have her smile, though.'

An awkward pause fell across the conversation. Daphne was shifting from foot to foot, not at all certain what to say to the duke, when Nigel exhibited stellar timing for the first time in his life, and sat up. 'Daphne?' he said, blinking as if he couldn't see straight. 'Daphne, is that you?'

'Good God, Miss Bridgerton,' the duke swore, 'how hard did you hit him?'

'Hard enough to knock him down, but no worse than that, I swear!' Her brow furrowed. 'Maybe he is drunk.'

'Oh, Daphne,' Nigel moaned.

The duke crouched next to him, then reeled back, coughing.

'Is he drunk?' Daphne asked.

The duke staggered back. 'He must have drunk an entire bottle of whiskey just to get up the nerve to propose.'

'Who would have thought I could be so terrifying?' Daphne murmured, thinking of all the men who thought of her as a jolly good friend and nothing more. 'How wonderful.'

Simon stared at her as if she were insane, then muttered, 'I'm not even going to question that statement.'

Daphne ignored his comment. 'Should we set our plan into action?'

Simon planted his hands on his hips and reassessed the scene. Nigel was trying to rise to his feet, but it didn't appear, to Simon's eye at least, that he was going to find success anytime in the near future. Still, he was probably lucid enough to make trouble, and certainly lucid enough to make noise, which he was doing. Quite well, actually.

'Oh, Daphne. I luff you so much, Daffery.' Nigel managed

to raise himself to his knees, weaving around as he shuffled toward Daphne, looking rather like a sotted churchgoer attempting to pray. 'Please marry me, Duffne. You have to.'

'Buck up, man,' Simon grunted, grabbing him by the collar. 'This is getting embarrassing.' He turned to Daphne. 'I'm going to have to take him outside now. We can't leave him here in the hall. He's liable to start moaning like a sickened cow—'

'I rather thought he'd already started,' Daphne said.

Simon felt one corner of his mouth twist up in a reluctant smile. Daphne Bridgerton might be a marriageable female and thus a disaster waiting to happen for any man in his position, but she was certainly a good sport.

She was, it occurred to him in a rather bizarre moment of clarity, the sort of person he'd probably call friend if she were a man.

But since it was abundantly obvious – to both his eyes and his body – that she wasn't a man, Simon decided it was in both of their best interests to wrap up this 'situation' as soon as possible. Aside from the fact that Daphne's reputation would suffer a deadly blow if they were discovered, Simon wasn't positive that he could trust himself to keep his hands off of her for very much longer.

It was an unsettling feeling, that. Especially for a man who so valued his self-control. Control was everything. Without it he'd never have stood up to his father or taken a first at university. Without it, he'd—

Without it, he thought grimly, he'd still be speaking like an idiot.

'I'll haul him out of here,' he said suddenly. 'You go back to the ballroom.'

Daphne frowned, glancing over her shoulder to the hall that led back to the party. 'Are you certain? I thought you wanted me to go to the library.'

'That was when we were going to leave him here while I summoned the carriage. But we can't do that if he's awake.'

She nodded her agreement, and asked, 'Are you sure you can do it? Nigel's a rather large man.'

'I'm larger.'

She cocked her head. The duke, although lean, was powerfully built, with broad shoulders and firmly muscled thighs. (Daphne knew she wasn't supposed to notice such things, but, really, was it her fault that current fashions dictated such snug breeches?) More to the point, he had a certain air about him, something almost predatory, something that hinted of tightly controlled strength and power.

Daphne decided she had no doubt that he'd be able to move Nigel.

'Very well,' she said, giving him a nod. 'And thank you. It's very kind of you to help me in this way.'

'I'm rarely kind,' he muttered.

'Really?' she murmured, allowing herself a tiny smile. 'How odd. I couldn't possibly think of anything else to call it. But then again, I've learned that men—'

'You do seem to be the expert on men,' he said, somewhat acerbically, then grunted as he hauled Nigel to his feet.

Nigel promptly reached for Daphne, practically sobbing her name. Simon had to brace his legs to keep him from lunging at her.

Daphne darted back a step. 'Yes, well, I do have four brothers. A better education I cannot imagine.'

There was no way of knowing if the duke had intended to answer her, because Nigel chose that moment to regain his energy (although clearly not his equilibrium) and yanked himself free of Simon's grip. He threw himself onto Daphne, making incoherent, drunken noises all the way.

If Daphne hadn't had her back to the wall, she would have been knocked to the ground. As it was, she hit the wall with a bone-jarring thud, knocking all the breath from her body.

'Oh, for the love of Christ,' the duke swore, sounding

supremely disgusted. He hauled Nigel off Daphne, then turned to her, and asked, 'Can I hit him?'

'Oh, please do go ahead,' she replied, still gasping for breath. She'd tried to be kind and generous toward her erstwhile suitor, but really, enough was enough.

The duke muttered something that sounded like 'good' and landed a stunningly powerful blow on Nigel's chin.

Nigel went down like a stone.

Daphne regarded the man on the floor with equanimity. 'I don't think he's going to wake up this time.'

Simon shook out his fist. 'No.'

Daphne blinked and looked back up. 'Thank you.'

'It was my pleasure,' he said, scowling at Nigel.

'What shall we do now?' Her gaze joined his on the man on the floor – now well and truly unconscious.

'Back to the original plan,' he said crisply. 'We leave him here while you wait in the library. I'd rather not have to drag him out until I've a carriage waiting.'

Daphne gave him a sensible nod. 'Do you need help righting him, or should I proceed directly to the library?'

The duke was silent for a moment. His head tilted this way and that as he analyzed Nigel's position on the floor. 'Actually, a bit of help would be greatly appreciated.'

'Really?' Daphne asked, surprised. 'I was sure you'd say no.'

That earned her a faintly amused and superior look from the duke. 'And is that why you asked?'

'No, of course not,' Daphne replied, slightly offended. 'I'm not so stupid as to offer help if I have no intention of giving it. I was merely going to point out that men, in my experience—'

'You have too much experience,' the duke muttered under his breath.

'What?!'

'I beg your pardon,' he amended. 'You think you have too much experience.'

Daphne glared at him, her dark eyes smoldering nearly to black. 'That is not true, and who are you to say, anyway?'

'No, that's not quite right, either,' the duke mused, completely ignoring her furious question. 'I think it's more that I think you think you have too much experience.'

'Why you – You – ' As retorts went, it wasn't especially effective, but it was all Daphne could manage to get out. Her powers of speech tended to fail her when she was angry.

And she was really angry.

Simon shrugged, apparently unmoved by her furious visage. 'My dear Miss Bridgerton—'

'If you call me that one more time, I swear I shall scream.'

'No, you won't,' he said with a rakish smile. 'That would draw a crowd, and if you recall, you don't want to be seen with me.'

'I am considering risking it,' Daphne said, each word squeezed out between her teeth.

Simon crossed his arms and leaned lazily against the wall. 'Really?' he drawled. 'This I should like to see.'

Daphne nearly threw up her arms in frustration. 'Forget it. Forget me. Forget this entire evening. I'm leaving.'

She turned around, but before she could even take a step, her movement was arrested by the sound of the duke's voice.

'I thought you were going to help me.'

Drat. He had her there. She turned slowly around. 'Why, yes,' she said, her voice patently false, 'I'd be delighted.'

'You know,' he said innocently, 'if you didn't want to help you shouldn't have—'

'I said I'd help,' she snapped.

Simon smiled to himself. She was such an easy mark. 'Here is what we are going to do,' he said. 'I'm going to haul him to his feet and drape his right arm over my shoulders. You will go around to the other side and shore him up.'

Daphne did as she was bid, grumbling to herself about his autocratic attitude. But she didn't voice a single complaint. After all, for all his annoying ways, the Duke of Hastings was helping her out of a possibly embarrassing scandal.

Of course if anyone found her in this position, she'd find herself in even worse straits.

'I have a better idea,' she said suddenly. 'Let's just leave him here.'

The duke's head swung around to face her, and he looked as if he'd dearly like to toss her through a window – preferably one that was still closed. 'I thought,' he said, clearly working hard to keep his voice even, 'that you didn't want to leave him on the floor.'

'That was before he knocked me into the wall.'

'Could you possibly have notified me of your change of heart before I expended my energy to lift him?'

Daphne blushed. She hated that men thought that women were fickle, changeable creatures, and she hated even more that she was living up to that image right then.

'Very well,' he said simply, and dropped Nigel.

The sudden weight of him nearly took Daphne down to the floor as well. She let out a surprised squeal as she ducked out of the way.

'Now may we leave?' the duke asked, sounding insufferably patient.

She nodded hesitantly, glancing down at Nigel. 'He looks rather uncomfortable, don't you think?'

Simon stared at her. Just stared at her. 'You're concerned for his comfort?' he finally asked.

She gave her head a nervous shake, then a nod, then went back to the shake. 'Maybe I should – That is to say – Here, just wait a moment.' She crouched and untwisted Nigel's legs so he lay flat on his back. 'I didn't think he deserved a trip home in your carriage,' she explained as she rearranged his coat, 'but it seemed rather cruel to leave him here in this position. There, now I'm done.' She stood and looked up.

And just managed to catch sight of the duke as he walked away, muttering something about Daphne and something about women in general and something else entirely that Daphne didn't quite catch.

But maybe that was for the best. She rather doubted it had been a compliment.

4

London is awash these days with Ambitious Mamas. At Lady Worth's ball last week This Author saw no fewer than eleven Determined Bachelors, cowering in corners and eventually fleeing the premises with those Ambitious Mamas hot on their heels.

It is difficult to determine who, precisely, is the worst of the lot, although This Author suspects the contest may come down to a near draw between Lady Bridgerton and Mrs. Featherington, with Mrs. F edging Lady B out by a nose. There are three Featherington misses on the market right now, after all, whereas Lady Bridgerton need only worry about one.

It is recommended, however, that all safety-minded people stay far, far away from the latest crop of unmarried men when Bridgerton daughters E, F, and H come of age. Lady B is not likely to look both ways when she barrels across a ballroom with three daughters in tow, and the Lord help us all should she decide to don metal-toed boots.

LADY WHISTLEDOWN'S SOCIETY PAPERS,
28 APRIL 1813

The night, Simon decided, couldn't possibly get much worse. He wouldn't have believed it at the time, but his bizarre encounter with Daphne Bridgerton was definitely turning out to be the evening's high point. Yes, he'd been horrified to discover that he'd been lusting – even briefly – after his best friend's younger sister. Yes, Nigel Berbrooke's oafish attempts at seduction had offended every one of his rakish sensibilities. And yes, Daphne had finally exasperated him beyond endurance with her indecision over whether to treat Nigel like a criminal or care for him as she would her dearest friend.

But none of that – not one bit – compared to the torture that he'd been about to endure.

His oh-so-clever plan of slipping into the ballroom, giving his regards to Lady Danbury, and leaving unnoticed had fallen into instant ruin. He'd taken no more than two steps into the ballroom when he'd been recognized by an old friend from Oxford, who, much to Simon's dismay, had recently married. The wife was a perfectly charming young woman, but unfortunately one with rather high social aspirations, and she had quickly determined that her road to happiness lay in her position as the one to introduce the new duke to society. And Simon, even though he fancied himself a world-weary, cynical sort, discovered that he wasn't quite rude enough to directly insult the wife of his old university friend.

And so, two hours later, he'd been introduced to every unmarried lady at the ball, *every* mother of every unmarried lady at the ball, and, of course, every older married sister of every unmarried lady at the ball. Simon couldn't decide which set of women was the worst. The unmarried ladies were decidedly boring, the mothers were annoyingly ambitious, and the *sisters* – well, the sisters were so forward Simon began to wonder if he'd stumbled into a brothel. Six of them had made extremely suggestive remarks, two had slipped him notes inviting him to their boudoirs, and one had actually run her hand down his thigh.

In retrospect, Daphne Bridgerton was starting to look very good, indeed.

And speaking of Daphne, where the hell was she? He'd thought he'd caught a glimpse of her about an hour earlier, surrounded by her rather large and forbidding brothers. (Not that Simon found them individually forbidding, but he'd quickly decided that any man would have to be an imbecile to provoke them as a group.)

But since then she seemed to have disappeared. Indeed, he thought she might have been the only unmarried female at the party to whom he *hadn't* been introduced.

Simon wasn't particularly worried about her being bothered by Berbrooke after he'd left them in the hall. He'd delivered a solid punch to the man's jaw and had no doubt that he'd be out for several minutes. Probably longer, considering the vast quantities of alcohol Berbrooke had consumed earlier in the evening. And even if Daphne had been foolishly tenderhearted when it came to her clumsy suitor, she wasn't stupid enough to remain in the hallway with him until he woke up.

Simon glanced back over to the corner where the Bridgerton brothers were gathered, looking as if they were having a grand old time. They had been accosted by almost as many young women and old mothers as Simon, but at least there seemed to be some safety in numbers. Simon noticed that the young debutantes didn't seem to spend half as much time in the Bridgertons' company as they did in his.

Simon sent an irritated scowl in their direction.

Anthony, who was leaning lazily against a wall, caught the expression and smirked, raising a glass of red wine in his direction. Then he cocked his head slightly, motioning to Simon's left. Simon turned, just in time to be detained by yet another mother, this one with a trio of daughters, all of whom were dressed in monstrously fussy frocks, replete with tucks and flounces, and of course, heaps and heaps of lace.

He thought of Daphne, with her simple sage green gown. Daphne, with her direct brown eyes and wide smile . . .

'Your grace!' the mother shrilled. 'Your grace!'

Simon blinked to clear his vision. The lace-covered family

had managed to surround him with such efficiency that he wasn't even able to shoot a glare in Anthony's direction.

'Your grace,' the mother repeated, 'it is such an honor to make your acquaintance.'

Simon managed a frosty nod. Words were quite beyond him. The family of females had pressed in so close he feared he might suffocate.

'Georgiana Huxley sent us over,' the woman persisted. 'She said I simply must introduce my daughters to you.'

Simon didn't remember who Georgiana Huxley was, but he thought he might like to strangle her.

'Normally I should not be so bold,' the woman went on, 'but your dear, dear papa was such a friend of mine.'

Simon stiffened.

'He was truly a marvelous man,' she continued, her voice like nails to Simon's skull, 'so conscious of his duties to the title. He must have been a marvelous father.'

'I wouldn't know,' Simon bit off.

'Oh!' The woman had to clear her throat several times before managing to say, 'I see. Well. My goodness.'

Simon said nothing, hoping an aloof demeanor would prompt her to take her leave. Damn it, where was Anthony? It was bad enough having these women acting as if he were some prize horse to be bred, but to have to stand here and listen to this woman tell him what a good father the old duke had been . . .

Simon couldn't possibly bear it.

'Your grace! Your grace!'

Simon forced his icy eyes back to the lady in front of him and told himself to be more patient with her. After all, she was probably only complimenting his father because she thought it was what he wanted to hear.

'I merely wanted to remind you,' she said, 'that we were introduced several years ago, back when you were still Clyvedon.'

'Yes,' Simon murmured, looking for any break in the

barricade of ladies through which he might make his escape.

'These are my daughters,' the woman said, motioning to the three young ladies. Two were pleasant-looking, but the third was still cloaked in baby fat and an orangey gown which did nothing for her complexion. She didn't appear to be enjoying the evening.

'Aren't they lovely?' the lady continued. 'My pride and joy. And so even-tempered.'

Simon had the queasy feeling that he'd heard the same words once when shopping for a dog.

'Your grace, may I present Prudence, Philipa, and Penelope.'

The girls made their curtsies, not a one of them daring to meet his eye.

'I have another daughter at home,' the lady continued. 'Felicity. But she's a mere ten years of age, so I do not bring her to such events.'

Simon could not imagine why she felt the need to share this information with him, but he just kept his tone carefully bored (this, he'd long since learned, was the best way not to show anger) and prompted, 'And you are . . . ?'

'Oh, beg pardon! I am Mrs. Featherington, of course. My husband passed on three years ago, but he was your papa's, er, dearest friend.' Her voice trailed off at the end of her sentence, as she remembered Simon's last reaction to mention of his father.

Simon nodded curtly.

'Prudence is quite accomplished on the pianoforte,' Mrs. Featherington said, with forced brightness.

Simon noted the oldest girl's pained expression and quickly decided never to attend a musicale chez Featherington.

'And my darling Philipa is an expert watercolorist.'

Philipa beamed.

'And Penelope?' some devil inside Simon forced him to ask.

Mrs. Featherington shot a panicked look at her youngest

daughter, who looked quite miserable. Penelope was not terribly attractive, and her somewhat pudgy figure was not improved by her mother's choice of attire for her. But she seemed to have kind eyes.

'Penelope?' Mrs. Featherington echoed, her voice a touch shrill. 'Penelope is . . . ah . . . well, she's Penelope!' Her mouth wobbled into a patently false grin.

Penelope looked as if she wanted to dive under a rug. Simon decided that if he was forced to dance, he'd ask Penelope.

'Mrs. Featherington,' came a sharp and imperious voice that could only belong to Lady Danbury, 'are you pestering the duke?'

Simon wanted to answer in the affirmative, but the memory of Penelope Featherington's mortified face led him to murmur, 'Of course not.'

Lady Danbury raised a brow as she moved her head slowly toward him. 'Liar.'

She turned back to Mrs. Featherington, who had gone quite green. Mrs. Featherington said nothing. Lady Danbury said nothing. Mrs. Featherington finally mumbled something about seeing her cousin, grabbed her three daughters, and scurried off.

Simon crossed his arms, but he wasn't able to keep his face completely free of amusement. 'That wasn't very well done of you,' he said.

'Bah. She's feathers for brains, and so do her girls, except maybe that unattractive young one.' Lady Danbury shook her head. 'If they'd only put her in a different color . . . '

Simon fought a chuckle and lost. 'You never did learn to mind your own business, did you?'

'Never. And what fun would that be?' She smiled. Simon could tell she didn't want to, but she smiled. 'And as for you,' she continued. 'You are a monstrous guest. One would have thought you'd possess the manners to greet your hostess by now.'

'You were always too well surrounded by your admirers for me to dare even approach.'

'So glib,' she commented.

Simon said nothing, not entirely certain how to interpret her words. He'd always had the suspicion that she knew his secret, but he'd never been quite sure.

'Your friend Bridgerton approaches,' she said.

Simon's eyes followed the direction of her nod. Anthony ambled over, and was only half a second in their presence before Lady Danbury called him a coward.

Anthony blinked. 'I beg your pardon?'

'You could have come over and saved your friend from the Featherington quartet ages ago.'

'But I was so enjoying his distress.'

'Hmmph.' And without another word (or another grunt) she walked away.

'Strangest old woman,' Anthony said. 'I wouldn't be surprised if she's that cursed Whistledown woman.'

'You mean the gossip columnist?'

Anthony nodded as he led Simon around a potted plant to the corner where his brothers were waiting. As they walked, Anthony grinned, and said, 'I noticed you speaking with a number of very proper young ladies.'

Simon muttered something rather obscene and unflattering under his breath.

But Anthony only laughed. 'You can't say I didn't warn you, can you?'

'It is galling to admit that you might be right about anything, so please do not ask me to do so.'

Anthony laughed some more. 'For that comment I shall start introducing you to the debutantes myself.'

'If you do,' Simon warned, 'you shall soon find yourself dying a very slow and painful death.'

Anthony grinned. 'Swords or pistols?'

'Oh, poison. Very definitely poison.'

'Ouch.' Anthony stopped his stroll across the ballroom

in front of two other Bridgerton men, both clearly marked by their chestnut hair, tall height, and excellent bone structure. Simon noted that one had green eyes and the other brown like Anthony, but other than that, the dim evening light made the three men practically interchangeable.

'You do remember my brothers?' Anthony queried politely. 'Benedict and Colin. Benedict I'm sure you recall from Eton. He was the one who dogged our footsteps for three months when he first arrived.'

'Not true!' Benedict said with a laugh.

'I don't know if you've met Colin, actually,' Anthony continued. 'He was probably too young to have crossed your path.'

'Pleased to meet you,' Colin said jovially.

Simon noted the rascally glint in the young man's green eyes and couldn't help but smile in return.

'Anthony here has said such insulting things about you,' Colin continued, his grin growing quite wicked, 'that I know we're sure to be great friends.'

Anthony rolled his eyes. 'I'm certain you can understand why my mother is convinced that Colin will be the first of her children to drive her to insanity.'

Colin said, 'I pride myself on it, actually.'

'Mother, thankfully, has had a brief respite from Colin's tender charms,' Anthony continued. 'He is actually just returned from a grand tour of the Continent.'

'Just this evening,' Colin said with a boyish grin. He had a devil-may-care youthful look about him. Simon decided he couldn't be much older than Daphne.

'I have just returned from travels as well,' Simon said.

'Yes, except yours spanned the globe, I hear,' Colin said. 'I should love to hear about them someday.'

Simon nodded politely. 'Certainly.'

'Have you met Daphne?' Benedict inquired. 'She's the only Bridgerton in attendance who's unaccounted for.'

Simon was pondering how best to answer that question

when Colin let out a snort, and said, 'Oh, Daphne's accounted for. Miserable, but accounted for.'

Simon followed his gaze across the ballroom, where Daphne was standing next to what had to be her mother, looking, just as Colin had promised, as miserable as could be.

And then it occurred to him – Daphne was one of those dreaded unmarried young ladies being paraded about by her mother. She'd seemed far too sensible and forthright to be such a creature, and yet of course that was what she had to be. She couldn't have been more than twenty, and as her name was still Bridgerton she was clearly a maiden. And since she had a mother – well, of course she'd be trapped into an endless round of introductions.

She looked every bit as pained by the experience as Simon had been. Somehow that made him feel a good deal better.

'One of us should save her,' Benedict mused.

'Nah,' Colin said, grinning. 'Mother's only had her over there with Macclesfield for ten minutes.'

'Macclesfield?' Simon asked.

'The earl,' Benedict replied. 'Castleford's son.'

'Ten minutes?' Anthony asked. 'Poor Macclesfield.'

Simon shot him a curious look.

'Not that Daphne is such a chore,' Anthony quickly added, 'but when Mother gets it in her head to, ah . . .'

'Pursue,' Benedict filled in helpfully.

'—a gentleman,' Anthony continued with a nod of thanks toward his brother, 'she can be, ah . . . '

'Relentless,' Colin said.

Anthony smiled weakly. 'Yes. Exactly.'

Simon looked back over toward the trio in question. Sure enough, Daphne looked miserable, Macclesfield was scanning the room, presumably looking for the nearest exit, and Lady Bridgerton's eyes held a gleam so ambitious that Simon cringed in sympathy for the young earl.

'We should save Daphne,' Anthony said.

'We really should,' Benedict added.

'And Macclesfield,' Anthony said.

'Oh, certainly,' Benedict added.

But Simon noticed that no one was leaping into action.

'All talk, aren't you?' Colin chortled.

'I don't see *you* marching over there to save her,' Anthony shot back.

'Hell no. But I never said we should. *You,* on the other hand . . . '

'What the devil is going on?' Simon finally asked.

The three Bridgerton brothers looked at him with identical guilty expressions.

'We *should* save Daff,' Benedict said.

'We really should,' Anthony added.

'What my brothers are too lily-livered to tell you,' Colin said derisively, 'is that they are terrified of my mother.'

'It's true,' Anthony said with a helpless shrug.

Benedict nodded. 'I freely admit it.'

Simon thought he'd never seen a more ludicrous sight. These were the Bridgerton brothers, after all. Tall, handsome, athletic, with every miss in the nation setting her cap after them, and here they were, completely cowed by a mere slip of a woman.

Of course, it was their mother. Simon supposed one had to make allowances for that.

'If I save Daff,' Anthony explained, 'Mother might get me into her clutches, and then I'm done for.'

Simon choked on laughter as his mind filled with a vision of Anthony being led around by his mother, moving from unmarried lady to unmarried lady.

'Now you see why I avoid these functions like the plague,' Anthony said grimly. 'I'm attacked from both directions. If the debutantes and their mothers don't find me, *my* mother makes certain I find *them.*'

'Say!' Benedict exclaimed. 'Why don't *you* save her, Hastings?'

Simon took one look at Lady Bridgerton (who at that point had her hand firmly wrapped around Macclesfield's forearm) and decided he'd rather be branded an eternal coward. 'Since we haven't been introduced, I'm sure it would be most improper,' he improvised.

'I'm sure it wouldn't,' Anthony returned. 'You're a duke.'

'So?'

'So?' Anthony echoed. 'Mother would forgive any impropriety if it meant gaining an audience for Daphne with a duke.'

'Now look here,' Simon said hotly, 'I'm not some sacrificial lamb to be slaughtered on the altar of your mother.'

'You *have* spent a lot of time in Africa, haven't you?' Colin quipped.

Simon ignored him. 'Besides, your sister said—'

All three Bridgerton heads swung round in his direction. Simon immediately realized he'd blundered. Badly.

'You've met Daphne?' Anthony queried, his voice just a touch too polite for Simon's comfort.

Before Simon could even reply, Benedict leaned in ever-so-slightly closer, and asked, 'Why didn't you mention this?'

'Yes,' Colin said, his mouth utterly serious for the first time that evening. 'Why?'

Simon glanced from brother to brother and it became perfectly clear why Daphne must still be unmarried. This belligerent trio would scare off all but the most determined – or stupid – of suitors.

Which would probably explain Nigel Berbrooke.

'Actually,' Simon said, 'I bumped into her in the hall as I was making my way into the ballroom. It was' – he glanced rather pointedly at the Bridgertons – 'rather obvious that she was a member of your family, so I introduced myself.'

Anthony turned to Benedict. 'Must have been when she was fleeing Berbrooke.'

Benedict turned to Colin. 'What did happen to Berbrooke? Do you know?'

Colin shrugged. 'Haven't the faintest. Probably left to nurse his broken heart.'

Or broken head, Simon thought acerbically.

'Well, that explains everything, I'm sure,' Anthony said, losing his overbearing big-brother expression and looking once again like a fellow rake and best friend.

'Except,' Benedict said suspiciously, 'why he didn't mention it.'

'Because I didn't have the chance,' Simon bit off, about ready to throw his arms up in exasperation. 'In case you hadn't noticed, Anthony, you have a ridiculous number of siblings, and it takes a ridiculous amount of time to be introduced to all of them.'

'There are only two of us present,' Colin pointed out.

'I'm going home,' Simon announced. 'The three of you are mad.'

Benedict, who had seemed to be the most protective of the brothers, suddenly grinned. 'You don't have a sister, do you?'

'No, thank God.'

'If you ever have a daughter, you'll understand.'

Simon was rather certain he would never have a daughter, but he kept his mouth shut.

'It can be a trial,' Anthony said.

'Although Daff is better than most,' Benedict put in. 'She doesn't have that many suitors, actually.'

Simon couldn't imagine why not.

'I'm not really sure why,' Anthony mused. 'I think she's a perfectly nice girl.'

Simon decided this wasn't the time to mention that he'd been one inch away from easing her up against the wall, pressing his hips against hers, and kissing her senseless. If he hadn't discovered that she was a Bridgerton, frankly, he might have done exactly that.

'Daff's the best,' Benedict agreed.

Colin nodded. 'Capital girl. Really good sport.'

There was an awkward pause, and then Simon said, 'Well, good sport or not, I'm not going over there to save her, because she told me quite specifically that your mother forbade her ever to be seen in my presence.'

'Mother said *that?*' Colin asked. 'You must really have a black reputation.'

'A good portion of it undeserved,' Simon muttered, not entirely certain why he was defending himself.

'That's too bad,' Colin murmured. 'I'd thought to ask you to take me 'round.'

Simon foresaw a long and terrifyingly roguish future for the boy.

Anthony's fist found its way to the small of Simon's back, and he started to propel him forward. 'I'm sure Mother will change her mind given the proper encouragement. Let's go.'

Simon had no choice but to walk toward Daphne. The alternative required making a really big scene, and Simon had long since learned that he didn't do well with scenes. Besides, if he'd been in Anthony's position, he probably would have done the exact same thing.

And after an evening with the Featherington sisters and the like, Daphne didn't sound half-bad.

'Mother!' Anthony called out in a jovial voice as they approached the viscountess. 'I haven't seen you all evening.'

Simon noticed that Lady Bridgerton's blue eyes lit up when she saw her son approaching. Ambitious Mama or not, Lady Bridgerton clearly loved her children.

'Anthony!' she said in return. 'How nice to see you. Daphne and I were just chatting with Lord Macclesfield.'

Anthony sent Lord Macclesfield a commiserating look. 'Yes, I see.'

Simon caught Daphne's eye for a moment and gave his

head the tiniest shake. She responded with an even tinier nod, sensible girl that she was.

'And who is this?' Lady Bridgerton inquired, her eyes lighting upon Simon's face.

'The new Duke of Hastings,' Anthony replied. 'Surely you remember him from my days at Eton and Oxford.'

'Of course,' Lady Bridgerton said politely.

Macclesfield, who had been keeping scrupulously quiet, quickly located the first lull in the conversation, and burst in with, 'I think I see my father.'

Anthony shot the young earl an amused and knowing glance. 'Then by all means, go to him.'

The young earl did, with alacrity.

'I thought he detested his father,' Lady Bridgerton said with a confused expression.

'He does,' Daphne said baldly.

Simon choked down a laugh. Daphne raised her brows, silently daring him to comment.

'Well, he had a terrible reputation, anyway,' Lady Bridgerton said.

'There seems to be quite a bit of that in the air these days,' Simon murmured.

Daphne's eyes widened, and this time Simon got to raise *his* brows, silently daring *her* to comment.

She didn't, of course, but her mother gave him a sharp look, and Simon had the distinct impression that she was trying to decide whether his newly acquired dukedom made up for his bad reputation.

'I don't believe I had the chance to make your acquaintance before I left the country, Lady Bridgerton,' Simon said smoothly, 'but I am very pleased to do so now.'

'As am I.' She motioned to Daphne. 'My daughter Daphne.'

Simon took Daphne's gloved hand and laid a scrupulously polite kiss on her knuckles. 'I am honored to officially make your acquaintance, Miss Bridgerton.'

'Officially?' Lady Bridgerton queried.

Daphne opened her mouth, but Simon cut in before she could say anything. 'I already told your brother about our *brief* meeting earlier this evening.'

Lady Bridgerton's head turned rather sharply in Daphne's direction. 'You were introduced to the duke earlier this evening? Why did you not say anything?'

Daphne smiled tightly. 'We were rather occupied with the earl. And before that, with Lord Westborough. And before that, with—'

'I see your point, Daphne,' Lady Bridgerton ground out.

Simon wondered how unforgivably rude it would be if he laughed.

Then Lady Bridgerton turned the full force of her smile on him – and Simon quickly learned where Daphne got that wide, wide smile from – and Simon realized that Lady Bridgerton had decided that his bad reputation could be overlooked.

A strange light appeared in her eye, and her head bobbed back and forth between Daphne and Simon.

Then she smiled again.

Simon fought the urge to flee.

Anthony leaned over slightly, and whispered in his ear, 'I am *so* sorry.'

Simon said between clenched teeth, 'I may have to kill you.'

Daphne's icicle glare said that she'd heard both of them and was not amused.

But Lady Bridgerton was blissfully oblivious, her head presumably already filling with images of a grand wedding.

Then her eyes narrowed as she focused on something behind the men. She looked so overwhelmingly annoyed that Simon, Anthony, and Daphne all twisted their necks to see what was afoot.

Mrs. Featherington was marching purposefully in their direction, Prudence and Philipa right behind. Simon noticed that Penelope was nowhere to be seen.

Desperate times, Simon quickly realized, called for desperate measures. 'Miss Bridgerton,' he said, whipping his head around to face Daphne, 'would you care to dance?'

5

Were you at Lady Danbury's ball last night? If not, shame on you. You missed witnessing quite the most remarkable coup of the season. It was clear to all partygoers, and especially to This Author, that Miss Daphne Bridgerton has captured the interest of the newly returned to England Duke of Hastings.

One can only imagine the relief of Lady Bridgerton. How mortifying it will be if Daphne remains on the shelf for yet another season! And Lady B – with three more daughters to marry off. Oh, the horror.

LADY WHISTLEDOWN'S SOCIETY PAPERS,
30 APRIL 1813

There was no way Daphne could refuse.

First of all, her mother was impaling her with her deadly I-Am-Your-Mother-Don't-You-Dare-Defy-Me gaze.

Secondly, the duke had clearly not given Anthony the entire story of their meeting in the dimly lit hallway; to make a show of refusing to dance with him would certainly raise undue speculation.

Not to mention that Daphne really didn't particularly relish getting drawn into a conversation with the Featheringtons, which was sure to happen if she didn't make immediate haste for the dance floor.

And finally, she kind of sort of just a little teeny bit actually *wanted to* dance with the duke.

Of course the arrogant boor didn't even give her the

chance to accept. Before Daphne could manage an 'I'd be delighted,' or even a mere, 'Yes,' he had her halfway across the room.

The orchestra was still producing those awful noises it makes while the musicians were getting ready to begin, so they were forced to wait a moment before they actually danced.

'Thank God you didn't refuse,' the duke said with great feeling.

'When would I have had the opportunity?'

He grinned at her.

Daphne answered that with a scowl. 'I wasn't given the opportunity to accept, either, if you recall.'

He raised a brow. 'Does that mean I must ask you again?'

'No, of course not,' Daphne replied, rolling her eyes. 'That would be rather childish of me, don't you think? And besides, it would cause a terrible scene, which I don't think either of us desires.'

He cocked his head and gave her a rather assessing glance, as if he had analyzed her personality in an instant and decided she might just be acceptable. Daphne found the experience somewhat unnerving.

Just then the orchestra ceased its discordant warm-up and struck the first notes of a waltz.

Simon groaned. 'Do young ladies still need permission to waltz?'

Daphne found herself smiling at his discomfort. 'How long have you been away?'

'Five years. Do they?'

'Yes.'

'Do you have it?' He looked almost pained at the prospect of his escape plan falling apart.

'Of course.'

He swept her into his arms and whirled her into the throng of elegantly clad couples. 'Good.'

They had made a full circle of the ballroom before Daphne

asked, 'How much of our meeting did you reveal to my brothers? I saw you with them, you know.'

Simon only smiled.

'What are you grinning about?' she asked suspiciously.

'I was merely marveling at your restraint.'

'I beg your pardon?'

He shrugged slightly, his shoulders rising as his head tilted to the right. 'I hadn't thought you the most patient of ladies,' he said, 'and here it took you a full three and a half minutes before asking me about my conversation with your brothers.'

Daphne fought a blush. The truth was, the duke was a most accomplished dancer, and she'd been enjoying the waltz too much even to think of conversation.

'But since you asked,' he said, mercifully sparing her from having to make a comment, 'all I told them was that I ran into you in the hall and that, given your coloring, I instantly recognized you as a Bridgerton and introduced myself.'

'Do you think they believed you?'

'Yes,' he said softly, 'I rather think they did.'

'Not that we have anything to hide,' she added quickly.

'Of course not.'

'If there is any villain in this piece it is most certainly Nigel.'

'Of course.'

She chewed on her lower lip. 'Do you think he's still out in the hall?'

'I certainly have no intention of finding out.'

There was an awkward moment of silence, and then Daphne said, 'It has been some time since you have attended a London ball, has it not? Nigel and I must have been quite a welcome.'

'You were a welcome sight. He was not.'

She smiled slightly at the compliment. 'Aside from our little escapade, have you been enjoying your evening?'

Simon's answer was so unequivocally in the negative that he actually snorted a laugh before saying it.

'Really?' Daphne replied, her brows arching with curiosity. 'Now *that* is interesting.'

'You find my agony interesting? Remind me never to turn to you should I ever fall ill.'

'Oh, please,' she scoffed. 'It can't have been that bad.'

'Oh, it can.'

'Certainly not as bad as *my* evening.'

'You did look rather miserable with your mother and Macclesfield,' he allowed.

'How kind of you to point it out,' she muttered.

'But I still think my evening was worse.'

Daphne laughed, a light musical sound that warmed Simon's bones. 'What a sad pair we are,' she said. 'Surely we can manage a conversation on a topic other than our respective terrible evenings.'

Simon said nothing.

Daphne said nothing.

'Well, I can't think of anything,' he said.

Daphne laughed again, this time with more gaiety, and Simon once again found himself mesmerized by her smile.

'I give in,' she gasped. 'What has turned your evening into such a dreadful affair?'

'What or *whom?*'

'"Whom"?' she echoed, tilting her head as she looked at him. 'This grows even more interesting.'

'I can think of any number of adjectives to describe all of the "whoms" I have had the pleasure of meeting this evening, but "interesting" is not one of them.'

'Now, now,' she chided, 'don't be rude. I did see you chatting with my brothers, after all.'

He nodded gallantly, tightening his hand slightly at her waist as they swung around in a graceful arc. 'My apologies. The Bridgertons are, of course, excluded from my insults.'

'We are all relieved, I'm sure.'

Simon cracked a smile at her deadpan wit. 'I live to make Bridgertons happy.'

'Now *that is* a statement that may come back to haunt you,' she chided. 'But in all seriousness, what has you in such a dither? If your evening has gone that far downhill since our interlude with Nigel, you're in sad straits, indeed.'

'How shall I put this,' he mused, 'so that I do not completely offend you?'

'Oh, go right ahead,' she said blithely. 'I promise not to be offended.'

Simon grinned wickedly. 'A statement that may come back to haunt *you.*'

She blushed slightly. The color was barely noticeable in the shadowy candlelight, but Simon had been watching her closely. She didn't say anything, however, so he added, 'Very well, if you must know, I have been introduced to every single unmarried lady in the ballroom.'

A strange snorting sound came from the vicinity of her mouth. Simon had the sneaking suspicion that she was laughing at him.

'I have also,' he continued, 'been introduced to all of their mothers.'

She gurgled. She actually gurgled.

'Bad show,' he scolded. 'Laughing at your dance partner.'

'I'm sorry,' she said, her lips tight from trying not to smile.

'No, you're not.'

'All right,' she admitted, 'I'm not. But only because I have had to suffer the same torture for two years. It's difficult to summon too much pity for a mere evening's worth.'

'Why don't you just find someone to marry and put yourself out of your misery?'

She shot him a sharp look. 'Are you asking?'

Simon felt the blood leave his face.

'I thought not.' She took one look at him and let out an impatient exhale. 'Oh, for goodness sake. You can start breathing now, your grace. I was only teasing.'

Simon wanted to make some sort of dry, cutting, and utterly ironic comment, but the truth was, she has so startled him that he couldn't utter a word.

'To answer your question,' she continued, her voice a touch more brittle than he was accustomed to hearing from her, 'a lady must consider her options. There is Nigel, of course, but I think we must agree he is not a suitable candidate.'

Simon shook his head.

'Earlier this year there was Lord Chalmers.'

'Chalmers?' He frowned. 'Isn't he—'

'On the darker side of sixty? Yes. And since I would someday like to have children, it seemed—'

'Some men that age can still sire brats,' Simon pointed out.

'It wasn't a risk I was prepared to take,' she returned. 'Besides—' She shuddered slightly, a look of revulsion passing over her features. 'I didn't particularly care to have children with *him*.'

Much to his annoyance, Simon found himself picturing Daphne in bed with the elderly Chalmers. It was a disgusting image, and it left him feeling faintly furious. At whom, he didn't know; maybe at himself for even bothering to imagine the damned thing, but—

'Before Lord Chalmers,' Daphne continued, thankfully interrupting his rather unpleasant thought process, 'there were two others, both just as repulsive.'

Simon looked at her thoughtfully. 'Do you want to marry?'

'Well, of course.' Her face registered her surprise. 'Doesn't everyone?'

'I don't.'

She smiled condescendingly. 'You think you don't. All men think they don't. But you will.'

'No,' he said emphatically. 'I will never marry.'

She gaped at him. Something in the duke's tone of voice told her that he truly meant what he said. 'What about your title?'

Simon shrugged. 'What about it?'

'If you don't marry and sire an heir, it will expire. Or go to some beastly cousin.'

That caused him to raise an amused brow. 'And how do you know that my cousins are beastly?'

'All cousins who are next in line for a title are beastly.' She cocked her head in a mischievous manner. 'Or at least they are according to the men who actually *possess* the title.'

'And this is information you've gleaned from your extensive knowledge of men?' he teased.

She shot him a devastatingly superior grin. 'Of course.'

Simon was silent for a moment, and then he asked, 'Is it worth it?'

She looked bemused by his sudden change of subject. 'Is what worth it?'

He let go of her hand just long enough to wave at the crowd. 'This. This endless parade of parties. Your mother nipping at your heels.'

Daphne let out a surprised chuckle. 'I doubt she'd appreciate the metaphor.' She fell silent for a moment, her eyes taking on a faraway look as she said, 'But yes, I suppose it is worth it. It has to be worth it.'

She snapped back to attention and looked back to his face, her dark eyes meltingly honest. 'I want a husband. I want a family. It's not so silly when you think about it. I'm fourth of eight children. All I know are large families. I shouldn't know how to exist outside of one.'

Simon caught her gaze, his eyes burning hot and intense into hers. A warning bell sounded in his mind. He wanted her. He wanted her so desperately he was straining against his clothing, but he could never, ever so much as touch her. Because to do so would be to shatter every last one of her dreams, and rake or not, Simon wasn't certain he could live with himself if he did that.

He would never marry, never sire a child, and that was all she wanted out of life.

He might enjoy her company; he wasn't certain he could deny himself that. But he had to leave her untouched for another man.

'Your grace?' she asked quietly. When he blinked, she smiled and said, 'You were woolgathering.'

He inclined his head graciously. 'Merely pondering your words.'

'And did they meet with your approval?'

'Actually, I can't remember the last time I conversed with someone with such obvious good sense.' He added in a slow voice, 'It's good to know what you want out of life.'

'Do you know what you want?'

Ah, how to answer that. There were some things he knew he could not say. But it was so easy to talk to this girl. Something about her put his mind at ease, even as his body tingled with desire. By all rights they should not have been having such a frank conversation so soon into an acquaintance, but somehow it just felt natural.

Finally, he just said, 'I made some decisions when I was younger. I try to live my life according to those vows.'

She looked ravenously curious, but good manners prevented her from questioning him further. 'My goodness,' she said with a slightly forced smile, 'we've grown serious. And here I thought all we meant to debate was whose evening was less pleasant.'

They were both trapped, Simon realized. Trapped by their society's conventions and expectations.

And that's when an idea popped into his mind. A strange, wild, and appallingly wonderful idea. It was probably also a dangerous idea, since it would put him in her company for long periods of time, which would certainly leave him in a perpetual state of unfulfilled desire, but Simon valued his self-control above all else, and he was certain he could control his baser urges.

'Wouldn't you like a respite?' he asked suddenly.

'A respite?' she echoed bemusedly. Even as they twirled across the floor, she looked from side to side. 'From this?'

'Not precisely. This, you'd still have to endure. What I envision is more of a respite from your mother.'

Daphne choked on her surprise. 'You're going to remove my mother from the social whirl? Doesn't that seem a touch extreme?'

'I'm not talking about removing your mother. Rather, I want to remove you.'

Daphne tripped over her feet, and then, just as soon as she'd regained her balance, she tripped over his. 'I beg your pardon?'

'I had hoped to ignore London society altogether,' he explained, 'but I'm finding that may prove to be impossible.'

'Because you've suddenly developed a taste for ratafia and weak lemonade?' she quipped.

'No,' he said, ignoring her sarcasm, 'because I've discovered that half of my university friends married in my absence, and their wives seem to be obsessed with throwing the perfect party—'

'And you've been invited?'

He nodded grimly.

Daphne leaned in close, as if she were about to tell him a grave secret. 'You're a duke,' she whispered. 'You can say no.'

She watched with fascination as his jaw tightened. 'These men,' he said, 'their husbands – they are my friends.'

Daphne felt her lips moving into an unbidden grin. 'And you don't want to hurt their wives' feelings.'

Simon scowled, clearly uncomfortable with the compliment.

'Well, I'll be,' she said mischievously. 'You might just be a nice person after all.'

'I'm hardly nice,' he scoffed.

'Perhaps, but you're hardly cruel, either.'

The music drew to a close, and Simon took her arm and guided her to the perimeter of the ballroom. Their dance had deposited them on the opposite side of the room from Daphne's family, so they had time to continue their conversation as they walked slowly back to the Bridgertons.

'What I was trying to say,' he said, 'before you so skillfully diverted me, was that it appears I must attend a certain number of London events.'

'Hardly a fate worse than death.'

He ignored her editorial. 'You, I gather, must attend them as well.'

She gave him a single regal nod.

'Perhaps there is a way that I might be spared the attentions of the Featheringtons and the like, and at the same time, you might be spared the matchmaking efforts of your mother.'

She looked at him intently. 'Go on.'

'We' – he leaned forward, his eyes mesmerizing hers – 'will form an attachment.'

Daphne said nothing. Absolutely nothing. She just stared at him as if she were trying to decide if he were the rudest man on the face of the earth or simply mad in the head.

'Not a true attachment,' Simon said impatiently. 'Good God, what sort of man do you think I am?'

'Well, I was warned about your reputation,' she pointed out. 'And you yourself tried to terrify me with your rakish ways earlier this evening.'

'I did no such thing.'

'Of course you did.' She patted his arm. 'But I forgive you. I'm sure you couldn't help it.'

Simon gave her a startled look. 'I don't believe I have ever been condescended to by a woman before.'

She shrugged. 'It was probably past time.'

'Do you know, I'd thought that you were unmarried because your brothers had scared off all your suitors, but now I wonder if you did it all on your own.'

Much to his surprise, she just laughed. 'No,' she said, 'I'm unmarried because everyone sees me as a friend. No one ever has any romantic interest in me.' She grimaced. 'Except Nigel.'

Simon pondered her words for a few moments, then realized that his plan could work to her benefit even more than he'd originally imagined. 'Listen,' he said, 'and listen quickly because we're almost back to your family, and Anthony looks as if he's about to bolt in our direction any minute now.'

They both glanced quickly to the right. Anthony was still trapped in conversation with the Featheringtons. He did not look happy.

'Here is my plan,' Simon continued, his voice low and intense. 'We shall pretend to have developed a tendre for each other. I won't have quite so many debutantes thrown in my direction because it will be perceived that I am no longer available.'

'No it won't,' Daphne replied. 'They won't believe you're unavailable until you're standing up before the bishop, taking your vows.'

The very thought made his stomach churn. 'Nonsense,' he said. 'It may take a bit of time, but I'm sure I will eventually be able to convince society that I am not anyone's candidate for marriage.'

'Except mine,' Daphne pointed out.

'Except yours,' he agreed, 'but we will know that isn't true.'

'Of course,' she murmured. 'Frankly, I do not believe that this will work, but if you're convinced . . . '

'I am.'

'Well, then, what do I gain?'

'For one thing, your mother will stop dragging you from man to man if she thinks you have secured my interest.'

'Rather conceited of you,' Daphne mused, 'but true.'

Simon ignored her gibe. 'Secondly,' he continued, 'men are always more interested in a woman if they think other men are interested.'

'Meaning?'

'Meaning, quite simply, and pardon my *conceit*' – he shot her a sardonic look to show that he hadn't missed her earlier sarcasm – 'but if all the world thinks I intend to make you my duchess, all of those men who see you as nothing more than an affable friend will begin to view you in a new light.'

Her lips pursed. 'Meaning that once you throw me over, I shall have hordes of suitors at my beck and call?'

'Oh, I shall allow you to be the one to cry off,' he said gallantly.

He noticed she didn't bother to thank him.

'I still think I'm gaining much more from this arrangement than you,' she said.

He squeezed her arm slightly. 'Then you'll do it?'

Daphne looked at Mrs. Featherington, who looked like a bird of prey, and then at her brother, who looked as if he had swallowed a chicken bone. She'd seen those expressions dozens of times before – except on the faces of her own mother and some hapless potential suitor.

'Yes,' she said, her voice firm. 'Yes, I'll do it.'

'What do you suppose is taking them so long?'

Violet Bridgerton tugged on her eldest son's sleeve, unable to take her eyes off of her daughter – who appeared to have thoroughly captured the attention of the Duke of Hastings – only one week in London and already the catch of the season.

'I don't know,' Anthony replied, looking gratefully at the backs of the Featheringtons as they moved on to their next victim, 'but it feels as if it's been hours.'

'Do you think he likes her?' Violet asked excitedly. 'Do you think our Daphne truly has a chance to be a duchess?'

Anthony's eyes filled with a mixture of impatience and disbelief. 'Mother, you told Daphne she wasn't even to be seen with him, and now you're thinking of marriage?'

'I spoke prematurely,' Violet said with a blithe wave of

her hand. 'Clearly he is a man of great refinement and taste. And how, may I ask, do you know what I said to Daphne?'

'Daff told me, of course,' Anthony lied.

'Hmmph. Well, I am certain that Portia Featherington won't be forgetting this evening anytime soon.'

Anthony's eyes widened. 'Are you trying to marry Daphne off so that she might be happy as a wife and a mother, or are you just trying to beat Mrs. Featherington to the altar?'

'The former, of course,' Violet replied in a huff, 'and I am offended you would even imply otherwise.' Her eyes strayed off of Daphne and the duke for just long enough to locate Portia Featherington and her daughters. 'But I certainly shan't mind seeing the look on her face when she realizes that *Daphne* will make the season's greatest match.'

'Mother, you are hopeless.'

'Certainly not. Shameless, perhaps, but never hopeless.'

Anthony just shook his head and muttered something under his breath.

'It's impolite to mumble,' Violet said, mostly just to annoy him. Then she spotted Daphne and the duke. 'Ah, here they come. Anthony, behave yourself. Daphne! Your grace!' She paused as the couple made their way to her side. 'I trust you enjoyed your dance.'

'Very much,' Simon murmured. 'Your daughter is as graceful as she is lovely.'

Anthony let out a snort.

Simon ignored him. 'I hope we may have the pleasure of dancing together again very soon.'

Violet positively glowed. 'Oh, I'm *sure* Daphne would *adore* that.' When Daphne didn't answer with all possible haste, she added, quite pointedly, 'Wouldn't you, Daphne?'

'Of course,' Daphne said demurely.

'I'm certain your mother would never be so lax as to allow me a second waltz,' Simon said, looking every inch the debonair duke, 'but I do hope she will permit us to take a stroll around the ballroom.'

'You just took a stroll around the ballroom,' Anthony pointed out.

Simon ignored him again. He said to Violet, 'We shall, of course, remain in your sight at all times.'

The lavender silk fan in Violet's hand began to flutter rapidly. 'I should be delighted. I mean, Daphne should be delighted. Shouldn't you, Daphne?'

Daphne was all innocence. 'Oh, I should.'

'And I,' Anthony snapped, 'should take a dose of laudanum, for clearly I am fevered. What the devil is going on?'

'Anthony!' Violet exclaimed. She turned hastily to Simon. 'Don't mind him.'

'Oh, I never do,' Simon said affably.

'Daphne,' Anthony said pointedly, 'I should be delighted to act as your chaperon.'

'Really, Anthony,' Violet cut in, 'they hardly need one if they are to remain here in the ballroom.'

'*Oh, I insist.*'

'You two run along,' Violet said to Daphne and Simon, waving her hand at them. 'Anthony will be with you in just a moment.'

Anthony tried to follow immediately, but Violet grabbed onto his wrist. Hard. 'What the devil do you think you're doing?' she hissed.

'Protecting my sister!'

'From the duke? He can't be that wicked. Actually, he reminds me of you.'

Anthony groaned. 'Then she definitely needs my protection.'

Violet patted him on the arm. 'Don't be so overprotective. If he attempts to spirit her out onto the balcony, I promise you may dash out to rescue her. But until that unlikely event occurs, please allow your sister her moment of glory.'

Anthony glared at Simon's back. 'Tomorrow I will kill him.'

'Dear me,' Violet said, shaking her head, 'I had no idea

you could be so high-strung. One would think, as your mother, I would know these things, especially since you are my firstborn, and thus I have known you for the longest of any of my children, but—'

'Is that Colin?' Anthony interrupted, his voice strangled.

Violet blinked, then squinted her eyes. 'Why, yes, it is. Isn't it lovely that he returned early? I could hardly believe my eyes when I saw him an hour ago. In fact, I—'

'I'd better go to him,' Anthony said quickly. 'He looks lonely. Good-bye, Mother.'

Violet watched as Anthony ran off, presumably to escape her chattering lecture. 'Silly boy,' she murmured to herself. None of her children seemed to be on to any of her tricks. Just blather on about nothing in particular, and she could be rid of any of them in a trice.

She let out a satisfied sigh and resumed her watch of her daughter, now on the other side of the ballroom, her hand nestled comfortably in the crook of the duke's elbow. They made a most handsome couple.

Yes, Violet thought, her eyes growing misty, her daughter would make an excellent duchess.

Then she let her gaze wander briefly over to Anthony, who was now right where she wanted him – out of her hair. She allowed herself a secret smile. Children were so easy to manage.

Then her smile turned to a frown as she noticed Daphne walking back toward her – on the arm of another man. Violet's eyes immediately scanned the ballroom until she found the duke.

Dash it all, what the devil was he doing dancing with Penelope Featherington?

6

It has been reported to This Author that the Duke of Hastings mentioned no fewer than six times yestereve that he has no plans to marry. If his intention was to discourage the Ambitious Mamas, he made a grave error in judgment. They will simply view his remarks as the greatest of challenges.

And in an interesting side note, his half dozen anti-matrimony remarks were all uttered before he made the acquaintance of the lovely and sensible Miss (Daphne) Bridgerton.

LADY WHISTLEDOWN'S SOCIETY PAPERS, 30 APRIL 1813

The following afternoon found Simon standing on the front steps of Daphne's home, one hand rapping the brass knocker on the door, the other wrapped around a large bouquet of fiendishly expensive tulips. It hadn't occurred to him that his little charade might require his attention during the daylight hours, but during their stroll about the ballroom the previous night, Daphne had sagely pointed out that if he did not call upon her the next day, no one – least of all her mother – would truly believe he was interested.

Simon accepted her words as truth, allowing that Daphne almost certainly had more knowledge in this area of etiquette than he did. He'd dutifully found some flowers and trudged across Grosvenor Square to Bridgerton House. He'd never courted a respectable woman before, so the ritual was foreign to him.

The door was opened almost immediately by the Bridgertons' butler. Simon gave him his card. The butler, a tall thin man with a hawkish nose, looked at it for barely a quarter second before nodding, and murmuring, 'Right this way, your grace.'

Clearly, Simon thought wryly, he had been expected.

What was unexpected, however, was the sight that awaited him when he was shown into the Bridgertons' drawing room.

Daphne, a vision in ice-blue silk, perched on the edge of Lady Bridgerton's green damask sofa, her face decorated with another one of those wide wide smiles.

It would have been a lovely sight, had she not been surrounded by at least a half dozen men, one of whom had actually descended to one knee, gales of poetry spewing from his mouth.

Judging from the florid nature of the prose, Simon fully expected a rosebush to sprout from the nitwit's mouth at any moment.

The entire scene, Simon decided, was most disagreeable.

He fixed his gaze on Daphne, who was directing her magnificent smile at the buffoon reciting poetry, and waited for her to acknowledge him.

She didn't.

Simon looked down at his free hand and noticed that it was curled into a tight fist. He scanned the room slowly, trying to decide on which man's face to use it.

Daphne smiled again, and again not at him.

The idiot poet. Definitely the idiot poet. Simon tilted his head slightly to the side as he analyzed the young swain's face. Would his fist fit best in the right eye socket or the left? Or maybe that was too violent. Maybe a light clip to the chin would be more appropriate. At the very least, it might actually shut the man up.

'This one,' the poet announced grandly, 'I wrote in your honor last night.'

Simon groaned. The last poem he had recognized as a rather grandiose rendition of a Shakespearean sonnet, but an original work was more than he could bear.

'Your grace!'

Simon looked up to realize that Daphne had finally noticed that he had entered the room.

He nodded regally, his cool look very much at odds with the puppy-dog faces of her other suitors. 'Miss Bridgerton.'

'How lovely to see you,' she said, a delighted smile crossing her face.

Ah, that was more like it. Simon straightened the flowers and started to walk toward her, only to realize that there were three young suitors in his path, and none appeared inclined to move. Simon pierced the first one with his haughtiest stare, which caused the boy – really, he looked all of twenty, hardly old enough to be called a *man* – *to* cough in a most unattractive manner and scurry off to an unoccupied window seat.

Simon moved forward, ready to repeat the procedure with the next annoying young man, when the viscountess suddenly stepped into his path, wearing a dark blue frock and a smile that might possibly rival Daphne's in its brightness.

'Your grace!' she said excitedly. 'What a pleasure to see you. You honor us with your presence.'

'I could hardly imagine myself anywhere else,' Simon murmured as he took her gloved hand and kissed it. 'Your daughter is an exceptional young lady.'

The viscountess sighed contentedly. 'And such lovely, lovely flowers,' she said, once she was finished with her little revel of maternal pride. 'Are they from Holland? They must have been terribly dear.'

'Mother!' Daphne said sharply. She extricated her hand from the grasp of a particularly energetic suitor and made her way over. 'What can the duke possibly say to that?'

'I could tell her how much I paid for them,' he said with a devilish half-smile.

'You wouldn't.'

He leaned forward, lowering his voice so that only Daphne could hear. 'Didn't you remind me last night that I'm a duke?' he murmured. 'I thought you told me I could do anything I wanted.'

'Yes, but not that,' Daphne said with a dismissive wave of her hand. 'You would never be so crass.'

'Of course the duke would not be crass!' her mother exclaimed, clearly horrified that Daphne would even mention the word in his presence. 'What are you talking about? Why would he be crass?'

'The flowers,' Simon said. 'The cost. Daphne thinks I shouldn't tell you.'

'Tell me later,' the viscountess whispered out of the side of her mouth, 'when she's not listening.' Then she moved back over to the green damask sofa where Daphne had been sitting with her suitors and cleared it out in under three seconds. Simon had to admire the military precision with which she managed the maneuver.

'There now,' the viscountess said. 'Isn't that convenient? Daphne, why don't you and the duke sit right there?'

'You mean where Lord Railmont and Mr. Crane were sitting just moments ago?' Daphne asked innocently.

'Precisely,' her mother replied, with what Simon considered to be an admirable lack of obvious sarcasm. 'Besides, Mr. Crane said that he has to meet his mother at Gunter's at three.'

Daphne glanced at the clock. 'It's only two, Mother.'

'The traffic,' Violet said with a sniff, 'is nothing short of dreadful these days. Far too many horses on the road.'

'It ill becomes a man,' Simon said, getting into the spirit of the conversation, 'to keep his mother waiting.'

'Well said, your grace.' Violet beamed. 'You can be sure

that I have expressed that very same sentiment to my own children.'

'And in case you're not sure,' Daphne said with a smile, 'I'd be happy to vouch for her.'

Violet merely smiled. 'If anyone should know, it would be you, Daphne. Now, if you will excuse me, I have business to attend to. Oh, Mr. Crane! Mr. Crane! Your mother would never forgive me if I did not shoo you out in time.' She bustled off, taking the hapless Mr. Crane by the arm and leading him toward the door, barely giving him time to say farewell.

Daphne turned to Simon with an amused expression. 'I can't quite decide if she is being terribly polite or exquisitely rude.'

'Exquisitely polite, perhaps?' Simon asked mildly.

She shook her head. 'Oh, definitely not that.'

'The alternative, of course, is—'

'Terribly rude?' Daphne grinned and watched as her mother looped her arm through Lord Railmont's, pointed him toward Daphne so that he could nod his good-bye, and led him from the room. And then, as if by magic, the remaining beaux murmured their hasty farewells and followed suit.

'Remarkably efficient, isn't she?' Daphne murmured.

'Your mother? She's a marvel.'

'She'll be back, of course.'

'Pity. And here I thought I had you well and truly in my clutches.'

Daphne laughed. 'I don't know how anyone considered you a rake. Your sense of humor is far too superb.'

'And here we rakes thought we were so wickedly droll.'

'A rake's humor,' Daphne stated, 'is essentially cruel.'

Her comment surprised him. He stared at her intently, searching her brown eyes, and yet not really knowing what it was he was looking for. There was a narrow ring of green just outside her pupils, the color as deep and rich as moss.

He'd never seen her in the daylight before, he realized.

'Your grace?' Daphne's quiet voice snapped him out of his daze.

Simon blinked. 'I beg your pardon.'

'You looked a thousand miles away,' she said, her brow wrinkling.

'I've been a thousand miles away.' He fought the urge to return his gaze to her eyes. 'This is entirely different.'

Daphne let out a little laugh, the sound positively musical. 'You have, haven't you? And here I've never even been past Lancashire. What a provincial I must seem.'

He brushed aside her remark. 'You must forgive my wool-gathering. We were discussing my lack of humor, I believe?'

'We were not, and you well know it.' Her hands found their way to her hips. 'I specifically told you that you were in possession of a sense of humor far superior to that of the average rake.'

One of his brows lifted in a rather superior manner. 'And you wouldn't classify your brothers as rakes?'

'They only *think they* are rakes,' she corrected. 'There is a considerable difference.'

Simon snorted. 'If Anthony isn't a rake, I pity the woman who meets the man who is.'

'There is more to being a rake than seducing legions of women,' Daphne said blithely. 'If a man can't do more than poke his tongue into a woman's mouth and kiss—'

Simon felt his throat close up, but somehow he managed to sputter, 'You should not be speaking of such things.'

She shrugged.

'You shouldn't even *know* about them,' he grunted.

'Four brothers,' she said by way of an explanation. 'Well, three, I suppose. Gregory is too young to count.'

'Someone ought to tell them to hold their tongues around you.'

She shrugged again, this time with only one shoulder. 'Half the time they don't even notice I'm there.'

Simon couldn't imagine *that.*

'But we seem to have veered away from the original subject,' she said. 'All I meant to say is that a rake's humor has its basis in cruelty. He needs a victim, for he cannot imagine ever laughing at himself. You, your grace, are rather clever with the self-deprecating remark.'

'I just don't know whether to thank you or throttle you.'

'Throttle me? Good heavens, why?' She laughed again, a rich, throaty sound that Simon felt deep in his gut.

He exhaled slowly, the long whoosh of air just barely steadying his pulse. If she continued laughing, he wasn't going to be able to answer to the consequences.

But she just kept looking at him, her wide mouth curved into one of those smiles that looked as if it were perpetually on the verge of laughter.

'I am going to throttle you,' he growled, 'on general principle.'

'And what principle is that?'

'The general principle of *man,*' he blustered.

Her brows lifted dubiously. 'As opposed to the general principle of woman?'

Simon looked around. 'Where is your brother? You're far too cheeky. Surely someone needs to take you in hand.'

'Oh, I'm sure you'll be seeing more of Anthony. In fact I'm rather surprised he hasn't made an appearance yet. He was quite irate last night. I was forced to listen to a full hour's lecture on your many faults and sins.'

'The sins are almost certainly exaggerated.'

'And the faults?'

'Probably true,' Simon admitted sheepishly.

That remark earned him another smile from Daphne. 'Well, true or not,' she said, 'he thinks you're up to something.'

'I *am* up to something.'

Her head tilted sarcastically as her eyes rolled upward. 'He thinks you're up to something nefarious.'

'I'd like to be up to something nefarious,' he muttered.

‘What was that?’

‘Nothing.’

She frowned. ‘I think we should tell Anthony about our plan.’

‘And what could possibly be the benefit to that?’

Daphne remembered the full-hour grilling she’d endured the previous night, and just said, ‘Oh, I think I’ll let you figure that out for yourself.’

Simon merely raised his brows. ‘My dear Daphne . . . ’

Her lips parted slightly in surprise.

‘Surely you’re not going to force me to call you Miss Bridgerton.’ He sighed dramatically. ‘After all that we’ve been through.’

‘We’ve been through nothing, you ridiculous man, but I suppose you may call me Daphne nonetheless.’

‘Excellent.’ He nodded in a condescending manner. ‘You may call me “your grace.”’

She swatted him.

‘Very well,’ he replied, his lips twitching at the corners. ‘Simon, if you must.’

‘Oh I must,’ Daphne said, rolling her eyes, ‘clearly, I must.’

He leaned toward her, something odd and slightly hot sparking in the depths of his pale eyes. ‘Must you?’ he murmured. ‘I should be very excited to hear it.’

Daphne had the sudden sense that he was talking about something far more intimate than the mere mention of his given name. A strange, tingling sort of heat shot down her arms, and without thinking, she jumped back a step. ‘Those flowers are quite lovely,’ she blurted out.

He regarded them lazily, rotating the bouquet with his wrist. ‘Yes, they are, aren’t they?’

‘I adore them.’

‘They’re not for you.’

Daphne choked on air.

Simon grinned. ‘They’re for your mother.’

Her mouth slowly opened in surprise, a short little gasp

of air passing through her lips before she said, 'Oh, you clever clever man. She will positively melt at your feet. But this will come back to haunt you, you know.'

He gave her an arch look. 'Oh really?'

'Really. She will be more determined than ever to drag you to the altar. You shall be just as beleaguered at parties as if we hadn't concocted this scheme.'

'Nonsense,' he scoffed. 'Before I would have had to endure the attentions of dozens of Ambitious Mamas. Now I must deal with only one.'

'Her tenacity might surprise you,' Daphne muttered. Then she twisted her head to look out the partially open door. 'She must truly like you,' she added. 'She's left us alone far longer than is proper.'

Simon pondered that and leaned forward to whisper, 'Could she be listening at the door?'

Daphne shook her head. 'No, we would have heard her shoes clicking down the hall.'

Something about that statement made him smile, and Daphne found herself smiling right along with him. 'I really should thank you, though,' she said, 'before she returns.'

'Oh? Why is that?'

'Your plan is a brilliant success. At least for me. Did you notice how many suitors came to call this morning?'

He crossed his arms, the tulips dangling upside down. 'I noticed.'

'It's brilliant, really. I've never had so many callers in a single afternoon before. Mother was beside herself with pride. Even Humboldt – he's our butler – was beaming, and I've never seen him so much as smile before. Ooops! Look, you're dripping.' She leaned down and righted the flowers, her forearm grazing the front of his coat. She immediately jumped back, startled by both the heat and power of him.

Good God, if she could sense all that through his shirt and coat, what must he be like—

Daphne colored red. Deep, dark red.

'I should give my entire fortune for those thoughts,' Simon said, his brows rising in question.

Thankfully, Violet chose that moment to sail into the room. 'I'm terribly sorry for abandoning you for so long,' she said, 'but Mr. Crane's horse threw a shoe, so naturally I had to accompany him to the stables and find a groom to repair the damage.'

In all their years together – which, Daphne thought acerbically, naturally constituted her entire life – Daphne had never known her mother to step foot in the stables.

'You are truly an exceptional hostess,' Simon said, holding out the flowers. 'Here, these are for you.'

'For me?' Violet's mouth fell open in surprise, and a strange little breathy sound escaped her lips. 'Are you certain? Because I – ' She looked over at Daphne, and then at Simon, and then finally back at her daughter. 'Are you certain?'

'Absolutely.'

Violet blinked rapidly, and Daphne noticed that there were actually tears in her mother's eyes. No one ever gave her flowers, she realized. At least not since her father had died ten years earlier. Violet was such a mother – Daphne had forgotten that she was a woman as well.

'I don't know what to say,' Violet sniffled.

'Try "thank you," Daphne whispered in her ear, her grin lending warmth to her voice.

'Oh, Daff, you are the worst.' Violet swatted her in the arm, looking more like a young woman than Daphne had ever seen her. 'But thank you, your grace. These are beautiful blooms, but more importantly, it was a most thoughtful gesture. I shall treasure this moment always.'

Simon looked as if he were about to say something, but in the end he just smiled and inclined his head.

Daphne looked at her mother, saw the unmistakable joy in her cornflower blue eyes, and realized with a touch of shame that none of her own children had ever acted in such a thoughtful manner as this man standing beside her.

The Duke of Hastings. Daphne decided then and there that she'd be a fool if she didn't fall in love with him.

Of course it would be nice if he returned the sentiment.

'Mother,' Daphne said, 'would you like me to fetch you a vase?'

'What?' Violet was still too busy sniffing blissfully at her flowers to pay attention to her daughter's words. 'Oh. Yes, of course. Ask Humboldt for the cut crystal from my grandmother.'

Daphne flashed a grateful smile at Simon and headed for the door, but before she could take more than two steps, the large and forbidding form of her eldest brother materialized in the doorway.

'Daphne,' Anthony growled. 'Just the person I needed to see.'

Daphne decided the best strategy was simply to ignore his churlish mood. 'In just a moment, Anthony,' she said sweetly. 'Mother has asked me to fetch a vase. Hastings has brought her flowers.'

'Hastings is here?' Anthony looked past her to the duo further in the room. 'What are you doing here, Hastings?'

'Calling on your sister.'

Anthony pushed past Daphne and strode into the room, looking rather like a thundercloud on legs. 'I did not give you leave to court my sister,' he bellowed.

'I did,' Violet said. She shoved the flowers in Anthony's face, wiggling them so as to deposit the greatest amount of pollen on his nose. 'Aren't these lovely?'

Anthony sneezed and pushed them aside. 'Mother, I am trying to have a conversation with the duke.'

Violet looked at Simon. 'Do you want to have this conversation with my son?'

'Not particularly.'

'Fine, then. Anthony, be quiet.'

Daphne clapped her hand over her mouth, but a snuffly-giggly sound escaped nonetheless.

'You!' Anthony jabbed a finger in her direction. 'Be quiet.'

'Perhaps I should fetch that vase,' Daphne mused.

'And leave me to the tender mercies of your brother?' Simon said in a mild voice. 'I think not.'

Daphne raised a brow. 'Do you imply that you are not man enough to deal with him?'

'Nothing of the sort. Merely that he ought to be your problem, not mine, and—'

'What the *hell is* going on here?' Anthony roared.

'Anthony!' Violet exclaimed. 'I will not tolerate such unbecoming language in my drawing room.'

Daphne smirked.

Simon did nothing more than cock his head, regarding Anthony with a curious stare.

Anthony threw a dark scowl at both of them before turning his attention to his mother. 'He is not to be trusted. Do you have any idea what is happening here?' he demanded.

'Of course I do,' Violet replied. 'The duke is paying a call upon your sister.'

'And I brought flowers for your mother,' Simon said helpfully.

Anthony gazed longingly at Simon's nose. Simon had the distinct impression that Anthony was imagining smashing it in.

Anthony whipped his head around to face his mother. 'Do you understand the extent of his reputation?'

'Reformed rakes make the best husbands,' Violet said.

'Rubbish and you know it.'

'He's not a true rake, anyway,' Daphne added.

The look Anthony shot at his sister was so comically malevolent Simon nearly laughed. He managed to restrain himself, but mostly just because he was fairly certain that any show of humor would cause Anthony's fist to lose its battle with his brain, with Simon's face emerging as the conflict's primary casualty.

'You don't know,' Anthony said, his voice low and nearly shaking with rage. 'You don't know what he has done.'

'No more than what you have done, I'm sure,' Violet said slyly.

'Precisely!' Anthony roared. 'Good God, I know *exactly* what is going on in his brain right now, and it has nothing to do with poetry and roses.'

Simon pictured laying Daphne down on a bed of rose petals. 'Well, maybe roses,' he murmured.

'I'm going to kill him,' Anthony announced.

'These are tulips, anyway,' Violet said primly, 'from Holland. And Anthony, you really must summon control of your emotions. This is most unseemly.'

'He is not fit to lick Daphne's boots.'

Simon's head filled with more erotic images, this time of himself licking her toes. He decided not to comment.

Besides, he had already decided that he wasn't going to allow his thoughts to wander in such directions. Daphne was Anthony's sister, for God's sake. He couldn't seduce her.

'I refuse to listen to another disparaging word about his grace,' Violet stated emphatically, 'and that is the end of the subject.'

'But—'

'I don't like your tone, Anthony Bridgerton!'

Simon thought he heard Daphne choke on a chuckle, and he wondered what that was all about.

'If it would please Your Motherhood,' Anthony said in excruciatingly even tones, 'I would like a private word with his grace.'

'This time I'm really going to get that vase,' Daphne announced, and dashed from the room.

Violet crossed her arms, and said to Anthony, 'I will not have you mistreat a guest in my home.'

'I shan't lay so much as a hand on him,' Anthony replied. 'I give you my word.'

Having never had a mother, Simon was finding this exchange fascinating. Bridgerton House was, after all, technically Anthony's house, not his mother's, and Simon was impressed that Anthony had refrained from pointing this out. 'It's quite all right, Lady Bridgerton,' he interjected. 'I'm sure Anthony and I have much to discuss.'

Anthony's eyes narrowed. 'Much.'

'Very well,' Violet said. 'You're going to do what you want no matter what I say, anyway. But I'm not leaving.' She plopped down onto the sofa. 'This is my drawing room, and I'm comfortable here. If the two of you want to engage in that asinine interchange that passes for conversation among the males of our species, you may do so elsewhere.'

Simon blinked in surprise. Clearly there was more to Daphne's mother than met the eye.

Anthony jerked his head toward the door, and Simon followed him into the hall.

'My study is this way,' Anthony said.

'You have a study here?'

'*I am* the head of the family.'

'Of course,' Simon allowed, 'but you do reside elsewhere.'

Anthony paused and turned an assessing stare on Simon. 'It cannot have escaped your notice that my position as head of the Bridgerton family carries with it serious responsibilities.'

Simon looked him evenly in the eye. 'Meaning Daphne?'

'Precisely.'

'If I recall,' Simon said, 'earlier this week you told me you wanted to introduce us.'

'That was before I thought you'd be interested in her!'

Simon held his tongue as he preceded Anthony into his study, remaining silent until Anthony shut the door. 'Why,' he asked softly, 'would you assume I would not be interested in your sister?'

'Besides the fact that you have sworn to me that you will never marry?' Anthony drawled.

He had a good point. Simon hated that he had such a good point. 'Besides that,' he snapped.

Anthony blinked a couple of times, then said, 'No one is interested in Daphne. At least no one we'd have her marry.'

Simon crossed his arms and leaned back against the wall. 'You don't hold her in terribly high regard, do y—?'

Before he could even finish the query, Anthony had him by throat. 'Don't you dare insult my sister.'

But Simon had learned quite a bit about self-defense on his travels, and it took him only two seconds to reverse their positions. 'I wasn't insulting your sister,' he said in a malevolent voice. 'I was insulting you.'

Strange gurgling sounds were coming from Anthony's throat, so Simon let him go. 'As it happens,' he said, brushing his hands against each other, 'Daphne explained to me why she has not attracted any suitable suitors.'

'Oh?' Anthony asked derisively.

'Personally, I think it has everything to do with your and your brothers' apelike ways, but she tells me it is because all London views her as a friend, and none sees her as a romantic heroine.'

Anthony was silent for a long moment before saying, 'I see.' Then, after another pause, he added thoughtfully, 'She's probably right.'

Simon said nothing, just watched his friend as he sorted all of this out. Finally, Anthony said, 'I still don't like your sniffing about her.'

'Good God, you make me sound positively canine.'

Anthony crossed his arms, 'Don't forget, we ran in the same pack after we left Oxford. I know exactly what you've done.'

'Oh, for the love of Christ, Bridgerton, we were twenty! All men are idiots at that age. Besides, you know damn well that h-h—'

Simon felt his tongue grow awkward, and faked a coughing fit to cover his stammer. Damn. This happened so infrequently these days, but when it did, it was always when he was upset or angry. If he lost control over his emotions, he lost control over his speech. It was as simple as that.

And unfortunately, episodes such as this only served to make him upset and angry with himself, which in turn exacerbated the stammer. It was the worst sort of vicious circle.

Anthony looked at him quizzically. 'Are you all right?'

Simon nodded. 'Just a bit of dust in my throat,' he lied.

'Shall I ring for tea?'

Simon nodded again. He didn't particularly want tea, but it seemed the sort of thing one would ask for if one truly did have dust in one's throat.

Anthony tugged at the bellpull, then turned back to Simon and asked, 'You were saying?'

Simon swallowed, hoping the gesture would help him to regain control over his ire. 'I merely meant to point out that you know better than anyone that at least half of my reputation is undeserved.'

'Yes, but I was there for the half that was deserved, and while I don't mind your occasionally socializing with Daphne, I don't want you courting her.'

Simon stared at his friend – or at least the man he thought was his friend – in disbelief. 'Do you really think I'd seduce your sister?'

'I don't know what to think. I know you plan never to marry. I know that Daphne does.' Anthony shrugged. 'Frankly, that's enough for me to keep you two on opposite sides of the dance floor.'

Simon let out a long breath. While Anthony's attitude was irritating as hell, he supposed it was understandable, and in fact even laudable. After all, the man was only acting in the best interests of his sister. Simon had difficulty imagining being responsible for anyone save himself, but he supposed that if he had a sister, he'd be damned picky about who courted her as well.

Just then, a knock sounded at the door.

'Enter!' Anthony called out.

Instead of the maid with tea, Daphne slipped into the room. 'Mother told me that the two of you are in beastly moods, and I should leave you alone, but I thought I ought to make certain neither of you had killed the other.'

'No,' Anthony said with a grim smile, 'just a light strangle.'

To Daphne's credit, she didn't bat an eyelash. 'Who strangled whom?'

'I strangled him,' her brother replied, 'then he returned the favor.'

'I see,' she said slowly. 'I'm sorry to have missed the entertainment.'

Simon couldn't suppress a smile at her remark. 'Daff,' he began.

Anthony whirled around. 'You call her Daff?' His head snapped back to Daphne. 'Did you give him permission to use your given name?'

'Of course.'

'But—'

'I think,' Simon interrupted, 'that we are going to have to come clean.'

Daphne nodded somberly. 'I think you're right. If you recall, I told you so.'

'How genteel of you to mention it,' Simon murmured.

She smiled gamely. 'I could not resist. With four brothers, after all, one must always seize the moment when one may say, "I told you so."'

Simon looked from sibling to sibling. 'I don't know which one of you I pity more.'

'What the devil is going on?' Anthony demanded, and then added as an aside, 'And as for your remark, pity me.

I am a far more amiable brother than she is a sister.'

'Not true!'

Simon ignored the squabble and focused his attention on Anthony. 'You want to know what the devil is going on? It's like this . . . '

7

Men are sheep. Where one goes, the rest will soon follow.

LADY WHISTLEDOWN'S SOCIETY PAPERS,
30 APRIL 1813

All in all, Daphne thought, Anthony was taking this rather well. By the time Simon had finished explaining their little plan (with, she had to admit, frequent interruptions on her part), Anthony had raised his voice only seven times.

That was about seven fewer than Daphne would have predicted.

Finally, after Daphne begged him to hold his tongue until she and Simon were done with their story, Anthony gave a curt nod, crossed his arms, and clamped his mouth shut for the duration of the explanation. His frown was enough to shake the plaster off the walls, but true to his word, he remained utterly silent.

Until Simon finished with, 'And that's that.'

There was silence. Dead silence. For a full ten seconds, nothing but silence, although Daphne would have sworn she could hear her eyes moving in their sockets as they darted back from Anthony to Simon.

And then finally, from Anthony: 'Are you mad?'

'I thought this might be his reaction,' Daphne murmured.

'Are you both completely, irrevocably, abominably insane?' Anthony's voice rose to a roar. 'I don't know which of you is more clearly the idiot.'

'Will you hush!' Daphne hissed. 'Mother will hear you.'

'Mother would perish of heart failure if she knew what you were about,' Anthony retorted, but he did use a softer tone.

'But *Mother is* not going to hear of it, is she?' Daphne shot back.

'No, she's not,' Anthony replied, his chin jutting forward, 'because your little scheme is finished as of this very moment.'

Daphne crossed her arms. 'You can't do anything to stop me.'

Anthony jerked his head toward Simon. 'I can kill *him.*'

'Don't be ridiculous.'

'Duels have been fought for less.'

'By idiots!'

'I'm not disputing the title as regards to *him.*'

'If I might interrupt,' Simon said quietly.

'He's your best friend!' Daphne protested.

'Not,' Anthony said, the single syllable brimming with barely contained violence, 'anymore.'

Daphne turned to Simon with a huff. 'Aren't you going to say anything?'

His lips quirked into an amused half-smile. 'And when would I have had the chance?'

Anthony turned to Simon. 'I want you out of this house.'

'Before I may defend myself?'

'It's my house, too,' Daphne said hotly, 'and I want him to stay.'

Anthony glared at his sister, exasperation evident in every inch of his posture. 'Very well,' he said, 'I'll give you two minutes to state your case. No more.'

Daphne glanced hesitantly at Simon, wondering if he'd want to use the two minutes himself. But all he did was shrug, and say, 'Go right ahead. He's *your* brother.'

She took a fortifying breath, planted her hands on her hips without even realizing it, and said, 'First of all, I must point out that I have far more to gain from this alliance than his grace. He says he wishes to use me to keep the other women—'

'And their mothers,' Simon interrupted.

'—and their mothers at bay. But frankly' – Daphne glanced at Simon as she said this – 'I think he's wrong. The women aren't going to stop pursuing him just because they think he might have formed an attachment with another young lady – especially when that young lady is *me*.'

'And what is wrong with you?' Anthony demanded.

Daphne started to explain, but then she caught a strange glance pass between the two men. 'What was that all about?'

'Nothing,' Anthony muttered, looking a trifle sheepish.

'I explained to your brother your theory on why you have not had more suitors,' Simon said gently.

'I see.' Daphne pursed her lips as she tried to decide whether that was something she ought to be irritated about. 'Hmmph. Well, he should have figured that out on his own.'

Simon made an odd snorting sound that might have been a laugh.

Daphne leveled a sharp look at both men. 'I do hope my two minutes do not include all of these interruptions.'

Simon shrugged. 'He's the timekeeper.'

Anthony clutched at the edge of the desk, probably, Daphne thought, to keep himself from going for Simon's throat. 'And *he,*' he said menacingly, 'is going to find himself headfirst through the goddamned window if he doesn't shut up.'

'Did you know I have always suspected that men were idiots,' Daphne ground out, 'but I was never positive until today.'

Simon grinned.

'Allowing for interruptions,' Anthony bit off, shooting yet another deadly glare in Simon's direction even as he spoke to Daphne, 'you have a minute and a half left.'

'Fine,' she snapped. 'Then I'll reduce this conversation

to one single fact. Today I had six callers. Six! Can you recall the last time I had six callers?'

Anthony just stared at her blankly.

'I can't,' Daphne continued, in fine form now. 'Because it *has never happened*. Six men marched up our steps, knocked on our door, and gave Humboldt their cards. Six men brought me flowers, engaged me in conversation, and one even recited poetry.'

Simon winced.

'And do you know *why?*' she demanded, her voice rising dangerously. 'Do you?'

Anthony, in his somewhat belatedly arrived wisdom, held his tongue.

'It is all because *he*' – she jabbed her forefinger toward Simon – 'was kind enough to feign interest in me last night at Lady Danbury's ball.'

Simon, who had been leaning casually against the edge of the desk, suddenly straightened. 'Well, now,' he said quickly, 'I wouldn't quite put it that way.'

She turned to him, her eyes remarkably steady. 'And how would you put it?'

He didn't get much past, 'I—' before she added, 'Because I can assure you those men have never seen fit to call on me before.'

'If they are so myopic,' Simon said quietly, 'why do you care for their regard?'

She fell silent, drawing back slightly. Simon had the sinking suspicion that he might have said something very, very wrong, but he wasn't positive until he saw her blinking rapidly.

Oh, damn.

Then she wiped one of her eyes. She coughed as she did it, trying to hide the maneuver by pretending to cover her mouth, but Simon still felt like the worst sort of heel.

'Now look what you've done,' Anthony snapped. He placed a comforting hand on his sister's arm, all the while glaring at Simon. 'Pay him no mind, Daphne. He's an ass.'

'Maybe,' she sniffled. 'But he's an intelligent ass.'

Anthony's mouth fell open.

She shot him a testy look. 'Well, if you didn't want me to repeat it, you shouldn't have said it.'

Anthony let out a weary sigh. 'Were there really six men here this afternoon?'

She nodded. 'Seven including Hastings.'

'And,' he asked carefully, 'were any of them men you might be interested in marrying?'

Simon realized that his fingers were gouging small holes in his thigh and forced himself to move his hand to the desk.

Daphne nodded again. 'They are all men with whom I have enjoyed a previous friendship. It is only that they never viewed me as a candidate for romance before Hastings led the way. I might, if given the opportunity, develop an attachment for one of them.'

'But—' Simon quickly shut his mouth.

'But what?' Daphne asked, turning to him with curious eyes.

It occurred to him that what he wanted to say was that if those men had only noticed Daphne's charms because a duke had shown interest in her, then they were idiots, and thus she shouldn't even contemplate marrying them. But considering that he had been the one to originally point out that his interest would gain her more suitors – well, frankly, it seemed a bit self-defeating to mention it.

'Nothing,' he finally said, raising a hand in a don't-mind-me motion. 'It doesn't signify.'

Daphne looked at him for a few moments, as if waiting for him to change his mind, and then turned back to her brother. 'Do you admit the wisdom of our plan, then?'

'"Wisdom" might be a bit of a stretch, but' – Anthony looked pained to say it – 'I can see where you might think it might benefit you.'

'Anthony, I have to find a husband. Besides the fact that Mother is pestering me to death, I want a *husband*. I want to marry and have a family of my own. I want it more than you could ever know. And thus far, no one acceptable has asked.'

Simon had no idea how Anthony could possibly hold out against the warm pleading in her dark eyes. And sure enough, Anthony sagged against the desk and let out a weary groan. 'Very well,' he said, closing his eyes as if he couldn't believe what he was saying, 'I shall agree to this if I must.'

Daphne jumped up and threw her arms around him. 'Oh, Anthony, I knew you were the very best of brothers.' She gave him a kiss on the cheek. 'You're just occasionally misguided.'

Anthony's eyes floated heavenward before focusing on Simon. 'Do you see what I have to put up with?' he asked with a shake of his head. His tone was that particular timbre used only from one beleaguered male to another.

Simon chuckled to himself as he wondered when he'd turned from evil seducer back into good friend.

'But,' Anthony said loudly, causing Daphne to back up, 'I am placing some conditions on this.'

Daphne didn't say anything, just blinked as she waited for her brother to continue.

'First of all, this goes no further than this room.'

'Agreed,' she said quickly.

Anthony looked pointedly at Simon.

'Of course,' he replied.

'Mother would be devastated if she learned the truth.'

'Actually,' Simon murmured, 'I rather think your mother would applaud our ingenuity, but since you have quite obviously known her longer, I bow to your discretion.'

Anthony shot him a frosty look. 'Second, under no circumstances are the two of you to be alone together. Ever.'

'Well, that should be easy,' Daphne said, 'as we wouldn't be allowed to be alone if we were courting in truth, anyway.'

Simon recalled their brief interlude in the hall at Lady Danbury's house, and found it a pity that he wasn't to be allowed any more private time with Daphne, but he recognized a brick wall when he saw one, especially when said wall happened to be named Anthony Bridgerton. So he just nodded and murmured his assent.

'Third—'

'There is a third?' Daphne asked.

'There would be thirty if I could think of them,' Anthony growled.

'Very well,' she acceded, looking most aggrieved. 'If you must.'

For a split second Simon thought Anthony might strangle her.

'What are you laughing about?' Anthony demanded.

It was only then that Simon realized that he had snorted a laugh. 'Nothing,' he said quickly.

'Good,' Anthony grunted, 'because the third condition is this: If I ever, even once, catch you in any behavior that compromises her . . . If I ever even catch you kissing her bloody hand without a chaperone, I shall tear your head off.'

Daphne blinked. 'Don't you think that's a bit excessive?'

Anthony leveled a hard stare in her direction. 'No.'

'Oh.'

'Hastings?'

Simon had no choice but to nod.

'Good,' Anthony replied gruffly. 'And now that we're done with that, you' – he cocked his head rather abruptly toward Simon – 'can leave.'

'Anthony!' Daphne exclaimed.

'I assume this means I am disinvited for supper this evening?' Simon asked.

'Yes.'

'No!' Daphne jabbed her brother in the arm. 'Is Hastings invited for supper? Why did you not say something?'

'It was days ago,' Anthony grumbled. 'Years.'

'It was Monday,' Simon said.

'Well, then you must join us,' Daphne said firmly. 'Mother will be so delighted. And you' – she poked her brother in the arm – 'stop thinking about how you may poison him.'

Before Anthony could reply, Simon waved off her words with a chuckle. 'Do not worry on my behalf, Daphne. You forget that I attended school with him for nearly a decade. He never did understand the principles of chemistry.'

'I shall kill him,' Anthony said to himself. 'Before the week is out, I shall kill him.'

'No you won't,' Daphne said blithely. 'By tomorrow you will have forgotten all of this and will be smoking cheroots at White's.'

'I don't think so,' Anthony said ominously.

'Of course you will. Don't you agree, Simon?'

Simon studied his best friend's face and realized he was seeing something new. Something in his eyes. Something serious.

Six years ago, when Simon had left England, he and Anthony had been boys. Oh, they'd thought they were men. They'd gambled and whored and strutted about society, consumed with their own importance, but now they were different.

Now they were men in truth.

Simon had felt the change within himself during his travels. It had been a slow transformation, wrought over time as he faced new challenges. But now he realized that he'd returned to England still picturing Anthony as that twenty-two-year-old boy he'd left behind.

He'd done his friend a great disservice, he'd realized, in failing to realize that he, too, had grown up. Anthony had responsibilities Simon had never even dreamed of. He had brothers to guide, sisters to protect. Simon had a dukedom, but Anthony had a family.

There was a grave difference, and Simon found that he

couldn't fault his friend for his overprotective and indeed somewhat mulish behavior.

'I think,' Simon said slowly, finally answering Daphne's question, 'that your brother and I are both different people than we were when we ran wild six years ago. And I think that might not be such a bad thing.'

Several hours later, the Bridgerton household was in chaos.

Daphne had changed into an evening dress of dark green velvet that someone had once said almost made her eyes look not quite brown, and was presently idling about in the great hall, trying to find a way to calm her mother's racing nerves.

'I cannot *believe,*' Violet said, one hand fluttering on her chest, 'that Anthony forgot to tell me he invited the duke to dinner. I had no time to prepare. None at all.'

Daphne eyed the menu in her hand, which began with turtle soup and marched through three more courses before finishing with lamb a la bechamel (followed, of course, by a choice of four desserts). She tried to keep her voice free of sarcasm as she said, 'I do not think the duke will have cause to complain.'

'I pray that he won't,' Violet replied. 'But if I had known he was coming, I would have made sure we had a beef dish as well. One cannot entertain without a beef dish.'

'He knows this is an informal meal.'

Violet shot her an acerbic look. 'No meal is informal when a duke is calling.'

Daphne regarded her mother thoughtfully. Violet was wringing her hands and gnashing her teeth. 'Mother,' Daphne said, 'I don't think the duke is the sort to expect us to dramatically alter our family supper plans on his behalf.'

'He might not expect it,' Violet said, 'but I do. Daphne, there are certain rules in society. Expectations. And frankly, I do not understand how you can be quite so calm and disinterested.'

'I'm not disinterested!'

'You certainly don't look nervous.' Violet eyed her suspiciously. 'How can you not be nervous? For goodness sake, Daphne, this man is thinking of marrying you.'

Daphne caught herself just before she groaned. 'He has never said as much, Mother.'

'He didn't have to. Why else would he have danced with you last night? The only other lady he so honored was Penelope Featherington, and we both know that that had to be out of pity.'

'I *like* Penelope,' Daphne said.

'I like Penelope, too,' Violet returned, 'and I long for the day her mother realizes that a girl of her complexion cannot be dressed in tangerine satin, but that is beside the point.'

'What is the point?'

'I don't know!' Violet very nearly wailed.

Daphne shook her head. 'I'm going to find Eloise.'

'Yes, do that,' Violet said distractedly, 'and make sure Gregory is clean. He never washes behind his ears. And Hyacinth – Good God, what are we to do about Hyacinth? Hastings will not expect a ten-year-old at the table.'

'Yes, he will,' Daphne replied patiently. 'Anthony told him we were dining as a family.'

'Most families do not allow their younger children to dine with them,' Violet pointed out.

'Then that is their problem.' Daphne finally gave in to her exasperation and let out a loud sigh. 'Mother, I spoke to the duke. He understands that this is not a formal meal. And he specifically told me that he was looking forward to a change of pace. He has no family himself, so he has never experienced anything like a Bridgerton family dinner.'

'God help us.' Violet's face went utterly pale.

'Now, Mother,' Daphne said quickly, 'I know what you're thinking, and I assure you that you don't have to worry about Gregory putting creamed potatoes on Francesca's chair again. I'm certain he has outgrown such childish behavior.'

'He did it last week!'

'Well, then,' Daphne said briskly, not missing a beat, 'then I'm sure he's learned his lesson.'

The look Violet gave her daughter was dubious in the extreme.

'Very well, then,' Daphne said, her tone considerably less businesslike, 'then I will simply threaten him with death if he does anything to upset you.'

'Death won't scare him,' Violet mused, 'but perhaps I can threaten to sell his horse.'

'He'll never believe you.'

'No, you're right. I'm far too softhearted.' Violet frowned. 'But he might believe me if I told him he would be forbidden to go on his daily ride.'

'That might work,' Daphne agreed.

'Good. I shall go off and scare some sense into him.' Violet took two steps then turned around. 'Having children is such a challenge.'

Daphne just smiled. She knew it was a challenge her mother adored.

Violet cleared her throat softly, signaling a more serious turn of conversation. 'I do hope this supper goes well, Daphne. I think Hastings might be an excellent match for you.'

'"Might"?' Daphne teased. 'I thought dukes were good matches even if they had two heads and spit while they talked.' She laughed. 'Out of both mouths!'

Violet smiled benignly. 'You might find this difficult to believe, Daphne, but I don't want to see you married off to just anyone. I may introduce you to no end of eligible men, but that is only because I would like you to have as many suitors as possible from which to choose a husband.' Violet smiled wistfully. 'It is my fondest dream to see you as happy as I was with your father.'

And then, before Daphne could reply, Violet disappeared down the hall.

Leaving Daphne with second thoughts.

Maybe this plan with Hastings wasn't such a good idea, after all. Violet was going to be crushed when they broke off their faux alliance. Simon had said that Daphne might be the one to do the jilting, but she was beginning to wonder if perhaps it wouldn't be better the other way around. It would be mortifying for Daphne to be thrown over by Simon, but at least that way she wouldn't have to endure Violet's bewildered chorus of 'Why?'

Violet was going to think she was insane for letting him get away.

And Daphne would be left wondering if maybe her mother was right.

Simon had not been prepared for supper with the Bridgertons. It was a loud, raucous affair, with plenty of laughter and thankfully, only one incident involving a flying pea.

(It had looked as if the pea in question had originated at Hyacinth's end of the table, but the littlest Bridgerton had looked so innocent and angelic that Simon had difficulty believing she had actually aimed the legume at her brother.)

Thankfully, Violet had not noticed the flying pea, even though it sailed right over her head in a perfect arc.

But Daphne, who was sitting directly across from him, most certainly had, because her napkin flew up to cover her mouth with remarkable alacrity. Judging from the way her eyes were crinkling at the corners, she was definitely laughing under the square of linen.

Simon spoke little throughout the meal. Truth be told, it was far easier to listen to the Bridgertons than actually to try to converse with them, especially considering the number of malevolent stares he was receiving from Anthony and Benedict.

But Simon had been seated clear at the opposite end of the table from the two eldest Bridgertons (no accident on Violet's part, he was sure) so it was relatively simple to ignore them and instead enjoy Daphne's interactions with the rest of her family. Every now and then one of them would ask him a direct question, and he would answer, and then he would return to his demeanor of quiet observation.

Finally, Hyacinth, who was seated to Daphne's right, looked him straight in the eye, and said, 'You don't talk much, do you?'

Violet choked on her wine.

'The duke,' Daphne said to Hyacinth, 'is being far more polite than we are, constantly jumping into the conversation and interrupting one another as if we're afraid we might not be heard.'

'I'm not afraid I might not be heard,' Gregory said.

'I'm not afraid of that, either,' Violet commented dryly. 'Gregory, eat your peas.'

'But Hyacinth—'

'Lady Bridgerton,' Simon said loudly, 'may I trouble you for another helping of those delicious peas?'

'Why certainly.' Violet shot an arch look at Gregory. 'Notice how the duke is eating his peas.'

Gregory ate his peas.

Simon smiled to himself as he spooned another portion of peas onto his plate, thankful that Lady Bridgerton had not decided to serve dinner *a la russe*. It would have been difficult to stave off Gregory's certain accusation of Hyacinth as a pea-tosser if he'd had to summon a footman to serve him.

Simon busied himself with his peas, since he really had no choice but to finish off every last one. He stole a glance at Daphne, however, who was wearing a secret little smile. Her eyes were brimming with infectious good humor, and Simon soon felt the corners of his mouth turning up as well.

'Anthony, why are you scowling?' asked one of the other Bridgerton girls – Simon thought it might be Francesca, but it was hard to say. The two middle ones looked amazingly alike, right down to their blue eyes, so like their mother's.

'I'm not scowling,' Anthony snapped, but Simon, having been on the receiving end of those scowls for the better part of an hour, rather thought he was lying.

'You are, too,' either Francesca or Eloise said.

Anthony's tone of reply was condescending in the extreme. 'If you think I am going to say, "Am not," you are sadly mistaken.'

Daphne laughed into her napkin again.

Simon decided life was more amusing than it had been in ages.

'Do you know,' Violet suddenly announced, 'that I think this might be one of the most pleasant evenings of the year. Even' – she sent a knowing glance down the table at Hyacinth – 'if my youngest is tossing peas down the table.'

Simon looked up just as Hyacinth cried out, 'How did you know?'

Violet shook her head as she rolled her eyes. 'My dear children,' she said, 'when will you learn that I know everything?'

Simon decided he had a great deal of respect for Violet Bridgerton.

But even still, she managed to completely confuse him with a question and a smile. 'Tell me, your grace,' she said, 'are you busy tomorrow?'

Despite her blond and blue-eyed coloring, she looked so like Daphne as she asked him this question that he was momentarily befuddled. Which had to be the only reason he didn't bother to think before he stammered, 'N-no. Not that I recall.'

'Excellent!' Violet exclaimed, beaming. 'Then you must join us on our outing to Greenwich.'

'Greenwich?' Simon echoed.

'Yes, we've been planning a family outing for several weeks now. We thought we'd take a boat, then perhaps have a picnic on the shores of the Thames.' Violet smiled at him confidently. 'You'll come, won't you?'

‘Mother,’ Daphne interjected, ‘I’m certain the duke has any number of commitments.’

Violet gave Daphne a look so frigid Simon was surprised that neither one of them turned to ice. ‘Nonsense,’ Violet replied. ‘He just said himself that he wasn’t busy.’ She turned back to Simon. ‘And we shall be visiting the Royal Observatory as well, so you needn’t worry that this will be a mindless jaunt. It’s not open to the public, of course, but my late husband was a great patron, so we are assured entry.’

Simon looked at Daphne. She just shrugged and apologized with her eyes.

He turned back to Violet. ‘I’d be delighted.’

Violet beamed and patted him on the arm.

And Simon had the sinking sensation that his fate had just been sealed.

8

It has reached This Author's ears that the entire Bridgerton family (plus one duke!) embarked upon a journey to Greenwich on Saturday.

It has also reached This Author's ears that the aforementioned duke, along with a certain member of the Bridgerton family, returned to London very wet indeed.

LADY WHISTLEDOWN'S SOCIETY PAPERS,
3 MAY 1813

'If you apologize to me one more time,' Simon said, leaning his head back against his hands, 'I may have to kill you.'

Daphne shot him an irritated look from her position in her deck chair on the small yacht her mother had commissioned to take the entire family – and the duke, of course – to Greenwich. 'Pardon me,' she said, 'if I am polite enough to apologize for my mother's quite obvious manipulations. I thought that the purpose of our little charade was to shield you from the tender mercies of matchmaking mothers.'

Simon waved off her comment, as he settled deeper into his own chair. 'It would only be a problem if I were not enjoying myself.'

Daphne's chin lurched backward slightly in surprise. 'Oh,' she said (stupidly, in her opinion). 'That's nice.'

He laughed. 'I am inordinately fond of boat travel, even if it is just down to Greenwich, and besides, after spending so much time at sea, I rather fancy a visit to the Royal Observatory to see the Greenwich Meridian.' He cocked his head in her direction. 'Do you know much about navigation and longitude?'

She shook her head. 'Very little, I'm afraid. I must confess I'm not even certain what this meridian here at Greenwich is.'

'It's the point from which all longitude is measured. It used to be that sailors and navigators measured longitudinal distance from their point of departure, but in the last century, the astronomer royal decided to make Greenwich the starting point.'

Daphne raised her brows. 'That seems rather self-important of us, don't you think, positioning ourselves at the center of the world?'

'Actually, it's quite convenient to have a universal reference point when one is attempting to navigate the high seas.'

She still looked doubtful. 'So everyone simply agreed on Greenwich? I find it difficult to believe that the French wouldn't have insisted upon Paris, and the Pope, I'm sure, would have preferred Rome . . . '

'Well, it wasn't an agreement, precisely,' he allowed with a laugh. 'There was no official treaty, if that is what you mean. But the Royal Observatory publishes an excellent set of charts and tables each year – it's called the *Nautical Almanac*. And a sailor would have to be insane to attempt to navigate the ocean without one on board. And since the *Nautical Almanac* measures longitude with Greenwich as zero . . . well, everyone else has adopted it as well.'

'You seem to know quite a bit about this.'

He shrugged. 'If you spend enough time on a ship, you learn.'

'Well, I'm afraid it wasn't the sort of thing one learned in the Bridgerton nursery.' She cocked her head to the side in a somewhat self-deprecating manner. 'Most of my learning was restricted to what my governess knew.'

'Pity,' he murmured. Then he asked, 'Only most?'

'If there was something that interested me, I could usually find several books to read on the topic in our library.'

'I would wager then, that your interests did not lie in abstract mathematics.'

Daphne laughed. 'Like you, you mean? Hardly, I'm afraid. My mother always said that it was a wonder I could add high enough to put shoes on my feet.'

Simon winced.

'I know, I know,' she said, still smiling. 'You sorts who excel at arithmetic simply don't understand how we lesser mortals can look at a page of numbers and not know the answer – or at least how to *get* to the answer – instantly. Colin is the same way.'

He smiled, because she was exactly right. 'What, then, were your favorite subjects?'

'Hmm? Oh, history and literature. Which was fortunate, since we had no end of books on those topics.'

He took another sip of his lemonade. 'I've never had any great passion for history.'

'Really? Why not, do you think?'

Simon pondered that for a moment, wondering if perhaps his lack of enthusiasm for history was due to his distaste for his dukedom and all the tradition that wrapped around it. His father had been so passionate about the title . . .

But of course all he said was, 'Don't know, really. Just didn't like it, I suppose.'

They fell into a few moments of companionable silence, the gentle river wind ruffling their hair. Then Daphne smiled, and said, 'Well, I won't apologize again, since I'm too fond of my life to sacrifice it needlessly at your hands, but I am glad that you're not miserable after my mother browbeat you into accompanying us.'

The look he gave her was vaguely sardonic. 'If I hadn't wanted to join you, there is nothing your mother could have said that would have secured my presence.'

She snorted. 'And this from a man who is feigning a courtship to *me,* of all people, all because he's too polite to refuse invitations from his friends' new wives.'

A rather irritable scowl immediately darkened his features. 'What do you mean, *you* of all people?'

'Well, I . . . ' She blinked in surprise. She had no idea *what* she meant. 'I don't know,' she finally said.

'Well, stop saying it,' he grumbled, then settled back into his chair.

Daphne's eyes inexplicably focused on a wet spot on the railing as she fought to keep an absurd smile off her face. Simon was so sweet when he was grumpy.

'What are you looking at?' he asked.

Her lips twitched. 'Nothing.'

'Then what are you smiling about?'

That she most certainly was not going to reveal. 'I'm not smiling.'

'If you're not smiling,' he muttered, 'then you're either about to suffer a seizure or sneeze.'

'Neither,' she said in a breezy voice. 'Just enjoying the excellent weather.'

Simon was leaning his head against the back of the chair, so he just rolled it to the side so he could look at her. 'And the company's not that bad,' he teased.

Daphne shot a pointed look at Anthony, who was leaning against the rail on the opposite side of the deck, glowering at them both. '*All* of the company?' she asked.

'If you mean your belligerent brother,' Simon replied, 'I'm actually finding his distress most amusing.'

Daphne fought a smile and didn't win. 'That's not very kindhearted of you.'

'I never said I was kind. And look—' Simon tipped his head ever so slightly in Anthony's direction. Anthony's scowl had, unbelievably, turned even blacker. 'He knows we're talking about him. It's killing him.'

'I thought you were friends.'

'We are *friends.* This is what friends do to one another.'

'Men are mad.'

'Generally speaking,' he agreed.

She rolled her eyes. 'I thought the primary rule of friendship was that one was not supposed to dally with one's friend's sister.'

'Ah, but I'm not dallying. I'm merely *pretending to* dally.'

Daphne nodded thoughtfully and glanced at Anthony. 'And it's still killing him – even though he knows the truth of the matter.'

'I know.' Simon grinned. 'Isn't it brilliant?'

Just then Violet came sailing across the deck. 'Children!' she called out. 'Children! Oh, pardon me, your grace,' she added when she spied him. 'It's certainly not fair for me to lump you with my children.'

Simon just smiled and waved off her apology.

'The captain tells me we're nearly there,' Violet explained. 'We should gather up our things.'

Simon rose to his feet and extended a helpful hand to Daphne, who took it gratefully, wobbling as she stood.

'I haven't my sea legs yet,' she laughed, clutching his arm to steady herself.

'And here we're merely on the river,' he murmured.

'Beast. You're not supposed to point out my lack of grace and balance.'

As she spoke, she turned her face toward his, and in that instant, with the wind catching her hair and painting her cheeks pink, she looked so enchantingly lovely that Simon nearly forgot to breathe.

Her lush mouth was caught somewhere between a laugh and a smile, and the sun glinted almost red on her hair. Here on the water, away from stuffy ballrooms, with the fresh air swirling about them, she looked natural and beautiful and just being in her presence made Simon want to grin like an idiot.

If they hadn't been about to pull into dock, with her entire family running around them, he would have kissed her. He knew he couldn't dally with her, and he knew he would never marry her, and still he found himself leaning toward her. He didn't even realize what he was doing until he suddenly felt off-balance and lurched back upright.

Anthony, unfortunately, caught the entire episode, and he rather brusquely insinuated himself between Simon and Daphne, grasping her arm with far more strength than grace. 'As your eldest brother,' he growled, 'I believe it is my honor to escort you ashore.'

Simon just bowed and let Anthony have his way, too shaken and angered by his momentary loss of control to argue.

The boat settled next to the dock, and a gangplank was put into place. Simon watched as the entire Bridgerton family disembarked, then he brought up the rear, following them onto the grassy banks of the Thames.

At the top of the hill stood the Royal Observatory, a stately old building of rich red brick. Its towers were topped with gray domes, and Simon had the sense that he was, as Daphne had put it, at the very center of the world. Everything, he realized, was measured from this point.

After having crossed a good portion of the globe, the thought was rather humbling.

'Do we have everyone?' the viscountess called out. 'Hold still, everyone, so I may be sure we are all present and accounted for.' She started counting heads, finally ending on herself with a triumphant, 'Ten! Good, we're all here.'

'Just be glad she doesn't make us line up by age any longer.'

Simon looked to the left to see Colin grinning at him.

'As a method of keeping order, age worked when it still corresponded with height. But then Benedict gained an inch on Anthony, and then Gregory outgrew Francesca—' Colin shrugged. 'Mother simply gave up.'

Simon scanned the crowd and lifted one shoulder in a shrug. 'I'm just trying to figure out where I'd fit in.'

'Somewhere near Anthony, if I had to hazard a guess,' Colin replied.

'God forbid,' Simon muttered.

Colin glanced at him with a mix of amusement and curiosity.

'Anthony!' Violet called out. 'Where's Anthony?'

Anthony indicated his location with a rather ill-tempered grunt.

'Oh, there you are, Anthony. Come and escort me in.'

Anthony reluctantly let go of Daphne's arm and walked to his mother's side.

'She's shameless, isn't she?' Colin whispered.

Simon thought it best not to comment.

'Well, don't disappoint her,' Colin said. 'After all her machinations, the least you can do is go and take Daphne's arm.'

Simon turned to Colin with a quirked eyebrow. 'You might be just as bad as your mother.'

Colin just laughed. 'Yes, except that at least I don't *pretend* to be subtle.'

Daphne chose that moment to walk over. 'I find myself without an escort,' she said.

'Imagine that,' Colin returned. 'Now, if the two of you will excuse me, I'm off to find Hyacinth. If I'm forced to escort Eloise, I may have to swim back to London. She's been a wretch ever since she attained the age of fourteen.'

Simon blinked in confusion. 'Didn't you just return from the Continent last week?'

Colin nodded. 'Yes, but Eloise's fourteenth birthday was a year and a half ago.'

Daphne swatted him on the elbow. 'If you're lucky, I won't tell her you said that.'

Colin just rolled his eyes and disappeared into the small crowd, bellowing Hyacinth's name.

Daphne laid her hand in the crook of Simon's elbow as he offered her his arm, then asked, 'Have we scared you off yet?'

'I beg your pardon?'

She offered him a rueful smile. 'There is nothing quite as exhausting as a Bridgerton family outing.'

'Oh, that.' Simon stepped quickly to the right to avoid Gregory, who was racing after Hyacinth, yelling something about mud and revenge. 'It's, ah, a new experience.'

'Very politely put, your grace,' Daphne said admiringly. 'I'm impressed.'

'Yes, well—' He jumped back as Hyacinth barreled by, squealing at such a pitch that Simon was certain that dogs would start howling from there to London. 'I have no siblings, after all.'

Daphne let out a dreamy sigh. 'No siblings,' she mused. 'Right now it sounds like heaven.' The faraway look remained in her eyes for a few more seconds, then she straightened and shook off her reverie. 'Be that as it may, however—' Her hand shot out just as Gregory ran past, catching the boy firmly by the upper arm. 'Gregory Bridgerton,' she scolded, 'you should know better than to run thus through a crowd. You're liable to knock someone over.'

'How did you do that?' Simon asked.

'What, catch him?'

'Yes.'

She shrugged. 'I have years of practice.'

'Daphne!' Gregory whined. His arm, after all, was still attached to her hand.

She let go. 'Now, slow down.'

He took two exaggerated steps then broke into a trot.

'No scolding for Hyacinth?' Simon asked.

Daphne motioned over her shoulder. 'It appears my mother has Hyacinth in hand.'

Simon saw that Violet was shaking her finger quite vehemently at Hyacinth. He turned back to Daphne. 'What were you about to say before Gregory appeared on the scene?'

She blinked. 'I have no idea.'

'I believe you were about to go into raptures at the thought of having no siblings.'

‘Oh, of course.’ She let out a little laugh as they followed the rest of the Bridgertons up the hill toward the observatory. ‘Actually, believe it or not, I was going to say that while the concept of eternal solitude is, at times, tempting, I think I would be quite lonely without family.’

Simon said nothing.

‘I cannot imagine having only one child myself,’ she added.

‘Sometimes,’ Simon said in a dry voice, ‘one has little choice in the matter.’

Daphne’s cheeks turned an immediate red. ‘Oh, I’m so sorry,’ she stammered, her feet absolutely refusing to take a step. ‘I’d forgotten. Your mother . . . ’

Simon paused beside her. ‘I didn’t know her,’ he said with a shrug. ‘I didn’t mourn her.’

But his blue eyes were strangely hollow and shuttered, and Daphne somehow knew that his words were false.

And at the same time, she knew that he believed them one hundred percent.

And she wondered – what could have happened to this man to make him lie to himself for so many years?

She studied his face, her head tilting slightly as she took in his features. The wind had brought color to his cheeks and ruffled his dark hair. He looked rather uncomfortable under her scrutiny, and finally he just grunted, and said, ‘We’re falling behind.’

Daphne looked up the hill. Her family was a good distance ahead of them. ‘Yes, of course,’ she said, straightening her shoulders. ‘We should get going.’

But as she trudged up the hill, she wasn’t thinking of her family, or of the observatory, or even of longitude. Instead, she was wondering why she had the most bizarre urge to throw her arms around the duke and never let go.

Several hours later, they were all back on the grassy banks of the Thames, enjoying the last bites of an elegant yet simple luncheon that had been prepared by the Bridgertons' cook. As he had the night before, Simon spoke little, instead observing the often boisterous interactions of Daphne's family.

But Hyacinth apparently had other ideas.

'Good day, your grace,' she said, seating herself next to him on the blanket one of the footmen had laid out for their picnic. 'Did you enjoy your tour of the observatory?'

Simon couldn't quite suppress a smile as he answered, 'Indeed I did, Miss Hyacinth. And you?'

'Oh, very much so. I especially appreciated your lecture on longitude and latitude.'

'Well, I don't know that I'd call it a *lecture,*' Simon said, the word making him feel just the slightest bit old and stodgy.

Across the blanket, Daphne was grinning at his distress.

Hyacinth just smiled flirtatiously – *flirtatiously?* – and said, 'Did you know that Greenwich also has a most romantic history?'

Daphne started to shake with laughter, the little traitor.

'Really?' Simon managed to get out.

'Indeed,' Hyacinth replied, using such cultured tones that Simon briefly wondered if there were actually a forty-year-old matron inside her ten-year-old body. 'It was here that Sir Walter Raleigh laid his cloak upon the ground so that Queen Elizabeth would not have to dirty her slippers in a puddle.'

'Is that so?' Simon stood and scanned the area.

'Your grace!' Hyacinth's face reverted to ten-year-old impatience as she jumped to her feet. 'What are you doing?'

'Examining the terrain,' he replied. He cast a secret glance at Daphne. She was looking up at him with mirth and humor and something else that made him feel about ten feet tall.

'But what are you looking for?' Hyacinth persisted.

'Puddles.'

'Puddles?' Her face slowly transformed into one of utter delight as she grasped his meaning. 'Puddles?'

'Indeed. If I'm going to have to ruin a cloak to save your slippers, Miss Hyacinth, I'd like to know about it in advance.'

'But you're not wearing a cloak.'

'Heavens above,' Simon replied, in such a voice that Daphne burst into laughter below him. 'You do not mean that I will be forced to remove my *shirt?*'

'No!' Hyacinth squealed. 'You don't have to remove anything! There aren't any puddles.'

'Thank heavens,' Simon breathed, clasping one hand to his chest for added effect. He was having far more fun with this than he would have ever dreamed possible. 'You Bridgerton ladies are very demanding, did you know that?'

Hyacinth viewed him with a mixture of suspicion and glee. Suspicion finally won out. Her hands found their way to her little hips as she narrowed her eyes and asked, 'Are you funning me?'

He smiled right at her. 'What do you think?'

'I think you are.'

'I think I'm lucky there aren't any puddles about.'

Hyacinth pondered that for a moment. 'If you decide to marry my sister—' she said.

Daphne choked on a biscuit.

'—then you have my approval.'

Simon choked on air.

'But if you don't,' Hyacinth continued, smiling shyly, 'then I'd be much obliged if you'd wait for me.'

Luckily for Simon, who had little experience with young girls and not a clue how to respond, Gregory came dashing by and yanked on Hyacinth's hair. She immediately took off after him, her eyes narrowed with the single-minded determination to get even.

'I never thought I'd say this,' Daphne said, laughter in her voice, 'but I believe you have just been saved by my younger brother.'

'How old is your sister?' Simon asked.

'Ten, why?'

He shook his head in bewilderment. 'Because for a moment, I could have sworn she was forty.'

Daphne smiled. 'Sometimes she is so like my mother it's frightening.'

At that moment, the woman in question stood and began to summon her children back to the boat. 'Come along!' Violet called out. 'It's growing late!'

Simon looked at his pocket watch. 'It's three.'

Daphne shrugged as she rose to her feet. 'To her that's late. According to Mother, a lady should always be home at five o'clock.'

'Why?'

She reached down to pick up the blanket. 'I have no idea. To get ready for the evening, I suppose. It's one of those rules I've grown up with and deemed best not to question.' She straightened, holding the soft blue blanket to her chest, and smiled. 'Are we ready to go?'

Simon held out his arm. 'Certainly.'

They took a few steps toward the boat, and then Daphne said, 'You were very good with Hyacinth. You must have spent a great deal of time with children.'

'None,' he said tersely.

'Oh,' she said, a puzzled frown decorating her face. 'I knew you had no siblings, but I had assumed you must have met some children on your travels.'

'No.'

Daphne held silent for a moment, wondering if she should pursue the conversation. Simon's voice had grown hard and forbidding, and his face . . .

He didn't look like the same man who had teased Hyacinth mere minutes earlier.

But for some reason – maybe because it had been such a lovely afternoon, maybe it was just because the weather was fine – she faked a sunny smile and said, 'Well, experience or no, you clearly have the touch. Some adults don't know how to talk to children, you know.'

He said nothing.

She patted his arm. 'You'll make some lucky child an excellent father someday.'

His head whipped around to face her, and the look in his eyes nearly froze her heart. 'I believe I told you I have no intention of marrying,' he bit off. 'Ever.'

'But surely you—'

'Therefore it is unlikely that I shall ever have children.'

'I . . . I see.' Daphne swallowed and attempted a shaky smile, but she had a feeling she didn't manage anything more than a slight quivering of her lips. And even though she knew that their courtship was nothing more than a charade, she felt a vague sense of disappointment.

They reached the edge of the dock, where most of the rest of the Bridgertons were milling about. A few had already boarded, and Gregory was dancing on the gangplank.

'Gregory!' Violet called out, her voice sharp. 'Stop that at once!'

He stilled, but didn't move from his position.

'Either get on the boat or come back to the dock.'

Simon slipped his arm from Daphne's, muttering, 'That gangplank looks wet.' He started moving forward.

'You heard Mother!' Hyacinth called out.

'Oh, Hyacinth,' Daphne sighed to herself. 'Can't you just keep out of it?'

Gregory stuck out his tongue.

Daphne groaned, then noticed that Simon was still walking toward the gangplank. She hurried to his side, whispering, 'Simon, I'm sure he'll be fine.'

'Not if he slips and gets caught in the ropes.' He motioned with his chin to a tangled mess of ropes that were hanging off the boat.

Simon reached the end of the gangplank, walking casually, as if he hadn't a worry in the world. 'Are you going to get moving?' he called out, stepping out onto the narrow piece of wood. 'So that I might cross?'

Gregory blinked. 'Don't you have to escort Daphne?'

Simon groaned and moved forward, but just then, Anthony, who had already boarded the small yacht, appeared at the top of the gangplank.

'Gregory!' he called out sharply. 'Get on this boat at once!'

From down on the dock, Daphne watched with horror as Gregory spun around in surprise, losing his footing on the slippery wood. Anthony leapt forward, making a frantic grab with his arms, but Gregory had already slid to his bottom, and Anthony caught only air.

Anthony fought for balance as Gregory slid down the gangplank, clipping Simon rather neatly in the shins.

'Simon!' Daphne croaked, running forward.

Simon went tumbling into the murky water of the Thames, just as Gregory wailed a heartfelt, 'I'm sorry!' He scooted up the gangplank backwards on his behind – rather like a crab, actually – not at all looking where he was going.

Which probably explained why he had no idea that Anthony – who had almost managed to regain his balance – was only a few short feet behind him.

Gregory rammed into Anthony with a thud on his part and a grunt on Anthony's, and before anyone knew it, Anthony was sputtering in the water, right next to Simon.

Daphne clapped a hand to her mouth, her eyes wide as saucers.

Violet yanked on her arm. 'I highly suggest you don't laugh.'

Daphne pinched her lips together in an effort to comply, but it was difficult. '*You're* laughing,' she pointed out.

'I'm not,' Violet lied. Her entire neck was quivering with the exertion required to keep her laughter inside. 'And besides, I'm a *mother*. They wouldn't dare do anyme.'

Anthony and Simon came stalking out of the water, dripping and glaring at each other.

Gregory crawled the rest of the way up the gangplank and disappeared over the edge.

'Maybe you should intercede,' Violet suggested.

'Me?' Daphne squeaked.

'It looks as if they might come to blows.'

'But why? It was all Gregory's fault.'

'Of course,' Violet said impatiently, 'but they're *men,* and they're both furious and embarrassed, and they can't very well take it out on a boy of twelve.'

Sure enough, Anthony was muttering, 'I could have taken care of him,' just as Simon growled, 'If you hadn't surprised him . . . '

Violet rolled her eyes, and said to Daphne, 'Any man, you'll soon learn, has an insurmountable need to blame someone else when he is made to look a fool.'

Daphne rushed forward, fully intending to attempt to reason with the two men, but one close look at their faces told her that nothing she could possibly say could imbue them with as much intelligence and sensibility as a woman would have in such a situation, so she simply pasted on a bright smile, grabbed Simon's arm, and said, 'Escort me up?'

Simon glared at Anthony.

Anthony glared at Simon.

Daphne yanked.

'This isn't over, Hastings,' Anthony hissed.

'Far from it,' Simon hissed back.

Daphne realized that they were simply looking for an excuse to come to blows. She yanked harder, prepared to dislocate Simon's shoulder if need be.

After one last burning glare, he acquiesced and followed her up into the boat.

It was a very long trip home.

Later that night, as Daphne prepared for bed, she found herself oddly restless. Sleep, she could already tell, would prove impossible, so she pulled on a robe and wandered downstairs in search of warm milk and some company. With so many siblings, she thought wryly, surely *someone* had to be up and about.

On her way to the kitchen, however, she heard rustlings in Anthony's study, so she poked her head in. Her eldest brother was hunched over his desk, ink spots on his fingers from the correspondence he was answering. It was uncommon to find him here so late into the evening. He'd preferred to keep his study at Bridgerton House even after he'd moved into his bachelor's lodgings, but he usually took care of his business matters during the day.

'Don't you have a secretary to do that?' Daphne asked with a smile.

Anthony looked up. 'Damned fool got married and moved to Bristol,' he muttered.

'Ah.' She walked into the room and perched on a chair opposite the desk. 'That would explain your presence here in the wee hours of the morning.'

Anthony glanced up at the clock. 'Midnight is hardly wee. And besides, it took me all afternoon just to get the Thames out of my hair.'

Daphne tried not to smile.

'But you're right,' Anthony said with a sigh, setting down his quill. 'It's late, and there's nothing here that won't keep until the morning.' He leaned back and stretched out his neck. 'What are you doing up and about?'

'Couldn't sleep,' Daphne explained with a shrug. 'I came downstairs for some hot milk and heard you cursing.'

Anthony let out a grunt. 'It's this bloody quill. I swear I—' He smiled sheepishly. 'I suppose "I swear" pretty much takes care of it, eh?'

Daphne smiled in return. Her brothers had never minded their language around her. 'So you'll be heading home soon, then?'

He nodded. 'Although that warm milk you mentioned sounds rather nice. Why don't you ring for it?'

Daphne stood. 'I've a better idea. Why don't we get it ourselves? We're not complete idiots. We should be able to warm some milk. And besides, the servants are probably in bed.'

Anthony followed her out the door. 'Very well, but you shall have to do all the work. I haven't the faintest idea how to boil milk.'

'I don't think one is supposed to let it boil,' Daphne said with a frown. She rounded the last corner on the way to the kitchen and pushed open the door. The room was dark, save for moonlight glowing through the windows. 'Find a lamp while I find some milk,' she said to Anthony. Her face took on a slight smirk. 'You *can* light a lamp, can't you?'

'Oh, I believe I can manage that,' he said good-naturedly.

Daphne smiled to herself as she fumbled about in the dark, pulling a small pot from the hanging rack above her. She and Anthony usually had an easy, joking relationship, and it was nice to see him back to his normal self again. He'd been in such a beastly mood for the past week, with most of his sour temper directed squarely at her.

And Simon, of course, but Simon was rarely present to receive Anthony's scowls.

A light flickered to life behind her, and Daphne turned to see Anthony smiling triumphantly. 'Have you found the milk,' he asked, 'or must I venture out in search of a cow?'

She laughed and held up a bottle. 'Found it!' She wandered over to the enclosed range, a rather modern-looking contraption that Cook had purchased earlier in the year. 'Do you know how to work this?' she asked.

'No idea. You?'

Daphne shook her head. 'None.' She reached forward and gingerly touched the surface of the stove top. 'It's not hot.'

'Not even a little bit?'

She shook her head. 'It's rather cold, actually.'

Brother and sister were silent for a few seconds.

'You know,' Anthony finally said, 'cold milk might be quite refreshing.'

'I was just thinking that very thing!'

Anthony grinned and found two mugs. 'Here, you pour.'

Daphne did, and soon they were seated on stools, gulping down the fresh milk. Anthony drained his mug in short order, and poured another. 'You need some more?' he asked, wiping off his milk mustache.

'No, I'm barely halfway to the bottom,' Daphne said, taking another sip. She licked at her lips, fidgeting in her chair. Now that she was alone with Anthony, and he seemed like he was back in his usual good humor, it seemed like a good time to . . . Well, the truth was . . .

Oh, blast, she thought to herself, *just go ahead and ask him.*

'Anthony?' she said, a touch hesitantly. 'Could I ask you a question?'

'Of course.'

'It's about the duke.'

Anthony's mug hit the table with a loud thunk. 'What about the duke?'

'I know you don't like him . . . ' she began, her words trailing off.

'It's not that I don't like him,' Anthony said with a weary sigh. 'He's one of my closest friends.'

Daphne's brows rose. 'One would be hard-pressed to deduce that based on your recent behavior.'

'I just don't trust him around women. Around you in particular.'

'Anthony, you must know that that is one of the silliest things you have ever said. The duke might have been a rake – I suppose he might still be a rake for all I know – but he would never seduce me, if only because I'm your sister.'

Anthony looked unconvinced.

'Even if there weren't some male code of honor about such things,' Daphne persisted, barely resisting the urge to roll her eyes, 'he knows you'd kill him if he touched me. The man isn't stupid.'

Anthony refrained from commenting, instead saying, 'What was it you wanted to ask me?'

'Actually,' Daphne said slowly, 'I was wondering if you knew why the duke was so opposed to marriage.'

Anthony spit his milk halfway across the table. 'For Christ's sake, Daphne! I thought we agreed that this was just a charade! Why are you even thinking about marrying him?'

'I'm not!' she insisted, thinking that she might be lying but unwilling to examine her feelings closely enough to be sure. 'I'm just curious,' she muttered defensively.

'You had better not be thinking about trying to get him to marry you,' Anthony said with a grunt, 'because I'll tell you right now he'll never do it. Never. Do you understand me, Daphne? He won't marry you.'

'I would have to be a half-wit not to understand you,' she grumbled.

'Good. Then that's the end of it.'

'No, it's not!' she returned. 'You still haven't answered my question.'

Anthony leveled a stony stare at her across the table.

'About why he won't get married,' she prodded.

'Why are you so interested?' he asked wearily.

The truth, Daphne feared, lay a little too close to Anthony's accusations, but she just said, 'I'm curious, and besides, I think I have a right to know, since, if I don't find an acceptable suitor soon, I may become a pariah after the duke drops me.'

'I thought *you* were supposed to jilt *him,*' Anthony said suspiciously.

Daphne snorted. 'Who is going to believe that?'

Anthony didn't immediately jump to her defense, which Daphne found vaguely annoying. But he did say, 'I don't know why Hastings refuses to marry. All I know is that he has maintained this opinion for as long as I've known him.'

Daphne opened her mouth to speak, but Anthony cut her off by adding, '*And* he's stated it in such a way so that I do not believe his is the weak vow of the beleaguered bachelor.'

'Meaning?'

'Meaning that unlike most men, when he says he will never marry, he means it.'

'I see.'

Anthony let out a long, tired breath, and Daphne noticed tiny lines of concern around his eyes that she'd never seen before. 'Choose a man from your new crowd of suitors,' he said, 'and forget Hastings. He's a good man, but he's not for you.'

Daphne latched on to the first part of his sentence. 'But you think he's a good—'

'He's not for you,' Anthony repeated.

But Daphne couldn't help thinking that maybe, just maybe, Anthony might be wrong.

9

The Duke of Hastings was espied yet again with Miss Bridgerton. (That is Miss Daphne Bridgerton, for those of you who, like This Author, find it difficult to differentiate between the multitudes of Bridgerton offspring.) It has been some time since This Author has seen a couple so obviously devoted to one another.

It does seem odd, however, that, with the exception of the Bridgerton family outing to Greenwich, which was reported in this newspaper ten days earlier, they are seen together only at evening functions. This Author has it on the best authority that while the duke called upon Miss Bridgerton at her home a fortnight ago, this courtesy has not been repeated, and indeed, they have not been seen riding together in Hyde Park even once!

LADY WHISTLEDOWN'S SOCIETY PAPERS,
14 MAY 1813

Two weeks later, Daphne found herself in Hampstead Heath, standing on the fringes of Lady Trowbridge's ballroom, far away from the fashionable crowd. She was quite content with her position.

She didn't want to be at the center of the party. She didn't want to be found by the dozens of suitors now clamoring to claim her in a dance. In all truth, she didn't want to be in Lady Trowbridge's ballroom at all.

Because Simon was not there.

This did not mean that she was destined to spend the evening as a wallflower. All of Simon's predictions in regard to her burgeoning popularity had proven correct, and Daphne, who had always been the girl everyone liked but no one adored, was suddenly proclaimed the season's Incomparable. Everyone who cared to air an opinion on the subject (and this being the *ton,* that meant everyone) declared that they always knew that Daphne was special and were just waiting for everyone else to notice. Lady Jersey told everyone who would listen that she had been predicting Daphne's success for months, and the only mystery was why no one had listened to her sooner.

Which was, of course, hogwash. While Daphne had certainly never been the object of Lady Jersey's scorn, not one Bridgerton could recall ever hearing Lady Jersey refer to her (as she was presently doing) as 'Tomorrow's Treasure.'

But even though Daphne's dance card was now full within minutes of her arrival at any ball, and even though men fought for the privilege of fetching her a glass of lemonade (Daphne had almost laughed out loud the first time *that* had happened), she found that no evening was truly memorable unless Simon was at her side.

It didn't matter that he seemed to find it necessary to mention at least once every evening that he was adamantly opposed to the institution of marriage. (Although, to his credit, he usually mentioned this in conjunction with his thankfulness to Daphne for saving him from the multitudes of Ambitious Mamas.) And it didn't matter that he occasionally fell silent and was even almost rude to certain members of society.

All that seemed to matter were those moments when they were not quite alone (they were never alone), but still somehow left to their own devices. A laughing conversation in a corner, a waltz around a ballroom. Daphne could look into his pale blue eyes and almost forget that she was surrounded by five hundred onlookers, all of whom were inordinately interested in the state of her courtship.

And she could almost forget that her courtship was a complete sham.

Daphne hadn't tried to talk to Anthony about Simon again. Her brother's hostility was apparent every time the duke's name was brought up in conversation. And when he and Simon actually met – well, Anthony usually managed a certain level of cordiality, but that was all he seemed able to muster.

And yet even amidst all this anger, Daphne could see faint glimmers of the old friendship between them. She could only hope that when all this was over – and she was married off to some boring but affable earl who never quite managed to make her heart sing – that the two men would be friends again.

At Anthony's somewhat forceful request, Simon had elected not to attend every social event to which Violet and Daphne had RSVPed in the affirmative. Anthony said that the only reason he had agreed to this ridiculous scheme was so that Daphne might find a husband among all her new suitors. Unfortunately, in Anthony's opinion (and fortunately in Daphne's) none of these eager young gentlemen dared to approach her in Simon's presence.

'A fat lot of good this is doing,' were Anthony's exact words.

Actually, those exact words had been appended a fair amount of cursing and invective, but Daphne had seen no reason to dwell on this. Ever since the incident at – or rather *in* – the Thames, Anthony had spent a great deal of time applying expletives to Simon's name.

But Simon had seen Anthony's point, and Simon had told Daphne that he wanted her to find a suitable husband.

And so Simon stayed away.

And Daphne was miserable.

She supposed she should have known that this was going

to happen. She should have realized the dangers of being courted – even falsely – by the man society had recently dubbed The Devastating Duke.

The moniker had begun when Philipa Featherington had pronounced him 'devastatingly handsome,' and since Philipa didn't know the meaning of the word 'whisper,' all the *ton* bore witness to her statement. Within minutes some droll young buck just down from Oxford had shortened and alliterated, and The Devastating Duke was born.

Daphne found the name woefully ironic. For The Devastating Duke was devastating her heart.

Not that he meant to. Simon treated her with nothing but respect and honor and good humor. Even Anthony was forced to admit that he'd been given no cause to complain in that quarter. Simon never tried to get Daphne alone, never did anything more than kiss her gloved hand (and much to Daphne's dismay, that had only happened twice).

They had become the best of companions, their conversations ranging from comfortable silences to the wittiest of repartee. At every party, they danced together twice – the maximum permitted without scandalizing society.

And Daphne knew, without a shadow of a doubt, that she was falling in love.

The irony was exquisite. She had, of course, begun spending so much time in Simon's company specifically so that she might attract other men. For his part, Simon had begun spending time in her company so that he might avoid marriage.

Come to think of it, Daphne thought, sagging against the wall, the irony was exquisitely painful.

Although Simon was still quite vocal on the subject of marriage and his determination never to enter that blessed state, she did on occasion catch him looking at her in ways that made her think he might desire her. He never repeated any of the risque comments he'd made before he'd learned she was a Bridgerton, but sometimes she caught him looking at her in the same hungry, feral way he'd done that first evening. He turned away, of course, as soon as she noticed, but it was always enough to set her skin tingling and shorten her breath with desire.

And his eyes! Everyone likened their color to ice, and when Daphne watched him converse with other members of society, she could see why. Simon wasn't as loquacious with others as he was with her. His words were more clipped, his tone more brusque, and his eyes echoed the hardness in his demeanor.

But when they were laughing together, just the two of them poking fun at some silly society rule, his eyes changed. They grew softer, gentler, more at ease. In her more fanciful moments, she almost thought they looked as if they were melting.

She sighed, leaning even more heavily against the wall. It seemed her fanciful moments were coming closer and closer together these days.

'Ho, there, Daff, why are you skulking in the corner?'

Daphne looked up to see Colin approaching, his usual cocky smile firmly in place on his handsome face. Since his return to London, he had taken the town by storm, and Daphne could easily name a dozen young ladies who were *positive* they were in love with him and *desperate* for his attention. She wasn't worried about her brother's returning any of their affections, however; Colin obviously had many more wild oats to sow before he settled down.

'I'm not skulking,' she corrected. 'I'm avoiding.'

'Avoiding whom? Hastings?'

'No, of course not. He's not here tonight, anyway.'

'Yes, he is.'

Since this was Colin, whose primary purpose in life (after chasing loose women and betting on horses, of course) was to torment his sister, Daphne meant to act blase, but still she lurched to attention as she asked, 'He is?'

Colin nodded slyly and motioned with his head toward the

ballroom entrance. 'I saw him enter not fifteen minutes ago.'

Daphne narrowed her eyes. 'Are you bamming me? He told me quite specifically that he wasn't planning to attend tonight.'

'And you still came?' Colin laid both his hands on his cheeks and faked surprise.

'Of course I did,' she retorted. 'My life does not revolve around Hastings.'

'Doesn't it?'

Daphne had the sinking feeling that he was not being facetious. 'No, it doesn't,' she replied, lying through her teeth. Her life might not revolve around Simon, but her thoughts certainly did.

Colin's emerald eyes grew uncharacteristically serious. 'You've got it bad, don't you?'

'I have no idea what you mean.'

He smiled knowingly. 'You will.'

'Colin!'

'In the meantime' – he motioned back toward the ballroom's entrance – 'why don't you go and locate him? Clearly my scintillating company pales in comparison. I can see that your feet are already inching away from me.'

Horrified that her body would betray her in such a way, Daphne looked down.

'Ha! Made you look.'

'Colin Bridgerton,' Daphne ground out, 'sometimes I swear I think you're no more than three years old.'

'An interesting concept,' he mused, 'and one that would place you at the tender age of one and a half, little sister.'

Lacking a suitably cutting retort, Daphne just fixed upon him her blackest scowl.

But Colin only laughed. 'An attractive expression to be sure, sis, but one you might want to remove from your cheeks. His Devastatingness is heading this way.'

Daphne refused to fall for his bait this time. He wasn't going to Make Her Look.

Colin leaned forward and whispered conspiratorially, 'This time I'm not kidding, Daff.'

Daphne held her scowl.

Colin chuckled.

'Daphne!' Simon's voice. Right at her ear.

She whirled around.

Colin's chuckles grew more heartfelt. 'You really ought to have more faith in your favorite brother, dear sis.'

'*He's* your favorite brother?' Simon asked, one dark brow raised in disbelief.

'Only because Gregory put a toad in my bed last night,' Daphne bit off, 'and Benedict's standing has never recovered from the time he beheaded my favorite doll.'

'Makes me wonder what Anthony's done to deny him even an honorable mention,' Colin murmured.

'Don't you have somewhere else to be?' Daphne asked pointedly.

Colin shrugged. 'Not really.'

'Didn't,' she asked through clenched teeth, 'you just tell me you promised a dance to Prudence Featherington?'

'Gads, no. You must have misheard.'

'Perhaps Mother is looking for you, then. In fact, I'm certain I hear her calling your name.'

Colin grinned at her discomfort. 'You're not supposed to be so obvious,' he said in a stage whisper, purposely loud enough for Simon to hear. 'He'll figure out that you like him.'

Simon's entire body jerked with barely contained mirth.

'It's not his company I'm trying to secure,' Daphne said acidly. 'It's yours I'm trying to avoid.'

Colin clapped a hand over his heart. 'You wound me, Daff.' He turned to Simon. 'Oh, how she wounds me.'

'You missed your calling, Bridgerton,' Simon said genially. 'You should have been on the stage.'

'An interesting idea,' Colin replied, 'but one that would surely give my mother the vapors.' His eyes lit up. 'Now that's an idea. And just when the party was growing tedious. Good eve to you both.' He executed a smart bow and walked off.

Daphne and Simon remained silent as they watched Colin disappear into the crowd. 'The next shriek you hear,' Daphne said blandly, 'will surely be my mother's.'

'And the thud will be her body hitting the floor in a dead faint?'

Daphne nodded, a reluctant smile playing across her lips. 'But of course.' She waited a moment before saying, 'I wasn't expecting you this evening.'

He shrugged, the black cloth of his evening jacket wrinkling slightly with the movement. 'I was bored.'

'You were bored so you decided to come all the way out to Hampstead Heath to attend Lady Trowbridge's annual ball?' Her eyebrows arched up. Hampstead Heath was a good seven miles from Mayfair, at least an hour's drive in the best of conditions, more on nights like tonight, when all the ton was clogging the roads. 'Forgive me if I start to question your sanity.'

'I'm starting to question it myself,' he muttered.

'Well, whatever the case,' she said with a happy sigh, 'I'm glad you're here. It's been a ghastly evening.'

'Really?'

She nodded. 'I have been plagued by questions about you.'

'Well, now, this grows interesting.'

'Think again. The first person to interrogate me was my mother. She wants to know why you never call upon me in the afternoon.'

Simon frowned. 'Do you think it's necessary? I rather thought my undivided attention at these evening affairs would be enough to perpetrate the ruse.'

Daphne surprised herself by managing not to growl in frustration. He didn't need to make this sound like such a chore. 'Your undivided attention,' she said, 'would have been enough to fool anyone but my mother. And she probably wouldn't have said anything except that your lack of calls was reported in *Whistledown.*'

'Really?' Simon asked with great interest.

'Really. So now you'd better call tomorrow or everyone will start to wonder.'

'I'd like to know who that woman's spies are,' Simon murmured, 'and then I'd like to hire them for myself.'

'What do you need spies for?'

'Nothing. But it seems a shame to let such stellar talent go to waste.'

Daphne rather doubted that the fictitious Lady Whistledown would agree that any talents were being wasted, but she didn't particularly want to get into a discussion of the merits and evils of that newspaper, so she just shrugged off his comment. 'And then,' she continued, 'once my mother was through with me, everyone else set in, and they were even worse.'

'Heaven forfend.'

She turned an acerbic look on him. 'All but one of the questioners were female, and although they all vehemently professed their happiness on my behalf, they were clearly trying to deduce the probability of our not becoming betrothed.'

'You told them all I was desperately in love with you, I assume?'

Daphne felt something lurch in her chest. 'Yes,' she lied, offering him a too-sweet smile. 'I have a reputation to maintain, after all.'

Simon laughed. 'So then, who was the lone male doing the questioning?'

Daphne pulled a face. 'It was another duke, actually. A bizarre old man who claimed to have been friends with your father.'

Simon's face went suddenly tight.

She just shrugged, not having seen the change in his

expression. 'He went on and on about what a *good duke* your father was.' She let out a little laugh as she tried to imitate the old man's voice. 'I had no idea you dukes had to look out for one another so much. We don't want an incompetent duke making the title look bad, after all.'

Simon said nothing.

Daphne tapped her finger against her cheek in thought. 'Do you know, I've never heard you mention your father, actually.'

'That is because I don't choose to discuss him,' Simon said curtly.

She blinked with concern. 'Is something wrong?'

'Not at all,' he said, his voice clipped.

'Oh.' She caught herself chewing on her lower lip and forced herself to stop. 'I won't mention it then.'

'I said *nothing wrong.*'

Daphne kept her expression impassive. 'Of course.'

There was a long, uncomfortable silence. Daphne picked awkwardly at the fabric of her skirts before finally saying, 'Lovely flowers Lady Trowbridge used for decoration, don't you think?'

Simon followed the motion of her hand toward a large arrangement of pink and white roses. 'Yes.'

'I wonder if she grew them.'

'I haven't the faintest.'

Another awkward silence.

'Roses are so difficult to grow.'

This time his reply was just a grunt.

Daphne cleared her throat, and then, when he didn't even so much as look at her, asked, 'Have you tried the lemonade?'

'I don't drink lemonade.'

'Well, I do,' she snapped, deciding she'd had enough. 'And I'm thirsty. So if you will excuse me, I'm going to fetch myself a glass and leave you to your black mood. I'm certain you can find someone more entertaining than I.'

She turned to leave, but before she could take a step, she felt a heavy hand on her arm. She looked down, momentarily mesmerized by the sight of his white-gloved hand resting against the peach silk of her gown. She stared at it, almost waiting for it to move, to travel down the length of her arm until it reached the bare skin of her elbow.

But of course he wouldn't do that. He only did such things in her dreams.

'Daphne, please,' he said, 'turn around.'

His voice was low, and there was an intensity to it that made her shiver.

She turned, and as soon as her eyes met his, he said, 'Please accept my apologies.'

She nodded.

But he clearly felt the need to explain further. 'I did not . . . ' He stopped and coughed quietly into his hand. 'I was not on good terms with my father. I – I don't like to talk about him.'

Daphne stared at him in fascination. She'd never seen him at such a loss for words.

Simon let out an irritated exhale. It was strange, Daphne thought, because it seemed as if he were irritated with himself.

'When you brought him up . . . ' He shook his head, as if deciding to try a different avenue of conversation. 'It grabs at my mind. I can't stop thinking about him. It – it – it makes me extremely angry.'

'I'm sorry,' she said, knowing her confusion must show on her face. She thought she should say more, but she didn't know what words to use.

'Not at you,' he said quickly, and as his pale blue eyes focused on hers, something seemed to clear in them. His face seemed to relax as well, especially the tight lines that had formed around his mouth. He swallowed uncomfortably. 'I'm angry at myself.'

'And apparently at your father as well,' she said softly.

He said nothing. She hadn't expected him to, she realized. His hand was still on her arm, and she covered it with her own. 'Would you like to get a bit of air?' she asked gently. 'You look as if you might need it.'

He nodded. 'You stay. Anthony will have my head if I take you out onto the terrace.'

'Anthony can hang for all I care.' Daphne's mouth tightened with irritation. 'I'm sick of his constant hovering, anyway.'

'He is only trying to be a good brother to you.'

Her lips parted in consternation. 'Whose side are you on, anyway?'

Deftly ignoring her question, he said, 'Very well. But just a short walk. Anthony I can take on, but if he enlists the aid of your brothers, I'm a dead man.'

There was a door leading out to the terrace a few yards away. Daphne nodded toward it, and Simon's hand slid down her arm and around the crook of her elbow.

'There are probably dozens of couples out on the terrace, anyway,' she said. 'He'll have nothing about which to complain.'

But before they could make their way outside, a loud male voice sounded from behind them. 'Hastings!'

Simon halted and turned around, grimly realizing that he had grown used to the name. In no time, he'd be thinking of it as his own.

Somehow that concept made him ill.

An older man leaning on a cane hobbled his way toward them. 'That's the duke I told you about,' Daphne said. 'Of Middlethorpe, I believe.'

Simon nodded curtly, having no desire to speak.

'Hastings!' the old man said, patting him on the arm. 'I have wanted to make your acquaintance for so very long. I am Middlethorpe. Your father was a good friend of mine.'

Simon just nodded again, the motion almost military in its precision.

'He missed you, you know. While you were off traveling.'

A rage began to build in his mouth, a rage that rendered his tongue swollen and his cheeks tight and rigid. He knew, beyond a shadow of a doubt, that if he tried to speak, he would sound just as he'd done when he was a lad of eight.

And there was no way he'd shame himself in such a way in front of Daphne.

Somehow – he'd never know how, maybe it was because he'd never had much trouble with vowels aside from 'I' – he managed to say, 'Oh?' He was pleased that his voice came out sharp and condescending.

But if the old man heard the rancor in his tone, he made no reaction to it. 'I was with him when he died,' Middlethorpe said.

Simon said nothing.

Daphne – bless her – leapt into the fray with a sympathetic, 'My goodness.'

'He asked me to pass along some messages to you. I have several letters in my house.'

'Burn them.'

Daphne gasped and grabbed Middlethorpe by the arm. 'Oh, no, don't do that. He might not want to see them now, but surely he will change his mind in the future.'

Simon blasted her with an icy glare before turning back to Middlethorpe. 'I said burn them.'

'I – ah—' Middlethorpe looked hopelessly confused. He must have been aware that the Basset father and son were not on good terms, but clearly the late duke had not revealed to him the true depth of the estrangement. He looked to Daphne, sensing a possible ally, and said to her, 'In addition to the letters, there were things he asked me to tell him. I could tell them to him now.'

But Simon had already dropped Daphne's arm and stalked outside.

'I'm so sorry,' Daphne said to Middlethorpe, feeling the

need to apologize for Simon's atrocious behavior. 'I'm sure he doesn't mean to be rude.'

Middlethorpe's expression told her that he *knew* Simon meant to be rude.

But Daphne still said, 'He's a bit sensitive about his father.'

Middlethorpe nodded. 'The duke warned me he'd react this way. But he laughed as he said it, then made a joke about the Basset pride. I must confess I didn't think he was completely serious.'

Daphne looked nervously through the open door to the terrace. 'Apparently he was,' she murmured. 'I had best see to him.'

Middlethorpe nodded.

'Please don't burn those letters,' she said.

'I would never dream of it. But—'

Daphne had already taken a step toward the terrace door and turned around at the halting tone of the old man's voice. 'What is it?' she asked.

'I'm not a well man,' Middlethorpe said. 'I – The doctor says it could be anytime now. May I trust the letters into your safekeeping?'

Daphne stared at the duke with a mix of shock and horror. Shock because she could not believe he would trust such personal correspondence to a young woman he'd known for barely an hour. Horror because she knew that if she accepted them, Simon might never forgive her.

'I don't know,' she said in a strained voice. 'I'm not sure I'm the right person.'

Middlethorpe's ancient eyes crinkled with wisdom. 'I think you might be exactly the right person,' he said softly. 'And I believe you'll know when the time is right to give him the letters. May I have them delivered to you?'

Mutely, she nodded. She didn't know what else to do.

Middlethorpe lifted his cane and pointed it out toward the terrace. 'You'd best go to him.'

Daphne caught his gaze, nodded, and scurried outside.

The terrace was lit by only a few wall sconces, so the night air was dim, and it was only with the aid of the moon that she saw Simon off in the corner. His stance was wide and angry, and his arms were crossed across his chest. He was facing the endless lawn that stretched out past the terrace, but Daphne sincerely doubted he saw anything aside from his own raging emotions.

She moved silently toward him, the cool breeze a welcome change from the stagnant air in the overcrowded ballroom. Light murmurs of voices drifted through the night, indicating that they were not alone on the terrace, but Daphne saw no one else in the dim light. Clearly the other guests had elected to sequester themselves in dark corners. Or maybe they had descended the steps to the garden and were sitting on the benches below.

As she walked to him, she thought about saying something like, 'You were very rude to the duke,' or 'Why are you so angry at your father?' but in the end she decided this was not the time to probe into Simon's feelings, and so when she reached his side, she just leaned against the balustrade, and said, 'I wish I could see the stars.'

Simon looked at her, first with surprise, then with curiosity.

'You can never see them in London,' she continued, keeping her voice purposefully light. 'Either the lights are too bright, or the fog has rolled in. Or sometimes the air is just too filthy to see through it.' She shrugged and glanced back up at the sky, which was overcast. 'I'd hoped that I'd be able to see them here in Hampstead Heath. But alas, the clouds do not cooperate.'

There was a very long moment of silence. Then Simon cleared his throat, and asked, 'Did you know that the stars are completely different in the southern hemisphere?'

Daphne hadn't realized how tense she was until she felt her entire body relax at his query. Clearly, he was trying to force their evening back into normal patterns, and she was happy to let him. She looked at him quizzically, and said, 'You're joking.'

'I'm not. Look it up in any astronomy book.'

'Hmmm.'

'The interesting thing,' Simon continued, his voice sounding less strained as he moved further into the conversation, 'is that even if you're not a scholar of astronomy – and I'm not—'

'And obviously,' Daphne interrupted with a self-deprecating smile, 'neither am I.'

He patted her hand, and smiled, and Daphne noticed with relief that his happiness reached his eyes. Then her relief turned into something a little more precious – joy. Because she had been the one to chase the shadows from his eyes. She wanted to banish them forever, she realized.

If only he would let her . . .

'You'd notice the difference anyway,' he said. 'That's what's so strange. I never cared to learn the constellations and yet when I was in Africa, I looked up into the sky – and the night was so clear. You've never seen a night like that.'

Daphne stared at him, fascinated.

'I looked up into the sky,' he said with a bewildered shake of his head, 'and it looked wrong.'

'How can a sky look wrong?'

He shrugged, lifting one of his hands in an unknowing gesture. 'It just did. All the stars were in the wrong place.'

'I suppose I should want to see the southern sky,' Daphne mused. 'If I were exotic and dashing, and the sort of female men write poetry about, I suppose I should want to travel.'

'You *are* the sort of female men write poetry about,' Simon reminded her with a slightly sarcastic tilt to his head. 'It was just bad poetry.'

Daphne laughed. 'Oh, don't tease. It was exciting. My first day with six callers and Neville Binsby actually wrote poetry.'

'Seven callers,' Simon corrected, 'including me.'

'Seven including you. But you don't really count.'

'You wound me,' he teased, doing a fair imitation of Colin. 'Oh, how you wound me.'

'Perhaps you should consider a career in the theater as well.'

'Perhaps not,' he replied.

She smiled gently. 'Perhaps not. But what I was going to say is that, boring English girl that I am, I have no desire to go anywhere else. I'm happy here.'

Simon shook his head, a strange, almost electric light appearing in his eyes. 'You're not boring. And' – his voice dropped down to an emotional whisper – 'I'm glad you're happy. I haven't known many truly happy people.'

Daphne looked up at him, and it slowly dawned on her that he had moved closer. Somehow she doubted he even realized it, but his body was swaying toward hers, and she was finding it nigh near impossible to pull her eyes from his.

'Simon?' she whispered.

'There are people here,' he said, his voice oddly strangled.

Daphne turned her head to the corners of the terrace. The murmuring voices she'd heard earlier were gone, but that just might mean that their erstwhile neighbors were eavesdropping.

In front of her the garden beckoned. If this were a London ball, there would have been no place to go past the terrace, but Lady Trowbridge prided herself on being different, and thus always hosted her annual ball at her second residence in Hampstead Heath. It was less than ten miles from Mayfair, but it might as well have been in another world. Elegant homes dotted wide patches of green, and in Lady Trowbridge's garden, there were trees and flowers, shrubs and hedges – dark corners where a couple could lose themselves.

Daphne felt something wild and wicked take hold. 'Let's walk in the garden,' she said softly.

'We can't.'

'We must.'

'We *can't.*'

The desperation in Simon's voice told her everything she needed to know. He wanted her. He desired her. He was *mad* for her.

Daphne felt as if her heart was singing the aria from *The Magic Flute,* somersaulting wildly as it tripped past high C.

And she thought – what if she kissed him? What if she pulled him into the garden and tilted her head up and felt his lips touch hers? Would he realize how much she loved him? How much he could grow to love her? And maybe – just maybe he'd realize how happy she made him.

Then maybe he'd stop talking about how determined he was to avoid marriage.

'I'm going for a walk in the garden,' she announced. 'You may come if you wish.'

As she walked away – slowly, so that he might catch up with her – she heard him mutter a heartfelt curse, then she heard his footsteps shortening the distance between them.

'Daphne, this is insanity,' Simon said, but the hoarseness in his voice told her he was trying harder to convince himself of that than he was her.

She said nothing, just slipped farther into the depths of the garden.

'For the love of God, woman, will you listen to me?' His hand closed hard around her wrist, whirling her around. 'I promised your brother,' he said wildly. 'I made a vow.'

She smiled the smile of a woman who knows she is wanted. 'Then leave.'

'You know I can't. I can't leave you out in the garden unprotected. Someone could try to take advantage of you.'

Daphne gave her shoulders a dainty little shrug and tried to wiggle her hand free of his grasp.

But his fingers only tightened.

And so, although she knew it was not his intention, she

let herself be drawn to him, slowly moving closer until they were but a foot apart.

Simon's breathing grew shallow. 'Don't do this, Daphne.'

She tried to say something witty; she tried to say something seductive. But her bravado failed her at the last moment. She'd never been kissed before, and now that she had all but invited him to be the first, she didn't know what to do.

His fingers loosened slightly around her wrist, but then they tugged, pulling her along with him as he stepped behind a tall, elaborately carved hedge.

He whispered her name, touched her cheek.

Her eyes widened, lips parted.

And in the end, it was inevitable.

10

Many a woman has been ruined by a single kiss.

LADY WHISTLEDOWN'S SOCIETY PAPERS,
14 MAY 1813

Simon wasn't sure at what moment he knew he was going to kiss her. It was probably something he never knew, just something he felt.

Up until that very last minute he'd been able to convince himself that he was only pulling her behind the hedge to scold her, upbraid her for careless behavior that would only land both of them in serious trouble.

But then something had happened – or maybe it had been happening all along, and he'd just been trying too hard not to notice it. Her eyes changed; they almost glowed. And she opened her mouth – just the tiniest bit, barely enough for a breath, but it was enough that he couldn't take his eyes off of her.

His hand snaked up her arm, over the pale satin fabric of her glove, across bare skin, and then finally past the wispy silk of her sleeve. It stole around to her back, pulling her closer, squeezing out the distance between them. He wanted her closer. He wanted her around him, atop him, beneath him. He wanted her so much it terrified him.

He molded her to him, his arms wrapping around her like a vise. He could feel the length of her now, every last inch. She was considerably shorter than he was, so her breasts flattened against the bottom of his ribs, and his thigh—

He shuddered with desire.

His thigh wedged between her legs, his firm muscles feeling the heat that was pouring from her skin.

Simon groaned, a primitive sound that mixed need with frustration. He wasn't going to be able to have her this night – he wasn't able to have her ever, and he needed to make this touch last him a lifetime.

The silk of her dress was soft and flimsy beneath his fingers, and as his hands roved along her back, he could feel every elegant line of her.

And then somehow – to his dying day he would never know how – he stepped away from her. Just an inch, but it was enough for the cool night air to slide between their bodies.

'No!' she cried out, and he wondered if she had any idea the invitation she made with that simple word.

His hands cupped her cheeks, holding her steady so that he might drink in the sight of her. It was too dark to see the exact colors that made her unforgettable face, but Simon knew that her lips were soft and pink, with just a tinge of peach at the corners. He knew that her eyes were made up of dozens of shades of brown, with that one enchanting circle of green constantly daring him to take a closer look, to see if it was really there or just a figment of his imagination.

But the rest – how she would feel, how she would taste – he could only imagine.

And Lord, how he'd been imagining it. Despite his composed demeanor, despite all of his promises to Anthony, he burned for her. When he saw her across a crowded room, his skin grew hot, and when he saw her in his dreams, he went up in flames.

Now – now that he had her in his arms, her breath fast and uneven with desire, her eyes glazed with need she couldn't possibly comprehend – now he thought he might explode.

And so kissing her became a matter of self-preservation.

It was simple. If he did not kiss her now, if he did not consume her, he would die. It sounded melodramatic, but at the moment he would have sworn it to be true. The hand of desire twisting around his gut would burst into flame and take him along with it.

He needed her that much.

When his lips finally covered hers, he was not gentle. He was not cruel, but the pulse of his blood was too ragged, too urgent, and his kiss was that of a starving lover, not that of a gentle suitor.

He would have forced her mouth open, but she, too, was caught up in the passion of the moment, and when his tongue sought entry, he found no resistance.

'Oh, my God, Daphne,' he moaned, his hands biting into the soft curve of her buttocks, pulling her closer, needing her to feel the pulse of desire that had pooled in his groin. 'I never knew . . . I never dreamed . . . '

But that was a lie. He had dreamed. He'd dreamed in vivid detail. But it was nothing next to the real thing.

Every touch, every movement made him want her even more, and as each second passed, he felt his body wresting control from his mind. It no longer mattered what was right, what was proper. All that mattered was that she was here, in his arms, and he wanted her.

And, his body realized, she wanted him, too.

His hands clutched at her, his mouth devoured her. He couldn't get enough.

He felt her gloved hand slide hesitantly over his upper back, lightly resting at the nape of his neck. His skin prickled where she touched him, then burned.

And it wasn't enough. His lips left her mouth, trailing down her neck to the soft hollow above her collarbone. She moaned at each touch, the soft mewling sounds firing his passion even more.

With shaking hands, he reached for the delicately scalloped neckline of her gown. It was a gentle fit, and he knew it would take no more than the lightest push to ease the delicate silk down over the swell of her breast.

It was a sight he had no right to see, a kiss he did not deserve to make, but he couldn't help himself.

He gave her the opportunity to stop him. He moved with agonizing slowness, stopping before he bared her to give her one last chance to say no. But instead of maidenly dismay, she arched her back and let out the softest, most arousing rush of breath.

Simon was undone.

He let the fabric of her dress fall away, and in a staggering, shuddering moment of desire, just gazed at her. And then, as his mouth descended to claim her as his prize, he heard—

'You bastard!'

Daphne, recognizing the voice before he did, shrieked and jerked away. 'Oh, my God,' she gasped. 'Anthony!'

Her brother was only ten feet away, and closing the distance fast. His brows were knit together into a mask of utter fury, and as he launched himself at Simon, he let out a primeval warrior cry unlike anything Daphne had ever heard in her life. It barely sounded human.

She just had time to cover herself before Anthony's body crashed into Simon's with such force that she, too, was knocked to the ground by someone's flailing arm.

'I'll kill you, you bloody—' The rest of Anthony's rather violent curse was lost as Simon flipped him over, knocking the breath from him.

'Anthony, no! Stop!' Daphne cried, still clutching at the bodice of her gown, even though she'd already yanked it up and it was in no danger of falling down.

But Anthony was a man possessed. He pummeled Simon, his rage showing on his face, in his fists, in the primitive grunts of fury that emanated from his mouth.

And as for Simon – he was defending himself, but he wasn't really fighting back.

Daphne, who had been standing aside, feeling like a helpless idiot, suddenly realized that she had to intervene. Otherwise, Anthony was going to kill Simon, right there in Lady Trowbridge's garden. She reached down to try to wrest her brother away from the man she loved, but at that moment they suddenly rolled over in a quick flipping motion, clipping Daphne in the knees and sending her sprawling into the hedge.

'Yaaaaaaaahhhhhhh!' she howled, pain stabbing her in more parts of her body than she would have thought possible.

Her cry must have contained a sharper note of agony than she'd thought she'd let slip, because both men immediately stilled.

'Oh, my God!' Simon, who had been at the top of the altercation when Daphne fell over, rushed to her aid. 'Daphne! Are you all right?'

She just whimpered, trying not to move. The brambles were cutting into her skin, and every movement just elongated the scratches.

'I think she's hurt,' Simon said to Anthony, his voice sharp with worry. 'We need to lift her straight out. If we twist, she's likely to become even more entangled.'

Anthony gave a curt, businesslike nod, his fury at Simon temporarily put aside. Daphne was in pain, and she had to come first.

'Just hold still, Daff,' Simon crooned, his voice soft and soothing. 'I'm going to put my arms around you. Then I'm going to lift you forward and pull you out. Do you understand?'

She shook her head. 'You'll scratch yourself.'

'I have long sleeves. Don't worry about me.'

'Let me do it,' Anthony said.

But Simon ignored him. While Anthony stood by helplessly, Simon reached into the tangled bramble of the hedge, and slowly pushed his gloved hands through the mess, trying to wedge his coat-covered arms between the prickly branches and Daphne's bare, tortured skin. When he reached her sleeves, however, he had to stop to disentangle the razor-sharp points from the silk of her dress. Several branches had poked straight through the fabric and were biting her skin.

'I can't get you completely loose,' he said. 'Your dress will tear.'

She nodded, the movement jerky. 'I don't care,' she gasped. 'It's already ruined.'

'But—' Even though Simon had just been in the process of pulling that very same dress down to her waist, he still felt uncomfortable pointing out that the fabric was likely to fall right off her body once the branches were done tearing through the silk. Instead, he turned to Anthony, and said, 'She'll need your coat.'

Anthony was already shrugging out of it.

Simon turned back to Daphne and locked his eyes on hers. 'Are you ready?' he asked softly.

She nodded, and maybe it was his imagination, but he thought she seemed a little calmer now that her eyes were focused on his face.

After making sure that no branches were still stuck to her skin, he pushed his arms farther back into the bramble, and then around her body until his hands met and locked together behind her back.

'On the count of three,' he murmured.

She nodded again. 'One . . . Two . . . '

He yanked her up and out, the force sending them both sprawling.

'You said three!' Daphne yelled.

'I lied. I didn't want you to tense up.'

Daphne might have wanted to pursue the argument, but it was at that moment that she realized that her dress was in tatters, and she squealed as her arms flew up to cover herself.

'Take this,' Anthony said, thrusting his coat at her. Daphne gratefully accepted and wrapped herself in Anthony's superfine coat. It fit him to perfection, but on her it hung so loose that she could easily wrap herself up.

'Are you all right?' he asked gruffly.

She nodded.

'Good.' Anthony turned to Simon. 'Thank you for pulling her out.'

Simon said nothing, but his chin dipped in acknowledgment of Anthony's remark.

Anthony's eyes darted back to Daphne. 'Are you certain you're all right?'

'It stings a little,' she admitted, 'and I'll surely need to apply a salve when I get home, but it's nothing I can't bear.'

'Good,' Anthony said again. Then he drew back his fist and slammed it into Simon's face, easily knocking his unsuspecting friend to the ground.

'That,' Anthony spat out, 'is for defiling my sister.'

'Anthony!' Daphne shrieked. 'Stop this nonsense right now! He didn't defile me.'

Anthony swung around and glared at her, his eyes burning. 'I saw your—'

Daphne's stomach churned, and for a moment she feared she'd actually cast up her accounts. Good God, Anthony had seen her breast! Her brother! It was unnatural.

'Stand up,' Anthony grunted, 'so I can hit you again.'

'Are you mad?' Daphne cried out, jumping between him and Simon, who was still on the ground, his hand clutching his injured eye. 'Anthony, I swear if you hit him again, I shall not forgive you.'

Anthony pushed her aside, and not gently. 'The next one,' he spit, 'is for betraying our friendship.'

Slowly, and to Daphne's horror, Simon rose to his feet.

'No!' she yelled, jumping back between them.

'Get out of the way, Daphne,' Simon ordered softly. 'This is between us.'

'It most certainly is not! In case no one recalls, I'm the

one who—' She stopped herself in mid-sentence. There was no point in speaking. Neither man was listening to her.

'Get out of the way, Daphne,' Anthony said, his voice frighteningly still. He didn't even look at her; his gaze remained focused over her head, straight into Simon's eyes.

'This is ridiculous! Can we not all discuss this like adults?' She looked from Simon to her brother, then whipped her head back to Simon. 'Merciful heavens! Simon! Look at your eye!'

She hurried to him, reaching up to his eye, which was already swelling shut.

Simon remained impassive, not moving even a muscle under her concerned touch. Her fingers skimmed lightly over his swollen skin, oddly soothing. He ached for her still, although this time not with desire. She felt so good next to him, good and honorable and pure.

And he was about to do the most dishonorable thing he'd ever done in his life.

When Anthony finished with his violence, finished with his fury, and finally demanded that Simon marry his sister, Simon was going to say no.

'Move out of the way, Daphne,' he said, his voice strange in his own ears.

'No, I—'

'*Move!*' he roared.

She fled, pressing her back up against the very hedge in which she'd been caught, staring in horror at the two men.

Simon nodded grimly at Anthony. 'Hit me.'

Anthony looked stunned by the request.

'Do it,' Simon said. 'Get it over with.'

Anthony's fist fell slack. He didn't move his head, but his eyes flitted to Daphne. 'I can't,' he blurted out. 'Not when he's just standing there asking for it.'

Simon took a step forward, bringing his face mockingly close. 'Do it now. Make me pay.'

'You'll pay at the altar,' Anthony replied.

Daphne gasped, the sound drawing Simon's attention. Why was she surprised? Surely she understood the consequences of, if not their actions, their stupidity in getting caught?

'I won't force him,' Daphne said.

'I will,' Anthony bit out.

Simon shook his head. 'By tomorrow I'll be on the Continent.'

'You're leaving?' Daphne asked. The stricken sound of her voice sliced a guilty knife through Simon's heart.

'If I stay, you'll forever be tainted by my presence. It's best if I'm gone.'

Her lower lip was trembling. It killed him that it was trembling. A single word fell from her lips. It was his name, and it was filled with a longing that squeezed his heart in two.

It took Simon a moment to summon the words: 'I can't marry you, Daff.'

'Can't or won't?' Anthony demanded.

'Both.'

Anthony punched him again.

Simon hit the ground, stunned by the force of the blow to his chin. But he deserved every sting, every shot of pain. He didn't want to look at Daphne, didn't want to catch even the barest of glances at her face, but she knelt beside him, her gentle hand sliding behind his shoulder to help him right himself.

'I'm sorry, Daff,' he said, forcing himself to look at her. He felt odd and off-balance, and he could see out of only one eye, but she'd come to his aid, even after he'd rejected her, and he owed her that much. 'I'm so sorry.'

'Save your pathetic words,' Anthony spat. 'I'll see you at dawn.'

'No!' Daphne cried out.

Simon looked up at Anthony and gave him the briefest of nods. Then he turned back to Daphne, and said, 'If it c-could be anybody, Daff, it would be you. I p-promise you that.'

'What are you talking about?' she asked, bewilderment turning her dark eyes to frantic orbs. 'What do you mean?'

Simon just closed his eye and sighed. By this time tomorrow he'd be dead, because he sure as hell wasn't going to raise a pistol at Anthony, and he rather doubted that Anthony's temper would have cooled enough for him to shoot into the air.

And yet – in a bizarre, pathetic sort of way, he would be getting what he'd always wanted out of life. He'd have his final revenge against his father.

Strange, but even so, this wasn't how he'd thought it would end. He'd thought – Well, he didn't know what he'd thought – most men avoided trying to predict their own deaths – but it wasn't this. Not with his best friend's eyes burning with hatred. Not on a deserted field at dawn.

Not with dishonor.

Daphne's hands, which had been stroking him so gently, wrapped around his shoulders and shook. The motion jolted his watery eye open, and he saw that her face was very close to his – close and furious.

'What is the matter with you?' she demanded. Her face was like he'd never seen it before, eyes flashing with anger, and anguish, and even a little desperation. 'He's going to kill you! He's going to meet you on some godforsaken field tomorrow and shoot you dead. And you're acting like you want him to.'

'I d-don't w-w-want to d-die,' he said, too exhausted in mind and body to even care that he'd stammered. 'B-but I can't marry you.'

Her hands fell off his shoulders, and she lurched away. The look of pain and rejection in her eyes was almost impossible to bear. She looked so forlorn, wrapped up in her brother's too-big coat, pieces of twigs and brambles still caught in her dark hair. When she opened her mouth to speak, it looked as if her words were ripped from her very soul. 'I-I've always known that I wasn't the sort of woman men dream of, but I never thought anyone would prefer death to marriage with me.'

'No!' Simon cried out, scrambling to his feet despite the dull aches and stinging pains that jolted his body. 'Daphne, it's not like that.'

'You've said enough,' Anthony said in a curt voice, stepping between them. He placed his hands on his sister's shoulders, steering her away from the man who had broken her heart and possibly damaged her reputation for eternity.

'Just one more thing,' Simon said, hating the pleading, pathetic look he knew must be in his eyes. But he had to talk to Daphne. He had to make sure she understood.

But Anthony just shook his head.

'Wait.' Simon laid a hand on the sleeve of the man who had once been his closest friend. 'I can't fix this. I've made—' He let out a ragged breath, trying to collect his thoughts. 'I've made vows, Anthony. I can't marry her. I can't fix this. But I can tell her—'

'Tell her what?' Anthony asked with a complete lack of emotion.

Simon lifted his hand from Anthony's sleeve and raked it through his hair. He couldn't tell Daphne. She wouldn't understand. Or worse, she would, and then all he'd have was her pity. Finally, aware that Anthony was looking at him with an impatient expression, he said, 'Maybe I can make it just a little bit better.'

Anthony didn't move.

'Please.' And Simon wondered if he'd ever put such depth of meaning behind that word before.

Anthony was still for several seconds, and then he stepped aside.

'Thank you,' Simon said in a solemn voice, sparing Anthony the briefest of glances before focusing on Daphne.

He'd thought perhaps that she'd refuse to look at him,

insulting him with her scorn, but instead he found her chin up, eyes defiant and daring. Never had he admired her more.

'Daff,' he began, not at all sure what to say but hoping that the words somehow came out right and in one piece. 'It – it isn't you. If it could be anyone it would be you. But marriage to me would destroy you. I could never give you what you want. You'd die a little every day, and it would kill me to watch.'

'You could never hurt me,' she whispered.

He shook his head. 'You have to trust me.'

Her eyes were warm and true as she said softly, 'I do trust you. But I wonder if you trust me.'

Her words were like a punch to the gut, and Simon felt impotent and hollow as he said, 'Please know that I never meant to hurt you.'

She remained motionless for so long that Simon wondered if she'd stopped breathing. But then, without even looking at her brother, she said, 'I'd like to go home now.'

Anthony put his arms around her and turned her away, as if he could protect her simply by shielding her from the sight of him. 'We'll get you home,' he said in soothing tones, 'tuck you into bed, give you some brandy.'

'I don't want brandy,' Daphne said sharply, 'I want to think.'

Simon thought Anthony looked a bit bewildered by the statement, but to his credit, all he did was give her upper arm an affectionate squeeze, and say, 'Very well, then.'

And Simon just stood there, battered and bloodied, until they disappeared into the night.

11

Lady Trowbridge's annual ball at Hampstead Heath on Saturday evening was, as always, a highlight of the gossip season. This Author spied Colin Bridgerton dance with all three of the Featherington sisters (not at once, of course) although it must be said that this most dashing Bridgerton did not appear to be charmed by his fate. Additionally, Nigel Berbrooke was seen courting a woman who was not Miss Daphne Bridgerton – perhaps Mr. Berbrooke has finally realized the futility of his pursuit.

And speaking of Miss Daphne Bridgerton, she made an early departure. Benedict Bridgerton informed the curious that she had the headache, but This Author spied her earlier in the evening, while she was talking to the elderly Duke of Middlethorpe, and she appeared to be in perfect health

LADY WHISTLEDOWN'S SOCIETY PAPERS,
17 MAY 1813

It was, of course, impossible to sleep.

Daphne paced the length of her room, her feet wearing treads in the blue-and-white carpet that had lain in her room since childhood. Her mind was spinning in a dozen different directions, but one thing was clear.

She had to stop this duel.

She did not, however, underestimate the difficulties involved in carrying out that task. For one thing, men tended to be mulish idiots when it came to things like honor and duels, and she rather doubted that either Anthony or Simon would appreciate her interference. Secondly, she didn't even know where the duel was to take place. The men hadn't discussed that out in Lady Trowbridge's garden. Daphne assumed that Anthony would send word to Simon by a servant. Or maybe Simon got to choose the location since he was the one who'd been challenged. Daphne was certain there had to be some sort of etiquette surrounding duels, but she certainly didn't know what it was.

Daphne paused by the window and pushed the curtain aside to peer out. The night was still young by the standards of the *ton;* she and Anthony had left the party prematurely. As far as she knew, Benedict, Colin, and her mother were all still at Lady Trowbridge's house. The fact that they had not yet returned (Daphne and Anthony had been home for nearly two hours) Daphne took as a good sign. If the scene with Simon had been witnessed, surely the gossip would have raged across the ballroom in seconds, causing her mother to rush home in disgrace.

And maybe Daphne would make it through the night with only her dress in shreds – and *not* her reputation.

But concern for her good name was the least of her worries. She needed her family home for another reason. There was no way she'd be able to stop this duel on her own. Only an idiot would ride through London in the wee hours of the morning and try to reason with two belligerent men by herself. She was going to need help.

Benedict, she feared, would immediately take Anthony's side of the whole thing; in fact, she'd be surprised if Benedict didn't act as Anthony's second.

But Colin – Colin might come around to her way of thinking. Colin would grumble, and Colin would probably say that Simon deserved to be shot at dawn, but if Daphne begged, he would help her.

And the duel had to be stopped. Daphne didn't understand

what was going on in Simon's head, but he was clearly anguished about something, probably something having to do with his father. It had long been obvious to her that he was tortured by some inner demon. He hid it well, of course, especially when he was with her, but too often she'd seen a desperate bleak look in his eyes. And there had to be a reason why he fell silent with such frequency. Sometimes it seemed to Daphne that she was the only person with whom he was ever truly relaxed enough to laugh and joke and make small talk.

And maybe Anthony. Well, maybe Anthony before all of *this*.

But despite it all, despite Simon's rather fatalistic attitude in Lady Trowbridge's garden, she didn't think he wanted to die.

Daphne heard the sound of wheels on cobbles and rushed back to the open window just in time to see the Bridgerton carriage rolling past the house on its way to the mews.

Wringing her hands, she hurried across the room and pressed her ear to the door. It wouldn't do for her to go downstairs; Anthony thought she was asleep, or at least tucked into her bed and contemplating her actions of the evening.

He'd said he wasn't going to say anything to their mother. Or at least he wasn't until he could determine what she knew. Violet's delayed return home led Daphne to believe that there hadn't been any huge or dreadful rumors circulating about her, but that didn't mean that she was off scot-free. There would be whispers. There were always whispers. And whispers, if left unchecked, could quickly grow into roars.

Daphne knew that she would have to face her mother eventually. Sooner or later Violet would hear something. The *ton* would make certain she heard something. Daphne just hoped that by the time Violet was assaulted by rumors – most of them regrettably true – her daughter would already be safely betrothed to a duke.

People would forgive anything if one was connected to a duke.

And that would be the crux of Daphne's strategy to save Simon's life. He wouldn't save himself, but he might save *her.*

Colin Bridgerton tiptoed down the hall, his boots moving silently over the runner carpet that stretched across the floor. His mother had gone off to bed, and Benedict was ensconced with Anthony in the latter's study. But he wasn't interested in any of them. It was Daphne he wanted to see.

He knocked softly on her door, encouraged by the pale shaft of light that glowed at the bottom. Clearly she'd left several candles burning. Since she was far too sensible ever to fall asleep without snuffing her candles, she was still awake.

And if she were still awake, then she'd have to talk to him.

He raised his hand to knock again, but the door swung open on well-oiled hinges, and Daphne silently motioned for him to enter.

'I need to talk to you,' she whispered, her words coming out in a single, urgent rush of air.

'I need to talk to you, too.'

Daphne ushered him in, and then, after a quick glance up and down the hall, shut the door. 'I'm in big trouble,' she said.

'I know.'

The blood drained from her face. 'You do?'

Colin nodded, his green eyes for once deadly serious. 'Do you remember my friend Macclesfield?'

She nodded. Macclesfield was the young earl her mother had insisted upon introducing her to a fortnight ago. The very night she'd met Simon.

'Well, he saw you disappear into the gardens tonight with Hastings.'

Daphne's throat felt suddenly scratchy and swollen, but she managed to get out, 'He did?'

Colin nodded grimly. 'He won't say anything. I'm sure of it. We've been friends for nearly a decade. But if he saw you, someone else might have as well. Lady Danbury was looking at us rather queerly when he was telling me what he'd seen.'

'Lady Danbury saw?' Daphne asked sharply.

'I don't know if she did or if she didn't. All I know is that' – Colin shuddered slightly – 'she was looking at me as if she knew my every transgression.'

Daphne gave her head a little shake. 'That's just her way. And if she did see anything, she won't say a word.'

'Lady Danbury?' Colin asked doubtfully.

'She's a dragon, and she can be rather cutting, but she isn't the sort to ruin someone just for the fun of it. If she saw something, she'll confront me directly.'

Colin looked unconvinced.

Daphne cleared her throat several times as she tried to figure out how to phrase her next question. 'What exactly did he see?'

Colin eyed her suspiciously. 'What do you mean?'

'Exactly what I said,' Daphne very nearly snapped, her nerves stretched taut by the long and stressful evening. 'What did he see?'

Colin's back straightened and his chin jolted back in a defensive manner. 'Exactly what I said,' he retorted. 'He saw you disappear into the gardens with Hastings.'

'But that's all?'

'That's all?' he echoed. His eyes widened, then narrowed. 'What the hell happened out there?'

Daphne sank onto an ottoman and buried her face in her hands, 'Oh, Colin, I'm in such a tangle.'

He didn't say anything, so she finally wiped her eyes, which weren't exactly crying but did feel suspiciously wet, and looked up. Her brother looked older – and harder – than she'd ever before seen him. His arms were crossed, his legs spread in a wide and implacable stance, and his eyes, normally so merry and mischievous, were as hard as emeralds. He'd clearly been waiting for her to look up before speaking.

'Now that you're done with your display of self-pity,' he said sharply, 'suppose you tell me what you and Hastings did tonight in Lady Trowbridge's garden.'

'Don't use that tone of voice with me,' Daphne snapped back, 'and don't accuse me of indulging in self-pity. For the love of God, a man is going to die tomorrow. I'm entitled to be a little upset.'

Colin sat down on a chair opposite her, his face immediately softening into an expression of extreme concern. 'You'd better tell me everything.'

Daphne nodded and proceeded to relate the events of the evening. She didn't, however, explain the precise extent of her disgrace. Colin didn't need to know exactly what Anthony had seen; the fact that she'd been caught in a compromising position ought to be enough.

She finished with, 'And now there is going to be a duel, and Simon is going to die!'

'You don't know that, Daphne.'

She shook her head miserably. 'He won't shoot Anthony. I'd bet my life on it. And Anthony – ' Her voice caught, and she had to swallow before continuing. 'Anthony is so furious. I don't think he'll delope.'

'What do you want to do?'

'I don't know. I don't even know where the duel is to be held. All I know is that I have to stop it!'

Colin swore under his breath, then said softly, 'I don't know if you can, Daphne.'

'I must!' she cried out. 'Colin, I can't sit here and stare at the ceiling while Simon dies.' Her voice broke, and she added, 'I love him.'

He blanched. 'Even after he rejected you?'

She nodded dejectedly. 'I don't care if that makes me a

pathetic imbecile, but I can't help it. I still love him. He needs me.'

Colin said quietly, 'If that were true, don't you think he would have agreed to marry you when Anthony demanded it?'

Daphne shook her head. 'No. There's something else I don't know about. I can't really explain it, but it was almost as if a part of him wanted to marry me.' She could feel herself growing agitated, feel her breath starting to come in jerky gasps, but still she continued. 'I don't know, Colin. But if you could have seen his face, you'd understand. He was trying to protect me from something. I'm sure of it.'

'I don't know Hastings nearly as well as Anthony,' Colin said, 'or even as well as you, but I've never even heard the barest hint of a whisper about some deep, dark secret. Are you certain – ' He broke off in the middle of his sentence, and let his head fall into his hands for a moment before looking back up. When he spoke again, his voice was achingly gentle. 'Are you certain you might not be imagining his feelings for you?'

Daphne took no offense. She knew her story sounded a fantasy. But she knew in her heart that she was right. 'I don't want him to die,' she said in a low voice. 'In the end, that's all that's important.'

Colin nodded, but then asked one last question. 'You don't want him to die, or you don't want him to die on your account?'

Daphne stood on shaky feet. 'I think you'd better leave,' she said, using every last bit of her energy to keep her voice steady. 'I can't believe you just asked that of me.'

But Colin didn't leave. He just reached over and squeezed his sister's hand. 'I'll help you, Daff. You know I'd do anything for you.'

And Daphne just fell into his arms and let out all the tears she'd been keeping so valiantly inside.

*

Thirty minutes later, her eyes were dried and her mind was clear. She'd needed to cry; she realized that. There'd been too much trapped inside her – too much feeling, too much confusion, hurt, and anger. She'd had to let it out. But now there was no more time for emotion. She needed to keep a cool head and remain focused on her goal.

Colin had gone off to question Anthony and Benedict, whom he'd said were talking in low and intense voices in Anthony's study. He'd agreed with her that Anthony had most probably asked Benedict to act as his second. It was Colin's job to get them to tell him where the duel was to take place. Daphne had no doubt that Colin would succeed. He'd always been able to get anybody to tell him anything.

Daphne had dressed in her oldest, most comfortable riding habit. She had no idea how the morning would play out, but the last thing she wanted was to be tripping over lace and petticoats.

A swift knock on her door brought her to attention, and before she could even reach for the knob, Colin entered the room. He, too, had changed out of his evening clothes.

'Did you find out everything?' Daphne asked urgently.

His nod was sharp and brief. 'We don't have much time to lose. I assume you want to try to get there before anyone else arrives?'

'If Simon gets there before Anthony, maybe I can convince him to marry me before anyone even pulls out a gun.'

Colin let out a tense breath. 'Daff,' he began, 'have you considered the possibility that you might not succeed?'

She swallowed, her throat feeling like it had a cannonball lodged in it. 'I'm trying not to think about that.'

'But—'

Daphne cut him off. 'If I think about it,' she replied in a strained voice, 'I might lose my focus. I might lose my nerve. And I can't do that. For Simon's sake, I can't do that.'

'I hope he knows what he has in you,' Colin said quietly.

'Because if he doesn't, I may have to shoot him myself.'

Daphne just said, 'We'd better go.'

Colin nodded, and they were off.

Simon guided his horse along Broad Walk, making his way to the farthest, most remote corner in the new Regent's Park. Anthony had suggested, and he had agreed, that they carry out their business far from Mayfair. It was dawn, of course, and no one was likely to be out, but there was no reason to be flaunting a duel in Hyde Park.

Not that Simon much cared that dueling was illegal. After all, he wouldn't be around to suffer the legal consequences.

It was, however, a damned distasteful way to die. But Simon didn't see any alternatives. He had disgraced a gently bred lady whom he could not marry, and now he must suffer the consequences. It was nothing Simon had not known before he'd kissed her.

As he made his way to the designated field, he saw that Anthony and Benedict had already dismounted and were waiting for him. Their chestnut hair ruffled in the breeze, and their faces looked grim.

Almost as grim as Simon's heart.

He brought his horse to a halt a few yards away from the Bridgerton brothers and dismounted.

'Where is your second?' Benedict called out.

'Didn't bother with it,' Simon replied.

'But you have to have a second! A duel isn't a duel without one.'

Simon just shrugged. 'There didn't seem a point. You brought the guns. I trust you.'

Anthony walked toward him. 'I don't want to do this,' he said.

'You don't have a choice.'

'But you do,' Anthony said urgently. 'You could marry her. Maybe you don't love her, but I know you like her well enough. Why won't you marry her?'

Simon thought about telling them everything, all the reasons he'd sworn never to take a wife and perpetuate his line. But they wouldn't understand. Not the Bridgertons, who only knew that family was good and kind and true. They didn't know anything about cruel words and shattered dreams. They didn't know the impossible feeling of rejection.

Simon then thought about saying something cruel, something that would make Anthony and Benedict despise him and get this mockery of a duel over with more quickly. But that would require him to malign Daphne, and he just couldn't do that.

And so, in the end, all he did was look up into the face of Anthony Bridgerton, the man who had been his friend since his earliest days at Eton, and said, 'Just know it isn't Daphne. Your sister is the finest woman I've ever had the privilege to know.'

And then, with a nod to both Anthony and Benedict, he picked up one of the two pistols in the case Benedict had laid on the ground, and began his long walk to the north side of the field.

'Waaaaaaaaaaaiiiiiiittttttttt!'

Simon gasped and whirled around. Dear God, it was Daphne!

She was bent low over her mare, in full gallop as she raced across the field, and for one stunned moment Simon forgot to be absolutely furious with her for interfering with the duel and instead just marveled at how utterly magnificent she looked in the saddle.

By the time she yanked on the reins and brought the horse to a halt right in front of him, however, his rage was back in full force.

'What the hell do you think you're doing?' he demanded.

'Saving your miserable life!' Her eyes flashed fire at him, and he realized he'd never seen her so angry.

Almost as angry as he was. 'Daphne, you little idiot. Do you realize how dangerous this little stunt was?' Without realizing what he was doing, his hands wrapped around her shoulders and started to shake. 'One of us could have shot you.'

'Oh, please,' she scoffed. 'You hadn't even reached your end of the field.'

She had a point, but he was far too furious to acknowledge it. 'And riding here in the dead of night by yourself,' he yelled. 'You should know better.'

'I do know better,' she shot back. 'Colin escorted me.'

'Colin?' Simon's head whipped back and forth as he looked for the youngest of her older brothers. 'I'm going to kill him!'

'Would that be before or after Anthony shoots you through the heart?'

'Oh, definitely before,' Simon growled. 'Where is he? Bridgerton!' he bellowed.

Three chestnut heads swiveled in his direction.

Simon stomped across the grass, murder in his eyes. 'I meant the idiot Bridgerton.'

'That, I believe,' Anthony said mildly, tilting his chin toward Colin, 'would refer to you.'

Colin turned a deadly stare in his direction. 'And I was supposed to let her stay at home and cry her eyes out?'

'Yes!' This came from three different sources.

'Simon!' Daphne yelled, tripping across the grass after him. 'Get back here!'

Simon turned to Benedict. 'Get her out of here.'

Benedict looked undecided.

'Do it,' Anthony ordered.

Benedict held still, his eyes darting back and forth between his brothers, his sister, and the man who'd shamed her.

'For the love of Christ,' Anthony swore.

'She deserves to have her say,' Benedict said, and crossed his arms.

'What the hell is wrong with you two?' Anthony roared, glaring at his two younger brothers.

‘Simon,’ Daphne said, gasping for breath after her race across the field, ‘you must listen to me.’

Simon tried to ignore her tugs on his sleeve. ‘Daphne, leave it. There’s nothing you can do.’

Daphne looked pleadingly at her brothers. Colin and Benedict were obviously sympathetic, but there was little they could do to help her. Anthony still looked like an angry god.

Finally she did the only thing she could think of to delay the duel. She punched Simon.

In his good eye.

Simon howled in pain as he staggered back. ‘What the hell was that for?’

‘Fall down, you idiot,’ she hissed. If he was prostrate on the ground, Anthony couldn’t very well shoot him.

‘I am certainly not going to fall down!’ He clutched his eye as he muttered, ‘Good God, being felled by a woman. Intolerable.’

‘Men,’ Daphne grunted. ‘Idiots, all.’ She turned to her brothers, who were staring at her with identical expressions of openmouthed shock. ‘What are you looking at?’ she snapped.

Colin started to clap.

Anthony smacked him in the shoulder.

‘Might I have one, single, tiny, ever-so-brief moment with his grace?’ she asked, half the words mere hisses.

Colin and Benedict nodded and walked away. Anthony didn’t move.

Daphne glared at him. ‘I’ll hit you, too.’

And she might have done it too, except that Benedict returned and nearly yanked Anthony’s arm out of the socket as he pulled him away.

She stared at Simon, who was pressing his fingers against his eyebrow, as if that might lessen the pain in his eye.

‘I can’t believe you punched me,’ he said.

She glanced back at her brothers to make sure they’d moved out of earshot. ‘It seemed like a good idea at the time.’

'I don't know what you hoped to accomplish here,' he said.

'I should think that would be abundantly obvious.'

He sighed, and in that moment he looked weary and sad and infinitely old. 'I've already told you I cannot marry you.'

'*You have to.*'

Her words emerged with such urgency and force that he looked up, his eyes on sharp alert. 'What do you mean?' he asked, his voice a study in control.

'I mean that we were seen.'

'By whom?'

'Macclesfield.'

Simon relaxed visibly. 'He won't talk.'

'But there were others!' Daphne bit her lip. It wasn't necessarily a lie. There might have been others. In fact, there probably *were* others.

'Whom?'

'I don't know,' she admitted. 'But I've heard rumblings. By tomorrow it will be all over London.'

Simon swore so viciously that Daphne actually took a step back.

'If you don't marry me,' she said in a low voice, 'I will be ruined.'

'That's not true.' But his voice lacked conviction.

'It is true, and you know it.' She forced her eyes to meet his. Her entire future – and his life! – was riding on this moment. She couldn't afford to falter. 'No one will have me. I shall be packed away to some godforsaken corner of the country—'

'You know your mother would never send you away.'

'But I will never marry. You know that.' She took a step forward, forcing him to acknowledge her nearness. 'I will be forever branded as used goods. I'll never have a husband, never bear children—'

'Stop!' Simon fairly yelled. 'For the love of God, just stop.'

Anthony, Benedict, and Colin all started at his shout, but Daphne's frantic shake of her head kept them in their places.

'Why can't you marry me?' she asked in a low voice. 'I know you care for me. What is it?'

Simon wrapped his hand across his face, his thumb and forefinger pressing mercilessly into his temples. Christ, he had a headache. And Daphne – dear God, she kept moving closer. She reached out and touched his shoulder, then his cheek. He wasn't strong enough. Dear God, he wasn't going to be strong enough.

'Simon,' she pleaded, 'save me.'

And he was lost.

12

A duel, a duel, a duel. Is there anything more exciting, more romantic . . . or more utterly moronic?

It has reached This Author's ears that a duel took place earlier this week in Regent's Park. Because dueling is illegal, This Author shall not reveal the names of the perpetrators, but let it be known that This Author frowns heavily upon such violence.

Of course, as this issue goes to press, it appears that the two dueling idiots (I am loath to call them gentlemen; that would imply a certain degree of intelligence, a quality which, if they ever possessed it, clearly eluded them that morning) are both unharmed.

One wonders if perhaps an angel of sensibility and rationality smiled down upon them that fateful morn.

If so, it is the belief of This Author that This Angel ought to shed her influence on a great many more men of the ton. Such an action could only make for a more peaceful and amiable environment, leading to a vast improvement of our world.

LADY WHISTLEDOWN'S SOCIETY PAPERS,
19 MAY 1813

Simon raised ravaged eyes to meet hers. 'I'll marry you,' he said in a low voice, 'but you need to know—'

His sentence was rendered incomplete by her exultant shout and fierce hug. 'Oh, Simon, you won't be sorry,' she said, her words coming out in a relieved rush. Her eyes sparkled with unshed tears, but they glowed with joy. 'I'll make you happy. I promise you. I'll make you so happy. You won't regret this.'

'Stop!' Simon ground out, pushing her away. Her unfeigned joy was too much to bear. 'You have to listen to me.'

She stilled, and her face grew apprehensive.

'You listen to what I have to say,' he said in a harsh voice, 'and then decide if you want to marry me.'

Her bottom lip caught between her teeth, and she gave the barest of nods.

Simon took in a shaky breath. How to tell her? What to tell her? He couldn't tell her the truth. Not all of it, at least. But she had to understand . . . If she married him . . .

She'd be giving up more than she'd ever dreamed.

He had to give her the opportunity to refuse him. She deserved that much. Simon swallowed, guilt sliding uncomfortably down his throat. She deserved much more than that, but that was all he could give her.

'Daphne,' he said, her name as always soothing his frazzled mouth, 'if you marry me . . . '

She stepped toward him and reached out her hand, only to pull it back at his burning glare of caution. 'What is it?' she whispered. 'Surely nothing could be so awful that—'

'I can't have children.'

There. He'd done it. And it was almost the truth.

Daphne's lips parted, but other than that, there was no indication that she'd even heard him.

He knew his words would be brutal, but he saw no other way to force her understanding. 'If you marry me, you will never have children. You will never hold a baby in your arms and know it is yours, that you created it in love. You will never—'

'How do you know?' she interrupted, her voice flat and unnaturally loud.

'I just do.'

'But—'

'I cannot have children,' he repeated cruelly. 'You need to understand that.'

'I see.' Her mouth was quivering slightly, as if she wasn't quite sure if she had anything to say, and her eyelids seemed to be blinking a bit more than normal.

Simon searched her face, but he couldn't read her emotions the way he usually could. Normally her expressions were so open, her eyes startlingly honest – it was as if he could see to her very soul and back. But right now she looked shuttered and frozen.

She was upset – that much was clear. But he had no idea what she was going to say. No idea how she would react.

And Simon had the strangest feeling that Daphne didn't know, either.

He became aware of a presence to his right, and he turned to see Anthony, his face torn between anger and concern.

'Is there a problem?' Anthony asked softly, his eyes straying to his sister's tortured face.

Before Simon could reply, Daphne said, 'No.'

All eyes turned to her.

'There will be no duel,' she said. 'His grace and I will be getting married.'

'I see.' Anthony looked as if he wanted to react with considerably more relief, but his sister's solemn face forced a strange quietude on the scene. 'I'll tell the others,' he said, and walked off.

Simon felt a rush of something utterly foreign fill his lungs. It was air, he realized dumbly. He'd been holding his breath. He hadn't even realized he'd been holding his breath.

And something else filled him as well. Something hot and terrible, something triumphant and wonderful. It was emotion, pure and undiluted, a bizarre mix of relief and joy and desire and dread. And Simon, who'd spent most of his life avoiding such messy feelings, had no idea what to do about it.

His eyes found Daphne's. 'Are you certain?' he asked, his voice whisper soft.

She nodded, her face strangely devoid of emotion. 'You're worth it.' Then she walked slowly back to her horse.

And Simon was left wondering if he had just been snatched up into heaven – or perhaps led to the darkest corner of hell.

Daphne spent the rest of the day surrounded by her family. Everyone was, of course, thrilled by the news of her engagement. Everyone, that was, except her older brothers, who while happy for her, were somewhat subdued. Daphne didn't blame them. She felt rather subdued herself. The events of the day had left them all exhausted.

It was decided that the wedding must take place with all possible haste. (Violet had been informed that Daphne *might* have been seen kissing Simon in Lady Trowbridge's garden, and that was enough for her to immediately send a request to the archbishop for a special license.) Violet had then immersed herself in a whirlwind of party details; just because the wedding was to be small, she'd announced, it didn't have to be shabby.

Eloise, Francesca, and Hyacinth, all vastly excited at the prospect of dressing up as bridesmaids, kept up a steady stream of questions. How had Simon proposed? Did he get down on one knee? What color would Daphne wear and when would he give her a ring?

Daphne did her best to answer their questions, but she could barely concentrate on her sisters, and by the time afternoon slipped into the eve, she was reduced to monosyllables. Finally, after Hyacinth asked her what color roses she wanted for her bouquet, and Daphne answered, 'Three,' her sisters gave up talking to her and left her alone.

The enormity of her actions had left Daphne nearly speechless. She had saved a man's life. She had secured a promise of marriage from the man she adored. And she had committed herself to a life without children.

All in one day.

She laughed, somewhat desperately. It made one wonder what she could do tomorrow as an encore.

She wished she knew what had gone through her head in those last moments before she'd turned to Anthony, and said, 'There will be no duel,' but in all truth, she wasn't sure it was anything she could possibly remember. Whatever had been racing through her mind – it hadn't been made up of words or sentences or conscious thought. It had been as if she was enveloped by color. Reds and yellows, and a swirling mishmash of orange where they met. Pure feeling and instinct. That's all there had been. No reason, no logic, nothing even remotely rational or sane.

And somehow, as all of that churned violently within her, she'd known what she had to do. She might be able to live without the children she hadn't yet borne, but she couldn't live without Simon. The children were amorphous, unknown beings she couldn't picture or touch.

But Simon – Simon was real and he was here. She knew how it felt to touch his cheek, to laugh in his presence. She knew the sweet taste of his kiss, and the wry quirk of his smile.

And she loved him.

And although she barely dared think it, maybe he was wrong. Maybe he *could* have children. Maybe he'd been misled by an incompetent surgeon, or maybe God was just waiting for the right time to bestow a miracle. She'd be unlikely to mother a brood the size of the Bridgertons, but if she could have even one child she knew she'd feel complete.

She wouldn't mention these thoughts to Simon, though. If he thought she was holding out even the tiniest hope for a child, he wouldn't marry her. She was sure of it. He'd gone to such lengths to be brutally honest. He wouldn't allow her to make a decision if he didn't think she had the facts absolutely straight.

'Daphne?'

Daphne, who had been sitting listlessly on the sofa in the Bridgerton's drawing room, looked up to see her mother gazing at her with an expression of deep concern.

'Are you all right?' Violet asked.

Daphne forced a weary smile. 'I'm just tired,' she replied. And she was. It hadn't even occurred to her until that very moment that she hadn't slept in over thirty-six hours.

Violet sat beside her. 'I thought you'd be more excited. I know how much you love Simon.'

Daphne turned surprised eyes to her mother's face.

'It's not hard to see,' Violet said gently. She patted her on the hand. 'He's a good man. You've chosen well.'

Daphne felt a wobbly smile coming on. She *had* chosen well. And she would make the best of her marriage. If they weren't blessed with children – well, she reasoned, she might have turned out to be barren, anyway. She knew of several couples who had never had children, and she doubted any of them had known of their deficiencies prior to their marriage vows. And with seven brothers and sisters, she was sure to have plenty of nieces and nephews to hug and spoil.

Better to live with the man she loved than to have children with one she didn't.

'Why don't you take a nap?' Violet suggested. 'You look terribly tired. I hate seeing such dark smudges below your eyes.'

Daphne nodded and stumbled to her feet. Her mother knew best. Sleep was what she needed. 'I'm sure I'll feel much better in an hour or two,' she said, a wide yawn escaping her mouth.

Violet stood and offered her daughter her arm. 'I don't think you're going to be able to make it up the stairs on your own,' she said, smiling as she led Daphne out of the room and up the stairs. 'And I sincerely doubt we'll see you in an hour or two. I shall give everyone explicit instructions that you are not to be disturbed until morning.'

Daphne nodded sleepily. 'Thaz good,' she mumbled, stumbling into her room. 'Morningsh good.'

Violet steered Daphne to the bed and helped her into it. The shoes she pulled off, but that was all. 'You might as well sleep in your clothes,' she said softly, then bent to kiss her daughter on the forehead. 'I can't imagine I'll be able to move you enough to get you out of them.'

Daphne's only reply was a snore.

Simon, too, was exhausted. It wasn't every day that a man resigned himself to death. And then to be saved by – and betrothed to! – the woman who had occupied his every dream for the past two weeks.

If he weren't sporting two black eyes and a sizable bruise on his chin, he'd have thought he'd dreamed the whole thing.

Did Daphne realize what she'd done? What she was denying herself? She was a levelheaded girl, not given to foolish dreams and flights of fancy; he didn't think she would have agreed to marry him without sorting through all the consequences.

But then again, she'd reached her decision in under a minute. How could she have thought everything through in under a minute?

Unless she fancied herself in love with him. Would she give up her dream of a family because she loved him?

Or maybe she did it out of guilt. If he'd died in that duel, he was sure Daphne could come up with some line of reasoning that would make it seem her fault. Hell, he liked Daphne. She was one of the finest people he knew. He didn't think he could live with her death on his conscience. Perhaps she felt the same way about him.

But whatever her motives, the simple truth was that come this Saturday (Lady Bridgerton had already sent him a note informing him that the engagement would not be an extended one) he would be bound to Daphne for life.

And she to him.

There was no stopping it now, he realized. Daphne would never back out of the marriage at this point, and neither would he. And to his utter surprise, this almost fatalistic certainty felt . . .

Good.

Daphne would be his. She knew of his shortcomings, she knew what he could not give her, and she had still chosen him.

It warmed his heart more than he would ever have thought possible.

'Your grace?'

Simon looked up from his slouchy position in his study's leather chair. Not that he needed to; the low, even voice was obviously that of his butler. 'Yes, Jeffries?'

'Lord Bridgerton is here to see you. Shall I inform him that you are not at home?'

Simon pulled himself to his feet. Damn, but he was tired. 'He won't believe you.'

Jeffries nodded. 'Very well, sir.' He took three steps, then turned around. 'Are you certain you wish to receive a guest? You do seem to be a trifle, er, indisposed.'

Simon let out a single humorless chuckle. 'If you are referring to my eyes, Lord Bridgerton would be the one responsible for the larger of the two bruises.'

Jeffries blinked like an owl. 'The larger, your grace?'

Simon managed a half-smile. It wasn't easy. His entire face hurt. 'I realize it's difficult to discern, but my right eye is actually a touch worse off than the left.'

Jeffries swayed closer, clearly intrigued.

'Trust me.'

The butler straightened. 'Of course. Shall I show Lord Bridgerton to the drawing room?'

'No, bring him here.' At Jeffries's nervous swallow, Simon added, 'And you needn't worry for my safety. Lord Bridgerton isn't likely to add to my injuries at this juncture. Not,' he added in a mutter, 'that he'd find it easy to find a spot he hasn't already injured.'

Jeffries's eyes widened, and he scurried out of the room.

A moment later Anthony Bridgerton strode in. He took one look at Simon, and said, 'You look like hell.'

Simon stood and raised a brow – not an easy feat in his current condition. 'This surprises you?'

Anthony laughed. The sound was a little mirthless, a little hollow, but Simon heard a shadow of his old friend. A shadow of their old friendship. He was surprised by how grateful he was for that.

Anthony motioned to Simon's eyes. 'Which one is mine?'

'The right,' Simon replied, gingerly touching his abused skin. 'Daphne packs quite a punch for a girl, but she lacks your size and strength.'

'Still,' Anthony said, leaning forward to inspect his sister's handiwork, 'she did quite a nice job.'

'You should be proud of her,' Simon grunted. 'Hurts like the devil.'

'Good.'

And then they were silent, with so much to say and no idea how to say it.

'I never wanted it to be like this,' Anthony finally said.

'Nor I.'

Anthony leaned against the edge of Simon's desk, but he shifted uncomfortably, looking oddly ill at ease in his own body. 'It wasn't easy for me to let you court her.'

'You knew it wasn't real.'

'You *made it* real last night.'

What was he to say? That Daphne had been the seducer, not he? That she'd been the one to lead him off the terrace and dance into the darkness of the night? None of that mattered. He was far more experienced than Daphne. He should have been able to stop.

He said nothing.

'I hope we may put this behind us,' Anthony said.

'I'm certain that would be Daphne's fondest wish.'

Anthony's eyes narrowed. 'And is it now your aim in life to grant her fondest wishes?'

All but one, Simon thought. *All but the one that really matters.* 'You know that I will do everything in my capabilities to keep her happy,' he said quietly.

Anthony nodded. 'If you hurt her—'

'I will never hurt her,' Simon vowed, his eyes blazing.

Anthony regarded him with a long and even stare. 'I was prepared to kill you for dishonoring her. If you damage her soul, I guarantee you will never find peace as long as you live. Which,' he added, his eyes turning slightly harder, 'would not be long.'

'Just long enough to put me in excruciating pain?' Simon asked mildly.

'Exactly.'

Simon nodded. Even though Anthony was threatening torture and death, Simon could not help but respect him for it. Devotion to one's sister was an honorable thing.

Simon wondered if Anthony perhaps saw something in him that no one else did. They had known each other for over half of their lives. Did Anthony somehow see the darkest corners of his soul? The anguish and fury he tried so hard to keep hidden?

And if so, was that why he worried for his sister's happiness?

'I give you my word,' Simon said. 'I will do everything in my power to keep Daphne safe and content.'

Anthony nodded curtly. 'See that you do.' He pushed himself away from the desk and walked to the door. 'Or you'll be seeing me.'

He left.

Simon groaned and sank back into the leather chair. When had his life grown so damned complicated? When had friends become enemies and flirtations grown to lust?

And what the hell was he going to do with Daphne? He

didn't want to hurt her, couldn't bear to hurt her, actually, and yet he was doomed to do so simply by marrying her. He burned for her, ached for the day when he could lay her down and cover her body with his, slowly entering her until she moaned his name—

He shuddered. Such thoughts could not possibly be advantageous to his health.

'Your grace?'

Jeffries again. Simon was too tired to look up, so he just made an acknowledging motion with his hand.

'Perhaps you would like to retire for the evening, your grace.'

Simon managed to look at the clock, but that was only because he didn't have to move his head to do it. It was barely seven in the evening. Hardly his usual bedtime. 'It's early yet,' he mumbled.

'Still,' the butler said pointedly, 'perhaps you'd like to retire.'

Simon closed his eyes. Jeffries had a point. Maybe what he needed was a long engagement with his feather mattress and fine linen sheets. He could escape to his bedroom, where he might manage to avoid seeing a Bridgerton for an entire night.

Hell, the way he felt, he might hole up there for days.

13

It's marriage for the Duke of Hastings and Miss Bridgerton!

This Author must take this opportunity to remind you, dear reader, that the forthcoming nuptials were predicted in this very column. It has not escaped the note of This Author that when this newpaper reports a new attachment between an eligible gentleman and an unmarried lady, the odds in the betting books at gentleman's clubs change within hours, and always in favor of marriage.

Although This Author is not allowed in White's, she has reason to believe that the official odds concerning the marriage of the duke and Miss Bridgerton were 2-1 for.

LADY WHISTLEDOWN'S SOCIETY PAPERS,
21 MAY 1813

The rest of the week flew by in a rush. Daphne didn't see Simon for several days. She might have thought he'd left town, except that Anthony told her he'd been over to Hastings House to settle the details of the marriage contract.

Much to Anthony's surprise, Simon had refused to accept even a penny as dowry. Finally, the two men had decided that Anthony would put the money his father had put aside for Daphne's marriage in a separate estate with himself as the trustee. It would be hers to spend or save as she liked.

'You can pass it along to your children,' Anthony suggested.

Daphne only smiled. It was either that or cry.

A few days after that, Simon called upon Bridgerton House in the afternoon. It was two days before the wedding.

Daphne waited in the drawing room after Humboldt announced his arrival. She sat primly on the edge of the damask sofa, her back straight and her hands clasped together in her lap. She looked, she was sure, the very model of genteel English womanhood.

She felt a bundle of nerves.

Correction, she thought, as her stomach turned itself inside out, a bundle of nerves with frayed edges.

She looked down at her hands and realized that her fingernails were leaving red, crescent-shaped indentations on her palms.

Second correction, a bundle of nerves with frayed edges with an arrow stuck through them. Maybe a flaming arrow at that.

The urge to laugh was almost as overwhelming as it was inappropriate. She had never felt nervous at seeing Simon before. In fact, that had been possibly the most remarkable aspect of their friendship. Even when she caught him gazing at her with smoldering heat, and she was sure that her eyes reflected the same need, she had felt utterly comfortable with him. Yes, her stomach flipped and her skin tingled, but those were symptoms of desire, not of unease. First and foremost, Simon had been her friend, and Daphne knew that the easy, happy feeling she'd experienced whenever he was near was not something to be taken for granted.

She was confident that they would find their way back to that sense of comfort and companionship, but after the scene in Regent's Park, she very much feared that this would occur later rather than sooner.

'Good day, Daphne.'

Simon appeared in the doorway, filling it with his marvelous presence. Well, perhaps his presence wasn't quite as marvelous as usual. His eyes still sported matching purple bruises, and the one on his chin was starting to turn an impressive shade of green.

Still, it was better than a bullet in the heart.

'Simon,' Daphne replied. 'How nice to see you. What brings you to Bridgerton House?'

He gave her a surprised look. 'Aren't we betrothed?'

She blushed. 'Yes, of course.'

'It was my impression that men were supposed to visit their betrothed.' He sat down across from her. 'Didn't Lady Whistledown say something to that effect?'

'I don't think so,' Daphne murmured, 'but I'm certain my mother must have done.'

They both smiled, and for a moment Daphne thought that all would be well again, but as soon as the smiles faded, an uncomfortable silence fell across the room.

'Are your eyes feeling any better?' she finally asked. 'They don't look quite as swollen.'

'Do you think?' Simon turned so that he was facing a large gilt mirror. 'I rather think the bruises have turned a spectacular shade of blue.'

'Purple.'

He leaned forward, not that that brought him appreciably closer to the mirror. 'Purple then, but I suppose it might be a debatable fact.'

'Do they hurt?'

He smiled humorlessly. 'Only when someone pokes at them.'

'I shall refrain from doing so, then,' she murmured, her lips quirking in a telltale twitch. 'It shall be difficult, of course, but I shall persevere.'

'Yes,' he said, with a perfectly deadpan expression, 'I've often been told I make women want to poke me in the eye.'

Daphne's smile was one of relief. Surely if they could joke about such things, everything would go back to the way it was.

Simon cleared his throat. 'I did have a specific reason for coming to see you.'

Daphne gazed at him expectantly, waiting for him to continue.

He held out a jewelers' box. 'This is for you.'

Her breath caught in her throat as she reached for the small, velvet-covered box. 'Are you certain?' she asked.

'I believe betrothal rings are considered quite de rigueur,' he said quietly.

'Oh. How stupid of me. I didn't realize . . . '

'That it was a betrothal ring? What did you think it was?'

'I wasn't thinking,' she admitted sheepishly. He'd never given her a gift before. She'd been so taken aback by the gesture she'd completely forgotten that he owed her a betrothal ring.

'Owed.' She didn't like that word, didn't like that she'd even thought it. But she was fairly certain that that was what Simon must have been thinking when he'd picked out the ring.

This depressed her.

Daphne forced a smile. 'Is this a family heirloom?'

'No!' he said, with enough vehemence to make her blink.

'Oh.'

Yet another awkward silence.

He coughed, then said, 'I thought you might like something of your own. All of the Hastings jewelry was chosen for someone else. This I chose for you.'

Daphne thought it a wonder she didn't melt on the spot. 'That's so sweet,' she said, just barely managing to stifle a sentimental sniffle.

Simon squirmed in his seat, which didn't surprise her. Men did so hate to be called sweet.

'Aren't you going to open it?' he grunted.

'Oh, yes, of course.' Daphne shook her head slightly as she snapped back to attention. 'How silly of me.' Her eyes had glazed over slightly as she stared at the jeweler's box.

Blinking a few times to clear her vision, she carefully released the box's clasp and opened it.

And couldn't possibly say anything besides, 'Oh, my goodness,' and even that came out with more breath than voice.

Nestled in the box was a stunning band of white gold, adorned with a large marquis-cut emerald, flanked on either side by a single, perfect diamond. It was the most beautiful piece of jewelry Daphne had ever seen, brilliant but elegant, obviously precious but not overly showy.

'It's beautiful,' she whispered. 'I love it.'

'Are you certain?' Simon removed his gloves, then leaned forward and took the ring out of the box. 'Because it is your ring. You shall be the one to wear it, and it should reflect your tastes, not mine.'

Daphne's voice shook slightly as she said, 'Clearly, our tastes coincide.'

Simon breathed a small sigh of relief and picked up her hand. He hadn't realized how much it meant to him that she liked the ring until that very moment. He hated that he felt so nervous around her when they'd been such easy friends for the past few weeks. He hated that there were silences in their conversations, when before she'd been the only person with whom he never felt the need to pause and take stock of his words.

Not that he was having any trouble speaking now. It was just that he didn't seem to know what to say.

'May I put it on?' he asked softly.

She nodded and started to remove her glove.

But Simon stilled her fingers with his own, then took over the task. He gave the tip of each finger a tug, then slowly slid the glove from her hand. The motion was unabashedly erotic, clearly an abbreviated version of what he wanted to do: remove every stitch from her body.

Daphne gasped as the edge of the glove trailed past the tips of her fingers. The sound of her breath rushing across her lips made him want her all the more.

With tremulous hands, he slid the ring on her finger, easing it over her knuckle until it rested in place.

'It fits perfectly,' she said, moving her hand this way and that so that she could see how it reflected the light.

Simon, however, didn't let go of her hand. As she moved, her skin slid along his, creating a warmth that was oddly soothing. Then he lifted her hand to his mouth and dropped a gentle kiss on her knuckles. 'I'm glad,' he murmured. 'It suits you.'

Her lips curved – a hint of that wide smile he'd come to adore. Maybe a hint that all would be well between them.

'How did you know I like emeralds?' she asked.

'I didn't,' he admitted. 'They reminded me of your eyes.'

'Of my—' Her head cocked slightly as her mouth twisted into what could only be described as a scolding grin. 'Simon, my eyes are brown.'

'They're mostly brown,' he corrected.

She twisted until she was facing the gilt mirror he'd used earlier to inspect his bruises and blinked a few times. 'No,' she said slowly, as if she were speaking to a person of considerably small intellect, 'they're brown.'

He reached out and brushed one gentle finger along the bottom edge of her eye, her delicate lashes tickling his skin like a butterfly kiss. 'Not around the edge.'

She gave him a look that was mostly dubious, but a little bit hopeful, then let out a funny little breath and stood. 'I'm going to look for myself.'

Simon watched with amusement as she stood and marched over to the mirror and put her face close to the glass. She blinked several times, then held her eyes open wide, then blinked some more.

'Oh, my goodness!' she exclaimed. 'I've never seen that!'

Simon stood and moved to her side, leaning with her against the mahogany table that stood in front of the mirror. 'You'll soon learn that I am always right.'

She shot him a sarcastic look. 'But how did you notice that?'

He shrugged. 'I looked very closely.'

'You . . . ' She seemed to decide against finishing her statement, and leaned back against the table, opening her eyes wide to inspect them again. 'Fancy that,' she murmured. 'I have green eyes.'

'Well, I wouldn't go so far as to say—'

'For today,' she interrupted, 'I refuse to believe they are anything but green.'

Simon grinned. 'As you wish.'

She sighed. 'I was always so jealous of Colin. Such beautiful eyes wasted on a man.'

'I'm sure the young ladies who fancy themselves in love with him would disagree.'

Daphne gave him a smirky glance. 'Yes, but they don't signify, do they?'

Simon caught himself wanting to laugh. 'Not if you say so.'

'You'll soon learn,' she said archly, 'that I am always right.'

This time he did laugh. There was no way he could have held it in. He finally stopped, realizing that Daphne was silent. She was regarding him warmly, though, her lips curved into a nostalgic smile.

'This was nice,' she said, placing her hand on his. 'Almost like it used to be, don't you think?'

He nodded, turning his hand palm up so that he could clasp hers.

'It will be like this again, won't it?' Her eyes showed a flicker of trepidation. 'We'll go back to the way it was, won't we? Everything will be exactly the same.'

'Yes,' he said, even though he knew it could not be true. They might find contentment, but it would never be just as it was.

She smiled, closed her eyes, and rested her head against his shoulder. 'Good.'

Simon watched their reflection for several minutes. And he almost believed he would be able to make her happy.

The next evening – Daphne's last night as Miss Bridgerton – Violet knocked on her bedroom door.

Daphne was sitting on her bed, mementos of her childhood spread out before her, when she heard the rap. 'Come in!' she called out.

Violet poked her head in, an awkward smile pasted on her face. 'Daphne,' she said, sounding queasy, 'do you have a moment?'

Daphne looked at her mother with concern. 'Of course.' She stood as Violet edged into the room. Her mother's skin was a remarkable match with her yellow dress.

'Are you quite all right, Mother?' Daphne inquired. 'You look a little green.'

'I'm fine. I just—' Violet cleared her throat and steeled her shoulders. 'It's time we had a talk.'

'Ohhhhhh,' Daphne breathed, her heart racing with anticipation. She'd been waiting for this. All her friends had told her that the night before one's wedding, one's mother delivered all the secrets of marriage. At the last possible moment, one was admitted into the company of womanhood, and told all those wicked and delicious facts that were kept so scrupulously from the ears of unmarried girls. Some of the young ladies of her set had, of course, already married, and Daphne and her friends had tried to get them to reveal what no one else would, but the young matrons had just giggled and smiled, saying, 'You'll find out soon.'

'Soon' had become 'now,' and Daphne couldn't wait.

Violet, on the other hand, looked as if she might lose the contents of her stomach at any moment.

Daphne patted a spot on her bed. 'Would you like to sit here, Mother?'

Violet blinked in a rather distracted manner. 'Yes, yes,

that would be fine.' She sat down, half-on and half-off the bed. She didn't look very comfortable.

Daphne decided to take pity on her and begin the conversation. 'Is this about marriage?' she asked gently.

Violet's nod was barely perceptible.

Daphne fought to keep the fascinated glee out of her voice. 'The wedding night?'

This time Violet managed to bob her chin up and down an entire inch. 'I really don't know how to tell this to you. It's highly indelicate.'

Daphne tried to wait patiently. Eventually her mother would get to the point.

'You see,' Violet said haltingly, 'there are things you need to know. Things that will occur tomorrow night. Things' – she coughed – 'that involve your husband.'

Daphne leaned forward, her eyes widening.

Violet scooted back, clearly uncomfortable with Daphne's obvious interest. 'You see, your husband . . .

that is to say, Simon, of course, since he will be your husband . . . '

Since Violet showed no sign of finishing that thought, Daphne murmured, 'Yes, Simon will be my husband.'

Violet groaned, her cornflower blue eyes glancing everywhere but Daphne's face. 'This is very difficult for me.'

'Apparently so,' Daphne muttered.

Violet took a deep breath and sat up straight, her narrow shoulders thrown back as if she were steeling herself for the most unpleasant task. 'On your wedding night,' she began, 'your husband will expect you to do your marital duty.'

This was nothing Daphne didn't already know.

'Your marriage must be consummated.'

'Of course,' Daphne murmured.

'He will join you in your bed.'

Daphne nodded. She knew this as well.

'And he will perform certain' – Violet groped for a word,

her hands actually waving through the air – '*intimacies* upon your person.'

Daphne's lips parted slightly, her short indrawn breath the room's only sound. This was finally getting interesting.

'I am here to tell you,' Violet said, her voice turning quite brisk, 'that your marital duty need not be unpleasant.'

But what *was it?*

Violet's cheeks blazed. 'I know that some women find the, er, act distasteful, but—'

'They do?' Daphne asked curiously. 'Then why do I see so many maids sneaking off with the footmen?'

Violet instantly went into outraged employer mode. 'Which maid was that?' she demanded.

'Don't try to change the subject,' Daphne warned. 'I've been waiting for this all week.'

Some of the steam went out of her mother. 'You have?'

Daphne's look was pure what-did-you-expect. 'Well, of course.'

Violet sighed and mumbled, 'Where was I?'

'You were telling me that some women find their marital duty unpleasant.'

'Right. Well. Hmmm.'

Daphne looked down at her mother's hands and noticed that she'd practically shredded a handkerchief.

'All I really want you to know,' Violet said, the words tumbling out as if she could not wait to be rid of them, 'is that it needn't be unpleasant at all. If two people care for one another – and I believe that the duke cares for you very much—'

'And I for him,' Daphne interrupted softly.

'Of course. Right. Well, you see, given that you do care for each other, it will probably be a very lovely and special moment.' Violet started scooting to the foot of the bed, the pale yellow silk of her skirts spreading along the quilts as she moved. 'And you shouldn't be nervous. I'm sure the duke will be very gentle.'

Daphne thought of Simon's scorching kiss. 'Gentle' didn't seem to apply. 'But—'

Violet stood up like a shot. 'Very well. Have a good night. That's what I came here to say.'

'*That's all?*'

Violet dashed for the door. 'Er, yes.' Her eyes shifted guiltily. 'Were you expecting something else?'

'Yes!' Daphne ran after her mother and threw herself against the door so she couldn't escape. 'You can't leave telling me only that!'

Violet glanced longingly at the window. Daphne gave thanks that her room was on the second floor; otherwise, she wouldn't have put it past her mother to try to make a getaway that way.

'Daphne,' Violet said, her voice sounding rather strangled.

'But what do I *do?*'

'Your husband will know,' Violet said primly.

'I don't want to make a fool of myself, Mother.'

Violet groaned. 'You won't. Trust me. Men are . . . '

Daphne seized upon the half-finished thought. 'Men are what? What, Mother? What were you going to say?'

By now Violet's entire face had turned bright red, and her neck and ears had progressed well into the pinks. 'Men are easily pleased,' she mumbled. 'He won't be disappointed.'

'But—'

'But enough!' Violet finally said firmly. 'I have told you everything my mother told me. Don't be a nervous ninny, and do it enough so you'll have a baby.'

Daphne's jaw dropped. '*What?*'

Violet chuckled nervously. 'Did I forget to mention the bit about the baby?'

'Mother!'

'Very well. Your marital duty – the, er, consummation, that is – is how you have a baby.'

Daphne sank against the wall. 'So you did this eight times?' she whispered.

'No!'

Daphne blinked in confusion. Her mother's explanations had been impossibly vague, and she still didn't know what marital duty was, precisely, but something wasn't adding up. 'But wouldn't you have had to do it eight times?'

Violet began to fan herself furiously. 'Yes. No! Daphne, this is very personal.'

'But how could you have had eight children if you—'

'I did it more than eight times,' Violet ground out, looking as if she wanted to melt right into the walls.

Daphne stared at her mother in disbelief. 'You did?'

'Sometimes,' Violet said, barely even moving her lips, and certainly not moving her eyes off a single spot on the floor, 'people just do it because they like to.'

Daphne's eyes grew very wide. 'They do?' she breathed.

'Er, yes.'

'Like when men and women kiss?'

'Yes, exactly,' Violet said, sighing with relief. 'Very much like – ' Her eyes narrowed. 'Daphne,' she said, her voice suddenly shrill, 'have you kissed the duke?'

Daphne felt her skin turning a shade that rivaled her mother's. 'I might have done,' she mumbled.

Violet shook her finger at her daughter. 'Daphne Bridgerton, I cannot believe you would do such a thing. You know very well I warned you about allowing men such liberties!'

'It hardly signifies now that we're to be married!'

'But still – ' Violet gave a deflating sigh. 'Never mind. You're right. It doesn't signify. You're to be married, and to a duke no less, and if he kissed you, well, then, that was to be expected.'

Daphne just stared at her mother in disbelief. Violet's nervous, halting chatter was very much out of character.

'Now then,' Violet announced, 'as long as you don't have any more questions, I'll just leave you to your, er,' – she glanced distractedly at the mementos Daphne had been shuffling through – 'whatever it is that you're doing.'

'But I do have more questions!'

Violet, however, had already made her escape.

And Daphne, no matter how desperately she wanted to learn the secrets of the marital act, wasn't about to chase her mother down the hall – in full view of all the family and servants – to find out.

Besides, her mother's talk had raised a new set of worries. Violet had said that the marital act was a requirement for the creation of children. If Simon couldn't have children, did that mean he couldn't perform those intimacies her mother had mentioned?

And dash it all, what were those intimacies? Daphne suspected they had something to do with kissing, since society seemed so determined to make sure that young ladies keep their lips pure and chaste. And, she thought, a blush stealing over her cheeks as she remembered her time in the gardens with Simon, they might have something to do with a woman's breasts as well.

Daphne groaned. Her mother had practically ordered her not to be nervous, but she didn't see how she could be otherwise – not when she was expected to enter into this contract without the slightest idea of how to perform her duties.

And what of Simon? If he could not consummate the marriage, would it even *be* a marriage?

It was enough to make a new bride very apprehensive, indeed.

In the end, it was the little details of the wedding that Daphne remembered. There were tears in her mother's eyes (and then eventually on her face), and Anthony's voice had been oddly hoarse when he stepped forward to give her away. Hyacinth had strewn her rose petals too quickly, and there were none left by the time she reached the altar. Gregory sneezed three times before they even got to their vows.

And she remembered the look of concentration on Simon's face as he repeated his vows. Each syllable was uttered slowly and carefully. His eyes burned with intent, and his voice was low but true. To Daphne, it sounded as if nothing in the world could possibly be as important as the words he spoke as they stood before the archbishop.

Her heart found comfort in this; no man who spoke his vows with such intensity could possibly view marriage as a mere convenience.

Those whom God hath joined together, let no man put asunder.

A shiver raced down Daphne's spine, causing her to sway. In just a moment, she would belong to this man forever.

Simon's head turned slightly, his eyes darting to her face. Are you all right? his eyes asked.

She nodded, a tiny little jog of her chin that only he could see. Something blazed in his eyes – could it be relief?

I now pronounce you—

Gregory sneezed for a fourth time, then a fifth and sixth, completely obliterating the archbishop's 'man and wife.' Daphne felt a horrifying bubble of mirth pushing up her throat. She pressed her lips together, determined to maintain an appropriately serious facade. Marriage, after all, was a solemn institution, and not one to be treating as a joke.

She shot a glance at Simon, only to find that he was looking at her with a queer expression. His pale eyes were focused on her mouth, and the corners of his lips began to twitch.

Daphne felt that bubble of mirth rising ever higher.

You may kiss the bride.

Simon grabbed her with almost desperate arms, his mouth crashing down on hers with a force that drew a collective gasp from the small assemblage of guests.

And then both sets of lips – bride and groom – burst into laughter, even as they remained entwined.

Violet Bridgerton later said it was the oddest kiss she'd ever been privileged to view.

Gregory Bridgerton – when he finished sneezing – said it was disgusting.

The archbishop, who was getting on in years, looked perplexed.

But Hyacinth Bridgerton, who at ten should have known the least about kisses of anyone, just blinked thoughtfully, and said, 'I think it's nice. If they're laughing now, they'll probably be laughing forever.' She turned to her mother. 'Isn't that a good thing?'

Violet took her youngest daughter's hand and squeezed it. 'Laughter is always a good thing, Hyacinth. And thank you for reminding us of that.'

And so it was that the rumor was started that the new Duke and Duchess of Hastings were the most blissfully happy and devoted couple to be married in decades. After all, who could remember another wedding with so much laughter?

14

We are told that the wedding of the Duke of Hastings and the former Miss Bridgerton, while small, was most eventful. Miss Hyacinth Bridgerton (ten years of age) whispered to Miss Felicity Featherington (also aged ten) that the bride and groom actually laughed aloud during the ceremony. Miss Felicity then repeated this information to her mother, Mrs. Featherington, who then repeated it to the world.

This Author shall have to trust Miss Hyacinth's account, since This Author was not invited to view the ceremony.

LADY WHISTLEDOWN'S SOCIETY PAPERS,
24 MAY 1813

There was to be no wedding trip. There hadn't, after all, been any time to plan one. Instead, Simon had made arrangements for them to spend several weeks at Clyvedon Castle, the Bassets' ancestral seat. Daphne thought this a fine idea; she was eager to get away from London and the inquiring eyes and ears of the ton.

Besides, she was oddly eager to see the place where Simon had grown up.

She found herself imagining him as a young boy. Had he been as irrepressible as he now was with her? Or had he been a quiet child, with the reserved demeanor he showed to most of society?

The new couple left Bridgerton House amidst cheers and

hugs, and Simon quickly bundled Daphne into his finest carriage. Although it was summer, there was a chill in the air, and he carefully tucked a blanket over her lap. Daphne laughed. 'Isn't that a bit much?' she teased. 'I'm unlikely to catch a chill on the few short blocks to your home.'

He regarded her quizzically. 'We travel to Clyvedon.'

'Tonight?' She could not disguise her surprise. She had assumed they would embark on their journey the following day. The village of Clyvedon was located near Hastings, all the way down on England's southeastern coast. It was already late afternoon; by the time they reached the castle, it would be the middle of the night.

This was not the wedding night Daphne had envisioned.

'Wouldn't it make more sense to rest here in London for one night, and then travel on to Clyvedon?' she asked.

'The arrangements have already been made,' he grunted.

'I . . . see.' Daphne made a valiant attempt to hide her disappointment. She was silent for a full minute as the carriage lurched into motion, the well-sprung wheels unable to disguise the bumps from the uneven cobbles beneath them. As they swung around the corner to Park Lane, she asked, 'Will we be stopping at an inn?'

'Of course,' Simon replied. 'We need to eat supper. It wouldn't do for me to starve you on our first day of our marriage, would it?'

'Will we be spending the night at this inn?' Daphne persisted.

'No, we – ' Simon's mouth clamped shut into a firm line, then inexplicably softened. He turned to her with an expression of heart-melting tenderness. 'I've been a bear, haven't I?'

She blushed. She always blushed when he looked at her like that. 'No, no, it's just that I was surprised that—'

'No, you're right. We will rest the night at an inn. I know of a good one halfway down to the coast. The Hare and Hounds. The food is hot, and the beds are clean.' He touched her on the chin. 'I shan't abuse you by forcing you to make the entire trip to Clyvedon in one day.'

'It's not that I'm not hardy enough for the trip,' she said, her face coloring even further as she considered her next words. 'It's just that we did get married today, and if we don't stop at an inn, we'll be here in the carriage when night falls, and—'

'Say no more,' he said, placing a finger to her lips.

Daphne nodded gratefully. She didn't really wish to discuss their wedding night like this. Besides, it seemed the sort of topic that the husband ought to bring up, not the wife. After all, Simon was certainly the more knowledgeable of the two on that subject.

He couldn't possibly be anyless knowledgeable, she thought with a disgruntled grimace. Her mother, despite all her hemming and hawing, had managed to tell her absolutely nothing. Well, except for the bit about the creation of children, not that Daphne understood any of the particulars. But on the other hand, maybe—

Daphne's breath caught in her throat. What if Simon couldn't – Or what if he didn't want to—

No, she decided firmly, he definitely wanted to. Moreover, he definitely wanted *her*. She hadn't imagined the fire in his eyes or the fierce pounding of his heart that night in the gardens.

She glanced out the window, watching as London melted into the countryside. A woman could go mad obsessing over such things. She was going to put this from her mind. She was absolutely, positively, forever going to put this from her mind.

Well, at least until that night.

Her wedding night.

The thought made her shiver.

Simon glanced over at Daphne – his wife, he reminded himself, although it was still a bit difficult to believe. He'd never planned to have a wife. In fact, he'd planned quite specifically not to have one. And yet here he was, with Daphne Bridgerton – no, Daphne *Basset.* Hell, she was the Duchess of Hastings, that's what she was.

That was probably the strangest of all. His dukedom hadn't had a duchess in his lifetime. The title sounded odd, rusty.

Simon let out a long, calming exhale, letting his eyes rest on Daphne's profile. Then he frowned. 'Are you cold?' he asked. She'd been shivering.

Her lips were slightly parted, so he saw her tongue press up against the roof of her mouth to make an N sound, then she moved ever so slightly and said, 'Yes. Yes, but just a touch. You needn't—'

Simon tucked the blanket a bit more closely around her, wondering why on earth she would lie about such an innocuous fact. 'It's been a long day,' he murmured, not because he felt it – although, when he did stop to think about it, it had been a long day – but because it seemed like the right type of soothing remark for the moment.

He'd been thinking a lot about soothing remarks and gentle consideration. He was going to try to be a good husband to her. She deserved at least that much. There were a lot of things he wasn't going to be able to give Daphne, true and complete happiness unfortunately among them, but he could do his best to keep her safe and protected and relatively content.

She had chosen him, he reminded himself. Even knowing that she would never have children, she had chosen him. Being a good and faithful husband seemed the least he could do in return.

'I enjoyed it,' Daphne said softly.

He blinked and turned to her with a blank expression. 'I beg your pardon?'

A shadow of a smile touched her lips. It was a sight to behold, something warm and teasing and just a little bit mischievous. It sent jolts of desire straight to his midsection, and it was all he could do to concentrate on her words as she said, 'You said it had been a long day. I said I enjoyed it.'

He looked at her blankly.

Her face screwed up with such enchanting frustration that Simon felt a smile tugging at his lips. 'You said it had been a long day,' she said yet again. 'I said I enjoyed it.' When he still didn't speak, she let out a little snort and added, 'Perhaps this will all seem more clear if I point out that I implied the words "yes" and "but" as in "Yeeeessss, but I enjoyed it.'

'I see,' he murmured, with all the solemnity he could muster.

'I suspect you see a great deal,' she muttered, 'and ignore at least half of it.'

He quirked a brow, which caused her to grumble to herself, which of course caused him to want to kiss her.

Everything made him want to kiss her.

It was starting to grow quite painful, that.

'We should be at the inn by nightfall,' he said crisply, as if a businesslike mien would relieve his tension.

It didn't, of course. All it did was remind him that he'd put off his wedding night by a full day. A full day of wanting, needing, of his body screaming for release. But he was damned if he was going to take her in some roadside inn, no matter how clean and tidy it might be.

Daphne deserved better. This was her one and only wedding night, and he *would* make it perfect for her.

She shot him a slightly startled look at the sudden change of subject. 'That will be nice.'

'The roads really aren't safe these days after dark,' he added, trying not to remind himself that he'd originally planned on pushing straight through to Clyvedon.

'No,' she agreed.

'And we'll be hungry.'

'Yes,' she said, starting to look puzzled at his current obsession with their newly scheduled stop at the inn. Simon couldn't blame her, but it was either discuss the travel plans to death or grab her and take her right there in the carriage.

Which was *not an* option.

So he said, 'They have good food.'

She blinked, once, before pointing out, 'You said that.'

'So I did.' He coughed. 'I believe I'll take a nap.'

Her dark eyes widened, and her entire face actually bobbed forward as she asked, 'Right now?'

Simon gave a brisk nod. 'I do seem to be repeating myself, but I did, as you so thoughtfully reminded me, say it had been a long day.'

'Indeed.' She watched him curiously as he shifted in his seat, looking for the most comfortable position. Finally, she asked, 'Are you truly going to be able to fall asleep here in the moving carriage? Don't you find the ride a bit bumpy?'

He shrugged. 'I'm quite good at falling asleep whenever I wish to. Learned how on my travels.'

'It's a talent,' she murmured.

'Jolly good one,' he agreed. Then he closed his eyes and faked sleep for the better part of three hours.

Daphne stared at him. Hard. He was faking it. With seven siblings, she knew every trick in the book, and Simon was definitely *not* asleep.

His chest was rising and falling in an admirably even manner, and his breath contained just the right amount of whoosh and wheeze to sound like he was almost but not quite snoring.

But Daphne knew better.

Every time she moved, made a rustling sound, or breathed just a little too loudly, his chin moved. It was barely perceptible, but it was there. And when she yawned, making a low, sleepy, moaning noise, she saw his eyes move under his closed lids.

There was something to admire, however, in the fact that he'd managed to keep up the charade for over two hours.

She'd never lasted past twenty minutes herself.

If he wanted to feign sleep, she decided in a rare fit of magnanimity, she might as well let him. Far be it from her to ruin such a marvelous performance.

With one last yawn – a loud one, just to watch his eyes snap to attention under his eyelids – she turned to the carriage window, drawing the heavy velvet curtain back so she could peer outside. The sun sat orange and fat on the western horizon, about one-third of it already resting below the edge of the earth.

If Simon had been correct in his estimation of their traveling time – and she had the feeling that he was frequently correct about such things; people who liked mathematics usually were – then they should be almost at the halfway point of their journey. Almost to The Hare and Hounds.

Almost to her wedding night.

Good God, she was going to have to stop thinking in such melodramatic terms. This was getting ridiculous.

'Simon?'

He didn't move. This irritated her.

'Simon?' A little louder this time.

The corner of his mouth twitched slightly, pulling down into a tiny frown. Daphne was positive he was trying to decide if she'd spoken too loudly for him to continue to feign sleep.

'Simon!' She poked him. Hard, right where his arm joined with his chest. There was no way he could possibly think a person could sleep through that.

His eyelids fluttered open, and he made a funny little breathy sound – the sort people made when they woke up.

He was *good,* Daphne thought with reluctant admiration.

He yawned. 'Daff?'

She didn't mince words. 'Are we there yet?'

He rubbed nonexistent sleep from his eyes. 'I beg your pardon?'

'Are we *there* yet?'

'Uhhh . . . ' He glanced around the inside of carriage, not that that would tell him anything. 'Aren't we still moving?'

'Yes, but we could be close.'

Simon let out a little sigh and peered out the window. He was facing east, so the sky looked considerably darker than it had through Daphne's window. 'Oh,' he said, sounding surprised. 'Actually, it's just up ahead.'

Daphne did her best not to smirk.

The carriage rolled to a halt, and Simon hopped down. He exchanged some words with the driver, presumably informing him that they had changed their plans and now intended to spend the night. Then he reached up for Daphne's hand and helped her down.

'Does this meet with your approval?' he asked, with a nod and a wave toward the inn.

Daphne didn't see how she could render judgment without seeing the interior, but she said yes, anyway. Simon led her inside, then deposited her by the door when he went to deal with the innkeeper.

Daphne watched the comings and goings with great interest. Right now a young couple – they looked to be landed gentry – were being escorted into a private dining room, and a mother was ushering her brood of four up the stairs. Simon was arguing with the innkeeper, and a tall, lanky gentleman was leaning against a—

Daphne swung her head back toward her husband. Simon was arguing with the innkeeper? Why on earth would he do that? She craned her neck. The two men were speaking in low tones, but it was clear that Simon was most displeased. The innkeeper looked as if he might die of shame at his inability to please the Duke of Hastings.

Daphne frowned. This didn't look right.

Should she intervene?

She watched them argue a few moments longer. Clearly, she should intervene.

Taking steps that weren't hesitant yet could never be called determined, she made her way over to her husband's side. 'Is anything amiss?' she inquired politely.

Simon spared her a brief glance. 'I thought you were waiting by the door.'

'I was.' She smiled brightly. 'I moved.'

Simon scowled and turned back to the innkeeper.

Daphne let out a little cough, just to see if he would turn around. He didn't. She frowned. She didn't like being ignored. 'Simon?' She poked him in the back. 'Simon?'

He turned slowly around, his face pure thundercloud.

Daphne smiled again, all innocence. 'What is the problem?'

The innkeeper held his hands up in supplication and spoke before Simon could make any explanations. 'I have but one room left,' he said, his voice a study in abject apology. 'I had no idea his grace planned to honor us with his presence this eve. Had I known, I would never have let that last room out to Mrs. Weatherby and her brood. I assure you' – the innkeeper leaned forward and gave Daphne a commiserating look – 'I would have sent them right on their way!'

The last sentence was accompanied by a dramatic whooshing wave of both hands that made Daphne a touch seasick. 'Is Mrs. Weatherby the woman who just walked by here with four children?'

The innkeeper nodded. 'If it weren't for the children, I'd—'

Daphne cut him off, not wanting to hear the remainder of a sentence that would obviously involve booting an innocent woman out into the night. 'I see no reason why we cannot make do with one room. We are certainly not as high in the instep as that.'

Beside her, Simon's jaw clenched until she would swear she could hear his teeth grinding.

He wanted separate rooms, did he? It was enough to make a new bride feel extremely unappreciated.

The innkeeper turned to Simon and waited for his approval. Simon gave a curt nod, and the innkeeper clapped his hands together in delight (and presumably relief; there was little worse for business than an irate duke on one's premises). He grabbed the key and scurried out from behind his desk. 'If you'll follow me . . .'

Simon motioned for Daphne to go first, so she swept past him and climbed the stairs behind the innkeeper. After only a couple of twists and turns, they were deposited in a large, comfortably furnished room with a view of the village.

'Well, now,' Daphne said, once the innkeeper had seen himself out, 'this seems nice enough.'

Simon's reply was a grunt.

'How articulate of you,' she murmured, then disappeared behind the dressing screen.

Simon watched her for several seconds before it occurred to him where she'd gone. 'Daphne?' he called out, his voice strangling on itself. 'Are you changing your clothing?'

She poked her head out. 'No. I was just looking around.'

His heart continued to thud, although perhaps not at quite as rapid a pace. 'Good,' he grunted. 'We'll be wanting to go down for supper soon.'

'Of course.' She smiled – a rather annoyingly winning and confident smile, in his opinion. 'Are you hungry?' she asked.

'Extremely.'

Her smile wobbled just a touch at his curt tone. Simon gave himself a mental scolding. Just because he was irate with himself didn't mean he had to extend the anger toward her. She'd done nothing wrong. 'And you?' he asked, keeping his voice gentle.

She emerged fully from behind the screen and perched

at the end of the bed. 'A bit,' she admitted. She swallowed nervously. 'But I'm not certain I could eat any

'The food was excellent the last time I ate here. I assure you—'

'It's not the quality of the food that worries me,' she interrupted. 'It's my nerves.'

He stared at her blankly.

'Simon,' she said, obviously trying to hide the impatience in her voice (but not, in Simon's opinion, succeeding), 'we were married this morning.'

Realization finally dawned. 'Daphne,' he said gently, 'you needn't worry.'

She blinked. 'I needn't?'

He drew a ragged breath. Being a gentle, caring husband was not as easy as it sounded. 'We will wait until we reach Clyvedon to consummate the marriage.'

'We will?'

Simon felt his eyes widen in surprise. Surely she didn't sound disappointed? 'I'm not going to take you in some roadside inn,' he said. 'I have more respect for you than that.'

'You're not? You do?'

His breath stopped. She *did* sound disappointed.

'Uh, no.'

She inched forward. 'Why not?'

Simon stared at her face for several moments, just sat there on the bed and stared at her. Her dark eyes were huge as they returned his regard, filled with tenderness and curiosity and a touch of hesitation. She licked her lips – surely just another sign of nerves, but Simon's frustrated body reacted to the seductive movement with an instant quickening.

She smiled tremulously but didn't quite meet his eye. 'I wouldn't mind.'

Simon remained frozen, curiously rooted to the spot as his body screamed, Tackle her! Haul her onto the bed! Do anything, just get her under you!

And then, just when his urges began to outweigh his honor, she let out a small, tortured cry and jumped to her feet, turning her back on him as she covered her mouth with her hand.

Simon, who had just swiped one arm through the air to yank her to him, found himself off-balance and facedown on the bed. 'Daphne?' he mumbled into the mattress.

'I should have known,' she whimpered. 'I'm so sorry.'

She was sorry? Simon pushed himself back up. She was whimpering? What the hell was going on? Daphne never whimpered.

She turned back around, regarding him with stricken eyes. Simon would have been more concerned, except that he couldn't even begin to imagine what had so suddenly upset her. And if he couldn't imagine it, he tended to believe it wasn't serious.

Arrogant of him, but there you had it.

'Daphne,' he said with controlled gentleness, 'what is wrong?'

She sat down opposite him and placed a hand on his cheek. 'I'm so insensitive,' she whispered. 'I should have known. I should never have said anything.'

'Should have known what?' he ground out.

Her hand fell away. 'That you can't – that you couldn't—'

'Can't *what?*'

She looked down at her lap, where her hands were attempting to wring each other to shreds. 'Please don't make me say it,' she said.

'This,' Simon muttered, 'has got to be why men avoid marriage.'

His words were meant more for his ears than hers, but she heard them and, unfortunately, reacted to them with another pathetic moan.

'What the hell is going on?' he finally demanded.

'You're unable to consummate the marriage,' she whispered.

It was a wonder his erection didn't die off in that instant. Frankly, it was a wonder he was even able to strangle out the words: 'I beg your pardon?'

She hung her head. 'I'll still be a good wife to you. I'll never tell a soul, I promise.'

Not since childhood, when his stuttering and stammering had attacked his every word, had Simon been so at a loss for speech.

She thought he was *impotent?*

'Why – why – why – ?' A stutter? Or plain old shock? Simon thought shock. His brain didn't seem able to focus on anything other than that single word.

'I know that men are very sensitive about such things,' Daphne said quietly.

'Especially when it's not true!' Simon burst out.

Her head jerked up. 'It's not?'

His eyes narrowed to slits. 'Did your brother tell you this?'

'No!' She slid her gaze away from his face. 'My mother.'

'Your mother?' Simon choked out. Surely no man had ever suffered so on his wedding night. 'Your mother told you I'm *impotent?*'

'Is that the word for it?' Daphne asked curiously. And then, at his thunderous glare, she hastily added, 'No, no, she didn't say it in so many words.'

'What,' Simon asked, his voice clipped, 'did she say, exactly?'

'Well, not much,' Daphne admitted. 'It was rather annoying, actually, but she did explain to me that the marital act—'

'She called it an act?'

'Isn't that what everyone calls it?'

He waved off her question. 'What else did she say?'

'She told me that the, ah, whatever it is *you* wish to call it—'

Simon found her sarcasm oddly admirable under the circumstances.

'—is related in some manner to the procreation of children, and—'

Simon thought he might choke on his tongue. 'In some manner?'

'Well, yes.' Daphne frowned. 'She really didn't provide me with any specifics.'

'Clearly.'

'She did try her best,' Daphne pointed out, thinking she ought at least to try to come to her mother's defense. 'It was very embarrassing for her.'

'After eight children,' he muttered, 'you'd think she'd be over that by now.'

'I don't think so,' Daphne said, shaking her head. 'And then when I asked her if she'd participated in this' – she looked up at him with an exasperated expression. 'I really don't know what else to call it but an act.'

'Go right ahead,' he said with a wave, his voice sounding awfully strained.

Daphne blinked with concern. 'Are you all right?'

'Just fine,' he choked.

'You don't sound fine.'

He waved his hand some more, giving Daphne the odd impression that he couldn't speak.

'Well,' she said slowly, going back to her earlier story, 'I asked her if that meant she'd participated in this act eight times, and she became very embarrassed, and—'

'You asked her that?' Simon burst out, the words escaping his mouth like an explosion.

'Well, yes.' Her eyes narrowed. 'Are you laughing?'

'No,' he gasped.

Her lips twisted into a small scowl. 'You certainly look as if you're laughing.'

Simon just shook his head in a decidedly frantic manner.

'Well,' Daphne said, clearly disgruntled. 'I thought my question made perfect sense, seeing as she has eight children. But then she told me that—'

He shook his head and held up a hand, and now he looked like he didn't know whether to laugh or cry. 'Don't tell me. I beg of you.'

'Oh.' Daphne didn't know what to say to that, so she just clamped her hands together in her lap and shut her mouth.

Finally, she heard Simon take a long, ragged breath, and say, 'I know I'm going to regret asking you this. In fact, I regret it already, but *why* exactly did you assume I was' – he shuddered – 'unable to perform?'

'Well, you said you couldn't have children.'

'Daphne, there are many, many other reasons why a couple might be unable to have children.'

Daphne had to force herself to stop grinding her teeth. 'I really *hate* how stupid I feel right now,' she muttered.

He leaned forward and pried her hands apart. 'Daphne,' he said softly, massaging her fingers with his, 'do you have any idea what happens between a man and a woman?'

'I haven't a clue,' she said frankly. 'You'd think I would, with three older brothers, and I thought I'd finally learn the truth last night when my mother—'

'Don't say anything more,' he said in the oddest voice. 'Not another word. I couldn't bear it.'

'But—'

His head fell into his hands, and for a moment Daphne thought he might be crying. But then, as she sat there castigating herself for making her husband weep on his wedding day, she realized that his shoulders were shaking with laughter.

The fiend.

'Are you laughing at me?' she growled.

He shook his head, not looking up.

'Then what are you laughing about?'

'Oh, Daphne,' he gasped, 'you have a lot to learn.'

'Well, I never disputed *that,*' she grumbled. Really, if people weren't so intent on keeping young women completely ignorant of the realities of marriage, scenes like this could be avoided.

He leaned forward, his elbows resting on his knees. His eyes grew positively electric. 'I can teach you,' he whispered.

Daphne's stomach did a little flip.

Never once taking his eyes off of hers, Simon took her hand and raised it to her lips. 'I assure you,' he murmured, flicking his tongue down the line of her middle finger, 'I am perfectly able to satisfy you in bed.'

Daphne suddenly found it difficult to breathe. And when had the room grown so hot? 'I-I'm not sure I know what you mean.'

He yanked her into his arms. 'You will.'

15

London seems terribly quiet this week, now that society's favorite duke and that duke's favorite duchess have departed for the country. This Author could report that Mr. Nigel Berbrooke was seen asking Miss Penelope Featherington to dance, or that Miss Penelope, despite her mother's gleeful urging and her eventual acceptance of his offer, did not seem terribly enamored with the notion.

But really, who wants to read about Mr. Berbrooke or Miss Penelope? Let us not fool ourselves. We are all still ravenously curious about the duke and duchess.

LADY WHISTLEDOWN'S SOCIETY PAPERS,
28 MAY 1813

It was like being in Lady Trowbridge's garden all over again, Daphne thought wildly, except that this time there would be no interruptions – no furious older brothers, no fear of discovery, nothing but a husband, a wife, and the promise of passion.

Simon's lips found hers, gentle but demanding. With each touch, each flick of his tongue, she felt flutterings within her, tiny spasms of need that were building in pitch and frequency.

'Have I told you,' he whispered, 'how enamored I am of the corner of your mouth?'

'N-no,' Daphne said tremulously, amazed that he'd ever even once examined it.

'I adore it,' he murmured, and then went to show her

how. His teeth scraped along her lower lip until his tongue darted out and traced the curve of the corner of her mouth.

It tickled, and Daphne felt her lips spreading into a wide, openmouthed smile. 'Stop,' she giggled.

'Never,' he vowed. He pulled back, cradling her face in his hands. 'You have the most beautiful smile I've ever seen.'

Daphne's initial reaction was to say, 'Don't be silly,' but then she thought – *Why ruin such a moment?* – and so she just said, 'Really?'

'Really.' He dropped a kiss on her nose. 'When you smile it takes up half your face.'

'Simon!' she exclaimed. 'That sounds horrible.'

'It's enchanting.'

'Distorted.'

'Desirable.'

She grimaced, but somehow she laughed at the same time. 'Clearly, you have no knowledge of the standards of female beauty.'

He arched a brow. 'As pertains to you, my standards are the only ones that count any longer.'

For a moment she was speechless, then she collapsed against him, a torrent of laughter shaking both of their bodies. 'Oh, Simon,' she gasped, 'you sounded so fierce. So wonderfully, perfectly, absurdly fierce.'

'Absurd?' he echoed. 'Are you calling me absurd?'

Her lips tightened to prevent another giggle, but they weren't entirely successful.

'It's almost as bad as being called impotent,' he grumbled.

Daphne was instantly serious. 'Oh, Simon, You know I didn't . . . ' She gave up trying to explain, and instead just said, 'I'm so sorry about that.'

'Don't be.' He waved off her apology. 'Your mother I may have to kill, but you have nothing to apologize for.'

A horrified giggle escaped her lips. 'Mother did try her best, and if I hadn't been confused because you said—'

'Oh, so now it's all my fault?' he said with mock outrage.

But then his expression grew sly, seductive. He moved closer, angling his body so that she had to arch backwards. 'I suppose I'll just have to work doubly hard to prove my capabilities.'

One of his hands slid to the small of her back, supporting her as he lowered her onto the bed. Daphne felt the breath leave her body as she looked up into his intensely blue eyes. The world seemed somehow different when one was lying down. Darker, more dangerous. And all the more thrilling because Simon was looming above her, filling her vision.

And in that moment, as he slowly closed the distance between them, he became her entire world.

This time his kiss wasn't light. He didn't tickle; he devoured. He didn't tease; he possessed.

His hands slipped under her, cradling her derriere, pressing it up against his arousal. 'Tonight,' he whispered, his voice hoarse and hot in her ear, 'I will make you mine.'

Daphne's breath started coming faster and faster, each little gasp of air impossibly loud to her ears. Simon was so close, every inch of him covering her intimately. She'd imagined this night a thousand times since that moment in Regent's Park when he'd said he would marry her, but it had never occurred to her that the sheer weight of his body on hers would be so thrilling. He was large and hard and exquisitely muscled; there was no way she could escape his seductive onslaught, even if she'd wanted to.

How strange it was to feel such titillating joy at being so powerless. He could do with her whatever he desired – and she wanted to let him.

But when his body shuddered, and his lips tried to say her name but didn't get beyond 'D-D-Daph—' she realized that she possessed her own kind of control. He wanted her so much he couldn't breathe, needed her so badly he couldn't speak.

And somehow, as she reveled in her newfound strength,

she found that her body seemed to know what to do. Her hips arched up to meet his, and as his hands pushed her skirts up over her waist, her legs snaked around his, pulling him ever closer to the cradle of her femininity.

'My God, Daphne,' Simon gasped, hauling his shaking body up on his elbows. 'I want to – I can't—'

Daphne grabbed at his back, trying to pull him back down to her. The air felt cool where his body had just been.

'I can't go slow,' he grunted.

'I don't care.'

'I do.' His eyes burned with wicked intention. 'We seem to be getting ahead of ourselves.'

Daphne just stared at him, trying to catch her breath. He'd sat up, and his eyes were raking across her body as one of his hands slid up the length of her leg to her knee.

'First of all,' he murmured, 'we need to do something about all of your clothes.'

Daphne gasped with shock as he stood, pulling her to her feet along with him. Her legs were weak, her balance nonexistent, but he held her upright, his hands bunching her skirts around her waist. He whispered in her ear, 'It's difficult to strip you naked when you're lying down.'

One of his hands found the curve of her buttocks, and started massaging her in a circular motion. 'The question,' he mused, 'is do I push the dress up, or pull it down?'

Daphne prayed that he wasn't expecting her to actually answer his question, because she couldn't make a sound.

'Or,' he said slowly, one finger slipping under the ribboned bodice of her dress, 'both?'

And then, before she had even a moment to react, he'd pushed her dress down so that the entire garment encircled her waist. Her legs were bare, and were it not for her thin silk chemise, she would have been completely naked.

'Now this is a surprise,' Simon murmured, palming one of her breasts through the silk. 'Not an entirely unwelcome one, of course. Silk is never as soft as skin, but it does have its advantages.'

Daphne's breath fled as she watched him slide the silk slowly from side to side, the sweet friction causing her nipples to pucker and harden.

'I had no idea,' Daphne whispered, her every breath sliding hot and moist across her lips.

Simon went to work on her other breast. 'No idea of what?'

'That you were so wicked.'

He smiled, slow and full of the devil. His lips moved to her ear, whispering, 'You were my best friend's sister. Utterly forbidden. What was I to do?'

Daphne shivered with desire. His breath touched only her ear, but her skin prickled across her entire body.

'I could do nothing,' he continued, edging one strap of her chemise off her shoulder, 'except imagine.'

'You thought about me?' Daphne whispered, her body thrilling at the notion. 'You thought about this?'

His hand at her hip grew tight. 'Every night. Every moment before I fell asleep, until my skin burned and my body begged for release.'

Daphne felt her legs wobble, but he held her up.

'And then when I was asleep . . . ' He moved to her neck, his hot breath as much of a kiss as the touch of his lips. 'That's when I was truly naughty.'

A moan escaped her lips, strangled and incoherent and full of desire.

The second chemise strap fell off her shoulder just as Simon's lips found the tantalizing hollow between her breasts. 'But tonight—' he whispered, pushing the silk down until one breast was bared, and then the other. 'Tonight all of my dreams come true.'

Daphne had time only to gasp before his mouth found her breast and fastened on her hardened nipple.

'This is what I wanted to do in Lady Trowbridge's garden,' he said. 'Did you know that?'

She shook her head wildly, grabbing on to his shoulders for support. She was swaying from side to side, barely able to hold her head straight. Spasms of pure feeling were shooting through her body, robbing her of breath, of balance, even of thought.

'Of course you didn't,' he murmured. 'You're such an innocent.'

With deft and knowing fingers, Simon slid the rest of her clothes from her body, until she was nude in his arms. Gently, because he knew she had to be almost as nervous as she was excited, he lowered her onto the bed.

His motions were uncontrolled and jerky as he yanked at his own clothing. His skin was on fire, his entire body burning with need. Never once, however, did he take his eyes off of her. She lay sprawled on the bed, a temptation like none he'd ever seen. Her skin glowed peachy smooth in the flickering candlelight, and her hair, long since released from its coiffure, fell around her face in wild abandon.

His fingers, which had removed her clothing with such finesse and speed, now felt awkward and clumsy as he tried to make sense of his own buttons and knots.

As his hands moved to his trousers, he saw that she was pulling the bedsheets over her. 'Don't,' he said, barely recognizing his own voice.

Her eyes met his, and he said, 'I'll be your blanket.'

He peeled the rest of his clothing off, and before she could utter a word, he moved to the bed, covering her body with his. He felt her gasp with surprise at the feel of him, and then her body stiffened slightly.

'Shhh,' he crooned, nuzzling her neck while one of his hands made soothing circles on the side of her thigh. 'Trust me.'

'I do trust you,' she said in a shaky voice. 'It's just that—'

His hand moved up to her hip. 'Just that what?'

He could hear the grimace in her voice as she said, 'Just that I wish I weren't so utterly ignorant.'

A low rumble of a laugh shook his chest.

'Stop that,' she griped, swatting him on the shoulder.

'I'm not laughing at you,' Simon insisted.

'You're certainly laughing,' she muttered, 'and don't tell me you're laughing *with me,* because that excuse *never* works.'

'I was laughing,' he said softly, lifting himself up on his elbows so that he could look into her face, 'because I was thinking how very glad *I* am of your ignorance.' He lowered his face down until his lips brushed hers in a feather-light caress. 'I am honored to be the only man to touch you thus.'

Her eyes shone with such purity of feeling that Simon was nearly undone. 'Truly?' she whispered.

'Truly,' he said, surprised by how gruff his voice sounded. 'Although honor is most likely only the half of it.'

She said nothing, but her eyes were enchantingly curious.

'I might have to kill the next man who so much as looks at you sideways,' he grumbled.

To his great surprise, she burst out laughing. 'Oh, Simon,' she gasped, 'it is so perfectly splendidly *wonderful* to be the object of such irrational jealousy. Thank you.'

'You'll thank me later,' he vowed.

'And perhaps,' she murmured, her dark eyes suddenly far more seductive than they had any right to be, 'you'll thank me as well.'

Simon felt her thighs slide apart as he settled his body against hers, his manhood hot against her belly. 'I already do,' he said, his words melting into her skin as he kissed the hollow of her shoulder. 'Believe me, I already do.'

Never had he been so thankful for the hard-won control he had learned to exert over himself. His entire body ached to plunge into her and finally make her his in truth, but he knew that this night – their wedding night – was for Daphne, not for him.

This was her first time. He was her first lover – her only lover, he thought with uncharacteristic savagery – and it was his responsibility to make certain that this night brought her nothing but exquisite pleasure.

He knew she wanted him. Her breath was erratic, her eyes glazed with need. He could hardly bear to look at her face, for every time he saw her lips, half-open and panting with desire, the urge to slam into her nearly overwhelmed him.

So instead he kissed her. He kissed her everywhere, and ignored the fierce pounding of his blood every time he heard her gasp or mewl with desire. And then finally, when she was writhing and moaning beneath him, and he knew she was mad for him, he slipped his hand between her legs and touched her.

The only sound he could make was her name, and even that came out as a half-groan. She was more than ready for him, hotter and wetter than he'd ever dreamed. But still, just to be sure – or maybe it was because he couldn't resist the perverse impulse to torture himself – he slid one long finger inside her, testing her warmth, tickling her sheath.

'Simon!' she gasped, bucking beneath him. Already her muscles were tightening, and he knew that she was nearly to completion. Abruptly, he removed his hand, ignoring her whimper of protest.

He used his thighs to nudge hers further apart, and with a shuddering groan, positioned himself to enter her. 'This m-may hurt a little,' he whispered hoarsely, 'but I p-promise you—'

'Just *do* it,' she groaned, her head tossing wildly from side to side.

And so he did. With one powerful thrust, he entered her fully. He felt her maidenhead give way, but she didn't seem to flinch from pain. 'Are you all right?' he groaned, his every muscle tensing just to keep himself from moving within her.

She nodded, her breath coming in shallow gasps. 'It feels very odd,' she admitted.

'But not bad?' he asked, almost ashamed by the desperate note in his voice.

She shook her head, a tiny, feminine smile touching her lips. 'Not bad at all,' she whispered. 'But before . . .

when you . . . with your fingers . . . '

Even in the dull candlelight he could see that her cheeks burned with embarrassment. 'Is this what you want?' he whispered, pulling out until he was only halfway within her.

'No!' she cried out.

'Then perhaps *this* is what you want.' He plunged back in.

She gasped. 'Yes. No. Both.'

He began to move within her, his rhythm deliberately slow and even. With each thrust, he pushed a gasp from her lips, each little moan the perfect pitch to drive him wild.

And then her moans grew into squeals and her gasps into pants, and he knew that she was near her peak. He moved ever faster, his teeth gritted as he fought to maintain his control as she spiralled toward completion.

She moaned his name, and then she screamed it, and then her entire body went rigid beneath him. She clutched at his shoulders, her hips rising off the bed with a strength he could barely believe. Finally, with one last, powerful shudder, she collapsed beneath him, oblivious to everything but the power of her own release.

Against his better judgment, Simon allowed himself one last thrust, burying himself to the hilt, savoring the sweet warmth of her body.

Then, taking her mouth in a searingly passionate kiss, he pulled out and spent himself on the sheets next to her.

It was to be only the first of many nights of passion. The newlyweds traveled down to Clyvedon, and then, much to Daphne's extreme embarrassment, sequestered themselves in the master suite for more than a week.

(Of course Daphne was not so embarrassed that she made

anything more than a halfhearted attempt to actually *leave* the suite.)

Once they emerged from their honeymoonish seclusion, Daphne was given a tour of Clyvedon – which was much needed, since all she'd seen upon arrival was the route from the front door to the duke's bedroom. She then spent several hours introducing herself to the upper servants. She had, of course, been formally intoduced to the staff upon her arrival, but Daphne thought it best to meet the more important members of the staff in a more individual manner.

Since Simon had not resided at Clyvedon for so many years, many of the newer servants did not know him, but those who had been at Clyvedon during his childhood seemed – to Daphne – to be almost ferociously devoted to her husband. She laughed about it to Simon as they privately toured the garden, and had been started to find herself on the receiving end of a decidedly shuttered stare.

'I lived here until I went to Eton,' was all he said, as if that ought to be explanation enough.

Daphne was made instantly uncomfortable by the flatness in his voice. 'Did you never travel to London? When we were small, we often—'

'I lived here exclusively.'

His tone signaled that he desired – no, *required* – an end to the conversation, but Daphne threw caution to the winds, and decided to pursue the topic, anyway. 'You must have been a darling child,' she said in a deliberately blithe voice, 'or perhaps an extremely mischievous one, to have inspired such long-standing devotion.'

He said nothing.

Daphne plodded on. 'My brother – Colin, you know – is much the same way. He was the very devil when he was small, but so insufferably charming that all servants adored him. Why, one time—'

Her mouth froze, half-open. There didn't seem much point in continuing. Simon had turned on his heel and walked away.

He wasn't interested in roses. And he'd never pondered the existence of violets one way or another, but now Simon found himself leaning on a wooden fence, gazing out over Clyvedon's famed flower garden as if he were seriously considering a career in horticulture.

All because he couldn't face Daphne's questions about his childhood.

But the truth was, he hated the memories. He despised the reminders. Even staying here at Clyvedon was uncomfortable. The only reason he'd brought Daphne down to his childhood home was because it was the only one of his residences within a two-day drive from London that was ready for immediate occupancy.

The memories brought back the feelings. And Simon didn't want to feel like that young boy again. He didn't want to remember the number of times he'd sent letters to his father, only to wait in vain for a response. He didn't want to remember the kind smiles of the servants – kind smiles that were always accompanied by pitying eyes. They'd loved him, yes, but they'd also felt sorry for him.

And the fact that they'd hated his father on his behalf – well, somehow that had never made him feel better. He hadn't been – and, to be honest, still wasn't – so noble-minded that he didn't take a certain satisfaction in his father's lack of popularity, but that never took away the embarrassment or the discomfort.

Or the shame.

He'd wanted to be admired, not pitied. And it hadn't been until he'd struck out on his own by traveling unheralded to Eton that he'd had his first taste of success.

He'd come so far; he'd travel to hell before he went back to the way he'd been.

None of this, of course, was *Daphne's* fault. He knew

she had no ulterior motives when she asked about his childhood. How could she? She knew nothing of his occasional difficulties with speech. He'd worked damned hard to hide it from her.

No, he thought with a weary sigh, he'd rarely had to work hard at all to hide it from Daphne. She'd always set him at ease, made him feel free. His stammer rarely surfaced these days, but when it did it was always during times of stress and anger.

And whatever life was about when he was with Daphne, it wasn't stress and anger.

He leaned more heavily against the fence, guilt forcing his posture into a slouch. He'd treated her abominably. It seemed he was fated to do that time and again.

'Simon?'

He'd felt her presence before she'd spoken. She'd approached from behind, her booted feet soft and silent on the grass. But he knew she was there. He could smell her gentle fragrance and hear the wind whispering through her hair.

'These are beautiful roses,' she said. It was, he knew, her way of soothing his peevish mood. He knew she was dying to ask more. But she was wise beyond her years, and much as he liked to tease her about it, she did know a lot about men and their idiot tempers. She wouldn't say anything more. At least not today.

'I'm told my mother planted them,' he replied. His words came out more gruffly than he would have liked, but he hoped she saw them as the olive branch he'd meant them to be. When she didn't say anything, he added by way of an explanation, 'She died at my birth.'

Daphne nodded. 'I'd heard. I'm sorry.'

Simon shrugged. 'I didn't know her.'

'That doesn't mean it wasn't a loss.'

Simon considered his childhood. He had no way of knowing if his mother would have been more sympathetic to his difficulties than his father had been, but he figured there was no way she could have made it worse. 'Yes,' he murmured, 'I suppose it was.'

Later that day, while Simon was going over some estate accounts, Daphne decided it was as good a time as any to get to know Mrs. Colson, the housekeeper. Although she and Simon had not yet discussed where they would reside, Daphne couldn't imagine that they wouldn't spend some time there at Clyvedon, Simon's ancestral home, and if there was one thing she'd learned from her mother, it was that a lady simply had to have a good working relationship with her housekeeper.

Not that Daphne was terribly worried about getting along with Mrs. Colson. She had met the housekeeper briefly when Simon had introduced her to the staff, and it had been quickly apparent that she was a friendly, talkative sort.

She stopped by Mrs. Colson's office – a tiny little room just off the kitchen – a bit before teatime. The housekeeper, a handsome woman in her fifties, was bent over her small desk, working on the week's menus.

Daphne gave the open door a knock. 'Mrs. Colson?'

The housekeeper looked up and immediately stood. 'Your grace,' she said, bobbing into a small curtsy. 'You should have called for me.'

Daphne smiled awkwardly, still unused to her elevation from the ranks of mere misses. 'I was already up and about,' she said, explaining her unorthodox appearance in the servants' domain. 'But if you have a moment, Mrs. Colson, I was hoping we might get to know one another better, since you have lived here for many years, and I hope to do so for many to come.'

Mrs. Colson smiled at Daphne's warm tone. 'Of course, your grace. Was there anything in particular about which you cared to inquire?'

'Not at all. But I still have much to learn about Clyvedon

if I am to manage it properly. Perhaps we could take tea in the yellow room? I do so enjoy the decor. It's so warm and sunny. I had been hoping to make that my personal parlor.'

Mrs. Colson gave her an odd look. 'The last duchess felt the same way.'

'Oh,' Daphne replied, not certain whether that ought to make her feel uncomfortable.

'I've given special care to that room over the years,' Mrs. Colson continued. 'It does get quite a bit of sun, being on the south side. I had all of the furniture reupholstered three years ago.' Her chin rose in a slightly proud manner. 'Went all the way to London to get the same fabric.'

'I see,' Daphne replied, leading the way out of the office. 'The late duke must have loved his wife very much, to order such a painstaking conservation of her favorite room.'

Mrs. Colson didn't quite meet her eyes. 'It was my decision,' she said quietly. 'The duke always gave me a certain budget for the upkeep of the house. I thought it the most fitting use of the money.'

Daphne waited while the housekeeper summoned a maid and gave her instructions for the tea. 'It's a lovely room,' she announced once they had exited the kitchen, 'and although the current duke never had the opportunity to know his mother, I'm sure he'll be quite touched that you have seen fit to preserve her favorite room.'

'It was the least I could do,' Mrs. Colson said as they strolled across the hall. 'I have not always served the Basset family, after all.'

'Oh?' Daphne asked curiously. Upper servants were notoriously loyal, often serving a single family for generations.

'Yes, I was the duchess's personal maid.' Mrs. Colson waited outside the doorway of the yellow room to allow Daphne to precede her. 'And before that her companion. My mother was her nurse. Her grace's family was kind enough to allow me to share her lessons.'

'You must have been quite close,' Daphne murmured.

Mrs. Colson nodded. 'After she died I occupied a number of different positions here at Clyvedon until I finally became housekeeper.'

'I see.' Daphne smiled at her and then took a seat on the sofa. 'Please sit,' she said, motioning to the chair across from her.

Mrs. Colson seemed hesitant with such familiarity, but eventually sat. 'It broke my heart when she died,' she said. She gave Daphne a slightly apprehensive look. 'I hope you don't mind my telling you so.'

'Of course not,' Daphne said quickly. She was ravenously curious about Simon's childhood. He said so little, and yet she sensed that it all meant so much. 'Please, tell me more. I would love to hear about her.'

Mrs. Colson's eyes grew misty. 'She was the kindest, gentlest soul this earth has ever known. She and the duke – well, it wasn't a love match, but they got on well enough. They were friends in their own way.' She looked up. 'They were both very much aware of their duties as duke and duchess. Took their responsibilities quite seriously.'

Daphne nodded understandingly.

'She was so determined to give him a son. She kept trying even after the doctors all told her she mustn't. She used to cry in my arms every month when her courses came.'

Daphne nodded again, hoping the motion would hide her suddenly strained expression. It was difficult to listen to stories about not being able to have children. But she supposed she was going to have to get used to it. It was going to be even more strenuous to answer questions about it.

And there *would be* questions. Painfully tactful and hideously pitying questions.

But Mrs. Colson thankfully didn't notice Daphne's distress. She sniffled as she continued her story. 'She was always saying things like how was she to be a proper duchess if she couldn't give him a son. It broke my heart. Every month it broke my heart.'

Daphne wondered if her own heart would shatter every month. Probably not. She, at least, knew for a fact that she wouldn't have children. Simon's mother had her hopes crushed every four weeks.

'And of course,' the housekeeper continued, 'everyone talked as if it were *her* fault there was no baby. How could they know that, I ask you? It's not always the woman who is barren. Sometimes it's the man's fault, you know.'

Daphne said nothing.

'I told her this time and again, but still she felt guilty. I said to her—' The housekeeper's face turned pink. 'Do you mind if I speak frankly?'

'Please do.'

She nodded. 'Well, I said to her what my mother said to me. A womb won't quicken without strong, healthy seed.'

Daphne held her face in an expressionless mask. It was all she could manage.

'But then she finally had Master Simon.' Mrs. Colson let out a maternal sigh, then looked to Daphne with an apprehensive expression. 'I beg your pardon,' she said hastily. 'I shouldn't be calling him that. He's the duke now.'

'Don't stop on my account,' Daphne said, happy to have something to smile about.

'It's hard to change one's ways at my age,' Mrs. Colson said with a sigh. 'And I'm afraid a part of me will always remember him as that poor little boy.' She looked up at Daphne and shook her head. 'He would have had a much easier time of it if the duchess had lived.'

'An easier time of it?' Daphne murmured, hoping that would be all the encouragement Mrs. Colson would need to explain further.

'The duke just never understood that poor boy,' the housekeeper said forcefully. 'He stormed about and called him stupid, and—'

Daphne's head snapped up. 'The duke thought Simon was stupid?' she interrupted. That was preposterous. Simon was one of the smartest people she knew. She'd once asked him a bit about his studies at Oxford and had been stunned to learned that his brand of mathematics didn't even use *numbers*.

'The duke never could see the world beyond his own nose,' Mrs. Colson said with a snort. 'He never gave that boy a chance.'

Daphne felt her body leaning forward, her ears straining for the housekeeper's words. What had the duke done to Simon? And was this the reason he turned to ice every time his father's name was mentioned?

Mrs. Colson pulled out a handkerchief and dabbed at her eyes. 'You should have seen the way that boy worked to improve himself. It broke my heart. It simply broke my heart.'

Daphne's hands clawed at the sofa. Mrs. Colson was never going to get to the point.

'But nothing he ever did was good enough for the duke. This is just my opinion of course, but—'

Just then a maid entered with tea. Daphne nearly screamed with frustration. It took a good two minutes for the tea to be set up and poured, and all the while Mrs. Colson chitchatted about the biscuits, and did Daphne prefer them plain or with coarse sugar on top.

Daphne had to pry her hands off the sofa, lest she puncture holes in the upholstery Mrs. Colson had worked so hard to preserve. Finally, the maid left, and Mrs. Colson took a sip of her tea, and said, 'Now then, where were we?'

'You were talking about the duke,' Daphne said quickly. 'The late duke. That nothing my husband did was ever good enough for him and in your opinion—'

'My goodness, you *were* listening.' Mrs. Colson beamed. 'I'm so flattered.'

'But you were saying . . . ' Daphne prompted.

'Oh yes, of course. I was simply going to say that I have long held the opinion that the late duke never forgave his son for not being perfect.'

'But Mrs. Colson,' Daphne said quietly, 'none of us is perfect.'

'Of course not, but—' The housekeeper's eyes floated up for a brief second in an expression of disdain toward the late duke. 'If you'd known his grace, you would understand. He'd waited so long for a son. And in his mind, the Basset name was synonymous with perfection.'

'And my husband wasn't the son he wanted?' Daphne asked.

'He didn't want a son. He wanted a perfect little replica of himself.'

Daphne could no longer contain her curiosity. 'But what did Simon do that was so repugnant to the duke?'

Mrs. Colson's eyes widened in surprise, and one of her hands floated to her chest. 'Why, you don't know,' she said softly. 'Of course you wouldn't know.'

'*What?*'

'He couldn't speak.'

Daphne's lips parted in shock. 'I beg your pardon?'

'He couldn't speak. Not a word until he was four, and then it was all stutters and stammers. It broke my heart every time he opened his mouth. I could see that there was a bright little boy inside. He just couldn't get the words out right.'

'But he speaks so well now,' Daphne said, surprised by the defensiveness in her voice. 'I've never heard him stammer. Or if I have, I-I-I didn't notice it. See! Look, I just did it myself. Everyone stammers a bit when they're flustered.'

'He worked very hard to improve himself. It was seven years, I recall. For seven years he did nothing but practice his speech with his nurse.' Mrs. Colson's face wrinkled with thought. 'Let's see, what was her name? Oh yes, Nurse Hopkins. She was a saint, she was. As devoted to that boy as if he'd been her own. I was the housekeeper's assistant at the time, but she often let me come up and help him practice his speech.'

‘Was it difficult for him?’ Daphne whispered.

‘Some days I thought he’d surely shatter from the frustration of it. But he was so stubborn. Heavens, but he was a stubborn boy. I’ve never seen a person so single-minded.’ Mrs. Colson shook her head sadly. ‘And his father still rejected him. It—’

‘Broke your heart,’ Daphne finished for her. ‘It would have broken mine, as well.’

Mrs. Colson took a sip of her tea during the long, uncomfortable silence that followed. ‘Thank you very much for allowing me to take tea with you, your grace,’ she said, misinterpreting Daphne’s quietude for displeasure. ‘It was highly irregular of you to do so, but very . . . ’

Daphne looked up as Mrs. Colson searched for the correct word.

‘Kind,’ the housekeeper finally finished. ‘It was very kind of you.’

‘Thank you,’ Daphne murmured distractedly.

‘Oh, but I haven’t answered any of your questions about Clyvedon,’ Mrs. Colson said suddenly.

Daphne gave her head a little shake. ‘Another time, perhaps,’ she said softly. She had too much to think on just then.

Mrs. Colson, sensing her employer desired privacy, stood, bobbed a curtsy, and silently left the room.

16

The stifling heat in London this week has certainly put a crimp in society functions. This author saw Miss Prudence Featherington swoon at the Huxley ball, but it is impossible to discern whether this temporary lack of verticality was due to the heat or the presence of Mr. Colin Bridgerton, who has been cutting quite a swash through society since his return from the Continent.

The unseasonable heat has also made a casualty of Lady Danbury, who quit London several days ago, claiming that her cat (a long-haired, bushy beast) could not tolerate the weather. It is believed that she has retired to her country home in Surrey.

One would guess that the Duke and Duchess of Hastings are unaffected by these rising temperatures; they are down on the coast, where the sea wind is always a pleasure. But This Author cannot be certain of their comfort; contrary to popular belief, This Author does not have spies in all the important households, and certainly not outside of London!

LADY WHISTLEDOWN'S SOCIETY PAPERS,
2 JUNE 1813

It was odd, Simon reflected, how they'd not been married even a fortnight and yet had already fallen into comfortable patterns and routines. Just now, he stood barefoot in the doorway of his dressing room, loosening his cravat as he watched his wife brush her hair.

And he'd done the exact same thing yesterday. There was something oddly comforting in that.

And both times, he thought with a hint of a leer, he'd been planning how to seduce her into bed. Yesterday, of course, he'd been successful.

His once expertly tied cravat lying limp and forgotten on the floor, he took a step forward.

Today he'd be successful, too.

He stopped when he reached Daphne's side, perching on the edge of her vanity table. She looked up and blinked owlishly.

He touched his hand to hers, both of their fingers wrapped around the handle of the hairbrush. 'I like to watch you brush your hair,' he said, 'but I like to do it myself better.'

She stared at him in an oddly intent fashion. Slowly, she relinquished the brush. 'Did you get everything done with your accounts? You were tucked away with your estate manager for quite a long time.'

'Yes, it was rather tedious but necessary, and – ' His face froze. 'What are you looking at?'

Her eyes slid from his face. 'Nothing,' she said, her voice unnaturally staccato.

He gave his head a tiny shake, the motion directed more at himself than at her, then he began to brush her hair. For a moment it had seemed as if she were staring at his mouth.

He fought the urge to shudder. All through his childhood, people had stared at his mouth. They'd gazed in horrified fascination, occasionally forcing their eyes up to his, but always returning to his mouth, as if unable to believe that such a normal-looking feature could produce such gibberish.

But he had to be imagining things. Why would Daphne be looking at his mouth?

He pulled the brush gently through her hair, allowing his fingers to trail through the silky strands as well. 'Did you have a nice chat with Mrs. Colson?' he asked.

She flinched. It was a tiny movement, and she hid it quite

well, but he noticed it nonetheless. 'Yes,' she said, 'she's very knowledgeable.'

'She should be. She's been here forev – *what* are you looking at?'

Daphne practically jumped in her chair. 'I'm looking at the mirror,' she insisted.

Which was true, but Simon was still suspicious. Her eyes had been fixed and intent, focused on a single spot.

'As I was saying,' Daphne said hastily, 'I'm certain Mrs. Colson will prove invaluable as I adjust to the management of Clyvedon. It's a large estate, and I have much to learn.'

'Don't make too much of an effort,' he said. 'We won't spend much time here.'

'We won't?'

'I thought we would make London our primary residence.' At her look of surprise, he added, 'You'll be closer to your family, even when they retire to the country. I thought you'd like that.'

'Yes, of course,' she said. 'I do miss them. I've never been away from them for so long before. Of course I've always known that when I married I would be starting my own family, and—'

There was an awful silence.

'Well, you're my family now,' she said, her voice sounding just a bit forlorn.

Simon sighed, the silver-backed hairbrush halting its path through her dark hair. 'Daphne,' he said, 'your family will always be your family. I can never take their place.'

'No,' she agreed. She twisted around to face him, her eyes like warm chocolate as she whispered, 'But you can be something more.'

And Simon realized that all his plans to seduce his wife were moot, because clearly *she* was planning to seduce him.

She stood, her silk robe slipping from her shoulders. Underneath she wore a matching negligee, one that revealed almost as much as it hid.

One of Simon's large hands found its way to the side of her breast, his fingers in stark contrast with the sage green fabric of her nightgown. 'You like this color, don't you?' he said in a husky voice.

She smiled, and he forgot to breathe.

'It's to match my eyes,' she teased. 'Remember?'

Simon managed a returning smile, although how he didn't know. He'd never before thought it possible to smile when one was about to expire from lack of oxygen. Sometimes the need to touch her was so great it hurt just to look at her.

He pulled her closer. He *had* to pull her closer. He would have gone insane if he hadn't. 'Are you telling me,' he murmured against her neck, 'that you purchased this just for me?'

'Of course,' she replied, her voice catching as his tongue traced her earlobe. 'Who else is going to see me in it?'

'No one,' he vowed, reaching around to the small of her back and pressing her firmly against his arousal. 'No one. Not ever.'

She looked slightly bemused by his sudden burst of possessiveness. 'Besides,' she added, 'it's part of my trousseau.'

Simon groaned. 'I love your trousseau. I adore it. Have I told you that?'

'Not in so many words,' she gasped, 'but it hasn't been too difficult to figure it out.'

'Mostly,' he said, nudging her toward the bed as he tore off his shirt, 'I like you out of your trousseau.'

Whatever Daphne had meant to say – and he was certain she'd meant to say something, because her mouth opened in a most delightful manner – was lost as she toppled onto the bed.

Simon covered her in an instant. He put his hands on either side of her hips, then slid them up, pushing her arms over her head. He paused on the bare skin of her upper arms, giving them a gentle squeeze.

'You're very strong,' he said. 'Stronger than most women.'

The look Daphne gave him was just a bit arch. 'I don't want to hear about most women.'

Despite himself, Simon chuckled. Then, with movements quick as lightning, his hands flew to her wrists and pinned them above her head. 'But not,' he drawled, 'as strong as I.'

She gasped with surprise, a sound he found particularly thrilling, and he quickly circled both her wrists with one of his hands, leaving the other free to roam her body.

And roam he did.

'If you aren't the perfect woman,' he groaned, sliding the hem of her nightgown up over her hips, 'then the world is—'

'Stop,' she said shakily. 'You know I'm not perfect.'

'I do?' His smile was dark and wicked as he slid his hand under one of her buttocks. 'You must be misinformed, because this' – he gave her a squeeze – 'is perfect.'

'Simon!'

'And as for these—' He reached up and covered one of her breasts with his hand, tickling the nipple through the silk. 'Well, I don't need to tell you how I feel about these.'

'You're mad.'

'Quite possibly,' he agreed, 'but I have excellent taste. And you' – he leaned down quite suddenly and nipped at her mouth – 'taste quite good.'

Daphne giggled, quite unable to help herself.

Simon wiggled his brows. 'Dare you mock me?'

'Normally I would,' she replied, 'but not when you've got both my arms pinned over my head.'

Simon's free hand went to work on the fastenings of his trousers. 'Clearly I married a woman of great sense.'

Daphne gazed at him with pride and love as she watched his words trip effortlessly from his lips. To hear him speak now, one could never guess that he'd stammered as a child.

What a remarkable man she'd married. To take such a hindrance and beat it with sheer force of will – he had to be the strongest, most disciplined man she knew.

'I am so glad I married you,' she said in a rush of tenderness. 'So very proud you're mine.'

Simon stilled, obviously surprised by her sudden gravity. His voice grew low and husky. 'I'm proud you're mine as well.' He yanked at his trousers. 'And I'd show you how proud,' he grunted, 'if I could get these damned things off.'

Daphne felt another bubble of laughter welling up in her throat. 'Perhaps if you used two hands . . . ' she suggested.

He gave her an I'm-not-as-stupid-asthat sort of look. 'But that would require my letting you go.'

She cocked her head coyly. 'What if I promised not to move my arms?'

'I wouldn't even begin to believe you.'

Her smile turned wickedly suggestive. 'What if I promised I *would* move them?'

'Now, *that* sounds interesting.' He leapt off the bed with an odd combination of grace and frantic energy and managed to get himself naked in under three seconds. Hopping back on, he stretched out on his side, all along the length of her. 'Now then, where were we?'

Daphne giggled again. 'Right about here, I believe.'

'A-ha,' he said with a comically accusing expression. 'You haven't been paying attention. We were right' – he slid atop her, his weight pressing her into the mattress – 'here.'

Her giggles exploded into full-throated laughter.

'Didn't anyone tell you not to laugh at a man when he's trying to seduce you?'

If she'd had any chance of stopping her laughter before, it was gone now. 'Oh, Simon,' she gasped, 'I do love you.'

He went utterly still. 'What?'

Daphne just smiled and touched his cheek. She understood him so much better now. After facing such rejection as a child, he probably didn't realize he was worthy of love. And he probably wasn't certain how to give it in return. But she could wait. She could wait forever for this man.

'You don't have to say anything,' she whispered. 'Just know that I love you.'

The look in Simon's eyes was somehow both overjoyed and stricken. Daphne wondered if anyone had ever said the words 'I love you' to him before. He'd grown up without a family, without the cocoon of love and warmth she'd taken for granted.

His voice, when he found it, was hoarse and nearly broken, 'D-Daphne, I—'

'Shhh,' she crooned, placing a finger to his lips. 'Don't say anything now. Wait until it feels right.'

And then she wondered if perhaps she had said the most hurtful words imaginable – for Simon, did speaking *ever* feel right?

'Just kiss me,' she whispered hurriedly, eager to move past what she was afraid might be an awkward moment. 'Please, kiss me.'

And he did.

He kissed her with ferocious intensity, burning with all the passion and desire that flowed between them. His lips and hands left no spot untouched, kissing, squeezing, and caressing until her nightgown lay tossed on the floor and the sheets and blankets were twisted into coils at the foot of the bed.

But unlike every other night, he never did quite render her senseless. She'd been given too much to think about that day – nothing, not even the fiercest cravings of her body, could stop the frantic pace of her thoughts. She was swimming in desire, every nerve expertly brought to a fever pitch of need, and yet still her mind whirred and analyzed.

When his eyes, so blue they glowed even in the candle-light, burned into hers, she wondered if that intensity were due to emotions he didn't know how to express through words. When he gasped her name, she couldn't help but listen for another tiny stammer. And when he sank into her, his head thrown back until the cords of his neck stood out in harsh relief, she wondered why he looked like he was in so much pain.

Pain?

'Simon?' she asked tentatively, worry putting a very slight damper on her desire. 'Are you all right?'

He nodded, his teeth gritted together. He fell against her, his hips still moving in their ancient rhythm, and whispered against her ear, 'I'll take you there.'

It wouldn't be that difficult, Daphne thought, her breath catching as he captured the tip of her breast in his mouth. It was never that difficult. He seemed to know exactly how to touch her, when to move, and when to tease by remaining tauntingly in place. His fingers slipped between their bodies, tickling her hot skin until her hips were moving and grinding with the same force as his.

She felt herself sliding toward that familiar oblivion. And it felt so good . . .

'Please,' he pleaded, sliding his other hand underneath her so that he might press her even more tightly against him. 'I need you to – Now, Daphne, now!'

And she did. The world exploded around her, her eyes squeezing so tightly shut that she saw spots, and stars, and brilliant streaming bursts of light. She heard music – or maybe that was just her own high-pitched moan as she reached completion, providing a melody over the powerful pounding of her heart.

Simon, with a groan that sounded as if it were ripped from his very soul, yanked himself out of her with barely a second to spare before he spilled himself – as he always did – on the sheets at the edge of the bed.

In a moment he would turn to her and pull her into his arms. It was a ritual she'd come to cherish. He would hold her tightly against him, her back to his front, and nuzzle his face in her hair. And then, after their breathing had settled down to an even sigh, they would sleep.

Except tonight was different. Tonight Daphne felt oddly restless. Her body was blissfully weary and sated, but something felt wrong. Something niggled at the back of her mind, teasing her subconscious.

Simon rolled over and scooted his body next to hers, pushing her toward the clean side of the bed. He always did that, using his body as a barrier so that she would never roll into the mess he made. It was a thoughtful gesture, actually, and—

Daphne's eyes flew open. She almost gasped.

A womb won't quicken without strong, healthy seed.

Daphne hadn't given a thought to Mrs. Colson's words when the housekeeper had uttered the saying that afternoon. She'd been too consumed with the tale of Simon's painful childhood, too concerned with how she could bring enough love into his life to banish the bad memories forever.

Daphne sat up abruptly, the blankets falling to her waist. With shaking fingers she lit the candle that sat on her bedside table.

Simon opened a sleepy eye. 'What's wrong?'

She said nothing, just stared at the wet spot on the other side of the bed.

His seed.

'Daff?'

He'd told her he couldn't have children. He'd lied to her.

'Daphne, what's wrong?' He sat up. His face showed his concern.

Was that, too, a lie?

She pointed. 'What is that?' she asked, her voice so low it was barely audible.

'What is what?' His eyes followed the line of her finger and saw only bed. 'What are you talking about?'

'Why can't you have children, Simon?'

His eyes grew shuttered. He said nothing.

'*Why,* Simon?' She practically shouted the words.

'The details aren't important, Daphne.'

His tone was soft, placating, with just a hint of condescension. Daphne felt something inside of her snap.

'Get out,' she ordered.

His mouth fell open. 'This is my bedroom.'

'Then I'll get out.' She stormed out of the bed, whipping one of the bedsheets around her.

Simon was on her heels in a heartbeat. 'Don't you *dare* leave this room,' he hissed.

'You lied to me.'

'I never—'

'You lied to me,' she screamed. 'You lied to me, and I will never forgive you for that!'

'Daphne—'

'You took advantage of my stupidity.' She let out a disbelieving breath, the kind that came from the back of one's throat, right before it closed up in shock. 'You must have been so delighted when you realized how little I knew about marital relations.'

'It's called making love, Daphne,' he said.

'Not between us, it's not.'

Simon nearly flinched at the rancor in her voice. He stood, utterly naked, in the middle of the room, desperately trying to come up with some way to salvage the situation. He still wasn't even certain what she knew, or what she *thought* she knew. 'Daphne,' he said, very slowly so that he would not let his emotions trip up his words, 'perhaps you should tell me exactly what this is about.'

'Oh, we're going to play *that* game, are we?' She snorted derisively. 'Very well, let me tell you a story. Once upon a time, there was—'

The scathing anger in her voice was like a dagger in his gut. 'Daphne,' he said, closing his eyes and shaking his head, 'don't do it like this.'

'Once upon a time,' she said, louder this time, 'there was a young lady. We'll call her Daphne.'

Simon strode to his dressing room and yanked on a robe.

There were some things a man didn't want to deal with naked.

'Daphne was very, very stupid.'

'Daphne!'

'Oh, very well.' She flipped her hand through the air dismissively. 'Ignorant, then. She was very, very ignorant.'

Simon crossed his arms.

'Daphne knew nothing about what happened between a man and a woman. She didn't know what they did, except that they did it in a bed, and that at some point, the result would be a baby.'

'This is enough, Daphne.'

The only sign that she heard him was the dark, flashing fury in her eyes. 'But you see, she didn't really know how that baby was made, and so when her husband told her he couldn't have children—'

'I told you that before we married. I gave you every option to back out. Don't you forget that,' he said hotly. 'Don't you *dare* forget it.'

'You made me feel sorry for you!'

'Oh now, *that's* what a man wants to hear,' he sneered.

'For the love of God, Simon,' she snapped, 'you know I didn't marry you *because* I felt sorry for you.'

'Then why?'

'Because I loved you,' she replied, but the acid in her voice made the declaration rather brittle. 'And because I didn't want to see you die, which you seemed stupidly bent upon doing.'

He had no ready comment, so he just snorted and glared at her.

'But don't try to make this about me,' she continued hotly. 'I'm not the one who lied. You said you can't have children, but the truth is you just *won't* have them.'

He said nothing, but he knew the answer was in his eyes.

She took a step toward him, advancing with barely controlled fury. 'If you truly couldn't have children, it wouldn't matter where your seed landed, would it? You wouldn't be so frantic every night to make certain it ended up anywhere but inside me.'

'You don't know anything ab-bout this, Daphne.' His words were low and furious, and only slightly damaged.

She crossed her arms. 'Then tell me.'

'I will never have children,' he hissed. '*Never.* Do you understand?'

'No.'

He felt rage rising within him, roiling in his stomach, pressing against his skin until he thought he would burst. It wasn't rage against her, it wasn't even against himself. It was, as always, directed at the man whose presence – or lack thereof – had always managed to rule his life.

'My father,' Simon said, desperately fighting for control, 'was not a loving man.'

Daphne's eyes held his. 'I know about your father,' she said.

That caught him by surprise. 'What do you know?'

'I know that he hurt you. That he rejected you.' Something flickered in her dark eyes – not quite pity, but close to it. 'I know that he thought you were stupid.'

Simon's heart slammed in his chest. He wasn't certain how he was able to speak – he wasn't certain how he was able to breathe – but he somehow managed to say, 'Then you know about—'

'Your stammer?' she finished for him.

He thanked her silently for that. Ironically, 'stutter' and 'stammer' were two words he'd never been able to master.

She shrugged. 'He was an idiot.'

Simon gaped at her, unable to comprehend how she could dismiss decades of rage with one blithe statement. 'You don't understand,' he said, shaking his head. 'You couldn't possibly. Not with a family like yours. The only thing that mattered to him was blood. Blood and the title. And when I didn't turn out to be perfect – Daphne, he told people I was dead!'

The blood drained from her face. 'I didn't know it was like that,' she whispered.

'It was worse,' he bit off. 'I sent him letters. Hundreds of letters, begging him to come visit me. He didn't answer one.'

'Simon—'

'D-did you know I didn't speak until I was four? No? Well, I didn't. And when he visited, he shook me, and threatened to beat my voice out of me. That was my f-father.'

Daphne tried not to notice that he was beginning to stumble over his words. She tried to ignore the sick feeling in her stomach, the anger that rose within her at the hideous way Simon had been treated. 'But he's gone now,' she said in a shaky voice. 'He's gone, and you're here.'

'He said he couldn't even b-bear to look at me. He'd spent years praying for an heir. Not a son,' he said, his voice rising dangerously, 'an heir. And f-for what? Hastings would go to a half-wit. His precious dukedom would b-be ruled by an idiot!'

'But he was wrong,' Daphne whispered.

'I don't care if he was wrong!' Simon roared. 'All he cared about was the title. He never gave a single thought to me, about how I must feel, trapped with a m-mouth that didn't w-work!'

Daphne stumbled back a step, unsteady in the presence of such anger. This was the fury of decades-old resentment.

Simon very suddenly stepped forward and pressed his face very close to hers. 'But do you know what?' he asked in an awful voice. 'I shall have the last laugh. He thought that there could be nothing worse than Hastings going to a half-wit—'

'Simon, you're not—'

'Are you even listening to me?' he thundered.

Daphne, frightened now, scurried back, her hand reaching for the doorknob in case she needed to escape.

‘Of course I know I’m not an idiot,’ he spat out, ‘and in the end, I think h-he knew it, too. And I’m sure that brought him g-great comfort. Hastings was safe. N-never mind that I was not suffering as I once had. Hastings – *that’s* what mattered.’

Daphne felt sick. She knew what was coming next.

Simon suddenly smiled. It was a cruel, hard expression, one she’d never seen on his face before. ‘But Hastings dies with me,’ he said. ‘All those cousins he was so worried about inheriting . . . ’ He shrugged and let out a brittle laugh. ‘They all had girls. Isn’t that something?’

Simon shrugged. ‘Maybe that was why my f-father suddenly decided I wasn’t such an idiot. He knew I was his only hope.’

‘He knew he’d been wrong,’ Daphne said with quiet determination. She suddenly remembered the letters she’d been given by the Duke of Middlethorpe. The ones written to him by his father. She’d left them at Bridgerton House, in London. Which was just as well, since that meant she didn’t have to decide what to do with them yet.

‘It doesn’t matter,’ Simon said flippantly. ‘After I die, the title becomes extinct. And I for one couldn’t be h-happier.’

With that, he stalked out of the room, exiting through his dressing room, since Daphne was blocking the door.

Daphne sank down onto a chair, still wrapped in the soft linen sheet she’d yanked from the bed. What was she going to do?

She felt tremors spread through her body, a strange shaking over which she had no control. And then she realized she was crying. Without a sound, without even a caught breath, she was crying.

Dear God, *what* was she going to do?

17

To say that men can be bullheaded would be insulting to the bull.

LADY WHISTLEDOWN'S SOCIETY PAPERS,
2 JUNE 1813

In the end, Daphne did the only thing she knew how to do. The Bridgertons had always been a loud and boisterous family, not a one of them prone to keeping secrets or holding grudges.

So she tried to talk to Simon. To reason with him.

The following morning (she had no idea where he had spent the night; wherever it was, it hadn't been their bed) she found him in his study. It was a dark, overbearingly masculine room, probably decorated by Simon's father. Daphne was frankly surprised that Simon would feel comfortable in such surroundings; he hated reminders of the old duke.

But Simon, clearly, was not uncomfortable. He was sitting behind his desk, his feet insolently propped up on the leather blotter that protected the rich cherry wood of the desktop. In his hand he was holding a smoothly polished stone, turning it over and over in his hands. There was a bottle of whiskey on the desk next to him; she had a feeling it had been there all night.

He hadn't, however, drunk much of it. Daphne was thankful for small favors.

The door was ajar, so she didn't knock. But she wasn't

quite so brave as to stride boldly in. 'Simon?' she asked, standing back near the door.

He looked up at her and quirked a brow.

'Are you busy?'

He set down the stone. 'Obviously not.'

She motioned to it. 'Is that from your travels?'

'The Caribbean. A memento of my time on the beach.'

Daphne noticed that he was speaking with perfect elocution. There was no hint of the stammer that had become apparent the night before. He was calm now. Almost annoyingly so. 'Is the beach very different there than it is here?' she asked.

He raised an arrogant brow. 'It's warmer.'

'Oh. Well, I'd assumed as much.'

He looked at her with piercing, unwavering eyes. 'Daphne, I know you didn't seek me out to discuss the tropics.'

He was right, of course, but this wasn't going to be an easy conversation, and Daphne didn't think she was so much of a coward for wanting to put it off by a few moments.

She took a deep breath. 'We need to discuss what happened last night.'

'I'm sure you think we do.'

She fought the urge to lean forward and smack the bland expression from his face. 'I don't *think* we do. I *know* we do.'

He was silent for a moment before saying, 'I'm sorry if you feel that I have betrayed—'

'It's not that, exactly.'

'—but you must remember that I tried to avoid marrying you.'

'That's certainly a nice way of putting it,' she muttered.

He spoke as if delivering a lecture. 'You know that I had intended never to marry.'

'That's not the point, Simon.'

'It's exactly the point.' He dropped his feet to the floor, and his chair, which had been balancing on its two back legs, hit the ground with a loud thunk. 'Why do you think I avoided marriage with such determination? It was because I didn't want to take a wife and then hurt her by denying her children.'

'You were never thinking of your potential wife,' she shot back. 'You were thinking of yourself.'

'Perhaps,' he allowed, 'but when that potential wife became you, Daphne, everything changed.'

'Obviously not,' she said bitterly.

He shrugged. 'You know I hold you in the highest esteem. I never wanted to hurt you.'

'You're hurting me right now,' she whispered.

A flicker of remorse crossed his eyes, but it was quickly replaced with steely determination. 'If you recall, I refused to offer for you even when your brother demanded it. Even,' he added pointedly, 'when it meant my own death.'

Daphne didn't contradict him. They both knew he would have died on that dueling field. No matter what she thought of him now, how much she despised the hatred that was eating him up, Simon had too much honor ever to have shot at Anthony.

And Anthony placed too much value on his sister's honor to have aimed anywhere but at Simon's heart.

'I did that,' Simon said, 'because I knew I could never be a good husband to you. I knew you wanted children. You'd told me so on a number of occasions, and I certainly don't blame you. You come from a large and loving family.'

'You could have a family like that, too.'

He continued as if he hadn't heard her. 'Then, when you interrupted the duel, and begged me to marry you, I warned you. I told you I wouldn't have children—'

'You told me you *couldn't* have children,' she interrupted, her eyes flashing with anger. 'There's a very big difference.'

'Not,' Simon said coldly, 'to me. I *can't* have children. My soul won't allow it.'

'I see.' Something shriveled inside Daphne at that moment,

and she was very much afraid it was her heart. She didn't know how she was meant to argue with such a statement. Simon's hatred of his father was clearly far stronger than any love he might learn to feel for her.

'Very well,' she said in a clipped voice. 'This is obviously not a subject upon which you are open to discussion.'

He gave her one curt nod.

She gave him one in return. 'Good day, then.'

And she left.

Simon kept to himself for most of the day. He didn't particularly want to see Daphne; that did nothing but make him feel guilty. Not, he assured himself, that he had anything to feel guilty about. He had told her before their marriage that he could not have children. He had given her every opportunity to back out, and she had chosen to marry him, anyway. He had not forced her into anything. It was not *his* fault if she had misinterpreted his words and thought that he was physically unable to sire brats.

Still, even though he was plagued by this nagging sense of guilt every time he thought of her (which pretty much meant all day), and even though his gut twisted every time he saw her stricken face in his mind (which pretty much meant he spent the day with an upset stomach), he felt as if a great weight had been lifted from his shoulders now that everything was out in the open.

Secrets could be deadly, and now there were no more between them. Surely that had to be a good thing.

By the time night fell, he had almost convinced himself that he had done nothing wrong. Almost, but not quite. He had entered this marriage convinced that he would break Daphne's heart, and that had never sat well with him. He liked Daphne. Hell, he probably liked her better than any human being he'd ever known, and that was why he'd been so reluctant to marry her. He hadn't wanted to shatter her dreams. He hadn't wanted to deprive her of the family she so desperately wanted. He'd been quite prepared to step aside and watch her marry someone else, someone who would give her a whole houseful of children.

Simon suddenly shuddered. The image of Daphne with another man was not nearly as tolerable as it had been just a month earlier.

Of course not, he thought, trying to use the rational side of his brain. She was his wife now. She was his.

Everything was different now.

He had known how desperately she had wanted children, and he had married her, knowing full well that he would not give her any.

But, he told himself, *you warned her.* She'd known exactly what she was getting into.

Simon, who had been sitting in his study, tossing that stupid rock back and forth between his hands since supper, suddenly straightened. He had not deceived her. Not truly. He had told her that they wouldn't have children, and she had agreed to marry him, anyway. He could see where she would feel a bit upset upon learning his reasons, but she could not say that she had entered this marriage with any foolish hopes or expectations.

He stood. It was time they had another talk, this one at his behest. Daphne hadn't attended dinner, leaving him to dine alone, the silence of the night broken only by the metallic clink of his fork against his plate. He hadn't seen his wife since that morning; it was high time he did.

She was his *wife,* he reminded himself. He ought to be able to see her whenever he damn well pleased.

He marched down the hall and swung open the door to the duke's bedroom, fully prepared to lecture her about *something* (the topic, he was sure, would come to him when necessary), but she wasn't there.

Simon blinked, unable to believe his eyes. Where the hell was she? It was nearly midnight. She should be in bed.

The dressing room. She had to be in the dressing-room.

The silly chit insisted upon donning her nightrobe every night, even though Simon wiggled her out of it mere minutes later.

'Daphne?' he barked, crossing to the dressing room door. 'Daphne?'

No answer. And no light shining in the crack between the door and the floor. Surely she wouldn't dress in the dark.

He pulled the door open. She most definitely wasn't present.

Simon yanked on the bellpull. Hard. Then he strode out into the hall to await whichever servant was unfortunate enough to have answered his summons.

It was one of the upstairs maids, a little blond thing whose name he could not recall. She took one look at his face and blanched.

'Where is my wife?' he barked.

'Your wife, your grace?'

'Yes,' he said impatiently, 'my wife.'

She stared at him blankly.

'I assume you know about whom I am speaking. She's about your height, long dark hair . . . ' Simon would have said more, but the maid's terrified expression made him rather ashamed of his sarcasm. He let out a long, tense breath. 'Do you know where she is?' he asked, his tone softer, although not what anyone would describe as gentle.

'Isn't she in bed, your grace?'

Simon jerked his head toward his empty room. 'Obviously not.'

'But that's not where she sleeps, your grace.'

His eyebrows snapped together. 'I beg your pardon.'

'Doesn't she—' The maid's eyes widened in horror, then shot frantically around the hall. Simon had no doubt that she was looking for an escape route. Either that or someone who might possibly save her from his thunderous temper.

'Spit it out,' he barked.

The maid's voice was very small. 'Doesn't she inhabit the duchess's bedchamber?'

'The duchess's . . . ' He pushed down an unfamiliar bolt of rage. 'Since when?'

'Since today, I suppose, your grace. We had all assumed that you would occupy separate rooms at the end of your honeymoon.'

'You did, did you?' he growled.

The maid started to tremble. 'Your parents did, your grace, and—'

'*We are not my parents!*' he roared.

The maid jumped back a step.

'And,' Simon added in a deadly voice, 'I am not my father.'

'Of-of course, your grace.'

'Would you mind telling me which room my wife has chosen to designate as the duchess's bedchamber?'

The maid pointed one shaking finger at a door down the hall.

'Thank you.' He took four steps away, then whirled around. 'You are dismissed.' The servants would have plenty to gossip about on the morrow, what with Daphne moving out of their bedroom; he didn't need to give them any more by allowing this maid to witness what was sure to be a colossal argument.

Simon waited until she had scurried down the stairs, then he moved on angry feet down the hall to Daphne's new bedroom. He stopped outside her door, thought about what he'd say, realized he had no idea, and then went ahead and knocked.

No response.

He pounded.

No response.

He raised his fist to pound again, when it occurred to him that maybe she hadn't even locked the door. Wouldn't he feel like a fool if—

He twisted the knob.

She had *locked* it. Simon swore swiftly and fluently under his breath. Funny how he'd never once in his life stuttered on a curse.

'Daphne! Daphne!' His voice was somewhere between a call and a yell. 'Daphne!'

Finally, he heard footsteps moving in her room. 'Yes?' came her voice.

'Let me in.'

A beat of silence, and then, 'No.'

Simon stared at the sturdy wooden door in shock. It had never occurred to him that she would disobey a direct order. She was his wife, damn it. Hadn't she promised to obey him?

'Daphne,' he said angrily, 'open this door this instant.'

She must have been very close to the door, because he actually heard her sigh before saying, 'Simon, the only reason to let you into this room would be if I were planning to let you into my bed, which I'm not, so I would appreciate it – indeed I believe the entire household would appreciate it – if you would take yourself off and go to sleep.'

Simon's mouth actually fell open. He began to mentally weigh the door and compute how many foot-pounds per second would be required to bash the bloody thing in.

'Daphne,' he said, his voice so calm it frightened even him, 'if you do not open the door this instant I shall break it down.'

'You wouldn't.'

He said nothing, just crossed his arms and glared, confident that she would know exactly what sort of expression he wore on his face.

'Wouldn't you?'

Again, he decided that silence was the most effective answer.

'I *wish* you wouldn't,' she added in a vaguely pleading voice.

He stared at the door in disbelief.

'You'll hurt yourself,' she added.

'Then open the damned door,' he ground out.

Silence, followed by a key slowly turning in the lock. Simon had just enough presence of mind not to throw the door violently open; Daphne was almost certainly directly on the other side. He shoved his way in and found her about five paces away from him, her arms crossed, her legs in a wide, militant stance.

'Don't you ever lock a door against me again,' he spat out.

She shrugged. She actually shrugged! 'I desired privacy.'

Simon advanced several steps. 'I want your things moved back into our bedroom by morning. And *you* will be moving back tonight.'

'No.'

'What the hell do you mean, no?'

'What the hell do you think I mean?' she countered.

Simon wasn't sure what shocked and angered him more – that she was defying him or that she was cursing aloud.

'No,' she continued in a louder voice, 'means no.'

'You are my wife!' he roared. 'You will sleep with me. In *my* bed.'

'No.'

'Daphne, I'm warning you . . . '

Her eyes narrowed to slits. 'You have chosen to withhold something from me. Well, I have chosen to withhold something from you. Me.'

He was speechless. Utterly speechless.

She, however, was not. She marched to the door and motioned rather rudely for him to go through it. 'Get out of my room.'

Simon started to shake with rage. 'I own this room,' he growled. 'I own *you.*'

'You own nothing but your father's title,' she shot back. 'You don't even own yourself.'

A low roar filled his ears – the roar of red-hot fury. Simon staggered back a step, fearing that if he did not he might actually do something to hurt her. 'What the hell do you m-mean?' he demanded.

She shrugged again, damn her. 'You figure it out,' she said.

All of Simon's good intentions fled the room, and he charged forward, grabbing her by her upper arms. He knew his grip was too tight, but he was helpless against the searing rage that flooded his veins. 'Explain yourself,' he said – between his teeth because he couldn't unclench his jaw. 'Now.'

Her eyes met his with such a level, knowing gaze that he was nearly undone. 'You are not your own man,' she said simply. 'Your father is still ruling you from the grave.'

Simon shook with untold fury, with unspoken words.

'Your actions, your choices – ' she continued, her eyes growing very sad, 'They have nothing to do with you, with what you want, or what you need. Everything you do, Simon, every move you make, every word you speak – it's all just to thwart him.' Her voice broke as she finished with, 'And he's not even *alive.*'

Simon moved forward with a strange, predatory grace. 'Not every move,' he said in a low voice. 'Not every word.'

Daphne backed up, unnerved by the feral expression in his eyes. 'Simon?' she asked hesitantly, suddenly devoid of the courage and bravado that had enabled her to stand up to him, a man twice her size and possibly thrice her strength.

The tip of his index finger trailed down her upper arm. She was wearing a silk robe, but the heat and power of him burned through the fabric. He came closer, and one of his hands stole around her until it cupped her buttock and squeezed. 'When I touch you like this,' he whispered, his voice perilously close to her ear, 'it has nothing to do with him.'

Daphne shuddered, hating herself for wanting him. Hating him for making her want him.

'When my lips touch your ear,' he murmured, catching

her lobe between his teeth, 'it has nothing to do with him.'

She tried to push him away, but when her hands found his shoulders, all they could do was clutch.

He started to push her, slowly, inexorably, toward the bed. 'And when I take you to bed,' he added, his words hot against the skin of her neck, 'and we are skin to skin, it is just the two of—'

'No!' she cried out, shoving against him with all her might. He stumbled back, caught by surprise.

'When you take me to bed,' she choked out, 'it is never just the two of us. Your father is *always* there.'

His fingers, which had crept up under the wide sleeve of her dressing gown, dug into her flesh. He said nothing, but he didn't have to. The icy anger in his pale blue eyes said everything.

'Can you look me in the eye,' she whispered, 'and tell me that when you pull from my body and give yourself instead to the bed you're thinking about *me?*'

His face was drawn and tight, and his eyes were focused on her mouth.

She shook her head and shook herself from his grasp, which had gone slack. 'I didn't think so,' she said in a small voice.

She moved away from him, but also away from the bed. She had no doubt that he could seduce her if he so chose. He could kiss her and caress her and bring her to dizzying heights of ecstasy, and she would hate him in the morning.

She would hate herself even more.

The room was deadly silent as they stood across from each other. Simon was standing with his arms at his sides, his face a heartbreaking mixture of shock and hurt and fury. But mostly, Daphne thought, her heart cracking a little as she met his eyes, he looked confused.

'I think,' she said softly, 'that you had better leave.'

He looked up, his eyes haunted. 'You're my wife.'

She said nothing.

'Legally, I own you.'

Daphne just stared at him as she said, 'That's true.'

He closed the space between them in a heartbeat, his hands finding her shoulders. 'I can make you want me,' he whispered.

'I know.'

His voice dropped even lower, hoarse and urgent. 'And even if I couldn't, you're mine. You belong to me. I could force you to let me stay.'

Daphne felt about a hundred years old as she said, 'You would never do that.'

And he knew she was right, so all he did was wrench himself away from her and storm out of the room.

18

Is This Author the only one who has noticed, or have the (gentle)men of the ton been imbibing more than usual these days?

LADY WHISTLEDOWN'S SOCIETY PAPERS, 4 JUNE 1813

Simon went out and got drunk. It wasn't something he did often. It wasn't even something he particularly enjoyed, but he did it anyway.

There were plenty of pubs down near the water, only a few miles from Clyvedon. And there were plenty of sailors there, too, looking for fights. Two of them found Simon.

He thrashed them both.

There was an anger in him, a fury that had simmered deep in his soul for years. It had finally found its way to the surface, and it had taken very little provocation to set him to fighting.

He was drunk enough by then so that when he punched, he saw not the sailors with their sun-reddened skin but his father. Every fist was slammed into that constant sneer of rejection. And it felt good. He'd never considered himself a particularly violent man, but damn, it felt good.

By the time Simon was through with the two sailors, no one else dared approach him. The local folk recognized strength, but more importantly they recognized rage. And they all knew that of the two, the latter was the more deadly.

Simon remained in the pub until the first lights of dawn streaked the sky. He drank steadily from the bottle he'd paid for, and then, when it was time to go, rose on unsteady legs, tucked the bottle into his pocket, and made his way back home.

He drank as he rode, the bad whiskey burning straight to his gut. And as he got drunker and drunker, only one thought managed to burst through his haze.

He wanted Daphne back.

She was his wife, damn her. He'd gotten used to having her around. She couldn't just up and move out of their bedroom.

He'd get her back. He'd woo her and he'd win her, and—

Simon let out a loud, unattractive belch. Well, it was going to have to be enough to woo her and win her. He was far too intoxicated to think of anything else.

By the time he reached Castle Clyvedon, he had worked himself into a fine state of drunken self-righteousness. And by the time he stumbled up to Daphne's door, he was making enough noise to raise the dead.

'Daphneeeeeeeeeeee!' he yelled, trying to hide the slight note of desperation in his voice. He didn't need to sound pathetic.

He frowned thoughtfully. On the other hand, maybe if he sounded desperate, she'd be more likely to open the door. He sniffled loudly a few times, then yelled again, 'Daphneeeeeeeee!'

When she didn't respond in under two seconds, he leaned against the heavy door (mostly because his sense of balance was swimming in whiskey). 'Oh, Daphne,' he sighed, his forehead coming to rest against the wood, 'If you—'

The door opened and Simon went tumbling to the ground.

'Didja . . . didja hafta open it so . . . so *fast?*' he mumbled.

Daphne, who was still yanking on her dressing gown,

looked at the human heap on the floor and just barely recognized it as her husband. 'Good God, Simon,' she said, 'What did you—' She leaned down to help him, then lurched back when he opened his mouth and breathed on her. 'You're drunk!' she accused.

He nodded solemnly. ''Fraid so.'

'Where have you been?' she demanded.

He blinked and looked at her as if he'd never heard such a stupid question. 'Out getting foxed,' he replied, then burped.

'Simon, you should be in bed.'

He nodded again, this time with considerably more vigor and enthusiasm. 'Yesh, yesh I should.' He tried to rise to his feet, but only made it as far as his knees before he tripped and fell back down onto the carpet. 'Hmmm,' he said, peering down at the lower half of his body. 'Hmmm, that's strange.' He lifted his face back to Daphne's and looked at her in utter confusion. 'I could have sworn those were my legs.'

Daphne rolled her eyes.

Simon tried out his legs again, with the same results. 'My limbs don't sheem to be working properly,' he commented.

'Your *brain* isn't working properly!' Daphne returned. 'What am I to do with you?'

He looked her way and grinned. 'Love me? You said you loved me, you know.' He frowned. 'I don't think you can take that back.'

Daphne let out a long sigh. She should be furious with him – blast it all, she *was* furious with him! – but it was difficult to maintain appropriate levels of anger when he looked so pathetic.

Besides, with three brothers, she'd had some experience with drunken nitwits. He was going to have to sleep it off, that's all there was to it. He'd wake up with a blistering headache, which would probably serve him right, and then he would insist upon drinking some noxious concoction that he was absolutely positive would eliminate his hangover completely.

'Simon?' she asked patiently. 'How drunk are you?'

He gave her a loopy grin. 'Very.'

'I thought as much,' she muttered under her breath. She bent down and shoved her hands under his arms. 'Up with you now, we've got to get you to bed.'

But he didn't move, just sat there on his fanny and looked up at her with an extremely foolish expression. 'WhydulI need t'get up?' he slurred. 'Can't you sit wi' me?' He threw his arms around her in a sloppy hug. 'Come'n sit wi' me, Daphne.'

'Simon!'

He patted the carpet next to him. 'It's nice down here.'

'Simon, no, I cannot sit with you,' she ground out, struggling out of his heavy embrace. 'You have to go to bed.' She tried to move him again, with the same, dismal outcome. 'Heavens above,' she said under her breath, 'why did you have to go out and get so drunk?'

He wasn't supposed to hear her words, but he must have done, because he cocked his head, and said, 'I wanted you back.'

Her lips parted in shock. They both knew what he had to do to win her back, but Daphne thought he was far too intoxicated for her to conduct any kind of conversation on the topic. So she just tugged at his arm and said, 'We'll talk about it tomorrow, Simon.'

He blinked several times in rapid succession. 'Think it already is tomorrow.' He craned his neck this way and that, peering toward the windows. The curtains were drawn, but the light of the new day was already filtering through. 'Iz day all right,' he mumbled. 'See?' He waved his arm toward the window. 'Tomorrow already.'

'Then we'll talk about it in the evening,' she said, a touch desperately. She already felt as if her heart had been pushed through a windmill; she didn't think she could bear any more just then. 'Please, Simon, let's just leave it be for now.'

'The thing is, Daphrey—' He shook his head in much the same manner a dog shakes off water. 'DaphNe,' he said carefully. 'DaphNe DaphNe.'

Daphne couldn't quite stop a smile at that. 'What, Simon?'

'The problem, y'see' – he scratched his head – 'you just don't understand.'

'What don't I understand?' she said softly.

'Why I can't do it,' he said. He raised his face until it was level with hers, and she nearly flinched at the haunted misery in his eyes.

'I never wanted to hurt you, Daff,' he said hoarsely. 'You know that, don't you?'

She nodded. 'I know that, Simon.'

'Good, because the thing is – ' He drew a long breath that seemed to shake his entire body. 'I can't do what you want.'

She said nothing.

'All my life,' Simon said sadly, 'all my life he won. Didjou know that? He always won. This time I get to win.' In a long, awkward movement he swung his arm in a horizontal arc and jabbed his thumb against his chest. 'Me. I want to win for once.'

'Oh, Simon,' she whispered. 'You won long ago. The moment you exceeded his expectations you won. Every time you beat the odds, made a friend, or traveled to a new land you won. You did all the things he never wanted for you.' Her breath caught, and she gave his shoulders a squeeze. 'You beat him. You won. Why can't you see that?'

He shook his head. 'I don't want to become what he wanted,' he said. 'Even though—' He hiccuped. 'Even though he never expected it of m-me, what he w-wanted was a perfect son, someone who'd be the perfect d-duke, who'd then m-marry the perfect duchess, and have p-perfect children.'

Daphne's lower lip caught between her teeth. He was stuttering again. He must be truly upset. She felt her heart breaking for him, for the little boy who'd wanted nothing other than his father's approval.

Simon cocked his head to the side and regarded her with a surprisingly steady gaze. 'He would have approved of you.'

'Oh,' Daphne said, not sure how to interpret that.

'But' – he shrugged and gave her a secret, mischievous smile – 'I married you anyway.'

He looked so earnest, so boyishly serious, that it was a hard battle not to throw her arms around him and attempt to comfort him. But no matter how deep his pain, or how wounded his soul, he was going about this all wrong. The best revenge against his father would simply be to live a full and happy life, to achieve all those heights and glories his father had been so determined to deny him.

Daphne swallowed a heavy sob of frustration. She didn't see how he could possibly lead a happy life if all of his choices were based on thwarting the wishes of a dead man.

But she didn't want to get into all of that just then. She was tired and he was drunk and this just wasn't the right time. 'Let's get you to bed,' she finally said.

He stared at her for a long moment, his eyes filling with an ages-old need for comfort. 'Don't leave me,' he whispered.

'Simon,' she choked out.

'Please don't. He left. Everyone left. Then I left.' He squeezed her hand. 'You stay.'

She nodded shakily and rose to her feet. 'You can sleep it off in my bed,' she said. 'I'm sure you'll feel better in the morning.'

'But you'll stay with me?'

It was a mistake. She knew it was a mistake, but still she said, 'I'll stay with you.'

'Good.' He wobbled himself upright. 'Because I couldn't – I really – ' He sighed and turned anguished eyes to her. 'I need you.'

She led him to her bed, nearly falling over with him when he tumbled onto the mattress. 'Hold still,' she ordered, kneeling to pull off his boots. She'd done this for her brothers before, so she knew to grab the heel, not the toe, but they were a snug fit, and she went sprawling on the ground when his foot finally slipped out.

'Good gracious,' she muttered, getting up to repeat the aggravating procedure. 'And they say women are slaves to fashion.'

Simon made a noise that sounded suspiciously like a snore.

'Are you asleep?' Daphne asked incredulously. She yanked at the other boot, which came off with a bit more ease, then lifted his legs – which felt like deadweights – up onto the bed.

He looked young and peaceful with his dark lashes resting against his cheeks. Daphne reached out and brushed his hair off his forehead. 'Sleep well, my sweet,' she whispered.

But when she started to move, one of his arms shot out and wrapped around her. 'You said you would stay,' he said accusingly.

'I thought you were asleep!'

'Doesn't give you the right to break your promise.' He tugged her at her arm, and Daphne finally gave up resisting and settled down next to him. He was warm, and he was hers, and even if she had grave fears for their future, at that moment she couldn't resist his gentle embrace.

Daphne awoke an hour or so later, surprised that she'd fallen asleep at all. Simon still lay next to her, snoring softly. They were both dressed, he in his whiskey-scented clothes, and she in her nightrobe.

Gently, she touched his cheek. 'What am I to do with

you?' she whispered. 'I love you, you know. I love you, but I hate what you're doing to yourself.' She drew a shaky breath. 'And to me. I hate what you're doing to me.'

He shifted sleepily, and for one horrified moment, she was afraid that he'd woken up. 'Simon?' she whispered, then let out a relieved exhale when he didn't answer. She knew she shouldn't have spoken words aloud that she wasn't quite ready for him to hear, but he'd looked so innocent against the snowy white pillows. It was far too easy to spill her innermost thoughts when he looked like that.

'Oh, Simon,' she sighed, closing her eyes against the tears that were pooling in her eyes. She should get up. She should absolutely positively get up now and leave him to his rest. She understood why he was so dead set against bringing a child into this world, but she hadn't forgiven him, and she certainly didn't agree with him. If he woke up with her still in his arms, he might think she was willing to settle for his version of a family.

Slowly, reluctantly, she tried to pull away. But his arms tightened around her, and his sleepy voice mumbled, 'No.'

'Simon, I—'

He pulled her closer, and Daphne realized that he was thoroughly aroused.

'Simon?' she whispered, her eyes flying open. 'Are you even awake?'

His response was another sleepy mumble, and he made no attempts at seduction, just snuggled her closer.

Daphne blinked in surprise. She hadn't realized that a man could want a woman in his sleep.

She pulled her head back so she could see his face, then reached out and touched the line of his jaw. He let out a little groan. The sound was hoarse and deep, and it made her reckless. With slow, tantalizing fingers, she undid the buttons of his shirt, pausing just once to trace the outline of his navel.

He shifted restlessly, and Daphne felt the strangest, most intoxicating surge of power. He was in her control, she realized. He was asleep, and probably still more than a little bit drunk, and she could do whatever she wanted with him.

She could *have* whatever she wanted.

A quick glance at his face told her that he was still sleeping, and she quickly undid his trousers. Underneath, he was hard and needy, and she wrapped her hand around him, feeling his blood leap beneath her fingers.

'Daphne,' he gasped. His eyes fluttered open, and he let out a ragged groan. 'Oh, God. That feels so damned good.'

'Shhhh,' she crooned, slipping out of her silken robe. 'Let me do everything.'

He lay on his back, his hands fisted at his sides as she stroked him. He'd taught her much during their two short weeks of marriage, and soon he was squirming with desire, his breath coming in short pants.

And God help her, but she wanted him, too. She felt so powerful looming over him. She was in control, and that was the most stunning aphrodisiac she could imagine. She felt a fluttering in her stomach, then a strange sort of quickening, and she knew that she needed him.

She wanted him inside her, filling her, giving her everything a man was meant to give to a woman.

'Oh, Daphne,' he moaned, his head tossing from side to side. 'I need you. I need you *now.*'

She moved atop him, pressing her hands against his shoulders as she straddled him. Using her hand, she guided him to her entrance, already wet with need.

Simon arched beneath her, and she slowly slid down his shaft, until he was almost fully within her.

'More,' he gasped. 'Now.'

Daphne's head fell back as she moved down that last inch. Her hands clutched at his shoulders as she gasped for breath. Then he was completely within her, and she thought she would die from the pleasure. Never had she felt so full, nor so completely a woman.

She keened as she moved above him, her body arching and writhing with delight. Her hands splayed flat against her stomach as she twisted and turned, then slid upward toward her breasts.

Simon let out a guttural moan as he watched her, his eyes glazing over as his breath came hot and heavy over his parted lips. 'Oh, my God,' he said in a hoarse, raspy voice. 'What are you doing to me? What have you – ' Then she touched one of her nipples, and his entire body bucked upwards. 'Where did you learn that?'

She looked down and gave him a bewildered smile. 'I don't know.'

'More,' he groaned. 'I want to watch you.'

Daphne wasn't entirely certain what to do, so she just let instinct take over. She ground her hips against his in a circular motion as she arched her back, causing her breasts to jut out proudly. She cupped both in her hands, squeezing them softly, rolling the nipples between her fingers, never once taking her eyes off Simon's face.

His hips started to buck in a frantic, jerky motion, and he grasped desperately at the sheets with his large hands. And Daphne realized that he was almost there. He was always so careful to please her, to make certain that she reached her climax before he allowed himself the same privilege, but this time, he was going to explode first.

She was close, but not as close as he was.

'Oh, Christ!' he suddenly burst out, his voice harsh and primitive with need. 'I'm going to – I can't – ' His eyes pinned upon her with a strange, pleading sort of look, and he made a feeble attempt to pull away.

Daphne bore down on him with all her might.

He exploded within her, the force of his climax lifting his hips off the bed, pushing her up along with him. She planted her hands underneath him, using all of her strength to hold him against her. She would not lose him this time. She would not lose this chance.

Simon's eyes flew open as he came, as he realized too late what he had done. But his body was too far gone; there was no stopping the power of his climax. If he'd been on top, he might have found the strength to pull away, but lying there under her, watching her tease her own body into a mass of desire, he was helpless against the raging force of his own need.

As his teeth clenched and his body bucked, he felt her small hands slip underneath him, pressing him more tightly against the cradle of her womb. He saw the expression of pure ecstasy on her face, and then he suddenly realized – she had done this on purpose. She had planned this.

Daphne had aroused him in his sleep, taken advantage of him while he was still slightly intoxicated, and held him to her while he poured his seed into her.

His eyes widened and fixed on hers. 'How could you?' he whispered.

She said nothing, but he saw her face change, and he knew she'd heard him.

Simon pushed her from his body just as he felt her begin to tighten around him, savagely denying her the ecstasy he'd just had for himself. 'How could you?' he repeated. 'You knew. You knew th-that that I-I-I—'

But she had just curled up in a little ball, her knees tucked against her chest, obviously determined not to lose a single drop of him.

Simon swore viciously as he yanked himself to his feet. He opened his mouth to pour invective over her, to castigate her for betraying him, for taking advantage of him, but his throat tightened, and his tongue swelled, and he couldn't even begin a word, much less finish one.

'Y-y-you – ' he finally managed.

Daphne stared at him in horror. 'Simon?' she whispered.

He didn't want this. He didn't want her looking at him like he was some sort of freak. Oh God, oh God, he felt seven years old again. He couldn't speak. He couldn't make his mouth work. He was lost.

Daphne's face filled with concern. Unwanted, pitying concern. 'Are you all right?' she whispered. 'Can you breathe?'

'D-d-d-d-d – ' It was a far cry from *don't pity me*, but it was all he could do. He could feel his father's mocking presence, squeezing at his throat, choking his tongue.

'Simon?' Daphne said, hurrying to his side. Her voice grew panicked. 'Simon, say something!'

She reached out to touch his arm, but he threw her off. 'Don't touch me!' he exploded.

She shrank back. 'I guess there are still some things you can say,' she said in a small, sad voice.

Simon hated himself, hated the voice that had forsaken him, and hated his wife because she had the power to reduce his control to rubble. This complete loss of speech, this choking, strangling feeling – he had worked his entire life to escape it, and now she had brought it all back with a vengeance.

He couldn't let her do this. He couldn't let her make him like he'd once been.

He tried to say her name, couldn't get anything out.

He had to leave. He couldn't look at her. He couldn't be with her. He didn't even want to be with himself, but that, unfortunately, was beyond his meager control.

'D-don't c-come n-near me,' he gasped, jabbing his finger at her as he yanked on his trousers. 'Y-y-y-you did this!'

'Did what?' Daphne cried, pulling a sheet around her. 'Simon, stop this. What did I do that was so wrong? You wanted me. You know you wanted me.'

'Th-th-this!' he burst out, pointing at his throat. Then he pointed toward her abdomen. 'Th-th-that.'

Then, unable to bear the sight of her any longer, he stormed from the room.

If only he could escape himself with the same ease.

Ten hours later Daphne found the following note:

Pressing business at another of my estates requires my attention. I trust you will notify me if your attempts at conception were successful.

My steward will give you my direction, should you need it.

Simon

The single sheet of paper slipped from Daphne's fingers and floated slowly to the floor. A harsh sob escaped her throat, and she pressed her fingers to her mouth, as if that might possibly stem the tide of emotion that was churning within her.

He'd left her. He'd actually left her. She'd known he was angry, known he might not even forgive her, but she hadn't thought he would actually leave.

She'd thought – oh, even when he'd stormed out the door she'd thought that they might be able to resolve their differences, but now she wasn't so sure.

Maybe she'd been too idealistic. She'd egotistically thought that she could heal him, make his heart whole. Now she realized that she'd imbued herself with far more power than she actually possessed. She'd thought her love was so good, so shining, so pure that Simon would immediately abandon the years of resentment and pain that had fueled his very existence.

How self-important she'd been. How stupid she felt now.

Some things were beyond her reach. In her sheltered life, she'd never realized that until now. She hadn't expected the world to be handed to her upon a golden platter, but she'd always assumed that if she worked hard enough for something, treated everyone the way she would like to be treated, then she would be rewarded.

But not this time. Simon was beyond her reach.

The house seemed preternaturally quiet as Daphne made her way down to the yellow room. She wondered if all the servants had learned of her husband's departure and were now studiously avoiding her. They had to have heard bits and pieces of the argument the night before.

Daphne sighed. Grief was even more difficult when one had a small army of onlookers.

Or invisible onlookers, as the case may be, she thought as she gave the bellpull a tug. She couldn't see them, but she knew they were there, whispering behind her back and pitying her.

Funny how she'd never given much thought to servants' gossip before. But now – she plopped down on the sofa with a pained little moan – now she felt so wretchedly alone. What else was she supposed to think about?

'Your grace?'

Daphne looked up to see a young maid standing hesitantly in the doorway. She bobbed a little curtsy and gave Daphne an expectant look.

'Tea, please,' Daphne said quietly. 'No biscuits, just tea.'

The young girl nodded and ran off.

As she waited for the maid to return, Daphne touched her abdomen, gazing down at herself with gentle reverence. Closing her eyes, she sent up a prayer. *Please God please,* she begged, *let there be a child.*

She might not get another chance.

She wasn't ashamed of her actions. She supposed she should be, but she wasn't.

She hadn't planned it. She hadn't looked at him while he was sleeping and thought – *he's probably still drunk. I can make love to him and capture his seed and he'll never know.*

It hadn't happened that way.

Daphne wasn't quite sure how it had happened, but one moment she was above him, and the next she'd realized that he wasn't going to withdraw in time, and she'd made certain he *couldn't*. . .

Or maybe – She closed her eyes. Tight. Maybe it had happened the other way. Maybe she *had* taken advantage of more than the moment, maybe she had taken advantage of *him*.

She just didn't know. It had all melted together. Simon's stutter, her desperate wish for a baby, his hatred of his father – it had all swirled and mixed in her mind, and she couldn't tell where one ended and the other began.

And she felt so alone.

She heard a sound at the door and turned, expecting the timid young maid back with tea, but in her stead was Mrs. Colson. Her face was drawn and her eyes were concerned.

Daphne smiled wanly at the housekeeper. 'I was expecting the maid,' she murmured.

'I had things to attend to in the next room, so I thought I'd bring the tea myself,' Mrs. Colson replied.

Daphne knew she was lying, but she nodded anyway.

'The maid said no biscuits,' Mrs. Colson added, 'but I knew you'd skipped breakfast, so I put some on the tray, anyway.'

'That's very thoughtful of you.' Daphne didn't recognize the timbre of her own voice. It sounded rather flat to her, almost as if it belonged to someone else.

'It was no trouble, I assure you.' The housekeeper looked as if she wanted to say more, but eventually she just straightened and asked, 'Will that be all?'

Daphne nodded.

Mrs. Colson made her way to the door, and for one brief moment Daphne almost called out to her. She almost said her name, and asked her to sit with her, and share her tea. And she would have spilled her secrets and her shame, and then she would have spilled her tears.

And not because she was particularly close to the housekeeper, just because she had no one else.

But she didn't call out, and Mrs. Colson left the room.

Daphne picked up a biscuit and bit into it. Maybe, she thought, it was time to go home.

19

The new Duchess of Hastings was spotted in Mayfair today. Philipa Featherington saw the former Miss Daphne Bridgerton taking a bit of air as she walked briskly around the block. Miss Featherington called out to her, but the duchess pretended not to hear.

And we know the duchess must have been pretending, for after all, one would have to be deaf to let one of Miss Featherington's shouts go unnoticed.

LADY WHISTLEDOWN'S SOCIETY PAPERS, 9 JUNE 1813

Heartache, Daphne eventually learned, never really went away; it just dulled. The sharp, stabbing pain that one felt with each breath eventually gave way to a blunter, lower ache – the kind that one could almost – but never quite – ignore.

She left Castle Clyvedon the day after Simon's departure, heading to London with every intention of returning to Bridgerton House. But going back to her family's house somehow seemed like an admission of failure, and so at the last minute, she instructed the driver to take her to Hastings House instead. She would be near her family if she felt the need for their support and companionship, but she was a married woman now; she should reside in her own home.

And so she introduced herself to her new staff, who accepted her without question (but not without a considerable amount of curiosity), and set about her new life as an abandoned wife.

Her mother was the first to come calling. Daphne hadn't bothered to notify anyone else of her return to London, so this was not terribly surprising.

'Where is he?' Violet demanded without preamble.

'My husband, I presume?'

'No, your great-uncle Edmund,' Violet practically snapped. 'Of course I mean your husband.'

Daphne didn't quite meet her mother's eyes as she said, 'I believe that he is tending to affairs at one of his country estates.'

'You *believe?*'

'Well, I know,' Daphne amended.

'And do you *know* why you are not with him?'

Daphne considered lying. She considered brazening it out and telling her mother some nonsense about an emergency involving tenants and maybe some livestock or disease or *anything.* But in the end, her lip quivered, and her eyes started to prick with tears, and her voice was terribly small, as she said, 'Because he did not choose to take me with him.'

Violet took her hands. 'Oh, Daff,' she sighed, 'what happened?'

Daphne sank onto a sofa, pulling her mother along with her. 'More than I could ever explain.'

'Do you want to try?'

Daphne shook her head. She'd never, not even once in her life, kept a secret from her mother. There had never been anything she didn't feel she could discuss with her.

But there had never been this.

She patted her mother's hand. 'I'll be all right.'

Violet looked unconvinced. 'Are you certain?'

'No.' Daphne stared at the floor for a moment. 'But I have to believe it, anyway.'

Violet left, and Daphne placed her hand on her abdomen and prayed.

* * *

Colin was the next to visit. About a week later, Daphne returned from a quick walk in the park to find him standing in her drawing room, arms crossed, expression furious.

'Ah,' Daphne said, pulling off her gloves, 'I see you've learned of my return.'

'What the hell is going on?' he demanded.

Colin, Daphne reflected wryly, had clearly not inherited their mother's talent for subtlety in speech.

'Speak!' he barked.

She closed her eyes for a moment. Just a moment to try to relieve the headache that had been plaguing her for days. She didn't want to tell her woes to Colin. She didn't even want to tell him as much as she told her mother, although she supposed he already knew. News always traveled fast at Bridgerton House.

She wasn't really sure where she got the energy, but there was a certain fortifying benefit to putting up a good front, so she squared her shoulders, raised a brow, and said, 'And by that you mean . . . ?'

'I mean,' Colin growled, 'where is your husband?'

'He is otherwise occupied,' Daphne replied. It sounded so much better than, 'He left me.'

'Daphne . . .' Colin's voice held no end of warning.

'Are you here alone?' she asked, ignoring his tone.

'Anthony and Benedict are in the country for the month, if that's what you mean,' Colin said.

Daphne very nearly sighed with relief. The last thing she needed just then was to face her eldest brother. She'd already prevented him from killing Simon once; she wasn't sure if she'd be able to manage the feat a second time. Before she could say anything, however, Colin added, 'Daphne, I am ordering you right now to tell me where the bastard is hiding.'

Daphne felt her spine stiffening. She might have the right to call her errant husband nasty names, but her brother certainly didn't. 'I assume,' she said icily, 'that by "that bastard" you refer to my husband.'

'You're damned right I—'

'I'm going to have to ask you to leave.'

Colin looked at her as if she'd suddenly sprouted horns. 'I beg your pardon?'

'I don't care to discuss my marriage with you, so if you cannot refrain from offering your unsolicited opinions, you're going to have to leave.'

'You can't ask me to leave,' he said in disbelief.

She crossed her arms. 'This is my house.'

Colin stared at her, then looked around the room – the drawing room of the Duchess of Hastings – then looked back at Daphne, as if just realizing that his little sister, whom he'd always viewed as rather jolly extension of himself, had become her own woman.

He reached out and took her hand. 'Daff,' he said quietly, 'I'll let you handle this as you see fit.'

'Thank you.'

'*For now,*' he warned. 'Don't think I'll let this situation continue indefinitely.'

But it wouldn't, Daphne thought a half hour later as Colin left the house. It couldn't continue indefinitely. Within a fortnight, she would know.

Every morning Daphne woke to find she was holding her breath. Even before her courses were due to arrive, she bit her lip, said a little prayer, and gingerly peeled back the covers of her bed and looked for blood.

And every morning she saw nothing but snowy white linen.

A week after her courses were due, she allowed herself the first glimmerings of hope. Her courses had never been perfectly punctual; they could, she reasoned, still arrive at any time. But still, she had never been quite *this* late . . .

After another week, though, she found herself smiling each morning, holding on to her secret as she would a treasure. She wasn't ready to share this with anyone yet.

Not her mother, not her brothers, and certainly not Simon.

She didn't feel terribly guilty about withholding the news from him. After all, he had withheld his seed from her. But more importantly, she feared that his reaction would be explosively negative, and she just wasn't ready to let his displeasure ruin her perfect moment of joy. She did, however, jot off a note to his steward, asking that he forward Simon's new address to her.

But then finally, after the third week, her conscience got the better of her, and she sat down at her desk to write him a letter.

Unfortunately for Daphne, the sealing wax hadn't even dried on her missive when her brother Anthony, obviously returned from his sojourn in the country, came crashing into the room. Since Daphne was upstairs, in her private chamber, where she was *not* supposed to receive visitors, she didn't even want to think about how many servants he had injured on his way up.

He looked furious, and she knew she probably shouldn't provoke him, but he always made her slightly sarcastic, so she asked, 'And how did you get up here? Don't I have a butler?'

'You *had* a butler,' he growled.

'Oh, dear.'

'Where is he?'

'Not here, obviously.' There didn't seem any point in pretending she didn't know exactly who he was talking about.

'I'm going to kill him.'

Daphne stood, eyes flashing. 'No, you're not!'

Anthony, who had been standing with his hands on his hips, leaned forward and speared her with a stare. 'I made a vow to Hastings before he married you, did you know that?'

She shook her head.

'I reminded him that I had been prepared to kill him for

damaging your reputation. Heaven help him if he damages your soul.'

'He hasn't damaged my soul, Anthony.' Her hand strayed to her abdomen. 'Quite the opposite, actually.'

But if Anthony found her words odd, she would never know, because his eyes strayed to her writing table, then narrowed. 'What is that?' he asked.

Daphne followed his line of vision to the small pile of paper that constituted her discarded attempts at a letter to Simon. 'It's nothing,' she said, reaching forward to grab the evidence.

'You're writing him a letter, aren't you?' Anthony's already stormy expression grew positively thunderous. 'Oh, for the love of God, don't try to lie about it. I saw his name at the top of the paper.'

Daphne crumpled the wasted papers and dropped them into a basket under the desk. 'It's none of your business.'

Anthony eyed the basket as if he were about to lunge under the desk and retrieve the half-written notes. Finally, he just looked back at Daphne, and said, 'I'm not going let him get away with this.'

'Anthony, this isn't your affair.'

He didn't dignify that with a reply. 'I'll find him, you know. I'll find him, and I'll kill—'

'Oh, for goodness sake,' Daphne finally exploded. 'This is my marriage, Anthony, not yours. And if you interfere in my affairs, so help me God, I swear I will never speak to you again.'

Her eyes were steady, and her tone was forceful, and Anthony looked slightly shaken by her words. 'Very well,' he muttered, 'I won't kill him.'

'Thank you,' Daphne said, rather sarcastically.

'But I will find him,' Anthony vowed. 'And I will make my disapproval clear.'

Daphne took one look at his face and knew that he meant it. 'Very well,' she said, reaching for the completed letter that she'd tucked away in a drawer. 'I'll let you deliver this.'

'Good.' He reached for the envelope.

Daphne moved it out of his reach. 'But only if you make me two promises.'

'Which are . . . ?'

'First, you must promise that you won't read this.'

He looked mortally affronted that she'd even suggested he would.

'Don't try that "I'm so honorable' expresssion with me," Daphne said with a snort. 'I know you, Anthony Bridgerton, and I know that you would read this in a second if you thought you could get away with it.'

Anthony glared at her.

'But I also know,' she continued, 'that you would never break an explicit promise made to me. So I'll need your promise, Anthony.'

'This is hardly necessary, Daff.'

'Promise!' she ordered.

'Oh, all right,' he grumbled, 'I promise.'

'Good.' She handed him the letter. He looked at it longingly.

'Secondly,' Daphne said loudly, forcing his attention back to her, 'you must promise not to hurt him.'

'Oh, now, wait one second, Daphne,' Anthony burst out. 'You ask far too much.'

She held out her hand. 'I'll be taking that letter back.'

He shoved it behind his back. 'You already gave it to me.'

She smirked. 'I didn't give you his address.'

'I can get his address,' he returned.

'No, you can't, and you know it,' Daphne shot back. 'He has no end of estates. It'd take you weeks to figure out which one he's visiting.'

'A-ha!' Anthony said triumphantly. 'So he's at one of his estates. You, my dear, let slip a vital clue.'

'Is this a *game?*' Daphne asked in amazement.

'Just tell me where he is.'

'Not unless you promise – no violence, Anthony.' She crossed her arms. 'I mean it.'

'All right,' he mumbled.

'Say it.'

'You're a hard woman, Daphne Bridgerton.'

'It's Daphne Basset, and I've had good teachers.'

'I promise,' he said – barely. His words weren't precisely crisp.

'I need a bit more than that,' Daphne said. She uncrossed her arms and twisted her right hand in a rolling manner, as if to draw forth the words from his lips. 'I promise not to . . . '

'I promise not to hurt your bloody idiot of a husband,' Anthony spat out. 'There. Is that good enough?'

'Certainly,' Daphne said congenially. She reached into a drawer and pulled out the letter she'd received earlier that week from Simon's steward, giving his address. 'Here you are.'

Anthony took it with a decidedly ungraceful – and ungrateful – swipe of his hand. He glanced down, scanned the lines, then said, 'I'll be back in four days.'

'You're leaving today?' Daphne asked, surprised.

'I don't know how long I can keep my violent impulses in check,' he drawled.

'Then by all means, go today,' Daphne said.

He did.

'Give me one good reason why I shouldn't pull your lungs out through your mouth.'

Simon looked up from his desk to see a travel-dusty Anthony Bridgerton, fuming in the doorway to his study. 'It's nice to see you, too, Anthony,' he murmured.

Anthony entered the room with all the grace of a thunderstorm, planted his hands on Simon's desk and leaned forward menacingly. 'Would you mind telling me why my sister is in London, crying herself to sleep every night, while you're in – ' He looked around the office and scowled. 'Where the hell are we?'

'Wiltshire,' Simon supplied.

'While you're in Wiltshire, puttering around an inconsequential estate?'

'Daphne's in London?'

'You'd think,' Anthony growled, 'that as her husband you'd know that.'

'You'd think a lot of things,' Simon muttered, 'but most of the time, you'd be wrong.' It had been two months since he'd left Clyvedon. Two months since he'd looked at Daphne and not been able to utter a word. Two months of utter emptiness.

In all honesty, Simon was surprised it had taken Daphne this long to get in touch with him, even if she had elected to do so through her somewhat belligerent older brother. Simon wasn't exactly certain why, but he'd thought she would have contacted him sooner, if only to blister his ears. Daphne wasn't the sort to stew in silence when she was upset; he'd half expected her to track him down and explain in six different ways why he was an utter fool.

And truth be told, after about a month, he'd half wished she would.

'I would tear your bloody head off,' Anthony growled, breaking into Simon's thoughts with considerable force, 'if I hadn't promised Daphne I wouldn't do you bodily harm.'

'I'm sure that wasn't a promise easily made,' Simon said.

Anthony crossed his arms and settled a heavy stare on Simon's face. 'Nor easily kept.'

Simon cleared his throat as he tried to figure out some way to ask about Daphne without seeming too obvious. He missed her. He felt like an idiot, he felt like a fool, but he missed her. He missed her laugh and her scent and the way, sometimes in the middle of the night, she always managed to tangle her legs with his.

Simon was used to being alone, but he wasn't used to being this lonely.

'Did Daphne send you to fetch me back?' he finally asked.

'No.' Anthony reached into his pocket, pulled out a small, ivory envelope, and slapped it down on the desk. 'I caught her summoning a messenger to send you this.'

Simon stared at the envelope with growing horror. It could only mean one thing. He tried to say something neutral, such as 'I see,' but his throat closed up.

'I told her I'd be happy to conduct the letter to you,' Anthony said, with considerable sarcasm.

Simon ignored him. He reached for the envelope, hoping that Anthony would not see how his fingers were shaking.

But Anthony did see. 'What the devil is wrong with you?' he asked in an abrupt voice. 'You look like hell.'

Simon snatched the envelope and pulled it to him. 'Always a pleasure to see you, too,' he managed to quip.

Anthony gazed steadily at him, the battle between anger and concern showing clearly on his face. Clearing his throat a few times, Anthony finally asked, in a surprisingly gentle tone, 'Are you ill?'

'Of course not.'

Anthony went pale. 'Is Daphne ill?'

Simon's head snapped up. 'Not that she's told me. Why? Does she look ill? Has she—'

'No, she looks fine.' Anthony's eyes filled with curiosity. 'Simon,' he finally asked, shaking his head, 'what are you doing here? It's obvious you love her. And much as I can't comprehend it, she seems to love you as well.'

Simon pressed his fingers to his temples, trying to stave off the pounding headache he never seemed to be without these days. 'There are things you don't know,' he said wearily, shutting his eyes against the pain. 'Things you could never understand.'

Anthony was silent for a full minute. Finally, just when

Simon opened his eyes, Anthony pushed away from the desk and walked back to the door. 'I won't drag you back to London,' he said in a low voice. 'I should but I won't. Daphne needs to know you came for her, not because her older brother had a pistol at your back.'

Simon almost pointed out that that was why he'd married her, but he bit his tongue. That wasn't the truth. Not all of it, at least. In another lifetime, he'd have been on bended knee, begging for her hand.

'You should know, however,' Anthony continued, 'that people are starting to talk. Daphne returned to London alone, barely a fortnight after your rather hasty marriage. She's keeping a good face about it, but it's got to hurt. No one has actually come out and insulted her, but there's only so much well-meaning pity a body can take. And that damned Whistledown woman has been writing about her.'

Simon winced. He'd not been back in England long, but it was long enough to know that the fictitious Lady Whistledown could inflict a great deal of damage and pain.

Anthony swore in disgust. 'Get yourself to a doctor, Hastings. And then get yourself back to your wife.' With that, he strode out the door.

Simon stared at the envelope in his hands for many minutes before opening it. Seeing Anthony had been a shock. Knowing he'd just been with Daphne made Simon's heart ache.

Bloody hell. He hadn't expected to miss her.

This was not to say, however, that he wasn't still furious with her. She'd taken something from him that he quite frankly hadn't wanted to give. He didn't want children. He'd told her that. She'd married him knowing that. And she'd tricked him.

Or had she? He rubbed his hands wearily against his eyes and forehead as he tried to remember the exact details of that fateful morning. Daphne had definitely been the leader in their lovemaking, but he distinctly recalled his own voice, urging her on. He should not have encouraged what he knew he could not stop.

She probably wasn't pregnant, anyway, he reasoned. Hadn't it taken his own mother over a decade to produce a single living child?

But when he was alone, lying in bed at night, he knew the truth. He hadn't fled just because Daphne had disobeyed him, or because there was a chance he'd sired a child.

He'd fled because he couldn't bear the way he'd been with her. She'd reduced him to the stuttering, stammering fool of his childhood. She'd rendered him mute, brought back that awful, choking feeling, the horror of not being able to say what he felt.

He just didn't know if he could live with her if it meant going back to being the boy who could barely speak. He tried to remind himself of their courtship – their mock-courtship, he thought with a smile – and to remember how easy it had been to be with her, to talk with her. But every memory was tainted by where it had all led – to Daphne's bedroom that hideous morning, with him tripping over his tongue and choking on his own throat.

And he hated himself like that.

So he'd fled to another of his country estates – as a duke, he had a number of them. This particular house was in Wiltshire, which, he had reasoned, wasn't too terribly far from Clyvedon. He could get back in a day and a half if he rode hard enough. It wasn't so much like he'd run away, if he could go back so easily.

And now it looked like he was going to have to go back.

Taking a deep breath, Simon picked up his letter opener and slit the envelope. He pulled out a single sheet of paper and looked down.

Simon,

My efforts, as you termed them, were met with success. I have removed myself to London, so that I might

be near my family, and await your directive there.
Yours,
Daphne

Simon didn't know how long he sat there behind his desk, barely breathing, the cream-colored slip of paper hanging from his fingers. Then finally, a breeze washed over him, or perhaps the light changed, or the house creaked – but something broke him out of his reverie and he jumped to his feet, strode into the hall, and bellowed for his butler.

'Have my carriage hitched,' he barked when the butler appeared. 'I'm going to London.'

20

The marriage of the season seems to have gone sour. The Duchess of Hastings (formerly Miss Bridgerton) returned to London nearly two months ago, and This Author has seen neither hide nor hair of her new husband, the duke.

Rumor has it that he is not at Clyvedon, where the once happy couple took their honeymoon. Indeed, This Author cannot find anyone who professes to know his whereabouts. (If her grace knows, she is not telling, and furthermore, one rarely has the opportunity to ask, as she has shunned the company of all except her rather large and extensive family.)

It is, of course, This Author's place and indeed duty to speculate on the source of such rifts, but This Author must confess that even she is baffled. They seemed so very much in love . . .

LADY WHISTLEDOWN'S SOCIETY PAPERS,
2 AUGUST 1813

The trip took two days, which was two days longer than Simon would have liked to be alone with his thoughts. He'd brought a few books to read, hoping to keep himself distracted during the tedious journey, but whenever he managed to open one it sat unread in his lap.

It was difficult to keep his mind off Daphne.

It was even more difficult to keep his mind off the prospect of fatherhood.

Once he reached London, he gave his driver instructions to take him directly to Bridgerton House. He was travel-weary, and probably could use a change of clothing, but he'd done nothing for the past two days but play out his upcoming confrontation with Daphne – it seemed foolish to put it off any longer than he had to.

Once admitted to Bridgerton House, however, he discovered that Daphne wasn't there.

'What do you mean,' Simon asked in a deadly voice, not particularly caring that the butler had done little to earn his ire, 'the duchess isn't here?'

The butler took his deadly voice and raised him one curled upper lip. 'I mean, your grace' – this was not said with particular graciousness – 'that she is not in residence.'

'I have a letter from my wife – ' Simon thrust his hand into his pocket, but – damn it – didn't come up with the paper. 'Well, I have a letter from her somewhere,' he grumbled. 'And it specifically states that she has removed herself to London.'

'And she has, your grace.'

'Then where the hell is she?' Simon ground out.

The butler merely raised a brow. 'At Hastings House, your grace.'

Simon clamped his mouth shut. There was little more humiliating than being bested by a butler.

'After all,' the butler continued, clearly enjoying himself now, 'she is married to you, is she not?'

Simon glared at him. 'You must be quite secure in your position.'

'Quite.'

Simon gave him a brief nod (since he couldn't quite bring himself to thank the man) and stalked off, feeling very much like a fool. Of course Daphne would have gone to Hastings House. She hadn't *left* him, after all; she just wanted to be near her family.

If he could have kicked himself on the way back to the carriage, he would have done so.

Once inside, however, he did kick himself. He lived just across Grosvenor Square from the Bridgertons. He could have walked across the blasted green in half the time.

Time, however, proved not to be particularly of the essence, because when he swung open the door to Hastings House and stomped into the hall, he discovered that his wife was not at home.

'She's riding,' Jeffries said.

Simon stared at his butler in patent disbelief. 'She's riding?' he echoed.

'Yes, your grace,' Jeffries replied. 'Riding. On a horse.'

Simon wondered what the penalty was for strangling a butler. 'Where,' he bit off, 'did she go?'

'Hyde Park, I believe.'

Simon's blood began to pound, and his breath grew uneven. Riding? Was she bloody insane? She was pregnant, for God's sake. Even *he* knew that pregnant women weren't supposed to ride.

'Have a horse saddled for me,' Simon ordered. 'Immediately.'

'Any particular horse?' Jeffries inquired.

'A fast one,' Simon snapped. 'And do it now. Or better yet, I'll do it.' With that, he turned on his heel and marched out of the house.

But about halfway to the stables, his panic seeped from his blood to his very bones, and Simon's determined stride turned into a run.

It wasn't the same as riding astride, Daphne thought, but at least she was going *fast.*

In the country, when she'd been growing up, she'd always borrowed Colin's breeches and joined her brothers on their hell-for-leather rides. Her mother usually suffered an attack of the vapors every time she saw her eldest daughter return covered with mud, and quite frequently sporting a new and startling bruise, but Daphne hadn't cared. She hadn't cared where they were riding to or what they were riding from. It had all been about speed.

In the city, of course, she couldn't don breeches and thus was relegated to the sidesaddle, but if she took her horse out early enough, when fashionable society was still abed, and if she made certain to limit herself to the more remote areas of Hyde Park, she could bend over her saddle and urge her horse to a gallop. The wind whipped her hair out of its bun and stung her eyes to tears, but at least it made her forget.

Atop her favorite mare, tearing across the fields, she felt free. There was no better medicine for a broken heart.

She'd long since ditched her groom, pretending she hadn't heard him when he'd yelled, 'Wait! Your grace! Wait!'

She'd apologize to him later. The grooms at Bridgerton House were used to her antics and well aware of her skill atop a horse. This new man – one of her husband's servants – would probably worry.

Daphne felt a twinge of guilt – but only a twinge. She needed to be alone. She needed to move fast.

She slowed down as she reached a slightly wooded area and took a deep breath of the crisp autumn air. She closed her eyes for a moment, letting the sounds and smells of the park fill her senses. She thought of a blind man she'd once met, who'd told her that the rest of his senses had grown sharper since he'd lost his sight. As she sat there and inhaled the scents of the forest, she thought he might be right.

She listened hard, first identifying the high-pitched chirp of the birds, then the soft, scurrying feet of the squirrels as they hoarded nuts for the winter. Then—

She frowned and opened her eyes. Damn. That was definitely the sound of another rider approaching.

Daphne didn't want company. She wanted to be alone with her thoughts and her pain, and she certainly didn't want to have to explain to some well-meaning society member why she was alone in the park. She listened again, identified the location of the oncoming rider, and took off in the other direction.

She kept her horse to a steady trot, thinking that if she just got out of the other rider's way, he'd pass her by. But whichever way she went, he seemed to follow.

She picked up speed, more speed than she should have in this lightly wooded area. There were too many low branches and protruding tree roots. But now Daphne was starting to get scared. Her pulse pounded in her ears as a thousand horrifying questions rocked through her head.

What if this rider wasn't, as she'd originally supposed, a member of the *ton?* What if he was a criminal? Or a drunk? It was early; there was no one about. If Daphne screamed, who would hear her? Was she close enough to her groom? Had he stayed put where she'd left him or had he tried to follow? And if he had, had he even gone in the right direction?

Her groom! She nearly cried out in relief. It had to be her groom. She swung her mare around to see if she could catch a glimpse of the rider. The Hastings livery was quite distinctly red; surely she'd be able to see if—

Smack!

Every bit of air was violently forced from her body as a branch caught her squarely in the chest. A strangled grunt escaped her lips, and she felt her mare moving forward without her. And then she was falling . . . falling . . .

She landed with a bone-jarring thud, the autumn brown leaves on the ground providing scant cushioning. Her body immediately curled into a fetal position, as if by making herself as small as possible, she could make the hurt as small as possible.

And, oh God, she hurt. Damn it, she hurt everywhere. She squeezed her eyes shut and concentrated on breathing. Her mind flooded with curses she'd never dared speak aloud. But it hurt. Bloody hell, it hurt to breathe.

But she had to. Breathe. *Breathe, Daphne,* she ordered. *Breathe. Breathe. You can do it.*

'Daphne!'

Daphne made no response. The only sounds she seemed able to make were whimpers. Even groans were beyond her capability.

'Daphne! Christ above, Daphne!'

She heard someone jump off a horse, then felt movement in the leaves around her.

'Daphne?'

'Simon?' she whispered in disbelief. It made no sense that he was here, but it was his voice. And even though she still hadn't pried her eyes open, it *felt* like him. The air changed when he was near.

His hands touched her lightly, checking for broken bones. 'Tell me where it hurts,' he said.

'Everywhere,' she gasped.

He swore under his breath, but his touch remained achingly gentle and soothing. 'Open your eyes,' he ordered softly. 'Look at me. Focus on my face.'

She shook her head. 'I can't.'

'You *can*.'

She heard him strip off his gloves, and then his warm fingers were on her temples, smoothing away the tension. He moved to her eyebrows, then the bridge of her nose. 'Shhhh,' he crooned. 'Let it go. Just let the pain go. Open your eyes, Daphne.'

Slowly, and with great difficulty, she did so. Simon's face filled her vision, and for the moment she forgot everything that had happened between them, everything but the fact that she loved him, and he was here, and he was making the hurt go away.

'Look at me,' he said again, his voice low and insistent. 'Look at me and don't take your eyes off of mine.'

She managed the tiniest of nods. She focused her eyes on his, letting the intensity of his gaze hold her still.

'Now, I want you to relax,' he said. His voice was soft but commanding, and it was exactly what she needed. As he spoke, his hands moved across her body, checking for breaks or sprains.

His eyes never once left hers.

Simon kept speaking to her in low, soothing tones as he examined her body for injuries. She didn't appear to have suffered anything worse than a few bad bruises and having the wind knocked out of her, but one could never be too careful, and with the baby . . .

The blood drained from his face. In his panic for Daphne, he'd forgotten all about the child she was carrying. His child.

Their child.

'Daphne,' he said slowly. Carefully. 'Do you think you're all right?'

She nodded.

'Are you still in pain?'

'Some,' she admitted, swallowing awkwardly as she blinked. 'But it's getting better.'

'Are you certain?'

She nodded again.

'Good,' he said calmly. He was silent for several seconds and then he fairly yelled, '*What in God's name did you think you were doing?*'

Daphne's jaw dropped, and her eyelids started opening and closing with great rapidity. She made a strangled sort of sound that might have metamorphosed into an actual word, but Simon cut her off with more bellows.

'What the hell were you doing out here with no groom? And why were you galloping here, where the terrain clearly does not allow it?' His eyebrows slammed together. 'And for the love of God, woman, what were you doing on a horse?'

'Riding?' Daphne answered weakly.

'Don't you even care about our child? Didn't you give even a moment's thought to its safety?'

'Simon,' Daphne said, her voice very small.

'A pregnant woman shouldn't even get within ten feet of a horse! You should know better.'

When she looked at him her eyes looked old. 'Why do you care?' she asked flatly. 'You didn't want this baby.'

'No, I didn't, but now that it's here I don't want you to *kill* it.'

'Well, don't worry.' She bit her lip. 'It's not here.'

Simon's breath caught. 'What do you mean?'

Her eyes flitted to the side of his face. 'I'm not pregnant.'

'You're – ' He couldn't finish the sentence. The strangest feeling sank into his body. He didn't think it was disappointment, but he wasn't quite sure. 'You lied to me?' he whispered.

She shook her head fiercely as she sat up to face him. 'No!' she cried. 'No, I never lied. I swear. I thought I'd conceived. I truly thought I had. But – ' She choked on a sob, and squeezed her eyes shut against an onslaught of tears. She hugged her legs to her body and pressed her face against her knees.

Simon had never seen her like this, so utterly stricken with grief. He stared at her, feeling agonizingly helpless. All he wanted was to make her feel better, and it didn't much help to know that *he* was the cause of her pain. 'But what, Daff?' he asked.

When she finally looked up at him, her eyes were huge, and full of grief. 'I don't know. Maybe I wanted a child so badly that I somehow willed my courses away. I was so happy last month.' She let out a shaky breath, one that teetered precariously on the edge of a sob. 'I waited and waited, even got my woman's padding ready, and nothing happened.'

'Nothing?' Simon had never heard of such a thing.

'Nothing.' Her lips trembled into a faintly self-mocking smile. 'I've never been so happy in my life to have nothing happen.'

'Did you feel queasy?'

She shook her head. 'I felt no different. Except that I didn't bleed. But then two days ago . . . '

Simon laid his hand on hers. 'I'm sorry, Daphne.'

'No you're not,' she said bitterly, yanking her hand away. 'Don't pretend something you don't feel. And for God's sake, don't lie to me again. You never wanted this baby.' She let out a hollow, brittle laugh. '*This* baby? Good God, I talk as if it ever actually existed. As if it were ever more than a product of my imagination.' She looked down, and when she spoke again, her voice was achingly sad. 'And my dreams.'

Simon's lips moved several times before he managed to say, 'I don't like to see you so upset.'

She looked at him with a combination of disbelief and regret. 'I don't see how you could expect anything else.'

'I – I – I – ' He swallowed, trying to relax his throat, and finally he just said the only thing in his heart. 'I want you back.'

She didn't say anything. Simon silently begged her to say something, but she didn't. And he cursed at the gods for her silence, because it meant that he would have to say more.

'When we argued,' he said slowly, 'I lost control. I—

I couldn't speak.' He closed his eyes in agony as he felt his jaw tighten. Finally, after a long and shaky exhale, he said, 'I hate myself like that.'

Daphne's head tilted slightly as furrows formed in her brow. 'Is that why you left?'

He nodded once.

'It wasn't about – what I did?'

His eyes met hers evenly. 'I didn't like what you did.'

'But that wasn't why you left?' she persisted.

There was a beat of silence, and then he said, 'It wasn't why I left.'

Daphne hugged her knees to her chest, pondering his words. All this time she'd thought he'd abandoned her because he hated her, hated what she'd done, but in truth, the only thing he hated was himself.

She said softly, 'You know I don't think less of you when you stammer.'

'I think less of myself.'

She nodded slowly. Of course he would. He was proud and stubborn, and all the *ton* looked up to him. Men curried his favor, women flirted like mad. And all the while he'd been terrified every time he'd opened his mouth.

Well, maybe not every time, Daphne thought as she gazed into his face. When they were together, he usually spoke so freely, answered her so quickly that she knew he couldn't possibly be concentrating on every word.

She put her hand on his. 'You're not the boy your father thought you were.'

'I know that,' he said, but his eyes didn't meet hers.

'Simon, look at me,' she gently ordered. When he did, she repeated her words. 'You're not the boy your father thought you were.'

'I know that,' he said again, looking puzzled and maybe just a bit annoyed.

'Are you sure?' she asked softly.

'Damn it, Daphne, I know – ' His words tumbled into silence as his body began to shake. For one startling moment, Daphne thought he was going to cry. But the tears that pooled in his eyes never fell, and when he looked up at her, his body shuddering, all he said was, 'I hate him, Daphne. I h-h-h—'

She moved her hands to his cheeks and turned his face to hers, forcing him to meet her steady gaze. 'That's all right,' she said. 'It sounds as if he was a horrid man. But you have to let it go.'

'I can't.'

'You *can.* It's all right to have anger, but you can't let that be the ruling factor in your life. Even now, you're letting him dictate your choices.'

Simon looked away.

Daphne's hands dropped from his face, but she made sure they rested on his knees. She needed this connection. In a strange way she feared that if she let go of him right now she'd lose him forever. 'Did you ever stop to wonder if you wanted a family? If *you* wanted a child of your own? You'd be such a wonderful father, Simon, and yet you won't even let yourself consider the notion. You think you're getting your revenge, but you're really just letting him control you from the grave.'

'If I give him a child, he wins,' Simon whispered.

'No, if you give *yourself* a child, *you* win.' She swallowed convulsively. 'We all win.'

Simon said nothing, but she could see his body shaking.

'If you don't want a child because *you* don't want one, that's one thing. But if you deny yourself the joy of fatherhood because of a dead man, then you're a coward.'

Daphne winced as the insult crossed her lips, but it had to be said. 'At some point you've got to leave him behind and live your own life. You've got to let go of the anger and—'

Simon shook his head, and his eyes looked lost and hopeless. 'Don't ask me to do that. It's all I had. Don't you see, it's *all I had?*'

'I don't understand.'

His voice rose in volume. 'Why do you think I learned to speak properly? What do you think drove me? It was anger. It was always anger, always to show him.'

'Simon—'

A bubble of mocking laughter erupted from his throat. 'Isn't that just too amusing? I hate him. I hate him so much, and yet he's the one reason I've managed to succeed.'

Daphne shook her head. 'That's not true,' she said fervently, 'you would have succeeded no matter what. You're stubborn and brilliant, and *I know you.* You learned to speak because of you, not because of him.' When he said nothing, she added in a soft voice, 'If he'd shown you love, it would have made it all the easier.'

Simon started to shake his head, but she cut him off by taking his hand and squeezing it. 'I was shown love,' she whispered. 'I knew nothing but love and devotion when I was growing up. Trust me, it makes everything easier.'

Simon sat very still for several minutes, the only sound the low whoosh of his breath as he fought to control his emotions. Finally, just when Daphne was beginning to fear she'd lost him, he looked up at her with shattered eyes.

'I want to be happy,' he whispered.

'You will be,' she vowed, wrapping her arms around him. 'You will be.'

21

The Duke of Hastings is back!

LADY WHISTLEDOWN'S SOCIETY PAPERS,
6 AUGUST 1813

Simon didn't speak as they slowly rode home. Daphne's mare had been found munching contentedly on a patch of grass about twenty yards away, and even though Daphne had insisted that she was fit to ride, Simon had insisted that he didn't care. After tying the mare's reins to his own gelding, he had boosted Daphne into his saddle, hopped up behind her, and headed back to Grosvenor Square.

Besides, he needed to hold her.

He was coming to realize that he needed to hold on to something in life, and maybe she was right – maybe anger wasn't the solution. Maybe – just maybe he could learn to hold on to love instead.

When they reached Hastings House, a groom ran out to take care of the horses, and so Simon and Daphne trudged up the front steps and entered the hall.

And found themselves being stared down by the three older Bridgerton brothers.

'What the hell are you doing in my house?' Simon demanded. All he wanted to do was scoot up the stairs and make love to his wife, and instead he was greeted by this belligerent trio. They were standing with identical postures – legs spread, hands on hips, chins jutted out. If Simon hadn't been so damned irritated with the lot of them, he probably would have had the presence of mind to have been slightly alarmed.

Simon had no doubt that he could hold his own against one of them – *maybe* two – but against all three he was a dead man.

'We heard you were back,' Anthony said.

'So I am,' Simon replied. 'Now leave.'

'Not so fast,' Benedict said, crossing his arms.

Simon turned to Daphne. 'Which one of them may I shoot first?'

She threw a scowl at her brothers. 'I have no preference.'

'We have a few demands before we'll let you keep Daphne,' Colin said.

'What?' Daphne howled.

'*She is my wife!*' Simon roared, effectively obliterating Daphne's angry query.

'She was our sister first,' Anthony growled, 'and you've made her miserable.'

'This isn't any of your business,' Daphne insisted.

'*You're* our business,' Benedict said.

'She's *my* business,' Simon snapped, 'so now get the hell out of my house.'

'When the three of you have marriages of your own, then you can presume to offer me advice,' Daphne said angrily, 'but in the meantime, keep your meddling impulses to yourselves.'

'I'm sorry, Daff,' Anthony said, 'but we're not budging on this.'

'On what?' she snapped. 'You have no place to budge one way or the other. This isn't your affair!'

Colin stepped forward. 'We're not leaving until we're convinced he loves you.'

The blood drained from Daphne's face. Simon had never once told her that he loved her. He'd shown it, in a thousand different little ways, but he'd never said the words. When they came, she didn't want them at the hands of her overbearing brothers; she wanted them free and felt, from Simon's heart.

'Don't do this, Colin,' she whispered, hating the pathetic, pleading note of her voice. 'You have to let me fight my own battles.'

'Daff—'

'Please,' she pleaded.

Simon marched between them. 'If you will excuse us,' he said to Colin, and by extension, to Anthony and Benedict. He ushered Daphne to the other end of the hall, where they might talk privately. He would have liked to have moved to another room altogether, but he had no confidence that her idiot brothers wouldn't follow.

'I'm so sorry about my brothers,' Daphne whispered, her words coming out in a heated rush. 'They're boorish idiots, and they had no business invading your house. If I could disown them I would. After this display I wouldn't be surprised if you *never* want children—'

Simon silenced her with a finger to her lips. 'First of all, it's our house, not my house. And as for your brothers – they annoy the hell out of me, but they're acting out of love.' He leaned down, just an inch, but it brought him close enough so that she could feel his breath on her skin. 'And who can blame them?' he murmured.

Daphne's heart stopped.

Simon moved ever closer, until his nose rested on hers. 'I love you, Daff,' he whispered.

Her heart started again, with a vengeance. 'You do?'

He nodded, his nose rubbing against hers. 'I couldn't help it.'

Her lips wobbled into a hesitant smile. 'That's not terribly romantic.'

'It's the truth,' he said, with a helpless shrug. 'You know better than anyone that I didn't want any of this. I didn't want a wife, I didn't want a family, and *I definitely* didn't want to fall in love.' He brushed his mouth softly against hers, sending shivers down both of their bodies. 'But what I found' – his lips touched hers again – 'much to my dismay' – and again – 'was that it's quite impossible *not* to love you.'

Daphne melted into his arms. 'Oh, Simon,' she sighed.

His mouth captured hers, trying to show her with his kiss what he was still learning to express in words. He loved her. He worshipped her. He'd walk across fire for her. He—

—still had the audience of her three brothers.

Slowly breaking the kiss, he turned his face to the side. Anthony, Benedict, and Colin were still standing in the foyer. Anthony was studying the ceiling, Benedict was pretending to inspect his fingernails, and Colin was staring quite shamelessly.

Simon tightened his hold on Daphne, even as he shot a glare down the hall. 'What the hell are the three of you still doing in my house?'

Not surprisingly, none of them had a ready answer.

'*Get out,*' Simon growled.

'Please.' Daphne's tone didn't exactly suggest politeness.

'Right,' Anthony replied, smacking Colin on the back of the head. 'I believe our work here is done, boys.'

Simon started steering Daphne toward the stairs. 'I'm sure you can show yourselves out,' he said over his shoulder.

Anthony nodded and nudged his brothers toward the door.

'Good,' Simon said tersely. 'We'll be going upstairs.'

'Simon!' Daphne squealed.

'It's not as if they don't know what we're going to do,' he whispered in her ear.

'But still – They're my *brothers!*'

'God help us,' he muttered.

But before Simon and Daphne could even reach the landing, the front door burst open, followed by a stream of decidedly feminine invective.

'Mother?' Daphne said, the word croaking in her throat.

But Violet only had eyes for her sons. 'I knew I'd find you here,' she accused. 'Of all the stupid, bullheaded—'

Daphne didn't hear the rest of her mother's speech. Simon was laughing too hard in her ear.

'He made her miserable!' Benedict protested. 'As her brothers, it's our duty to—'

'Respect her intelligence enough to let her solve her own problems,' Violet snapped. 'And she doesn't look particularly unhappy right now.'

'That's because—'

'And if you say that's because you lot barged into her home like a herd of mentally deficient sheep, I'm disowning all three of you.'

All three men shut their mouths.

'Now then,' Violet continued briskly, 'I believe it's time we left, don't you?' When her sons didn't move quickly enough to suit her, she reached out and—

'Please, Mother!' Colin yelped. 'Not the—'

She grabbed him by his ear.

'Ear,' he finished glumly.

Daphne grabbed Simon's arm. He was laughing so hard now, she was afraid he'd tumble down the steps.

Violet herded her sons out the door with a loud, 'March!' and then turned back to Simon and Daphne on the stairs.

'Glad to see you in London, Hastings,' she called, gifting him with a wide, brilliant smile. 'Another week and I would have dragged you here myself.'

Then she stepped outside and shut the door behind her.

Simon turned to Daphne, his body still shaking with laughter. 'Was that your mother?' he asked, smiling.

'She has hidden depths.'

'Clearly.'

Daphne's face grew serious. 'I'm sorry if my brothers forced—'

'Nonsense,' he said cutting her off. 'Your brothers could never force me to say something I don't feel.' He cocked his head and pondered that for a moment. 'Well, not without a pistol.'

Daphne smacked him in the shoulder.

Simon ignored her and pulled her body against his. 'I meant what I said,' he murmured, wrapping his arms around her waist. 'I love you. I've known it for some time now, but—'

'It's all right,' Daphne said, laying her cheek against his chest. 'You don't need to explain.'

'Yes, I do,' he insisted. 'I – .' But the words wouldn't come. There was too much emotion inside, too many feelings rocking within him. 'Let me show you,' he said hoarsely. 'Let me show you how much I love you.'

Daphne answered by tilting her face up to receive his kiss. And as their lips touched, she sighed, 'I love you, too.'

Simon's mouth took hers with hungry devotion, his hands clutching at her back as if he were afraid she might disappear at any moment. 'Come upstairs,' he whispered. 'Come with me now.'

She nodded, but before she could take a step, he swept her into the cradle of his arms and carried her up the stairs.

By the time Simon reached the second floor, his body was rock hard and straining for release. 'Which room have you been using?' he gasped.

'Yours,' she replied, sounding surprised that he'd even asked.

He grunted his approval and moved swiftly into his – no, *their* – room, kicking the door shut behind him. 'I love you,' he said as they tumbled onto the bed. Now that he'd said the words once, they were bursting within him, demanding a voice. He needed to tell her, make sure she knew, make sure she understood what she meant to him.

And if it took a thousand sayings, he didn't care.

'I love you,' he said again, his fingers frantically working on the fastenings of her dress.

'I know,' she said tremulously. She cupped his face in her hands and caught his eyes with hers. 'I love you, too.'

Then she pulled his mouth down to hers, kissing him with a sweet innocence that set him afire.

'If I ever, ever hurt you again,' he said fervently, his mouth moving to the corner of hers, 'I want you to kill me.'

'Never,' she answered, smiling.

His lips moved to the sensitive spot where her jaw met her earlobe. 'Then maim me,' he murmured. 'Twist my arm, sprain my ankle.'

'Don't be silly,' she said, touching his chin and turning his face back to hers. 'You won't hurt me.'

Love for this woman filled him. It flooded his chest, made his fingers tingle, and stole his very breath. 'Sometimes,' he whispered, 'I love you so much it scares me. If I could give you the world, you know I would do it, don't you?'

'All I want is you,' she whispered. 'I don't need the world, just your love. And maybe,' she added with a wry smile, 'for you to take off your boots.'

Simon felt his face erupt into a grin. Somehow his wife always seemed to know exactly what he needed. Just when his emotions were choking him, bringing him dangerously close to tears, she lightened the mood, made him smile. 'Your wish is my command,' he said, and rolled to her side to yank the offending footwear off.

One boot tumbled to the floor, the other skittered across the room.

'Anything else, your grace?' he asked.

She cocked her head coyly. 'Your shirt could go, too, I suppose.'

He complied, and the linen garment landed on the nightstand.

'Will that be all?'

'These,' she said, hooking her finger around the waistband of his breeches, 'are definitely in the way.'

'I agree,' he murmured, shrugging them off. He crawled over her, on his hands and knees, his body a hot prison around her. 'Now what?'

Her breath caught. 'Well, you're quite naked.'

'That is true,' he concurred, his eyes burning down on hers.

'And I'm not.'

'That is also true.' He smiled like a cat. 'And a pity it is.'

Daphne nodded, completely without words.

'Sit up,' he said softly.

She did, and seconds later her dress was whipped over her head.

'Now that,' he said hoarsely, staring hungrily at her breasts, 'is an improvement.'

They were now kneeling across from each other on the massive four-poster bed. Daphne stared at her husband, her pulse quickening at the sight of his broad chest, rising and falling with each heavy breath. With a trembling hand, she reached out and touched him, her fingers lightly skimming over his warm skin.

Simon stopped breathing until her forefinger touched his nipple, and then his hand shot up to cover hers. 'I want you,' he said.

Her eyes flicked downward, and her lips curved ever so slightly. 'I know.'

'No,' he groaned, pulling her closer. 'I want to be in your heart. I want – ' His entire body shuddered when their skin touched. 'I want to be in your soul.'

'Oh, Simon,' she sighed, sinking her fingers in his thick, dark hair. 'You're already there.'

And then there were no more words, only lips and hands and flesh against flesh.

Simon worshipped her in every way he knew how. He ran his hands along her legs and kissed the back of her knees. He squeezed her hips and tickled her navel. And when he was poised to enter her, his entire body straining against the most all-consuming desire he'd ever felt, he gazed down upon her with a reverence that brought tears to her eyes.

'I love you,' he whispered. 'In all my life, it's been only you.'

Daphne nodded and although she made no sound, her mouth formed the words, 'I love you, too.'

He pushed forward, slowly, inexorably. And when he was settled fully within her body, he knew he was home.

He looked down at her face. Her head was thrown back, her lips parted as she struggled for breath. He grazed her flushed cheeks with his lips. 'You're the most beautiful thing I've ever seen,' he whispered. 'I've never – I don't know how – '

She arched her back in response. 'Just love me,' she gasped. 'Please, love me.'

Simon began to move, his hips rising and falling in time's most ancient rhythm. Daphne's fingers pressed into his back, her nails digging into his skin every time he thrust further into her body.

She moaned and mewled, and his body burned at the sounds of her passion. He was spiraling out of control, his movements growing jerky, more frenetic. 'I can't hold on much longer,' he gasped. He wanted to wait for her, needed to know that he'd brought her bliss before he allowed himself his own release.

But then, just when he thought his body would shatter from the effort of his restraint, Daphne shook beneath him, her most intimate muscles squeezing around him as she cried out his name.

Simon's breath stopped in his throat as he watched her face. He'd always been so busy making sure he didn't spill his seed inside of her that he'd never seen her face as she climaxed. Her head was thrown back, the elegant lines of her throat straining as her mouth opened in a silent scream.

He was awestruck.

'I love you,' he said. 'Oh, God, how I love you.' Then he plunged deeper.

Daphne's eyes fluttered open as he resumed his rhythm. 'Simon?' she asked, her voice tinged with touch of urgency. 'Are you sure?'

They both knew what she meant.

Simon nodded.

'I don't want you to do this just for me,' she said. 'It has to be for you, too.'

The strangest lump formed in his throat – it was nothing like his stutters, nothing like his stammers. It was, he realized, nothing but love. Tears stabbed at his eyes, and he nodded, utterly unable to speak.

He plunged forward, exploding within her. It felt good. Oh God, it felt good. Nothing in life had ever felt that good before.

His arms finally gave out, and he collapsed atop her, the only sound in the room the rasp of his ragged breathing.

And then Daphne smoothed his hair from his forehead and kissed his brow. 'I love you,' she whispered. 'I will always love you.'

Simon buried his face into her neck, breathing in the scent of her. She surrounded him, enveloped him, and he was complete.

Many hours later, Daphne's eyelids fluttered open. She stretched her arms above her as she noticed that the curtains had all been pulled shut. Simon must have done that, she thought with a yawn. Light filtered around the edges, bathing the room with a soft glow.

She twisted her neck, working the kinks out, then slid

out of bed and padded to the dressing room to fetch her robe. How unlike her to sleep in the middle of the day. But, she supposed, this hadn't been an ordinary day.

She pulled on her robe, tying the silken sash around her waist. Where had Simon gone off to? She didn't think he'd left the bed too long before she had; she had a sleepy memory of lying in his arms that somehow seemed too fresh.

The master suite consisted of five rooms altogether: two bedrooms, each with its own dressing room off to the side, connected by a large sitting room. The door to the sitting room was ajar, and bright sunlight streamed through the aperture, suggesting that the curtains inside had been pulled open. Moving on deliberately quiet feet, Daphne walked to the open doorway and peered inside.

Simon was standing by the window, staring out over the city. He'd donned a lush burgundy dressing gown, but his feet were still bare. His pale blue eyes held a reflective look, unfocused and just the slightest bit bleak.

Daphne's brow wrinkled with concern. She crossed the room toward him, quietly saying, 'Good afternoon,' when she was but a foot away.

Simon turned at the sound of her voice, and his haggard face softened at the sight of her. 'Good afternoon to you, too,' he murmured, pulling her into his arms. Somehow she ended up with her back pressed up against his broad chest, gazing out over Grosvenor Square as Simon rested his chin on the top of her head.

It took Daphne several moments before she worked up the courage to ask, 'Any regrets?'

She couldn't see him, but she felt his chin rub against her scalp as he shook his head.

'No regrets,' he said softly. 'Just . . . thoughts.'

Something about his voice didn't sound quite right, and so Daphne twisted in his arms until she could see his face. 'Simon, what's wrong?' she whispered.

'Nothing.' But his eyes didn't meet hers.

Daphne led him to a loveseat, and sat, tugging on his arm until he settled in beside her. 'If you're not ready to be a father yet,' she whispered, 'that's all right.'

'It's not that.'

But she didn't believe him. He'd answered too quickly, and there'd been a choked sound to his voice that made her uneasy. 'I don't mind waiting,' she said. 'Truth be told,' she added shyly, 'I wouldn't mind having a little time just for the two of us.'

Simon didn't say anything, but his eyes grew pained, and then he closed them as he brought his hand to his brow and rubbed.

A ripple of panic washed over Daphne, and she started talking faster. 'It wasn't so much that I wanted a baby right away,' she said. 'I just . . . would like one eventually, that's all, and I think you might, too, if you let yourself consider it. I was upset because I hated that you were denying us a family just to spite your father. It's not—'

Simon laid a heavy hand on her thigh. 'Daphne, stop,' he said. 'Please.'

His voice held just enough agonized emotion to silence her immediately. She caught her lower lip between her teeth and chewed nervously. It was his turn to speak. There was obviously something big and difficult squeezing at his heart, and if it took all day for him to find the words to explain it, she could wait.

She could wait forever for this man.

'I can't say I'm excited about having a child,' Simon said slowly.

Daphne noticed his breathing was slightly labored, and she placed her hand on his forearm to offer comfort.

He turned to her with eyes that pleaded for understanding. 'I've spent so long intending never to have one, you see.' He swallowed. 'I d-don't know even how to begin to think about it.'

Daphne offered him a reassuring smile that in retrospect, she realized was meant for both of them. 'You'll learn,' she whispered. 'And I'll learn with you.'

'I-it's not that,' he said, shaking his head. He let out an impatient breath. 'I don't . . . want . . . to live my life j-just to spite my father.'

He turned to her, and Daphne was nearly undone by the sheer emotion burning on his face. His jaw was trembling, and a muscle worked frantically in his cheek. There was incredible tension in his neck, as if every ounce of his energy was devoted to the task of delivering this speech.

Daphne wanted to hold him, to comfort the little boy inside. She wanted to smooth his brow, and squeeze his hand. She wanted to do a thousand things, but instead she just held silent, encouraging him with her eyes to continue.

'You were right,' he said, the words tumbling from his mouth. 'All along, you've been right. About my father. Th-that I was letting him win.'

'Oh, Simon,' she murmured.

'B-but what – ' His face – his strong, handsome face, which was always so firm, always so in control – crumpled. 'What if . . . if we have a child, a-a-and it comes out like me?'

For a moment Daphne couldn't speak. Her eyes tingled with unshed tears, and her hand moved unbidden to her mouth, covering lips that had parted in shock.

Simon turned away from her, but not before she saw the utter torment in his eyes. Not before she heard his breath catch, or the shaky exhale he finally expelled in an attempt to hold himself together.

'If we have a child who stutters,' Daphne said carefully, 'then I shall love him. And help him. And – ' She swallowed convulsively, praying that she was doing the right thing. 'And I shall turn to you for advice, because obviously you have learned how to overcome it.'

He turned to face her with surprising swiftness. 'I don't want my child to suffer as I have suffered.'

A strange little smile moved across Daphne's face without her even realizing it, as if her body had realized before her mind that she knew exactly what to say. 'But he wouldn't suffer,' she said, 'because you'll be his father.'

Simon's face did not change expression, but his eyes shone with an odd, new, almost hopeful light.

'Would you reject a child who stuttered?' Daphne asked quietly.

Simon's negative reply was strong, swift, and accompanied by just a touch of blasphemy.

She smiled softly. 'Then I have no fears for our children.'

Simon held still for one moment more, and then in a rush of movement pulled her into his arms, burying his face in the crook of her neck. 'I love you,' he choked out. 'I love you so much.'

And Daphne was finally certain that everything was going to be all right.

Several hours later, Daphne and Simon were still sitting on the love seat in the sitting room. It had been an afternoon for holding hands, for resting one's head on the other's shoulder. Words hadn't been necessary; for both it had been enough simply to be next to the other. The sun was shining, the birds were chirping, and they were together.

It was all they needed.

But something was niggling at the back of Daphne's brain, and it wasn't until her eyes fell on a writing set on the desk that she remembered.

The letters from Simon's father.

She closed her eyes and exhaled, summoning the courage she knew she'd need to hand them over to Simon. The Duke of Middlethorpe had told her, when he'd asked her to take the packet of letters, that she'd know when the time was right to give them to him.

She disentangled herself from Simon's heavy arms and padded over to the duchess's chamber.

'Where are you going?' Simon asked sleepily. He'd been dozing in the warm afternoon sun.

'I – I have to get something.'

He must have heard the hesitation in her voice, because he opened his eyes and craned his body around to look at her. 'What are you getting?' he asked curiously.

Daphne avoided answering his question by scurrying into the next room. 'I'll just be a moment,' she called out.

She'd kept the letters, tied together by a red-and-gold ribbon – the ancestral colors of Hastings – in the bottom drawer of her desk. She'd actually forgotten about them for her first few weeks back in London, and they'd lain untouched in her old bedroom at Bridgerton House. But she'd stumbled across them on a visit to see her mother. Violet had suggested she go upstairs to gather a few of her things, and while Daphne was collecting old perfume bottles and the pillowcase she'd stitched at age ten, she found them again.

Many a time she'd been tempted to open one up, if only to better understand her husband. And truth be told, if the envelopes hadn't been closed with sealing wax, she probably would have tossed her scruples over her shoulder and read them.

She picked up the bundle and walked slowly back to the sitting room. Simon was still on the couch, but he was up and alert, and watching her curiously.

'These are for you,' she said, holding up the bundle as she walked to his side.

'What are they?' he asked.

But from the tone of his voice, she was fairly certain he already knew.

'Letters from your father,' she said. 'Middlethorpe gave them to me. Do you remember?'

He nodded. 'I also remember giving him orders to burn them.'

Daphne smiled weakly. 'He apparently disagreed.'

Simon stared at the bundle. Anywhere but at her face. 'And so, apparently, did you,' he said in a very quiet voice.

She nodded and sat next to him. 'Do you want to read them?'

Simon thought about his answer for several seconds and finally settled on complete honesty. 'I don't know.'

'It might help you to finally put him behind you.'

'Or it might make it worse.'

'It might,' she agreed.

He stared at the letters, bundled up by a ribbon, resting innocently in her hands. He expected to feel animosity. He expected to feel rage. But instead, all he felt was . . .

Nothing.

It was the strangest sensation. There before him was a collection of letters, all written in his father's hand. And yet he felt no urge to toss them in the fire, or tear them to bits.

And at the same time no urge to read them.

'I think I'll wait,' Simon said with a smile.

Daphne blinked several times, as if her eyes could not believe her ears. 'You don't want to read them?' she asked.

He shook his head.

'And you don't want to burn them?'

He shrugged. 'Not particularly.'

She looked down at the letters, then back at his face. 'What do you want to do with them?'

'Nothing.'

'Nothing?'

He grinned. 'That's what I said.'

'Oh.' She looked quite adorably befuddled. 'Do you want me to put them back in my desk?'

'If you like.'

'And they'll just sit there?'

He caught hold of the sash on her dressing robe and starting pulling her toward him. 'Mmm-hmm.'

'But – ' she spluttered. 'But – but – '

'One more "but," he teased, 'and you're going to start to sound like me.'

Daphne's mouth fell open. Simon wasn't surprised by her reaction. It was the first time in his life he'd ever been able to make a joke out of his difficulties.

'The letters can wait,' he said, just as they fell off her lap onto the floor. 'I've just finally managed – thanks to you – to boot my father from my life.' He shook his head, smiling as he did so. 'Reading those now would just invite him back in.'

'But don't you want to see what he had to say?' she persisted. 'Maybe he apologized. Maybe he even groveled at your feet!' She bent down for the bundle, but Simon pulled her tightly against him so she couldn't reach.

'Simon!' she yelped.

He arched one brow. 'Yes?'

'What are you doing?'

'Trying to seduce you. Am I succeeding?'

Her face colored. 'Probably,' she mumbled.

'Only probably? Damn. I must be losing my touch.'

His hand slid under her bottom, which prompted a little squeal. 'I think your touch is just fine,' she said hastily.

'Only fine?' He pretended to wince. '"Fine" is so pale a word, don't you think? Almost wan.'

'Well,' she allowed, 'I might have misspoken.'

Simon felt a smile forming in his heart. By the time it spread to his lips, he was on his feet, and tugging his wife in the general direction of his four-poster bed.

'Daphne,' he said, trying to sound businesslike, 'I have a proposition.'

'A proposition?' she queried, raising her brows.

'A request,' he amended. 'I have a request.'

She cocked her head and smiled. 'What kind of request?'

He nudged her through the doorway and into the bedroom. 'It's actually a request in two parts.'

'How intriguing.'

'The first part involves you, me, and' – he picked her up and tossed her onto the bed amidst a fit of giggles – 'this sturdy antique of a bed.'

'Sturdy?'

He growled as he crawled up beside her. 'It had better be sturdy.'

She laughed and squealed as she scooted out of his grasp. 'I think it's sturdy. What's the second part of your request?'

'That, I'm afraid involves a certain commitment of time on your part.'

Her eyes narrowed, but she was still smiling. 'What sort of commitment of time?'

In one stunningly swift move, he pinned her to the mattress. 'About nine months.'

Her lips softened with surprise. 'Are you sure?'

'That it takes nine months?' He grinned. 'That's what I've always been told.'

But the levity had left her eyes. 'You know that's not what I mean,' she said softly.

'I know,' he replied, meeting her serious gaze with one of his own. 'But yes, I'm sure. And I'm scared to death. And thrilled to the marrow. And a hundred other emotions I never let myself feel before you came along.'

Tears pricked her eyes. 'That's the sweetest thing you've ever said to me.'

'It's the truth,' he vowed. 'Before I met you I was only half-alive.'

'And now?' she whispered.

'And now?' he echoed. '"Now" suddenly means happiness, and joy, and a wife I adore. But do you know what?'

She shook her head, too overcome to speak.

He leaned down and kissed her. '"Now" doesn't even compare to tomorrow. And tomorrow couldn't possibly compete with the next day. As perfect as I feel this very moment, tomorrow is going to be even better. Ah, Daff,' he murmured, moving his lips to hers, 'every day I'm going to love you more. I promise you that. Every day . . . '

Epilogue

It's a boy for the Duke and Duchess of Hastings!

After three girls, society's most besotted couple has finally produced an heir. This Author can only imagine the level of relief in the Hastings household; after all, it is a truth universally acknowledged that a married man in possession of a good fortune must be in want of an heir.

The name of the new babe has yet to be made public, although This Author feels herself uniquely qualified to speculate. After all, with sisters named Amelia, Belinda, and Caroline, could the new Earl Clyvedon be called anything but David?

LADY WHISTLEDOWN'S SOCIETY PAPERS, 15 DECEMBER 1817

Simon threw up his arms in amazement, the single-sheet newspaper flying across the room. 'How does she know this?' he demanded. 'We've told no one of our decision to name him David.'

Daphne tried not to smile as she watched her husband sputter and storm about the room. 'It's just a lucky guess, I'm sure,' she said, turning her attention back to the newborn in her arms. It was far too early to know if his eyes would remain blue or turn brown like his older sisters', but already he looked so like his father; Daphne couldn't imagine that his eyes would spoil the effect by darkening.

'She must have a spy in our household,' he said, planting his hands on his hips. 'She must.'

'I'm sure she doesn't have a spy in our household,' Daphne said without looking up at him. She was too interested in the way David's tiny hand was gripping her finger.

'But—'

Daphne finally lifted her head. 'Simon, you're being ridiculous. It's just a gossip column.'

'Whistledown – ha!' he grumbled. 'I've never heard of any Whistledowns. I'd like to know who this blasted woman is.'

'You and the rest of London,' Daphne said under her breath.

'Someone should put her out of business once and for all.'

'If you wish to put her out of business,' Daphne could not resist pointing out, 'you shouldn't support her by buying her newspaper.'

'I—'

'And don't even try to say that you buy *Whistledown* for me.'

'You read it,' Simon muttered.

'And so do you.' Daphne dropped a kiss on the top of David's head. 'Usually well before I can get my hands on it. Besides, I'm rather fond of Lady Whistledown these days.'

Simon looked suspicious. 'Why?'

'Did you read what she wrote about us? She called us London's most besotted couple.' Daphne smiled wickedly. 'I rather like that.'

Simon groaned. 'That's only because Philipa Featherington—'

'She's Philipa Berbrooke now,' Daphne reminded him.

'Well, whatever her name, she has the bloodiest big mouth in London, and ever since she heard me calling you "Dear Heart" at the theater last month, I have not been able to show my face at my clubs.'

‘Is it so very unfashionable to love one’s wife, then?’ Daphne teased.

Simon pulled a face, looking rather like a disgruntled young boy.

‘Never mind,’ Daphne said. ‘I don’t want to hear your answer.’

Simon’s smile was an endearing cross between sheepish and sly.

‘Here,’ she said, holding David up. ‘Do you want to hold him?’

‘Of course.’ Simon crossed the room and took the baby into his arms. He cuddled him for several moments, then glanced over at Daphne and grinned. ‘I think he looks like me.’

‘I know he does.’

Simon kissed him on the nose, and whispered, ‘Don’t you worry, my little man. I shall love you always. I’ll teach you your letters and your numbers, and how to sit on a horse. And I shall protect you from all the awful people in this world, especially that Whistledown woman . . . ’

And in a small, elegantly furnished chamber, not so very far from Hastings House, a young woman sat at her desk with a quill and a pot of ink and pulled out a piece of paper.

With a smile on her face, she set her quill to paper and wrote:

Lady Whistledown’s Society Papers
19 December 1817
Ah Gentle Reader, This Author is pleased to report . . .

Watch out for other titles in Julia Quinn's delightful Bridgerton Series *available now from Piatkus:*

THE VISCOUNT WHO LOVED ME

Anthony Bridgerton needs a wife. Having spent his twenties in a rakish pursuit of pleasure (whilst taking care to ensure the financial security of his mother and seven younger siblings and mother) he knows it's high time he settled down and ensured the continuation of the Bridgerton line.

Edwina Sheffield is considered the most beautiful debutante of the current season. She is also sweet, innocent and eminently biddable – Anthony is sure she'll make a perfectly acceptable wife and vows to make her his.

The only obstacle in his way is Edwina's older sister, Kate. Kate is determined to do all she can to allow her sister the chance to marry for love rather than convenience. And the roguish viscount is beginning to think he may have met his match in Kate's keen wit and sharp tongue. Until, that is, he makes the mistake of kissing her . . .

AN OFFER FROM A GENTLEMAN

'This year's most sought-after invitation must surely be that of the Bridgerton masquerade ball, to be held Monday next.'
Lady Whistledown's Society Papers, 31 May 1815

As the illegitimate daughter of the Earl of Penwood, Sophie Beckett has never been accepted in polite society. And since her father's untimely death, her step-mother has made her life doubly hard, forcing her to work as an unpaid servant. Sophie's days are pure drudgery, until one night her fellow servants conspire to help her attend the Bridgerton masquerade ball.

There she meets her very own Prince Charming, handsome Benedict Bridgerton and falls head over heels in love. Benedict is equally smitten, but when the clock strikes midnight Sophie is forced to flee the ballroom, leaving only her glove in his hand . . .

978-0-7499-3659-4

ROMANCING MR BRIDGERTON

Penelope Featherington has secretly adored her best friend's brother for . . . well, it feels like forever. After half a lifetime of watching Colin Bridgerton from afar, she thinks she knows everything about him, until she stumbles across his deepest secret – and fears she doesn't know him at all.

Colin Bridgerton is tired of being thought nothing but an empty-headed charmer, tired of the ton's preoccupation with the notorious gossip columnist Lady Whistledown. But when Colin returns to London from a trip abroad he discovers nothing in his life is quite the same – especially Penelope Featherington! Only then he discovers that Penelope has secrets of her own, and this elusive bachelor must decide . . . is she his biggest threat – or his promise of a happy ending?

978-0-7499-3660-0

TO SIR PHILLIP, WITH LOVE

'My dear Miss Bridgerton, Forgive me if I am too bold, but I am writing to invite you to visit me here at Romney Hall. It is my hope that after a suitable period of time, you will consent to be my wife . . .'

Sir Phillip knew from his correspondence with his dead wife's distant cousin that Eloise Bridgerton was a spinster, and so he'd proposed, figuring that she'd be homely and unassuming, and more than a little desperate for an offer of marriage. Except . . . she wasn't. The beautiful woman on his doorstep was anything but quiet, and when she stopped talking long enough to close her mouth, all he wanted to do was kiss her . . .

Eloise Bridgerton couldn't marry a man she had never met! But then she started thinking . . . and wondering . . . and before she knew it, she was in a hired carriage in the middle of the night, on her way to meet the man she hoped might be her perfect match. Except he wasn't. Her perfect husband wouldn't be so moody and ill-mannered. And he certainly should have mentioned that he had two young – and decidedly unruly – children, as much in need of a mother as Phillip is in need of a wife.

978-0-7499-3661-7

***Praise for Julia Quinn*:**

'Quinn has a smart, funny touch . . . that's reminiscent of Helen Fielding'
Time Magazine

'Delightful'
Nora Roberts

'Julia Quinn is truly our contemporary Jane Austen'
Jill Barnett

'Refreshing and radiant'
Lisa Kleypas

'Ms. Quinn writes delightfully fast-paced, funny, sparkling, and bright romance'
Romantic Times

'Writers like Quinn are reinventing the romance novel for the post-feminist generation'
Time Magazine

'Captivating and alluring'
Romantic Times

'Julia Quinn's witty Regency-set romantic comedies are the next best thing to Georgette Heyer'
Gloss

Julia Quinn started writing her first book one month after finishing university and has been tapping away at her keyboard ever since. The No. 1 *New York Times* bestselling author of more than two dozen novels, she is a graduate of Harvard and Radcliffe Colleges and is one of only sixteen authors ever to be inducted in the Romance Writers of America Hall of Fame. She lives in the Pacific Northwest with her family.

Please visit Julia Quinn online:

www.juliaquinn.com
www.facebook.com/AuthorJuliaQuinn
@JQAuthor

By Julia Quinn

The Rokesby Series:
Because of Miss Bridgerton
The Girl with the Make-Believe Husband
The Other Miss Bridgerton
First Comes Scandal

The Smythe-Smith Quartet:
Just Like Heaven
A Night Like This
The Sum of All Kisses
The Secrets of Sir Richard Kenworthy

The Bevelstoke Series:
The Secret Diaries of Miss Miranda Cheever
What Happens in London
Ten Things I Love About You

The Two Dukes of Wyndham:
The Lost Duke of Wyndham
Mr Cavendish, I Presume

Blydon Family Saga:
Splendid
Dancing at Midnight
Minx

Agents for the Crown:
To Catch an Heiress
How to Marry a Marquis

Bridgerton Series:
The Duke and I
The Viscount Who Loved Me
An Offer from a Gentleman
Romancing Mr Bridgerton
To Sir Phillip, With Love
When He Was Wicked
It's In His Kiss
On the Way to the Wedding
The Bridgertons: Happily Ever After

The Lyndon Sisters:
Everything and the Moon
Brighter than the Sun

The Ladies Most (written with Eloisa James and Connie Brockway):
The Lady Most Likely
The Lady Most Willing

The Wit and Wisdom of Bridgerton: Lady Whistledown's Official Guide

Miss Butterworth and the Mad Baron (graphic novel)

BRIDGERTON

THE VISCOUNT WHO LOVED ME

JULIA QUINN

PIATKUS

PIATKUS

First published in the US in 2000 by Avon Books,
An imprint of Harper Collins, New York
First published in Great Britain in 2006 by Piatkus Books
This paperback edition published in 2021 by Piatkus
by arrangement with Avon

20

A CIP catalogue record for this book
is available from the British Library.

ISBN 978-0-349-42979-3

Printed and bound in Great Britain by Clays Ltd, Elcograf S.p.A.

Papers used by Piatkus are from well-managed forests
and other responsible sources.

MIX
Paper from
responsible sources
FSC® C104740

Piatkus
An imprint of
Little, Brown Book Group
Carmelite House
50 Victoria Embankment
London EC4Y 0DZ

Hachette Ireland
8 Castlecourt Centre
Castleknock
Dublin 15

An Hachette UK Company
www.hachette.co.uk

www.littlebrown.co.uk

For Little Goose Twist,
who kept me company
throughout the writing of this book.
I can't wait to meet you!

And also for Paul,
even though he is allergic to musicals.

Prologue

Anthony Bridgerton had always known he would die young.

Oh, not as a child. Young Anthony had never had cause to ponder his own mortality. His early years had been a young boy's perfection, right from the very day of his birth.

It was true that Anthony was the heir to an ancient and wealthy viscountcy, but unlike most other aristocratic couples, Lord and Lady Bridgerton were very much in love, and they saw their son's birth not as the arrival of an heir, but rather that of a child.

And so there were no parties, no fêtes, no celebration other than that of mother and father staring in wonderment at their new son.

The Bridgertons were young parents—Edmund barely twenty and Violet just eighteen—but they were sensible and they were strong, and they loved their son with a fierceness and devotion that was rarely seen in their social circles. Much to her own mother's horror, Violet insisted upon nursing the boy herself, and Edmund never subscribed to the prevailing attitude that fathers should neither see nor hear their children. He took the infant on long hikes across the fields of Kent, spoke to him of philosophy and poetry before he could possibly understand the words, and told him a bedtime story every night.

Because the viscount and viscountess were so young

and so very much in love, it came as no surprise to anyone when, just two years after Anthony's birth, he was joined by a younger brother, christened Benedict. Edmund immediately adjusted his daily routine to take two sons on his hikes, and he spent a week holed up in the stables, working with his leatherworker to devise a special pack that would hold Anthony on his back while he held the baby Benedict in his arms.

They walked across fields and streams, and he told them of wondrous things, of perfect flowers and clear blue skies, of knights in shining armor and damsels in distress. Violet used to laugh when they returned all windblown and sun-kissed, and Edmund would say, "See? Here is our damsel in distress. Clearly we must save her." And Anthony would throw himself into his mother's arms, giggling as he swore he'd protect her from the fire-breathing dragon they'd seen just *two miles down the road* in the village.

"Two miles down the road in the village?" Violet would breathe, keeping her voice carefully laden with horror. "Heaven above, what would I do without three strong men to protect me?"

"Benedict's a baby," Anthony would reply.

"But he'll grow up," she'd always say, tousling his hair, "just as you did. And just as you still will."

Edmund always treated his children with equal affection and devotion, but late at night, when Anthony cradled the Bridgerton pocket watch to his chest (given to him on his eighth birthday by his father, who had received it on his eighth birthday from *his* father), he liked to think that his relationship with his father was just a little bit special. Not because Edmund loved him best; by that point the Bridgerton siblings numbered four (Colin and Daphne had arrived fairly close together) and Anthony knew very well that all the children were well loved.

No, Anthony liked to think that his relationship with his father was special simply because he'd known him the longest. After all, no matter how long Benedict had known their father, Anthony would always have two years on him. And six on Colin. And as for Daphne, well, besides the fact that she was a girl (the horror!), she'd known Father a full eight years less than he had and, he liked to remind himself, always would.

Edmund Bridgerton was, quite simply, the very center of Anthony's world. He was tall, his shoulders were broad, and he could ride a horse as if he'd been born in the saddle. He always knew the answers to arithmetic questions (even when the tutor didn't), he saw no reason why his sons should not have a tree house (and then he went and built it himself), and his laugh was the sort that warmed a body from the inside out.

Edmund taught Anthony how to ride. He taught Anthony how to shoot. He taught him to swim. He took him off to Eton himself, rather than sending him in a carriage with servants, as most of Anthony's future friends arrived, and when he saw Anthony glancing nervously about the school that would become his new home, he had a heart-to-heart talk with his eldest son, assuring him that everything would be all right.

And it was. Anthony knew it would be. His father, after all, never lied.

Anthony loved his mother. Hell, he'd probably bite off his own arm if it meant keeping her safe and well. But growing up, everything he did, every accomplishment, every goal, every single hope and dream—it was all for his father.

And then one day, everything changed. It was funny, he reflected later, how one's life could alter in an instant, how one minute everything could be a certain way, and the next it's simply . . . not.

It happened when Anthony was eighteen, home for the summer and preparing for his first year at Oxford. He was to belong to All Souls College, as his father had before him, and his life was as bright and dazzling as any eighteen-year-old had a right to enjoy. He had discovered women, and perhaps more splendidly, they had discovered him. His parents were still happily reproducing, having added Eloise, Francesca, and Gregory to the family, and Anthony did his best not to roll his eyes when he passed his mother in the hall—pregnant with her *eighth* child! It was all a bit unseemly, in Anthony's opinion, having children at their age, but he kept his opinions to himself.

Who was he to doubt Edmund's wisdom? Maybe he, too, would want more children at the advanced age of thirty-eight.

When Anthony found out, it was late afternoon. He was returning from a long and bruising ride with Benedict and had just pushed through the front door of Aubrey Hall, the ancestral home of the Bridgertons, when he saw his ten-year-old-sister sitting on the floor. Benedict was still in the stables, having lost some silly bet with Anthony, the terms of which required him to rub down both horses.

Anthony stopped short when he saw Daphne. It was odd enough that his sister was sitting in the middle of the floor in the main hall. It was even more odd that she was crying.

Daphne never cried.

"Daff," he said hesitantly, too young to know what to do with a crying female and wondering if he'd ever learn, "what—"

But before he could finish his question, Daphne lifted her head, and the shattering heartbreak in her large brown eyes cut through him like a knife. He stumbled back a step, knowing something was wrong, terribly wrong.

"He'd dead," Daphne whispered. "Papa is dead."

For a moment Anthony was sure he'd misheard. His father couldn't be dead. Other people died young, like Uncle Hugo, but Uncle Hugo had been small and frail. Well, at least smaller and frailer than Edmund.

"You're wrong," he told Daphne. "You must be wrong."

She shook her head. "Eloise told me. He was . . . it was . . ."

Anthony knew he shouldn't shake his sister while she

sobbed, but he couldn't help himself. "It was *what,* Daphne?"

"A bee," she whispered. "He was stung by a bee."

For a moment Anthony could do nothing but stare at her. Finally, his voice hoarse and barely recognizable, he said, "A man doesn't die from a bee sting, Daphne."

She said nothing, just sat there on the floor, her throat working convulsively as she tried to control her tears.

"He's been stung before," Anthony added, his voice rising in volume. "I was with him. We were both stung. We came across a nest. I was stung on the shoulder." Unbidden, his hand rose to touch the spot where he'd been stung so many years before. In a whisper he added, "He on his arm."

Daphne just stared at him with an eerily blank expression.

"He was fine," Anthony insisted. He could hear the panic in his voice and knew he was frightening his sister, but he was powerless to control it. "A man can't die from a bee sting!"

Daphne shook her head, her dark eyes suddenly looking about a hundred years old. "It was a bee," she said in a hollow voice. "Eloise saw it. One minute he was just standing there, and the next he was . . . he was . . ."

Anthony felt something very strange building within him, as if his muscles were about to jump through his skin. "The next he was *what,* Daphne?"

"Gone." She looked bewildered by the word, as bewildered as he felt.

Anthony left Daphne sitting in the hall and took the stairs three at a time up to his parents' bedchamber. Surely his father wasn't dead. A man couldn't die from a bee sting. It was impossible. Utterly mad. Edmund Bridgerton was young, he was strong. He was tall, his shoulders were broad, his muscles were powerful, and by God, no insignificant honeybee could have felled him.

But when Anthony reached the upstairs hall, he could

tell by the utter and complete silence of the dozen or so hovering servants that the situation was grim.

And their pitying faces . . . for the rest of his life he'd be haunted by those pitying faces.

He'd thought he'd have to push his way into his parents' room, but the servants parted as if they were drops in the Red Sea, and when Anthony pushed open the door, he knew.

His mother was sitting on the edge of the bed, not weeping, not even making a sound, just holding his father's hand as she rocked slowly back and forth.

His father was still. Still as . . .

Anthony didn't even want to think the word.

"Mama?" he choked out. He hadn't called her that for years; she'd been "Mother" since he'd left for Eton.

She turned, slowly, as if hearing his voice through a long, long tunnel.

"What happened?" he whispered.

She shook her head, her eyes hopelessly far away. "I don't know," she said. Her lips remained parted by an inch or so, as if she'd meant to say something more but then forgotten to do it.

Anthony took a step forward, his movements awkward and jerky.

"He's gone," Violet finally whispered. "He's gone and I . . . oh, God, I . . ." She placed a hand on her belly, full and round with child. "I told him—oh, Anthony, I told him—"

She looked as if she might shatter from the inside out. Anthony choked back the tears that were burning his eyes and stinging his throat and moved to her side. "It's all right, Mama," he said.

But he knew it wasn't all right.

"I told him this had to be our last," she gasped, sobbing onto his shoulder. "I told him I couldn't carry another, and we'd have to be careful, and . . . Oh, God, Anthony, what I'd do to have him here and give him another child. I don't understand. I just don't understand. . . ."

Anthony held her while she cried. He said nothing; it seemed useless to try to make any words fit the devastation in his heart.

He didn't understand, either.

The doctors came later that evening and pronounced themselves baffled. They'd heard of such things before, but never in one so young and strong. He was so vital, so powerful; nobody could have known. It was true that the viscount's younger brother Hugo had died quite suddenly the year before, but such things did not necessarily run in families, and besides, even though Hugo had died by himself out-of-doors, no one had noticed a bee sting on his skin.

Then again, nobody had looked.

Nobody could have known, the doctors kept saying, over and over until Anthony wanted to strangle them all. Eventually he got them out of the house, and he put his mother to bed. They had to move her into a spare bedroom; she grew agitated at the thought of sleeping in the bed she'd shared for so many years with Edmund. Anthony managed to send his six siblings to bed as well, telling them that they'd all talk in the morning, that everything would be well, and he would take care of them as their father would have wanted.

Then he walked into the room where his father's body still lay and looked at him. He looked at him and looked at him, staring at him for hours, barely blinking.

And when he left the room, he left with a new vision of his own life, and new knowledge about his own mortality.

Edmund Bridgerton had died at the age of thirty-eight. And Anthony simply couldn't imagine ever surpassing his father in any way, even in years.

Chapter 1

The topic of rakes has, of course, been previously discussed in this column, and This Author has come to the conclusion that there are rakes, and there are Rakes.

Anthony Bridgerton is a Rake.

A rake (lower-case) is youthful and immature. He flaunts his exploits, behaves with utmost idiocy, and thinks himself dangerous to women.

A Rake (upper-case) knows *he is dangerous to women.*

He doesn't flaunt his exploits because he doesn't need to. He knows he will be whispered about by men and women alike, and in fact, he'd rather they didn't whisper about him at all. He knows who he is and what he has done; further recountings are, to him, redundant.

He doesn't behave like an idiot for the simple reason that he isn't an idiot (any moreso than must be expected among all members of the male gender). He has little patience for the foibles of society, and quite frankly, most of the time This Author cannot say she blames him.

And if that doesn't describe Viscount Bridgerton—surely this season's most eligible bachelor—to perfection, This Author shall retire Her quill immediately. The only question is: Will 1814 be the season he finally succumbs to the exquisite bliss of matrimony?

This Author Thinks . . .
Not.

LADY WHISTLEDOWN'S SOCIETY PAPERS, 20 APRIL 1814

"Please don't tell me," Kate Sheffield said to the room at large, "that she is writing about Viscount Bridgerton again."

Her half-sister Edwina, younger by almost four years, looked up from behind the single-sheet newspaper. "How could you tell?"

"You're giggling like a madwoman."

Edwina giggled, shaking the blue damask sofa on which they both sat.

"See?" Kate said, giving her a little poke in the arm. "You always giggle when she writes about some reprehensible rogue." But Kate grinned. There was little she liked better than teasing her sister. In a good-natured manner, of course.

Mary Sheffield, Edwina's mother, and Kate's stepmother for nearly eighteen years, glanced up from her embroidery and pushed her spectacles farther up the bridge of her nose. "What are you two laughing about?"

"Kate's in a snit because Lady Whistledown is writing about that rakish viscount again," Edwina explained.

"I'm not in a snit," Kate said, even though no one was listening.

"Bridgerton?" Mary asked absently.

Edwina nodded. "Yes."

"She always writes about him."

"I think she just likes writing about rakes," Edwina commented.

"Of course she likes writing about rakes," Kate retorted. "If she wrote about boring people, no one would buy her newspaper."

"That's not true," Edwina replied. "Just last week she

wrote about us, and heaven knows we're not the most interesting people in London."

Kate smiled at her sister's naïveté. Kate and Mary might not be the most interesting people in London, but Edwina, with her buttery-colored hair and startlingly pale blue eyes, had already been named the Incomparable of 1814. Kate, on the other hand, with her plain brown hair and eyes, was usually referred to as "the Incomparable's older sister."

She supposed there were worse monikers. At least no one had yet begun to call her "the Incomparable's spinster sister." Which was a great deal closer to the truth than any of the Sheffields cared to admit. At twenty (nearly twenty-one, if one was going to be scrupulously honest about it), Kate was a bit long in the tooth to be enjoying her first season in London.

But there hadn't really been any other choice. The Sheffields hadn't been wealthy even when Kate's father had been alive, and since he'd passed on five years earlier, they'd been forced to economize even further. They certainly weren't ready for the poorhouse, but they had to mind every penny and watch every pound.

With their straitened finances, the Sheffields could manage the funds for only one trip to London. Renting a house—and a carriage—and hiring the bare minimum of servants for the season cost money. More money than they could afford to spend twice. As it was, they'd had to save for five solid years to be able to afford this trip to London. And if the girls weren't successful on the Marriage Mart . . . well, no one was going to clap them into debtor's prison, but they would have to look forward to a quiet life of genteel poverty at some charmingly small cottage in Somerset.

And so the two girls were forced to make their debuts in the same year. It had been decided that the most logical time would be when Edwina was just seventeen and Kate almost twenty-one. Mary would have liked to have waited until Edwina was eighteen, and a bit more mature, but that would have made Kate nearly twenty-two, and heavens, but who would marry her then?

Kate smiled wryly. She hadn't even wanted a season. She'd known from the outset that she wasn't the sort who would capture the attention of the *ton*. She wasn't pretty enough to overcome her lack of dowry, and she'd never learned to simper and mince and walk delicately, and do all those things other girls seemed to know how to do in the cradle. Even Edwina, who didn't have a devious bone in her body, somehow knew how to stand and walk and sigh so that men came to blows just for the honor of helping her cross the street.

Kate, on the other hand, always stood with her shoulders straight and tall, couldn't sit still if her life depended upon it, and walked as if she were in a race—and why not? she always wondered. If one was going somewhere, what could possibly be the point in not getting there quickly?

As for her current season in London, she didn't even like the city very much. Oh, she was having a good enough time, and she'd met quite a few nice people, but a London season seemed a horrible waste of money to a girl who would have been perfectly content to remain in the country and find some sensible man to marry there.

But Mary would have none of that. "When I married your father," she'd said, "I vowed to love you and bring you up with all the care and affection I'd give to a child of my own blood."

Kate had managed to get in a single, "But—" before Mary carried on with, "I have a responsibility to your poor mother, God rest her soul, and part of that responsibility is to see you married off happily and securely."

"I could be happy and secure in the country," Kate had replied.

Mary had countered, "There are more men from which to choose in London."

After which Edwina had joined in, insisting that she

would be utterly miserable without her, and since Kate never could bear to see her sister unhappy, her fate had been sealed.

And so here she was—sitting in a somewhat faded drawing room in a rented house in a section of London that was almost fashionable, and . . .

She looked about mischievously.

. . . and she was about to snatch a newspaper from her sister's grasp.

"Kate!" Edwina squealed, her eyes bugging out at the tiny triangle of newsprint that remained between her right thumb and forefinger. "I wasn't done yet!"

"You've been reading it forever," Kate said with a cheeky grin. "Besides, I want to see what she has to say about Viscount Bridgerton today."

Edwina's eyes, which were usually compared to peaceful Scottish lochs, glinted devilishly. "You're *awfully* interested in the viscount, Kate. Is there something you're not telling us?"

"Don't be silly. I don't even know the man. And if I did, I would probably run in the opposite direction. He is exactly the sort of man the two of us should avoid at all costs. He could probably seduce an iceberg."

"Kate!" Mary exclaimed.

Kate grimaced. She'd forgotten her stepmother was listening. "Well, it's true," she added. "I've heard he's had more mistresses than I've had birthdays."

Mary looked at her for a few seconds, as if trying to decide whether or not she wanted to respond, and then finally she said, "Not that this is an appropriate topic for your ears, but many men have."

"Oh." Kate flushed. There was little less appealing than being decisively contradicted while one was trying to make a grand point. "Well, then, he's had twice as many. Whatever the case, he's far more promiscuous than most men, and not the sort Edwina ought to allow to court her."

"*You* are enjoying a season as well," Mary reminded her.

Kate shot Mary the most sarcastic of glances. They all knew that if the viscount chose to court a Sheffield, it would not be Kate.

"I don't think there is anything in there that's going to alter your opinion," Edwina said with a shrug as she leaned toward Kate to get a better view of the newspaper. "She doesn't say very much about *him,* actually. It's more of a treatise on thc topic of rakes."

Kate's eyes swept over the typeset words. "Hmmph," she said, her favorite expression of disdain. "I'll wager she's correct. He probably won't come up to scratch this year."

"You always think Lady Whistledown is correct," Mary murmured with a smile.

"She usually is," Kate replied. "You must admit, for a gossip columnist, she displays remarkable good sense. She has certainly been correct in her assessment of all the people I have met thus far in London."

"You should make your own judgments, Kate," Mary said lightly. "It is beneath you to base your opinions on a gossip column."

Kate knew her stepmother was right, but she didn't want to admit it, and so she just let out another "Hmmph" and turned back to the paper in her hands.

Whistledown was, without a doubt, the most interesting reading material in all London. Kate wasn't entirely certain when the gossip column had begun—sometime the previous year, she'd heard—but one thing was certain. Whoever Lady Whistledown was (and no one *really* knew who she was), she was a well-connected member of the *ton.* She had to be. No interloper could ever uncover all the gossip she printed in her columns every Monday, Wednesday, and Friday.

Lady Whistledown always had all the latest *on-dits*, and unlike other columnists, she wasn't hesitant about using people's full names. Having decided last week, for example, that Kate didn't look good in yellow, she wrote, clear as day: "The color yellow makes the dark-haired Miss Katharine Sheffield look like a singed daffodil."

Kate hadn't minded the insult. She'd heard it said on more than one occasion that one could not consider oneself "arrived" until one had been insulted by Lady Whistledown. Even Edwina, who was a huge social success by anyone's measure, had been jealous that Kate had been singled out for an insult.

And even though Kate didn't particularly want to be in London for a season, she figured that if she had to participate in the social whirl, she might as well not be a complete and utter failure. If getting insulted in a gossip column was to be her only sign of success, well then, so be it. Kate would take her triumphs where she may.

Now when Penelope Featherington bragged about being likened to an overripe citrus fruit in her tangerine satin, Kate could wave her arm and sigh with great drama, "Yes, well, I am a singed daffodil."

"Someday," Mary announced out of the blue, giving her spectacles yet another push with her index finger, "someone is going to discover that woman's true identity, and then she's going to be in trouble."

Edwina looked at her mother with interest. "Do you really think someone will ferret her out? She has managed to keep her secret for over a year now."

"Nothing that big can stay a secret forever," Mary replied. She jabbed her embroidery with her needle, pulling a long strand of yellow thread through the fabric. "Mark my words. It's all going to come out sooner or later, and when it does, a scandal the likes of which you have never seen is going to erupt all over town."

"Well, if I knew who she was," Kate announced, flipping the single-sheet newspaper over to page two, "I'd probably make her my best friend. She's fiendishly entertaining. And no matter what anyone says, she's almost always right."

Just then, Newton, Kate's somewhat overweight corgi, trotted into the room.

"Isn't that dog supposed to stay outside?" Mary asked. Then she yelped, "Kate!" as the dog angled over to her feet and panted as if waiting for a kiss.

"Newton, come here this minute," Kate ordered.

The dog gazed longingly at Mary, then waddled over to Kate, hopped up onto the sofa, and laid his front paws across her lap.

"He's covering you with fur," Edwina said.

Kate shrugged as she stroked his thick, caramel-colored coat. "I don't mind."

Edwina sighed, but she reached out and gave Newton a quick pat, anyway. "What else does she say?" she asked, leaning forward with interest. "I never did get to see page two."

Kate smiled at her sister's sarcasm. "Not much. A little something about the Duke and Duchess of Hastings, who apparently arrived in town earlier this week, a list of the food at Lady Danbury's ball, which she proclaimed 'surprisingly delicious,' and a rather unfortunate description of Mrs. Featherington's gown Monday last."

Edwina frowned. "She does seem to pick on the Featheringtons quite a bit."

"And no wonder," Mary said, setting down her embroidery as she stood up. "That woman wouldn't know how to pick out a dress color for her girls if a rainbow wrapped itself right around her neck."

"Mother!" Edwina exclaimed.

Kate clapped a hand over her mouth, trying not to laugh. Mary rarely made such opinionated pronouncements, but when she did, they were always marvelous.

"Well, it's true. She keeps dressing her youngest in tangerine. Anyone can see that poor girl needs a blue or a mint green."

"You dressed me in yellow," Kate reminded her.

"And I'm sorry I did. That will teach me to listen to a shopgirl. I should never have doubted my own judgment. We'll simply have to have that one cut down for Edwina."

Since Edwina was a full head shorter than Kate, and several shades more delicate, this would not be a problem.

"When you do," Kate said, turning to her sister, "make sure you eliminate the ruffle on the sleeve. It's dreadfully distracting. *And* it itches. I had half a mind to rip it off right there at the Ashbourne ball."

Mary rolled her eyes. "I am both surprised and thankful that you saw fit to restrain yourself."

"I am surprised but not thankful," Edwina said with a mischievous smile. "Just think of the fun Lady Whistledown would have had with *that*."

"Ah, yes," Kate said, returning her grin. "I can see it now. 'The singed daffodil rips off her petals.' "

"I am going upstairs," Mary announced, shaking her head at her daughters' antics. "Do try not to forget that we have a party to attend this evening. You girls may want to get a bit of rest before we go out. It's sure to be another late night for us."

Kate and Edwina nodded and murmured promises to that effect as Mary gathered her embroidery and left the room. As soon as she was gone, Edwina turned to Kate and asked, "Have you decided what you're going to wear tonight?"

"The green gauze, I think. I should wear white, I know, but I fear it does not suit me."

"If you don't wear white," Edwina said loyally, "then neither shall I. I shall wear my blue muslin."

Kate nodded her approval as she glanced back at the newspaper in her hand, trying to balance Newton, who had flipped over onto his back and was angling to have his belly rubbed. "Just last week Mr. Berbrooke said you are an angel in blue. On account of it matching your eyes so well."

Edwina blinked in surprise. "Mr. Berbrooke said that? To you?"

Kate looked back up. "Of course. All of your beaux try to pass on their compliments through me."

"They do? Whyever?"

Kate smiled slowly and indulgently. "Well, now, Edwina, it might have something to do with the time you announced to the entire audience at the Smythe-Smith musicale that you could never marry without your sister's approval."

Edwina's cheeks turned just the slightest bit pink. "It wasn't the entire audience," she mumbled.

"It might as well have been. The news traveled faster than fire on rooftops. I wasn't even in the room at the time and it only took two minutes for me to hear about it."

Edwina crossed her arms and let out a "Hmmph" that made her sound rather like her older sister. "Well, it's true, and I don't care who knows it. I know I'm expected to make a grand and brilliant match, but I don't have to marry someone who will ill treat me. Anyone with the fortitude to actually impress *you* would have to be up to snuff."

"Am I so difficult to impress, then?"

The two sisters looked at each other, then answered in unison, "Yes."

But as Kate laughed along with Edwina, a niggling sense of guilt rose within her. All three Sheffields knew that it would be Edwina who would snag a nobleman or marry into a fortune. It would be Edwina who would ensure that her family would not have to live out their lives in genteel poverty. Edwina was a beauty, while Kate was . . .

Kate was Kate.

Kate didn't mind. Edwina's beauty was simply a fact of life. There were certain truths Kate had long since come to accept. Kate would never learn to waltz without trying to take the lead; she'd always be afraid of electrical storms, no matter how often she told herself she was being silly; and no matter what she wore, no matter how she dressed her hair or pinched her cheeks, she'd never be as pretty as Edwina.

Besides, Kate wasn't certain that she'd like all the attention Edwina received. Nor, she was coming to realize, would she relish the responsibility of having to marry well to provide for her mother and sister.

"Edwina," Kate said softly, her eyes growing serious, "you don't have to marry anyone you don't like. You know that."

Edwina nodded, suddenly looking as if she might cry.

"If you decide there isn't a single gentleman in London who is good enough for you, then so be it. We shall simply go back to Somerset and enjoy our own company. There's no one I like better, anyway."

"Nor I," Edwina whispered.

"And if you do find a man who sweeps you off your feet, then Mary and I shall be delighted. You should not worry about leaving us, either. We shall get on fine with each other for company."

"You might find someone to marry as well," Edwina pointed out.

Kate felt her lips twist into a small smile. "I might," she allowed, knowing that it probably wasn't true. She didn't want to remain a spinster her entire life, but she doubted she would find a husband here in London. "Perhaps one of your lovesick suitors will turn to me once he realizes you are unattainable," she teased.

Edwina swatted her with a pillow. "Don't be silly."

"But I'm not!" Kate protested. And she wasn't. Quite frankly, this seemed to her the most likely avenue by which she might actually find a husband in town.

"Do you know what sort of man I'd like to marry?" Edwina asked, her eyes turning dreamy.

Kate shook her head.

"A scholar."

"A *scholar*?"

"A scholar," Edwina said firmly.

Kate cleared her throat. "I'm not certain you'll find many of those in town for the season."

"I know." Edwina let out a little sigh. "But the truth is—and you know this even if I am not supposed to let on in public—I'm really rather bookish. I'd much rather spend my day in a library than gadding about in Hyde Park. I think I should enjoy life with a man who enjoyed scholarly pursuits as well."

"Right. Hmmm . . ." Kate's mind worked frantically. Edwina wasn't likely to find a scholar back in Somerset, either. "You know, Edwina, it might be difficult to find you a true scholar outside the university towns. You might have to settle for a man who likes to read and learn as you do."

"That would be all right," Edwina said happily. "I'd be quite content with an amateur scholar."

Kate breathed a sigh of relief. Surely they could find someone in London who liked to read.

"And do you know what?" Edwina added. "You truly cannot tell a book by its cover. All sorts of people are amateur scholars. Why, even that Viscount Bridgerton Lady Whistledown keeps talking about might be a scholar at heart."

"Bite your tongue, Edwina. You are not to have anything to do with Viscount Bridgerton. Everyone knows he is the worst sort of rake. In fact, he's the worst rake, period. In all London. In the entire country!"

"I know, I was just using him as an example. Besides, he's not likely to choose a bride this year, anyway. Lady Whistledown said so, and you yourself said that she is almost always right."

Kate patted her sister on the arm. "Don't worry. We will find you a suitable husband. But *not*—not not not not not Viscount Bridgerton!"

At that very moment, the subject of their discussion was relaxing at White's with two of his three younger brothers, enjoying a late afternoon drink.

Anthony Bridgerton leaned back in his leather chair, regarded his scotch with a thoughtful expression as he swirled it about, and then announced, "I'm thinking about getting married."

Benedict Bridgerton, who had been indulging in a habit his mother detested—tipping his chair drunkenly on the back two legs—fell over.

Colin Bridgerton started to choke.

Luckily for Colin, Benedict regained his seat with enough time to smack him soundly on the back, sending a green olive sailing across the table.

It narrowly missed Anthony's ear.

Anthony let the indignity pass without comment. He was all too aware that his sudden declaration had come as a bit of a surprise.

Well, perhaps more than a bit. "Complete," "total," and "utter" were words that came to mind.

Anthony knew that he did not fit the image of a man who had settling down on his mind. He'd spent the last decade as the worst sort of rake, taking pleasure where he may. For as he well knew, life was short and certainly meant to be enjoyed. Oh, he'd had a certain code of honor. He never dallied with well-bred young women. Anyone who might have any right to demand marriage was strictly off-limits.

With four younger sisters of his own, Anthony had a healthy degree of respect for the good reputations of gently bred women. He'd already nearly fought a duel for one of his sisters, all over a slight to her honor. And as for the other three . . . he freely admitted that he broke out in a cold sweat at the mere thought of their getting involved with a man who bore a reputation like his.

No, he certainly wasn't about to despoil some other gentleman's younger sister.

But as for the other sort of women—the widows and actresses who knew what they wanted and what they were getting into—he'd enjoyed their company and enjoyed it well. Since the day he left Oxford and headed west to London, he'd not been without a mistress.

Sometimes, he thought wryly, he'd not been without two.

He'd ridden in nearly every horse race society had to offer, he'd boxed at Gentleman Jackson's, and he'd won more card games than he could count. (He'd lost a few, too, but he disregarded those.) He'd spent the decade of his twenties in a mindful pursuit of pleasure, tempered only by his overwhelming sense of responsibility to his family.

Edmund Bridgerton's death had been both sudden and unexpected; he'd not had a chance to make any final requests of his eldest son before he perished. But if he had, Anthony was certain that he would have asked him to care for his mother and siblings with the same diligence and affection Edmund had displayed.

And so in between Anthony's rounds of parties and horse races, he'd sent his brothers to Eton and Oxford, gone to a mind-numbing number of piano recitals given by his sisters (no easy feat; three out of four of them were tone deaf), and kept a close and watchful eye on the family finances. With seven brothers and sisters, he saw it as his duty to make sure there was enough money to secure all of their futures.

As he grew closer to thirty, he'd realized that he was spending more and more time tending to his heritage and family and less and less in his old pursuit of decadence and pleasure. And he'd realized that he liked it that way. He still kept a mistress, but never more than one at a time, and he discovered that he no longer felt the need to enter every horse race or stay late at a party just to win that last hand of cards.

His reputation, of course, stayed with him. He didn't mind that, actually. There were certain benefits to being thought England's most reprehensible rake. He was nearly universally feared, for example.

That was always a good thing.

But now it was time for marriage. He ought to settle

down, have a son. He had a title to pass on, after all. He did feel a rather sharp twinge of regret—and perhaps a touch of guilt as well—over the fact that it was unlikely that he'd live to see his son into adulthood. But what could he do? He was the firstborn Bridgerton of a firstborn Bridgerton of a firstborn Bridgerton eight times over. He had a dynastic responsibility to be fruitful and multiply.

Besides, he took some comfort in knowing that he'd leave three able and caring brothers behind. They'd see to it that his son was brought up with the love and honor that every Bridgerton enjoyed. His sisters would coddle the boy, and his mother might spoil him . . .

Anthony actually smiled a bit as he thought of his large and often boisterous family. His son would not need a father to be well loved.

And whatever children he sired—well, they probably wouldn't remember him after he was gone. They'd be young, unformed. It had not escaped Anthony's notice that of all the Bridgerton children, he, the eldest, was the one most deeply affected by their father's death.

Anthony downed another sip of his scotch and straightened his shoulders, pushing such unpleasant ruminations from his mind. He needed to focus on the matter at hand, namely, the pursuit of a wife.

Being a discerning and somewhat organized man, he'd made a mental list of requirements for the position. First, she ought to be reasonably attractive. She needn't be a raving beauty (although that would be nice), but if he was going to have to bed her, he figured a bit of attraction ought to make the job more pleasant.

Second, she couldn't be stupid. This, Anthony mused, might be the most difficult of his requirements to fill. He was not universally impressed by the mental prowess of London debutantes. The last time he'd made the mistake of engaging a young chit fresh out of the schoolroom in conversation, she'd been unable to discuss anything other than food (she'd had a plate of strawberries in her hand at the time) and the weather (and she hadn't even gotten *that* right; when Anthony had asked if she thought the weather was going to turn inclement, she'd replied, "I'm sure I don't know. I've never been to Clement.")

He might be able to avoid conversation with a wife who was less than brilliant, but he did *not* want stupid children.

Third—and this was the most important—she couldn't be anyone with whom he might actually fall in love.

Under no circumstances would this rule be broken.

He wasn't a complete cynic; he knew that true love existed. Anyone who'd ever been in the same room with his parents knew that true love existed.

But love was a complication he wished to avoid. He had no desire for his life to be visited by that particular miracle.

And since Anthony was used to getting what he wanted, he had no doubt that he would find an attractive, intelligent woman with whom he would never fall in love. And what was the problem with that? Chances were he wouldn't have found the love of his life even if he had been looking for her. Most men didn't.

"Good God, Anthony, what has you frowning so? Not that olive. I saw it clearly and it didn't even touch you."

Benedict's voice broke him out of his reverie, and Anthony blinked a few times before answering, "Nothing. Nothing at all."

He hadn't, of course, shared his thoughts about his own mortality with anyone else, even his brothers. It was not the sort of thing one wanted to advertise. Hell, if someone had come up to him and said the same thing, he probably would have laughed him right out the door.

But no one else could understand the depth of the bond he'd felt with his father. And no one could possibly understand the way Anthony felt it in his bones, how he simply knew that he could not live longer than his father had done. Edmund had been everything to him. He'd always aspired to be as great a man as his father, knowing that

that was unlikely, yet trying all the same. To actually achieve more than Edmund had—in any way—that was nothing short of impossible.

Anthony's father was, quite simply, the greatest man he'd ever known, possibly the greatest man who'd ever lived. To think that he might be more than that seemed conceited in the extreme.

Something had happened to him the night his father had died, when he'd remained in his parents' bedroom with the body, just sitting there for hours, watching his father and trying desperately to remember every moment they'd shared. It would be so easy to forget the little things—how Edmund would squeeze Anthony's upper arm when he needed encouragement. Or how he could recite from memory Balthazar's entire "Sigh No More" song from *Much Ado About Nothing,* not because he thought it particularly meaningful but just because he liked it.

And when Anthony finally emerged from the room, the first streaks of dawn pinking the sky, he somehow knew that his days were numbered, and numbered in the same way Edmund's had been.

"Spit it out," Benedict said, breaking into his thoughts once again. "I won't offer you a penny for your thoughts, since I know they can't possibly be worth that much, but what are you thinking about?"

Anthony suddenly sat up straighter, determined to force his attention back to the matter at hand. After all, he had a bride to choose, and that was surely serious business. "Who is considered the diamond of this season?" he asked.

His brothers paused for a moment to think on this, and then Colin said, "Edwina Sheffield. Surely you've seen her. Rather petite, with blond hair and blue eyes. You can usually spot her by the sheeplike crowd of lovesick suitors following her about."

Anthony ignored his brother's attempts at sarcastic humor. "Has she a brain?"

Colin blinked, as if the question of a woman with a brain were one that had never occurred to him. "Yes, I rather think she does. I once heard her discussing mythology with Middlethorpe, and it sounded as if she had the right of it."

"Good," Anthony said, letting his glass of scotch hit the table with a thunk. "Then I'll marry her."

Chapter 2

At the Hartside ball Wednesday night, Viscount Bridgerton was seen dancing with more than one eligible young lady. This behavior can only be termed "startling" as Bridgerton normally avoids proper young misses with a perseverance that would be impressive were it not so utterly frustrating to all marriage-minded Mamas.

Can it be that the viscount read This Author's most recent column and, in that perverse manner all males of the species seem to endorse, decided to prove This Author wrong?

It may seem that This Author is ascribing to herself far more importance than She actually wields, but men have certainly made decisions based on far, far less.

LADY WHISTLEDOWN'S SOCIETY PAPERS, 22 APRIL 1814

By eleven o'clock that evening, all of Kate's fears had been realized.

Anthony Bridgerton had asked Edwina to dance.

Even worse, Edwina had accepted.

Even worse, Mary was gazing at the couple as if she'd like to reserve a church that minute.

"Will you stop that?" Kate hissed, poking her stepmother in the ribs.

"Stop what?"

"Looking at them like that!"

Mary blinked. "Like what?"

"Like you're planning the wedding breakfast."

"Oh." Mary's cheeks turned pink. A guilty sort of pink.

"Mary!"

"Well, I might have been," Mary admitted. "And what's wrong with that, I might ask? He'd be a superb catch for Edwina."

"Were you listening this afternoon in the drawing room? It's bad enough that Edwina has any number of rakes and rogues sniffing about her. You cannot imagine the amount of time it has taken me to sort the good suitors from the bad. But Bridgerton!" Kate shuddered. "He's quite possibly the worst rake in all London. You cannot want her to marry a man like him."

"Don't you presume to tell me what I can and cannot do, Katharine Grace Sheffield," Mary said sharply, stiffening her spine until she'd straightened to her full height—which was still a full head shorter than Kate. "I am still your mother. Well, your stepmother. And that counts for something."

Kate immediately felt like a worm. Mary was all she'd ever known as a mother, and she'd never, not even once, made Kate feel any less her daughter than Edwina was. She'd tucked Kate into bed at night, told her stories, kissed her, hugged her, helped her through the awkward years between childhood and adulthood. The only thing she had not done was ask Kate to call her "Mother."

"It counts," Kate said in a quiet voice, letting her gaze fall shamefully down to her feet. "It counts for a lot. And you *are* my mother. In every way that matters."

Mary stared at her for a long moment, then started to blink rather furiously. "Oh, dear," she choked out, reaching into her reticule for a handkerchief. "Now you've gone and turned me into a watering pot."

"I'm sorry," Kate murmured. "Oh, here, turn around so no one sees you. There you are."

Mary pulled out a white square of linen and dabbed at her eyes, the exact same blue as Edwina's. "I do love you, Kate. You know that, don't you?"

"Of course!" Kate exclaimed, shocked that Mary would even ask. "And you know . . . you know that I . . ."

"I know." Mary patted her arm. "Of course I know. It's just that when you agree to be mother to a child you haven't borne, your responsibility is twice as great. You must work even harder to ensure that child's happiness and welfare."

"Oh, Mary, I do love you. And I love Edwina."

At the mention of Edwina's name, they both turned and looked out across the ballroom at her, dancing prettily with the viscount. As usual, Edwina was a vision of petite loveliness. Her blond hair was swept atop her head, a few stray curls left to frame her face, and her form was the epitome of grace as she moved through the steps of the dance.

The viscount, Kate noted with irritation, was blindingly handsome. Dressed in stark black and white, he eschewed the garish colors that had become popular among the more foppish members of the *ton*. He was tall, stood straight and proud, and had thick chestnut hair that tended to fall forward over his brow.

He was, on the surface at least, everything a man was meant to be.

"They make a handsome couple, don't they?" Mary murmured.

Kate bit her tongue. She actually bit her tongue.

"He's a trifle tall for her, but I don't see that as an insurmountable obstacle, do you?"

Kate clasped her hands together and let her nails bite into her skin. It said a great deal about the strength of her grip that she could feel them all the way through her kid gloves.

Mary smiled. A rather sly smile, Kate thought. She gave her stepmother a suspicious look.

"He dances well, don't you think?" Mary asked.

"He is not going to marry Edwina!" Kate burst out.

Mary's smile slid straight into a grin. "I was wondering how long you'd manage to hold your silence."

"Far longer than was my natural inclination," Kate retorted, practically biting each word.

"Yes, that much was clear."

"Mary, you know he is not the sort of man we want for Edwina."

Mary cocked her head slightly to the side and raised her brows. "I believe the question ought to be whether he is the sort of man *Edwina* wants for Edwina."

"He's not that, either!" Kate replied heatedly. "Just this afternoon she told me that she wanted to marry a scholar. A scholar!" She jerked her head toward the dark-haired cretin dancing with her sister. "Does he look like a scholar to you?"

"No, but then again, you don't look particularly like an accomplished watercolorist, and yet I know that you are." Mary smirked a bit, which needled Kate to no end, and waited for her reply.

"I'll allow," Kate said through clenched teeth, "that one ought not judge a person merely on his outer appearance, but surely you must agree. From all that we have heard of him, he does not seem the sort to spend his afternoons bent over musty books in a library."

"Perhaps not," Mary mused, "but I had a lovely chat with his mother earlier this evening."

"His mother?" Kate fought to follow the conversation. "What has that to do with anything?"

Mary shrugged. "I find it difficult to believe that such a gracious and intelligent lady could have raised anything but the finest of gentlemen, regardless of his reputation."

"But Mary—"

"When you are a mother," she said loftily, "you will understand what I mean."

"But—"

"Have I told you," Mary said, the purposeful tone of her voice indicating that she'd meant to interrupt, "how lovely you look in that green gauze? I'm so glad we chose it."

Kate looked dumbly down at her dress, wondering why on earth Mary had changed the subject so suddenly.

"The color suits you well. Lady Whistledown shall not be calling you a singed blade of grass in Friday's column!"

Kate stared at Mary in dismay. Perhaps her stepmother had become overheated. It *was* crowded in the ballroom, and the air had grown thick.

Then she felt Mary's finger jabbing her directly below her left shoulder blade, and she knew something else was afoot entirely.

"Mr. Bridgerton!" Mary suddenly exclaimed, sounding as gleeful as a young girl.

Horrified, Kate jerked her head up to see a startlingly handsome man approach them. A startlingly handsome man who looked startlingly like the viscount currently dancing with her sister.

She swallowed. It was either that or let her jaw hang open.

"Mr. Bridgerton!" Mary said again. "How nice to see you. This is my daughter Katharine."

He took her limp, gloved hand and brushed an airy kiss across her knuckles. So airy, in fact, that Kate rather suspected he hadn't kissed her at all.

"Miss Sheffield," he murmured.

"Kate," Mary continued, "this is Mr. Colin Bridgerton. I met him earlier this evening while I was talking with his mother, Lady Bridgerton." She turned to Colin and beamed. "Such a lovely lady."

He grinned back. "We think so."

Mary tittered. Tittered! Kate thought she might gag.

"Kate," Mary said again, "Mr. Bridgerton is brother to the viscount. Who is dancing with Edwina," she added unnecessarily.

"I gathered," Kate replied.

Colin Bridgerton shot her a sideways glance, and she knew instantly that he had not missed the vague sarcasm in her tone.

"It is a pleasure to meet you, Miss Sheffield," he said politely. "I do hope you will favor me with one of your dances this evening."

"I— Of course." She cleared her throat. "I would be honored."

"Kate," Mary said, nudging her softly, "show him your dance card."

"Oh! Yes, of course." Kate fumbled for her dance card, which was tied prettily to her wrist with a green ribbon. That she had to fumble for anything actually tied to her body was a bit alarming, but Kate decided to blame her lack of composure on the sudden and unexpected appearance of a heretofore unknown Bridgerton brother.

That, and the unfortunate fact that even under the best of circumstances she was never the most graceful girl in the room.

Colin filled his name in for one of the dances later that evening, then asked if she might like to walk with him to the lemonade table.

"Go, go," Mary said, before Kate could reply. "Don't worry about me. I'll be just fine without you."

"I can bring you back a glass," Kate offered, trying to figure out if it was possible to glare at her stepmother without Mr. Bridgerton noticing.

"Not necessary. I really should get back to my position with all the other chaperones and mamas." Mary whipped her head around frantically until she spied a familiar face. "Oh, look, there is Mrs. Featherington. I must be off. Portia! Portia!"

Kate watched her stepmother's rapidly retreating form

for a moment before turning back to Mr. Bridgerton. "I think," she said dryly, "that she doesn't want any lemonade."

A sparkle of humor glinted in his emerald green eyes. "Either that or she's planning to run all the way to Spain to pick the lemons herself."

Despite herself, Kate laughed. She didn't want to like Mr. Colin Bridgerton. She didn't much want to like any Bridgerton after all she'd read about the viscount in the newspaper. But she allowed that it probably wasn't fair to judge a man based on his brother's misdeeds, so she forced herself to relax a bit.

"And are you thirsty," she asked, "or were you merely being polite?"

"I am always polite," he said with a wicked grin, "but I am thirsty as well."

Kate took one look at that grin, lethally combined with those devastating green eyes, and nearly groaned. "You are a rake as well," she said with a sigh.

Colin choked—on what, she did not know, but he choked nonetheless. "I beg your pardon?"

Kate's face flushed as she realized with horror that she'd spoken aloud. "No, it is I who should beg your pardon. Please forgive me. That was unforgivably rude."

"No, no," he said quickly, looking terribly interested and not a little bit amused, "do continue."

Kate swallowed. There was really no way to get out of it now. "I was merely—" She cleared her throat. "If I might be frank . . ."

He nodded, his sly grin telling her that he could not imagine her being anything *but* frank.

Kate cleared her throat yet again. Really, this was getting ridiculous. She was starting to sound as if she'd swallowed a toad. "It had occurred to me that you might be rather like your brother, that is all."

"My brother?"

"The viscount," she said, thinking it must be obvious.

"I have three brothers," he explained.

"Oh." Now she felt stupid. "I'm sorry."

"I'm sorry, too," he said with great feeling. "Most of the time they're a dreadful nuisance."

Kate had to cough to cover up her small gasp of surprise.

"But at least you were not comparing me to Gregory," he said with a dramatic sigh of relief. He shot her a cheeky, sideways look. "He's thirteen."

Kate caught the smile in his eyes and realized he'd been bamming her all along. This was not a man who wished his brothers off to perdition. "You're rather devoted to your family, aren't you?" she asked.

His eyes, which had been laughing throughout the conversation, turned dead serious without even a blink. "Utterly."

"As am I," Kate said pointedly.

"And that means?"

"It means," she said, knowing she should hold her tongue but speaking anyway, "that I will not allow anyone to break my sister's heart."

Colin remained silent for a moment, slowly turning his head to watch his brother and Edwina, who were just then finishing up their dance. "I see," he murmured.

"Do you?"

"Oh, indeed." They arrived at the lemonade table, and he reached out and took two glasses, handing one to her. She'd already had three glasses of lemonade that evening, a fact of which she was sure Mary had been aware before she'd insisted Kate have some more. But it was hot in the ballroom—it was always hot in ballrooms—and she was thirsty again.

Colin took a leisurely sip, watching her over the rim of his glass, then said, "My brother has it in his mind to settle down this year."

Two could play at this game, Kate thought. She took a sip of her lemonade—slowly—before speaking. "Is that so?"

"I would certainly be in a position to know."

"He is reputed to be quite a rake."

Colin looked at her assessingly. "That is true."

"It is difficult to imagine so notorious a rogue settling down with one woman and finding happiness in marriage."

"You seem to have given such a scenario a great deal of thought, Miss Sheffield."

She leveled a frank stare directly at his face. "Your brother is not the first man of questionable character to court my sister, Mr. Bridgerton. And I assure you, I do not take my sister's happiness lightly."

"Surely any girl would find happiness in marriage to a wealthy and titled gentleman. Isn't that what a season in London is all about?"

"Perhaps," Kate allowed, "but I'm afraid that line of thinking does not address the true problem at hand."

"Which is?"

"Which is that a husband can break a heart with far greater intensity than a mere suitor." She smiled—a small, knowing sort of smile—then added, "Don't you think?"

"Having never been married, I am certainly not in a position to speculate."

"Shame, shame, Mr. Bridgerton. That was the worst sort of evasion."

"Was it? I rather thought it might be the best. I am clearly losing my touch."

"That, I fear, will never be a worry." Kate finished the rest of her lemonade. It was a small glass; Lady Hartside, their hostess, was notoriously stingy.

"You are far too generous," he said.

She smiled, a real smile this time. "I am rarely accused of that, Mr. Bridgerton."

He laughed. Right out loud in the middle of the ballroom. Kate realized with discomfort that they were suddenly the object of numerous curious stares.

"You," he said, still sounding most heartily amused, "must meet my brother."

"The viscount?" she asked with disbelief.

"Well, you might enjoy Gregory's company as well," he allowed, "but as I said, he is only thirteen and likely to put a frog on your chair."

"And the viscount?"

"Is not likely to put a frog on your chair," he said with an utterly straight face.

How Kate managed not to laugh she would never know. Keeping her lips completely straight and serious, she replied, "I see. He has a great deal to recommend him, then."

Colin grinned. "He's not such a bad sort."

"I am much relieved. I shall begin planning the wedding breakfast immediately."

Colin's mouth fell open. "I didn't mean— You shouldn't— That is to say, such a move would be premature—"

Kate took pity on him and said, "I was joking."

His face flushed slightly. "Of course."

"Now, if you'll excuse me, I must make my farewell."

He raised a brow. "Not leaving so early, are you, Miss Sheffield?"

"Not at all." But she wasn't about to tell him she had to go relieve herself. Four glasses of lemonade tended to do that to a body. "I promised a friend I would meet her for a moment."

"It has been a pleasure." He executed a smart bow. "May I see you to your destination?"

"No, thank you. I shall be quite all right on my own." And with a smile over her shoulder, she made her retreat from the ballroom.

Colin Bridgerton watched her go with a thoughtful expression, then made his way to his older brother, who was leaning against a wall, arms crossed in an almost belligerent manner.

"Anthony!" he called out, slapping his brother on the back. "How was your dance with the lovely Miss Sheffield?"

"She'll do," was Anthony's terse reply. They both knew what that meant.

"Really?" Colin's lips twitched ever so slightly. "You should meet the sister, then."

"I beg your pardon?"

"Her sister," Colin repeated, starting to laugh. "You simply must meet her sister."

Twenty minutes later, Anthony was confident he'd gotten the whole story on Edwina Sheffield from Colin. And it seemed that the road to Edwina's heart and hand in marriage lay squarely through her sister.

Edwina Sheffield apparently would not marry without the approval of her older sister. According to Colin, this was common knowledge, and had been for at least a week, ever since Edwina had made an announcement to this effect at the annual Smythe-Smith musicale. The Bridgerton brothers had all missed this momentous statement, as they avoided Smythe-Smith musicales like the plague (as did anyone with any affection for Bach, Mozart, or music in any form.)

Edwina's older sister, one Katharine Sheffield, more commonly known as Kate, was also making her debut this year, even though she was reputed to be at least one and twenty. Such timing led Anthony to believe that the Sheffields must be among the less wealthy ranks of the *ton,* a fact which suited him nicely. He had no need of a bride with a great dowry, and a bride without one might have more need of *him.*

Anthony believed in using all of his advantages.

Unlike Edwina, the elder Miss Sheffield had not immediately taken the *ton* by storm. According to Colin, she was generally well liked, but she lacked Edwina's dazzling beauty. She was tall where Edwina was tiny, and dark where Edwina was fair. She also lacked Edwina's dazzling grace. Again, according to Colin (who, though recently arrived in London for the season, was a veritable font of knowledge and gossip), more than one gentleman had reported sore feet after a dance with Katharine Sheffield.

The entire situation seemed a bit absurd to Anthony. After all, who had ever heard of a girl requiring her sister's approval for a husband? A father, yes, a brother, or even a mother, but a sister? It was unfathomable. And furthermore, it seemed odd that Edwina would look to Katharine for guidance when Katharine clearly did not know what she was about in matters of the *ton.*

But Anthony didn't particularly feel like searching out another suitable candidate to court, so he conveniently decided this simply meant that family was important to Edwina. And since family was all-important to him, this was one more indication that she would make an excellent choice as a wife.

So now it appeared that all he had to do was charm the sister. And how difficult could that be?

"You'll have no trouble winning her over," Colin predicted, a confident smile lighting his face. "No trouble at all. A shy, aging spinster? She's probably never received attentions from such a man as you. She'll never know what hit her."

"I don't want her to fall in love with me," Anthony retorted. "I just want her to recommend me to her sister."

"You can't fail," Colin said. "You simply can't fail. Trust me, I spent a few minutes in conversation with her earlier this evening, and she could not say enough about you."

"Good." Anthony pushed himself up off the wall and gazed out with an air of determination. "Now, where is she? I need you to introduce us."

Colin scanned the room for a minute or so, then said, "Ah, there she is. She's coming this way, as a matter of fact. What a marvelous coincidence."

Anthony was coming to believe that nothing within five yards of his younger brother was ever a coincidence, but he followed his gaze nonetheless. "Which one is she?"

"In the green," Colin said, motioning toward her with a barely perceptible nod of his chin.

She was not at all what he'd expected, Anthony realized as he watched her pick her way through the crowds. She was certainly no ape-leading amazon; it was only when compared to Edwina, who barely touched five feet, that she would appear so tall. In fact, Miss Katharine Sheffield was quite pleasant-looking, with thick, medium brown hair and dark eyes. Her skin was pale, her lips pink, and she held herself with an air of confidence he could not help but find attractive.

She would certainly never be considered a diamond of the first water like her sister, but Anthony didn't see why she shouldn't be able to find a husband of her own. Perhaps after he married Edwina he'd provide a dowry for her. It seemed the very least a man could do.

Beside him, Colin strode forward, pushing through the crowd. "Miss Sheffield! Miss Sheffield!"

Anthony swept along in Colin's wake, mentally preparing himself to charm Edwina's older sister. An underappreciated spinster, was she? He'd have her eating out of his hand in no time.

"Miss Sheffield," Colin was saying, "what a delight to see you again."

She looked a bit perplexed, and Anthony didn't blame her. Colin was making it sound as if they'd bumped into each other accidentally, when they all knew he'd trampled at least a half dozen people to reach her side.

"And it's lovely to see you again as well, sir," she replied wryly. "And so unexpectedly soon after our last encounter."

Anthony smiled to himself. She had a sharper wit than he'd been led to believe.

Colin grinned winningly, and Anthony had the distinct

and unsettling impression that his brother was up to something. "I can't explain why," Colin said to Miss Sheffield, "but it suddenly seemed imperative that I introduce you to my brother."

She looked abruptly to Colin's right and stiffened as her gaze settled on Anthony. In fact, she rather looked as if she'd just swallowed an antidote.

This, Anthony thought, was odd.

"How kind of you," Miss Sheffield murmured—between her teeth.

"Miss Sheffield," Colin continued brightly, motioning to Anthony, "my brother Anthony, Viscount Bridgerton. Anthony, Miss Katharine Sheffield. I believe you made the acquaintance of her sister earlier this evening."

"Indeed," Anthony said, becoming aware of an overwhelming desire—no, *need*—to strangle his brother.

Miss Sheffield bobbed a quick, awkward curtsy. "Lord Bridgerton," she said, "it is an honor to make your acquaintance."

Colin made a noise that sounded suspiciously like a snort. Or maybe a laugh. Or maybe both.

And Anthony suddenly *knew*. One look at his brother's face should have given it all away. This was no shy, retiring, underappreciated spinster. And whatever she had said to Colin earlier that evening, it had contained no compliments about Anthony.

Fratricide was legal in England, wasn't it? If not, it damn well should have been.

Anthony belatedly realized that Miss Sheffield had held out her hand to him, as was only polite. He took it and brushed a light kiss across her gloved knuckles. "Miss Sheffield," he murmured unthinkingly, "you are as lovely as your sister."

If she had seemed uncomfortable before, her bearing now turned downright hostile. And Anthony realized with a mental slap that he'd said *exactly* the wrong thing. Of course he should not have compared her to her sister.

It was the one compliment she could never have believed.

"And you, Lord Bridgerton," she replied in a tone that could have frozen champagne, "are almost as handsome as your brother."

Colin snorted again, only this time it sounded as if he were being strangled.

"Are you all right?" Miss Sheffield asked.

"He's fine," Anthony barked.

She ignored him, keeping her attention on Colin. "Are you certain?"

Colin nodded furiously. "Tickle in my throat."

"Or perhaps a guilty conscience?" Anthony suggested.

Colin turned deliberately from his brother to Kate. "I think I might need another glass of lemonade," he gasped.

"Or maybe," said Anthony, "something stronger. Hemlock, perhaps?"

Miss Sheffield clapped a hand over her mouth, presumably to stifle a burst of horrified laughter.

"Lemonade will do just fine," Colin returned smoothly.

"Would you like me to fetch you a glass?" she asked. Anthony noticed that she'd already stepped out with one foot, looking for any excuse to flee.

Colin shook his head. "No, no, I'm quite capable. But I do believe I had reserved this next dance with you, Miss Sheffield."

"I shall not hold you to it," she said with a wave of her hand.

"Oh, but I could not live with myself were I to leave you unattended," he replied.

Anthony could see Miss Sheffield growing worried at the devilish gleam in Colin's eye. He took a rather uncharitable pleasure in this. His reaction was, he knew, a touch out of proportion. But something about this Miss Katharine Sheffield sparked his temper and made him positively *itch* to do battle with her.

And win. That much went without saying.

"Anthony," Colin said, sounding so deucedly innocent and earnest that it was all Anthony could do not to kill him on the spot, "you're not engaged for this dance, are you?"

Anthony said nothing, just glared at him.

"Good. Then you will dance with Miss Sheffield."

"I'm sure that's not necessary," the woman in question blurted out.

Anthony glared at his brother, then for good measure at Miss Sheffield, who was looking at him as if he'd just despoiled ten virgins in her presence.

"Oh, but it is," Colin said with great drama, ignoring the optical daggers being hurled across their little threesome. "I could never dream of abandoning a young lady in her hour of need. How"—he shuddered—"ungentlemanly."

Anthony thought seriously about pursuing some ungentlemanly behavior himself. Perhaps planting his fist in Colin's face.

"I assure you," Miss Sheffield said quickly, "that being left to my own devices would be far preferable to dan—"

Enough, Anthony thought savagely, was really enough. His own brother had already played him for a fool; he was not going to stand idly by while he was insulted by Edwina's sharp-tongued spinster sister. He laid a heavy hand on Miss Sheffield's arm and said, "Allow me to prevent you from making a grievous mistake, Miss Sheffield."

She stiffened. How, he did not know; her back was already ramrod straight. "I beg your pardon," she said.

"I believe," he said smoothly, "that you were about to say something you would soon regret."

"No," she said, sounding deliberately thoughtful, "I don't think regrets were in my future."

"They will be," he said ominously. And then he grabbed her arm and practically dragged her onto the ballroom floor.

Chapter 3

Viscount Bridgerton was also seen dancing with Miss Katharine Sheffield, elder sister to the fair Edwina. This can only mean one thing, as it has not escaped the notice of This Author that the elder Miss Sheffield has been in much demand on the dance floor ever since the younger Miss Sheffield made her bizarre and unprecedented announcement at the Smythe-Smith musicale last week.

Whoever heard of a girl needing her sister's permission to choose a husband?

And perhaps more importantly, whoever decided that the words "Smythe-Smith" and "musicale" might be used in the same sentence? This Author has attended one of these gatherings in the past, and heard nothing that might ethically be termed "music."

LADY WHISTLEDOWN'S SOCIETY PAPERS, 22 APRIL 1814

There was really nothing she could do, Kate realized with dismay. He was a viscount, and she was a mere nobody from Somerset, and they were both in the middle of a crowded ballroom. It didn't matter if she'd disliked him on sight. She *had* to dance with him.

"There is no need to drag me," she hissed.

He made a great show of loosening his grip.

Kate ground her teeth together and swore to herself that this man would never take her sister as his bride. His manner was too cold, too superior. He was, she thought a touch unfairly, too handsome as well, with velvety brown eyes that matched his hair to perfection. He was tall, certainly over six feet, although probably not by more than an inch, and his lips, while classically beautiful (Kate had studied enough art to regard herself qualified to make such a judgment) were tight at the corners, as if he did not know how to smile.

"Now then," he said, once their feet began to move in the familiar steps, "suppose you tell me why you hate me."

Kate trod on his foot. Lord, he was direct. "I beg your pardon?"

"There is no need to maim me, Miss Sheffield."

"It was an accident, I assure you." And it *was,* even if she didn't really mind this particular example of her lack of grace.

"Why," he mused, "do I find I have difficulty believing you?"

Honesty, Kate quickly decided, would be her best strategy. If he could be direct, well then, so could she. "Probably," she answered with a wicked smile, "because you know that had it occurred to me to step on your foot on purpose, I would have done so."

He threw back his head and laughed. It was not the reaction she'd been either expecting or hoping for. Come to think of it, she had no idea what sort of reaction she'd been hoping for, but this *certainly* wasn't what she'd been expecting.

"Will you stop, my lord?" she whispered urgently. "People are starting to stare."

"People started to stare two minutes ago," he returned. "It's not often a man such as I dances with a woman such as you."

As barbs went, this one was well aimed, but sadly for him, also incorrect. "Not true," she replied jauntily. "You are certainly not the first of Edwina's besotted idiots to attempt to gain her favor through me."

He grinned. "Not suitors, but idiots?"

She caught his gaze with hers and was surprised to find true mirth in his eyes. "Surely you're not going to hand me such a delicious piece of bait as that, my lord?"

"And yet you did not take it," he mused.

Kate looked down to see if there was some way she might discreetly step on his foot again.

"I have very thick boots, Miss Sheffield," he said.

Her head snapped back up in surprise.

One corner of his mouth curved up in a mockery of a smile. "And quick eyes as well."

"Apparently so. I shall have to watch my step around you, to be sure."

"My goodness," he drawled, "was that a compliment? I might expire from the shock of it."

"If you'd like to consider that a compliment, I give you leave to do so," she said airily. "You're not likely to receive many more."

"You wound me, Miss Sheffield."

"Does that mean that your skin is not as thick as your boots?"

"Oh, not nearly."

She felt herself laugh before she realized she was amused. "That I find difficult to believe."

He waited for her smile to melt away, then said, "You did not answer my question. Why do you hate me?"

A rush of air slipped through Kate's lips. She hadn't expected him to repeat the question. Or at least she'd hoped that he would not. "I do not hate you, my lord," she replied, choosing her words with great care. "I do not even know you."

"Knowing is rarely a prerequisite for hating," he said softly, his eyes settling on hers with lethal steadiness. "Come now, Miss Sheffield, you don't seem a coward to me. Answer the question."

Kate held silent for a full minute. It was true, she had not been predisposed to like the man. She *certainly* wasn't about to give her blessing to his courtship of Edwina. She didn't believe for one second that reformed rakes made the best husbands. She wasn't even sure that a rake could be properly reformed in the first place.

But he might have been able to overcome her preconceptions. He could have been charming and sincere and straightforward, and been able to convince her that the stories about him in *Whistledown* were an exaggeration, that he was not the worst rogue London had seen since the turn of the century. He might have convinced her that he held to a code of honor, that he was a man of principles and honesty . . .

If he hadn't gone and compared her to Edwina.

For nothing could have been more obvious a lie. She knew she wasn't an antidote; her face and form were pleasing enough. But there was simply no way she could be compared to Edwina in this measure and emerge as her equal. Edwina was truly a diamond of the first water, and Kate could never be more than average and unremarkable.

And if this man was saying otherwise, then he had some ulterior motive, because it was obvious he wasn't blind.

He could have offered her any other empty compliment and she would have accepted it as a gentleman's polite conversation. She might have even been flattered if his words had struck anywhere close to the truth. But to compare her to Edwina . . .

Kate adored her sister. She truly did. And she knew better than anyone that Edwina's heart was as beautiful and radiant as her face. She didn't like to think herself jealous, but still . . . somehow the comparison stung right to the core.

"I do not hate you," she finally replied. Her eyes were trained on his chin, but she had no patience for cowardice, especially within herself, so she forced herself to meet his gaze when she added, "But I find I cannot like you."

Something in his eyes told her that he appreciated her stark honesty. "And why is that?" he asked softly.

"May I be frank?"

His lips twitched. "Please do."

"You are dancing with me right now because you wish to court my sister. This does not bother me," she hastened to assure him. "I am well used to receiving attentions from Edwina's suitors."

Her mind was clearly not on her feet. Anthony pulled his foot out of the way of hers before she could injure him again. He noticed with interest that she was back to referring to them as suitors rather than idiots. "Please continue," he murmured.

"You are not the sort of man I would wish my sister to marry," she said simply. Her manner was direct, and her intelligent brown eyes never left his. "You are a rake. You are a rogue. You are, in fact, notorious for being both. I would not allow my sister within ten feet of you."

"And yet," he said with a wicked little smile, "I waltzed with her earlier this evening."

"An act which shall not be repeated, I can assure you."

"And is it your place to decide Edwina's fate?"

"Edwina trusts my judgment," she said primly.

"I see," he said in what he hoped was his most mysterious manner. "That is very interesting. I thought Edwina was an adult."

"Edwina is but seventeen years old!"

"And you are so ancient at, what, twenty years of age?"

"Twenty-one," she bit off.

"Ah, that makes you a veritable expert on men, and husbands in particular. Especially since you have been married yourself, yes?"

"You know I am unwed," she ground out.

Anthony stifled the urge to smile. Good Lord, but it was *fun* baiting the elder Miss Sheffield. "I think," he said, keeping his words slow and deliberate, "that you have found it relatively easy to manage most of the men who have come knocking on your sister's door. Is that true?"

She kept her stony silence.

"Is it?"

Finally she gave him one curt nod.

"I thought so," he murmured. "You seem the sort who would."

She glared at him with such intensity that it was all he could do to keep from laughing. If he weren't dancing, he probably would have stroked his chin in an affectation of deep thought. But since his hands were otherwise engaged, he had to settle for a ponderous tilt of his head, combined with an arch raise of his eyebrows. "But I also think," he added, "that you made a grave mistake when you thought to manage *me*."

Kate's lips were set in a grim, straight line, but she managed to say, "I do not seek to manage you, Lord Bridgerton. I only seek to keep you away from my sister."

"Which just goes to show, Miss Sheffield, how very little you know of men. At least of the rakish, roguish variety." He leaned in closer, letting his hot breath brush against her cheek.

She shivered. He'd known she'd shiver.

He smiled wickedly. "There is very little we relish more than a challenge."

The music drew to a close, leaving them standing in the middle of the ballroom floor, facing one another. Anthony took her arm, but before he led her back to the perimeter of the room, he put his lips very close to her ear and whispered, "And you, Miss Sheffield, have issued to me a most delicious challenge."

Kate stepped on his foot. Hard. Enough to make him let out a small, decidedly unrakish, unroguish squeak.

When he glared at her, though, she just shrugged and said, "It was my only defense."

His eyes darkened. "You, Miss Sheffield, are a menace."

"And you, Lord Bridgerton, need thicker boots."

His grasp tightened on her arm. "Before I return you to the sanctuary of the chaperones and spinsters, there is one thing we need to make clear."

Kate held her breath. She did not like the hard tone of his voice.

"I am going to court your sister. And should I decide that she will make a suitable Lady Bridgerton, I will make her my wife."

Kate whipped her head up to face him, fire flashing in her eyes. "And I suppose, then, that you think it is *your* place to decide Edwina's fate. Do not forget, my lord, that even if you decide she will make a *suitable*"—she sneered the word—"Lady Bridgerton, she might choose otherwise."

He looked down at her with the confidence of a male who is never crossed. "Should I decide to ask Edwina, she will not say no."

"Are you trying to tell me that no woman has ever been able to resist you?"

He did not answer, just raised one supercilious brow and let her draw her own conclusions.

Kate wrenched her arm free and strode back to her stepmother, shaking with fury, resentment, and not a little bit of fear.

Because she had an awful feeling that he did not lie. And if he really did turn out to be irresistible . . .

Kate shuddered. She and Edwina were going to be in big, big trouble.

The next afternoon was like any following a major ball. The Sheffields' drawing room was filled to bursting with flower bouquets, each one accompanied by a crisp white card bearing the name, "Edwina Sheffield."

A simple "Miss Sheffield" would have sufficed, Kate thought with a grimace, but she supposed one couldn't really fault Edwina's suitors for wanting to make certain the flowers went to the correct Miss Sheffield.

Not that *anyone* was likely to make a mistake on that measure. Floral arrangements generally went to Edwina. In fact, there was nothing general about it; every bouquet that had arrived at the Sheffield residence in the last month had gone to Edwina.

Kate liked to think she had the last laugh, however. Most of the flowers made Edwina sneeze, so they tended to end up in Kate's chamber, anyway.

"You beautiful thing," she said, lovingly fingering a fine orchid. "I think you belong right on my bedstand. And you"—she leaned forward and sniffed at a bouquet of perfect white roses—"you will look smashing on my dressing table."

"Do you always talk to flowers?"

Kate whirled around at the sound of a deep male voice. Good heavens, it was Lord Bridgerton, looking sinfully handsome in a blue morning coat. What the devil was *he* doing here?

No sense in not asking.

"What the dev—" She caught herself just in time. She would not let this man reduce her to cursing aloud, no matter how often she did it in her head. "What are *you* doing here?"

He raised a brow as he adjusted the huge bouquet of flowers he had tucked under his arm. Pink roses, she noted. Perfect buds. They were lovely. Simple and elegant. Exactly the sort of thing she'd choose for herself.

"I believe it's customary for suitors to call upon young women, yes?" he murmured. "Or did I misplace my etiquette book?"

"I meant," Kate growled, "how did you get in? No one alerted me to your arrival."

He cocked his head toward the hall. "The usual manner. I knocked on your front door."

Kate's look of irritation at his sarcasm did not prevent him from continuing with, "Amazingly enough, your butler answered. Then I gave him my card, he took a look at it, and showed me to the drawing room. Much as I'd like to claim some sort of devious, underhanded subterfuge," he continued, maintaining a rather impressively supercilious tone, "it was actually quite aboveboard and straightforward."

"Infernal butler," Kate muttered. "He's supposed to see if we're 'at home' before showing you in."

"Maybe he had previous instructions that you would be 'at home' for me under any circumstances."

She bristled. "I gave him no such instructions."

"No," Lord Bridgerton said with a chuckle, "I wouldn't have thought so."

"And I know Edwina didn't."

He smiled. "Perhaps your mother?"

Of course. "Mary," she groaned, a world of accusation in the single word.

"You call her by her given name?" he asked politely.

She nodded. "She's actually my stepmother. Although she's really all I know. She married my father when I was but three. I don't know why I still call her Mary." She gave her head a little shake as her shoulders lifted into a perplexed shrug. "I just do."

His brown eyes remained fixed on her face, and she realized she'd just let this man—her nemesis, really—into a small corner of her life. She felt the words "I'm sorry" bubbling on her tongue—a reflexive reaction, she supposed, for having spoken too freely. But she didn't want to apologize to this man for anything, so instead she just said, "Edwina is out, I'm afraid, so your visit was for nothing."

"Oh, I don't know about that," he replied. He grasped

the bouquet of flowers—which had been tucked under his right arm—with his other hand, and as he brought it forward Kate saw that it was not one massive bouquet, but three smaller ones.

"This," he said, putting one of the bouquets down on a side table, "is for Edwina. And this"—he did the same with the second—"is for your mother."

He was left with a single bouquet. Kate stood frozen with shock, unable to take her eyes off the perfect pink blooms. She knew what he had to be about, that the only reason he'd included her in the gesture was to impress Edwina, but blast it, no one had ever brought her flowers before, and she hadn't known until that very moment how badly she'd wanted someone to do so.

"These," he said finally, holding out the final arrangement of pink roses, "are for you."

"Thank you," she said hesitantly, taking them into her arms. "They're lovely." She leaned down to sniff them, sighing with pleasure at the thick scent. Glancing back up, she added, "It was very thoughtful of you to think of Mary and me."

He nodded graciously. "It was my pleasure. I must confess, a suitor for my sister's hand once did the same for my mother, and I don't believe I've ever seen her more delighted."

"Your mother or your sister?"

He smiled at her pert question. "Both."

"And what happened to this suitor?" Kate asked.

Anthony's grin turned devilish in the extreme. "He married my sister."

"Hmmph. Don't think history is likely to repeat itself. But—" Kate coughed, not particularly wanting to be honest with him but quite incapable of doing anything otherwise. "But the flowers are truly lovely, and—and it was a lovely gesture on your part." She swallowed. This wasn't easy for her. "And I do appreciate them."

He leaned forward slightly, his dark eyes positively melting. "A kind sentence," he mused. "And directed at me, no less. There now, that wasn't so difficult, was it?"

Kate went from bending lovingly over the flowers to standing uncomfortably straight in an instant. "You do seem to have a knack for saying the *exact* wrong thing."

"Only where you're concerned, my dear Miss Sheffield. Other women, I assure you, hang on my every word."

"So I've read," she muttered.

His eyes lit up. "Is that where you've developed your opinions of me? Of course! The estimable Lady Whistledown. I should have known. Lud, I'd like to strangle the woman."

"I find her rather intelligent and quite on the mark," Kate said primly.

"You would," he returned.

"Lord Bridgerton," Kate ground out, "I'm sure you did not come calling to insult me. May I leave a message for Edwina for you?"

"I think not. I don't particularly trust that it would reach her unadulterated."

That was really too much. "I would *never* stoop to interfering with another person's correspondence," Kate somehow managed to say. Her entire body was shaking with rage, and if she'd been a less controlled sort of woman, her hands would surely have been wrapped around his throat. "How dare you imply otherwise."

"When all is said and done, Miss Sheffield," he said with annoying calmness, "I really don't know you very well. What I do know consists of your fervent avowals that I will never find myself within ten feet of your sister's saintly presence. You tell me, would *you* feel confident to leave a note if you were me?"

"If you are attempting to gain my sister's favor through me," Kate replied icily, "you are not doing a very good job of it."

"I'm aware of that," he said. "I really shouldn't provoke

you. It's not very well done of me, is it? But I'm afraid I just can't help myself." He grinned roguishly and held up his hands in a helpless manner. "What can I say? You do something to me, Miss Sheffield."

His smile, Kate realized with dismay, was truly a force to be reckoned with. She suddenly felt faint. A seat . . . yes, what she needed to do was sit down. "Please, have a seat," she said, waving at the blue damask sofa as she scrambled across the room to a chair. She didn't particularly want him to linger, but she couldn't very well sit without offering him a seat as well, and her legs were starting to feel *awfully* wobbly.

If the viscount thought oddly of her sudden burst of politeness, he did not say anything. Instead he removed a long black case off the sofa and placed it on a table, then sat down in its place. "Is that a musical instrument?" he queried, motioning to the case.

Kate nodded. "A flute."

"Do you play?"

She shook her head, then cocked her head slightly and nodded. "I'm trying to learn. I took it up just this year."

He nodded in reply, and that, apparently, was to be the end of the subject, because he then politely asked, "When do you expect Edwina to return?"

"Not for at least an hour, I should think. Mr. Berbrooke took her out for a ride in his curricle."

"Nigel Berbrooke?" He practically choked on the name.

"Yes, why?"

"The man has more hair than wit. A great deal more."

"But he's going bald," she couldn't resist pointing out.

He grimaced. "And if that doesn't prove my point, I don't know what will."

Kate had reached much the same conclusion about Mr. Berbrooke's intelligence (or lack thereof), but she said, "Isn't it considered bad form to insult one's fellow suitors?"

Anthony let out a little snort. "It wasn't an insult. It was the truth. He courted my sister last year. Or tried to. Daphne did her best to discourage him. He's a nice enough fellow, I'll grant you that, but not someone you'd want building you a boat were you stranded on a desert island."

Kate had a strange and unwelcome image of the viscount stranded on a desert island, clothes in tatters, skin kissed by the sun. It left her feeling uncomfortably warm.

Anthony cocked his head, regarding her with a quizzical gaze. "I say, Miss Sheffield, are you feeling all right?"

"Fine!" she practically barked. "Never better. You were saying?"

"You look a bit flushed." He leaned in, watching her closely. She really didn't look well.

Kate fanned herself. "It's a bit hot in here, don't you think?"

Anthony shook his head slowly. "Not at all."

She gazed longingly out the door. "I wonder where Mary is."

"Are you expecting her?"

"It's unlike her to leave me unchaperoned for so long," she explained.

Unchaperoned? The ramifications were frightening. Anthony had a sudden vision of being trapped into marriage with Miss Sheffield the elder, and it made him break out in a cold sweat. Kate was so unlike any debutante he'd ever met that he'd quite forgotten that they even needed a chaperone. "Perhaps she's not aware I'm here," he said quickly.

"Yes, that must be it." She sprang to her feet and crossed the room to the bellpull. Giving it a firm yank, she said, "I'll just ring for someone to alert her. I'm sure she won't want to miss you."

"Good. Perhaps she can keep us company while we wait for your sister to return."

Kate froze halfway back to her chair. "You're planning to wait for Edwina?"

He shrugged, enjoying her discomfort. "I have no other plans for the afternoon."

"But she might be hours!"

"An hour at most, I'm sure, and besides—" He cut himself off, noting the arrival of a maid in the doorway.

"You rang, miss?" the maid queried.

"Yes, thank you, Annie," Kate replied. "Would you please inform Mrs. Sheffield that we have a guest?"

The maid bobbed a curtsy and departed.

"I'm sure Mary will be down at any moment," Kate said, quite unable to stop tapping her foot. "Any minute now. I'm sure of it."

He just smiled in that annoying manner, looking terribly relaxed and comfortable on the sofa.

An awkward silence fell across the room. Kate offered him a tight smile. He just raised a brow in return.

"I'm sure she'll be here—"

"Any minute now," he finished for her, sounding heartily amused.

She sank back into her chair, trying not to grimace. She probably didn't succeed.

Just then a small commotion broke out in the hall—a few decidedly canine barks, followed by a high-pitched shriek of, "Newton! Newton! Stop that at once!"

"Newton?" the viscount queried.

"My dog," Kate explained, sighing as she rose to her feet. "He doesn't—"

"NEWTON!"

"—get along with Mary very well, I'm afraid." Kate moved to the door. "Mary? Mary?"

Anthony rose when Kate did, wincing as the dog let out three more earsplitting barks, which were immediately followed by another terrified shriek from Mary. "What is he," he muttered, "a mastiff?" It had to be a mastiff. Miss

Sheffield the elder seemed exactly the sort to keep a man-eating mastiff at her beck and call.

"No," Kate said, rushing out into the hall as Mary let out another shriek. "He's a—"

But Anthony missed her words. It didn't matter much, anyway, because one second later, in trotted the most benign-looking corgi he'd ever seen, with thick caramel-colored fur and a belly that almost dragged on the ground.

Anthony froze with surprise. *This* was the fearsome creature from the hall? "Good day, dog," he said firmly.

The dog stopped in its tracks, sat right down, and . . .

Smiled?

Chapter 4

This Author was, sadly, unable to determine all the details, but there was a considerable to-do Thursday last near The Serpentine in Hyde Park involving Viscount Bridgerton, Mr. Nigel Berbrooke, both the Misses Sheffield, and an unnamed dog of indeterminate breed.

This Author was not an eyewitness, but all accounts seem to indicate that the unnamed dog emerged the victor.

LADY WHISTLEDOWN'S SOCIETY PAPERS, 25 APRIL 1814

Kate stumbled back into the drawing room, knocking arms with Mary as they both squeezed through the doorway at the same time. Newton was seated happily in the middle of the room, shedding on the blue-and-white rug as he grinned up at the viscount.

"I think he likes you," Mary said, somewhat accusingly.

"He likes you, too, Mary," Kate said. "The problem is that *you* don't like *him*."

"I'd like him better if he didn't try to accost me every time I come through the hall."

"I thought you said Mrs. Sheffield and the dog didn't get along," Lord Bridgerton said.

"They don't," Kate replied. "Well, they do. Well, they don't *and* they do."

"That clears things up immeasurably," he murmured.

Kate ignored his quiet sarcasm. "Newton adores Mary," she explained, "but Mary doesn't adore Newton."

"I'd adore him a bit more," Mary interrupted, "if he'd adore me a bit less."

"*So*," Kate continued determinedly, "poor Newton regards Mary as something of a challenge. So when he sees her . . ." She shrugged helplessly. "Well, I'm afraid he simply adores her *more*."

As if on cue, the dog caught sight of Mary and bounded straight over to her feet.

"Kate!" Mary exclaimed.

Kate rushed to her stepmother's side, just as Newton rose on his hind legs and planted his front paws just above Mary's knees. "Newton, down!" she scolded. "Bad dog. Bad dog."

The dog sat back down with a little whine.

"Kate," Mary said in an extremely no-nonsense voice, "that dog *must* be taken for a walk. Now."

"I had been planning to when the viscount arrived," Kate replied, motioning to the man across the room. Really, it was remarkable the number of things she could blame on the insufferable man if she put her mind to it.

"Oh!" Mary yelped. "I beg your pardon, my lord. How rude of me not to greet you."

"It is of no concern," he said smoothly. "You were a bit preoccupied upon your arrival."

"Yes," Mary grumbled, "that beastly dog. . . . Oh, but where are my manners? May we offer you tea? Something to eat? It is so kind of you to call upon us."

"No, thank you. I've just been enjoying your daughter's invigorating company while I await Miss Edwina's arrival."

"Ah, yes," Mary answered. "Edwina's off with Mr. Berbrooke, I believe. Isn't that so, Kate?"

Kate nodded stonily, not sure she liked being called "invigorating."

"Do you know Mr. Berbrooke, Lord Bridgerton?" Mary asked.

"Ah, yes," he said, with what Kate thought was fairly surprising reticence. "Yes, I do."

"I wasn't sure if I should have allowed Edwina to go off with him for a ride. Those curricles are terribly difficult to drive, aren't they?"

"I believe that Mr. Berbrooke has a steady hand with his horses," Anthony replied.

"Oh, good," Mary replied, letting out a much-relieved sigh. "You have surely set my mind at rest."

Newton let out a staccato bark, simply to remind everyone of his presence.

"I had better find his lead and take him for a walk," Kate said hurriedly. She certainly could use a bit of fresh air. And it would be nice to finally escape the viscount's fiendish company. "If you'll excuse me . . ."

"But wait, Kate!" Mary called out. "You cannot leave Lord Bridgerton here with me. I'm sure I'll bore him to tears."

Kate slowly turned around, dreading Mary's next words.

"You could never bore me, Mrs. Sheffield," the viscount said, debonair rake that he was.

"Oh, but I could," she assured him. "You've never been trapped in conversation with me for an hour. Which is about how long it will be before Edwina returns."

Kate stared at her stepmother, her jaw actually hanging open with shock. What on earth did Mary think she was doing?

"Why don't you go with Kate to take Newton for a walk?" Mary suggested.

"Oh, but I could never ask Lord Bridgerton to accompany me on a *chore*," Kate said quickly. "It would be beyond rudeness, and after all, he is our esteemed guest."

"Don't be silly," Mary answered, before the viscount could get even half of a word in. "I'm sure he wouldn't look upon it as a chore. Would you, my lord?"

"Of course not," he murmured, looking utterly sincere. But really, what else could he say?

"There. That settles it," Mary said, sounding inordinately pleased with herself. "And who knows? You may stumble across Edwina in your travels. Wouldn't that be convenient?"

"Indeed," Kate said under her breath. It would be lovely to be rid of the viscount, but the last thing she wanted to do was deliver Edwina into his clutches. Her sister was still young and impressionable. What if she couldn't resist one of his smiles? Or his glib tongue?

Even Kate was willing to admit that Lord Bridgerton exuded considerable charm, and she didn't even like the man! Edwina, with her less suspicious nature, would surely be overwhelmed.

She turned to the viscount. "You shouldn't feel you must accompany me while I walk Newton, my lord."

"I'd be delighted," he said with a wicked smile, and Kate had the distinct impression he was agreeing to go for the sole purpose of vexing her. "Besides," he continued, "as your mother said, we might see Edwina, and wouldn't that be a delightful coincidence?"

"Delightful," Kate returned flatly. "Just delightful."

"Excellent!" Mary said, clapping her hands together with joy. "I saw Newton's lead on the hall table. Here, I'll go and get it for you."

Anthony watched Mary leave, then turned to Kate and said, "That was very neatly done."

"I'll say," Kate muttered.

"Do you suppose," he whispered, leaning toward her, "that her matchmaking is directed toward Edwina or you?"

"Me?" Kate all but croaked. "Surely you jest."

Anthony rubbed his chin thoughtfully, gazing at the doorway through which Mary had just exited. "I'm not certain," he mused, "but—" He closed his mouth upon hearing Mary's footsteps drawing back near.

"Here you are," Mary said, holding the lead out to Kate. Newton barked enthusiastically and drew back as if preparing to lunge at Mary—undoubtedly to shower her with all sorts of unpalatable love—but Kate kept a firm hold on his collar.

"Here," Mary quickly amended, handing the lead instead to Anthony. "Why don't you give this to Kate? I'd rather not get too close."

Newton barked and gazed longingly at Mary, who inched farther away.

"You," Anthony said forcefully to the dog. "Sit down and be quiet."

Much to Kate's surprise, Newton obeyed, settling his plump bottom onto the rug with almost comical alacrity.

"There," Anthony said, sounding rather pleased with himself. He held out the lead toward Kate. "Shall you do the honors or shall I?"

"Oh, go right ahead," she replied. "You seem to have such an affinity for canines."

"Clearly," he shot back, keeping his voice low so that Mary could not hear, "they are not so very different from women. Both breeds hang on my every word."

Kate stepped on his hand as he knelt to fasten the lead to Newton's collar. "Oops," she said, rather insincerely. "I'm so sorry."

"Your tender solicitude quite unmans me," he returned, standing back up. "I might break into tears."

Mary's head bobbed back and forth between Kate and Anthony. She couldn't hear what they were saying but was clearly fascinated. "Is something wrong?" she queried.

"Not at all," Anthony replied, just as Kate gave a firm, "No."

"Good," Mary said briskly. "Then I'll see you to the door." At Newton's enthusiastic bark, she added, "Then again, maybe not. I don't really want to get within ten feet of that dog. But I'll wave you off."

"What would I do," Kate said to Mary as she passed her, "without you to wave me off?"

Mary smiled slyly. "I surely don't know, Kate. I surely don't know."

Which left Kate with a queasy feeling in her stomach and a vague suspicion that Lord Bridgerton might have been correct. Maybe Mary was playing matchmaker with more than just Edwina this time around.

It was a horrifying thought.

With Mary standing in the hall, Kate and Anthony exited out the doorway and headed west on Milner Street. "I usually stay to the smaller streets and make my way up to Brompton Road," Kate explained, thinking that he might not be very familiar with this area of town, "then take that to Hyde Park. But we can walk straight up Sloane Street, if you prefer."

"Whatever you wish," he demurred. "I shall follow your direction."

"Very well," Kate replied, marching determinedly up Milner Street toward Lenox Gardens. Maybe if she kept her eyes ahead of her and moved briskly, he'd be discouraged from conversation. Her daily walks with Newton were supposed to be her time for personal reflection. She did not appreciate having to drag him along.

Her strategy worked quite well for several minutes. They walked in silence all the way to the corner of Hans Crescent and Brompton Road, and then he quite suddenly said, "My brother played us for fools last night."

That stopped her in her tracks. "I beg your pardon?"

"Do you know what he told me about you before he introduced us?"

Kate stumbled a step before shaking her head, no. Newton hadn't stopped in *his* tracks, and he was tugging on the lead like mad.

"He told me you couldn't say enough about me."

"Wellll," Kate stalled, "if one doesn't want to put too fine a point on it, that's not entirely untrue."

"He implied," Anthony added, "that you could not say enough *good* about me."

She shouldn't have smiled. "*That's* not true."

He probably shouldn't have smiled, either, but Kate was glad he did. "I didn't think so," he replied.

They turned up Brompton Road toward Knightsbridge and Hyde Park, and Kate asked, "Why would he do such a thing?"

Anthony shot her a sideways look. "You don't have a brother, do you?"

"No, just Edwina, I'm afraid, and she's decidedly female."

"He did it," Anthony explained, "purely to torture me."

"A noble pursuit," Kate said under her breath.

"I heard that."

"I rather thought you would," she added.

"And I expect," he continued, "that he wanted to torture you as well."

"Me?" she exclaimed. "Whyever? What could I possibly have done to him?"

"You might have provoked him ever so slightly by denigrating his beloved brother," he suggested.

Her brows arched. "Beloved?"

"Much-admired?" he tried.

She shook her head. "That one doesn't wash, either."

Anthony grinned. Miss Sheffield the elder, for all her annoyingly managing ways, did have an admirable wit. They'd reached Knightsbridge, so he took her arm as they crossed over the thoroughfare and took one of the smaller pathways that led to South Carriage Road within Hyde Park. Newton, clearly a country dog at heart, picked up his pace considerably as they entered greener surroundings, although it would be difficult to imagine the portly canine moving with anything that might correctly be termed speed.

Still, the dog seemed rather jolly and certainly interested in every flower, small animal, or passerby that crossed their path. The spring air was crisp, but the sun was warm, and the sky was a surprisingly clear blue after so many typical London days of rain. And while the woman on his arm was not the woman he planned to take to wife, nor, in fact, was she a woman he planned to take to anything, Anthony felt a rather easy sense of contentment wash over him.

"Shall we cross over to Rotten Row?" he asked Kate.

"Hmmm?" was her distracted reply. She had her face tipped up to the sun and was basking in its warmth. And for one extremely disconcerting moment, Anthony felt a sharp stab of . . . *something*.

Something? He gave his head a little shake. It couldn't possibly be desire. Not for this woman.

"Did you say something?" she murmured.

He cleared his throat and took a deep breath, hoping it would clear his head. Instead, he simply got an intoxicating whiff of her scent, which was an odd combination of exotic lilies and sensible soap. "You seem to be enjoying the sun," he said.

She smiled, turning to face him with a clear-eyed gaze. "I know that's not what you said, but yes, I am. It's been so dreadfully rainy of late."

"I thought young ladies were not supposed to let sun on their faces," he teased.

She shrugged, looking only the slightest bit sheepish as she replied, "They're not. That is to say, we're not. But it does feel heavenly." She let out a little sigh, and a look of longing crossed her face, so intense that Anthony almost ached for her. "I do wish I could remove my bonnet," she said wistfully.

Anthony nodded his agreement, feeling much the same way about his hat. "You could probably push it back just a bit without anyone noticing," he suggested.

"Do you think?" Her entire face lit up at the prospect, and that strange stab of *something* pierced his gut again.

"Of course," he murmured, reaching up to adjust the

rim of the bonnet. It was one of those bizarre confections women seemed to favor, all ribbons and lace, and tied in such a way that no reasonable man could ever make sense of it. "Here, just hold still for a moment. I'll fix it."

Kate held still, just as he'd gently ordered, but when his fingers accidentally brushed the skin on her temple she stopped breathing as well. He was so very close, and there was something very odd about it. She could feel the heat of his body, and smell the clean, soapy scent of him.

And it sent a prickle of awareness straight through her.

She hated him, or at least she heartily disliked and disapproved of him, and yet she had the most absurd inclination to lean forward slightly, until the space between their bodies was squeezed into nothingness, and . . .

She swallowed and forced herself to draw back. Good God, what had come over her?

"Hold for a moment," he said. "I haven't finished."

Kate reached up with frantic fingers to adjust her bonnet. "I'm sure it's just fine. You needn't—you needn't worry yourself."

"Can you feel the sun any better?" he asked.

She nodded, even though she was so distracted she wasn't even sure if it was true. "Yes, thank you. It's lovely. I— Oh!"

Newton let out a loud stream of barks and yanked on the lead. Hard.

"Newton!" she called out, jerking forward with the lead. But the dog already had something in his sights—Kate had no idea what—and was bounding enthusiastically forward, pulling her along until she was stumbling over her feet, her entire body pulled into a diagonal line, with her shoulder decidedly in front of the rest of her. "Newton!" she called out again, rather helplessly. "Newton! Stop!"

Anthony watched with amusement as the dog barreled forward, moving with more speed than he would have ever guessed its short, pudgy legs could have managed.

Kate was making a valiant attempt to keep her grip on the lead, but Newton was now barking like mad, and running with equal vigor.

"Miss Sheffield, allow me to take the lead," he boomed, striding forward to aid her. It wasn't the most glamorous manner in which to play the hero, but anything would do when one was trying to impress the sister of one's future bride.

But just as Anthony caught up with her, Newton gave the lead a vicious tug, and it went flying from her grasp. Kate let out a shriek and dashed forward, but the dog was off and running, the lead snaking along the grass behind him.

Anthony didn't know whether to laugh or groan. Newton clearly did not intend to be caught.

Kate froze for a moment, one hand clasped over her mouth. Then her eyes caught Anthony's, and he had the worst sort of feeling that he knew what she intended to do.

"Miss Sheffield," he said quickly, "I'm sure—"

But she was off and running, hollering, "Newton!" with a decided lack of decorum. Anthony let out a weary sigh and began running after her. He couldn't very well let her chase the dog on her own and still presume to call himself a gentleman.

She had a bit of a head start on him, though, and when he caught up with her around the corner, she'd stopped. She was breathing hard, her hands on her hips as she scanned her surroundings.

"Where'd he go?" Anthony asked, trying to forget that there was something rather arousing about a woman who was panting.

"I don't know." She paused to catch her breath. "I think he's chasing a rabbit."

"Oh, now, well, *that* will make it easy to catch him," he said. "Since rabbits always stick to the well-trod paths."

She scowled at his sarcasm. "What are we to do?"

Anthony had half a mind to answer, "Go home and get

a *real* dog," but she looked so worried he bit his tongue. Actually, upon closer inspection she looked more irritated than worried, but there was definitely a bit of worry in the mix.

So instead he said, "I propose we wait until we hear someone shriek. Any minute now he's bound to dash right across some young lady's feet and scare her out of her very wits."

"Do you think?" She didn't look convinced. "Because he's not the scariest dog to look at. He thinks he is, and it's really quite sweet, actually, but the truth is, he's—"

"Eeeeeeeeeeeeeeaaaaaaaaaahhhhhk!"

"I believe we have our answer," Anthony said dryly, and he took off in the direction of the anonymous lady's scream.

Kate hurried after him, cutting right across the grass toward Rotten Row. The viscount was running in front of her, and all she could think was that he must really want to marry Edwina, because despite the fact that he was clearly a splendid athlete, he looked most undignified dashing through the park after a rotund corgi. Even worse, they were going to have to run right across Rotten Row, the *ton*'s favorite spot for riding and driving.

Everyone was going to see them. A less determined man would have given up ages ago.

Kate kept running on after them, but she was losing ground. She hadn't spent much time in breeches, but she was fairly certain it was easier to run in them than in skirts. Especially when one was out in public and could not hitch them up above one's ankles.

She tore across Rotten Row, refusing to make eye contact with any of the fashionable ladies and gentlemen out with their horses. There was always the chance she wouldn't be recognized as the hoydenish miss racing through the park as if someone had set fire to her shoes. Not much of a chance, but a chance nonetheless.

When she reached the grass again, she stumbled for a second and had to pause to take a few deep breaths. Then horror dawned. They were almost to The Serpentine.

Oh, *no*.

There was little Newton liked better than to jump in a lake. And the sun was just warm enough that it might look tempting, especially if one happened to be a creature covered with thick, heavy fur, a creature who'd been running at breakneck speed for five minutes. Well, breakneck for an overweight corgi.

Which was still, Kate noted with some interest, fast enough to keep a six-foot-tall viscount at bay.

Kate hitched up her skirts an inch or so—hang the onlookers, she couldn't afford to be fussy right now—and took off running again. There was no way she'd catch up with Newton, but maybe she could catch up with Lord Bridgerton before he killed Newton.

Murder *had* to be on his mind by now. The man would have to be a saint not to want to murder the dog.

And if one percent of what had been written about him in *Whistledown* was true, he was no saint.

Kate gulped. "Lord Bridgerton!" she called out, intending to tell him to call off the hunt. She'd simply have to wait for Newton to exhaust himself. With four-inch-tall legs, that had to come sooner rather than later. "Lord Bridgerton! We can just—"

Kate stumbled in her tracks. Was that Edwina over there by The Serpentine? She squinted. It *was* Edwina, standing gracefully with her hands clasped in front of her. And it appeared that the hapless Mr. Berbrooke was making some sort of repair to his curricle.

Newton stopped short for one moment, spying Edwina at the same moment Kate did, and abruptly changed his course, barking joyfully as he ran toward his beloved.

"Lord Bridgerton!" Kate called out again. "See, look! There's—"

Anthony turned around at the sound of her voice, then

followed her pointed finger toward Edwina. So that was why the damned dog spun on its heel and made a ninety-degree change of course. Anthony had nearly slipped on the mud and fallen on his bum trying to maneuver such a sharp turn.

He was going to kill that dog.

No, he was going to kill Kate Sheffield.

No, maybe—

Anthony's gleeful thoughts of vengeance were broken by Edwina's sudden shriek of, "Newton!"

Anthony liked to think of himself as a man of decisive action, but when he saw that dog launch himself in the air and hurtle himself toward Edwina, he was quite simply frozen with shock. Shakespeare himself could not have devised a more appropriate ending to this farce, and it was all playing out right before Anthony's eyes as if at half speed.

And there was nothing he could do about it.

The dog was going to hit Edwina straight in the chest. Edwina was going to topple backward.

Straight into The Serpentine.

"Nooooooo!" he yelled, charging forward even though he knew all attempts at heroics on his part were utterly useless.

Splash!

"Dear God!" Berbrooke exclaimed. "She's all wet!"

"Well, don't just stand there," Anthony snapped, reaching the scene of the accident and charging forward into the waters. "Do something to help!"

Berbrooke clearly did not quite understand what that meant, because he just stood there, bug-eyed, as Anthony reached down, grasped Edwina's hand, and hauled her to her feet.

"Are you all right?" he asked gruffly.

She nodded, sputtering and sneezing too hard to answer.

"Miss Sheffield," he roared, seeing Kate skid to a halt

on the banks. "No, not you," he added, when he felt Edwina jerk to attention at his side. "Your sister."

"Kate?" she asked, blinking the filthy water from her eyes. "Where's Kate?"

"Dry as a bone on the embankment," he muttered, followed by a holler in Kate's direction of, "Rein in your bloody dog!"

Newton had cheerfully splashed back out of the Serpentine and was now sitting on the grass, his tongue hanging happily out of his mouth. Kate scurried to his side and grabbed the lead. Anthony noticed that she had no pithy comeback to his roared order. Good, he thought viciously. He wouldn't have thought the bloody woman would have had the sense to keep her mouth shut.

He turned back to Edwina, who, astoundingly, still managed to look lovely even while dripping with pond water. "Let me get you out of here," he said gruffly, and before she had a chance to react, he scooped her into his arms and carried her to dry ground.

"I've never seen anything like that," Berbrooke said, shaking his head.

Anthony made no reply. He didn't think he'd be able to speak without tossing the idiot into the water. What was he thinking, just standing there while Edwina was submerged by that pathetic excuse for a dog?

"Edwina?" Kate asked, walking forward as far as Newton's lead would allow. "Are you all right?"

"I think you've done enough," Anthony bit out, advancing upon her until they were barely a foot apart.

"Me?" she gasped.

"Look at her," he snapped, thrusting a pointed finger in Edwina's direction even while his full attention was focused on Kate. "Just look at her!"

"But it was an accident!"

"I'm really fine!" Edwina called out, sounding a little panicked by the level of anger simmering between her sister and the viscount. "Cold, but fine!"

"See?" Kate returned, swallowing convulsively as she took in the disheveled sight of her sister. "It was an accident."

He merely crossed his arms and arched a brow.

"You don't believe me," she breathed. "I can't believe you don't believe me."

Anthony said nothing. It was inconceivable to him that Kate Sheffield, for all her wit and intelligence, could *not* be jealous of her sister. And even if there was nothing she could have done to prevent this mishap, surely she must be taking a bit of pleasure in the fact that she was dry and comfortable while Edwina looked like a drowned rat. An attractive rat, to be sure, but certainly a drowned one.

But Kate clearly wasn't done with the conversation. "Aside from the fact," she scorned, "that I would never ever do anything to harm Edwina, how do you propose I managed this amazing feat?" She clapped her free hand to her cheek in an expression of mock discovery. "Oh, yes, I know the secret language of the corgis. I ordered the dog to yank the lead from my hand and then, since I have the second sight, I knew that Edwina was standing right here by the Serpentine, so then I said to the dog—through our powerful mind-to-mind connection, since he was much too far away to hear my voice at this point—to change his direction, head for Edwina, and topple her into the lake."

"Sarcasm doesn't become you, Miss Sheffield."

"*Nothing* becomes you, Lord Bridgerton."

Anthony leaned forward, his chin jutting out in a most menacing manner. "Women should not keep pets if they cannot control them."

"And men should not take women with pets for a walk in the park if they cannot control either," she shot back.

Anthony could actually feel the tips of his ears turning red with barely leashed rage. "You, madam, are a menace to society."

She opened her mouth as if to return the insult, but instead she just offered him an almost frighteningly devious smile and turned to the dog and said, "Shake, Newton."

Newton looked up at her finger, pointed right at Anthony, and obediently trotted a few steps closer to him before allowing himself a full-body shake, spraying pond water everywhere.

Anthony went for her throat. "I . . . am . . . going . . . to . . . KILL YOU!" he roared.

Kate ducked nimbly out of the way, dashing over to Edwina's side. "Now, now, Lord Bridgerton," she taunted, seeking safety behind her sister's dripping form. "It would not do to lose your temper in front of the fair Edwina."

"Kate?" Edwina whispered urgently. "What is going on? Why are you being so mean to him?"

"Why is he being so mean to *me*?" Kate hissed back.

"I say," Mr. Berbrooke suddenly said, "that dog got me wet."

"He got all of us wet," Kate replied. Including her. But it had been worth it. Oh, it had been worth it to see the look of surprise and rage on that pompous aristocrat's face.

"You!" Anthony roared, jabbing a furious finger at Kate. "Be quiet."

Kate held her silence. She wasn't foolhardy enough to provoke him any further. He looked as if his head might explode at any moment. And he'd certainly lost whatever claim to dignity he'd had at the beginning of the day. His right sleeve was dripping wet from when he'd hauled Edwina out of the water, his boots looked to be ruined forever, and the rest of him was spotted with water, thanks to Newton's expert shaking prowess.

"I'll tell you what we're going to do," he continued in a low, deadly voice.

"What I need to do," Mr. Berbrooke said jovially, clearly unaware that Lord Bridgerton was likely to murder the first person who opened his mouth, "is finish repairing this curricle. Then I can take Miss Sheffield home." He pointed at Edwina, just in case anyone didn't understand to which Miss Sheffield he referred.

"Mr. Berbrooke," Anthony ground out, "do you know how to fix a curricle?"

Mr. Berbrooke blinked a few times.

"Do you even know what is *wrong* with your curricle?"

Berbrooke's mouth opened and closed a few more times, and then he said, "I have a few ideas. Shouldn't take terribly long to figure out which is the actual problem."

Kate stared at Anthony, fascinated by the vein leaping in his throat. She had never before seen a man so clearly pushed to his limit. Feeling not a little apprehensive at the impending explosion, she took a prudent half step behind Edwina.

She didn't like to think herself a coward, but self-preservation was another matter entirely.

But the viscount somehow managed to keep himself under control, and his voice was terrifyingly even as he said, "This is what we're going to do."

Three pairs of eyes widened in expectation.

"I am going to walk over there"—he pointed at a lady and gentleman about twenty yards away who were trying not to stare but not succeeding—"and ask Montrose if I might borrow his carriage for a few minutes."

"I say," Berbrooke said, craning his neck, "is that Geoffrey Montrose? Haven't seen him for an age."

A second vein started leaping, this time on Lord Bridgerton's temple. Kate grasped Edwina's hand for moral support and held tight.

But Bridgerton, to his credit, ignored Berbrooke's exceedingly inappropriate interjection and continued with, "Since he will say yes—"

"Are you sure?" Kate blurted out.

Somehow his brown eyes resembled icicles. "Am I sure of what?" he bit off.

"Nothing," she mumbled, ready to kick herself. "Please continue."

"As I was saying, since as a friend and a gentleman"—he glared at Kate—"he will say yes, I will take Miss Sheffield home and then *I* will return home and have one of my men return Montrose's curricle."

No one bothered to ask which Miss Sheffield he was talking about.

"What about Kate?" Edwina inquired. After all, the curricle could only seat two.

Kate gave her hand a squeeze. Dear, sweet Edwina.

Anthony looked straight at Edwina. "Mr. Berbrooke will escort your sister home."

"But I can't," Berbrooke said. "Got to finish with the curricle, you know."

"Where do you live?" Anthony snapped.

Berbrooke blinked with surprise but gave his address.

"I will stop by your house and fetch a servant to wait with your conveyance while you escort Miss Sheffield to her home. Is that clear?" He paused and looked at everyone—including the dog—with a rather hard expression. Except for Edwina, of course, who was the only person present who had not lit a fuse directly under his temper.

"Is that clear?" he repeated.

Everyone nodded, and his plan was set into motion. Minutes later, Kate found herself watching Lord Bridgerton and Edwina ride off into the horizon—the very two people she had vowed should never even be in the same room together.

Even worse, she was left alone with Mr. Berbrooke and Newton.

And it took only two minutes to discern that of the two, Newton was the finer conversationalist.

Chapter 5

It has come to This Author's attention that Miss Katharine Sheffield took offense at the labeling of her beloved pet, "an unnamed dog of indeterminate breed."

This Author is, to be sure, prostrate with shame at this grievous and egregious error and begs of you, dear reader, to accept this abject apology and pay attention to the first ever correction in the history of this column.

Miss Katharine Sheffield's dog is a corgi. It is called Newton, although it is difficult to imagine that England's great inventor and physicist would have appreciated being immortalized in the form of a short, fat canine with poor manners.

LADY WHISTLEDOWN'S SOCIETY PAPERS, 27 APRIL 1814

By that evening, it had become apparent that Edwina had not come through her (albeit brief) ordeal unscathed. Her nose turned red, her eyes began to water, and it was apparent to anyone who glimpsed her puffy face for even a second that, while not seriously ill, she'd caught a bad cold.

But even while Edwina was tucked into bed with a hot water bottle between her feet and a therapeutic potion brewed up by the cook in a mug on her bedside table, Kate was determined to have a conversation with her.

"What did he say to you on the ride home?" Kate demanded, perching on the edge of her sister's bed.

"Who?" Edwina replied, sniffing fearfully at the remedy. "Look at this," she said, holding it forward. "It's giving off fumes."

"The viscount," Kate ground out. "Who else would have spoken to you on the ride home? And don't be a ninny. It's not giving off fumes. That's just steam."

"Oh." Edwina took another sniff and pulled a face. "It doesn't smell like steam."

"It's *steam*," Kate ground out, gripping the mattress until her knuckles hurt. "What did he *say*?"

"Lord Bridgerton?" Edwina asked blithely. "Oh, just the usual sort of things. You know what I mean. Polite conversation and all that."

"He made polite conversation while you were dripping wet?" Kate asked doubtfully.

Edwina took a hesitant sip, then nearly gagged. "What is *in* this?"

Kate leaned over and sniffed at the contents. "It smells a bit like licorice. And I think I see a raisin at the bottom." But as she sniffed, she thought she heard rain pattering against the glass of the window, and so she sat back up. "Is it raining?"

"I don't know," Edwina said. "It might be. It was rather cloudy when the sun set earlier." She gave the glass one more dubious look, then set it back on the table. "If I drink that, I *know* it will make me sicker," she stated.

"But what else did he say?" Kate persisted, getting up to check out the window. She pushed the curtain aside and peered out. It was raining, but only lightly, and it was too early to tell whether the precipitation would be accompanied by any thunder or lightning.

"Who, the viscount?"

Kate thought herself a saint for not shaking her sister senseless. "Yes, the viscount."

Edwina shrugged, clearly not as interested in the conversation as Kate. "Not much. He asked for my welfare, of course. Which was only reasonable, considering that I had just been dunked in The Serpentine. Which, I might add, was perfectly wretched. Aside from being cold, the water was most certainly not clean."

Kate cleared her throat and sat back down, preparing to ask a most scandalous question, but one which, in her opinion, simply had to be asked. Trying to keep her voice devoid of the complete and total fascination that was coursing through her veins, she asked, "Did he make any untoward advances?"

Edwina lurched back, her eyes growing round with shock. "Of course not!" she exclaimed. "He was a perfect gentleman. Really, I don't see what has you so excited. It wasn't a very interesting conversation. I can't even remember half of what was said."

Kate just stared at her sister, unable to fathom that she could have been trapped in conversation with that odious rake for a good ten minutes and it *didn't* make an indelible impression on her. Much to her own everlasting dismay, every single awful word he'd said to her was etched permanently on her brain.

"By the way," Edwina added, "how was your time with Mr. Berbrooke? It took you nearly an hour to return."

Kate shuddered visibly.

"That bad?"

"I'm sure he will make some woman a good husband," Kate said. "Just not one with a brain."

Edwina let out a little giggle. "Oh, Kate, you are awful."

Kate sighed. "I know. I know. That was terribly cruel of me. The poor man hasn't an unkind bone in his body. It's just that—"

"He hasn't an intelligent bone, either," Edwina finished.

Kate raised her brows. It was most unlike Edwina to make such a judgmental comment.

"I know," Edwina said with a sheepish smile. "Now I am the unkind one. I really shouldn't have said a word, but truly, I thought I would perish on our curricle ride."

Kate straightened with concern. "Was he a dangerous driver?"

"Not at all. It was his conversation."

"Boring?"

Edwina nodded, her blue eyes slightly bewildered. "He was so hard to follow it was almost fascinating to try to figure out how his mind works." She let out a stream of coughs, then added, "But it made my brain hurt."

"So he's not to be your perfect scholar-husband?" Kate said with an indulgent smile.

Edwina coughed some more. "I'm afraid not."

"Maybe you should try a bit more of that brew," Kate suggested, motioning to the lonely mug sitting on Edwina's bedside table. "Cook swears by it."

Edwina shook her head violently. "It tastes like death."

Kate waited a few moments, then had to ask, "Did the viscount say anything about me?"

"You?"

"No, some other me," Kate practically snapped. "Of course *me*. How many other people may I correctly refer to as 'me'?"

"No need to get upset about it."

"I'm not upset—"

"But actually, no, he didn't mention you."

Kate suddenly felt upset.

"He had a lot to say about Newton, though."

Kate's lips parted with dismay. It was never flattering to be passed over for a dog.

"I assured him that Newton is truly the perfect pet, and that I was not at all angry with him, but he was rather charmingly upset on my behalf."

"How charming," Kate muttered.

Edwina grabbed a handkerchief and blew her nose. "I say, Kate, you're rather interested in the viscount."

"I did spend practically the entire afternoon trapped in conversation with him," Kate replied, as if that ought to explain everything.

"Good. Then you've had a chance to see how polite and charming he can be. He's very wealthy, too." Edwina let out a loud sniffle, then fumbled around for a fresh handkerchief. "And while I don't think that one can choose a husband based entirely on finances, given our lack of funds, I would be remiss not to consider it, don't you think?"

"Well . . ." Kate hedged, knowing that Edwina was absolutely correct but not wanting to say anything that might be construed as approval of Lord Bridgerton.

Edwina brought the handkerchief to her face and gave her nose a rather unfeminine blow. "I think we should add him to our list," she said, snuffling over the words.

"Our list," Kate echoed, her voice strangled.

"Yes, of possible matches. I think he and I would suit very well."

"But I thought you wanted a scholar!"

"I did. I do. But you yourself pointed out the unlikelihood of my finding a true scholar. Lord Bridgerton seems intelligent enough. I'll just have to devise a way to discover if he likes to read."

"I'd be surprised if that boor *can* read," Kate muttered.

"Kate Sheffield!" Edwina exclaimed with a laugh. "Did you just say what I think you said?"

"No," Kate said baldly, because of course the viscount could read. But he was just so awful in every other way.

"You did," Edwina accused. "You are the *worst,* Kate." She smiled. "But you do make me laugh."

A low rumble of distant thunder echoed in the night, and Kate forced a smile on her face, trying not to flinch. She was usually all right when the thunder and lightning were far away. It was only when they came one on top of each other, and both seemingly on top of her, that she felt as if she were about to burst from her skin.

"Edwina," Kate said, needing to have this discussion with her sister but also needing to say something that would take her mind off the approaching storm, "you must put the viscount from your mind. He is absolutely not the sort of husband who would make you happy. Aside from the fact that he is the worst sort of rake and would probably flaunt a dozen mistresses in your face—"

At Edwina's frown, Kate cut off the rest of her sentence and decided to expand upon this point. "He would!" she said with great drama. "Haven't you been reading *Whistledown*? Or listening to anything any of the other young ladies' mamas have to say? The ones who have been on the social circuit for several years and know what's what. They *all* say he is a terrible rake. That his only saving grace is how nicely he treats his family."

"Well, that would be a mark in his favor," Edwina pointed out. "Since a wife would be family, yes?"

Kate nearly groaned. "A wife isn't the same as a blood relative. Men who would never dream of uttering a cross word in front of their mothers trample all over their wives' feelings every day."

"And how would you know this?" Edwina demanded.

Kate's mouth fell open. She couldn't remember the last time Edwina had questioned her judgment on an important matter, and unfortunately, the only answer she could think of on such short notice was, "I just do."

Which, even she had to admit, really didn't pass muster.

"Edwina," she said in a placating voice, deciding to steer the topic in a different direction, "aside from all that, I don't think you would even like the viscount if you got to know him."

"He seemed pleasant enough while driving me home."

"But he was on his best behavior!" Kate persisted. "Of course he'd seem nice. He wants you to fall in love with him."

Edwina blinked. "So you think it was all an act."

"Exactly!" Kate exclaimed, pouncing on the concept.

"Edwina, between last night and this afternoon, I spent several hours in his company, and I can assure you, he was *not* on his best behavior with me."

Edwina gasped with horror and maybe a little titillation. "Did he kiss you?" she breathed.

"No!" Kate howled. "Of course not! Where on earth would you get that idea?"

"You said he wasn't on his best behavior."

"What I meant," Kate ground out, "was that he wasn't polite. Nor was he very nice. In fact, he was insufferably arrogant and dreadfully rude and insulting."

"That's interesting," Edwina murmured.

"It wasn't the least bit interesting. It was horrible!"

"No, that's not what I meant," Edwina said, thoughtfully scratching her chin. "It's very odd that he would have behaved rudely to you. He must have heard that I shall be looking to your judgment when I choose a husband. One would think he'd go out of his way to be nice to you. Why," she mused, "would he behave the churl?"

Kate's face colored a dull red—thankfully not so noticeable in the candlelight—as she muttered, "He said he couldn't help himself."

Edwina's mouth fell open, and for one second she sat utterly frozen, as if suspended in time. Then she fell back onto her pillows, hooting with laughter. "Oh, Kate!" she gasped. "That is splendid! Oh, what a tangle. Oh, I love it!"

Kate glared at her. "It's not funny."

Edwina wiped at her eyes. "It might be the funniest thing I've heard all month. All year! Oh, my goodness." She let out a short stream of coughs, brought on by her laughing fit. "Oh, Kate, I do believe you might have cleared out my nose."

"Edwina, that's disgusting."

Edwina brought her handkerchief to her face and blew her nose. "But true," she said triumphantly.

"It won't last," Kate muttered. "You'll be sick as a dog by morning."

"You're probably right," Edwina agreed, "but oh, what fun. He said he couldn't help himself? Oh, Kate, that is just rich."

"There is no need to dwell on it," Kate grumbled.

"Do you know, but he might be the very first gentleman we've met all season you haven't been able to manage."

Kate's lips twisted into a grimace. The viscount had used the same word, and they were both correct. She'd indeed spent the season managing men—managing them for Edwina. And she suddenly wasn't so sure she liked this role of mother hen she'd been thrust into.

Or maybe she'd thrust herself into it.

Edwina saw the play of emotion on her sister's face and immediately turned apologetic. "Oh, dear," she murmured. "I'm sorry, Kate. I didn't mean to tease."

Kate arched a brow.

"Oh, very well, I did mean to tease, but never to actually hurt your feelings. I had no idea Lord Bridgerton had upset you so."

"Edwina, I just don't like the man. And I don't think you should even consider marrying him. I don't care how ardently or how persistently he pursues you. He will not make a good husband."

Edwina was silent for a moment, her magnificent eyes utterly sober. Then she said, "Well, if you say so, it must be true. I have certainly never been steered wrong by your judgment before. And, as you said, you have spent more time in his company than have I, so you would know better."

Kate let out a long and ill-disguised sigh of relief. "Good," she said firmly. "And when you are feeling more the thing, we shall look among your current suitors for a better match."

"And maybe you could look for a husband, too," Edwina suggested.

"Of course I'm always looking," Kate insisted. "What

would be the point of a London season if I weren't looking?"

Edwina looked dubious. "I don't think you *are* looking, Kate. I think that all you do is interview possibilities for me. And there is no reason you shouldn't find a husband as well. You need a family of your own. I certainly can't imagine anyone more suited to be a mother than you."

Kate bit her lip, not wanting to respond directly to Edwina's point. Because behind those lovely blue eyes and perfect face, Edwina was quite the most perceptive person she knew. And Edwina was right. Kate hadn't been looking for a husband. But why should she? No one was considering her for marriage, either.

She sighed, glancing toward the window. The storm seemed to have passed without striking her area of London. She supposed she ought to be thankful for small favors.

"Why don't we see about you first," Kate finally said, "since I think we both agree that you are more likely to receive a proposal before I do, and then we'll think about my prospects?"

Edwina shrugged, and Kate knew that her deliberate silence meant that she did not agree.

"Very well," Kate said, rising to her feet. "I'll leave you to your rest. I'm sure you'll need it."

Edwina coughed as a reply.

"And drink that remedy!" Kate said with a laugh, heading out the door.

As she shut the door behind her, she heard Edwina mutter, "I'd rather die."

Four days later, Edwina was dutifully drinking Cook's remedy, although not without considerable grumbling and complaint. Her health had improved, but only to the point where she was *almost* better. She was still stuck in bed, still coughing, and very irritable.

Mary had declared that Edwina could not attend any social functions until Tuesday at the earliest. Kate had taken that to mean that they all would receive a respite (because really, what was the point of attending a ball without Edwina?), but after Kate spent a blessedly uneventful Friday, Saturday, and Sunday with nothing to do but read and take Newton for walks, Mary suddenly declared that the two of them would attend Lady Bridgerton's musicale Monday evening, and—

(Kate tried to interject a vehement argument about why this was not a good idea at this point.)

—that was *final*.

Kate gave in fairly quickly. There was really no point in arguing any further, especially since Mary turned on her heel and walked away directly after uttering the word, "final."

Kate did have certain standards, and they included not arguing with closed doors.

And so Monday evening she found herself dressed in ice blue silk, fan in hand, as she and Mary rolled through the streets of London in their inexpensive carriage, on their way to Bridgerton House in Grosvenor Square.

"Everyone will be very surprised to see us without Edwina," Kate said, her left hand fiddling with the black gauze of her cloak.

"You are looking for a husband as well," Mary replied.

Kate held silent for a moment. She couldn't very well argue that point, since, after all, it was supposed to be true.

"And stop crumpling your cloak," Mary added. "It will be wrinkled all evening."

Kate's hand went limp. She then tapped the right one rhythmically against the seat for several seconds, until Mary blurted out, "Good heavens, Kate, can't you sit still?"

"You know I can't," Kate said.

Mary just sighed.

After another long silence, punctuated only by the tapping of her foot, Kate added, "Edwina will be lonely without us."

Mary didn't even bother to look at her as she answered, "Edwina has a novel to read. The latest by that Austen woman. She won't even notice we're gone."

That much was also true. Edwina probably wouldn't notice if her bed caught on fire while she was reading a book.

So Kate said, "The music will probably be dreadful. After that Smythe-Smith affair . . ."

"The Smythe-Smith musicale was performed by the Smythe-Smith daughters," Mary replied, her voice starting to hold an edge of impatience. "Lady Bridgerton has hired a professional opera singer, visiting from Italy. We are honored simply to receive an invitation."

Kate knew without a doubt that the invitation was for Edwina; she and Mary were surely included only out of politeness. But Mary's teeth were beginning to clench together, and so Kate vowed to hold her tongue for the remainder of the ride.

Which wouldn't be so difficult, after all, as they were presently rolling up in front of Bridgerton House.

Kate's mouth dropped open as she looked out the window. "It's huge," she said dumbly.

"Isn't it?" Mary replied, gathering her things together. "I understand that Lord Bridgerton doesn't live there. Even though it belongs to him, he remains in his bachelor's lodgings so that his mother and siblings may reside at Bridgerton House. Isn't that thoughtful of him?"

Thoughtful and *Lord Bridgerton* were not two expressions Kate would have thought to use in the same sentence, but she nodded nonetheless, too awed by the size and grace of the stone building to make an intelligent comment.

The carriage rolled to a halt, and Mary and Kate were helped down by one of the Bridgerton footmen, who rushed to open the door. A butler took their invitation and admitted them, taking their wraps and pointing them toward the music room, which was just at the end of the hall.

Kate had been inside enough grand London homes not to publicly gape at the obvious wealth and beauty of the furnishings, but even she was impressed by the interiors, decorated with elegance and restraint in the Adam style. Even the ceilings were works of art—done up in pale shades of sage and blue, the colors separated by white plasterwork so intricate it almost appeared to be a more solid form of lace.

The music room was just as lovely, the walls painted a friendly shade of lemon yellow. Rows of chairs had been set up for attendees, and Kate quickly steered her stepmother toward the back. Truly, there could be no reason why she'd want to put herself in a noticeable position. Lord Bridgerton was sure to be in attendance—if all the tales about his devotion to his family were true—and if Kate was lucky, maybe he wouldn't even notice her presence.

Quite to the contrary, Anthony knew exactly when Kate stepped out of her carriage and entered his family home. He had been in his study, having a solitary drink before heading down to his mother's annual musicale. In a bid for privacy, he'd chosen not to live at Bridgerton House while still a bachelor, but he did keep his study here. His position as head of the Bridgerton family carried with it serious responsibilities, and Anthony generally found it easier to attend to these responsibilities while in close proximity to the rest of his family.

The study's windows looked out over Grosvenor Square, however, and so he had been amusing himself watching the carriages arrive and the guests alight. When Kate Sheffield had stepped down, she'd looked up at the facade of Bridgerton House, tipping her face up in much the same manner she'd done while enjoying the warmth of the sun in Hyde Park. The light from the sconces on either side of the front door had filtered onto her skin, bathing her with a flickering glow.

And Anthony's breath was sucked right out of him.

His glass tumbler landed on the wide windowsill with a heavy thunk. This was getting ridiculous. He wasn't self-delusional enough to mistake the tightening of his muscles as anything other than desire.

Bloody hell. He didn't even like the woman. She was too bossy, too opinionated, too quick to jump to conclusions. She wasn't even beautiful—at least not compared to quite a few of the ladies flitting about London for the season, her sister most especially included.

Kate's face was a touch too long, her chin a hair too pointed, her eyes a shade too big. Everything about her was too *some*thing. Even her mouth, which vexed him to no end with its endless stream of insults and opinions, was too full. It was a rare event when she actually had it closed and was treating him to a moment of blessed silence, but if he happened to look at her in that split second (for surely she could not be silent for much longer than that) all he saw were her lips, full and pouty, and—provided that she kept them shut and didn't actually speak—eminently kissable.

Kissable?

Anthony shuddered. The thought of kissing Kate Sheffield was terrifying. In fact, the mere fact that he'd even *thought* of it ought to be enough to have him locked up in an asylum.

And yet . . .

Anthony collapsed in a chair.

And yet he'd dreamed about her.

It had happened after the fiasco at The Serpentine. He'd been so furious with her he could barely speak. It was a wonder he'd managed to say anything at all to Edwina during the short ride back to her house. Polite conversation was all he'd been able to get out—mindless words so familiar they tripped from his tongue as if by rote.

A blessing indeed, since his mind most definitely had not been where it should be: on Edwina, his future wife.

Oh, she hadn't agreed to marry him. He hadn't even asked. But she fit his requirements for a wife in every possible way; he'd already decided that she would be the one to whom he would finally propose marriage. She was beautiful, intelligent, and even-tempered. Attractive without making his blood rush. They would spend enjoyable years together, but he'd never fall in love with her.

She was exactly what he needed.

And yet . . .

Anthony reached for his drink and downed the rest of its contents in one gasping gulp.

And yet he'd dreamed about her sister.

He tried not to remember. He tried not to remember the details of the dream—the heat and the sweat of it—but he'd only had this one drink this evening, certainly not enough to impair his memory. And although he'd had no intention of having more than this one drink, the concept of sliding into mindless oblivion was starting to sound appealing.

Anything would be appealing if it meant he wouldn't remember.

But he didn't feel like drinking. He'd not overimbibed in years. It seemed such the young man's game, not at all attractive as one neared thirty. Besides, even if he did decide to seek temporary amnesia in a bottle, it wouldn't come fast enough to make the memory of *her* go away.

Memory? Ha. It wasn't even a real memory. Just a dream, he reminded himself. Just a dream.

He'd fallen asleep quickly upon returning home that evening. He'd stripped naked and soaked in a hot bath for nearly an hour, trying to remove the chill from his bones. He hadn't been completely submerged in The Serpentine as had Edwina, but his legs had been soaked, as had one of his sleeves, and Newton's strategic shake had guaranteed that not one inch of his body remained warm during the windy ride home in the borrowed curricle.

After his bath he'd crawled into bed, not particularly caring that it was still light outside, and would be for a good hour yet. He was exhausted, and he'd had every intention of falling into a deep, dreamless sleep, not to be awakened until the first streaks of dawn touched the morning.

But sometime in the night, his body had grown restless and hungry. And his treacherous mind had filled with the most awful of images. He'd watched it as if floating near the ceiling, and yet he felt everything—his body, naked, moving over a lithe female form; his hands stroking and squeezing warm flesh. The delectable tangle of arms and legs, the musky scent of two bodies in love—it had all been there, hot and vivid in his mind.

And then he'd shifted. Just the tiniest bit, perhaps to kiss the faceless woman's ear. Except as he moved to the side, she was no longer faceless. First appeared a thick lock of dark brown hair, softly curling and tickling at his shoulder. Then he moved even farther . . .

And he saw her.

Kate Sheffield.

He'd awakened in an instant, sitting bolt upright in bed and shaking from the horror of it. It had been the most vivid erotic dream he'd ever experienced.

And his worst nightmare.

He'd felt frantically around the sheets with one of his hands, terrified that he'd find the proof of his passion. God help him if he'd actually ejaculated while dreaming of quite the most awful woman of his acquaintance.

Thankfully, his sheets were clean, and so, with beating heart and heavy breath, he'd lain back against his pillows, his movements slow and careful, as if that would somehow prevent a recurrence of the dream.

He'd stared at the ceiling for hours, first conjugating

Latin verbs, then counting to a thousand, all in an attempt to keep his brain on anything but Kate Sheffield.

And amazingly, he'd exorcised her image from his brain and fallen asleep.

But now she was back. Here. In his home.

It was a terrifying thought.

And where the hell was Edwina? Why hadn't she accompanied her mother and sister?

The first strains of a string quartet drifted under his door, discordant and jumbled, no doubt the warm-up of the musicians his mother had hired to accompany Maria Rosso, the latest soprano to take London by storm.

Anthony certainly hadn't told his mother, but he and Maria had enjoyed a pleasant interlude the last time she'd been in town. Maybe he ought to consider renewing their friendship. If the sultry Italian beauty didn't cure what ailed him, nothing would.

Anthony stood and straightened his shoulders, aware that he probably looked as if he were girding himself for battle. Hell, that's how he *felt*. Maybe, if he was lucky, he'd be able to avoid Kate Sheffield entirely. He couldn't imagine she'd go out of her way to engage him in conversation. She'd made it abundantly clear that she held him in just as much esteem as he did her.

Yes, that's exactly what he would do. Avoid her. How difficult could that be?

Chapter 6

Lady Bridgerton's musicale proved to be a decidedly musical affair (not, This Author assures you, always the norm for musicales). The guest performer was none other than Maria Rosso, the Italian soprano who made her debut in London two years ago and has returned after a brief stint on the Vienna stage.

With thick, sable hair and flashing dark eyes, Miss Rosso proved as lovely in form as she did in voice, and more than one (indeed, more than a dozen) of society's so-called gentlemen found it difficult indeed to remove their eyes from her person, even after the performance had concluded.

LADY WHISTLEDOWN'S SOCIETY PAPERS, 27 APRIL 1814

Kate knew the minute he walked in the room.

She tried to tell herself it had nothing to do with a heightened awareness of the man. He was excruciatingly handsome; that was fact, not opinion. She couldn't imagine that every woman didn't notice him immediately.

He arrived late. Not very—the soprano couldn't have been more than a dozen bars into her piece. But late enough so that he tried to be quiet as he slipped into a chair toward the front near his family. Kate remained motionless in her position at the back, fairly certain that he didn't see her as he settled in for the performance. He didn't look her way, and besides, several candles had been snuffed, leaving the room bathed in a dim, romantic glow. The shadows surely obscured her face.

Kate tried to keep her eyes on Miss Rosso throughout the performance. Kate's disposition was not improved, however, by the fact that the singer could not take her eyes off of Lord Bridgerton. At first Kate had thought she must be imagining Miss Rosso's fascination with the viscount, but by the time the soprano was halfway done, there could be no doubt. Maria Rosso was issuing the viscount a sultry invitation with her eyes.

Why this bothered Kate so much, she didn't know. After all, it was just another piece of proof that he was every bit the licentious rake she'd always known him to be. She should have felt smug. She should have felt vindicated.

Instead, all she felt was disappointment. It was a heavy, uncomfortable feeling around her heart, one that left her slumping slightly in her chair.

When the performance was done, she couldn't help but notice that the soprano, after graciously accepting her applause, walked brazenly up to the viscount and offered him one of those seductive smiles—the sort Kate would never learn to do if she had a dozen opera singers trying to teach her. There was no mistaking what the singer meant by that smile.

Good heavens, the man didn't even need to chase women. They practically dropped at his feet.

It was disgusting. Really, truly disgusting.

And yet Kate couldn't stop watching.

Lord Bridgerton offered the opera singer a mysterious half-smile of his own. Then he reached out and actually tucked an errant lock of her raven hair behind her ear.

Kate shivered.

Now he was leaning forward, whispering something in

her ear. Kate felt her own ears straining in their direction, even though it was quite obviously impossible for her to hear a thing from so far away.

But still, was it truly a crime to be ravenously curious? And—

Good heavens, did he just kiss her neck? Surely he wouldn't do that in his mother's home. Well, she supposed Bridgerton House was technically *his* home, but his mother lived here, as did many of his siblings. Truly, the man should know better than that. A little decorum in the company of his family would not be remiss.

"Kate? Kate?"

It may have been a small kiss, just a feather-light brush of his lips against the opera singer's skin, but it was still a kiss.

"Kate!"

"Right! Yes?" Kate nearly jumped half a foot as she whirled around to face Mary, who was watching her with a decidedly irritated expression.

"Stop watching the viscount," Mary hissed.

"I wasn't—well, all right, I was, but did you see him?" Kate whispered urgently. "He's shameless."

She looked back over at him. He was still flirting with Maria Rosso, and he obviously didn't care who saw them.

Mary's lips pursed into a tight line before she said, "I'm sure his behavior isn't any of our business."

"Of course it's our business. He wants to marry Edwina."

"We don't know that for sure."

Kate thought back over her conversations with Lord Bridgerton. "I'd say it's a very, very good bet."

"Well, stop watching him. I'm certain he wants nothing to do with you after that fiasco in Hyde Park. And besides, there are any number of eligible gentlemen here. You'd do well to stop thinking of Edwina all the time and start looking around for yourself."

Kate felt her shoulders sag. The mere thought of trying

to attract a suitor was exhausting. They were all interested in Edwina, anyway. And even though she wanted nothing to do with the viscount, it still stung when Mary said she was *certain* he wanted nothing to do with *her*.

Mary grasped her arm with a grip that brooked no protest. "Come now, Kate," she said quietly. "Let us go forward to greet our hostess."

Kate swallowed. Lady Bridgerton? She had to meet Lady Bridgerton? The viscount's mother? It was hard enough to believe that a creature such as he even *had* a mother.

But manners were manners, and no matter how much Kate would have liked to slip out into the hall and depart, she knew she must thank her hostess for staging such a lovely performance.

And it had been lovely. Much as Kate was loath to admit it, especially while the woman in question was hanging all over the viscount, Maria Rosso did possess the voice of an angel.

With Mary's arm firmly guiding her, Kate reached the front of the room and waited her turn to meet the viscountess. She seemed a lovely woman, with fair hair and light eyes, and rather petite to have mothered such large sons. The late viscount must have been a tall man, Kate decided.

Finally they reached the front of the small crowd, and the viscountess grasped Mary's hand. "Mrs. Sheffield," she said warmly, "what a delight to see you again. I so enjoyed our meeting at the Hartside ball last week. I am very glad you decided to accept my invitation."

"We would not dream of spending the evening anywhere else," Mary replied. "And may I present my daughter?" She motioned to Kate, who stepped forward and bobbed a dutiful curtsy.

"It is a pleasure to meet you, Miss Sheffield," Lady Bridgerton said.

"And I am likewise honored," Kate replied.

Lady Bridgerton motioned to a young lady at her side. "And this is my daughter, Eloise."

Kate smiled warmly at the girl, who looked to be about the same age as Edwina. Eloise Bridgerton had the exact same color hair as her older brothers, and her face was lit by a friendly, wide smile. Kate liked her instantly.

"How do you do, Miss Bridgerton," Kate said. "Is this your first season?"

Eloise nodded. "I'm not officially out until next year, but my mother has been allowing me to attend functions here at Bridgerton House."

"How lucky for you," Kate replied. "I should have loved to have attended a few parties last year. Everything was so new when I arrived in London this spring. The mind boggles at the simple attempt to remember everyone's name."

Eloise grinned. "Actually, my sister Daphne came out two years ago, and she always described everyone and everything to me in such detail, I feel as if I already recognize almost everyone."

"Daphne is your eldest daughter?" Mary asked Lady Bridgerton.

The viscountess nodded. "She married the Duke of Hastings last year."

Mary smiled. "You must have been delighted."

"Indeed. He is a duke, but more importantly, he is a good man and loves my daughter. I only hope the rest of my children make such excellent matches." Lady Bridgerton cocked her head slightly to the side and turned back to Kate. "I understand, Miss Sheffield, that your sister was not able to attend this evening."

Kate fought a groan. Clearly Lady Bridgerton was already pairing up Anthony and Edwina for a walk down the aisle. "I'm afraid she caught a chill last week."

"Nothing serious, I hope?" the viscountess said to Mary, in a rather mother-to-mother sort of tone.

"No, not at all," Mary replied. "In fact, she is nearly

back to sorts. But I thought she should have one more day of recuperation before venturing out. It would not do for her to suffer a relapse."

"No, of course not." Lady Bridgerton paused, then smiled. "Well, that is too bad. I was so looking forward to meeting her. Edwina is her name, yes?"

Kate and Mary both nodded.

"I've heard she is lovely." But even as Lady Bridgerton said the words, she was glancing at her son—who was flirting madly with the Italian opera singer—and frowning.

Kate felt something very uneasy in her stomach. According to recent issues of *Whistledown,* Lady Bridgerton was on a mission to get her son married off. And while the viscount didn't seem the sort of man to bend to his mother's will (or anyone's, for that matter), Kate had a feeling that Lady Bridgerton would be able to exert quite a bit of pressure if she so chose.

After a few more moments of polite chatter, Mary and Kate left Lady Bridgerton to greet the rest of her guests. They were soon accosted by Mrs. Featherington, who, as the mother of three unmarried young women herself, always had a lot to say to Mary on a wide variety of topics. But as the stout woman bore down on them, her eyes were focused firmly on Kate.

Kate immediately began to assess possible escape routes.

"Kate!" Mrs. Featherington boomed. She had long since declared herself on a first-name basis with the Sheffields. "What a surprise to see you here."

"And why is that, Mrs. Featherington?" Kate asked, puzzled.

"Surely you read *Whistledown* this morning."

Kate smiled weakly. It was either that or wince. "Oh, you mean that little incident involving my dog?"

Mrs. Featherington's brows rose a good half inch. "From what I hear, it was more than a 'little incident.' "

"It was of little consequence," Kate said firmly,

although truth be told, she was finding it difficult not to growl at the meddlesome woman. "And I must say I resent Lady Whistledown referring to Newton as a dog of indeterminate breed. I'll have you know he is a full-blooded corgi."

"It was truly of no matter," Mary said, finally coming to Kate's defense. "I'm surprised it even warranted a mention in the column."

Kate offered Mrs. Featherington her blandest smile, fully aware that both she and Mary were lying through their teeth. Dunking Edwina (and nearly dunking Lord Bridgerton) in The Serpentine was not an incident of "little consequence," but if Lady Whistledown hadn't seen fit to report the full details, Kate certainly wasn't about to fill the gap.

Mrs. Featherington opened her mouth, a sharp intake of breath telling Kate that she was preparing to launch into a lengthy monologue on the topic of the importance of good deportment (or good manners, or good breeding, or good whatever the day's topic was), so Kate quickly blurted out, "May I fetch you two some lemonade?"

The two matrons said yes and thanked her, and Kate slipped away. Once she returned, however, she smiled innocently and said, "But I have only two hands, so now I must return for a glass for myself."

And with that, she took her leave.

She stopped briefly at the lemonade table, just in case Mary was looking, then darted out of the room and into the hall, where she sank onto a cushioned bench about ten yards from the music room, eager to get a bit of air. Lady Bridgerton had left the music room's French doors open to the small garden at the back of the house, but it was such a crush that the air was stifling, even with the slight breeze from outside.

She remained where she sat for several minutes, more than pleased that the other guests had not chosen to spill out into the hall. But then she heard one particular voice rise slightly above the low rumble of the crowd, followed by decidedly musical laughter, and Kate realized with horror that Lord Bridgerton and his would-be mistress were leaving the music room and entering the hall.

"Oh, no," she groaned, trying to keep her voice to herself. The last thing she wanted was for the viscount to stumble across her sitting alone in the hall. She knew she was by herself by choice, but he'd probably think she'd fled the gathering because she was a social failure and all the *ton* shared his opinion of her—that she was an impertinent, unattractive menace to society.

Menace to society? Kate's teeth clamped together. It would take a long, long time before she'd forgive him *that* insult.

But still, she was tired, and she didn't feel like facing him just then, so she hitched up her skirts by a few inches to save her from tripping and ducked into the doorway next to her bench. With any luck, he and his paramour would walk on by, and she could scoot back into the music room, no one being the wiser.

Kate looked around quickly as she shut the door. There was a lighted lantern on a desk, and as her eyes adjusted to the dimness, she realized she was in some sort of office. The walls were lined with books, although not enough for this to be the Bridgertons' library, and the room was dominated by a massive oak desk. Papers lay on top in neat piles, and a quill and inkpot still sat on the blotter.

Clearly this office was not just for show. Someone actually worked here.

Kate wandered toward the desk, her curiosity getting the better of her, and idly ran her fingers along the wooden rim. The air still smelled faintly of ink, and maybe the slightest hint of pipe smoke.

All in all, she decided, it was a lovely room. Comfortable and practical. A person could spend hours here in lazy contemplation.

But just as Kate leaned back against the desk, savoring her quiet solitude, she heard an *awful* sound.

The click of a doorknob.

With a frantic gasp, she dove under the desk, squeezing herself into the empty cube of space and thanking the heavens that the desk was completely solid, rather than the sort that rested on four spindly legs.

Barely breathing, she listened.

"But I had heard this would be the year we would finally see the notorious Lord Bridgerton fall into the parson's mousetrap," came a lilting feminine voice.

Kate bit her lip. It was a lilting feminine voice with an *Italian* accent.

"And where did you hear that?" came the unmistakable voice of the viscount, followed by another awful click of the doorknob.

Kate shut her eyes in agony. She was trapped in the office with a pair of lovers. Life simply could not get any worse than this.

Well, she could be discovered. *That* would be worse. Funny how that didn't make her feel much better about her present predicament, though.

"It is all over town, my lord," Maria replied. "Everyone is saying you have decided to settle down and choose a bride."

There was a silence, but Kate could swear she could *hear* him shrug.

Some footsteps, most probably drawing the lovers closer together, then Bridgerton murmured, "It is probably past time."

"You are breaking my heart, did you know that?"

Kate thought she might gag.

"Now, now, my sweet signorina"—the sound of lips on skin—"we both know that your heart is impervious to any of my machinations."

Next came a rustling sound, which Kate took to be

Maria pulling coyly away, followed by, "But I am not inclined for a dalliance, my lord. I do not look for marriage, of course—that would be most foolish. But when I next choose a protector, it shall be for, shall we say, the long term."

Footsteps. Perhaps Bridgerton was closing the distance between them again?

His voice was low and husky as he said, "I fail to see the problem."

"Your wife may see a problem."

Bridgerton chuckled. "The only reason to give up one's mistress is if one happens to love one's wife. And as I do not intend to choose a wife with whom I might fall in love, I see no reason to deny myself the pleasures of a lovely woman like you."

And you want to marry Edwina? It was all Kate could do not to scream. Truly, if she weren't squatting like a frog with her hands wrapped around her ankles, she probably would have emerged like a Fury and tried to murder the man.

Then followed a few unintelligible sounds, which Kate dearly prayed were not the prelude to something considerably more intimate. After a moment, though, the viscount's voice emerged clearly. "Would you care for something to drink?"

Maria murmured her assent, and Bridgerton's forceful stride echoed along the floor, growing closer and closer, until . . .

Oh, *no.*

Kate spied the decanter, sitting on the windowsill, directly opposite her hiding spot under the desk. If he just kept his face to the window as he poured, she might escape detection, but if he turned so much as halfway . . .

She froze. Utterly froze. Completely stopped breathing.

Eyes wide and unblinking (could eyelids make a sound?) she watched with utter and complete horror as

Bridgerton came into view, his athletic frame displayed to surprising benefit from her vantage point on the floor.

The tumblers clinked slightly together as he set them down, then he pulled the stopper from the decanter and poured two fingers of amber liquid into each glass.

Don't turn around. Don't turn around.

"Is everything all right?" Maria called out.

"Perfect," Bridgerton answered, although he sounded vaguely distracted. He lifted the glasses, humming slightly to himself as his body slowly began to turn.

Keep walking. Keep walking. If he walked away from her while he turned, he'd go back to Maria and she'd be safe. But if he turned, and *then* walked, Kate was as good as dead.

And she had no doubt that he *would* kill her. Frankly, she was surprised he hadn't made an attempt last week at The Serpentine.

Slowly, he turned. And turned. And didn't walk.

And Kate tried to think of all the reasons why dying at the age of twenty-one was really not such a bad thing.

Anthony knew quite well why he'd brought Maria Rosso back to his study. Surely no warm-blooded man could be immune to her charms. Her body was lush, her voice was intoxicating, and he knew from experience that her touch was equally potent.

But even as he took in that silky sable hair and those full, pouting lips, even as his muscles tightened at the memory of other full, pouting parts of her body, he knew that he was using her.

He felt no guilt that he would be using her for his own pleasure. In that regard, she was using him as well. And she at least would be compensated for it, whereas he would be out several jewels, a quarterly allowance, and the rent on a fashionable townhouse in a fashionable (but not too fashionable) part of town.

No, if he felt uneasy, if he felt frustrated, if he felt like he wanted to put his damned fist through a brick wall, it was because he was using Maria to banish the nightmare that was Kate Sheffield from his mind. He never wanted to wake up hard and tortured again, knowing that Kate Sheffield was the cause. He wanted to drown himself in another woman until the very memory of the dream dissolved and faded into nothingness.

Because God knew he was never going to act on that particular erotic fantasy. He didn't even *like* Kate Sheffield. The thought of bedding her made him break out in a cold sweat, even as it swirled a ripple of desire right through his gut.

No, the only way that dream was going to come true was if he were delirious with fever . . . and maybe she'd have to be delirious as well . . . and perhaps they would both have to be stranded on a desert isle, or sentenced to be executed in the morning, or . . .

Anthony shuddered. It simply wasn't going to happen.

But bloody hell, the woman must have bewitched him. There could be no other explanation for the dream—no, make that a nightmare—and besides that, even now he could swear that he could *smell* her. It was that maddening combination of lilies and soap, that beguiling scent that had washed over him while they were out in Hyde Park last week.

Here he was, pouring a glass of the finest whiskey for Maria Rosso, one of the few women of his acquaintance who knew how to appreciate both a fine whiskey and the devilish intoxication that followed, and all he could smell was the damned scent of Kate Sheffield. He knew she was in the house—and he was half ready to kill his mother for that—but this was ridiculous.

"Is everything all right?" Maria called out.

"Perfect," Anthony said, his voice sounding tight to his ears. He began to hum, something he'd always done to relax himself.

He turned and started to take a step forward. Maria was waiting for him, after all.

But there was that damned scent again. Lilies. He could swear it was lilies. And soap. The lilies were intriguing, but the soap made sense. A practical sort of woman like Kate Sheffield would scrub herself clean with soap.

His foot hesitated in midair, and his step forward proved to be a small one instead of his usual long stride. He couldn't quite escape the smell, and he kept turning, his nose instinctively twisting his eyes toward where he knew there couldn't be lilies, and yet the scent was, impossibly, there.

And then he saw her.

Under his desk.

It was impossible.

Surely this was a nightmare. Surely if he closed his eyes and opened them again, she'd be gone.

He blinked. She was still there.

Kate Sheffield, the most maddening, irritating, diabolical woman in all England, was crouching like a frog under his desk.

It was a wonder he didn't drop the whiskey.

Their eyes met, and he saw hers widen with panic and fright. Good, he thought savagely. She *should* be frightened. He was going to tan her bloody hide until her hide was bloody well bloody.

What the *hell* was she doing here? Wasn't dousing him with the filthy water of The Serpentine enough for her bloodthirsty spirit? Wasn't she satisfied with her attempts to stymie his courtship of her sister? Did she need to spy on him as well?

"Maria," he said smoothly, moving forward toward the desk until he was stepping on Kate's hand. He didn't step hard, but he heard her squeak.

This gave him immense satisfaction.

"Maria," he repeated, "I have suddenly remembered an

urgent matter of business that must be dealt with immediately."

"This very night?" she asked, sounding quite dubious.

"I'm afraid so. Euf!"

Maria blinked. "Did you just grunt?"

"No," Anthony lied, trying not to choke on the word. Kate had removed her glove and wrapped her hand around his knee, digging her nails straight through his breeches and into his skin. Hard.

At least he hoped it was her nails. It could have been her teeth.

"Are you sure there is nothing amiss?" Maria inquired.

"Nothing . . . at"—whatever body part Kate was sinking into his leg sank a little farther—"all!" The last word came out as more of a howl, and he kicked his foot forward, connecting with something he had a sneaking suspicion was her stomach.

Normally, Anthony would die before striking a woman, but this truly seemed to be an exceptional case. In fact, he took not a little bit of pleasure in kicking her while she was down.

She was biting his leg, after all.

"Allow me to walk you to the door," he said to Maria, shaking Kate off his ankle.

But Maria's eyes were curious, and she took a few steps forward. "Anthony, is there an animal under your desk?"

Anthony let out a bark of laughter. "You could say that."

Kate's fist came down on his foot.

"Is it a dog?"

Anthony seriously considered answering in the affirmative, but even he was not that cruel. Kate obviously appreciated his uncharacteristic tact, because she let go of his leg.

Anthony took advantage of his release to quickly step out from behind the desk. "Would I be unforgivably rude," he asked, striding to Maria's side and taking her arm, "if I merely walked you to the door and not back to the music room?"

She laughed, a low, sultry sound that should have seduced him. "I am a grown woman, my lord. I believe I can manage the short distance."

"Forgive me?"

She stepped through the door he held open for her. "I suspect there isn't a woman alive who could deny you forgiveness for that smile."

"You are a rare woman, Maria Rosso."

She laughed again. "But not, apparently, rare enough."

She floated out, and Anthony shut the door with a decisive click. Then, some devil on his shoulder surely prodding him, he turned the key in the lock and pocketed it.

"You," he boomed, eliminating the distance to the desk in four long strides. "Show yourself."

When Kate didn't scramble out quickly enough, he reached down, clamped his hand around her upper arm, and hauled her to her feet.

"Explain yourself," he hissed.

Kate's legs nearly buckled as the blood rushed back to her knees, which had been bent for nearly a quarter of an hour. "It was an accident," she said, grabbing on to the edge of the desk for support.

"Funny how those words seem to emerge from your mouth with startling frequency."

"It's true!" she protested. "I was sitting in the hall, and—" She gulped. He had stepped forward and was now very, very close. "I was sitting in the hall," she said again, her voice sounding crackly and hoarse, "and I heard you coming. I was just trying to avoid you."

"And so you invaded my private office?"

"I didn't know it was your office. I—" Kate sucked in her breath. He'd moved even closer, his crisp, wide lapels now only inches from the bodice of her dress. She knew his proximity was deliberate, that he sought to intimidate rather than seduce, but that didn't do anything to quell the frantic beating of her heart.

"I think perhaps you did know that this was my office," he murmured, letting his forefinger trail down the side of her cheek. "Perhaps you did not seek to avoid me at all."

Kate swallowed convulsively, long past the point of trying to maintain her composure.

"Mmmm?" His finger slid along the line of her jaw. "What do you say to that?"

Kate's lips parted, but she couldn't have uttered a word if her life had depended on it. He wore no gloves—he must have removed them during his tryst with Maria—and the touch of his skin against hers was so powerful it seemed to control her body. She breathed when he paused, stopped when he moved. She had no doubt that her heart was beating in time to his pulse.

"Maybe," he whispered, so close now that his breath kissed her lips, "you desired something else altogether."

Kate tried to shake her head, but her muscles refused to obey.

"Are you sure?"

This time, her head betrayed her and gave a little shake.

He smiled, and they both knew he had won.

Chapter 7

Also in attendance at Lady Bridgerton's musicale: Mrs. Featherington and the three elder Featherington daughters (Prudence, Philippa, and Penelope, none of whom wore colors beneficial to their complexions); Mr. Nigel Berbrooke (who, as usual, had much to say, although no one save Philippa Featherington seemed interested); and, of course, Mrs. Sheffield and Miss Katharine Sheffield.

This Author assumes that the Sheffields' invitation had also included Miss Edwina Sheffield, but she was not present. Lord Bridgerton seemed in fine spirits despite the younger Miss Sheffield's absence, but alas, his mother appeared disappointed.

But then again, Lady Bridgerton's matchmaking tendencies are legendary, and surely she must be at loose ends now that her daughter has married the Duke of Hastings.

LADY WHISTLEDOWN'S SOCIETY PAPERS, 27 APRIL 1814

Anthony knew he had to be insane.

There could be no other explanation. He'd meant to scare her, terrify her, make her understand that she could never hope to meddle in his affairs and win, and instead . . .

He kissed her.

Intimidation had been his intention, and so he'd moved closer and closer until she, an innocent, could only be cowed by his presence. She wouldn't know what it was like to have a man so near that the heat of his body seeped through her clothes, so close that she couldn't tell where his breath ended and hers began.

She wouldn't recognize the first prickles of desire, nor would she understand that slow, swirling heat in the core of her being.

And that slow, swirling heat was there. He could see it in her face.

But she, a complete innocent, would never comprehend what he could see with one look of his experienced eyes. All she would know was that he was looming over her, that he was stronger, more powerful, and that she had made a dreadful mistake by invading his private sanctuary.

He was going to stop right there and leave her bothered and breathless. But when there was barely an inch between them, the pull grew too strong. Her scent was too beguiling, the sound of her breath too arousing. The prickles of desire he'd meant to spark within her suddenly ignited within *him,* sending a warm claw of need to the very tips of his toes. And the finger he'd been trailing along her cheek—just to torture her, he told himself—suddenly became a hand that cupped the back of her head as his lips took hers in an explosion of anger and desire.

She gasped against his mouth, and he took advantage of her parted lips by sliding his tongue between them. She was stiff in his arms, but it seemed more to do with surprise than anything else, and so Anthony pressed his suit further by allowing one of his hands to slide down her back and cup the gentle curve of her derriere.

"This is madness," he whispered against her ear. But he made no move to let her go.

Her reply was an incoherent, confused moan, and her body became slightly more pliant in his arms, allowing him to mold her even closer to his form. He knew he should stop, knew he damned well shouldn't have started, but his blood was racing with need, and she felt so . . . so . . .

So *good.*

He groaned, his lips leaving hers to taste the slightly salty skin of her neck. There was something about her that suited him like no woman ever had before, as if his body had discovered something his mind utterly refused to consider.

Something about her was . . . right.

She felt right. She smelled right. She tasted right. And he knew that if he stripped off all of her clothes and took her there on the carpet on the floor of his study, she would fit underneath him, fit around him—just right.

It occurred to Anthony that when she wasn't arguing with him, Kate Sheffield might bloody well be the finest woman in England.

Her arms, which had been imprisoned in his embrace, slowly edged up, until her hands were hesitantly resting on his back. And then her lips moved. It was a tiny thing, actually, a movement barely felt on the thin skin of his forehead, but she was definitely kissing him back.

A low, triumphant growl emerged from Anthony's mouth as he moved his mouth back to hers, kissing her fiercely, daring her to continue what she'd begun. "Oh, Kate," he moaned, nudging her back until she was leaning against the edge of the desk. "God, you taste so good."

"Bridgerton?" Her voice was tremulous, the word more of a question than anything else.

"Don't say anything," he whispered. "Whatever you do, don't say anything."

"But—"

"Not a word," he interrupted, pressing a finger to her lips. The last thing he wanted was for her to ruin this perfectly good moment by opening her mouth and arguing.

"But I—" She planted her hands on his chest and

wrenched herself away, leaving him off balance and panting.

Anthony let out a curse, and not a mild one.

Kate scurried away, not all the way across the room, but over to a tall wingback chair, far enough away so that she was not in arms' reach. She gripped the stiff back of the chair, then darted around it, thinking that it might be a good idea to have a nice solid piece of furniture between them.

The viscount didn't look to be in the best of tempers.

"Why did you do that?" she said, her voice so low it was almost a whisper.

He shrugged, suddenly looking a little less angry and a little more uncaring. "Because I wanted to."

Kate just gaped at him for a moment, unable to believe that he could have such a simple answer to what was, despite its simple phrasing, such a complicated question. Finally, she blurted out, "But you can't have."

He smiled. Slowly. "But I did."

"But you don't like me!"

"True," he allowed.

"And I don't like you."

"So you've been telling me," he said smoothly. "I'll have to take your word for it, since it wasn't particularly apparent a few seconds ago."

Kate felt her cheeks flush with shame. She had responded to his wicked kiss, and she hated herself for it, almost as much as she hated him for initiating the intimacy.

But he didn't have to taunt her. That was the act of a cad. She gripped the back of the chair until her knuckles turned white, no longer certain if she was using it as a defense against Bridgerton or as a means to stop herself from lunging forward to strangle him.

"I am not going to let you marry Edwina," she said in a very low voice.

"No," he murmured, moving slowly forward until he

was just on the other side of the chair. "I didn't think you were."

Her chin lifted a notch. "And *I* am certainly not going to marry you."

He planted his hands on the armrests and leaned forward until his face was only a few inches from hers. "I don't recall asking."

Kate lurched backward. "But you just kissed me!"

He laughed. "If I offered marriage to every woman I'd kissed, I'd have been thrown into jail for bigamy long ago."

Kate could feel herself begin to shake, and she held on to the back of the chair for dear life. "You, sir," she nearly spat out, "have no honor."

His eyes blazed and one of his hands shot out to grip her chin. He held her that way for several seconds, forcing her to meet his gaze. "That," he said in a deadly voice, "is not true, and were you a man, I'd call you out for it."

Kate remained still for what seemed like a very long time, her eyes locked on his, the skin on her cheek burning where his powerful fingers held her motionless. Finally she did the one thing she'd sworn she would never do with this man.

She begged.

"Please," she whispered, "let me go."

He did, his hand releasing her with a startling abruptness. "My apologies," he said, sounding the slightest bit . . . surprised?

No, that was impossible. Nothing could surprise this man.

"I didn't mean to hurt you," he added softly.

"Didn't you?"

He gave his head a small shake. "No. To scare you, perhaps. But not to hurt you."

Kate stepped backward on shaky legs. "You're nothing but a rake," she said, wishing her voice had emerged with a bit more disdain and a bit less quavering.

"I know," he said with a shrug, the intense fire in his eyes draining down to light amusement. "It's in my nature."

Kate took another step back. She didn't have the energy to try to keep up with his abrupt changes of mood. "I'm leaving now."

"Go," he said affably, waving toward the door.

"You can't stop me."

He smiled. "I wouldn't dream of it."

She began to edge away, walking slowly backward, afraid that if she took her eyes off him for one second he might pounce. "I'm leaving now," she said again, unnecessarily.

But when her hand was an inch away from the doorknob, he said, "I suppose I'll see you next time I call upon Edwina."

Kate went white. Not that she could actually see her face, of course, but for the first time in her life, she actually felt the blood drain from her skin. "You said you were going to leave her alone," she said accusingly.

"No," he replied, leaning rather insolently against the side of the chair, "I said that I didn't think you were likely to 'let' me marry her. Which doesn't really signify, as I have no plans to let you manage my life."

Kate suddenly felt as if a cannonball were lodged in her throat. "But you can't possibly want to marry her after you—after I—"

He took a few steps toward her, his movements slow and sleek like a cat. "After you kissed me?"

"I didn't—" But the words burned the back of her throat, because they were so obviously a lie. She had not initiated the kiss, but she had, in the end, participated in it.

"Oh, come now, Miss Sheffield," he said, standing up straight and crossing his arms. "Let's not go down that road. We don't like each other, that much is true, but I do respect you in an odd, perverted sort of way, and I know you're not a liar."

She said nothing. Really, what could she say? How did one respond to a statement that contained the words "respect" *and* "perverted"?

"You kissed me back," he said with a small, satisfied smile. "Not with any great enthusiasm, I'll admit, but that would be just a matter of time."

She shook her head, unable to believe what she was hearing. "How can you talk of such things not even a minute after declaring your intention to court my sister?"

"This does put a bit of a crimp in my plans, that is true," he commented, his voice light and thoughtful, as if he were considering the purchase of a new horse, or perhaps deciding which neckcloth to wear.

Maybe it was his casual posture, maybe it was the way he stroked his chin as if pretending to give the matter some thought. But something ignited a fuse inside of Kate, and without even thinking, she launched forward, all the furies of the world collecting in her soul as she threw herself against him, pounding his chest with her fists. "You will never marry her!" she cried out. "Never! Do you hear me?"

He raised one arm to ward off a blow to his face. "I'd have to be deaf not to." Then he expertly captured her wrists, holding her arms immobile while her body heaved and shook with rage.

"I won't let you make her unhappy. I won't let you ruin her life," she said, the words choking in her throat. "She is everything that is good and honorable and pure. And she deserves better than you."

Anthony watched her closely, his eyes trained on her face, somehow rendered beautiful by the force of her anger. Her cheeks were high with color, her eyes shone with tears she was fighting hard to keep off her face, and he was beginning to feel like he might be the worst sort of cad.

"Why, Miss Sheffield," he said softly, "I do believe you truly love your sister."

"Of course I love her!" she burst out. "Why do you

think I have gone to such efforts to keep her away from *you*? Did you think I did it for amusement? Because I can assure you, my lord, I can think of many things more amusing than being held captive in your study."

Abruptly, he let go of her wrists.

"I should think," she said with a sniffle, rubbing her reddened, abused flesh, "that my love for Edwina would be the one thing about me you could understand with perfect clarity. You, who are supposedly so devoted to your own family."

Anthony said nothing, just watched her, and wondered if perhaps there was a great deal more to this woman than he'd originally estimated.

"If you were Edwina's brother," Kate said with deadly accuracy, "would you allow her to marry a man like you?"

He did not speak for a very long moment, long enough so that the silence rang awkwardly in his own ears. Finally he said, "That is beside the point."

To her credit, she did not smile. She did not crow, nor did she taunt. When she spoke, her words were quiet and true. "I believe I have my answer." Then she turned on her heel and began to walk away.

"My sister," he said, loudly enough to halt her progress toward the door, "married the Duke of Hastings. Are you familiar with his reputation?"

She paused, but she did not turn around. "He is reputed to be quite devoted to his wife."

Anthony chuckled. "Then you are not familiar with his reputation. At least not as it was before he married."

Kate turned slowly around. "If you are attempting to convince me that reformed rakes make the best husbands, you will meet with no success. It was in this very room, not fifteen minutes ago, that you told Miss Rosso that you saw no reason to give up a mistress for a wife."

"I believe I said that was the case only if one does not love one's wife."

A funny little sound emerged from her nose—not quite

a snort, but more than a breath, and it was abundantly clear, in that moment at least, that she had no respect for him. With a sharp amusement in her eyes, she asked, "And do you love my sister, Lord Bridgerton?"

"Of course not," he replied. "And I would never insult your intelligence by saying otherwise. *But*," he said loudly, warding off the interruption he knew was sure to come, "I have known your sister but a week. I have no reason to believe that I would not come to love her were we to spend many years in holy matrimony."

She crossed her arms. "Why is it that I cannot believe a word out of your mouth?"

He shrugged. "I'm sure I do not know." But he did know. The very reason he'd selected Edwina for his wife was that he knew he'd never come to love her. He liked her, he respected her, and he was confident that she'd make an excellent mother to his heirs, but he'd never love her. The spark simply was not there.

She shook her head, disappointment in her eyes. Disappointment that somehow made him feel less of a man. "I hadn't thought you a liar, either," she said softly. "A rake and a rogue, and perhaps a whole host of other things, but not a liar."

Anthony felt her words like blows. Something unpleasant squeezed around his heart—something that made him want to lash out, to hurt her, or at least to show her she hadn't the power to hurt him. "Oh, Miss Sheffield," he called out, his voice a rather cruel drawl, "you won't get far without *this*."

Before she had a chance to react, he reached into his pocket, pulled out the key to the study, and tossed it in her direction, deliberately aiming it at her feet. Given no warning, her reflexes were not sharp, and when she thrust out her hands to catch the key, she missed it entirely. Her hands made a hollow clapping sound as they connected, followed by the dull thud of the key hitting the carpet.

She stood there for a moment, staring at the key, and he

could tell the instant she realized he had not intended for her to catch it. She remained utterly still, and then she brought her eyes to his. They were blazing with hatred, and something worse.

Disdain.

Anthony felt as if he'd been punched in the gut. He fought the most ridiculous impulse to leap forward and grab the key from the carpet, to get down on one knee and hand it to her, to apologize for his conduct and beg her forgiveness.

But he would do none of those things. He did not want to mend this breach; he did not want her favorable opinion.

Because that elusive spark—the one so noticeably absent with her sister, whom he intended to marry—crackled and burned so strongly it seemed the room ought to be as light as day.

And nothing could have terrified him more.

Kate remained motionless for far longer than he would have thought, obviously loath to kneel before him, even if it was to gather up the key that would provide her with the escape she so obviously desired.

Anthony just forced a smile, lowering his gaze to the floor and then back up to her face. "Don't you want to leave, Miss Sheffield?" he said, too smoothly.

He watched as her chin trembled, as her throat worked a convulsive swallow. And then, abruptly, she crouched down and scooped up the key. "You will never marry my sister," she vowed, her low, intense voice sending chills to his very bones. "Never."

And then, with a decisive click of the lock, she was gone.

Two days later, Kate was still furious. It didn't help that the afternoon following the musicale, a large bouquet of flowers had arrived for Edwina, the card reading, "With my wishes for a speedy recovery. Last night was dull indeed without your shining presence. —Bridgerton."

Mary had ooohed and aahed over the note—so poetic, she'd sighed, so lovely, so obviously the words of a man truly smitten. But Kate had known the truth. The note was more of an insult toward her than it was a compliment toward Edwina.

Dull indeed, she fumed, eyeing that note—enshrined now on a table in the sitting room—and wondering how she might make it look an accident if it somehow found itself torn into pieces. She might not know very much about matters of the heart and the affairs of men and women, but she'd bet her life that whatever the viscount had been feeling that night in the study, it had not been boredom.

He hadn't, however, come to call. Kate couldn't imagine why, since taking Edwina out for a drive would be an even bigger slap in the face than the note had been. In her most fanciful moments, she liked to flatter herself that he hadn't stopped by because he was afraid to face her, but she knew that was patently untrue.

That man wasn't afraid of anyone. Least of all, a plain, aging spinster he'd probably kissed out of a mix of curiosity, anger, and pity.

Kate crossed over to a window and gazed out over Milner Street; not the most picturesque view in London, but at least it stopped her from staring at the note. It was the pity that truly ate at her. She prayed that whatever had gone into that kiss, the curiosity and the anger had outweighed the pity.

She didn't think she could bear it if he pitied her.

But Kate didn't have very long to obsess over the kiss and what it might and might not have meant, because that afternoon—the afternoon after the flowers—arrived an invitation far more unsettling than anything Lord Bridgerton might have issued himself. The Sheffields' presence, it seemed, was desired at a country house party being rather spontaneously hosted in one week's time by Lady Bridgerton.

The mother of the devil himself.

And there was no way that Kate could possibly get out of going. Nothing short of an earthquake combined with a hurricane combined with a tornado—none of which were likely to occur in Great Britain, although Kate was still holding out hope for the hurricane, as long as there was no thunder or lightning involved—would prevent Mary from showing up on the Bridgertons' bucolic doorstep with Edwina in tow. And Mary certainly wasn't going to allow Kate to remain alone in London, left to her own devices. Not to mention that there was no way Kate was going to allow Edwina to go without her.

The viscount had no scruples. He'd probably kiss Edwina just as he'd kissed Kate, and Kate couldn't imagine that Edwina would have the fortitude to resist such an advance. She'd probably think it beyond romantic and fall in love with him on the spot.

Even Kate had had difficulty keeping her head when his lips had been on hers. For one blissful moment, she'd forgotten everything. She'd known nothing but an exquisite sensation of being cherished and wanted—no, *needed*—and it had been heady stuff, indeed.

Almost enough to make a lady forget that the man doing the kissing was a worthless cad.

Almost . . . but not quite.

Chapter 8

As any regular reader of this column knows, there are two sects in London who shall forever remain in the utmost opposition: Ambitious Mamas and Determined Bachelors.

The Ambitious Mama has daughters of marriageable age. The Determined Bachelor does not want a wife. The crux of the conflict should be obvious to those with half a brain, or, in other words, approximately fifty percent of This Author's readership.

This Author has not yet seen a guest list for Lady Bridgerton's country house party, but informed sources indicate that nearly every eligible young lady of marriageable age will be gathering in Kent next week.

This surprises no one. Lady Bridgerton has never made a secret of her desire to see her sons favorably married. This sentiment has made her a favorite among the Ambitious Mama set, who despairingly view the Bridgerton brothers as the worst sort of Determined Bachelors.

If one is to trust the betting books, then at least one of the Bridgerton brothers shall be witness to wedding bells before the year is through.

As much as it pains This Author to agree with the betting books (they are written by men, and thus inherently flawed), This Author must concur in the prediction.

Lady Bridgerton will soon have her daughter-in-law. But who she will be—and to which brother she shall find herself married—ah, Gentle Reader, that is still anyone's guess.

LADY WHISTLEDOWN'S SOCIETY PAPERS, 29 APRIL 1814

One week later, Anthony was in Kent— in his private suite of offices, to be precise—awaiting the start of his mother's country house party.

He'd seen the guest list. There could be no doubt that his mother had decided to host this party for one reason and one reason only: to get one of her sons married off, preferably him. Aubrey Hall, the ancestral seat of the Bridgertons, would be filled to the brim with eligible young ladies, each lovelier and more empty-headed than the last. To keep numbers even, Lady Bridgerton had had to invite a number of gentlemen, to be sure, but none were as wealthy or well connected as her own sons, save for the few who were married.

His mother, Anthony thought ruefully, had never been known for her subtlety. At least not when the well-being (*her* definition of well-being, that is) of her children was concerned.

He had not been surprised to see that an invitation had been extended to the Misses Sheffield. His mother had mentioned—several times—how much she liked Mrs. Sheffield. And he had been forced to listen to his mother's "Good Parents Make Good Children" theory too many times not to know what *that* meant.

He'd actually felt a resigned sort of satisfaction upon the sight of Edwina's name on the list. He was eager to propose to her and be done with it. He did feel a measure of uneasiness over what had happened with Kate, but there seemed little to be done now unless he wanted to go to the trouble of finding another prospective bride.

Which he did not. Once Anthony made a decision—in this case to finally get married—he saw no reason in courting delays. Procrastination was for those with a bit more time to live out their lives. Anthony might have avoided the parson's mousetrap for nearly a decade, but now that he'd decided it was time for a bride, there seemed little sense in tarrying.

Marry, procreate, and die. Such was the life of a noble Englishman, even one whose father and uncle had not dropped unexpectedly dead at the ages of thirty-eight and thirty-four, respectively.

Clearly, all he could do at this point was to avoid Kate Sheffield. An apology would probably also be in order. It wouldn't be easy, since the last thing he wanted to do was humble himself to that woman, but the whispers of his conscience had risen to a dull roar, and he knew she deserved the words, "I'm sorry."

She probably deserved more, but Anthony was unwilling to contemplate what that might be.

Not to mention that unless he went and spoke to her, she was likely to block a union between him and Edwina to her dying breath.

Now was clearly the time to take action. If there ever was a romantic spot for a proposal of marriage, Aubrey Hall was it. Built in the early 1700s of warm yellow stone, it sat comfortably on a wide green lawn, surrounded by sixty acres of parkland, a full ten of which were flowering gardens. Later in the summer the roses would be out, but now the grounds were carpeted with grape hyacinths and the brilliant tulips his mother had had imported from Holland.

Anthony gazed across the room and out the window, where ancient elms rose majestically around the house. They shaded the drive and, he liked to think, made the hall seem a bit more like it was a part of nature and a bit less like the typical country homes of the aristocracy—man-made monuments to wealth, position, and power. There were several ponds, a creek, and countless hills and hollows, each one with its own special memories of childhood.

And his father.

Anthony closed his eyes and exhaled. He loved coming home to Aubrey Hall, but the familiar sights and smells brought his father to mind with a clarity so vivid it was almost painful. Even now, nearly twelve years after Edmund Bridgerton's death, Anthony still expected to see him come bounding around the corner, the smallest of the Bridgerton children screaming with delight as he rode on his father's shoulders.

The image made Anthony grin. The child on the shoulders might be a boy or a girl; Edmund had never discriminated between his children when it came to horseplay. But no matter who held the coveted spot at the top of the world, they would surely be chased after by a nurse, insisting that they stop this nonsense at once, and that a child's place was in the nursery and certainly *not* on her father's shoulders.

"Oh, Father," Anthony whispered, looking up at the portrait of Edmund that hung over the fireplace, "how on earth will I ever live up to your achievements?"

And surely that had to have been Edmund Bridgerton's greatest achievement—presiding over a family filled with love and laughter and everything that was so often absent from aristocratic life.

Anthony turned away from his father's portrait and crossed over to the window, watching the coaches pull up the drive. The afternoon had brought a steady stream of arrivals, and every conveyance seemed to carry yet another fresh-faced young lady, her eyes alight with happiness at having been gifted with an invitation to the Bridgerton house party.

Lady Bridgerton didn't often elect to fill her country home with guests. When she did, it was always the event of the season.

Although, truth be told, none of the Bridgertons spent much time at Aubrey Hall any longer. Anthony suspected that his mother suffered the same malady he did—memories of Edmund around every corner. The younger children had few memories of the place, having been raised primarily in London. They certainly didn't recall the long hikes across fields, or the fishing, or the treehouse.

Hyacinth, who was now just eleven, had never even been held in her father's arms. Anthony had tried to fill the gap as best as he could, but he knew he was a very pale comparison.

With a weary sigh, Anthony leaned heavily against the window frame, trying to decide whether or not he wanted to pour himself a drink. He was staring out over the lawn, his eyes focusing on absolutely nothing, when a carriage decidedly shabbier than the rest rolled down the drive. Not that there was anything shoddy about it; it was obviously well made and sturdy. But it lacked the gilded crests that graced the other carriages, and it seemed to bump along a tiny bit more than the rest, as if it weren't quite well sprung enough for comfort.

This would be the Sheffields, Anthony realized. Everyone else on the guest list was in possession of a respectable fortune. Only the Sheffields would have had to hire a carriage for the season.

Sure enough, when one of the Bridgerton footmen, dressed in stylish powder-blue livery, leaped forward to open the door, out stepped Edwina Sheffield, looking a veritable vision in a pale yellow traveling dress and matching bonnet. Anthony was not close enough to see her face clearly, but it was easy enough to imagine. Her cheeks would be soft and pink, and her exquisite eyes would mirror the cloudless sky.

The next to emerge was Mrs. Sheffield. It was only when she took her place next to Edwina that he realized how closely they resembled one another. Both were charmingly graceful and petite, and as they spoke, he could see that they held themselves in the same manner. The tilt of the head was identical, as were their posture and stance.

Edwina would not outgrow her beauty. This would clearly be a good attribute in a wife, although—Anthony threw a rueful glance at his father's portrait—he wasn't likely to be around to watch her age.

Finally, Kate stepped down.

And Anthony realized he'd been holding his breath.

She didn't move like the two other Sheffield women. They had been dainty, leaning on the footman, putting their hands in his with a graceful arch of the wrist.

Kate, on the other hand, practically hopped right down. She took the footman's proffered arm, but she certainly didn't appear to need his assistance. As soon as her feet touched the ground, she stood tall and lifted her face to gaze at the facade of Aubrey Hall. Everything about her was direct and straightforward, and Anthony had no doubt that if he were close enough to gaze into her eyes, he would find them utterly forthright.

Once she saw him, however, they would fill with disdain, and perhaps a touch of hatred as well.

Which was really all he deserved. A gentleman did not treat a lady as he had Kate Sheffield and expect her continued good favor.

Kate turned to her mother and sister and said something, causing Edwina to laugh and Mary to smile indulgently. Anthony realized he hadn't had much opportunity to watch the three of them interact before. They were a true family, comfortable in each other's presence, and there was a warmth one sensed in their faces when they conversed. It was especially fascinating since he knew that Mary and Kate were not blood relatives.

There were some bonds, he was coming to realize, that were stronger than those of blood. These were not bonds he had room for in his life.

Which was why, when he married, the face behind the veil would have to be Edwina Sheffield's.

Kate had expected to be impressed by Aubrey Hall. She had not expected to be enchanted.

The house was smaller than she'd expected. Oh, it was still far, far larger than anything she'd ever had the honor to call home, but the country manor was not a hulking behemoth rising out of the landscape like a misplaced medieval castle.

Rather, Aubrey Hall seemed almost cozy. It seemed a bizarre word to use to describe a house with surely fifty rooms, but its fanciful turrets and crenellations almost made it seem like something out of a fairy story, especially with the late afternoon sun giving the yellow stone an almost reddish glow. There was nothing austere or imposing about Aubrey Hall, and Kate liked it immediately.

"Isn't it lovely?" Edwina whispered.

Kate nodded. "Lovely enough to make a week spent in the company of that awful man almost bearable."

Edwina laughed and Mary scolded, but even Mary could not resist an indulgent smile. But she did say, casting an eye to the footman, who had gone around the back of the coach to unload their luggage, "You should not say such things, Kate. One never knows who is listening, and it is unbecoming to speak thusly about our host."

"Have no fear, he didn't hear me," Kate replied. "And besides, I thought Lady Bridgerton was our hostess. She *did* issue the invitation."

"The viscount owns the house," Mary returned.

"Very well," Kate acceded, motioning to Aubrey Hall with a dramatic wave of her arm. "The moment I enter those hallowed halls, I shall be nothing but sweetness and light."

Edwina snorted. "That will certainly be a sight to behold."

Mary shot Kate a knowing look. " 'Sweetness and light' applies to the gardens as well," she said.

Kate just smiled. "Truly, Mary, I shall be on my best behavior. I promise."

"Just do your best to avoid the viscount."

"I will," Kate promised. *As long as he does his best to avoid Edwina.*

A footman appeared at their side, his arm sweeping toward the hall in a splendid arc. "If you will step inside," he said, "Lady Bridgerton is eager to greet her guests."

The three Sheffields immediately turned and made their way to the front door. As they mounted the shallow steps, however, Edwina turned to Kate with a mischievous grin and whispered, "Sweetness and light begins here, sister mine."

"If we weren't in public," Kate returned, her voice equally hushed, "I might have to hit you."

Lady Bridgerton was in the main hall when they stepped inside, and Kate could see the ribboned hems of walking dresses disappearing up the stairs as the previous carriage's occupants made their way to their rooms.

"Mrs. Sheffield!" Lady Bridgerton called out, crossing over toward them. "How lovely to see you. And Miss Sheffield," she added, turning to Kate, "I am so glad you were able to join us."

"It was kind of you to invite us," Kate replied. "And it is truly a pleasure to escape the city for a week."

Lady Bridgerton smiled. "You are a country girl at heart, then?"

"I'm afraid so. London is exciting, and always worth a visit, but I do prefer the green fields and fresh air of the countryside."

"My son is much the same way," Lady Bridgerton said. "Oh, he spends his time in the city, but a mother knows the truth."

"The viscount?" Kate asked doubtfully. He seemed such the consummate rake, and everyone knew a rake's natural habitat was the city.

"Yes, Anthony. We lived here almost exclusively when he was a child. We went to London during the season, of course, since I do love to attend parties and balls, but never for more than a few weeks. It was only after my husband passed away that we moved our primary residence to town."

"I'm sorry for your loss," Kate murmured.

The viscountess turned to her with a wistful expression in her blue eyes. "That is very sweet of you. He has been gone for many years, but I do still miss him each and every day."

Kate felt a lump forming in her throat. She remembered how well Mary and her father had loved each other, and she knew that she was in the presence of another woman who had experienced true love. And suddenly she felt so very sad. Because Mary had lost her husband and the viscountess had lost hers as well, and . . .

And maybe most of all because she would probably never know the bliss of true love herself.

"But we're becoming so maudlin," Lady Bridgerton suddenly said, smiling a little too brightly as she turned back to Mary, "and here I haven't even met your other daughter."

"Have you not?" Mary asked, her brow furrowing. "I suppose that must be true. Edwina was not able to attend your musicale."

"I have, of course, seen you from afar," Lady Bridgerton said to Edwina, bestowing upon her a dazzling smile.

Mary made the introductions, and Kate could not help but notice the appraising manner in which Lady Bridgerton regarded Edwina. There could be no doubt about it. She'd decided Edwina would make an excellent addition to her family.

After a few more moments of chitchat, Lady Bridgerton offered them tea while their bags were being delivered to their rooms, but they declined, as Mary was tired and wanted to lie down.

"As you wish," Lady Bridgerton said, signaling to a housemaid. "I shall have Rose show you to your rooms. Dinner is at eight. Is there anything else I may do for you before you retire?"

Mary and Edwina both shook their heads no, and Kate started to follow suit, but at the last minute she blurted out, "Actually, if I might ask you a question."

Lady Bridgerton smiled warmly. "Of course."

"I noticed when we arrived that you have extensive flower gardens. Might I explore them?"

"Then you are a gardener as well?" Lady Bridgerton inquired.

"Not a very good one," Kate admitted, "but I do admire the hand of an expert."

The viscountess blushed. "I should be honored if you explored the gardens. They are my pride and joy. I don't have much a hand in them now, but when Edmund was al—" She stopped and cleared her throat. "That is to say, when I spent more time here, I was always up to my elbows in dirt. It used to drive my mother positively mad."

"And the gardener, too, I imagine," Kate said.

Lady Bridgerton's smile erupted into laughter. "Oh, indeed! He was a terrible sort. Always saying that the only thing women knew about flowers was how to accept them as a gift. But he had the greenest thumb you could ever imagine, so I learned to put up with him."

"And he learned to put up with you?"

Lady Bridgerton smiled wickedly. "No, he never did, actually. But I didn't let that stop me."

Kate grinned, instinctively warming to the older woman.

"But don't let me keep you any longer," Lady Bridgerton said. "Let Rose take you up and get you settled in. And Miss Sheffield," she said to Kate, "if you like, I should be happy to give you a tour of the gardens later in the week. I'm afraid I'm too busy greeting guests right now, but I would be delighted to make time for you at a later date."

"I would like that, thank you," Kate said, and then she and Mary and Edwina followed the maid up the stairs.

Anthony emerged from his position behind his ever-so-slightly ajar door and strode down the hall toward his mother. "Was that the Sheffields I saw you greeting?" he asked, even though he knew very well it was. But his offices were too far down the hall for him to have heard anything the quartet of women had actually said, so he decided that a brief interrogation was in order.

"Indeed it was," Violet replied. "Such a lovely family, don't you think?"

Anthony just grunted.

"I'm so glad I invited them."

Anthony said nothing, although he considered grunting again.

"They were a last-minute addition to the guest list."

"I didn't realize," he murmured.

Violet nodded. "I had to scrounge up three more gentlemen from the village to even the numbers."

"So we may expect the vicar at supper this eve?"

"And his brother, who is visiting for a spell, and his son."

"Isn't young John only sixteen?"

Violet shrugged. "I was desperate."

Anthony pondered this. His mother was indeed desperate to have the Sheffields join the house party if it meant inviting a spotty-faced sixteen-year-old to supper. Not that she wouldn't have invited him for a family meal; when not formally entertaining, the Bridgertons broke with accepted standards and had all the children eat in the dining room, regardless of age. Indeed, the first time Anthony had gone to visit a friend, he'd been shocked that he was expected to take his meals in the nursery.

But still, a house party was a house party, and even Violet Bridgerton did not allow children at the table.

"I understand you've made the acquaintance of both Sheffield girls," Violet said.

Anthony nodded.

"I find them both delightful myself," she continued. "They haven't much in the way of fortune, but I've always maintained that when choosing a spouse, fortune is not as important as character, provided, of course, that one isn't in desperate straits."

"Which I," Anthony drawled, "as I am sure you are about to point out, am not."

Violet sniffed and shot him a haughty look. "I should not be so quick to mock me, my son. I merely point out the truth. You should be down on your hands and knees thanking your maker every day that you don't *have* to marry an heiress. Most men don't have the luxury of free will when it comes to marriage, you know."

Anthony just smiled. "I should be thanking my maker? Or my mother?"

"You are a beast."

He clucked her gently under the chin. "A beast you raised."

"And it wasn't an easy task," she muttered. "I can assure you of that."

He leaned forward and dropped a kiss on her cheek. "Have fun greeting your guests, Mother."

She scowled at him, but her heart clearly wasn't in it. "Where are you going?" she asked as he started to move away.

"For a walk."

"Really?"

He turned around, a bit bewildered over her interest. "Yes, really. Is there a problem with that?"

"Not at all," she replied. "Just that you haven't taken a walk—for the simple sake of taking a walk—in ages."

"I haven't been in the country in ages," he commented.

"True," she conceded. "In that case, you should really head out to the flower gardens. The early species are just beginning to bloom, and it's simply spectacular. Like nothing you can ever see in London."

Anthony nodded. "I shall see you for supper."

Violet beamed and waved him off, watching as he disappeared back into his offices, which wrapped around the corner of Aubrey Hall and had French doors leading out to the side lawn.

Her eldest son's interest in the Sheffields was most intriguing. Now, if she could only figure out which Sheffield he was interested in. . . .

About a quarter of an hour later, Anthony was out strolling through his mother's flower gardens, enjoying the contradiction of the warm sun and the cool breeze, when he heard the light sound of a second set of footsteps on a nearby path. This piqued his curiosity. The guests were all settling in their rooms, and it was the gardener's day off. Frankly, he'd been anticipating solitude.

He turned toward the direction of the footfall, moving silently until he reached the end of his path. He looked to the right, then to the left, and then he saw . . .

Her.

Why, he wondered, was he surprised?

Kate Sheffield, dressed in a pale lavender frock, blending in charmingly with the irises and grape hyacinths. She was standing beside a decorative wooden arch, which, later in the year, would be covered with climbing pink and white roses.

He watched her for a moment as she trailed her fingers along some fuzzy plant he could never remember the name of, then bent down to sniff at a Dutch tulip.

"They don't have a scent," he called out, slowly making his way toward her.

She straightened immediately, her entire body reacting before she'd turned to see him. He could tell she'd recognized his voice, which left him feeling rather oddly satisfied.

As he approached her side, he motioned to the brilliant red bloom and said, "They're lovely and somewhat rare in an English garden, but alas, with no perfume."

She waited longer to reply than he would have expected, then she said, "I've never seen a tulip before."

Something about that made him smile. "Never?"

"Well, not in the ground," she explained. "Edwina has received many bouquets, and the bulb flowers are quite the rage this time of year. But I've never actually seen one growing."

"They are my mother's favorite," Anthony said, reaching down and plucking one. "That and hyacinths, of course."

She smiled curiously. "Of course?" she echoed.

"My youngest sister is named Hyacinth," he said, handing her the flower. "Or didn't you know that?"

She shook her head. "I didn't."

"I see," he murmured. "We are quite famously named in alphabetical order, from Anthony right down to Hyacinth. But then, perhaps I know a great deal more about you than you know of me."

Kate's eyes widened in surprise at his enigmatic statement, but all she said was, "That may very well be true."

Anthony quirked a brow. "I'm shocked, Miss Sheffield. I had donned all my armor and was expecting you to return with, 'I know quite enough.' "

Kate tried not to make a face at his imitation of her voice. But her expression was wry in the extreme as she said, "I promised Mary I would be on my best behavior."

Anthony let out a loud hoot of laughter.

"Strangely enough," Kate muttered, "Edwina had a similar reaction."

He leaned one hand against the arch, carefully avoiding the thorns on the climbing rose vine. "I find myself insanely curious as to what constitutes good behavior."

She shrugged and fiddled with the tulip in her hand. "I expect I shall figure that out as I go along."

"But you're not supposed to argue with your host, correct?"

Kate shot him an arch look. "There was some debate

over whether or not you qualify as our host, my lord. After all, the invitation was issued by your mother."

"True," he acceded, "but I do own the house."

"Yes," she muttered, "Mary said as much."

He grinned. "This is killing you, isn't it?"

"Being nice to you?"

He nodded.

"It's not the easiest thing I've ever done."

His expression changed slightly, as if he might be done teasing her. As if he might have something entirely different on his mind. "But it's not the hardest thing, either, now, is it?" he murmured.

"I don't like you, my lord," she blurted out.

"No," he said with an amused smile. "I didn't think you did."

Kate started to feel very strange, much like she had in his study, right before he'd kissed her. Her throat suddenly felt a bit tight, and her palms grew very warm. And her insides—well, there was really nothing to describe the tense, prickly feeling that tightened through her abdomen. Instinctively, and perhaps out of self-preservation, she took a step back.

He looked amused, as if he knew exactly what she was thinking.

She fiddled with the flower some more, then blurted out, "You shouldn't have picked this."

"You should have a tulip," he said matter-of-factly. "It isn't right that Edwina receives all the flowers."

Kate's stomach, already tense and prickly, did a little flip. "Nonetheless," she managed to say, "your gardener will surely not appreciate the mutilation of his work."

He smiled devilishly. "He'll blame one of my younger siblings."

She couldn't help but smile. "I *should* think less of you for such a ploy," she said.

"But you don't?"

She shook her head. "But then again, it's not as if my opinion of you could sink very much lower."

"Ouch." He shook a finger at her. "I thought you were supposed to be on your best behavior."

Kate looked around. "It doesn't count if there is no one nearby to hear me, right?"

"*I* can hear you."

"*You* certainly don't count."

His head dipped a little closer in her direction. "I should think I was the *only* one who did."

Kate said nothing, not wanting even to meet his eyes. Whenever she allowed herself one glimpse into those velvety depths, her stomach started flipping anew.

"Miss Sheffield?" he murmured.

She looked up. Big mistake. Her stomach flipped again.

"Why did you seek me out?" she asked.

Anthony pushed off the wooden post and stood straight. "I didn't, actually. I was just as surprised to see you as you were me." Although, he thought acerbically, he shouldn't have been. He should have realized his mother was up to something the moment she actually suggested where he take his walk.

But could she possibly be steering him to the *wrong* Miss Sheffield? Surely she wouldn't choose Kate over Edwina as a prospective daughter-in-law.

"But now that I have found you," he said, "I did have something I wanted to say."

"Something you haven't already said?" she quipped. "I can't imagine."

He ignored her jibe. "I wanted to apologize."

That got her attention. Her lips parted with shock, and her eyes grew round. "I beg your pardon?" she said. Anthony thought her voice sounded rather like a frog.

"I owe you an apology for my behavior the other night," he said. "I treated you most rudely."

"You're apologizing for the kiss?" she asked, still looking rather dazed.

The kiss? He hadn't even considered apologizing for the kiss. He'd never apologized for a kiss, never before kissed someone for whom an apology might be necessary. He'd actually been thinking more of the unpleasant things he'd said to her after the kiss. "Er, yes," he lied, "the kiss. And for what I said, as well."

"I see," she murmured. "I didn't think rakes apologized."

His hand flexed, then made a tight fist. It was damned annoying, this habit of hers always to jump to conclusions about him. "This rake does," he said in clipped tones.

She took a deep breath, then let it out in a long, steady exhale. "Then I accept your apology."

"Excellent," he said, offering his most winning smile. "May I escort you back to the house?"

She nodded. "But don't think this means that I will suddenly change my mind about you and Edwina."

"I would never dream of considering you so easily swayed," he said, quite honestly.

She turned to him, her eyes startlingly direct, even for her. "The fact remains that you kissed me," she said bluntly.

"And you kissed me," he could not resist returning.

Her cheeks turned a delightful shade of pink. "The fact remains," she repeated determinedly, "that it happened. And should you marry Edwina—regardless of your reputation, which I do not consider inconsequential—"

"No," he murmured, interrupting her with velvet soft tones, "I didn't think you would."

She glared at him. "Regardless of your reputation, *it* would always be between us. Once something happens, you can't take it away."

The devil in Anthony nearly compelled him to drawl the word, "It?" forcing her to repeat the words, "The kiss," but instead he took pity on her and let it go. Besides, she had a good point. The kiss would always be between them. Even now, with her cheeks pinkened by embarrassment and her lips pursed with irritation, he found himself wondering how she'd feel if he pulled her into his arms, how she'd taste if he traced the outline of her lips with his tongue.

Would she smell like the garden? Or would that maddening scent of lilies and soap still cling to her skin?

Would she melt into his embrace? Or would she push him away and run for the house?

There was only one way to find out, and doing so would ruin his chances with Edwina forever.

But as Kate had pointed out, maybe marrying Edwina would bring with it far too many complications. It would not do to be lusting after one's sister-in-law, after all.

Maybe the time had come to search out a new bride, tedious though the prospect may be.

Maybe the time was right to kiss Kate Sheffield again, here in the perfect beauty of Aubrey Hall's gardens, with the flowers grazing their legs and the smell of lilac hanging in the air.

Maybe . . .

Maybe . . .

Chapter 9

Men are contrary creatures. Their heads and their hearts are never in agreement. And as women know all too well, their actions are usually governed by a different aspect altogether.

LADY WHISTLEDOWN'S SOCIETY PAPERS, 29 APRIL 1814

Or maybe not.

Just as Anthony was plotting the best course to her lips, he heard the perfectly awful sound of his younger brother's voice.

"Anthony!" Colin shouted out. "There you are."

Miss Sheffield, blissfully unaware of how close she'd come to having been kissed utterly senseless, turned to watch Colin approach.

"One of these days," Anthony muttered, "I'm going to have to kill him."

Kate turned back. "Did you say something, my lord?"

Anthony ignored her. It was probably his best option, since *not* ignoring her tended to leave him rather desperately lusting after her, which was, as he well knew, a short, straight road to utter disaster.

In all truth, he probably should have thanked Colin for

his untimely interruption. A few more seconds, and he would have kissed Kate Sheffield, which would have been the greatest mistake of his life.

One kiss with Kate could probably be excused, especially considering how far she'd provoked him the other night in his study. But two . . . well, two would have required any man of honor to withdraw his courtship of Edwina Sheffield.

And Anthony wasn't quite ready to give up on the concept of honor.

He couldn't believe how close he'd come to tossing aside his plan to marry Edwina. What was he thinking? She was the perfect bride for his purposes. It was only when her meddlesome sister was around that his brain grew confused.

"Anthony," Colin said again as he drew near, "and Miss Sheffield." He eyed them curiously; he well knew they didn't get along. "What a surprise."

"I was just exploring your mother's gardens," Kate said, "and I stumbled upon your brother."

Anthony gave a single nod of agreement.

"Daphne and Simon are here," Colin said.

Anthony turned to Kate and explained, "My sister and her husband."

"The duke?" she inquired politely.

"The very one," he grumbled.

Colin laughed at his brother's pique. "He was opposed to the marriage," he said to Kate. "It kills him that they're happy."

"Oh, for the love of—" Anthony snapped, catching himself just before he blasphemed in front of Kate. "I'm very happy that my sister is happy," he ground out, not sounding particularly happy. "It's simply that I should have had one more opportunity to beat the tar out of that bas—bounder before they embarked on 'happily ever after.'"

Kate choked on a laugh. "I see," she said, fairly certain that she had *not* kept the straight face she'd been aiming for.

Colin shot her a grin before turning back to his brother.

"Daff suggested a game of Pall Mall. What do you say? We haven't played for ages. And, if we set off soon, we can escape the milksop misses Mother has invited for us." He turned back to Kate with the sort of grin that could win forgiveness for anything. "Present company excluded, of course."

"Of course," she murmured.

Colin leaned forward, his green eyes flashing with mischief. "*No one* would make the mistake of calling you a milksop miss," he added.

"Is that a compliment?" she asked acerbically.

"Without a doubt."

"Then I shall accept it with grace and good favor."

Colin laughed and said to Anthony, "I like her."

Anthony didn't look amused.

"Have you ever played Pall Mall, Miss Sheffield?" Colin asked.

"I'm afraid not. I'm not even sure what it is."

"It's a lawn game. Brilliant fun. More popular in France than it is here, although they call it *Paille Maille*."

"How does one play?" Kate asked.

"We set out wickets on a course," Colin explained, "then hit wooden balls through them with mallets."

"That sounds simple enough," she mused.

"Not," he said with a laugh, "when you're playing with the Bridgertons."

"And what does *that* mean?"

"It means," Anthony cut in, "that we've never seen the need to set out a regulation course. Colin sets out the wickets over tree roots—"

"And you aimed yours toward the lake," Colin interrupted. "We never did find the red ball after Daphne sank it."

Kate knew she shouldn't be committing herself to an afternoon in the company of Viscount Bridgerton, but dash it all, Pall Mall sounded fun. "Might there be room for one more player?" she inquired. "Since we've already excluded me from the ranks of the milksops?"

"Of course!" Colin said. "I suspect you'll fit right in with the rest of us schemers and cheaters."

"Coming from you," Kate said with a laugh, "I *know* that was a compliment."

"Oh, for certain. Honor and honesty has its time and place, but *not* in a game of Pall Mall."

"And," Anthony cut in, a smug expression on his face, "we shall have to invite your sister as well."

"Edwina?" Kate choked out. Drat. She'd just played right into his hand. She'd been doing her best to keep the two of them apart, and now she'd practically arranged an afternoon out. There was no way she could exclude Edwina after all but inviting herself into the game.

"Do you have another sister?" he asked mildly.

She just scowled at him. "She might not wish to play. I think she was resting in her room."

"I'll instruct the maid to knock very lightly on her door," Anthony said, obviously lying.

"Excellent!" Colin said brightly. "We shall be evenly matched. Three men and three women."

"Does one play on teams?" Kate asked.

"No," he replied, "but my mother has always been adamant that one must be evenly matched in all things. She'll be quite disturbed if we go out in odd numbers."

Kate couldn't imagine the lovely and gracious woman she'd chatted with just an hour earlier getting upset over a game of Pall Mall, but she figured it wasn't her place to comment.

"I'll see to fetching Miss Sheffield," Anthony murmured, looking insufferably smug. "Colin, why don't you see *this* Miss Sheffield down to the field and I'll meet you there in half an hour?"

Kate opened her mouth to protest the arrangements that would leave Edwina alone in the viscount's company, even for so short a time as a walk down to the field, but in the end she remained silent. There was no reasonable excuse she could give to prevent it, and she knew it.

Anthony caught her fishlike spluttering and quirked one corner of his mouth in the most obnoxious manner before he said, "I'm pleased to see you agree with me, Miss Sheffield."

She just grumbled. If she'd formed words, they wouldn't have been polite ones.

"Excellent," Colin said. "We'll see you then."

And then he looped his arm through hers and led her away, leaving Anthony smirking behind them.

Colin and Kate walked about a quarter of a mile from the house to a somewhat uneven clearing bordered on one side by a lake.

"Home of the prodigal red ball, I presume?" Kate queried, motioning to the water.

Colin laughed and nodded. "It's a pity, because we used to have equipment enough for eight players; Mother had insisted on our purchasing a set that could accommodate all of her children."

Kate wasn't certain whether to smile or frown. "Yours is a very close family, isn't it?"

"The best," Colin said simply, walking over to a nearby shed.

Kate trailed after him, tapping her hand idly against her thigh. "Do you know what time it is?" she called out.

He paused, pulled out his pocket watch, and flipped it open. "Ten minutes past three."

"Thank you," Kate replied, making a mental note of it. They'd probably left Anthony at five to three, and he'd promised to deliver Edwina to the Pall Mall field within thirty minutes, so they should be down at twenty-five past the hour.

Half three at the very latest. Kate was willing to be generous and allow for unavoidable delays. If the viscount had Edwina down by half three, she wouldn't quibble.

Colin resumed his trek to the shed, Kate watching with

interest as he wrenched open the door. "It sounds rusty," she commented.

"It's been a while since we've been out here to play," he said.

"Really? If I had a house like Aubrey Hall, I would never go to London."

Colin turned around, his hand still on the half-open door to the shed. "You're a lot like Anthony, did you know that?"

Kate gasped. "Surely you're joking."

He shook his head, a strange little smile on his lips. "Perhaps it's because you're both the eldest. The Lord knows I'm thankful every day I wasn't born in Anthony's shoes."

"What do you mean?"

Colin shrugged. "I simply wouldn't want his responsibilities, that's all. The title, the family, the fortune—it's a great deal to fit on one man's shoulders."

Kate didn't particularly want to hear how well the viscount had assumed the responsibilities of his title; she didn't want to hear anything that might change her opinion of him, although she had to confess that she'd been impressed by the apparent sincerity of his apology earlier that afternoon. "What has this to do with Aubrey Hall?" she inquired.

Colin stared at her blankly for a moment, as if he'd forgotten that the conversation had started with her innocent comment about how lovely his country home was. "Nothing, I suppose," he said finally. "And everything as well. Anthony loves it here."

"But he spends all his time in London," Kate said. "Doesn't he?"

"I know." Colin shrugged. "Odd, isn't it?"

Kate had no reply, so she just watched as he pulled the door to the shed all the way open. "Here we are," he said, pulling out a wheeled cart that had been specially constructed to fit eight mallets and wooden balls. "A bit musty, but none the worse for the wear."

"Except for the loss of the red ball," Kate said with a smile.

"I blame that entirely on Daphne," Colin replied. "I blame everything on Daphne. It makes my life much easier."

"I heard that!"

Kate turned to see an attractive young couple approaching. The man was devastatingly handsome, with dark, dark hair and light, light eyes. The woman could only be a Bridgerton, with the same chestnut hair as both Anthony and Colin. Not to mention the same bone structure and smile. Kate had heard that all the Bridgertons looked rather alike, but she'd never fully believed it until now.

"Daff!" Colin called out. "You're just in time to help us put out the wickets."

She gave him an arch smile. "You didn't think I'd let you set up the course yourself, do you?" She turned to her husband. "I don't trust him as far as I can throw him."

"Don't listen to her," Colin said to Kate. "She's very strong. I'd wager she could toss me clear into the lake."

Daphne rolled her eyes and turned to Kate. "Since I'm sure my miserable brother won't do the honors, I'll introduce myself. I am Daphne, Duchess of Hastings, and this is my husband Simon."

Kate bobbed a quick curtsy. "Your grace," she murmured, then turned to the duke and said again, "Your grace."

Colin waved his hand toward her as he bent down to retrieve the wickets from the Pall Mall cart. "This is Miss Sheffield."

Daphne looked confused. "I just passed by Anthony at the house. I thought he said he was on his way to fetch Miss Sheffield."

"My sister," Kate explained. "Edwina. I am Katharine. Kate to my friends."

"Well, if you are brave enough to play Pall Mall with the Bridgertons, I definitely want you as my friend," Daphne said with a wide smile. "Therefore you must call me Daphne. And my husband Simon. Simon?"

"Oh, of course," he said, and Kate had the distinct

impression that he would have said the same had she just declared the sky orange. Not that he wasn't listening to her, just that it was clear he adored her to distraction.

This, Kate thought, was what she wanted for Edwina.

"Let me take half of those," Daphne said, reaching for the wickets in her brother's hand. "Miss Sheffield and I . . . that is, Kate and I"—she flashed Kate a friendly grin—"will set up three of them, and you and Simon can do the rest."

Before Kate could even venture an opinion, Daphne had taken her by the arm and was leading her toward the lake.

"We have to make absolutely certain that Anthony loses his ball in the water," Daphne muttered. "I have never forgiven him for last time. I thought Benedict and Colin were going to die laughing. And Anthony was the worst. He just stood there smirking. Smirking!" She turned to Kate with a most beleaguered expression. "No one smirks quite like my eldest brother."

"I know," Kate muttered under her breath.

Thankfully, the duchess hadn't heard her. "If I could have killed him, I vow I would have."

"What will happen once all your balls are lost in the lake?" Kate couldn't resist asking. "I haven't played with you lot yet, but you do seem rather competitive, and it seems . . ."

"That it would be inevitable?" Daphne finished for her. She grinned. "You're probably right. We have no sense of sportsmanship when it comes to Pall Mall. When a Bridgerton picks up a mallet, we become the worst sorts of cheaters and liars. Truly, the game is less about winning than making sure the other players lose."

Kate fought for words. "It sounds . . ."

"Awful?" Daphne grinned. "It's not. You'll never have more fun, I guarantee it. But at the rate we're going, the entire set will end up in the lake ere long. I suppose we'll have to send to France for another set." She jammed a wicket into the ground. "It seems a waste, I know, but worth it to humiliate my brothers."

Kate tried not to laugh, but she didn't succeed.

"Do you have any brothers, Miss Sheffield?" Daphne asked.

Since the duchess had forgotten to use her given name, Kate deemed it best to revert to formal manners. "None, your grace," she replied. "Edwina is my only sibling."

Daphne shaded her eyes with her hand and scanned the area for a devilish wicket location. When she spied one—sitting right atop a tree root—she marched away, leaving Kate no choice but to follow.

"Four brothers," Daphne said, shoving the wicket into the ground, "provide quite a marvelous education."

"The things you must have learned," Kate said, quite impressed. "Can you give a man a black eye? Knock him to the ground?"

Daphne grinned wickedly. "Ask my husband."

"Ask me what?" the duke called out from where he and Colin were placing a wicket on a tree root on the opposite side of the tree.

"Nothing," the duchess called out innocently. "I've also learned," she whispered to Kate, "when it's best just to keep one's mouth shut. Men are much easier to manage once you understand a few basic facts about their nature."

"Which are?" Kate prompted.

Daphne leaned forward and whispered behind her cupped hand, "They're not as smart as we are, they're not as intuitive as we are, and they certainly don't need to know about fifty percent of what we do." She looked around. "He didn't hear that, did he?"

Simon stepped out from behind the tree. "Every word."

Kate choked on a laugh as Daphne jumped a foot. "But it's true," Daphne said archly.

Simon crossed his arms. "I'll let you think so." He turned to Kate. "I've learned a thing or two about women over the years."

"Really?" Kate asked, fascinated.

He nodded and leaned in, as if imparting a grave state secret. "They're much easier to manage if one allows them to believe that they are smarter and more intuitive than men. And," he added with a superior glance at his wife, "our lives are much more peaceful if we pretend that we're only aware of about fifty percent of what they do."

Colin approached, swinging a mallet in a low arc. "Are they having a spat?" he asked Kate.

"A discussion," Daphne corrected.

"God save me from such discussions," Colin muttered. "Let's choose colors."

Kate followed him back to the Pall Mall set, her fingers drumming against her thigh. "Do you have the time?" she asked him.

Colin pulled out his pocket watch. "A bit after half three, why?"

"I just thought that Edwina and the viscount would be down by now, that's all," she said, trying not to look too concerned.

Colin shrugged. "They should be." Then, completely oblivious to her distress, he motioned to the Pall Mall set. "Here. You're the guest. You choose first. What color do you want?"

Without giving it much thought, Kate reached in and grabbed a mallet. It was only when it was in her hand that she realized it was black.

"The mallet of death," Colin said approvingly. "I knew she'd make a fine player."

"Leave the pink one for Anthony," Daphne said, reaching for the green mallet.

The duke pulled the orange mallet out of the set, turning to Kate as he said, "You are my witness that I had nothing to do with Bridgerton's pink mallet, yes?"

Kate smiled wickedly. "I noticed that *you* didn't choose the pink mallet."

"Of course not," he returned, his grin even more devious than hers. "My wife had already chosen it for him. I could not gainsay her, now, could I?"

"Yellow for me," Colin said, "and blue for Miss Edwina, don't you think?"

"Oh, yes," Kate replied. "Edwina loves blue."

The foursome stared down at the two mallets left: pink and purple.

"He's not going to like either one," Daphne said.

Colin nodded. "But he'll like pink even less." And with that, he picked up the purple mallet and tossed it into the shed, then reached down and sent the purple ball in after it.

"I say," the duke said, "where *is* Anthony?"

"That's a very good question," Kate muttered, tapping her hand against her thigh.

"I suppose you'll want to know what time it is," Colin said slyly.

Kate flushed. She'd already asked him to check his pocket watch twice. "I'm fine, thank you," she answered, lacking a witty retort.

"Very well. It's just that I've learned that once you start moving your hand like that—"

Kate's hand froze.

"—you're usually about ready to ask me what time it is."

"You've learned quite a lot about me in the past hour," Kate said dryly.

He grinned. "I'm an observant fellow."

"Obviously," she muttered.

"But in case you wanted to know, it's a quarter of an hour before four."

"They're past due," Kate said.

Colin leaned forward and whispered, "I highly doubt that my brother is ravishing your sister."

Kate lurched back. "Mr. Bridgerton!"

"What are you two talking about?" Daphne asked.

Colin grinned. "Miss Sheffield is worried that Anthony is compromising the other Miss Sheffield."

"Colin!" Daphne exclaimed. "That isn't the least bit funny."

"And certainly not true," Kate protested. Well, almost not true. She didn't think the viscount was compromising Edwina, but he was probably doing his very best to charm her silly. And *that* was dangerous in and of itself.

Kate pondered the mallet in her hand and tried to figure out how she might bring it down upon the viscount's head and make it look like an accident.

The mallet of death, indeed.

Anthony checked the clock on the mantel in his study. Almost half three. They were going to be late.

He grinned. Oh, well, nothing to do about it.

Normally he was a stickler for punctuality, but when tardiness resulted in the torture of Kate Sheffield, he didn't much mind a late arrival.

And Kate Sheffield was surely writhing in agony by now, horrified at the thought of her precious younger sister in his evil clutches.

Anthony looked down at his evil clutches—hands, he reminded himself, hands—and grinned anew. He hadn't had this much fun in ages, and all he was doing was loitering about his office, picturing Kate Sheffield with her jaw clenched together, steam pouring from her ears.

It was a highly entertaining image.

Not, of course, that this was even his fault. He would have left right on time if he hadn't had to wait for Edwina. She'd sent word down with the maid that she would join him in ten minutes. That was twenty minutes ago. He couldn't help it if she was late.

Anthony had a sudden image of the rest of his life—waiting for Edwina. Was she the sort who was chronically late? That might grow vexing after a while.

As if on cue, he heard the patter of footsteps in the hall, and when he looked up, Edwina's exquisite form was framed by the doorway.

She was, he thought dispassionately, a vision. Utterly lovely in every way. Her face was perfection, her posture the epitome of grace, and her eyes were the most radiant shade of blue, so vivid that one could not help but be surprised by their hue every time she blinked.

Anthony waited for some sort of reaction to rise up within him. Surely no man could be immune to her beauty.

Nothing. Not even the slightest urge to kiss her. It almost seemed a crime against nature.

But maybe this was a good thing. After all, he didn't want a wife with whom he'd fall in love. Desire would have been nice, but desire could be dangerous. Desire certainly had a greater chance of sliding into love than did disinterest.

"I'm terribly sorry I'm late, my lord," Edwina said prettily.

"It was no trouble whatsoever," he replied, feeling a bit brightened by his recent set of rationalizations. She'd still work just fine as a bride. No need to look elsewhere. "But we should be on our way. The others will have the course set up already."

He took her arm and they strolled out of the house. He remarked on the weather. She remarked on the weather. He remarked on the previous day's weather. She agreed with whatever he'd said (he couldn't even remember, one minute later).

After exhausting all possible weather-related topics, they fell into silence, and then finally, after a full three minutes of neither of them having anything to say, Edwina blurted out, "What did you study at university?"

Anthony looked at her oddly. He couldn't remember ever being asked such a question by a young lady. "Oh, the usual," he replied.

"But what," she ground out, looking most uncharacteristically impatient, "is the usual?"

"History, mostly. A bit of literature."

"Oh." She pondered that for a moment. "I love to read."

"Do you?" He eyed her with renewed interest. He wouldn't have taken her for a bluestocking. "What do you like to read?"

She seemed to relax as she answered the question. "Novels if I'm feeling fanciful. Philosophy if I'm in the mood for self-improvement."

"Philosophy, eh?" Anthony queried. "Never could stomach the stuff myself."

Edwina let out one of her charmingly musical laughs. "Kate is the same way. She is forever telling me that she knows perfectly well how to live her life and doesn't need a dead man to give her instructions."

Anthony thought about his experiences reading Aristotle, Bentham, and Descartes at university. Then he thought about his experiences *avoiding* reading Aristotle, Bentham, and Descartes at university. "I think," he murmured, "that I would have to agree with your sister."

Edwina grinned. "*You,* agree with Kate? I feel I should find a notebook and record the moment. Surely this must be a first."

He gave her a sideways, assessing sort of glance. "You're more impertinent than you let on, aren't you?"

"Not half as much as Kate."

"*That* was never in doubt."

He heard Edwina let out a little giggle, and when he looked over at her, she appeared to be trying her hardest to maintain a straight face. They rounded the final corner to the field, and as they came over the rise, they saw the rest of the Pall Mall party waiting for them, idly swinging their mallets to and fro as they waited.

"Oh, bloody hell," Anthony swore, completely forgetting that he was in the company of the woman he planned to make his wife. "She's got the mallet of death."

Chapter 10

The country house party is a very dangerous event. Married persons often find themselves enjoying the company of one other than one's spouse, and unmarried persons often return to town as rather hastily engaged persons.

Indeed, the most surprising betrothals are announced on the heels of these spells of rustication.

LADY WHISTLEDOWN'S SOCIETY PAPERS, 2 MAY 1814

"You certainly took your time getting here," Colin remarked as soon as Anthony and Edwina reached the group. "Here, we're ready to go. Edwina, you're blue." He handed her a mallet. "Anthony, you're pink."

"I'm pink and *she*"—he jabbed a finger toward Kate—"gets to have the mallet of death?"

"I gave her first pick," Colin said. "She is our guest, after all."

"Anthony is usually black," Daphne explained. "In fact, he gave the mallet its name."

"You shouldn't have to be pink," Edwina said to Anthony. "It doesn't suit you at all. Here"—she held out her mallet—"why don't we trade?"

"Don't be silly," Colin interjected. "We specifically decided that you must be blue. To match your eyes."

Kate thought she heard Anthony groan.

"I will be pink," Anthony announced, grabbing the offending mallet rather forcefully from Colin's hand, "and I will still win. Let's begin, shall we?"

As soon as the necessary introductions were made between the duke and duchess and Edwina, they all plopped their wooden balls down near the starting point and prepared to play.

"Shall we play youngest to oldest?" Colin suggested, with a gallant bow in Edwina's direction.

She shook her head. "I should rather go last, so that I might have a chance to observe the play of those more experienced than I."

"A wise woman," Colin murmured. "Then we shall play oldest to youngest. Anthony, I believe you're the most ancient among us."

"Sorry, brother dear, but Hastings has a few months on me."

"Why," Edwina whispered in Kate's ear, "do I get the feeling I am intruding upon a family spat?"

"I think the Bridgertons take Pall Mall very seriously," Kate whispered back. The three Bridgerton siblings had assumed bulldog faces, and they all appeared rather single-mindedly determined to win.

"Eh eh eh!" Colin scolded, waving a finger at them. "No collusion allowed."

"We wouldn't even begin to know where to collude," Kate commented, "as no one has seen fit to even explain to us the rules of play."

"Just follow along," Daphne said briskly. "You'll figure it out as you go."

"I think," Kate whispered to Edwina, "that the object is to sink your opponents' balls into the lake."

"Really?"

"No. But I think that's how the Bridgertons see it."

"You're still whispering!" Colin called out without

sparing a glance in their direction. Then, to the duke, he barked, "Hastings, hit the bloody ball. We haven't all day."

"Colin," Daphne cut in, "don't curse. There are ladies present."

"You don't count."

"There are two ladies present who are not me," she ground out.

Colin blinked, then turned to the Sheffield sisters. "Do you mind?"

"Not at all," Kate replied, utterly fascinated. Edwina just shook her head.

"Good." Colin turned back to the duke. "Hastings, get moving."

The duke nudged his ball a bit forward from the rest of the pile. "You do realize," he said to no one in particular, "that I have never played Pall Mall before?"

"Just give the ball a good whack in that direction, darling," Daphne said, pointing to the first wicket.

"Isn't that the last wicket?" Anthony asked.

"It's the first."

"It *ought* to be the last."

Daphne's jaw jutted out. "I set up the course, and it's the first."

"I think this might get bloody," Edwina whispered to Kate.

The duke turned to Anthony and flashed him a false smile. "I believe I'll take Daphne's word for it."

"She did set up the course," Kate cut in.

Anthony, Colin, Simon, and Daphne all looked at her in shock, as if they couldn't quite believe she'd had the nerve to enter the conversation.

"Well, she did," Kate said.

Daphne looped her arm through hers. "I do believe I adore you, Kate Sheffield," she announced.

"God help me," Anthony muttered.

The duke drew back his mallet, let fly, and soon the orange ball was hurtling along the lawn.

"Well done, Simon!" Daphne cried out.

Colin turned and looked at his sister with disdain. "One never cheers one's opponents in Pall Mall," he said archly.

"He's never played before," she said. "He's not likely to win."

"Doesn't matter."

Daphne turned to Kate and Edwina and explained, "Bad sportsmanship is a requirement in Bridgerton Pall Mall, I'm afraid."

"I'd gathered," Kate said dryly.

"My turn," Anthony barked. He gave the pink ball a disdainful glance, then gave it a good whack. It sailed splendidly over the grass, only to slam into a tree and drop like a stone to the ground.

"Brilliant!" Colin exclaimed, getting ready to take his turn.

Anthony muttered a few things under his breath, none of which were suitable for gentle ears.

Colin sent the yellow ball toward the first wicket, then stepped aside to let Kate try her hand.

"Might I have a practice swing?" she inquired.

"No." It was a rather loud no, coming, as it did, from three mouths.

"Very well," she grumbled. "Stand back, all of you. I won't be held responsible if I injure anyone on the first try." She drew back on her mallet with all her might and slammed it into the ball. It sailed through the air in a rather impressive arc, then smacked into the same tree that had foiled Anthony and plopped on the ground right next to his ball.

"Oh, dear," Daphne said, setting her aim by drawing back on her mallet a few times without actually hitting the ball.

"Why 'oh, dear'?" Kate asked worriedly, not reassured by the duchess's faintly pitying smile.

"You'll see." Daphne took her turn, then marched off in the direction of her ball.

Kate looked over at Anthony. He looked very, very pleased with the current state of affairs.

"What are you going to do to me?" she asked.

He leaned forward devilishly. "What am I *not* going to do to you might be a more appropriate question."

"I believe it's my turn," Edwina said, stepping up to the starting point. She gave her ball an anemic hit, then groaned when it traveled only a third as far as the rest.

"Put a bit more muscle into it next time," Anthony said before stalking over to his ball.

"Right," Edwina muttered at his back. "I never would have figured that out."

"Hastings!" Anthony yelled. "It's your turn."

While the duke tapped his ball toward the next wicket, Anthony leaned against the tree with crossed arms, his ridiculous pink mallet hanging from one hand, and waited for Kate.

"Oh, Miss Sheffield," he finally called out. "Play of the game dictates that one follow one's ball!"

He watched her tromp over to his side. "There," she grumbled. "Now what?"

"You really ought to treat me with more respect," he said, offering her a slow, sly smile.

"After you tarried with Edwina?" she shot back. "What I ought to do is have you drawn and quartered."

"Such a bloodthirsty wench," he mused. "You'll do well at Pall Mall . . . eventually."

He watched, utterly entertained, as her face grew red, then white. "What do you mean?" she asked.

"For the love of God, Anthony," Colin yelled. "Take your bloody turn."

Anthony looked down to where the wooden balls sat

kissing on the grass, hers black, his appallingly pink. "Right," he murmured. "Wouldn't want to keep dear, sweet Colin waiting." And with that, he put his foot atop his ball, drew back his mallet—

"What are you doing?" Kate shrieked.

—and let fly. His ball remained firmly in place under his boot. Hers went sailing down the hill for what seemed like miles.

"You fiend," she growled.

"All's fair in love and war," he quipped.

"I am going to *kill* you."

"You can try," he taunted, "but you'll have to catch up with me first."

Kate pondered the mallet of death, then pondered his foot.

"Don't even think about it," he warned.

"It's so very, very tempting," she growled.

He leaned forward menacingly. "We have witnesses."

"And that is the only thing saving your life right now."

He merely smiled. "I believe your ball is down the hill, Miss Sheffield. I'm sure we'll see you in a half hour or so, when you catch up."

Just then Daphne marched by, following her ball, which had sailed unnoticed past their feet. "That was why I said 'oh, dear,' " she said—rather unnecessarily, in Kate's opinion.

"You'll pay for this," Kate hissed at Anthony.

His smirk said more than words ever could.

And then she marched down the hill, letting out a loud and extremely unladylike curse when she realized her ball was lodged under a hedge.

Half an hour later Kate was still two wickets behind the next-to-last player. Anthony was winning, which irked her to no end. The only saving grace was that she was so far behind she couldn't see his gloating face.

Then as she was twiddling her thumbs and waiting for her turn (there was precious little else to do while waiting for her turn, as no other players were remotely near her), she heard Anthony let out an aggrieved shout.

This immediately got her attention.

Beaming with anticipation at his possible demise, she looked eagerly about until she saw the pink ball hurtling along the grass, straight at her.

"Urp!" Kate gurgled, jumping up and darting quickly to the side before she lost a toe.

Looking back up, she saw Colin leaping into the air, his mallet swinging wildly above him, as he cried out exultantly, "Woo-hoo!"

Anthony looked as if he might disembowel his brother on the spot.

Kate would have done a little victory dance herself—if she couldn't win, the next best thing was knowing that *he* wouldn't—except now it seemed that he'd be stuck back with her for a few turns. And while her solitude wasn't terribly entertaining, it was better than having to make conversation with *him*.

Still, it was difficult not to look just a little bit smug when he came tromping over toward her, scowling as if a thundercloud had just lodged itself in his brain.

"Bad luck there, my lord," Kate murmured.

He glared at her.

She sighed—just for effect, of course. "I'm sure you'll still manage to place second or third."

He leaned forward menacingly and made a sound suspiciously like a growl.

"Miss Sheffield!" came Colin's impatient holler from up the hill. "It's your turn!"

"So it is," Kate said, analyzing her possible shots. She could aim for the next wicket or she could attempt to sabotage Anthony even further. Unfortunately, his ball wasn't touching hers, so she couldn't attempt the foot-on-the-ball maneuver he'd used on her earlier in the game. Which was probably for the best. With her luck, she'd end up missing the ball entirely and instead breaking her foot.

"Decisions, decisions," she murmured.

Anthony crossed his arms. "The only way you're going to ruin my game is to ruin yours as well."

"True," she acceded. If she wanted to send him into oblivion, she'd have to send herself there as well, since she'd have to hit hers with all she was worth just to get his to move. And since she couldn't hold hers in place, heaven only knew where she'd end up.

"But," she said, looking up at him and smiling innocently, "I really have no chance of winning the game, anyway."

"You could come in second or third," he tried.

She shook her head. "Unlikely, don't you think? I'm so far behind as it is, and we are nearing the end of play."

"You don't want to do this, Miss Sheffield," he warned.

"Oh," she said with great feeling, "I *do*. I really, really do." And then, with quite the most evil grin her lips had ever formed, she drew back her mallet and smacked her ball with every ounce of every single emotion within her. It knocked into his with stunning force, sending it hurtling even farther down the hill.

Farther . . .

Farther . . .

Right into the lake.

Openmouthed with delight, Kate just stared for a moment as the pink ball sank into the lake. Then something rose up within her, some strange and primitive emotion, and before she knew what she was about, she was jumping about like a crazy woman, yelling, "Yes! Yes! I win!"

"You don't win," Anthony snapped.

"Oh, it *feels* like I've won," she reveled.

Colin and Daphne, who had come dashing down the hill, skidded to a halt before them. "Well done, Miss

Sheffield!" Colin exclaimed. "I knew you were worthy of the mallet of death."

"Brilliant," Daphne agreed. "Absolutely brilliant."

Anthony, of course, had no choice but to cross his arms and scowl mightily.

Colin gave her a congenial pat on the back. "Are you certain you're not a Bridgerton in disguise? You have truly lived up to the spirit of the game."

"I couldn't have done it without you," Kate said graciously. "If you hadn't hit his ball down the hill . . ."

"I had been hoping you would pick up the reins of his destruction," Colin said.

The duke finally approached, Edwina at his side. "A rather stunning conclusion to the game," he commented.

"It's not over yet," Daphne said.

Her husband gave her a faintly amused glance. "To continue the play now seems rather anticlimactic, don't you think?"

Surprisingly, even Colin agreed. "I certainly can't imagine anything topping it."

Kate beamed.

The duke glanced up at the sky. "Furthermore, it's starting to cloud over. I want to get Daphne in before it starts to rain. Delicate condition and all, you know."

Kate looked in surprise at Daphne, who had started to blush. She didn't look the least bit pregnant.

"Very well," Colin said. "I move we end the game and declare Miss Sheffield the winner."

"I was two wickets behind the rest of you," Kate demurred.

"Nevertheless," Colin said, "any true aficionado of Bridgerton Pall Mall understands that sending Anthony into the lake is far more important than actually sending one's ball through all the wickets. Which makes you our winner, Miss Sheffield." He looked about, then straight at Anthony. "Does anyone disagree?"

No one did, although Anthony looked close to violence.

"Excellent," Colin said. "In that case, Miss Sheffield is our winner, and Anthony, *you* are our loser."

A strange, muffled sound burst from Kate's mouth, half laugh and half choke.

"Well, someone has to lose," Colin said with a grin. "It's tradition."

"It's true," Daphne agreed. "We're a bloodthirsty lot, but we do like to follow tradition."

"You're all mad in the head is what you are," the duke said affably. "And on that note, Daphne and I must bid you farewell. I do want to get her inside before it begins to rain. I trust no one will mind if we leave without helping to clear the course?"

No one minded, of course, and soon the duke and duchess were on their way back to Aubrey Hall.

Edwina, who had kept silent throughout the exchange (although she had been looking at the various Bridgertons as if they'd recently escaped from an asylum), suddenly cleared her throat. "Do you think we should try to retrieve the ball?" she asked, squinting down the hill toward the lake.

The rest of the party just stared at the calm waters as if they'd never considered such a bizarre notion.

"It's not as if it landed in the middle," she added. "It just rolled in. It's probably right by the edge."

Colin scratched his head. Anthony continued to glower.

"Surely you don't want to lose another ball," Edwina persisted. When no one had a reply, she threw down her mallet and threw up arms, saying, "Fine! I'll get the silly old ball."

That certainly roused the men from their stupor, and they jumped to help her.

"Don't be silly, Miss Sheffield," Colin said gallantly as he started to walk down the hill, "I'll get it."

"For the love of Christ," Anthony muttered. "I'll get the bloody ball." He strode down the hill, quickly overtaking his brother. For all his ire, he couldn't really blame Kate for her actions. He would have done the very same thing, although he would have hit the ball with enough force to sink hers in the middle of the lake.

Still, it was damned humiliating to be bested by a female, especially *her*.

He reached the edge of the lake and peered in. The pink ball was so brightly colored that it ought to show through the water, provided it had settled at a shallow enough level.

"Do you see it?" Colin asked, coming to a halt beside him.

Anthony shook his head. "It's a stupid color, anyway. No one ever wanted to be pink."

Colin nodded his agreement.

"Even the purple was better," Anthony continued, moving a few steps to the right so that he could inspect another stretch of shoreline. He looked up suddenly, glaring at his brother. "What the hell happened to the purple mallet, anyway?"

Colin shrugged. "I'm sure I have no idea."

"And I'm sure," Anthony muttered, "that it will miraculously reappear in the Pall Mall set tomorrow evening."

"You might very well be right," Colin said brightly, moving a bit past Anthony, keeping his eyes on the water the whole way. "Perhaps even this afternoon, if we're lucky."

"One of these days," Anthony said matter-of-factly, "I'm going to kill you."

"Of that I have no doubt." Colin scanned the water, then suddenly pointed with his index finger. "I say! There it is."

Sure enough, the pink ball sat in the shallow water, about two feet out from the edge of the lake. It looked to be only a foot or so deep. Anthony swore under his breath. He was going to have to take off his boots and wade in. It seemed Kate Sheffield was forever forcing him to take off his boots and wade into bodies of water.

No, he thought wearily, he hadn't had time to remove

his boots when he'd charged into The Serpentine to save Edwina. The leather had been completely ruined. His valet had nearly fainted from the horror of it.

With a groan he sat on a rock to pull off his footwear. To save Edwina he supposed it was worth a pair of good boots. To save a stupid pink Pall Mall ball—frankly, it didn't even seem worth getting his feet wet.

"You seem to have this well in hand," Colin said, "so I'm going to go help Miss Sheffield pull up the wickets."

Anthony just shook his head in resignation and waded in.

"Is it cold?" came a feminine voice.

Good God, it was *her*. He turned around. Kate Sheffield was standing on the shore.

"I thought you were pulling up wickets," he said, somewhat testily.

"That's Edwina."

"Too bloody many Miss Sheffields," he muttered under his breath. There ought to be a law against letting sisters come out in the same season.

"I beg your pardon?" she asked, cocking her head to the side.

"I said it's freezing," he lied.

"Oh. I'm sorry."

That got his attention. "No, you're not," he finally said.

"Well, no," she admitted. "Not for your losing, anyway. But I didn't intend for you to freeze your toes off."

Anthony was suddenly gripped by the most insane desire to see her toes. It was a horrible thought. He had no business lusting after this woman. He didn't even like her.

He sighed. That wasn't true. He supposed he did like her in an odd, paradoxical sort of way. And he thought, strangely enough, she might be beginning to like him in much the same manner.

"You would have done the same thing if you were me," she called out.

He said nothing, just continued his slow wade.

"You would have!" she insisted.

He leaned down and scooped up the ball, getting his sleeve wet in the process. Damn. "I know," he replied.

"Oh," she said, sounding surprised, as if she hadn't expected him to admit it.

He waded back out, thankful that the ground by the shore was firmly packed, so that dirt didn't stick to his feet.

"Here," she said, holding out what looked like a blanket. "It was in the shed. I stopped by on my way down. I thought you might need something to dry your feet."

Anthony opened his mouth, but oddly enough, no sound emerged. Finally, he managed, "Thank you," and took the blanket from her hands.

"I'm not such a terrible person, you know," she said with a smile.

"Neither am I."

"Perhaps," she allowed, "but you shouldn't have tarried so long with Edwina. I know you did it just to vex me."

He lifted a brow as he sat on the rock so he could dry his feet, dropping the ball onto the ground next to him. "Don't you think it's possible that my delay had anything to do with my wanting to spend time with the woman I'm considering making my wife?"

She colored slightly, but then muttered, "This has to be the most self-centered thing I've ever said, but no, I think you just wanted to vex me."

She was right, of course, but he wasn't going to tell her so. "As it happens," he said, "Edwina was delayed. Why, I do not know. I deemed it impolite to seek her out in her room and demand that she hurry along, so I waited in my study until she was ready."

There was a long moment of silence, then she said, "Thank you for telling me that."

He smiled wryly. "I'm not such a terrible person, you know."

She sighed. "I know."

Something about her resigned expression made him grin. "But maybe a little terrible?" he teased.

She brightened, their return to levity obviously making her much more comfortable with the conversation. "Oh, for certain."

"Good. I'd hate to be boring."

Kate smiled, watching him as he pulled on his stockings and boots. She reached down and picked up the pink ball. "I'd better carry this back to the shed."

"In case I'm overcome by an uncontrollable urge to toss it back in the lake?"

She nodded. "Something like that."

"Very well." He stood. "I'll take the blanket, then."

"A fair trade." She turned to walk up the hill, then spied Colin and Edwina disappearing into the distance. "Oh!"

Anthony turned quickly around. "What is it? Oh, I see. It seems your sister and my brother have decided to head back without us."

Kate scowled at their errant siblings, then shrugged in resignation as she started trudging up the hill. "I suppose I can tolerate your company for a few more minutes if you can tolerate mine."

He didn't say anything, which surprised her. It seemed just the sort of comment to which he'd have a witty and perhaps even cutting comeback. She looked up at him, then drew back slightly in surprise. He was staring at her in the *oddest* manner . . .

"Is—is everything all right, my lord?" she asked hesitantly.

He nodded. "Fine." But he sounded rather distracted.

The rest of the trip to the shed was met with silence. Kate set the pink ball in its spot in the Pall Mall cart, noting that Colin and Edwina had cleared the course and put everything neatly away, including the errant purple mallet and ball. She stole a glance at Anthony and had to smile. It was obvious from his beleaguered frown that he'd noticed as well.

"The blanket goes in here, my lord," she said with a hidden grin, stepping out of his way.

Anthony shrugged. "I'll bring it up to the house. It probably needs a good cleaning."

She nodded in agreement, and they shut the door and were off.

Chapter 11

There is nothing like a spot of competition to bring out the worst in a man—or the best in a woman.

LADY WHISTLEDOWN'S SOCIETY PAPERS, 4 MAY 1814

Anthony whistled as they ambled up the path to the house, stealing glances at Kate when she wasn't looking. She really was quite an attractive woman in her own right. He didn't know why this always surprised him, but it did. His memory of her never quite lived up to the enchanting reality of her face. She was always in motion, always smiling or frowning or pursing her lips. She'd never master the placid, serene expression to which young ladies were meant to aspire.

He'd fallen into the same trap as had the rest of society—of thinking of her only in terms of her younger sister. And Edwina was so stunning, so amazingly, startlingly beautiful that anyone near to her couldn't help but fade into the background. It was, Anthony allowed, difficult to look at anyone else when Edwina was in the room.

And yet . . .

He frowned. And yet he'd barely spared Edwina a glance through the entire Pall Mall game. This might have been understandable simply because it was Bridgerton

Pall Mall, and it brought out the worst in anyone named Bridgerton; hell, he probably wouldn't have spared a glance for the Prince Regent if he'd deigned to join the game.

But that explanation wouldn't wash, for his mind was filled with other images. Kate bending over her mallet, her face tense with concentration. Kate giggling as someone missed a shot. Kate cheering on Edwina when her ball rolled through the wicket—a very un-Bridgerton-like trait, that. And, of course, Kate smiling wickedly in that last second before she'd sent his ball flying into the lake.

Clearly, even if he hadn't been able to spare a glance for Edwina, he'd been sparing plenty for Kate.

That ought to have been disturbing.

He glanced back over at her again. This time her face was tilted slightly toward the sky, and she was frowning.

"Is something wrong?" he inquired politely.

She shook her head. "Just wondering if it's going to rain."

He looked up. "Not anytime soon, I imagine."

She nodded slowly in agreement. "I hate the rain."

Something about the expression on her face—rather reminiscent of a frustrated three-year-old—made him laugh. "You live in the wrong country, then, Miss Sheffield."

She turned to him with a sheepish smile. "I don't mind a gentle rain. It's just when it grows violent that I don't like it."

"I've always rather enjoyed thunderstorms," he murmured.

She shot him a startled look but didn't say anything, then returned her gaze to the pebbles at her feet. She was kicking one along the path as they walked, occasionally breaking her stride or stepping to the side just so she could give it a kick and keep it flying ahead of her. There was something charming about it, something rather sweet about the way her booted foot peeked out from under the hem of her dress at such regular intervals and connected with the pebble.

Anthony watched her curiously, forgetting to pull his eyes off her face when she looked back up.

"Do you think— *Why* are you looking at me like that?" she asked.

"Do I think what?" he returned, deliberately ignoring the second part of her question.

Her lips settled into a peevish line. Anthony felt his own quivering, wanting to smile with amusement.

"Are you laughing at me?" she asked suspiciously.

He shook his head.

Her feet ground to a halt. "I think you are."

"I assure you," he said, sounding even to himself as if he wanted to laugh, "that I am not laughing at you."

"You're lying."

"I'm not—" He had to stop. If he spoke any further he knew he'd explode with laughter. And the strangest thing was—he hadn't a clue why.

"Oh, for heaven's sake," she muttered. "What is the problem?"

Anthony sank against the trunk of a nearby elm, his entire body shaking with barely contained mirth.

Kate planted her hands on her hips, the expression in her eyes a little bit curious, a little bit furious. "What's so funny?"

He finally gave in to the laughter and barely managed to lift his shoulders into a shrug. "I don't know," he gasped. "The expression on your face . . . it's . . ."

He noticed that she smiled. He loved that she smiled.

"The expression on your face is not exactly unamusing yourself, my lord," she remarked.

"Oh, I'm sure." He took a few deep breaths and then, when he was satisfied that he had regained control, straightened. He caught sight of her face, still vaguely suspicious, and suddenly he realized that he had to know what she thought of him.

It couldn't wait until the next day. It couldn't wait until that evening.

He wasn't sure how it had come about, but her good opinion meant a great deal to him. Of course he needed her approval in his much-neglected suit of Edwina, but there was more to it than that. She'd insulted him, she'd nearly dunked him in The Serpentine, she'd humiliated him at Pall Mall, and yet he craved her good opinion.

Anthony couldn't remember the last time someone's regard had meant so much, and frankly, it was humbling.

"I think you owe me a boon," he said, pushing off the tree and standing straight. His mind was whirring. He needed to be clever about this. He had to know what she thought. And yet, he didn't want her knowing how much it meant to him. Not until he understood *why* it meant so much to him.

"I beg your pardon?"

"A boon. For the Pall Mall game."

She let out a ladylike snort as she leaned against the tree and crossed her arms. "If anyone owes anyone else a boon, then you owe one to me. I did win, after all."

"Ah, but I was the one humiliated."

"True," she acceded.

"You would not be yourself," he said in an extremely dry voice, "if you resisted the urge to agree."

Kate gave him a demure glance. "A lady should be honest in all things."

When she raised her eyes to his face, one corner of his mouth was curved into a rather knowing smile. "I was hoping you'd say that," he murmured.

Kate felt immediately uneasy. "And why is that?"

"Because my boon, Miss Sheffield, is to ask you a question—any question of my choosing—and you must answer with the utmost honesty." He planted one hand against the tree trunk, rather close to her face, and leaned forward. Kate suddenly felt trapped, even though it would be easy enough to dart away.

With a touch of dismay—and a shiver of excitement—she realized that she felt trapped by his eyes, which were burning rather dark and hot into hers.

"Do you think you can do that, Miss Sheffield?" he murmured.

"Wh-what is your question?" she asked, not realizing that she was whispering until she heard her voice, breathy and crackling like the wind.

He cocked his head slightly to the side. "Now, remember, you have to answer honestly."

She nodded. Or at least she thought she nodded. She *meant* to nod. In all truth, she wasn't entirely convinced of her ability to move.

He leaned forward, not so much that she could feel his breath, but close enough to make her shiver. "Here, Miss Sheffield, is my question."

Her lips parted.

"Do you"—he moved closer—"still"—and another inch—"hate me?"

Kate swallowed convulsively. Whatever she'd been expecting him to ask, it hadn't been this. She licked her lips, preparing to speak, even though she had no idea what she'd say, but not a sound emerged.

His lips curved into a slow, masculine smile. "I'll take that as a no."

And then, with an abruptness that left her head spinning, he pushed off the tree and said briskly, "Well, then, I do believe it's time we went inside and prepared for the evening, don't you?"

Kate sagged against the tree, completely devoid of energy.

"You wish to remain outside for a few moments?" He planted his hands on his hips and looked up at the sky, his demeanor pragmatic and efficient—one hundred and eighty degrees changed from the slow, lazy seducer he'd been just ten seconds earlier. "You might as well. It doesn't look like it's going to rain, after all. At least not in the next few hours."

She just stared at him. Either he'd lost his mind or she'd forgotten how to talk. Or maybe both.

"Very well. I've always admired a woman who appreciates fresh air. I shall see you at supper, then?"

She nodded. She was surprised she even managed that.

"Excellent." He reached out and took her hand, dropping a searing kiss on the inside of her wrist, upon the single band of bare flesh that peeked out between her glove and the hem of her sleeve. "Until tonight, Miss Sheffield."

And then he strode off, leaving her with the oddest feeling that something rather important had just taken place.

But for the life of her, she had no idea what.

At half seven that night, Kate considered falling dreadfully ill. At quarter to eight, she'd refined her goal to an apoplectic fit. But at five minutes to the hour, as the dinner bell sounded, alerting guests that it was time to assemble in the drawing room, she squared her shoulders and walked into the hall outside her bedroom door to meet Mary.

She refused to be a coward.

She *wasn't* a coward.

And she could make it through the evening. Besides, she told herself, she wasn't likely to be seated anywhere near Lord Bridgerton. He was a viscount and the man of the house, and would therefore be at the head of the table. As the daughter of a baron's second son, she held little rank compared to the other guests, and would most certainly be seated so far down the table that she wouldn't even be able to see him without developing a crick in her neck.

Edwina, who was sharing a room with Kate, had already gone to Mary's chamber to help her choose a necklace, and so Kate found herself alone in the hall. She supposed she could enter Mary's room and wait for the two of them there, but she didn't feel terribly conversational, and Edwina had already noticed her odd, reflective mood. The last thing Kate needed was a round of "Whatever can be wrong's" from Mary.

And the truth was—Kate didn't even *know* what was wrong. All she knew was that that afternoon, something had changed between her and the viscount. Something was different, and she freely admitted (to herself, at least) that it frightened her.

Which was normal, right? People always feared what they didn't understand.

And Kate *definitely* didn't understand the viscount.

But just as she was beginning to truly enjoy her solitude, the door across the hall opened, and out walked another young lady. Kate recognized her instantly as Penelope Featherington, the youngest of the three famed Featherington sisters—well, the three who were out in society. Kate had heard that there was a fourth still in the schoolroom.

Unfortunately for the Featherington sisters, they were famed for their lack of success on the marriage mart. Prudence and Philippa had been out for three years now, without a single proposal between the two of them. Penelope was in the midst of her second season and could usually be found at social functions trying to avoid her mother and sisters, who were universally regarded as ninnies.

Kate had always liked Penelope. The two had formed a bond ever since they'd both been skewered by Lady Whistledown for wearing gowns of an unflattering color.

Kate noted with a sad sigh that Penelope's current gown of lemon yellow silk made the poor girl look hopelessly sallow. And if that weren't bad enough, it had been cut with far too many frills and flounces. Penelope wasn't a tall girl, and the gown positively overwhelmed her.

It was a pity, because she might be quite attractive if

someone could convince her mother to stay away from the modiste and let Penelope choose her own clothing. She had a rather pleasing face, with the pale, pale skin of a redhead, except that her hair was truly more auburn than red, and if one really wanted to put a fine point on it, more brownish red than auburn.

Whatever you called it, Kate thought with dismay, it didn't go with lemon yellow.

"Kate!" Penelope called out, after closing her door behind her. "What a surprise. I didn't realize you were attending."

Kate nodded. "I think we might have been issued a late invitation. We met Lady Bridgerton only just last week."

"Well, I know I just said I was surprised, but I'm actually not surprised. Lord Bridgerton has been paying much attention to your sister."

Kate flushed. "Er, yes," she stammered. "He has."

"That is what the gossips say, at least," Penelope continued. "But then again, one can't always trust the gossips."

"I have rarely known Lady Whistledown to be incorrect," Kate said.

Penelope just shrugged and then looked down at her gown with disgust. "She certainly is never incorrect about *me*."

"Oh, don't be silly," Kate said quickly, but they both knew she was just being polite.

Penelope gave her head a weary shake. "My mother is convinced that yellow is a *happy* color and that a *happy* girl will snare a husband."

"Oh, dear," Kate said, snorting a giggle.

"What she doesn't grasp," Penelope continued wryly, "is that such a *happy* shade of yellow makes me look rather *un*happy and positively repels the gentlemen."

"Have you suggested green?" Kate inquired. "I think you'd be smashing in green."

Penelope shook her head. "She doesn't like green. Says it's melancholy."

"Green?" Kate asked with disbelief.

"I don't even try to understand her."

Kate, who was wearing green, held up her sleeve near Penelope's face, blocking the yellow as best as she could. "Your whole face lights up," she said.

"Don't tell me that. It will only make the yellow more painful."

Kate offered her a sympathetic smile. "I would loan you one of mine, but I'm afraid it would drag on the floor."

Penelope waved away her offer. "That's very kind of you, but I'm resigned to my fate. At least it's better than last year."

Kate raised a brow.

"Oh, that's right. You weren't out last year." Penelope winced. "I weighed nearly two stone more than I do now."

"Two stone?" Kate echoed. She couldn't believe it.

Penelope nodded and made a face. "Baby fat. I begged Mama not to force me to come out until I turned eighteen, but she thought a head start might be good for me."

Kate only had to take one look at Penelope's face to know that it hadn't been good for her. She felt a certain kinship with this girl, even though Penelope was nearly three years younger. Both of them knew the singular feeling of not being the most popular girl in the room, knew the exact expression you put on your face when you weren't asked to dance but you wanted to look as if you didn't care.

"I say," Penelope said, "why don't the two of us go down to supper together? It seems your family and mine are both delayed."

Kate wasn't in much of a rush to reach the drawing room and the inevitable company of Lord Bridgerton, but waiting for Mary and Edwina would delay the torture by only a few minutes, so she decided she might as well head down with Penelope.

They both poked their heads into their respective

mother's room, informed them of the change in plans, and linked arms, heading down the hall.

When they reached the drawing room, much of the company was already in attendance, milling about and chatting as they waited for the rest of the guests to come down. Kate, who had never attended a country house party before, noted with surprise that nearly everyone seemed more relaxed and a bit more animated than they did in London. It must be the fresh air, she thought with a smile. Or perhaps distance relaxed the strict rules of the capital. Whatever the case, she decided she preferred this atmosphere to that of a London dinner party.

She could see Lord Bridgerton across the room. Or rather she supposed she could sense him. As soon as she spotted him standing over by the fireplace, she'd kept her gaze scrupulously averted.

But she could feel him nonetheless. She knew she had to be crazy, but she'd swear she knew when he tilted his head, and heard him when he spoke and when he laughed.

And she definitely knew when his eyes were on her back. Her neck felt as if it were about to go up in flames.

"I didn't realize Lady Bridgerton had invited so many people," Penelope said.

Careful to keep her eyes away from the fireplace, Kate did a sweep of the room to see who was there.

"Oh, no," Penelope half whispered, half moaned. "Cressida Cowper is here."

Kate discreetly followed Penelope's gaze. If Edwina had any competition for the role of 1814's reigning beauty, it was Cressida Cowper. Tall, slender, with honey-blond hair and sparkling green eyes, Cressida was almost never without a small bevy of admirers. But where Edwina was kind and generous, Cressida was, in Kate's estimation, a self-centered, ill-mannered witch who took her joy in the torment of others.

"She hates me," Penelope whispered.

"She hates everyone," Kate replied.

"No, she *really* hates me."

"Whyever?" Kate turned to her friend with curious eyes. "What could you possibly have done to her?"

"I bumped into her last year and caused her to spill punch all over herself *and* the Duke of Ashbourne."

"That's all?"

Penelope rolled her eyes. "It was enough for Cressida. She's convinced he would have proposed if she hadn't appeared clumsy."

Kate let out a snort that didn't even pretend to be ladylike. "Ashbourne isn't about to get hitched anytime soon. Everyone knows that. He's nearly as bad a rake as Bridgerton."

"Who is most probably going to get married this year," Penelope reminded her. "If the gossips are correct."

"Bah," Kate scoffed. "Lady Whistledown herself wrote that she doesn't think he'll marry this year."

"That was *weeks* ago," Penelope replied with a dismissive wave of her hand. "Lady Whistledown changes her mind all the time. Besides, it's obvious to everyone that the viscount is courting your sister."

Kate bit her tongue before she muttered, "Don't remind me."

But her wince of pain was drowned out by Penelope's hoarse whisper of, "Oh, *no*. She's coming this way."

Kate gave her arm a reassuring squeeze. "Don't worry about her. She's no better than you."

Penelope shot her a sarcastic look. "I *know* that. But that doesn't make her any less unpleasant. And she always goes out of her way to make sure that I *have* to deal with her."

"Kate. Penelope," Cressida trilled, drawing up alongside them, giving her shiny hair an affected shake. "What a surprise to see you here."

"And why is that?" Kate asked.

Cressida blinked, obviously surprised that Kate had even questioned her pronouncement. "Well," she said slowly, "I suppose it is not such a surprise to see *you* here, as your sister is very much in demand, and we all know that you must go where she goes, but Penelope's presence . . ." She shrugged daintily. "Well, who am I to judge? Lady Bridgerton is a most kindhearted woman."

The comment was so rude that Kate could not help but gape. And while she was staring at Cressida, open-mouthed with shock, Cressida went in for the kill.

"That's a lovely gown, Penelope," she said, her smile so sweet that Kate would swear she could taste sugar in the air. "I do love yellow," she added, smoothing down the pale yellow fabric of her own gown. "It takes a very special complexion to wear it, don't you think?"

Kate ground her teeth together. Naturally Cressida looked brilliant in her gown. Cressida would look brilliant in a sackcloth.

Cressida smiled again, this time reminding Kate of a serpent, then turned slightly to motion to someone across the room. "Oh, Grimston, Grimston! Come over here for a moment."

Kate looked over her shoulder to see Basil Grimston approaching and just barely managed to stifle a groan. Grimston was the perfect male counterpart to Cressida—rude, supercilious, and self-important. Why a lovely lady like Viscountess Bridgerton had invited him, she'd never know. Probably to even up the numbers with so many young ladies invited.

Grimston slithered over and lifted one corner of his mouth in a mockery of a smile. "Your servant," he said to Cressida after sparing Kate and Penelope a fleeting, disdainful glance.

"Don't you think dear Penelope looks fetching in that gown?" Cressida said. "Yellow truly must be the color of the season."

Grimston did a slow, insulting perusal of Penelope, from the top of her head to the tips of her feet and back. He barely moved his head, letting his eyes travel up and down her frame. Kate fought a spasm of revulsion so strong it nearly brought on a wave of nausea. More than anything, she wanted to throw her arms around Penelope and give the poor girl a hug. But such attention would only single her out further as someone who was weak and easily bullied.

When Grimston was finally done with his rude inspection, he turned to Cressida and shrugged, as if he couldn't think of anything complimentary to say.

"Don't you have somewhere else to be?" Kate blurted out.

Cressida looked shocked. "Why, Miss Sheffield, I can hardly countenance your impertinence. Mr. Grimston and I were merely admiring Penelope's appearance. That shade of yellow does so much for her complexion. And it is so nice to see her looking so well after last year."

"Indeed," Grimston drawled, his oily tone making Kate feel positively unclean.

Kate could feel Penelope shaking next to her. She hoped it was with anger, not with pain.

"I can't imagine what you mean," Kate said in icy tones.

"Why, surely you know," Grimston said, his eyes glittering with delight. He leaned forward and then said in a whisper that was louder than his usual voice, loud enough so that a great many people could hear, "She was *fat*."

Kate opened her mouth to give a scathing retort, but before she could make a sound, Cressida added, "It was such a pity, because there were so many more men in town last year. Of course most of us still never lack for a dance partner, but I do feel for poor Penelope when I see her sitting with the dowagers."

"The dowagers," Penelope ground out, "are often the only people in the room with a modicum of intelligence."

Kate wanted to jump up and cheer.

Cressida made a breathy little "Oh" sound, as if she had

any right to be offended. "Still, one cannot help but . . . Oh! Lord Bridgerton!"

Kate moved to the side to allow the viscount into their small circle, noticing with disgust that Cressida's entire demeanor changed. Her eyelids began to flutter and her mouth made a pretty little cupid's bow.

It was so appalling Kate forgot to be self-conscious around the viscount.

Bridgerton shot Cressida a hard look but did not say anything. Instead, he turned quite deliberately to Kate and Penelope and murmured their names in greeting.

Kate nearly gasped with glee. He'd given Cressida Cowper the cut direct!

"Miss Sheffield," he said smoothly, "I hope you will excuse us as I escort Miss Featherington in to dinner."

"But you can't escort her in!" Cressida blurted out.

Bridgerton gave her an icy stare. "I'm sorry," he said in a voice that said he was anything but. "Had I included you in the conversation?"

Cressida shrank back, obviously mortified by her outburst. Still, it was beyond irregular for him to escort Penelope. As the man of the house, it was his duty to escort the highest-ranking woman. Kate wasn't sure who that happened to be this evening, but it certainly wasn't Penelope, whose father had been a mere mister.

Bridgerton offered Penelope his arm, turning his back on Cressida in the process. "I do hate a bully, don't you?" he murmured.

Kate clapped her hand over her mouth, but she couldn't stifle her giggle. Bridgerton offered her a small, secret smile over Penelope's head, and in that moment Kate had the oddest feeling that she understood this man completely.

But even stranger—suddenly she wasn't so certain that he was the soulless, reprehensible rake she'd taken such comfort in believing him.

"Did you see that?"

Kate, who, along with the rest of the assembled company, had been staring openmouthed as Bridgerton led Penelope from the room, his head bent to hers as if she were the most fascinating woman ever to walk the earth, turned to see Edwina standing next to her.

"I saw the whole thing," Kate said in a dazed voice. "I heard the whole thing."

"What happened?"

"He was . . . he was . . ." Kate stumbled over her words, unsure of how to describe what exactly he'd done. And then she said something she'd never thought possible: "He was a hero."

Chapter 12

A man with charm is an entertaining thing, and a man with looks is, of course, a sight to behold, but a man with honor—ah, he is the one, dear reader, to which the young ladies should flock.

LADY WHISTLEDOWN'S SOCIETY PAPERS, 2 MAY 1814

Later that night, after supper was done and the men went off to drink their port before rejoining the ladies with superior expressions on their faces, as if they had just talked about something weightier than which horse was likely to win the Royal Ascot; after the assembled company had played a sometime tedious and sometime hilarious round of charades; after Lady Bridgerton had cleared her throat and discreetly suggested that it might be time to turn in; after the ladies had taken their candles and headed off to bed; after the gentlemen had presumably followed . . .

Kate couldn't sleep.

Clearly, it was to be one of those stare-at-the-cracks-in-the-ceiling sort of nights. Except that there were no cracks in the ceiling at Aubrey Hall. And the moon wasn't even out, so there wasn't any light filtering through the curtains, which meant that even if there were cracks, she wouldn't be able to see them, and . . .

Kate groaned as she pushed back her covers and rose to her feet. One of these days she was going to have to learn how to force her brain to stop racing in eight different directions at once. She'd already lain in bed for nearly an hour, staring up into the dark, inky night, shutting her eyes every now and then and trying to will herself to sleep.

It wasn't working.

She couldn't stop thinking about the expression on Penelope Featherington's face when the viscount had swooped in to her rescue. Her own expression, Kate was sure, must have been somewhat similar—a bit stunned, a little delighted, and a lot as if she were about to melt onto the floor at that very minute.

Bridgerton had been *that* magnificent.

Kate had spent the entire day either watching or interacting with the Bridgertons. And one thing had become clear: Everything that had been said about Anthony and his devotion to his family—it was all true.

And while she wasn't quite ready to relinquish her opinion that he was a rake and a rogue, she was starting to realize that he might be all that and something else as well.

Something good.

Something that, if she were trying to be utterly objective about the matter, which she admitted was difficult to do, really ought not disqualify him as a potential husband for Edwina.

Oh, why why why did he have to go and be *nice*? Why couldn't he have just stayed the suave but shallow libertine it had been so easy to believe him? Now he was something else altogether, someone she feared she might actually come to care for.

Kate felt her face flush, even in the dark. She had to stop thinking about Anthony Bridgerton. At this rate she wasn't going to get any sleep for a week.

Maybe if she had something to read. She'd seen a rather

large and extensive library earlier that evening; surely the Bridgertons had some tome in there that would be guaranteed to put her to sleep.

She pulled on her robe and tiptoed to the door, careful not to wake Edwina. Not that that would have been an easy task. Edwina had always slept like the dead. According to Mary, she'd even slept through the night as a baby—from the very first day of her birth.

Kate slid her feet into a pair of slippers, then moved quietly into the hall, careful to look this way and that before shutting the door behind her. This was her first country house visit, but she'd heard a thing or two about these sorts of gatherings, and the last thing she wanted to do was run into someone on his way to a bedroom not his own.

If someone was carrying on with someone not his spouse, Kate decided, she didn't want to know about it.

A single lantern lit the hall, giving the dark air a dim, flickering glow. Kate had grabbed a candle on her way out, so she walked over and flipped the lid of the lantern to light her wick. Once the flame was steady, she started toward the stairs, making sure to pause at every corner and check carefully for passersby.

A few minutes later she found herself in the library. It wasn't large by *ton* standards, but the walls were covered floor to ceiling with bookcases. Kate pushed the door until it was almost closed—if someone was up and about, she didn't want to alert them to her presence by letting the door click shut—and made her way to the nearest bookcase, peering at the titles.

"Hmmm," she murmured to herself, pulling out a book and looking at the front cover, "botany." She did love gardening, but somehow a textbook on the subject didn't sound terribly exciting. Should she seek out a novel, which would capture her imagination, or should she go for a dry text, which would be more likely to put her to sleep?

Kate replaced the book and moved over to the next bookcase, setting her candle down on a nearby table. It appeared to be the philosophy section. "Definitely not," she muttered, sliding her candle along the table as she moved one bookcase to the right. Botany might put her to sleep, but philosophy was likely to leave her in a stupor for days.

She moved the candle a bit to the right, leaning forward to peer at the next set of books, when a bright and completely unexpected flash of lightning lit up the room.

A short, staccato scream burst forth from her lungs, and she jumped backward, bumping her behind against the table. *Not now*, she silently pleaded, *not here*.

But as her mind formed the word, "here," the entire room exploded with a dull boom of thunder.

And then it was dark again, leaving Kate shaking, her fingers gripping the table so hard that her joints locked. She hated this. Oh, how she hated this. She hated the noise and the streaks of light, and the crackling tension in the air, but most of all she hated what it made her feel.

So terrified that eventually she couldn't feel anything at all.

It had been this way all her life, or at least as long as she could remember. When she'd been small, her father or Mary had comforted her whenever it had stormed. Kate had many memories of one of them sitting on the edge of her bed, holding her hand and whispering soothing words as thunder and lightning crashed around her. But as she grew older, she managed to convince people that she was over her affliction. Oh, everyone knew that she still hated storms. But she'd managed to keep the extent of her terror to herself.

It seemed the worst sort of weakness—one with no apparent cause, and unfortunately, one with no clear cure.

She didn't hear any rain against the windows; maybe the storm wouldn't be so bad. Maybe it had started far away and was moving even farther. Maybe it was—

Another flash illuminated the room, squeezing out a second scream from Kate's lungs. And this time the thunder had arrived even closer to the lightning, indicating that the storm was pulling closer.

Kate felt herself sink to the floor.

It was too loud. Too loud, and too bright, and too—

BOOM!

Kate huddled under the table, her legs folded up, her arms about her knees, waiting in terror for the next round.

And then the rain began.

It was a bit past midnight, and all the guests (who were keeping somewhat to country hours) had gone to bed, but Anthony was still in his study, tapping his fingers against the edge of his desk in time with the rain beating against his window. Every now and then a bolt of lightning lit up the room in a flash of brilliance, and each clap of thunder was so loud and unexpected, he jumped in his chair.

God, he loved thunderstorms.

Hard to tell why. Maybe it was just the proof of nature's power over man. Maybe it was the sheer energy of the light and sound that pounded around him. Whatever the case, it made him feel alive.

He hadn't been particularly tired when his mother had suggested they all turn in, and so it had seemed silly not to use these few moments of solitude to go over the Aubrey Hall books his steward had left out for him. The Lord knew his mother would have his every minute crammed with activities involving eligible young women on the morrow.

But after an hour or so of painstaking checking, the dry tip of a quill tapping against each number in the ledger as he added and subtracted, multiplied and occasionally divided, his eyelids began to droop.

It had been a long day, he allowed, closing the ledger but leaving a piece of paper sticking out to mark his place. He'd spent much of the morning visiting tenants and inspecting buildings. One family needed a door repaired. Another was having trouble harvesting their crops and paying their rent, due to the father's broken leg. Anthony had heard and settled disputes, admired new babies, and even helped to fix a leaky roof. It was all part of being a landowner, and he enjoyed it, but it was tiring.

The Pall Mall game had been an enjoyable interlude, but once back at the house, he'd been thrust into the role of host for his mother's party. Which had been almost as exhausting as the tenant visits. Eloise was barely seventeen and clearly had needed someone to watch over her, that bitchy Cowper girl had been tormenting poor Penelope Featherington, and someone had had to do something about that, and . . .

And then there was Kate Sheffield.

The bane of his existence.

And the object of his desires.

All at once.

What a muddle. He was supposed to be courting her sister, for God's sake. Edwina. The belle of the season. Lovely beyond compare. Sweet and generous and even-tempered.

And instead he couldn't stop thinking about Kate. Kate, who, much as she infuriated him, couldn't help but command his respect. How could he not admire one who clung so steadfastly to her convictions? And Anthony had to admit that the crux of her convictions—devotion to family—was the one principle he held above all else.

With a yawn, Anthony got up from behind his desk and stretched his arms. It was definitely time for bed. With any luck, he'd fall asleep the moment his head hit the pillow. The last thing he wanted was to find himself staring at the ceiling, thinking of Kate.

And of all the things he wanted to do *to* Kate.

Anthony picked up a candle and headed out into the empty hall. There was something peaceful and intriguing about a quiet house. Even with the rain beating against the walls, he could hear every click of his boots against the floor—heel, toe, heel, toe. And except for when the lightning streaked through the sky, his candle provided the only illumination in the hall. He rather enjoyed waving the flame this way and that, watching the play of shadows against the walls and furniture. It was a rather odd feeling of control, but—

One of his brows rose up in question. The library door was a few inches ajar, and he could see a pale strip of candlelight shining from within.

He was fairly certain no one else was up. And there certainly wasn't a sound coming from the library. Someone must have gone in for a book and left a candle burning. Anthony frowned. It was a damned irresponsible thing to do. Fire could devastate a house faster than anything else, even in the middle of a rainstorm, and the library—filled to the brim with books—was the ideal place to spark a flame.

He pushed the door open and entered the room. One entire wall of the library was taken up by tall windows, so the sound of the rain was much louder here than it had been in the hall. A crack of thunder shook the floor, then, practically on top of that, a flash of lightning split the night.

The electricity of the moment made him grin, and he crossed over to where the offending candle had been left burning. He leaned over, blew it out, and then . . .

He heard something.

It was the sound of breath. Panicked, labored, with the slightest touch of a whimper.

Anthony looked purposefully around the room. "Is someone here?" he called out. But he could see no one.

Then he heard it again. From below.

Holding his own candle steady, he crouched down to peer under the table.

And his breath was sucked right out of his body.

"My God," he gasped. "Kate."

She was curled up into a ball, her arms wrapped around her bent legs so tightly it looked as if she were about to shatter. Her head was bent down, her eye sockets resting on her knees, and her entire body was shaking with fast, intense tremors.

Anthony's blood ran to ice. He'd never seen someone shake like that.

"Kate?" he said again, setting his candle down on the floor as he moved closer. He couldn't tell if she could hear him. She seemed to have retreated into herself, desperate to escape something. Was it the storm? She'd said she hated the rain, but this went far deeper. Anthony knew that most people didn't thrive on electrical storms as he did, but he'd never heard of someone being reduced to this.

She looked as if she'd break into a million brittle pieces if he so much as touched her.

Thunder shook the room, and her body flinched with such torment that Anthony felt it in his gut. "Oh, Kate," he whispered. It broke his heart to see her thus. With a careful and steady hand, he reached out to her. He still wasn't sure if she'd even registered his presence; startling her might be like waking a sleepwalker.

Gently he set his hand on her upper arm and gave it the tiniest of squeezes. "I'm here, Kate," he murmured. "Everything will be all right."

Lightning tore through the night, flashing the room with a sharp burst of light, and she squeezed herself into an even tighter ball, if that was possible. It occurred to him that she was trying to shield her eyes by keeping her face to her knees.

He moved closer and took one of her hands in his. Her skin was like ice, her fingers stiff from terror. It was difficult to pry her arm from around her legs, but eventually he was able to bring her hand to his mouth, and he pressed his lips against her skin, trying to warm her.

"I'm here, Kate," he repeated, not really sure what else to say. "I'm here. It will be all right."

Eventually he managed to scoot himself under the table so that he was sitting beside her on the floor, with his arm around her trembling shoulders. She seemed to relax slightly at his touch, which left him with the oddest feeling—almost a sense of pride that he had been the one to be able to help her. That, and a bone-deep feeling of relief, because it was killing him to see her in such torment.

He whispered soothing words in her ear and softly caressed her shoulder, trying to comfort her with his mere presence. And slowly—very, slowly; he had no idea how many minutes he sat under that table with her—he could feel her muscles begin to unwind. Her skin lost that awful clammy feeling, and her breathing, while still rushed, no longer sounded quite so panicked.

Finally, when he felt she might be ready, he touched two fingers to the underside of her chin, using the softest pressure imaginable to lift her face so that he could see her eyes. "Look at me, Kate," he whispered, his voice gentle but suffused with authority. "If you just look at me, you will know that you are safe."

The tiny muscles around her eyes quivered for a good fifteen seconds before her lids finally fluttered. She was trying to open her eyes, but they were resisting. Anthony had little experience with this sort of terror, but it seemed to make sense to him that her eyes just wouldn't want to open, that they simply wouldn't want to see whatever it was that so frightened her.

After several more seconds of fluttering, she finally managed to open her eyes all the way and met his gaze.

Anthony felt as if he'd been punched in the gut.

If eyes were truly the windows to the soul, something had shattered within Kate Sheffield that night. She looked haunted, hunted, and utterly lost and bewildered.

"I don't remember," she whispered, her voice barely audible.

He took her hand, which he'd never relinquished his

hold on, and brought it to his lips again. He pressed a gentle, almost paternal kiss on her palm. "You don't remember what?"

She shook her head. "I don't know."

"Do you remember coming to the library?"

She nodded.

"Do you remember the storm?"

She closed her eyes for a moment, as if the act of keeping them open had required more energy than she possessed. "It's still storming."

Anthony nodded. That was true. The rain was still beating against the windows with just as much ferocity as before, but it had been several minutes since the last bout of thunder and lightning.

She looked at him with desperate eyes. "I can't . . . I don't . . ."

Anthony squeezed her hand. "You don't have to say anything."

He felt her body shudder and relax, then heard her whisper, "Thank you."

"Do you want me to talk to you?" he asked.

She shut her eyes—not as tightly as before—and nodded.

He smiled, even though he knew she could not see it. But maybe she could sense it. Maybe she'd be able to hear his smile in his voice. "Let's see," he mused, "what can I tell you about?"

"Tell me about the house," she whispered.

"This house?" he asked in surprise.

She nodded.

"Very well," he replied, feeling rather absurdly pleased that she was interested in the one pile of stone and mortar that meant so much to him. "I grew up here, you know."

"Your mother told me."

Anthony felt a spark of something warm and powerful in his chest as she spoke. He'd told her she didn't have to say anything, and she'd been quite obviously thankful for that, but now she was actually taking part in the conversation. Surely that had to mean she was beginning to feel better. If she'd open her eyes—if they weren't sitting under a table—it might seem almost normal.

And it was stunning how much he wanted to be the one to make her feel better.

"Shall I tell you about the time my brother drowned my sister's favorite doll?" he asked.

She shook her head, then flinched when the wind picked up, causing the rain to beat against the windows with new ferocity. But she steeled her chin and said, "Tell me something about you."

"All right," Anthony said slowly, trying to ignore the vague, uncomfortable feeling that spread in his chest. It was so much easier to tell a tale of his many siblings than to talk about himself.

"Tell me about your father."

He froze. "My father?"

She smiled, but he was too shocked by her request to notice. "You must have had one," she said.

Anthony's throat began to feel very tight. He didn't often talk about his father, not even with his family. He'd told himself that it was because it was so much water under the bridge; Edmund had been dead for over ten years. But the truth was that some things simply hurt too much.

And there were some wounds that didn't heal, not even in ten years.

"He—he was a great man," he said softly. "A great father. I loved him very much."

Kate turned to look at him, the first time she'd met his gaze since he'd lifted her chin with his fingers many minutes earlier. "Your mother speaks of him with great affection. That was why I asked."

"We all loved him," he said simply, turning his head and staring out across the room. His eyes focused on the leg of a chair, but he didn't really see it. He didn't see anything but the memories in his mind. "He was the finest father a boy could ever want."

"When did he die?"

"Eleven years ago. In the summer. When I was eighteen. Right before I left for Oxford."

"That's a difficult time for a man to lose his father," she murmured.

He turned sharply to look at her. "Any time is a difficult time for a man to lose his father."

"Of course," she quickly agreed, "but some times are worse than others, I think. And surely it must be different for boys and girls. My father passed on five years ago, and I miss him terribly, but I don't think it's the same."

He didn't have to voice his question. It was there in his eyes.

"My father was wonderful," Kate explained, her eyes warming as she reminisced. "Kind and gentle, but stern when he needed to be. But a boy's father—well, he has to teach his son how to be a man. And to lose a father at eighteen, when you're just learning what all that means . . ." She let out a long exhale. "It's probably presumptuous for me even to discuss it, as I'm not a man and therefore couldn't possibly put myself in your shoes, but I think . . ." She paused, pursing her lips as she considered her words. "Well, I just think it would be very difficult."

"My brothers were sixteen, twelve, and two," Anthony said softly.

"I would imagine it was difficult for them as well," she replied, "although your youngest brother probably doesn't remember him."

Anthony shook his head.

Kate smiled wistfully. "I don't remember my mother, either. It's an odd thing."

"How old were you when she died?"

"It was on my third birthday. My father married Mary only a few months later. He didn't observe the proper mourning period, and it shocked some of the neighbors, but he thought I needed a mother more than he needed to follow etiquette."

For the first time, Anthony wondered what would have happened if it had been his mother who had died young, leaving his father with a house full of children, several of them infants and toddlers. Edmund wouldn't have had an easy time of it. None of them would have.

Not that it had been easy for Violet. But at least she'd had Anthony, who'd been able to step in and try to act the role of surrogate father to his younger siblings. If Violet had died, the Bridgertons would have been left completely without a maternal figure. After all, Daphne—the eldest of the Bridgerton daughters—had been only ten at Edmund's death. And Anthony was certain that his father would not have remarried.

No matter how his father would have wanted a mother for his children, he would not have been able to take another wife.

"How did your mother die?" Anthony asked, surprised by the depth of his curiosity.

"Influenza. Or at least that's what they thought. It could have been any sort of lung fever." She rested her chin on her hand. "It was very quick, I'm told. My father said I fell ill as well, although mine was a mild case."

Anthony thought about the son he hoped to sire, the very reason he had finally decided to marry. "Do you miss a parent you never knew?" he whispered.

Kate considered his question for some time. His voice had held a hoarse urgency that told her there was something critical about her reply. Why, she couldn't imagine, but something about her childhood clearly rang a chord within his heart.

"Yes," she finally answered, "but not in the way you would think. You can't really miss her, because you didn't know her, but there's still a hole in your life—a big empty spot, and you know who was supposed to fit there, but you can't remember her, and you don't know what she was like, and so you don't know *how* she would have filled that hole." Her lips curved into a sad sort of smile. "Does this make any sense?"

Anthony nodded. "It makes a great deal of sense."

"I think losing a parent once you know and love them is harder," Kate added. "And I know, because I've lost both."

"I'm sorry," he said quietly.

"It's all right," she assured him. "That old adage—time heals all wounds—it's really true."

He stared at her intently, and she could tell from his expression that he didn't agree.

"It really is more difficult when you're older. You're blessed because you had the chance to know them, but the pain of the loss is more intense."

"It was as if I'd lost an arm," Anthony whispered.

She nodded soberly, somehow knowing that he hadn't spoken of his sorrow to many people. She licked nervously at her lips, which had gone quite dry. Funny how that happened. All the rain in the world pounding outside, and here she was, parched as a bone.

"Perhaps it was better for me, then," Kate said softly, "losing my mother so young. And Mary has been wonderful. She loves me as a daughter. In fact—" She broke off, startled by the sudden wetness in her eyes. When she finally found her voice again, it was an emotional whisper. "In fact, she has never once treated me differently than she has Edwina. I—I don't think I could have loved my own mother any better."

Anthony's eyes burned into hers. "I'm so glad," he said, his voice low and intense.

Kate swallowed. "She's so funny about it sometimes. She visits my mother's grave, just to tell her how I'm doing. It's very sweet, actually. When I was small, I would go with her, to tell my mother how Mary was doing."

Anthony smiled. "And was your report favorable?"

"Always."

They sat in companionable silence for a moment, both staring at the candle flame, watching the wax drip down the taper to the candlestick. When the fourth drop of wax rolled down the candle, sliding along the column until it hardened in place, Kate turned to Anthony and said, "I'm sure I sound insufferably optimistic, but I think there must be some master plan in life."

He turned to her and quirked a brow.

"Everything really does work out in the end," she explained. "I lost my mother, but I gained Mary. And a sister I love dearly. And—"

A flash of lightning lit the room. Kate bit her lip, trying to force slow and even breaths through her nose. The thunder would come, but she'd be ready for it, and—

The room shook with noise, and she was able to keep her eyes open.

She let out a long exhale and allowed herself a proud smile. That hadn't been so difficult. It certainly hadn't been *fun,* but it hadn't been impossible. It might have been Anthony's comforting presence next to her, or simply that the storm was moving away, but she'd made it through without her heart jumping through her skin.

"Are you all right?" Anthony asked.

She looked over at him, and something inside of her melted at the concerned look on his face. Whatever he'd done in the past, however they'd argued and fought, in this moment he truly cared about her.

"Yes," she said, hearing surprise in her voice even though she hadn't intended it. "Yes, I think I am."

He gave her hand a squeeze. "How long have you been like this?"

"Tonight? Or in my life?"

"Both."

"Tonight since the first clap of thunder. I get quite nervous when it begins to rain, but as long as there is no thunder and lightning, I'm all right. It's not the rain, actually, which upsets me, but just the fear that it might grow into something more." She swallowed, licking her dry lips before she continued. "To answer your other query, I can't remember a time I wasn't terrified by storms. It's simply a part of me. It's quite foolish, I know—"

"It's not foolish," he interjected.

"You're very sweet to think so," she said with a sheepish half-smile, "but you're wrong. Nothing could be more foolish than to fear something with no reason."

"Sometimes . . ." Anthony said in a halting voice, "sometimes there are reasons for our fears that we can't quite explain. Sometimes it's just something we feel in our bones, something we know to be true, but would sound foolish to anyone else."

Kate stared at him intently, watching his dark eyes in the flickering candlelight, and catching her breath at the flash of pain she saw in the brief second before he looked away. And she knew—with every fiber of her being—that he wasn't speaking of intangibles. He was talking about his own fears, something very specific that haunted him every minute of every day.

Something she knew she did not have the right to ask him about. But she wished—oh, how she wished—that when he was ready to face his fears, she could be the one to help him.

But that wasn't to be. He would marry someone else, maybe even Edwina, and only his wife would have the right to talk to him about such personal matters.

"I think I might be ready to go upstairs," she said. Suddenly it was too hard to be in his presence, too painful to know that he would belong to someone else.

His lips quirked into a boyish smile. "Are you saying I might finally crawl out from under this table?"

"Oh, goodness!" She clapped one of her hands to her cheek in a sheepish expression. "I'm so sorry. I stopped noticing where we were sitting ages ago, I'm afraid. What a ninny you must think me."

He shook his head, still smiling. "Never a ninny, Kate.

Even when I thought you the most insufferable female creature on the planet, I had no doubts about your intelligence."

Kate, who had been in the process of scooting out from under the table, paused. "I just don't know if I should feel complimented or insulted by that statement."

"Probably both," he admitted, "but for friendship's sake, let's decide upon complimented."

She turned to look at him, aware that she presented an awkward picture on her hands and knees, but the moment seemed too important to delay. "Then we are friends?" she whispered.

He nodded as he stood. "Hard to believe, but I think we are."

Kate smiled as she took his helping hand and rose to her feet. "I'm glad. You're—you're really not the devil I'd originally thought you."

One of his brows lifted, and his face suddenly took on a very wicked expression.

"Well, maybe you are," she amended, thinking he probably was every bit the rake and rogue that society had painted him. "But maybe you're also a rather nice person as well."

"Nice seems so bland," he mused.

"*Nice,*" she said emphatically, "is nice. And given what I used to think of you, you ought to be delighted by the compliment."

He laughed. "One thing about you, Kate Sheffield, is that you are never boring."

"Boring is so bland," she quipped.

He smiled—a true grin, not that ironic curve he used at society functions, but the real thing. Kate's throat suddenly felt very tight.

"I'm afraid I cannot walk you back to your room," he said. "If someone should come across us at this hour . . ."

Kate nodded. They'd forged an unlikely friendship, but she didn't want to get trapped into marriage with him, right? And it went without saying that *he* didn't want to marry *her*.

He motioned to her. "And especially with you dressed like that. . . ."

Kate looked down and gasped, yanking her robe more tightly around her. She'd completely forgotten that she wasn't properly dressed. Her nightclothes certainly weren't risqué or revealing, especially with her thick robe, but they *were* nightclothes.

"Will you be all right?" he asked softly. "It's still raining."

Kate stopped and listened to the rain, which had softened to a gentle patter against the windows. "I think the storm is over."

He nodded and peered out into the hall. "It's empty," he said.

"I should go."

He stepped aside to let her pass.

She moved forward, but when she reached the doorway she stopped and turned around. "Lord Bridgerton?"

"Anthony," he said. "You should call me Anthony. I believe I've already called you Kate."

"You did?"

"When I found you." He waved a hand. "I don't think you heard anything I said."

"You're probably right." She smiled hesitantly. "Anthony." His name sounded strange on her tongue.

He leaned forward slightly, an odd, almost devilish light in his eyes. "Kate," he said in return.

"I just wanted to say thank you," she said. "For helping me tonight. I—" She cleared her throat. "It would have been a great deal more difficult without you."

"I didn't do anything," he said gruffly.

"No, you did everything." And then, before she'd be tempted to stay, she hurried down the hall and up the stairs.

Chapter 13

There is little to report in London with so many people away in Kent at the Bridgerton house party. This Author can only imagine all the gossip that will soon reach town. There will be a scandal, yes? There is always a scandal at a house party.

LADY WHISTLEDOWN'S SOCIETY PAPERS, 4 MAY 1814

The following morning was the sort that usually follows a violent storm—bright and clear, but with a fine, damp mist that settled cold and refreshing on the skin.

Anthony was oblivious to the weather, having spent most of the night staring into the darkness and seeing nothing but Kate's face. He'd finally fallen asleep as the first streaks of dawn fingered across the sky. By the time he woke, it was well past noon, but he did not feel rested. His body was suffused with a strange combination of exhaustion and nervous energy. His eyes felt heavy and dull in their sockets, and yet his fingers kept drumming the bed, inching toward the edge as if they alone could pull him out and to his feet.

Finally, when his stomach growled so loudly that he could swear he saw the plaster on the ceiling shake, he staggered upright and pulled on his robe. With a wide, loud yawn, he moved to the window, not because he was looking for anyone or anything in particular, but simply because the view was better than anything else in his room.

And yet in the quarter second before he looked down and gazed upon the grounds, he somehow knew what he would see.

Kate. Walking slowly across the lawn, far more slowly than he'd ever seen her walk before. Usually, she walked as if in a race.

She was much too far away for him to see her face—just a sliver of her profile, the curve of her cheek. And yet he could not take his eyes off of her. There was so much magic in her form—a strange grace in the way her arm swung as she walked, an artistry in the posture of her shoulders.

She was walking toward the garden, he realized.

And he knew he had to join her.

The weather remained in its contradictory state for most of the day, dividing the house party neatly in half, between those who insisted the bright sunshine beckoned outdoor play, and those who eschewed the wet grass and damp air for the warmer, drier clime of the drawing room.

Kate was firmly in the former group, although she was not in the mood for company. Her mind was in far too reflective a mood to make polite conversation with people she barely knew, and so she stole away once again to Lady Bridgerton's spectacular gardens and found herself a quiet spot on a bench near the rose arbor. The stone was cold and just a little bit damp beneath her bottom, but she hadn't slept particularly well the night before, and she was tired, and it was better than standing.

And it was, she realized with a sigh, just about the only place where she might be left to her own company. If she remained in the house, she'd surely be roped into joining the group of ladies chatting in the drawing room while they wrote correspondence to friends and family, or worse, she'd be stuck with the coterie who'd retired to the orangery to pursue their embroidery.

As for the outdoor enthusiasts, they'd also broken into two groups. One had hied off to the village to shop and see whatever sights there were to be found, and the other was taking a constitutional walk to the lake. As Kate had no interest in shopping (and she was already quite familiar with the lake) she'd eschewed their company as well.

Hence, her solitude in the garden.

She sat for several minutes, just staring off into space, her eyes focusing somewhat blindly on the tightly furled bud of a nearby rose. It was nice to be alone, where she didn't have to cover her mouth or stifle the loud sleepy noises she made when she yawned. Nice to be alone, where no one was going to comment on the dark circles beneath her eyes or her uncommon quietude and lack of conversation.

Nice to be alone, where she could sit and attempt to sort through her muddle of thoughts about the viscount. It was a daunting task, and one she'd rather put off, but it had to be done.

But there really wasn't all that much to sort out. Because everything she had learned in the past few days pointed her conscience in one, singular direction. And she knew that she could no longer oppose Bridgerton's courtship of Edwina.

In the past few days he'd proven himself sensitive, caring, and principled. Even, she thought with a glimmer of a smile as she recalled the light in Penelope Featherington's eyes when he'd saved her from the verbal talons of Cressida Cowper, heroic.

He was devoted to family.

He had used his social position and power not to lord over others but simply to spare another person insult.

He had helped her through one of her phobic attacks with a grace and sensitivity that, now that she could view it with a clear head, stunned her.

He might have been a rake and a rogue—he might still *be* a rake and a rogue—but clearly his behavior to those ends did not define the man. And the only objection Kate had to his marrying Edwina was . . .

She swallowed painfully. There was a lump the size of a cannonball in her throat.

Because deep in her heart, she wanted him for herself.

But that was selfish, and Kate had spent her life trying to be unselfish, and she knew she could never ask Edwina not to marry Anthony for such a reason. If Edwina knew that Kate was even the tiniest bit infatuated with the viscount, she would put an end to his courtship at once. And what purpose would that serve? Anthony would just find some other beautiful, eligible woman to pursue. There were plenty to choose from in London.

It wasn't as if he were going to ask *her* instead, so what would she have to gain by preventing a match between him and Edwina?

Nothing except the agony of having to see him married to her sister. And that would fade in time, wouldn't it? It had to; she herself had just said the night before that time truly did heal all wounds. Besides, it would probably hurt just as much to see him married to some other lady; the only difference would be that she would not have to see him at holidays and christenings and the like.

Kate let out a sigh. A long, sad, weary sigh that stole every breath from her lungs and left her shoulders sagging, her posture drooping.

Her heart aching.

And then a voice filled her ears. *His* voice, low and smooth, like a warm swirl around her. "My goodness, you sound serious."

Kate stood so suddenly that the backs of her legs knocked into the edge of the stone bench, setting her off balance and causing her to stumble. "My lord," she blurted out.

His lips curved with the barest hint of a smile. "I thought I might find you here."

Her eyes widened at the realization that he'd deliberately sought her out. Her heart started beating faster as well, but at least that was something she could keep hidden from him.

He glanced briefly down to the stone bench, signaling that she should feel free to resume her seat. "Actually, I saw you from my window. I wanted to make certain that you were feeling better," he said quietly.

Kate sat down, disappointment rising in her throat. He was merely being polite. Of *course* he was merely being polite. Silly of her to dream—even for a moment—that there might be something more. He was, she'd finally realized, a nice person, and any nice person would want to make sure that she was feeling better after what had transpired the night before.

"I am," she replied. "Very much. Thank you."

If he thought anything of her broken, staccato sentences, he did not make any discernible reaction of it. "I'm glad," he said as he sat beside her. "I worried about you for much of the night."

Her heart, which had already been pounding much too quickly, skipped a beat. "You did?"

"Of course. How could I not?"

Kate swallowed. There it was, that infernal politeness again. Oh, she didn't doubt that his interest and concern were real and true. It just hurt that they were prompted by his natural kindness of spirit, not any special feeling for her.

Not that she had expected anything different. But she'd found it impossible not to hope, anyway.

"I'm sorry to have bothered you so late at night," she said quietly, mostly because she thought she should. In truth, she was desperately glad that he'd been there.

"Don't be silly," he said, straightening slightly and fixing upon her a rather stern sort of look. "I hate to think of you all alone during a storm. I'm glad I was there to comfort you."

"I'm usually alone during storms," she admitted.

Anthony frowned. "Your family does not offer you comfort during storms?"

She looked a little sheepish as she said, "They do not know that I still fear them."

He nodded slowly. "I see. There are times—" Anthony paused to clear his throat, a diversionary tactic he frequently employed when he wasn't quite certain what it was he wanted to say. "I think you would gain comfort by seeking the aid of your mother and sister, but I know—" He cleared his throat again. He knew well the singularly strange sensation of loving one's family to distraction, and yet not feeling quite able to share one's deepest and most intractable fears. It brought on an uncanny sense of isolation, of being remarkably alone in a loud and loving crowd.

"I know," he said again, his voice purposely even and subdued, "that it can often be most difficult to share one's fears with those one most deeply loves."

Her brown eyes, wise and warm and undeniably perceptive, focused on his. For one split moment he had the bizarre thought that she somehow knew everything about him, every last detail from the moment of his birth to his certainty of his own death. It seemed, in that second, with her face tipped up toward his and her lips slightly parted, that she, more than anyone else who would ever walk this earth, truly *knew* him.

It was thrilling.

But more than that, it was terrifying.

"You're a very wise man," she whispered.

It took him a moment to remember what they'd been talking about. Ah yes, fears. He knew fears. He tried to laugh off her compliment. "Most of the time I'm a very foolish man."

She shook her head. "No. I think you've hit the nail squarely on its proverbial head. Of course I would not tell Mary and Edwina. I do not want to trouble them." She chewed on her lip for a moment—a funny little movement with her teeth that he found oddly seductive.

"Of course," she added, "if I am to be true to myself, I must confess that my motives are not entirely unselfish. Surely, an equal part of my reluctance lies in my desire not to be seen as weak."

"That's not such a terrible sin," he murmured.

"Not as far as sins go, I suppose," Kate said with a smile. "But I would hazard a guess that it is one from which you, too, suffer."

He didn't say anything, just nodded his assent.

"We all have our roles to play in life," she continued, "and mine has always been to be strong and sensible. Cringing under a table during an electrical storm is neither."

"Your sister," he said quietly, "is probably a great deal stronger than you think."

Her eyes flew to his face. Was he trying to tell her that he'd fallen in love with Edwina? He'd complimented her sister's grace and beauty before, but never had he referred to her inner person.

Kate's eyes searched his for as long as she dared, but she found nothing that revealed his true feelings. "I did not mean to imply that she wasn't," she finally replied. "But I am her older sister. I have always had to be strong for her. Whereas she has only had to be strong for herself." She brought her eyes back up to his, only to find that he was staring at her with an odd intensity, almost as if he could see past her skin and into her very soul. "You are the oldest as well," she said. "I'm sure you know what I mean."

He nodded, and his eyes looked amused and resigned at the same time. "Exactly."

She gave him an answering smile, the kind that passed between people who know similar experiences and trials. And as she felt herself growing more at ease next to him, almost as if she could sink into his side and bury herself against the warmth of his body, she knew that she could put off her task no longer.

She had to tell him that she'd withdrawn her opposition to his match with Edwina. It wasn't fair to anyone to keep it to herself, just because she wanted to keep *him* to herself, if only for a few perfect moments right here in the gardens.

She took a deep breath, straightened her shoulders, and turned to him.

He looked at her expectantly. It was obvious, after all, that she had something to say.

Kate's lips parted. But nothing came out.

"Yes?" he asked, looking rather amused.

"My lord," she blurted out.

"Anthony," he corrected gently.

"Anthony," she repeated, wondering why the use of his given name made this all the more difficult. "I did need to speak with you about something."

He smiled. "I'd gathered."

Her eyes became inexplicably fastened on her right foot, which was tracing half-moons on the packed dirt of the path. "It's . . . um . . . it's about Edwina."

Anthony's brows rose and he followed her gaze to her foot, which had left half-moons behind and was now drawing squiggly lines. "Is something amiss with your sister?" he inquired gently.

She shook her head, looking back up. "Not at all. I believe she's in the drawing room, writing a letter to our cousin in Somerset. Ladies like to do that, you know."

He blinked. "Do what?"

"Write letters. I'm not a very good correspondent

myself," she said, her words coming forth in an oddly rushed fashion, "as I rarely have the patience to sit still at a desk long enough to write an entire letter. Not to mention that my penmanship is abysmal. But most ladies spend a goodly portion of every day drafting letters."

He tried not to smile. "You wanted to warn me that your sister likes to write letters?"

"No, of course not," she mumbled. "It's just that you asked if she was all right, and I said of course, and I told you where she was, and then we were entirely off the topic, and—"

He laid his hand across hers, effectively cutting her off. "What is it you needed to tell me, Kate?"

He watched with interest as she steeled her shoulders and clenched her jaw. She looked as if she were preparing for a hideous task. Then, in one big rush of a sentence, she said, "I just wanted you to know that I have withdrawn my objections to your suit of Edwina."

His chest suddenly felt a bit hollow. "I . . . see," he said, not because he did see, just because he had to say something.

"I admit to a strong prejudice against you," she continued quickly, "but I have come to know you since my arrival at Aubrey Hall, and in all conscience, I could not allow you to go on thinking that I would stand in your way. It would—it would not be right of me."

Anthony just stared at her, completely at a loss. There was, he realized dimly, something a bit deflating about her willingness to marry him off to her sister, since he'd spent the better part of the last two days fighting the urge to kiss her rather senseless.

On the other hand, wasn't this what he wanted? Edwina would make the perfect wife.

Kate would not.

Edwina fit all the criteria he'd laid out when he'd finally decided it was time to wed.

Kate did not.

And he certainly couldn't dally with Kate if he meant to marry Edwina.

She was giving him what he wanted—*exactly*, he reminded himself, what he wanted; with her sister's blessing, Edwina would marry him next week if he so desired.

Then why the devil did he want to grab her by the shoulders and shake and shake and shake until she took back every bloody little annoying word?

It was that spark. That damnable spark that never seemed to dim between them. That awful prickle of awareness that burned every time she entered a room, or took a breath, or pointed a toe. That sinking feeling that he could, if he let himself, love her.

Which was the one thing he feared most.

Perhaps the only thing he feared at all.

It was ironic, but death was the one thing he wasn't afraid of. Death wasn't frightening to a man alone. The great beyond held no terror when one had managed to avoid attachments here on earth.

Love was truly a spectacular, sacred thing. Anthony knew that. He'd seen it every day of his childhood, every time his parents had shared a glance or touched hands.

But love was the enemy of the dying man. It was the only thing that could make the rest of his years intolerable—to taste bliss and know that it would all be snatched away. And that was probably why, when Anthony finally reacted to her words, he didn't yank her to him and kiss her until she was gasping, and he didn't press his lips to her ear and burn his breath against her skin, making sure she understood that he was on fire for her, and not her sister.

Never her sister.

Instead, he just looked at her impassively, his eyes far, far steadier than his heart, and said, "I am much relieved," all the while having the strangest feeling that he wasn't really there, but rather watching the entire scene—nothing more than a farce, really—from outside of his body, all the while wondering what the hell was going on.

She smiled weakly and said, "I thought you might feel that way."

"Kate, I—"

She'd never know what he meant to say. In all truth, *he* wasn't even sure what he intended to say. He hadn't even realized that he was going to speak until her name passed over his lips.

But his words would remain forever unspoken, because at that moment, he heard it.

A low buzz. A whine, really. It was the sort of sound most people found mildly annoying.

Nothing, to Anthony, could have been more terrifying.

"Don't move," he whispered, his voice harsh with fear.

Kate's eyes narrowed, and of course she moved, trying to twist about. "What are you talking about? What is wrong?"

"Just don't move," he repeated.

Her eyes slid to the left, then her chin followed by a quarter of an inch or so. "Oh, it's just a bee!" Her face broke out in a relieved grin, and she lifted her hand to swat it away. "For goodness' sake, Anthony, don't do that again. You had me scared for a moment."

Anthony's hand shot out and grasped her wrist with painful force. "I said don't move," he hissed.

"Anthony," she said, laughing, "it's a *bee*."

He held her immobile, his grasp hard and painful, his eyes never leaving the loathsome creature, watching as it buzzed purposefully around her head. He was paralyzed by fear, and fury, and something else he couldn't quite put his finger on.

It wasn't as if he hadn't come into contact with bees in the eleven years since his father's death. One couldn't reside in England, after all, and expect to avoid them altogether.

Until now, in fact, he'd forced himself to flirt with them in an odd, fatalistic manner. He'd always suspected that he might be doomed to follow in his father's footsteps in all respects. If he was going to be brought down by a humble insect, by God he'd do it standing firm and holding his ground. He was going to die sooner or . . . well, sooner, and he wasn't going to run from some bloody bug. And so when one flew by, he laughed, he mocked, he cursed, and he swatted it away with his hand, daring it to retaliate.

And he'd never been stung.

But seeing one fly so dangerously close to Kate, brushing by her hair, landing on the lacy sleeve of her dress—it was terrifying, almost hypnotizing. His mind raced ahead, and he saw the tiny monster sink its stinger into her soft flesh, he saw her gasping for air, sinking to the ground.

He saw her here at Aubrey Hall, laid out on the same bed that had served as his father's first coffin.

"Just be quiet," he whispered. "We're going to stand—*slowly*. Then we're going to walk away."

"Anthony," she said, her eyes crinkling in an impatiently confused manner, "what is *wrong* with you?"

He tugged on her hand, trying to force her to rise, but she resisted. "It's a *bee*," she said in an exasperated voice. "Stop acting so strangely. For heaven's sake, it's not going to kill me."

Her words hung heavy in the air, almost like solid objects, ready to crash to the ground and shatter them both. Then, finally, when Anthony felt his throat relax enough to speak, he said in a low, intense voice, "It might."

Kate froze, not because she meant to follow his orders, but because something in his aspect, something in his eyes, frightened her to the bone. He looked changed, possessed by some unknown demon. "Anthony," she said in what she hoped was an even, authoritative voice, "let go of my wrist this instant."

She pulled, but he did not relent, and the bee kept buzzing relentlessly about her.

"Anthony!" she exclaimed. "Stop this right—"

The rest of her sentence was lost as she somehow managed to yank her hand from his crushing grasp. The sudden freedom left her off balance, and her arm flailed up and about, the inside of her elbow knocking into the bee, which let out a loud, angry buzz as the force of the blow sent it hurtling through space, smashing right into the strip of bare skin above the lace-edged bodice of her afternoon dress.

"Oh, for the love of— Ow!" Kate let out a howl as the bee, no doubt infuriated by its abuse, sank its stinger into her flesh. "Oh, damn," she swore, completely past any pretensions toward proper language. It was just a bee sting, of course, and nothing she hadn't suffered several times before, but bloody hell, it *hurt*.

"Oh, bother," she grumbled, pulling her chin against her chest so she could look down and get the best view of the red welt rising right along the edge of her bodice. "Now I'll have to go inside for a poultice, and it'll get all over my dress." With a disdainful sniff, she brushed the dead carcass of the bee from her skirt, muttering, "Well, at least he's dead, the vexing thing. It's probably the only justice in the—"

That was when she looked up and spied Anthony's face. He'd gone white. Not pale, not even bloodless, but white. "Oh, my God," he whispered, and the oddest thing was that his lips didn't even move. "Oh, my God."

"Anthony?" she asked, leaning forward and momentarily forgetting about the painful sting on her chest. "Anthony, what is wrong?"

Whatever trance he was in suddenly snapped, and he leaped forward, roughly grabbing one of her shoulders with one hand while his other grappled with the bodice of her gown, pulling it down to better expose her wound.

"My lord!" Kate shrieked. "Stop!"

He said nothing, but his breath was ragged and fast as he pinned her against the back of the bench, still holding her dress down, not low enough to expose her, but certainly lower than decency allowed.

"Anthony!" she tried, hoping that the use of his given name might get his attention. She didn't know this man; he wasn't the one who had sat at her side just two minutes earlier. He was crazed, frantic, and completely heedless of her protestations.

"Will you shut up?" he hissed, never once looking up at her. His eyes were focused on the red, swollen circle of flesh on her chest, and with trembling hands he plucked the stinger from her skin.

"Anthony, I'm fine!" she insisted. "You must—"

She gasped. He'd moved one of his hands slightly as he used the other to yank a handkerchief from his pocket, and it now rather indelicately cupped her entire breast.

"Anthony, what are you doing?" She grabbed at his hand, trying to remove it from her person, but his strength was beyond her.

He pinned her even more firmly against the back of the bench, his hand nearly pressing her breast flat. "Be still!" he barked, and then he took the handkerchief and began to press against the swollen sting.

"What are you doing?" she asked, still trying to scoot away.

He didn't look up. "Expressing the venom."

"*Is* there venom?"

"There must be," he muttered. "There has to be. Something is killing you."

Her mouth fell open. "Something is *killing me*? Are you mad? Nothing is killing me. It's a bee sting."

But he ignored her, too focused on his self-appointed task of treating her wound.

"Anthony," she said in a placating voice, trying to reason with him. "I appreciate your concern, but I've been stung by bees at least a half dozen times, and I—"

"He'd been stung before, too," he interrupted.

Something about his voice sent a shiver down her spine. "Who?" she whispered.

He pressed more firmly against the raised hive, dabbing the handkerchief against the clear liquid that oozed out. "My father," he said flatly, "and it killed him."

She couldn't quite believe it. "A bee?"

"Yes, a bee," he snapped. "Haven't you been listening?"

"Anthony, a little bee cannot kill a man."

He actually paused in his ministrations for a brief second to glance up at her. His eyes were hard, haunted. "I assure you that it can," he bit off.

Kate couldn't quite believe that his words were true, but she also didn't think he was lying, and so she held still for a moment, recognizing that he needed to treat her bee sting far more than she needed to scoot away from his attentions.

"It's still swollen," he muttered, pressing harder with the handkerchief. "I don't think I got it all out."

"I'm sure I'll be fine," she said gently, her ire with him turning into an almost maternal concern. His brow was wrinkled with concentration, and his movements still carried an air of frantic energy. He was petrified, she realized, scared that she would drop dead right there on the garden bench, felled by a tiny little bee.

It seemed unfathomable, and yet it was true.

He shook his head. "It's not good enough," he said hoarsely. "I have to get it all out."

"Anthony, I— What are you *doing*?"

He'd tipped her chin back and his head was closing the distance between them, almost as if he meant to kiss her.

"I'm going to have to suck the venom out," he said grimly. "Just hold still."

"Anthony!" she shrieked. "You can't—" She gasped, completely unable to finish her sentence once she felt his lips settling on her skin, applying a gentle, yet inexorable pressure, pulling her into his mouth. Kate didn't know how to respond, didn't know whether to push him away or pull him toward her.

But in the end she just froze. Because when she lifted her head and looked over his shoulder, she saw a group of three women staring at them with equal expressions of shock.

Mary.

Lady Bridgerton.

And Mrs. Featherington, arguably the *ton*'s biggest gossip.

And Kate knew, beyond a shadow of a doubt, that her life would never be the same.

Chapter 14

And indeed, if a scandal does erupt at Lady Bridgerton's party, those of us who remain in London may be assured that any and all titillating news shall reach our tender ears with all possible haste. With so many notorious gossips in attendance, we are all but guaranteed a full and detailed report.

LADY WHISTLEDOWN'S SOCIETY PAPERS, 4 MAY 1814

For a split second, everyone remained frozen as if in a tableau. Kate stared at the three matrons in shock. They stared back at her in utter horror.

And Anthony kept trying to suck the venom from Kate's bee sting, completely oblivious to the fact that they had an audience.

Of the quintet, Kate found her voice—and her strength—first, shoving with all her might against Anthony's shoulder as she let out an impassioned cry of, "Stop!"

Caught off guard, he proved surprisingly easy to dislodge, and he landed on his bum on the ground, his eyes still burning with determination to save her from what he perceived as her deathly fate.

"Anthony?" Lady Bridgerton gasped, her voice quavering on her son's name, as if she couldn't quite believe what she was seeing.

He twisted around. "Mother?"

"Anthony, what were you doing?"

"She was stung by a bee," he said grimly.

"I'm fine," Kate insisted, then yanked up her dress. "I told him I was fine, but he wouldn't listen to me."

Lady Bridgerton's eyes misted over with understanding. "I see," she said in a small, sad voice, and Anthony knew that she did see. She was, perhaps, the only person who *could* see.

"Kate," Mary finally said, choking on her words, "he had his lips on your . . . on your—"

"On her breast," Mrs. Featherington said helpfully, folding her arms over her ample bosom. A disapproving frown crossed her face, but it was clear that she was enjoying herself immensely.

"He did not!" Kate exclaimed, struggling to her feet, which wasn't the easiest task, since Anthony had landed on one of them when she'd shoved him off the bench. "I was stung right here!" With a frantic finger, she pointed at the round red welt that was still rising on the thin skin covering her collarbone.

The three older ladies stared at her bee sting, their skin assuming identical blushes of faint crimson.

"It's not anywhere near my breast!" Kate protested, too horrified by the direction of the conversation to remember to feel embarrassed at her rather anatomical language.

"It isn't *far,*" Mrs. Featherington pointed out.

"Will someone shut her up?" Anthony snapped.

"Well!" Mrs. Featherington huffed. "I never!"

"No," Anthony replied. "You *always.*"

"What does he mean by that?" Mrs. Featherington demanded, poking Lady Bridgerton in the arm. When the viscountess did not respond, she turned to Mary and repeated the question.

But Mary had eyes only for her daughter. "Kate," she ordered, "come here this instant."

Dutifully, Kate moved to Mary's side.

"Well?" Mrs. Featherington asked. "What are we going to do?"

Four sets of eyes turned on her in disbelief.

" 'We'?" Kate questioned faintly.

"I fail to see how *you* have any say in the matter," Anthony bit off.

Mrs. Featherington just let out a loud, disdainful, and rather nasal sniff. "You have to marry the chit," she announced.

"What?" The word was ripped from Kate's throat. "You must be mad."

"I must be the only sensible one in the garden is what I must be," Mrs. Featherington said officiously. "Lud, girl, he had his mouth on your bubbies, and we all saw it."

"He did not!" Kate moaned. "I was stung by a bee. A bee!"

"Portia," Lady Bridgerton interjected, "I hardly think there is need for such graphic language."

"There's little use for delicacy now," Mrs. Featherington replied. "It's going to make a tidy piece of gossip no matter how you describe it. The *ton*'s most fervent bachelor, brought down by a bee. I must say, my lord, it's not how I imagined it."

"There is not going to be any gossip," Anthony growled, advancing on her with a menacing air, "because no one is going to say a word. I will not see Miss Sheffield's reputation besmirched in any way."

Mrs. Featherington's eyes bugged out with disbelief. "You think you can keep something like this quiet?"

"*I'm* not going to say anything, and I rather doubt that Miss Sheffield will, either," he said, planting his hands on his hips as he glared down at her. It was the sort of stare that brought grown men to their knees, but Mrs. Featherington was either impervious or simply stupid, so he continued with, "Which leaves our respective mothers, who would seem to have a vested interest in protecting our reputations. Which then leaves you, Mrs. Featherington, as the only member of our cozy little group who might prove herself a gossipy, loudmouthed fishwife over this."

Mrs. Featherington turned a dull red. "Anyone could have seen from the house," she said bitterly, clearly loath to lose such a prime piece of gossip. She'd be fêted for a month as the only eyewitness to such a scandal. The only eyewitness who'd talk, that is.

Lady Bridgerton glanced up at the house, her face going pale. "She's right, Anthony," she said. "You were in full view of the guest wing."

"It was a bee," Kate practically wailed. "Just a bee! Surely we can't be forced to marry because of a bee!"

Her outburst was met with silence. She looked from Mary to Lady Bridgerton, both of whom were gazing at her with expressions hovering between concern, kindness, and pity. Then she looked at Anthony, whose expression was hard, closed, and utterly unreadable.

Kate closed her eyes in misery. This wasn't how it was supposed to happen. Even as she had told him he might marry her sister, she'd secretly wished he could be hers, but not like this.

Oh, dear Lord, not like this. Not so he'd feel trapped. Not so he'd spend the rest of his life looking at her and wishing she were someone else.

"Anthony?" she whispered. Maybe if he spoke to her, maybe if he just looked at her she might glean some clue as to what he was thinking.

"We will marry next week," he stated. His voice was firm and clear, but otherwise devoid of emotion.

"Oh, good!" Lady Bridgerton said with great relief, clapping her hands together. "Mrs. Sheffield and I will begin preparations immediately."

"Anthony," Kate whispered again, this time with more

urgency, "are you certain?" She grabbed his arm and tried to pull him away from the matrons. She gained only a few inches, but at least now they weren't facing them.

He gazed at her with implacable eyes. "We will marry," he said simply, his voice that of the consummate aristocrat, brooking no protest and expecting to be obeyed. "There is nothing else to do."

"But you don't want to marry me," she said.

This caused him to raise a brow. "And do you want to marry me?"

She said nothing. There was nothing she could say, not if she wanted to maintain even a shred of pride.

"I suspect we shall suit well enough," he continued, his expression softening slightly. "We've become friends of a sort, after all. That's more than most men and women have at the beginning of a union."

"You can't want this," she persisted. "You wanted to marry Edwina. What are you going to say to Edwina?"

He crossed his arms. "I never made any promises to Edwina. And I imagine we'll simply tell her we fell in love."

Kate felt her eyes rolling of their own volition. "She'll never believe *that*."

He shrugged. "Then tell her the truth. Tell her you were stung by a bee, and I was trying to aid you, and we were caught in a compromising position. Tell her whatever you want. She's your sister."

Kate sank back down onto the stone bench, sighing. "No one is going to believe you wanted to marry me," she said. "Everyone will think you were trapped."

Anthony shot a pointed glare at the three women, who were still staring at them with interest. At his, "Would you mind?" both his and Kate's mothers stepped back several feet and turned around to afford them more privacy. When Mrs. Featherington did not follow immediately, Violet reached forward and nearly pulled her arm out of the socket.

Sitting down next to Kate, he said, "There is little we can do to prevent people from talking, especially with Portia Featherington as a witness. I don't trust that woman to keep her mouth shut any longer than it takes her to return to the house." He leaned back and propped his left ankle on his right knee. "So we might as well make the best of it. I have to get married this year—"

"Why?"

"Why what?"

"Why do you have to get married this year?"

He paused for a moment. There wasn't really an answer to that question. So he said, "Because I decided I would, and that's a good enough reason for me. As for you, you have to get married eventually—"

She interrupted him again with, "To be honest, I rather assumed I wouldn't."

Anthony felt his muscles tense, and it took him several seconds to realize that what he was feeling was rage. "You planned to live your life as a spinster?"

She nodded, her eyes innocent and frank at the same time. "It seemed a definite possibility, yes."

Anthony held himself still for several seconds, thinking he might like to murder all those men and women who had compared her to Edwina and found her lacking. Kate truly had no idea that she might be attractive and desirable in her own right.

When Mrs. Featherington had announced that they must marry, his initial reaction had been the same as Kate's—utter horror. Not to mention a rather pricked sense of pride. No man liked to be forced into marriage, and it was particularly galling to be forced by a *bee*.

But as he stood there, watching Kate howl in protest (not, he thought, the most flattering of reactions, but he supposed she was allowed her pride as well), a strange sense of satisfaction washed over him.

He wanted her.

He wanted her desperately.

He wouldn't, in a million years, have allowed himself to choose her as a wife. She was far, far too dangerous to his peace of mind.

But fate had intervened, and now that it looked like he *had* to marry her . . . well, there didn't seem much use in putting up a big fuss. There were worse fates than finding oneself married to an intelligent, entertaining woman whom one happened to lust after around the clock.

All he had to do was make certain he didn't actually fall in love with her. Which shouldn't prove impossible, right? The Lord knew she drove him crazy half the time with her incessant arguing. He could have a pleasant marriage with Kate. He'd enjoy her friendship and enjoy her body and keep it at that. It didn't have to go any deeper.

And he couldn't have asked for a better woman to serve as mother to his sons after he was gone. That was certainly worth a great deal.

"This will work," he said with great authority. "You'll see."

She looked doubtful, but she nodded. Of course, there was little else she could do. She'd just been caught by the biggest gossip in London with a man's mouth on her chest. If he hadn't offered to marry her, she'd have been ruined forever.

And if she'd refused to marry him . . . well, then she'd be branded a fallen woman *and* an idiot.

Anthony suddenly stood. "Mother!" he barked, leaving Kate on the bench as he strode over to her. "My fiancée and I desire a bit of privacy here in the garden."

"Of course," Lady Bridgerton murmured.

"Do you think that's wise?" Mrs. Featherington asked.

Anthony leaned forward, placed his mouth very close to his mother's ear, and whispered, "If you do not remove her from my presence within the next ten seconds, I shall murder her on the spot."

Lady Bridgerton choked on a laugh, nodded, and managed to say, "Of course."

In under a minute, Anthony and Kate were alone in the garden.

He turned to face her; she'd stood and taken a few steps toward him. "I think," he murmured, slipping his arm through hers, "that we ought to consider moving out of sight of the house."

His steps were long and purposeful, and she stumbled to keep up with him until she found her stride. "My lord," she asked, hurrying along, "do you think this is wise?"

"You sound like Mrs. Featherington," he pointed out, not breaking his pace, even for a second.

"Heaven forbid," Kate muttered, "but the question still stands."

"Yes, I do think it's very wise," he replied, pulling her into a gazebo. Its walls were partially open to the air, but it was surrounded by lilac bushes and afforded them considerable privacy.

"But—"

He smiled. Slowly. "Did you know you argue too much?"

"You brought me here to tell me *that*?"

"No," he drawled, "I brought you here to do *this*."

And then, before she had a chance to utter a word, before she even had a chance to draw breath, his mouth swooped down and captured hers in a hungry, searing kiss. His lips were voracious, taking everything she had to give and then demanding even more. The fire that glowed within her burned and crackled even hotter than what he'd stoked that night in his study, hotter by a tenfold.

She was melting. Dear God, she was melting, and she wanted so much more.

"You shouldn't do this to me," he whispered against her mouth. "You shouldn't. Everything about you is absolutely wrong. And yet . . ."

Kate gasped as his hands stole around to her backside and pressed her harshly against his arousal.

"Do you see?" he said raggedly, his lips moving along

her cheek. "Do you feel?" He chuckled hoarsely, an odd mocking sound. "Do you even understand?" He squeezed mercilessly, then nibbled the tender skin of her ear. "Of course you don't."

Kate felt herself sliding into him. Her skin was starting to burn, and her traitorous arms stole up and around his neck. He was stoking a fire in her, something she could not even begin to control. She'd been possessed by some primitive urge, something hot and molten which needed nothing so much as the touch of his skin against hers.

She wanted him. Oh, how she wanted him. She shouldn't want him, shouldn't desire this man who was marrying her for all the wrong reasons.

And yet she wanted him with a desperation that left her breathless.

It was wrong, so very wrong. She had grave doubts about this marriage, and she knew she ought to maintain a clear head. She kept trying to remind herself of that, but it didn't stop her lips from parting to allow his entry, nor her own tongue from shyly flicking out to taste the corner of his mouth.

And the desire pooling in her belly—and surely that was what this strange, prickly, swirling feeling had to be—it just kept getting stronger and stronger.

"Am I a terrible person?" she whispered, more for her ears than for his. "Does this mean I am fallen?"

But he heard her, and his voice was hot and moist on the skin of her cheek.

"*No*."

He moved to her ear and made her listen more closely.

"*No*."

He traveled to her lips and forced her to swallow the word.

"*No*."

Kate felt her head fall back. His voice was low and seductive, and it almost made her feel like she'd been born for this moment.

"You're perfect," he whispered, his large hands moving urgently over her body, one settling on her waist and the other moving up toward the gentle swell of her breast. "Right here, right now, in this moment, in this garden, you're perfect."

Kate found something unsettling about his words, as if he were trying to tell her—and perhaps himself as well—that she might not be perfect tomorrow, and perhaps even less so the next day. But his lips and hands were persuasive, and she forced the unpleasant thoughts from her head, instead reveling in the heady bliss of the moment.

She felt beautiful. She felt . . . perfect. And right there, right then, she couldn't help but adore the man who made her feel that way.

Anthony slid the hand at her waist to the small of her back, supporting her as his other hand found her breast and squeezed her flesh through the thin muslin of her dress. His fingers seemed beyond his control, tight and spasmodic, gripping her as if he were falling off a cliff and had finally found purchase. Her nipple was hard and tight against his palm, even through the fabric of her dress, and it took everything in him, every last ounce of restraint, not to reach around to the back of her frock and slowly pull each button from its prison.

He could see it all in his mind, even as his lips met hers in another searing kiss. Her dress would slip from her shoulders, the muslin doing a tantalizing slide along her skin until her breasts were bared. He could picture those in his mind, too, and he somehow knew they, too, would be perfect. He'd cup one, lifting the nipple to the sun, and slowly, ever so slowly, he'd bend his head toward her until he could just barely touch her with his tongue.

She'd moan, and he'd tease her some more, holding her tightly so that she couldn't wriggle away. And then, just when her head dropped back and she was gasping, he'd replace his tongue with his lips and suckle her until she screamed.

Dear God, he wanted that so badly he thought he might explode.

But this wasn't the time or the place. It wasn't that he felt a need to wait for his marriage vows. As far as he was concerned, he'd declared himself in public, and she was his. But he wasn't going to tumble her in his mother's garden gazebo. He had more pride—and more respect for her—than that.

With great reluctance, he slowly tore himself away from her, letting his hands rest on her slim shoulders and straightening his arms to keep himself far enough away so that he wouldn't be tempted to continue where he'd left off.

And the temptation was there. He made the mistake of looking at her face, and in that moment he would have sworn that Kate Sheffield was every bit as beautiful as her sister.

Hers was a different sort of attraction. Her lips were fuller, less in fashion but infinitely more kissable. Her lashes—how had he not noticed before how long they were? When she blinked they seemed to rest on her cheeks like a carpet. And when her skin was tinged with the pinks of desire, she glowed. Anthony knew he was being fanciful, but when he gazed upon her face, he could not help thinking of the new dawn, of that exact moment when the sun was creeping over the horizon, painting the sky with its subtle palette of peaches and pinks.

They stood that way for a full minute, both catching their breath, until Anthony finally let his arms drop, and they each took a step back. Kate lifted a hand to her mouth, her fore, middle, and ring fingers just barely touching her lips. "We shouldn't have done that," she whispered.

He leaned back against one of the gazebo posts, looked extremely satisfied with his lot. "Why not? We're betrothed."

"We're not," she admitted. "Not really."

He quirked a brow.

"No agreements have been made," Kate explained hastily. "Or papers signed. And I have no dowry. You should know that I have no dowry."

This caused him to smile. "Are you trying to get rid of me?"

"Of course not!" She fidgeted slightly, shifting her weight from foot to foot.

He took a step toward her. "Surely you're not trying to provide me with a reason to be rid of *you*?"

Kate flushed. "N-no," she lied, even though that was exactly what she had been doing. It was, of course, the utmost stupidity on her part. If he backed out of this marriage, she'd be ruined forever, not just in London, but also in her little village in Somerset. News of a fallen woman always traveled fast.

But it was never easy to be the second choice, and a part of her almost wanted him to confirm all of her suspicions—that he didn't want her as his bride, that he'd much prefer Edwina, that he was only marrying her because he had to. It would hurt dreadfully, but if he would just say it, she would know, and knowing—even if the knowledge was bitter—was always better than not knowing.

At least then she would know exactly where she stood. As it was, she felt as if her feet were planted firmly in quicksand.

"Let us make one thing clear," Anthony said, capturing her attention with his decisive tone. His eyes caught hers, burning with such intensity that she could not look away. "I said I was going to marry you. I am a man of my word. Any further speculation on the subject would be highly insulting."

Kate nodded. But she couldn't help thinking: *Be careful what you wish for . . . be careful what you wish for.*

She'd just agreed to marry the very man with whom she

feared she was falling in love. And all she could wonder was: *Does he think of Edwina when he kisses me?*

Be careful what you wish for, her mind thundered.

You just might get it.

Chapter 15

Once again, This Author has been proven correct. Country house parties do result in the most surprising of betrothals.

Yes indeed, dear reader, you are surely reading it here first: Viscount Bridgerton is to marry Miss Katharine Sheffield. Not Miss Edwina, as gossips had speculated, but Miss Katharine.

As to how the betrothal came about, details have been surprisingly difficult to obtain. This Author has it on the best authority that the new couple was caught in a compromising position, and that Mrs. Featherington was a witness, but Mrs. F has been uncharacteristically close-lipped about the entire affair. Given that lady's propensity for gossip, This Author can only assume that the viscount (never known for lacking a spine) threatened bodily injury upon Mrs. F should she even breathe a syllable.

Lady Whistledown's Society Papers, 11 May 1814

Kate soon realized that notoriety did not agree with her.

The remaining two days in Kent had been bad enough; once Anthony had announced their engagement at supper following their somewhat precipitous betrothal, she had scarcely a chance to breathe between all the congratulations, questions, and innuendos that were being tossed her way by Lady Bridgerton's guests.

The only time she felt truly at ease was when, a few hours after Anthony's announcement, she finally had a chance to talk privately with Edwina, who'd thrown her arms around her sister and declared herself "thrilled," "overjoyed," and "not even one tiny bit surprised."

Kate had expressed *her* surprise that Edwina was not surprised, but Edwina had just shrugged and said, "It was obvious to me that he was smitten. I do not know why no one else saw it."

Which had left Kate rather puzzled, since she'd been fairly certain that Anthony had had his matrimonial sights set on Edwina.

Once Kate returned to London, the speculation was even worse. Every single member of the *ton*, it seemed, found it imperative to stop by the Sheffields' small rented home on Milner Street to call on the future viscountess. Most managed to infuse their congratulations with a healthy dose of unflattering implication. No one believed it possible that the viscount might actually *want* to marry Kate, and no one seemed to realize how rude it was to say as much to her face.

"My goodness, you were lucky," said Lady Cowper, the mother of the infamous Cressida Cowper, who, for her part, did not say two words to Kate, just sulked in the corner and glared daggers in her direction.

"I had no *idea* he was interested in you," gushed Miss Gertrude Knight, with a facial expression that clearly said she still didn't believe it, and perhaps even hoped that the betrothal might still prove to be a sham, announcement in the *London Times* notwithstanding.

And from Lady Danbury, who'd never been known to mince words: "Don't know how you trapped him, but it must have been a neat trick. There are a few gels out there who wouldn't mind taking lessons from you, mark my words."

Kate just smiled (or tried to, at least; she suspected that her attempts at gracious and friendly response were not always convincing) and nodded, and murmured, "I am a fortunate girl," whenever Mary poked her in the side.

As for Anthony, the lucky man had been able to avoid the harsh scrutiny she'd been forced to endure. He had told her he needed to remain at Aubrey Hall to take care of a few estate details before the wedding, which had been set for the following Saturday, only nine days after the incident in the garden. Mary had worried that such hastiness would lead to "talk," but Lady Bridgerton had rather pragmatically explained that there would be "talk" no matter what, and that Kate would be less subject to unflattering innuendo once she had the protection of Anthony's name.

Kate suspected that the viscountess—who had gained a certain reputation for her single-minded desire to see her adult children married off—simply wanted to get Anthony in front of the bishop before he had the chance to change his mind.

Kate found herself in agreement with Lady Bridgerton. As nervous as she was about the wedding and the marriage to follow, she'd never been the sort to put things off. Once she made a decision—or, in this case, had one made for her—she saw no reason for delay. And as for the "talk," a hasty wedding might increase its volume, but Kate suspected that the sooner she and Anthony were married, the sooner it would die down, and the sooner she might hope to return to the normal obscurity of her own life.

Of course, her life would not be her own for much longer. She was going to have to get used to that.

Not that it felt like her own even now. Her days were a whirlwind of activity, with Lady Bridgerton dragging her from shop to shop, spending an enormous amount of

Anthony's money for her trousseau. Kate had quickly learned that resistance was useless; when Lady Bridgerton—or Violet, as she had now been instructed to call her—made up her mind, heaven help the fool who got in her way. Mary and Edwina had accompanied them on a few of the outings, but they had quickly declared themselves exhausted by Violet's indefatigable energy and gone off to Gunter's for a flavored ice.

Finally, a mere two days before the wedding, Kate received a note from Anthony, asking her to be at home at four that afternoon so that he might pay her a call. Kate was a little nervous at seeing him again; somehow everything seemed different—more formal—in town. Nonetheless, she seized upon the opportunity to avoid another afternoon on Oxford Street, at the dressmaker, and the milliner, and the glovemaker, and to whomever else Violet had it in mind to drag her.

And so, while Mary and Edwina were out running errands—Kate had conveniently forgotten to mention that the viscount was expected—she sat down in the drawing room, Newton sleeping contentedly at her feet, and waited.

Anthony had spent most of the week thinking. Not surprisingly, all of his thoughts were of Kate and their upcoming union.

He'd been worried that he could, if he let himself, love her. The key, it seemed, was simply not to let himself. And the more he thought about it, the more convinced he was that this would not pose a problem. He was a man, after all, and well in control of his actions and emotions. He was no fool; he knew that love existed. But he also believed in the power of the mind, and perhaps even more importantly, the power of the will. Frankly, he saw no reason why love should be an involuntary thing.

If he didn't want to fall in love, then by damn, he wasn't going to. It was as simple as that. It *had* to be as simple as that. If it weren't, then he wasn't much of a man, was he?

He would, however, have to have a talk with Kate on this measure prior to the wedding. There were certain things about their marriage that needed to be made clear. Not rules, exactly, but . . . *understandings*. Yes, that was a good word for it.

Kate needed to understand exactly what she could expect from him, and what he expected in return. Theirs was not a love match. And it wasn't going to grow into one. That simply was not an option. He didn't think she had any delusions on that measure, but just in case, he wanted to make it clear now, before any misunderstandings had the chance to grow into full-fledged disasters.

It was best to lay everything out on the proverbial table so that neither party would be unpleasantly surprised later on. Surely Kate would agree. She was a practical girl. She'd want to know where she stood. She wasn't the sort who liked to be kept guessing.

At precisely two minutes before four, Anthony rapped twice on the Sheffields' front door, trying to ignore the half dozen members of the *ton* who just *happened* to be strolling along Milner Street that afternoon. They were, he thought with a grimace, a bit far from their usual haunts.

But he wasn't surprised. He might be recently returned to London, but he was well aware that his betrothal was the current scandal *du jour*. *Whistledown* was delivered all the way in Kent, after all.

The butler opened the door quickly and ushered him in, showing him to the nearby drawing room. Kate was waiting on the sofa, her hair swept up into a neat something-or-other (Anthony never could remember the names of all those coiffures the ladies seemed to favor) and topped with a ridiculous little cap of some sort that he supposed was meant to match the white trim on her pale blue afternoon dress.

The cap, he decided, would be the first thing to go once they were married. She had lovely hair, long and lustrous and thick. He knew that good manners dictated that she wear bonnets when she was out and about, but really, it seemed a crime to cover it up in the comfort of her own home.

Before he could open his mouth, however, even in greeting, she motioned to a silver tea service on the table in front of her and said, "I took the liberty of ordering tea. There's a slight chill in the air and I thought you might like some. If you don't, I'd be happy to ring for something else."

There hadn't been a chill in the air, at least not one that Anthony had detected, but he nonetheless said, "That would be lovely, thank you."

Kate nodded and picked up the pot to pour. She tipped it about an inch, then righted it, frowning as she said, "I don't even know how you take your tea."

Anthony felt one corner of his mouth tipping up slightly. "Milk. No sugar."

She nodded, setting the pot down in favor of the milk. "It seems a thing a wife should know."

He sat down in a chair that sat at a right angle to the sofa. "And now you do."

She took a deep breath and then let it go. "Now I do," she murmured.

Anthony cleared his throat as he watched her pour. She wasn't wearing gloves, and he found he liked to watch her hands as she worked. Her fingers were long and slender, and they were incredibly graceful, which surprised him, considering how many times she'd trod on his toes while dancing.

Of course some of those missteps had been done on purpose, but not, he suspected, as many as she would have liked to have him believe.

"Here you are," she murmured, holding out his tea. "Be careful, it's hot. I've never been one for lukewarm tea."

No, he thought with a smile, she wouldn't be. Kate wasn't the sort to do anything in half measures. It was one of the things he liked best about her.

"My lord?" she said politely, moving the tea a few inches farther in his direction.

Anthony grasped the saucer, allowing his gloved fingers to brush against her bare ones. He kept his eyes on her face, noticing the faint pink stain of blush that touched her cheeks.

For some reason that pleased him.

"Did you have something specific you wanted to ask me, my lord?" she asked, once her hand was safely away from his and her fingers wrapped around the handle of her own teacup.

"It's Anthony, as I'm sure you recall, and I can't call upon my fiancée merely for the pleasure of her company?"

She gave him a shrewd look over the rim of her cup. "Of course you can," she replied, "but I don't think you are."

He raised a brow at her impertinence. "As it happens, you're right."

She murmured something. He didn't quite catch it, but he had a sneaking suspicion it had been, "I usually am."

"I thought we ought to discuss our marriage," he said.

"I beg your pardon?"

He leaned back in his chair. "We're both practical people. I think we'll find ourselves more at ease once we understand what we can expect from one another."

"Of—of course."

"Good." He set his teacup down in the saucer, then set both down on the table in front of him. "I'm glad you feel that way."

Kate nodded slowly but didn't say anything, instead choosing to keep her eyes trained on his face as he cleared his throat. He looked as if he were preparing for a parliamentary speech.

"We did not get off to the most favorable of starts," he said, scowling slightly when she nodded her agreement, "but I feel—and I hope that you do as well—that we have since reached a friendship of sorts."

She nodded again, thinking that she might make it all the way through the conversation doing nothing but nodding.

"Friendship between the husband and the wife is of the utmost importance," he continued, "even more important, in my opinion, than love."

This time she didn't nod.

"Our marriage will be one based on mutual friendship and respect," he pontificated, "and I for one could not be more pleased."

"Respect," Kate echoed, mostly because he was looking at her expectantly.

"I will do my best to be a good husband to you," he said. "And, provided that you do not bar me from your bed, I shall be faithful to both you and our vows."

"That's rather enlightened of you," she murmured. He was saying nothing she did not expect, and yet she found it somewhat needling all the same.

His eyes narrowed. "I hope you're taking me seriously, Kate."

"Oh, very much so."

"Good." But he gave her a funny look, and she wasn't sure if he believed her. "In return," he added, "I expect that you will not behave in any manner that will sully my family's name."

Kate felt her spine stiffen. "I would not dream of it."

"I didn't think you would. That is one of the reasons I am so pleased with this marriage. You will make an excellent viscountess."

It was meant as a compliment, Kate knew, but still it felt a bit hollow, and maybe a touch condescending. She'd much rather have been told that she'd make an excellent wife.

"We shall have friendship," he announced, "and we

shall have mutual respect, and children—intelligent children, thank God, since you are quite the most intelligent woman of my acquaintance."

That made up for his condescension, but Kate had barely time to smile at his compliment before he added, "But you should not expect love. This marriage will not be about love."

An awful lump rose in Kate's throat, and she found herself nodding yet again, except this time every movement of her neck somehow brought pain to her heart.

"There are certain things I cannot give you," Anthony said, "and love, I'm afraid, is one of them."

"I see."

"Do you?"

"Of course," she practically snapped. "You could not make it any plainer if you wrote it on my arm."

"I had never planned to marry for love," he said.

"That is not what you told me when you were courting Edwina."

"When I was courting Edwina," he returned, "I was trying to impress *you*."

Her eyes narrowed. "You are not impressing me now."

He let out a long breath. "Kate, I did not come here to argue. I merely thought it best if we were honest with one another before the wedding on Saturday morning."

"Of course," she sighed, forcing herself to nod. His intention hadn't been to insult her, and she shouldn't have overreacted. She knew him well enough now to know that he was merely acting out of concern. He knew he would never love her; better to make that clear in the beginning.

But still it hurt. She didn't know if she loved him, but she was fairly certain she *could* love him, and deathly afraid that after a few weeks of marriage, she *would* love him.

And it would be so nice if he could just love her back.

"It is best that we understand each other now," he said softly.

Kate just kept nodding. A body in motion tended to

remain in motion, and she was afraid that if she stopped, she might do something really stupid, like cry.

He reached across the table and took her hand, which made her flinch. "I didn't want you to enter this marriage with any delusions," he said. "I didn't think you'd want that."

"Of course not, my lord," she said.

He frowned. "I thought I told you to call me Anthony."

"You did," she said, "my lord."

He withdrew his hand. Kate watched as he returned it to his own lap, feeling strangely bereft.

"Before I go," he said, "I have something for you." Without taking his eyes off of her face, he reached into his pocket and pulled out a small jeweler's box. "I must apologize for being so delayed in presenting you with a betrothal ring," he murmured, handing it to her.

Kate smoothed her fingers over the blue velvet covering before flipping the box open. Inside lay a rather simple gold ring, adorned by a single round-cut diamond.

"It's a Bridgerton heirloom," he said. "There are several betrothal rings in the collection, but I thought you'd like this one best. The others were rather heavy and fussy."

"It's beautiful," Kate said, quite unable to take her eyes off of it.

He reached out and took the box from her. "May I?" he murmured, plucking the ring from its velvet nest.

She held out her hand, cursing at herself when she realized she was trembling—not a great deal, but surely enough for him to notice. He didn't say a word, though, just steadied her hand with his as he used the other to slip the ring on her finger.

"Looks rather nice, don't you think?" he asked, still holding the tips of her fingers with his.

Kate nodded, unable to take her eyes off of it. She'd never been one for rings; this would be the first she wore with any regularity. It felt strange on her finger, heavy and cold and very, very solid. It somehow made everything that had happened in the past week seem more real. More final. It occurred to her as she was staring at the ring that she'd been half expecting a bolt of lightning to come down from heaven and stop the proceedings before they actually said their vows.

Anthony moved closer, then brought her newly adorned fingers to his lips. "Perhaps we should seal the bargain with a kiss?" he murmured.

"I'm not sure. . . ."

He pulled her onto his lap and grinned devilishly. "I am."

But as Kate tumbled onto him, she accidentally kicked Newton, who let out a loud, whiny bark, obviously distressed at having his nap so rudely interrupted.

Anthony raised a brow and peered over Kate at Newton. "I didn't even see him here."

"He was taking a nap," Kate explained. "He's a very sound sleeper."

But once awake, Newton refused to be left out of the action, and with a slightly more awake bark, he leaped up onto the chair, landing on Kate's lap.

"Newton!" she squealed.

"Oh, for the love of—" But Anthony's mutterings were cut short by a big, sloppy kiss from Newton.

"I think he likes you," Kate said, so amused by Anthony's disgusted expression that she forgot to be self-conscious about her position on his lap.

"Dog," Anthony ordered, "get down on the floor this instant."

Newton hung his head and whined.

"Now!"

Letting out a big sigh, Newton turned about and plopped down onto the floor.

"My goodness," Kate said, peering down at the dog, who was now moping under the table, his snout lying sorrowfully on the carpet, "I'm impressed."

"It's all in the tone of voice," Anthony said archly,

snaking a viselike arm around her waist so that she could not get up.

Kate looked at his arm, then looked at his face, her brows arching in question. "Why," she mused, "do I get the impression you find that tone of voice effective on women as well?"

He shrugged and leaned toward her with a heavy-lidded smile. "It usually is," he murmured.

"Not this one." Kate planted her hands on the arms of the chair and tried to wrench herself up.

But he was far too strong. "Especially this one," he said, his voice dropping to an impossibly low purr. With his free hand, he cupped her chin and turned her face to his. His lips were soft but demanding, and he explored her mouth with a thoroughness that left her breathless.

His mouth moved along the line of her jaw to her neck, pausing only to whisper, "Where is your mother?"

"Out," Kate gasped.

His teeth tugged at the edge of her bodice. "For how long?"

"I don't know." She let out a little squeal as his tongue dipped below the muslin and traced an erotic line on her skin. "Good heavens, Anthony, what are you doing?"

"How long?" he repeated.

"An hour. Maybe two."

Anthony glanced up to make sure he'd shut the door when he had entered earlier. "Maybe two?" he murmured, smiling against her skin. "Really?"

"M-maybe just one."

He hooked a finger under the edge of her bodice up near her shoulder, making sure to catch the edge of her chemise as well. "One," he said, "is still quite splendid." Then, pausing only to bring his mouth to hers so that she could not utter any protest, he swiftly pulled her dress down, taking the chemise along with it.

He felt her gasp into his mouth, but he just deepened

the kiss as he palmed the round fullness of her breast. She was perfect under his fingers, soft and pert, filling his hand as if she'd been made for him.

When he felt the last of her resistance melt away, he moved his kiss to her ear, nibbling softly on her lobe. "Do you like this?" he whispered, squeezing gently with his hand.

She nodded jerkily.

"Mmmm, good," he murmured, letting his tongue do a slow sweep of her ear. "It would make things very difficult if you did not."

"H-how?"

He fought the bubble of mirth that was rising in his throat. This absolutely wasn't the time to laugh, but she was so damned innocent. He'd never made love to a woman like her before; he was finding it surprisingly delightful. "Let's just say," he said, "that I like it very much."

"Oh." She offered him the most tentative of smiles.

"There's more, you know," he whispered, letting his breath caress her ear.

"I'm sure there must be," she replied, her voice mere breath.

"You are?" he asked teasingly, squeezing her again.

"I'm not so green that I think one can make a baby from what we've been doing."

"I'd be happy to show you the rest," he murmured.

"Not— Oh!"

He'd squeezed again, this time allowing his fingers to tickle her skin. He loved that she couldn't think when he touched her breasts. "You were saying?" he prompted, nibbling on her neck.

"I—I was?"

He nodded, the faint stubble of his beard brushing her throat. "I'm sure you were. But then again, perhaps I'd rather not hear. You'd begun with the word 'not.' Surely," he added with a flick of his tongue against the underside of her chin, "not a word that belongs between us at a time like this. But"—his tongue moved down the line of her throat to the hollow above her collarbone—"I digress."

"You—you do?"

He nodded. "I believe I was trying to determine what pleases you, as all good husbands should do."

She said nothing, but her breathing quickened.

He smiled against her skin. "What, for example, about this?" He flattened his hand so that he was no longer cupping her, instead just letting his palm graze lightly over her nipple.

"Anthony!" she choked out.

"Good," he said, moving to her neck, nudging her chin up so that she was more open to him. "I'm glad we're back to Anthony. 'My lord' is so formal, don't you think? Far too formal for *this*."

And then he did what he'd been fantasizing about for weeks. He lowered his head to her breast and took her into his mouth, tasting, suckling, teasing, reveling in each gasp he heard spill forth from her lips, each spasm of desire he felt shivering across her body.

He loved that she reacted this way, thrilled that he did this to her. "So good," he murmured, his breath hot and moist against her skin. "You taste so damn good."

"Anthony," she said, her voice hoarse, "Are you sure—"

He put a finger to her lips without even lifting his face to look at her. "I have no idea what you're asking, but whatever it is"—he moved his attention to her other breast—"I'm sure."

She made a soft little moaning sound, the sort that came from the very bottom of one's throat. Her body arched under his ministrations, and with renewed fervor, he teased her nipple, grazing it gently between her teeth.

"Oh, my—oh, Anthony!"

He ran his tongue around the aureole. She was perfect, simply perfect. He loved the sound of her voice, hoarse and broken with desire, and his body tingled at the thought of their wedding night, of her cries of passion and need. She'd be an inferno beneath him, and he relished the prospect of making her explode.

He pulled away so that he could see her face. She was flushed and her eyes were dazed and dilated. Her hair was starting to come undone from that hideous cap.

"This," he said, plucking it from her head, "has got to go."

"My lord!"

"Promise me you'll never wear it again."

She twisted in her seat—on his lap, actually, which did little to help the rather urgent state of his groin—to look over the edge of the chair. "I'll do no such thing," she retorted. "I quite like that cap."

"You can't possibly," he said in all seriousness.

"I can and— Newton!"

Anthony followed her line of vision and broke out into loud laughter, shaking the both of them in their seats. Newton was happily munching away on Kate's cap. "Good dog!" he said on a laugh.

"I would make you buy me another," Kate muttered, yanking her dress back up, "except that you've already spent a fortune on me this week."

This amused him. "I have?" he inquired mildly.

She nodded. "I've been shopping with your mother."

"Ah. Good. I'm sure she didn't let you pick out anything like *that*." He motioned toward the now mangled cap in Newton's mouth.

When he looked back at her, her mouth was twisted into a fetchingly disgruntled line. He couldn't help but smile. She was so easy to read. His mother hadn't let her buy such an unattractive cap, and it was killing her that she couldn't offer a retort to his last statement.

He sighed rather contentedly. Life with Kate wasn't going to be dull.

But it was getting late, and he should probably be going. Kate had said her mother wasn't expected for at least an hour, but Anthony knew better than to trust the female sense of time. Kate could be wrong, or her mother could have changed her mind, or any number of things might have happened, and even though he and Kate were due to be married in just two days, it didn't seem particularly prudent to get caught in the drawing room in such a compromising position.

With great reluctance—sitting in the chair with Kate and doing nothing but hold her was surprisingly satisfying—he stood, lifting her in his arms as he did so, and then set her back in the chair.

"This has been a delightful interlude," he murmured, leaning down to drop a kiss on her forehead. "But I fear your mother's early return. I shall see you Saturday morning?"

She blinked. "Saturday?"

"A superstition of my mother's," he said with a sheepish smile. "She thinks it's bad luck for the bride and groom to see one another the day before the wedding."

"Oh." She rose to her feet, self-consciously smoothing her dress and hair. "And do you believe it as well?"

"Not at all," he said with a snort.

She nodded. "It's very sweet of you to indulge your mother, then."

Anthony paused for a moment, well aware that most men of his reputation did not want to appear tied to apron strings. But this was Kate, and he knew that she valued devotion to family as much as he did, so he finally said, "There is little I would not do to keep my mother content."

She smiled shyly. "It is one of the things I like best about you."

He made some sort of gesture designed to change the subject, but she interrupted with, "No, it's true. You're far more caring a person than you'd like people to believe."

Since he wasn't going to be able to win the argument with her—and there was little point in contradicting a woman when she was being complimentary—he put a finger to his lips and said, "Shhh. Don't tell anyone." And then, with one last kiss to her hand and a murmured, "Adieu," he made his way out the door and outside.

Once on his horse and on his way back to his small townhouse across town, he allowed himself to assess the visit. It went well, he thought. Kate had seemed to understand the limits he had set upon their marriage, and she'd reacted to his lovemaking with a desire that was sweet and fierce at the same time.

All in all, he thought with a satisfied smile, the future looked bright. His marriage would be a success. As for his previous concerns—well, it was clear he had nothing to worry about.

Kate was worried. Anthony had been practically tripping over himself to make certain that she understood that he would never love her. And he certainly didn't seem to want her love in return.

Then he'd gone and kissed her as if there were no tomorrow, as if she were the most beautiful woman on earth. She'd be the first to admit that she had little experience with men and their desires, but he'd certainly seemed to desire her.

Or was he simply wishing she was someone else? She was not his first choice for a wife. She'd do well to remember that fact.

And even if she did fall in love with him—well, she'd simply have to keep it to herself. There was really nothing else to do.

Chapter 16

It has come to This Author's attention that the wedding of Lord Bridgerton and Miss Sheffield is to be a small, intimate, and private affair.

In other words, This Author is not invited.

But have no fear, dear reader, This Author is at her most resourceful at times such as these, and promises to uncover the details of the ceremony, both the interesting and the banal.

The wedding of London's most eligible bachelor is surely something which must be reported in This Author's humble column, don't you agree?

LADY WHISTLEDOWN'S SOCIETY PAPERS, 13 MAY 1814

The night before the wedding, Kate was sitting on her bed in her favorite dressing gown, looking dazedly at the multitude of trunks strewn across the floor. Her every belonging was packed away, neatly folded or stored, ready for transport to her new home.

Even Newton had been prepared for the journey. He'd been bathed and dried, a new collar had been affixed to his neck, and his favorite toys were loaded into a small satchel that now sat in the front hall, right next to the delicately carved wooden chest Kate had had since she was a baby.

The chest was filled with Kate's childhood toys and treasures, and she'd found tremendous comfort in their presence here in London. It was silly and sentimental, but to Kate it made her upcoming transition a little less scary. Bringing her things—funny little items that meant nothing to anyone but her—to Anthony's home made it seem more like it would truly be her home as well.

Mary, who always seemed to understand what Kate needed before she understood it herself, had sent word to friends back in Somerset as soon as Kate had become betrothed, asking them to ship the chest to London in time for the wedding.

Kate stood and wandered about the room, stopping to run her fingers across a nightgown that was folded and laid upon a table, awaiting transfer to the last of her trunks. It was one that Lady Bridgerton—Violet, she had to start thinking of her as Violet—had picked out, modest in cut but sheer in fabric. Kate had been mortified throughout the entire visit to the lingerie maker. This was her betrothed's mother, after all, selecting items for the wedding night!

As Kate picked up the gown and set it carefully in a trunk, she heard a knock at the door. She called out her greeting, and Edwina poked her head in. She, too, was dressed for bed, her pale hair pulled back into a sloppy bun at the nape of her neck.

"I thought you might like some hot milk," Edwina said.

Kate smiled gratefully. "That sounds heavenly."

Edwina reached down and picked up the ceramic mug she'd set on the floor. "Can't hold two mugs and twist the doorknob at the same time," she explained with a smile. Once inside, she kicked the door shut and handed one of the mugs to Kate. Eyes trained on Kate, Edwina asked without preamble, "Are you scared?"

Kate took a gingerly sip, checking the temperature before gulping it down. It was hot but not scalding, and it somehow comforted her. She'd been drinking hot milk since childhood, and the taste and feel of it always made her feel warm and secure.

"Not scared precisely," she finally replied, sitting down on the edge of her bed, "but nervous. Definitely nervous."

"Well, of course you're nervous," Edwina said, her free hand waving animatedly through the air. "Only an idiot wouldn't be nervous. Your whole life is going to change. Everything! Even your name. You'll be a married woman. A viscountess. After tomorrow, you will not be the same woman, Kate, and after tomorrow *night*—"

"That's enough, Edwina," Kate interrupted.

"But—"

"You are *not* doing anything to ease my mind."

"Oh." Edwina offered her a sheepish smile. "Sorry."

"It's all right," Kate assured her.

Edwina managed to hold her tongue for about four seconds before she asked, "Has Mother been in to speak with you?"

"Not yet."

"She must, don't you think? Tomorrow is your wedding day, and I'm sure there are all sorts of things one needs to know." Edwina took a big gulp of her milk, leaving a rather incongruous white mustache on her upper lip, then perched on the edge of the bed across from Kate. "I know there are all sorts of things *I* don't know. And unless you've been up to something I don't know about, I don't see how *you* could know them, either."

Kate wondered if it would be impolite to muzzle her sister with some of the lingerie Lady Bridgerton had picked out. There seemed to be some rather nice poetic justice in such a maneuver.

"Kate?" Edwina asked, blinking curiously. "Kate? Why are you looking at me so strangely?"

Kate gazed at the lingerie longingly. "You don't want to know."

"Hmmph. Well, I—"

Edwina's mutterings were cut short by a soft knock at

the door. "That'll be Mother," Edwina said with a wicked grin. "I can't wait."

Kate rolled her eyes at Edwina as she rose to open the door. Sure enough, Mary was standing in the hall, holding two steaming mugs. "I thought you might like some hot milk," she said with a weak smile.

Kate lifted her mug in response. "Edwina had the same notion."

"What is Edwina doing here?" Mary asked, entering the room.

"Since when do I need a reason to talk with my sister?" Edwina asked with a snort.

Mary shot her a peevish look before turning her attention back to Kate. "Hmmm," she mused. "We do seem to have a surfeit of hot milk."

"This one's gone lukewarm, anyway," Kate said, setting her mug down on one of the already-closed-up trunks and replacing it with the warmer one in Mary's hand. "Edwina can take the other one down to the kitchen when she leaves."

"Beg pardon?" Edwina asked, vaguely distracted. "Oh, of course. I'm happy to help." But she didn't rise to her feet. In fact, she didn't even twitch, save for the back and forth of her head as she looked from Mary to Kate and back again.

"I need to speak with Kate," Mary said.

Edwina nodded enthusiastically.

"Alone."

Edwina blinked. "I have to leave?"

Mary nodded and held out the lukewarm mug.

"Now?"

Mary nodded again.

Edwina looked stricken, then her expression melted into a wary smile. "You're joking, right? I may stay, right?"

"Wrong," Mary replied.

Edwina turned pleading eyes to Kate.

"Don't look to me," Kate said with a barely suppressed smile. "It's her decision. She'll be doing the talking, after all. I'll just be listening."

"And asking questions," Edwina pointed out. "And I have questions, too." She turned to her mother. "Lots of questions."

"I'm sure you do," Mary said, "and I'll be happy to answer them all the night before you get married."

Edwina groaned her way upright. "This isn't fair," she grumbled, snatching the mug out of Mary's hand.

"Life isn't fair," Mary said with a grin.

"I'll say," Edwina muttered, dragging her feet as she crossed the room.

"And no listening at the door!" Mary called out.

"I wouldn't dream of it," Edwina drawled. "Not that you'd talk loudly enough for me to hear a thing, anyway."

Mary sighed as Edwina stepped out into the hall and shut the door, her movements punctuated by a constant stream of unintelligible grumbles. "We shall have to whisper," she said to Kate.

Kate nodded, but she did feel enough loyalty toward her sister to say, "She *might* not be eavesdropping."

The look Mary gave her was dubious in the extreme. "Do you want to swing the door open to find out?"

Kate grinned despite herself. "Point taken."

Mary sat down in the spot Edwina had just vacated and gave Kate a rather direct look. "I'm sure you know why I'm here."

Kate nodded.

Mary took a sip of her milk and was silent for a long moment before she said, "When I married—for the first time, not to your father—I knew nothing of what to expect in the marriage bed. It was not—" She closed her eyes briefly, and for a moment she looked to be in pain. "My lack of knowledge made it all the more difficult," she finally said, the slowness of her carefully chosen words telling Kate that "difficult" was probably a euphemism.

"I see," Kate murmured.

Mary looked up sharply. "No, you don't see. And I hope you never do. But that is beside the point. I always swore that no daughter of mine would enter into marriage ignorant of what occurs between a husband and wife."

"I'm already aware of the basics of the maneuver," Kate admitted.

Clearly surprised, Mary asked, "You are?"

Kate nodded. "It can't be very much different from animals."

Mary shook her head, her lips pursed into a slightly amused smile. "No, it's not."

Kate pondered how best to phrase her next question. From what she'd seen on her neighbor's farm back in Somerset, the act of procreation didn't look terribly enjoyable at all. But when Anthony kissed her, she felt as if she were losing her mind. And when he kissed her twice, she wasn't even sure if she wanted it back! Her entire body tingled, and she suspected that if their recent encounters had occurred in more suitable locales, she would have let him have his way with her with nary a protest.

But then there was that awful screaming mare at the farm. . . . Frankly, the various pieces of the puzzle didn't seem to reconcile.

Finally, after much clearing of her throat, she said, "It doesn't look very pleasant."

Mary closed her eyes again, her face taking on that same look as before—as if she were remembering something she'd rather keep tucked away in the darkest recesses of her mind. When she opened her eyes again, she said, "A woman's enjoyment depends entirely on her husband."

"And a man's?"

"The act of love," Mary said, blushing, "can and should be a pleasant experience for both man and woman. But—" She coughed and took a sip of her milk. "I would be remiss if I did not tell you that a woman does not always find pleasure in the act."

"But a man does?"

Mary nodded.

"That doesn't seem fair."

Mary's smile was wry. "I believe I just told Edwina that life wasn't always fair."

Kate frowned, staring down into her milk. "Well, this *really* doesn't seem fair."

"This doesn't mean," Mary hastened to add, "that the experience is necessarily distasteful to the woman. And I'm certain it won't be distasteful to you. I assumed the viscount has kissed you?"

Kate nodded without looking up.

When Mary spoke, Kate could hear the smile in her voice. "I'll assume from your blush," Mary said, "that you enjoyed it."

Kate nodded again, her cheeks now burning.

"If you enjoyed his kiss," Mary said, "then I am certain you won't be upset by his further attentions. I'm sure that he will be gentle and attentive with you."

"Gentle" didn't quite capture the essence of Anthony's kisses, but Kate didn't think that was the sort of thing one was meant to share with one's mother. Truly, the entire conversation was embarrassing enough as it was.

"Men and women are very different," Mary continued, as if that weren't completely obvious, "and a man—even one who is faithful to his wife, which I'm sure the viscount will be to you—can find his pleasure with almost any woman."

This was disturbing, and not what Kate had wanted to hear. "And a woman?" she had prompted.

"It is different for a woman. I have heard that wicked women find their pleasure like a man, in the arms of any who will satisfy, but I do not believe it. I think that a woman must care for her husband in order to enjoy the marriage bed."

Kate was silent for a moment. "You did not love your first husband, did you?"

Mary shook her head. "It makes all the difference, sweet one. That, and a husband's regard for his wife. But I have seen the viscount in your company. I realize that your match was sudden and unexpected, but he treats you with care and respect. You will have nothing to fear, I'm sure of it. The viscount will treat you well."

And with that, Mary kissed Kate upon the forehead and bade her good night, picking up both empty milk mugs as she left the room. Kate sat on her bed, staring sightlessly at the wall for several minutes.

Mary was wrong. Kate was sure of it. She had much to fear.

She hated that she was not Anthony's first choice for a wife, but she was practical, and she was pragmatic, and she knew that certain things in life simply had to be accepted as fact. But she'd been consoling herself with the memory of the desire she had felt—and she thought Anthony had felt—when she was in his arms.

Now it seemed that this desire wasn't even necessarily for her, but rather some primitive urge that every man felt for every woman.

And Kate would never know if, when Anthony snuffed the candles and took her to bed, he closed his eyes . . .

And pictured another woman's face.

The wedding, which was held in the drawing room of Bridgerton House, was a small, private affair. Well, as small as one could expect with the entire Bridgerton family in attendance, from Anthony all the way down to little eleven-year-old Hyacinth, who'd taken her role as flower girl *very* seriously. When her brother Gregory, aged thirteen, had tried to tip her basket of rose petals, she'd walloped him in the chin, delaying the ceremony by a good ten minutes but interjecting a much-needed note of levity and laughter.

Well, for everyone except Gregory, who'd been quite put out by the entire episode and certainly *wasn't* laughing, even though he was, as Hyacinth was quick to point out to anyone who would listen (and her voice was loud enough so that one didn't really have the option of *not* listening), the one who'd started it.

Kate had seen it all from her vantage point in the hall, where she'd been peeking through a crack in the door. It had made her smile, which was much appreciated, since her knees had been knocking for over an hour. She could only thank her lucky stars that Lady Bridgerton had not insisted upon a large, grand affair. Kate, who'd never thought of herself as a nervous sort of person before, would probably have passed out from fright.

Indeed, Violet had mentioned the possibility of a huge wedding as a method by which to combat the rumors that were circulating about Kate, Anthony, and their rather sudden engagement. Mrs. Featherington was, true to her word, remaining mostly silent on the details of the matter, but she'd let enough innuendo slip that *everyone* knew that the betrothal had not come about in the usual matter.

As a result, *everyone* was talking, and Kate knew it was only a matter of time before Mrs. Featherington could no longer restrain herself and everyone learned the true story of her downfall at the hands—or rather, the stinger—of a bee.

But in the end Violet had decided that a quick marriage was best, and since one couldn't throw together a grand party in one week, the guest list had been limited to family. Kate was attended by Edwina, Anthony by his brother Benedict, and in due course they were man and wife.

It was strange, Kate thought later that afternoon as she stared at the gold band that had joined the diamond on her left hand, how quickly one's life could change. The ceremony had been brief, rushing by in a crazy blur, and yet her life was forever altered. Edwina had been correct. Everything was different. She was a married woman now, a viscountess.

Lady Bridgerton.

She chewed on her lower lip. It sounded like someone else. How long would it take before someone said, "Lady Bridgerton," and she actually thought they were talking to *her,* and not Anthony's mother?

She was a wife now, with a wife's responsibilities.

It terrified her.

Now that the wedding was done, Kate reflected upon Mary's words from the previous night and knew that she was right. In many respects, she was the luckiest woman alive. Anthony would treat her well. He would treat any woman well. And that was the problem.

And now she was in a carriage, traveling the short distance between Bridgerton House, where the reception had been held, and Anthony's private residence, which she supposed could no longer be referred to as "bachelor's lodgings."

She stole a glance at her new husband. He was facing straight ahead, his face oddly serious.

"Do you plan to move into Bridgerton House now that you are married?" she inquired quietly.

Anthony started, almost as if he'd forgotten she was there. "Yes," he replied, turning to face her, "although not for several months. I thought we could do with a bit of privacy at the start of our marriage, don't you think?"

"Of course," Kate murmured. She looked down at her hands, which were fidgeting in her lap. She tried to still them, but it was impossible. It was a wonder she had not burst out of her gloves.

Anthony followed the line of her gaze and placed one of his large hands over both of hers. She went still instantly.

"Are you nervous?" he inquired.

"Did you think I wouldn't be?" she replied, trying to keep her voice dry and ironic.

He smiled in response. "There is nothing to fear."

Kate nearly burst out in jittery laughter. It seemed she

was destined to hear that platitude over and over again. "Perhaps," she allowed, "but still much about which to be nervous."

His smile broadened. "Touché, my dear wife."

Kate swallowed convulsively. It was strange to be someone's wife, especially strange to be this man's wife. "And are *you* nervous?" she countered.

He leaned in toward her, his dark eyes hot and heavy with the promise of things to come. "Oh, desperately," he murmured. He closed the rest of the distance between them, his lips finding the sensitive hollow of her ear. "My heart is pounding," he whispered.

Kate's body seemed to stiffen and melt at the same time. And then she blurted out, "I think we should wait."

He nibbled on her ear. "Wait for what?"

She tried to wiggle away. He didn't understand. If he'd understood, he'd be furious, and he didn't seem particularly upset.

Yet.

"F-for the marriage," she stammered.

That seemed to amuse him, and he playfully wiggled the rings that now rested on her gloved fingers. "It's a bit late for that, don't you think?"

"For the wedding night," she clarified.

He drew back, his dark brows flattening into a straight, and perhaps a little bit angry, line. "No," he said simply. But he did not move to embrace her again.

Kate tried to think of words that would make him understand, but it wasn't easy; she wasn't so sure that she understood herself. And she was rather certain that he would not believe her if she told him that she'd not intended to make this request; it had just burst forth from within her, born of a panic she hadn't even known was there until that very moment.

"I'm not asking for forever," she said, hating the tremor that shook her words. "Just a week."

This caught his attention, and one of his brows rose in ironic query. "And what, pray tell, do you hope to gain by a week?"

"I don't know," she answered quite honestly.

His eyes focused onto hers, hard, hot, and sardonic. "You're going to have to do better than that," he said.

Kate didn't want to look at him, didn't want the intimacy he forced upon her when she was caught in his dark gaze. It was easy to hide her feelings when she could keep her focus on his chin or his shoulder, but when she had to look straight into his eyes . . .

She was afraid he could see into her very soul.

"This has been a week of a great many changes in my life," she began, wishing she knew where she was going with the statement.

"For me as well," he interjected softly.

"Not so much for you," she returned. "The intimacies of marriage are nothing new to you."

One corner of his mouth quirked into a lopsided, slightly arrogant smile. "I assure you, my lady, that I have never before been married."

"That's not what I meant, and you know it."

He did not contradict her.

"I simply would like a bit of time to prepare," she said, primly folding her hands in her lap. But she couldn't keep her thumbs still, and they twiddled anxiously, giving proof to the state of her nerves.

Anthony stared at her for a long moment, then leaned back, propping his left ankle rather casually on his right knee. "Very well," he allowed.

"Really?" She straightened with surprise. She had not expected him to capitulate with such ease.

"Provided . . ." he continued.

She slumped. She should have known that there would be a contingency.

". . . that you edify me on one point."

She gulped. "And what would that be, my lord?"

He leaned forward, the very devil in his eyes. "How, precisely, do you plan to prepare?"

Kate glanced out the window, then swore under her breath when she realized they weren't even to Anthony's street. There would be no escaping his question; she was stuck in the carriage for at least another five minutes. "We-e-e-e-ll," she stalled, "I'm sure I don't understand what you mean."

He chuckled. "I'm sure you don't, either."

Kate scowled at him. There was nothing worse than being the butt of someone else's joke, and it seemed especially inappropriate when one happened to be a bride on her wedding day. "Now you're having fun with me," she accused.

"No," he said with what could only have been called a leer, "I'd *like* to have fun with you. There's quite a difference."

"I wish you wouldn't talk like that," she grumbled. "You know I don't understand."

His eyes focused on her lips as his tongue darted out to wet his own. "You would," he murmured, "if you'd simply give in to the inevitable and forget your silly request."

"I don't enjoy being condescended to," Kate said stiffly.

His eyes flashed. "And I don't like being denied my rights," he returned, his voice cold and his face a harsh rendition of aristocratic power.

"I'm not denying you anything," she insisted.

"Oh, really?" His drawl lacked all humor.

"I'm just asking for a reprieve. A brief, temporary, *brief*"—she repeated the word, just in case his brain was too dulled by single-minded male pride to have understood her the first time—"reprieve. Surely you would not deny me such a simple request."

"Of the two of us," he said, his voice clipped, "I don't think I'm the one doing the denying."

He was right, drat the man, and she had no idea what else to say. She knew she hadn't a leg to stand on with her spur-of-the-moment request; he had every right to toss her over his shoulder, drag her off to bed, and lock her in the room for a week if he so desired.

She was acting foolishly, a prisoner of her own insecurities—insecurities she hadn't even known she possessed until she'd met Anthony.

All her life, she'd been the one who'd received the second glance, the second greeting, the second kiss on the hand. As the elder daughter, it should have been her due to be addressed before her younger sister, but Edwina's beauty was so stunning, the pure and perfect blue of her eyes so startling, that people simply forgot themselves in her presence.

Introductions to Kate were usually met with an embarrassed, "Of course," and a polite murmured greeting while their eyes slid back to Edwina's pure and shining face.

Kate had never minded it much. If Edwina had been spoiled or bad-tempered it might have been difficult, and in all truth, most of the men she'd met were shallow and silly, and she hadn't much cared if they only took the time to acknowledge her after her sister.

Until now.

She wanted Anthony's eyes to light up when *she* entered the room. She wanted him to scan a crowd until he saw *her* face. She didn't need him to love her—or at least that's what she was telling herself—but she desperately wanted to be first in his affections, first in his desires.

And she had an awful, terrible feeling that all this meant she was falling in love.

Falling in love with one's husband—who would have thought it could be such a disaster?

"I see you have no response," Anthony said quietly.

The carriage rolled to a halt, thankfully sparing her from having to make a reply. But when a liveried footman rushed forward and attempted to open the door, Anthony yanked it back shut, never once taking his eyes off of her face.

"How, my lady?" he repeated.

"How . . ." she echoed. She'd quite forgotten what he was asking.

"How," he said yet again, his voice hard as ice but hot as flame, "do you plan to prepare for your wedding night?"

"I—I had not considered," Kate replied.

"I thought not." He let go of the door handle, and the door swung open, revealing the faces of two footmen who were obviously trying very hard not to look curious. Kate remained silent as Anthony helped her down and led her into the house.

His household staff was assembled in the small entry hall, and Kate murmured her greetings as each member was introduced to her by the butler and housekeeper. The staff wasn't very extensive, as the house was small by *ton* standards, but the introductions took a good twenty minutes.

Twenty minutes which, unfortunately, did little to calm her nerves. By the time he placed his hand at the small of her back and guided her toward the stairs, her heart was racing, and for the first time in her life, she thought she might actually pass out.

It wasn't that she feared the marriage bed.

It wasn't even that she feared not pleasing her husband. Even an innocent virgin such as herself could tell that his actions and reactions when they kissed were proof enough of his desire. He would show her what to do; of that she had no doubt.

What she feared . . .

What she feared . . .

She caught her throat closing, choking, and she brought her fist to her mouth, biting on the knuckle to steady her stomach, as if that might actually do something to help the awful churning that had her in knots.

"My God," Anthony whispered as the reached the landing. "You're terrified."

"No," she lied.

He took her by the shoulders and twisted her to face him, staring deeply into her eyes. Cursing under his breath, he grabbed her hand and pulled her into his bedroom, muttering, "We need privacy."

When they reached his chamber—a richly appointed, masculine room exquisitely decorated in shades of burgundy and gold—he planted his hands on his hips and demanded, "Didn't your mother tell you about . . . ah . . . about . . ."

Kate would have laughed at his flailings if she hadn't been so nervous. "Of course," she said quickly. "Mary explained everything."

"Then what the hell is the problem?" He cursed again, then apologized. "I beg your pardon," he said stiffly. "That certainly is not the way to set you at ease."

"I can't say," she whispered, her eyes sliding to the floor, focusing on the intricate pattern of the carpet until they swam with tears.

A strange, horrible choking noise emerged from Anthony's throat. "Kate?" he asked hoarsely. "Did someone . . . has a man . . . ever forced unwelcome attentions on you?"

She looked up, and the concern and terror on his face nearly made her heart melt. "No!" she cried out. "It isn't that. Oh, don't look that way, I can't bear it."

"*I* can't bear it," Anthony whispered, closing the distance between them as he took her hand and raised it to his lips. "You must tell me," he said, his voice oddly choked. "Do you fear me? Do I repulse you?"

Kate shook her head frantically, unable to believe that he could possibly think any woman would find him repulsive.

"Tell me," he whispered, his lips pressing against her ear. "Tell me how to make it right. For I don't think I can grant you your reprieve." He molded his body against hers, his strong arms holding her close as he groaned, "I can't wait a week, Kate. I simply cannot do it."

"I . . ." Kate made the mistake of looking up into his eyes, and she forgot everything she'd meant to say. He was staring at her with a burning intensity that forged a fire in the very center of her being, leaving her breathless, hungry, and desperate for something she did not quite understand.

And she knew that she could not make him wait. If she looked into her own soul, and looked with honesty and without delusion, she was forced to admit that she did not wish to wait, either.

For what could be the point? Maybe he would never love her. Maybe his desire would never be focused as single-mindedly on her as hers was for him.

But she could pretend. And when he held her in his arms and pressed his lips to her skin, it was so, so easy to pretend.

"Anthony," she whispered, his name a benediction, a plea, a prayer all in one.

"Anything," he replied raggedly, dropping to his knees before her, his lips trailing a hot path along her skin as his fingers frantically worked to release her from her gown. "Ask me anything," he groaned. "Anything in my power, I give to you."

Kate felt her head fall back, felt the last of her resistance melting away. "Just love me," she whispered. "Just love me."

His only answer was a low growl of need.

Chapter 17

The deed is done! Miss Sheffield is now Katharine, Viscountess Bridgerton.

This Author extends the very best of wishes to the happy couple. Sensible and honorable people are surely scarce among the ton, and it's certainly gratifying to see two of this rare breed joined in marriage.

LADY WHISTLEDOWN'S SOCIETY PAPERS, 16 MAY 1814

Until that moment, Anthony had not even realized just how badly he'd needed for her to say yes, to admit to her need. He clutched her to him, his cheek pressing against the gentle curve of her belly. Even in her wedding gown she smelled of lilies and soap, that maddening scent that had haunted him for weeks.

"I need you," he growled, not sure if his words were getting lost in the layers of silk that still kept her from him. "I need you now."

He rose to his feet and lifted her in his arms, taking remarkably few steps to reach the large four-poster bed that dominated his bedroom. He'd never taken a woman there before, always preferring to conduct his liaisons elsewhere, and suddenly he was absurdly glad of that fact.

Kate was different, special, his wife. He wanted no

other memories to intrude upon this or any night.

He laid her down on the mattress, his eyes never leaving her charmingly disheveled form as he methodically stripped off his clothing. First his gloves, one by one, then his coat, already rumpled by his ardor.

He caught her eyes, dark and large and filled with wonder, and he smiled, slowly and with satisfaction. "You've never seen a naked man before, have you?" he murmured.

She shook her head.

"Good." He leaned forward and plucked one of her slippers from her foot. "You'll never see another."

He moved to the buttons of his shirt, slowly slipping each from its buttonhole, his desire increased tenfold when he saw her tongue dart out to wet her lips.

She wanted him. He knew enough of women to be positive of that. And by the time this night was through, she wouldn't be able to live without him.

That *he* might not be able to live without *her* was something he refused to consider. What smoldered in the bedroom and what whispered in his heart were two different things. He could keep them separate. He *would* keep them separate.

He might not wish to love his wife, but that did not mean they could not enjoy each other thoroughly in bed.

His hands slid to the top button of his trousers and unfastened it, but stopped there. She was still fully clothed, and still fully an innocent. She wasn't yet ready to see the proof of his desire.

He climbed onto the bed and, like a feral cat, crawled toward her, inching closer and closer until her elbows, which had been propping her up, slid out from under her and she was flat on her back, staring up at him, her breath coming fast and shallow through her parted lips.

There was nothing, he decided, more breathtaking than Kate's face when flushed with desire. Her hair, dark and silky and thick, was already pulling free of the pins and fasteners that had held her elaborate wedding day coiffure in place. Her lips, always a bit too full for conventional beauty, had taken on a dusky pink color in the slanted light of the late afternoon. And her skin—never had it seemed so flawless, so luminescent. A pale blush tinted her cheeks, denying her the bloodless complexion that the fashionable ladies always seemed to desire, but Anthony found the color enchanting. She was real, human, and trembling with desire. He couldn't have wished for more.

With a reverent hand, he stroked her cheek with the backs of his fingers, then slid them down her neck to the tender skin that peeked above the edge of her bodice. Her gown was fastened by a maddening row of buttons at the back, but he'd already undone nearly a third of them, and it was now loose enough to slide the silken fabric over her breasts.

If anything, they looked even more beautiful than they had two days earlier. Her nipples were rosy pink, cresting breasts that he knew fit his hands to perfection. "No chemise?" he murmured appreciatively, running his finger along the prominent line of her collarbone.

She shook her head, her voice breathy as she answered, "The cut of the gown didn't allow it."

One side of his mouth lifted into a very male smile. "Remind me to send a bonus to your modiste."

His hand moved ever lower, and he cupped one of her breasts, squeezing it softly, feeling a groan of desire rise up within him as he heard a similar moan escape her lips.

"So lovely," he murmured, lifting his hand and letting his eyes caress her. It had never occurred to him that there could be such pleasure from the simple act of gazing at a woman. Lovemaking had always been about touch and taste; for the first time sight was equally seductive.

She was so perfect, so utterly beautiful to him, and he felt a rather strange and primitive sense of satisfaction that most men were blind to her beauty. It was as if a certain side of her were visible only to him. He loved that her charms were hidden to the rest of the world.

It made her seem more *his*.

Suddenly eager to be touched as he was touching, he lifted one of her hands, still wrapped in a long satin glove, and brought it to his chest. He could feel the heat of her skin even through the fabric, but it wasn't enough. "I want to feel you," he whispered, then removed the two rings that rested on her fourth finger. He laid them in the hollow between her breasts, a space made shallow by her supine position.

Kate gasped and shivered at the touch of the cold metal against her skin, then watched with breathless fascination as Anthony went to work on her glove, tugging gently at each finger until it was loose, then sliding the length of it down her arm and over her hand. The rush of satin was like an endless kiss, raising goose bumps over her entire body.

Then, with a tenderness that nearly brought tears to her eyes, he replaced the rings on her finger, one by one, stopping only to kiss the sensitive palm of her hand in between.

"Give me your other hand," he gently ordered.

She did, and he repeated the same exquisite torture, tugging and sliding the satin along her skin. But this time, when he was through, he brought her pinkie finger to his mouth, then drew it between his lips and sucked, swirling his tongue around the tip.

Kate felt an answering tug of desire pulling through her arm, shivering through her chest, snaking through her until it pooled, hot and mysterious, between her legs. He was awakening something within her, something dark and maybe just a little bit dangerous, something that had lain dormant for years, just waiting for a single kiss from this man.

Her entire life had been preparation for this very moment, and she didn't even know what to expect next.

His tongue slid down the inner length of her finger, then traced the lines on her palm. "Such lovely hands," he murmured, nibbling on the fleshy part of her thumb as his fingers entwined with hers. "Strong, and yet so graceful and delicate."

"You're talking nonsense," Kate said self-consciously. "My hands—"

But he silenced her with a finger to her lips. "Shhh," he admonished. "Haven't you learned that you should never ever contradict your husband when he is admiring your form?"

Kate shivered with delight.

"For example," he continued, the very devil in his voice, "if I want to spend an hour examining the inside of your wrist"—with lightning-quick movements, his teeth grazed the delicate thin skin on the inside of her wrist—"it is certainly my prerogative, don't you think?"

Kate had no response, and he chuckled, the sound low and warm in her ears.

"And don't think I won't," he warned, using the pad of his finger to trace the blue veins that pulsed under her skin. "I may decide to spend *two* hours examining your wrist."

Kate watched with fascination as his fingers, touching her so softly that she tingled from the contact, made their way to the inside of her elbow, then stopped to twirl circles on her skin.

"I can't imagine," he said softly, "that I could spend two hours examining your wrist and *not* find it lovely." His hand made the jump to her torso, and he used his palm to lightly graze the tip of her puckered breast. "I should be most aggrieved were you to disagree."

He leaned down and captured her lips in a brief, yet searing kiss. Lifting his head just an inch, he murmured, "It is a wife's place to agree with her husband in all things, hmmm?"

His words were so absurd that Kate finally managed to find her voice. "If," she said with an amused smile, "his opinions are agreeable, my lord."

One of his brows arched imperiously. "Are you arguing with me, my lady? And on my wedding night, no less."

"It's my wedding night, too," she pointed out.

He made a clucking noise and shook his head. "I may have to punish you," he said. "But how? By touching?" His hand skimmed over one breast, then the next. "Or not touching?"

He lifted his hands from her skin, but he leaned down, and through pursed lips, blew a soft stream of air over her nipple.

"Touching," Kate gasped, arching off the bed. "Definitely touching."

"You think?" He smiled, slowly like a cat. "I never thought I'd say this, but not touching has its appeal."

Kate stared up at him. He loomed over her on his hands and knees like some primitive hunter coming in for the final kill. He looked feral, triumphant, and powerfully possessive. His thick chestnut hair fell over his forehead, giving him an oddly boyish air, but his eyes burned and gleamed with a very adult desire.

He wanted her. It was thrilling. He might be a man, and thus able to find his satisfaction with any woman, but right now, in this moment, he wanted her. Kate was sure of it.

And it made her feel like the most beautiful woman alive.

Emboldened by the knowledge of his desire, she reached up and cupped one hand around the back of his head, drawing him down until his lips were just a whisper away from hers. "Kiss me," she ordered, surprised by the imperiousness of her voice. "Kiss me now."

He smiled in vague disbelief, but his words, in that last second before their lips met, were, "Anything you wish, Lady Bridgerton. Anything you wish."

And then it all seemed to happen at once. His lips were on hers, teasing and devouring, while his hands were lifting her up into a seated position. His fingers worked nimbly at the buttons of her gown, and she could feel the cool brush of the air on her skin as the fabric slipped down, inch by inch, exposing her rib cage, then her navel, and then . . .

And then his hands slid beneath her hips, and he was lifting her up, yanking the dress out from underneath her. Kate gasped at the intimacy of it. She was clad only in her unmentionables, stockings, and garters. She'd never felt so exposed in her life, and yet she thrilled in every moment, every sweep of his eyes over her body.

"Lift your leg," Anthony ordered softly.

She did, and with a slowness that was exquisite and agonizing at the same time, he rolled one of her silk stockings down to her toes. The other soon followed, and then her drawers came next, and before she knew it she was nude, completely bared before him.

His hand skimmed softly over her stomach, then he said, "I think I'm a little overdressed, don't you?"

Kate's eyes widened as he left the bed and stripped off the rest of his clothing. His body was perfection, his chest finely muscled, his arms and legs powerful, and his—

"Oh, my God," she gasped.

He grinned. "I'll take that as a compliment."

Kate swallowed convulsively. No wonder those animals on her neighbor's farm hadn't looked as if they were enjoying the act of procreation. At least not the female ones. Surely this wasn't going to work.

But she didn't want to seem naive and foolish, so she didn't say anything, just gulped and tried to smile.

Anthony caught the flash of terror in her eyes and smiled gently. "Trust me," he murmured, sliding onto the bed beside her. His hands settled on the curve of her hip as he nuzzled her neck. "Just trust me."

He felt her nod, and he propped himself up on one of his elbows, using his free hand to idly trace circles and swirls on her abdomen, moving lower and lower, until he brushed the edge of the dark thatch of hair nestling between her legs.

Her muscles quivered, and he heard a rush of indrawn breath pass over her lips. "Shhhh," he said soothingly, leaning down to distract her with a kiss. The last time he'd lain with a virgin he'd been one himself, and he was relying on instinct to guide him with Kate. He wanted this, her first time, to be perfect. Or if not perfect, then at least damn good.

While his lips and tongue explored her mouth, his hand dipped ever lower, until he reached the moist heat of her womanhood. She gasped again, but he was relentless, teasing and tickling, delighting in each of her squirms and moans.

"What are you doing?" she whispered against his lips.

He gave her a lopsided grin, as one of his fingers slid inside. "Making you feel really, really good?"

She moaned, which pleased him. If she'd managed intelligible speech he would have known he wasn't doing his job correctly.

He moved over her, nudging her legs farther apart with one of his thighs, and letting out a moan of his own as his manhood settled against her hip. Even there, she felt perfect, and he was nearly bursting at the thought of sinking within her.

He was trying to hold his control, trying to make sure that he remained slow and gentle, but his need was getting stronger and stronger, and his own breath was growing fast and ragged.

She was ready for him, or at least as ready as she was going to be. He knew that this first time would bring her pain, but he prayed it wouldn't last more than a moment.

He fitted himself against her opening, using his arms to brace his body a few inches above hers. He whispered her name, and her dark eyes, hazed by passion, focused on his.

"I'm going to make you mine now," he said, inching forward as he spoke. Her body tightened spasmodically around him; the feeling was so exquisite he had to grit his teeth against it. It would be so, so easy to lose himself in the moment, to plunge forward and seek only his own pleasure.

"Tell me if it hurts," he whispered hoarsely, allowing himself to move forward only by tiny increments. She was certainly aroused, but she was very small, and he knew he needed to give her time to adjust to his intimate invasion.

She nodded.

He froze, barely able to comprehend the stab of pain in his chest. "It hurts?"

She shook her head. "No, I only meant I'll tell you if it does. It doesn't hurt, but it feels so very . . . odd."

Anthony fought a smile and he leaned down to kiss the tip of her nose. "I don't know that I've ever been called odd while making love to a woman before."

For a moment it looked as if she were afraid that she'd insulted him, then her mouth quivered into a small smile. "Perhaps," she said softly, "you've been making love to the wrong women."

"Perhaps so," he replied, moving forward yet another inch.

"May I tell you a secret?" she asked.

He nudged farther. "Of course," he murmured.

"When I first saw you . . . tonight, I mean . . ."

"In all my glory?" he teased, lifting his brows into an arrogant arch.

She shot him a rather enchanting scowl. "I didn't think this could possibly work."

He moved forward. He was close, so close to embedding himself fully within her. "May I tell *you* a secret?" he returned.

"Of course."

"Your secret"—one more little thrust and he was resting against her maidenhead—"wasn't very much of a secret."

Her brows drew together in question.

He grinned. "It was written all over your face."

She scowled again, and it made him want to explode in

laughter. "But now," he said, keeping a scrupulously straight face, "I have a question for you."

She gazed at him in response, clearly waiting for him to elucidate further.

He leaned down, brushed his lips against her ear, and whispered, "What do you think now?"

For a moment she didn't respond in any way, then he felt her start in surprise when she finally figured out what he was asking. "Are we done?" she asked in clear disbelief.

This time he did burst out in laughter. "Far from it, my dear wife," he gasped, wiping his eyes with one hand as he tried to hold himself up with the other. "Far, far from it." His eyes growing serious, he added, "This is where it might hurt a little, Kate. But I promise you, the pain will never be repeated."

She nodded, but he could feel her body tense up, which he knew would only make it worse. "Shhh," he crooned. "Relax."

She nodded, her eyes shut. "I am relaxed."

He was glad she couldn't see him smile. "You are most definitely *not* relaxed."

Her eyes flew open. "Yes, I am."

"I can't believe this," Anthony said, as if there were someone else in the room to hear him. "She's arguing with me on our wedding night."

"I'm—"

He cut her off with a finger to her lips. "Are you ticklish?"

"Am I *ticklish*?"

He nodded. "Ticklish."

Her eyes narrowed suspiciously. "Why?"

"That sounds like a yes to me," he said with a grin.

"Not at— Oooohhh!" She let out a squeal as one of his hands found a particularly sensitive spot under arm. "Anthony, stop!" she gasped, squirming desperately beneath him. "I can't bear it! I—"

He plunged forward.

"Oh," she breathed. "Oh, my."

He groaned, barely able to believe just how good it felt to be buried completely within her. "Oh, my, indeed."

"We're not done now, are we?"

He shook his head slowly as his body began to move in an ancient rhythm. "Not even close," he murmured.

His mouth took hers as one of his hands snaked up to caress her breast. She was utter perfection beneath him, her hips rising to meet his, moving tentatively at first, then with a vigor that matched her rising passion.

"Oh, God, Kate," he moaned, his ability to form flowery sentences completely lost in the primitive heat of the moment. "You're so good. So good."

Her breath was coming faster and faster, and each little wispy gasp inflamed his passion even more. He wanted to possess her, to own her, to hold her beneath him and never let her go. And with each thrust it was getting more difficult to put her needs before his. His mind screamed that this was her first time and he had to have a care for her, but his body demanded release.

With a ragged groan, he forced himself to stop thrusting and catch his breath. "Kate?" he said, barely recognizing his own voice. It sounded hoarse, detached, desperate.

Her eyes, which had been closed as her head tossed from side to side, flew open. "Don't stop," she gasped, "please don't stop. I'm so close to something . . . I don't know what."

"Oh, God," he groaned, plunging back in to the hilt, throwing his head back as his spine arched. "You're so beautiful, so unbelievably— Kate?"

She'd stiffened beneath him, and not in climax.

He froze. "What's wrong?" he whispered.

He saw a brief flash of pain—the emotional sort, not the physical—flash across her face before she hid it and whispered, "Nothing."

"That's not true," he said in a low voice. His arms were

straining from holding himself above her, but he barely noticed. Every fiber of his being was focused on her face, which was shuttered and pained, despite her obvious attempts to hide it.

"You called me beautiful," she whispered.

For a good ten seconds he just stared at her. For the life of him, he couldn't understand how that was a bad thing. But then again, he'd never professed to understand the female mind. He thought he should simply reaffirm the statement, that she *was* beautiful, and what the hell was the problem, but a little voice inside warned him that this was one of *those* moments, and no matter what he said, it would be the wrong thing, so he decided to tread very, very carefully, and he just murmured her name, which he had a feeling might be the only word guaranteed not to get him into trouble.

"I'm not beautiful," she whispered, her eyes meeting his. She looked shattered and broken, but before he could contradict her, she asked, "Who were you picturing?"

He blinked. "I beg your pardon?"

"Who do you think of when you make love to me?"

Anthony felt as if he'd been punched in the gut. The breath whooshed from his body. "Kate," he said slowly. "Kate, you're mad, you're—"

"I know a man doesn't have to feel desire for a woman to find pleasure with her," she cried out.

"You think I don't desire you?" he choked out. God in heaven, he was ready to explode right now within her and he hadn't even moved for the last thirty seconds.

Her lower lip trembled between her teeth, and a muscle spasmed in her neck. "Do you—do you think of Edwina?"

Anthony froze. "How could I *possibly* confuse the two of you?"

Kate felt her face crumple, felt hot tears stinging at her eyes. She didn't want to cry in front of him, oh, God, especially not now, but it hurt, it hurt so much, and—

His hand grasped her cheeks with stunning speed, forcing her to look up at him.

"Listen to me," he said, his voice even and intense, "and listen well, because I'm only going to say this once. I desire you. I burn for you. I can't sleep at night for wanting you. Even when I didn't *like* you, I lusted for you. It's the most maddening, beguiling, damnable thing, but there it is. And if I hear one more word of nonsense from your lips, I'm going to have to tie you to the bloody bed and have my way with you a hundred different ways, until you finally get it through your silly skull that you are the most beautiful and desirable woman in England, and if everyone else doesn't see that, then they're all bloody fools."

Kate wouldn't have thought it possible for her mouth to fall open while she was lying down, but somehow it did.

One of his brows arched into what had to be the most arrogant expression ever to grace a face. "Is that understood?"

She just stared at him, not quite able to form a response.

He leaned down until his nose was a mere inch from hers. "Is that understood?"

She nodded.

"Good," he grunted, and then, before she had a moment even to catch her breath, his lips were devouring hers in a kiss so fierce she was clutching the bed just to keep from screaming. His hips ground into hers, frenzied in their power, thrusting, rotating, stroking her until she was certain she must be on fire.

She clutched at him, not certain whether she was trying to bind him to her or tear him away. "I can't do this," she moaned, certain she would shatter. Her muscles were stiff, tense, and it was getting hard to breathe.

But if he'd heard her, he didn't care. His face was a harsh mask of concentration, sweat beading on his brow.

"Anthony," she gasped, "I can—"

One of his hands slipped between them and touched her intimately, and she screamed. He slammed forward one last time, and her world simply fell apart. She was stiff, then shaking, then she thought she must be falling. She couldn't breathe, couldn't even gasp. Her throat had to be closing, and her head fell back as her hands grabbed at the mattress with a ferocity she'd never have believed she possessed.

He went utterly still above her, his mouth open in a silent scream, and then he collapsed, the weight of him pressing her farther into the mattress.

"Oh, my God," he gasped, his body now shaking. "Never . . . it's never . . . so good . . . it's never been so good."

Kate, who'd had a few seconds longer to recover, smiled as she smoothed his hair. A wicked thought came to her, a perfectly wonderful wicked thought. "Anthony?" she murmured.

How he lifted his head she would never know, because it looked like it took a Herculean effort just to open his eyes and grunt his response.

She smiled, slowly, and with a womanly seductiveness she'd learned just that evening. Letting one of her fingers trail down the angular edge of his jaw, she whispered, "Are we done yet?"

For a second he made no response, then his lips broke into a smile far more devilish than she could ever have imagined. "For now," he murmured huskily, rolling onto his side and pulling her along with him. "But only for now."

Chapter 18

Although gossip still surrounds the hasty marriage of Lord and Lady Bridgerton (formerly Miss Katharine Sheffield, for those of you who have been in hibernation for these past few weeks), This Author is of the firm opinion that theirs was a love match. Viscount Bridgerton does not escort his wife to every society function (but then again, what husband does?), but when he is present, This Author cannot fail to note that he always seems to be murmuring something in his lady's ear, and that something always seems to make her smile and blush.

Furthermore, he always dances with her one more time than is considered de rigueur. Considering how many husbands don't like to dance with their wives at all, this is romantic stuff, indeed.

Lady Whistledown's Society Papers, 10 June 1814

The next few weeks flew by in a delirious rush. After a brief stay in the country at Aubrey Hall, the newlyweds returned to London, where the season was in full swing. Kate had hoped to use her afternoons to resume her flute lessons, but she quickly discovered that she was in great demand, and her days were filled with social calls, shopping excursions with her family, and the occasional ride in the park. Her evenings were a whirlwind of balls and parties.

But her nights were for Anthony alone.

Marriage, she decided, agreed with her. She saw less of Anthony than she would have liked, but she understood and accepted that he was a very busy man. His many concerns, both in Parliament and on his estates, took up a great deal of his time. But when he returned home at night and met her in the bedroom (no separate bedchambers for Lord and Lady Bridgerton!) he was marvelously attentive, asking about her day, telling her of his, and making love to her until the wee hours of the night.

He'd even taken the time to listen to her practice her flute. She'd managed to hire a musician to come and tutor her two mornings a week. Considering the (not very expert) level of play which Kate had achieved, Anthony's willingness to sit through an entire thirty minutes of rehearsal could only be interpreted as a sign of great affection.

Of course, it did not escape her notice that he'd never repeated the gesture.

Hers was a fine existence, a far better marriage than most women of her station could expect. If her husband did not love her, if he would never love her, then at least he did a good job of making her feel cared for and appreciated. And for now Kate was able to content herself with that.

And if he seemed distant during the day, well, he certainly wasn't distant at night.

The rest of society, however, and Edwina in particular, had gotten it into their heads that Lord and Lady Bridgerton's marriage was a love match. Edwina had taken to visiting in the afternoons, and this day was no exception. She and Kate were sitting in the drawing room, sipping tea and nibbling on biscuits, enjoying a rare moment of privacy now that Kate had bidden farewell to her daily swarm of visitors.

Everyone, it seemed, wanted to see how the new viscountess was getting along, and Kate's drawing room was almost never empty in the afternoon.

Newton had hopped up onto the sofa beside Edwina, and she was idly stroking his fur as she said, "Everyone is talking about you today."

Kate didn't even pause as she lifted her tea to her lips and took a sip. "Everyone is always talking about me," she said with a shrug. "They'll soon find another topic."

"Not," Edwina replied, "as long as your husband keeps looking at you the way he did last night."

Kate felt her cheeks grow warm. "He did nothing out of the ordinary," she murmured.

"Kate, he was positively smoldering!" Edwina shifted her position as Newton shifted his, letting her know with a little whine that he wanted his belly rubbed. "I personally saw him push Lord Haveridge out of the way in his haste to reach your side."

"We arrived separately," Kate explained, although her heart was filling with a secret—and most probably foolish—joy. "I'm sure he just had something he needed to tell me."

Edwina looked dubious. "And did he?"

"Did he what?"

"*Tell* you something," Edwina said with palpable exasperation. "You just said you were sure he just had something he needed to tell you. If that were the case, wouldn't he have told you whatever it was? And then you'd *know* he had something to tell you, right?"

Kate blinked. "Edwina, you're making me dizzy."

Edwina's lips smooshed together in a disgruntled frown. "You never tell me anything."

"Edwina, there's nothing to tell!" Kate reached forward, grabbed a biscuit, and took a large, extremely uncouth bite so that her mouth would be too full to speak. What was she supposed to say to her sister—that before they'd even wed, her husband had informed her in a most matter-of-fact and straightforward manner that he would never love her?

That would make for charming conversation over tea and biscuits.

"Well," Edwina finally announced, after watching Kate chew for an improbable full minute, "I actually had another reason for coming here today. I have something I wish to tell you."

Kate swallowed gratefully. "Really?"

Edwina nodded, then blushed.

"What is it?" Kate implored, sipping at her tea. Her mouth was awfully dry after all that chewing.

"I think I'm in love."

Kate nearly spit out her tea. "With whom?"

"Mr. Bagwell."

Try as she might, Kate could not for the life of her recall who Mr. Bagwell was.

"He's a scholar," Edwina said with a dreamy sigh. "I met him at Lady Bridgerton's country house party."

"I don't recall meeting him," Kate said, her brow knitting into thoughtful lines.

"You were rather busy throughout the visit," Edwina replied in an ironic voice. "Getting yourself betrothed and all that."

Kate pulled the sort of face one could only display with a sibling. "Just tell me about Mr. Bagwell."

Edwina's eyes grew warm and bright. "He's a second son, I'm afraid, so he cannot expect much in the way of income. But now that you've married so well, I needn't worry about that."

Kate felt an unexpected welling of tears in her eyes. She hadn't realized just how pressured Edwina must have felt earlier that season. She and Mary had been careful to assure Edwina that she might marry anyone she liked, but they had all known exactly where their finances stood, and they had certainly all been guilty of making jokes about how it was just as easy to fall in love with a wealthy man as it was with a poor one.

It only took one look at Edwina's face to realize that a huge burden had been lifted from her shoulders.

"I'm glad you've found someone who suits you," Kate murmured.

"Oh, he does. I know that we shall not have much in the way of money, but truly, I don't need silks and jewels." Her eyes fell on the glittering diamond on Kate's hand. "Not that I think you do, of course!" she quickly interjected, her face growing red. "Just that—"

"Just that it's nice not to have to worry about supporting your sister and mother," Kate finished for her in a gentle voice.

Edwina let out a huge sigh. "Exactly."

Kate reached across the table and took her sister's hands in hers. "You certainly needn't worry about me, and I'm sure that Anthony and I will always be able to provide for Mary, should she ever need assistance."

Edwina's lips curved into a wobbly smile.

"As for you," Kate added, "I think it's high time you were able to think only of yourself for a change. To make a decision based on what *you* desire, not what you think others need."

Edwina pulled one of her hands free to brush back a tear. "I really like him," she whispered.

"Then I am certain I will like him as well," Kate said firmly. "When may I meet him?"

"He is in Oxford for the next fortnight, I'm afraid. He has prior commitments which I should not want him to break on my account."

"Of course not," Kate murmured. "You wouldn't want to marry the sort of gentleman who does not honor his commitments."

Edwina nodded in agreement. "I received a letter from him this morning, though, and he says he will come down to London at the end of the month and hopes that he might call on me."

Kate smiled wickedly. "He's already sending you letters?"

Edwina nodded and blushed. "Several per week," she admitted.

"And what is his area of study?"

"Archaeology. He's quite brilliant. He has been to Greece. Twice!"

Kate hadn't thought that her sister—already renowned throughout the land for her beauty—could possibly grow any lovelier, but when Edwina spoke of her Mr. Bagwell, her face shone with a radiance that was nothing short of heart-stopping.

"I cannot wait to meet him," Kate announced. "We must have an informal dinner party with him as our guest of honor."

"That would be wonderful."

"And perhaps the three of us might go for a ride in the park ahead of time so that we might become better acquainted. Now that I am an old married lady, I qualify as a suitable chaperone." Kate let out a little laugh. "Isn't that funny?"

A very amused, very male voice sounded from the doorway: "Isn't what funny?"

"Anthony!" Kate exclaimed, surprised to see her husband in the middle of the day. He always seemed to have appointments and meetings that kept him from their home. "How delightful to see you."

He smiled slightly as he nodded toward Edwina in greeting. "I found myself with an unexpected block of free time."

"Would you care to join us for tea?"

"I'll join you," he murmured as he crossed the room and picked up a crystal decanter that sat on a mahogany side table, "but I believe I'll have a brandy instead."

Kate watched as he poured himself a drink, then

swirled it absently in his hand. It was at times like these that she found it so difficult to keep her heart out of her eyes. He was so handsome in the late afternoon. She wasn't sure why; maybe it was the faint hint of stubble on his cheeks or the fact that his hair was always slightly mussed from whatever it was he did all day. Or maybe it was simply that she didn't often get to see him this time of day; she'd once read a poem that said the unexpected moment was always sweeter.

As Kate gazed upon her husband, she rather thought that poet might be right.

"So," Anthony said after taking a sip of his drink, "what have you two ladies been discussing?"

Kate looked to her sister for permission to share her news, and when Edwina nodded, she said, "Edwina has met a gentleman she fancies."

"Really?" Anthony asked, sounding interested in a strangely paternal sort of manner. He perched on the arm of Kate's chair, a relaxed, overstuffed piece of furniture that was not at all in fashion but well loved nonetheless in the Bridgerton household for its uncommon comfort. "I should like to meet him," he added.

"You should?" Edwina echoed, blinking like an owl. "You would?"

"Of course. In fact, I insist upon it." When neither lady commented, he scowled a bit and added, "I am the head of the family, after all. That's what we do."

Edwina's lips parted with surprise. "I—I hadn't realized you felt a responsibility toward me."

Anthony looked at her as if she'd gone momentarily insane. "You're Kate's sister," he said, as if that should explain everything.

Edwina's blank expression remained fixed on her face for another second, and then it melted into a rather radiant delight. "I have always wondered what it would be like to have a brother," she said.

"I hope I pass muster," Anthony grunted, not entirely comfortable with the sudden outpouring of emotion.

She beamed at him. "Brilliantly. I vow I do not understand why Eloise complains so much."

Kate turned to Anthony and explained, "Edwina and your sister have become fast friends since our marriage."

"God help us," he muttered. "And what, may I ask, could Eloise possibly have to complain about?"

Edwina smiled innocently. "Oh, nothing, really. Just that you can, at times, be a touch overprotective."

"That's ridiculous," he scoffed.

Kate choked on her tea. She was quite certain that by the time their daughters were of marriageable age, Anthony would have converted to Catholicism just so that he could lock them in a convent with twelve-foot walls!

Anthony glanced at her with narrowed eyes. "What are you laughing about?"

Kate quickly patted her mouth with a napkin, mumbling, "Nothing," under the folds of the cloth.

"Hmmmph."

"Eloise says that you were quite the bear when Daphne was being courted by Simon," Edwina said.

"Oh, did she?"

Edwina nodded. "She says the two of you dueled!"

"Eloise talks too much," Anthony grumbled.

Edwina nodded happily. "She always knows everything. Everything! Even more than Lady Whistledown."

Anthony turned to Kate with an expression that was one part beleaguered and one part pure irony. "Remind me to buy a muzzle for my sister," he said drolly. "And one for your sister as well."

Edwina let out a musical laugh. "I never dreamed a brother would be as much fun to tease as a sister. I'm so glad you decided to marry him, Kate."

"I didn't have much choice in the matter," Kate said

with a dry smile, "but I'm rather pleased with the way things turned out myself."

Edwina stood, waking up Newton, who had fallen into blissful sleep next to her on the sofa. He let out an affronted whine and toddled to the floor, where he promptly curled up under a table.

Edwina watched the dog and chuckled before saying, "I should be going. No, don't see me out," she added when both Kate and Anthony stood to escort her to the front door. "I can make my own way."

"Nonsense," Kate said, linking her arm in Edwina's. "Anthony, I shall be right back."

"I shall be counting the seconds," he murmured, and then, as he took another sip of his drink, the two ladies left the room, followed by Newton, who was now barking enthusiastically, presumably guessing that someone was going to take him for a walk.

Once the two sisters were gone, he settled into the comfortable chair so recently vacated by Kate. It was still warm from her body, and he rather fancied that he could smell her scent in the fabric. More soap than lilies this time, he thought with a careful sniff. Perhaps the lilies were a perfume, something she added at night.

He wasn't entirely sure why he'd returned home this afternoon; he certainly hadn't intended to. Contrary to what he'd been telling Kate, his many meetings and responsibilities did not require him to be away from the house all the day long; quite a few of his appointments could easily have been scheduled at home. And while he was indeed a busy man—he'd never subscribed to the indolent lifestyle of so many of the *ton*—he'd spent many a recent afternoon at White's, reading the paper and playing cards with his friends.

He'd thought it best. It was important to keep a certain distance from one's wife. Life—or at least *his* life—was meant to be compartmentalized, and a wife fit rather neatly in the sections he'd mentally labeled "society affairs" and "bed."

But when he'd reached White's that afternoon, there was no one there with whom he felt a particular urge to converse. He'd skimmed through the paper, but there was very little of interest in the most recent edition. And as he sat by the window, trying to enjoy his own company (but finding it pathetically lacking), he'd been struck by the most ridiculous urge to return home and see what Kate was up to.

One afternoon couldn't hurt. He wasn't likely to fall in love with his wife for having spent one afternoon in her presence. Not that he thought there was a danger of his falling in love with her at all, he reminded himself sternly. He'd been married nearly a month now and he'd managed to keep his life blessedly free of such entanglements. There was no reason to think that he could not maintain the status quo indefinitely.

Feeling rather satisfied with himself, he took another sip of his brandy, looking up when he heard Kate reenter the room.

"I do think Edwina might be in love," she said, her entire face lit up with a radiant smile.

Anthony felt his body tighten in response. It was rather ridiculous, actually, how he reacted to her smiles. Happened all the time, and it was a damned nuisance.

Well, most of the time it was a nuisance. He didn't mind it much when he was able to follow it with a nudge and a trip to the bedroom.

But Kate's mind was obviously not lodged as firmly in the gutter as his, since she chose to sit in the chair opposite him, even though there was plenty of room in his chair, provided they didn't mind squeezing next to each other. Even the chair kitty-corner to his would have been better; at least then he could have yanked her up and hauled her onto his lap. If he tried that maneuver where she was seated across the table, he'd have to drag her through the middle of the tea service.

Anthony narrowed his eyes as he assessed the situation, trying to guess exactly how much tea would spill on the rug, and then how much it would cost to replace the rug, and then whether he really cared about such a piddling amount of money, anyway . . .

"Anthony? Are you listening to me?"

He looked up. Kate was resting her arms on her knees as she leaned forward to talk with him. She looked very intent and just a little bit irritated.

"Were you?" she persisted.

He blinked.

"Listening to me?" she ground out.

"Oh." He grinned. "No."

She rolled her eyes but didn't bother to scold him any further than that. "I was saying that we should have Edwina and her young man over for dinner one night. To see if we think they suit. I have never before seen her so interested in a gentleman, and I do so want her to be happy."

Anthony reached for a biscuit. He was hungry, and he'd pretty much given up on the prospect of getting his wife into his lap. On the other hand, if he managed to clear off the cups and saucers, yanking her across the table might not have such messy consequences . . .

He surreptitiously pushed the tray bearing the tea service to the side. "Hmmm?" he grunted, chewing on the biscuit. "Oh, yes, of course. Edwina should be happy."

Kate eyed him suspiciously. "Are you certain you don't want some tea with that biscuit? I'm not a great aficionado of brandy, but I would imagine that tea would taste better with shortbread."

Actually, Anthony thought, the brandy did quite well with shortbread, but it certainly couldn't hurt to empty out the teapot a bit, just in case he toppled it over. "Capital idea," he said, grabbing a teacup and thrusting it toward her. "Tea's just the thing. Can't imagine why I didn't think of it earlier."

"I can't imagine, either," she murmured acerbically—if one could murmur in an acerbic manner, and after hearing Kate's low sarcasm, Anthony rather thought one could.

But he just gave her a jovial smile as he reached out and took his teacup from her outstretched hand. "Thank you," he said, checking to see that she'd added milk. She had, which didn't surprise him; she was very good at remembering such details.

"Is it still hot enough?" Kate asked politely.

Anthony drained the cup. "Perfect," he replied, letting out a satisfied exhale. "Might I trouble you for some more?"

"You seem to be developing quite a taste for tea," she said dryly.

Anthony eyed the teapot, wondering how much was left and whether he'd be able to finish it off without being attacked by an urgent need to relieve himself. "You should have some more, too," he suggested. "You look a bit parched."

Her eyebrows shot up. "Is that so?"

He nodded, then worried he might have laid it on a little too thick. "Just a bit, of course," he said.

"Of course."

"Is there enough tea left for me to have another cup?" he asked, as nonchalantly as he could manage.

"If there isn't, I'm sure I could have Cook brew another pot."

"Oh, no, I'm sure that won't be necessary," he exclaimed, probably a little too loudly. "I'll just take whatever is left."

Kate tipped the pot until the last dregs of tea swirled in his cup. She added a dollop of milk, then handed it back to him in silence, although her arched eyebrows spoke volumes.

As he sipped at his tea—his belly was a little too full to gulp it down as quickly as the last cup—Kate cleared her throat and asked, "Do you know Edwina's young man?"

"I don't even know who he *is*."

"Oh. I'm sorry. I must have forgotten to mention his name. It's Mr. Bagwell. I don't know his Christian name, but Edwina said he's a second son, if that's helpful. She met him at your mother's party."

Anthony shook his head. "Never heard of him. He's probably one of the poor chaps my mother invited to even out the numbers. My mother invited a bloody lot of women. She always does, hoping that one of us might actually fall in love, but then she has to find a pack of unremarkable men to even up the numbers."

"Unremarkable?" Kate echoed.

"So that the women don't fall in love with them instead of us," he replied, his grin rather lopsided.

"She's rather desperate to marry the lot of you off, isn't she?"

"All I know," Anthony said with a shrug, "is that my mother invited so many eligible women last time that she had to go down to the vicar's and beg his sixteen-year-old son to come up for supper."

Kate winced. "I think I met him."

"Yes, he's painfully shy, poor fellow. The vicar told me he had hives for a week after ending up seated next to Cressida Cowper at supper."

"Well, that would give anyone hives."

Anthony grinned. "I knew you had a mean streak in you."

"I'm not being mean!" Kate protested. But her smile was sly. "It was nothing more than the truth."

"Don't defend yourself on my account." He finished the tea; it was bitterly strong from having sat in the pot for so long, but the milk made it almost palatable. Setting the cup down, he added, "Your mean streak is one of the things I like best about you."

"Goodness," she muttered, "I should hate to know what you like least."

Anthony just waved a dismissive hand in the air. "But getting back to your sister and her Mr. Bugwell—"

"Bagwell."

"Pity."

"Anthony!"

He ignored her. "I've actually been thinking I ought to provide Edwina with a dowry."

The irony of the gesture was not lost on him. Back when he'd intended to wed Edwina, he'd planned to provide a dowry for *Kate*.

He peeked over at Kate to see her reaction.

He hadn't, of course, made the offer just to gain her good favor, but he wasn't so noble that he couldn't admit to himself that he'd been hoping for a little more than the stunned silence she was displaying.

Then he realized she was near tears.

"Kate?" he asked, not certain whether to be delighted or worried.

She wiped her nose rather inelegantly with the back of her hand. "That's the nicest thing anyone has ever done for me," she sniffled.

"I actually did it for Edwina," he mumbled, never comfortable with weepy females. But inside, she was making him feel about eight feet tall.

"Oh, Anthony!" she practically wailed. And then, much to his extreme surprise, she jumped to her feet and leaped across the table and into his arms, the heavy hem of her afternoon dress sweeping three teacups, two saucers, and a spoon onto the floor.

"You are so sweet," she said, wiping at her eyes as she landed rather solidly in his lap. "The nicest man in London."

"Well, I don't know about that," he returned, sliding his arm around her waist. "The most dangerous, perhaps, or handsome—"

"Nicest," she interrupted firmly, tucking her head into the crook of his neck. "Definitely the nicest."

"If you insist," he murmured, not at all unhappy with the recent turn of events.

"It's a good thing we finished that tea," Kate said, eyeing the cups on the floor. "It would have made a dreadful mess."

"Oh, indeed." He smiled to himself as he pulled her closer. There was something warm and comfortable about holding Kate. Her legs were dangling over the arm of the chair and her back was resting against the curve of his arm. They fit together nicely, he realized. She was just the right size for a man of his proportions.

There were a lot of things about her that were just right. It was the sort of realization that usually terrified him, but at that moment he was so damned *happy* just sitting here with her in his lap that he simply refused to think about the future.

"You are so good to me," she murmured.

Anthony thought of all the times he'd purposely stayed away, all the times he'd left her to her own devices, but he pushed away the guilt. If he was forcing a distance between them, it was for her own good. He didn't want her to fall in love with him. It would make it that much harder for her when he died.

And if he fell in love with her . . .

He didn't even want to think about how much harder it would be for him.

"Do we have any plans for this evening?" he whispered in her ear.

She nodded; the motion caused her hair to tickle his cheek. "A ball," she said. "At Lady Mottram's."

Anthony couldn't resist the soft silkiness of her hair, and he threaded two fingers through it, letting it slide across his hand and wrap around his wrist. "Do you know what I think?" he murmured.

He heard her smile as she asked, "What?"

"I think I've never cared that much for Lady Mottram. And do you know what else I think?"

Now he heard her trying not to giggle. "What?"

"I think we should go upstairs."

"You do?" she asked, clearly feigning ignorance.

"Oh, indeed. This very minute, as a matter of fact."

She wiggled her bottom, the minx, ascertaining for herself just how quickly he needed to go upstairs. "I see," she murmured gravely.

He pinched her hip lightly. "I rather thought you *felt*."

"Well, that, too," she admitted. "It was quite enlightening."

"I'm sure it was," he muttered. Then, with a very wicked smile, he nudged her chin until they were nose to nose. "Do you know what *else* I think?" he said huskily.

Her eyes widened. "I'm sure I can't imagine."

"I think," he said, one of his hands creeping under her dress and slithering up her leg, "that if we don't go upstairs this instant, I might be content to remain right here."

"Here?" she squeaked.

His hand found the edge of her stockings. "Here," he affirmed.

"Now?"

His fingers tickled her soft thatch of hair, then sank into the very core of her womanhood. She was soft and wet and felt like heaven. "Oh, most definitely now," he said.

"Here?"

He nibbled on her lips. "Didn't I already answer that question?"

And if she had any further questions, she didn't voice them for the next hour.

Or maybe it was just that he was trying his damnedest to rob her of speech.

And if a man could judge from the little squeals and mewls that slipped from her mouth, he was doing a ripping good job.

Chapter 19

Lady Mottram's annual ball was a crush, as always, but society watchers could not fail to note that Lord and Lady Bridgerton did not make an appearance. Lady Mottram insists that they had promised to attend, and This Author can only speculate as to what kept the newlyweds at home . . .

LADY WHISTLEDOWN'S SOCIETY PAPERS, 13 JUNE 1814

Much later that night, Anthony was lying on his side in bed, cradling his wife, who had snuggled her back up to his front and was presently sleeping soundly.

Which was fortunate, he realized, because it had started to rain.

He tried to nudge the covers up over her exposed ear so that she would not hear the drops beating against the windows, but she was as fidgety in sleep as she was when awake, and he could not manage to pull the coverlet much above the level of her neck before she shook it off.

He couldn't yet tell whether the storm would grow electrical in nature, but the force of the rain had increased, and the wind had picked up until it howled through the night, rattling the tree branches against the side of the house.

Kate was growing a little more restless at his side, and

he made shhhh-ing sounds as he smoothed her hair with his hand. The storm hadn't woken her up, but it had definitely intruded upon her slumber. She had begun to mumble in her sleep, tossing and turning until she was curled on her opposite side, facing him.

"What happened to make you hate the rain so?" he whispered, tucking one dark lock of hair behind her ear. But he did not judge her for her terrors; he knew well the frustration of unfounded fears and premonitions. His certainty of his own impending death, for example, had haunted him since the moment he'd picked up his father's limp hand and laid it gently on his unmoving chest.

It wasn't something he could explain, or even something he could understand. It was just something he *knew*.

He'd never feared death, though, not really. The knowledge of it had been a part of him for so long that he merely accepted it, just as other men accepted the other truths that made up the cycle of life. Spring followed winter, and summer after that. For him, death was much the same way.

Until now. He'd been trying to deny it, trying to shut the niggling notion from his mind, but death was beginning to show a frightening face.

His marriage to Kate had sent his life down an alternate path, no matter how much he tried to convince himself that he could restrict their marriage to nothing but friendship and sex.

He cared about her. He cared about her far too much. He craved her company when they were apart, and he dreamed about her at night, even as he held her in his arms.

He wasn't ready to call it love, but it terrified him all the same.

And whatever it was that burned between them, he didn't want it to end.

Which was, of course, the cruelest irony of all.

Anthony closed his eyes as he let out a weary and nervous exhale, wondering what the hell he was going to do about the complication that lay beside him in the bed. But even while his eyes were shut, he saw the flash of lightning that lit up the night, turning the black of the inside of his eyelids into a bloody red-orange.

Opening his eyes, he saw that they'd left the drapes partway open when they'd retired to bed earlier in the evening. He'd have to shut those; they'd help to keep the lightning from illuminating the room.

But when he shifted his weight and tried to nudge his way out from under the covers, Kate grabbed his arm, her fingers pressing frantically into his muscles.

"Shhhh, now, it's all right," he whispered, "I'm only going to close the drapes."

But she did not let go, and the whimper that escaped her lips when a clap of thunder shook the night nearly broke his heart.

A pale sliver of moonlight filtered through the window, just enough to illuminate the tense, drawn lines of her face. Anthony peered down to assure himself that she was still sleeping, then pried her hands from his arm and got up to close the drapes. He suspected that the flashes of lightning would still sneak into the room, though, so when he was done with the drapes, he lit a lone candle and set it on his nightstand. It didn't give off enough light to wake her up—at least he hoped it wouldn't—but at the same time it saved the room from utter blackness.

And there was nothing quite so startling as a streak of lightning cutting through utter blackness.

He crawled back into bed and regarded Kate. She was still sleeping, but not peacefully. She'd curled into a semi-fetal position and her breathing was labored. The lightning didn't seem to bother her much, but every time the room shook with thunder she flinched.

He took her hand and smoothed her hair, and for several minutes he simply lay with her, trying to soothe her as she slept. But the storm was increasing in intensity, with the thunder and lightning practically coming on top of each other. Kate was growing more restless by the second, and then, as a particularly loud clap of thunder exploded in the air, her eyes flew open, her face a mask of utter panic.

"Kate?" Anthony whispered.

She sat up, scrambling back until her spine was pressed against the solid headboard of the bed. She looked like a statue of terror, her body stiff and frozen into place. Her eyes were still open, barely blinking, and though she did not move her head, they flicked frantically back and forth, scanning the entire room, but not seeing anything.

"Oh, Kate," he whispered. This was far, far worse than what she'd been through that night in the library at Aubrey Hall. And he could feel the force of her pain slicing right through his heart.

No one should feel terror like this. And especially not his wife.

Moving slowly, so as not to startle her, he made his way to her side, then carefully laid an arm over her shoulders. She was shaking, but she did not push him away.

"Are you even going to remember any of this in the morning?" he whispered.

She made no response, but then, he hadn't expected her to.

"There, there," he said gently, trying to remember the soothing nonsense words his mother used whenever one of her children was upset. "It's all right now. You'll be fine."

Her tremors seemed to slow a bit, but she was still very clearly disturbed, and when the next clap of thunder shook the room, her entire body flinched, and she buried her face in the crook of her neck.

"No," she moaned, "no, no."

"Kate?" Anthony blinked several times, then gazed at her intently. She sounded different, not awake but more lucid, if that was possible.

"No, no."

And she sounded very . . .

"No, no, don't go."

. . . *young*.

"Kate?" He held her tightly, unsure of what to do. Should he wake her? Her eyes might be open, but she was clearly asleep and dreaming. Part of him longed to break her of her nightmare, but once she woke, she'd still be in the same place—in bed in the middle of a horrible electrical storm. Would she even feel any better?

Or should he let her sleep? Perhaps if she rode out the nightmare he might actually gain some idea as to what had caused her terror.

"Kate?" he whispered, as if she herself might actually give him a clue as to how to proceed.

"No," she moaned, growing more agitated by the second. "Nooooo."

Anthony pressed his lips to her temple, trying to soothe her with his presence.

"No, please. . . ." She started to sob, her body racked with huge gasps of air as her tears drenched his shoulder. "No, oh, no . . . *Mama*!"

Anthony stiffened. He knew that Kate always referred to her stepmother as Mary. Could she actually be speaking of her true mother, the woman who had given her life and then died so many years ago?

But as he pondered that question, Kate's entire body stiffened and she let out a shrill, high-pitched scream.

The scream of a very young girl.

In an instant, she turned about, and then she leaped into his arms, grabbing at him, clutching his shoulders with a terrifying desperation. "No, Mama," she wailed, her entire body heaving from the exertion of her cries. "No, you can't go! Oh, Mama Mama Mama Mama Mama Mama . . ."

If Anthony hadn't had his back to the headboard, she would have knocked him over, the force of her fervor was that strong.

"Kate?" he blurted out, surprised by the slight note of panic in his voice. "Kate? It's all right. You're all right. You're fine. Nobody is going anywhere. Do you hear me? No one."

But her words had melted away, and all that was left was the low sound of a weeping that came from deep in her soul. Anthony held her, and then when she'd calmed a bit, he eased her down until she was lying on her side again, and then he held her some more, until she drifted back into sleep.

Which, he noticed ironically, was right about the time the last of the thunder and lightning split the room.

When Kate woke the following morning, she was surprised to see her husband sitting up in bed, staring down at her with the oddest look . . . a combination of concern, and curiosity, and maybe even the barest hint of pity. He didn't say anything when her eyes opened, even though she could see that he was watching her face intently. She waited, to see what he would do, and then finally she just said, somewhat hesitantly, "You look tired."

"I didn't sleep well," he admitted.

"You didn't?"

He shook his head. "It rained."

"It did?"

He nodded. "And thundered."

She swallowed nervously. "And lightninged as well, I suppose."

"It did," he said, nodding again. "It was quite a storm."

There was something very profound in the way he was speaking in short, concise sentences, something that raised the hair on the back of her neck. "H-how fortunate that I missed it, then," she said. "You know I don't do well with strong storms."

"I know," he said simply.

But there was a wealth of meaning behind those two

short words, and Kate felt her heartbeat speed up slightly. "Anthony," she asked, not certain she wanted to know the answer, "what happened last night?"

"You had a nightmare."

She closed her eyes for a second. "I didn't think I had those any longer."

"I didn't realize you'd ever suffered from nightmares."

Kate let out a long exhale and sat up, pulling the covers along with her and tucking them under arms. "When I was small. Whenever it stormed, I'm told. I don't know for a fact; I never remembered anything. I thought I'd—" She had to stop for a moment; her throat felt like it was closing up, and her words seemed to choke her.

He reached out and took her hand. It was a simple gesture, but somehow it touched her heart far more than any words would have done. "Kate?" he asked quietly. "Are you all right?"

She nodded. "I thought I'd stopped, that's all."

He didn't say anything for a moment, and the room was so quiet that Kate was sure she could hear both of their heartbeats. Finally, she heard the slight rush of indrawn breath across Anthony's lips, and he asked, "Did you know that you speak in your sleep?"

She hadn't been facing him, but at that comment, her head jerked quite suddenly to the right, her eyes colliding with his. "I do?"

"You did last night."

Her fingers clutched the coverlet. "What did I say?"

He hesitated, but when his words emerged, they were steady and even. "You called out to your mother."

"Mary?" she whispered.

He shook his head. "I don't think so. I've never heard you call Mary anything but Mary; last night you were crying for 'Mama.' You sounded . . ." He paused and took a slightly ragged breath. "You sounded quite young."

Kate licked her lips, then chewed on the bottom one. "I don't know what to tell you," she finally said, afraid to press into the deepest recesses of her memory. "I have no idea why I'd be calling out to my mother."

"I think," he said gently, "that you should ask Mary."

Kate gave her head a quick and immediate shake. "I didn't even know Mary when my mother died. Neither did my father. She couldn't know why I was calling out to her."

"Your father might have told her something," he said, lifting her hand to his lips and giving it a reassuring kiss.

Kate let her eyes drop to her lap. She wanted to understand why she was so afraid of the storms, but prying into one's deepest fears was almost as terrifying as the fear itself. What if she discovered something she didn't want to know? What if—

"I'll go with you," Anthony said, breaking into her thoughts.

And somehow that made everything all right.

Kate looked to him and nodded, tears in her eyes. "Thank you," she whispered. "Thank you so much."

Later that day, the two of them walked up the steps to Mary's small townhouse. The butler showed them into the drawing room, and Kate sat on the familiar blue sofa while Anthony walked over to the window, leaning on the sill as he peered out.

"See something interesting?" she asked.

He shook his head, smiling sheepishly as he turned to face her. "I just like looking out windows, that's all."

Kate thought there was something awfully sweet about that, although she couldn't really put her finger on what. Every day seemed to reveal some new little quirk to his character, some uniquely endearing habit that bound them ever closer. She *liked* knowing strange little things about him, like how he always doubled up his pillow before going to sleep, or that he detested orange marmalade but adored the lemon.

"You look rather introspective."

Kate jerked to attention. Anthony was staring at her quizzically. "You drifted off," he said with an amused expression, "and you had the dreamiest smile on your face."

She shook her head, blushed, and mumbled, "It was nothing."

His answering snort was dubious, and as he walked over to the sofa, he said, "I'd give a hundred pounds for those thoughts."

Kate was saved from having to comment by Mary's entrance. "Kate!" Mary exclaimed. "What a lovely surprise. And Lord Bridgerton, how nice to see you both."

"You really should call me Anthony," he said somewhat gruffly.

Mary smiled as he took her hand in greeting. "I shall endeavor to remember to do so," she said. She sat across from Kate, then waited for Anthony to take his place on the sofa before saying, "Edwina is out, I'm afraid. Her Mr. Bagwell came rather unexpectedly down to town. They've gone for a walk in the park."

"We should lend them Newton," Anthony said affably. "A more capable chaperone I cannot imagine."

"We actually came to see you, Mary," Kate said.

Kate's voice held an uncommon note of seriousness, and Mary responded instantly. "What is it?" she asked, her eyes flicking back and forth from Kate to Anthony. "Is everything all right?"

Kate nodded, swallowing as she searched for the right words. Funny how she'd been rehearsing what to ask all morning, and now she was speechless. But then she felt Anthony's hand on hers, the weight and the warmth of it strangely comforting, and she looked up and said to Mary, "I'd like to ask you about my mother."

Mary looked a little startled, but she said, "Of course. But you know that I did not know her personally. I only know what your father told me of her."

Kate nodded. "I know. And you might not have the

answers to any of my questions, but I don't know who else to ask."

Mary shifted in her seat, her hands clasped primly in her lap. But Kate noticed that her knuckles had gone white.

"Very well," Mary said. "What is it you wish to learn? You know that I will tell you anything I know."

Kate nodded again and swallowed, her mouth having gone dry. "How did she die, Mary?"

Mary blinked, then sagged slightly, perhaps with relief. "But you know that already. It was influenza. Or some sort of lung fever. The doctors were never certain."

"I know, but . . ." Kate looked to Anthony, who gave her a reassuring nod. She took a deep breath and plunged on. "I'm still afraid of storms, Mary. I want to know why. I don't want to be afraid any longer."

Mary's lips parted, but she was silent for many seconds as she stared at her stepdaughter. Her skin slowly paled, taking on an odd, translucent hue, and her eyes grew haunted. "I didn't realize," she whispered. "I didn't know you still—"

"I hid it well," Kate said softly.

Mary reached up and touched her temple, her hands shaking. "If I'd known, I'd have . . ." Her fingers moved to her forehead, smoothing over worry lines as she fought for words. "Well, I don't know what I'd have done. Told you, I suppose."

Kate's heart stopped. "Told me what?"

Mary let out a long breath, both of her hands at her face now, pressing against the upper edge of her eye sockets. She looked as if she had a terrible headache, the weight of the world pounding against her skull, from the inside out.

"I just want you to know," she said in a choked voice, "that I didn't tell you because I thought you didn't remember. And if you didn't remember, well, it didn't seem right to *make* you remember."

She looked up, and there were tears streaking her face.

"But obviously you do," she whispered, "or you wouldn't be so afraid. Oh, Kate. I'm so sorry."

"I am sure there is nothing for you to be sorry about," Anthony said softly.

Mary looked at him, her eyes momentarily startled, as if she'd forgotten he was in the room. "Oh, but there is," she said sadly. "I didn't know that Kate was still suffering from her fears. I should have known. It's the sort of thing a mother should sense. I may not have given her life, but I have tried to be a true mother to her—"

"You have," Kate said fervently. "The very best."

Mary turned back to her, holding her silence for a few seconds before saying, in an oddly detached voice, "You were three when your mother died. It was your birthday, actually."

Kate nodded, mesmerized.

"When I married your father I made three vows. There was the vow I made to him, before God and witnesses, to be his wife. But in my heart I made two other vows. One was to you, Kate. I took one look at you, so lost and forlorn with those huge brown eyes—and they were sad, oh, they were so sad, eyes no child should have—and I vowed that I would love you as my own, and raise you with everything I had within me."

She paused to wipe her eyes, gratefully accepting the handkerchief that Anthony handed to her. When she continued, her voice was barely a whisper. "The other vow was to your mother. I visited her grave, you know."

Kate's nod was accompanied by a wistful smile. "I know. I went with you on several occasions."

Mary shook her head. "No. I mean before I married your father. I knelt there, and that was when I made my third vow. She had been a good mother to you; everyone said so, and any fool could see that you missed her with everything in your heart. So I promised her all the same things I promised you, to be a good mother, to love and cherish you as if you were of my own flesh." She lifted her head, and her eyes were utterly clear and direct when she said, "And I'd like to think that I brought her some peace. I don't think any mother can die in peace leaving behind a child so young."

"Oh, Mary," Kate whispered.

Mary looked at her and smiled sadly, then turned to Anthony. "And that, my lord, is why I am sorry. I should have known, should have seen that she suffered."

"But Mary," Kate protested, "I didn't want you to see. I hid in my room, under my bed, in the closet. Anything to keep it from you."

"But why, sweetling?"

Kate sniffed back a tear. "I don't know. I didn't want to worry you, I suppose. Or maybe I was afraid of appearing weak."

"You've always tried to be so strong," Mary whispered. "Even when you were a tiny thing."

Anthony took Kate's hand, but he looked at Mary. "She is strong. And so are you."

Mary gazed at Kate's face for a long minute, her eyes nostalgic and sad, and then, in a low, even voice, she said, "When your mother died, it was . . . I wasn't there, but when I married your father, he told the story to me. He knew that I loved you already, and he thought it might help me to understand you a bit better.

"Your mother's death was very quick. According to your father, she fell ill on a Thursday and died on a Tuesday. And it rained the whole time. It was one of those awful storms that never ends, just beats the ground mercilessly until the rivers flood and the roads become impassable.

"He said that he was sure she would turnabout if only the rain would stop. It was silly, he knew, but every night he'd go to bed praying for the sun to peek out from the clouds. Praying for anything that might give him a little hope."

"Oh, Papa," Kate whispered, the words slipping unbidden from her lips.

"You were confined to the house, of course, which apparently rankled you to no end." Mary looked up and smiled at Kate, the sort of smile that spoke of years of memories. "You've always loved to be outdoors. Your father told me that your mother used to bring your cradle outside and rock you in the fresh air."

"I didn't know that," Kate whispered.

Mary nodded, then continued with her story. "You didn't realize your mother was ill right away. They kept you from her, fearing contagion. But eventually you must have sensed that something was wrong. Children always do.

"The night she died the rain had grown worse, and I'm told the thunder and lightning were as terrifying as anyone had ever seen." She paused, then tilted her head slightly to the side as she asked, "Do you remember the old gnarled tree in the back garden—the one you and Edwina always used to scramble on?"

"The one that was split in two?" Kate whispered.

Mary nodded. "It happened that night. Your father said it was the most terrifying sound he'd ever heard. The thunder and lightning were coming on top of each other, and a bolt split the tree at the exact moment that the thunder shook the earth.

"I suppose you couldn't sleep," she continued. "I remember that storm, even though I lived in the next county. I don't know how anyone could have slept through it. Your father was with your mother. She was dying, and everyone knew it, and in their grief they'd forgotten about you. They'd been so careful to keep you out, but on that night, their attention was elsewhere.

"Your father told me that he was sitting by your mother's side, trying to hold her hand as she passed. It wasn't a gentle death, I'm afraid. Lung disease often isn't." Mary looked up. "My mother died the same way. I know. The end wasn't peaceful. She was gasping for breath, suffocating before my very eyes."

Mary swallowed convulsively, then trained her eyes on

Kate's. "I can only assume," she whispered, "that you witnessed the same thing."

Anthony's hand tightened on Kate's.

"But where I was five and twenty at my mother's death," Mary said, "you were but three. It's not the sort of thing a child should see. They tried to make you leave, but you would not go. You bit and clawed and screamed and screamed and screamed, and then—"

Mary stopped, choking on her words. She lifted the handkerchief Anthony had given her to her face, and several moments passed before she was able to continue.

"Your mother was near death," she said, her voice so low it was nearly a whisper. "And just as they found someone strong enough to remove such a wild child, a flash of lightning pierced the room. Your father said—"

Mary stopped and swallowed. "Your father told me that what happened next was the most eerie and awful moment he'd ever experienced. The lightning—it lit the room up as bright as day. And the flash wasn't over in an instant, as it should be; it almost seemed to hang in the air. He looked at you, and you were frozen. I'll never forget the way he described it. He said it was as if you were a little statue."

Anthony jerked.

"What is it?" Kate asked, turning to him.

He shook his head disbelievingly. "That's how you looked last night," he said. "Exactly how you looked. I thought those very words."

"I . . ." Kate looked from Anthony to Mary. But she didn't know what to say.

Anthony gave her hand another squeeze as he turned to Mary and urged, "Please, go on."

She nodded once. "Your eyes were fixed on your mother, and so your father turned to see what had horrified you so, and that's when he . . . when he saw . . ."

Kate gently disengaged her hand from Anthony's grasp and got up to sit beside Mary, pulling an ottoman down next to her chair. She took one of Mary's hands in both of her own. "It's all right, Mary," she murmured. "You can tell me. I need to know."

Mary nodded. "It was the moment of her death. She sat upright. Your father said she hadn't lifted her body from the pillows for days, and yet she sat bolt upright. He said she was stiff, her head thrown back, and her mouth was open as if she were screaming, but she couldn't make a sound. And then the thunder came, and you must have thought the sound came from her mouth, because you screamed like nothing anyone had ever heard and came running forward, jumping onto the bed and throwing your arms around her.

"They tried to pry you off, but you just wouldn't let go. You kept screaming and screaming and calling her name, and then there was a terrible crash. Glass shattering. A bolt of lightning severed a branch from a tree, and it crashed right through the window. There was glass everywhere, and wind, and rain, and thunder, and more lightning, and through the whole thing you didn't stop screaming. Even after she was dead and had fallen back onto the pillows, your little arms were still clutched around her neck, and you screamed and sobbed and begged for her to wake up, and not to leave.

"And you just wouldn't let go," Mary whispered. "Finally they had to wait until you wore yourself out and fell asleep."

The room was hung with silence for a full minute, and then Kate finally whispered, "I didn't know. I didn't know that I'd witnessed that."

"Your father said you wouldn't speak of it," Mary said. "Not that you could, right away. You slept for hours and hours, and then when you woke up, it was clear that you'd caught your mother's illness. Not with the same gravity; your life was never in danger. But you were ill, and not in any state to talk about your mother's death. And when you were well, you *wouldn't* talk about it. Your father tried, but he said that every time he mentioned it, you shook your head and clamped your hands over your ears. And eventually he stopped trying."

Mary gave Kate an intent gaze. "He said you seemed happier when he stopped trying. He did what he thought was best."

"I know," Kate whispered. "And at the time, it probably *was* best. But now I needed to know." She turned to Anthony, not for reassurance exactly, but for some sort of validation, and she repeated, "I needed to know."

"How do you feel now?" he asked, his words soft and direct.

She thought about that for a moment. "I don't know. Good, I think. A little lighter." And then, without even realizing what she was doing, she smiled. It was a hesitant, slow thing, but nonetheless a smile. She turned to Anthony with astonished eyes. "I feel as if a huge weight has been lifted from my shoulders."

"Do you remember now?" Mary asked.

Kate shook her head. "But I still feel better. I can't explain it, really. It's good to know, even if I can't remember."

Mary made a choked sort of sound and then she was out of her chair and next to Kate on the ottoman, embracing her with all her might. And they both were crying, the odd, energetic sort of sobs that were mixed with laughter. There were tears, but they were happy tears, and when Kate finally pulled away and looked at Anthony, she saw that he, too, was wiping at the corner of his eye.

He pulled his hand away, of course, and assumed a dignified mien, but she'd seen him. And in that moment, she knew she loved him. With every thought, every emotion, every piece of her being, she loved him.

And if he never loved her back—well, she didn't want to think about that. Not now, not in this profound moment.

Probably not ever.

Chapter 20

Has anyone besides This Author noticed that Miss Edwina Sheffield has been very distracted of late? Rumor has it that she has lost her heart, although no one seems to know the identity of the lucky gentleman.

Judging from Miss Sheffield's behavior at parties, however, This Author feels it is safe to assume that the mystery gentleman is not someone currently residing here in London. Miss Sheffield has shown no marked interest in any one gentleman, and indeed, even sat out the dancing at Lady Mottram's ball Friday last.

Could her suitor be someone she met in the country last month? This Author will have to do a bit of sleuthing to uncover the truth.

LADY WHISTLEDOWN'S SOCIETY PAPERS, 13 JUNE 1814

"Do you know what I think?" Kate asked, as she sat at her vanity table later that night, brushing her hair.

Anthony was standing by the window, one hand leaning against the frame as he gazed out. "Mmmm?" was his reply, mostly because he was too distracted by his own thoughts to formulate a more coherent word.

"I think," she continued in a cheery voice, "that next time it storms, I'm going to be just fine."

He turned slowly around. "Really?" he asked.

She nodded. "I don't know why I think that. A gut feeling, I suppose."

"Gut feelings," he said, in a voice that sounded strange and flat even to his own ears, "are often the most accurate."

"I feel the strangest sense of optimism," she said, waving her silver-backed hairbrush in the air as she spoke. "All my life, I've had this awful thing hanging over my head. I didn't tell you—I never told anyone—but every time it stormed, and I fell to pieces, I thought . . . well, I didn't just *think*, I somehow *knew* . . ."

"What, Kate?" he asked, dreading the answer without even having a clue why.

"Somehow," she said thoughtfully, "as I shook and sobbed, I just knew that I was going to die. I knew it. There was just no way I could feel that awful and live to see the next day." Her head cocked slightly to the side, and her face took on a vaguely strained expression, as if she weren't sure how to say what she needed to say.

But Anthony understood all the same. And it made his blood run to ice.

"I'm sure you'll think it's the silliest thing imaginable," she said, her shoulders rising and falling in a sheepish shrug. "You're so rational, so levelheaded and practical. I don't think you could understand something like this."

If she only knew. Anthony rubbed at his eyes, feeling strangely drunk. He staggered to a chair, hoping she wouldn't notice how off balance he was, and sat down.

Luckily, her attention had returned to the various bottles and trinkets on her vanity table. Or maybe she was just too embarrassed to look at him, thinking he'd scoff at her irrational fears.

"Whenever the storm passed," she continued, talking down at her table, "I knew how foolish I'd been and how ridiculous the notion was. After all, I'd endured thunderstorms before, and none had ever killed me. But knowing that in my rational mind never seemed to help. Do you know what I mean?"

Anthony tried to nod. He wasn't sure if he actually did.

"When it rained," she said, "nothing really existed except for the storm. And, of course, my fear. Then the sun would come out, and I'd realize again how silly I'd been, but the next time it stormed, it was just like before. And once again, I knew I would die. I just knew it."

Anthony felt sick. His body felt strange, not his own. He couldn't have said anything if he'd tried.

"In fact," she said, raising her head to look at him, "the only time I felt I might actually live to see the next day was in the library at Aubrey Hall." She stood and walked to his side, resting her cheek on his lap as she knelt before him. "With you," she whispered.

He lifted his hand to stroke her hair. The motion was more out of reflex than anything else. He certainly wasn't conscious of his actions.

He'd had no idea that Kate had any sense of her own mortality. Most people didn't. It was something that had lent Anthony an odd sense of isolation through the years, as if he understood some basic, awful truth that eluded the rest of society.

And while Kate's sense of doom wasn't the same as his—hers was fleeting, brought on by a temporary burst of wind and rain and electricity, whereas his was with him always, and would be until the day he died—she, unlike him, had beaten it.

Kate had fought her demons and she had won.

And Anthony was so damned jealous.

It was not a noble reaction; he knew that. And, caring for her as he did, he was thrilled and relieved and overjoyed and every good and pure emotion imaginable that she had beaten the terrors that came with the storms, but he was still jealous. So goddamned jealous.

Kate had won.

Whereas he, who had acknowledged his demons but

refused to fear them, was now petrified with terror. And all because the one thing he swore would never happen had come to pass.

He had fallen in love with his wife.

He had fallen in love with his wife, and now the thought of dying, of leaving her, of knowing that their moments together would form a short poem and not a long and lusty novel—it was more than he could bear.

And he didn't know where to set the blame. He wanted to point his finger at his father, for dying young and leaving him as the bearer of this awful curse. He wanted to rail at Kate, for coming into his life and making him fear his own end. Hell, he would have blamed a stranger on the street if he'd thought there'd be any use to it.

But the truth was, there was no one to blame, not even himself. It would make him feel so much better if he could point his finger at someone—anyone—and say, "This is *your* fault." It was juvenile, he knew, this need to assign blame, but everyone had a right to childish emotions from time to time, didn't they?

"I'm so happy," Kate murmured, her head still resting on his lap.

And Anthony wanted to be happy, too. He wanted so damned much for everything to be uncomplicated, for happiness just to be happiness and nothing more. He wanted to rejoice in her recent victories without any thought to his own worries. He wanted to lose himself in the moment, to forget about the future, to hold her in his arms and . . .

In one abrupt, unpremeditated movement, he hauled them both to their feet.

"Anthony?" Kate queried, blinking in surprise.

In answer, he kissed her. His lips met hers in an explosion of passion and need that blurred the mind until he could be ruled by body alone. He didn't want to think, he didn't want to be *able* to think. All he wanted was this very moment.

And he wanted this moment to last forever.

He swept his wife into his arms and stalked to the bed, depositing her on the mattress half a second before his body came down to cover hers. She was stunning beneath him, soft and strong, and consumed by the same fire that raged within his own body. She might not understand what had prompted his sudden need, but she felt it and shared it all the same.

Kate had already dressed for bed, and her nightrobe fell open easily under his experienced fingers. He had to touch her, to feel her, to assure himself that she was there beneath him and he was there to make love to her. She was wearing a silky little confection of ice blue that tied at the shoulders and hugged her curves. It was the sort of gown designed to reduce men to liquid fire, and Anthony was no exception.

There was something desperately erotic about the feel of her warm skin through the silk, and his hands roamed over her body relentlessly, touching, squeezing, doing anything he could to bind her to him.

If he could have drawn her within him, he would have done it and kept her there forever.

"Anthony," Kate gasped, in that brief moment when he removed his mouth from hers, "are you all right?"

"I want you," he grunted, bunching her gown up around the tops of her legs. "I want you now."

Her eyes widened with shock and excitement, and he sat up, straddling her, his weight on his knees so as not to crush her. "You are so beautiful," he whispered. "So unbelievably gorgeous."

Kate glowed at his words, and her hands went up to his face, smoothing her fingers over his faintly stubbled cheeks. He caught one of her hands and turned his face into it, kissing her palm as her other hand trailed down the muscled cords of his neck.

His fingers found the delicate straps at her shoulders, tied into loose bow-tie loops. It took the barest of tugs to release the knots, but once the silky fabric slid over her breasts, Anthony lost all semblance of patience, and he yanked at the garment until it pooled at her feet, leaving her completely and utterly naked under his gaze.

With a ragged groan he tore at his shirt, buttons flying as he pulled it off, and it took mere seconds to divest himself of his trousers. And then, when there was finally nothing in the bed but glorious skin, he covered her again, one muscular thigh nudging her legs apart.

"I can't wait," he said hoarsely. "I can't make this good for you."

Kate let out a fevered groan as she grabbed him by the hips, steering him toward her entrance. "It *is* good for me," she gasped. "And I don't want you to wait."

And at that point, words ceased. Anthony let out a primitive, guttural cry as he plunged into her, burying himself fully with one long and powerful stroke. Kate's eyes flew wide open, and her mouth formed a little *Oh* of surprise at the shock of his swift invasion. But she'd been ready for him—more than ready for him. Something about the relentless pace of his lovemaking had stirred a passion deep within her, until she needed him with a desperation that left her breathless.

They weren't delicate, and they weren't gentle. They were hot, and sweaty, and needy, and they held on to each other as if they could make time last forever by sheer force of will. When they climaxed, it was fiery and it was simultaneous, both their bodies arching as their cries of release mingled in the night.

But when they were done, curled in each other's arms as they fought for control over their labored breath, Kate closed her eyes in bliss and surrendered to an overwhelming lassitude.

Anthony did not.

He stared at her as she drifted off, then watched her as she slumbered. He watched the way her eyes sometimes moved under her sleepy eyelids. He measured the pace of her breathing by counting the gentle rise and fall of her chest. He listened for each sigh, each mumble.

There were certain memories a man wanted to sear on his brain, and this was one of them.

But just when he was sure that she was totally and completely asleep, she made a funny, warm sort of noise as she snuggled more deeply into his embrace, and her eyelids fluttered slowly open.

"You're still awake," she murmured, her voice scratchy and mellow with sleep.

He nodded, wondering if he was holding her too tightly. He didn't want to let go. He never wanted to let go.

"You should sleep," she said.

He nodded again, but he couldn't seem to make his eyes close.

She yawned. "This is nice."

He kissed her forehead, making an "Mmmm" sound of agreement.

She arched her neck and kissed him back, full on the lips, then settled into her pillow. "I hope we'll be like this always," she murmured, yawning yet again as sleep overtook her. "Always and forever."

Anthony froze.

Always.

She couldn't know what that word meant to him. Five years? Six? Maybe seven or eight.

Forever.

That was a word that had no meaning, something he simply couldn't comprehend.

Suddenly he couldn't breathe.

The coverlet felt like a brick wall atop him, and the air grew thick.

He had to get out of there. He had to go. He had to—

He vaulted from the bed, and then, stumbling and choking, he reached for his clothes, tossed so recklessly to the floor, and started thrusting his limbs into the appropriate holes.

"Anthony?"

His head jerked up. Kate was pushing herself upright in

the bed, yawning. Even in the dim light, he could see that her eyes were confused. And hurt.

"Are you all right?" she asked.

He gave her one curt nod.

"Then why are you trying to put your leg into the armhole of your shirt?"

He looked down and bit off a curse he'd never before even considered uttering in front of a female. With yet another choice expletive, he balled the offending piece of linen into a wrinkled mess and threw it on the floor, pausing for barely a second before yanking his trousers on.

"Where are you going?" Kate asked anxiously.

"I have to go out," he grunted.

"Now?"

He didn't answer because he didn't know how to answer.

"Anthony?" She stepped out of bed and reached for him, but a split second before her hand touched his cheek he flinched, stumbling backward until his back hit the bedpost. He saw the hurt on her face, the pain of his rejection, but he knew that if she touched him in tenderness, he'd be lost.

"Damn it all," he bit off. "Where the hell are my shirts?"

"In your dressing room," she said nervously. "Where they always are."

He stalked off in search of a fresh shirt, unable to bear the sound of her voice. No matter what she said, he kept hearing *always* and *forever*.

And it was killing him.

When he emerged from his dressing room, coat and shoes on their proper places on his body, Kate was on her feet, pacing the floor and anxiously fidgeting with the wide blue sash on her dressing gown.

"I have to go," he said tonelessly.

She didn't make a sound, which was what he'd thought he wanted, but instead he just found himself standing there, waiting for her to speak, unable to move until she did.

"When will you be back?" she finally asked.

"Tomorrow."

"That's . . . good."

He nodded. "I can't be here," he blurted out. "I have to go."

She swallowed convulsively. "Yes," she said, her voice achingly small, "you've said as much."

And then, without a backward glance and without a clue as to where he was going, he left.

Kate walked slowly to the bed and stared at it. Somehow it seemed wrong to climb in alone, to pull the covers around her and make a little huddle of one. She thought she should cry, but no tears pricked her eyes. So finally she moved to the window, pushed aside the drapes, and stared out, surprising herself with a soft prayer for a storm.

Anthony was gone, and while she was certain he'd return in body, she was not so confident about his spirit. And she realized that she needed something—she needed the storm—to prove to herself that she could be strong, by herself and for herself.

She didn't want to be alone, but she might not have a choice in that matter. Anthony seemed determined to maintain a distance. There were demons within him—demons she feared he would never choose to face in her presence.

But if she was destined to be alone, even with a husband at her side, then by God she'd be alone and strong.

Weakness, she thought as she let her forehead rest against the smooth, cool glass of her window, never got anyone anywhere.

Anthony had no recollection of his off-balance stumble through the house, but somehow he found himself tripping down the front steps, made slippery by the light fog that hung in the air. He crossed the street, not having a clue where he was going, only knowing that he needed to be *away*. But when he reached the opposite pavement, some devil within him forced his eyes upward toward his bedroom window.

He shouldn't have seen her was his rather inane thought. She should have been in bed or the drapes should have been pulled or he should have been halfway to his club by now.

But he did see her and the dull ache in his chest grew sharper, more viciously unrelenting. His heart felt as if it had been sliced wide open—and he had the most unsettling sensation that the hand wielding the knife had been his own.

He watched her for a minute—or maybe it was an hour. He didn't think she saw him; nothing in her posture gave any indication that she was aware of his presence. She was too far away for him to see her face, but he rather thought her eyes were closed.

Probably hoping it doesn't storm, he thought, glancing up at the murky sky. She'd most likely be out of luck. The mist and fog were already coalescing into drops of moisture on his skin, and it seemed only a quick transition to out-and-out rain.

He knew he should leave, but some invisible cord kept him rooted to the spot. Even after she'd left her position at the window, he remained in place, staring up at the house. The pull back inside was nearly impossible to deny. He wanted to run back into the house, fall to his knees before her, and beg her forgiveness. He wanted to sweep her into his arms and make love to her until the first streaks of dawn touched the sky. But he knew he couldn't do any of those things.

Or maybe it was that he *shouldn't*. He just didn't know anymore.

And so, after standing frozen in place for nearly an hour, after the rain came, after the wind blew gusts of chilly air down the street, Anthony finally left.

He left, not feeling the cold, not feeling the rain, which had begun to fall with surprising force.

He left, not feeling anything.

Chapter 21

It has been whispered that Lord and Lady Bridgerton were forced to marry, but even if that is true, This Author refuses to believe that theirs is anything but a love match.
LADY WHISTLEDOWN'S SOCIETY PAPERS, 15 JUNE 1814

It was strange, Kate thought as she looked at the morning repast laid upon the side table in the small dining room, how one could feel utterly famished and at the same time have no appetite. Her stomach was rumbling and churning, demanding food now, and yet everything—from the eggs to the scones to the kippers to the roast pork—looked awful.

With a dejected sigh, she reached for a solitary triangle of toast and sank into her chair with a cup of tea.

Anthony had not come home last night.

Kate took a nibble of the toast and forced it down. She'd been hoping that he might at least make an appearance in time for breakfast. She'd delayed the meal as long as she could—it was already nearly eleven in the morning and she usually ate at nine—but her husband was still absent.

"Lady Bridgerton?"

Kate looked up and blinked. A footman was standing

before her bearing a small cream-colored envelope.

"This arrived for you a few minutes ago," he said.

Kate murmured her thanks and reached for the envelope, which had been secured with a neat dollop of pale pink sealing wax. Bringing it closer to her eyes, she made out the initials *EOB*. One of Anthony's relations? The E would be Eloise, of course, since all of the Bridgertons had been named in alphabetical order.

Kate carefully broke the seal and slipped out the contents—a single piece of paper, neatly folded in half.

Kate—

Anthony is here. He looks a wreck. It is, of course, none of my business, but I thought you might like to know.

Eloise

Kate stared at the note a few seconds longer, then shoved her chair back and stood. It was time she paid a call upon Bridgerton House.

Much to Kate's surprise, when she knocked at Bridgerton House, the door was swung open not by the butler but by Eloise, who immediately said, "That was fast!"

Kate looked around the hall, half expecting another Bridgerton sibling or two to jump out at her. "Were you waiting for me?"

Eloise nodded. "And you don't have to knock at the door, you know. Bridgerton House belongs to Anthony, after all. And you *are* his wife."

Kate smiled weakly. She didn't feel much like a wife this morning.

"I hope you don't think me a hopeless meddler," Eloise continued, linking her arm through Kate's and guiding her down the hall, "but Anthony does look awful, and I had a sneaking suspicion you didn't know he was here."

"Why would you think that?" Kate couldn't help asking.

"Well," Eloise said, "he didn't go to any great pains to tell any of *us* that he was here."

Kate eyed her sister-in-law suspiciously. "Meaning?"

Eloise had the grace to blush a faint pink. "Meaning, ah, that the only reason I know he's here is that I was spying upon him. I don't think my mother even knows he's in residence."

Kate felt her eyelids blink in rapid succession. "You've been spying upon us?"

"No, of course not. But I happened to be up and about rather early this morning, and I heard someone come in, and so I went to investigate and I saw light coming from under the door in his study."

"How, then, do you know he looks awful?"

Eloise shrugged. "I figured he'd have to emerge eventually to eat or relieve himself, so I waited on the steps for an hour or so—"

"Or so?" Kate echoed.

"Or three," Eloise admitted. "It's really not that long when one is interested in one's subject, and besides, I had a book with me to while away the time."

Kate shook her head in reluctant admiration. "What time did he come in last night?"

"Around four or so."

"What were you doing up so late?"

Eloise shrugged again. "I couldn't sleep. I often can't. I'd gone down to get a book to read from the library. Finally, at around seven—well, I suppose it was a bit before seven, so it wasn't quite three hours I waited—"

Kate began to feel dizzy.

"—he emerged. He didn't head in the direction of the breakfast room, so I can only assume it was for other reasons. After a minute or two, he reemerged and headed back into his study. Where," Eloise finished with a flourish, "he has been ever since."

Kate stared at her for a good ten seconds. "Have you

ever considered offering your services to the War Department?"

Eloise grinned, a smile so like Anthony's Kate almost cried. "As a spy?" she asked.

Kate nodded.

"I'd be brilliant, don't you think?"

"Superb."

Eloise gave Kate a spontaneous hug. "I'm so glad you married my brother. Now go and see what is wrong."

Kate nodded, straightened her shoulders, and took a step toward Anthony's study. Turning around, she pointed a finger at Eloise and said, "You will not be listening at the door."

"I wouldn't dream of it," Eloise replied.

"I mean it, Eloise!"

Eloise sighed. "It's time I went up to bed, anyway. I could use a nap after staying up all night."

Kate waited until the younger girl had disappeared up the stairs, then made her way to Anthony's study door. She put her hand on the knob, whispering, "Don't be locked," as she gave it a twist. To her extreme relief, it turned, and the door swung open.

"Anthony?" she called out. Her voice was soft and hesitant, and she found she didn't like the sound of it. She wasn't used to being soft and hesitant.

There was no reply, so Kate stepped farther into the room. The drapes were tightly closed, and the heavy velvet admitted little light. Kate scanned the room until her eyes fell on the figure of her husband, slouched over his desk, sound asleep.

Kate walked quietly across the room to the windows and pulled the drapes partway open. She didn't want to blind Anthony when he woke up, but at the same time, she wasn't going to conduct such an important conversation in the dark. Then she walked back over to his desk and gently shook his shoulder.

"Anthony?" she whispered. "Anthony?"

His reply was closer to a snore than anything else.

Frowning impatiently, she shook a little harder. "Anthony?" she said softly. "Anthon—"

"Yibbledeedad—!" He came awake in one sudden movement, an incoherent rush of speech bursting forth as his torso snapped upright.

Kate watched as he blinked himself into coherency, then focused on her. "Kate," he said, his voice hoarse and husky with sleep and something else—maybe alcohol. "What are you doing here?"

"What are *you* doing here?" she countered. "The last time I checked, we lived nearly a mile away."

"I didn't want to disturb you," he mumbled.

Kate didn't believe that for one second, but she decided not to argue the point. Instead, she opted for the direct approach and asked, "Why did you leave last night?"

A long stretch of silence was followed by a weary, tired sigh, and Anthony finally said, "It's complicated."

Kate fought the urge to cross her arms. "I'm an intelligent woman," she said in a purposefully even voice. "I'm generally able to grasp complex concepts."

Anthony didn't look pleased by her sarcasm. "I don't want to go into this now."

"When *do* you want to go into it?"

"Go home, Kate," he said softly.

"Do you plan to come with me?"

Anthony let out a little groan as he raked a hand through his hair. Christ, she was like a dog with a bone. His head was pounding, his mouth tasted like wool, all he really wanted to do was splash some water on his face and clean his teeth, and here his wife would not stop *interrogating him. . . .*

"Anthony?" she persisted.

That was *enough.* He stood so suddenly that his chair tipped back and slammed into the floor with a resounding crash. "You will cease your questions this instant," he bit off.

Her mouth settled into a flat, angry line. But her eyes. . . .

Anthony swallowed against the acidic taste of guilt that flooded his mouth.

Because her eyes were awash with pain.

And the anguish in his own heart grew tenfold.

He wasn't ready. Not yet. He didn't know what to do with her. He didn't know what to do with himself. All his life—or at least since his father had died—he'd known that certain things were true, that certain things *had* to be true. And now Kate had gone and turned his world upside down.

He hadn't wanted to love her. Hell, he hadn't wanted to love anyone. It was the one thing—the only thing—that could make him fear his own mortality. And what about Kate? He'd promised to love and protect her. How could he do that, all the while knowing he would leave her? He certainly couldn't tell her of his odd convictions. Aside from the fact that she'd probably think he was crazy, all it would do was subject her to the same pain and fear that wracked him. Better to let her live in blissful ignorance.

Or was it even better if she didn't love him at all?

Anthony just didn't know the answer. And he needed more time. And he couldn't think with her standing there before him, those pain-filled eyes raking his face. And—

"Go," he choked out. "Just go."

"No," she said with a quiet determination that made him love her all the more. "Not until you tell me what is bothering you."

He strode out from behind his desk and took her arm. "I can't be with you right now," he said hoarsely, his eyes avoiding hers. "Tomorrow. I'll see you tomorrow. Or the next day."

"Anthony—"

"I need time to think."

"About *what*?" she cried out.

"Don't make this any harder than—"

"How could it possibly get any harder?" she demanded. "I don't even know what you're talking about."

"I just need a few days," he said, feeling like an echo. Just a few days to think. To figure out what he was going to do, how he was going to live his life.

But she twisted around until she was facing him, and then her hand was on his cheek, touching him with a tenderness that made his heart ache. "Anthony," she whispered, "please . . ."

He couldn't form a word, couldn't make a sound.

Her hand slipped to the back of his head, and then she was drawing him closer . . . closer . . . and he couldn't help himself. He wanted her so damned badly, wanted to feel her body pressed against his, to taste the faint salt of her skin. He wanted to smell her, to touch her, to hear the rasp of her breath in his ear.

Her lips touched his, soft and seeking, and her tongue tickled the corner of her mouth. It would be so easy to lose himself in her, to sink down to the carpet and . . .

"No!" The word was ripped from his throat, and by God, he'd had no idea it was there until it burst forth.

"No," he said again, pushing her away. "Not now."

"But—"

He didn't deserve her. Not right now. Not yet. Not until he understood how he was meant to live out the rest of his life. And if it meant he had to deny himself the one thing that might bring him salvation, so be it.

"Go," he ordered, his voice sounding a bit more harsh than he'd intended. "Go now. I'll see you later."

And this time, she did go.

She went, without looking back.

And Anthony, who'd only just learned what it was to love, learned what it was to die inside.

By the following morning, Anthony was drunk. By afternoon, he was hungover.

His head was pounding, his ears were ringing, and his

brothers, who had been surprised to discover him in such a state at their club, were talking *far* too loudly.

Anthony put his hands over his ears and groaned. *Everyone* was talking far too loudly.

"Kate boot you out of the house?" Colin asked, grabbing a walnut from a large pewter dish in the middle their table and splitting it open with a viciously loud crack.

Anthony lifted his head just far enough to glare at him.

Benedict watched his brother with raised brows and the vaguest hint of a smirk. "She definitely booted him out," he said to Colin. "Hand me one of those walnuts, will you?"

Colin tossed one across the table. "Do you want the crackers as well?"

Benedict shook his head and grinned as he held up a fat, leather-bound book. "Much more satisfying to smash them."

"Don't," Anthony bit out, his hand shooting out to grab the book, "even think about it."

"Ears a bit sensitive this afternoon, are they?"

If Anthony had had a pistol, he would have shot them both, hang the noise.

"If I might offer you a piece of advice?" Colin said, munching on his walnut.

"You might not," Anthony replied. He looked up. Colin was chewing with his mouth open. As this had been strictly forbidden while growing up in their household, Anthony could only deduce that Colin was displaying such poor manners only to make more noise. "Close your damned mouth," he muttered.

Colin swallowed, smacked his lips, and took a sip of his tea to wash it all down. "Whatever you did, apologize for it. I know you, and I'm getting to know Kate, and knowing what I know—"

"What the hell is he talking about?" Anthony grumbled.

"I think," Benedict said, leaning back in his chair, "that he's telling you you're an ass."

"Just so!" Colin exclaimed.

Anthony just shook his head wearily. "It's more complicated than you think."

"It always is," Benedict said, with sincerity so false it almost managed to sound sincere.

"When you two idiots find women gullible enough to actually marry you," Anthony snapped, "then you may presume to offer me advice. But until then . . . *shut up*."

Colin looked at Benedict. "Think he's angry?"

Benedict quirked a brow. "That or drunk."

Colin shook his head. "No, not drunk. Not anymore, at least. He's clearly hungover."

"Which would explain," Benedict said with a philosophical nod, "why he's so angry."

Anthony spread one hand over his face and pressed hard against his temples with his thumb and middle finger. "God above," he muttered. "What would it take to get you two to leave me alone?"

"Go home, Anthony," Benedict said, his voice surprisingly gentle.

Anthony closed his eyes and let out a long breath. There was nothing he wanted to do more, but he wasn't sure what to say to Kate, and more importantly, he had no idea how he'd feel once he got there.

"Yes," Colin agreed. "Just go home and tell her that you love her. What could be more simple?"

And suddenly it *was* simple. He had to tell Kate that he loved her. Now. This very day. He had to make sure she *knew*, and he vowed to spend every last minute of his miserably short life proving it to her.

It was too late to change the destiny of his heart. He'd tried not to fall in love, and he'd failed. Since he wasn't likely to fall back *out* of love, he might as well make the best of the situation. He was going to be haunted by the premonition of his own death whether or not Kate knew of his love for her. Wouldn't he be happier during these last few years if he spent them loving her openly and honestly?

He was fairly certain she'd fallen in love with him as well; surely she'd be glad to hear that he felt the same way. And when a man loved a woman, truly loved her from the depths of her soul to the tips of her toes, wasn't it his God-given duty to try to make her happy?

He wouldn't tell her of his premonitions, though. What would be the point? He might suffer the knowledge that their time together would be cut short, but why should she? Better she be struck by sharp and sudden pain at his death than suffer the anticipation of it beforehand.

He was going to die. Everyone died, he reminded himself. He was just going to have to do it sooner rather than later. But by God, he was going to enjoy his last years with every breath of his being. It might have been more convenient not to have fallen in love, but now that he had, he wasn't going to hide from it.

It was simple. His world was Kate. If he denied that, he might as well stop breathing right now.

"I have to go," he blurted out, standing up so suddenly that his thighs hit the edge of the table, sending walnut shell shards skittering across the tabletop.

"I thought you might," Colin murmured.

Benedict just smiled and said, "Go."

His brothers, Anthony realized, were a bit smarter than they let on.

"We'll speak to you in a week or so?" Colin asked.

Anthony had to grin. He and his brothers had met at their club every day for the past fortnight. Colin's oh-so-innocent query could only imply one thing—that it was obvious that Anthony had completely lost his heart to his wife and planned to spend at least the next seven days proving it to her. And that the family he was creating had grown as important as the one he'd been born into.

"Two weeks," Anthony replied, yanking on his coat. "Maybe three."

His brothers just grinned.

* * *

But when Anthony pushed through the door of his home, slightly out of breath from taking the front steps three at a time, he discovered that Kate was not in.

"Where did she go?" he asked the butler. Stupidly, he'd never once considered that she might not be at home.

"Out for a ride in the park," the butler replied, "with her sister and a Mr. Bagwell."

"Edwina's suitor," Anthony muttered to himself. Damn. He supposed he ought to be happy for his sister-in-law, but the timing was bloody annoying. He'd just made a life-altering decision regarding his wife; it would have been nice if she'd been home.

"Her *creature* went as well," the butler said with a shudder. He'd never been able to tolerate what he considered the corgi's invasion into his home.

"She took Newton, eh?" Anthony murmured.

"I imagine they'll be back within an hour or two."

Anthony tapped his booted toe against the marble floor. He didn't want to wait an hour. Hell, he didn't want to wait even a minute. "I'll find them myself," he said impatiently. "It can't be that difficult."

The butler nodded and motioned through the open doorway to the small carriage in which Anthony had ridden home. "Will you be needing another carriage?"

Anthony gave his head a single shake. "I'll go on horseback. It'll be quicker."

"Very well." The butler bent into a small bow. "I'll have a mount brought 'round."

Anthony watched the butler make his slow and sedate way toward the rear of the house for about two seconds before impatience set in. "I'll take care of it myself," he barked.

And the next thing he knew, he was dashing out of the house.

Anthony was in jaunty spirits by the time he reached Hyde Park. He was eager to find his wife, to hold her in his arms and watch her face as he told her he loved her. He prayed that she would offer words returning the sentiment. He thought she would; he'd seen her heart in her eyes on more than one occasion. Perhaps she was just waiting for him to say something first. He couldn't blame her if that was the case; he'd made a rather big fuss about how theirs would *not* be a love match right before their wedding.

What an idiot he'd been.

Once he entered the park, he made the decision to turn his mount and head over to Rotten Row. The busy path seemed the most likely destination for the threesome; Kate certainly would have no reason to encourage a more private route.

He nudged his horse into as fast a trot as he could safely manage within the confines of the park, trying to ignore the calls and waves of greeting that were directed his way by other riders and pedestrians.

Then, just when he thought he'd made it through without delay, he heard an aged, female, and very imperious voice call out his name.

"Bridgerton! I say, Bridgerton! Stop at once. I'm speaking to you!"

He groaned as he turned about. Lady Danbury, the dragon of the *ton*. There was simply no way he could ignore her. He had no idea how old she was. Sixty? Seventy? Whatever her age, she was a force of nature, and *no one* ignored her.

"Lady Danbury," he said, trying not to sound resigned as he reined in his mount. "How nice to see you."

"Good gad, boy," she barked, "you sound as if you've just taken an antidote. Perk up!"

Anthony smiled weakly.

"Where's your wife?"

"I'm looking for her right now," he replied, "or at least I *was*."

Lady Danbury was far too sharp to miss his pointed

hint, so he could only deduce that she ignored him apurpose when she said, "I like your wife."

"I like her, too."

"Never could understand why you were so set on courting her sister. Nice gel, but clearly not for you." She rolled her eyes and let out an indignant huff. "The world would be a much happier place if people would just listen to me before they up and got married," she added. "I could have the entire Marriage Mart matched up in a week."

"I'm sure you could."

Her eyes narrowed. "Are you patronizing me?"

"I wouldn't dream of it," Anthony said with complete honesty.

"Good. You always seemed like the sensible sort. I . . ." Her mouth fell open. "What the devil is that?"

Anthony followed Lady Danbury's horrified gaze until his eyes fell on an open-topped carriage careening out of control as it rounded a corner on two wheels. It was still too far to see the faces of the occupants, but then he heard a shriek, and then the terrified bark of a dog.

Anthony's blood froze in his veins.

His wife was in that carriage.

With nary a word to Lady Danbury, he kicked his horse into motion and galloped full speed ahead. He wasn't sure what he'd do once he reached the carriage. Maybe he'd grab the reins from the hapless driver. Maybe he'd be able to pull someone to safety. But he knew that he could not sit still and watch while the vehicle crashed before his eyes.

And yet that was exactly what happened.

Anthony was halfway to the drunken carriage when it veered off the path and ran up over a large rock, upsetting the balance and sending it tumbling onto its side.

And Anthony could only watch in horror as his wife died before his eyes.

Chapter 22

Contrary to popular opinion, This Author is aware that she is viewed as something of a cynic.

But that, Dear Reader, could not be further from the truth. This Author likes nothing better than a happy ending. And if that makes her a romantic fool, so be it.

LADY WHISTLEDOWN'S SOCIETY PAPERS, 15 JUNE 1814

By the time Anthony reached the overturned carriage, Edwina had managed to crawl from the wreckage and was clawing at a mangled piece of wood, trying to open a hole on the other side of the carriage. The sleeve of her dress was torn, and the hem was ragged and dirty, but she seemed not to notice as she tugged frantically at the door. Newton was jumping and squirming at her feet, his barks sharp and frenzied.

"What happened?" Anthony asked, his voice curt and panicked as he leapt from his horse.

"I don't know," Edwina gasped, wiping at the streaky tears that ran down her face. "Mr. Bagwell's not such an experienced driver, I think, and then Newton got loose, and then I don't know *what* happened. One minute we were rolling along, and the next—"

"Where is Bagwell?"

She motioned to the other side of the carriage. "He was thrown. He hit his head. But he'll be all right. But Kate . . ."

"What about Kate?" Anthony dropped to his knees as he tried to peer into the wreckage. The entire carriage had overturned, smashing the right side of the vehicle as it had rolled. "Where is she?"

Edwina swallowed convulsively, and her voice barely rose above a whisper as she said, "I think she's trapped beneath the carriage."

In that moment Anthony tasted death. It was bitter in his throat, metallic and hard. It scraped his flesh like a knife, choking and squeezing, pulling the air from his very lungs.

Anthony yanked viciously at the wreckage, trying to open a wider hole. It wasn't as bad as it had looked during the crash, but that did little to calm his racing heart. "Kate!" he yelled, trying to sound calm and unworried. "Kate, can you hear me?"

The only sound he heard in reply, however, was the frantic whinny of the horses. Damn. He'd have to get them unharnessed and loose before they panicked and started trying to drag the debris. "Edwina?" Anthony called sharply, looking over his shoulder.

She hurried over, wringing her hands. "Yes?"

"Do you know how to unharness the horses?"

She nodded. "I'm not very fast, but I can do it."

Anthony flicked his head toward the onlookers who were hurrying over. "See if you can find someone to help you."

She nodded again and quickly got to work.

"Kate?" Anthony yelled again. He couldn't see anyone; a dislodged bench was blocking the opening. "Can you hear me?"

Still no response.

"Try the other side," came Edwina's frantic voice. "The opening isn't as crushed."

Anthony jumped to his feet and ran around the back of the carriage to the other side. The door had already come off its hinges, leaving a hole just large enough for him to stuff his upper body into. "Kate?" he called out, trying not to notice the sharp sound of panic in his voice. Every breath from his lips seemed overloud, reverberating in the tight space, reminding him that he wasn't hearing the same sounds from Kate.

And then, as he carefully moved a seat cushion that had turned sideways, he saw her. She was terrifyingly still, but her head didn't appear to be stuck in an unnatural position, and he didn't see any blood.

That had to be a good sign. He didn't know much of medicine, but he held on to that thought like a miracle.

"You can't die, Kate," he said as his terrified fingers yanked away at the wreckage, desperate to open the hole until it was wide enough to pull her through. "Do you hear me? *You can't die!*"

A jagged piece of wood sliced open the back of his hand, but Anthony didn't notice the blood running over his skin as he pulled on another broken beam. "You had better be breathing," he warned, his voice shaking and precariously close to a sob. "This wasn't supposed to be you. It was never supposed to be you. It isn't your time. Do you understand me?"

He tore away another broken piece of wood and reached through the newly widened hole to grasp her hand. His fingers found her pulse, which seemed steady enough to him, but it was still impossible to tell if she was bleeding, or had broken her back, or had hit her head, or had . . .

His heart shuddered. There were so many ways to die. If a bee could bring down a man in his prime, surely a carriage accident could steal the life of one small woman.

Anthony grabbed the last piece of wood that stood in his way and heaved, but it didn't budge. "Don't do this to me," he muttered. "Not now. It isn't her time. Do you hear me? It isn't her time!" He felt something wet on his cheeks and dimly realized that it was tears. "It was supposed to be me," he said, choking on the words. "It was always supposed to be me."

And then, just as he was preparing to give that last piece of wood another desperate yank, Kate's fingers tightened like a claw around his wrist. His eyes flew to her face, just in time to see her eyes open wide and clear, with nary a blink.

"What the devil," she asked, sounding quite lucid and utterly awake, "are you talking about?"

Relief flooded his chest so quickly it was almost painful. "Are you all right?" he asked, his voice wobbling on every syllable.

She grimaced, then said, "I'll be fine."

Anthony paused for the barest of seconds as he considered her choice of words. "But are you fine right now?"

She let out a little cough, and he fancied he could hear her wince with pain. "I did something to my leg," she admitted. "But I don't think I'm bleeding."

"Are you faint? Dizzy? Weak?"

She shook her head. "Just in pain. What are you doing here?"

He smiled through his tears. "I came to find you."

"You did?" she whispered.

He nodded. "I came to— That is to say, I realized . . ." He swallowed convulsively. He'd never dreamed that the day would come when he'd say these words to a woman, and they'd grown so big in his heart he could barely squeeze them out. "I love you, Kate," he said chokingly. "It took me a while to figure it out, but I do, and I had to tell you. Today."

Her lips wobbled into a shaky smile as she motioned to the rest of her body with her chin. "You've bloody good timing."

Amazingly, he found himself grinning in return. "Almost makes you glad I waited so long, eh? If I'd told you last week, I wouldn't have followed you out to the park today."

She stuck out her tongue, which, considering the circumstances, made him love her even more. "Just get me out," she said.

"Then you'll tell me you love me?" he teased.

She smiled, wistful and warm, and nodded.

It was, of course, as good as a declaration, and even though he was crawling through the wreckage of an overturned carriage, even though Kate was *stuck* in the cursed carriage, with what might very well be a broken leg, he was suddenly consumed with an overwhelming sense of contentment and peace.

And he realized he hadn't felt that way for nearly twelve years, not since that fateful afternoon when he'd walked into his parents' bedroom and seen his father laid out on the bed, cold and still.

"I'm going to pull you through now," he said, sliding his arms beneath her back. "It'll hurt your leg, I'm afraid, but it can't be avoided."

"My leg already hurts," she said, smiling bravely. "I just want to get out."

Anthony gave her a single, serious nod, then curved his hands around her side and began to pull. "How is that?" he asked, his heart stopping every time he saw her wince with pain.

"Fine," she gasped, but he could tell she was merely putting up a brave front.

"I'm going to have to turn you," he said, eyeing a broken and jagged piece of wood that stuck down from above. It was going to be difficult to maneuver her around it. He couldn't care less if he tore her clothing—hell, he'd buy her a hundred new dresses if she'd only promise never again to step into a carriage if it was being driven by anyone other than himself. But he couldn't bear the thought of scratching even an inch of her skin. She'd been through enough already. She didn't need more.

"I need to pull you out headfirst," he told her. "Do you think you can wiggle yourself around? Just enough so I can grasp under your arms."

She nodded, gritting her teeth as she painstakingly turned herself inch by inch, lifting herself up on her hands as she scooted her hips around clockwise.

"There you are," Anthony said encouragingly. "Now I'm going to—"

"Just do it," Kate ground out. "You don't need to explain."

"Very well," he replied, inching backward until his knees found purchase on the grass. On a mental count of three, he gritted his teeth and began to pull her out.

And stopped a second later, as Kate let out an earsplitting scream. If he hadn't been so convinced that he'd die within the next nine years, he would have sworn she'd just taken ten off his life.

"Are you all right?" he asked urgently.

"I'm fine," she insisted. But she was breathing hard, puffing through pursed lips, and her face was tense with pain.

"What happened?" came a voice from just outside the carriage. It was Edwina, done with the horses and sounding frantic. "I heard Kate scream."

"Edwina?" Kate asked, twisting her neck as she tried to see out. "Are you all right?" She yanked on Anthony's sleeve. "Is Edwina all right? Is she hurt? Does she need a doctor?"

"Edwina's fine," he replied. "*You* need a doctor."

"And Mr. Bagwell?"

"How's Bagwell?" Anthony asked Edwina, his voice curt as he concentrated on maneuvering Kate around the debris.

"A bump on his head, but he's back on his feet."

"It's nothing. Can I help?" came a worried male voice.

Anthony had a feeling that the accident had been as much Newton's fault as Bagwell's, but still, the young man had been in control of the reins, and Anthony wasn't inclined to feel charitable toward him just now. "I'll let you know," he said curtly, before turning back to Kate and saying, "Bagwell's fine."

"I can't believe I forgot to ask after them."

"I'm sure your lapse will be pardoned, given the circumstances," Anthony said, edging farther back until he was nearly entirely out of the carriage. Kate was now positioned at the opening, and it would take only one more—rather long and almost certainly painful—tug to get her out.

"Edwina? Edwina?" Kate was calling out. "Are you sure you're not injured?"

Edwina jammed her face into the opening. "I'm fine," she said reassuringly. "Mr. Bagwell was thrown clear, and I was able to—"

Anthony elbowed her out of the way. "Grit your teeth, Kate," he ordered.

"What? I— *Aaaaaaaargh*!"

With one single tug, he freed her completely from the wreckage, both of them landing on the ground, both of them breathing hard. But where Anthony's hyperventilation was from exertion, Kate's was obviously from intense pain.

"Good God!" Edwina nearly yelled. "Look at her leg!"

Anthony glanced over at Kate and felt his stomach drop down clear to his toes. Her lower leg was crooked and bent, and more than obviously broken. He swallowed convulsively, trying not to let his concern show. Legs could be set, but he'd also heard of men who'd lost limbs due to infection and bad medical care.

"What's wrong with my leg?" Kate asked. "It hurts, but— Oh, my God!"

"Best not to look," Anthony said, trying to tip her chin in the other direction.

Her breathing, which was already rapid from trying to control the pain, grew erratic and panicked. "Oh, my

God," she gasped. "It hurts. Didn't realize how much it hurt until I saw—"

"Don't look," Anthony ordered.

"Oh, my God. Oh, my God."

"Kate?" Edwina asked in a concerned voice, leaning in. "Are you all right?"

"Look at my leg!" Kate nearly shrieked. "Does it look all right?"

"I was actually speaking of your face. You look a bit green."

But Kate couldn't reply. She was hyperventilating too hard. And then, with Anthony, Edwina, Mr. Bagwell, and Newton all staring down at her, her eyes rolled back in her head, and she fainted.

Three hours later, Kate was installed in her bed, certainly not comfortable but at least in a bit less pain thanks to the laudanum Anthony had forced down her throat the minute they'd gotten home. Her leg had been expertly set by the three surgeons Anthony had summoned (not, as all three surgeons had pointed out, that more than one was needed to set a bone, but Anthony had crossed his arms implacably and stared them all down until they'd shut up), and a physician had stopped by to leave several prescriptions that he swore would hasten the bone-knitting process.

Anthony had fussed over her like a mother hen, second-guessing every move from every doctor until one of them had actually had the audacity to ask him when he'd received his license from the Royal College of Physicians.

Anthony had not been amused.

But after much haranguing, Kate's leg was set and splinted, and she was told to look forward to at least a month of confinement in bed.

"Look forward?" she groaned to Anthony once the last of the surgeons had gone. "How can I look forward to that?"

"You'll be able to catch up on your reading," he suggested.

She let out an impatient exhale through her nose; it was hard to breathe through her mouth while clenching her teeth. "I wasn't aware I was behind on my reading."

If he'd been tempted to laugh, he did a good job of hiding it. "Perhaps you could take up needlework," he suggested.

She just glared at him. As if the prospect of needlework were going to make her feel better.

He sat gingerly on the edge of her bed and patted the back of her hand. "I'll keep you company," he said with an encouraging smile. "I'd already decided to cut back on the time I spent at my club."

Kate sighed. She was tired and cranky and in pain, and she was taking it out on her husband, which really wasn't fair. She turned her hand over so that their palms met and then entwined her fingers through his. "I love you, you know," she said softly.

He squeezed her hands and nodded, the warmth of his eyes on hers saying more than words ever could.

"You told me not to," Kate said.

"I was an ass."

She didn't argue; a quirk of his lips told her that he noticed her lack of contradiction. After a moment of silence, she said, "You were saying some odd things in the park."

Anthony's hand remained in hers, but his body pulled back slightly. "I don't know what you mean," he replied.

"I think you do," she said softly.

Anthony closed his eyes for a moment, then stood, his fingers trailing through her grasp until finally they were no longer touching at all. For so many years he'd been careful to keep his odd convictions to himself. It seemed best. Either people would believe him and then worry or they wouldn't and then think him insane.

Neither option was particularly appealing.

But now, in the heat of one terrified moment, he'd blurted it out to his wife. He couldn't even remember exactly what he'd said. But it had been enough to make her curious. And Kate wasn't the sort to let go of a curiosity. He could practice all the avoidance he wanted, but eventually she'd get it out of him. A more stubborn woman had never been born.

He walked to the window and leaned against the sill, gazing blankly in front of him as if he could actually see the streetscape through the heavy burgundy drapes that had long since been pulled shut. "There is something you should know about me," he whispered.

She didn't say anything, but he knew she'd heard. Maybe it was the sound of her changing her position in bed, maybe it was the sheer electricity in the air. But somehow he knew.

He turned around. It would have been easier to speak his words to the curtains, but she deserved better from him. She was sitting up in bed, her leg propped up on pillows, her eyes wide and filled with a heartbreaking mix of curiosity and concern.

"I don't know how to tell you this without sounding ridiculous," he said.

"Sometimes the easiest way is just to say it," she murmured. She patted an empty spot on the bed. "Do you want to sit beside me?"

He shook his head. Proximity would only make it that much more difficult. "Something happened to me when my father died," he said.

"You were very close to him, weren't you?"

He nodded. "Closer than I'd ever been to anyone, until I met you."

Her eyes glistened. "What happened?"

"It was very unexpected," he said. His voice was flat, as if he were recounting an obscure news item and not the single most disturbing event of his life. "A bee, I told you."

She nodded.

"Who would have thought a bee could kill a man?" Anthony said with a caustic laugh. "It would have been funny if it weren't so tragic."

She didn't say anything, just looked at him with a sympathy that made his heart break.

"I stayed with him throughout the night," he continued, turning slightly so that he would not have to look into her eyes. "He was dead, of course, but I needed a little more time. I just sat beside him and watched his face." Another short burst of angry laughter escaped his lips. "God, what a fool I was. I think I half expected him to open his eyes at any moment."

"I don't think that's foolish," Kate said softly. "I've seen death, too. It's hard to believe that someone is gone when he looks so normal and at peace."

"I don't know when it happened," Anthony said, "but by morning I was sure."

"That he was dead?" she asked.

"No," he said roughly, "that I would be, too."

He waited for her to comment, he waited for her to cry, to do anything, but she just sat there staring at him with no perceptible change of expression, until finally he had to say, "I'm not as great a man as my father was."

"He might choose to disagree," she said quietly.

"Well, he's not here to do that, is he?" Anthony snapped.

Again, she said nothing. Again, he felt like a heel.

He cursed under his breath and pressed his fingers against his temples. His head was starting to throb. He was starting to feel dizzy, and he realized that he couldn't remember the last time he'd eaten. "It's my judgment to make," he said in a low voice. "You didn't know him."

He sagged against a wall with a long, weary exhale, and said, "Just let me tell you. Don't talk, don't interrupt, don't judge. It's hard enough to get it out as it is. Can you do that for me?"

She nodded.

Anthony took a shaky breath. "My father was the greatest man I've ever known. Not a day goes by when I don't realize that I'm not living up to his standards. I knew that he was everything to which I could aspire. I might not ever match his greatness, but if I could come close I'd be satisfied. That's all I ever wanted. Just to come close."

He looked at Kate. He wasn't sure why. Maybe for reassurance, maybe for sympathy. Maybe just to see her face.

"If there was one thing I knew," he whispered, somehow finding the courage to keep his eyes focused on hers, "it was that I would never surpass him. Not even in years."

"What are you trying to tell me?" she whispered.

He shrugged helplessly. "I know it makes no sense. I know I can offer no rational explanation. But since that night when I sat with my father's dead body, I knew I couldn't possibly live any longer than he had."

"I see," she said quietly.

"Do you?" And then, as if a dam had burst, the words poured forth. It all gushed out of him—why he'd been so dead set against marrying for love, the jealousy he'd felt when he'd realized that she'd managed to fight her demons and win.

He watched as she brought one of her hands to her mouth and bit the end of her thumb. He'd seen her do that before, he realized—whenever she was disturbed or deep in thought.

"How old was your father when he died?" she asked.

"Thirty-eight."

"How old are you now?"

He looked at her curiously; she knew his age. But he said it anyway. "Twenty-nine."

"So by your estimation, we have nine years left."

"At most."

"And you truly believe this."

He nodded.

She pursed her lips and let out a long breath through her nose. Finally, after what felt like an endless silence, she looked back up at him with clear, direct eyes, and said, "Well, you're wrong."

Oddly enough, the straightforward tone of her voice was rather reassuring. Anthony even felt one corner of his mouth lift up in the palest of smiles. "You think I'm unaware of how ludicrous it all sounds?"

"I don't think it sounds ludicrous at all. It sounds like a perfectly normal reaction, actually, especially considering how much you adored your father." She lifted her shoulders in a rather self-aware shrug as her head tipped to the side. "But it's still wrong."

Anthony didn't say anything.

"Your father's death was an accident," Kate said. "An accident. A terrible, horrible twist of fate that no one could have predicted."

Anthony shrugged fatalistically. "I'll probably go the same way."

"Oh, for the love of—" Kate managed to bite her tongue a split second before she blasphemed. "Anthony, I could die tomorrow as well. I could have died today when that carriage rolled on top of me."

He paled. "Don't ever remind me of that."

"My mother died when she was my age," Kate reminded him harshly. "Did you ever think of that? By your laws, I should be dead by my next birthday."

"Don't be—"

"Silly?" she finished for him.

Silence reigned for a full minute.

Finally, Anthony said, his voice barely above a whisper, "I don't know if I can get past this."

"You don't have to get past it," Kate said. She caught her lower lip, which had begun to tremble, between her teeth, and then laid her hand on an empty spot on the bed. "Could you come over here so I can hold your hand?"

Anthony responded instantly; the warmth of her touch

flooded him, seeping through his body until it caressed his very soul. And in that moment he realized that this was about more than love. This woman made him a better person. He'd been good and strong and kind before, but with her at his side, he was something more.

And together they could do anything.

It almost made him think that forty might not be such an impossible dream.

"You don't have to get past it," she said again, her words blowing softly between them. "To be honest, I don't see how you *could* get completely past it until you turn thirty-nine. But what you *can* do"—she gave his hand a squeeze, and Anthony somehow felt even stronger than he had just moments before—"is refuse to allow it to rule your life."

"I realized that this morning," he whispered, "when I knew I had to tell you I loved you. But somehow now—now I *know* it."

She nodded, and he saw that her eyes were filling with tears. "You have to live each hour as if it's your last," she said, "and each day as if you were immortal. When my father grew ill, he had so many regrets. There were so many things he wished he'd done, he told me. He'd always assumed he had more time. That's something I've always carried with me. Why on earth do you think I decided to attempt the flute at such an advanced age? Everyone told me I was too old, that to be truly good at it I had to have started as a child. But that's not the point, really. I don't need to be truly good. I just need to enjoy it for myself. And I need to know I tried."

Anthony smiled. She was a terrible flutist. Even Newton couldn't bear to listen.

"But the opposite is true as well," Kate added softly. "You can't shun new challenges or hide yourself from love just because you think you might not be here to carry your dreams to completion. In the end, you'll have just as many regrets as did my father."

"I didn't want to love you," Anthony whispered. "It was

the one thing I feared above all. I'd grown rather used to my rather odd little outlook on life. Almost comfortable, actually. But love—" His voice caught; the choking sound seemed unmanly, it made him vulnerable. But he didn't care, because this was Kate.

And it didn't matter if she saw his deepest fears, because he knew she'd love him no matter what. It was a sublimely freeing feeling.

"I've seen true love," he continued. "I wasn't the cynical jade society made me out to be. I knew love existed. My mother—my father—" He stopped, sucking in a ragged breath. This was the hardest thing he'd ever done. And yet he knew the words had to be said. He knew, no matter how difficult it was to get them out, that in the end, his heart would soar.

"I was so sure that it was the one thing that could make this . . . this . . . I don't really know what to call it—this knowledge of my own mortality . . ." He raked his hand through his hair, fighting for words. "Love was the only thing that was going to make that unbearable. How could I love someone, truly and deeply, knowing that it was doomed?"

"But it's not doomed," Kate said, squeezing his hand.

"I know. I fell in love with you, and then I knew. Even if I am right, even if I'm fated to live only as long as my father did before me, I'm not doomed." He leaned forward and brushed a feather-light kiss on her lips. "I have you," he whispered, "and I'm not going to waste a single moment we have together."

Kate's lips spread into a smile. "What does that mean?"

"It means that love isn't about being afraid that it will all be snatched away. Love's about finding the one person who makes your heart complete, who makes you a better person than you ever dreamed you could be. It's about looking in the eyes of your wife and knowing, all the way to your bones, that she's simply the best person you've ever known."

"Oh, Anthony," Kate whispered, tears streaming down her cheeks. "That's how I feel about you."

"When I thought you'd died—"

"Don't say it," she choked out. "You don't have to relive that."

"No," he said. "I do. I have to tell you. It was the first time—even after all these years of expecting my own death—that I truly knew what it meant to die. Because with you gone . . . there was nothing left for me to live for. I don't know how my mother did it."

"She had her children," Kate said. "She couldn't leave you."

"I know," he whispered, "but the pain she must have endured . . ."

"I think the human heart must be stronger than we could ever imagine."

Anthony stared at her for a long moment, his eyes locking with hers until he felt they must be one person. Then, with a shaking hand, he cupped the back of her head and leaned down to kiss her. His lips worshiped hers, offering her every ounce of love and devotion and reverence and prayer that he felt in his soul.

"I love you, Kate," he whispered, his lips brushing the words against her mouth. "I love you so much."

She nodded, unable to make a sound.

"And right now I wish . . . I wish . . ."

And then the strangest thing happened. Laughter bubbled up inside of him. He was overtaken by the pure joy of the moment, and it was all he could do not to pick her up and twirl her grandly through the air.

"Anthony?" she asked, sounding equal parts confused and amused.

"Do you know what else love means?" he murmured, planting his hands on either side of her body and letting his nose rest against hers.

She shook her head. "I couldn't possibly even hazard a guess."

"It means," he grumbled, "that I'm finding this broken leg of yours a damned nuisance."

"Not half so much as I, my lord," she said, casting a rueful glance at her splinted leg.

Anthony frowned. "No vigorous exercise for two months, eh?"

"At least."

He grinned, and in that moment he looked every inch the rake she'd once accused him of being. "Clearly," he murmured, "I shall have to be very, very gentle."

"Tonight?" she croaked.

He shook his head. "Even I haven't the talent to express myself with *that* light a touch."

Kate giggled. She couldn't help herself. She loved this man and he loved her and whether he knew it or not, they were going to grow very, very old together. It was enough to make a girl—even a girl with a broken leg—positively giddy.

"Are you laughing at me?" he queried, one of his brows arching arrogantly as he slid his body into place next to her.

"I wouldn't dream of it."

"Good. Because I have some very important things to tell you."

"Really?"

He nodded gravely. "I may not be able to show you how much I love you this eve, but I can tell you."

"I should never tire of hearing it," she murmured.

"Good. Because when I'm done telling you, I'm going to tell you how I'd like to *show* you."

"Anthony!" she squeaked.

"I think I'd start with your earlobe," he mused. "Yes, definitely the earlobe. I'd kiss it, and then nibble it, and then . . ."

Kate gasped. And then she squirmed. And then she fell in love with him all over again.

And as he whispered sweet nothings in her ear, she had the strangest sensation, almost as if she could see her entire future laid out before her. Each day was richer and fuller than the last, and every day she was falling, falling, falling . . .

Was it possible to fall in love with the same man over and over again, every single day?

Kate sighed as she settled into the pillows, letting his wicked words wash over her.

By God, she was going to try.

Epilogue

Lord Bridgerton celebrated his birthday—This Author believes that it was his thirty-ninth—at home with his family.

This Author was not invited.

Nonetheless, details of the fête have reached This Author's always attentive ears, and it sounds to have been a most amusing party. The day began with a short concert: Lord Bridgerton on the trumpet and Lady Bridgerton on the flute. Mrs. Bagwell (Lady Bridgerton's sister) apparently offered to mediate on the pianoforte, but her offer was refused.

According to the dowager viscountess, a more discordant concert has never been performed, and we are told that eventually young Miles Bridgerton stood atop his chair and begged his parents to cease.

We are also told that no one scolded the boy for his rudeness, but rather just heaved huge sighs of relief when Lord and Lady Bridgerton laid down their instruments.

LADY WHISTLEDOWN'S SOCIETY PAPERS, 17 SEPTEMBER 1823

"She must have a spy in the family," Anthony said to Kate, shaking his head.

Kate laughed as she brushed her hair, readying herself

for bed. "She didn't realize that today is your birthday, not yesterday."

"A trifling matter," he grumbled. "She must have a spy. There's no other explanation."

"She did get everything else right," Kate couldn't help noting. "I tell you, I've always admired that woman."

"We weren't that bad," Anthony protested.

"We were dreadful." She set the brush down and walked to his side. "We're always dreadful. But at least we try."

Anthony wound his arms around his wife's waist and settled his chin on the top of her head. There was little that brought him more peace than simply holding her in his arms. He didn't know how any man survived without a woman to love.

"It's almost midnight," Kate murmured. "Your birthday is almost over."

Anthony nodded. Thirty-nine. He'd never thought he'd see the day.

No, that wasn't true. Since the moment he'd let Kate into his heart, his fears had been slowly melting away. But still, it was nice to be thirty-nine. Settling. He'd spent a goodly portion of the day in his study, staring up at his father's portrait. And he'd found himself talking. For hours on end, he'd talked to his father. He told him of his three children, of his siblings' marriages and their children. He told him of his mother, and how she'd recently taken up painting with oils, and that she was actually quite good. And he told him of Kate, and how she'd freed his soul, and how he loved her so damn much.

It was, Anthony realized, what his father had always wanted for him.

The clock on the mantel began to chime, and neither Anthony nor Kate spoke until the twelfth bell rang.

"That's it, then," Kate whispered.

He nodded. "Let's go to bed."

She moved away, and he could see that she was smiling. "That's how you want to celebrate?"

He took her hand and raised it to his lips. "I can think of no better way. Can you?"

Kate shook her head, then giggled as she ran for the bed. "Did you read what else she wrote in her column?"

"That Whistledown woman?"

She nodded.

Anthony planted his hands on either side of his wife and leered down at her. "Was it about us?"

Kate shook her head.

"Then I don't care."

"It was about Colin."

Anthony let out a little sigh. "She does seem to write about Colin a great deal."

"Maybe she has a *tendre* for him," Kate suggested.

"Lady Whistledown?" Anthony rolled his eyes. "That old biddy?"

"She might not be old."

Anthony snorted derisively. "She's a wrinkled old crone and you know it."

"I don't know," Kate said, scooting out of his grasp and crawling under the covers. "I think she might be young."

"And *I* think," Anthony announced, "that I don't much want to talk about Lady Whistledown just now."

Kate smiled. "You don't?"

He slid into place next to her, his fingers settling around the curve of her hip. "I have much better things to do."

"You do?"

"Much." His lips found her ear. "Much, much, *much* better."

And in a small, elegantly furnished chamber, not so very far from Bridgerton House, a woman—no longer in the first blush of youth, but certainly not wrinkled and old—

sat at her desk with a quill and a pot of ink and pulled out a piece of paper.

Stretching her neck from side to side, she set her quill to paper and wrote:

Lady Whistledown's Society Papers, 19 September, 1823
Ah, Gentle Reader, it has come to This Author's attention . . .

Author's Note

Anthony's reaction to his father's untimely death is a very common one, especially among men. (To a much lesser degree, women whose mothers die young react in a similar fashion.) Men whose fathers die at a very young age are very often gripped by a certainty that they, too, will suffer the same fate. Such men usually know their fears are irrational, but it is nearly impossible to get past these fears until one has reached (and passed) the age of one's father's death.

Since my readers are almost exclusively women, and Anthony's issue is such (to use a very modern phrase) a "guy thing," I worried that you might not be able to relate to his problem. As a writer of romance, I constantly find myself walking a fine line between making my heroes utterly and completely heroic, and making them real. With Anthony, I hope I struck a balance. It's easy to scowl at a book and grumble, "Get over it already!" but the truth is, for most men, it's not so easy to "get over" the sudden and premature loss of a beloved father.

Sharp-eyed readers will note that the bee sting that killed Edmund Bridgerton was actually the second sting he'd received in his life. This is medically accurate; bee sting allergies generally don't manifest themselves until the second sting. Since Anthony has only been stung once in his life, it's impossible to know whether or not he's allergic. As the author of this book, however, I'd like to think I have a certain creative control over the medical conditions of my characters, so I've decided that Anthony has no allergies of any kind, and furthermore will live to the ripe old age of 92.

My very best wishes,

Turn the page for a sneak preview of the next wonderfully romantic novel from Julia Quinn:

An Offer From A Gentleman

Now available from Piatkus . . .

Prologue

Everyone knew that Sophie Beckett was a bastard.

The servants all knew it. But they loved little Sophie, had loved her since she'd arrived at Penwood Park at the age of three, a small bundle wrapped in a too-big coat, left on the doorstep on a rainy July night. And because they loved her, they pretended that she was exactly what the sixth Earl of Penwood said she was—the orphaned daughter of an old friend. Never mind that Sophie's moss green eyes and dark blond hair matched the earl's precisely. Never mind that the shape of her face looked remarkably like that of the earl's recently deceased mother, or that her smile was an exact replica of the earl's sister's. No one wanted to hurt Sophie's feelings—or risk their livelihoods—by pointing that out.

The earl, one Richard Gunningworth, never discussed Sophie or her origins, but he must have known she was his bastard. No one knew what had been in the letter the housekeeper had fished from Sophie's pocket when she'd been discovered that rainy midnight; the earl had burned the missive mere seconds after reading it. He'd watched the paper shrivel and curl in the flames, then ordered a room made up for Sophie near the nursery. She'd remained there ever since. He called her Sophia, and she called him "my lord," and they saw each other a few times a year, whenever the earl returned home from London, which wasn't very often.

But perhaps most importantly, Sophie knew she was a bastard. She wasn't entirely certain how she knew it, just that she did, and probably had her entire life. She had few memories of her life before her arrival at Penwood Park, but she could remember a long coach journey across England, and she could remember her grandmother, coughing and wheezing and looking terribly thin, telling her she was going to live with her father. And most of all, she could remember standing on the doorstep in the rain, knowing that her grandmother was hiding in the bushes, waiting to see if Sophie was taken inside.

The earl had touched his fingers to the little girl's chin, tipped her face up to the light, and in that moment they both knew the truth.

Everyone knew Sophie was a bastard, and no one talked about it, and they were all quite happy with this arrangement.

Until the earl decided to marry.

Sophie had been quite pleased when she'd heard the news. The housekeeper had said that the butler had said that the earl's secretary had said that the earl planned to spend more time at Penwood Park now that he would be a family man. And while Sophie didn't exactly miss the earl when he was gone—it was hard to miss someone who didn't pay her much attention even when he was there—she rather thought she *might* miss him if she got to know him better, and if she got to know him better, maybe he wouldn't go away so often. Plus, the upstairs maid had said that the housekeeper had said that the neighbors' butler had said that the earl's intended wife already had two daughters, and they were near in age to Sophie.

After seven years alone in the nursery, Sophie was delighted. Unlike the other children in the district, she was never invited to local parties and events. No one actually came out and called her a bastard—to do so was tantamount to calling the earl, who had made one declaration that Sophie was his ward and then never revisited the subject, a liar. But at the same time, the earl never made any great attempt to force Sophie's acceptance. And so at the age of ten, Sophie's best friends were maids and footmen, and her parents might as well have been the housekeeper and butler.

But now she was getting sisters for real.

Oh, she knew she could not call them her sisters. She knew that she would be introduced as Sophia Maria Beckett, the earl's ward, but they would *feel* like sisters. And that was what really mattered.

And so, one February afternoon, Sophie found herself waiting in the great hall along with the assembled servants, watching out the window for the earl's carriage to pull up the drive, carrying in it the new countess and her two daughters. And, of course, the earl.

"Do you think she'll like me?" Sophie whispered to Mrs. Gibbons, the housekeeper. "The earl's wife, I mean."

"Of course she'll like you, dearling," Mrs. Gibbons whispered back. But her eyes hadn't been as certain as her tone. The new countess might not take kindly to the presence of her husband's by-blow.

"And I'll take lessons with her daughters?"

"No point in having you take your lessons separately."

Sophie nodded thoughtfully, then started to squirm when she saw the carriage rolling up the drive. "They're here!" she whispered.

Mrs. Gibbons reached out to pat her on the head, but Sophie had already dashed off to the window, practically pressing her face up to the glass.

The earl stepped down first, then reached in and helped down two young girls. They were dressed in matching black coats. One wore a pink ribbon in her hair; the other yellow. Then, as the two girls stepped aside, the earl reached up to help one last person from the carriage.

Sophie's breath caught in her throat as she waited for the new countess to emerge. Her little fingers crossed and a single, "Please," whispered over her lips.

Please let her love me.

Maybe if the countess loved her, then the earl would love her as well, and maybe, even if he didn't actually call her daughter, he'd treat her as one, and they'd be a family truly.

As Sophie watched through the window, the new countess stepped down from the carriage, her every movement so graceful and pure that Sophie was reminded of the delicate lark that occasionally came to splash in the birdbath in the garden. Even the countess's hat was adorned by a long feather, its turquoise plume glittering in the hard winter sun.

"She's beautiful," Sophie whispered. She darted a quick look back at Mrs. Gibbons to gauge her reaction, but the housekeeper was standing at strict attention, eyes straight ahead, waiting for the earl to bring his new family inside for introductions.

Sophie gulped, not exactly certain where she was meant to stand. Everyone else seemed to have a designated place. The servants were lined up according to rank, from the butler right down to the lowliest scullery maid. Even the dogs were sitting dutifully in the corner, their leads held tight by the Keeper of the Hounds.

But Sophie was rootless. If she were truly the daughter of the house, she'd be standing with her governess, awaiting the new countess. If she were truly the earl's ward, she'd be in much the same place. But Miss Timmons had caught a head cold and refused to leave the nursery and come downstairs. None of the servants believed for a second that the governess was truly ill. She'd been fine the night before, but no one blamed her for the deception. Sophie was, after all, the earl's bastard, and no one wanted to be the one to offer potential insult to the new countess by introducing her to her husband's by-blow.

And the countess would have to be blind, stupid, or both not to realize in an instant that Sophie was something more than the earl's ward.

Suddenly overcome with shyness, Sophie shrank into a corner as two footmen threw open the front doors with a flourish. The two girls entered first, then stepped to the side as the earl led the countess in. The earl introduced the countess and her daughters to the butler, and the butler introduced them to the servants.

And Sophie waited.

The butler presented the footmen, the chef, the housekeeper, the grooms.

And Sophie waited.

He presented the kitchen maids, the upstairs maids, the scullery maids.

And Sophie waited.

And then finally the butler—Rumsey was his name—presented the lowliest of the lowest of maids, a scullery girl named Dulcie who had been hired a mere week earlier. The earl nodded and murmured his thanks, and Sophie was still waiting, completely unsure of what to do.

So she cleared her throat and stepped forward, a nervous smile on her face. She didn't spend much time with the earl, but she was trotted out before him whenever he visited Penwood Park, and he always gave her a few minutes of his time, asking about her lessons before shooing her back up to the nursery.

Surely he'd still want to know how her studies were progressing, even now that he'd married. Surely he'd want to know that she'd mastered the science of multiplying fractions, and that Miss Timmons had recently declared her French accent, "perfection."

But he was busy saying something to the countess's daughters, and he didn't hear her. Sophie cleared her throat again, this time more loudly, and said, "My lord?" in a voice that came out a bit more squeaky than she'd intended.

The earl turned around. "Ah, Sophia," he murmured, "I didn't realize you were in the hall."

Sophie beamed. He hadn't been ignoring her, after all.

"And who might this be?" the countess asked, stepping forward to get a better look.

"My ward," the earl replied. "Miss Sophia Beckett."

The countess speared Sophie with an assessing look, then her eyes narrowed.

And narrowed.

And narrowed some more.

"I see," she said.

And everyone in the room knew instantly that she *did* see.

"Rosamund," the countess said, turning to her two girls, "Posy, come with me."

The girls moved immediately to their mother's side. Sophie hazarded a smile in their direction. The smaller one smiled back, but the older one, whose hair was the color of spun gold, took her cue from her mother, pointed her nose in the air, and looked firmly away.

Sophie gulped and smiled again at the friendly girl, but this time the little girl chewed on her lower lip in indecision, then cast her eyes toward the floor.

The countess turned her back on Sophie and said to the earl, "I assume you have had rooms prepared for Rosamund and Posy."

He nodded. "Near the nursery. Right next to Sophie."

There was a long silence, and then the countess must have decided that certain battles should not be conducted before the servants, because all she said was, "I would like to go upstairs now."

And she left, taking the earl and her daughters along with her.

Sophie watched the new family walk up the stairs, and then, as they disappeared onto the landing, she turned to Mrs. Gibbons and asked, "Do you think I should go up to help? I could show the girls the nursery."

Mrs. Gibbons shook her head. "They looked tired," she lied. "I'm sure they'll be needing a nap."

Sophie frowned. She'd been told that Rosamund was

eleven and Posy was ten. Surely that was a bit old for taking naps.

Mrs. Gibbons patted her on the back. "Why don't you come with me? I could use a bit of company, and Cook told me that she just made a fresh batch of shortbread. I think it's still warm."

Sophie nodded and followed her out of the hall. She'd have plenty of time that evening to get to know the two girls. She'd show them the nursery, and then they'd become friends, and before long they'd be as sisters.

Sophie smiled. It would be glorious to have sisters.

As it happened, Sophie did not encounter Rosamund and Posy—or the earl and countess, for that matter—until the next day. When Sophie entered the nursery to take her supper, she noticed that the table had been set for two, not four, and Miss Timmons (who had miraculously recovered from her ailment) said that the new countess had told her that Rosamund and Posy were too tired from their travels to eat that evening.

But the girls had to have their lessons, and so the next morning they arrived in the nursery, trailing the countess by one step each. Sophie had been working at her lessons for an hour already, and she looked up from her arithmetic with great interest. She didn't smile at the girls this time. Somehow it seemed best not to.

"Miss Timmons," the countess said.

Miss Timmons bobbed a curtsy, murmuring, "My lady."

"The earl tells me you will teach my daughters."

"I will do my best, my lady."

The countess motioned to the older girl, the one with golden hair and cornflower eyes. She looked, Sophie thought, as pretty as the porcelain doll the earl had sent up from London for her seventh birthday.

"This," the countess said, "is Rosamund. She is eleven. And this"—she then motioned to the other girl, who had not taken her eyes off of her shoes—"is Posy. She is ten."

Sophie looked at Posy with great interest. Unlike her mother and sister, her hair and eyes were quite dark, and her cheeks were a bit pudgy.

"Sophie is also ten," Miss Timmons replied.

The countess's lips thinned. "I would like you to show the girls around the house and garden."

Miss Timmons nodded. "Very well. Sophie, put your slate down. We can return to arithmetic—"

"Just *my* girls," the countess interrupted, her voice somehow hot and cold at the same time. "I will speak with Sophie alone."

Sophie gulped and tried to bring her eyes to the countess's, but she only made it as far as her chin. As Miss Timmons ushered Rosamund and Posy out of the room she stood up, awaiting further direction from her father's new wife.

"I know who you are," the countess said the moment the door clicked shut.

"M-my lady?"

"You're his bastard, and don't try to deny it."

Sophie said nothing. It was the truth, of course, but no one had ever said it aloud. At least not to her face.

The countess grabbed her chin and squeezed and pulled until Sophie was forced to look her in the eye. "You listen to me," she said in a menacing voice. "You might live here at Penwood Park, and you might share lessons with my daughters, but you are nothing but a bastard, and that is all you will ever be. Don't you ever, *ever* make the mistake of thinking you are as good as the rest of us."

Sophie let out a little moan. The countess's fingernails were biting into the underside of her chin.

"My husband," the countess continued, "feels some sort of misguided duty to you. It's admirable of him to see to his mistakes, but it is an insult to me to have you in my home—fed, clothed, and educated as if you were his real daughter."

But she *was* his real daughter. And it had been her home much longer than the countess's.

Abruptly, the countess let go of her chin. "I don't want to see you," she hissed. "You are never to speak to me, and you shall endeavor never to be in my company. Furthermore, you are not to speak to Rosamund and Posy except during lessons. They are the daughters of the house now, and should not have to associate with the likes of *you*. Do you have any questions?"

Sophie shook her head.

"Good."

And with that, she swept out of the room, leaving Sophie with wobbly legs and a quivering lip.

And an awful lot of tears.

In time, Sophie learned a bit more about her precarious position in the house. The servants always knew everything, and it all reached Sophie's ears eventually.

The countess, whose given name was Araminta, had insisted that very first day that Sophie be removed from the house. The earl had refused. Araminta didn't have to love Sophie, he'd said coolly. She didn't even have to like her. But she had to put up with her. He had owned up to his responsibility to the girl for seven years, and he wasn't going to stop now.

Rosamund and Posy took their cues from Araminta and treated Sophie with hostility and disdain, although Posy's heart clearly wasn't into torture and cruelty in the way Rosamund's was. Rosamund liked nothing better than to pinch and twist the skin on the back of Sophie's hand when Miss Timmons wasn't looking. Sophie never said anything; she rather doubted that Miss Timmons would have the courage to reprimand Rosamund (who would surely run to Araminta with a false tale), and if anyone noticed that Sophie's hands were perpetually black-and-blue, no one ever said so.

Posy showed her the occasional kindness, although

more often than not she just sighed, and said, "My mummy says I'm not to be nice to you."

As for the earl, he never intervened.

Sophie's life continued in this vein for four years, until the earl surprised everyone by clutching his hand to his chest while taking tea in the rose garden, letting out one ragged gasp, and falling facefirst to the stone cobbles.

He never regained consciousness.

Everyone was quite shocked. The earl was only forty years old. Who could have known that his heart would give out at such a young age? No one was more stunned than Araminta, who had been trying quite desperately since her wedding night to conceive the all-important heir.

"I might be with child!" she hastened to tell the earl's solicitors. "You can't give the title over to some distant cousin. I could very well be with child."

But she wasn't with child, and when the earl's will was read one month later (the solicitors had wanted to be sure to give the countess enough time to know for sure if she was pregnant) Araminta was forced to sit next to the new earl, a rather dissolute young man who was more often drunk than not.

Most of the earl's wishes were standard fare. He left bequests to loyal servants. He settled funds on Rosamund, Posy, and even Sophie, ensuring that all three girls would have respectable dowries.

And then the solicitor reached Araminta's name.

To my wife, Araminta Gunningworth, Countess of Penwood, I leave a yearly income of two thousand pounds—

"That's all?" Araminta cried out.

—unless she agrees to shelter and care for my

ward, Miss Sophia Maria Beckett, until the latter reaches the age of twenty, in which case her yearly income shall be trebled to six thousand pounds.

"I don't want her," Araminta whispered.

"You don't have to take her," the solicitor reminded her. "You can—"

"Live on a measly two thousand a year?" she snapped. "I don't think so."

The solicitor, who lived on considerably less than two thousand a year, said nothing.

The new earl, who'd been drinking steadily throughout the meeting, just shrugged.

Araminta stood.

"What is your decision?" the solicitor asked.

"I'll take her," she said in a low voice.

"Shall I find the girl and tell her?"

Araminta shook her head. "I'll tell her myself."

But when Araminta found Sophie, she left out a few important facts . . .

Chapter 1

This year's most sought-after invitation must surely be that of the Bridgerton masquerade ball, to be held Monday next. Indeed, one cannot take two steps without being forced to listen to some society mama speculating on who will attend, and perhaps more importantly, who will wear what.

Neither of the aforementioned topics, however, are nearly as interesting as that of the two unmarried Bridgerton brothers, Benedict and Colin. (Before anyone points out that there is a third unmarried Bridgerton brother, let This Author assure you that she is fully aware of the existence of Gregory Bridgerton. He is, however, fourteen years of age, and therefore not pertinent to this particular column, which concerns, as This Author's columns often do, that most sacred of sports: husband-hunting.)

Although the Misters Bridgerton are just that—merely Misters—they are still considered two of the prime catches of the season. It is a well-known fact that both are possessed of respectable fortunes, and it does not require perfect sight to know that they also possess, as do all eight of the Bridgerton offspring, the Bridgerton good looks.

Will some fortunate young lady use the mystery of a masquerade night to snare one of the eligible bachelors?

This Author isn't even going to attempt to speculate.

LADY WHISTLEDOWN'S SOCIETY PAPERS, 31 MAY 1815

"Sophie! Sophieeeeeeeeeeeeeee!"

As screeches went, it was enough to shatter glass. Or at least an eardrum.

"Coming, Rosamund! I'm coming!" Sophie hitched up the hem of her coarse woolen skirts and hurried up the stairs, slipping on the fourth step and only just barely managing to grab the bannister before landing on her bottom. She should have remembered that the stairs would be slick; she'd helped the downstairs maid wax them just that morning.

Skidding to a halt in the doorway to Rosamund's bedroom and still catching her breath, Sophie said, "Yes?"

"My tea is cold."

What Sophie wanted to say was, "It was warm when I brought it an hour ago, you lazy fiend."

What she did say was, "I'll get you another pot."

Rosamund sniffed. "See that you do."

Sophie stretched her lips into what the nearly blind might call a smile and picked up the tea service. "Shall I leave the biscuits?" she asked.

Rosamund gave her pretty head a shake. "I want fresh ones."

Shoulders slightly stooped from the weight of the overloaded tea service, Sophie exited the room, careful not to start grumbling until she'd safely reached the hall. Rosamund was forever ordering tea, then not bothering to drink it until an hour passed. By then, of course, it was cold, so she had to order a fresh pot.

Which meant Sophie was forever running up and down the stairs, up and down, up and down. Sometimes it seemed that was all she did with her life.

Up and down, up and down.

And of course the mending, the pressing, the hairdressing, the shoe polishing, the darning, the bed-making . . .

"Sophie!"

Sophie turned around to see Posy heading toward her.

"Sophie, I've been meaning to ask you, do you think this color is becoming on me?"

Sophie assessed Posy's mermaid costume. The cut wasn't quite right for Posy, who had never lost all of her baby fat, but the color did indeed bring out the best in her complexion. "It is a lovely shade of green," Sophie replied quite honestly. "It makes your cheeks very rosy."

"Oh, good. I'm so glad you like it. You do have such a knack for picking out my clothing." Posy smiled as she reached out and plucked a sugared biscuit from the tray. "Mother has been an absolute bear all week about the masquerade ball, and I know I shall never hear the end of it if I do not look my best. Or"—Posy's face twisted into a grimace—"if she *thinks* I do not look my best. She is determined that one of us snare one of the remaining Bridgerton brothers, you know."

"I know."

"And to make matters worse, that Whistledown woman has been writing about them again. It only"—Posy finished chewing and paused while she swallowed—"whets her appetite."

"Was the column very good this morning?" Sophie asked, shifting the tray to rest on her hip. "I haven't had a chance to read it yet."

"Oh, the usual stuff," Posy said with a wave of her hand. "Really, it can be quite humdrum, you know."

Sophie tried to smile and failed. She'd like nothing more than to live a day of Posy's humdrum life. Well, perhaps she wouldn't want Araminta for a mother, but she wouldn't mind a life of parties, routs, and musicales.

"Let's see," Posy mused. "There was a review of Lady Worth's recent ball, a bit about Viscount Guelph, who seems rather smitten with some girl from Scotland, and then a longish piece on the upcoming Bridgerton masquerade."

Sophie sighed. She'd been reading about the upcoming masquerade for weeks, and even though she was nothing but a lady's maid (and occasionally a housemaid as well, whenever Araminta decided she wasn't working hard enough) she couldn't help but wish that she could attend the ball.

"I for one will be thrilled if that Guelph viscount gets himself engaged," Posy remarked, reaching for another biscuit. "It will mean one fewer bachelor for Mother to go on and on about as a potential husband. It's not as if I have any hope of attracting his attention anyway." She took a bite of the biscuit; it crunched loudly in her mouth. "I do hope Lady Whistledown is right about him."

"She probably is," Sophie answered. She had been reading *Lady Whistledown's Society Papers* since it had debuted in 1813, and the gossip columnist was almost always correct when it came to matters of the Marriage Mart.

Not, of course, that Sophie had ever had the chance to see the Marriage Mart for herself. But if one read *Whistledown* often enough, one could almost feel a part of London Society without actually attending any balls.

In fact, reading *Whistledown* was really Sophie's one true enjoyable pastime. She'd already read all of the novels in the library, and as neither Araminta, Rosamund, nor Posy was particularly enamored of reading, Sophie couldn't look forward to a new book entering the house.

But *Whistledown* was great fun. No one actually knew the columnist's true identity. When the single-sheet newspaper had debuted two years earlier, speculation had been rampant. Even now, whenever Lady Whistledown reported a particularly juicy bit of gossip, people starting talking and guessing anew, wondering who on earth was able to report with such speed and accuracy.

And for Sophie, *Whistledown* was a tantalizing glimpse into the world that might have been hers, had her parents actually made their union legal. She would have been an earl's daughter, not an earl's bastard; her name Gunningworth instead of Beckett.

Just once, she'd like to be the one stepping into the coach and attending the ball.

Instead, she was the one dressing others for their nights on the town, cinching Posy's corset or dressing Rosamund's hair or polishing a pair of Araminta's shoes.

But she could not—or at least should not—complain. She might have to serve as maid to Araminta and her daughters, but at least she had a home. Which was more than most girls in her position had.

When her father had died, he'd left her nothing. Well, nothing but a roof over her head. His will had ensured that she could not be turned out until she was twenty. There was no way that Araminta would forfeit four thousand pounds a year by giving Sophie the boot.

But that four thousand pounds was Araminta's, not Sophie's, and Sophie hadn't ever seen a penny of it. Gone were the fine clothes she'd used to wear, replaced by the coarse wool of the servants. And she ate what the rest of the maids ate—whatever Araminta, Rosamund, and Posy chose to leave behind.

Sophie's twentieth birthday, however, had come and gone almost a year earlier, and here she was, still living at Penwood House, still waiting on Araminta hand and foot. For some unknown reason—probably because she didn't want to train (or pay) a new maid—Araminta had allowed Sophie to remain in her household.

And Sophie had stayed. If Araminta was the devil she knew, then the rest of the world was the devil she didn't. And Sophie had no idea which would be worse.

"Isn't that tray getting heavy?"

Sophie blinked her way out of her reverie and focused on Posy, who was reaching for the last biscuit on the tray. Drat. She'd been hoping to snitch it for herself. "Yes," she murmured. "Yes, it is quite. I should really be getting to the kitchen with it."

Julia Quinn started writing her first book one month after finishing university and has been tapping away at her keyboard ever since. The No. 1 *New York Times* bestselling author of more than two dozen novels, she is a graduate of Harvard and Radcliffe Colleges and is one of only sixteen authors ever to be inducted in the Romance Writers of America Hall of Fame. She lives in the Pacific Northwest with her family.

Please visit Julia Quinn online:

www.juliaquinn.com
www.facebook.com/AuthorJuliaQuinn
@JQAuthor

By Julia Quinn

The Rokesby Series:
Because of Miss Bridgerton
The Girl with the Make-Believe Husband
The Other Miss Bridgerton
First Comes Scandal

The Smythe-Smith Quartet:
Just Like Heaven
A Night Like This
The Sum of All Kisses
The Secrets of Sir Richard Kenworthy

The Bevelstoke Series:
The Secret Diaries of Miss Miranda Cheever
What Happens in London
Ten Things I Love About You

The Two Dukes of Wyndham:
The Lost Duke of Wyndham
Mr Cavendish, I Presume

Blydon Family Saga:
Splendid
Dancing at Midnight
Minx

Agents for the Crown:
To Catch an Heiress
How to Marry a Marquis

Bridgerton Series:
The Duke and I
The Viscount Who Loved Me
An Offer from a Gentleman
Romancing Mr Bridgerton
To Sir Phillip, With Love
When He Was Wicked
It's In His Kiss
On the Way to the Wedding
The Bridgertons: Happily Ever After

The Lyndon Sisters:
Everything and the Moon
Brighter than the Sun

The Ladies Most (written with Eloisa James and Connie Brockway):
The Lady Most Likely
The Lady Most Willing

An Offer from a Gentleman

Julia Quinn

PIATKUS

PIATKUS

First published in the US in 2001 by Avon Books,
An imprint of HarperCollins, New York
First published in Great Britain in 2006 by Piatkus
This paperback edition published in 2021 by Piatkus

22

A CIP catalogue record for this book
is available from the British Library.

ISBN 978-0-349-42944-1

Printed and bound in Great Britain by Clays Ltd, Elcograf S.p.A.

Papers used by Piatkus are from well-managed forests
and other responsible sources.

FSC www.fsc.org MIX Paper from responsible sources FSC® C104740

Piatkus
An imprint of
Little, Brown Book Group
Carmelite House
50 Victoria Embankment
London EC4Y 0DZ

Hachette Ireland
8 Castlecourt Centre
Castleknock
Dublin 15

An Hachette UK Company
www.hachette.co.uk

www.littlebrown.co.uk

For Cheyenne,
and the memory of a Frappucino summer.

And also for Paul,
even though he doesn't see anything wrong
with watching open heart surgery on TV
while we're eating spaghetti.

Prologue

Everyone knew that Sophie Beckett was a bastard.

The servants all knew it. But they loved little Sophie, had loved her since she'd arrived at Penwood Park at the age of three, a small bundle wrapped in a too-big coat, left on the doorstep on a rainy July night. And because they loved her, they pretended that she was exactly what the sixth Earl of Penwood said she was—the orphaned daughter of an old friend. Never mind that Sophie's moss green eyes and dark blond hair matched the earl's precisely. Never mind that the shape of her face looked remarkably like that of the earl's recently deceased mother, or that her smile was an exact replica of the earl's sister's. No one wanted to hurt Sophie's feelings—or risk their livelihoods—by pointing that out.

The earl, one Richard Gunningworth, never discussed Sophie or her origins, but he must have known she was his bastard. No one knew what had been in the letter the housekeeper had fished from Sophie's pocket when she'd been discovered that rainy midnight; the earl had burned the missive mere seconds after reading it. He'd watched the paper shrivel and curl in the flames, then ordered a room made up for Sophie near the nursery. She'd remained there ever since. He called her Sophia, and she called him "my lord," and they saw each other a few times a year, whenever the earl returned home from London, which wasn't very often.

But perhaps most importantly, Sophie knew she was a bastard. She wasn't entirely certain how she knew it, just that she did, and probably had her entire life. She had few memories of her life before her arrival at Penwood Park, but she could remember a long coach journey across England, and she could remember her grandmother, coughing and wheezing and looking terribly thin, telling her she was going to live with her father. And most of all, she could remember standing on the doorstep in the rain, knowing that her grandmother was hiding in the bushes, waiting to see if Sophie was taken inside.

The earl had touched his fingers to the little girl's chin, tipped her face up to the light, and in that moment they both knew the truth.

Everyone knew Sophie was a bastard, and no one talked about it, and they were all quite happy with this arrangement.

Until the earl decided to marry.

Sophie had been quite pleased when she'd heard the news. The housekeeper had said that the butler had said that the earl's secretary had said that the earl planned to spend more time at Penwood Park now that he would be a family man. And while Sophie didn't exactly miss the earl when he was gone—it was hard to miss someone who didn't pay her much attention even when he was there—she rather thought she *might* miss him if she got to know him better, and if she got to know him better, maybe he wouldn't go away so often. Plus, the upstairs maid had said that the housekeeper had said that the neighbors' butler had said that the earl's intended wife already had two daughters, and they were near in age to Sophie.

After seven years alone in the nursery, Sophie was delighted. Unlike the other children in the district, she was never invited to local parties and events. No one actually came out and called her a bastard—to do so was tantamount to calling the earl, who had made one declaration that Sophie was his ward and then never revisited the subject, a liar. But at the same time, the earl never made any great attempt to force Sophie's acceptance. And so at the age of ten, Sophie's best friends were maids and footmen, and her parents might as well have been the housekeeper and butler.

But now she was getting sisters for real.

Oh, she knew she could not call them her sisters. She knew that she would be introduced as Sophia Maria Beckett, the earl's ward, but they would *feel* like sisters. And that was what really mattered.

And so, one February afternoon, Sophie found herself waiting in the great hall along with the assembled servants, watching out the window for the earl's carriage to pull up the drive, carrying in it the new countess and her two daughters. And, of course, the earl.

"Do you think she'll like me?" Sophie whispered to Mrs. Gibbons, the housekeeper. "The earl's wife, I mean."

"Of course she'll like you, dearling," Mrs. Gibbons whispered back. But her eyes hadn't been as certain as her tone. The new countess might not take kindly to the presence of her husband's by-blow.

"And I'll take lessons with her daughters?"

"No point in having you take your lessons separately."

Sophie nodded thoughtfully, then started to squirm when she saw the carriage rolling up the drive. "They're here!" she whispered.

Mrs. Gibbons reached out to pat her on the head, but Sophie had already dashed off to the window, practically pressing her face up to the glass.

The earl stepped down first, then reached in and helped down two young girls. They were dressed in matching black coats. One wore a pink ribbon in her hair; the other yellow. Then, as the two girls stepped aside, the earl reached up to help one last person from the carriage.

Sophie's breath caught in her throat as she waited for the new countess to emerge. Her little fingers crossed and a single, "Please," whispered over her lips.

Please let her love me.

Maybe if the countess loved her, then the earl would love her as well, and maybe, even if he didn't actually call her daughter, he'd treat her as one, and they'd be a family truly.

As Sophie watched through the window, the new countess stepped down from the carriage, her every movement so graceful and pure that Sophie was reminded of the delicate lark that occasionally came to splash in the birdbath in the garden. Even the countess's hat was adorned by a long feather, its turquoise plume glittering in the hard winter sun.

"She's beautiful," Sophie whispered. She darted a quick look back at Mrs. Gibbons to gauge her reaction, but the housekeeper was standing at strict attention, eyes straight ahead, waiting for the earl to bring his new family inside for introductions.

Sophie gulped, not exactly certain where she was meant to stand. Everyone else seemed to have a designated place. The servants were lined up according to rank, from the butler right down to the lowliest scullery maid. Even the dogs were sitting dutifully in the corner, their leads held tight by the Keeper of the Hounds.

But Sophie was rootless. If she were truly the daughter of the house, she'd be standing with her governess, awaiting the new countess. If she were truly the earl's ward, she'd be in much the same place. But Miss Timmons had caught a head cold and refused to leave the nursery and come downstairs. None of the servants believed for a second that the governess was truly ill. She'd been fine the night before, but no one blamed her for the deception. Sophie was, after all, the earl's bastard, and no one wanted to be the one to offer potential insult to the new countess by introducing her to her husband's by-blow.

And the countess would have to be blind, stupid, or both not to realize in an instant that Sophie was something more than the earl's ward.

Suddenly overcome with shyness, Sophie shrank into a corner as two footmen threw open the front doors with a flourish. The two girls entered first, then stepped to the side as the earl led the countess in. The earl introduced the countess and her daughters to the butler, and the butler introduced them to the servants.

And Sophie waited.

The butler presented the footmen, the chef, the housekeeper, the grooms.

And Sophie waited.

He presented the kitchen maids, the upstairs maids, the scullery maids.

And Sophie waited.

And then finally the butler—Rumsey was his name—presented the lowliest of the lowest of maids, a scullery girl named Dulcie who had been hired a mere week earlier. The earl nodded and murmured his thanks, and Sophie was still waiting, completely unsure of what to do.

So she cleared her throat and stepped forward, a nervous smile on her face. She didn't spend much time with the earl, but she was trotted out before him whenever he visited Penwood Park, and he always gave her a few minutes of his time, asking about her lessons before shooing her back up to the nursery.

Surely he'd still want to know how her studies were progressing, even now that he'd married. Surely he'd want to know that she'd mastered the science of multiplying fractions, and that Miss Timmons had recently declared her French accent, "perfection."

But he was busy saying something to the countess's daughters, and he didn't hear her. Sophie cleared her throat again, this time more loudly, and said, "My lord?" in a voice that came out a bit more squeaky than she'd intended.

The earl turned around. "Ah, Sophia," he murmured, "I

didn't realize you were in the hall."

Sophie beamed. He hadn't been ignoring her, after all.

"And who might this be?" the countess asked, stepping forward to get a better look.

"My ward," the earl replied. "Miss Sophia Beckett."

The countess speared Sophie with an assessing look, then her eyes narrowed.

And narrowed.

And narrowed some more.

"I see," she said.

And everyone in the room knew instantly that she *did* see.

"Rosamund," the countess said, turning to her two girls, "Posy, come with me."

The girls moved immediately to their mother's side. Sophie hazarded a smile in their direction. The smaller one smiled back, but the older one, whose hair was the color of spun gold, took her cue from her mother, pointed her nose in the air, and looked firmly away.

Sophie gulped and smiled again at the friendly girl, but this time the little girl chewed on her lower lip in indecision, then cast her eyes toward the floor.

The countess turned her back on Sophie and said to the earl, "I assume you have had rooms prepared for Rosamund and Posy."

He nodded. "Near the nursery. Right next to Sophie."

There was a long silence, and then the countess must have decided that certain battles should not be conducted before the servants, because all she said was, "I would like to go upstairs now."

And she left, taking the earl and her daughters along with her.

Sophie watched the new family walk up the stairs, and then, as they disappeared onto the landing, she turned to Mrs. Gibbons and asked, "Do you think I should go up to help? I could show the girls the nursery."

Mrs. Gibbons shook her head. "They looked tired," she

lied. "I'm sure they'll be needing a nap."

Sophie frowned. She'd been told that Rosamund was eleven and Posy was ten. Surely that was a bit old for taking naps.

Mrs. Gibbons patted her on the back. "Why don't you come with me? I could use a bit of company, and Cook told me that she just made a fresh batch of shortbread. I think it's still warm."

Sophie nodded and followed her out of the hall. She'd have plenty of time that evening to get to know the two girls. She'd show them the nursery, and then they'd become friends, and before long they'd be as sisters.

Sophie smiled. It would be glorious to have sisters.

As it happened, Sophie did not encounter Rosamund and Posy—or the earl and countess, for that matter—until the next day. When Sophie entered the nursery to take her supper, she noticed that the table had been set for two, not four, and Miss Timmons (who had miraculously recovered from her ailment) said that the new countess had told her that Rosamund and Posy were too tired from their travels to eat that evening.

But the girls had to have their lessons, and so the next morning they arrived in the nursery, trailing the countess by one step each. Sophie had been working at her lessons for an hour already, and she looked up from her arithmetic with great interest. She didn't smile at the girls this time. Somehow it seemed best not to.

"Miss Timmons," the countess said.

Miss Timmons bobbed a curtsy, murmuring, "My lady."

"The earl tells me you will teach my daughters."

"I will do my best, my lady."

The countess motioned to the older girl, the one with golden hair and cornflower eyes. She looked, Sophie thought, as pretty as the porcelain doll the earl had sent up from London for her seventh birthday.

"This," the countess said, "is Rosamund. She is eleven. And this"—she then motioned to the other girl, who had not taken her eyes off of her shoes—"is Posy. She is ten."

Sophie looked at Posy with great interest. Unlike her mother and sister, her hair and eyes were quite dark, and her cheeks were a bit pudgy.

"Sophie is also ten," Miss Timmons replied.

The countess's lips thinned. "I would like you to show the girls around the house and garden."

Miss Timmons nodded. "Very well. Sophie, put your slate down. We can return to arithmetic—"

"Just *my* girls," the countess interrupted, her voice somehow hot and cold at the same time. "I will speak with Sophie alone."

Sophie gulped and tried to bring her eyes to the countess's, but she only made it as far as her chin. As Miss Timmons ushered Rosamund and Posy out of the room she stood up, awaiting further direction from her father's new wife.

"I know who you are," the countess said the moment the door clicked shut.

"M-my lady?"

"You're his bastard, and don't try to deny it."

Sophie said nothing. It was the truth, of course, but no one had ever said it aloud. At least not to her face.

The countess grabbed her chin and squeezed and pulled until Sophie was forced to look her in the eye. "You listen to me," she said in a menacing voice. "You might live here at Penwood Park, and you might share lessons with my daughters, but you are nothing but a bastard, and that is all you will ever be. Don't you ever, *ever* make the mistake of thinking you are as good as the rest of us."

Sophie let out a little moan. The countess's fingernails were biting into the underside of her chin.

"My husband," the countess continued, "feels some sort of misguided duty to you. It's admirable of him to see to his mistakes, but it is an insult to me to have you in my home—fed, clothed, and educated as if you were his real daughter."

But she *was* his real daughter. And it had been her home much longer than the countess's.

Abruptly, the countess let go of her chin. "I don't want to see you," she hissed. "You are never to speak to me, and you shall endeavor never to be in my company. Furthermore, you are not to speak to Rosamund and Posy except during lessons. They are the daughters of the house now, and should not have to associate with the likes of *you*. Do you have any questions?"

Sophie shook her head.

"Good."

And with that, she swept out of the room, leaving Sophie with wobbly legs and a quivering lip.

And an awful lot of tears.

In time, Sophie learned a bit more about her precarious position in the house. The servants always knew everything, and it all reached Sophie's ears eventually.

The countess, whose given name was Araminta, had insisted that very first day that Sophie be removed from the house. The earl had refused. Araminta didn't have to love Sophie, he'd said coolly. She didn't even have to like her. But she had to put up with her. He had owned up to his responsibility to the girl for seven years, and he wasn't going to stop now.

Rosamund and Posy took their cues from Araminta and treated Sophie with hostility and disdain, although Posy's heart clearly wasn't into torture and cruelty in the way Rosamund's was. Rosamund liked nothing better than to pinch and twist the skin on the back of Sophie's hand when Miss Timmons wasn't looking. Sophie never said anything; she rather doubted that Miss Timmons would have the courage to reprimand Rosamund (who would surely run to

Araminta with a false tale), and if anyone noticed that Sophie's hands were perpetually black-and-blue, no one ever said so.

Posy showed her the occasional kindness, although more often than not she just sighed, and said, "My mummy says I'm not to be nice to you."

As for the earl, he never intervened.

Sophie's life continued in this vein for four years, until the earl surprised everyone by clutching his hand to his chest while taking tea in the rose garden, letting out one ragged gasp, and falling facefirst to the stone cobbles.

He never regained consciousness.

Everyone was quite shocked. The earl was only forty years old. Who could have known that his heart would give out at such a young age? No one was more stunned than Araminta, who had been trying quite desperately since her wedding night to conceive the all-important heir.

"I might be with child!" she hastened to tell the earl's solicitors. "You can't give the title over to some distant cousin. I could very well be with child."

But she wasn't with child, and when the earl's will was read one month later (the solicitors had wanted to be sure to give the countess enough time to know for sure if she was pregnant) Araminta was forced to sit next to the new earl, a rather dissolute young man who was more often drunk than not.

Most of the earl's wishes were standard fare. He left bequests to loyal servants. He settled funds on Rosamund, Posy, and even Sophie, ensuring that all three girls would have respectable dowries.

And then the solicitor reached Araminta's name.

To my wife, Araminta Gunningworth, Countess of Penwood, I leave a yearly income of two thousand pounds—

"That's all?" Araminta cried out.

—unless she agrees to shelter and care for my ward, Miss Sophia Maria Beckett, until the latter reaches the age of twenty, in which case her yearly income shall be trebled to six thousand pounds.

"I don't want her," Araminta whispered.

"You don't have to take her," the solicitor reminded her. "You can—"

"Live on a measly two thousand a year?" she snapped. "I don't think so."

The solicitor, who lived on considerably less than two thousand a year, said nothing.

The new earl, who'd been drinking steadily throughout the meeting, just shrugged.

Araminta stood.

"What is your decision?" the solicitor asked.

"I'll take her," she said in a low voice.

"Shall I find the girl and tell her?"

Araminta shook her head. "I'll tell her myself."

But when Araminta found Sophie, she left out a few important facts . . .

Part One

Chapter 1

This year's most sought-after invitation must surely be that of the Bridgerton masquerade ball, to be held Monday next. Indeed, one cannot take two steps without being forced to listen to some society mama speculating on who will attend, and perhaps more importantly, who will wear what.

Neither of the aforementioned topics, however, are nearly as interesting as that of the two unmarried Bridgerton brothers, Benedict and Colin. (Before anyone points out that there is a third unmarried Bridgerton brother, let This Author assure you that she is fully aware of the existence of Gregory Bridgerton. He is, however, fourteen years of age, and therefore not pertinent to this particular column, which concerns, as This Author's columns often do, that most sacred of sports: husband-hunting.)

Although the Misters Bridgerton are just that—merely Misters—they are still considered two of the prime catches of the season. It is a well-known fact that both are possessed of respectable fortunes, and it does not require perfect sight to know that they also possess, as do all eight of the Bridgerton offspring, the Bridgerton good looks.

Will some fortunate young lady use the mystery of a masquerade night to snare one of the eligible bachelors?

This Author isn't even going to attempt to speculate.

LADY WHISTLEDOWN'S SOCIETY PAPERS, 31 MAY 1815

"Sophie! Sophieeeeeeeeeeeeeeee!"

As screeches went, it was enough to shatter glass. Or at least an eardrum.

"Coming, Rosamund! I'm coming!" Sophie hitched up the hem of her coarse woolen skirts and hurried up the stairs, slipping on the fourth step and only just barely managing to grab the bannister before landing on her bottom. She should have remembered that the stairs would be slick; she'd helped the downstairs maid wax them just that morning.

Skidding to a halt in the doorway to Rosamund's bedroom and still catching her breath, Sophie said, "Yes?"

"My tea is cold."

What Sophie wanted to say was, "It was warm when I brought it an hour ago, you lazy fiend."

What she did say was, "I'll get you another pot."

Rosamund sniffed. "See that you do."

Sophie stretched her lips into what the nearly blind might call a smile and picked up the tea service. "Shall I leave the biscuits?" she asked.

Rosamund gave her pretty head a shake. "I want fresh ones."

Shoulders slightly stooped from the weight of the overloaded tea service, Sophie exited the room, careful not to start grumbling until she'd safely reached the hall. Rosamund was forever ordering tea, then not bothering to drink it until an hour passed. By then, of course, it was cold, so she had to order a fresh pot.

Which meant Sophie was forever running up and down the stairs, up and down, up and down. Sometimes it seemed that was all she did with her life.

Up and down, up and down.

And of course the mending, the pressing, the hairdressing, the shoe polishing, the darning, the bedmaking . . .

"Sophie!"

Sophie turned around to see Posy heading toward her.

"Sophie, I've been meaning to ask you, do you think this color is becoming on me?"

Sophie assessed Posy's mermaid costume. The cut wasn't quite right for Posy, who had never lost all of her baby fat, but the color did indeed bring out the best in her complexion. "It is a lovely shade of green," Sophie replied quite honestly. "It makes your cheeks very rosy."

"Oh, good. I'm so glad you like it. You do have such a knack for picking out my clothing." Posy smiled as she reached out and plucked a sugared biscuit from the tray. "Mother has been an absolute bear all week about the masquerade ball, and I know I shall never hear the end of it if I do not look my best. Or"—Posy's face twisted into a grimace—"if she *thinks* I do not look my best. She is determined that one of us snare one of the remaining Bridgerton brothers, you know."

"I know."

"And to make matters worse, that Whistledown woman has been writing about them again. It only"—Posy finished chewing and paused while she swallowed—"whets her appetite."

"Was the column very good this morning?" Sophie asked, shifting the tray to rest on her hip. "I haven't had a chance to read it yet."

"Oh, the usual stuff," Posy said with a wave of her hand. "Really, it can be quite humdrum, you know."

Sophie tried to smile and failed. She'd like nothing more than to live a day of Posy's humdrum life. Well, perhaps she wouldn't want Araminta for a mother, but she wouldn't mind a life of parties, routs, and musicales.

"Let's see," Posy mused. "There was a review of Lady Worth's recent ball, a bit about Viscount Guelph, who seems rather smitten with some girl from Scotland, and then a longish piece on the upcoming Bridgerton masquerade."

Sophie sighed. She'd been reading about the upcoming masquerade for weeks, and even though she was nothing but a lady's maid (and occasionally a housemaid as well, whenever Araminta decided she wasn't working hard enough) she couldn't help but wish that she could attend the ball.

"I for one will be thrilled if that Guelph viscount gets himself engaged," Posy remarked, reaching for another biscuit. "It will mean one fewer bachelor for Mother to go on and on about as a potential husband. It's not as if I have any hope of attracting his attention anyway." She took a bite of the biscuit; it crunched loudly in her mouth. "I do hope Lady Whistledown is right about him."

"She probably is," Sophie answered. She had been reading *Lady Whistledown's Society Papers* since it had debuted in 1813, and the gossip columnist was almost always correct when it came to matters of the Marriage Mart.

Not, of course, that Sophie had ever had the chance to see the Marriage Mart for herself. But if one read *Whistledown* often enough, one could almost feel a part of London Society without actually attending any balls.

In fact, reading *Whistledown* was really Sophie's one true enjoyable pastime. She'd already read all of the novels in the library, and as neither Araminta, Rosamund, nor Posy was particularly enamored of reading, Sophie couldn't look forward to a new book entering the house.

But *Whistledown* was great fun. No one actually knew the columnist's true identity. When the single-sheet newspaper had debuted two years earlier, speculation had been rampant. Even now, whenever Lady Whistledown reported a particularly juicy bit of gossip, people starting talking and guessing anew, wondering who on earth was able to report with such speed and accuracy.

And for Sophie, *Whistledown* was a tantalizing glimpse into the world that might have been hers, had her parents actually made their union legal. She would have been an earl's daughter, not an earl's bastard; her name Gunningworth instead of Beckett.

Just once, she'd like to be the one stepping into the coach and attending the ball.

Instead, she was the one dressing others for their nights on the town, cinching Posy's corset or dressing Rosamund's hair or polishing a pair of Araminta's shoes.

But she could not—or at least should not—complain. She might have to serve as maid to Araminta and her daughters, but at least she had a home. Which was more than most girls in her position had.

When her father had died, he'd left her nothing. Well, nothing but a roof over her head. His will had ensured that she could not be turned out until she was twenty. There was no way that Araminta would forfeit four thousand pounds a year by giving Sophie the boot.

But that four thousand pounds was Araminta's, not Sophie's, and Sophie hadn't ever seen a penny of it. Gone were the fine clothes she'd used to wear, replaced by the coarse wool of the servants. And she ate what the rest of the maids ate—whatever Araminta, Rosamund, and Posy chose to leave behind.

Sophie's twentieth birthday, however, had come and gone almost a year earlier, and here she was, still living at Penwood House, still waiting on Araminta hand and foot. For some unknown reason—probably because she didn't want to train (or pay) a new maid—Araminta had allowed Sophie to remain in her household.

And Sophie had stayed. If Araminta was the devil she knew, then the rest of the world was the devil she didn't. And Sophie had no idea which would be worse.

"Isn't that tray getting heavy?"

Sophie blinked her way out of her reverie and focused on Posy, who was reaching for the last biscuit on the tray. Drat. She'd been hoping to snitch it for herself. "Yes," she murmured. "Yes, it is quite. I should really be getting to the kitchen with it."

Posy smiled. "I won't keep you any longer, but when you're done with that, could you press my pink gown? I'm going to wear it tonight. Oh, and I suppose the matching shoes should be readied as well. I got a bit of dirt on them last time I wore them, and you know how Mother is about shoes. Never mind that you can't even see them under my skirt. She'll notice the tiniest speck of dirt the instant I lift my hem to climb a step."

Sophie nodded, mentally adding Posy's requests to her daily list of chores.

"I'll see you later, then!" Biting down on that last biscuit, Posy turned and disappeared into her bedchamber.

And Sophie trudged down to the kitchen.

A few days later, Sophie was on her knees, pins clamped between her teeth as she made last-minute alterations on Araminta's masquerade costume. The Queen Elizabeth gown had, of course, been delivered from the dressmaker as a perfect fit, but Araminta insisted that it was now a quarter inch too large in the waist.

"How is that?" Sophie asked, speaking through her teeth so the pins wouldn't fall.

"Too tight."

Sophie adjusted a few pins. "What about that?"

"Too loose."

Sophie pulled out a pin and stuck it back in precisely the same spot. "There. How does that feel?"

Araminta twisted this way and that, then finally declared, "It'll do."

Sophie smiled to herself as she stood to help Araminta out of the gown.

"I'll need it done in an hour if we're to get to the ball on time," Araminta said.

"Of course," Sophie murmured. She'd found it easiest just to say "of course" on a regular basis in conversations with Araminta.

"This ball is very important," Araminta said sharply. "Rosamund must make an advantageous match this year. The new earl—" She shuddered with distaste; she still considered the new earl an interloper, never mind that he was the old earl's closest living male relative. "Well, he has told me that this is the last year we may use Penwood House in London. The nerve of the man. I am the dowager countess, after all, and Rosamund and Posy are the earl's daughters."

Stepdaughters, Sophie silently corrected.

"We have every right to use Penwood House for the season. What he plans to do with the house, I'll never know."

"Perhaps he wishes to attend the season and look for a wife," Sophie suggested. "He'll be wanting an heir, I'm sure."

Araminta scowled. "If Rosamund doesn't marry into money, I don't know what we'll do. It is so difficult to find a proper house to rent. And so expensive as well."

Sophie forbore to point out that at least Araminta didn't have to pay for a lady's maid. In fact, until Sophie had turned twenty, she'd received four thousand pounds per year, just for *having* a lady's maid.

Araminta snapped her fingers. "Don't forget that Rosamund will need her hair powdered."

Rosamund was attending dressed as Marie Antoinette. Sophie had asked if she was planning to put a ring of faux blood around her neck. Rosamund had not been amused.

Araminta pulled on her dressing gown, cinching the sash with swift, tight movements. "And Posy—" Her nose wrinkled. "Well, Posy will need your help in some manner or other, I'm sure."

"I'm always glad to help Posy," Sophie replied.

Araminta narrowed her eyes as she tried to figure out if Sophie was being insolent. "Just see that you do," she finally said, her syllables clipped. She stalked off to the washroom.

Sophie saluted as the door closed behind her.

"Ah, there you are, Sophie," Rosamund said as she bustled into the room. "I need your help immediately."

"I'm afraid it'll have to wait until—"

"I said immediately!" Rosamund snapped.

Sophie squared her shoulders and gave Rosamund a steely look. "Your mother wants me to alter her gown."

"Just pull the pins out and tell her you pulled it in. She'll never notice the difference."

Sophie had been considering the very same thing, and she groaned. If she did as Rosamund asked, Rosamund would tattle on her the very next day, and then Araminta would rant and rage for a week. Now she would definitely have to do the alteration.

"What do you need, Rosamund?"

"There is a tear at the hem of my costume. I have no idea how it happened."

"Perhaps when you tried it on—"

"Don't be impertinent!"

Sophie clamped her mouth shut. It was far more difficult to take orders from Rosamund than from Araminta, probably because they'd once been equals, sharing the same schoolroom and governess.

"It must be repaired immediately," Rosamund said with an affected sniff.

Sophie sighed. "Just bring it in. I'll do it right after I finish with your mother's. I promise you'll have it in plenty of time."

"I won't be late for this ball," Rosamund warned. "If I am, I shall have *your* head on a platter."

"You won't be late," Sophie promised.

Rosamund made a rather huffy sound, then hurried out the door to retrieve her costume.

"Ooof!"

Sophie looked up to see Rosamund crashing into Posy, who was barreling through the door.

"Watch where you're going, Posy!" Rosamund snapped.

"You could watch where you're going, too," Posy pointed out.

"I *was* watching. It's impossible to get out of *your* way, you big oaf."

Posy's cheeks stained red, and she stepped aside.

"Did you need something, Posy?" Sophie asked, as soon as Rosamund had disappeared.

Posy nodded. "Could you set aside a little extra time to dress my hair tonight? I found some green ribbons that look a little like seaweed."

Sophie let out a long breath. The dark green ribbons weren't likely to show up very well against Posy's dark hair, but she didn't have the heart to point that out. "I'll try, Posy, but I have to mend Rosamund's dress and alter your mother's."

"Oh." Posy looked crestfallen. It nearly broke Sophie's heart. Posy was the only person who was even halfway nice to her in Araminta's household, save for the servants. "Don't worry," she assured her. "I'll make sure your hair is lovely no matter how much time we have."

"Oh, thank you, Sophie! I—"

"Haven't you gotten started on my gown yet?" Araminta thundered as she returned from the washroom.

Sophie gulped. "I was talking with Rosamund and Posy. Rosamund tore her gown and—"

"Just get to work!"

"I will. Immediately." Sophie plopped down on the settee and turned the gown inside out so that she could take in the waist. "Faster than immediately," she muttered. "Faster than a hummingbird's wings. Faster than—"

"What are you chattering about?" Araminta demanded.

"Nothing."

"Well, cease your prattle immediately. I find the sound of your voice particularly grating."

Sophie ground her teeth together.

"Mama," Posy said, "Sophie is going to dress my hair tonight like—"

"Of course she's going to dress your hair. Quit your dilly-dallying this minute and go put compresses on your eyes so they don't look so puffy."

Posy's face fell. "My eyes are puffy?"

Sophie shook her head on the off chance that Posy decided to look down at her.

"Your eyes are always puffy," Araminta replied. "Don't you think so, Rosamund?"

Posy and Sophie both turned toward the door. Rosamund had just entered, carrying her Marie Antoinette gown. "Always," she agreed. "But a compress will help, I'm sure."

"You look stunning tonight," Araminta told Rosamund. "And you haven't even started getting ready. That gold in your gown is an exquisite match to your hair."

Sophie shot a sympathetic look at the dark-haired Posy, who never received such compliments from her mother.

"You shall snare one of those Bridgerton brothers," Araminta continued. "I'm sure of it."

Rosamund looked down demurely. It was an expression she'd perfected, and Sophie had to admit it looked lovely on her. But then again, most everything looked lovely on Rosamund. Her golden hair and blue eyes were all the rage that year, and thanks to the generous dowry settled upon her by the late earl, it was widely assumed that she would make a brilliant match before the season was through.

Sophie glanced back over at Posy, who was staring at her mother with a sad, wistful expression. "You look lovely, too, Posy," Sophie said impulsively.

Posy's eyes lit up. "Do you think so?"

"Absolutely. And your gown is terribly original. I'm sure there won't be any other mermaids."

"How would you know, Sophie?" Rosamund asked with a laugh. "It's not as if you've ever been out in society."

"I'm sure you'll have a lovely time, Posy," Sophie said

pointedly, ignoring Rosamund's jibe. "I'm terribly jealous. I do wish I could go."

Sophie's little sigh and wish was met with absolute silence . . . followed by the raucous laughter of both Araminta and Rosamund. Even Posy giggled a bit.

"Oh, that's rich," Araminta said, barely able to catch her breath. "Little Sophie at the Bridgerton ball. They don't allow bastards out in society, you know."

"I didn't say I expected to go," Sophie said defensively, "just that I wish I *could*."

"Well, you shouldn't even bother doing that," Rosamund chimed in. "If you wish for things you can't possibly hope for, you're only going to be disappointed."

But Sophie didn't hear what she had to say, because in that moment, the oddest thing happened. As she was turning her head toward Rosamund, she caught sight of the housekeeper standing in the doorway. It was Mrs. Gibbons, who had come up from Penwood Park in the country when the town housekeeper had passed away. And when Sophie's eyes met hers, she winked.

Winked!

Sophie didn't think she'd ever seen Mrs. Gibbons wink.

"Sophie! Sophie! Are you listening to me?"

Sophie turned a distracted eye toward Araminta. "I'm sorry," she murmured. "You were saying?"

"I was saying," Araminta said in a nasty voice, "that you had better get to work on my gown this instant. If we are late for the ball, *you* will answer for it tomorrow."

"Yes, of course," Sophie said quickly. She jabbed her needle into the fabric and started sewing but her mind was still on Mrs. Gibbons.

A wink?

Why on earth would she wink?

Three hours later, Sophie was standing on the front steps of Penwood House, watching first Araminta, then Rosamund, then Posy each take the footman's hand and climb up into the carriage. Sophie waved at Posy, who waved back, then watched the carriage roll down the street and disappear around the corner. It was barely six blocks to Bridgerton House, where the masquerade was to be held, but Araminta would have insisted upon the carriage if they'd lived right next door.

It was important to make a grand entrance, after all.

With a sigh, Sophie turned around and made her way back up the steps. At least Araminta had, in the excitement of the moment, forgotten to leave her with a list of tasks to complete while she was gone. A free evening was a luxury indeed. Perhaps she'd reread a novel. Or maybe she could find today's edition of *Whistledown*. She'd thought she'd seen Rosamund take it into her room earlier that afternoon.

But as Sophie stepped through the front door of Penwood House, Mrs. Gibbons materialized as if from nowhere and grabbed her arm. "There's no time to lose!" the housekeeper said.

Sophie looked at her as if she'd lost her mind. "I beg your pardon?"

Mrs. Gibbons tugged at her elbow. "Come with me."

Sophie allowed herself to be led up the three flights of stairs to her room, a tiny little chamber tucked under the eaves. Mrs. Gibbons was acting in a most peculiar manner, but Sophie humored her and followed along. The housekeeper had always treated her with exceptional kindness, even when it was clear that Araminta disapproved.

"You'll need to get undressed," Mrs. Gibbons said as she grasped the doorknob.

"What?"

"We really must rush."

"Mrs. Gibbons, you . . ." Sophie's mouth fell open, and her words trailed off as she took in the scene in her bedroom. A steaming tub of water lay right in the center, and all three housemaids were bustling about. One was pouring a pitcher of water into the tub, another was fiddling with the lock on a rather mysterious-looking trunk, and the third was holding a towel and saying, "Hurry! Hurry!"

Sophie cast bewildered eyes at the lot of them. "What is going on?"

Mrs. Gibbons turned to her and beamed. "You, Miss Sophia Maria Beckett, are going to the masquerade!"

One hour later, Sophie was transformed. The trunk had held dresses belonging to the late earl's mother. They were all fifty years out of date, but that was no matter. The ball was a masquerade; no one expected the gowns to be of the latest styles.

At the very bottom of the trunk they'd found an exquisite creation of shimmering silver, with a tight, pearl-encrusted bodice and the flared skirts that had been so popular during the previous century. Sophie felt like a princess just touching it. It was a bit musty from its years in the trunk, and one of the maids quickly took it outside to dab a bit of rosewater on the fabric and air it out.

She'd been bathed and perfumed, her hair had been dressed, and one of the housemaids had even applied a touch of rouge to her lips. "Don't tell Miss Rosamund," the maid had whispered. "I nicked it from her collection."

"Ooooh, look," Mrs. Gibbons said. "I found matching gloves."

Sophie looked up to see the housekeeper holding up a pair of long, elbow-length gloves. "Look," she said, taking one from Mrs. Gibbons and examining it. "The Penwood crest. And it's monogrammed. Right at the hem."

Mrs. Gibbons turned over the one in her hand. "SLG. Sarah Louisa Gunningworth. Your grandmother."

Sophie looked at her in surprise. Mrs. Gibbons had never referred to the earl as her father. No one at Penwood Park had ever verbally acknowledged Sophie's blood ties to the Gunningworth family.

"Well, she *is* your grandmother," Mrs. Gibbons declared. "We've all danced around the issue long enough. It's a crime the way Rosamund and Posy are treated like daughters of the house, and you, the earl's true blood, must sweep and serve like a maid!"

The three housemaids nodded in agreement.

"Just once," Mrs. Gibbons said, "for just one night, *you* will be the belle of the ball." With a smile on her face, she slowly turned Sophie around until she was facing the mirror.

Sophie's breath caught. "Is that me?"

Mrs. Gibbons nodded, her eyes suspiciously bright. "You look lovely, dearling," she whispered.

Sophie's hand moved slowly up to her hair.

"Don't muss it!" one of the maids yelped.

"I won't," Sophie promised, her smile wobbling a bit as she fought back a tear. A touch of shimmery powder had been sprinkled onto her hair, so that she sparkled like a fairy princess. Her dark blond curls had been swept atop her head in a loose topknot, with one thick lock allowed to slide down the length of her neck. And her eyes, normally moss green, shone like emeralds.

Although Sophie suspected that might have had more to do with her unshed tears than anything else.

"Here is your mask," Mrs. Gibbons said briskly. It was a demi-mask, the sort that tied at the back so that Sophie would not have to use one of her hands to hold it up. "Now all we need are shoes."

Sophie glanced ruefully at her serviceable and ugly work shoes that sat in the corner. "I have nothing suitable for such finery, I'm afraid."

The housemaid who had rouged Sophie's lips held up a pair of white slippers. "From Rosamund's closet," she said.

Sophie slid her right foot into one of the slippers and just as quickly slid it back out. "It's much too big," she said, glancing up at Mrs. Gibbons. "I'll never be able to walk in them."

Mrs. Gibbons turned to the maid. "Fetch a pair from Posy's closet."

"Hers are even bigger," Sophie said. "I know. I've cleaned enough scuff marks from them."

Mrs. Gibbons let out a long sigh. "There's nothing for it, then. We shall have to raid Araminta's collection."

Sophie shuddered. The thought of walking anywhere in Araminta's shoes was somewhat creepy. But it was either that or go without, and she didn't think that bare feet would be acceptable at a fancy London masquerade.

A few minutes later the maid returned with a pair of white satin slippers, stitched in silver and adorned with exquisite faux-diamond rosettes.

Sophie was still apprehensive about wearing Araminta's shoes, but she slipped one of her feet in, anyway. It fit perfectly.

"And they match, too," one of the maids said, pointing to the silver stitching. "As if they were made for the dress."

"We don't have time for admiring shoes," Mrs. Gibbons suddenly said. "Now listen to these instructions very carefully. The coachman has returned from taking the countess and her girls, and he will take you to Bridgerton House. But he has to be waiting outside when they wish to depart, which means you must leave by midnight and not a second later. Do you understand?"

Sophie nodded and looked at the clock on the wall. It was a bit after nine, which meant she'd have more than two hours at the masquerade. "Thank you," she whispered. "Oh, thank you so much."

Mrs. Gibbons dabbed her eyes with a handkerchief. "You just have a good time, dearling. That's all the thanks I need."

Sophie looked again at the clock. Two hours.

Two hours that she'd have to make last a lifetime.

Chapter 2

The Bridgertons are truly a unique family. Surely there cannot be anyone in London who does not know that they all look remarkably alike, or that they are famously named in alphabetical order: Anthony, Benedict, Colin, Daphne, Eloise, Francesca, Gregory, and Hyacinth.

It does make one wonder what the late viscount and (still very-much alive) dowager viscountess would have named their next child had their offspring numbered nine. Imogen? Inigo?

Perhaps it is best they stopped at eight.

LADY WHISTLEDOWN'S SOCIETY PAPERS, 2 JUNE 1815

Benedict Bridgerton was the second of eight children, but sometimes it felt more like a hundred.

This ball his mother had insisted upon hosting was supposed to be a masquerade, and Benedict had dutifully donned a black demi-mask, but everyone knew who he was. Or rather, they all *almost* knew.

"A Bridgerton!" they would exclaim, clapping their hands together with glee.

"You must be a Bridgerton!"

"A Bridgerton! I can spot a Bridgerton anywhere."

Benedict was a Bridgerton, and while there was no family to which he'd rather belong, he sometimes wished he were considered a little less a Bridgerton and a little more himself.

Just then, a woman of somewhat indeterminate age dressed as a shepherdess sauntered over. "A Bridgerton!" she trilled. "I'd recognize that chestnut hair anywhere. Which are you? No, don't say. Let me guess. You're not the viscount, because I just saw him. You must be Number Two or Number Three."

Benedict eyed her coolly.

"Which one? Number Two or Number Three?"

"Two," he bit off.

She clapped her hands together. "That's what I thought! Oh, I must find Portia. I told her you were Number Two—"

Benedict, he nearly growled.

"—but she said, no, he's the younger one, but I—"

Benedict suddenly had to get away. It was either that or kill the twittering ninnyhammer, and with so many witnesses, he didn't think he could get away with it. "If you'll excuse me," he said smoothly. "I see someone with whom I must speak."

It was a lie, but he didn't much care. With a curt nod toward the overage shepherdess, he made a beeline toward the ballroom's side door, eager to escape the throng and sneak into his brother's study, where he might find some blessed peace and quiet and perhaps a glass of fine brandy.

"Benedict!"

Damn. He'd nearly made a clean escape. He looked up to see his mother hurrying toward him. She was dressed in some sort of Elizabethan costume. He supposed she was meant to be a character in one of Shakespeare's plays, but for the life of him, he had no idea which.

"What can I do for you, Mother?" he asked. "And don't say 'Dance with Hermione Smythe-Smith.' Last time I did that I nearly lost three toes in the process."

"I wasn't going to ask anything of the sort," Violet replied. "I was going to ask you to dance with Prudence Featherington."

"Have mercy, Mother," he moaned. "She's even worse."

"I'm not asking you to marry the chit," she said. "Just dance with her."

Benedict fought a groan. Prudence Featherington, while essentially a nice person, had a brain the size of a pea and a laugh so grating he'd seen grown men flee with their hands over their ears. "I'll tell you what," he wheedled. "I'll dance with Penelope Featherington if you keep Prudence at bay."

"That'll do," his mother said with a satisfied nod, leaving Benedict with the sinking sensation that she'd wanted him to dance with Penelope all along.

"She's over there by the lemonade table," Violet said, "dressed as a leprechaun, poor thing. The color is good for her, but someone really must take her mother in hand next time they venture out to the dressmaker. A more unfortunate costume, I can't imagine."

"You obviously haven't seen the mermaid," Benedict murmured.

She swatted him lightly on the arm. "No poking fun at the guests."

"But they make it so easy."

She shot him a look of warning before saying, "I'm off to find your sister."

"Which one?"

"One of the ones who isn't married," Violet said pertly. "Viscount Guelph might be interested in that Scottish girl, but they aren't betrothed yet."

Benedict silently wished Guelph luck. The poor bloke was going to need it.

"And thank you for dancing with Penelope," Violet said pointedly.

He gave her a rather ironic half smile. They both knew that her words were meant as a reminder, not as thanks.

His arms crossed in a somewhat forbidding stance, he watched his mother depart before drawing a long breath and turning to make his way to the lemonade table. He adored his mother to distraction, but she did tend to err on the side of meddlesome when it came to the social lives of her children. And if there was one thing that bothered her even more than Benedict's unmarried state, it was the sight of a young girl's glum face when no one asked her to dance. As a result, Benedict spent a lot of time on the ballroom floor, sometimes with girls she wanted him to marry, but more often with the overlooked wallflowers.

Of the two, he rather thought he preferred the wallflowers. The popular girls tended to be shallow and, to be frank, just a little bit dull.

His mother had always had a particular soft spot for Penelope Featherington, who was on her . . . Benedict frowned. On her *third* season? It must be her third. And with no marriage prospects in sight. Ah, well. He might as well do his duty. Penelope was a nice enough girl, with a decent wit and personality. Someday she'd find herself a husband. It wouldn't be *him*, of course, and in all honesty it probably wouldn't be anyone he even knew, but surely she'd find *some*one.

With a sigh, Benedict started to make his way toward the lemonade table. He could practically taste that brandy, smooth and mellow in his mouth, but he supposed that a glass of lemonade would tide him over for a few minutes.

"Miss Featherington!" he called out, trying not to shudder when three Miss Featheringtons turned around. With what he knew could not possibly be anything but the weakest of smiles, he added, "Er, Penelope, that is."

From about ten feet away, Penelope beamed at him, and Benedict was reminded that he actually *liked* Penelope Featherington. Truly, she wouldn't be considered so antidotal if she weren't always lumped together with her unfortunate sisters, who could easily make a grown man wish himself aboard a ship to Australia.

He'd nearly closed the gap between them when he heard a low rumble of whispers rippling across the ballroom behind him. He knew he ought to keep going and get this duty-dance over with, but God help him, his curiosity got the best of him and he turned around.

And found himself facing what had to be the most breathtaking woman he'd ever seen.

He couldn't even tell if she was beautiful. Her hair was a rather ordinary dark blond, and with her mask tied securely around her head he couldn't even see half of her face.

But there was something about her that held him mesmerized. It was her smile, the shape of her eyes, the way she held herself and looked about the ballroom as if she'd never seen a more glorious sight than the silly members of the *ton* all dressed up in ridiculous costumes.

Her beauty came from within.

She shimmered. She glowed.

She was utterly radiant, and Benedict suddenly realized that it was because she looked so damned *happy*. Happy to be where she was, happy to be *who* she was.

Happy in a way Benedict could barely remember. His was a good life, it was true, maybe even a great life. He had seven wonderful siblings, a loving mother, and scores of friends. But this woman—

This woman knew joy.

And Benedict had to know *her*.

Penelope forgotten, he pushed his way through the crowd until he was but a few steps from her side. Three other gentlemen had beaten him to his destination and were presently showering her with flattery and praise. Benedict watched her with interest; she did not react as any woman of his acquaintance might.

She did not act coy. Nor did she act as if she expected their compliments as her due. Nor was she shy, or tittering, or arch, or ironic, or any of those things one might expect from a woman.

She just smiled. Beamed, actually. Benedict supposed that compliments were meant to bring a measure of happiness to the receiver, but never had he seen a woman react with such pure, unadulterated joy.

He stepped forward. He wanted that joy for himself.

"Excuse me, gentlemen, but the lady has already promised this dance to me," he lied.

Her mask's eye-holes were cut a bit large, and he could see that her eyes widened considerably, then crinkled with amusement. He held out his hand to her, silently daring her to call his bluff.

But she just smiled at him, a wide, radiant grin that pierced his skin and traveled straight to his soul. She put her hand in his, and it was only then that Benedict realized he'd been holding his breath.

"Have you permission to dance the waltz?" he murmured once they reached the dance floor.

She shook her head. "I do not dance."

"You jest."

"I'm afraid I do not. The truth is—" She leaned forward and with a glimmer of a smile said, "I don't know how."

He looked at her with surprise. She moved with an inborn grace, and furthermore, what gently bred lady could reach her age without learning how to dance? "There is only one thing to do, then," he murmured. "I shall teach you."

Her eyes widened, then her lips parted, and a surprised laugh burst forth.

"What," he asked, trying to sound serious, "is so funny?"

She grinned at him—the sort of grin one expects from an old school chum, not a debutante at a ball. Still smiling, she said, "Even I know that one does not conduct dancing lessons at a ball."

"What does that mean, I wonder," he murmured, *"even you?"*

She said nothing.

"I shall have to take the upper hand, then," he said, "and force you to do my bidding."

"Force me?"

But she was smiling as she said it, so he knew she took no offense, and he said, "It would be ungentlemanly of me to allow this sorrowful state of affairs to continue."

"Sorrowful, you say?"

He shrugged. "A beautiful lady who cannot dance. It seems a crime against nature."

"If I allow you to teach me . . ."

"*When* you allow me to teach you."

"*If* I allow you to teach me, where shall you conduct the lesson?"

Benedict lifted his chin and scanned the room. It wasn't difficult to see over the heads of most of the partygoers; at an inch above six feet, he was one of the tallest men in the room. "We shall have to retire to the terrace," he said finally.

"The terrace?" she echoed. "Won't it be terribly crowded? It's a warm night, after all."

He leaned forward. "Not the *private* terrace."

"The private terrace, you say?" she asked, amusement in her voice. "And how, pray tell, would you know of a private terrace?"

Benedict stared at her in shock. Could she possibly not know who he was? It wasn't that he held such a high opinion of himself that he expected all of London to be aware of his identity. It was just that he was a Bridgerton, and if a person met one Bridgerton, that generally meant he could recognize another. And as there was no one in London who had not crossed paths with one Bridgerton or another, Benedict was generally recognized everywhere. Even, he thought ruefully, when that recognition was simply as "Number Two."

"You did not answer my question," his mystery lady reminded him.

"About the private terrace?" Benedict raised her hand to his lips and kissed the fine silk of her glove. "Let us just say that I have my ways."

She appeared undecided, and so he tugged at her fingers, pulling her closer—only by an inch, but somehow it seemed she was only a kiss away. "Come," he said. "Dance with me."

She took a step forward, and he knew his life had been changed forever.

Sophie hadn't seen him when she'd first walked into the room, but she'd felt magic in the air, and when he'd appeared before her, like some charming prince from a children's tale, she somehow knew that *he* was the reason she'd stolen into the ball.

He was tall, and what she could see of his face was very handsome, with lips that hinted of irony and smiles, and skin that was just barely touched by the beginnings of a beard. His hair was a dark, rich brown, and the flickering candlelight lent it a faint reddish cast.

People seemed to know who he was, as well. Sophie noticed that when he moved, the other partygoers stepped out of his path. And when he'd lied so brazenly and claimed her for a dance, the other men had deferred and stepped away.

He was handsome and he was strong, and for this one night, he was hers.

When the clock struck midnight, she'd be back to her life of drudgery, of mending and washing, and attending to Araminta's every wish. Was she so wrong to want this one heady night of magic and love?

She felt like a princess—a reckless princess—and so when he asked her to dance, she put her hand in his. And even though she knew that this entire evening was a lie, that she was a nobleman's bastard and a countess's maid, that her dress was borrowed and her shoes practically stolen—none of that seemed to matter as their fingers twined.

For a few hours, at least, Sophie could pretend that this gentleman could be *her* gentleman, and that from this moment on, her life would be changed forever.

It was nothing but a dream, but it had been so terribly long since she'd let herself dream.

Banishing all caution, she allowed him to lead her out of the ballroom. He walked quickly, even as he wove through the pulsing crowd, and she found herself laughing as she tripped along after him.

"Why is it," he said, halting for a moment when they reached the hall outside the ballroom, "that you always seem to be laughing at me?"

She laughed again; she couldn't help it. "I'm happy," she said with a helpless shrug. "I'm just so happy to be here."

"And why is that? A ball such as this must be routine for one such as yourself."

Sophie grinned. If he thought she was a member of the *ton*, an alumna of dozens of balls and parties, then she must be playing her role to perfection.

He touched the corner of her mouth. "You keep smiling," he murmured.

"I like to smile."

His hand found her waist, and he pulled her toward him. The distance between their bodies remained respectable, but the increasing nearness robbed her of breath.

"I like to watch you smile," he said. His words were low and seductive, but there was something oddly hoarse about his voice, and Sophie could almost let herself believe that he really meant it, that she wasn't merely that evening's conquest.

But before she could respond, an accusing voice from down the hall suddenly called out, "There you are!"

Sophie's stomach lurched well into her throat. She'd been found out. She'd be thrown into the street, and tomorrow probably into jail for stealing Araminta's shoes, and—

And the man who'd called out had reached her side and

was saying to her mysterious gentleman, "Mother has been looking all over for you. You weaseled out of your dance with Penelope, and *I* had to take your place."

"So sorry," her gentleman murmured.

That didn't seem to be enough of an apology for the newcomer, because he scowled mightily as he said, "If you flee the party and leave me to that pack of she-devil debutantes, I swear I shall exact revenge to my dying day."

"A chance I'm willing to take," her gentleman said.

"Well, I covered up for you with Penelope," the other man grumbled. "You're just lucky that I happened to be standing by. The poor girl's heart looked broken when you turned away."

Sophie's gentleman had the grace to blush. "Some things are unavoidable, I'm afraid."

Sophie looked from one man to the other. Even under their demi-masks, it was more than obvious that they were brothers, and she realized in a blinding flash that they must be the Bridgerton brothers, and this must be their house, and—

Oh, good Lord, had she made a total and utter fool of herself by asking him how he knew of a private terrace?

But which brother was he? Benedict. He had to be Benedict. Sophie sent a silent thank-you to Lady Whistledown, who'd once written a column completely devoted to the task of telling the Bridgerton siblings apart. Benedict, she recalled, had been singled out as the tallest.

The man who made her heart flip in triple time stood a good inch above his brother—

—who Sophie suddenly realized was looking at her quite intently.

"I see why you departed," Colin said (for he must be Colin; he certainly wasn't Gregory, who was only fourteen, and Anthony was married, so he wouldn't care if Benedict fled the party and left him to fend off the debutantes by himself.) He looked at Benedict with a sly expression. "Might I request an introduction?"

Benedict raised a brow. "You can try your best, but I doubt you'll meet with success. I haven't learned her name yet myself."

"You haven't asked," Sophie could not help pointing out.

"And would you tell me if I did?"

"I'd tell you *some*thing," she returned.

"But not the truth."

She shook her head. "This isn't a night for truth."

"My favorite kind of night," Colin said in a jaunty voice.

"Don't you have somewhere to *be*?" Benedict asked.

Colin shook his head. "I'm sure Mother would prefer that I *be* in the ballroom, but it's not exactly a requirement."

"*I* require it," Benedict returned.

Sophie felt a giggle bubbling in her throat.

"Very well," Colin sighed. "I shall take myself off."

"Excellent," Benedict said.

"All alone, to face the ravenous wolves . . ."

"Wolves?" Sophie queried.

"Eligible young ladies," Colin clarified. "A pack of ravenous wolves, the lot of them. Present company excluded, of course."

Sophie thought it best not to point out that she was not an "eligible young lady" at all.

"My mother—" Colin began.

Benedict groaned.

"—would like nothing better than to see my dear elder brother married off." He paused and pondered his words. "Except, perhaps, to see *me* married off."

"If only to get you out of the house," Benedict said dryly.

This time Sophie *did* giggle.

"But then again, he's considerably more ancient," Colin continued, "so perhaps we should send him to the gallows—er, altar first."

"Do you have a *point*?" Benedict growled.

"None whatsoever," Colin admitted. "But then again, I

rarely do."

Benedict turned to Sophie. "He speaks the truth."

"So then," Colin said to Sophie with a grand flourish of his arm, "will you take pity on my poor, long-suffering mother and chase my dear brother up the aisle?"

"Well, he hasn't asked," Sophie said, trying to join the humor of the moment.

"How much have you had to drink?" Benedict grumbled.

"Me?" Sophie queried.

"Him."

"Nothing at all," Colin said jovially, "but I'm thinking quite seriously of remedying that. In fact, it might be the only thing that will make this eve bearable."

"If the procurement of drink removes you from my presence," Benedict said, "then it will certainly be the only thing that will make *my* night bearable as well."

Colin grinned, gave a jaunty salute, and was gone.

"It's nice to see two siblings who love each other so well," Sophie murmured.

Benedict, who had been staring somewhat menacingly at the doorway through which his brother had just disappeared, snapped his attention back to her. "You call *that* love?"

Sophie thought of Rosamund and Posy, who were forever sniping at each other, and not in jest. "I do," she said firmly. "It's obvious you would lay your life down for him. And vice versa."

"I suppose you're right." Benedict let out a beleaguered sigh, then ruined the effect by smiling. "Much as it pains me to admit it." He leaned against the wall, crossing his arms and looking terribly sophisticated and urbane. "So tell me," he said, "have you any siblings?"

Sophie pondered that question for a moment, then gave a decisive, "No."

One of his brows rose into a curiously arrogant arch. He cocked his head very slightly to the side as he said, "I find myself rather curious as to why it took you so long to determine the answer to that question. One would think the answer would be an easy one to reach."

Sophie looked away for a moment, not wanting him to see the pain that she knew must show in her eyes. She had always wanted a family. In fact, there was nothing in life she had ever wanted more. Her father had never recognized her as his daughter, even in private, and her mother had died at her birth. Araminta treated her like the plague, and Rosamund and Posy had certainly never been sisters to her. Posy had occasionally been a friend, but even she spent most of the day asking Sophie to mend her dress, or style her hair, or polish her shoes . . .

And in all truth, even though Posy asked rather than ordered, as her sister and mother did, Sophie didn't exactly have the option of saying no.

"I am an only child," Sophie finally said.

"And that is all you're going to say on the subject," Benedict murmured.

"And that is all I'm going to say on the subject," she agreed.

"Very well." He smiled, a lazy masculine sort of smile. "What, then, am I permitted to ask you?"

"Nothing, really."

"Nothing at all?"

"I suppose I might be induced to tell you that my favorite color is green, but beyond that I shall leave you with no clues to my identity."

"Why so many secrets?"

"If I answered that," Sophie said with an enigmatic smile, truly warming to her role as a mysterious stranger, "then that would be the end of my secrets, wouldn't it?"

He leaned forward ever so slightly. "You could always develop new secrets."

Sophie backed up a step. His gaze had grown hot, and she had heard enough talk in the servants' quarters to know what that meant. Thrilling as that was, she was not quite as daring as she pretended to be. "This entire night," she said, "is secret enough."

"Then ask me a question," he said. "I have no secrets."

Her eyes widened. "None? Truly? Doesn't everyone have secrets?"

"Not I. My life is hopelessly banal."

"*That* I find difficult to believe."

"It's true," he said with a shrug. "I've never seduced an innocent, or even a married lady, I have no gambling debts, and my parents were completely faithful to one another."

Meaning he wasn't a bastard. Somehow the thought brought an ache to Sophie's throat. Not, of course, because he was legitimate, but rather because she knew he would never pursue her—at least not in an honorable fashion—if he knew that she wasn't.

"You haven't asked me a question," he reminded her.

Sophie blinked in surprise. She hadn't thought he'd been serious. "A-all right," she half stammered, caught off guard. "What, then, is your favorite color?"

He grinned. "You're going to waste your question on that?"

"I only get one question?"

"More than fair, considering you're granting me none." Benedict leaned forward, his dark eyes glinting. "And the answer is blue."

"Why?"

"Why?" he echoed.

"Yes, why? Is it because of the ocean? Or the sky? Or perhaps just because you like it?"

Benedict eyed her curiously. It seemed such an odd question—*why* his favorite color was blue. Everyone else would have taken blue for an answer and left it at that. But this woman—whose name he still didn't even know—went deeper, beyond the whats and into the whys.

"Are you a painter?" he queried.

She shook her head. "Just curious."

"Why is your favorite color green?"

She sighed, and her eyes grew nostalgic. "The grass, I suppose, and maybe the leaves. But mostly the grass. The way it feels when one runs barefoot in the summer. The smell of it after the gardeners have gone through with their scythes and trimmed it even."

"What does the feel and smell of grass have to do with the color?"

"Nothing, I suppose. And maybe everything. I used to live in the country, you see . . ." She caught herself. She hadn't meant to tell him even that much, but there didn't seem to be harm in his knowing such an innocent fact.

"And you were happier there?" he asked quietly.

She nodded, a faint rush of awareness shivering across her skin. Lady Whistledown must never have had a conversation with Benedict Bridgerton beyond the superficial, because she'd never written that he was quite the most perceptive man in London. When he looked into her eyes, Sophie had the oddest sense that he could see straight into her soul.

"You must enjoy walking in the park, then," he said.

"Yes," Sophie lied. She never had time to go to the park. Araminta didn't even give her a day off like the other servants received.

"We shall have to take a stroll together," Benedict said.

Sophie avoided a reply by reminding him, "You never did tell me why your favorite color is blue."

His head cocked slightly to the side, and his eyes narrowed just enough so that Sophie knew that he had noticed her evasion. But he simply said, "I don't know. Perhaps, like you, I'm reminded of something I miss. There is a lake at Aubrey Hall—that is where I grew up, in Kent—but the water always seemed more gray than blue."

"It probably reflects the sky," Sophie commented.

"Which is, more often than not, more gray than blue," Benedict said with a laugh. "Perhaps that is what I miss—

blue skies and sunshine."

"If it weren't raining," Sophie said with a smile, "this wouldn't be England."

"I went to Italy once," Benedict said. "The sun shone constantly."

"It sounds like heaven."

"You'd think," he said. "But I found myself missing the rain."

"I can't believe it," she said with a laugh. "I feel like I spend half my life staring out the window and grumbling at the rain."

"If it were gone, you'd miss it."

Sophie grew pensive. Were there things in her life she'd miss if they were gone? She wouldn't miss Araminta, that was for certain, and she wouldn't miss Rosamund. She'd probably miss Posy, and she'd definitely miss the way the sun shone through the window in her attic room in the mornings. She'd miss the way the servants laughed and joked and occasionally included her in their fun, even though they all knew she was the late earl's bastard.

But she wasn't going to miss these things—she wouldn't even have the opportunity to miss them—because she wasn't going anywhere. After this evening—this one amazing, wonderful, magical evening—it would be back to life as usual.

She supposed that if she were stronger, braver, she'd have left Penwood House years ago. But would that have really made much difference? She might not like living with Araminta, but she wasn't likely to improve her lot in life by leaving. She might have liked to have been a governess, and she was certainly well qualified for the position, but jobs were scarce for those without references, and Araminta certainly wasn't going to give her one.

"You're very quiet," Benedict said softly.

"I was just thinking."

"About?"

"About what I'd miss—and what I wouldn't miss—should my life drastically change."

His eyes grew intense. "And do you expect it to drastically change?"

She shook her head and tried to keep the sadness out of her voice when she answered, "No."

His voice grew so quiet it was almost a whisper. "Do you want it to change?"

"Yes," she sighed, before she could stop herself. "Oh, *yes*."

He took her hands and brought them to his lips, gently kissing each one in turn. "Then we shall begin right now," he vowed. "And tomorrow you shall be transformed."

"Tonight I am transformed," she whispered. "Tomorrow I shall disappear."

Benedict drew her close and dropped the softest, most fleeting of kisses onto her brow. "Then we must pack a lifetime into this very night."

Chapter 3

This Author waits with bated breath to see what costumes the ton will choose for the Bridgerton masquerade. It is rumored that Eloise Bridgerton plans to dress as Joan of Arc, and Penelope Featherington, out for her third season and recently returned from a visit with Irish cousins, will don the costume of a leprechaun. Miss Posy Reiling, stepdaughter to the late Earl of Penwood, plans a costume of mermaid, which This Author personally cannot wait to behold, but her elder sister, Miss Rosamund Reiling, has been very close-lipped about her own attire.

As for the men, if previous masquerade balls are any indication, the portly will dress as Henry VIII, the more fit as Alexander the Great or perhaps the devil, and the bored (the eligible Bridgerton brothers sure to be among these ranks) as themselves—basic black evening kit, with only a demi-mask as a nod to the occasion.

LADY WHISTLEDOWN'S SOCIETY PAPERS, 5 JUNE 1815

"Dance with me," Sophie said impulsively.

His smile was amused, but his fingers twined tightly with hers as he murmured, "I thought you didn't know how."

"You said you would teach me."

He stared at her for a long moment, his eyes boring into hers, then he tugged on her hand and said, "Come with me."

Pulling her along behind him, they slipped down a hallway, climbed a flight of stairs, and then rounded a corner, emerging in front of a pair of French doors. Benedict jiggled the wrought-iron handles and swung the doors open, revealing a small private terrace, adorned with potted plants and two chaise lounges.

"Where are we?" Sophie asked, looking around.

"Right above the ballroom terrace." He shut the doors behind them. "Can't you hear the music?"

Mostly, what Sophie could hear was the low rumble of endless conversation, but if she strained her ears, she could hear the faint lilt of the orchestra. "Handel," she said with a delighted smile. "My governess had a music box with this very tune."

"You loved your governess very much," he said quietly.

Her eyes had been closed as she hummed along with the music, but when she heard his words, she opened them in a startled fashion. "How did you know?"

"The same way I knew you were happier in the country." Benedict reached out and touched her cheek, one gloved finger trailing slowly along her skin until it reached the line of her jaw. "I can see it in your face."

She held silent for a few moments, then pulled away, saying, "Yes, well, I spent more time with her than with anyone else in the household."

"It sounds a lonely upbringing," he said quietly.

"Sometimes it was." She walked over to the edge of the balcony and rested her hands on the balustrade as she stared out into the inky night. "Sometimes it wasn't." Then she turned around quite suddenly, her smile bright, and Benedict knew that she would not reveal anything more about her childhood.

"Your upbringing must have been the complete opposite

of lonely," she said, "with so many brothers and sisters about."

"You know who I am," he stated.

She nodded. "I didn't at first."

He walked over to the balustrade and leaned one hip against it, crossing his arms. "What gave me away?"

"It was your brother, actually. You looked so alike—"

"Even with our masks?"

"Even with your masks," she said with an indulgent smile. "Lady Whistledown writes about you quite often, and she never passes up an opportunity to comment upon how alike you look."

"And do you know which brother I am?"

"Benedict," she replied. "If indeed Lady Whistledown is correct when she says that you are tallest among your brothers."

"You're quite the detective."

She looked slightly embarrassed. "I merely read a gossip sheet. It makes me no different from the rest of the people here."

Benedict watched her for a moment, wondering if she realized that she'd revealed another clue to the puzzle of her identity. If she'd recognized him only from *Whistledown*, then she'd not been out in society for long, or perhaps not at all. Either way, she was not one of the many young ladies to whom his mother had introduced him.

"What else do you know about me from *Whistledown*?" he asked, his smile slow and lazy.

"Are you fishing for compliments?" she asked, returning the half smile with the vaguest tilt of her lips. "For you must know that the Bridgertons are almost always spared her rapier quill. Lady Whistledown is nearly always complimentary when writing about your family."

"It's led to quite a bit of speculation about her identity," he admitted. "Some think she must be a Bridgerton."

"Is she?"

He shrugged. "Not that I'm aware of. And you didn't answer my question."

"Which question was that?"

"What you know of me from *Whistledown*."

She looked surprised. "Are you truly interested?"

"If I cannot know anything about *you*, at least I might know what you know about *me*."

She smiled, and touched the tip of her index finger to her lower lip in an endearingly absentminded gesture. "Well, let's see. Last month you won some silly horse race in Hyde Park."

"It wasn't the least bit silly," he said with a grin, "and I'm a hundred quid richer for it."

She shot him an arch look. "Horse races are almost always silly."

"Spoken just like a woman," he muttered.

"Well—"

"Don't point out the obvious," he interrupted.

That made her smile.

"What else do you know?" he asked.

"From *Whistledown*?" She tapped her finger against her cheek. "You once lopped the head off your sister's doll."

"And I'm still trying to figure out how she knew about that," Benedict muttered.

"Maybe Lady Whistledown is a Bridgerton, after all."

"Impossible. Not," he added rather forcefully, "that we're not smart enough to pull it off. Rather, the rest of the family would be too smart not to figure it out."

She laughed out loud at that, and Benedict studied her, wondering if she was aware that she'd given away yet another tiny clue to her identity. Lady Whistledown had written of the doll's unfortunate encounter with a guillotine two years earlier, in one of her very earliest columns. Many people now had the gossip sheet delivered all the way out in the country, but in the beginning, *Whistledown* had been strictly for Londoners.

Which meant that his mystery lady had been in London two years ago. And yet she hadn't known who he was until she'd met Colin.

She'd been in London, but she'd not been out in society. Perhaps she was the youngest in her family, and had been reading *Whistledown* while her older sisters enjoyed their seasons.

It wasn't enough to figure out who she was, but it was a start.

"What else do you know?" he asked, eager to see if she'd inadvertently reveal anything else.

She chuckled, clearly enjoying herself. "Your name has not been seriously linked with any young lady, and your mother despairs of ever seeing you married."

"The pressure has lessened a bit now that my brother's gone and got himself a wife."

"The viscount?"

Benedict nodded.

"Lady Whistledown wrote about that as well."

"In great detail. Although—" He leaned toward her and lowered his voice. "She didn't get all the facts."

"Really?" she asked with great interest. "What did she leave out?"

He tsked-tsked and shook his head at her. "I'm not about to reveal the secrets of my brother's courtship if you won't reveal even your name."

She snorted at that. "*Courtship* might be too strong a word. Why, Lady Whistledown wrote—"

"Lady Whistledown," he interrupted with a vaguely mocking half smile, "is not privy to all that goes on in London."

"She certainly seems privy to *most*."

"Do you think?" he mused. "I tend to disagree. For example, I suspect that if Lady Whistledown were here on the terrace, she would not know your identity."

Her eyes widened under her mask. Benedict took some satisfaction in that.

He crossed his arms. "Is that true?"

She nodded. "But I am so well disguised that no one would recognize me right now."

He raised a brow. "What if you removed your mask? Would she recognize you then?"

She pushed herself away from the railing and took a few steps toward the center of the terrace. "I'm not going to answer that."

He followed her. "I didn't think you would. But I wanted to ask, nonetheless."

Sophie turned around, then caught her breath as she realized he was mere inches away. She'd heard him following her, but she hadn't thought he was quite that close. She parted her lips to speak, but to her great surprise, she hadn't a thing to say. All she could seem to do was stare up at him, at those dark, dark eyes peering at her from behind his mask.

Speech was impossible. Even breathing was difficult.

"You still haven't danced with me," he said.

She didn't move, just stood there as his large hand came to rest at the small of her back. Her skin tingled where he touched her, and the air grew thick and hot.

This was desire, Sophie realized. This was what she'd heard the maids whispering about. This was what no gently bred lady was even supposed to *know* about.

But she was no gently bred lady, she thought defiantly. She was a bastard, a nobleman's by-blow. She was not a member of the *ton* and never would be. Did she really have to abide by their rules?

She'd always sworn that she would never become a man's mistress, that she'd never bring a child into this world to suffer her fate as a bastard. But she wasn't planning anything quite so brazen. This was one dance, one evening, perhaps one kiss.

It was enough to ruin a reputation, but what sort of reputation did she have to begin with? She was outside society, beyond the pale. And she wanted one night of fantasy.

She looked up.

"You're not going to run, then," he murmured, his dark eyes flaring with something hot and exciting.

She shook her head, realizing that once again, he'd known what she was thinking. It should have scared her that he so effortlessly read her thoughts, but in the dark seduction of the night, with the wind tugging at the loose strands of her hair, and the music floating up from below, it was somehow thrilling instead. "Where do I put my hand?" she asked. "I want to dance."

"Right here on my shoulder," he instructed. "No, just a touch lower. There you are."

"You must think me the veriest ninny," she said, "not knowing how to dance."

"I think you're very brave, actually, for admitting it." His free hand found hers and slowly lifted it into the air. "Most women of my acquaintance would have feigned an injury or disinterest."

She looked up into his eyes even though she knew it would leave her breathless. "I haven't the acting skills to feign disinterest," she admitted.

The hand at the small of her back tightened.

"Listen to the music," he instructed, his voice oddly hoarse. "Do you feel it rising and falling?"

She shook her head.

"Listen harder," he whispered, his lips drawing closer to her ear. "*One*, two, three; *one*, two, three."

Sophie closed her eyes and somehow filtered out the endless chatter of the guests below them until all she heard was the soft swell of the music. Her breathing slowed, and she found herself swaying in time with the orchestra, her head rocking back and forth with Benedict's softly uttered numerical instructions.

"*One*, two, three; *one* two three."

"I feel it," she whispered.

He smiled. She wasn't sure how she knew that; her eyes were still closed. But she felt the smile, heard it in the tenor of his breath.

"Good," he said. "Now watch my feet and allow me to lead you."

Sophie opened her eyes and looked down.

"*One*, two, three; *one*, two, three."

Hesitantly, she stepped along with him—right onto his foot.

"Oh! I'm sorry!" she blurted out.

"My sisters have done far worse," he assured her. "Don't give up."

She tried again, and suddenly her feet knew what to do. "Oh!" she breathed in surprise. "This is wonderful!"

"Look up," he ordered gently.

"But I'll stumble."

"You won't," he promised. "I won't let you. Look into my eyes."

Sophie did as he asked, and the moment her eyes touched his, something inside her seemed to lock into place, and she could not look away. He twirled her in circles and spirals around the terrace, slowly at first, then picking up speed, until she was breathless and giddy.

And all the while, her eyes remained locked on his.

"What do you feel?" he asked.

"Everything!" she said, laughing.

"What do you hear?"

"The music." Her eyes widened with excitement. "I hear the music as I've never heard it before."

His hands tightened, and the space between them diminished by several inches. "What do you see?" he asked.

Sophie stumbled, but she never took her eyes off his. "My soul," she whispered. "I see my very soul."

He stopped dancing. "What did you say?" he whispered.

She held silent. The moment seemed too charged, too meaningful, and she was afraid she'd spoil it.

No, that wasn't true. She was afraid she'd make it even better, and that would make it hurt all the more when she returned to reality at midnight.

How on earth was she going to go back to polishing Araminta's shoes after this?

"I know what you said," Benedict said hoarsely. "I heard you, and—"

"Don't say anything," Sophie cut in. She didn't want him to tell her that he felt the same way, didn't want to hear anything that would leave her pining for this man forever.

But it was probably already too late for that.

He stared at her for an agonizingly long moment, then murmured, "I won't speak. I won't say a word." And then, before she even had a second to breathe, his lips were on hers, exquisitely gentle and achingly tender.

With deliberate slowness, he brushed his lips back and forth across hers, the bare hint of friction sending shivers and tingles spiraling through her body.

He touched her lips and she felt it in her toes. It was a singularly odd—and singularly wonderful—sensation.

Then his hand at the small of her back—the one that had guided her so effortlessly in their waltz—started to pull her toward him. The pressure was slow but inexorable, and Sophie grew hot as their bodies grew closer, then positively burned when she suddenly felt the length of him pressing against her.

He seemed very large, and very powerful, and in his arms she felt like she must be the most beautiful woman in the world.

Suddenly anything seemed possible, maybe even a life free of servitude and stigma.

His mouth grew more insistent, and his tongue darted out to tickle the corner of her mouth. His hand, which had still been holding hers in a waltz-pose, slid down the length of her arm and then up her back until it rested at the nape of her neck, his fingers tugging her hair loose from its coiffure.

"Your hair is like silk," he whispered, and Sophie actually giggled, because he was wearing gloves.

He pulled away. "What," he asked with an amused expression, "are you laughing about?"

"How can you know what my hair feels like? You're wearing gloves."

He smiled, a crooked, boyish sort of a smile that sent her stomach into flips and melted her heart. "I don't know how I know," he said, "but I do." His grin grew even more lopsided, and then he added, "But just to be sure, perhaps I'd better test with my bare skin."

He held out his hand before her. "Will you do the honors?"

Sophie stared at his hand for a few seconds before she realized what he meant. With a shaky, nervous breath, she took a step back and brought both of her hands to his. Slowly she pinched the end of each of the glove's fingertips and gave it a little tug, loosening the fine fabric until she could slide the entire glove from his hand.

Glove still dangling from her fingers, she looked up. He had the oddest expression in his eyes. Hunger . . . and something else. Something almost spiritual.

"I want to touch you," he whispered, and then his bare hand cupped her cheek, the pads of his fingers lightly stroking her skin, whispering upward until they touched the hair near her ear. He tugged gently until he pulled one lock loose. Freed from the coiffure, her hair sprang into a light curl, and Sophie could not take her eyes off it, wrapped golden around his index finger.

"I was wrong," he murmured. "It's softer than silk."

Sophie was suddenly gripped by a fierce urge touch him

in the same way, and she held out her hand. "It's my turn," she said softly.

His eyes flared, and then he went to work on her glove, loosening it at the fingers the same way she had done. But then, rather than pulling it off, he brought his lips to the edge of the long glove, all the way above her elbow, and kissed the sensitive skin on the inside of her arm. "Also softer than silk," he murmured.

Sophie used her free hand to grip his shoulder, no longer confident of her ability to stand.

He tugged at the glove, allowing it to slide off her arm with agonizing slowness, his lips following its progress until they reached the inside of her elbow. Barely breaking the kiss, he looked up and said, "You don't mind if I stay here for a bit."

Helplessly, Sophie shook her head.

His tongue darted out and traced the bend of her arm.

"Oh, my," she moaned.

"I thought you might like that," he said, his words hot against her skin.

She nodded. Or rather, she meant to nod. She wasn't sure if she actually did.

His lips continued their trail, sliding sensuously down her forearm until they reached the inside of her wrist. They remained there for a moment before finally coming to rest in the absolute center of her palm.

"Who are you?" he asked, lifting his head but not letting go of her hand.

She shook her head.

"I have to know."

"I can't say." And then, when she saw that he would not take no for an answer, she lied and added, "Yet."

He took one of her fingers and rubbed it gently against his lips. "I want to see you tomorrow," he said softly. "I want to call on you and see where you live."

She said nothing, just held herself steady, trying not to cry.

"I want to meet your parents and pet your damned dog," he continued, somewhat unsteadily. "Do you understand what I mean?"

Music and conversation still drifted up from below, but the only sound on the terrace was the harsh rasp of their breath.

"I want—" His voice dropped to a whisper, and his eyes looked vaguely surprised, as if he couldn't quite believe the truth of his own words. "I want your future. I want every little piece of you."

"Don't say anything more," she begged him. "*Please*. Not another word."

"Then tell me your name. Tell me how to find you tomorrow."

"I—" But then she heard a strange sound, exotic and ringing. "What is that?"

"A gong," he replied. "To signal the unmasking."

Panic rose within her. "What?"

"It must be midnight."

"Midnight?" she gasped.

He nodded. "Time to remove your mask."

One of Sophie's hands flew up to her temple, pressing the mask harshly against her skin, as if she could somehow glue it onto her face through sheer force of will.

"Are you all right?" Benedict asked.

"I have to go," she blurted out, and then, with no further warning, she hitched up her skirts and ran from the terrace.

"Wait!" she heard him call out, felt the rush of air as his arm swiped forward in a futile attempt to grab her dress.

But Sophie was fast, and perhaps more importantly, she was in a state of utter panic, and she tore down the stairs as if the fires of hell were nipping at her heels.

She plunged into the ballroom, knowing that Benedict would prove a determined pursuer, and she'd have the best chance of losing him in a large crowd. All she had to do was make it across the room, and then she could exit via the side door and scoot around the outside of the house to her waiting carriage.

The revelers were still removing their masks, and the party was loud with raucous laughter. Sophie pushed and jostled, anything to beat her way to the other side of the room. She threw one desperate glance over her shoulder. Benedict had entered the ballroom, his face intense as he scanned the crowd. He didn't seem to have seen her yet, but she knew that he would; her silver gown would make her an easy target.

Sophie kept shoving people out of her way. At least half of them didn't seem to notice; probably too drunk. "Excuse me," she muttered, elbowing Julius Caesar in the ribs. "Beg pardon," came out more like a grunt; that was when Cleopatra stepped on her toe.

"Excuse me, I—" And then the breath was quite literally sucked out of her, because she found herself face-to-face with Araminta.

Or rather, face to mask. Sophie was still disguised. But if anyone could recognize her, it would be Araminta. And—

"Watch where you're going," Araminta said haughtily. Then, while Sophie stood openmouthed, she swished her Queen Elizabeth skirts and swept away.

Araminta hadn't recognized her! If Sophie hadn't been so frantic about getting out of Bridgerton House before Benedict caught up with her, she would have laughed with delight.

Sophie glanced desperately behind her. Benedict had spotted her and was pushing his way through the crowd with considerably more efficiency than she had done. With an audible gulp and renewed energy, she pushed forth, almost knocking two Grecian goddesses to the ground before finally reaching the far door.

She looked behind her just long enough to see that Benedict had been waylaid by some elderly lady with a cane, then ran out of the building and around front, where the Penwood carriage was waiting, just as Mrs. Gibbons had said it would.

"Go, go, go!" Sophie shouted frantically to the driver.

And she was gone.

Chapter 4

More than one masquerade attendee has reported to This Author that Benedict Bridgerton was seen in the company of an unknown lady dressed in a silver gown.

Try as she might, This Author has been completely unable to discern the mystery lady's identity. And if This Author cannot uncover the truth, you may be assured that her identity is a well-kept secret indeed.

LADY WHISTLEDOWN'S SOCIETY PAPERS, 7 JUNE 1815

She was gone.

Benedict stood on the pavement in front of Bridgerton House, surveying the street. All of Grosvenor Square was a mad crush of carriages. She could be in any one of them, just sitting there on the cobbles, trying to escape the traffic. Or she could be in one of the three carriages that had just escaped the tangle and rolled around the corner.

Either way, she was gone.

He was half-ready to strangle Lady Danbury, who'd jammed her cane onto his toe and insisted upon giving him her opinion on most of the partygoers' costumes. By the time he'd managed to free himself, his mystery lady had disappeared through the ballroom's side door.

And he knew that she had no intention of letting him see her again.

Benedict let out a low and rather viciously uttered curse. With all the ladies his mother had trotted out before him—and there had been many—he'd never once felt the same soul-searing connection that had burned between him and the lady in silver. From the moment he'd seen her—no, from the moment *before* he'd seen her, when he'd only just felt her presence, the air had been alive, crackling with tension and excitement. And he'd been alive, too—alive in a way he hadn't felt for years, as if everything were suddenly new and sparkling and full of passion and dreams.

And yet . . .

Benedict cursed again, this time with a touch of regret.

And yet he didn't even know the color of her eyes.

They definitely hadn't been brown. Of that much he was positive. But in the dim light of the candled night, he'd been unable to discern whether they were blue or green. Or hazel or gray. And for some reason he found this the most upsetting. It ate at him, leaving a burning, hungry sensation in the pit of his stomach.

They said eyes were the windows to the soul. If he'd truly found the woman of his dreams, the one with whom he could finally imagine a family and a future, then by God he ought to know the color of her eyes.

It wasn't going to be easy to find her. It was never easy to find someone who didn't want to be found, and she'd made it more than clear that her identity was a secret.

His clues were paltry at best. A few dropped comments concerning Lady Whistledown's column and . . .

Benedict looked down at the single glove still clutched in his right hand. He'd quite forgotten that he'd been holding it as he'd dashed through the ballroom. He brought it to his face and inhaled its scent, but much to his surprise, it didn't smell of rosewater and soap, as had his mystery lady. Rather, its scent was a bit musty, as if it had been packed away in an attic trunk for many years.

Odd, that. Why would she be wearing an ancient glove?

He turned it over in his hand, as if the motion would somehow bring her back, and that was when he noticed a tiny bit of stitching at the hem.

SLG. Someone's initials.

Were they hers?

And a family crest. One he did not recognize.

But his mother would. His mother always knew that sort of thing. And chances were, if she knew the crest, she'd know who the initials SLG belonged to.

Benedict felt his first glimmer of hope. He would find her.

He would find her, and he would make her his. It was as simple as that.

It took a mere half hour to return Sophie to her regular, drab state. Gone were the dress, the glittering earbobs, and the fancy coiffure. The jeweled slippers were tucked neatly back in Araminta's closet, and the rouge the maid had used for her lips was resting in its place on Rosamund's dressing table. She'd even taken five minutes to massage the skin on her face, to remove the indentations left by the mask.

Sophie looked as she always looked before bed—plain, simple, and unassuming, her hair pulled into a loose braid, her feet tucked into warm stockings to keep out the chill night air.

She was back to looking what she was in truth—nothing more than a housemaid. Gone were all traces of the fairy princess she'd been for one short evening.

And saddest of all, gone was her fairy prince.

Benedict Bridgerton had been everything she'd read in *Whistledown*. Handsome, strong, debonair. He was the stuff of a young girl's dreams, but not, she thought glumly, of *her* dreams. A man like that didn't marry an earl's by-blow. And he certainly didn't marry a housemaid.

But for one night he'd been hers, and she supposed that would have to be enough.

She picked up a little stuffed dog she'd had since she'd been a small girl. She'd kept it all these years as a reminder of happier times. It usually sat on her dresser, but for some reason she wanted it closer right now. She crawled into bed, the little dog tucked under her arm, and curled up under the covers.

Then she squeezed her eyes shut, biting her lip as silent tears trickled onto her pillow.

It was a long, long night.

"Do you recognize this?"

Benedict Bridgerton was sitting next to his mother in her very feminine rose-and-cream drawing room, holding out his only link to the woman in silver. Violet Bridgerton took the glove and examined the crest. She needed only a second before she announced, "Penwood."

"As in 'Earl of'?"

Violet nodded. "And the G would be for Gunningworth. The title recently passed out of their family, if I recall correctly. The earl died without issue . . . oh, it must have been six or seven years ago. The title went to a distant cousin. And," she added with a disapproving nod of her head, "you forgot to dance with Penelope Featherington last night. You're lucky your brother was there to dance in your stead."

Benedict fought a groan and tried to ignore her scolding. "Who, then, is SLG?"

Violet's blue eyes narrowed. "Why are you interested?"

"I don't suppose," Benedict said on a groan, "that you will simply answer my question without posing one of your own."

She let out a ladylike snort. "You know me far better than that."

Benedict just managed to stop himself from rolling his eyes.

"Who," Violet asked, "does the glove belong to, Benedict?" And then, when he didn't answer quickly enough for her taste, she added, "You might as well tell me everything. You know I will figure it out on my own soon enough, and it will be far less embarrassing for you if I don't have to ask any questions."

Benedict sighed. He was going to have to tell her everything. Or at least, almost everything. There was little he enjoyed less than sharing such details with his mother—she tended to grab hold of any hope that he might actually marry and cling on to it with the tenacity of a barnacle. But he had little choice. Not if he wanted to find *her*.

"I met someone last night at the masquerade," he finally said.

Violet clapped her hands together with delight. "Really?"

"She's the reason I forgot to dance with Penelope."

Violet looked nearly ready to die of rapture. "Who? One of Penwood's daughters?" She frowned. "No, that's impossible. He had no daughters. But he did have two stepdaughters." She frowned again. "Although I must say, having met those two girls . . . well . . ."

"Well, what?"

Violet's brow wrinkled as she fumbled for polite words. "Well, I simply wouldn't have guessed you'd be interested in either of them, that's all. But if you *are*," she added, her face brightening considerably, "then I shall surely invite the dowager countess over for tea. It's the very least I can do."

Benedict started to say something, then stopped when he saw that his mother was frowning yet again. "What now?" he asked.

"Oh, nothing," Violet said. "Just that . . . well . . ."

"Spit it out, Mother."

She smiled weakly. "Just that I don't particularly *like* the dowager countess. I've always found her rather cold and ambitious."

"Some would say you're ambitious as well, Mother," Benedict pointed out.

Violet pulled a face. "Of course I have great ambition that my children marry well and happily, but I am not the sort who'd marry her daughter off to a seventy-year-old man just because he was a duke!"

"Did the dowager countess do that?" Benedict couldn't recall any seventy-year-old dukes making recent trips to the altar.

"No," Violet admitted, "but she would. Whereas I—"

Benedict bit back a smile as his mother pointed to herself with great flourish.

"I would allow my children to marry paupers if it would bring them happiness."

Benedict raised a brow.

"They would be well-principled and hardworking paupers, of course," Violet explained. "No gamblers need apply."

Benedict didn't want to laugh at his mother, so instead he coughed discreetly into his handkerchief.

"But you should not concern yourself with me," Violet said, giving her son a sideways look before punching him lightly in the arm.

"Of course I must," he said quickly.

She smiled serenely. "I shall put aside my feelings for the dowager countess if you care for one of her daughters . . ." She looked up hopefully. "Do you care for one of her daughters?"

"I have no idea," Benedict admitted. "I never got her name. Just her glove."

Violet gave him a stern look. "I'm not even going to ask how you obtained her glove."

"It was all very innocent, I assure you."

Violet's expression was dubious in the extreme. "I have far too many sons to believe *that,*" she muttered.

"The initials?" Benedict reminded her.

Violet examined the glove again. "It's rather old," she said.

Benedict nodded. "I thought so as well. It smelled a bit musty, as if it had been packed away for some time."

"And the stitches show wear," she commented. "I don't know what the L is for, but the S could very well be for Sarah. The late earl's mother, who has also passed on. Which would make sense, given the age of the glove."

Benedict stared down at the glove in his mother's hands for a moment before saying, "As I'm fairly certain I did not converse with a ghost last night, who do you think the glove might belong to?"

"I have no idea. Someone in the Gunningworth family, I imagine."

"Do you know where they live?"

"At Penwood House, actually," Violet replied. "The new earl hasn't given them the boot yet. Don't know why. Perhaps he's afraid they'll want to live with him once he takes up residence. I don't think he's even in town for the season. Never met him myself."

"Do you happen to know—"

"Where Penwood House is?" Violet cut in. "Of course I do. It's not far, only a few blocks away." She gave him directions, and Benedict, in his haste to be on his way, was already on his feet and halfway out the door before she finished.

"Oh, Benedict!" Violet called out, her smile very amused.

He turned around. "Yes?"

"The countess's daughters are named Rosamund and Posy. Just in case you're interested."

Rosamund and Posy. Neither seemed fitting, but what did he know? Perhaps he didn't seem a proper Benedict to people he met. He turned on his heel and tried to exit once again, but his mother stopped him with yet another, "Oh, Benedict!"

He turned around. "Yes, Mother?" he asked, sounding purposefully beleaguered.

"You will tell me what happens, won't you?"

"Of course, Mother."

"You're lying to me," she said with a smile, "but I forgive you. It's so nice to see you in love."

"I'm not—"

"Whatever you say, dear," she said with a wave.

Benedict decided there was little point in replying, so with nothing more than a roll of his eyes, he left the room and hurried out of the house.

"Sophieeeeeeeeeeeeeee!"

Sophie's chin snapped up. Araminta sounded even more irate than usual, if that were possible. Araminta was *always* upset with her.

"Sophie! Drat it, where is that infernal girl?"

"The infernal girl is right here," Sophie muttered, setting down the silver spoon she'd been polishing. As lady's maid to Araminta, Rosamund, and Posy, she shouldn't have had to add the polishing to her list of chores, but Araminta positively reveled in working her to the bone.

"Right here," she called out, rising to her feet and walking out into the hall. The Lord only knew what Araminta was upset about this time. She looked this way and that. "My lady?"

Araminta came storming around the corner. "What," she snapped, holding something up in her right hand, "is the meaning of *this*?"

Sophie's eyes fell to Araminta's hand, and she only just managed to stifle a gasp. Araminta was holding the shoes that Sophie had borrowed the night before. "I—I don't know what you mean," she stammered.

"These shoes are *brand-new*. Brand-new!"

Sophie stood quietly until she realized that Araminta required a reply. "Um, what is the problem?"

"Look at this!" Araminta screeched, jabbing her finger toward one of the heels. "It's scuffed. Scuffed! How could something like this happen?"

"I'm sure I don't know, my lady," Sophie said. "Perhaps—"

"There is no perhaps about it," Araminta huffed. "Someone has been wearing my shoes."

"I assure you no one has been wearing your shoes," Sophie replied, amazed that she was able to keep her voice even. "We all know how particular you are about your footwear."

Araminta narrowed her eyes suspiciously. "Are you being sarcastic?"

Sophie rather thought that if Araminta had to ask, then she was playing her sarcasm very well indeed, but she lied, and said, "No! Of course not. I merely meant that you take very good care of your shoes. They last longer that way."

Araminta said nothing, so Sophie added, "Which means you don't have to buy as many pairs."

Which was, of course, utter ridiculousness, as Araminta already owned more pairs of shoes than any one person could hope to wear in a lifetime.

"This is your fault," Araminta growled.

According to Araminta, everything was always Sophie's fault, but this time she was actually correct, so Sophie just gulped and said, "What would you like me to do about it, my lady?"

"I want to know who wore my shoes."

"Perhaps they were scuffed in your closet," Sophie suggested. "Maybe you accidentally kicked them last time you walked by."

"I never *accidentally* do anything," Araminta snapped.

Sophie silently agreed. Araminta was deliberate in all

things. "I can ask the maids," Sophie said. "Perhaps one of them knows something."

"The maids are a pack of idiots," Araminta replied. "What they know could fit on my littlest fingernail."

Sophie waited for Araminta to say, "Present company excluded," but of course she did not. Finally, Sophie said, "I can try to polish the shoe. I'm sure we can do something about the scuff mark."

"The heels are covered in satin," Araminta sneered. "If you can find a way to polish that, then we should have you admitted to the Royal College of Fabric Scientists."

Sophie badly wanted to ask if there even *existed* a Royal College of Fabric Scientists, but Araminta didn't have much of a sense of humor even when she wasn't in a complete snit. To poke fun now would be a clear invitation for disaster. "I could try to rub it out," Sophie suggested. "Or brush it."

"You do that," Araminta said. "In fact, while you're at it . . ."

Oh, *blast*. All bad things began with Araminta saying, "While you're at it."

". . . you might as well polish all of my shoes."

"All of them?" Sophie gulped. Araminta's collection must have numbered at least eighty pair.

"All of them. And while you're at it . . ."

Not *again*.

"Lady Penwood?"

Araminta blessedly stopped in mid-command to turn and see what the butler wanted.

"A gentleman is here to see you, my lady," he said, handing her a crisp, white card.

Araminta took it from him and read the name. Her eyes widened, and she let out a little, "Oh!" before turning back to the butler, and barking out, "Tea! And biscuits! The best silver. At once."

The butler hurried out, leaving Sophie staring at Araminta with unfeigned curiosity. "May I be of any help?" Sophie asked.

Araminta blinked twice, staring at Sophie as if she'd forgotten her presence. "No," she snapped. "I'm far too busy to bother with you. Go upstairs at once." She paused, then added, "What are you doing down here, anyway?"

Sophie motioned toward the dining room she'd recently exited. "You asked me to polish—"

"I asked you to see to my shoes," Araminta fairly yelled.

"All—all right," Sophie said slowly. Araminta was acting very odd, even for Araminta. "I'll just put away—"

"Now!"

Sophie hurried to the stairs.

"Wait!"

Sophie turned around. "Yes?" she asked hesitantly.

Araminta's lips tightened into an unattractive frown. "Make sure that Rosamund's and Posy's hair is properly dressed."

"Of course."

"Then you may instruct Rosamund to lock you in my closet."

Sophie stared at her. She actually wanted Sophie to give the order to have herself locked in the closet?

"Do you understand me?"

Sophie couldn't quite bring herself to nod. Some things were simply too demeaning.

Araminta marched over until their faces were quite close. "You didn't answer," she hissed. "Do you understand me?"

Sophie nodded, but just barely. Every day, it seemed, brought more evidence of the depth of Araminta's hatred for her. "Why do you keep me here?" she whispered before she had time to think better of it.

"Because I find you useful," was Araminta's low reply.

Sophie watched as Araminta stalked from the room, then

hurried up the stairs. Rosamund's and Posy's hair looked quite acceptable, so she sighed, turned to Posy, and said, "Lock me in the closet, if you will."

Posy blinked in surprise. "I beg your pardon?"

"I was instructed to ask Rosamund, but I can't quite bring myself to do so."

Posy peered in the closet with great interest. "May I ask why?"

"I'm meant to polish your mother's shoes."

Posy swallowed uncomfortably. "I'm sorry."

"So am I," Sophie said with a sigh. "So am I."

Chapter 5

And in other news from the masquerade ball, Miss Posy Reiling's costume as a mermaid was somewhat unfortunate, but not, This Author thinks, as dreadful as that of Mrs. Featherington and her two eldest daughters, who went as a bowl of fruit—Philippa as an orange, Prudence as an apple, and Mrs. Featherington as a bunch of grapes.

Sadly, none of the three looked the least bit appetizing.

LADY WHISTLEDOWN'S SOCIETY PAPERS, 7 JUNE 1815

What had his life come to, Benedict wondered, that he was obsessed with a glove? He'd patted his coat pocket about a dozen times since he'd taken a seat in Lady Penwood's sitting room, silently reassuring himself that it was still there. Uncharacteristically anxious, he wasn't certain what he planned to say to the dowager countess once she arrived, but he was usually fairly glib of tongue; surely he'd figure out something as he went along.

His foot tapping, he glanced over at the mantel clock. He'd given his card to the butler about fifteen minutes earlier, which meant that Lady Penwood ought to be down soon. It seemed an unwritten rule that all ladies of the *ton* must keep their callers waiting for at least fifteen minutes, twenty if they were feeling particularly peevish.

A bloody stupid rule, Benedict thought irritably. Why the rest of the world didn't value punctuality as he did, he would never know, but—

"Mr. Bridgerton!"

He looked up. A rather attractive, extremely fashionable blond woman in her forties glided into the room. She looked vaguely familiar, but that was to be expected. They'd surely attended many of the same society functions, even if they had not been introduced.

"You must be Lady Penwood," he murmured, rising to his feet and offering her a polite bow.

"Indeed," she replied with a gracious incline of her head. "I am so delighted that you have chosen to honor us with a call. I have, of course, informed my daughters of your presence. They shall be down shortly."

Benedict smiled. That was exactly what he'd hoped she'd do. He would have been shocked if she'd behaved otherwise. No mother of marriageable daughters ever ignored a Bridgerton brother. "I look forward to meeting them," he said.

Her brow furrowed slightly. "Then you have not yet met them?"

Blast. Now she'd be wondering why he was there. "I have heard such lovely things about them," he improvised, trying not to groan. If Lady Whistledown caught hold of this—and Lady Whistledown seemed to catch hold of everything—it would soon be all over town that he was looking for a wife, *and* that he'd zeroed in on the countess's daughters. Why else would he call upon two women to whom he had not even been introduced?

Lady Penwood beamed. "My Rosamund is considered one of the loveliest girls of the season."

"And your Posy?" Benedict asked, somewhat perversely.

The corners of her mouth tightened. "Posy is, er, delightful."

He smiled benignly. "I cannot wait to meet Posy."

Lady Penwood blinked, then covered up her surprise with a slightly hard smile. "I'm sure Posy will be delighted to meet you."

A maid entered with an ornate silver tea service, then set it down on a table at Lady Penwood's nod. Before the maid could depart, however, the countess said (somewhat sharply, in Benedict's opinion), "Where are the Penwood spoons?"

The maid bobbed a rather panicked curtsy, then replied, "Sophie was polishing the silver in the dining room, my lady, but she had to go upstairs when you—"

"Silence!" Lady Penwood cut in, even though she'd been the one to ask about the spoons in the first place. "I'm sure Mr. Bridgerton is not so high in the instep that he needs monogrammed spoons for his tea."

"Of course not," Benedict murmured, thinking that Lady Penwood must be a bit too high in the instep herself if she even thought to bring it up.

"Go! Go!" the countess ordered the maid, waving her briskly away. "Begone."

The maid hurried out, and the countess turned back to him, explaining, "Our better silver is engraved with the Penwood crest."

Benedict leaned forward. "Really?" he asked with obvious interest. This would be an excellent way to verify that the crest on the glove was indeed that of the Penwoods. "We don't have anything like that at Bridgerton House," he said, hoping he wasn't lying. In all truth, he'd never even noticed the pattern of the silver. "I should love to see it."

"Really?" Lady Penwood asked, her eyes lighting up. "I knew you were a man of taste and refinement."

Benedict smiled, mostly so he wouldn't groan.

"I shall have to send someone to the dining room to fetch a piece. Assuming, of course, that infernal girl managed to do her job." The corners of her lips turned down in a most unattractive manner, and Benedict noticed that her frown lines were deep indeed.

"Is there a problem?" he asked politely.

She shook her head and waved her hand dismissively. "Merely that it is so difficult to find good help. I'm sure your mother says the same thing all the time."

His mother never said any such thing, but that was probably because all of the Bridgerton servants were treated very well and thus were utterly devoted to the family. But Benedict nodded all the same.

"One of these days I'm going to have to give Sophie the boot," the countess said with a sniff. "She cannot do anything right."

Benedict felt a vague pang of pity for the poor, unseen Sophie. But the last thing he wanted to do was get into a discussion on servants with Lady Penwood, and so he changed the subject by motioning to the teapot, and saying, "I imagine it's well steeped by now."

"Of course, of course." Lady Penwood looked up and smiled. "How do you take yours?"

"Milk, no sugar."

As she prepared his cup, Benedict heard the clatter of feet coming down the stairs, and his heart began to race with excitement. Any minute now the countess's daughters would slip through the door, and surely one of them would be the woman he'd met the night before. It was true that he had not seen most of her face, but he knew her approximate size and height. And he was fairly certain that her hair was a long, light brown.

Surely he'd recognize her when he saw her. How could he not?

But when the two young ladies entered the room, he knew instantly that neither was the woman who'd haunted his every thought. One of them was far too blond, and besides, she held herself with a prissy, rather affected manner. There was no joy in her aspect, no mischief in her smile. The other looked friendly enough, but she was too chubby, and her hair was too dark.

Benedict did his best not to look disappointed. He smiled during the introductions and gallantly kissed each of their hands, murmuring some nonsense about how delighted he was to meet them. He made a point of fawning over the chubby one, if only because her mother so obviously preferred the other.

Mothers like that, he decided, didn't deserve to be mothers.

"And do you have any other children?" Benedict asked Lady Penwood, once the introductions were through.

She gave him an odd look. "Of course not. Else I would have brought them out to meet you."

"I thought you might have children still in the schoolroom," he demurred. "Perhaps from your union with the earl."

She shook her head. "Lord Penwood and I were not blessed with children. Such a pity it was that the title left the Gunningworth family."

Benedict could not help but notice that the countess looked more irritated than saddened by her lack of Penwood progeny. "Did your husband have any brothers or sisters?" he asked. Maybe his mystery lady was a Gunningworth cousin.

The countess shot him a suspicious look, which, Benedict had to admit, was well deserved, considering that his questions were not at all the usual fare for an afternoon call. "Obviously," she replied, "my late husband did not have any brothers, as the title passed out of the family."

Benedict knew he should keep his mouth shut, but something about the woman was so bloody irritating he had to say, "He could have had a brother who predeceased him."

"Well, he did not."

Rosamund and Posy were watching the exchange with great interest, their heads bobbing back and forth like balls at a tennis match.

"And any sisters?" Benedict inquired. "The only reason I ask is that I come from such a large family." He motioned to Rosamund and Posy. "I cannot imagine having only one sibling. I thought perhaps that your daughters might have cousins to keep them company."

It was, he thought, rather paltry as far as explanations went, but it would have to do.

"He did have one sister," the countess replied with a disdainful sniff. "But she lived and died a spinster. She was a woman of great faith," she explained, "and chose to devote her life to charitable works."

So much for *that* theory.

"I very much enjoyed your masquerade ball last night," Rosamund suddenly said.

Benedict looked at her in surprise. The two girls had been so silent he'd forgotten they could even speak. "It was really my mother's ball," he answered. "I had no part in the planning. But I shall convey your compliments."

"Please do," Rosamund said. "Did you enjoy the ball, Mr. Bridgerton?"

Benedict stared at her for a moment before answering. She had a hard look in her eyes, as if she was searching for a specific piece of information. "I did indeed," he finally said.

"I noticed you spent a great deal of time with one lady in particular," Rosamund persisted.

Lady Penwood twisted her head sharply to look at him, but she did not say anything.

"Did you?" Benedict murmured.

"She was wearing silver," Rosamund said. "Who was she?"

"A mystery woman," he said with an enigmatic smile. No need for them to know that she was a mystery to him as well.

"Surely you can share her name with us," Lady Penwood said.

Benedict just smiled and stood. He wasn't going to get any more information here. "I'm afraid I must be going, ladies," he said affably, offering them a smooth bow.

"You never did see the spoons," Lady Penwood reminded him.

"I'll have to save them for another time," Benedict said. It was unlikely that his mother would have incorrectly identified the Penwood crest, and besides, if he spent much more time in the company of the hard and brittle Countess of Penwood, he might retch.

"It has been lovely," he lied.

"Indeed," Lady Penwood said, rising to walk him to the door. "Brief, but lovely."

Benedict didn't bother to smile again.

"What," Araminta said as she heard the front door close behind Benedict Bridgerton, "do you suppose that was about?"

"Well," Posy said, "he might—"

"I didn't ask you," Araminta bit off.

"Well, then, who *did* you ask?" Posy returned with uncharacteristic gumption.

"Perhaps he saw me from afar," Rosamund said, "and—"

"He didn't see you from afar," Araminta snapped as she strode across the room.

Rosamund lurched backward in surprise. Her mother rarely spoke to her in such impatient tones.

Araminta continued, "You yourself said he was besotted with some woman in a silver dress."

"I didn't say 'besotted' precisely . . ."

"Don't argue with me over such trivialities. Besotted or not, he didn't come here looking for either of *you*," Araminta said with a fair amount of derision. "I don't know what he was up to. He . . ."

Her words trailed off as she reached the window. Pulling the sheer curtain back, she saw Mr. Bridgerton standing on the pavement, pulling something from his pocket. "What is he doing?" she whispered.

"I think he's holding a glove," Posy said helpfully.

"It's not a—" Araminta said automatically, too used to contradicting everything Posy had to say. "Why, it *is* a glove."

"I should think I know a glove when I see one," Posy muttered.

"What is he looking at?" Rosamund asked, nudging her sister out of the way.

"There's something on the glove," Posy said. "Perhaps it's a piece of embroidery. We've some gloves with the Penwood crest embroidered on the hem. Maybe that glove has the same."

Araminta went white.

"Are you feeling all right, Mother?" Posy asked. "You look rather pale."

"He came here looking for her," Araminta whispered.

"Who?" Rosamund asked.

"The woman in silver."

"Well, he isn't going to find her here," Posy replied, "as I was a mermaid and Rosamund was Marie Antoinette. And you, of course, were Queen Elizabeth."

"The shoes," Araminta gasped. "The shoes."

"What shoes?" Rosamund asked irritably.

"They were scuffed. Someone wore my shoes." Araminta's face, already impossibly pale, blanched even more. "It was *her*. How did she do it? It had to be her."

"Who?" Rosamund demanded.

"Mother, are you certain you're all right?" Posy asked again. "You're not at all yourself."

But Araminta had already run out of the room.

"Stupid, stupid shoe," Sophie grumbled, scrubbing at the heel of one of Araminta's older pieces of footwear. "She hasn't even worn this one for years."

She finished polishing the toe and put it back in its place in the neatly ordered row of shoes. But before she could reach for another pair, the door to the closet burst open, slamming against the wall with such force that Sophie nearly screamed with surprise.

"Oh, goodness, you gave me a fright," she said to Araminta. "I didn't hear you coming, and—"

"Pack your things," Araminta said in a low, cruel voice. "I want you out of this house by sunrise."

The rag Sophie had been using to polish the shoes fell from her hand. "What?" she gasped. "Why?"

"Do I really need a reason? We both know I ceased receiving any funds for your care nearly a year ago. It's enough that I don't want you here any longer."

"But where will I go?"

Araminta's eyes narrowed to nasty slits. "That's not my concern, now, is it?"

"But—"

"You're twenty years of age. Certainly old enough to make your way in the world. There will be no more coddling from me."

"You never coddled me," Sophie said in a low voice.

"Don't you dare talk back to me."

"Why not?" Sophie returned, her voice growing shrill. "What have I to lose? You're booting me out of the house, anyway."

"You might treat me with a little respect," Araminta hissed, planting her foot on Sophie's skirt so that she was pinned in her kneeling position, "considering that I have clothed and sheltered you this past year out of the goodness of my heart."

"You do nothing out of the goodness of your heart." Sophie tugged at her skirt, but it was firmly trapped under Araminta's heel. "Why did you really keep me here?"

Araminta cackled. "You're cheaper than a regular maid,

and I do enjoy ordering you about."

Sophie hated being Araminta's virtual slave, but at least Penwood House was home. Mrs. Gibbons was her friend, and Posy was usually sympathetic, and the rest of the world was . . . well . . . rather scary. Where would she go? What would she do? How would she support herself?

"Why now?" Sophie asked.

Araminta shrugged. "You're no longer useful to me."

Sophie looked at the long row of shoes she'd just polished. "I'm not?"

Araminta ground the pointy heel of her shoe into Sophie's skirt, tearing the fabric. "You went to the ball last night, didn't you?"

Sophie felt the blood drain from her face, and she knew that Araminta saw the truth in her eyes. "N-no," she lied. "How would I—"

"I don't know how you did it, but I know you were there." Araminta kicked a pair of shoes in Sophie's direction. "Put these on."

Sophie just stared at the shoes in dismay. They were white satin, stitched in silver. They were the shoes she'd worn the night before.

"Put them on!" Araminta screamed. "I know that Rosamund's and Posy's feet are too large. You're the only one who could have worn my shoes last night."

"And from that you think I went to the ball?" Sophie asked, her voice breathy with panic.

"Put on the shoes, Sophie."

Sophie did as she was told. They were, of course, a perfect fit.

"You have overstepped your bounds," Araminta said in a low voice. "I warned you years ago not to forget your place in this world. You are a bastard, a by-blow, the product of—"

"I *know* what a bastard is," Sophie snapped.

Araminta raised one haughty brow, silently mocking Sophie's outburst. "You are unfit to mingle with polite society," she continued, "and yet you *dared* to pretend you are as good as the rest of us by attending the masquerade."

"Yes, I dared," Sophie cried out, well past caring that Araminta had somehow discovered her secret. "I dared, and I'd dare again. My blood is just as blue as yours, and my heart far kinder, and—"

One minute Sophie was on her feet, screaming at Araminta, and the next she was on the floor, clutching her cheek, made red by Araminta's palm.

"Don't you ever compare yourself to me," Araminta warned.

Sophie remained on the floor. How could her father have done this to her, leaving her in the care of a woman who so obviously detested her? Had he cared so little? Or had he simply been blind?

"You will be gone by morning," Araminta said in a low voice. "I don't ever want to see your face again."

Sophie started to make her way to the door.

"But not," Araminta said, planting the heel of her hand against Sophie's shoulder, "until you finish the job I have assigned you."

"It will take me until morning just to finish," Sophie protested.

"That is your problem, not mine." And with that, Araminta slammed the door shut, turning the lock with a very loud click.

Sophie stared down at the flickering candle she'd brought in to help illuminate the long, dark closet. There was no way the wick would last until morning.

And there was no way—absolutely no way in hell—that she was going to polish the rest of Araminta's shoes.

Sophie sat down on the floor, arms crossed and legs crossed, and stared at the candle flame until her eyes crossed, too. When the sun rose tomorrow, her life would be forever altered. Penwood House might not have been terribly welcoming, but at least it was safe.

She had almost no money. She hadn't received so much as a farthing from Araminta in the past seven years. Luckily, she still had a bit of the pin money she'd received when her father had been alive and she'd been treated as his ward, not his wife's slave. There had been many opportunities to spend it, but Sophie had always known that this day might come, and it had seemed prudent to hold on to what little funds she possessed.

But her paltry few pounds wasn't going to get her very far. She needed a ticket out of London, and that cost money. Probably well over half what she had saved. She supposed she could stay in town for a bit, but the London slums were dirty and dangerous, and Sophie knew that her budget would not place her in any of the better neighborhoods. Besides, if she were going to be on her own, she might as well return to the countryside she loved.

Not to mention that Benedict Bridgerton was here. London was a large city, and Sophie had no doubt that she could successfully avoid him for years, but she was desperately afraid that she wouldn't *want* to avoid him, that she'd find herself gazing at his house, hoping for the merest of glimpses as he came through the front door.

And if he saw her . . . Well, Sophie didn't know what would happen. He might be furious at her deception. He might want to make her his mistress. He might not recognize her at all.

The only thing she was certain he would not do was to throw himself at her feet, declare his undying devotion, and demand her hand in marriage.

Sons of viscounts did not marry baseborn nobodies. Not even in romantic novels.

No, she'd have to leave London. Keep herself far from temptation. But she'd need more money, enough to keep her going until she found employment. Enough to—

Sophie's eyes fell on something sparkly—a pair of shoes tucked away in the corner. Except she'd cleaned those shoes just an hour earlier, and she knew that those sparklies weren't the shoes but a pair of jeweled shoe clips, easily detachable and small enough to fit in her pocket.

Did she dare?

She thought about all the money that Araminta had received for her upkeep, money Araminta had never seen fit to share.

She thought about all those years she'd toiled as a lady's maid, without drawing a single wage.

She thought about her conscience, then quickly squelched it. In times like these, she didn't have room for a conscience.

She took the shoe clips.

And then, several hours later when Posy came (against her mother's wishes) and let her out, she packed up all of her belongings and left.

Much to her surprise, she didn't look back.

Part Two

Chapter 6

It has now been three years since any of the Bridgerton siblings have wed, and Lady Bridgerton has been heard to declare on several occasions that she is nearing her wit's end. Benedict has not taken a bride (and it is the opinion of This Author that as he has attained the age of thirty, he is far past due), and neither has Colin, although he may be forgiven his tardiness, since he is, after all, merely six-and-twenty.

The dowager viscountess also has two girls about which she must worry. Eloise is nearly one-and-twenty and although she has received several proposals, she has shown no inclination to marry. Francesca is nearly twenty (the girls quite coincidentally share a birthday), and she, too, seems more interested in the season than she does in marriage.

This Author feels that Lady Bridgerton does not need to worry. It is inconceivable that any of the Bridgertons might not eventually make an acceptable match, and besides, her two married children have already given her a total of five grandchildren, and surely that is her heart's desire.

LADY WHISTLEDOWN'S SOCIETY PAPERS, 30 APRIL 1817

Alcohol and cheroots. Card games and lots of hired women. It was just the sort of party Benedict Bridgerton would have enjoyed immensely when he was fresh out of university.

Now he was just bored.

He wasn't even certain why he'd agreed to attend. More boredom, he supposed. The London season of 1817 had thus far been a repeat of the previous year, and he hadn't found 1816 terribly scintillating to begin with. To do the whole thing over again was beyond banal.

He didn't even really know his host, one Phillip Cavender. It was one of those friend of a friend of a friend situations, and now Benedict was fervently wishing he'd remained in London. He'd just gotten over a blistering head cold, and he should have used that as an excuse to cry off, but his friend—whom he hadn't even seen in the past four hours—had prodded and cajoled, and finally Benedict had given in.

Now he heartily regretted it.

He walked down the main hall of Cavender's parents' home. Through the doorway to his left he could see a high-stakes card game in process. One of the players was sweating profusely. "Stupid idiot," Benedict muttered. The poor bloke was probably just a breath away from losing his ancestral home.

The door to his right was closed, but he could hear the sound of feminine giggling, followed by masculine laughter, followed by some rather unattractive grunting and squealing.

This was madness. He didn't want to be here. He hated card games where the stakes were higher than the participants could afford, and he'd never had any interest in copulating in such a public manner. He had no idea what had happened to the friend who had brought him here, and he didn't much like any of the other guests.

"I'm leaving," he declared, even though there was no one in the hall to hear him. He had a small piece of property not so very far away, just an hour's ride, really. It wasn't much more than a cottage, but it was his, and right now it sounded like heaven.

But good manners dictated that he find his host and inform him of his departure, even if Mr. Cavender was so sotted that he wouldn't remember the conversation the next day.

After about ten minutes of fruitless searching, however, Benedict was beginning to wish that his mother had not been so adamant in her quest to instill good manners in all of her children. It would have been a great deal easier just to leave and be done with it. "Three more minutes," he grumbled. "If I don't find the bloody idiot in three more minutes, I'm leaving."

Just then, a pair of young men stumbled by, tripping over their own feet as they exploded in raucous laughter. Alcoholic fumes filled the air, and Benedict took a discreet step back, lest one of them was suddenly compelled to cast up the contents of his stomach.

Benedict had always been fond of his boots.

"Bridgerton!" one of them called out.

Benedict gave them a curt nod in greeting. They were both about five years younger than he was, and he didn't know them well.

"Tha's not a Bridgerton," the other fellow slurred. "Tha's a—why, it *is* a Bridgerton. Got the hair and the nose." His eyes narrowed. "But which Bridgerton?"

Benedict ignored his question. "Have you seen our host?"

"We have a host?"

"Course we have a host," the first man replied. "Cavender. Damned fine fellow, you know, t'let us use his house—"

"Hiss parents' house," the other one corrected. "Hasn't inherited yet, poor bloke."

"Just so! His parents' house. Still jolly of him."

"Have either of you *seen* him?" growled Benedict.

"Just outside," replied the one who previously hadn't recalled that they had a host. "In the front."

"Thank you," Benedict said shortly, then strode past them to the front door of the house. He'd head down the front steps, pay his respects to Cavender, then make his way to the stables to collect his phaeton. He'd barely even have to break his stride.

It was, thought Sophie Beckett, high time she found a new job.

It had been almost two years since she'd left London, two years since she'd finally stopped being Araminta's virtual slave, two years since she'd been completely on her own.

After she'd left Penwood House, she'd pawned Araminta's shoe clips, but the diamonds Araminta had liked to boast about had turned out not to be diamonds at all, but rather simple paste, and they hadn't brought much money. She'd tried to find a job as a governess, but none of the agencies she'd queried was willing to take her on. She was obviously well educated, but she'd had no references, and besides, most women did not like to hire someone quite so young and pretty.

Sophie had eventually purchased a ticket on a coach to Wiltshire, since that was as far as she could go while still reserving the bulk of her pin money for emergencies. Luckily, she'd found employment quickly, as an upstairs maid for Mr. and Mrs. John Cavender. They were an ordinary sort of couple, expecting good work from their servants but not demanding the impossible. After toiling for Araminta for so many years, Sophie found the Cavenders a positive vacation.

But then their son had returned from his tour of Europe, and everything had changed. Phillip was constantly cornering her in the hall, and when his innuendo and suggestions were rebuffed, he'd grown more aggressive. Sophie had just started to think that maybe she ought to find employment elsewhere when Mr. and Mrs. Cavender had left for a week to visit Mrs. Cavender's sister in Brighton, and Phillip had decided to throw a party for two dozen of his closest friends.

It had been difficult to avoid Phillip's advances before, but at least Sophie had felt reasonably protected. Phillip would never dare attack her while his mother was in residence.

But with Mr. and Mrs. Cavender gone, Phillip seemed to think that he could do and take anything he wanted, and his friends were no better.

Sophie knew she should have left the grounds immediately, but Mrs. Cavender had treated her well, and she didn't think it was polite to leave without giving two weeks' notice. After two hours of being chased around the house, however, she decided that good manners were not worth her virtue, and so she'd told the (thankfully sympathetic) housekeeper that she could not stay, packed her meager belongings in one small bag, stolen down the side stairs, and let herself out. It was a two-mile hike into the village, but even in the dead of night, the road to town seemed infinitely safer than remaining at the Cavender home, and besides, she knew of a small inn where she could get a hot meal and a room for a reasonable price.

She'd just come 'round the house and had stepped onto the front drive, however, when she heard a raucous shout.

She looked up. Oh, *blast*. Phillip Cavender, looking even drunker and meaner than usual.

Sophie broke into a run, praying that alcohol had impaired Phillip's coordination because she knew she could not match him for speed.

But her flight must have only served to excite him, because she heard him yell out with glee, then felt his footsteps rumbling on the ground, growing closer and closer until she felt his hand close round the back collar of her coat, jerking her to a halt.

Phillip laughed triumphantly, and Sophie had never been so terrified in her entire life.

"Look what I have here," he cackled. "Little Miss Sophie. I shall have to introduce you to my friends."

Sophie's mouth went dry, and she wasn't sure whether her heart started to beat double time or stopped altogether. "Let me go, Mr. Cavender," she said in her sternest voice. She knew that he liked her helpless and pleading, and she refused to cater to his wishes.

"I don't think so," he said, turning her around so that she was forced to watch his lips stretch into a slippery smile. He turned his head to the side and called out, "Heasley! Fletcher! Look what I have here!"

Sophie watched with horror as two more men emerged from the shadows. From the looks of them, they were just as drunk, or maybe even more so, than Phillip.

"You always host the best parties," one of them said in an oily voice.

Phillip puffed out with pride.

"Let me go!" Sophie said again.

Phillip grinned. "What do you think, boys? Should I do as the lady asks?"

"Hell, no!" came the reply from the younger of the two men.

" 'Lady,' " said the other—the same one who had told Phillip that he hosted the best parties, "might be a bit of a misnomer, don't you think?"

"Quite right!" Phillip replied. "This one's a housemaid, and as we all know, that breed is born to serve." He gave Sophie a shove, pushing her toward one of his friends. "Here. Have a look at the goods."

Sophie cried out as she was propelled forward, and she clutched tightly to her small bag. She was about to be raped; that much was clear. But her panicked mind wanted to hold on to some last shred of dignity, and she refused to allow these men to spill her every last belonging onto the cold ground.

The man who caught her fondled her roughly, then

shoved her toward the third one. He'd just snaked his hand around her waist, when she heard someone yell out, "Cavender!"

Sophie shut her eyes in agony. *A fourth man. Dear God, weren't three enough?*

"Bridgerton!" Phillip called out. "Come join us!"

Sophie's eyes snapped open. Bridgerton?

A tall, powerfully built man emerged from the shadows, moving forward with easy, confident grace.

"What have we here?"

Dear God, she'd recognize that voice anywhere. She heard it often enough in her dreams.

It was Benedict Bridgerton. Her Prince Charming.

The night air was chilly, but Benedict found it refreshing after being forced to breathe the alcohol and tobacco fumes inside. The moon was nearly full, glowing round and fat, and a gentle breeze ruffled the leaves on the trees. All in all, it was an excellent night to leave a boring party and ride home.

But first things first. He had to find his host, go through the motions of thanking him for his hospitality, and inform him of his departure. As he reached the bottom step, he called out, "Cavender!"

"Over here!" came the reply, and Benedict turned his head to the right. Cavender was standing under a stately old elm with two other gentlemen. They appeared to be having a bit of fun with a housemaid, pushing her back and forth between them.

Benedict groaned. He was too far away to determine whether the housemaid was enjoying their attentions, and if she was not, then he was going to have to save her, which was not how he'd planned to spend his evening. He'd never been particularly enamored of playing the hero, but he had far too many younger sisters—four, to be precise—to ignore any female in distress.

"Ho there!" he called out as he ambled over, keeping his posture purposefully casual. It was always better to move slowly and assess the situation than it was to charge in blindly.

"Bridgerton!" Cavender called out. "Come join us!"

Benedict drew close just as one of the men snaked an arm around the young woman's waist and pinned her to him, her back to his front. His other hand was on her bottom, squeezing and kneading.

Benedict brought his gaze to the maid's eyes. They were huge and filled with terror, and she was looking at him as if he'd just dropped fully formed from the sky.

"What have we here?" he asked.

"Just a bit of sport," Cavender chortled. "My parents were kind enough to hire this prime morsel as the upstairs maid."

"She doesn't appear to be enjoying your attentions," Benedict said quietly.

"She likes it just fine," Cavender replied with a grin. "Fine enough for me, anyway."

"But not," Benedict said, stepping forward, "for me."

"You can have your turn with her," Cavender said, ever jovial. "Just as soon as we're through."

"You misunderstand."

There was a hard edge to Benedict's voice, and the three men all froze, looking over at him with wary curiosity.

"Release the girl," he said.

Still stunned by the sudden change of atmosphere, and with reflexes most likely dulled by alcohol, the man holding the girl did nothing.

"I don't want to fight you," Benedict said, crossing his arms, "but I will. And I can assure you that the three-to-one odds don't frighten me."

"Now, see here," Cavender said angrily. "You can't come here and order me about on my own property."

"It's your parents' property," Benedict pointed out, reminding them all that Cavender was still rather wet behind the ears.

"It's my home," Cavender shot back, "and she's my maid. And she'll do what I want."

"I wasn't aware that slavery was legal in this country," Benedict murmured.

"She has to do what I say!"

"Does she?"

"I'll fire her if she doesn't."

"Very well," Benedict said with a tiny quirk of a smile. "Ask her then. Ask the girl if she wants to tup with all three of you. Because that is what you had in mind, isn't it?"

Cavender sputtered as he fought for words.

"Ask her," Benedict said again, grinning now, mostly because he knew his smile would infuriate the younger man. "And if she says no, you can fire her right here on the spot."

"I'm not going to ask her," Cavender whined.

"Well, then, you can't really expect her to do it, can you?" Benedict looked at the girl. She was a fetching thing, with a short bob of light brown curls and eyes that loomed almost too large in her face. "Fine," he said, sparing a brief glance back at Cavender. "I'll ask her."

The girl's lips parted slightly, and Benedict had the oddest sensation that they had met before. But that was impossible, unless she'd worked for some other aristocratic family. And even then, he would have only seen her in passing. His taste in women had never run to housemaids, and in all truth, he tended not to notice them.

"Miss . . ." He frowned. "I say, what's your name?"

"Sophie Beckett," she gasped, sounding as if there were a very large frog caught in her throat.

"Miss Beckett," he continued, "would you be so kind as to answer the following question?"

"No!" she burst out.

"You're not going to answer?" he asked, his eyes amused.

"No, I do *not* want to tup with these three men!" The words practically exploded from her mouth.

"Well, that seems to settle that," Benedict said. He glanced up at the man still holding her. "I suggest you release her so that Cavender here may relieve her of employment."

"And where will she go?" Cavender sneered. "I can assure you she won't work in this district again."

Sophie turned to Benedict, wondering much the same thing.

Benedict gave a careless shrug. "I'll find her a position in my mother's household." He looked over at her and raised a brow. "I assume that's acceptable?"

Sophie's mouth dropped open in horrified surprise. He wanted to take her to his *home*?

"That's not quite the reaction I expected," Benedict said dryly. "It will certainly be more pleasant than your employment here. At the very least, I can assure you you won't be raped. What do you say?"

Sophie glanced frantically at the three men who had intended to rape her. She really didn't have a choice. Benedict Bridgerton was her only means off the Cavender property. She knew she couldn't possibly work for his mother; to be in such close proximity to Benedict and still have to be a servant would be more than she could bear. But she could find a way to avoid that later. For now she just needed to get away from Phillip.

She turned to Benedict and nodded, still afraid to use her voice. She felt as if she were choking inside, although she wasn't certain whether that was from fear or relief.

"Good," he said. "Shall we be off?"

She gave a rather pointed look at the arm that was still holding her hostage.

"Oh, for the love of God," Benedict snarled. "Will you let go of her or will I have to shoot your damned hand off?"

Benedict wasn't even holding a gun, but the tone of his voice was such that the man let go instantly.

"Good," Benedict said, holding his arm out toward the maid. She stepped forward, and with trembling fingers placed her hand on his elbow.

"You can't just take her!" Phillip yelled.

Benedict gave him a supercilious look. "I just did."

"You'll be sorry you did this," Phillip said.

"I doubt it. Now get out of my sight."

Phillip made a huffy sound, then turned his friends and said, "Let's get out of here." Then he turned to Benedict and added, "Don't think you shall ever receive another invitation to one of my parties."

"My heart is breaking," Benedict drawled.

Phillip let out one more outraged snort, and then he and his two friends stalked back to the house.

Sophie watched them walk away, then slowly dragged her gaze back to Benedict. When she'd been trapped by Phillip and his leering friends, she'd known what they wanted to do to her, and she'd almost wanted to die. And then, all of a sudden, there was Benedict Bridgerton, standing before her like a hero from her dreams, and she'd thought maybe she *had* died, because why else would he be here with her unless she was in heaven?

She'd been so completely and utterly stunned, she'd almost forgotten that Phillip's friend still held her pinned against him and was grabbing her behind in a most humiliating manner. For one brief second the world had melted away, and the only thing she could see, the only thing she *knew*, was Benedict Bridgerton.

It had been a moment of perfection.

But then the world had come crashing back, and all she could think was—what on earth was he doing here? It was a disgusting party, full of drunkards and whores. When she'd met him two years ago, he hadn't seemed the sort who would frequent such events. But she'd only known him for a few short hours. Perhaps she'd misjudged him. She closed her eyes in agony. For the past two years, the memory of Benedict Bridgerton had been the brightest light in her drab and dreary life. If she'd misjudged him, if he was little better than Phillip and his friends, then she'd be left with nothing.

Not even a memory of love.

But he *had* saved her. That was irrefutable. Maybe it didn't really matter why he'd come to Phillip's party, only that he had, and he had saved her.

"Are you all right?" he suddenly asked.

Sophie nodded, looking him squarely in the eye, waiting for him to recognize her.

"Are you certain?"

She nodded again, still waiting. It had to happen soon.

"Good. They were handling you roughly."

"I'll be all right." Sophie chewed on her lower lip. She had no idea how he would react once he realized who she was. Would he be delighted? Furious? The suspense was killing her.

"How much time will it take for you to pack your things?"

Sophie blinked rather dumbly, then realized she was still holding her satchel. "It's all right here," she said. "I was trying to leave when they caught me."

"Smart girl," he murmured approvingly.

Sophie just stared at him, unable to believe he hadn't recognized her.

"Let's be off, then," he said. "It makes me ill just to be on Cavender's property."

Sophie said nothing, but her chin jutted slightly forward, and her head tilted to the side as she watched his face.

"Are you certain you're all right?" he asked.

And then Sophie started to think.

Two years ago, when she'd met him, half of her face had been covered by a mask.

Her hair had been lightly powdered, making it seem

blonder than it actually was. Furthermore, she'd since cut it and sold the locks to a wigmaker. Her previous long waves were now short curls.

Without Mrs. Gibbons to feed her, she'd lost nearly a stone.

And when one got right down to it, they'd only been in each other's company a mere hour and a half.

She stared at him, right into his eyes. And that was when she knew.

He wasn't going to recognize her.

He had no idea who she was.

Sophie didn't know whether to laugh or to cry.

Chapter 7

It was clear to all of the guests at the Mottram ball Thursday last that Miss Rosamund Reiling has set her cap for Mr. Phillip Cavender.

It is the opinion of This Author that the two are well matched indeed.

Lady Whistledown's Society Papers, 30 April 1817

Ten minutes later, Sophie was sitting next to Benedict Bridgerton in his phaeton.

"Is there something in your eye?" he asked politely.

That caught her attention. "I-I beg your pardon?"

"You keep blinking," he explained. "I thought perhaps you had something in your eye."

Sophie swallowed hard, trying to suppress a round of nervous laughter. What was she supposed to say to him? The truth? That she was blinking because she kept expecting to wake up from what could only be a dream? Or maybe a nightmare?

"Are you certain you're all right?" he asked.

She nodded.

"Just the aftereffects of shock, I imagine," he said.

She nodded again, letting him think that was all that affected her.

How could he not have recognized her? She'd been dreaming of this moment for years. Her Prince Charming had finally come to rescue her, and he didn't even know who she was.

"What was your name again?" he asked. "I'm terribly sorry. It always takes me twice to remember a name."

"Miss Sophia Beckett." There seemed little reason to lie; she hadn't told him her name at the masquerade.

"I'm pleased to meet you, Miss Beckett," he said, keeping his eyes on the dark road. "I'm Mr. Benedict Bridgerton."

Sophie acknowledged his greeting with a nod even though he wasn't looking at her. She held silent for a moment, mostly because she simply didn't know what to say in such an unbelievable situation. It was, she realized, the introduction that had never taken place two years earlier. Finally, she just said, "That was a very brave thing you did."

He shrugged.

"There were three of them and only one of you. Most men would not have intervened."

This time he did look at her. "I hate bullies," was all he said.

She nodded again. "They would have raped me."

"I know," he replied. And then he added, "I have four sisters."

She almost said "I know," but caught herself just in time. How was a housemaid from Wiltshire supposed to know that? So instead she said, "I expect that is why you were so sensitive to my plight."

"I would like to think another man would come to their aid, should they ever find themselves in a similar situation."

"I pray you never have to find out."

He nodded grimly. "As do I."

They rode on, silence cloaking the night. Sophie remembered the masquerade ball, when they hadn't lacked for conversation, even for a moment. It was different now, she realized. She was a housemaid, not a glorious woman of the *ton*. They had nothing in common.

But still, she kept waiting for him to recognize her, to yank the carriage to a halt, clasp her to his chest, and tell her he'd been looking for her for two years. But that wasn't going to happen, she soon realized. He couldn't recognize the lady in the housemaid, and in all truth, why should he?

People saw what they expected to see. And Benedict Bridgerton surely didn't expect to see a fine lady of the *ton* in the guise of a humble housemaid.

Not a day had gone by that she hadn't thought of him, hadn't remembered his lips on hers, or the heady magic of that costumed night. He had become the centerpiece of her fantasies, dreams in which she was a different person, with different parents. In her dreams, she'd met him at a ball, maybe her own ball, hosted by her devoted mother and father. He courted her sweetly, with fragrant flowers and stolen kisses. And then, on a mellow spring day, while the birds were singing and a gentle breeze ruffled the air, he got down on one knee and asked her to marry him, professing his everlasting love and adoration.

It was a fine daydream, surpassed only by the one in which they lived happily ever after, with three or four splendid children, born safely within the sacrament of marriage.

But even with all her fantasies, she never imagined she'd actually see him again, much less be rescued by him from a trio of licentious attackers.

She wondered if he ever thought of the mysterious woman in silver with whom he'd shared one passionate kiss. She liked to think that he did, but she doubted that it had meant as much to him as it had to her. He was a man, after all, and had most likely kissed dozens of women.

And for him, that one night had been much like any other. Sophie still read *Whistledown* whenever she could get her hands on it. She knew that he attended scores of balls. Why should one masquerade stand out in his memory?

Sophie sighed and looked down at her hands, still clutching the drawstring to her small bag. She wished she owned gloves, but her only pair had worn out earlier that year, and she hadn't been able to afford another. Her hands looked rough and chapped, and her fingers were growing cold.

"Is that everything you own?" Benedict asked, motioning to the bag.

She nodded. "I haven't much, I'm afraid. Just a change of clothing and a few personal mementos."

He was silent for a moment, then said, "You have quite a refined accent for a housemaid."

He was not the first to make that observation, so Sophie gave him her stock answer. "My mother was a housekeeper to a very kind and generous family. They allowed me to share some of their daughters' lessons."

"Why do you not work there?" With an expert twist of his wrists, he guided his team to the left side of the fork in the road. "I assume you do not speak of the Cavenders."

"No," she replied, trying to devise a proper answer. No one had ever bothered to probe deeper than her offered explanation. No one had ever been interested enough to care. "My mother passed on," she finally replied, "and I did not deal well with the new housekeeper."

He seemed to accept that, and they rode on for a few minutes. The night was almost silent, save for the wind and the rhythmic clip-clop of the horses' hooves. Finally, Sophie, unable to contain her curiosity, asked, "Where are we going?"

"I have a cottage not far away," he replied. "We'll stay there a night or two, then I'll take you to my mother's home. I'm certain she'll find a position for you in her household."

Sophie's heart began to pound. "This cottage of yours . . ."

"You will be properly chaperoned," he said with a faint smile. "The caretakers will be in attendance, and I assure you that Mr. and Mrs. Crabtree are not likely to let anything untoward occur in their house."

"I thought it was *your* house."

His smile grew deeper. "I have been trying to get them to think of it as such for years, but I have never been successful."

Sophie felt her lips tug up at the corners. "They sound like people I would like very much."

"I expect you would."

And then there was more silence. Sophie kept her eyes scrupulously straight ahead. She had the most absurd fear that if their eyes met, he would recognize her. But that was mere fancy. He'd already looked her squarely in the eye, more than once even, and he still thought her nothing but a housemaid.

After a few minutes, however, she felt the oddest tingling in her cheek, and as she turned to face him she saw that he kept glancing at her with an odd expression.

"Have we met?" he blurted out.

"No," she said, her voice a touch more choked than she would have preferred. "I don't believe so."

"I'm sure you're right," he muttered, "but still, you do seem rather familiar."

"All housemaids look the same," she said with a wry smile.

"I used to think so," he mumbled.

She turned her face forward, her jaw dropping. Why had she said that? Didn't she *want* him to recognize her? Hadn't she spent the last half hour hoping and wishing and dreaming and—

And that was the problem. She was dreaming. In her dreams he loved her. In her dreams he asked her to marry him. In reality, he might ask her to become his mistress, and that was something she'd sworn she would never do. In reality, he might feel honor bound to return her to Araminta, who would probably turn her straightaways over to the magistrate for stealing her shoe clips (and Sophie didn't for one moment think that Araminta hadn't noticed their disappearance.)

No, it was best if he did not recognize her. It would only complicate her life, and considering that she had no source of income, and in fact very little beyond the clothes on her back, her life did not need complications at this point.

And yet she felt unaccountably disappointed that he had not instantly known who she was.

"Is that a raindrop?" Sophie asked, eager to keep the conversation on more benign topics.

Benedict looked up. The moon was now obscured by clouds. "It didn't look like rain when we left," he murmured. A fat raindrop landed on his thigh. "But I do believe you're correct."

She glanced at the sky. "The wind has picked up quite a bit. I hope it doesn't storm."

"It's sure to storm," he said wryly, "as we are in an open carriage. If I had taken my coach, there wouldn't be a cloud in the sky."

"How close are we to your cottage?"

"About half an hour away, I should think." He frowned. "Provided we are not slowed by the rain."

"Well, I do not mind a bit of rain," she said gamely. "There are far worse things than getting wet."

They both knew exactly what she was talking about.

"I don't think I remembered to thank you," she said, her words quiet.

Benedict turned his head sharply. By all that was holy, there was something damned familiar about her voice. But when his eyes searched her face, all he saw was a simple housemaid. A very attractive housemaid, to be sure, but a housemaid nonetheless. No one with whom he would ever have crossed paths.

"It was nothing," he finally said.

"To you, perhaps. To me it was everything."

Uncomfortable with such appreciation, he just nodded and gave one of those grunts men tended to emit when they didn't know what to say.

"It was a very brave thing you did," she said.

He grunted again.

And then the heavens opened up in earnest.

It took about one minute for Benedict's clothes to be soaked through. "I'll get there as quickly as I can," he yelled, trying to make himself heard over the wind.

"Don't worry about me!" Sophie called back, but when he looked over at her, he saw that she was huddling into herself, her arms wrapped tightly over her chest as she tried to conserve the heat of her body.

"Let me give you my coat."

She shook her head and actually laughed. "It'll probably make me even wetter, soaked as it is."

He nudged the horses into a faster pace, but the road was growing muddy, and the wind was whipping the rain every which way, reducing the already mediocre visibility.

Bloody hell. This was just what he needed. He'd had a head cold all last week, and he probably wasn't completely recovered. A ride in the freezing rain would most likely set him back, and he'd spend the next month with a runny nose, watery eyes . . . all those infuriating, unattractive symptoms.

Of course . . .

Benedict couldn't quite contain a smile. Of course, if he were ill again, his mother couldn't try to cajole him into attending every single party in town, all in the hopes that he would find some suitable young lady and settle down into a quiet and happy marriage.

To his credit, he always kept his eyes open, was always on the lookout for a prospective bride. He certainly wasn't opposed to marriage on principle. His brother Anthony and his sister Daphne had made splendidly happy matches. But

Anthony's and Daphne's marriages were splendidly happy because they'd been smart enough to wed the right people, and Benedict was quite certain he had not yet met the right person.

No, he thought, his mind wandering back a few years, that wasn't entirely true. He'd once met someone . . .

The lady in silver.

When he'd held her in his arms and twirled her around the balcony in her very first waltz, he'd felt something different inside, a fluttering, tingling sensation. It should have scared the hell out of him.

But it hadn't. It had left him breathless, excited . . . and determined to have her.

But then she'd disappeared. It was as if the world were actually flat, and she'd fallen right off the edge. He'd learned nothing in that irritating interview with Lady Penwood, and when he'd queried his friends and family, no one knew anything about a young woman wearing a silver dress.

She hadn't arrived with anyone and she hadn't left with anyone. For all intents and purposes, she hadn't even existed.

He'd watched for her at every ball, party, and musicale he attended. Hell, he attended twice as many functions as usual, just in the hopes that he'd catch a glimpse of her.

But he'd always come home disappointed.

He'd thought he would stop looking for her. He was a practical man, and he'd assumed that eventually he would simply give up. And in some ways, he had. After a few months he found himself back in the habit of turning down more invitations than he accepted. A few months after that, he realized that he was once again able to meet women and not automatically compare them to her.

But he couldn't stop himself from watching for her. He might not feel the same urgency, but whenever he attended a ball or took a seat at a musicale, he found his eyes sweeping across the crowd, his ears straining for the lilt of her laughter.

She was out there somewhere. He'd long since resigned himself to the fact that he wasn't likely to find her, and he hadn't searched actively for over a year, but . . .

He smiled wistfully. He just couldn't stop from looking. It had become, in a very strange way, a part of who he was. His name was Benedict Bridgerton, he had seven brothers and sisters, was rather skilled with both a sword and a sketching crayon, and he always kept his eyes open for the one woman who had touched his soul.

He kept hoping . . . and wishing . . . and watching. And even though he told himself it was probably time to marry, he just couldn't muster the enthusiasm to do so.

Because what if he put his ring on some woman's finger, and the next day he saw *her*?

It would be enough to break his heart.

No, it would be more than that. It would be enough to shatter his soul.

Benedict breathed a sigh of relief as he saw the village of Rosemeade approaching. Rosemeade meant that his cottage was a mere five minutes away, and lud, but he couldn't wait to get inside and throw himself into a steaming tub of water.

He glanced over at Miss Beckett. She, too, was shivering, but, he thought with a touch of admiration, she hadn't let out even a peep of complaint. Benedict tried to think of another woman of his acquaintance who would have stood up to the elements with such fortitude and came up empty-handed. Even his sister Daphne, who was as good a sport as any, would have been howling about the cold by now.

"We're almost there," he assured her.

"I'm all—Oh! Are you all right?"

Benedict was gripped by wave of coughs, the deep, hacking kind that rumble down in one's chest. His lungs felt as if they were on fire, and his throat like someone had taken a razor blade to it.

"I'm fine," he gasped, jerking slightly on the reins to make up for the lack of direction he'd given the horses while he was coughing.

"You don't sound fine."

"Had a head cold last week," he said with a wince. Damn, but his lungs felt sore.

"That didn't sound like your head," she said, giving him what she obviously hoped was a teasing smile. But it didn't look like a teasing smile. In truth, she looked terribly concerned.

"Must've moved," he muttered.

"I don't want you getting sick on my account."

He tried to grin, but his cheekbones ached too much. "I would've been caught in the rain whether I'd taken you along or not."

"Still—"

Whatever she'd intended to say was lost under another stream of deep, chesty coughs.

"Sorry," he mumbled.

"Let me drive," she said, reaching for the reins.

He turned to her in disbelief. "This is a phaeton, not a single-horse wagon."

Sophie fought the urge to throttle him. His nose was running, his eyes were red, he couldn't stop coughing, and still he found the energy to act like an arrogant peacock. "I assure you," she said slowly, "that I know how to drive a team of horses."

"And where did you acquire that skill?"

"The same family that allowed me to share in their daughters' lessons," Sophie lied. "I learned to drive a team when the girls learned."

"The lady of the house must have taken quite a liking to you," he said.

"She did quite," Sophie replied, trying not to laugh. Araminta had been the lady of the house, and she'd fought tooth and nail every time her father had insisted that she be allowed to receive the same instruction as Rosamund and Posy. They'd all three learned how to drive teams the year before the earl had died.

"I'll drive, thank you," Benedict said sharply. Then he ruined the entire effect by launching into yet another coughing fit.

Sophie reached for the reins. "For the love of—"

"Here," he said, thrusting them toward her, as he wiped his eyes. "Take them. But I'll be watching you."

"I would expect no less," she said peevishly. The rain didn't exactly make for ideal driving conditions, and it had been years since she'd held reins in her hands, but she thought she acquitted herself rather nicely. There were some things one didn't forget, she supposed.

It felt rather nice, actually, to do something she hadn't done since her previous life, when she'd been, officially at least, an earl's ward. She'd had fine clothes then, and good food, and interesting lessons, and . . .

She sighed. It hadn't been perfect, but it had been better than anything that had come after.

"What's wrong?" Benedict asked.

"Nothing. Why should you think something is wrong?"

"You sighed."

"You heard me over the wind?" she asked incredulously.

"I've been paying close attention. I'm sick enough"—cough cough—"without you landing us in a ditch."

Sophie decided not even to credit him with a reply.

"Turn right up ahead," he directed. "It'll take us directly to my cottage."

She did as he asked. "Does your cottage have a name?"

"My Cottage."

"I might have known," she muttered.

He smirked. Quite a feat, in her opinion, since he looked sick as a dog. "I'm not kidding," he said.

Sure enough, in another minute they pulled up in front of an elegant country house, complete with a small, unobtrusive sign in front reading, MY COTTAGE.

"The previous owner coined the name," Benedict said as he directed her toward the stables, "but it seemed to fit me as well."

Sophie looked over at the house, which, while fairly small, was no humble dwelling. "You call this a cottage?"

"No, the previous owner did," he replied. "You should have seen his other house."

A moment later they were out of the rain, and Benedict had hopped down and was unhitching the horses. He was wearing gloves, but they were completely sodden and slipping on the bridle, and so he peeled them off and flung them away. Sophie watched him as he went about his work. His fingers were wrinkled like prunes and trembling from the cold. "Let me help," she said, stepping forward.

"I can do it."

"Of course you can," she said placatingly, "but you can do it faster with my help."

He turned, presumably to refuse her again, then doubled over as he was wracked by coughs. Sophie quickly rushed in and led him to a nearby bench. "Sit down, please," she implored him. "I'll finish up the job."

She thought he'd disagree, but this time he gave in. "I'm sorry," he said hoarsely. "I—"

"There's nothing to feel sorry about," she said, making quick work of the job. Or as quick as she could; her fingers were still numb, and bits of her skin had turned white from having been wet for so long.

"Not very . . ." He coughed again, this one lower and deeper than before. ". . . gentlemanly of me."

"Oh, I think I can forgive you this time, considering the

way you saved me earlier this evening." Sophie tried to give him a jaunty smile, but for some reason it wobbled, and without warning she found herself inexplicably near tears. She turned quickly away, not wanting him to see her face.

But he must have seen something, or maybe just sensed that something was wrong, because he called out, "Are you all right?"

"I'm fine!" she replied, but her voice came out strained and choked, and before she knew it, he was next to her, and she was in his arms.

"It's all right," he said soothingly. "You're safe now."

The tears burst forth. She cried for what could have been her fate that evening, and she cried for what had been her fate for the past nine years. She cried for the memory of when he'd held her in his arms at the masquerade, and she cried because she was in his arms right now.

She cried because he was so damned *nice*, and even though he was clearly ill, even though she was, in his eyes, nothing but a housemaid, he still wanted to care for her and protect her.

She cried because she hadn't let herself cry in longer than she could remember, and she cried because she felt so alone.

And she cried because she'd been dreaming of him for so very long, and he hadn't recognized her. It was probably best that he did not, but her heart still ached from it.

Eventually her tears subsided, and he stepped back, touching her chin as he said, "Do you feel better now?"

She nodded, surprised that it was true.

"Good. You had a scare, and—" He jerked away from her, doubling over as he coughed.

"We really need to get you inside," Sophie said, brushing away the last streaks of her tears. "Inside the house, that is."

He nodded. "I'll race you to the door."

Her eyes widened in shock. She couldn't believe that he had the spirit to make a joke of this, when he was obviously feeling so poorly. But she wrapped the drawstring of her bag around her hands, hitched up her skirts, and ran for the front door to the cottage. By the time she reached the steps, she was laughing from the exertion, giggling at the ridiculousness of running wildly to get out of the rain when she was already soaked to the bone.

Benedict had, not surprisingly, beaten her to the small portico. He might have been ill, but his legs were significantly longer and stronger. When she skidded to a halt at his side, he was banging on the front door.

"Don't you have a key?" Sophie yelled. The wind was still howling, making it difficult to be heard.

He shook his head. "I wasn't planning on stopping here."

"Do you think the caretakers will even hear you?"

"I bloody well hope so," he muttered.

Sophie wiped away the rivulets of water running over her eyes and peeked in a nearby window. "It's very dark," she told him. "Do you think they might not be home?"

"I don't know where else they'd be."

"Shouldn't there at least be a maid or a footman?"

Benedict shook his head. "I'm so rarely here it seemed foolish to hire a full staff. The maids only come in for the day."

Sophie grimaced. "I'd suggest we look for an open window, but that's rather unlikely in the rain."

"Not necessary," Benedict said grimly. "I know where the spare key is hidden."

Sophie looked at him in surprise. "Why do you sound so glum about it?"

He coughed several times before answering, "Because it means I have to go back out into the bloody storm."

Sophie knew he was truly reaching the end of his patience. He'd already sworn twice in front of her, and he didn't seem the sort to curse in front of a woman, even a mere housemaid.

"Wait here," he ordered, and then before she could reply, he'd left the shelter of the portico and dashed away.

A few minutes later she heard a key turning in the lock, and the front door swung open to reveal Benedict, holding a candle and dripping all over the floor. "I don't know where Mr. and Mrs. Crabtree are," he said, his voice raspy from all his coughing, "but they're definitely not here."

Sophie gulped. "We're alone?"

He nodded. "Completely."

She edged toward the stairs. "I'd better find the servants' quarters."

"Oh, no you won't," he growled, grabbing hold of her arm.

"I won't?"

He shook his head. "You, dear girl, aren't going anywhere."

Chapter 8

It seems one cannot take two steps at a London ball these days without stumbling across a society matron lamenting the difficulties of finding good help. Indeed, This Author thought that Mrs. Featherington and Lady Penwood were going to come to blows at last week's Smythe-Smith musicale. It seems that Lady Penwood stole Mrs. Featherington's lady's maid right out from under her nose one month ago, promising higher wages and free cast-off clothing. (It should be noted that Mrs. Featherington also gave the poor girl cast-off clothing, but anyone who has ever observed the attire of the Featherington girls would understand why the lady's maid would not view this as a benefit.)

The plot thickened, however, when the lady's maid in question fled back to Mrs. Featherington, begging to be rehired. It seemed that Lady Penwood's idea of a lady's maid included duties more accurately ascribed to the scullery maid, upstairs maid, and cook.

Someone ought to tell the woman that one girl cannot do the work of three.

LADY WHISTLEDOWN'S SOCIETY PAPERS, 2 MAY 1817

"We're going to build a fire," Benedict said, "and get warm before either of us goes off to bed. I didn't save you from Cavender just so you could die of influenza."

Sophie watched him cough anew, the spasms wracking his body and forcing him to bend over at the waist. "Begging your pardon, Mr. Bridgerton," she could not help commenting, "but of the two of us, I should think you're more in danger of contracting influenza."

"Just so," he gasped, "and I assure you I have no desire to be so afflicted, either. So—" He bent over again as he was once again engulfed by coughs.

"Mr. Bridgerton?" Sophie asked, concern in her voice.

He swallowed convulsively and barely managed to say, "Just help me get a fire blazing before I cough myself into oblivion."

Sophie's brow knit with worry. His coughing fits were coming closer and closer together, and each time they were deeper, more rumbly, as if they were coming from the very pit of his chest.

She made easy work of the fire; she'd certainly had enough experience setting them as a housemaid, and soon they were both holding their hands as close to the flames as they dared.

"I don't suppose your change of clothing remained dry," Benedict said, nodding toward Sophie's sodden satchel.

"I doubt it," she said ruefully. "But it's no matter. If I stand here long enough, I'll dry out."

"Don't be silly," he scoffed, turning around so that the fire might heat his back. "I'm sure I can find you a change of clothing."

"You have women's clothing here?" she asked doubtfully.

"You're not so fussy that you can't wear breeches and a shirt for one evening, are you?"

Until that very moment, Sophie had probably been *exactly* that fussy, but put that way, it did seem a little silly. "I suppose not," she said. Dry clothing certainly sounded appealing.

"Good," he said briskly. "Why don't you light the furnaces in two bedrooms, and I'll find us both some clothing?"

"I can stay in the servants' quarters," Sophie said quickly.

"Not necessary," he said, striding out of the room and motioning for her to follow. "I've extra rooms, and you are not a servant here."

"But I *am* a servant," she pointed out, hurrying after him.

"Do whatever you please then." He started to march up the stairs, but had to stop halfway up to cough. "You can find a tiny little room in the servants' quarters with a hard little pallet, or you can avail yourself of a guest bedroom, all of which I assure you come equipped with feather mattresses and goosedown coverlets."

Sophie knew that she should remember her place in the world and march right up the next flight of stairs to the attic, but by God above, a feather mattress and down coverlet sounded like heaven on earth. She hadn't slept in such comfort in years. "I'll just find a small guest bedroom," she acceded. "The, er, smallest you have."

Half of Benedict's mouth quirked up in a dry, I-told-you-so sort of smile. "Pick whichever room you like. But not that one," he said, pointing to the second door on the left. "That's mine."

"I'll get the furnace started in there immediately," she said. He needed the warmth more than she did, and besides, she found herself inordinately curious to see what the inside of his bedroom looked like. One could tell a lot about a person by the décor of his bedchamber. Provided, of course, she thought with a grimace, that one possessed enough funds to decorate in the manner one preferred. Sophie sincerely doubted that anyone could have told anything about her from her little attic turret at the Cavenders'—except for the fact that she had not a penny to her name.

Sophie left her satchel in the hall and scurried into Benedict's bedchamber. It was a lovely room, warm and masculine and very comfortable. Despite the fact that Benedict had said he was rarely in residence, there were all sorts of personal items on the desk and tables—miniatures of what had to be his brothers and sisters, leather-bound books, and even a small glass bowl filled with . . .

Rocks?

"How odd," Sophie murmured, moving forward even though she knew she was being dreadfully invasive and nosy.

"Each one is meaningful in some way," came a deep voice from behind her. "I've collected them since—" He stopped to cough. "Since I was a child."

Sophie's face flushed red at having been caught so shamelessly snooping, but her curiosity was still piqued, so she held one up. It was of a pinkish hue, with a ragged grey vein running straight through the middle. "What about this one?"

"I picked that one up on a hike," Benedict said softly. "It happened to be the day my father died."

"Oh!" Sophie dropped the rock back on the pile as if burned. "I'm so sorry."

"It was long ago."

"I'm still sorry."

He smiled sadly. "As am I." Then he coughed, so hard that he had to lean against the wall.

"You need to get warm," Sophie said quickly. "Let me get to work on that fire."

Benedict tossed a bundle of clothing onto the bed. "For you," he said simply.

"Thank you," she said, keeping her attention focused on the small furnace. It was dangerous to remain in the same room as him. She didn't think he was likely to make an untoward advance; he was far too much of a gentleman to foist himself on a woman he barely knew. No, the danger lay squarely within herself. Frankly, she was terrified that if she spent too much time in his company she might fall head over heels in love.

And what would that get her?

Nothing but a broken heart.

Sophie huddled in front of the small iron furnace for several minutes, stoking the flame until she was confident that it would not flicker out. "There," she announced once she was satisfied. She stood up, arching her back slightly as she stretched and turned around. "That should take care of—Oh my!"

Benedict Bridgerton looked positively green.

"Are you all right?" she asked, hurrying to his side.

"Don' feel too well," he slurred, leaning heavily against the bedpost. He sounded vaguely intoxicated, but Sophie had been in his company for at least two hours, and she knew that he had not been drinking.

"You need to get into bed," she said, stumbling under his weight when he decided to lean against her instead of the bedpost.

He grinned. "You coming?"

She lurched back. "Now I know you're feverish."

He lifted his hand to touch his forehead, but he smacked his nose instead. "Ow!" he yelped.

Sophie winced in sympathy.

His hand crept up to his forehead. "Hmmm, maybe I am a bit hot."

It was horribly familiar of her, but a man's health was at stake, so Sophie reached out and touched her hand to his brow. It wasn't burning, but it certainly wasn't cool. "You need to get out of those wet clothes," she said. "Immediately."

Benedict looked down, blinking as if the sight of his sodden clothing was a surprise. "Yes," he murmured thoughtfully. "Yes, I believe I do." His fingers went to the buttons on his shirt, but they were clammy and numb and kept slipping and sliding. Finally, he just shrugged at her and said helplessly, "I can't do it."

"Oh, dear. Here, I'll . . ." Sophie reached out to undo his buttons, jerked her hands back nervously, then finally gritted her teeth and reached out again. She made quick work of the buttons, doing her best to keep her gaze averted as each undone button revealed another two inches of his skin. "Almost done," she muttered. "Just a moment now."

He didn't say anything in reply, so she looked up. His eyes were closed, and his entire body was swaying slightly. If he weren't standing up, she'd have sworn that he was asleep.

"Mr. Bridgerton?" she asked softly. "Mr. Bridgerton!"

Benedict's head jerked up violently. "What? What?"

"You fell asleep."

He blinked confusedly. "Is there a reason that's bad?"

"You can't fall asleep in your clothing."

He looked down. "How'd my shirt get undone?"

Sophie ignored the question, instead nudging him until his behind was leaning against the mattress. "Sit," she ordered.

She must have sounded suitably bossy, because he did.

"Have you something dry we can change you into?" she asked.

He shrugged the shirt off, letting it land on the floor in a messy heap. "Never sleep with clothes."

Sophie felt her stomach lurch. "Well, tonight I think you should, and—*What* are you doing?"

He looked over at her as if she'd asked the most inane question in the world. "Taking my breeches off."

"Couldn't you at least wait until I'd turned my back?"

He stared at her blankly.

She stared back.

He stared some more. Finally, he said, "Well?"

"Well what?"

"Aren't you going to turn your back?"

"Oh!" she yelped, spinning around as if someone had lit a fire under her feet.

Benedict shook his head wearily as he sat on the edge of the bed and pulled off his stockings. God save him from prudish misses. She was a housemaid, for God's sake. Even if she was a virgin—and given her behavior, he rather suspected she was—she'd surely seen a male form before. Housemaids were always slipping in and out of rooms without knocking, carrying towels and sheets and what have you. It was inconceivable she'd never accidentally barged in on a naked man.

He stripped off his breeches—not an easy task considering they were still more than a little damp and he had quite literally to peel them from his skin. When he was well and truly naked, he quirked a brow in the direction of Sophie's back. She was standing rigidly, her hands fisted tightly at her sides.

With surprise, he realized the sight of her made him smile.

He was starting to feel a bit sluggish, and it took him two tries before he was able to lift his leg high enough to climb into bed. With considerable effort he leaned forward and grabbed the edge of his coverlet, dragging it over his body. Then, completely worn-out, he sagged back against the pillows and groaned.

"Are you all right?" Sophie called.

He made an effort to say, "Fine," but it came out more like, "Fmmph."

He heard her moving about, and when he summoned up the energy to lift one eyelid halfway open, he saw that she'd moved to the side of the bed. She looked concerned.

For some reason that seemed rather sweet. It had been quite a long time since any woman who wasn't related to him had been concerned for his welfare.

"I'm fine," he mumbled, trying to give her a reassuring smile. But his voice sounded like it was coming through a long, narrow tunnel. He reached up and tugged at his ear. His mouth felt like he was talking properly; the problem must be with his ears.

"Mr. Bridgerton? Mr. Bridgerton?"

He pried an eyelid open again. "Go da bed," he grunted. "Get dry."

"Are you certain?"

He nodded. It was getting too difficult to speak.

"Very well. But I'm going to leave your door open. If you need me in the night, just call out."

He nodded again. Or at least he tried to. Then he slept.

It took Sophie barely a quarter of an hour to get ready for bed. A surfeit of nervous energy kept her going as she changed into dry clothing and readied the furnace in her room, but once her head hit her pillow, she felt herself succumbing to an exhaustion so total it seemed to come from her very bones.

It had been a long day, she thought groggily. A really long day, between attending to her morning chores, dashing around the house to escape Cavender and his friends . . . Her eyelids drifted shut. It had been an extraordinarily long day, and . . .

Sophie sat up suddenly, her heart pounding. The fire in the furnace had burned low, so she must have fallen asleep. She'd been dead tired, though, so something must have woken her. Was it Mr. Bridgerton? Had he called out? He'd not looked well when she'd left him, but neither had he seemed at death's door.

Sophie hopped out of bed, grabbed a candle, then dashed toward the door of her room, grabbing hold of the waistband of the too-big breeches Benedict had lent her when they started to slip down her hips. When she reached the hall she heard the sound that must have woken her up.

It was a deep groan, followed by a thrashing noise, followed by what could only be called a whimper.

Sophie dashed into Benedict's room, stopping briefly at the furnace to light her candle. He was lying in his bed, almost preternaturally still. Sophie edged toward him, her eyes focusing on his chest. She knew he couldn't possibly be dead, but she'd feel an awful lot better once she saw his chest rise and fall.

"Mr. Bridgerton?" she whispered. "Mr. Bridgerton?"

No response.

She crept closer, leaning over the edge of the bed. "Mr. Bridgerton?"

His hand shot out and grabbed her shoulder, pulling her off-balance until she fell onto the bed.

"Mr. Bridgerton!" Sophie squealed. "Let go!"

But he'd started to thrash and moan, and there was enough heat coming off his body that Sophie knew he was in the grips of a fever.

She somehow managed to wrench herself free, and she went tumbling off the bed while he continued to toss and turn, mumbling streams of words that made no sense.

Sophie waited for a quiet moment, then darted her hand out to touch his forehead. It was on fire.

She chewed on her lower lip as she tried to decide what to do. She had no experience nursing the feverish, but it seemed to her that the logical thing would be to cool him off. On the other hand, sickrooms always seemed to be kept closed, stuffy, and warm, so maybe . . .

Benedict started to thrash again, and then, out of nowhere, he murmured, "Kiss me."

Sophie lost hold of her breeches; they fell to the floor. She let out a little yelp of surprise as she quickly bent to retrieve them. Clutching the waistband securely with her right hand, she reached out to pat his hand with her left, then thought the better of it. "You're just dreaming, Mr. Bridgerton," she told him.

"Kiss me," he repeated. But he did not open his eyes.

Sophie leaned in closer. Even by the light of one solitary

candle she could see his eyeballs moving quickly under his lids. It was bizarre, she thought, to see another person dream.

"God damn it!" he suddenly yelled. "Kiss me!"

Sophie lurched back in surprise, setting her candle hastily on the bedside table. "Mr. Bridgerton, I—" she began, fully intending to explain why she could not even begin to think about kissing him, but then she thought—*Why not?*

Her heart fluttering wildly, she leaned down and brushed the barest, lightest, most gentle of kisses on his lips.

"I love you," she whispered. "I've always loved you."

To Sophie's everlasting relief, he didn't move. It wasn't the sort of moment she wanted him to remember in the morning. But then, just when she was convinced that he'd settled back into a deep sleep, his head began to toss from side to side, leaving deep indentations in his feather pillow.

"Where'd you go?" he grunted hoarsely. "Where'd you go?"

"I'm right here," Sophie replied.

He opened his eyes, and for the barest of seconds appeared completely lucid, as he said, "Not *you*." Then his eyes rolled back and his head started tossing from side to side again.

"Well, I'm all you've got," Sophie muttered. "Don't go anywhere," she said with a nervous laugh. "I'll be right back."

And then, her heart pounding with fear and nerves, she ran out of the room.

If there was one thing Sophie had learned in her days as a housemaid, it was that most households were run in essentially the same way. It was for that reason that she had no trouble at all finding spare linens to replace Benedict's sweat-soaked sheets. She also scavenged a pitcher full of cool water and a few small towels for dampening his brow.

Upon her return to his bedroom, she found him lying still again, but his breathing was shallow and rapid. Sophie reached out and touched his brow again. She couldn't be certain, but it seemed to her that it was growing warmer.

Oh, dear. This was not good, and she was singularly unqualified to care for a feverish patient. Araminta, Rosamund, and Posy had never had a sick day in their lives, and the Cavenders had all been uncommonly healthy as well. The closest she'd ever come to nursing had been helping Mrs. Cavender's mother, who'd been unable to walk. But she'd never taken care of someone with a fever.

She dunked a cloth in the pitcher of water, then wrung it out until it was no longer dripping from the corners. "This ought to make you feel a little better," she whispered, placing it gingerly on his brow. Then she added, in a rather unconfident voice, "At least I hope it will."

He didn't flinch when she touched him with the cloth. Sophie took that as an excellent sign, and she prepared another cool towel. She had no idea where to put it, though. His chest somehow didn't seem right, and she certainly wasn't going to allow the bedsheet to drift any lower than his waist unless the poor man was at death's door (and even then, she wasn't certain what she could possibly do down there that would resurrect him.) So she finally just dabbed with it behind his ears, and a little on the sides of his neck.

"Does that feel better?" she asked, not expecting any sort of an answer but feeling nonetheless that she ought to continue with her one-sided conversation. "I really don't know very much about caring for the ill, but it just *seems* to me like you'd want something cool on your brow. I know if *I* were sick, that's how I'd feel."

He shifted restlessly, mumbling something utterly incoherent.

"Really?" Sophie replied, trying to smile but failing miserably. "I'm glad you feel that way."

He mumbled something else.

"No," she said, dabbing the cool cloth on his ear, "I'd have to agree with what you said the first time."

He went still again.

"I'd be happy to reconsider," she said worriedly. "Please don't take offense."

He didn't move.

Sophie sighed. One could only converse so long with an unconscious man before one started to feel extremely silly. She lifted up the cloth she'd placed on his forehead and touched his skin. It felt kind of clammy now. Clammy and still warm, which was a combination she wouldn't have thought possible.

She decided to leave the cloth off for now, and she laid it over the top of the pitcher. There seemed little she could do for him at that very moment, so Sophie stretched her legs and walked slowly around his room, shamelessly examining everything that wasn't nailed down, and quite a bit that was.

The collection of miniatures was her first stop. There were nine on the writing desk; Sophie surmised that they were of Benedict's parents and seven brothers and sisters. She started to put the siblings in order according to their ages, but then it occurred to her that the miniatures most likely hadn't been painted all at the same time, so she could be looking at a likeness of his older brother at fifteen and younger brother at twenty.

She was struck by how alike they all were, with the same deep chestnut hair, wide mouths, and elegant bone structure. She looked closely to try to compare eye color but found it impossible in the dim candlelight, and besides, eye color often wasn't easily discerned on a miniature, anyway.

Next to the miniatures was the bowl with Benedict's rock collection. Sophie picked a few of them up in turn, rolling them lightly over her palm. "Why are these so special to you, I wonder?" she whispered, placing them carefully back in the bowl. They just looked like rocks to her, but she supposed that they might appear more interesting and unique to Benedict if they represented special memories for him.

She found a small wooden box that she absolutely could not open; it must have been one of those trick boxes she'd heard about that came from the Orient. And most intriguing, leaning against the side of the desk was a large sketchbook, filled with pencil drawings, mostly of landscapes but with a few portraits as well. Had Benedict drawn them? Sophie squinted at the bottom of each drawing. The small squiggles certainly looked like two Bs.

Sophie sucked in her breath, an unbidden smile lighting her face. She'd never dreamed that Benedict was an artist. There had never even been a peep about it in *Whistledown*, and it seemed like the sort of thing the gossip columnist would have figured out over the years.

Sophie drew the sketchbook closer to her candle and flipped through the pages. She wanted to sit with the book and spend ten minutes perusing each sketch, but it seemed too intrusive to examine his drawings in such detail. She was probably just trying to justify her nosiness, but somehow it didn't seem as bad just to give them a glance.

The landscapes were varied. Some were of My Cottage (or should she call it His Cottage?) and some were of a larger house, which Sophie supposed was the country home of the Bridgerton family. Most of the landscapes featured no architecture at all, just a babbling brook, or a windswept tree, or a rain-dappled meadow. And the amazing thing about his drawings was that they seemed to capture the whole and true moment. Sophie could swear that she could hear that brook babbling or the wind ruffling the leaves on that tree.

The portraits were fewer in number, but Sophie found them infinitely more interesting. There were several of what had to be his littlest sister, and a few of what she thought must be his mother. One of Sophie's favorites was of what appeared to be some kind of outdoor game. At least five

Bridgerton siblings were holding long mallets, and one of the girls was depicted at the forefront, her face screwed up in determination as she tried to aim a ball through a wicket.

Something about the picture almost made Sophie laugh out loud. She could feel the merriment of the day, and it made her long desperately for a family of her own.

She glanced back at Benedict, still sleeping quietly in his bed. Did he realize how lucky he was to have been born into such a large and loving clan?

With a sigh, Sophie flipped through a few more pages until she reached the end of the book. The very last sketch was different from the rest, if only because it appeared to be of a night scene, and the woman in it was holding her skirts above her ankles as she ran across—

Good God! Sophie gasped, thunderstruck. It was her!

She brought the sketch closer to her face. He'd gotten the details of her dress—that wonderful, magical silver concoction that had been hers for only a single evening—perfectly. He'd even remembered her long, elbow-length gloves and the exact manner in which her hair had been styled. Her face was a little less recognizable, but one would have to make allowances for that given that he'd never actually seen it in its entirety.

Well, not until now.

Benedict suddenly groaned, and when Sophie glanced over she saw that he was shifting restlessly in the bed. She closed up the sketchbook and put it back into its place before hurriedly making her way to his side.

"Mr. Bridgerton?" she whispered. She wanted desperately to call him Benedict. That was how she thought of him; that was what she'd called him in her dreams these long two years. But that would be inexcusably familiar and certainly not in keeping with her position as a servant.

"Mr. Bridgerton?" she whispered again. "Are you all right?"

His eyelids fluttered open.

"Do you need anything?"

He blinked several times, and Sophie couldn't be sure whether he'd heard her or not. He looked so unfocused, she couldn't even be sure whether he'd truly seen her.

"Mr. Bridgerton?"

He squinted. "Sophie," he said hoarsely, his throat sounding terribly dry and scratchy. "The housemaid."

She nodded. "I'm here. What do you need?"

"Water," he rasped.

"Right away." Sophie had been dunking the cloths into the water in the pitcher, but she decided that now was no time to be fussy, so she grabbed hold of the glass she'd brought up from the kitchen and filled it. "Here you are," she said, handing it to him.

His fingers were shaky, so she did not let go of the glass as he brought it to his lips. He took a couple of sips, then sagged back against his pillows.

"Thank you," he whispered.

Sophie reached out and touched his brow. It was still quite warm, but he seemed lucid once again, and she decided to take that as a sign that the fever had broken. "I think you'll be better in the morning."

He laughed. Not hard, and not with anything approaching vigor, but he actually laughed. "Not likely," he croaked.

"Well, not recovered," she allowed, "but I think you'll feel better than you do right now."

"It would certainly be hard to feel worse."

Sophie smiled at him. "Do you think you can scoot to one side of your bed so I can change your sheets?"

He nodded and did as she asked, closing his weary eyes as she changed the bed around him. "That's a neat trick," he said when she was done.

"Mrs. Cavender's mother often came to visit," Sophie explained. "She was bedridden, so I had to learn how to change the sheets without her leaving the bed. It's not terribly difficult."

He nodded. "I'm going back to sleep now."

Sophie gave his shoulder a reassuring pat. She just couldn't help herself. "You'll feel better in the morning," she whispered. "I promise."

Chapter 9

It has oft been said that physicians make the worst patients, but it is the opinion of This Author that any man makes a terrible patient. One might say it takes patience to be a patient, and heaven knows, the males of our species lack an abundance of patience.

LADY WHISTLEDOWN'S SOCIETY PAPERS, 2 MAY 1817

The first thing Sophie did the following morning was scream.

She'd fallen asleep in the straight-backed chair next to Benedict's bed, her limbs sprawled most inelegantly and her head cocked to the side in a rather uncomfortable position. Her sleep had been light at first, her ears perked to listen for any sign of distress from the sickbed. But after an hour or so of complete, blessed silence, exhaustion claimed her, and she fell into a deeper slumber, the kind from which one ought to awaken in peace, with a restful, easy smile on one's face.

Which may have been why, when she opened her eyes and saw two strange people staring at her, she had such a fright that it took a full five minutes for her heart to stop racing.

"Who are you?" The words tumbled out of Sophie's mouth before she realized exactly who they must be: Mr. and Mrs. Crabtree, the caretakers of My Cottage.

"Who are *you*?" the man demanded, not a little bit belligerently.

"Sophie Beckett," she said with a gulp. "I . . ." She pointed desperately at Benedict. "He . . ."

"Spit it out, girl!"

"Don't torture her," came a croak from the bed.

Three heads swiveled in Benedict's direction. "You're awake!" Sophie exclaimed.

"Wish to God I weren't," he muttered. "My throat feels like it's on fire."

"Would you like me to fetch you some more water?" Sophie asked solicitously.

He shook his head. "Tea. Please."

She shot to her feet. "I'll go get it."

"*I'll* get it," Mrs. Crabtree said firmly.

"Would you like help?" Sophie asked timidly. Something about this pair made her feel like she were ten years old. They were both short and squat, but they positively exuded authority.

Mrs. Crabtree shook her head. "A fine housekeeper I am if I can't prepare a pot of tea."

Sophie gulped. She couldn't tell whether Mrs. Crabtree was miffed or joking. "I never meant to imply—"

Mrs. Crabtree waved off her apology. "Shall I bring you a cup?"

"You shouldn't fetch anything for me," Sophie said. "I'm a ser—"

"Bring her a cup," Benedict ordered.

"But—"

He jabbed his finger at her, grunting, "Be quiet," before turning to Mrs. Crabtree and bestowing upon her a smile that could have melted an ice cap. "Would you be so kind as to include a cup for Miss Beckett on the tray?"

"Of course, Mr. Bridgerton," she replied, "but may I say—"

"You can say anything you please once you return with the tea," he promised.

She gave him a stern look. "I have a lot to say."

"Of that I have no doubt."

Benedict, Sophie, and Mr. Crabtree waited in silence while Mrs. Crabtree left the room, and then, when she was safely out of earshot, Mr. Crabtree positively chortled, and said, "You're in for it now, Mr. Bridgerton!"

Benedict smiled weakly.

Mr. Crabtree turned to Sophie and explained, "When Mrs. Crabtree has a lot to say, she has a *lot* to say."

"Oh," Sophie replied. She would have liked to have said something slightly more articulate, but "oh" was truly the best she could come up with on such short notice.

"And when she has a lot to say," Mr. Crabtree continued, his smile growing wide and sly, "she likes to say it with great vigor."

"Fortunately," Benedict said in a dry voice, "we'll have our tea to keep us occupied."

Sophie's stomach grumbled loudly.

"And," Benedict continued, shooting her an amused glance, "a fair bit of breakfast, too, if I know Mrs. Crabtree."

Mr. Crabtree nodded. "Already prepared, Mr. Bridgerton. We saw your horses in the stables when we returned from our daughter's house this morning, and Mrs. Crabtree got to work on breakfast straightaway. She knows how you love your eggs."

Benedict turned to Sophie and gave her a conspiratorial sort of smile. "I do love eggs."

Her stomach grumbled again.

"We didn't know there'd be two of you, though," Mr. Crabtree said.

Benedict chuckled, then winced at the pain. "I can't imagine that Mrs. Crabtree didn't make enough to feed a small army."

"Well, she didn't have time to prepare a proper breakfast with beef pie and fish," Mr. Crabtree said, "but I believe she has bacon and ham and eggs and toast."

Sophie's stomach positively growled. She clapped a hand to her belly, just barely resisting the urge to hiss, "Be quiet!"

"You should have told us you were coming," Mr. Crabtree added, shaking a finger at Benedict. "We never would have gone visiting if we'd known to expect you."

"It was a spur-of-the-moment decision," Benedict said, stretching his neck from side to side. "Went to a bad party and decided to leave."

Mr. Crabtree jerked his head toward Sophie. "Where'd she come from?"

"She was at the party."

"I wasn't *at* the party," Sophie corrected. "I just happened to be there."

Mr. Crabtree squinted at her suspiciously. "What's the difference?"

"I wasn't attending the party. I was a servant at the house."

"You're a servant?"

Sophie nodded. "That's what I've been trying to tell you."

"You don't look like a servant." Mr. Crabtree turned to Benedict. "Does she look like a servant to you?"

Benedict shrugged helplessly. "I don't know *what* she looks like."

Sophie scowled at him. It might not have been an insult, but it certainly wasn't a compliment.

"If she's somebody else's servant," Mr. Crabtree persisted, "then what's she doing here?"

"May I save my explanations until Mrs. Crabtree returns?" Benedict asked. "Since I'm certain she'll repeat all of your questions?"

Mr. Crabtree looked at him for a moment, blinked, nodded, then turned back to Sophie. "Why're you dressed like that?"

Sophie looked down and realized with horror that she'd completely forgotten she was wearing men's clothes. Men's clothes so big that she could barely keep the breeches from falling to her feet. "My clothes were wet," she explained, "from the rain."

Mr. Crabtree nodded sympathetically. "Quite a storm last night. That's why we stayed over at our daughter's. We'd planned to come home, you know."

Benedict and Sophie just nodded.

"She doesn't live terribly far away," Mr. Crabtree continued. "Just on the other side of the village." He glanced over at Benedict, who nodded immediately.

"Has a new baby," he added. "A girl."

"Congratulations," Benedict said, and Sophie could see from his face that he was not merely being polite. He truly meant it.

A loud clomping sound came from the stairway; surely Mrs. Crabtree returning with breakfast. "I ought to help," Sophie said, jumping up and dashing for the door.

"Once a servant, always a servant," Mr. Crabtree said sagely.

Benedict wasn't sure, but he thought he saw Sophie wince.

A minute later, Mrs. Crabtree entered, bearing a splendid silver tea service.

"Where's Sophie?" Benedict asked.

"I sent her down to get the rest," Mrs. Crabtree replied. "She should be up in no time. Nice girl," she added in a matter-of-fact tone, "but she needs a belt for those breeches you lent her."

Benedict felt something squeeze suspiciously in his chest at the thought of Sophie-the-housemaid, with her breeches 'round her ankles. He gulped uncomfortably when he realized the tight sensation might very well be desire.

Then he groaned and grabbed at his throat, because uncomfortable gulps were even more uncomfortable after a night of harsh coughing.

"You need one of my tonics," Mrs. Crabtree said.

Benedict shook his head frantically. He'd had one of her tonics before; it had had him retching for three hours.

"I won't take no for an answer," she warned.

"She never does," Mr. Crabtree added.

"The tea will work wonders," Benedict said quickly, "I'm sure."

But Mrs. Crabtree's attention had already been diverted. "Where is that girl?" she muttered, walking back to the door and looking out. "Sophie! Sophie!"

"If you can keep her from bringing me a tonic," Benedict whispered urgently to Mr. Crabtree, "it's a fiver in your pocket."

Mr. Crabtree beamed. "Consider it done!"

"There she is," Mrs. Crabtree declared. "Oh, heaven above."

"What is it, dearie?" Mr. Crabtree asked, ambling toward the door.

"The poor thing can't carry a tray and keep her breeches up at the same time," she replied, clucking sympathetically.

"Aren't you going to help her?" Benedict asked from the bed.

"Oh yes, of course." She hurried out.

"I'll be right back," Mr. Crabtree said over his shoulder. "Don't want to miss this."

"Someone get the bloody girl a belt!" Benedict yelled grumpily. It didn't seem quite fair that everyone got to go out to the hall and watch the sideshow while he was stuck in bed.

And he definitely was stuck there. Just the thought of getting up made him dizzy.

He must have been sicker than he'd realized the night before. He no longer felt the urge to cough every few seconds, but his body felt worn-out, exhausted. His muscles ached, and his throat was damned sore. Even his teeth didn't feel quite right.

He had vague recollections of Sophie taking care of him. She'd put cool compresses on his forehead, watched over him, even sung him a lullaby. But he'd never quite seen her face. Most of the time he hadn't had the energy to open his eyes, and even when he had, the room had been dark, always leaving her in shadows, reminding him of—

Benedict sucked in his breath, his heart thumping crazily in his chest as, in a sudden flash of clarity, he remembered his dream.

He'd dreamed of *her*.

It was not a new dream, although it had been months since he'd been visited by it. It was not a fantasy for the innocent, either. Benedict was no saint, and when he dreamed of the woman from the masquerade, she was not wearing her silver dress.

She was not, he thought with a wicked smile, wearing anything.

But what perplexed him was why this dream would return now, after so many months of dormancy. Was there something about Sophie that had triggered it? He'd thought—he'd hoped—that the disappearance of the dream had meant he was over her.

Obviously not.

Sophie certainly didn't look like the woman he'd danced with two years earlier. Her hair was all wrong, and she was far too thin. He distinctly remembered the lush, curvy feel of the masked woman in his arms; in comparison, Sophie could only be called scrawny. He supposed their voices were a bit similar, but he had to admit to himself that as time passed, his memories of that night grew less vivid, and he could no longer recall his mystery woman's voice with perfect clarity. Besides, Sophie's accent, while exceptionally refined for a housemaid, was not as upper-crust as *hers* had been.

Benedict let out a frustrated snort. How he hated calling her *her*. That seemed the cruelest of her secrets. She'd kept from him even her name. Part of him wished she'd just lied and given him a false name. At least then he'd have something to think of her by in his mind.

Something to whisper in the night, when he was staring out the window, wondering where in hell she was.

Benedict was saved from further reflection by the sounds of stumbling and bumbling in the hallway. Mr. Crabtree was the first to return, staggering under the weight of the breakfast tray.

"What happened to the rest?" Benedict asked suspiciously, eyeing the door.

"Mrs. Crabtree went off to find Sophie some proper clothing," Mr. Crabtree replied, setting the tray down on Benedict's desk. "Ham or bacon?"

"Both. I'm famished. And what the devil does she mean by 'proper clothing'?"

"A dress, Mr. Bridgerton. That's what women wear."

Benedict seriously considered lobbing a candle stump at him. "I meant," he said with what he considered saintly patience, "where is she going to *find* a dress?"

Mr. Crabtree walked over with a plate of food on a footed tray that would fit over Benedict's lap. "Mrs. Crabtree has several extras. She's always happy to share."

Benedict choked on the bite of egg he'd shoveled into his mouth. "Mrs. Crabtree and Sophie are hardly the same size."

"Neither are you," Mr. Crabtree pointed out, "and she wore your clothes just fine."

"I thought you said the breeches fell off in the hall."

"Well, we don't have to worry about that with the dress, do we? I hardly think her shoulders are going to slip through the neck hole."

Benedict decided it was safer for his sanity to mind his own business, and he turned his full attention to his breakfast. He was on his third plate when Mrs. Crabtree bustled in.

"Here we are!" she announced.

Sophie slunk in, practically drowning in Mrs. Crabtree's voluminous dress. Except, of course, at her ankles. Mrs. Crabtree was a good five inches shorter than Sophie.

Mrs. Crabtree beamed. "Doesn't she look smashing?"

"Oh, yes," Benedict replied, lips twitching.

Sophie glared at him.

"You'll have plenty of room for breakfast," he said gamely.

"It's only until I get her clothing cleaned up," Mrs. Crabtree explained. "But at least it's decent." She waddled over to Benedict. "How is your breakfast, Mr. Bridgerton?"

"Delicious," he replied. "I haven't eaten so well in months."

Mrs. Crabtree leaned forward and whispered, "I like your Sophie. May we keep her?"

Benedict choked. On what, he didn't know, but he choked nonetheless. "I beg your pardon?"

"Mr. Crabtree and I aren't as young as we used to be. We could use another set of hands around here."

"I, ah, well . . ." He cleared his throat. "I'll think about it."

"Excellent." Mrs. Crabtree crossed back to the other side of the room and grabbed Sophie's arm. "You come with me. Your stomach has been growling all morning. When was the last time you ate?"

"Er, sometime yesterday, I should think."

"When yesterday?" Mrs. Crabtree persisted.

Benedict hid a smile under his napkin. Sophie looked utterly overwhelmed. Mrs. Crabtree tended to do that to a person.

"Er, well, actually—"

Mrs. Crabtree planted her hands on her hips. Benedict grinned. Sophie was in for it now.

"Are you going to tell me that you didn't eat yesterday?" Mrs. Crabtree boomed.

Sophie shot a desperate look at Benedict. He replied with a don't-look-to-*me*-for-help shrug. Besides, he rather enjoyed watching Mrs. Crabtree fuss over her. He'd be willing to bet that the poor girl hadn't been fussed over in years.

"I was very busy yesterday," Sophie hedged.

Benedict frowned. She'd probably been busy running from Phillip Cavender and the pack of idiots he called friends.

Mrs. Crabtree shoved Sophie into the seat behind the desk. "Eat," she ordered.

Benedict watched as Sophie tucked into the food. It was obvious that she was trying to put on her best manners, but eventually hunger must have gotten the best of her, because after a minute she was practically shoveling the food into her mouth.

It was only when Benedict noticed that his jaw was clamped together like a vise that he realized he was absolutely furious. At whom, he wasn't precisely certain. But he did *not* like seeing Sophie so hungry.

They had an odd little bond, he and the housemaid. He'd saved her and she'd saved him. Oh, he doubted his fever from the night before would have killed him; if it had been truly serious, he'd still be battling it now. But she had cared for him and made him comfortable and probably hastened his road to recovery.

"Will you make certain she eats at least another plateful?" Mrs. Crabtree asked Benedict. "I'm going to make up a room for her."

"In the servants' quarters," Sophie said quickly.

"Don't be a silly. Until we hire you on, you're not a servant here."

"But—"

"Nothing more about it," Mrs. Crabtree interrupted.

"Would you like my help, dearie?" Mr. Crabtree asked.

Mrs. Crabtree nodded, and in a moment the couple was gone.

Sophie paused in her quest to consume as much food as humanly possible to stare at the door through which they'd just disappeared. She supposed they considered her one of their own, because if she'd been anything but a servant, they'd never have left her alone with Benedict. Reputations could be ruined on far less.

"You didn't eat at all yesterday, did you?" Benedict asked quietly.

Sophie shook her head.

"Next time I see Cavender," he growled, "I'm going to beat him to a bloody pulp."

If she were a better person, she would have been horrified, but Sophie couldn't quite prevent a smile at the thought of Benedict further defending her honor. Or of seeing Phillip Cavender with his nose relocated to his forehead.

"Fill up your plate again," Benedict said. "If only for my sake. I assure you that Mrs. Crabtree counted how many eggs and strips of bacon were on the platter when she left, and she'll have my head if the numbers haven't gone down by the time she returns."

"She's a very nice lady," Sophie said, reaching for the eggs. The first plate of food had barely touched upon her hunger; she needed no further urging to eat.

"The best."

Sophie expertly balanced a slice of ham between a serving fork and spoon and moved it to her plate. "How are you feeling this morning, Mr. Bridgerton?"

"Very well, thank you. Or if not well, then at least a damn sight better than I did last night."

"I was very worried about you," she said, spearing a corner of the ham with her fork and then cutting a piece off with her knife.

"It was very kind of you to care for me."

She chewed, swallowed, then said, "It was nothing, really. Anyone would have done it."

"Perhaps," he said, "but not with such grace and good humor."

Sophie's fork froze in midair. "Thank you," she said softly. "That is a lovely compliment."

"I didn't . . . er . . ." He cleared his throat.

Sophie eyed him curiously, waiting for him to finish whatever it was he wanted to say.

"Never mind," he mumbled.

Disappointed, she put a piece of ham in her mouth.

"I didn't do anything for which I ought to apologize, did I?" he suddenly blurted out.

Sophie spat the ham out into her napkin.

"I'll take that as a yes," he muttered.

"No!" she said quickly. "Not at all. You merely startled me."

His eyes narrowed. "You wouldn't lie to me about this, would you?"

Sophie shook her head as she remembered the single, perfect kiss she'd given him. He hadn't done anything that required an apology, but that didn't mean that *she* hadn't.

"You're blushing," he accused.

"No, I'm not."

"Yes," he said, "you are."

"If I'm blushing," she replied pertly, "it's because I'm wondering why *you* would think you had any reason to apologize."

"You have a rather smart mouth for a servant," he said.

"I'm sorry," Sophie said quickly. She had to remember her place. But that was hard to do with this man, the one member of the *ton* who had treated her—if only for a few hours—as an equal.

"I meant it as a compliment," he said. "Do not stifle yourself on my account."

She said nothing.

"I find you rather . . ." He paused, obviously searching for the correct word. "Refreshing."

"Oh." She set her fork down. "Thank you."

"Have you plans for the rest of the day?" he asked.

She looked down at her huge garments and grimaced. "I thought I'd wait for my clothes to be readied, and then I suppose I'll see if any of the nearby houses are in need of housemaids."

Benedict scowled at her. "I told you I would find you a position with my mother."

"And I do appreciate that," she said quickly. "But I would prefer to stay in the country."

He shrugged the shrug of one who has never been thrown one of life's great stumbles. "You can work at Aubrey Hall, then. In Kent."

Sophie chewed on her lower lip. She couldn't exactly come out and say she didn't want to work for his mother because then she'd have to see *him*.

She couldn't think of a torture that would be more exquisitely painful.

"You shouldn't think of me as your responsibility," she finally said.

He gave her a rather superior glance. "I told you I would find you a new position."

"But—"

"What could there possibly be to discuss?"

"Nothing," she grumbled. "Nothing at all." Clearly, it was no use arguing with him just then.

"Good." He leaned back contentedly against his pillows. "I'm glad you see it my way."

Sophie stood. "I should be going."

"To do what?"

She felt rather stupid as she said, "I don't know."

He grinned. "Have fun with it, then."

Her hand tightened around the handle of the serving spoon.

"Don't do it," he warned.

"Do what?"

"Throw the spoon."

"I wouldn't dream of it," she said tightly.

He laughed aloud. "Oh, yes you would. You're dreaming of it right now. You just wouldn't *do* it."

Sophie's hand was gripping the spoon so hard it shook.

Benedict was chuckling so hard his bed shook.

Sophie stood, still holding the spoon.

Benedict smiled. "Are you planning to take that with you?"

Remember your place, Sophie was screaming at herself. *Remember your place*.

"Whatever could you be thinking," Benedict mused, "to look so adorably ferocious? No, don't tell me," he added. "I'm sure it involves my untimely and painful demise."

Slowly and carefully, Sophie turned her back to him and put the spoon down on the table. She didn't want to risk any sudden movements. One false move and she knew she'd be hurling it at his head.

Benedict raised his brows approvingly. "That was very mature of you."

Sophie turned around slowly. "Are you this charming with everyone or only me?"

"Oh, only you." He grinned. "I shall have to make sure you take me up on my offer to find you employment with my mother. You do bring out the best in me, Miss Sophie Beckett."

"This is the best?" she asked with obvious disbelief.

"I'm afraid so."

Sophie just shook her head as she walked to the door. Conversations with Benedict Bridgerton could be exhausting.

"Oh, Sophie!" he called out.

She turned around.

He smiled slyly. "I knew you wouldn't throw the spoon."

What happened next was surely not Sophie's fault. She was, she was convinced, temporarily and fleetingly possessed by a demon. Because she absolutely did not recognize the hand that shot out to the small table next to her and picked up a stump of a candle. True, the hand appeared to be connected quite firmly to her arm, but it didn't look the least bit familiar as it drew back and hurled the stump across the room.

Straight at Benedict Bridgerton's head.

Sophie didn't even wait to see if her aim had been true. But as she stalked out the door, she heard Benedict explode with laughter. Then she heard him shout out, "Well done, Miss Beckett!"

And she realized that for the first time in years, her smile was one of pure, unadulterated joy.

Chapter 10

Although he responded in the affirmative (or so says Lady Covington) Benedict Bridgerton did not make an appearance at the annual Covington Ball. Complaints were heard from young women (and their mamas) across the ballroom.

According to Lady Bridgerton (his mother, not his sister-in-law), Mr. Bridgerton left for the country last week and has not been heard from since. Those who might fear for Mr. Bridgerton's health and well-being should not fret; Lady Bridgerton sounded more annoyed than worried. Last year no less than four couples met their future spouses at the Covington Ball; the previous year, three.

Much to Lady Bridgerton's dismay, if any matches are made at this year's Covington Ball, her son Benedict will not be among the grooms.

LADY WHISTLEDOWN'S SOCIETY PAPERS, 5 MAY 1817

There were advantages, Benedict soon discovered, to a long, drawn-out recovery.

The most obvious was the quantity and variety of most excellent food brought forth from Mrs. Crabtree's kitchen. He'd always been fed well at My Cottage, but Mrs. Crabtree truly rose to the occasion when she had someone tucked away in the sickroom.

And even better, Mr. Crabtree had managed to intercept all of Mrs. Crabtree's tonics and replace them with Benedict's best brandy. Benedict dutifully drank every drop, but the last time he looked out the window, it appeared that three of his rosebushes had died, presumably where Mr. Crabtree had dumped the tonic.

It was a sad sacrifice, but one Benedict was more than willing to make after his last experience with Mrs. Crabtree's tonics.

Another perk of staying abed was the simple fact that, for the first time in years, he could enjoy some quiet time. He read, sketched, and even closed his eyes and just daydreamed—all without feeling guilty for neglecting some other task or chore.

Benedict soon decided that he'd be perfectly happy leading the life of the indolent.

But the best part of his recovery, by far, was Sophie. She popped into his room several times a day, sometimes to fluff his pillows, sometimes to bring him food, sometimes just to read to him. Benedict had a feeling that her industriousness was due to her desire to feel useful, and to thank him with deeds for saving her from Phillip Cavender.

But he didn't much care why she came to visit; he just liked it that she did.

She'd been quiet and reserved at first, obviously trying to adhere to the standard that servants should be neither seen nor heard. But Benedict had had none of that, and he'd purposefully engaged her in conversation, just so she couldn't leave. Or he'd goad and needle her, simply to get a rise out of her, because he liked her far better when she was spitting fire than when she was meek and submissive.

But mostly he just enjoyed being in the same room with her. It didn't seem to matter if they were talking or if she was just sitting in a chair, leafing through a book while he stared out the window. Something about her presence brought him peace.

A sharp knock at the door broke him out of his thoughts, and he looked up eagerly, calling out, "Enter!"

Sophie poked her head in, her shoulder-length curls shaking slightly as they brushed against the edge of the door. "Mrs. Crabtree thought you might like tea."

"Tea? Or tea and biscuits?"

Sophie grinned, pushing the door open with her hip as she balanced the tray. "Oh, the latter, to be sure."

"Excellent. And will you join me?"

She hesitated, as she always did, but then she nodded, as she also always did. She'd long since learned that there was no arguing with Benedict when he had his mind set on something.

Benedict rather liked it that way.

"The color is back in your cheeks," she commented as she set the tray down on a nearby table. "And you don't look nearly so tired. I should think you'll be up and out of bed soon,"

"Oh, soon, I'm sure," he said evasively.

"You're looking healthier every day."

He smiled gamely. "Do you think so?"

She lifted the teapot and paused before she poured. "Yes," she said with an ironic smile. "I wouldn't have said so otherwise."

Benedict watched her hands as she prepared his tea. She moved with an innate sense of grace, and she poured the tea as if she'd been to the manner born. Clearly the art of afternoon tea had been another one of those lessons she'd learned from her mother's generous employers. Or maybe she'd just watched other ladies closely while they'd prepared tea. Benedict had noticed that she was a very observant woman.

They'd enacted this ritual often enough that she didn't have to ask how he liked his tea. She handed him his cup—

milk, no sugar—and then placed a selection of biscuits and scones on a plate.

"Fix yourself a cup," Benedict said, biting into a biscuit, "and come sit by me."

She hesitated again. He knew she'd hesitate, even though she'd already agreed to join him. But he was a patient man, and his patience was rewarded with a soft sigh as she reached out and plucked another cup off the tray.

After she'd fixed her own cup—two lumps of sugar, just the barest splash of milk—she sat in the velvet-covered, straight-backed chair by his bed, regarding him over the rim of her teacup as she took a sip.

"No biscuits for you?" Benedict asked.

She shook her head. "I had a few straight out of the oven."

"Lucky you. They're always best when they're warm." He polished off another biscuit, brushed a few crumbs off of his sleeve, and reached for another. "And how have you spent your day?"

"Since I last saw you two hours earlier?"

Benedict shot her a look that said he recognized her sarcasm but chose not to respond to it.

"I helped Mrs. Crabtree in the kitchen," Sophie said. "She's making a beef stew for supper and needed some potatoes peeled. Then I borrowed a book from your library and read in the garden."

"Really? What did you read?"

"A novel."

"Was it good?"

She shrugged. "Silly, but romantic. I enjoyed it."

"And do you long for romance?"

Her blush was instantaneous. "That's a rather personal question, don't you think?"

Benedict shrugged and started to say something utterly flip, like, "It was worth a try," but as he watched her face, her cheeks turning delightfully pink, her eyes cast down to her lap, the strangest thing happened.

He realized he wanted her.

He really, really wanted her.

He wasn't certain why this so surprised him. Of course he *wanted* her. He was as red-blooded as any man, and one couldn't spend a protracted amount of time around a woman as gamine and adorable as Sophie without wanting her. Hell, he wanted half the women he met, in a purely low-intensity, non-urgent sort of way.

But in that moment, with this woman, it became urgent.

Benedict changed positions. Then he bunched the coverlet up over his lap. Then he changed positions again.

"Is your bed uncomfortable?" Sophie asked. "Do you need me to fluff your pillows?"

Benedict's first urge was to reply in the affirmative, grab her as she leaned across him, and then have his wicked way with her, since they would, rather conveniently, be in bed.

But he had a sneaking suspicion that that particular plan would not go over well with Sophie, so instead he said, "I'm fine," then winced when he realized his voice sounded oddly squeaky.

She smiled as she eyed the biscuits on his plate, saying, "Maybe just one more."

Benedict moved his arm out of the way to allow her easy access to his plate, which was, he realized somewhat belatedly, resting on his lap. The sight of her hand reaching toward his groin—even if she was aiming for a plate of biscuits—did funny things to him, to his groin, to be precise.

Benedict had a sudden vision of things . . . *shifting* down there, and he hastily grabbed the plate, lest it become unbalanced.

"Do you mind if I take the last—"

"Fine!" he croaked.

She plucked a ginger biscuit off the plate and frowned. "You look better," she said, giving the biscuit a little sniff, "but you don't sound better. Is your throat bothering you?"

Benedict took a quick sip of his tea. "Not at all. I must've swallowed a piece of dust."

"Oh. Drink some more tea, then. That shouldn't bother you for long." She set her teacup down. "Would you like me to read to you?"

"Yes!" Benedict said quickly, bunching up his coverlet around his waist. She might try to take away the strategically placed plate, and then where would he be?

"Are you certain you're all right?" she asked, looking far more suspicious than concerned.

He smiled tightly. "Just fine."

"Very well," she said, standing up. "What would you like me to read?"

"Oh, anything," he said with a blithe wave of his hand.

"Poetry?"

"Splendid." He would have said, "Splendid," had she offered to read a dissertation on botany in the arctic tundra.

Sophie wandered over to a recessed bookshelf and idly perused its contents. "Byron?" she asked. "Blake?"

"Blake," he said quite firmly. A hour's worth of Byron's romantic drivel would probably send him quite over the edge.

She slid a slim volume of poetry off the shelf and returned to her chair, swishing her rather unattractive skirts before she sat down.

Benedict frowned. He'd never really noticed before how ugly her dress was. Not as bad as the one Mrs. Crabtree had lent her, but certainly not anything designed to bring out the best in a woman.

He ought to buy her a new dress. She would never accept it, of course, but maybe if her current garments were accidentally *burned* . . .

"Mr. Bridgerton?"

But how could he manage to burn her dress? She'd have to not be wearing it, and that posed a certain challenge in and of itself . . .

"Are you even listening to me?" Sophie demanded.

"Hmmm?"

"You're *not* listening to me."

"Sorry," he admitted. "My apologies. My mind got away from me. Please continue."

She began anew, and in his attempt to show how much attention he was paying her, he focused his eyes on her lips, which proved to be a *big* mistake.

Because suddenly those lips were all he could see, and he couldn't stop thinking about kissing her, and he knew—absolutely knew—that if one of them didn't leave the room in the next thirty seconds, he was going to do something for which he'd owe her a thousand apologies.

Not that he didn't plan to seduce her. Just that he'd rather do it with a bit more finesse.

"Oh, dear," he blurted out.

Sophie gave him an odd look. He didn't blame her. He sounded like a complete idiot. He didn't think he'd uttered the phrase, "Oh, dear," in years. If ever.

Hell, he sounded like his mother.

"Is something wrong?" Sophie asked.

"I just remembered something," he said, rather stupidly, in his opinion.

She raised her brows in question.

"Something that I'd forgotten," Benedict said.

"The things one remembers," she said, looking exceedingly amused, "are most often things one had forgotten."

He scowled at her. "I'll need a bit of privacy."

She stood instantly. "Of course," she murmured.

Benedict fought off a groan. Damn. She looked hurt. He hadn't meant to injure her feelings. He just needed to get her out of the room so that he didn't yank her into the bed. "It's a personal matter," he told her, trying to make her feel better but suspecting that all he was doing was making himself look like a fool.

"Ohhhhh," she said knowingly. "Would you like me to bring you the chamber pot?"

"I can walk to the chamber pot," he retorted, forgetting that he didn't need to use the chamber pot.

She nodded and stood, setting the book of poetry onto a nearby table. "I'll leave you to your business. Just ring the bellpull when you need me."

"I'm not going to summon you like a servant," he growled.

"But I *am* a—"

"Not for me you're not," he said. The words emerged a little more harshly than was necessary, but he'd always detested men who preyed on helpless female servants. The thought that he might be turning into one of those repellent creatures was enough to make him gag.

"Very well," she said, her words meek like a servant. Then she nodded like a servant—he was fairly certain she did it just to annoy him—and left.

The minute she was gone, Benedict leapt out of the bed and ran to the window. Good. No one was in sight. He shrugged off his dressing gown, replaced it with a pair of breeches and a shirt and jacket, and looked out the window again. Good. Still no one.

"Boots, boots," he muttered, glancing around the room. Where the hell were his boots? Not his good boots—the pair for mucking around in the mud . . . ah, there they were. He grabbed the boots and yanked them on.

Back to the window. Still no one. Excellent. Benedict threw one leg over the sill, then another, then grabbed hold of the long, sturdy branch that jutted out from a nearby elm tree. From there it was an easy shimmy, wiggle, and balancing act down to the ground.

And from there it was straight to the lake. To the very cold lake.

To take a very cold swim.

* * *

“If he needed the chamber pot,” Sophie muttered to herself, “he could have just said so. It’s not as if I haven’t fetched chamber pots before.”

She stamped down the stairs to the main floor, not entirely certain why she was going downstairs (she had nothing specific to do there) but heading in that direction simply because she couldn’t think of anything better to do.

She didn’t understand why he had so much trouble treating her like what she was—a servant. He kept insisting that she didn’t work for him and didn’t have to do anything to earn her keep at My Cottage, and then in the same breath assured her that he would find her a position in his mother’s household.

If he would just treat her like a servant, she’d have no trouble remembering that she was an illegitimate nobody and he was a member of one of the *ton*’s wealthiest and most influential families. Every time he treated her like a real person (and it was her experience that most aristocrats did not treat servants like anything remotely approaching a real person) it brought her back to the night of the masquerade, when she’d been, for one perfect evening, a lady of glamour and grace—the sort of woman who had a right to dream about a future with Benedict Bridgerton.

He acted as if he actually liked her and enjoyed her company. And maybe he did. But that was the cruelest twist of all, because he was making her love him, making a small part of her think she had the right to dream about him.

And then, inevitably, she had to remind herself of the truth of the situation, and it hurt so damned much.

“Oh, there you are, Miss Sophie!”

Sophie lifted up her eyes, which had been absently following the cracks in the parquet floor, to see Mrs. Crabtree descending the stairs behind her.

“Good day, Mrs. Crabtree,” Sophie said. “How is that beef stew coming along?”

"Fine, fine," Mrs. Crabtree said absently. "We were a bit short on carrots, but I think it will be tasty nonetheless. Have you seen Mr. Bridgerton?"

Sophie blinked in surprise at the question. "In his room. Just a minute ago."

"Well, he's not there now."

"I think he had to use the chamber pot."

Mrs. Crabtree didn't even blush; it was the sort of conversation servants often had about their employers. "Well, if he did use it, he didn't *use* it, if you know what I mean," she said. "The room smelled as fresh as a spring day."

Sophie frowned. "And he wasn't there?"

"Neither hide nor hair."

"I can't imagine where he might have gone."

Mrs. Crabtree planted her hands on her ample hips. "I'll search the downstairs and you search the up. One of us is bound to find him."

"I'm not sure that's such a good idea, Mrs. Crabtree. If he's left his room, he probably had a good reason. Most likely, he doesn't want to be found."

"But he's ill," Mrs. Crabtree protested.

Sophie considered that, then pictured his face in her mind. His skin had held a healthy glow and he hadn't looked the least bit tired. "I'm not so certain about that, Mrs. Crabtree," she finally said. "I think he's malingering on purpose."

"Don't be silly," Mrs. Crabtree scoffed. "Mr. Bridgerton would never do something like that."

Sophie shrugged. "I wouldn't have thought so, but truly, he doesn't look the least bit ill any longer."

"It's my tonics," Mrs. Crabtree said with a confident nod. "I told you they'd speed up his recovery."

Sophie had seen Mr. Crabtree dump the tonics in the rosebushes; she'd also seen the aftermath. It hadn't been a pretty sight. How she managed to smile and nod, she'd never know.

"Well, I for one would like to know where he went," Mrs.

Crabtree continued. "He shouldn't be out of bed, and he knows it."

"I'm sure he'll return soon," Sophie said placatingly. "In the meantime, do you need any help in the kitchen?"

Mrs. Crabtree shook her head. "No, no. All that stew needs to do now is cook. And besides, Mr. Bridgerton has been scolding me for allowing you to work."

"But—"

"No arguments, if you please," Mrs. Crabtree cut in. "He's right, of course. You're a guest here, and you shouldn't have to lift a finger."

"I'm not a guest," Sophie protested.

"Well, then, what are you?"

That gave Sophie pause. "I have no idea," she finally said, "but I'm definitely not a guest. A guest would be . . . A guest would be . . ." She struggled to make sense of her thoughts and feelings. "I suppose a guest would be someone who is of the same social rank, or at least close to it. A guest would be someone who has never had to wait upon another person, or scrub floors, or empty chamber pots. A guest would be—"

"Anyone the master of the house chooses to invite as a guest," Mrs. Crabtree retorted. "That's the beauty of being the master of the house. You can do anything you please. And you should stop belittling yourself. If Mr. Bridgerton chooses to regard you as a houseguest, then you should accept his judgment and enjoy yourself. When was the last time you were able to live in comfort without having to work your fingers to the bone in return?"

"He can't truly regard me as a houseguest," Sophie said quietly. "If he did, he would have installed a chaperone for the protection of my reputation."

"As if *I* would allow anything untoward in my house," Mrs. Crabtree bristled.

"Of course you wouldn't," Sophie assured her. "But where reputations are at stake, appearance is just as important as fact. And in the eyes of society, a housekeeper does not qualify as a chaperone, no matter how strict and pure her morals may be."

"If that's true," Mrs. Crabtree protested, "then you need a chaperone, Miss Sophie."

"Don't be silly. I don't need a chaperone because I'm not of his class. No one cares if a housemaid lives and works in the household of a single man. No one thinks any less of her, and certainly no one who would consider her for marriage would consider her ruined." Sophie shrugged. "It's the way of the world. And obviously it's the way Mr. Bridgerton thinks, whether he'll admit it or not, because he has never once said a word about it being improper for me to be here."

"Well, I don't like it," Mrs. Crabtree announced. "I don't like it one bit."

Sophie just smiled, because it was so sweet of the housekeeper to care. "I think I'm going to take myself off for a walk," she said, "as long as you're certain you don't need any help in the kitchen. And," she added with a sly grin, "as long as I'm in this strange, hazy position. I might not be a guest, but it is the first time in years I'm not a servant, and I'm going to enjoy my free time while it lasts."

Mrs. Crabtree gave her a hearty pat on the shoulder. "You do that, Miss Sophie. And pick a flower for me while you're out there."

Sophie grinned and headed out the front door. It was a lovely day, unseasonably warm and sunny, and the air held the gentle fragrance of the first blooms of spring. She couldn't recall the last time she'd taken a walk for the simple pleasure of enjoying the fresh air.

Benedict had told her about a nearby pond, and she thought she might amble that way, maybe even dip her toes in the water if she was feeling particularly daring.

She smiled up at the sun. The air might be warm, but the water was surely still freezing, so early in May. Still, it would feel good. Anything felt good that represented leisure time and peaceful, solitary moments.

She paused for a moment, frowning thoughtfully at the horizon. Benedict had mentioned that the lake was south of My Cottage, hadn't he? A southward route would take her right through a rather densely wooded patch, but a bit of a hike certainly wouldn't kill her.

Sophie picked her way through the forest, stepping over tree roots, and pushing aside low-lying branches, letting them snap back behind her with reckless abandon. The sun barely squeaked through the canopy of leaves above her, and down at ground level, it felt more like dusk than midday.

Up ahead, she could see a clearing, which she assumed must be the pond. As she drew closer, she saw the glint of sunlight on water, and she breathed a little sigh of satisfaction, happy to know that she'd gone in the correct direction.

But as she drew even closer, she heard the sound of someone splashing about, and she realized with equal parts terror and curiosity that she was not alone.

She was only ten or so feet from the edge of the pond, easily visible to anyone in the water, so she quickly flattened herself behind the trunk of a large oak. If she had a sensible bone in her body, she'd turn right around and run back to the house, but she just couldn't quite keep herself from peeking around the tree and looking to see who might be mad enough to splash about in a lake so early in the season.

With slow, silent movements, she crept out from behind the tree, trying to keep as much of herself concealed as possible.

And she saw a man.

A *naked* man.

A naked . . .

Benedict?

Chapter 11

The housemaid wars rage on in London. Lady Penwood called Mrs. Featherington a conniving, ill-bred thief in front of no less than three society matrons, including the very popular dowager Viscountess Bridgerton!

Mrs. Featherington responded by calling Lady Penwood's home no better than a workhouse, citing the ill treatment of her lady's maid (whose name, This Author has learned, is not Estelle as was originally claimed, and furthermore, she is not remotely French. The girl's name is Bess, and she hails from Liverpool.)

Lady Penwood stalked away from the altercation in quite a huff, followed by her daughter, Miss Rosamund Reiling. Lady Penwood's other daughter, Posy (who was wearing an unfortunate green gown) remained behind with a somewhat apologetic look in her eyes until her mother returned, grabbed her by the sleeve, and dragged her off.

This Author certainly does not make up the guest lists at society parties, but it is difficult to imagine that the Penwoods will be invited to Mrs. Featherington's next soirée.

LADY WHISTLEDOWN'S SOCIETY PAPERS, 7 MAY 1817

It was wrong of her to stay.

So wrong.

So very, very wrong.

And yet she did not move an inch.

She found a large, bald-pated rock, mostly obscured by a short, squat bush, and sat down, never once taking her eyes off of him.

He was *naked*. She still couldn't quite believe it.

He was, of course, partially submerged, with the edge of the water rippling against his rib cage.

The *lower*—she thought giddily—edge of his rib cage.

Or perhaps if she were to be honest with herself, she'd have to rephrase her previous thought to: He was, *unfortunately*, partially submerged.

Sophie was as innocent as the next . . . as, well, the next innocent, but dash it all, she was curious, and she was more than halfway in love with this man. Was it so very wicked to wish for a huge gust of wind, powerful enough to create a small tidal wave that would whip the water away from his body and deposit it somewhere else? Anywhere else?

Very well, it was wicked. *She* was wicked, and she didn't care.

She'd spent her life taking the safe road, the prudent path. Only one night in her short life had she completely thrown caution to the wind. And that night had been the most thrilling, the most magical, the most stupendously wonderful night of her life.

And so she decided to remain right where she was, stay the course, and see what she saw. It wasn't as if she had anything to lose. She had no job, no prospects save for Benedict's promise to find her a position in his mother's household (and she had a feeling that would be a very bad idea, anyway.)

And so she sat back, tried not to move a muscle, and kept her eyes wide, wide open.

* * *

Benedict had never been a superstitious man, and he'd certainly never thought himself the sort with a sixth sense, but once or twice in his life, he'd experienced a strange surge of awareness, a sort of mystical tingling feeling that warned him that something important was afoot.

The first time had been the day his father had died. He'd never told anyone about this, not even his older brother Anthony, who'd been utterly devastated by their father's death, but that afternoon, as he and Anthony had raced across the fields of Kent in some silly horse race, he'd felt an odd, numb feeling in his arms and legs, followed by the strangest pounding in his head. It hadn't hurt, precisely, but it had sucked the air from his lungs and left him with the most intense sensation of terror he could ever imagine.

He'd lost the race, of course; it was difficult to grip reins when one's fingers refused to work properly. And when he'd returned home, he'd discovered that his terror had not been unwarranted. His father was already dead, having collapsed after being stung by a bee. Benedict still had difficulty believing that a man as strong and vital as his father could be felled by a bee, but there had been no other explanation.

The second time it had happened, however, the feeling had been completely different. It had been the night of his mother's masquerade, right before he'd seen the woman in the silver dress. Like the time before, the sensation had started in his arms and legs, but instead of feeling numb, this time he felt an odd tingling, as if he'd just suddenly come alive after years of sleepwalking.

Then he'd turned and seen her, and he'd known she was the reason he was there that night; the reason he lived in England; hell, the very reason he'd been born.

Of course, she had gone and proven him wrong by disappearing into thin air, but at the time he'd believed all that, and if she'd let him, he would have proven it to her as well.

Now, as he stood in the pond, the water lapping at his

midriff, just above his navel, he was struck once again by that odd sense of somehow being more alive than he'd been just seconds earlier. It was a good feeling, an exciting, breathless rush of emotion.

It was like before. When he'd met *her*.

Something was about to happen, or maybe someone was near.

His life was about to change.

And he was, he realized with wry twist of his lips, naked as the day he was born. It didn't exactly put a man at an advantage, at least not unless he was in between a pair of silk sheets with an attractive young woman at his side.

Or underneath.

He took a step into slightly deeper waters, the soft sludge of the pondbottom squishing between his toes. Now the water reached a couple of inches higher. He was bloody well freezing, but at least he was mostly covered up.

He scanned the shore, looking up into trees and down in the bushes. There had to be someone there. Nothing else could account for the strange, tingling feeling that had now spread throughout his body.

And if his body could tingle while submerged in a lake so cold, he was terrified to see his own privates (the poor things felt like they'd shrunk to nothing, which was *not* what a man liked to imagine), then it must be a very strong tingle indeed.

"Who is out there?" he called out.

No answer. He hadn't really expected one, but it had been worth a try.

He squinted as he searched the shore again, turning a full three hundred and sixty degrees as he watched for any sign of movement. He saw nothing but the gentle ruffling of the leaves in the wind, but as he finished his sweep of the area, he somehow *knew*.

"Sophie!"

He heard a gasp, followed by a huge flurry of activity.

"Sophie Beckett," he yelled, "if you run from me right now, I swear I will follow you, and I will not take the time to don my clothing."

The noises coming from the shore slowed.

"I *will* catch up with you," he continued, "because I'm stronger and faster. And I might very well feel compelled to tackle you to the ground, just to be certain you do not escapc."

The sounds of her movement ceased.

"Good," he grunted. "Show yourself."

She didn't.

"Sophie," he warned.

There was a beat of silence, followed by the sound of slow, hesitant footsteps, and then he saw her, standing on the shore in one of those awful dresses he'd like to see sunk to the bottom of the Thames.

"What are you doing here?" he demanded.

"I went for a walk. What are *you* doing here?" she countered. "You're supposed to be ill. That"—she waved her arm toward him and, by extension, the pond—"can't possibly be good for you."

He ignored her question and comment. "Were you following me?"

"Of course not," she replied, and he rather believed her. He didn't think she possessed the acting talents to fake that level of righteousness.

"I would never follow you to a swimming hole," she continued. "It would be indecent."

And then her face went completely red, because they both knew she hadn't a leg to stand on with that argument. If she had truly been concerned about decency, she'd have left the pond the second she'd seen him, accidentally or not.

He lifted one hand from the water and pointed toward her, twisting his wrist as he motioned for her to turn around. "Give me your back while you wait for me," he ordered. "It will only take me a moment to pull on my clothing."

"I'll go home right now," she offered. "You'll enjoy greater privacy, and—"

"You'll stay," he said firmly.

"But—"

He crossed his arms. "Do I look like a man in the mood to be argued with?"

She stared at him mutinously.

"If you run," he warned, "I *will* catch you."

Sophie eyed the distance between them, then tried to judge the distance back to My Cottage. If he stopped to pull on his clothing she might have a chance of escaping, but if he *didn't* . . .

"Sophie," he said, "I can practically see the steam coming out of your ears. Stop taxing your brain with useless mathematical computations and do as I asked."

One of her feet twitched. Whether it was itching to run home or merely turn around, she'd never know.

"Now," he ordered.

With a loud sigh and grumble, Sophie crossed her arms and turned around to stare at a knothole in the tree trunk in front of her as if her very life depended on it. The infernal man wasn't being particularly quiet as he went about his business, and she couldn't seem to keep herself from listening to and trying to identify every sound that rustled and splashed behind her. Now he was emerging from the water, now he was reaching for his breeches, now he was . . .

It was no use. She had a dreadfully wicked imagination, and there was no getting around it.

He should have just let her return to the house. Instead she was forced to wait, utterly mortified, while he dressed. Her skin felt like it was on fire, and she was certain her cheeks must be eight different shades of red. A gentleman would have let her weasel out of her embarrassment and hole up in her room back at the house for at least three days in hopes that he'd just forget about the entire affair.

But Benedict Bridgerton was obviously determined not to

be a gentleman this afternoon, because when she moved one of her feet—just to flex her toes, which were falling asleep in her shoes, honest!—barely half a second passed before he growled, "Don't even think about it."

"I wasn't!" she protested. "My foot was falling asleep. And hurry up! It can't possibly take so long to get dressed."

"Oh?" he drawled.

"You're doing this just to torture me," she grumbled.

"You may feel free to face me at any time," he said, his voice laced with quiet amusement. "I assure you that I asked you to turn your back for the sake of *your* sensibilities, not mine."

"I'm just fine where I am," she replied.

After what seemed like an hour but what was probably only three minutes, she heard him say, "You may turn around now."

Sophie was almost afraid to do so. He had just the sort of perverse sense of humor that would compel him to order her around before he'd donned his clothing.

But she decided to trust him—not, she was forced to admit, that she had much choice in the matter—and so she turned around. Much to her relief and, if she was to be honest with herself, a fair bit of disappointment, he was quite decently dressed, save for a smattering of damp spots where the water from his skin had seeped through the fabric of his clothing.

"Why didn't you just let me run home?" she asked.

"I wanted you here," he said simply.

"But why?" she persisted.

He shrugged. "I don't know. Punishment, perhaps, for spying on me."

"I wasn't—" Sophie's denial was automatic, but she cut herself off halfway through, because of course she'd been spying on him.

"Smart girl," he murmured.

She scowled at him. She would have liked to have said

something utterly droll and witty, but she had a feeling that anything emerging from her mouth just then would have been quite the opposite, so she held her tongue. Better to be a silent fool than a talkative one.

"It's very bad form to spy on one's host," he said, planting his hands on his hips and somehow managing to look both authoritative and relaxed at the same time.

"It was an accident," she grumbled.

"Oh, I believe you there," he said. "But even if you didn't intend to spy on me, the fact remains that when the opportunity arose, you took it."

"Do you blame me?"

He grinned. "Not at all. I would have done precisely the same thing."

Her mouth fell open.

"Oh, don't pretend to be offended," he said.

"I'm not pretending."

He leaned a bit closer. "To tell the truth, I'm quite flattered."

"It was academic curiosity," she ground out. "I assure you."

His smile grew sly. "So you're telling me that you would have spied upon any naked man you'd come across?"

"Of course not!"

"As I said," he drawled, leaning back against a tree, "I'm flattered."

"Well, now that we have that settled," Sophie said with a sniff, "I'm going back to Your Cottage."

She made it only two steps before his hand shot out and grabbed a small measure of the fabric of her dress. "I don't think so," he said.

Sophie turned back around with a weary sigh. "You have already embarrassed me beyond repair. What more could you possibly wish to do to me?"

Slowly, he reeled her in. "That's a very interesting question," he murmured.

Sophie tried to plant her heels into the ground, but she was no match for the inexorable tug of his hand. She stumbled slightly, then found herself mere inches away from him. The air suddenly felt hot, very hot, and Sophie had the bizarre sense that she no longer quite knew how to work her hands and feet. Her skin tingled, her heart raced, and the bloody man was just staring at her, not moving a muscle, not pulling her the final few inches against him.

Just staring at her.

"Benedict?" she whispered, forgetting that she still called him Mr. Bridgerton.

He smiled. It was a small, knowing sort of smile, one that sent chills right down her spine to another area altogether. "I like when you say my name," he said.

"I didn't mean to," she admitted.

He touched a finger to her lips. "Shhh," he admonished. "Don't tell me that. Don't you know that's not what a man wishes to hear?"

"I don't have much experience with men," she said.

"Now that's what a man wishes to hear."

"Really?" she asked dubiously. She knew men wanted innocence in their wives, but Benedict wasn't about to marry a girl like her.

He touched her cheek with one fingertip. "It's what I want to hear from *you*."

A soft rush of air crossed Sophie's lips as she gasped. He was going to kiss her.

He was going to kiss her. It was the most wonderful and awful thing that could possibly happen.

But oh, how she wanted this.

She knew she was going to regret this tomorrow. She let out a smothered, choking sort of laugh. Who was she kidding? She'd regret it in ten minutes. But she had spent the last two years remembering what it felt like to be in his arms, and she wasn't sure she'd make it through the rest of her days without at least one more memory to keep her going.

His finger floated across her cheek to her temple, and then from there traced her eyebrow, ruffling the soft hairs as it moved to the bridge of her nose. "So pretty," he said softly, "like a storybook fairy. Sometimes I think you couldn't possibly be real."

Her only reply was a quickening of breath.

"I think I'm going to kiss you," he whispered.

"You think?"

"I think I *have* to kiss you," he said, looking as if he couldn't quite believe his own words. "It's rather like breathing. One doesn't have much choice in the matter."

Benedict's kiss was achingly tender. His lips brushed across hers in a feather-light caress, back and forth with just the barest hint of friction. It was utterly breathtaking, but there was something more, something that made her dizzy and weak. Sophie clutched at his shoulders, wondering why she felt so off-balance and strange, and then it suddenly came to her—

It was just like before.

The way his lips brushed hers so soft and sweet, the way he began with gentle titillation, rather than forcing entry—it was just what he'd done at the masquerade. After two years of dreams, Sophie was finally reliving the single most exquisite moment of her life.

"You're crying," Benedict said, touching her cheek.

Sophie blinked, then reached up to wipe away the tears she hadn't even known were falling.

"Do you want me to stop?" he whispered.

She shook her head. No, she didn't want him to stop. She wanted him to kiss her just as he had at the masquerade, the gentle caress giving way to a more passionate joining. And then she wanted him to kiss her some more, because this time the clock wasn't going to strike midnight, and she wouldn't have to flee.

And she wanted him to know that she was the woman from the masquerade. And she desperately prayed that he would never recognize her. And she was just so bloody confused, and . . .

And he kissed her.

Really kissed her, with fierce lips and probing tongue, and all the passion and desire a woman could ever want. He made her feel beautiful, precious, priceless. He treated her like a woman, not some serving wench, and until that very moment, she hadn't realized just how much she missed being treated like a person. Gentry and aristocrats didn't see their servants, they tried not to hear them, and when they were forced to converse, they kept it as short and perfunctory as possible.

But when Benedict kissed her, she felt real.

And when he kissed her, he did so with his entire body. His lips, which had begun the intimacy with such gentle reverence, were now fierce and demanding on hers. His hands, so large and strong they seemed to cover half her back, held her to him with a strength that left her breathless. And his body—dear God, it ought to be illegal the way it was pressed against hers, the heat of it seeping through her clothing, searing her very soul.

He made her shiver. He made her melt.

He made her want to give herself to him, something she'd sworn she would never do outside the sacrament of marriage.

"Oh, Sophie," he murmured, his voice husky against her lips. "I've never felt—"

Sophie stiffened, because she was fairly certain he'd intended to say he'd never felt that way before, and she had no idea how she felt about that. On the one hand, it was thrilling to be the one woman who could bring him to his knees, make him dizzy with desire and need.

On the other hand, he'd kissed her before. Hadn't he felt the same exquisite torture then, too?

Dear God, was she jealous of herself?

He pulled back a half inch. "What's wrong?"

She gave her head a little shake. "Nothing."

Benedict touched his fingers to the tip of her chin and tilted her face up. "Don't lie to me, Sophie. What's wrong?"

"I'm—I'm only nervous," she stammered. "That's all."

His eyes narrowed with concerned suspicion. "Are you certain?"

"Absolutely certain." She tugged herself from his grasp and took a few steps away from him, her arms hugging over her chest. "I don't do this sort of thing, you know."

Benedict watched her walk away, studying the bleak line of her back. "I know," he said softly. "You're not the sort of girl who would."

She gave a little laugh at that, and even though he could not see her face, he could well imagine its expression. "How do you know that?" she asked.

"It's obvious in everything you do."

She didn't turn around. She didn't say anything.

And then, before he had any idea what he was saying, the most bizarre question tumbled from his mouth. "Who are you, Sophie?" he asked. "Who are you, really?"

She still didn't turn around, and when she spoke, her voice was barely above a whisper. "What do you mean?"

"Something isn't quite right about you," he said. "You speak too well to be a maid."

Her hand was nervously fidgeting with the folds of her skirt as she said, "Is it a crime to wish to speak well? One can't get very far in this country with a lowborn accent."

"One could make the argument," he said with deliberate softness, "that you haven't gotten very far."

Her arms straightened into sticks. Straight rigid sticks with little tight fists at the end. And then, while he waited for her to say something, she started walking away.

"Wait!" he called out, and he caught up with her in under three strides, grabbing hold of her wrist. He tugged at her until she was forced to turn around. "Don't go," he said.

"It is not my habit to remain in the company of people who insult me."

Benedict nearly flinched, and he knew he would be forever haunted by the stricken look in her eyes. "I wasn't insulting you," he said, "and you know it. I was speaking the truth. You're not meant to be a housemaid, Sophie. It's clear to me, and it ought to be clear to you."

She laughed—a hard, brittle sound he'd never thought to hear from her. "And what do you suggest I do, Mr. Bridgerton?" she asked. "Find work as a governess?"

Benedict thought that was a fine idea, and he started to tell her so, but she interrupted him, saying, "And who do you think will hire me?"

"Well . . ."

"No one," she snapped. "No one will hire me. I have no references, and I look far too young."

"And pretty," he said grimly. He'd never given much thought to the hiring of governesses, but he knew that the duty usually fell to the mother of the house. And common sense told him that no mother wanted to bring such a pretty young thing into her household. Just look what Sophie had had to endure at the hands of Phillip Cavender.

"You could be a lady's maid," he suggested. "At least then you wouldn't be cleaning chamber pots."

"You'd be surprised," she muttered.

"A companion to an elderly lady?"

She sighed. It was a sad, weary sound, and it nearly broke his heart. "You're very kind to try to help me," she said, "but I have already explored all of those avenues. Besides, I am not your responsibility."

"You could be."

She looked at him in surprise.

In that moment, Benedict knew that he had to have her. There was a connection between them, a strange, inexplicable bond that he'd felt only one other time in his life, with the mystery lady from the masquerade. And while she was gone, vanished into thin air, Sophie was very real. He was tired of mirages. He wanted someone he could see, someone he could touch.

And she needed him. She might not realize it yet, but she needed him. Benedict took her hand and tugged, catching her off-balance and wrapping her to him when she fell against his body.

"Mr. Bridgerton!" she yelped.

"Benedict," he corrected, his lips at her ear.

"Let me—"

"Say my name," he persisted. He could be very stubborn when it suited his interests, and he wasn't going to let her go until he heard his name cross her lips.

And maybe not even then.

"Benedict," she finally relented. "I—"

"Hush." He silenced her with his mouth, nibbling at the corner of her lips. When she went soft and compliant in his arms, he drew back, just far enough so that he could focus on her eyes. They looked impossibly green in the late-afternoon light, deep enough to drown in.

"I want you to come back to London with me," he whispered, the words tumbling forth before he had a chance to consider them. "Come back and live with me."

She looked at him in surprise.

"Be mine," he said, his voice thick and urgent. "Be mine right now. Be mine forever. I'll give you anything you want. All I want in return is you."

Chapter 12

Speculation continues to abound concerning the disappearance of Benedict Bridgerton. According to Eloise Bridgerton, who as his sister ought to know, he was due back in town several days ago.

But as Eloise must be the first to admit, a man of Mr. Bridgerton's age and stature need hardly report his whereabouts to his younger sister.

LADY WHISTLEDOWN'S SOCIETY PAPERS, 9 MAY 1817

"You want me to be your mistress," she said flatly.

He gave her a confused look, although she couldn't be sure whether that was because her statement was so obvious or because he objected to her choice of words. "I want you to be with me," he persisted.

The moment was so staggeringly painful and yet she found herself almost smiling. "How is that different from being your mistress?"

"Sophie—"

"How is it different?" she repeated, her voice growing strident.

"I don't know, Sophie." He sounded impatient. "Does it matter?"

"It does to me."

"Fine," he said in a short voice. "Fine. Be my mistress, and have *this*."

Sophie had just enough time to gasp before his lips descended on hers with a ferocity that turned her knees to water. It was like no kiss they'd ever shared, harsh with need, and laced with an odd, strange anger.

His mouth devoured hers in a primitive dance of passion. His hands seemed to be everywhere, on her breasts, around her waist, even under her skirt. He touched and squeezed, caressed and stroked.

And all the while, he had her pressed up so tightly against him she was certain she'd melt into his skin.

"I want you," he said roughly, his lips finding the hollow at the base of her throat. "I want you right now. I want you here."

"Benedict—"

"I want you in my bed," he growled. "I want you tomorrow. And I want you the next day."

She was wicked, and she was weak, and she gave in to the moment, arching her neck to allow him greater access. His lips felt so good against her skin, sending shivers and tingles to the very center of her being. He made her long for him, long for all the things she couldn't have, and curse the things she could.

And then somehow she was on the ground, and he was there with her, half-on and half-off of her body. He seemed so large, so powerful, and in that moment, so perfectly *hers*. A very small part of Sophie's mind was still functioning, and she knew that she had to say no, had to put a stop to the madness, but God help her, she couldn't. Not yet.

She'd spent so long dreaming about him, trying desperately to remember the scent of his skin, the sound of his voice. There had been many nights when the fantasy of him had been all that had kept her company.

She had been living on dreams, and she wasn't a woman

for whom many had come true. She didn't want to lose this one just yet.

"Benedict," she murmured, touching the crisp silkiness of his hair and pretending—pretending that he hadn't just asked her to be his mistress, that she was someone else—anyone else.

Anyone but the bastard daughter of a dead earl, with no means of support besides waiting on others.

Her murmurings seemed to embolden him, and his hand, which had been tickling her knee for so long, started to inch upward, squeezing the soft skin of her thigh. Years of hard work had made her lean, not fashionably curvy, but he didn't seem to mind. In fact, she could feel his heart begin to beat even more rapidly, hear his breath coming in hoarser gasps.

"Sophie, Sophie, Sophie," he groaned, his lips moving frantically along her face until they found her mouth again. "I need you." He pressed his hips hotly against hers. "Do you feel how I need you?"

"I need you, too," she whispered. And she did. There was a fire burning within her that had been simmering quietly for years. The sight of him had ignited it anew, and his touch was like kerosene, sending her into a conflagration.

His fingers wrestled with the large, poorly made buttons on back of her dress. "I'm going to burn this," he grunted, his other hand relentlessly stroking the tender skin at the back of her knee. "I'll dress you in silks, in satins." He moved to her ear, nipping at her lobe, then licking the tender skin where her ear met her cheek. "I'll dress you in nothing at all."

Sophie stiffened in his arms. He'd managed to say the one thing that could remind her why she was here, why he was kissing her. It wasn't love, or any of those tender emotions she'd dreamed about, but lust. And he wanted to make her a kept woman.

Just as her mother had been.

Oh, God, it was so tempting. So impossibly tempting. He was offering her a life of ease and luxury, a life with *him*.

At the price of her soul.

No, that wasn't entirely true, or entirely a problem. She might be able to live as a man's mistress. The benefits—and how could she consider life with Benedict anything but a benefit—might outweigh the drawbacks. But while she might be willing to make such decisions with her own life and reputation, she would not do so for a child. And how could there not be a child? All mistresses eventually had children.

With a tortured cry, she gave him a shove and wrenched herself away, rolling to the side until she found herself on her hands and knees, stopping to catch her breath before hauling herself to her feet.

"I can't do this, Benedict," she said, barely able to look at him.

"I don't see why not," he muttered.

"I can't be your mistress."

He rose to his feet. "And why is that?"

Something about him pricked at her. Maybe it was the arrogance of his tone, maybe it was the insolence in his posture. "Because I don't want to," she snapped.

His eyes narrowed, not with suspicion, but with anger. "You wanted to just a few seconds ago."

"You're not being fair," she said in a low voice. "I wasn't thinking."

His chin jutted out belligerently. "You're not supposed to be thinking. That's the point of it."

She blushed as she redid her buttons. He'd done a very good job of making her not think. She'd almost thrown away a lifetime of vows and morals, all at one wicked kiss. "Well, I won't be your mistress," she said again. Maybe if she said it enough, she'd feel more confident that he wouldn't be able to break down her defenses.

"And what are you going to do instead?" he hissed. "Work as a housemaid?"

"If I have to."

"You'd rather wait on people—polish their silver, scrub out their damned chamber pots—than come and live with me."

She said only one word, but it was low and true. "Yes."

His eyes flashed furiously. "I don't believe you. No one would make that choice."

"I did."

"You're a fool."

She said nothing.

"Do you understand what you're giving up?" he persisted, his arm waving wildly as he spoke. She'd hurt him, she realized. She'd hurt him and insulted his pride, and he was lashing out like a wounded bear.

Sophie nodded, even though he wasn't looking at her face.

"I could give you whatever you wanted," he bit off. "Clothes, jewels—Hell, forget about the clothes and jewels, I could give you a bloody roof over your head, which is more than you have now."

"That is true," she said quietly.

He leaned forward, his eyes burning hot into hers. "I could give you everything."

Somehow she managed to stand up straight, and somehow she managed not to cry. And somehow she even managed to keep her voice even as she said, "If you think that's everything, then you probably wouldn't understand why I must refuse."

She took a step back, intending to head to His Cottage and pack her meager bag, but he obviously wasn't through with her yet, because he stopped her with a strident, "Where are you going?"

"Back to the cottage," she said. "To pack my bag."

"And where do you think you're going to go with that bag?"

Her mouth fell open. Surely he didn't expect her to *stay*.

"Do you have a job?" he demanded. "A place to go?"

"No," she replied, "but—"

He planted his hands on his hips and glared at her. "And you think I'm going to just let you leave here, with no money or prospects?"

Sophie was so surprised she started to blink uncontrollably. "W-well," she stammered, "I didn't think—"

"No, you *didn't* think," he snapped.

She just stared at him, eyes wide and lips parted, unable to believe what she was hearing.

"You bloody fool," he swore. "Do you have any idea how dangerous it is in the world for a woman alone?"

"Er, yes," she managed. "Actually, I do."

If he heard her, he gave no indication, just went on about "men who take advantage" and "helpless women" and "fates worse than death." Sophie wasn't positive, but she thought she even heard the phrase, "roast beef and pudding." About halfway through his tirade, she lost all ability to focus on his words. She just kept watching his mouth and hearing the tone of his voice, all the while trying to comprehend the fact that he seemed remarkably concerned for her welfare, considering that she'd just summarily rejected him.

"Are you even listening to a word I'm saying?" Benedict demanded.

Sophie didn't nod or shake her head, instead doing an odd combination of both.

Benedict swore under his breath. "That's it," he announced. "You're coming back to London with me."

That seemed to wake her up. "I just said I'm not!"

"You don't have to be my damned mistress," he bit off. "But I'm not leaving you to fend for yourself."

"I was fending for myself quite adequately before I met you."

"Adequately?" he sputtered. "At the Cavenders'? You call that adequate?"

"You're not being fair!"

"And you're not being intelligent."

Benedict thought that his argument was most reasonable, if a little overbearing, but Sophie obviously did not agree, because, much to his surprise, he found himself lying faceup on the ground, having been felled by a remarkably quick right hook.

"Don't you ever call me stupid," she hissed.

Benedict blinked, trying to get his eyesight back to the point where he only saw one of her. "I wasn't—"

"Yes, you were," she replied in a low, angry voice. Then she turned on her heel, and in the split second before she stalked away, he realized he had only one way to stop her. He certainly wasn't going to make it to his feet with anything resembling speed in his current befuddled state, so he reached out and grabbed one of her ankles with both of his hands, sending her sprawling onto the ground right next to him.

It wasn't a particularly gentlemanly maneuver, but beggars really couldn't be choosers, and besides, she had thrown the first punch.

"You're not going anywhere," he growled.

Sophie slowly lifted her head, spitting out dirt as she glared at him. "I cannot believe," she said scathingly, "that you just did that."

Benedict let go of her foot and hauled himself to a crouching position. "Believe it."

"You—"

He held up a hand. "Don't say anything now. I beg you."

Her eyes bugged out. "You're begging me?"

"I hear your voice," he informed her, "therefore you must be speaking."

"But—"

"And as for begging you," he said, effectively cutting her off again, "I assure you it was merely a figure of speech."

She opened her mouth to say something, then obviously thought the better of it, clamping her lips shut with the petulant look of a three-year-old. Benedict let out a short breath, then offered her his hand. She was, after all, still sitting in the dirt and not looking especially happy about it.

She stared at his hand with remarkable revulsion, then moved her gaze to his face and glared at him with such ferocity that Benedict wondered if he had recently sprouted horns. Still not saying a word, she ignored his offer of help and hefted herself to her feet.

"As you like," he murmured.

"A poor choice of words," she snapped, then started marching away.

As Benedict was on his feet this time, he felt no need to incapacitate her. Instead, he dogged her every step, remaining a mere (and annoying, he was sure) two paces behind her. Finally, after about a minute, she turned around and said, "Please leave me alone."

"I'm afraid I can't," he said.

"Can't or won't?"

He thought about that for a moment. "Can't."

She scowled at him and kept walking.

"I find it as difficult to believe as you do," Benedict called out, keeping pace with her.

She stopped and turned around. "That is impossible."

"I can't help it," he said with a shrug. "I find myself completely unwilling to let you go."

" 'Unwilling' is a far cry from 'can't.' "

"I didn't save you from Cavender just to let you squander your life away."

"That isn't your choice to make."

She had a point there, but he wasn't inclined to give it to her. "Perhaps," he allowed, "but I'm going to make it, anyway. You're coming with me to London. We will discuss it no further."

"You're trying to punish me," she said, "because I refused you."

"No," he said slowly, considering her words even as he answered. "No, I'm not. I'd like to punish you, and in my current state of mind I'd even go so far as to say you deserve to be punished, but that's not why I'm doing it."

"Then why are you?"

"It's for your own good."

"That's the most condescending, patronizing—"

"I'm sure you're right," he allowed, "but nonetheless, in this particular case, at this particular moment, I know what's best for you, and you clearly don't, so—*don't* hit me again," he warned.

Sophie looked down at her fist, which she hadn't even realized was pulled back and ready to fly. He was turning her into a monster. There was no other explanation. She didn't think she'd ever hit anyone in her life, and here she was ready to do it for the second time that day.

Eyes never leaving her hand, she slowly unclenched her fist, stretching her fingers out like a starfish and holding them there for the count of three. "How," she said in a very low voice, "do you intend to stop me from going my way?"

"Does it really matter?" he asked, shrugging nonchalantly. "I'm sure I'll think of something."

Her mouth fell open. "Are you saying you'd tie me up and—"

"*I* didn't say anything of the sort," he cut in with a wicked grin. "But the idea certainly has its charms."

"You are despicable," she spat.

"And you sound like the heroine of a very poorly written novel," he replied. "What did you say you were reading this morning?"

Sophie felt the muscles working frenetically in her cheek, felt her jaw clenching to the point where she was certain her teeth would shatter. How Benedict managed to be the most wonderful and the most awful man in the world at the very same time, she would never understand. Right now, though, the awful side seemed to be winning, and she was quite certain—logic aside—that if she remained in his company one more second, her head would explode.

"I'm leaving!" she said, with, in her opinion, great drama and resolve.

But he just answered her with a sly half smile, and said, "I'm following."

And the bloody man remained two strides behind her the entire way home.

Benedict didn't often go out of his way to annoy people (with the notable exception of his siblings), but Sophie Beckett clearly brought out the devil in him. He stood in the doorway to her room as she packed, casually lounging against the doorframe. His arms were crossed in a manner that he somehow knew would vex her, and his right leg was slightly bent, the toe of his boot stubbed up against the floor.

"Don't forget your dress," he said helpfully.

She glared at him.

"The ugly one," he added, as if clarification were necessary.

"They're both ugly," she spat out.

Ah, a reaction. "I know."

She went back to shoving her belongings into her satchel.

He waved an arm expansively. "Feel free to take a souvenir."

She straightened, her hands planted angrily on her hips. "Does that include the silver tea service? Because I could live for several years on what that would fetch."

"You may certainly take the tea service," he replied genially, "as you will not be out of my company."

"I will not be your mistress," she hissed. "I told you, I won't do it. I *can't* do it."

Something about her use of the word "can't" struck him

as significant. He mulled that over for a few moments while she gathered up the last of her belongings and cinched shut the drawstring to her satchel.

"That's it," he murmured.

She ignored him, instead marching toward the door and giving him a pointed look.

He knew she wanted him to get out of the way so she could depart. He didn't move a muscle, save for one finger that thoughtfully stroked the side of his jaw. "You're illegitimate," he said.

The blood drained from her face.

"You are," he said, more to himself than to her. Strangely, he felt rather relieved by the revelation. It explained her rejection of him, made it into something that had nothing to do with him and everything to do with her.

It took the sting out.

"I don't care if you're illegitimate," he said, trying not to smile. It was a serious moment, but by God, he wanted to break out in a grin because now she'd come to London with him and be his mistress. There were no more obstacles, and—

"You don't understand anything," she said, shaking her head. "It's not about whether I'm good enough to be your mistress."

"I would care for any children we might have," he said solemnly, pushing himself away from the doorframe.

Her stance grew even more rigid, if that were possible. "And what about your wife?"

"I don't have a wife."

"Ever?"

He froze. A vision of the masquerade lady danced through his mind. He'd pictured her many ways. Sometimes she wore her silver ballgown, sometimes nothing at all.

Sometimes she wore a wedding dress.

Sophie's eyes narrowed as she watched his face, then she snorted derisively as she stalked past him.

He followed. "That's not a fair question, Sophie," he said, dogging her heels.

She moved down the hall, not even pausing when she reached the stairs. "I think it's more than fair."

He raced down the stairs until he was below her, halting her progress. "I have to marry someday."

Sophie stopped. She had to; he was blocking her path. "Yes, you do," she said. "But I don't have to be anyone's mistress."

"Who was your father, Sophie?"

"I don't know," she lied.

"Who was your mother?"

"She died at my birth."

"I thought you said she was a housekeeper."

"Clearly I misrepresented the truth," she said, past the point of caring that she'd been caught in a lie.

"Where did you grow up?"

"It's of no interest," she said, trying to squirm her way past him.

One of his hands wrapped itself around her upper arm, holding her firmly in place. "I find it very interesting."

"Let me go!"

Her cry pierced the silence of the hall, loud enough so that the Crabtrees would certainly come running to save her. Except that Mrs. Crabtree had gone to the village, and Mr. Crabtree was outside, out of earshot. There was no one to help her, and she was at his mercy.

"I can't let you go," he whispered. "You're not cut out for a life of servitude. It will kill you."

"If it were going to kill me," she returned, "it would have done so years ago."

"But you don't have to do this any longer," he persisted.

"Don't you dare try to make this about me," she said, nearly shaking with emotion. "You're not doing this out of concern for my welfare. You just don't like being thwarted."

"That is true," he admitted, "but I also won't see you cast adrift."

"I have been adrift all my life," she whispered, and she felt the traitorous sting of tears prick her eyes. God above, she didn't want to cry in front of this man. Not now, not when she felt so off-balance and weak.

He touched her chin. "Let me be your anchor."

Sophie closed her eyes. His touch was painfully sweet, and a not very small part of her was aching to accept his offer, to leave the life she'd been forced to live and cast her lot with him, this marvelous, wonderful, infuriating man who had haunted her dreams for years.

But the pain of her childhood was still too fresh. And the stigma of her illegitimacy felt like a brand on her soul.

She would not do this to another child.

"I can't," she whispered. "I wish—"

"What do you wish?" he asked urgently.

She shook her head. She'd been about to tell him that she wished that she could, but she knew that such words would be unwise. He would only latch on to them, and press his cause anew.

And that would make it all the harder to say no.

"You leave me no choice, then," he stated grimly.

Her eyes met his.

"Either you come with me to London, and—" He held up a silencing hand when she tried to protest. "And I will find you a position in my mother's household," he added pointedly.

"Or?" she asked, her voice sullen.

"Or I will have to inform the magistrate that you have stolen from me."

Her mouth abruptly tasted like acid. "You wouldn't," she whispered.

"I certainly don't want to."

"But you would."

He nodded. "I would."

"They'd hang me," she said. "Or send me to Australia."

"Not if I requested otherwise."

"And what would you request?"

His brown eyes looked strangely flat, and she suddenly realized that he wasn't enjoying the conversation any more than she was.

"I would request," he said, "that you be released into my custody."

"That would be very convenient for you."

His fingers, which had been touching her chin all the while, slid down to her shoulder. "I'm only trying to save you from yourself."

Sophie walked to a nearby window and looked out, surprised that he hadn't tried to stop her. "You're making me hate you, you know," she said.

"I can live with that."

She gave him a curt nod. "I will wait for you in the library, then. I would like to leave today."

Benedict watched her walk away, stood utterly still as the door to the library closed behind her. He knew she would not flee. She was not the sort to go back on her word.

He couldn't let this one go. *She* had left—the great and mysterious "she," he thought with a bitter smile—the one woman who had touched his heart.

The same woman who had not even given him her name.

But now there was Sophie, and she *did* things to him. Things he hadn't felt since *her*. He was sick of pining for a woman who practically didn't exist. Sophie was here, and Sophie would be his.

And, he thought with grim determination, Sophie was *not* going to leave him.

"I can live with you hating me," he said to the closed door. "I just can't live without *you*."

Chapter 13

It was previously reported in this column that This Author predicted a possible match between Miss Rosamund Reiling and Mr. Phillip Cavender. This Author can now say that this is not likely to occur. Lady Penwood (Miss Reiling's mother) has been heard to say that she will not settle for a mere mister, even though Miss Reiling's father, while certainly wellborn, was not a member of the aristocracy.

Not to mention, of course, that Mr. Cavender has begun to show a decided interest in Miss Cressida Cowper.

LADY WHISTLEDOWN'S SOCIETY PAPERS, 9 MAY 1817

Sophie started feeling ill the minute the carriage departed My Cottage. By the time they stopped for the night at an inn in Oxfordshire, she was downright queasy. And when they reached the outskirts of London . . . Well, she was quite convinced she would throw up.

Somehow she managed to keep the contents of her stomach where they belonged, but as their carriage wended farther into the tangled streets of London, she was filled with an intense sense of apprehension.

No, not apprehension. Doom.

It was May, which meant that the season was in full

swing. Which meant that Araminta was in residence.

Which meant that Sophie's arrival was a bad, bad idea.

"Very bad," she muttered.

Benedict looked up. "Did you say something?"

She crossed her arms mutinously. "Just that you're a very bad man."

He chuckled. She'd known he would chuckle, and it still irritated her.

He pulled the curtain away from the window and looked out. "We're nearly there," he said.

He'd said that he was taking her directly to his mother's residence. Sophie remembered the grand house in Grosvenor Square as if she'd been there the night before. The ballroom was huge, with hundreds of sconces on the walls, each adorned by a perfect beeswax candle. The smaller rooms had been decorated in the Adam style, with exquisitely scalloped ceilings and pale, pastel walls.

It had been Sophie's dream house, quite literally. In all her dreams of Benedict and their fictional future together, she'd always seen herself in that house. It was silly, she knew, since he was a second son and thus not in line to inherit the property, but still, it was the most beautiful home she'd ever beheld, and dreams weren't meant to be about reality, anyway. If Sophie had wanted to dream her way right into Kensington Palace, that was her prerogative.

Of course, she thought with a wry smile, she wasn't likely ever to see the interior of Kensington Palace.

"What are you smiling about?" Benedict demanded.

She didn't bother to glance up as she replied, "I'm plotting your demise."

He grinned—not that she was looking at him, but it was one of those smiles she could hear in the way he breathed.

She hated that she was that sensitive to his every nuance. Especially since she had a sneaking suspicion that he was the same way about her.

"At least it sounds entertaining," he said.

"What does?" she asked, finally moving her eyes from the lower hem of the curtain, which she'd been staring at for what seemed like hours.

"My demise," he said, his smile crooked and amused. "If you're going to kill me, you might as well enjoy yourself while you're at it, because Lord knows, I won't."

Her jaw dropped a good inch. "You're mad," she said.

"Probably." He shrugged rather casually before settling back in his seat and propping his feet up on the bench across from him. "I've all but kidnapped you, after all. I should think that would qualify as the maddest thing I've ever done."

"You could let me go now," she said, even though she knew he never would.

"Here in London? Where you could be attacked by footpads at any moment? That would be most irresponsible of me, don't you think?"

"It hardly compares to abducting me against my will!"

"I didn't abduct you," he said, idly examining his fingernails. "I blackmailed you. There's a world of difference."

Sophie was saved from having to reply by the jolt of the carriage as it ground to a halt.

Benedict flipped back the curtains one last time, then let them fall into place. "Ah. Here we are."

Sophie waited while he disembarked, then moved to the doorway. She briefly considered ignoring his outstretched hand and jumping down herself, but the carriage was quite high off the ground, and she really didn't wish to make a fool of herself by tripping and landing in the gutter.

It would be nice to insult him, but not at the cost of a sprained ankle.

With a sigh, she took his hand.

"Very smart of you," Benedict murmured.

Sophie looked at him sharply. How did he know what she'd been thinking?

"I almost always know what you're thinking," he said.

She tripped.

"Whoa!" he called out, catching her expertly before she landed in the gutter.

He held her just a moment longer than was necessary before depositing her on the pavement. Sophie would have said something, except that her teeth were ground together far too tightly for words.

"Doesn't the irony just kill you?" Benedict asked, smiling wickedly.

She pried open her jaw. "No, but it may very well kill *you*."

He laughed, the blasted man. "Come along," he said. "I'll introduce you to my mother. I'm sure she'll find some position or another for you."

"She may not have any openings," Sophie pointed out.

He shrugged. "She loves me. She'll make an opening."

Sophie held her ground, refusing to take a single step alongside him until she'd made her point. "I'm not going to be your mistress."

His expression was remarkably bland as he murmured, "Yes, you've said as much."

"No, I mean, your plan isn't going to work."

He was all innocence. "I have a plan?"

"Oh, please," she scoffed. "You're going to try to wear me down in hopes that eventually I'll give in."

"I would never dream of it."

"I'm sure you dream of quite a bit more," she muttered.

He must have heard her, because he chuckled. Sophie crossed her arms mutinously, not caring that she looked most undignified in such a position, standing right there on the pavement in full view of the world. No one would pay her half a mind, anyway, dressed as she was in the coarse woolens of a servant. She supposed she ought to adopt a brighter outlook and approach her new position with a more optimistic attitude, but drat it all, she *wanted* to be sullen just then.

Frankly, she thought she'd earned it. If anyone had a right to be sullen and disgruntled, it was she.

"We *could* stand here on the pavement all day," Benedict said, his voice lightly laced with sarcasm.

She started to shoot him an angry glare, but that was when she noticed where they were standing. They weren't in Grosvenor Square. Sophie wasn't even certain where they were. Mayfair, to be sure, but the house before them definitely wasn't the house at which she'd attended the masquerade.

"Er, is this Bridgerton House?" she asked.

He quirked a brow. "How did you know my home is called Bridgerton House?"

"You've mentioned it." Which was, thankfully, true. He'd talked about both Bridgerton House, and the Bridgertons' country residence, Aubrey Hall, several times during their conversations.

"Oh." He seemed to accept that. "Well, no, actually, it's not. My mother moved out of Bridgerton House nearly two years ago. She hosted one last ball—it was a masquerade, actually—and then turned the residence over to my brother and his wife. She'd always said she would leave just as soon as he married and started a family of his own. I believe his first child was born a mere month after she left."

"Was it a boy or a girl?" she asked, even though she knew the answer. Lady Whistledown always reported such things.

"A boy. Edmund. They had another son, Miles, earlier this year."

"How nice for them," Sophie murmured, even though it felt like her heart were strangling. She wasn't likely to have children of her own, and that was one of the saddest realizations she'd ever reached. Children required a husband, and marriage seemed a pipe dream. She hadn't been raised to be a servant, and thus she had very little in common with most of the men she met in her daily life. Not that the other servants weren't good and honorable people, but it was difficult to imagine sharing her life with someone who, for example, couldn't read.

Sophie didn't need to marry someone of particularly high birth, but even the middle class was out of her reach. No self-respecting man in trade would marry a housemaid.

Benedict motioned for her to follow him, and she did, until they reached the front steps.

Sophie shook her head. "I'll use the side entrance."

His lips thinned. "You'll use the front entrance."

"I'll use the side entrance," she said firmly. "No woman of breeding will hire a maid who enters through the front."

"You're with me," he ground out. "You'll use the front entrance."

A bubble of mirth escaped her lips. "Benedict, just yesterday you wanted me to become your mistress. Would you dare bring your mistress to meet your mother through the front door?"

She'd confounded him with that. Sophie grinned as she watched his face twist with frustration.

She felt better than she had in days.

"Would you," she continued, mostly just to torture him further, "bring your mistress to meet her at all?"

"You're not my mistress," he bit off.

"Indeed."

His chin jutted out, and his eyes bored into hers with barely leashed fury. "You're a bloody little housemaid," he said, his voice low, "because you've insisted upon being a housemaid. And as a housemaid, you are, if somewhat low on the social scale, still utterly respectable. Certainly respectable enough for my mother."

Sophie's smile faltered. She might have pushed him too far.

"Good," Benedict grunted, once it was clear that she was not going to argue the point any further. "Come with me."

Sophie followed him up the steps. This might actually

work to her advantage. Benedict's mother surely would not hire a maid who had the effrontery to use the front door. And since she had steadfastly refused to be Benedict's mistress, he would have to accept defeat and allow her to return to the country.

Benedict pushed open the front door, holding it until Sophie entered before him. The butler arrived within seconds.

"Wickham," Benedict said, "kindly inform my mother that I am here."

"I will indeed, Mr. Bridgerton," Wickham replied. "And might I take the liberty of informing you that she has been rather curious as to your whereabouts this past week?"

"I would be shocked if she hadn't been," Benedict replied.

Wickham nodded toward Sophie with an expression that hovered somewhere between curiosity and disdain. "Might I inform her of your guest's arrival?"

"Please do."

"Might I inform her of your guest's identity?"

Sophie looked over at Benedict with great interest, wondering what he'd say.

"Her name is Miss Beckett," Benedict replied. "She is here to seek employment."

One of Wickham's brows rose. Sophie was surprised. She didn't think that butlers were supposed to show any expression whatsoever.

"As a maid?" Wickham inquired.

"As whatever," Benedict said, his tone beginning to show the first traces of impatience.

"Very good, Mr. Bridgerton," Wickham said, and then he disappeared up the staircase.

"I don't think he thought it was very good at all," Sophie whispered to Benedict, careful to hide her smile.

"Wickham is not in charge here."

Sophie let out a little whatever-you-say sort of sigh. "I imagine Wickham would disagree."

He looked at her with disbelief. "He's the butler."

"And I'm a housemaid. I know all about butlers. More, I daresay, than you do."

His eyes narrowed. "You act less like a housemaid than any woman of my acquaintance."

She shrugged and pretended to inspect a still life painting on the wall. "You bring out the worst in me, Mr. Bridgerton."

"Benedict," he hissed. "You've called me by my given name before. Use it now."

"Your mother is about to descend the stairs," she reminded him, "and you are insisting that she hire me as a housemaid. Do many of your servants call you by your given name?"

He glared at her, and she knew he knew she was right. "You can't have it both ways, Mr. Bridgerton," she said, allowing herself a tiny smile.

"I only wanted it *one* way," he growled.

"Benedict!"

Sophie looked up to see an elegant, petite woman descending the stairs. Her coloring was fairer than Benedict's, but her features marked her clearly as his mother.

"Mother," he said, striding to meet her at the bottom of the stairs. "It is good to see you."

"It would be better to see you," she said pertly, "had I known where you were this past week. The last I'd heard you'd gone off to the Cavender party, and then everyone returned without you."

"I left the party early," he replied, "then went off to My Cottage."

His mother sighed. "I suppose I can't expect you to notify me of your every movement now that you're thirty years of age."

Benedict gave her an indulgent smile.

She turned to Sophie. "This must be your Miss Beckett."

"Indeed," Benedict replied. "She saved my life while I was at My Cottage."

Sophie started. "I didn't—"

"She did," Benedict cut in smoothly. "I took ill from driving in the rain, and she nursed me to health."

"You would have recuperated without me," she insisted.

"But not," Benedict said, directing his words at his mother, "with such speed or in such comfort."

"Weren't the Crabtrees at home?" Violet asked.

"Not when we arrived," Benedict replied.

Violet looked at Sophie with such obvious curiosity that Benedict was finally forced to explain, "Miss Beckett had been employed by the Cavenders, but certain circumstances made it impossible for her to stay."

"I . . . see," Violet said unconvincingly.

"Your son saved me from a most unpleasant fate," Sophie said quietly. "I owe him a great deal of thanks."

Benedict looked to her in surprise. Given the level of her hostility toward him, he hadn't expected her to volunteer complimentary information. But he supposed he should have done; Sophie was highly principled, not the sort to let anger interfere with honesty.

It was one of the things he liked best about her.

"I see," Violet said again, this time with considerably more feeling.

"I was hoping you might find her a position in your household," Benedict said.

"But not if it's too much trouble," Sophie hastened to add.

"No," Violet said slowly, her eyes settling on Sophie's face with a curious expression. "No, it wouldn't be any trouble at all, but . . ."

Both Benedict and Sophie leaned forward, awaiting the rest of the sentence.

"Have we met?" Violet suddenly asked.

"I don't think so," Sophie said, stammering slightly. How

could Lady Bridgerton think she knew her? She was positive their paths had not crossed at the masquerade. "I can't imagine how we could have done."

"I'm certain you're right," Lady Bridgerton said with a wave of her hand. "There is something vaguely familiar about you. But I'm sure it's just that I've met someone with similar features. It happens all the time."

"Especially to me," Benedict said with a crooked smile.

Lady Bridgerton looked to her son with obvious affection. "It's not my fault all my children ended up looking remarkably alike."

"If the blame can't be placed with you," Benedict asked, "then where may we place it?"

"Entirely upon your father," Lady Bridgerton replied jauntily. She turned to Sophie. "They all look just like my late husband."

Sophie knew she should remain silent, but the moment was so lovely and comfortable that she said, "I think your son resembles you."

"Do you think?" Lady Bridgerton asked, clasping her hands together with delight. "How lovely. And here I've always just considered myself a vessel for the Bridgerton family."

"Mother!" Benedict said.

She sighed. "Am I speaking too plainly? I do that more and more in my old age."

"You are hardly elderly, Mother."

She smiled. "Benedict, why don't you go visit with your sisters while I take your Miss Bennett—"

"Beckett," he interrupted.

"Yes, of course, Beckett," she murmured. "I shall take her upstairs and get her settled in."

"You need only take me to the housekeeper," Sophie said. It was most odd for a lady of the house to concern herself with the hiring of a housemaid. Granted, the entire situation was unusual, what with Benedict asking that she be hired on, but it was very strange that Lady Bridgerton would take a personal interest in her.

"Mrs. Watkins is busy, I'm sure," Lady Bridgerton said. "Besides, I believe we have need for another lady's maid upstairs. Have you any experience in that area?"

Sophie nodded.

"Excellent. I thought you might. You speak very well."

"My mother was a housekeeper," Sophie said automatically. "She worked for a very generous family and—" She broke off in horror, belatedly remembering that she'd told Benedict the truth—that her mother had died at her birth. She shot him a nervous look, and he answered it with a vaguely mocking tilt of his chin, silently telling her that he wasn't going to expose her lie.

"The family she worked for was very generous," Sophie continued, a relieved rush of air passing across her lips, "and they allowed me to share many lessons with the daughters of the house."

"I see," Lady Bridgerton said. "That explains a great deal. I find it difficult to believe you've been toiling as a housemaid. You are clearly educated enough to pursue loftier positions."

"She reads quite well," Benedict said.

Sophie looked to him in surprise.

He ignored her, instead saying to his mother, "She read to me a great deal during my recuperation."

"Do you write, as well?" Lady Bridgerton asked.

Sophie nodded. "My penmanship is quite neat."

"Excellent. It is always handy to have an extra pair of hands at my disposal when we are addressing invitations. And we do have a ball coming up later in the summer. I have two girls out this year," she explained to Sophie. "I'm hopeful that one of them will choose a husband before the season is through."

"I don't think Eloise wants to marry," Benedict said.

"Quiet your mouth," Lady Bridgerton said.

"Such a statement is sacrilege around here," Benedict said to Sophie.

"Don't listen to him," Lady Bridgerton said, walking toward the stairs. "Here, come with me, Miss Beckett. What did you say your given name was?"

"Sophia. Sophie."

"Come with me, Sophie. I'll introduce you to the girls. And," she added, her nose crinkling with distaste, "we'll find you something new to wear. I cannot have one of our maids dressed so shabbily. A person would think we didn't pay you a fair wage."

It had never been Sophie's experience that members of the *ton* were concerned about paying their servants fairly, and she was touched by Lady Bridgerton's generosity.

"You," Lady Bridgerton said to Benedict. "Wait for me downstairs. We have much to discuss, you and I."

"I'm quaking in my boots," he deadpanned.

"Between him and his brother, I don't know which one of them will kill me first," Lady Bridgerton muttered.

"Which brother?" Sophie asked.

"Either. Both. All three. Scoundrels, the lot of them."

But they were scoundrels she clearly loved. Sophie could hear it in the way she spoke, see it in her eyes when they lit with joy upon seeing her son.

And it made Sophie lonely and wistful and jealous. How different her life might have been had her mother lived through childbirth. They might have been unrespectable, Mrs. Beckett a mistress and Sophie a bastard, but Sophie liked to think that her mother would have loved her.

Which was more than she received from any other adult, her father included.

"Come along, Sophie," Lady Bridgerton said briskly.

Sophie followed her up the stairs, wondering why, if she

were merely about to begin a new job, she felt as if she were entering a new family.

It felt . . . nice.

And it had been a long, long while since her life had felt nice.

Chapter 14

Rosamund Reiling swears that she saw Benedict Bridgerton back in London. This Author is inclined to believe the veracity of the account; Miss Reiling can spot an unmarried bachelor at fifty paces.

Unfortunately for Miss Reiling, she can't seem to land one.

Lady Whistledown's Society Papers, 12 May 1817

Benedict had barely taken two steps toward the sitting room when his sister Eloise came dashing down the hall. Like all the Bridgertons, she had thick, chestnut hair and a wide smile. Unlike Benedict, however, her eyes were a clear, crisp gray, a shade quite unlike that possessed by any of her brothers and sisters.

The exact shade, it occurred to him, of Sophie's.

"Benedict!" she called out, throwing her arms rather exuberantly around him. "Where have you been? Mother has been grumbling all week, wondering where you'd gone off to."

"Funny, when I spoke to Mother, not two minutes ago, her grumbles were about *you*, wondering when you were finally planning to marry."

Eloise pulled a face. "When I meet someone worth marrying, that's when. I do wish someone new would move to town. I feel as though I meet the same hundred or so people over and over again."

"You *do* meet the same hundred or so people over and over again."

"Exactly my point," she said. "There are no secrets left in London. I already know everything about everyone."

"Really?" Benedict asked, with no small measure of sarcasm.

"Mock me all you want," she said, jabbing her finger toward him in a manner he was *sure* his mother would deem unladylike, "but I am not exaggerating."

"Not even a little bit?" he grinned.

She scowled at him. "Where *were* you this past week?"

He walked into the sitting room and plopped down on a sofa. He probably should have waited for her to sit, but she was just his sister, after all, and he'd never felt the need to stand on ceremony when they were alone. "Went to the Cavender party," he said, propping his feet up on a low table. "It was abominable."

"Mother will kill you if she catches you with your feet up," Eloise said, sitting down in a chair that was kitty-corner to him. "And why was the party so dreadful?"

"The company." He looked at his feet and decided to leave them where they were. "A more boring bunch of lazy louts, I've never met."

"As long as you don't mince words."

Benedict raised a brow at her sarcasm. "You are hereby forbidden from marrying anyone who was in attendance."

"An order I shall probably have no difficulty obeying." She tapped her hands against the arms of her chair. Benedict had to smile; Eloise had always been a bundle of nervous energy.

"But," she said, looking up with narrowed eyes, "that doesn't explain where you were all *week*."

"Has anyone ever told you that you are exceedingly nosy?"

"Oh, all the time. Where were you?"

"And persistent, too."

"It's the only way to be. Where were you?"

"Have I mentioned I'm considering investing in a company that manufactures human-sized muzzles?"

She threw a pillow at him. "Where *were* you?"

"As it happens," he said, gently tossing the pillow back in her direction, "the answer isn't the least bit interesting. I was at My Cottage, recuperating from a nasty cold."

"I thought you'd already recuperated."

He regarded her with an expression that was an unlikely cross between amazement and distaste. "How do you *know* that?"

"I know everything. You should know that by now." She grinned. "Colds can be so nasty. Did you have a setback?"

He nodded. "After driving in the rain."

"Well, that wasn't very smart of you."

"Is there any reason," he asked, glancing about the room as if he were directing his question at someone other than Eloise, "why I am allowing myself to be insulted by my ninnyhammer of a younger sister?"

"Probably because I do it so well." She kicked at his foot, trying to knock it off the table. "Mother will be here at any second, I'm sure."

"No, she won't," he returned. "She's busy."

"Doing what?"

He waved his hand toward the ceiling. "Orienting the new maid."

She sat up straight. "We have a new maid? Nobody told me about it."

"Heavens," he drawled, "something has happened and Eloise doesn't know about it."

She leaned back in her chair, then kicked his foot again. "Housemaid? Lady's maid? Scullery?"

"Why do you care?"

"It's always good to know what's what."

"Lady's maid, I believe."

Eloise took all of one half second to digest that. "And how do you know?"

Benedict figured he might as well tell her the truth. The Lord knew, she'd know the whole story by sundown, even if he didn't. "Because I brought her here."

"The maid?"

"No, Mother. Of course the maid."

"Since when do you trouble yourself with the hiring of servants?"

"Since this particular young lady nearly saved my life by nursing me while I was ill."

Eloise's mouth fell open. "You were *that* ill?"

Might as well let her believe he'd been at death's door. A little pity and concern might work to his advantage next time he needed to wheedle her into something. "I have felt better," he said mildly. "Where are you going?"

She'd already risen to her feet. "To go find Mother and meet the new maid. She's probably going to wait on Francesca and me, now that Marie is gone."

"You lost your maid?"

Eloise scowled. "She left us for that odious Lady Penwood."

Benedict had to grin at her description. He remembered his one meeting with Lady Penwood quite well; he, too, had found her odious.

"Lady Penwood is notorious for mistreating her servants. She's gone through three lady's maids this year. Stole Mrs. Featherington's right out from under her nose, but the poor girl only lasted a fortnight."

Benedict listened patiently to his sister's tirade, amazed that he was even interested. And yet for some strange reason, he was.

"Marie will come crawling back in a week, asking us to take her back on, you mark my words," Eloise said.

"I always mark your words," he replied, "I just don't always care."

"You," Eloise returned, pointing her finger at him, "are going to regret that you said that."

He shook his head, smiling faintly. "Doubtful."

"Hmmph. I'm going upstairs."

"Do enjoy yourself."

She poked her tongue out at him—surely not appropriate behavior for a woman of twenty-one—and left the room. Benedict managed to enjoy just three minutes of solitude before footsteps once again sounded in the hall, tapping rhythmically in his direction. When he looked up, he saw his mother in the doorway.

He stood immediately. Certain manners could be ignored for one's sister, but never for one's mother.

"I saw your feet on the table," Violet said before he could even open his mouth.

"I was merely polishing the surface with my boots."

She raised her brows, then made her way to the chair so recently vacated by Eloise and sat down. "All right, Benedict," she said in an extremely no-nonsense voice. "Who is she?"

"Miss Beckett, you mean?"

Violet gave him one businesslike nod.

"I have no idea, save that she worked for the Cavenders and was apparently mistreated by their son."

Violet blanched. "Did he . . . Oh dear. Was she . . ."

"I don't think so," Benedict said grimly. "In fact, I'm certain she wasn't. But not for lack of trying on his part."

"The poor thing. How lucky for her that you were there to save her."

Benedict found he didn't like to relive that night on the Cavenders' lawn. Even though the escapade had ended quite favorably, he could not seem to stop himself from racing through the gamut of "what-ifs." What if he hadn't come along in time? What if Cavender and his friends had been a little less drunk and a little more obstinate? Sophie could have been raped. Sophie *would* have been raped.

And now that he knew Sophie, had grown to care about her, the very notion chilled him to the bone.

"Well," Violet said, "she is not who she says she is. Of that I'm certain."

Benedict sat up straight. "Why do you say that?"

"She is far too educated to be a housemaid. Her mother's employers may have allowed her to share in some of their daughters' lessons, but all of them? I doubt it. Benedict, the girl speaks French!"

"She does?"

"Well, I can't be positive," Violet admitted, "but I caught her looking at a book on Francesca's desk that was written in French."

"Looking is not the same as reading, Mother."

She shot him a peevish look. "I'm telling you, I was looking at the way her eyes were moving. She was reading it."

"If you say so, you must be correct."

Violet's eyes narrowed. "Are you being sarcastic?"

"Normally," Benedict said with a smile, "I would say yes, but in this case, I was speaking quite seriously."

"Perhaps she is the cast-off daughter of an aristocratic family," Violet mused.

"Cast-off?"

"For getting herself with child," she explained.

Benedict was not used to his mother speaking quite so frankly. "Er, no," he said, thinking about Sophie's steadfast refusal to become his mistress. "I don't think so."

But then he thought—why not? Maybe she refused to bring an illegitimate child into this world because she had already *had* an illegitimate child and didn't want to repeat the mistake.

Benedict's mouth suddenly tasted quite sour. If Sophie had had a child, then Sophie had had a lover.

"Or maybe," Violet continued, warming to the endeavor, "she's the illegitimate child of a nobleman."

That was considerably more plausible—and more palatable. "One would think he'd have settled enough funds on her so that she didn't have to work as a housemaid."

"A great many men completely ignore their by-blows," Violet said, her face wrinkling with distaste. "It's nothing short of scandalous."

"More scandalous than their having the by-blows in the first place?"

Violet's expression turned quite peevish.

"Besides," Benedict said, leaning back against the sofa and propping one ankle on the other knee, "if she were the bastard of a nobleman, and he'd cared for her enough to make sure she had schooling as a child, then why is she completely penniless now?"

"Hmmm, that's a good point." Violet tapped her index finger against her cheek, pursed her lips, then continued tapping. "But have no fear," she finally said, "I shall discover her identity within a month."

"I'd recommend asking Eloise for help," Benedict said dryly.

Violet nodded thoughtfully. "Good idea. That girl could get Napoleon to spill his secrets."

Benedict stood. "I must be going. I'm weary from the road and would like to get home."

"You can always avail yourself here."

He gave her a half smile. His mother liked nothing better than to have her children close at hand. "I need to get back to my own lodgings," he said, leaning down and dropping a kiss on her cheek. "Thank you for finding a position for Sophie."

"Miss Beckett, you mean?" Violet asked, her lips curving slyly.

"Sophie, Miss Beckett," Benedict said, feigning indifference. "Whatever you wish to call her."

When he left, he did not see his mother smiling broadly at his back.

Sophie knew that she should not allow herself to grow too comfortable at Bridgerton House—she would, after all, be leaving just as soon as she could make the arrangements—but as she looked around her room, surely the nicest any servant had ever been assigned, and she thought about Lady Bridgerton's friendly manner and easy smile . . .

She just couldn't help wishing that she could stay forever.

But that was impossible. She knew that as well as she knew that her name was Sophia Maria Beckett, not Sophia Maria Gunningworth.

First and foremost, there was always the danger that she'd come into contact with Araminta, especially now that Lady Bridgerton had elevated her from housemaid to lady's maid. A lady's maid might, for example, find herself acting as a chaperone or escort on outings outside the house. Outings to places where Araminta and the girls might choose to frequent.

And Sophie had no doubt that Araminta would find a way to make her life a living hell. Araminta hated her in a way that defied reason, went beyond emotion. If she saw Sophie in London, she would not be content simply to ignore her. Sophie had no doubt that Araminta would lie, cheat, and steal just to make Sophie's life more difficult.

She hated Sophie that much.

But if Sophie were to be honest with herself, the true reason she could not remain in London was not Araminta. It was Benedict.

How could she avoid him when she lived in his mother's household? She was furious with him right now—beyond furious, in all truth—but she knew, deep down, that anger could only be short-lived. How could she resist him, day in and day out, when the mere sight of him made her weak with longing? Someday soon he'd smile at her, one of those sideways, crooked sorts of smiles, and she'd find herself clutching on to the furniture, just to keep herself from melting into a pathetic pool on the floor.

She'd fallen in love with the wrong man. She could never have him on her terms, and she refused to go to him on his.

It was hopeless.

Sophie was saved from any further depressing thoughts by a brisk knock on her door. When she called out, "Yes?" the door opened, and Lady Bridgerton entered the room.

Sophie immediately jumped to her feet and bobbed a curtsy. "Was there anything you needed, my lady?" she asked.

"No, not at all," Lady Bridgerton replied. "I was merely checking to see if you were getting settled in. Is there anything I can get for you?"

Sophie blinked. Lady Bridgerton was asking *her* if *she* needed anything? Rather the reverse of the usual lady-servant relationship. "Er, no thank you," Sophie said. "I would be happy to get something for you, though."

Lady Bridgerton waved her offer way. "No need. You shouldn't feel you have to do anything for us today. I'd prefer that you get yourself settled in first so that you do not feel distracted when you begin."

Sophie cast her eyes toward her small bag. "I don't have much to unpack. Truly, I should be happy to begin work immediately."

"Nonsense. It's already nearly the end of the day, and we are not planning to go out this evening, anyway. The girls and I have made do with only one lady's maid for the past week; we shall certainly survive for one more night."

"But—"

Lady Bridgerton smiled. "No arguments, if you please. One last day free is the least I can do after you saved my son."

"I did very little," Sophie said. "He would have been fine without me."

"Nonetheless, you aided him when he needed help, and for that I am in your debt."

"It was my pleasure," Sophie replied. "It was the very least I owed him after what he did for me."

Then, to her great surprise, Lady Bridgerton walked forward and sat down in the chair behind Sophie's writing desk.

Writing desk! Sophie was still trying fathom that. What maid had ever been blessed with a writing desk?

"So tell me, Sophie," Lady Bridgerton said with a winning smile—one that instantly reminded her of Benedict's easy grin. "Where are you from?"

"East Anglia, originally," Sophie replied, seeing no reason to lie. The Bridgertons were from Kent; it was unlikely that Lady Bridgerton would be familiar with Norfolk, where Sophie had grown up. "Not so very far from Sandringham, if you know where that is."

"I do indeed," Lady Bridgerton said. "I haven't been, but I've heard that it is a lovely building."

Sophie nodded. "It is, quite. Of course, I've never been inside. But the exterior is beautiful."

"Where did your mother work?"

"Blackheath Hall," Sophie replied, this lie slipping easily off her tongue. She'd been asked that question often enough; she'd long since settled upon a name for her fictional home. "Are you familiar with it?"

Lady Bridgerton's brow furrowed. "No, I don't believe so."

"A bit north of Swaffham."

Lady Bridgerton shook her head. "No, I do not know it."

Sophie gave her a gentle smile. "Not many people do."

"Do you have any brothers or sisters?"

Sophie was unused to an employer wanting to know so much about her personal background; usually all they cared about were her employment record and references. "No," she said. "There was only me."

"Ah, well, at least you had the company of the girls with whom you shared lessons. That must have been nice for you."

"It was good fun," Sophie lied. In all truth, studying with Rosamund and Posy had been sheer torture. She'd much preferred lessons when she'd been alone with her governess, before they'd come to live at Penwood Park.

"I must say, it was very generous of your mother's employers—I'm sorry," Lady Bridgerton interrupted herself, her brow furrowing, "what did you say their name was?"

"Grenville."

Her forehead wrinkled again. "I'm not familiar with them."

"They don't often come to London."

"Ah, well, that explains it," Lady Bridgerton said. "But as I was saying, it was very generous of them to allow you to share in their daughters' lessons. What did you study?"

Sophie froze, not sure whether she was being interrogated or if Lady Bridgerton were truly interested. No one had ever cared to delve so deeply into the faux background she had created for herself. "Er, the usual subjects," she hedged. "Arithmetic and literature. History, a bit of mythology. French."

"French?" Lady Bridgerton asked, looking quite surprised. "How interesting. French tutors can be very dear."

"The governess spoke French," Sophie explained. "So it didn't cost any extra."

"How *is* your French?"

Sophie wasn't about to tell her the truth and say that it was perfect. Or almost perfect. She'd gotten out of practice these past few years and lost a bit of her fluency. "It's tolerable," she said. "Good enough to pass for a French maid, if that's what you desire."

"Oh, no," Lady Bridgerton said, laughing merrily. "Heavens, no. I know it is all the rage to have French maids, but I would never ask you to go about your chores trying to remember to speak with a French accent."

"That's very thoughtful of you," Sophie said, trying not to let her suspicion show on her face. She was sure that Lady Bridgerton was a nice lady; she'd *have* to be a nice lady to have raised such a nice family. But this was almost *too* nice.

"Well, it's—oh, good day, Eloise. What brings you up here?"

Sophie looked to the doorway and saw what could only be a Bridgerton daughter standing there. Her thick, chestnut hair was coiled elegantly at the back of her neck, and her mouth was wide and expressive, just like Benedict's.

"Benedict told me we have a new maid," Eloise said.

Lady Bridgerton motioned to Sophie. "This is Sophie Beckett. We were just chatting. I think we shall deal famously."

Eloise gave her mother an odd look—or at least Sophie thought it was an odd look. She supposed that it was possible that Eloise always looked at her mother with a slightly suspicious, slightly confused, sideways glance. But somehow Sophie didn't think so.

"My brother tells me you saved his life," Eloise said, turning from her mother to Sophie.

"He exaggerates," Sophie said, a faint smile touching her lips.

Eloise regarded her with an oddly shrewd glance, and Sophie had the distinct impression that Eloise was analyzing her smile, trying to decide whether or not she was poking fun at Benedict, and if so, whether it was in jest or unkindness.

The moment seemed suspended in time, and then Eloise's lips curved in a surprisingly sly manner. "I think my mother is correct," she said. "We shall deal famously."

Sophie rather thought she had just passed some sort of crucial test.

"Have you met Francesca and Hyacinth?" Eloise asked.

Sophie shook her head, just as Lady Bridgerton said, "They are not at home. Francesca is visiting Daphne, and Hyacinth is off at the Featheringtons. She and Felicity seem to be over their row and are once again inseparable."

Eloise chuckled. "Poor Penelope. I think she was enjoying the relative peace and quiet with Hyacinth gone. I know *I* was enjoying the respite from Felicity."

Lady Bridgerton turned to Sophie and explained, "My daughter Hyacinth can more often than not be found at the home of her best friend, Felicity Featherington. And when she is not, then Felicity can be found here."

Sophie smiled and nodded, wondering once again why they were sharing such tidbits with her. They were treating her like family, something even her own family had never done.

It was very odd.

Odd and wonderful.

Odd and wonderful and horrible.

Because it could never last.

But maybe she could stay just a little while. Not long. A few weeks—maybe even a month. Just long enough to get her affairs and thoughts in order. Just long enough to relax and pretend she was more than just a servant.

She knew she could never be a part of the Bridgerton family, but maybe she could be a friend.

And it had been so long since she had been anyone's friend.

"Is something wrong, Sophie?" Lady Bridgerton asked. "You have a tear in your eye."

Sophie shook her head. "Just a speck of dust," she mumbled, pretending to busy herself with the unpacking of her small bag of possessions. She knew that no one believed her, but she didn't much care.

And even though she had no idea where she intended to go from this moment on, she had the oddest feeling that her life had just begun.

Chapter 15

This Author is quite certain that the male half of the population will be uninterested in the following portion of the column, so you are all given leave to skip to the next section. However, for the ladies, let This Author be the first to inform you that the Bridgerton family was recently sucked into the battle of the maids that has been raging all season between Lady Penwood and Mrs. Featherington. It seems that the maid attending to the daughters Bridgerton has defected to the Penwoods, replacing the maid who fled back to the Featherington household after Lady Penwood forced her to polish three hundred pairs of shoes.

And in other Bridgerton news, Benedict Bridgerton is most definitely back in London. It seems he took ill while in the country and extended his stay. One wishes that there were a more interesting explanation (especially when one is, like This Author, dependent upon interesting stories to earn one's living), but sadly, that is all there is to it.

LADY WHISTLEDOWN'S SOCIETY PAPERS, 14 MAY 1817

By the following morning, Sophie had met five of Benedict's seven siblings. Eloise, Francesca, and Hyacinth all still lived with their mother, Anthony had stopped by with his young son for breakfast, and Daphne—who was now the Duchess of Hastings—had been summoned to help Lady Bridgerton plan the end-of-the-season ball. The only Bridgertons Sophie hadn't met were Gregory, who was off at Eton, and Colin, who was off, in Anthony's words, God-knows-where.

Although, if one wanted to put a fine point on it, Sophie already had met Colin—two years earlier at the masquerade. She was rather relieved that he was out of town. She doubted that he would recognize her; Benedict, after all, had not. But somehow the thought of meeting him again was quite stressful and unsettling.

Not that that should matter, she thought ruefully. Everything seemed quite stressful and unsettling these days.

Much to Sophie's extreme *lack* of surprise, Benedict showed up at his mother's home the following morning for breakfast. Sophie should have been able to avoid him completely, except that he was loitering in the hall as she tried to make her way down to the kitchen, where she planned to take her morning meal with the rest of the servants.

"And how was your first night at Number Five, Bruton Street?" he inquired, his smile lazy and masculine.

"Splendid," Sophie replied, stepping aside so that she might make a clean half circle around him.

But as she stepped to her left, he stepped to his right, effectively blocking her path. "I'm so glad you're enjoying yourself," he said smoothly.

Sophie stepped back to her right. "I *was*," she said pointedly.

Benedict was far too debonair to step back to his left, but he somehow managed to turn and lean against a table in just the right way to once again block her movement. "Have you been given a tour of the house?" he asked.

"By the housekeeper."

"And of the grounds?"

"There are no grounds."

He smiled, his brown eyes warm and melting. "There's a garden."

"About the size of a pound note," she retorted.

"Nonetheless . . ."

"Nonetheless," Sophie cut in, "I have to eat breakfast."

He stepped gallantly aside. "Until next time," he murmured.

And Sophie had the sinking feeling that next time would come quickly indeed.

Thirty minutes later, Sophie edged slowly out of the kitchen, half-expecting Benedict to jump out at her from around a corner. Well, maybe not half-expecting. Judging from the way she couldn't quite breathe, she was probably whole-expecting.

But he wasn't there.

She inched forward. Surely he would come bounding down the stairs at any moment, ambushing her with his very presence.

Still no Benedict.

Sophie opened her mouth, then bit her tongue when she realized she'd been about to call out his name.

"Stupid girl," she muttered.

"Who's stupid?" Benedict asked. "Surely not *you*."

Sophie nearly jumped a foot. "Where did you come from?" she demanded, once she'd almost caught her breath.

He pointed to an open doorway. "Right there," he answered, his voice all innocence.

"So now you're jumping out at me from *closets*?"

"Of course not." He looked affronted. "That was a staircase."

Sophie peered around him. It was the side staircase. The *servants'* staircase. Certainly not anyplace a family member would just *happen* to be walking. "Do you often creep down the side staircase?" she asked, crossing her arms.

He leaned forward, just close enough to make her slightly

uncomfortable, and, although she would never admit it to anyone, barely even herself, slightly excited. "Only when I want to sneak up on someone."

She attempted to brush past him. "I have to get to work."

"Now?"

She gritted her teeth. "Yes, now."

"But Hyacinth is eating breakfast. You can hardly dress her hair while she's eating."

"I also attend to Francesca and Eloise."

He shrugged, smiling innocently. "They're eating breakfast, too. Truly, you have nothing to do."

"Which shows how little you know about working for a living," she shot back. "I have ironing, mending, polishing—"

"They make you polish the silver?"

"Shoes!" she fairly yelled. "I have to polish shoes."

"Oh." He leaned back, one shoulder resting against the wall as he crossed his arms. "It sounds dull."

"It *is* dull," she ground out, trying to ignore the tears that suddenly pricked her eyes. *She* knew her life was dull, but it was painful to hear someone else point it out.

One corner of his mouth lifted into a lazy, seductive smile. "Your life doesn't *have* to be dull, you know."

She tried to step past him. "I prefer it dull."

He waved his arm grandly to the side, motioning for her to pass. "If that is how you wish it."

"I do." But the words didn't come out nearly as firmly as she'd intended. "I *do*," she repeated. Oh, very well, no use lying to herself. She didn't. Not entirely. But that was the way it had to be.

"Are you trying to convince yourself, or me?" he asked softly.

"I won't even dignify that with an answer," she replied. But she didn't meet his eyes as she said it.

"You'd best get yourself upstairs, then," he said, raising

one brow when she didn't move. "I'm sure you have a great many shoes to polish."

Sophie ran up the stairs—the servants' stairs—and didn't look back.

He next found her in the garden—that tiny patch of green she'd so recently (and accurately) mocked as the size of a pound note. The Bridgerton sisters had gone off to visit the Featherington sisters, and Lady Bridgerton was taking a nap. Sophie had all of their gowns pressed and ready for that evening's social event, hair ribbons were selected and matched to each dress, and enough shoes had been polished to last a week.

With all her work done, Sophie decided to take a short break and read in the garden. Lady Bridgerton had told her that she might borrow freely from her small library of books, so Sophie selected a recently published novel and settled herself into a wrought-iron chair on the small patio. She'd only read a chapter before she heard footsteps approaching from the house. Somehow she managed not to look up until a shadow fell across her. Predictably, it was Benedict.

"Do you *live* here?" Sophie asked dryly.

"No," he said, plopping down into the chair next to her, "although my mother is constantly telling me to make myself right at home."

She could think of no witty rejoinder, so she merely "hmmphed" and stuck her nose back in her book.

He plunked his feet on the small table in front. "And what are we reading today?"

"That question," she said, snapping the book shut but leaving her finger in to mark her place, "implies that I am actually reading, which I assure you I am unable to do while you are sitting here."

"My presence is that compelling, eh?"

"It's that *disturbing*."

"Better than dull," he pointed out.

"I like my life dull."

"If you like your life dull, then that can only mean that you do not understand the nature of excitement."

The condescension in his tone was appalling. Sophie gripped her book so hard her knuckles turned white. "I have had enough excitement in my life," she said through gritted teeth. "I assure you."

"I would be pleased to participate in this conversation to a greater degree," he drawled, "except that you have not seen fit to share with me *any* of the details of your life."

"It was not an oversight on my part."

He clucked disapprovingly. "So hostile."

Her eyes bugged out. "You abducted me—"

"Coerced," he reminded her.

"Do you *want* me to hit you?"

"I wouldn't mind it," he said mildly. "And besides, now that you're here, was it really so very terrible that I browbeat you into coming? You like my family, don't you?"

"Yes, but—"

"And they treat you fairly, right?"

"Yes, but—"

"Then what," he asked, his tone most supercilious, "is the problem?"

Sophie almost lost her temper. She almost jumped to her feet and grabbed his shoulders and shook and shook and shook, but at the last moment she realized that that was exactly what he wanted her to do. And so instead she merely sniffed and said, "If you cannot recognize the problem, there is no way that I could explain it to you."

He laughed, damn the man. "My goodness," he said, "that was an expert sidestep."

She picked up her book and opened it. "I'm reading."

"Trying, at least," he murmured.

She flipped a page, even though she hadn't read the last

two paragraphs. She was really just trying to make a show of ignoring him, and besides, she could always go back and read them later, after he left.

"Your book is upside down," he pointed out.

Sophie gasped and looked down. "It is not!"

He smiled slyly. "But you still had to look to be sure, didn't you?"

She stood up and announced, "I'm going inside."

He stood immediately. "And leave the splendid spring air?"

"And leave *you*," she retorted, even though his gesture of respect was not lost on her. Gentlemen did not ordinarily stand for mere servants.

"Pity," he murmured. "I was having such fun."

Sophie wondered how much injury he'd sustain if she threw the book at him. Probably not enough to make up for the loss to her dignity.

It amazed her how easily he could infuriate her. She loved him desperately—she'd long since given up lying to herself about that—and yet he could make her entire body shake with anger with one little quip.

"Good-*bye*, Mr. Bridgerton."

He waved her off. "I'll see you later, I'm sure."

Sophie paused, not sure she liked his dismissive demeanor.

"I thought you were leaving," he said, looking faintly amused.

"I am," she insisted.

He cocked his head to the side but didn't say anything. He didn't have to. The vaguely mocking expression in his eyes did the job quite well.

She turned and walked toward the door leading inside, but when she was about halfway to her destination, she heard him call out, "Your new dress is quite fetching."

She stopped and sighed. She might have gone from faux-guardian of an earl to a mere lady's maid, but good manners were good manners, and there was no way she could ignore a compliment. Turning around, she said, "Thank you. It was a gift from your mother. I believe it used to belong to Francesca."

He leaned against the fence, his posture deceptively lazy. "That's a custom, isn't it, to share frocks with one's maid?"

Sophie nodded. "When one is through with them, of course. No one would give a new frock away."

"I see."

Sophie eyed him suspiciously, wondering why on earth he cared about the status of her new dress.

"Didn't you want to go inside?" he inquired.

"What are you up to?" she asked.

"Why would you think I'm up to anything?"

Her lips pursed before she said, "You wouldn't be you if you weren't up to something."

He smiled at that. "I do believe that was a compliment."

"It wasn't necessarily intended as such."

"But nonetheless," he said mildly, "that's how I choose to take it."

She wasn't sure how best to respond, so she said nothing. She also didn't move toward the door. She wasn't sure why, since she'd been quite vocal about her desire to be alone. But what she said and what she felt weren't always one and the same. In her heart she longed for this man, dreamed of a life that could never be.

She shouldn't be so angry with him. He shouldn't have forced her against her wishes to come to London, that was true, but she couldn't fault him for offering her a position as his mistress. He had done what any man in his position would have done. Sophie had no illusions about her place in London society. She was a maid. A servant. And the only thing that separated her from other maids and servants was that she'd had a taste of luxury as a child. She'd been reared gently, if without love, and the experience had shaped her ideals and values. Now she was forever stuck between two worlds, with no clear place in either.

"You look very serious," he said quietly.

Sophie heard him, but she couldn't quite break herself from her thoughts.

Benedict stepped forward. He reached out to touch her chin, then checked himself. There was something untouchable about her just then, something unreachable. "I can't bear it when you look so sad," he said, surprised by his own words. He hadn't intended to say anything; it had just slipped out.

She looked up at that. "I'm not sad."

He gave his head the tiniest shake. "There's a sorrow deep in your eyes. It's rarely gone."

Her hand flew to her face, as if she could actually touch that sorrow, as if it were solid, something that could be massaged away.

Benedict took her hand and raised it to his lips. "I wish you would share your secrets with me."

"I have no—"

"Don't lie," he cut in, his tone harsher than he'd intended. "You have more secrets than any woman I've—" He broke off, a sudden image of the woman from the masquerade flashing through his mind. "More than almost any woman I've known," he finished.

Her eyes met his for the briefest of seconds, and then she looked away. "There is nothing wrong with secrets. If I choose—"

"Your secrets are eating you alive," he said sharply. He didn't want to stand there and listen to her excuses, and his frustration gnawed at his patience. "You have the opportunity to change your life, to reach out and grasp happiness, and yet you won't do it."

"I can't," she said, and the pain in her voice nearly unmanned him.

"Nonsense," he said. "You can do anything you choose. You just don't want to."

"Don't make this harder than it already is," she whispered.

When she said that, something snapped inside of him. He felt it palpably, a strange popping sensation that released a rush of blood, feeding the frustrated anger that had been simmering inside of him for days. "You think it's not hard?" he asked. "You think it's not *hard?*"

"I didn't say that!"

He grabbed her hand and pulled her body against his, so she could see for herself just how hard he was. "I burn for you," he said, his lips touching her ear. "Every night, I lie in bed, thinking of you, wondering why the hell you're here with my mother, of all people, and not with me."

"I didn't want—"

"You don't know what you want," he cut in. It was a cruel statement, condescending in the extreme, but he was beyond caring. She'd wounded him in a way he hadn't even known was possible, with a power he'd never dreamed she possessed. She'd chosen a life of drudgery over a life with him, and now he was doomed to see her almost every day, to see her and taste her and smell her just enough to keep his desire sharp and strong.

It was his own fault, of course. He could have let her stay in the country, could have saved himself this wrenching torture. But he'd surprised even himself by insisting that she come to London. It was odd, and he was almost afraid to analyze what it meant, but he needed to know that she was safe and protected more than he needed her for himself.

She said his name, but her voice was laced with longing, and he knew that she was not indifferent to him. She might not fully understand what it meant to want a man, but she wanted him all the same.

He captured her mouth with his, swearing to himself as he did so that if she said no, if she made any sort of indication that she didn't want this, he'd stop. It'd be the hardest thing he'd ever done, but he would do it.

But she didn't say no, and she didn't push against him or struggle or squirm. Instead, she positively melted into him, her hands twining in his hair as her lips parted beneath his. He didn't know why she'd suddenly decided to let him kiss her—no, to kiss *him*—but he wasn't about to lift his lips from hers to wonder why.

He seized the moment, tasting her, drinking her, *breathing* her. He was no longer quite so confident that he would be able to convince her to become his mistress, and it was suddenly imperative that this kiss be more than just a kiss. It might have to last him a lifetime.

He kissed her with renewed vigor, pushing away the niggling voice in his head, telling him that he'd been here, done this before. Two years earlier he'd danced with a woman, kissed her, and she'd told him that he'd have to pack a lifetime into a single kiss.

He'd been overconfident then; he hadn't believed her. And he'd lost her, maybe lost everything. He certainly hadn't met anyone since with whom he could even imagine building a life.

Until Sophie.

Unlike the lady in silver, she wasn't someone he could hope to marry, but also unlike the lady in silver, she was *here*.

And he wasn't going to let her get away.

She was here, with him, and she felt like heaven. The soft scent of her hair, the slight taste of salt on her skin—she was, he thought, born to rest in the shelter of his arms. And he was born to hold her.

"Come home with me," he whispered in her ear.

She said nothing, but he felt her stiffen.

"Come home with me," he repeated.

"I can't," she said, the breath of each word whispering across his skin.

"You *can*."

She shook her head, but she didn't pull away, so he took advantage of the moment and brought his lips to hers one more time. His tongue darted in, exploring the warm recesses of her mouth, tasting the very essence of her. His hand found the swell of her breast and he squeezed gently, his breath catching as he felt her pucker beneath him. But it wasn't enough. He wanted to feel her skin, not the fabric of her dress.

But this was not the place. They were in his mother's garden, for God's sake. Anyone could come across them, and to be frank, if he hadn't pulled her into the alcove right by the door, anyone could have seen them. It was the sort of thing that could cause Sophie to lose her job.

Maybe he should be pulling her out into the open, where all the world would see, because then she'd be on her own again, and she'd have no choice but to be his mistress.

Which was, he reminded himself, what he wanted.

But it occurred to him—and frankly, he was rather surprised he had the presence of mind at such a moment for *anything* to occur to him—that part of the reason he cared so much for her was her remarkably solid and unflinching sense of herself. She knew who she was, and unfortunately for him, that person didn't stray from the bounds of respectable society.

If he ruined her so publicly, in front of people she admired and respected, he'd break her spirit. And that would be an unforgivable crime.

Slowly, he pulled away. He still wanted her, and he still wanted her to be his mistress, but he wasn't going to force the issue by compromising her in his mother's household. When she came to him—and she *would*, he vowed—it would be of her own free will.

In the meantime, he would woo her, wear her down. In the meantime, he'd—

"You stopped," she whispered, looking surprised.

"This isn't the place," he replied.

For a moment her face showed no change of expression. Then, almost as if someone were pulling a shade over her face, horror dawned. It started in her eyes, which grew impossibly round and somehow even more green than usual, then it reached her mouth, her lips parting as a gasp of air rushed in.

"I didn't think," she whispered, more to herself than to him.

"I know." He smiled. "I know. I hate it when you think. It always ends badly for me."

"We can't do this again."

"We certainly can't do it *here*."

"No, I mean—"

"But—"

"You're spoiling it."

"But—"

"Humor me," he said, "and let me believe the afternoon ended without your telling me this will never happen again."

"But—"

He pressed a finger to her lips. "You're not humoring me."

"But—"

"Don't I deserve this one little fantasy?"

At last, he broke through. She smiled.

"Good," he said. "That's more like it."

Her lips quivered, then, amazingly, her smile grew.

"Excellent," he murmured. "Now then, I'm going to leave. And you have only one task while I go. You will stay right here, and you will keep smiling. Because it breaks my heart to see any other expression on your face."

"You won't be able to see me," she pointed out.

He touched her chin. "I'll know."

And then, before her expression could change from that enchanting combination of shock and adoration, he left.

Chapter 16

The Featheringtons hosted a small dinner party yesterday eve, and, although This Author was not privileged enough to attend, it has been said that the evening was deemed quite a success. Three Bridgertons attended, but sadly for the Featherington girls, none of the Bridgertons were of the male variety. The always amiable Nigel Berbrooke was there, paying great attention to Miss Philippa Featherington.

This Author is told that both Benedict and Colin Bridgerton were invited, but had to send their regrets.

LADY WHISTLEDOWN'S SOCIETY PAPERS, 19 MAY 1817

As the days melted into a week, Sophie discovered that working for the Bridgertons could keep a girl very busy indeed. Her job was to be maid to all three unmarried girls, and her days were filled with hairdressing, mending, pressing gowns, polishing shoes . . . She hadn't left the house even once—unless one counted time out in the back garden.

But where such a life under Araminta had been dreary and demeaning, the Bridgerton household was filled with laughter and smiles. The girls bickered and teased, but never with the malice Sophie had seen Rosamund show to Posy. And when tea was informal—upstairs, with only Lady Bridgerton and the girls in attendance—Sophie was always invited to partake. She usually brought her basket of mending and darned or sewed buttons while the Bridgertons chattered away, but it was so lovely to be able to sit and sip a fine cup of tea, with fresh milk and warm scones. And after a few days, Sophie even began to feel comfortable enough to occasionally add to the conversation.

It had become Sophie's favorite time of day.

"Where," Eloise asked, one afternoon about a week after what Sophie was now referring to as *the big kiss*, "do you suppose Benedict is?"

"Ow!"

Four Bridgerton faces turned to Sophie. "Are you all right?" Lady Bridgerton asked, her teacup suspended halfway between her saucer and her mouth.

Sophie grimaced. "I pricked my finger."

Lady Bridgerton's lips curved into a small, secret smile.

"Mother has told you," fourteen-year-old Hyacinth said, "at least a *thousand* times—"

"A thousand times?" Francesca asked with arched brows.

"A hundred times," Hyacinth amended, shooting an annoyed look at her older sister, "that you do not have to bring your mending to tea."

Sophie suppressed a smile of her own. "I should feel very lazy if I did not."

"Well, I'm not going to bring my embroidery," Hyacinth announced, not that anyone had asked her to.

"Feeling lazy?" Francesca queried.

"Not in the least," Hyacinth returned.

Francesca turned to Sophie. "You're making Hyacinth feel lazy."

"I do not!" Hyacinth protested.

Lady Bridgerton sipped at her tea. "You *have* been working on the same piece of embroidery for quite some time, Hyacinth. Since February, if my memory serves."

"Her memory always serves," Francesca said to Sophie.

Hyacinth glared at Francesca, who smiled into her teacup.

Sophie coughed to cover a smile of her own. Francesca, who at twenty was merely one year younger than Eloise, had a sly, subversive sense of humor. Someday Hyacinth would be her match, but not yet.

"Nobody answered my question," Eloise announced, letting her teacup clatter into its saucer. "Where is Benedict? I haven't seen him in an age."

"It's been a week," Lady Bridgerton said.

"Ow!"

"Do you need a thimble?" Hyacinth asked Sophie.

"I'm not usually this clumsy," Sophie muttered.

Lady Bridgerton lifted her cup to her lips and held it there for what seemed like a rather long time.

Sophie gritted her teeth together and returned to her mending with a vengeance. Much to her surprise, Benedict had not made even the barest of appearances since *the big kiss* last week. She'd found herself peering out windows, peeking around corners, always expecting to catch a glimpse of him.

And yet he was never there.

Sophie couldn't decide whether she was crushed or relieved. Or both.

She sighed. Definitely both.

"Did you say something, Sophie?" Eloise asked.

Sophie shook her head and murmured, "No," refusing to look up from her poor, abused index finger. Grimacing slightly, she pinched her skin, watching blood slowly bead up on her fingertip.

"Where *is* he?" Eloise persisted.

"Benedict is thirty years of age," Lady Bridgerton said in a mild voice. "He doesn't need to inform us of his every activity."

Eloise snorted loudly. "That's a fine about-face from last week, Mother."

"Whatever do you mean?"

" 'Where is Benedict?' " Eloise mocked, doing a more-than-fair imitation of her mother. " 'How dare he go off without a word? It's as if he's dropped off the face of the earth.' "

"That was different," Lady Bridgerton said.

"How so?" This, from Francesca, who was wearing her usual sly smile.

"He'd said he was going to that awful Cavender boy's party, and then never came back, whereas *this* time . . ." Lady Bridgerton stopped, pursing her lips. "*Why* am I explaining myself to you?"

"I can't imagine," Sophie murmured.

Eloise, who was sitting closest to Sophie, choked on her tea.

Francesca whacked Eloise on the back as she leaned forward to inquire, "Did you say something, Sophie?"

Sophie shook her head as she stabbed her needle into the dress she was mending, completely missing the hem.

Eloise gave her a dubious sideways glance.

Lady Bridgerton cleared her throat. "Well, I think—" She stopped, cocking her head to the side. "I say, is that someone in the hall?"

Sophie stifled a groan and looked over toward the doorway, expecting the butler to enter. Wickham always gave her a disapproving frown before imparting whatever news he was carrying. He didn't approve of the maid taking tea with the ladies of the house, and while he never vocalized his thoughts on the issue in front of the Bridgertons, he rarely took pains to keep his opinions from showing on his face.

But instead of Wickham, Benedict walked through the doorway.

"Benedict!" Eloise called out, rising to her feet. "We were just talking about you."

He looked at Sophie. "Were you?"

"*I* wasn't," Sophie muttered.

"Did you say something, Sophie?" Hyacinth asked.

"Ow!"

"I'm going to have to take that mending away from you," Lady Bridgerton said with an amused smile. "You'll have lost a pint of blood before the day is through."

Sophie lurched to her feet. "I'll get a thimble."

"You don't have a *thimble*?" Hyacinth asked. "I would never *dream* of doing mending without a thimble."

"Have you *ever* dreamed of mending?" Francesca smirked.

Hyacinth kicked her, nearly upsetting the tea service in the process.

"Hyacinth!" Lady Bridgerton scolded.

Sophie stared at the door, trying desperately to keep her eyes focused on anything but Benedict. She'd spent all week hoping for a glimpse, but now that he was here, all she wanted was to escape. If she looked at his face, her eyes inevitably strayed to his lips. And if she looked at his lips, her thoughts immediately went to their kiss. And if she thought about the kiss . . .

"I need that thimble," she blurted out, jumping to her feet. There were some things one just shouldn't think about in public.

"So you said," Benedict murmured, one of his eyebrows quirking up into a perfect—and perfectly arrogant—arch.

"It's downstairs," she muttered. "In my room."

"But your room is upstairs," Hyacinth said.

Sophie could have killed her. "That's what I said," she ground out.

"No," Hyacinth said in a matter-of-fact tone, "you didn't."

"Yes," Lady Bridgerton said, "she did. I heard her."

Sophie twisted her head sharply to look at Lady Bridgerton and knew in an instant that the older woman had lied. "I have to get that thimble," she said, for what seemed like the thirtieth time. She hurried toward the doorway, gulping as she grew close to Benedict.

"Wouldn't want you to hurt yourself," he said, stepping

aside to allow her through the doorway. But as she brushed past him, he leaned forward, whispering, "Coward."

Sophie's cheeks burned, and she was halfway down the stairs before she realized that she'd meant to go back to her room. Dash it all, she didn't want to march back up the stairs and have to walk past Benedict again. He was probably still standing in the doorway, and his lips would tilt upward as she passed—one of those faintly mocking, faintly seductive smiles that never failed to leave her breathless.

This was a disaster. There was no way she was going to be able to stay here. How could she remain with Lady Bridgerton, when every glimpse of Benedict turned her knees to water? She just wasn't strong enough. He was going to wear her down, make her forget all of her principles, all of her vows. She was going to have to leave. There was no other option.

And that was really too bad, because she *liked* working for the Bridgerton sisters. They treated her like a human being, not like some barely paid workhorse. They asked her questions and seemed to care about her answers.

Sophie knew she wasn't one of them, would never be one of them, but they made it so easy to pretend. And in all truth, all that Sophie had ever really wanted out of life was a family.

With the Bridgertons, she could almost pretend that she had one.

"Lost your way?"

Sophie looked up to see Benedict at the top of the stairs, leaning lazily against the wall. She looked down and realized that she was still standing on the stairs. "I'm going out," she said.

"To buy a thimble?"

"Yes," she said defiantly.

"Don't you need money?"

She could lie, and say that she had money in her pocket, or she could tell the truth, and show herself for the pathetic fool she was. Or she could just run down the stairs and out of the house. It was the cowardly thing to do, but . . .

"I have to go," she muttered, and dashed away so quickly that she completely forgot she ought to be using the servants' entrance. She skidded across the foyer and pushed open the heavy door, stumbling her way down the front steps. When her feet hit the pavement, she turned north, not for any particular reason, just because she had to go somewhere, and then she heard a voice.

An awful, horrible, terrible voice.

Dear God, it was Araminta.

Sophie's heart stopped, and she quickly pressed herself back against the wall. Araminta was facing the street, and unless she turned around, she'd never notice Sophie.

At least it was easy to remain silent when one couldn't even breathe.

What was she doing here? Penwood House was at least eight blocks away, closer to—

Then Sophie remembered. She'd read it in *Whistledown* last year, one of the few copies she'd been able to get her hands on while she was working for the Cavenders. The new Earl of Penwood had finally decided to take up residence in London. Araminta, Rosamund, and Posy had been forced to find new accommodations.

Next door to the Bridgertons? Sophie couldn't have imagined a worse nightmare if she tried.

"Where is that insufferable girl?" she heard Araminta said.

Sophie immediately felt sorry for the girl in question. As Araminta's former "insufferable girl," she knew that the position came with few benefits.

"Posy!" Araminta yelled, then marched into a waiting carriage.

Sophie chewed on her lip, her heart sinking. In that moment, she knew exactly what must have happened when she left. Araminta would have hired a new maid, and she was probably just beastly to the poor girl, but she wouldn't have been able to degrade and demean her in quite the same fashion she'd done with Sophie. You had to know a person, really hate them, to be so cruel. Any old servant wouldn't do.

And since Araminta had to put someone down—she didn't know how to feel good about herself without making someone else feel bad—she'd obviously chosen Posy as her whipping boy—or girl, as the case might be.

Posy came dashing out the door, her face pinched and drawn. She looked unhappy, and perhaps a bit heavier than she had been two years earlier. Araminta wouldn't like that, Sophie thought glumly. She'd never been able to accept that Posy wasn't petite and blond and beautiful like Rosamund and herself. If Sophie had been Araminta's nemesis, then Posy had always been her disappointment.

Sophie watched as Posy stopped at the top of the steps, then reached down to fiddle with the laces of her short boots. Rosamund poked her head out of the carriage, yelling, "Posy!" in what Sophie thought was a rather unattractively shrill voice.

Sophie ducked back, turning her head away. She was right in Rosamund's line of sight.

"I'm coming!" Posy called out.

"Hurry up!" Rosamund snapped.

Posy finished tying her laces, then hurried forward, but her foot slipped on the final step, and a moment later she was sprawled on the pavement. Sophie lurched forward, instinctively moving to help Posy, but she jammed herself back against the wall. Posy was unhurt, and there was nothing in life Sophie wanted less than for Araminta to know that she was in London, practically right next door.

Posy picked herself off the pavement, stopping to stretch her neck, first to the right, then to the left, then . . .

Then she saw her. Sophie was sure of it. Posy's eyes widened, and her mouth fell open slightly. Then her lips came together, pursed to make the "S" to begin "Sophie?"

Sophie shook her head frantically.

"Posy!" came Araminta's irate cry.

Sophie shook her head again, her eyes begging, pleading with Posy not to give her away.

"I'm coming, Mother!" Posy called. She gave Sophie a single short nod, then climbed up into the carriage, which thankfully rolled off in the opposite direction.

Sophie sagged against the building. She didn't move for a full minute.

And then she didn't move for another five.

Benedict didn't mean to take anything away from his mother and sisters, but once Sophie ran out of the upstairs sitting room, he lost his interest in tea and scones.

"I was just wondering where you'd been," Eloise was saying.

"Hmmm?" He craned his head slightly to the right, wondering how much of the streetscape he could see through the window from this angle.

"I said," Eloise practically hollered, "I was just wondering—"

"Eloise, lower your voice," Lady Bridgerton interjected.

"But he's not listening."

"If he's not listening," Lady Bridgerton said, "then shouting isn't going to get his attention."

"Throwing a scone might work," Hyacinth suggested.

"Hyacinth, don't you da—"

But Hyacinth had already lobbed the scone. Benedict ducked out of the way, barely a second before it would have bounced off the side of his head. He looked first to the wall, which now bore a slight smudge where the scone had hit, then to the floor, where it had landed, remarkably in one piece.

"I believe that is my cue to leave," he said smoothly, shooting a cheeky smile at his youngest sister. Her airborne scone had given him just the excuse he needed to duck out of the room and see if he couldn't trail Sophie to wherever it was she thought she was going.

"But you just got here," his mother pointed out.

Benedict immediately regarded her with suspicion. Unlike her usual moans of "But you just got here," she didn't sound the least bit upset at his leaving.

Which meant she was up to something.

"I could stay," he said, just to test her.

"Oh, no," she said, lifting her teacup to her lips even though he was fairly certain it was empty. "Don't let us keep you if you're busy."

Benedict fought to school his features into an impassive expression, or at least to hide his shock. The last time he'd informed his mother that he was "busy," she'd answered with, "Too busy for your mother?"

His first urge was to declare, "I'll stay," and park himself in a chair, but he had just enough presence of mind to realize that staying to thwart his mother was rather ridiculous when what he really wanted to do was leave. "I'll go, then," he said slowly, backing toward the door.

"Go," she said, shooing him away. "Enjoy yourself."

Benedict decided to leave the room before she managed to befuddle him any further. He reached down and scooped up the scone, gently tossing it to Hyacinth, who caught it with a grin. He then nodded at his mother and sisters and headed out into the hall, reaching the stairs just as he heard his mother say, "I thought he'd never leave."

Very odd, indeed.

With long, easy strides, he made his way down the steps and out the front door. He doubted that Sophie would still be near the house, but if she'd gone shopping, there was really only one direction in which she would have headed. He turned right, intending to stroll until he reached the small row of shops, but he'd only gone three steps before he saw

Sophie, pressed up against the brick exterior of his mother's house, looking as if she could barely remember how to breathe.

"Sophie?" Benedict rushed toward her. "What happened? Are you all right?"

She started when she saw him, then nodded.

He didn't believe her, of course, but there seemed little point in saying so. "You're shaking," he said, looking at her hands. "Tell me what happened. Did someone bother you?"

"No," she said, her voice uncharacteristically quavery. "I just . . . I, ah . . ." Her gaze fell on the stairs next to them. "I tripped on my way down the stairs and it scared me." She smiled weakly. "I'm sure you know what I mean. When you feel as if your insides have flipped upside down."

Benedict nodded, because of course he knew what she meant. But that didn't mean that he believed her. "Come with me," he said.

She looked up, and something in the green depths of her eyes broke his heart. "Where?" she whispered.

"Anywhere but here."

"I—"

"I live just five houses down," he said.

"You do?" Her eyes widened, then she murmured, "No one told me."

"I promise that your virtue will be safe," he interrupted. And then he added, because he couldn't quite help himself: "Unless *you* want it otherwise."

He had a feeling she would have protested if she weren't so dazed, but she allowed him to lead her down the street. "We'll just sit in my front room," he said, "until you feel better."

She nodded, and he led her up the steps and into his home, a modest town house just a bit south of his mother's.

Once they were comfortably ensconced, and Benedict had shut the door so that they wouldn't be bothered by any of his servants, he turned to her, prepared to say, "Now, why don't you tell me what really happened," but at the very last minute something compelled him to hold his tongue. He could ask, but he knew she wouldn't answer. She'd be put on the defensive, and that wasn't likely to help his cause any.

So instead, he schooled his face into a neutral mask and asked, "How are you enjoying your work for my family?"

"They are very nice," she replied.

"Nice?" he echoed, sure that his disbelief showed clearly on his face. "Maddening, perhaps. Maybe even exhausting, but nice?"

"I think they are very nice," Sophie said firmly.

Benedict started to smile, because he loved his family dearly, and he loved that Sophie was growing to love them, but then he realized that he was cutting off his nose to spite his face, because the more attached Sophie became to his family, the less likely she was to potentially shame herself in their eyes by agreeing to be his mistress.

Damn. He'd made a serious miscalculation last week. But he'd been so focused on getting her to come to London, and a position in his mother's household had seemed the only way to convince her to do it.

That, combined with a fair bit of coercion.

Damn. Damn. Damn. Why hadn't he coerced her into something that would segue a little more easily into his arms?

"You should thank your lucky stars that you have them," Sophie said, her voice more forceful than it had been all afternoon. "I'd give anything for—"

But she didn't finish her sentence.

"You'd give anything for what?" Benedict asked, surprised by how much he wanted to hear her answer.

She gazed soulfully out the window as she replied, "To have a family like yours."

"You have no one," he said, his words a statement, not a question.

"I've never had anyone."

"Not even your—" And then he remembered that she'd slipped and told him that her mother had died at her birth. "Sometimes," he said, keeping his voice purposefully light and gentle, "it's not so easy being a Bridgerton."

Her head slowly turned around. "I can't imagine anything nicer."

"There isn't anything nicer," he replied, "but that doesn't mean it's always easy."

"What do you mean?"

And Benedict found himself giving voice to feelings he'd never shared with any other living soul, not even—no, especially not his family. "To most of the world," he said, "I'm merely a Bridgerton. I'm not Benedict or Ben or even a gentleman of means and hopefully a bit of intelligence. I'm merely"—he smiled ruefully—"a Bridgerton. Specifically, Number Two."

Her lips trembled, then they smiled. "You're much more than that," she said.

"I'd like to think so, but most of the world doesn't see it that way."

"Most of the world are fools."

He laughed at that. There was nothing more fetching than Sophie with a scowl. "You will not find disagreement here," he said.

But then, just when he thought the conversation was over, she surprised him by saying, "You're nothing like the rest of your family."

"How so?" he asked, not quite meeting her gaze. He didn't want her to see just how important her reply was to him.

"Well, your brother Anthony . . ." Her face scrunched in thought. "His whole life has been altered by the fact that he's the eldest. He quite obviously feels a responsibility to your family that you do not."

"Now wait just one—"

"Don't interrupt," she said, placing a calming hand on his

chest. "I didn't say that you didn't love your family, or that you wouldn't give your life for any one of them. But it's different with your brother. He feels responsible, and I truly believe he would consider himself a failure if any of his siblings were unhappy."

"How many times have you met Anthony?" he muttered.

"Just once." The corners of her mouth tightened, as if she were suppressing a smile. "But that was all I needed. As for your younger brother, Colin . . . well, I haven't met him, but I've heard plenty—"

"From whom?"

"Everyone," she said. "Not to mention that he is forever being mentioned in *Whistledown*, which I must confess I've read for years."

"Then you knew about me before you met me," he said.

She nodded. "But I didn't *know* you. You're much more than Lady Whistledown realizes."

"Tell me," he said, placing his hand over hers. "What do you see?"

Sophie brought her eyes to his, gazed into those chocolatey depths, and saw something there she'd never dreamed existed. A tiny spark of vulnerability, of need.

He needed to know what she thought of him, that he was important to her. This man, so self-assured and so confident, needed her approval.

Maybe he needed *her*.

She curled her hand until their palms touched, then used her other index finger to trace circles and swirls on the fine kid of his glove. "You are . . ." she began, taking her time because she knew that every word weighed heavier in such a powerful moment. "You are not quite the man you present to the rest of the world. You'd like to be thought of as debonair and ironic and full of quick wit, and you *are* all those things, but underneath, you're so much more.

"You care," she said, aware that her voice had grown

raspy with emotion. "You care about your family, and you even care about me, although God knows I don't always deserve it."

"Always," he interrupted, raising her hand to his lips and kissing her palm with a fervency that sucked her breath away. "Always."

"And . . . and . . ." It was hard to continue when his eyes were on hers with such single-minded emotion.

"And what?" he whispered.

"Much of who you are comes from your family," she said, the words tumbling forth in a rush. "That much is true. You can't grow up with such love and loyalty and not become a better person because of it. But deep within you, in your heart, in your very soul, is the man you were born to be. *You*, not someone's son, not someone's brother. Just you."

Benedict watched her intently. He opened his mouth to speak, but he discovered that he had no words. There *were* no words for a moment like this.

"Deep inside," she murmured, "you've the soul of an artist."

"No," he said, shaking his head.

"Yes," she insisted. "I've seen your sketches. You're brilliant. I don't think I knew how much until I met your family. You captured them all perfectly, from the sly look in Francesca's smile to the mischief in the very way Hyacinth holds her shoulders."

"I've never shown anyone else my sketches," he admitted.

Her head snapped up. "You can't be serious."

He shook his head. "I haven't."

"But they're brilliant. *You're* brilliant. I'm sure your mother would love to see them."

"I don't know why," he said, feeling sheepish, "but I never wanted to share them."

"You shared them with me," she said softly.

"Somehow," he said, touching his fingers to her chin, "it felt right."

And then his heart skipped a beat, because all of a sudden *everything* felt right.

He loved her. He didn't know how it had happened, only that it was true.

It wasn't just that she was convenient. There had been lots of convenient women. Sophie was different. She made him laugh. She made him want to make *her* laugh. And when he was with her—Well, when he was with her he wanted her like hell, but during those few moments when his body managed to keep itself in check . . .

He was content.

It was strange, to find a woman who could make him happy just with her mere presence. He didn't even have to see her, or hear her voice, or even smell her scent. He just had to know that she was there.

If that wasn't love, he didn't know what was.

He stared down at her, trying to prolong the moment, to hold on to these few moments of complete perfection. Something softened in her eyes, and the color seemed to melt right then and there, from a shiny, glowing emerald to a soft and lilting moss. Her lips parted and softened, and he knew that he had to kiss her. Not that he wanted to, that he had to.

He needed her next to him, below him, on top of him.

He needed her in him, around him, a part of him.

He needed her the way he needed air.

And, he thought in that last rational moment before his lips found hers, he needed her right now.

Chapter 17

This Author has it on the finest authority that two days ago, whilst taking tea at Gunter's, Lady Penwood was hit on the side of her head with a flying biscuit.

This Author is unable to determine who threw the biscuit, but all suspicions point to the establishment's youngest patrons, Miss Felicity Featherington and Miss Hyacinth Bridgerton.

Lady Whistledown's Society Papers, 21 May 1817

Sophie had been kissed before—she had been kissed by Benedict before—but nothing, not a single moment of a single kiss, prepared her for this.

It wasn't a kiss. It was heaven.

He kissed her with an intensity she could barely comprehend, his lips teasing hers, stroking, nibbling, caressing. He stoked a fire within her, a desire to be loved, a need to love in return. And God help her, when he kissed her, all she wanted to do was kiss him back.

She heard him murmuring her name, but it barely registered over the roaring in her ears. This was desire. This was need. How foolish of her ever to think that she could deny this. How self-important to think that she could be stronger than passion.

"Sophie, Sophie," he said, over and over, his lips on her cheek, her neck, her ear. He said her name so many times it seemed to soak into her skin.

She felt his hands on the buttons of her dress, could feel the fabric loosening as each slipped through its buttonhole. This was everything she'd always sworn she would never do, and yet when her bodice tumbled to her waist, leaving her shamelessly exposed, she groaned his name and arched her back, offering herself to him like some sort of forbidden fruit.

Benedict stopped breathing when he saw her. He'd pictured this moment in his mind so many times—every night as he lay in bed, and in every dream when he actually slept. But this—reality—was far sweeter than a dream, and far more erotic.

His hand, which had been stroking the warm skin on her back, slowly slid over her rib cage. "You're so beautiful," he whispered, knowing that the words were hopelessly inadequate. As if mere words could describe what he felt. And then, when his trembling fingers finished their journey and cupped her breast, he let out a shuddering groan. Words were impossible now. His need for her was so intense, so primitive. It robbed him of his ability to speak. Hell, he could barely think.

He wasn't certain how this woman had come to mean so much to him. It seemed that one day she was a stranger, and the next she was as indispensable as air. And yet it hadn't happened in a blinding flash. It had been a slow, sneaky process, quietly coloring his emotions until he realized that without her, his life lacked all meaning.

He touched her chin, lifting her face until he could peer into her eyes. They seemed to glow from within, glistening with unshed tears. Her lips were trembling, too, and he knew that she was as affected by the moment as he.

He leaned forward . . . slowly, slowly. He wanted to give her the chance to say no. It would kill him if she did, but it would be far worse to listen to her regrets in the proverbial morning.

But she didn't say no, and when he was but a few inches away, her eyes closed and her head tilted slightly to the side, silently inviting him to kiss her.

It was remarkable, but every time he kissed her, her lips seemed to grow sweeter, her scent more beguiling. And his need grew, too. His blood was racing with desire, and it was taking his every last shred of restraint not to push her back onto the sofa and tear her clothes from her body.

That would come later, he thought with a secret smile. But this—surely her first time—would be slow and tender and everything a young girl dreamed.

Well, maybe not. His smile turned into an outright grin. Half the things he was going to do to her, she wouldn't have even *thought* to dream about.

"What are you smiling about?" she asked.

He drew back a few inches, cupping her face with both hands. "How did you know I was smiling?"

"I could feel it on my lips."

He brought a finger to those lips, tracing the outline, then running the edge of his fingernail along the plump skin. "You make me smile," he whispered. "When you don't make me want to scream, you make me smile."

Her lips trembled, and her breath was hot and moist against his finger. He took her hand and brought it to his mouth, rubbing one finger against his lips in much the same way he had done with hers. But as he watched her eyes widen, he dipped her finger into his mouth, softly sucking at the fingertip, tickling her skin with his teeth and tongue.

She gasped, and the sound was sweet and erotic at the same time.

There were a thousand things that Benedict wanted to ask her— How did she feel? What did she feel? But he was so damned afraid that she'd change her mind if he gave her the opportunity to put any of her thoughts into words. And so instead of questions, he gave her kisses, returning his lips to hers in a searing, barely controlled dance of desire.

He murmured her name like a benediction as he lowered her onto the sofa, her bare back rubbing up against the upholstery. "I want you," he groaned. "You have no idea. No idea."

Her only response was a soft mewling sound that came from deep in her throat. For some reason that was like oil on the fire within him, and his fingers clutched at her even tighter, pressing into her skin, as his lips traveled down the swanlike column of her throat.

He moved lower, lower, burning a hot trail on her skin, pausing only briefly when he reached the gentle swell of her breast. She was completely beneath him now, her eyes glazed with desire, and it was so much better than any of his dreams.

And oh, how he'd dreamed of her.

With a low, possessive growl, Benedict took her nipple into his mouth. She let out a soft squeal, and he was unable to suppress his own low rumble of satisfaction. "Shhh," he crooned, "just let me—"

"But—"

He pressed one of his fingers against her lips, probably a little too roughly, but it was getting harder and harder to control his movements. "Don't think," he murmured. "Just lie back and let me pleasure you."

She looked dubious, but when he moved his mouth to her other breast and renewed his sensual onslaught, her eyes grew dazed, her lips parted, and her head lolled back against the cushions.

"Do you like this?" he whispered, tracing the peak of her breast with his tongue.

Sophie couldn't quite manage to open her eyes, but she nodded.

"Do you like this?" Now his tongue moved to the underside of her breast, and he nibbled the sensitive skin over her rib cage.

Her breath shallow and fast, she nodded again.

"What about this?" He pushed her dress further down, nibbling a trail along her skin until he reached her navel.

This time Sophie couldn't even manage a nod. Dear God, she was practically naked before him, and all she could do was moan and sigh and beg for more.

"I need you," she panted.

His words were murmured into the soft skin of her abdomen. "I know."

Sophie squirmed beneath him, unnerved by this primitive need to move. Something very strange was growing within her, something hot and tingling. It was as if she were growing, getting ready to burst through her skin. It was as if, after twenty-two years of life, she were finally coming alive.

She wanted desperately to feel his skin, and she grabbed at the fine linen of his shirt, bunching it in her hands until it came loose of his breeches. She touched him, skimming her hands along his lower back, surprised and delighted when his muscles quivered beneath her fingers.

"Ah, Sophie," he grunted, shuddering as her hands slipped under his shirt to caress his skin.

His reaction emboldened her, and she stroked him more, moving up until she reached his shoulders, broad and firmly muscled.

He groaned again, then cursed under his breath as he lifted himself off of her. "Damn thing is in the way," he muttered, tearing the shirt off and flinging it across the room. Sophie had just an instant to stare at his bare chest before he was atop her again, and this time they were skin against skin.

It was the most glorious feeling she could ever imagine.

He was so warm, and even though his muscles were hard and powerful, his skin was seductively soft. He even smelled good, a warm masculine mixture of sandalwood and soap.

Sophie touched her fingers to his hair as he moved to nuzzle her neck. It was thick and springy, and it tickled her chin as he tickled her neck. "Oh, Benedict," she sighed. "This is so perfect. I can't imagine anything better."

He looked up, his dark eyes as wicked as his smile. "I can."

She felt her lips part and knew she must look terribly foolish, just lying there staring at him like an idiot.

"Just you wait," he said. "Just you wait."

"But— Oh!" She let out a squeal as he flipped off her shoes. One of his hands wrapped around her ankle, then teased its way up her leg.

"Did you imagine this?" he asked, tracing the crease at the back of her knee.

She shook her head frantically, trying not to squirm.

"Really?" he murmured. "Then I'm sure you didn't imagine *this*." He reached up and unsnapped her garters.

"Oh, Benedict, you mustn't—"

"Oh, no, I *must*." He slid her stockings down her legs with agonizing slowness. "I really must."

Sophie watched with openmouthed delight as he tossed them over his head. Her stockings weren't of the highest quality, but they were nonetheless fairly light, and they floated through the air like dandelion tufts until they landed, one on a lamp and the other on the floor.

Then, while she was still laughing and looking at the stocking, hanging drunkenly from the lampshade, he sneaked up on her, sliding his hands back up her legs until they reached all the way to her thighs.

"I daresay no one has ever touched you here," he said wickedly.

Sophie shook her head.

"And I daresay you never imagined it."

She shook her head again.

"If you didn't imagine this . . ." He squeezed her thighs, causing her to squeal and arch off the sofa. ". . . then I'm sure you won't have imagined *this*." He trailed his fingers ever upward as he spoke, the rounded curves of his nails lightly grazing her skin until he reached the soft thatch of her womanhood.

"Oh, no," she said, more out of reflex than anything else. "You can't—"

"Oh, but I can. I assure you."

"But— Ooooooh." It was suddenly as if her brain had flown right out the window, because it was near impossible to think of anything while his fingers were tickling her. Well, almost anything. She seemed able to think about how utterly naughty this was and how very much she didn't want him to stop.

"What are you doing to me?" she gasped, her every muscle tightening as he moved his fingers in a particularly wicked manner.

"Everything," he returned, capturing her lips with his. "Anything you want."

"I want— Oh!"

"Like that, do you?" His words were murmured against her cheek.

"I don't know what I want," she breathed.

"I do." He moved to her ear, nibbling softly on her lobe. "I know exactly what you want. Trust me."

And it was as easy as that. She gave herself over to him completely—not that she hadn't been nearly to that point already. But when he said, "Trust me," and she realized that she did, something changed slightly inside. She was ready for this. It was still wrong, but she was ready, and she wanted it, and for once in her life she was going to do something wild and crazy and completely out of character.

Just because she wanted to.

As if he'd read her thoughts, he pulled away a few inches and cupped one cheek with his large hand. "If you want me to stop," he said, his voice achingly hoarse, "you need to tell me now. Not in ten minutes, not even in one. It has to be now."

Touched that he would even take the time to ask, she reached up and cupped his cheek in the same way he held hers. But when she opened her mouth to speak, the only word she could manage was, "Please."

His eyes flared with need, and then, as if something snapped within him, he changed in an instant. Gone was the gentle, languorous lover. In his place was a man gripped by desire. His hands were everywhere, on her legs, around her waist, touching her face. And before Sophie knew it, her dress was gone, on the floor next to one of her stockings. She was completely nude, and it felt very odd but somehow also very right as long as he was touching her.

The sofa was narrow, but that didn't seem to matter as Benedict yanked off his boots and breeches. He perched alongside her as his boots went flying, unable to stop touching her, even as he divested himself of his clothing. It took longer to get naked, but on the other hand, he had the oddest notion that he might perish on the spot if he moved from her side.

He'd thought he'd wanted a woman before. He'd thought he'd needed one. But this—this went beyond both. This was spiritual. This was in his soul.

His clothes finally gone, he lay back on top of her, pausing for one shuddering moment to savor the feel of her beneath him, skin to skin, head to toe. He was hard as a rock, harder than he could ever remember, but he fought against his impulses, and tried to move slowly.

This was her first time. It had to be perfect.

Or if not perfect, then damn good.

He snaked a hand between them and touched her. She was ready—more than ready for him. He slipped one finger inside of her, grinning with satisfaction as her entire body jerked and tensed around him.

"That's very—" Her voice was raspy, her breathing labored. "Very—"

"Strange?" he finished for her.

She nodded.

He smiled. Slowly, like a cat. "You'll get used to it," he promised. "I plan to get you very used to it."

Sophie's head lolled back. This was madness. Fever. Something was building inside of her, deep in her gut, coiling, pulsing, making her rigid. It was something that needed release, something that grabbed at her, and yet even with all this pressure, it felt so spectacularly wonderful, as if she'd been born for this very moment.

"Oh, Benedict," she sighed. "Oh, my love."

He froze—just for a fraction of a second, but it was long enough for her to know that he'd heard her. But he didn't say a word, just kissed her neck and squeezed her leg as he positioned himself between her thighs and nudged at her entrance.

Her lips parted with shock.

"Don't worry," he said in an amused voice, reading her mind as always. "It will work."

"But—"

"Trust me," he said, the words murmured against her lips.

Slowly, she felt him entering her. She was being stretched, invaded, and yet she wouldn't say it felt bad, exactly. It was . . . It was . . .

He touched her cheek. "You look serious."

"I'm trying to decide how this feels," she admitted.

"If you have the presence of mind to do that, then I'm certainly not doing a good enough job."

Startled, she looked up. He was smiling at her, that crooked grin that never failed to reduce her to mush.

"Stop thinking so hard," he whispered.

"But it's difficult not to— Oh!" And then her eyes rolled back as she arched beneath him.

Benedict buried his head in her neck so she wouldn't see

his amused expression. It seemed the best way for him to keep her from overanalyzing a moment that should have been pure sensation and emotion was for him to keep moving.

And he did. Inexorably forward, sliding in and out until he reached the fragile barrier of her maidenhead.

He winced. He'd never been with a virgin before. He'd heard it hurt, that there was nothing a man could do to eliminate the pain for the woman, but surely if he was gentle, it would go easier for her.

He looked down. Her face was flushed, and her breath was rapid. Her eyes were glazed, dazed, clearly rapt with passion.

It fueled his own fire. God, he wanted her so badly his bones ached.

"This might hurt," he lied. It *would* hurt. But he was stuck between wanting to give her the truth so that she would be prepared and giving her the softer version so that she would not be nervous.

"I don't care," she gasped. "Please. I need you."

Benedict leaned down for one final, searing kiss as his hips surged forward. He felt her stiffen slightly around him as he broke through her maidenhead, and he bit—he actually *bit* his hand to keep himself from coming at that very second.

It was like he was a green lad of sixteen, not an experienced man of thirty.

She did this to him. Only her. It was a humbling thought.

Gritting his teeth against his baser urges, Benedict began to move within her, slowly stroking when what he really wanted to do was let go completely.

"Sophie, Sophie," he grunted, repeating her name, trying to remind himself that this time was about *her*. He was here to please *her* needs, not his own.

It would be perfect. It had to be perfect. He needed her to love this. He needed her to love *him*.

She was quickening beneath him, and every wiggle, every squirm whipped up his own frenzy of desire. He was trying to be extra gentle for her, but she was making it so damn hard to hold back. Her hands were everywhere—on his hips, on his back, squeezing his shoulders.

"Sophie," he moaned again. He couldn't hold off much longer. He wasn't strong enough. He wasn't noble enough. He wasn't—

"Ohhhhhhhhhhhh!"

She convulsed beneath him, her body arching off the sofa as she screamed. Her fingers bit into his back, nails raking his skin, but he didn't care. All he knew was that she'd found her release, and it was good, and for the love of God, he could finally—

"Ahhhhhhhhhhhh!"

He exploded. There was simply no other word for it.

He couldn't stop moving, couldn't stop shaking, and then, in an instant, he collapsed, dimly aware that he was probably crushing her, but unable to move a single muscle.

He should say something, tell her something about how wonderful it had been. But his tongue felt thick and his lips felt heavy, and on top of all that, he could barely open his eyes. Pretty words would have to wait. He was only a man, and he had to catch his breath.

"Benedict?" she whispered.

He flopped his hand slightly against her. It was the only thing he could manage to indicate that he'd heard.

"Is it always like this?"

He shook his head, hoping that she'd feel the motion and know what it meant.

She sighed and seemed to sink deeper into the cushions. "I didn't think so."

Benedict kissed the side of her head, which was all that he could reach. No, it wasn't always like this. He'd dreamed of her so many times, but this . . . This . . .

This was more than dreams.

* * *

Sophie wouldn't have thought it possible, but she must've dozed off, even with the thrilling weight of Benedict pressing her down against the sofa, making it slightly difficult to breathe. He must've fallen asleep, too, and she woke when he woke, aroused by the sudden rush of cool air when he lifted himself off of her body.

He placed a blanket on top of her before she even had a chance to be embarrassed by her nakedness. She smiled even as she blushed, for there was little that could be done to ease her embarrassment. Not that she regretted her actions. But a woman didn't lose her virginity on a sofa and not feel a little bit embarrassed. It simply wasn't possible.

Still, the blanket had been a thoughtful gesture. Not a surprising one, though. Benedict was a thoughtful man.

He obviously didn't share her modesty, though, because he made no attempt to cover himself as he crossed the room and gathered his carelessly flung garments. Sophie stared shamelessly as pulled on his breeches. He stood straight and proud, and the smile he gave her when he caught her watching was warm and direct.

God, how she loved this man.

"How do you feel?" he asked.

"Fine," she answered. "Good." She smiled shyly. "Splendid."

He picked up his shirt and stuck one arm into it. "I'll send someone over to collect your belongings."

Sophie blinked. "What do you mean?"

"Don't worry, I'll make sure he's discreet. I know it might be embarrassing for you now that you know my family."

Sophie clutched the blanket to her, wishing that her dress wasn't out of reach. Because she suddenly felt ashamed. She'd done the one thing she'd always sworn she would never do, and now Benedict assumed she would be his mistress. And why shouldn't he? It was a fairly natural assumption.

"Please don't send anyone over," she said, her voice small.

He glanced at her in surprise. "You'd rather go yourself?"

"I'd rather my things stayed where they were," she said softly. It was so much easier saying that than telling him directly that she would not become his mistress.

Once, she could forgive. Once, she could even cherish. But a lifetime with a man who was not her husband—that she knew she could not do.

Sophie looked down at her belly, praying that there would be no child to be brought into the world illegitimately.

"What are you telling me?" he said, his eyes intent upon her face.

Damn. He wasn't going to allow her to take the easy way out. "I'm saying," she said, gulping against the boulder-sized lump that had suddenly developed in her throat, "that I cannot be your mistress."

"What do you call this?" he asked in a tight voice, waving his arm at her.

"I call it a lapse in judgment," she said, not meeting his eyes.

"Oh, so I'm a lapse?" he said, his tone unnaturally pleasant. "How nice. I don't believe I've ever been someone's lapse before."

"You know that's not the way I meant it."

"Do I?" He grabbed one of his boots and perched on the arm of a chair so that he could yank it on. "Frankly, my dear, I have no idea what you mean anymore."

"I shouldn't have done this—"

He whipped his head around to face her, his hot, flashing eyes at odds with his bland smile. "Now I'm a *shouldn't?* Excellent. Even better than a lapse. Shouldn't sounds much naughtier, don't you think? A lapse is merely a mistake."

"There is no need to be so ugly about this."

He cocked his head to the side as if he were truly considering her words. "Is that what I'm being? I rather thought

I was acting in a most friendly and understanding manner. Look, no yelling, no histrionics . . ."

"I'd prefer yelling and histrionics to *this*."

He scooped up her dress and threw it at her, none too gently. "Well, we don't always get what we prefer, do we, Miss Beckett? I can certainly attest to that."

She grabbed her dress and stuffed it under the covers with her, hoping that she'd eventually find a way to don it without moving the blanket.

"It'll be a neat trick if you figure out how to do it," he said, giving her a condescending glance.

She glared at him. "I'm not asking you to apologize."

"Well, that's a relief. I doubt I could find the words."

"Please don't be so sarcastic."

His smile was mocking in the extreme. "You're hardly in a position to ask me anything."

"Benedict . . ."

He loomed over her, leering rudely. "Except, of course, to rejoin you, which I'd gladly do."

She said nothing.

"Do you understand," he said, his eyes softening slightly, "what it feels like to be pushed away? How many times do you expect you can reject me before I stop trying?"

"It's not that I want to—"

"Oh, stop with that old excuse. It's grown tired. If you wanted to be with me, you would be with me. When you say no, it's because you want to say no."

"You don't understand," she said in a low voice. "You've always been in a position where you could do what you wanted. Some of us don't have that luxury."

"Silly me. I thought I was offering you that very luxury."

"The luxury to be your mistress," she said bitterly.

He crossed his arms, his lips twisting as he said, "You won't have to do anything you haven't already done."

"I got carried away," Sophie said slowly, trying to ignore his insult. It was no more than she deserved. She had slept with him. Why shouldn't he think she would be his mistress? "I made a mistake," she continued. "But that doesn't mean I should do it again."

"I can offer you a better life," he said in a low voice.

She shook her head. "I won't be your mistress. I won't be any man's mistress."

Benedict's lips parted with shock as he digested her words. "Sophie," he said incredulously, "you know I cannot *marry* you."

"Of course I know that," she snapped. "I'm a servant, not an idiot."

Benedict tried for a moment to put himself in her shoes. He knew she wanted respectability, but she had to know that he could not give it to her. "It would be hard for you as well," he said softly, "even if I were to marry you. You would not be accepted. The *ton* can be cruel."

Sophie let out a loud, hollow laugh. "I know," she said, her smile utterly humorless. "Believe me, I know."

"Then why—"

"Grant me a favor," she interrupted, turning her face so that she was no longer looking at him. "Find someone to marry. Find someone acceptable, who will make you happy. And then leave me alone."

Her words struck a chord, and Benedict was suddenly reminded of the lady from the masquerade. She had been of his world, his class. She would have been acceptable. And he realized, as he stood there, staring down at Sophie, who was huddled on the sofa, trying not to look at him, that she was the one he'd always pictured in his mind, whenever he thought to the future. Whenever he imagined himself with a wife and children.

He'd spent the last two years with one eye on every door, always waiting for his lady in silver to enter the room. He felt silly sometimes, even stupid, but he'd never been able to erase her from his thoughts.

Or purge the dream—the one in which he pledged his troth to her, and they lived happily ever after.

It was a silly fantasy for a man of his reputation, sickly sweet and sentimental, but he hadn't been able to help himself. That's what came from growing up in a large and loving family—one tended to want the same for oneself.

But the woman from the masquerade had become barely more than a mirage. Hell, he didn't even know her name. And Sophie was *here*.

He couldn't marry her, but that didn't mean they couldn't be together. It would mean compromise, mostly on her part, he admitted. But they could do it. And they'd certainly be happier than if they remained apart.

"Sophie," he began, "I know the situation is not ideal—"

"Don't," she interrupted, her voice low, barely audible.

"If you'd only listen—"

"*Please*. Don't."

"But you're not—"

"Stop!" she said, her voice rising perilously in volume.

She was holding her shoulders so tightly they were practically at her ears, but Benedict forged on, anyway. He loved her. He needed her. He had to make her see reason. "Sophie, I know you'll agree if—"

"I won't have an illegitimate child!" she finally yelled, struggling to keep the blanket around her as she rose to her feet. "I won't do it! I love you, but not that much. I don't love anyone that much."

His eyes fell to her midsection. "It may very well be too late for that, Sophie."

"I know," she said quietly, "and it's already eating me up inside."

"Regrets have a way of doing that."

She looked away. "I don't regret what we did. I wish I could. I know I should. But I can't."

Benedict just stared at her. He wanted to understand her,

but he just couldn't grasp how she could be so adamant about not wanting to be his mistress and have his children and at the same time *not* regret their lovemaking.

How could she say she loved him? It made the pain that much more intense.

"If we don't have a child," she said quietly, "then I shall consider myself very lucky. And I won't tempt the fates again."

"No, you'll merely tempt *me*," he said, hearing the sneer in his voice and hating it.

She ignored him, drawing the blanket closer around her as she stared sightlessly at a painting on the wall. "I'll have a memory I will forever cherish. And that, I suppose, is why I can't regret what we did."

"It won't keep you warm at night."

"No," she agreed sadly, "but it will keep my dreams full."

"You're a coward," he accused. "A coward for not chasing after those dreams."

She turned around. "No," she said, her voice remarkably even considering the way he was glaring at her. "What I am is a bastard. And before you say you don't care, let me assure you that I do. And so does everyone else. Not a day has gone by that I am not in some way reminded of the baseness of my birth."

"Sophie . . ."

"If I have a child," she said, her voice starting to crack, "do you know how much I would love it? More than life, more than breath, more than anything. How could I hurt my own child the way I've been hurt? How could I subject her to the same kind of pain?"

"Would you reject your child?"

"Of course not!"

"Then she wouldn't feel the same sort of pain," Benedict said with a shrug. "Because I wouldn't reject her either."

"You don't understand," she said, the words ending on a whimper.

He pretended he hadn't heard her. "Am I correct in assuming that *you* were rejected by your parents?"

Her smile was tight and ironic. "Not precisely. Ignored would be a better description."

"Sophie," he said, rushing toward her and gathering her in his arms, "you don't have to repeat the mistakes of your parents."

"I know," she said sadly, not struggling in his embrace, but not returning it either. "And that's why I cannot be your mistress. I won't relive my mother's life."

"You wouldn't—"

"They say that a smart person learns from her mistakes," she interrupted, her voice forcefully ending his protest. "But a truly smart person learns from other people's mistakes." She pulled away, then turned to face him. "I'd like to think I'm a truly smart person. Please don't take that away from me."

There was a desperate, almost palpable, pain in her eyes. It hit him in the chest, and he staggered back a step.

"I'd like to get dressed," she said, turning away. "I think you should leave."

He stared at her back for several seconds before saying, "I could make you change your mind. I could kiss you, and you would—"

"You wouldn't," she said, not moving a muscle. "It isn't in you."

"It *is*."

"You would kiss me, and then you would hate yourself. And it would only take a second."

He left without another word, letting the click of the door signal his departure.

Inside the room, Sophie's quivering hands dropped the blanket, and she crumpled onto the sofa, forever staining its delicate fabric with her tears.

Chapter 18

Pickings have been slim this past fortnight for marriage-minded misses and their mamas. The crop of bachelors is low to begin with this season, as two of 1816's most eligible, the Duke of Ashbourne and the Earl of Macclesfield, got themselves leg-shackled last year.

To make matters worse, the two unmarried Bridgerton brothers (discounting Gregory, who is only sixteen and hardly in a position to aid any poor, young misses on the marriage mart) have made themselves very scarce. Colin, This Author is told, is out of town, possibly in Wales or Scotland (although no one seems to know why he would go to Wales or Scotland in the middle of the season). Benedict's story is more puzzling. He is apparently in London, but he eschews all polite social gatherings in favor of less genteel milieus.

Although if truth be told, This Author should not give the impression that the aforementioned Mr. Bridgerton has been spending his every waking hour in debauched abandon. If accounts are correct, he has spent most of the past fortnight in his lodgings on Bruton Street.

As there have been no rumors that he is ill, This Author can only assume that he has finally come to the conclusion that the London season is utterly dull and not worth his time.

Smart man, indeed.

Lady Whistledown's Society Papers, 9 June 1817

Sophie didn't see Benedict for a full fortnight. She didn't know whether to be pleased, surprised, or disappointed. She didn't know whether she *was* pleased, surprised, or disappointed.

She didn't know anything these days. Half the time she felt like she didn't even know herself.

She was certain that she had made the right decision in yet again refusing Benedict's offer. She knew it in her head, and even though she ached for the man she loved, she knew it in her heart. She had suffered too much pain from her bastardy ever to risk imposing the same on a child, especially one of her own.

No, that was not true. She had risked it once. And she couldn't quite make herself regret it. The memory was too precious. But that didn't mean she should do it again.

But if she was so certain that she'd done the right thing, why did it hurt so much? It was as if her heart were perpetually breaking. Every day, it tore some more, and every day, Sophie told herself that it could not get worse, that surely her heart was finished breaking, that it was finally well and fully broken, and yet every night she cried herself to sleep, aching for Benedict.

And every day she felt even worse.

Her tension was intensified by the fact that she was terrified to step outside the house. Posy would surely be looking for her, and Sophie thought it best if Posy didn't find her.

Not that she thought Posy was likely to reveal her presence here in London to Araminta; Sophie knew Posy well enough to trust that Posy would never deliberately break a promise. And Posy's nod when Sophie had been frantically shaking her head could definitely be considered a promise.

But as true of heart as Posy was when it came to keeping promises, the same could not, unfortunately, be said of her lips. And Sophie could easily imagine a scenario—many scenarios as a matter of fact—in which Posy would accidentally blurt out that she'd seen Sophie. Which meant that Sophie's one big advantage was that Posy didn't know where Sophie was staying. For all she knew, Sophie had just been out for a stroll. Or maybe Sophie had come to spy on Araminta.

In all truth, that seemed an awful lot more plausible than the truth, which was that Sophie just happened to have been blackmailed into taking a job as a lady's maid just down the street.

And so, Sophie's emotions kept darting back and forth from melancholy to nervous, brokenhearted to downright fearful.

She'd managed to keep most of this to herself, but she knew she had grown distracted and quiet, and she also knew that Lady Bridgerton and her daughters had noticed it. They looked at her with concerned expressions, spoke with an extra gentleness. And they kept wondering why she did not come to tea.

"Sophie! There you are!"

Sophie had been hurrying to her room, where a small pile of mending awaited, but Lady Bridgerton had caught her in the hall.

She stopped and tried to manage a smile of greeting as she bobbed a curtsy. "Good afternoon, Lady Bridgerton."

"Good afternoon, Sophie. I have been looking all over for you."

Sophie stared at her blankly. She seemed to do a lot of that lately. It was difficult to focus on anything. "You have?" she asked.

"Yes. I was wondering why you haven't been to tea all week. You know that you are always invited when we are taking it informally."

Sophie felt her cheeks grow warm. She'd been avoiding tea because it was just so hard to be in the same room with all those Bridgertons at once and not to think of Benedict.

They all looked so alike, and whenever they were together they were such a family.

It forced Sophie to remember everything that she didn't have, reminded her of what she'd never have: a family of her own.

Someone to love. Someone who'd love her. All within the bounds of respectability and marriage.

She supposed there were women who could throw over respectability for passion and love. A very large part of her wished she were one of those women. But she was not. Love could not conquer all. At least not for her.

"I've been very busy," she finally said to Lady Bridgerton.

Lady Bridgerton just smiled at her—a small, vaguely inquisitive smile, imposing a silence that forced Sophie to say more.

"With the mending," she added.

"How terrible for you. I wasn't aware that we'd poked holes in quite so many stockings."

"Oh, you haven't!" Sophie replied, biting her tongue the minute she said it. There went her excuse. "I have some mending of my own," she improvised, gulping as she realized how bad that sounded. Lady Bridgerton well knew that Sophie had no clothes other than the ones she had given her, which were all, needless to say, in perfect condition. And besides, it was very bad form for Sophie to be doing her own mending during the day, when she was meant to be waiting on the girls. Lady Bridgerton was an understanding employer; she probably wouldn't have minded, but it went against Sophie's own code of ethics. She'd been given a job—a good one, even if it did involve getting her heart broken on a day to day basis—and she took pride in her work.

"I see," Lady Bridgerton said, that enigmatic smile still in place on her face. "You may, of course, bring your own mending to tea."

"Oh, but I could not dream of it."

"But I am telling you that you *can*."

And Sophie could tell by the tone of her voice that what she was really saying was that she *must*.

"Of course," Sophie murmured, and followed her into the upstairs sitting room.

The girls were all there, in their usual places, bickering and smiling and tossing jokes (although thankfully no scones.) The eldest Bridgerton daughter, Daphne—now the Duchess of Hastings—was there as well, with her youngest daughter, Caroline, in her arms.

"Sophie!" Hyacinth said with a beam. "I thought you must have been ill."

"But you just saw me this morning," Sophie reminded her, "when I dressed your hair."

"Yes, but you didn't seem quite yourself."

Sophie had no suitable reply, since she really *hadn't* been quite herself. She couldn't very well contradict the truth. So she just sat in a chair and nodded when Francesca inquired if she wanted some tea.

"Penelope Featherington said she would drop by today," Eloise said to her mother just as Sophie was taking her first sip. Sophie had never met Penelope, but she was frequently written about in *Whistledown*, and she knew that she and Eloise were fast friends.

"Has anyone noticed that Benedict hasn't visited in some time?" Hyacinth asked.

Sophie jabbed her finger but thankfully managed to keep from yelping with pain.

"He hasn't been by to see Simon and me, either," Daphne said.

"Well, he told me he would help me with my arithmetic," Hyacinth grumbled, "and he has most certainly reneged on his word."

"I'm sure it has merely slipped his mind," Lady Bridgerton said diplomatically. "Perhaps if you sent him a note."

"Or simply banged on his door," Francesca said, giving her eyes a slight roll. "It's not as if he lives very far away."

"I am an unmarried female," Hyacinth said with a huff. "I cannot visit bachelor lodgings."

Sophie coughed.

"You're fourteen," Francesca said disdainfully.

"Nevertheless!"

"You should ask Simon for help, anyway," Daphne said. "He's much better with numbers than Benedict."

"You know, she's right," Hyacinth said, looking at her mother after shooting one last glare at Francesca. "Pity for Benedict. He's completely without use to me now."

They all giggled, because they knew she was joking. Except for Sophie, who didn't think she knew how to giggle anymore.

"But in all seriousness," Hyacinth continued, "what *is* he good at? Simon's better at numbers, and Anthony knows more of history. Colin's funnier, of course, and—"

"Art," Sophie interrupted in a sharp voice, a little irritated that Benedict's own family didn't see his individuality and strengths.

Hyacinth looked at her in surprise. "I beg your pardon?"

"He's good at art," Sophie repeated. "Quite a bit better than any of you, I imagine."

That got everyone's attention, because while Sophie had let them see her naturally dry wit, she was generally soft-spoken, and she certainly had never said a sharp word to any of them.

"I didn't even know he drew," Daphne said with quiet interest. "Or does he paint?"

Sophie glanced at her. Of the Bridgerton women, she knew Daphne the least, but it would have been impossible to miss the look of sharp intelligence in her eyes. Daphne was curious about her brother's hidden talent, she wanted to know why she didn't know about it, and most of all, she wanted to know why Sophie *did*.

In less than a second Sophie was able to see all of that in the young duchess's eyes. And in less than a second she decided that she'd made a mistake. If Benedict hadn't told his family about his art, then it wasn't her place to do so.

"He draws," she finally said, in a voice that she hoped was curt enough to prevent further questions.

It was. No one said a word, although five pairs of eyes remained focused quite intently on her face.

"He sketches," Sophie muttered.

She looked from face to face. Eloise's eyes were blinking rapidly. Lady Bridgerton wasn't blinking at all. "He's quite good," Sophie muttered, mentally kicking herself even as she said it. There was something about silence among the Bridgertons that compelled her to fill the void.

Finally, after the longest moment of silence ever to fill the space of a second, Lady Bridgerton cleared her throat and said, "I should like to see one of his sketches." She dabbed a napkin to her lips even though she hadn't taken a sip of her tea. "Provided, of course, that he cares to share it with me."

Sophie stood up. "I think I should go."

Lady Bridgerton speared her with her eyes. "Please," she said, in a voice that was velvet over steel, "stay."

Sophie sat back down.

Eloise jumped to her feet. "I think I hear Penelope."

"You do not," Hyacinth said.

"Why would I lie?"

"I certainly don't know, but—"

The butler appeared in the doorway. "Miss Penelope Featherington," he intoned.

"See," Eloise shot at Hyacinth.

"Is this a bad time?" Penelope asked.

"No," Daphne replied with a small, vaguely amused smile, "just an odd one."

"Oh. Well, I could come back later, I suppose."

"Of course not," Lady Bridgerton said. "Please sit down and have some tea."

Sophie watched as the young woman took a seat on the sofa next to Francesca. Penelope was no sophisticated beauty, but she was rather fetching in her own, uncomplicated way. Her hair was a brownish red, and her cheeks were lightly dusted with freckles. Her complexion was a touch sallow, although Sophie had a suspicion that that had more to do with her unattractive yellow frock than anything else.

Come to think of it, she rather thought that she'd read something in Lady Whistledown's column about Penelope's awful clothes. Pity the poor girl couldn't talk her mother into letting her wear blue.

But as Sophie surreptitiously studied Penelope, she became aware that Penelope was not-so-surreptitiously studying her.

"Have we met?" Penelope suddenly asked.

Sophie was suddenly gripped by an awful, premonition-like feeling. Or maybe it was déjà vu. "I don't think so," she said quickly.

Penelope's gaze didn't waver from her face. "Are you certain?"

"I—I don't see how we could have done."

Penelope let out a little breath and shook her head, as if clearing cobwebs from her mind. "I'm sure you're correct. But there is something terribly familiar about you."

"Sophie is our new lady's maid," Hyacinth said, as if that would explain anything. "She usually joins us for tea when we're only family."

Sophie watched Penelope as she murmured something in response, and then suddenly it hit her. She *had* seen Penelope before! It had been at the masquerade, probably no more than ten seconds before she'd met Benedict.

She'd just made her entrance, and the young men who had quickly surrounded her had still been making their way to her side. Penelope had been standing right there, dressed in some rather strange green costume with a funny hat. For some reason she hadn't been wearing a mask. Sophie had stared at her for a moment, trying to figure out what her costume was meant to be, when a young gentleman had bumped into Penelope, nearly knocking her to the floor.

Sophie had reached out and helped her up, and had just managed to say something like, "There you are," when several more gentlemen had rushed in, separating the two women.

Then Benedict had arrived, and Sophie had had eyes for no one but him. Penelope—and the abominable way she had been treated by the young gentlemen at the masquerade—had been forgotten until this very moment.

And clearly the event had remained buried at the back of Penelope's mind as well.

"I'm sure I must be mistaken," Penelope said as she accepted a cup of tea from Francesca. "It's not your looks, precisely, but rather the way you hold yourself, if that makes any sense."

Sophie decided that a smooth intervention was necessary and so she pasted on her best conversational smile, and said, "I shall take that as a compliment, since I am sure that the ladies of your acquaintance are gracious and kind indeed."

The minute she shut her mouth, however, she realized that that had been overkill. Francesca was looking at her as if she'd sprouted horns, and the corners of Lady Bridgerton's mouth were twitching as she said, "Why, Sophie, I vow that is the longest sentence you have uttered in a fortnight."

Sophie lifted her teacup to her face and mumbled, "I haven't been feeling well."

"Oh!" Hyacinth suddenly blurted out. "I hope you are not feeling too sickly, because I was hoping you could help me this evening."

"Of course," Sophie said, eager for an excuse to turn away from Penelope, who was still studying her as if she were a human puzzle. "What is it you need?"

"I have promised to entertain my cousins this eve."

"Oh, that's right," Lady Bridgerton said, setting her saucer down on the table. "I'd nearly forgotten."

Hyacinth nodded. "Could you help? There are four of them, and I'm sure to be overrun."

"Of course," Sophie said. "How old are they?"

Hyacinth shrugged.

"Between the ages of six and ten," Lady Bridgerton said with a disapproving expression. "You should know that, Hyacinth." She turned to Sophie and added, "They are the children of my youngest sister."

Sophie said to Hyacinth, "Fetch me when they arrive. I love children and would be happy to help."

"Excellent," Hyacinth said, clasping her hands together. "They are so young and active. They would have worn me out."

"Hyacinth," Francesca said, "you're hardly old and decrepit."

"When was the last time you spent two hours with four children under the age of ten?"

"Stop," Sophie said, laughing for the first time in two weeks. "I'll help. No one will be worn-out. And you should come, too, Francesca. We'll have a lovely time, I'm sure."

"Are you—" Penelope started to say something, then cut herself off. "Never mind."

But when Sophie looked over at her, she was still staring at her face with a most perplexed expression. Penelope opened her mouth, closed it, then opened it again, saying, "I *know* I know you."

"I'm sure she's right," Eloise said with a jaunty grin. "Penelope never forgets a face."

Sophie blanched.

"Are you quite all right?" Lady Bridgerton asked, leaning forward. "You don't look well."

"I think something didn't agree with me," Sophie hastily

lied, clutching her stomach for effect. "Perhaps the milk was off."

"Oh, dear," Daphne said with a concerned frown as she looked down at her baby. "I gave some to Caroline."

"It tasted fine to me," Hyacinth said.

"It might have been something from this morning," Sophie said, not wanting Daphne to worry. "But all the same, I think I had better lie down." She stood and took a step toward the door. "If that is agreeable to you, Lady Bridgerton."

"Of course," she replied. "I hope you feel better soon."

"I'm sure I will," Sophie said, quite truthfully. She'd feel better just as soon as she left Penelope Featherington's line of vision.

"I'll come get you when my cousins arrive," Hyacinth called out.

"If you're feeling better," Lady Bridgerton added.

Sophie nodded and hurried out of the room, but as she left, she caught sight of Penelope Featherington watching her with a most intent expression, leaving Sophie filled with a horrible sense of dread.

Benedict had been in a bad mood for two weeks. And, he thought as he trudged down the pavement toward his mother's house, his bad mood was about to get worse. He'd been avoiding coming here because he didn't want to see Sophie; he didn't want to see his mother, who was sure to sense his bad mood and question him about it; he didn't want to see Eloise, who was sure to sense his mother's interest and try to interrogate him; he didn't want to see—

Hell, he didn't want to see anyone. And considering the way he'd been snapping off the heads of his servants (verbally, to be sure, although occasionally quite literally in his dreams) the rest of the world would do well if they didn't care to see him, either.

But, as luck would have it, right as he placed his foot on

the first step, he heard someone call out his name, and when he turned around, both of his adult brothers were walking toward him along the pavement.

Benedict groaned. No one knew him better than Anthony and Colin, and they weren't likely to let a little thing like a broken heart go unnoticed or unmentioned.

"Haven't seen you in an age," Anthony said. "Where have you been?"

"Here and there," Benedict said evasively. "Mostly at home." He turned to Colin. "Where have *you* been?"

"Wales."

"Wales? Why?"

Colin shrugged. "I felt like it. Never been there before."

"Most people require a slightly more compelling reason to take off in the middle of the season," Benedict said.

"Not I."

Benedict stared at him. Anthony stared at him.

"Oh, very well," Colin said with a scowl. "I needed to get away. Mother has started in on me with this bloody marriage thing."

" 'Bloody marriage thing'?" Anthony asked with an amused smile. "I assure you, the deflowering of one's wife is not quite so gory."

Benedict kept his expression scrupulously impassive. He'd found a small spot of blood on his sofa after he'd made love to Sophie. He'd thrown a pillow over it, hoping that by the time any of the servants noticed, they'd have forgotten that he'd had a woman over. He liked to think that none of the staff had been listening at doors or gossiping, but Sophie herself had once told him that servants generally knew everything that went on in a household, and he tended to think that she was right.

But if he had indeed blushed—and his cheeks did feel a touch warm—neither of his brothers saw it, because they didn't say anything, and if there was anything in life as certain as, say, the sun rising in the east, it was that a Bridgerton never passed up the opportunity to tease and torment another Bridgerton.

"She's been talking about Penelope Featherington non-stop," Colin said with a scowl. "I tell you, I've known the girl since we were both in short pants. Er, since I was in short pants, at least. She was in . . ." He scowled some more, because both his brothers were laughing at him. "She was in whatever it is that young girls wear."

"Frocks?" Anthony supplied helpfully.

"Petticoats?" was Benedict's suggestion.

"The point is," Colin said forcefully, "that I have known her forever, and I can assure you I am not likely to fall in love with her."

Anthony turned to Benedict and said, "They'll be married within a year. Mark my words."

Colin crossed his arms. "Anthony!"

"Maybe two," Benedict said. "He's young yet."

"Unlike *you*," Colin retorted. "Why am I besieged by Mother, I wonder? Good God, you're thirty-one—"

"Thirty," Benedict snapped.

"Regardless, one would think you'd be getting the brunt of it."

Benedict frowned. His mother had been uncharacteristically reserved these past few weeks when it came to her opinions on Benedict and marriage and why the two ought to meet and soon. Of course, Benedict had been avoiding his mother's house like the plague, but even before that, she'd not mentioned a word.

It was most odd.

"At any rate," Colin was still grumbling, "I am not going to marry soon, and I am certainly not going to marry Penelope Featherington!"

"Oh!"

It was a feminine "oh," and without looking up, Benedict

somehow knew that he was about to experience one of life's most awkward moments. Heart filled with dread, he lifted his head and turned toward the front door. There, framed perfectly in the open doorway, was Penelope Featherington, her lips parted with shock, her eyes filled with heartbreak.

And in that moment, Benedict realized what he'd probably been too stupid (and stupidly male) to notice: Penelope Featherington was in love with his brother.

Colin cleared his throat. "Penelope," he squeaked, his voice sounding as if he'd regressed ten years and gone straight back to puberty, "uh . . . good to see you." He looked to his brothers to leap in and save him, but neither chose to intervene.

Benedict winced. It was one of those moments that simply could not be saved.

"I didn't know you were there," Colin said lamely.

"Obviously not," Penelope said, but her words lacked an edge.

Colin swallowed painfully. "Were you visiting Eloise?"

She nodded. "I was invited."

"I'm sure you were!" he said quickly. "Of course you were. You're a great friend of the family."

Silence. Horrible, awkward silence.

"As if you would come uninvited," Colin mumbled.

Penelope said nothing. She tried to smile, but she obviously couldn't quite manage it. Finally, just when Benedict thought she would brush by them all and flee down the street, she looked straight at Colin and said, "I never asked you to marry me."

Colin's cheeks turned a deeper red than Benedict would have thought humanly possible. Colin opened his mouth, but no sound came out.

It was the first—and quite possibly would be the only—moment of Benedict's recollection for which his younger brother was at a complete loss for words.

"And I never—" Penelope added, swallowing convulsively when the words came out a bit tortured and broken. "I never said to anyone that I wanted you to ask me."

"Penelope," Colin finally managed, "I'm so sorry."

"You have nothing to apologize for," she said.

"No," Colin insisted, "I do. I hurt your feelings, and—"

"You didn't know I was there."

"But nevertheless—"

"You are not going to marry me," she said hollowly. "There is nothing wrong with that. I am not going to marry your brother Benedict."

Benedict had been trying not to look, but he snapped to attention at that.

"It doesn't hurt his feeling when I announce that I am not going to marry him." She turned to Benedict, her brown eyes focusing on his. "Does it, Mr. Bridgerton?"

"Of course not," Benedict answered quickly.

"It's settled, then," she said tightly. "No feelings were hurt. Now then, if you will excuse me, gentlemen, I should like to go home."

Benedict, Anthony, and Colin parted as if drops in the Red Sea as she made her way down the steps.

"Don't you have a maid?" Colin asked.

She shook her head. "I live just around the corner."

"I know, but—"

"I'll escort you," Anthony said smoothly.

"That's really not necessary, my lord."

"Humor me," he said.

She nodded, and the two of them took off down the street.

Benedict and Colin watched their retreating forms in silence for a full thirty seconds before Benedict turned to his brother and said, "That was very well done of you."

"I didn't know she was there!"

"Obviously," Benedict drawled.

"Don't. I feel terrible enough already."

"As well you should."

"Oh, and you have never inadvertently hurt a woman's feelings before?" Colin's voice was defensive, just defensive enough so that Benedict knew he felt like an utter heel inside.

Benedict was saved from having to reply by the arrival of his mother, standing at the top of the steps, framed in the doorway much the same way Penelope had been just a few minutes earlier.

"Has your brother arrived yet?" Violet asked.

Benedict jerked his head toward the corner. "He is escorting Miss Featherington home."

"Oh. Well, that's very thoughtful of him. I—Where are you going, Colin?"

Colin paused briefly but didn't even turn his head as he grunted, "I need a drink."

"It's a bit early for—" She stopped mid-sentence when Benedict laid his hand on her arm.

"Let him go," he said.

She opened her mouth as if to protest, then changed her mind and merely nodded. "I'd hoped to gather the family for an announcement," she said with a sigh, "but I suppose that can wait. In the meantime, why don't you join me for tea?"

Benedict glanced at the clock in the hall. "Isn't it a bit late for tea?"

"Skip the tea then," she said with a shrug. "I was merely looking for an excuse to speak with you."

Benedict managed a weak smile. He wasn't in the mood to converse with his mother. To be frank, he wasn't in the mood to converse with any person, a fact to which anyone with whom he'd recently crossed paths would surely attest.

"It's nothing serious," Violet said. "Heavens, you look as if you're ready to go to the gallows."

It probably would have been rude to point out that that was exactly how he felt, so instead he just leaned down and kissed her on the cheek.

"Well, that's a nice surprise," she said, beaming up at him.

"Now come with me," she added, motioning toward the downstairs sitting room. "I have someone I want to tell you about."

"Mother!"

"Just hear me out. She's a lovely girl . . ."

The gallows indeed.

Chapter 19

Miss Posy Reiling (younger step-daughter to the late Earl of Penwood) isn't a frequent subject of this column (nor, This Author is sad to say, a frequent subject of attention at social functions) but one could not help but notice that she was acting very strangely at her mother's musicale on Tuesday eve. She insisted upon sitting by the window, and she spent most of the performance staring at the streetscape, as if looking for something . . . or perhaps someone?

LADY WHISTLEDOWN'S SOCIETY PAPERS, 11 JUNE 1817

Forty-five minutes later, Benedict was slouching in his chair, his eyes glazed. Every now and then he had to stop and make sure his mouth wasn't hanging open.

His mother's conversation was *that* boring.

The young lady she had wanted to discuss with him had actually turned out to be seven young ladies, each of which she *assured* him was better than the last.

Benedict thought he might go mad. Right there in his mother's sitting room he was going to go stark, raving mad. He'd suddenly pop out of his chair, fall to the floor in a frenzy, his arms and legs waving, mouth frothing—

"Benedict, are you even *listening* to me?"

He looked up and blinked. Damn. Now he would have to focus on his mother's list of possible brides. The prospect of losing his sanity had been infinitely more appealing.

"I was trying to tell you about Mary Edgeware," Violet said, looking more amused than frustrated.

Benedict was instantly suspicious. When it came to her children dragging their feet to the altar, his mother was never amused. "Mary who?"

"Edge—Oh, never mind. I can see that I cannot compete with whatever is plaguing you just now."

"Mother," Benedict said abruptly.

She cocked her head slightly to the side, her eyes intrigued and perhaps a bit surprised. "Yes?"

"When you met Father—"

"It happened in an instant," she said softly, somehow knowing what he'd meant to ask.

"So you knew that he was the one?"

She smiled, and her eyes took on a faraway, misty look. "Oh, I wouldn't have admitted it," she said. "At least not right away. I fancied myself a practical sort. I'd always scoffed at the notion of love at first sight." She paused for a moment, and Benedict knew she was no longer in the room with him, but at some long-ago ball, meeting his father for the first time. Finally, just when he thought she'd completely forgotten the conversation, she looked back up and said, "But I knew."

"From the first moment you saw him?"

"Well, from the first time we spoke, at least." She took his offered handkerchief and dabbed at her eyes, smiling sheepishly, as if embarrassed by her tears.

Benedict felt a lump forming in his throat, and he looked away, not wanting her to see the moisture forming in his own eyes. Would anyone cry for him more than a decade after he died? It was a humbling thing to be in the presence of true love, and Benedict suddenly felt so damned jealous—of his own *parents*.

They'd found love and had the good sense to recognize and cherish it. Few people were so fortunate.

"There was something about his voice that was so soothing, so warm," Violet continued. "When he spoke, you felt like you were the only person in the room."

"I remember," Benedict said with a warm, nostalgic smile. "It was quite a feat, to be able to do that with eight children."

His mother swallowed convulsively, then said, her voice once again brisk, "Yes, well, he never knew Hyacinth, so I suppose it was only seven."

"Still . . ."

She nodded. "Still."

Benedict reached out and patted her on the hand. He didn't know why; he hadn't planned to. But somehow it seemed the right thing to do.

"Yes, well," she said, giving his hand a little squeeze before returning hers to her lap. "Was there any particular reason you asked about your father?"

"No," he lied. "At least not . . . Well . . ."

She waited patiently, with that mildly expectant expression that made it impossible to keep one's feelings to oneself.

"What happens," he asked, as surprised by the words tumbling forth as she undoubtedly was, "when one falls in love with someone unsuitable?"

"Someone unsuitable," she repeated.

Benedict nodded painfully, immediately regretting his words. He should never have said anything to his mother, and yet . . .

He sighed. His mother had always been a remarkably good listener. And truly, for all her annoying matchmaking ways, she was more qualified to give advice on matters of the heart than anyone he knew.

When she spoke, she appeared to be choosing her words carefully. "What do you mean by unsuitable?"

"Someone . . ." He stopped, paused. "Someone someone like me probably shouldn't marry."

"Someone perhaps who is not of our social class?"

He glanced at a painting on the wall. "Someone like that."

"I see. Well . . ." Violet's brow scrunched a bit, then she said, "I suppose it would depend on how far out of our social class this person is."

"Far."

"A little bit far or quite a lot far?"

Benedict was convinced that no man of his age and reputation had ever had such a conversation with his mother, but he nonetheless answered, "Quite a lot."

"I see. Well, I would have to say . . ." She chewed on her lower lip for a moment before continuing. "I would have to say," she said, slightly more forcefully (although not, if one was judging in absolute terms, forceful at all).

"I would have to say," she said for a third time, "that I love you very much and will support you in all things." She cleared her throat. "If indeed we are talking about *you*."

It seemed useless to deny it, so Benedict just nodded.

"But," Violet added, "I would caution you to consider what you are doing. Love is, of course, the most important element in any union, but outside influences can put a strain on a marriage. And if you marry someone of, say"—she cleared her throat—"the servant class, then you will find yourself the subject of a great deal of gossip and no small amount of ostracism. And that will be difficult for one such as you to bear."

"One such as me?" he asked, bristling at her choice of words.

"You must know I mean no insult. But you and your brothers do lead charmed lives. You're handsome, intelligent, personable. Everyone likes you. I cannot tell you how happy that makes me." She smiled, but it was a wistful, slightly sad smile. "It is not easy to be a wallflower."

And suddenly Benedict understood why his mother was always forcing him to dance with the girls like Penelope Featherington. The ones who stood at the fringes of the ballroom, the ones who always pretended they didn't actually *want* to dance.

She had been a wallflower herself.

It was difficult to imagine. His mother was hugely popular now, with an easy smile and piles of friends. And if Benedict had heard the story correctly, his father had been considered the catch of the season.

"Only you will be able to make this decision," Violet continued, bringing Benedict's thoughts back to the here and now, "and I'm afraid it won't be an easy one."

He stared out the window, his silence his agreement.

"But," she added, "should you decide to join your life with someone not of our class, I will of course support you in every possible manner."

Benedict looked up sharply. There were few women of the *ton* who would say the same to their sons.

"You are my son," she said simply. "I would give my life for you."

He opened his mouth to speak but was surprised to find that he couldn't make a sound.

"I certainly wouldn't banish you for marrying someone unsuitable."

"Thank you," he said. It was all he could manage to say.

Violet sighed, loudly enough to regain his full attention. She looked tired, wistful. "I wish your father were here," she said.

"You don't say that very often," he said quietly.

"I always wish your father were here." She closed her eyes for a brief moment. "Always."

And then somehow it became clear. As he watched his mother's face, finally realizing—no, finally *understanding*—the depth of his parents' love for one another, it all became clear.

Love. He loved Sophie. That was all that should have mattered.

He'd thought he'd loved the woman from the masquerade. He'd thought he'd wanted to marry her. But he understood now that that had been nothing but a dream, a fleeting fantasy of a woman he barely knew.

But Sophie was . . .

Sophie was Sophie. And that was everything he needed.

Sophie wasn't a great believer in destiny or fate, but after one hour with Nicholas, Elizabeth, John, and Alice Wentworth, young cousins to the Bridgerton clan, she was beginning to think that maybe there was a reason she had never managed to obtain a position as a governess.

She was exhausted.

No, no, she thought, with more than a touch of desperation. Exhaustion didn't really provide an adequate description for the current state of her existence. Exhaustion didn't quite capture the slight edge of insanity the foursome had brought to her mind.

"No, no, no, that's *my* doll," Elizabeth said to Alice.

"It's mine," Alice returned.

"It is not!"

"Is too!"

"I'll settle this," ten-year-old Nicholas said, swaggering over with his hands on his hips.

Sophie groaned. She had a feeling that it was not a terribly good idea to allow the dispute to be settled by a ten-year-old boy who happened to think he was a pirate.

"Neither of you will want the doll," he said, with a devious gleam in his eye, "if I simply *lop* off its—"

Sophie leapt to intervene. "You will not lop off its head, Nicholas Wentworth."

"But then they'll stop—"

"No," Sophie said forcefully.

He looked at her, obviously assessing her commitment to

that particular course of action, then grumbled and walked away.

"I think we need a new game," Hyacinth whispered to Sophie.

"I *know* we need a new game," Sophie muttered.

"Let go of my soldier!" John screeched. "Let go let go let go!"

"I'm never having children," Hyacinth announced. "In fact, I may never get married."

Sophie forbore to point out that when Hyacinth married and had children, she would certainly have a flotilla of nurses and nannies to aid her with their keeping and care.

Hyacinth winced as John pulled Alice's hair, then swallowed uncomfortably as Alice slugged John in the stomach. "The situation is growing desperate," she whispered to Sophie.

"Blind man's bluff!" Sophie suddenly exclaimed. "What do you think, everyone? How about a game of blind man's bluff?"

Alice and John nodded enthusiastically, and Elizabeth gave a reluctant, "All right," after carefully considering the issue.

"What do you say, Nicholas?" Sophie asked, addressing the last remaining holdout.

"It could be fun," he said slowly, terrifying Sophie with the devilish gleam in his eye.

"Excellent," she said, trying to keep the wariness out of her voice.

"But *you* must be the blind man," he added.

Sophie opened her mouth to protest, but at that moment, the other three children started jumping up and down and squealing with delight. Then her fate was sealed when Hyacinth turned to her with a sly smile and said, "Oh, you must."

Sophie knew that protest was useless, so she let out a long-suffering sigh—exaggerated, just to delight the children—

and turned around so that Hyacinth could fasten a scarf over her eyes.

"Can you see?" Nicholas demanded.

"No," Sophie lied.

He turned to Hyacinth with a grimace. "She can see."

How could he tell?

"Add a second scarf," he said. "This one is too sheer."

"The indignity," Sophie muttered, but nonetheless, she leaned down slightly so that Hyacinth could tie another scarf over her eyes.

"She's blind now!" John hooted.

Sophie gave them all a sickly-sweet smile.

"All right now," Nicholas said, clearly in charge. "You wait ten seconds so that we can take our places."

Sophie nodded, then tried not to wince as she heard the sounds of a mad scramble around the room. "Try not to break anything!" she yelled, as if that would make any difference to an overexcited six-year-old.

"Are you ready?" she asked.

No response. That meant yes.

"Blind Man!" she called out.

"Bluff!" came five voices in unison.

Sophie frowned in concentration. One of the girls was definitely behind the sofa. She took a few baby steps to the right.

"Blind Man!"

"Bluff!" Followed, of course, by a few titters and chuckles.

"Blind M— OW!"

More hoots and squeals of laughter. Sophie grunted as she rubbed her bruised shin.

"Blind Man!" she called, with considerably less enthusiasm.

"Bluff!"

"Bluff!"

"BLUFF!"

"BLUFF!"

"BLUFF!"

"You are all mine, Alice," she muttered under her breath, deciding to go for the smallest and presumably weakest of the bunch. "All mine."

Benedict had nearly made a clean escape. After his mother had left the sitting room, he'd downed a much-needed glass of brandy and headed out toward the door, only to be caught by Eloise, who informed him that he absolutely *couldn't* leave yet, that Mother was trying *very* hard to assemble all of her children in one place because Daphne had an *important* announcement to make.

"With child again?" Benedict asked.

"Act surprised. You weren't supposed to know."

"I'm not going to act anything. I'm leaving."

She made a desperate leap forward and somehow managed to grab his sleeve. "You can't."

Benedict let out a long breath and tried to pry her fingers off of his arm, but she had his shirt in a death grip. "I am going to pick up one foot," he said in slow, tedious tones, "and step forward. Then I will pick up the next foot—"

"You promised Hyacinth you would help her with her arithmetic," Eloise blurted out. "She hasn't seen hide nor hair of you in two weeks."

"It's not as if she has a school to flunk out of," Benedict muttered.

"Benedict, that is a terrible thing to say!" Eloise exclaimed.

"I know," he groaned, hoping to stave off a lecture.

"Just because we of the female gender are not allowed to study at places like Eton and Cambridge doesn't mean our educations are any less precious," Eloise ranted, completely ignoring her brother's weak "I know."

"Furthermore—" she carried on.

Benedict sagged against the wall.

"—I am of the opinion that the reason we are *not* allowed access is that if we *were*, we would trounce you men in all subjects!"

"I'm sure you're right," he sighed.

"Don't patronize me."

"Believe me, Eloise, the last thing I would dream of doing is patronizing you."

She eyed him suspiciously before crossing her arms and saying, "Well, don't disappoint Hyacinth."

"I won't," he said wearily.

"I believe she's in the nursery."

Benedict gave her a distracted nod, turning toward the stairs.

But as he trudged on up, he didn't see Eloise turn toward his mother, who was peeking out of the music room, and give her a big wink and a smile.

The nursery was located on the second floor. Benedict didn't often come up that high; most of his siblings' bedrooms were on the first floor. Only Gregory and Hyacinth still lived adjacent to the nursery, and with Gregory off at Eton most of the year and Hyacinth usually terrorizing someone in some other section of the house, Benedict simply didn't have much reason to visit.

It didn't escape him that aside from the nursery, the second floor was home to bedrooms for the higher servants. Including the lady's maids.

Sophie.

She was probably off in some corner somewhere with her mending—certainly not in the nursery, which was the domain of nurses and nannies. A lady's maid would have no reason to—

"Heeheeheehahaha!"

Benedict raised his brows. That was most definitely the sound of childish laughter, not something likely to come out of fourteen-year-old Hyacinth's mouth.

Oh, right. His Wentworth cousins were visiting. His mother had mentioned something about that. Well, that would be a bonus. He hadn't seen them in a few months, and they were nice enough children, if a little high-spirited.

As he approached the nursery door, the laughter increased, with a few squeals thrown in for good measure. The sounds brought a smile to Benedict's face, and he turned when he reached the open doorway, and then—

He saw her.

Her.

Not Sophie.

Her.

And yet it *was* Sophie.

She was blindfolded, smiling as she groped her hands toward the giggling children. He could see only the bottom half of her face, and that's when he knew.

There was only one other woman in the world for whom he'd seen only the bottom half of her face.

The smile was the same. The gamine little point at the end of her chin was the same. It was *all* the same.

She was the woman in silver, the woman from the masquerade ball.

It suddenly made sense. Only twice in his life had he felt this inexplicable, almost mystical attraction to a woman. He'd thought it remarkable, to have found two, when in his heart he'd always believed there was only one perfect woman out there for him.

His heart had been right. There *was* only one.

He'd searched for her for months. He'd pined for her even longer. And here she'd been right under his nose.

And she hadn't told him.

Did she understand what she'd put him through? How many hours he'd lain awake, feeling that he was betraying the lady in silver—the woman he'd dreamed of marrying—all because he was falling in love with a housemaid?

Dear God, it bordered on the absurd. He'd finally decided

to let the lady in silver go. He was going to ask Sophie to marry him, social consequences be damned.

And they were one and the same.

A strange roaring filled his head, as if two enormous seashells had been clapped to his ears, whistling, whirring, humming; and the air suddenly smelled a bit acrid and everything looked a little bit red, and—

Benedict could not take his eyes off of her.

"Is something wrong?" Sophie asked. All the children had gone silent, staring at Benedict with open mouths and large, large eyes.

"Hyacinth," he bit off, "will you please evacuate the room?"

"But—"

"Now!" he roared.

"Nicholas, Elizabeth, John, Alice, come along now," Hyacinth said quickly, her voice cracking. "There are biscuits in the kitchen, and I know that . . ."

But Benedict didn't hear the rest. Hyacinth had managed to clear the room out in record time and her voice was disappearing down the hall as she ushered the children away.

"Benedict?" Sophie was saying, fumbling with the knot at the back of her head. "Benedict?"

He shut the door. The click was so loud she jumped. "What's wrong?" she whispered.

He said nothing, just watched her as she tore at the scarf. He liked it that she was helpless. He didn't feel terribly kind and charitable at the moment.

"Do you have something you need to tell me?" he asked. His voice was controlled, but his hands were shaking.

She went still, so still that he would have sworn that he could see the heat rise from her body. Then she cleared her throat—an uncomfortable, awkward sort of sound—and went back to work on the knot. Her movements tightened her dress around her breasts, but Benedict felt not one speck of desire.

It was, he thought ironically, the first time he *hadn't* felt desire for this woman, in either of her incarnations.

"Can you help me with this?" she asked. But her voice was hesitant.

Benedict didn't move.

"Benedict?"

"It's interesting to see you with a scarf tied around your head, Sophie," he said softly.

Her hands dropped slowly to her sides.

"It's almost like a demi-mask, wouldn't you say?"

Her lips parted, and the soft rush of air that crossed them was the room's only noise.

He walked toward her, slowly, inexorably, his footsteps just loud enough so that she had to know he was stalking her. "I haven't been to a masquerade in many years," he said.

She knew. He could see it in her face, the way she held her mouth, tight at the corners, and yet still slightly open. She knew that he knew.

He hoped she was terrified.

He took another two steps toward her, then abruptly turned to the right, his arm brushing past her sleeve. "Were you ever going to tell me that we'd met before?"

Her mouth moved, but she didn't speak.

"Were you?" he asked, his voice low and controlled.

"No," she said, her voice wavering.

"Really?"

She didn't make a sound.

"Any particular reason?"

"It—it didn't seem pertinent."

He whirled around. "It didn't seem *pertinent*?" he snapped. "I fell in love with you two years ago, and it didn't seem pertinent?"

"Can I please remove the scarf?" she whispered.

"You can remain blind."

"Benedict, I—"

"Like *I* was blind this past month," he continued angrily. "Why don't you see how you like it?"

"You didn't fall in love with me two years ago," she said, yanking at the too-tight scarf.

"How would you know? *You* disappeared."

"I *had* to disappear," she cried out. "I didn't have a choice."

"We always have choices," he said condescendingly. "We call it free will."

"That's easy for you to say," she snapped, tugging frantically at the blindfold. "You, who have everything! I had to— Oh!" With one wrenching movement, she somehow managed to yank down the scarves until they hung loosely around her neck.

Sophie blinked against the sudden onslaught of light. Then she caught sight of Benedict's face and stumbled back a step.

His eyes were on fire, burning with a rage, and yes, a hurt that she could barely comprehend. "It's good to see you, Sophie," he said in a dangerously low voice. "If indeed that is your real name."

She nodded.

"It occurs to me," he said, a little too casually, "if you were at the masquerade, then you are not exactly of the servant class, are you?"

"I didn't have an invitation," she said hastily. "I was a fraud. A pretender. I had no right to be there."

"You lied to me. Through everything, all this, you lied to me."

"I had to," she whispered.

"Oh, please. What could possibly be so terrible that you must conceal your identity from *me*?"

Sophie gulped. Here in the Bridgerton nursery, with him looming over her, she couldn't quite remember why she'd decided not to tell him that she was the lady at the masquerade.

Maybe she'd feared that he would want her to become his mistress.

Which had happened anyway.

Or maybe she hadn't said anything because by the time she'd realized that this wasn't going to be a chance meeting, that he wasn't about to let Sophie-the-housemaid out of his life, it was too late. She'd gone too long without telling him, and she feared his rage.

Which was exactly what had happened.

Proving her point. Of course, that was cold consolation as she stood across from him, watching his eyes go hot with anger and cold with disdain—all at the same time.

Maybe the truth—as unflattering as it might be—was that her pride had been stung. She'd been disappointed that he hadn't recognized her himself. If the night of the masquerade had been as magical for him as it had been for her, shouldn't he have known instantly who she was?

Two years she'd spent dreaming about him. Two years she'd seen his face every night in her mind. And yet when he'd seen hers, he'd seen a stranger.

Or maybe, just maybe, it hadn't been any of those things. Maybe it was simpler than that. Maybe she'd just wanted to protect her heart. She didn't know why, but she'd felt a little safer, a little less exposed as an anonymous housemaid. If Benedict had known who she was—or at least known that she'd been the woman at the masquerade—then he would have pursued her. Relentlessly.

Oh, he had certainly pursued her when he'd thought she'd been a maid. But it would have been different if he'd known the truth. Sophie was sure of it. He wouldn't have perceived the class differences as being quite so great, and Sophie would have lost an important barrier between them. Her social status, or lack thereof, had been a protective wall around her heart. She *couldn't* get too close because, quite honestly, she couldn't get too close. A man such as Benedict—son of and brother to viscounts—would never marry a servant.

But an earl's by-blow—now that was a much trickier situation. Unlike a servant, an aristocratic bastard could dream.

But like those of a servant, the dreams weren't likely to come true. Making the dreaming all that much more painful. And she'd known—every time it had been on the tip of her tongue to blurt out her secret she had known—that telling him the truth would lead straight to a broken heart.

It almost made Sophie want to laugh. Her heart couldn't possibly feel worse than it did now.

"I searched for you," he said, his low, intense voice cutting into her thoughts.

Her eyes widened, grew wet. "You did?" she whispered.

"For six bloody months," he cursed. "It was as if you fell right off the face of the earth."

"I had nowhere to go," she said, not sure why she was telling him that.

"You had *me*."

The words hung in the air, heavy and dark. Finally, Sophie, propelled by some perverse sense of belated honesty, said, "I didn't know you searched for me. But—but—" She choked on the word, closing her eyes tightly against the pain of the moment.

"But what?"

She swallowed convulsively, and when she did open her eyes, she did not look at his face. "Even if I'd known you were looking," she said, hugging her arms to her body, "I wouldn't have let you find me."

"Was I that repulsive to you?"

"No!" she cried out, her eyes flying to his face. There was hurt there. He hid it well, but she knew him well. There was hurt in his eyes.

"No," she said, trying to make her voice calm and even. "It wasn't that. It could never be that."

"Then what?"

"We're from different worlds, Benedict. Even then I knew that there could be no future for us. And it would have been torture. To tease myself with a dream that couldn't come true? I couldn't do that."

"Who are you?" he asked suddenly.

She just stared at him, frozen into inaction.

"Tell me," he bit off. "Tell me who you are. Because you're no damned lady's maid, that's for certain."

"I'm exactly who I said I was," she said, then, at his murderous glare, hastily added, "Almost."

He advanced on her. "Who *are* you?"

She backed up another step. "Sophia Beckett."

"Who are you?"

"I've been a servant since I was fourteen."

"And who were you before that?"

Her voice dropped to a whisper. "A bastard."

"Whose bastard?"

"Does it matter?"

His stance grew more belligerent. "It matters to me."

Sophie felt herself deflate. She hadn't expected him to ignore the duties of his birth and actually *marry* someone like her, but she'd hoped he wouldn't care quite that much.

"Who were your parents?" Benedict persisted.

"No one you know."

"Who were your parents?" he roared.

"The Earl of Penwood," she cried out.

He stood utterly still, not a muscle moving. He didn't even blink.

"I am a nobleman's bastard," she said harshly, years of anger and resentment pouring forth. "My father was the Earl of Penwood and my mother was a maid. Yes," she spat out when she saw his face grow pale, "my mother was a lady's maid. Just as I am a lady's maid."

A heavy pause filled the air, and then Sophie said in a low voice, "I won't be like my mother."

"And yet, if she'd behaved otherwise," he said, "you wouldn't be here to tell me about it."

"That's not the point."

Benedict's hands, which had been fisted at his sides, began to twitch. "You lied to me," he said in a low voice.

"There was no need to tell you the truth."

"Who the hell are you to decide?" he exploded. "Poor little Benedict, he can't handle the truth. He can't make up his own mind. He—"

He broke off, disgusted by the whiny edge to his voice. She was turning him into someone he didn't know, someone he didn't like.

He had to get out of there. He had to—

"Benedict?" She was looking at him oddly. Her eyes were concerned.

"I have to go," he muttered. "I can't see you right now."

"Why?" she asked, and he could see from her face that she instantly regretted the question.

"I am so angry right now," he said, each word a slow, staccato beat in the sentence, "that I don't know myself. I—" He looked down at his hands. They were shaking. He wanted to hurt her, he realized. No, he didn't want to hurt her. He would never want to hurt her. And yet . . .

And yet . . .

It was the first time in his life he'd felt so out of control. It scared him.

"I have to go," he said again, and he brushed roughly past her as he strode out the door.

Chapter 20

While we are on the topic, Miss Reiling's mother, the Countess of Penwood, has also been acting very strange of late. According to servants' gossip (which we all know is always the most reliable sort), the countess threw quite the tantrum last night, hurling no fewer than seventeen shoes at her servants.

One footman sports a bruised eye, but other than that, all remain in good health.

LADY WHISTLEDOWN'S SOCIETY PAPERS, 11 JUNE 1817

Within an hour, Sophie had her bag packed. She didn't know what else to do. She was gripped—painfully gripped—by nervous energy, and she could not sit still. Her feet kept moving and her hands were shaking, and every few minutes, she found herself taking a big spontaneous gulp of air, as if the extra breath could somehow calm her inside.

She could not imagine that she would be allowed to remain here in Lady Bridgerton's household after such a horrible falling-out with Benedict. Lady Bridgerton was fond of Sophie, it was true, but Benedict was her son. Blood really was thicker than just about anything else, especially when it was Bridgerton blood.

It was sad, really, she thought as she sat down on her bed, her hands still torturing a hopelessly mangled handkerchief. For all her inner turmoil over Benedict, she'd *liked* living in the Bridgerton household. Sophie had never before had the honor of living amongst a group of people who truly understood the meaning of the word family.

She would miss them.

She would miss Benedict.

And she would mourn the life she could not have.

Unable to sit still, she jumped back to her feet and walked to the window. "Damn you, Papa," she said, looking up at the skies. "There. I've called you Papa. You never let me do that. You never wanted to *be* that." She gasped convulsively, using the back of her hand to wipe at her nose. "I've called you Papa. How does it feel?"

But there was no sudden clap of thunder, no gray cloud appearing out of nowhere to cover up the sun. Her father would never know how angry she was with him for leaving her penniless, leaving her with Araminta. Most likely, he wouldn't have cared.

She felt rather weary, and she leaned against the window frame, rubbing her eyes with her hand. "You gave me a taste of another life," she whispered, "and then left me in the wind. It would have been so much easier if I'd been raised a servant.

"I wouldn't have wanted so much. It would have been easier."

She turned back around, her eyes falling upon her single, meager bag. She hadn't wanted to take any of the dresses that Lady Bridgerton and her daughters had given her, but she'd had little choice in the matter, as her old dresses had already been relegated to the rag bin. So she'd chosen only two, the same number with which she'd arrived—the one she happened to be wearing when Benedict had discovered her identity, and a spare, which she'd tucked in the bag. The rest had been left hanging, neatly pressed, in the wardrobe.

Sophie sighed, closing her eyes for a moment. It was time to go. Where, she didn't know, but she couldn't stay here.

She leaned down and picked up the bag. She had a little money saved. Not much, but if she worked and was frugal, she'd have enough funds for passage to America within a year. She'd heard that things were easier there for those of less-than-respectable birth, that the boundaries of class weren't quite as strict as they were here in England.

She poked her head out into the hall, which was blessedly vacant. She knew she was a coward, but she didn't want to have to say good-bye to the Bridgerton daughters. She might do something *really* stupid, like cry, and then she'd feel even worse. Never in her life had she had the chance to spend time with women of her own age who treated her with respect and affection. She'd once hoped that Rosamund and Posy would be her sisters, but that had never come to pass. Posy might have tried, but Araminta wouldn't allow it, and Posy, for all her sweetness, had never been strong enough to stand up to her mother.

But she did have to bid farewell to Lady Bridgerton. There was no getting around that. Lady Bridgerton had been kind to her far beyond any expectations, and Sophie would not thank her by sneaking out and disappearing like some criminal. If she was lucky, Lady Bridgerton would not yet have heard of her altercation with Benedict. Sophie could give her notice, bid her farewell, and be off.

It was late afternoon, well past tea time, so Sophie decided to take a chance and see if Lady Bridgerton was in the small office she kept off of her bedchamber. It was a warm and cozy little room, with a writing desk and several bookshelves—a place where Lady Bridgerton penned her correspondence and settled the household accounts.

The door was ajar, so Sophie knocked softly, allowing the door to swing open a few inches as her knuckles connected with the wood.

"Enter!" came Lady Bridgerton's bidding.

Sophie pushed the door open and poked her head in. "Am I interrupting?" she asked quietly.

Lady Bridgerton set down her quill. "Yes, but it's a welcome interruption. I've never enjoyed balancing the household accounts."

"I would—" Sophie bit her tongue. She had been about to say that she would have been happy to take over the task; she'd always been good with numbers.

"You were saying?" Lady Bridgerton asked, her eyes warm.

Sophie gave her head a little shake. "Nothing."

The room lapsed into silence until Lady Bridgerton gave Sophie a slightly amused smile, and asked, "Was there a specific reason you knocked on my door?"

Sophie took a deep breath that was meant to settle her nerves (but didn't) and said, "Yes."

Lady Bridgerton looked at her expectantly but didn't say anything.

"I'm afraid I must resign my position here," Sophie said.

Lady Bridgerton actually rose out of her seat. "But why? Aren't you happy? Have any of the girls been mistreating you?"

"No, no," Sophie hastened to assure her. "That could not be further from the truth. Your daughters are so lovely—in heart as well as in appearance. I've never— That is to say, no one has ever—"

"What is it, Sophie?"

Sophie clutched at the doorframe, desperately trying to find her balance. Her legs felt unsteady, her heart felt unsteady. Any moment now she was going to burst into tears, and why? Because the man she loved would never marry her? Because he hated her for lying to him? Because he'd broken her heart twice—once by asking her to be his mistress, and once by making her love his family and then forcing her to leave?

He might not have demanded that she go, but it couldn't have been more obvious that she could not stay.

"It's Benedict, isn't it?"

Sophie's head snapped up.

Lady Bridgerton smiled sadly. "It's obvious that there is some feeling between you," she said gently, answering the question that Sophie knew must show in her eyes.

"Why didn't you fire me?" Sophie whispered. She didn't think that Lady Bridgerton knew that Sophie and Benedict had been intimate, but no one of Lady Bridgerton's position would want her son pining for a housemaid.

"I don't know," Lady Bridgerton replied, looking more conflicted than Sophie could ever have imagined. "I probably should have done." She shrugged, her eyes strangely helpless. "But I like you."

The tears Sophie had been working so hard to keep in check began to roll down her face, but beyond that, she somehow managed to keep her composure. She didn't shake, and she didn't make a sound. She just stood there, utterly still, as the tears came forth.

When Lady Bridgerton spoke again, her words held a very careful and measured quality, as if she were choosing them with great care, searching for a specific reply. "You are," she said, her eyes never leaving Sophie's face, "the sort of woman I would like for my son. Our acquaintance has not been a long one, but I know your character and I know your heart. And I wish—"

A small, choked sob burst forth from Sophie's mouth, but she swallowed it down as quickly as she could.

"I wish that you were of a different background," Lady Bridgerton continued, acknowledging Sophie's cry with a sympathetic tilt of her head and a sad, slow blink of her eyes. "Not that I hold such a thing against you, or think the less of you, but it makes things very difficult."

"Impossible," Sophie whispered.

Lady Bridgerton didn't say anything, and Sophie knew

that in her heart she agreed—if not completely, then ninety-eight percent—with her assessment.

"Is it possible," Lady Bridgerton asked, her words even more measured and careful than before, "that your background is not quite what it seems?"

Sophie said nothing.

"There are things about you that don't add up, Sophie."

Sophie knew that she expected her to ask what, but she had a fair idea what Lady Bridgerton meant.

"Your accent is impeccable," Lady Bridgerton said. "I know you told me that you had lessons with the children your mother worked for, but that doesn't seem like enough of an explanation to me. Those lessons wouldn't have started until you were a bit older, six at the very earliest, and your speech patterns would have already been rather set by that point."

Sophie felt her eyes widen. She'd never seen that particular hole in her story, and she was rather surprised that no one else had until now. But then again, Lady Bridgerton was a good deal smarter than most of the people to whom she had told her fabricated history.

"And you know Latin," Lady Bridgerton said. "Don't try to deny it. I heard you muttering under your breath the other day when Hyacinth vexed you."

Sophie kept her gaze fixed firmly on the window just to Lady Bridgerton's left. She couldn't quite bring herself to meet her eyes.

"Thank you for not denying it," Lady Bridgerton said. And then she waited for Sophie to say something, waited so long that finally Sophie had to fill the interminable silence.

"I'm not a suitable match for your son," was all she said.

"I see."

"I really have to go." She had to get the words out quickly, before she changed her mind.

Lady Bridgerton nodded. "If that is your wish, there is

nothing I can do to stop you. Where is it you plan to go?"

"I have relatives in the north," Sophie lied.

Lady Bridgerton clearly didn't believe her, but she answered, "You will, of course, use one of our carriages."

"No, I couldn't possibly."

"You can't think I would permit you to do otherwise. I consider you to be my responsibility—at least for the next few days—and it is far too dangerous for you to leave unescorted. It's not safe for women alone in this world."

Sophie couldn't quite suppress a rueful smile. Lady Bridgerton's tone might be different, but her words were almost exactly those uttered by Benedict a few weeks earlier. And look where that had gotten her. She would never say that she and Lady Bridgerton were close friends, but she knew her well enough to know that she would not be budged on this issue.

"Very well," Sophie acceded. "Thank you." She could have the carriage drop her off somewhere, preferably not too far from a port where she could eventually book passage to America, and then decide where to go from there.

Lady Bridgerton offered her a small, sad smile. "I assume you already have your bags packed?"

Sophie nodded. It didn't seem necessary to point out that she only had one bag, singular.

"Havc you made all of your good-byes?"

Sophie shook her head. "I'd rather not," she admitted.

Lady Bridgerton stood and nodded. "Sometimes that is best," she agreed. "Why don't you await me in the front hall? I will see to having a coach brought 'round."

Sophie turned and started to walk out, but when she reached the doorway, she stopped and turned around. "Lady Bridgerton, I—"

The older lady's eyes lit up, as if she were expecting some good news. Or if not good, then at least something different. "Yes?"

Sophie swallowed. "I just wanted to thank you."

The light in Lady Bridgerton's eyes dimmed a little. "Whatever for?"

"For having me here, for accepting me, and allowing me to pretend I was a part of your family."

"Don't be sil—"

"You didn't have to let me take tea with you and the girls," Sophie interrupted. If she didn't get this all out now, she'd lose her courage. "Most women wouldn't have done. It was lovely . . . and new . . . and . . ." She gulped. "I will miss you all."

"You don't have to go," Lady Bridgerton said softly.

Sophie tried to smile, but it came out all wobbly, and it tasted like tears. "Yes," she said, almost choking on the word. "I do."

Lady Bridgerton stared at her for a very long moment, her pale blue eyes filled with compassion and then maybe a touch of realization. "I see," she said quietly.

And Sophie feared that she did see.

"I'll meet you downstairs," Lady Bridgerton said.

Sophie nodded as she stood aside to let the dowager viscountess pass. Lady Bridgerton paused in the hallway, looking down at Sophie's well-worn bag. "Is that all you have?" she asked.

"Everything in the world."

Lady Bridgerton swallowed uncomfortably, and her cheeks took on the slightest hue of pink, almost as if she were actually embarrassed by her riches—and Sophie's lack thereof.

"But that . . ." Sophie said, motioning to the bag, "that's not what's important. What you have . . ." She stopped and swallowed, doing battle with the lump in her throat. "I don't mean what you own . . ."

"I know what you mean, Sophie." Lady Bridgerton dabbed at her eyes with her fingers. "Thank you."

Sophie's shoulders rose and fell in a tiny shrug. "It's the truth."

"Let me give you some money before you go, Sophie," Lady Bridgerton blurted out.

Sophie shook her head. "I couldn't. I've already taken two of the dresses you gave me. I didn't want to, but—"

"It's all right," Lady Bridgerton assured her. "What else could you do? The ones you came with are gone." She cleared her throat. "But please, let me give you some money." She saw Sophie open her mouth to protest and said, "*Please.* It would make me feel better."

Lady Bridgerton had a way of looking at a person that truly made one want to do as she asked, and besides that, Sophie really did need the money. Lady Bridgerton was a generous lady; she might even give Sophie enough to book third-class passage across the ocean. Sophie found herself saying, "Thank you," before her conscience had a chance to grapple with the offer.

Lady Bridgerton gave her a brief nod and disappeared down the hall.

Sophie took a long, shaky breath, then picked up her bag and walked slowly down the stairs. She waited in the foyer for a moment, then decided she might as well wait outside. It was a fine spring day, and Sophie thought that a bit of sun on her nose might be just the thing to make her feel better. Well, at least a little bit better. Besides, she'd be less likely to run into one of the Bridgerton daughters, and much as she was going to miss them, she just didn't want to have to say good-bye.

Still clutching her bag in one hand, she pushed open the front door and descended the steps.

It shouldn't take too long for the coach to be brought around. Five minutes, maybe ten, maybe—

"Sophie Beckett!"

Sophie's stomach dropped right down to her ankles. Araminta. How could she have forgotten?

Frozen into inaction, she looked around and up the stairs, trying to figure out which way to flee. If she ran back into the Bridgerton house, Araminta would know where to find her, and if she took off on foot—

"Constable!" Araminta shrieked. "I want a constable!"

Sophie dropped her bag and took off running.

"Someone stop her!" Araminta screamed. "Stop thief! Stop thief!"

Sophie kept running, even though she knew it would make her look guilty. She ran with every last fiber in her muscles, with every gulp of air she could force into her lungs. She ran and she ran and she ran . . .

Until someone tackled her, thumping into her back and knocking her to the ground.

"I got her!" the man yelled. "I got her for you!"

Sophie blinked and gasped at the pain. Her head had hit the pavement with a stunning blow, and the man who had caught her was practically sitting on her abdomen.

"There you are!" Araminta crowed as she hurried over. "Sophie Beckett. The nerve!"

Sophie glared at her. Words didn't exist to express the loathing in her heart. Not to mention that she was in too much pain to speak.

"I've been looking for you," Araminta said, smiling evilly. "Posy told me she'd seen you."

Sophie closed her eyes for a longer than the usual blink. *Oh, Posy*. She doubted that she'd meant to give her away, but Posy's tongue had a way of getting ahead of her mind.

Araminta planted her foot very close to Sophie's hand—the one that was being held immobile by her captor's fingers around her wrist—then smiled as she moved her foot *onto* Sophie's hand. "You shouldn't have stolen from me," Araminta said, her blue eyes glinting.

Sophie just grunted. It was all she could manage.

"You see," Araminta continued gleefully, "now I can have you thrown in jail. I suppose I could have done so before, but now I have the truth on my side."

Just then, a man ran up, skidding to a halt before Araminta. "The authorities are on the way, milady. We'll have this thief taken away in no time."

Sophie caught her lower lip between her teeth, torn between praying that the authorities would be delayed until Lady Bridgerton came outside, and praying that they'd come right away, so that the Bridgertons would never see her shame.

And in the end, she got her wish. The latter one, that was. Not two minutes later the authorities arrived, threw her into a wagon, and carted her off to jail.

And all Sophie could think of as she rode away was that the Bridgertons would never know what had happened to her, and maybe that was for the best.

Chapter 21

La, but such excitement yesterday on the front steps of Lady Bridgerton's residence on Bruton Street!

First, Penelope Featherington was seen in the company of not one, not two, but THREE Bridgerton brothers, surely a heretofore impossible feat for the poor girl, who is rather infamous for her wallflower ways. Sadly (but perhaps predictably) for Miss Featherington, when she finally departed, it was on the arm of the viscount, the only married man in the bunch.

If Miss Featherington were to somehow manage to drag a Bridgerton brother to the altar, it would surely mean the end of the world as we know it, and This Author, who freely admits she would not know heads from tails in such a world, would be forced to resign her post on the spot.

If Miss Featherington's gathering weren't enough gossip, not three hours later, a woman was accosted right in front of the town house by the Countess of Penwood, who lives three doors down. It seems the woman, who This Author suspects was working in the Bridgerton household, used to work for Lady Penwood. Lady Penwood alleges that the unidentified woman stole from her two years ago and immediately had the poor thing carted off to jail.

This Author is not certain what the punishment is these days for theft, but one has to suspect that if one has the au-

dacity to steal from a countess, the punishment is quite strict. The poor girl in question is likely to be hanged, or at the very least, find herself transported.

The previous housemaid wars (reported last month in This Column) seem rather trivial now.

LADY WHISTLEDOWN'S SOCIETY PAPERS, 13 JUNE 1817

Benedict's first inclination the following morning was to pour himself a good, stiff drink. Or maybe three. It might have been scandalously early in the day for spirits, but alcoholic oblivion sounded rather appealing after the emotional skewering he'd received the previous evening at the hands of Sophie Beckett.

But then he remembered that he'd made a date that morning for a fencing match with his brother Colin. Suddenly, skewering his brother sounded rather appealing, no matter that he'd had nothing to do with Benedict's wretched mood.

That, Benedict thought with a grim smile as he pulled on his gear, was what brothers were for.

"I've only an hour," Colin said as he attached the safety tip to his foil. "I have an appointment this afternoon."

"No matter," Benedict replied, lunging forward a few times to loosen up the muscles in his leg. He hadn't fenced in some time; the sword felt good in his hand. He drew back and touched the tip to the floor, letting the blade bend slightly. "It won't take more than an hour to best you."

Colin rolled his eyes before he drew down his mask.

Benedict walked to the center of the room. "Are you ready?"

"Not quite," Colin replied, following him.

Benedict lunged again.

"I said I wasn't ready!" Colin hollered as he jumped out of the way.

"You're too slow," Benedict snapped.

Colin cursed under his breath, then added a louder, "Bloody hell," for good measure. "What's gotten into you?"

"Nothing," Benedict nearly snarled. "Why would you say so?"

Colin took a step backward until they were a suitable distance apart to start the match. "Oh, I don't know," he intoned, sarcasm evident. "I suppose it could be because you nearly took my head off."

"I've a tip on my blade."

"And you were slashing like you were using a sabre," Colin shot back.

Benedict gave a hard smile. "It's more fun that way."

"Not for my neck." Colin passed his sword from hand to hand as he flexed and stretched his fingers. He paused and frowned. "You sure you have a foil there?"

Benedict scowled. "For the love of God, Colin, I would never use a real weapon."

"Just making sure," Colin muttered, touching his neck lightly. "Are you ready?"

Benedict nodded and bent his knees.

"Regular rules," Colin said, assuming a fencer's crouch. "*No* slashing."

Benedict gave him a curt nod.

"En garde!"

Both men raised their right arms, twisting their wrists until their palms were up, foils gripped in their fingers.

"Is that new?" Colin suddenly asked, eyeing the handle of Benedict's foil with interest.

Benedict cursed at the loss of his concentration. "Yes, it's new," he bit off. "I prefer an Italian grip."

Colin stepped back, completely losing his fencing posture as he looked at his own foil, with a less elaborate French grip. "Might I borrow it some time? I wouldn't mind seeing if—"

"Yes!" Benedict snapped, barely resisting the urge to advance and lunge that very second. "Will you get back *en garde*?"

Colin gave him a lopsided smile, and Benedict just *knew* that he had asked about his grip simply to annoy him. "As you wish," Colin murmured, assuming position again.

They held still for one moment, and then Colin said, "Fence!"

Benedict advanced immediately, lunging and attacking, but Colin had always been particularly fleet of foot, and he retreated carefully, meeting Benedict's attack with an expert parry.

"You're in a bloody bad mood today," Colin said, lunging forward and just nearly catching Benedict on the shoulder.

Benedict stepped out of his way, lifting his blade to block the attack. "Yes, well, I had a bad"—he advanced again, his foil stretched straight forward—"*day.*"

Colin sidestepped his attack neatly. "Nice riposte," he said, touching his forehead with the handle of his foil in a mock salute.

"Shut up and fence," Benedict snapped.

Colin chuckled and advanced, swishing his blade this way and that, keeping Benedict on the retreat. "It must be a woman," he said.

Benedict blocked Colin's attack and quickly began his own advance. "None of your damned business."

"It's a woman," Colin said, smirking.

Benedict lunged forward, the tip of his foil catching Colin on the collarbone. "Point," he grunted.

Colin gave a curt nod. "Touch for you." They walked back to the center of the room. "Are you ready?" he asked.

Benedict nodded.

"*En garde*. Fence!"

This time Colin was the first to take the attack. "If you need some advice about women . . ." he said, driving Benedict back to the corner.

Benedict raised his foil, blocking Colin's attack with

enough force to send his younger brother stumbling backward. "If I need advice about women," he returned, "the last person I'd go to would be *you*."

"You wound me," Colin said, regaining his balance.

"No," Benedict drawled. "That's what the safety tip is for."

"I certainly have a better record with women than *you*."

"Oh really?" Benedict said sarcastically. He stuck his nose in the air, and in a fair imitation of Colin said, " 'I am certainly *not* going to marry Penelope Featherington!' "

Colin winced.

"You," Benedict said, "shouldn't be giving advice to anyone."

"I didn't know she was there."

Benedict lunged forward, just barely missing Colin's shoulder. "That's no excuse. You were in public, in broad daylight. Even if she hadn't been there, someone would have heard and the bloody thing would have ended up in *Whistledown*."

Colin met his lunge with a parry, then riposted with blinding speed, catching Benedict neatly in the belly. "My touch," he grunted.

Benedict gave him a nod, acknowledging the point.

"I was foolish," Colin said as they walked back to the center of the room. "You, on the other hand, are stupid."

"What the hell does that mean?"

Colin sighed as he pushed up his mask. "Why don't you just do us all a favor and marry the girl?"

Benedict just stared at him, his hand going limp around the handle of his sword. Was there any possibility that Colin didn't know who they were talking about?

He removed his mask and looked into his brother's dark green eyes and nearly groaned. Colin knew. He didn't know how Colin knew, but he definitely knew. He supposed he shouldn't have been surprised. Colin always knew everything. In fact, the only person who ever seemed to know more gossip than Colin was Eloise, and it never took her more than a few hours to impart all of her dubious wisdom to Colin.

"How did you know?" Benedict finally asked.

One corner of Colin's mouth tilted up into a crooked smile. "About Sophie? It's rather obvious."

"Colin, she's—"

"A maid? Who cares? What is going to happen to you if you marry her?" Colin asked with a devil-may-care shrug of his shoulders. "People you couldn't care less about will ostracize you? Hell, I wouldn't mind being ostracized by some of the people with whom I'm forced to socialize."

Benedict shrugged dismissively. "I'd already decided I didn't care about all that," he said.

"Then what in bloody hell is the problem?" Colin demanded.

"It's complicated."

"Nothing is ever as complicated as it is in one's mind."

Benedict mulled that over, planting the tip of his foil against the floor and allowing the flexible blade to wiggle back and forth. "Do you remember Mother's masquerade?" he asked.

Colin blinked at the unexpected question. "A few years ago? Right before she moved out of Bridgerton House?"

Benedict nodded. "That's the one. Do you remember meeting a woman dressed in silver? You came upon us in the hall."

"Of course. You were rather taken with—" Colin's eyes suddenly bugged out. "That wasn't *Sophie*?"

"Remarkable, isn't it?" Benedict murmured, his every inflection screaming understatement.

"But . . . How . . ."

"I don't know how she got there, but she's not a maid."

"She's not?"

"Well, she is a maid," Benedict clarified, "but she's also the bastard daughter of the Earl of Penwood."

"Not the current—"

"No, the one who died several years back."

"And you knew all this?"

"No," Benedict said, the word short and staccato on his tongue, "I did not."

"Oh." Colin caught his lower lip between his teeth as he digested the meaning of his brother's short sentence. "I see." He stared at Benedict. "What are you going to do?"

Benedict's sword, whose blade had been wiggling back and forth as he pressed the tip against the floor, suddenly sprang straight and skittered out of his hand. He watched it dispassionately as it slid across the floor, and didn't look back up as he said, "That's a very good question."

He was still furious with Sophie for her deception, but neither was he without blame. He shouldn't have demanded that Sophie be his mistress. It had certainly been his right to ask, but it had also been her right to refuse. And once she had done so, he should have let her be.

Benedict hadn't been brought up a bastard, and if her experience had been sufficiently wretched so that she refused to risk bearing a bastard herself—well, then, he should have respected that.

If he respected *her*, then he had to respect her beliefs.

He shouldn't have been so flip with her, insisting that anything was possible, that she was free to make any choice her heart desired. His mother was right; he *did* live a charmed life. He had wealth, family, happiness . . . and nothing was truly out of his reach. The only awful thing that had ever happened in his life was the sudden and untimely death of his father, and even then, he'd had his family to help him through. It was difficult for him to imagine certain pains and hurts because he'd never experienced them.

And unlike Sophie, he'd never been alone.

What now? He had already decided that he was prepared to brave social ostracism and marry her. The unrecognized bastard daughter of an earl was a slightly more acceptable match than a servant, but only slightly. London society might accept her if he forced them to, but they wouldn't go out of their way to be kind. He and Sophie would most likely have to live quietly in the country, eschewing the London society that would almost certainly shun them.

But it took his heart less than a second to know that a quiet life with Sophie was by far preferable to a public life without her.

Did it matter that she was the woman from the masquerade? She'd lied to him about her identity, but he knew her soul. When they kissed, when they laughed, when they simply sat and talked—she had never feigned a moment.

The woman who could make his heart sing with a simple smile, the woman who could fill him with contentment just through the simple act of sitting by him while he sketched—that was the real Sophie.

And he loved her.

"You look as if you've reached a decision," Colin said quietly.

Benedict eyed his brother thoughtfully. When had he grown so perceptive? Come to think of it, when had he grown up? Benedict had always thought of Colin as a youthful rascal, charming and debonair, but not one who had ever had to assume any sort of responsibility.

But when he regarded his brother now, he saw someone else. His shoulders were a little broader, his posture a little more steady and subdued. And his eyes looked wiser. That was the biggest change. If eyes truly were windows to the soul, then Colin's soul had gone and grown up on him when Benedict hadn't been paying attention.

"I owe her a few apologies," Benedict said.

"I'm sure she'll forgive you."

"She owes me several as well. More than several."

Benedict could tell that his brother wanted to ask, "What

for?" but to his credit, all Colin said was, "Are you willing to forgive her?"

Benedict nodded.

Colin reached out and plucked Benedict's foil from his hands. "I'll put this away for you."

Benedict stared at his brother's fingers for a rather stupidly long moment before snapping to attention. "I have to go," he blurted out.

Colin barely suppressed a grin. "I surmised as much."

Benedict stared at his brother and then, for no other reason than an overwhelming urge, he reached out and pulled him into a quick hug. "I don't say this often," he said, his voice starting to sound gruff in his ears, "but I love you."

"I love you, too, big brother." Colin's smile, always a little bit lopsided, grew. "Now get the hell out of here."

Benedict tossed his mask at his brother and strode out of the room.

"What do you mean, she's gone?"

"Just that, I'm afraid," Lady Bridgerton said, her eyes sad and sympathetic. "She's gone."

The pressure behind Benedict's temples began to build; it was a wonder his head didn't explode. "And you just let her *go*?"

"It would hardly have been legal for me to force her to stay."

Benedict nearly groaned. It had hardly been legal for him to force her to come to London, but he'd done it, anyway.

"Where did she go?" he demanded.

His mother seemed to deflate in her chair. "I don't know. I had insisted that she take one of our coaches, partly because I feared for her safety but also because I wanted to know where she went."

Benedict slammed his hands on the desk. "Well, then, what happened?"

"As I was *trying* to say, I attempted to get her to take one of our coaches, but it was obvious she didn't want to, and she disappeared before I could have the carriage brought 'round."

Benedict cursed under his breath. Sophie was probably still in London, but London was huge and hugely populated. It would be damn near impossible to find someone who didn't want to be found.

"I had assumed," Violet said delicately, "that the two of you had had a falling-out."

Benedict raked his hand through his hair, then caught sight of his white sleeve. "Oh, Jesus," he muttered. He'd run over here in his fencing clothes. He looked up at his mother with a roll of his eyes. "No lectures on blasphemy just now, Mother. Please."

Her lips twitched. "I wouldn't dream of it."

"Where am I going to find her?"

The levity left Violet's eyes. "I don't know, Benedict. I wish I did. I quite liked Sophie."

"She's Penwood's daughter," he said.

Violet frowned. "I suspected something like that. Illegitimate, I assume?"

Benedict nodded.

His mother opened her mouth to say something, but he never did find out what, because at that moment, the door to her office came flying open, slamming against the wall with an amazing crash. Francesca, who had obviously been running across the house, smashed into her mother's desk, followed by Hyacinth, who smashed into Francesca.

"What is wrong?" Violet asked, rising to her feet.

"It's Sophie," Francesca panted.

"I know," Violet said. "She's gone. We—"

"No!" Hyacinth cut in, slapping a piece of paper down on the desk. "Look."

Benedict tried to grab the paper, which he immediately

recognized as an issue of *Whistledown*, but his mother got there first. "What is it?" he asked, his stomach sinking as he watched her face pale.

She handed him the paper. He scanned it quickly, passing by bits about the Duke of Ashbourne, the Earl of Macclesfield, and Penelope Featherington before he reached the section about what had to be Sophie.

"Jail?" he said, the word mere breath on his lips.

"We must see her released," his mother said, throwing her shoulders back like a general girding for battle.

But Benedict was already out the door.

"Wait!" Violet yelled, dashing after him. "I'm coming, too."

Benedict stopped short just before he reached the stairs. "You are not coming," he ordered. "I will not have you exposed to—"

"Oh, please," Violet returned. "I'm hardly a wilting flower. And I can vouch for Sophie's honesty and integrity."

"I'm coming, too," Hyacinth said, skidding to a halt alongside Francesca, who had also followed them out into the upstairs hall.

"No!" came the simultaneous reply from her mother and brother.

"But—"

"I said *no*," Violet said again, her voice sharp.

Francesca let out a sullen snort. "I suppose it would be fruitless for me to insist upon—"

"Don't even finish that sentence," Benedict warned.

"As if you would let me even try."

Benedict ignored her and turned to his mother. "If you want to go, we leave immediately."

She nodded. "Have the carriage brought 'round, and I'll be waiting out front."

Ten minutes later, they were on their way.

Chapter 22

Such a scurry on Bruton Street. The dowager Viscountess Bridgerton and her son, Benedict Bridgerton, were seen dashing out of her house Friday morning. Mr. Bridgerton practically threw his mother into a carriage, and they took off at breakneck speed. Francesca and Hyacinth Bridgerton were seen standing in the doorway, and This Author has it on the best authority that Francesca was heard to utter a very unladylike word.

But the Bridgerton household was not the only one to see such excitement. The Penwoods also experienced a great deal of activity, culminating in a public row right on the front steps between the countess and her daughter, Miss Posy Reiling.

As This Author has never liked Lady Penwood, she can only say, "Huzzah for Posy!"

LADY WHISTLEDOWN'S SOCIETY PAPERS, 16 JUNE 1817

It was cold. Really cold. And there was an awful scurrying noise that definitely belonged to a small, four-legged creature. Or even worse, a large, four-legged creature. Or to be more precise, a large version of a small, four-legged creature.

Rats.

"Oh, God," Sophie moaned. She didn't often take the Lord's name in vain, but now seemed as good a time as any to start. Maybe He would hear, and maybe He would smite the rats. Yes, that would do very nicely. A big jolt of lightning. Huge. Of biblical proportions. It could hit the earth, spread little electrical tentacles around the globe, and sizzle all the rats dead.

It was a lovely dream. Right up there with the ones in which she found herself living happily ever after as Mrs. Benedict Bridgerton.

Sophie took a quick gasp as a sudden stab of pain pierced her heart. Of the two dreams, she feared that the genocide of the rats might be the more likely to come true.

She was on her own now. Well and truly on her own. She didn't know why this was so upsetting. In all truth, she'd always been on her own. Not since her grandmother had deposited her on the front steps of Penwood Park had she had a champion, someone who put her interests above—or even at the same level—as their own.

Her stomach growled, reminding her that she could add hunger to her growing list of miseries.

And thirst. They hadn't even brought her so much as a sip of water. She was starting to have very strange fantasies about tea.

Sophie let out a long, slow breath, trying to remember to breathe through her mouth when it came time to inhale. The stench was overwhelming. She'd been given a crude chamber pot to use for her bodily functions, but so far she'd been holding it in, trying to relieve herself with as little frequency as possible. The chamber pot had been emptied before it had been tossed into her cell, but it hadn't been cleaned, and in fact when Sophie had picked it up it had been wet, causing her to drop it immediately as her entire body shuddered with revulsion.

She had, of course, emptied many chamber pots in her

time, but the people she'd worked for had generally managed to hit their mark, so to speak. Not to mention that Sophie had always been able to wash her hands afterward.

Now, in addition to the cold and the hunger, she didn't feel clean in her own skin.

It was a horrible sensation.

"You have a visitor."

Sophie jumped to her feet at the warden's gruff, unfriendly voice. Could Benedict have found out where she was? Would he even wish to come to her aid? Did he—

"Well, well, well."

Araminta. Sophie's heart sank.

"Sophie Beckett," she clucked, approaching the cell and then holding a handkerchief to her nose, as if Sophie were the sole cause of the stench. "I would never have guessed that you would have the audacity to show your face in London."

Sophie clamped her mouth together in a mutinous line. She knew that Araminta wanted to get a rise out of her, and she refused to give her the satisfaction.

"Things aren't going well for you, I'm afraid," Araminta continued, shaking her head in a parody of sympathy. She leaned forward and whispered, "The magistrate doesn't take very kindly to thieves."

Sophie crossed her arms and stared stubbornly at the wall. If she so much as looked at Araminta, she probably wouldn't be able to restrain herself from lunging at her, and the metal bars of her cell were likely to do serious damage to her face.

"The shoe clips were bad enough," Araminta said, tapping her chin with her forefinger, "but he grew so very angry when I informed him of the theft of my wedding ring."

"I didn't—" Sophie caught herself before she yelled any more. That was exactly what Araminta wanted.

"Didn't you?" she returned, smiling slyly. She waggled her fingers in the air. "I don't appear to be wearing it, and it's your word against mine."

Sophie's lips parted, but not a sound emerged. Araminta was right. And no judge would take her word over the Countess of Penwood's.

Araminta smiled slightly, her expression vaguely feline. "The man in front—I think he said he was the warden—said you're not likely to be hanged, so you needn't worry on that score. Transportation is a much more likely outcome."

Sophie almost laughed. Just the day before she'd been considering emigrating to America. Now it seemed she'd be leaving for certain—except her destination would be Australia. And she'd be in chains.

"I'll plead for clemency on your behalf," Araminta said. "I don't want you killed, only . . . gone."

"A model of Christian charity," Sophie muttered. "I'm sure the justice will be touched."

Araminta brushed her fingers against her temple, idly pushing back her hair. "Won't he, though?" She looked directly at Sophie and smiled. It was a hard and hollow expression, and suddenly Sophie had to know—

"Why do you hate me?" she whispered.

Araminta did nothing but stare at her for a moment, and then she whispered, "Because he loved you."

Sophie was stunned into silence.

Araminta's eyes grew impossibly brittle. "I will never forgive him for that."

Sophie shook her head in disbelief. "He never loved me."

"He clothed you, he fed you." Araminta's mouth tightened. "He forced me to live with you."

"That wasn't love," Sophie said. "That was guilt. If he loved me he wouldn't have left me with *you*. He wasn't stupid; he had to have known how much you hated me. If he loved me he wouldn't have forgotten me in his will. If he loved me—" She broke off, choking on her own voice.

Araminta crossed her arms.

"If he loved me," Sophie continued, "he might have taken the time to talk to me. He might have asked me how my day went, or what I was studying, or did I enjoy my breakfast." She swallowed convulsively, turning away. It was too hard to look at Araminta just then. "He never loved me," she said quietly. "He didn't know how to love."

No words passed between the two women for many moments, and then Araminta said, "He was punishing me."

Slowly, Sophie turned back around.

"For not giving him an heir." Araminta's hands began to shake. "He hated me for that."

Sophie didn't know what to say. She didn't know if there was anything to say.

After a long moment, Araminta said, "At first I hated you because you were an insult to me. No woman should have to shelter her husband's bastard."

Sophie said nothing.

"But then . . . But then . . ."

To Sophie's great surprise, Araminta sagged against the wall, as if the memories were sucking away her very strength.

"But then it changed," Araminta finally said. "How could he have had you with some whore, and I could not give him a child?"

There seemed little point in Sophie's defending her mother.

"I didn't just hate *you,* you know," Araminta whispered. "I hated seeing you."

Somehow, that didn't surprise Sophie.

"I hated hearing your voice. I hated the fact that your eyes were his. I hated knowing that you were in my house."

"It was my house, too," Sophie said quietly.

"Yes," Araminta replied. "I know. I hated that, too."

Sophie turned quite sharply, looking Araminta in the eye. "Why are you here?" she asked. "Haven't you done enough? You've already ensured my transportation to Australia."

Araminta shrugged. "I can't seem to stay away. There's something so lovely about seeing you in jail. I shall have to bathe for three hours straight to rid myself of the stench, but it's worth it."

"Then excuse me if I go sit in the corner and pretend to read a book," Sophie spat out. "There is nothing lovely about seeing *you.*" She marched over to the wobbly three-legged stool that was her cell's only piece of furniture and sat down, trying not to look as miserable as she felt. Araminta had bested her, it was true, but her spirit had not been broken, and she refused to let Araminta think otherwise.

She sat, arms crossed, her back to the cell opening, listening for signs that Araminta was leaving.

But Araminta stayed.

Finally, after about ten minutes of this nonsense, Sophie jumped to her feet and yelled, "Would you *go?*"

Araminta cocked her head slightly to the side. "I'm thinking."

Sophie would have asked, "About what?" but she was rather afraid of the answer.

"I wonder what it is like in Australia," Araminta mused. "I've never been, of course; no civilized person of my acquaintance would even consider it. But I hear it is dreadfully warm. And you with your fair skin. That lovely complexion of yours isn't likely to survive the hot sun. In fact—"

But whatever Araminta had been about to say was cut off (*thankfully*—because Sophie feared she might be moved to attempt murder if she had to listen to another word) by a commotion erupting around the corner.

"What the devil . . . ?" Araminta said, taking a few steps back and craning her neck for a better view.

And then Sophie heard a very familiar voice.

"Benedict?" she whispered.

"What did you say?" Araminta demanded.

But Sophie had already jumped to her feet and had her face pressed up against the bars of her cell.

"I said," Benedict boomed, *"let us pass!"*

"Benedict!" Sophie yelled. She forgot that she didn't particularly want the Bridgertons to see her in such demeaning surroundings. She forgot that she had no future with him. All she could think was that he had come for her, and he was *here*.

If Sophie could have fit her head through the bars, she would have.

A rather sickening smack, obviously that of flesh against bone, echoed through the air, followed by a duller thud, most probably that of body against floor.

Running steps, and then . . .

"Benedict!"

"Sophie! My God, are you well?" His hands reached through the bars, cupping her cheeks. His lips found hers; the kiss was not one of passion but of terror and relief.

"Mr. Bridgerton?" Araminta squeaked.

Sophie somehow managed to pull her eyes off of Benedict and onto Araminta's shocked face. In the flurry of excitement, she'd quite forgotten that Araminta was still unaware of her ties to the Bridgerton family.

It was one of life's most perfect moments. Maybe it meant she was a shallow person. Maybe it meant that she didn't have her priorities in the proper order. But Sophie just *loved* that Araminta, for whom position and power were everything, had just witnessed Sophie being kissed by one of London's most eligible bachelors.

Of course, Sophie was also rather glad to see Benedict.

Benedict pulled away, his reluctant hands trailing lightly across Sophie's face as he drew back out of her cell. As he crossed his arms, he gave Araminta a glare that Sophie was convinced would scorch earth.

"What are your charges against her?" Benedict demanded.

Sophie's feelings for Araminta could best be categorized as "extreme dislike," but even so, she never would have described the older woman as stupid. She was now, however, prepared to reassess that judgment because Araminta, instead of quaking and cowering as any sane person might do under such fire, instead planted her hands on her hips and belted out, "Theft!"

At that very moment, Lady Bridgerton came scurrying around the corner. "I can't believe Sophie would do any such thing," she said, rushing to her son's side. Her eyes narrowed as she regarded Araminta. "And," she added rather peevishly, "I never liked you, Lady Penwood."

Araminta drew back and planted an affronted hand on her chest. "This is not about me," she huffed. "It is about that girl"—(said with a scathing glance toward Sophie)—"who had the audacity to steal my wedding band!"

"I never stole your wedding band, and you know it!" Sophie protested. "The last thing I would want of yours—"

"You stole my shoe clips!"

Sophie's mouth shut into a belligerent line.

"Ha! See!" Araminta looked about, trying to gauge how many people had seen. "A clear admission of guilt."

"She is your stepdaughter," Benedict ground out. "She should never have been in a position where she felt she had to—"

Araminta's face twisted and grew red. "Don't you *ever,*" she warned, "call her my stepdaughter. She is nothing to me. Nothing!"

"I beg your pardon," Lady Bridgerton said in a remarkably polite voice, "but if she truly meant nothing to you, you'd hardly be here in this filthy jail, attempting to have her hanged for theft."

Araminta was saved from having to reply by the arrival of the magistrate, who was followed by an extremely grumpy-looking warden, who also happened to be sporting a rather stunning black eye.

As the warden had spanked her on the bottom while shoving her into her cell, Sophie really couldn't help but smile.

"What is going on here?" the magistrate demanded.

"This woman," Benedict said, his loud, deep voice effectively blotting out all other attempts at an answer, "has accused my fiancée of theft."

Fiancée?

Sophie just managed to snap her mouth closed, but even so, she had to clutch tightly on to the bars of her cell, because her legs had turned to instant water.

"Fiancée?" Araminta gasped.

The magistrate straightened. "And precisely who are you, sir?" he asked, clearly aware that Benedict was someone important, even if he wasn't positive who.

Benedict crossed his arms as he said his name.

The magistrate paled. "Er, any relation to the viscount?"

"He's my brother."

"And she's"—he gulped as he pointed to Sophie—"your fiancée?"

Sophie waited for some sort of supernatural sign to stir the air, branding Benedict as a liar, but to her surprise, nothing happened. Lady Bridgerton was even nodding.

"You can't marry her," Araminta insisted.

Benedict turned to his mother. "Is there any reason I need to consult Lady Penwood about this?"

"None that I can think of," Lady Bridgerton replied.

"She is nothing but a whore," Araminta hissed. "Her mother was a whore, and blood runs—urp!"

Benedict had her by the throat before anyone was even aware that he had moved. "Don't," he warned, "make me hit you."

The magistrate tapped Benedict on the shoulder. "You really ought to let her go."

"Might I muzzle her?"

The magistrate looked torn, but eventually he shook his head.

With obvious reluctance, Benedict released Araminta.

"If you marry her," Araminta said, rubbing her throat, "I shall make sure everyone knows *exactly* what she is—the bastard daughter of a whore."

The magistrate turned to Araminta with a stern expression. "I don't think we need that sort of language."

"I can assure you I am not in the habit of speaking in such a manner," she replied, sniffing disdainfully, "but the occasion warrants strong speech."

Sophie actually bit her knuckle as she stared at Benedict, who was flexing and unflexing his fingers in a most menacing manner. Clearly *he* felt the occasion warranted strong fists.

The magistrate cleared his throat. "You accuse her of a very serious crime." He gulped. "And she's going to be married to a Bridgerton."

"I am the Countess of Penwood," she shrilled. "Countess!"

The magistrate looked back and forth between the occupants of the room. As a countess, Araminta outranked everyone, but at the same time, she was only one Penwood against two Bridgertons, one of whom was very large, visibly angry, and had already planted his fist in the warden's eye.

"She stole from me!"

"No, you stole from her!" Benedict roared.

The room fell into instant silence.

"You stole her very childhood," Benedict said, his body shaking with rage. There were huge gaps in his knowledge of Sophie's life, but somehow he knew that this woman had caused much of the pain that lurked behind her green eyes. And he'd have been willing to bet that her dear, departed papa was responsible for the rest.

Benedict turned to the magistrate and said, "My fiancée is the bastard daughter of the late Earl of Penwood. And that is why the dowager countess has falsely accused her of theft. It is revenge and hate, pure and simple."

The magistrate looked from Benedict to Araminta and

then finally to Sophie. "Is this true?" he asked her. "Have you been falsely accused?"

"She took the shoe clips!" Araminta shrieked. "I swear on my husband's grave, she took the shoe clips!"

"Oh, for the love of God, Mother, *I* took the shoe clips."

Sophie's mouth fell open. "Posy?"

Benedict looked at the newcomer, a short, slightly pudgy young woman who was obviously the countess's daughter, then glanced back to Sophie, who had gone white as a sheet.

"Get out of here," Araminta hissed. "You have no place in these proceedings."

"Obviously she does," the magistrate said, turning to Araminta, "if she took the shoe clips. Do you want to have her charged?"

"She's my daughter!"

"Put me in the cell with Sophie!" Posy said dramatically, clasping one of her hands to her breast with great effect. "If she is transported for theft, then I must be as well."

For the first time in several days, Benedict found himself smiling.

The warden took out his keys. "Sir?" he said hesitantly, nudging the magistrate.

"Put those away," the magistrate snapped. "We're not incarcerating the countess's daughter."

"Do not put those away," Lady Bridgerton cut in. "I want my future daughter-in-law released immediately."

The warden looked helplessly at the magistrate.

"Oh, very well," the magistrate said, jabbing his finger in Sophie's direction. "Let that one free. But no one is going anywhere until I have this sorted out."

Araminta bristled in protest, but Sophie was duly released. She started to run to Benedict, but the magistrate held out a restraining arm. "Not so fast," he warned. "We'll be having no lovey-dovey reunions until I figure out who is to be arrested."

"No one is to be arrested," Benedict growled.

"She is going to Australia!" Araminta cried out, pointing toward Sophie.

"Put me in the cell!" Posy sighed, placing the back of her hand against her brow. "I did it!"

"Posy, will you be quiet?" Sophie whispered. "Trust me, you do not want to be in that cell. It's dreadful. And there are rats."

Posy started inching away from the cell.

"You will never see another invitation again in this town," Lady Bridgerton said to Araminta.

"I am a countess!" Araminta hissed.

"And I am more popular," Lady Bridgerton returned, the snide words so out of character that both Benedict's and Sophie's mouths dropped open.

"Enough!" the magistrate said. He turned to Posy, pointing to Araminta as he said, "Is she your mother?"

Posy nodded.

"And you said you stole the shoe clips?"

Posy nodded again. "And no one stole her wedding ring. It's in her jewelry box at home."

No one gasped, because no one was terribly surprised.

But Araminta said, nonetheless, "It is not!"

"Your other jewelry box," Posy clarified. "The one you keep in the third drawer from the left."

Araminta paled.

The magistrate said, "You don't seem to have a very good case against Miss Beckett, Lady Penwood."

Araminta began to shake with rage, her outstretched arm quivering as she pointed one long finger at Sophie. "She stole from me," she said in a deadly low voice before turning furious eyes on Posy. "My daughter is lying. I do not know why, and I certainly do not know what she hopes to gain, but she is lying."

Something very uncomfortable began to churn in Sophie's stomach. Posy was going to be in horrible trouble when she went home. There was no telling what Araminta would do in retaliation for such public humiliation. She couldn't let Posy take the blame for her. She had to—

"Posy didn't—" The words burst forth from her mouth before she had a chance to think, but she didn't manage to finish her sentence because Posy elbowed her in the belly.

Hard.

"Did you say something?" the magistrate inquired.

Sophie shook her head, completely unable to speak. Posy had knocked her breath clear to Scotland.

The magistrate let out a weary sigh and raked his hand through his thinning blond hair. He looked at Posy, then at Sophie, then Araminta, then Benedict. Lady Bridgerton cleared her throat, forcing him to look at her, too.

"Clearly," the magistrate said, looking very much as if he'd rather be anywhere other than where he was, "this is about a great deal more than a stolen shoe clip."

"Shoe *clips*," Araminta sniffed. "There were two of them."

"Regardless," the magistrate ground out, "you all obviously detest one another, and I would like to know why before I go ahead and charge anyone."

For a second, no one spoke. Then everyone spoke.

"Silence!" the magistrate roared. "You," he said, pointing at Sophie, "start."

"Uhhhh . . ." Now that Sophie actually had the floor, she felt terribly self-conscious.

The magistrate cleared his throat. Loudly.

"What he said was correct," Sophie said quickly, pointing to Benedict. "I am the daughter of the Earl of Penwood, although I was never acknowledged as such."

Araminta opened her mouth to say something, but the magistrate sent her such a withering glare that she kept quiet.

"I lived at Penwood Park for seven years before she married the earl," she continued, motioning to Araminta. "The earl said that he was my guardian, but everyone knew the truth." She paused, remembering her father's face, and thinking that she ought not be so surprised that she couldn't picture him with a smile. "I look a great deal like him," she said.

"I knew your father," Lady Bridgerton said softly. "And your aunt. It explains why I've always thought you looked so familiar."

Sophie flashed her a small, grateful smile. Something in Lady Bridgerton's tone was very reassuring, and it made her feel a little warmer inside, a little more secure.

"Please continue," the magistrate said.

Sophie gave him a nod, then added, "When the earl married the countess, she didn't want me living there, but the earl insisted. I rarely saw him, and I don't think he thought very much of me, but he did see me as his responsibility, and he wouldn't allow her to boot me out. But when he died . . ."

Sophie stopped and swallowed, trying to get past the lump in her throat. She'd never actually told her story to anyone before; the words seemed strange and foreign coming from her mouth. "When he died," she continued, "his will specified that Lady Penwood's portion would be trebled if she kept me in her household until I turned twenty. So she did. But my position changed dramatically. I became a servant. Well, not really a servant." Sophie smiled wryly. "A servant is paid. So I was really more like a slave."

Sophie looked over at Araminta. She was standing with her arms crossed and her nose tipped in the air. Her lips were pursed tightly, and it suddenly struck Sophie how very many times before she had seen that exact same expression on Araminta's face. More times than she could dare to count. Enough times to have broken her soul.

Yet here she was, dirty and penniless to be sure, but with her mind and spirit still strong.

"Sophie?" Benedict asked, gazing at her with a concerned expression. "Is everything all right?"

She nodded slowly, because she was just coming to realize that everything *was* all right. The man she loved had (in a rather roundabout way) just asked her to marry him, Araminta was finally about to receive the drubbing she deserved—at the hands of the Bridgertons, no less, who would leave her in shreds by the time they were through, and Posy . . . now that might have been the loveliest of all. Posy, who had always wanted to be a sister to her, who had never quite had the courage to be herself, had stood up to her mother and quite possibly saved the day. Sophie was one hundred percent certain that if Benedict had not come and declared her his fiancée, Posy's testimony would have been the only thing to save her from transportation—or maybe even execution. And Sophie knew better than anyone that Posy would pay dearly for her courage. Araminta was probably already plotting how to make her life a living hell.

Yes, everything *was* all right, and Sophie suddenly found herself standing a little straighter as she said, "Allow me to finish my story. After the earl died, Lady Penwood kept me on as her unpaid lady's maid. Although in truth I was made to do the work of three maids."

"You know, Lady Whistledown said that very thing just last month!" Posy said excitedly. "I told Mother that she—"

"Posy, shut *up*!" Araminta snapped.

"When I turned twenty," Sophie continued, "she didn't turn me out. To this day I don't know why."

"I think we've heard enough," Araminta said.

"I don't think we've heard nearly enough," Benedict snapped.

Sophie looked to the magistrate for guidance. At his nod she continued. "I can only deduce that she rather enjoyed having someone to order about. Or maybe she just liked having a maid she didn't have to pay. There was nothing left from his will."

"That's not true," Posy blurted out.

Sophie turned to her in shock.

"He did leave you money," Posy insisted.

Sophie felt her jaw go slack. "That's not possible. I had nothing. My father saw to my welfare up to age twenty, but after that—"

"After that," Posy said rather forcefully, "you had a dowry."

"A dowry?" Sophie whispered.

"That's not true!" Araminta shrilled.

"It *is* true," Posy insisted. "You ought not leave incriminating evidence about, Mother. I read a copy of the earl's will last year." She turned to the rest of the room and said, "It was in the same box where she put her wedding band."

"You stole my dowry?" Sophie said, her voice barely more than breath. All these years she'd thought her father had left her with nothing. She'd known that he'd never loved her, that he saw her as little more than his responsibility, but it had stung that he'd left dowries for Rosamund and Posy—who were not even his blood daughters—and not for her.

She'd never really thought that he'd ignored her on purpose; in all truth, she'd mostly felt . . . forgotten.

Which had felt worse than a deliberate snub would have done.

"He left me a dowry," she said dazedly. Then to Benedict, "I have a dowry."

"I don't care if you have a dowry," Benedict replied. "I don't need it."

"I care," Sophie said. "I thought he'd forgotten me. All these years I'd thought he'd written up his will and simply forgotten about me. I know he couldn't really leave money to his bastard daughter, but he'd told all the world I was his ward. There was no reason he couldn't provide for his ward." For some reason she looked to Lady Bridgerton. "He could have provided for a ward. People do that all the time."

The magistrate cleared his throat and turned on Araminta, "And what has happened to her dowry?"

Araminta said nothing.

Lady Bridgerton cleared her throat. "I don't think it's terribly legal," she said, "to embezzle a young woman's dowry." She smiled—a slow, satisfied sort of smile. "Eh, Araminta?"

Chapter 23

Lady Penwood appears to have left town. So does Lady Bridgerton. Interesting . . .

LADY WHISTLEDOWN'S SOCIETY PAPERS, 18 JUNE 1817

Benedict decided he had never loved his mother more than he did at that very minute. He was trying not to grin, but it was exceedingly difficult with Lady Penwood gasping like a fish on land.

The magistrate's eyes bugged out. "You're not suggesting I arrest the *countess*?"

"No, of course not," Violet demurred. "She'd likely go free. The aristocracy rarely pays for its crimes. But," she added, tilting her head slightly to the side as she gave Lady Penwood a very pointed glance, "if you *were* to arrest her, it would be terribly embarrassing while she defended the charges."

"What are you trying to say?" Lady Penwood asked through decidedly clenched teeth.

Violet turned to the magistrate. "Might I have a few moments alone with Lady Penwood?"

"Of course, my lady." He gave her a gruff nod, then barked, "Everyone! Out!"

"No, no," Violet said with a sweet smile as she pressed something that looked suspiciously like a pound note into his palm. "My family may stay."

The magistrate blushed slightly, then grabbed the warden's arm and yanked him out of the room.

"There now," Violet murmured. "Where were we?"

Benedict beamed with pride as he watched his mother march right up to Lady Penwood and stare her down. He stole a glance at Sophie. Her mouth was hanging open.

"My son is going to marry Sophie," Violet said, "and you are going to tell anyone who will listen that she was the ward of your late husband."

"I will never lie for her," Lady Penwood shot back.

Violet shrugged. "Fine. Then you can expect my solicitors to begin looking for Sophie's dowry immediately. After all, Benedict will be entitled to it once he marries her."

Benedict slipped his arm around Sophie's waist and gave her a light squeeze.

"If someone asks me," Lady Penwood ground out, "I will confirm whatever story you bandy about. But do not expect me to go out of my way to help her."

Violet pretended to mull that over, then said, "Excellent. I do believe that will do nicely." She turned to her son. "Benedict?"

He gave her a sharp nod.

His mother turned back to Lady Penwood. "Sophie's father was named Charles Beckett and he was a distant cousin of the earl's, no?"

Lady Penwood looked as if she'd swallowed a bad clam, but she nodded nonetheless.

Violet pointedly turned her back on the countess, and said, "I'm sure some members of the *ton* will consider her a bit shabby, since obviously nobody will be familiar with her family, but at least she will be respectable. After all"—she turned back around and flashed a wide smile at Araminta—"there is that connection with the Penwoods."

Araminta let out a strange, growling sound. It was all Benedict could do not to laugh.

"Oh, magistrate!" Violet called out, and when he bustled back into the room, she smiled gamely at him and said, "I believe my work here is done."

He let out a sigh of relief, saying, "Then I don't have to arrest anyone?"

"It seems not."

He practically sagged against the wall.

"Well, I am leaving!" Lady Penwood announced, as if anyone might possibly miss her. She turned to her daughter with furious eyes. "Come along, Posy."

Benedict watched as the blood quite literally drained from Posy's face. But before he could intervene, Sophie jumped forward, blurting out, "Lady Bridgerton!" just as Araminta roared, *"Now!"*

"Yes, dear?"

Sophie grabbed Violet's arm and pulled her close enough to whisper something in her ear.

"Quite right," Violet said. She turned to Posy. "Miss Gunningworth?"

"Actually, it's Miss Reiling," Posy corrected. "The earl never adopted me."

"Of course. Miss Reiling. How old are you?"

"One-and-twenty, my lady."

"Well, that's certainly old enough to make your own decisions. Would you like to come to my home for a visit?"

"Oh, *yes*!"

"Posy, you may *not* go live with the Bridgertons!" Araminta ordered.

Violet ignored her completely as she said to Posy, "I believe I will quit London early this season. Would you care to join us for an extended stay in Kent?"

Posy nodded quickly. "I would be much obliged."

"That settles it, then."

"That does not settle it," Araminta snapped. "She is my daughter, and—"

"Benedict," Lady Bridgerton said in a rather bored voice, "what was the name of my solicitor?"

"Go!" Araminta spat at Posy. "And don't ever darken my door again."

For the first time that afternoon, Posy began to look a little scared. It didn't help when her mother stalked right up to her and hissed straight in her face, "If you go with them now, you are dead to me. Do you understand? *Dead!*"

Posy threw a panicked look at Violet, who immediately stepped forward and linked their arms together.

"It's all right, Posy," Violet said softly. "You may stay with us as long as you wish."

Sophie stepped forward and slid her arm through Posy's free one. "Now we will be sisters truly," she said, leaning forward and giving her a kiss on the cheek.

"Oh, Sophie," Posy cried out, a well of tears bursting forth. "I'm so sorry! I never stood up for you. I should have said something. I should have done something, but—"

Sophie shook her head. "You were young. I was young. And I know better than anyone how difficult it is to defy *her*." She threw a scathing glare at Araminta.

"Don't you speak to me that way," Araminta seethed, raising her hand as if to strike.

"Ah ah ah!" Violet cut in. "The solicitors, Lady Penwood. Don't forget the solicitors."

Araminta dropped her hand, but she looked as if she might spontaneously burst into flame at any moment.

"Benedict?" Violet called out. "How quickly could we be at the solicitors' office?"

Grinning inside, he gave his chin a thoughtful stroke. "They're not too terribly far away. Twenty minutes? Thirty if the roads are full."

Araminta shook with rage as she directed her words at Violet. "Take her then. She's never been anything to me but a disappointment. And you can expect to be stuck with her until your dying day, as no one is likely to offer for her. I have to bribe men just to ask her to dance."

And then the strangest thing occurred. Sophie began to shake. Her skin turned red, her teeth clenched, and the most amazing roar burst forth from her mouth. And before anyone could even think to intervene, she had planted her fist squarely into Araminta's left eye and sent the older woman sprawling.

Benedict had thought that nothing could have surprised him more than his mother's heretofore undetected Machiavellian streak.

He was wrong.

"That," Sophie hissed, "is *not* for stealing my dowry. It's not for all the times you tried to boot me out of my house before my father died. And it's not even for turning me into your personal slave."

"Er, Sophie," Benedict said mildly, "what, then, is it for?"

Sophie's eyes never wavered off of Araminta's face as she said, "*That* was for not loving your daughters equally."

Posy began to bawl.

"There's a special place in hell for mothers like you," Sophie said, her voice dangerously low.

"You know," the magistrate squeaked, "we really do need to clear this cell out for the next occupant."

"He's right," Violet said quickly, stepping in front of Sophie before she decided to start kicking Araminta. She turned to Posy. "Have you any belongings you wish to retrieve?"

Posy shook her head.

Violet's eyes turned sad as she gave Posy's hand a little squeeze. "We shall make new memories for you, my dear."

Araminta rose to her feet, gave Posy one last horrific glare, then stalked away.

"Well," Violet declared, planting her hands on her hips. "I thought she would never leave."

Benedict disengaged his arm from Sophie's waist with a murmur of, "Don't move a muscle," then walked quickly to his mother's side.

"Have I told you lately," he whispered in her ear, "how much I love you?"

"No," she said with a jaunty smile, "but I know, anyway."

"Have I mentioned that you're the best of mothers?"

"No, but I know that, too."

"Good." He leaned down and dropped a kiss on her cheek. "Thank you. It's a privilege to be your son."

His mother, who had held her own throughout the day, and indeed proven herself the most hardheaded and quick-witted of them all, burst into tears.

"What did you say to her?" Sophie demanded.

"It's all right," Violet said, sniffling mightily. "It's . . ." She threw her arms around Benedict. "I love you, too!"

Posy turned to Sophie and said, "This is a nice family."

Sophie turned to Posy and said, "I know."

One hour later Sophie was in Benedict's sitting room, perched on the very same sofa on which she had lost her innocence just a few weeks earlier. Lady Bridgerton had questioned the wisdom (and propriety) of Sophie's going to Benedict's home by herself, but he had given her such a look that she had quickly backed down, saying only, "Just have her home by seven."

Which gave them one hour together.

"I'm sorry," Sophie blurted out, the instant her bottom touched the sofa. For some reason they hadn't said anything during the carriage ride home. They'd held hands, and Benedict had brought her fingers to his lips, but they hadn't said anything.

Sophie had been relieved. She hadn't been ready for

words. It had been easy at the jail, with all the commotion and so many people, but now that they were alone . . .

She didn't know what to say.

Except, she supposed, "I'm sorry."

"No, I'm sorry," Benedict replied, sitting beside her and taking her hands in his.

"No, I'm—" She suddenly smiled. "This is very silly."

"I love you," he said.

Her lips parted.

"I want to marry you," he said.

She stopped breathing.

"And I don't care about your parents or my mother's bargain with Lady Penwood to make you respectable." He stared down at her, his dark eyes meltingly in love. "I would have married you no matter what."

Sophie blinked. The tears in her eyes were growing fat and hot, and she had a sneaking suspicion that she was about to make a fool of herself by blubbering all over him. She managed to say his name, then found herself completely lost from there.

Benedict squeezed her hands. "We couldn't have lived in London, I know, but we don't need to live in London. When I thought about what it was in life I really needed—not what I wanted, but what I needed—the only thing that kept coming up was you."

"I—"

"No, let me finish," he said, his voice suspiciously hoarse. "I shouldn't have asked you to be my mistress. It wasn't right of me."

"Benedict," she said softly, "what else would you have done? You thought me a servant. In a perfect world we could have married, but this isn't a perfect world. Men like you don't marry—"

"Fine. I wasn't wrong to ask, then." He tried to smile. It came out lopsided. "I would have been a fool not to ask. I wanted you so badly, and I think I already loved you, and—"

"Benedict, you don't have to—"

"Explain? Yes, I do. I should never have pressed the issue once you refused my offer. It was unfair of me to ask, especially when we both knew that I would eventually be expected to marry. I would die before sharing you. How could I ask you to do the same?"

She reached out and brushed something off of his cheek. Jesus, was he crying? He couldn't remember the last time he'd cried. When his father had died, perhaps? Even then, his tears had fallen in private.

"There are so many reasons I love you," he said, each word emerging with careful precision. He knew that he had won her. She wasn't going to run away; she *would* be his wife. But he still wanted this to be perfect. A man only got one shot at declaring himself to his true love; he didn't want to muck it up completely.

"But one of the things I love best," he continued, "is the fact that you know yourself. You know who you are, and what you value. You have principles, Sophie, and you stick by them." He took her hand and brought it to his lips. "That is so rare."

Her eyes were filling with tears, and all he wanted to do was hold her, but he knew he had to finish. So many words had been welling up inside of him, and they all had to be said.

"And," he said, his voice dropping in volume, "you took the time to see *me*. To know me. Benedict. Not Mr. Bridgerton, not 'Number Two.' Benedict."

She touched his cheek. "You're the finest person I know. I adore your family, but I love *you*."

He crushed her to him. He couldn't help it. He had to feel her in his arms, to reassure himself that she was there and that she would always be there. With him, by his side, until death did they part. It was strange, but he was driven by the oddest compulsion to hold her . . . just hold her.

He wanted her, of course. He always wanted her. But more than that, he wanted to hold her. To smell her, to feel her.

He was, he realized, comforted by her presence. They didn't need to talk. They didn't even need to touch (although he wasn't about to let go just then). Simply put, he was a happier man—and quite possibly a better man—when she was near.

He buried his face in her hair, inhaling her scent, smelling . . .

Smelling . . .

He drew back. "Would you care for a bath?"

Her face turned an instant scarlet. "Oh, no," she moaned, the words muffled into the hand she'd clapped over her mouth. "It was so filthy in jail, and I was forced to sleep on the ground, and—"

"Don't tell me any more," he said.

"But—"

"Please." If he heard more he might have to kill someone. As long as there had been no permanent damage, he didn't want to know the details.

"I think," he said, the first hint of a smile tugging at the left corner of his mouth, "that you should take a bath."

"Right." She nodded as she rose to her feet. "I'll go straight to your mother's—"

"Here."

"Here?"

The smile spread to the right corner of his mouth. "Here."

"But we told your mother—"

"That you'd be home by nine."

"I think she said seven."

"Did she? Funny, I heard nine."

"Benedict . . ."

He took her hand and pulled her toward the door. "Seven sounds an *awful* lot like nine."

"Benedict . . ."

"Actually, it sounds even more like eleven."

"Benedict!"

He deposited her right by the door. "Stay here."

"I beg your pardon?"

"Don't move a muscle," he said, touching his fingertip to her nose.

Sophie watched helplessly as he slipped out into the hall, only to return two minutes later. "Where did you go?" she asked.

"To order a bath."

"But—"

His eyes grew very, very wicked. "For two."

She gulped.

He leaned forward. "They happened to have water heating already."

"They did?"

He nodded. "It'll only take a few minutes to fill the tub."

She glanced toward the front door. "It's nearly seven."

"But I'm allowed to keep you until twelve."

"Benedict!"

He pulled her close. "You want to stay."

"I never said that."

"You don't have to. If you really disagreed with me, you'd have something more to say than, 'Benedict'!"

She had to smile; he did *that* good an imitation of her voice.

His mouth curved into a devilish grin. "Am I wrong?"

She looked away, but she knew her lips were twitching.

"I thought not," he murmured. He motioned with his head toward the stairs. "Come with me."

She went.

To Sophie's great surprise, Benedict vacated the room while she undressed for her bath. She held her breath as she pulled her dress over her head. He was right; she did smell rank.

The maid who had drawn the bath had scented it with oil and a sudsy soap that left bubbles floating on the surface.

Once Sophie had shed all of her clothing, she dipped her toe into the steaming water. The rest of her soon followed.

Heaven. It was hard to believe it had only been two days since she'd had a bath. One night in jail made it feel more like a year.

Sophie tried to clear her mind and enjoy the hedonism of the moment, but it was difficult to enjoy with the anticipation growing within her veins. She knew when she'd decided to stay that Benedict planned on joining her. She could have refused; for all his wheedling and cajoling, he would have taken her back home to his mother's.

But she had decided to stay. Somewhere between the sitting-room doorway and the base of the stairs she'd realized she *wanted* to stay. It had been such a long road to this moment, and she wasn't quite ready to relinquish him, even if it would only be until the following morning, when he was sure to come by his mother's for breakfast.

He would be here soon. And when he was . . .

She shivered. Even in the steaming hot tub, she shivered. And then, as she was sinking deeper into the water, allowing it to rise above her shoulders and neck, even right up to her nose, she heard the click of the door opening.

Benedict. He was wearing a dark green dressing gown, tied with a sash at his waist. His feet were bare, as were his legs from the knees down.

"I hope you don't mind if I have this destroyed," he said, glancing down at her dress.

She smiled at him and shook her head. It wasn't what she'd been expecting him to say, and she knew that he'd done it to set her at ease.

"I'll send someone to fetch you another," he said.

"Thank you." She shifted slightly in the water to make room for him, but he surprised her by walking to her end of the tub.

"Lean forward," he murmured.

She did, and sighed with pleasure as he began to wash her back.

"I've dreamed of doing this for years."

"Years?" she asked, amused.

"Mmm-hmm. I had *many* dreams about you after the masquerade."

Sophie was glad she was leaning forward, her forehead resting on her bent knees, because she blushed.

"Dunk your head so I can wash your hair," he ordered.

She slid under the water, then quickly came back up.

Benedict rubbed the bar of soap in his hands and then began to work the lather through her hair. "It was longer before," he commented.

"I had to cut it," she said. "I sold it to a wigmaker."

She wasn't sure, but she thought she might have heard him growl.

"It used to be much shorter," she added.

"Ready to rinse."

She dunked back in the tub, swishing her head this way and that under the water before coming back up for air.

Benedict cupped his hands and filled them with water. "You've still got some in the back," he said, letting the water pour over her hair.

Sophie let him repeat that process a few times, then finally asked, "Aren't you coming in?" It was dreadfully brazen of her, and she knew she must be blushing like a raspberry, but she simply had to know.

He shook his head. "I'd planned to, but this is too much fun."

"Washing me?" she asked doubtfully.

One corner of his mouth quirked into the faintest of half smiles. "I'm rather looking forward to drying you off as well." He reached down and picked up a large white towel. "Up you go."

Sophie chewed on her lower lip in indecision. She had, of

course, already been as close to him as two people could be, but she wasn't so sophisticated that she could rise naked from the tub without a large degree of embarrassment.

Benedict smiled faintly as he stood and unfolded the towel. Holding it wide, he averted his gaze and said, "I'll have you all wrapped up before I can see a thing."

Sophie took a deep breath and stood, somehow feeling that that one action might mark the beginning of the rest of her life.

Benedict gently wrapped the towel around her, his hands bringing the corners to her face when he was done. He dabbed at her cheeks, where light droplets of water were still clinging to her skin, then leaned down and kissed her nose. "I'm glad you're here," he murmured.

"I'm glad, too."

He touched her chin. His eyes never left hers, and she almost felt as if he'd touched those as well. And then, with the softest, most tender caress imaginable, he kissed her. Sophie didn't just feel loved; she felt revered.

"I should wait until Monday," he said, "but I don't want to."

"I don't want you to wait," she whispered.

He kissed her again, this time with a bit more urgency. "You're so beautiful," he murmured. "Everything I ever dreamed of."

His lips found her cheek, her chin, her neck, and every kiss, every nibble robbed her of balance and breath. She was sure her legs would give out, sure her strength would fail her under his tender onslaught, and just when she was convinced she'd crumple to the floor, he scooped her into his arms and carried her to the bed.

"In my heart," he vowed, settling her against the quilts and pillows, "you are my wife."

Sophie's breath caught.

"After our wedding it will be legal," he said, stretching out alongside her, "blessed by God and country, but right now—" His voice grew hoarse as he propped himself up on one elbow so that he could gaze into her eyes. "Right now it is *true*."

Sophie reached up and touched his face. "I love you," she whispered. "I have always loved you. I think I loved you before I even knew you."

He leaned down to kiss her anew, but she stopped him with a breathy, "No, wait."

He paused, mere inches from her lips.

"At the masquerade," she said, her voice uncharacteristically shaky, "even before I saw you, I *felt* you. Anticipation. Magic. There was something in the air. And when I turned, and you were there, it was as if you'd been waiting for me, and I knew that you were the reason I'd stolen into the ball."

Something wet hit her cheek. A single tear, fallen from his eye.

"You are the reason I exist," she said softly, "the very reason I was born."

He opened his mouth, and for a moment she was certain he would say something, but the only sound that emerged was a rough, halting noise, and she realized that he was overcome, that he could not speak.

She was undone.

Benedict kissed her again, trying to show in deeds what he could not say in words. He hadn't thought he could love her any more than he did just five seconds earlier, but when she'd said . . . when she'd told him . . .

His heart had grown, and he'd thought it might burst.

He loved her. Suddenly the world was a very simple place. He loved her, and that was all that mattered.

His robe and her towel melted away, and when they were skin to skin he worshipped her with his hands and lips. He wanted her to realize the extent of his need for her, and he wanted her to know the same desire.

"Oh, Sophie," he groaned, her name the only word he could manage to say. "Sophie, Sophie, Sophie."

She smiled up at him, and he was struck by the most remarkable desire to laugh. He was happy, he realized. So damned happy.

And it felt good.

He positioned himself over her, ready to enter her, ready to make her his. This was different from the last time, when they'd both been swept away by emotion. This time they had been deliberate. They had chosen more than passion; they had chosen each other.

"You're mine," he said, his eyes never leaving hers as he slid inside. "You're mine."

And much later, when they were exhausted and spent, lying in each other's arms, he brought his lips to her ear and whispered, "And I'm yours."

Several hours later, Sophie yawned and blinked herself awake, wondering why she felt so lovely and warm, and—

"Benedict!" she gasped. "What time is it?"

He didn't respond, so she clutched at his shoulder and shook hard. "Benedict! Benedict!"

He grunted as he rolled over. "I'm sleeping."

"What time is it?"

He buried his face in the pillow. "Haven't the foggiest."

"I'm supposed to be at your mother's by seven."

"Eleven," he mumbled.

"Seven!"

He opened one eye. It looked like it took a great deal of effort. "You knew you weren't going to make it back by seven when you decided to take a bath."

"I know, but I didn't think I'd be much past nine."

Benedict blinked a few times as he looked around the room. "I don't think you're going to make it—"

But she'd already caught sight of the mantel clock and was presently choking frantically.

"Are you all right?" he inquired.

"It's three in the morning!"

He smiled. "You might as well spend the night, then."

"Benedict!"

"You wouldn't want to put out any of the servants, would you? They're all quite asleep, I'm sure."

"But I—"

"Have mercy, woman," he finally declared. "I'm marrying you next week."

That got her attention. "Next week?" she squeaked.

He tried to assume a serious mien. "It's best to take care of these things quickly."

"Why?"

"Why?" he echoed.

"Yes, why?"

"Er, ah, stemming gossip and all that."

Her lips parted and her eyes grew round. "Do you think Lady Whistledown will write about me?"

"God, I hope not," he muttered.

Her face fell.

"Well, I suppose she *might*. Why on earth would you want her to?"

"I've been reading her column for years. I always dreamed of seeing my name there."

He shook his head. "You have very strange dreams."

"Benedict!"

"Very well, yes, I imagine Lady Whistledown will report our marriage, if not before the ceremony, then certainly very quickly after the fact. She's diabolical that way."

"I wish I knew who she was."

"You and half of London."

"Me and *all* of London, I should think." She sighed, then said, not very convincingly, "I really should go. Your mother is surely worried about me."

He shrugged. "She knows where you are."

"But she'll think less of me."

"I doubt it. She'll give you a bit of latitude, I'm sure, considering we're to be married in three days."

"Three days?" she yelped. "I thought you said next week."

"Three days *is* next week."

Sophie frowned. "Oh. You're right. Monday, then?"

He nodded, looking very satisfied.

"Imagine that," she said. "I'll be in *Whistledown*."

He propped himself up on one elbow, eyeing her suspiciously. "Are you looking forward to marrying me," he asked in an amused voice, "or is it merely the *Whistledown* mention that has you so excited?"

She gave him a playful swat on the shoulder.

"Actually," he said thoughtfully, "you've already been in *Whistledown*."

"I have? When?"

"After the masquerade. Lady Whistledown remarked that I'd been rather taken with a mystery woman in silver. Try as she might, she couldn't deduce your identity." He grinned. "It very well may be the only secret in London she *hasn't* uncovered."

Sophie's face went instantly serious and she scooted a foot or so away from him on the bed. "Oh, Benedict. I have to . . . I want to . . . That is to say . . ." She stopped, looking away for a few seconds before turning back. "I'm sorry."

He considered yanking her back into his arms, but she looked so damned earnest he had no choice but to take her seriously. "What for?"

"For not telling you who I was. It was wrong of me." She bit her lip. "Well, not *wrong* precisely."

He drew back slightly. "If it wasn't wrong, then what was it?"

"I don't know. I can't explain exactly why I did what I did, but it just . . ." She chewed on her lips some more. He started to think that she might do herself permanent harm.

She sighed. "I didn't tell you right away because it didn't seem to make any sense to do so. I was so sure we'd part ways just as soon as we left the Cavenders. But then you grew ill, and I had to care for you, and you didn't recognize me, and . . ."

He lifted a finger to her lips. "It doesn't matter."

Her brows rose. "It seemed to matter a great deal the other night."

He didn't know why, but he just didn't want to get into a serious discussion at that moment. "A lot has changed since then."

"Don't you want to know why I didn't tell you who I was?"

He touched her cheeks. "I know who you are."

She chewed on her lip.

"And do you want to hear the funniest part?" he continued. "Do you know one of the reasons I was so hesitant to give my heart completely to you? I'd been saving a piece of it for the lady from the masquerade, always hoping that one day I'd find her."

"Oh, Benedict," she sighed, thrilled by his words, and at the same time miserable that she had hurt him so.

"Deciding to marry you meant I had to abandon my dream of marrying *her*," he said quietly. "Ironic, isn't it?"

"I'm sorry I hurt you by not revealing my identity," she said, not quite looking at his face, "but I'm not sure that I'm sorry I did it. Does that make any sense?"

He didn't say anything.

"I think I would do the same thing again."

He still didn't say anything. Sophie started to feel very uneasy inside.

"It just seemed like the right thing to do at the time," she persisted. "Telling you that I'd been at the masquerade would have served no purpose."

"I would have known the truth," he said softly.

"Yes, and what would you have done with that truth?" She sat up, pulling the covers until they were tucked under her arms. "You would have wanted your mystery woman to be your mistress, just as you wanted the housemaid to be your mistress."

He said nothing, just stared at her face.

"I guess what I'm saying," Sophie said quickly, "is that if I'd known at the beginning what I know now, I would have said something. But I didn't know, and I thought I'd just be positioning myself for heartbreak, and—" She choked on her final words, frantically searching his face for some kind of clue to his feelings. "*Please* say something."

"I love you," he said.

It was all she needed.

Epilogue

Sunday's bash at Bridgerton House is sure to be the event of the season. The entire family will gather, along with a hundred or so of their closest friends, to celebrate the dowager vis countess's birthday.

It is considered crass to mention a lady's age, and so This Author will not reveal which birthday Lady Bridgerton is celebrating.

But have no fear . . . This Author knows!

LADY WHISTLEDOWN'S SOCIETY PAPERS, 9 APRIL 1824

"Stop! Stop!"

Sophie shrieked with laughter as she ran down the stone steps that led to the garden behind Bridgerton House. After three children and seven years of marriage, Benedict could still make her smile, still make her laugh . . . and he still chased her around the house any chance he could get.

"Where are the children?" she gasped, once he'd caught her at the base of the steps.

"Francesca is watching them."

"And your mother?"

He grinned. "I daresay Francesca is watching her, too."

"Anyone could stumble upon us out here," she said, looking this way and that.

His smile turned wicked. "Maybe," he said, catching hold of her green-velvet skirt and reeling her in, "we should adjourn to the *private* terrace."

The words were oh-so-familiar, and it was only a second before she was transported back nine years to the masquerade ball. "The private terrace, you say?" she asked, amusement dancing in her eyes. "And how, pray tell, would you know of a *private* terrace?"

His lips brushed against hers. "I have my ways," he murmured.

"And I," she returned, smiling slyly, "have my secrets."

He drew back. "Oh? And will you share?"

"We five," she said with a nod, "are about to be six."

He looked at her face, then looked at her belly. "Are you sure?"

"As sure as I was last time."

He took her hand and raised it to lips. "This one will be a girl."

"That's what you said last time."

"I know, but—"

"And the time before."

"All the more reason for the odds to favor me *this* time."

She shook her head. "I'm glad you're not a gambler."

He smiled at that. "Let's not tell anyone yet."

"I think a few people already suspect," Sophie admitted.

"I want to see how long it takes that Whistledown woman to figure it out," Benedict said.

"Are you serious?"

"The blasted woman knew about Charles, and she knew about Alexander, and she knew about William."

Sophie smiled as she let him pull her into the shadows. "Do you realize that I have been mentioned in Whistledown *two hundred* and thirty-two times?"

That stopped him cold. "You've been counting?"

"Two hundred and thirty-three if you include the time after the masquerade."

"I can't believe you've been counting."

She gave him a nonchalant shrug. "It's exciting to be mentioned."

Benedict thought it was a bloody nuisance to be mentioned, but he wasn't about to spoil her delight, so instead he just said, "At least she always writes nice things about you. If she didn't, I might have to hunt her down and run her out of the country."

Sophie couldn't help but smile. "Oh, *please*. I hardly think you could discover her identity when no one else in the *ton* has managed it."

He raised one arrogant brow. "That doesn't sound like wifely devotion and confidence to me."

She pretended to examine her glove. "You needn't expend the energy. She's obviously very good at what she does."

"Well, she won't know about Violet," Benedict vowed. "At least not until it's obvious to the world."

"Violet?" Sophie asked softly.

"It's time my mother had a grandchild named after her, don't you think?"

Sophie leaned against him, letting her cheek rest against the crisp linen of his shirt. "I think Violet is a lovely name," she murmured, nestling deeper into the shelter of his arms. "I just hope it's a girl. Because if it's a boy, he's never going to forgive us . . ."

Later that night, in a town house in the very best part of London, a woman picked up her quill and wrote:

Lady Whistledown's Society Papers
12 April 1824

Ah, Gentle Reader, This Author has learned that the Bridgerton grandchildren will soon number eleven . . .

But when she tried to write more, all she could do was close her eyes and sigh. She'd been doing this for so very long now. Could it have possibly been eleven years already?

Maybe it was time to move on. She was tired of writing about everyone else. It was time to live her own life.

And so Lady Whistledown set down her quill and walked to her window, pushing aside her sage green curtains and looking out into the inky night.

"Time for something new," she whispered. "Time to finally be me."

Can't get enough of the fabulous Bridgerton family?

**Want more glamorous masquerade balls,
rakish lords and wicked earls?**

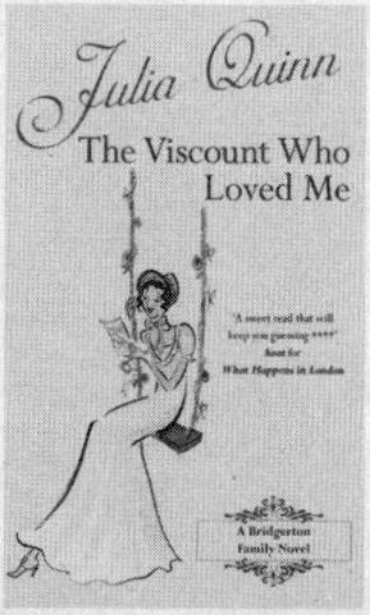

Make sure you've collected all the books in the series!

The Duke and I
The Viscount Who Loved Me
An Offer From a Gentleman
Romancing Mr Bridgerton
To Sir Phillip, With Love

**AVAILABLE AS BRAND NEW EDITIONS
FROM PIATKUS NOW**

The Duke And I

The irresistible Duke of Hastings has hatched a plan to keep himself free from the town's marriage-minded society mothers. He pretends to be engaged to the lovely Daphne Bridgerton. After all, it isn't as if the brooding rogue has any real plans to marry – though there is something about the alluring Miss Bridgerton that sets the Duke's heart beating a bit faster. And as for Daphne, surely the clever debutante will attract some very worthy suitors now that is seems a duke has declared her desirable.

But as Daphne waltzes across ballroom after ballroom with her 'fiancé', she soon forgets that their courtship is a complete sham. And now she has to do the impossible and keep herself from losing her heart and soul completely to the handsome hell-raiser who has sworn off marriage forever.

AVAILABLE FROM PIATKUS NOW!

The Viscount Who Loved Me

'1814 promises to be another eventful season, but not, This Author believes, for Anthony Bridgerton, London's most elusive bachelor, who has shown no indication that he plans to marry. And in all truth, why should he? When it comes to playing the consummate rake, nobody does it better . . .'

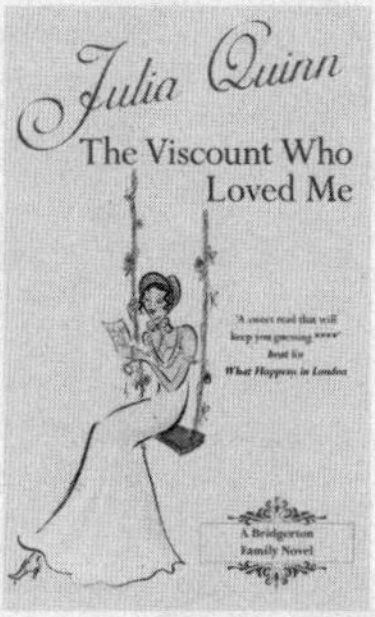

But this time the gossip columnists have it wrong. Anthony Bridgerton hasn't just decided to marry – he's even chosen a wife! The only obstacle is his intended's older sister, Kate Sheffield – the most meddlesome woman ever to grace a London ballroom. The spirited schemer is driving Anthony mad with her determination to stop the betrothal, but when he closes his eyes at night, Kate's the woman haunting his increasingly erotic dreams . . .

Contrary to popular belief, Kate is quite sure that reformed rakes do not make the best husbands – and Anthony Bridgerton is the most wicked rogue of them all. Kate's determined to protect her sister – but she fears her own heart is vulnerable. And when Anthony's lips touch hers, she's suddenly afraid she might not be able to resist the reprehensible rake herself . . .

AVAILABLE FROM PIATKUS NOW!

A Night Like This

Gareth St Clair has a father who hates him and who is determined to ruin the St Clair estates. Gareth's sole heirloom is an old family diary, which may or may not contain the secrets of his past . . . and the key to his future. The problem is – it's written in Italian, of which Gareth speaks not a word.

All the town agreed: there was no one quite like Hyacinth Bridgerton. She's fiendishly smart, devilishly outspoken and – according to Gareth – probably best in small doses. But there's something about her – something charming and vexing – that grabs him and won't quite let go . . . And Hyacinth – or so she claims – speaks Italian . . .

Romancing Mr Bridgerton

Everyone knows that Colin Bridgerton is the most charming man in London . . .

Penelope Featherington has secretly adored her best friend's brother for . . . well, it feels like forever. After half a lifetime of watching Colin Bridgerton from afar, she thinks she knows everything about him, until she stumbles across his deepest secret . . . and fears she doesn't know him at all.

Colin Bridgerton is tired of being thought of as nothing but an empty-headed charmer, tired of the notorious gossip columnist Lady Whistledown, who can't seem to publish an edition without mentioning him. But when Colin returns to London from a trip abroad, he discovers nothing in his life is quite the same – especially Penelope Featherington! The girl who was always simply there is suddenly the girl haunting his dreams. When he discovers that Penelope has secrets of her own, this elusive bachelor must decide . . . is she his biggest threat – or his promise of a happy ending?

AVAILABLE FROM PIATKUS NOW!

When He Was Wicked

If God ever wanted to smite a sinner, he couldn't do better than Michael Stirling. Michael Stirling, Sinner. He could see it on a calling card.

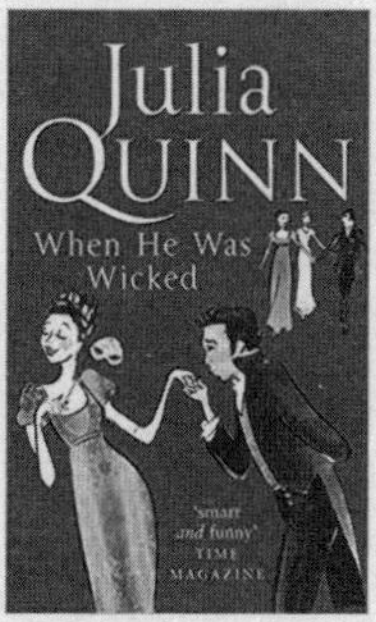

In every life there is a turning point. A moment so tremendous, so sharp and breath-taking, that one knows one's life will never be the same. For Michael Stirling, London's most infamous bachelor, that moment came the first time he laid eyes on Francesca Bridgerton.

After a lifetime of chasing women, of smiling slyly as they chased him, of allowing himself to be caught but never permitting his heart to become engaged, he took one look at Francesca Bridgerton and fell so fast and hard into love it was a wonder he managed to remain standing.

Unfortunately for Michael, however, Francesca's surname was to remain Bridgerton for only a mere thirty-six hours longer – the occasion of their meeting was, lamentably, a supper celebrating her imminent wedding to his cousin . . .

AVAILABLE FROM PIATKUS NOW!

To Sir Phillip, With Love

Sir Phillip Crane knew that Eloise Bridgerton was a spinster, and so he'd proposed, figuring that she'd be homely and unassuming, and more than a little desperate for an offer of marriage. Except . . . she wasn't. The beautiful woman on his doorstep was anything but quiet, and when she stopped talking long enough to close her mouth, all he wanted to do was kiss her . . . and more.

Did he think she was mad? Eloise Bridgerton couldn't marry a man she had never met! But then she started thinking . . . and wondering . . . and before she knew it, she was in a hired carriage in the middle of the night, on her way to meet the man she hoped might be her perfect match. Except . . . he wasn't. Her perfect husband wouldn't be so moody and ill-mannered, and while Phillip was certainly handsome, he was a large brute of a man, rough and rugged, and totally unlike the London gentlemen vying for her hand. But when he smiled . . . and when he kissed her . . . the rest of the world simply fell away, and she couldn't help but wonder . . . could this imperfect man be perfect for her?

AVAILABLE FROM PIATKUS NOW!

Julia Quinn started writing her first book one month after finishing university and has been tapping away at her keyboard ever since. The No. 1 *New York Times* bestselling author of more than two dozen novels, she is a graduate of Harvard and Radcliffe Colleges and is one of only sixteen authors ever to be inducted in the Romance Writers of America Hall of Fame. She lives in the Pacific Northwest with her family.

Please visit Julia Quinn online:

www.juliaquinn.com
www.facebook.com/AuthorJuliaQuinn
@JQAuthor

By Julia Quinn

The Rokesby Series:
Because of Miss Bridgerton
The Girl with the Make-Believe Husband
The Other Miss Bridgerton
First Comes Scandal

The Smythe-Smith Quartet:
Just Like Heaven
A Night Like This
The Sum of All Kisses
The Secrets of Sir Richard Kenworthy

The Bevelstoke Series:
The Secret Diaries of Miss Miranda Cheever
What Happens in London
Ten Things I Love About You

The Two Dukes of Wyndham:
The Lost Duke of Wyndham
Mr Cavendish, I Presume

Blydon Family Saga:
Splendid
Dancing at Midnight
Minx

Agents for the Crown:
To Catch an Heiress
How to Marry a Marquis

Bridgerton Series:
The Duke and I
The Viscount Who Loved Me
An Offer from a Gentleman
Romancing Mr Bridgerton
To Sir Phillip, With Love
When He Was Wicked
It's In His Kiss
On the Way to the Wedding
The Bridgertons: Happily Ever After

The Lyndon Sisters:
Everything and the Moon
Brighter than the Sun

The Ladies Most (written with Eloisa James and Connie Brockway):
The Lady Most Likely
The Lady Most Willing

Romancing Mr Bridgerton

Julia Quinn

PIATKUS

PIATKUS

First published in the US in 2002 by Avon Books,
An imprint of HarperCollins, New York
First published in Great Britain in 2006 by Piatkus
This paperback edition published in 2021 by Piatkus
by agreement with Avon

23

A CIP catalogue record for this book
is available from the British Library.

ISBN 978-0-349-42945-8

Printed and bound in Great Britain by Clays Ltd, Elcograf S.p.A.

Papers used by Piatkus are from well-managed forests
and other responsible sources.

FSC www.fsc.org MIX Paper from responsible sources FSC® C104740

Piatkus
An imprint of
Little, Brown Book Group
Carmelite House
50 Victoria Embankment
London EC4Y 0DZ

Hachette Ireland
8 Castlecourt Centre
Castleknock
Dublin 15

An Hachette UK Company
www.hachette.co.uk

www.littlebrown.co.uk

For the women on avonloop, colleagues and friends all—
thanks for giving me someone to talk to all day long.
Your support and friendship
have meant more to me than I could ever say.

And for Paul, even though the closest thing
you'd ever find to a romance in his field
is a lecture called "The Kiss of Death."

Acknowledgments

With utmost thanks to Lisa Kleypas and Stephanie Laurens for the gracious use of their characters.

Prologue

On the sixth of April, in the year 1812—precisely two days before her sixteenth birthday—Penelope Featherington fell in love.

It was, in a word, thrilling. The world shook. Her heart leaped. The moment was breathtaking. And, she was able to tell herself with some satisfaction, the man in question—one Colin Bridgerton—felt precisely the same way.

Oh, not the love part. He certainly didn't fall in love with her in 1812 (and not in 1813, 1814, 1815, or—oh, blast, not in all the years 1816–1822, either, and certainly not in 1823, when he was out of the country the whole time, anyway). But his earth shook, his heart leaped, and Penelope knew without a shadow of a doubt that his breath was taken away as well. For a good ten seconds.

Falling off a horse tended to do that to a man.

It happened thus:

She'd been out for a walk in Hyde Park with her mother and two older sisters when she felt a thunderous rumbling under her feet (see above: the bit about the earth shaking). Her mother wasn't paying much attention to her (her mother rarely did), so Penelope slipped away for a moment to see what was about. The rest of the Featheringtons were in rapt conversation with Viscountess Bridgerton and her daughter

Daphne, who had just begun her second season in London, so they were pretending to ignore the rumbling. The Bridgertons were an important family indeed, and conversations with them were *not* to be ignored.

As Penelope skirted around the edge of a particularly fat-trunked tree, she saw two riders coming her way, galloping along hell-for-leather or whatever expression people liked to use for fools on horseback who care not for their safety and well-being. Penelope felt her heart quicken (it would have been difficult to maintain a sedate pulse as a witness to such excitement, and besides, this allowed her to say that her heart leaped when she fell in love).

Then, in one of those inexplicable quirks of fate, the wind picked up quite suddenly and lifted her bonnet (which, much to her mother's chagrin, she had not tied properly since the ribbon chafed under her chin) straight into the air and, splat! right onto the face of one of the riders.

Penelope gasped (taking her breath away!), and then the man fell off his horse, landing most inelegantly in a nearby mud puddle.

She rushed forward, quite without thinking, squealing something that was meant to inquire after his welfare, but that she suspected came out as nothing more than a strangled shriek. He would, of course, be furious with her, since she'd effectively knocked him off his horse and covered him with mud—two things guaranteed to put any gentleman in the foulest of moods. But when he finally rose to his feet, brushing off whatever mud could be dislodged from his clothing, he didn't lash out at her. He didn't give her a stinging set-down, he didn't yell, he didn't even glare.

He laughed.

He laughed.

Penelope hadn't much experience with the laughter of men, and what little she *had* known had not been kind. But this man's eyes—a rather intense shade of green—were filled with mirth as he wiped a rather embarrassingly placed spot of mud off his cheek and said, "Well, that wasn't very well done of me, was it?"

And in that moment, Penelope fell in love.

When she found her voice (which, she was pained to note, was a good three seconds after a person of any intelligence would have replied), she said, "Oh, no, it is I who should apologize! My bonnet came right off my head, and . . ."

She stopped talking when she realized he hadn't actually apologized, so there was little point in contradicting him.

"It was no trouble," he said, giving her a somewhat amused smile. "I—Oh, good day, Daphne! Didn't know you were in the park."

Penelope whirled around to find herself facing Daphne Bridgerton, standing next to her mother, who promptly hissed, "What have you done, Penelope Featherington?" and Penelope couldn't even answer with her stock, *Nothing,* because in truth, the accident was completely her fault, and she'd just made a fool of herself in front of what was obviously—judging from the expression on her mother's face—a very eligible bachelor indeed.

Not that her mother would have thought that *she* had a chance with him. But Mrs. Featherington held high matrimonial hopes for her older girls. Besides, Penelope wasn't even "out" in society yet.

But if Mrs. Featherington intended to scold her any further, she was unable to do so, because that would have required that she remove her attention from the all-important Bridgertons, whose ranks, Penelope was quickly figuring out, included the man presently covered in mud.

"I hope your son isn't injured," Mrs. Featherington said to Lady Bridgerton.

"Right as rain," Colin interjected, making an expert sidestep before Lady Bridgerton could maul him with motherly concern.

Introductions were made, but the rest of the conversation was unimportant, mostly because Colin quickly and accurately sized up Mrs. Featherington as a matchmaking mama. Penelope was not at all surprised when he beat a hasty retreat.

But the damage had already been done. Penelope had discovered a reason to dream.

Later that night, as she replayed the encounter for about the thousandth time in her mind, it occurred to her that it would have been nice if she could have said that she'd fallen in love with him as he kissed her hand before a dance, his green eyes twinkling devilishly while his fingers held hers just a little more tightly than was proper. Or maybe it could have happened as he rode boldly across a windswept moor, the (aforementioned) wind no deterrent as he (or rather, his horse) galloped ever closer, his (Colin's, not the horse's) only intention to reach her side.

But no, she had to go and fall in love with Colin Bridgerton when he fell off a horse and landed on his bottom in a mud puddle. It was highly irregular, and *highly* unromantic, but there was a certain poetic justice in that, since nothing was ever going to come of it.

Why waste romance on a love that would never be returned? Better to save the windswept-moor introductions for people who might actually have a future together.

And if there was one thing Penelope knew, even then, at the age of sixteen years minus two days, it was that her future did not feature Colin Bridgerton in the role of husband.

She simply wasn't the sort of girl who attracted a man like him, and she feared that she never would be.

On the tenth of April, in the year 1813—precisely two days after her seventeenth birthday—Penelope Featherington made her debut into London society. She hadn't wanted to do it. She begged her mother to let her wait a year. She was at least two stone heavier than she ought to be, and her face still had an awful tendency to develop spots whenever she was nervous, which meant that she *always* had spots, since nothing in the world could make her as nervous as a London ball.

She tried to remind herself that beauty was only skin deep, but that didn't offer any helpful excuses when she was berating herself for never knowing what to *say* to people. There was nothing more depressing than an ugly girl with no personality. And in that first year on the marriage mart, that was exactly what Penelope was. An ugly girl with no—oh, very well, she had to give herself *some* credit—with very little personality.

Deep inside, she knew who she was, and that person was smart and kind and often even funny, but somehow her personality always got lost somewhere between her heart and her mouth, and she found herself saying the wrong thing or, more often, nothing at all.

To make matters even less attractive, Penelope's mother refused to allow Penelope to choose her own clothing, and when she wasn't in the requisite white that most young ladies wore (and which of course didn't flatter her complexion one bit), she was forced to wear yellow and red and orange, all of which made her look perfectly wretched. The one time Penelope had suggested green, Mrs. Featherington had planted her hands on her more-than-ample hips and declared that green was too melancholy.

Yellow, Mrs. Featherington declared, was a *happy* color and a *happy* girl would snare a husband.

Penelope decided then and there that it was best not to try to understand the workings of her mother's mind.

So Penelope found herself outfitted in yellow and orange and the occasional red, even though such colors made her look decidedly *un*happy, and in fact were positively ghastly with her brown eyes and red-tinged hair. There was nothing she could do about it, though, so she decided to grin and bear it, and if she couldn't manage a grin, at least she wouldn't cry in public.

Which, she took some pride in noting, she never did.

And if that weren't enough, 1813 was the year that the mysterious (and fictitious) Lady Whistledown began publishing her thrice-weekly *Society Papers.* The single-sheet newspaper became an instant sensation. No one knew who Lady Whistledown really was, but everyone seemed to have a theory. For weeks—no, months, really—London could speak of nothing else. The paper had been delivered for free for two weeks—just long enough to addict the *ton*—and then suddenly there was no delivery, just paperboys charging the outrageous price of five pennies a paper.

But by then, no one could live without the almost-daily dose of gossip, and everyone paid their pennies.

Somewhere some woman (or maybe, some people speculated, some man) was growing very rich indeed.

What set *Lady Whistledown's Society Papers* apart from any previous society newssheets was that the author actually listed her subjects' names in full. There was no hiding behind abbreviations such as Lord P——or Lady B——. If Lady Whistledown wanted to write about someone, she used his full name.

And when Lady Whistledown wanted to write about Penelope Featherington, she did. Penelope's first appearance in *Lady Whistledown's Society Papers* went as follows:

Miss Penelope Featherington's unfortunate gown left the unfortunate girl looking like nothing more than an overripe citrus fruit.

A rather stinging blow, to be sure, but nothing less than the truth.

Her second appearance in the column was no better.

Not a word was heard from Miss Penelope Featherington, and no wonder! The poor girl appeared to have drowned amidst the ruffles of her dress.

Not, Penelope was afraid, anything that would enhance her popularity.

But the season wasn't a complete disaster. There were a few people with whom she seemed able to speak. Lady Bridgerton, of all people, took a liking to her, and Penelope found that she could often tell things to the lovely viscountess that she would never dream of saying to her own mother. It was through Lady Bridgerton that she met Eloise Bridgerton, the younger sister of her beloved Colin. Eloise was also just turned seventeen, but her mother had wisely allowed her to delay her debut by a year, even though Eloise possessed the Bridgerton good looks and charm in abundance.

And while Penelope spent her afternoons in the green-and-cream drawing room at Bridgerton House (or, more often, up in Eloise's bedchamber where the two girls laughed and giggled and discussed everything under the sun with great earnestness), she found herself coming into occasional contact with Colin, who at two-and-twenty had not yet moved out of the family home and into bachelor lodgings.

If Penelope had thought she loved him before, that was nothing compared to what she felt after actually getting to know him. Colin Bridgerton was witty, he was dashing, he had a devil-may-care jokester quality to him that made women swoon, but most of all . . .

Colin Bridgerton was nice.

Nice. Such a silly little word. It should have been banal, but somehow it fit him to perfection. He always had something nice to say to Penelope, and when she finally worked up the courage to say something back (other than the very basic greetings and farewells), he actually listened. Which made it all the easier the next time around.

By the end of the season, Penelope judged that Colin Bridgerton was the only man with whom she'd managed an entire conversation.

This was love. Oh, this was love love love love love love. A silly repetition of words, perhaps, but that was precisely what Penelope doodled on a ridiculously expensive sheet of writing paper, along with the words, "Mrs. Colin Bridgerton" and "Penelope Bridgerton" and "Colin Colin Colin." (The paper went into the fire the moment Penelope heard footsteps in the hall.)

How wonderful it was to feel love—even the one-sided sort—for a nice person. It made one feel so positively sensible.

Of course, it didn't hurt that Colin possessed, as did all the Bridgerton men, fabulous good looks. There was that famous Bridgerton chestnut hair, the wide and smiling Bridgerton mouth, the broad shoulders, the six-foot height, and in Colin's case, the most devastating green eyes ever to grace a human face.

They were the sort of eyes that haunted a girl's dreams.

And Penelope dreamed and dreamed and dreamed.

April of 1814 found Penelope back in London for a second season, and even though she attracted the same number of suitors as the year before (zero), the season wasn't, in all honesty, quite so bad. It helped that she'd lost nearly two stone and could now call herself "pleasantly rounded" rather than "a hideous pudge." She was still nowhere near the slender ideal of womanhood that ruled the day, but at least she'd changed enough to warrant the purchase of a completely new wardrobe.

Unfortunately, her mother once again insisted on yellow, orange, and the occasional splash of red. And this time, Lady Whistledown wrote:

Miss Penelope Featherington (the least inane of the Featherington sisters) wore a gown of lemon yellow that left a sour taste in one's mouth.

Which at least seemed to imply that Penelope was the most intelligent member of her family, although the compliment was backhanded, indeed.

But Penelope wasn't the only one singled out by the acerbic gossip columnist. Dark-haired Kate Sheffield was likened to a singed daffodil in her yellow dress, and Kate went on to marry Anthony Bridgerton, Colin's older brother and a viscount to boot!

So Penelope held out hope.

Well, not really. She knew Colin wasn't going to marry her, but at least he danced with her at every ball, and he made her laugh, and every now and then she made him laugh, and she knew that that would have to be enough.

And so Penelope's life continued. She had her third season, then her fourth. Her two older sisters, Prudence and Philippa, finally found husbands of their own and moved away. Mrs. Featherington held out hope that Penelope might still make a match, since it had taken both Prudence and Philippa five seasons to snare husbands, but Penelope knew that she was destined to remain a spinster. It wouldn't be fair to marry someone when she was still so desperately in love with Colin. And maybe, in the far reaches of her mind—in the farthest-back corner, tucked away behind the French verb conjugations she'd never mastered and the arithmetic she never used—she still held out a tiny shred of hope.

Until *that* day.

Even now, seven years later, she still referred to it as *that* day.

She'd gone to the Bridgerton household, as she frequently did, to take tea with Eloise and her mother and sisters. It was right before Eloise's brother Benedict had married Sophie, only he didn't know who she really was, and—well, that didn't signify, except that it may have been the one truly great secret in the last decade that Lady Whistledown had never managed to unearth.

Anyway, she was walking through the front hall, listening to her feet tap along the marble tile as she saw herself out. She was adjusting her pelisse and preparing to walk the short distance to her own home (just around the corner, really) when she heard voices. Male voices. Male Bridgerton voices.

It was the three elder Bridgerton brothers: Anthony, Benedict, and Colin. They were having one of those conversations that men have, the kind in which they grumble a lot and poke fun at each other. Penelope had always liked to watch the Bridgertons interact in this manner; they were such a *family.*

Penelope could see them through the open front door, but she couldn't hear what they were saying until she'd reached the threshold. And in a testament to the bad timing that had plagued her throughout her life, the first voice she heard was Colin's, and the words were not kind.

"*. . . and I am certainly not going to marry Penelope Featherington!*"

"Oh!" The word slipped over her lips before she could even think, the squeal of it piercing the air like an off-key whistle.

The three Bridgerton men turned to face her with identical horrified faces, and Penelope knew that she had just entered into what would certainly be the most awful five minutes of her life.

She said nothing for what seemed like an eternity, and then, finally, with a dignity she never dreamed she possessed, she looked straight at Colin and said, "I never asked you to marry me."

His cheeks went from pink to red. He opened his mouth, but not a sound came out. It was, Penelope thought with wry satisfaction, probably the only time in his life he'd ever been at a loss for words.

"And I never—" She swallowed convulsively. "I never said to anyone that I wanted you to ask me."

"Penelope," Colin finally managed, "I'm so sorry."

"You have nothing to apologize for," she said.

"No," he insisted, "I do. I hurt your feelings, and—"

"You didn't know I was there."

"But nevertheless—"

"You are not going to marry me," she said, her voice sounding very strange and hollow to her ears. "There is nothing wrong with that. I am not going to marry your brother Benedict."

Benedict had clearly been trying not to look, but he snapped to attention at that.

Penelope fisted her hands at her sides. "It doesn't hurt his feelings when I announce that I am not going to marry him." She turned to Benedict, forcing her eyes directly on his. "Does it, Mr. Bridgerton?"

"Of course not," Benedict answered quickly.

"It's settled, then," she said tightly, amazed that, for once, *exactly* the right words were coming out of her mouth. "No feelings were hurt. Now, then, if you will excuse me, gentlemen, I should like to go home."

The three gentlemen immediately stood back to let her pass, and she would have made a clean escape, except that Colin suddenly blurted out, "Don't you have a maid?"

She shook her head. "I live just around the corner."

"I know, but—"

"I'll escort you," Anthony said smoothly.

"That's really not necessary, my lord."

"Humor me," he said, in a tone that told her quite clearly she hadn't any choice in the matter.

She nodded, and the two of them took off down the street. After they had passed about three houses, Anthony said in a strangely respectful voice, "He didn't know you were there."

Penelope felt her lips tighten at the corners—not out of anger, just out of a weary sense of resignation. "I know," she replied. "He's not the sort to be cruel. I expect your mother has been hounding him to get married."

Anthony nodded. Lady Bridgerton's intentions to see each and every one of her eight offspring happily married were legendary.

"She likes me," Penelope said. "Your mother, that is. She can't see beyond that, I'm afraid. But the truth is, it doesn't matter so much if she likes Colin's bride."

"Well, I wouldn't say *that,*" Anthony mused, sounding not so much like a highly feared and respected viscount and rather more like a well-behaved son. "I shouldn't like to be married to someone my mother didn't like." He shook his head in a gesture of great awe and respect. "She's a force of nature."

"Your mother or your wife?"

He considered that for about half a second. "Both."

They walked for a few moments, and then Penelope blurted out, "Colin should go away."

Anthony eyed her curiously. "I beg your pardon?"

"He should go away. Travel. He's not ready to marry, and your mother won't be able to restrain herself from pressuring him. She means well. . . ." Penelope bit her lip in horror. She hoped the viscount didn't think she was actually criticizing Lady Bridgerton. As far as she was concerned, there was no greater lady in England.

"My mother always means well," Anthony said with an indulgent smile. "But maybe you're right. Perhaps he should get away. Colin does enjoy travel. Although he did just return from Wales."

"Did he?" Penelope murmured politely, as if she didn't know perfectly well that he'd been in Wales.

"Here we are," he said as he nodded his reply. "This is your house, is it not?"

"Yes. Thank you for accompanying me home."

"It was my pleasure, I assure you."

Penelope watched as he left, then she went inside and cried.

The very next day, the following account appeared in *Lady Whistledown's Society Papers*:

La, but such excitement yesterday on the front steps of Lady Bridgerton's residence on Bruton Street!

First, Penelope Featherington was seen in the company of not one, not two, but THREE Bridgerton brothers, surely a heretofore impossible feat for the poor girl, who is rather infamous for her wallflower ways. Sadly (but perhaps predictably) for Miss Featherington, when she finally departed, it was on the arm of the viscount, the only married man in the bunch.

If Miss Featherington were to somehow manage to drag a Bridgerton brother to the altar, it would surely mean the end of the world as we know it, and This Author, who freely admits she would not know heads from tails in such a world, would be forced to resign her post on the spot.

It seemed even Lady Whistledown understood the futility of Penelope's feelings for Colin.

The years drifted by, and somehow, without realizing it, Penelope ceased to be a debutante and found herself sitting with the chaperones, watching her younger sister Felicity—surely the only Featherington sister blessed with both natural beauty and charm—enjoying her own London seasons.

Colin developed a taste for travel and began to spend more and more time outside of London; it seemed that every few months he was off to some new destination. When he was in town, he always saved a dance and a smile for Penelope, and somehow she managed to pretend that nothing had ever happened, that he'd never declared his distaste for her on a public street, that her dreams had never been shattered.

And when he was in town, which wasn't often, they seemed to settle into an easy, if not terribly deep, friendship. Which was all an almost twenty-eight-year-old spinster could hope for, right?

Unrequited love was never easy, but at least Penelope Featherington was used to it.

Chapter 1

Matchmaking mamas are united in their glee—Colin Bridgerton has returned from Greece!

For those gentle (and ignorant) readers who are new to town this year, Mr. Bridgerton is third in the legendary string of eight Bridgerton siblings (hence the name Colin, beginning with C; he follows Anthony and Benedict, and precedes Daphne, Eloise, Francesca, Gregory, and Hyacinth).

Although Mr. Bridgerton holds no noble title and is unlikely ever to do so (he is seventh in line for the title of Viscount Bridgerton, behind the two sons of the current viscount, his elder brother Benedict, and his three sons) he is still considered one of the prime catches of the season, due to his fortune, his face, his form, and most of all, his charm. It is difficult, however, to predict whether Mr. Bridgerton will succumb to matrimonial bliss this season; he is certainly of an age to marry (three-and-thirty), but he has never shown a decided interest in any lady of proper parentage, and to make matters even more complicated, he has an appalling tendency to leave London at the drop of a hat, bound for some exotic destination.

LADY WHISTLEDOWN'S SOCIETY PAPERS, 2 APRIL 1824

"Look at this!" Portia Featherington squealed. "Colin Bridgerton is back!"

Penelope looked up from her needlework. Her mother was clutching the latest edition of *Lady Whistledown's Society Papers* the way Penelope might clutch, say, a rope while hanging off a building. "I know," she murmured.

Portia frowned. She hated when someone—anyone—was aware of gossip before she was. "How did you get to *Whistledown* before I did? I told Briarly to set it aside for me and not to let anyone touch—"

"I didn't see it in *Whistledown,*" Penelope interrupted, before her mother went off to castigate the poor, beleaguered butler. "Felicity told me. Yesterday afternoon. Hyacinth Bridgerton told her."

"Your sister spends a great deal of time over at the Bridgerton household."

"As do I," Penelope pointed out, wondering where this was leading.

Portia tapped her finger against the side of her chin, as she always did when she was plotting or scheming. "Colin Bridgerton is of an age to be looking for a wife."

Penelope managed to blink just before her eyes bugged right out of her head. "Colin Bridgerton is not going to marry Felicity!"

Portia gave a little shrug. "Stranger things have happened."

"Not that I've ever seen," Penelope muttered.

"Anthony Bridgerton married that Kate Sheffield girl, and she was even less popular than *you*."

That wasn't exactly true; Penelope rather thought they'd been on equally low rungs of the social ladder. But there seemed little point in telling this to her mother, who probably thought she'd complimented her third daughter by saying she'd not been the least popular girl that season.

Penelope felt her lips tightening. Her mother's "compliments" had a habit of landing rather like wasps.

"Do not think I mean to criticize," Portia said, suddenly all concern. "In truth, I am glad for your spinsterhood. I am alone in this world save for my daughters, and it's comforting to know that one of you shall be able to care for me in my older years."

Penelope had a vision of the future—the future as described by her mother—and she had a sudden urge to run out and marry the chimney sweep. She'd long since resigned herself to a life of eternal spinsterhood, but somehow she'd always pictured herself off in her own neat little terrace house. Or maybe a snug cottage by the sea.

But lately Portia had been peppering her conversations with references to her old age and how lucky she was that Penelope could care for her. Never mind that both Prudence and Philippa had married well-heeled men and possessed ample funds to see to their mother's every comfort. Or that Portia was moderately wealthy in her own right; when her family had settled money on her as a dowry, one-fourth had been set aside for her own personal account.

No, when Portia talked about being "cared for," she wasn't referring to money. What Portia wanted was a slave.

Penelope sighed. She was being overly harsh with her mother, if only in her own mind. She did that too often. Her mother loved her. She knew her mother loved her. And she loved her mother back.

It was just that sometimes she didn't much *like* her mother.

She hoped that didn't make her a bad person. But truly, her mother could try the patience of even the kindest, gentlest of daughters, and as Penelope was the first to admit, she could be a wee bit sarcastic at times.

"Why don't you think Colin would marry Felicity?" Portia asked.

Penelope looked up, startled. She'd thought they were done with that subject. She should have known better. Her mother was nothing if not tenacious. "Well," she said slowly, "to begin with, she's twelve years younger than he is."

"Pfft," Portia said, waving her hand dismissively. "That's nothing, and you know it."

Penelope frowned, then yelped as she accidentally stabbed her finger with her needle.

"Besides," Portia continued blithely, "he's"—she looked back down at *Whistledown* and scanned it for his exact age—"three-and-thirty! How is he meant to avoid a twelve-year difference between him and his wife? Surely you don't expect him to marry someone *your* age."

Penelope sucked on her abused finger even though she knew it was hopelessly uncouth to do so. But she needed to put something in her mouth to keep her from saying something horrible *and* horribly spiteful.

Everything her mother said was true. Many *ton* weddings—maybe even most of them—saw men marrying girls a dozen or more years their junior. But somehow the age gap between Colin and Felicity seemed even larger, perhaps because . . .

Penelope was unable to keep the disgust off her face. "She's like a sister to him. A little sister."

"Really, Penelope. I hardly think—"

"It's almost incestuous," Penelope muttered.

"What did you say?"

Penelope snatched up her needlework again. "Nothing."

"I'm sure you said something."

Penelope shook her head. "I did clear my throat. Perhaps you heard—"

"I heard you saying something. I'm sure of it!"

Penelope groaned. Her life loomed long and tedious ahead of her. "Mother," she said, with the patience of, if not a saint, at least a very devout nun, "Felicity is practically engaged to Mr. Albansdale."

Portia actually began rubbing her hands together. "She won't be engaged to him if she can catch Colin Bridgerton."

"Felicity would *die* before chasing after Colin."

"Of course not. She's a smart girl. Anyone can see that Colin Bridgerton is a better catch."

"But Felicity loves Mr. Albansdale!"

Portia deflated into her perfectly upholstered chair. "There is that."

"And," Penelope added with great feeling, "Mr. Albansdale is in possession of a perfectly respectable fortune."

Portia tapped her index finger against her cheek. "True. Not," she said sharply, "as respectable as a Bridgerton portion, but it's nothing to sneeze at, I suppose."

Penelope knew it was time to let it go, but she couldn't stop her mouth from opening one last time. "In all truth, Mother, he's a wonderful match for Felicity. We should be delighted for her."

"I know, I know," Portia grumbled. "It's just that I so wanted one of my daughters to marry a Bridgerton. What a coup! I would be the talk of London for weeks. Years, maybe."

Penelope stabbed her needle into the cushion beside her. It was a rather foolish way to vent her anger, but the alternative was to jump to her feet and yell, *What about me?* Portia seemed to think that once Felicity was wed, her hopes for a Bridgerton union were forever dashed. But Penelope was still unmarried—didn't that count for anything?

Was it so much to wish that her mother thought of her with the same pride she felt for her other three daughters? Penelope knew that Colin wasn't going to choose her as his bride, but shouldn't a mother be at least a little bit blind to her children's faults? It was obvious to Penelope that neither Prudence, Philippa, nor even Felicity had ever had a chance with a Bridgerton. Why did her mother seem to think their charms so exceeded Penelope's?

Very well, Penelope had to admit that Felicity enjoyed a popularity that exceeded that of her three older sisters combined. But Prudence and Philippa had never been Incomparables. They'd hovered on the perimeters of ballrooms just as much as Penelope had.

Except, of course, that they were married now. Penelope wouldn't have wanted to cleave herself unto either of their husbands, but at least they were wives.

Thankfully, however, Portia's mind had already moved on to greener pastures. "I must pay a call upon Violet," she was saying. "She'll be so relieved that Colin is back."

"I'm sure Lady Bridgerton will be delighted to see you," Penelope said.

"That poor woman," Portia said, her sigh dramatic. "She worries about him, you know—"

"I know."

"Truly, I think it is more than a mother should be expected to bear. He goes gallivanting about, the good Lord only knows where, to countries that are positively *unheathen*—"

"I believe they practice Christianity in Greece," Penelope murmured, her eyes back down on her needlework.

"Don't be impertinent, Penelope Anne Featherington, and they're *Catholics*!" Portia shuddered on the word.

"They're not Catholics at all," Penelope replied, giving up on the needlework and setting it aside. "They're Greek Orthodox."

"Well, they're not Church of England," Portia said with a sniff.

"Seeing as how they're Greek, I don't think they're terribly worried about that."

Portia's eyes narrowed disapprovingly. "And how do you know about this Greek religion, anyway? No, don't tell me," she said with a dramatic flourish. "You read it somewhere."

Penelope just blinked as she tried to think of a suitable reply.

"I wish you wouldn't read so much," Portia sighed. "I probably could have married you off years ago if you had concentrated more on the social graces and less on . . . less on . . ."

Penelope had to ask. "Less on what?"

"I don't know. Whatever it is you do that has you staring into space and daydreaming so often."

"I'm just thinking," Penelope said quietly. "Sometimes I just like to stop and think."

"Stop what?" Portia wanted to know.

Penelope couldn't help but smile. Portia's query seemed to sum up all that was different between mother and daughter. "It's nothing, Mother," Penelope said. "Really."

Portia looked as if she wanted to say more, then thought the better of it. Or maybe she was just hungry. She did pluck a biscuit off the tea tray and pop it into her mouth.

Penelope started to reach out to take the last biscuit for herself, then decided to let her mother have it. She might as well keep her mother's mouth full. The last thing she wanted was to find herself in another conversation about Colin Bridgerton.

"Colin's back!"

Penelope looked up from her book—*A Brief History of Greece*—to see Eloise Bridgerton bursting into her room. As usual, Eloise had not been announced. The Featherington butler was so used to seeing her there that he treated her like a member of the family.

"Is he?" Penelope asked, managing to feign (in her opinion) rather realistic indifference. Of course, she did set *A Brief History of Greece* down behind *Mathilda*, the novel by S. R. Fielding that had been all the rage a year earlier. Everyone had a copy of *Mathilda* on their bedstand. And it was thick enough to hide *A Brief History of Greece*.

Eloise sat down in Penelope's desk chair. "Indeed, and he's very tanned. All that time in the sun, I suppose."

"He went to Greece, didn't he?"

Eloise shook her head. "He said the war there has worsened, and it was too dangerous. So he went to Cyprus instead."

"My, my," Penelope said with a smile. "Lady Whistledown got something wrong."

Eloise smiled that cheeky Bridgerton smile, and once again Penelope realized how lucky she was to have her as her closest friend. She and Eloise had been inseparable since the age of seventeen. They'd had their London seasons together, reached adulthood together, and, much to their mothers' dismay, had become spinsters together.

Eloise claimed that she hadn't met the right person.

Penelope, of course, hadn't been asked.

"Did he enjoy Cyprus?" Penelope inquired.

Eloise sighed. "He said it was brilliant. How I should love to travel. It seems everyone has been somewhere but me."

"And me," Penelope reminded her.

"And you," Eloise agreed. "Thank goodness for you."

"Eloise!" Penelope exclaimed, throwing a pillow at her. But she thanked goodness for Eloise, too. Every day. Many women went through their entire lives without a close female friend, and here she had someone to whom she could tell anything. Well, almost anything. Penelope had never told her of her feelings for Colin, although she rather thought Eloise suspected the truth. Eloise was far too tactful to mention it, though, which only validated Penelope's certainty that Colin would never love her. If Eloise had thought, for even one moment, that Penelope actually had a chance at snaring Colin as a husband, she would have been plotting her matchmaking strategies with a ruthlessness that would have impressed any army general.

When it came right down to it, Eloise was a rather managing sort of person.

". . . and then he said that the water was so choppy that he actually cast up his accounts over the side of the boat, and—" Eloise scowled. "You're not listening to me."

"No," Penelope admitted. "Well, yes, actually, parts of it. I cannot believe Colin actually told you he vomited."

"Well, I *am* his sister."

"He'd be furious with you if he knew you'd told me."

Eloise waved off her protest. "He won't mind. You're like another sister to him."

Penelope smiled, but she sighed at the same time.

"Mother asked him—of course—whether he was planning to remain in town for the season," Eloise continued, "and—of course—he was terribly evasive, but then I decided to interrogate him myself—"

"Terribly smart of you," Penelope murmured.

Eloise threw the pillow back at her. "And I finally got him to admit to me that yes, he thinks he will stay for at least a few months. But he made me promise not to tell Mother."

"Now, that's not"—Penelope cleared her throat—"terribly intelligent of him. If your mother thinks his time here is limited, she will redouble her efforts to see him married. I should think that was what he wanted most to avoid."

"It does seem his usual aim in life," Eloise concurred.

"If he lulled her into thinking that there was no rush, perhaps she might not badger him quite so much."

"An interesting idea," Eloise said, "but probably more true in theory than in practice. My mother is so determined to see him wed that it matters not if she increases her efforts. Her regular efforts are enough to drive him mad as it is."

"Can one go doubly mad?" Penelope mused.

Eloise cocked her head. "I don't know," she said. "I don't think I should want to find out."

They both fell silent for a moment (a rare occurrence, indeed) and then Eloise quite suddenly jumped to her feet and said, "I must go."

Penelope smiled. People who didn't know Eloise very well thought she had a habit of changing the subject frequently (and abruptly), but Penelope knew that the truth was something else altogether. When Eloise had her mind set on something, she was completely unable to let it go. Which meant that if Eloise suddenly wanted to leave, it probably had to do with something they'd been talking about earlier in the afternoon, and—

"Colin is expected for tea," Eloise explained.

Penelope smiled. She loved being right.

"You should come," Eloise said.

Penelope shook her head. "He'll want it to be just family."

"You're probably right," Eloise said, nodding slightly. "Very well, then, I must be off. Terribly sorry to cut my visit so short, but I wanted to be sure that you knew Colin was home."

"Whistledown," Penelope reminded her.

"Right. Where does that woman get her information?" Eloise said, shaking her head in wonder. "I vow sometimes she knows so much about my family I wonder if I ought to be frightened."

"She can't go on forever," Penelope commented, getting up to see her friend out. "Someone will eventually figure out who she is, don't you think?"

"I don't know." Eloise put her hand on the doorknob, twisted, and pulled. "I used to think so. But it's been ten years. More, actually. If she were going to be caught, I think it would have happened already."

Penelope followed Eloise down the stairs. "Eventually she'll make a mistake. She has to. She's only human."

Eloise laughed. "And here I thought she was a minor god."

Penelope found herself grinning.

Eloise stopped and whirled around so suddenly that Penelope crashed right into her, nearly sending both of them tumbling down the last few steps on the staircase. "Do you know what?" Eloise demanded.

"I couldn't begin to speculate."

Eloise didn't even bother to pull a face. "I'd wager that she *has* made a mistake," she said.

"I beg your pardon?"

"You said it yourself. She—or it could be he, I suppose—has been writing the column for over a decade. No one could do that for so long without making a mistake. Do you know what I think?"

Penelope just spread her hands in an impatient gesture.

"I think the problem is that the rest of us are too stupid to notice her mistakes."

Penelope stared at her for a moment, then burst out laughing. "Oh, Eloise," she said, wiping tears from her eyes. "I do love you."

Eloise grinned. "And it's a good thing you do, spinster that I am. We shall have to set up a household together when we are thirty and truly crones."

Penelope caught hold of the idea like a lifeboat. "Do you think we could?" she exclaimed. And then, in a hushed voice, after looking furtively up and down the hall, "Mother has begun to speak of her old age with alarming frequency."

"What's so alarming about that?"

"I'm in all of her visions, waiting on her hand and foot."

"Oh, dear."

"A milder expletive than had crossed my mind."

"Penelope!" But Eloise was grinning.

"I love my mother," Penelope said.

"I know you do," Eloise said, in a rather placating sort of voice.

"No, I really do."

The left corner of Eloise's mouth began to twitch. "I know you really do. Really."

"It's just that—"

Eloise put up a hand. "You don't need to say any more. I understand perfectly. I—Oh! Good day, Mrs. Featherington!"

"Eloise," Portia said, bustling down the hall. "I didn't realize you were here."

"I'm sneaky as always," Eloise said. "Cheeky, even."

Portia gave her an indulgent smile. "I heard your brother is back in town."

"Yes, we are all overjoyed."

"I'm sure you must be, especially your mother."

"Indeed. She is beside herself. I believe she is drawing up a list right now."

Portia's entire aspect perked up, as it did at the mention of anything that might be construed as gossip. "A list? What sort of list?"

"Oh, you know, the same list she has made for all of her adult children. Prospective spouses and all that."

"It makes me wonder," Penelope said in a dry voice, "what constitutes 'all that.' "

"Sometimes she includes one or two people who are hopelessly unsuitable so as to highlight the qualities of the *real* possibilities."

Portia laughed. "Perhaps she'll put you on Colin's list, Penelope!"

Penelope didn't laugh. Neither did Eloise. Portia didn't seem to notice.

"Well, I'd best be off," Eloise said, clearing her throat to cover a moment that was awkward to two of the three people in the hall. "Colin is expected for tea. Mother wants the entire family in attendance."

"Will you all fit?" Penelope asked. Lady Bridgerton's home was large, but the Bridgerton children, spouses, and grandchildren numbered twenty-one. It was a large brood, indeed.

"We're going to Bridgerton House," Eloise explained. Her mother had moved out of the Bridgertons' official London residence after her eldest son had married. Anthony, who had been viscount since the age of eighteen, had told Violet that she needn't go, but she had insisted that he and his wife needed their privacy. As a result, Anthony and Kate lived with their three children in Bridgerton House, while Violet lived with her unmarried children (with the exception of Colin, who kept his own lodgings) just a few blocks away at 5 Bruton Street. After a year or so of unsuccessful attempts to name Lady Bridgerton's new home, the family had taken to calling it simply Number Five.

"Do enjoy yourself," Portia said. "I must go and find Felicity. We are late for an appointment at the modiste."

Eloise watched Portia disappear up the stairs, then said to Penelope, "Your sister seems to spend a great deal of time at the modiste."

Penelope shrugged. "Felicity is going mad with all the fittings, but she's Mother's only hope for a truly grand match. I'm afraid she's convinced that Felicity will catch a duke if she's wearing the right gown."

"Isn't she practically engaged to Mr. Albansdale?"

"I imagine he'll make a formal offer next week. But until then, Mother is keeping her options open." She rolled her eyes. "You'd best warn your brother to keep his distance."

"Gregory?" Eloise asked in disbelief. "He's not even out of university."

"Colin."

"Colin?" Eloise exploded with laughter. "Oh, that's rich."

"That's what I told her, but you know how she is once she gets an idea in her head."

Eloise chuckled. "Rather like me, I imagine."

"Tenacious to the end."

"Tenacity can be a very good thing," Eloise reminded her, "at the proper time."

"Right," Penelope returned with a sarcastic smile, "and at the improper time, it's an absolute nightmare."

Eloise laughed. "Cheer up, friend. At least she let you rid yourself of all those yellow frocks."

Penelope looked down at her morning dress, which was, if she did say so herself, a rather flattering shade of blue. "She stopped choosing my clothing once she finally realized I was officially on the shelf. A girl with no marriage prospects isn't worth the time and energy it takes her to offer fashion advice. She hasn't accompanied me to the modiste in over a year! Bliss!"

Eloise smiled at her friend, whose complexion turned the loveliest peaches and cream whenever she wore cooler hues. "It was apparent to all, the moment you were allowed to choose your own clothing. Even Lady Whistledown commented upon it!"

"I hid that column from Mother," Penelope admitted. "I didn't want her feelings to be hurt."

Eloise blinked a few times before saying, "That was very kind of you, Penelope."

"I have my moments of charity and grace."

"One would think," Eloise said with a snort, "that a vital component of charity and grace is the ability not to draw attention to one's possession of them."

Penelope pursed her lips as she pushed Eloise toward the door. "Don't you need to go home?"

"I'm leaving! I'm leaving!"

And she left.

It was, Colin Bridgerton decided as he took a sip of some truly excellent brandy, rather nice to be back in England.

It was quite strange, actually, how he loved returning home just as much as he did the departure. In another few months—six at the most—he'd be itching to leave again, but for now, England in April was positively brilliant.

"It's good, isn't it?"

Colin looked up. His brother Anthony was leaning against the front of his massive mahogany desk, motioning to him with his own glass of brandy.

Colin nodded. "Hadn't realized how much I missed it until I returned. Ouzo has its charms, but this"—he lifted his glass—"is heaven."

Anthony smiled wryly. "And how long do you plan to remain this time?"

Colin wandered over to the window and pretended to look out. His eldest brother made little attempt to disguise his impatience with Colin's wanderlust. In truth, Colin really couldn't blame him. Occasionally, it was difficult to get letters home; he supposed that his family often had to wait a month or even two for word of his welfare. But while he knew that he would not relish being in their shoes—never knowing if a loved one was dead or alive, constantly waiting for the knock of the messenger at the front door—that just wasn't enough to keep his feet firmly planted in England.

Every now and then, he simply had to get *away*. There was no other way to describe it.

Away from the *ton,* who thought him a charming rogue and nothing else, away from England, which encouraged younger sons to enter the military or the clergy, neither of which suited his temperament. Even away from his family, who loved him unconditionally but had no clue that what he really wanted, deep down inside, was something to do.

His brother Anthony held the viscountcy, and with that came myriad responsibilities. He ran estates, managed the family's finances, and saw to the welfare of countless tenants and servants. Benedict, his elder by four years, had gained renown as an artist. He'd started with pencil and paper, but at the urging of his wife had moved on to oils. One of his landscapes now hung in the National Gallery.

Anthony would be forever remembered in family trees as the seventh Viscount Bridgerton. Benedict would live through his paintings, long after he left this earth.

But Colin had nothing. He managed the small property given to him by his family and he attended parties. He would never dream of claiming he didn't have fun, but sometimes he wanted something a little more than fun.

He wanted a purpose.

He wanted a legacy.

He wanted, if not to know then at least to hope, that when he was gone, he'd be memorialized in some manner other than in *Lady Whistledown's Society Papers.*

He sighed. No wonder he spent so much time traveling.

"Colin?" his brother prompted.

Colin turned to him and blinked. He was fairly certain Anthony had asked him a question, but somewhere in the meanderings of his mind, he'd forgotten what.

"Oh. Right." Colin cleared his throat. "I'll be here for the rest of the season, at least."

Anthony said nothing, but it was difficult to miss the satisfied expression on his face.

"If nothing else," Colin added, affixing his legendary crooked grin on his face, "someone has to spoil your children. I don't think Charlotte has nearly enough dolls."

"Only fifty," Anthony agreed in a deadpan voice. "The poor girl is horribly neglected."

"Her birthday is at the end of this month, is it not? I shall have to neglect her some more, I think."

"Speaking of birthdays," Anthony said, settling into the large chair behind his desk, "Mother's is a week from Sunday."

"Why do you think I hurried to return?"

Anthony raised a brow, and Colin had the distinct impression that he was trying to decide if Colin had truly rushed home for their mother's birthday, or if he was simply taking advantage of some very good timing.

"We're holding a party for her," Anthony said.

"She's letting you?" It was Colin's experience that women of a certain age did not enjoy birthday celebrations. And although his mother was still exceedingly lovely, she was definitely of a certain age.

"We were forced to resort to blackmail," Anthony admitted. "She agreed to the party or we revealed her true age."

Colin shouldn't have taken a sip of his brandy; he choked on it and just barely managed to avert spraying it all over his brother. "I should have liked to have seen *that*."

Anthony offered a rather satisfied smile. "It was a brilliant maneuver on my part."

Colin finished the rest of his drink. "What, do you think, are the chances she won't use the party as an opportunity to find me a wife?"

"Very small."

"I thought so."

Anthony leaned back in his chair. "You *are* thirty-three now, Colin . . ."

Colin stared at him in disbelief. "God above, don't *you* start on me."

"I wouldn't dream of it. I was merely going to suggest that you keep your eyes open this season. You needn't actively look for a wife, but there's no harm in remaining at least amenable to the possibility."

Colin eyed the doorway, intending to pass through it very shortly. "I assure you I am not averse to the idea of marriage."

"I didn't think you were," Anthony demurred.

"I see little reason to rush, however."

"There's never a reason to rush," Anthony returned. "Well, rarely, anyway. Just humor Mother, will you?"

Colin hadn't realized he was still holding his empty glass until it slipped through his fingers and landed on the carpet with a loud thunk. "Good God," he whispered, "is she ill?"

"No!" Anthony said, his surprise making his voice loud and forceful. "She'll outlive us all, I'm sure of it."

"Then what is this about?"

Anthony sighed. "I just want to see you happy."

"I am happy," Colin insisted.

"Are you?"

"Hell, I'm the happiest man in London. Just read Lady Whistledown. She'll tell you so."

Anthony glanced down at the paper on his desk.

"Well, maybe not this column, but anything from last year. I've been called charming more times than Lady Danbury has been called opinionated, and we both know what a feat *that* is."

"Charming doesn't necessarily equal happy," Anthony said softly.

"I don't have time for this," Colin muttered. The door had never looked so good.

"If you were truly happy," Anthony persisted, "you wouldn't keep leaving."

Colin paused with his hand on the doorknob. "Anthony, I *like* to travel."

"Constantly?"

"I must, or I wouldn't do it."

"That's an evasive sentence if ever I've heard one."

"And this"—Colin flashed his brother a wicked smile—"is an evasive maneuver."

"Colin!"

But he'd already left the room.

Chapter 2

It has always been fashionable among the ton to complain of ennui, but surely this year's crop of partygoers has raised boredom to an art form. One cannot take two steps at a society function these days without hearing the phrase "dreadfully dull," or "hopelessly banal." Indeed, This Author has even been informed that Cressida Twombley recently remarked that she was convinced that she might perish of eternal boredom if forced to attend one more off-key musicale.

(This Author must concur with Lady Twombley on that note; while this year's selection of debutantes are an amiable bunch, there is not a decent musician among them.)

If there is to be an antidote for the disease of tedium, surely it will be Sunday's fête at Bridgerton House. The entire family will gather, along with a hundred or so of their closest friends, to celebrate the dowager viscountess's birthday.

It is considered crass to mention a lady's age, and so This Author will not reveal which birthday Lady Bridgerton is celebrating.

But have no fear! This Author knows!

LADY WHISTLEDOWN'S SOCIETY PAPERS, 9 APRIL 1824

Spinsterhood was a word that tended to invoke either panic or pity, but Penelope was coming to realize that there were decided advantages to the unmarried state.

First of all, no one really expected the spinsters to dance at balls, which meant that Penelope was no longer forced to hover at the edge of the dance floor, looking this way and that, pretending that she didn't really want to dance. Now she could sit off to the side with the other spinsters and chaperones. She still wanted to dance, of course—she rather liked dancing, and she was actually quite good at it, not that anyone ever noticed—but it was much easier to feign disinterest the farther one got from the waltzing couples.

Second, the number of hours spent in dull conversation had been drastically reduced. Mrs. Featherington had officially given up hope that Penelope might ever snag a husband, and so she'd stopped thrusting her in the path of every third-tier eligible bachelor. Portia had never really thought Penelope had a prayer of attracting the attention of a first- or second-tier bachelor, which was probably true, but most of the third-tier bachelors were classified as such for a reason, and sadly, that reason was often personality, or lack thereof. Which, when combined with Penelope's shyness with strangers, didn't tend to promote sparkling conversation.

And finally, she could eat again. It was maddening, considering the amount of food generally on display at *ton* parties, but women on the hunt for husbands weren't supposed to exhibit anything more robust than a bird's appetite. This, Penelope thought gleefully (as she bit into what had to be the most heavenly éclair outside of France), had to be the best spinster perk of all.

"Good heavens," she moaned. If sin could take a solid form, surely it would be a pastry. Preferably one with chocolate.

"That good, eh?"

Penelope choked on the éclair, then coughed, sending a fine spray of pastry cream through the air. "Colin," she gasped, fervently praying the largest of the globs had missed his ear.

"Penelope." He smiled warmly. "It's good to see you."

"And you."

He rocked on his heels—once, twice, thrice—then said, "You look well."

"And you," she said, too preoccupied with trying to figure out where to set down her éclair to offer much variety to her conversation.

"That's a nice dress," he said, motioning to her green silk gown.

She smiled ruefully, explaining, "It's not yellow."

"So it's not." He grinned, and the ice was broken. It was strange, because one would think her tongue would be tied the tightest around the man she loved, but there was something about Colin that set everyone at ease.

Maybe, Penelope had thought on more than one occasion, part of the reason she loved him was that he made her feel comfortable with herself.

"Eloise tells me you had a splendid time in Cyprus," she said.

He grinned. "Couldn't resist the birthplace of Aphrodite, after all."

Penelope found herself smiling as well. His good humor was infectious, even if the last thing she wanted to do was take part in a discussion of the goddess of love. "Was it as sunny as everyone says?" she asked. "No, forget I asked. I can see from your face that it was."

"I did acquire a bit of a tan," he said with a nod. "My mother nearly fainted when she saw me."

"From delight, I'm sure," Penelope said emphatically. "She misses you terribly when you're gone."

He leaned in. "Come, now, Penelope, surely you're not going to start in on me? Between my mother, Anthony, Eloise, and Daphne, I'm liable to perish of guilt."

"Not Benedict?" she couldn't help quipping.

He shot her a slightly smirky look. "He's out of town."

"Ah, well, that explains his silence."

His narrowed eyes matched his crossed arms to perfection. "You've always been cheeky, did you know that?"

"I hide it well," she said modestly.

"It's easy to see," he said in a dry voice, "why you are such good friends with my sister."

"I'm assuming you intended that as a compliment?"

"I'm fairly certain I'd be endangering my health if I'd intended it any other way."

Penelope was standing there hoping she'd think of a witty rejoinder when she heard a strange, wet, splattish sound. She looked down to discover that a large yellowish blob of pastry cream had slid from her half-eaten éclair and landed on the pristine wooden floor. She looked back up to find Colin's oh-so-green eyes dancing with laughter, even as his mouth fought for a serious expression.

"Well, now, that's embarrassing," Penelope said, deciding that the only way to avoid dying of mortification was to state the painfully obvious.

"I suggest," Colin said, raising one brow into a perfectly debonair arch, "that we flee the scene."

Penelope looked down at the empty carcass of the éclair still in her hand. Colin answered her with a nod toward a nearby potted plant.

"No!" she said, her eyes growing wide.

He leaned in closer. "I dare you."

Her eyes darted from the éclair to the plant and back to Colin's face. "I couldn't," she said.

"As far as naughty things go, this one is fairly mild," he pointed out.

It was a dare, and Penelope was usually immune to such childish ploys, but Colin's half-smile was difficult to resist. "Very well," she said, squaring her shoulders and dropping the pastry onto the soil. She took a step back, examined her handiwork, looked around to see if anyone besides Colin was watching her, then leaned down and rotated the pot so that a leafy branch covered the evidence.

"I didn't think you'd do it," Colin said.

"As you said, it's not terribly naughty."

"No, but it is my mother's favorite potted palm."

"Colin!" Penelope whirled around, fully intending to sink her hand right back into the plant to retrieve the éclair. "How could you let me—Wait a second." She straightened, her eyes narrowed. "This isn't a palm."

He was all innocence. "It's not?"

"It's a miniature orange tree."

He blinked. "Is it, now?"

She scowled at him. Or at least she hoped it was a scowl. It was difficult to scowl at Colin Bridgerton. Even his mother had once remarked that it was nearly impossible to reprimand him.

He would just smile and look contrite and say something funny, and you just couldn't stay angry with him. You simply couldn't do it.

"You were trying to make me feel guilty," Penelope said.

"Anyone could confuse a palm with an orange tree."

She fought the urge to roll her eyes. "Except for the oranges."

He chewed on his lower lip, his eyes thoughtful. "Yes, hmmm, one would think they'd be a bit of a giveaway."

"You're a terrible liar, did you know that?"

He straightened, tugging slightly at his waistcoat as he lifted his chin. "Actually, I'm an excellent liar. But what I'm really good at is appearing appropriately sheepish and adorable after I'm caught."

What, Penelope wondered, was she meant to say to *that*? Because surely there was no one more adorably sheepish (sheepishly adorable?) than Colin Bridgerton with his hands clasped behind his back, his eyes flitting along the ceiling, and his lips puckered into an innocent whistle.

"When you were a child," Penelope asked, abruptly changing the subject, "were you ever punished?"

Colin immediately straightened to attention. "I beg your pardon?"

"Were you ever punished as a child?" she repeated. "Are you ever punished now?"

Colin just stared at her, wondering if she had any idea what she was asking. Probably not. "Errr . . ." he said, mostly because he hadn't anything else to say.

She let out a vaguely patronizing sigh. "I thought not."

If he were a less indulgent man, and if this were anyone but Penelope Featherington, whom he knew did not possess a malicious bone in her body, he might take offense. But he was an uncommonly easygoing fellow, and this *was* Penelope Featherington, who had been a faithful friend to his sister for God knows how many years, so instead of adopting a hard, cynical stare (which, admittedly, was an expression at which he'd never excelled), he merely smiled and murmured, "Your point being?"

"Do not think I mean to criticize your parents," she said with an expression that was innocent and sly at the same time. "I would never dream of implying that you were spoiled in any way."

He nodded graciously.

"It's just that"—she leaned in, as if imparting a grave secret—"I rather think you could get away with murder if you so chose."

He coughed—not to clear his throat and not because he wasn't feeling well, but rather because he was so damned startled. Penelope was such a funny character. No, that wasn't quite right. She was . . . *surprising*. Yes, that seemed to sum her up. Very few people really knew her; she had certainly never developed a reputation as a sterling conversationalist. He was fairly certain she'd made it through three-hour parties without ever venturing beyond words of a single syllable.

But when Penelope was in the company of someone with whom she felt comfortable—and Colin realized that he was probably privileged to count himself among that number—she had a dry wit, a sly smile, and evidence of a very intelligent mind, indeed.

He wasn't surprised that she'd never attracted any serious suitors for her hand; she wasn't a beauty by any stretch, although upon close examination she was more attractive than he'd remembered her to be. Her brown hair had a touch of red to it, highlighted nicely by the flickering candles. And her skin was quite lovely—that perfect peaches-and-cream complexion that ladies were always slathering their faces with arsenic to achieve.

But Penelope's attractiveness wasn't the sort that men usually noticed. And her normally shy and occasionally even stuttering demeanor didn't exactly showcase her personality.

Still, it was too bad about her lack of popularity. She would have made someone a perfectly good wife.

"So you're saying," he mused, steering his mind back to the matter at hand, "that I should consider a life of crime?"

"Nothing of the sort," she replied, a demure smile on her face. "Just that I rather suspect you could talk your way out of anything." And then, unexpectedly, her mien grew serious, and she quietly said, "I envy that."

Colin surprised himself by holding out his hand and saying, "Penelope Featherington, I think you should dance with me."

And then Penelope surprised *him* by laughing and saying, "That's very sweet of you to ask, but you don't have to dance with me any longer."

His pride felt oddly pricked. "What the devil do you mean by that?"

She shrugged. "It's official now. I'm a spinster. There's no longer a reason to dance with me just so that I don't feel left out."

"That's not why I danced with you," he protested, but he knew that it was exactly the reason. And half the time he'd only remembered to ask because his mother had poked him—*hard*—in the back and reminded him.

She gave him a faintly pitying look, which galled him, because he'd never thought to be pitied by Penelope Featherington.

"If you think," he said, feeling his spine grow stiff, "that I'm going to allow you to wiggle out of a dance with me *now*, you're quite delusional."

"You don't have to dance with me just to prove you don't mind doing it," she said.

"I *want* to dance with you," he fairly growled.

"Very well," she said, after what seemed to be a ridiculously long pause. "It would surely be churlish for me to refuse."

"It was probably churlish of you to doubt my intentions," he said as he took her arm, "but I'm willing to forgive you if you can forgive yourself."

She stumbled, which made him smile.

"I do believe I'll manage," she choked out.

"Excellent." He offered her a bland smile. "I'd hate to think of you living with the guilt."

The music was just beginning, so Penelope took his hand and curtsied as they began the minuet. It was difficult to talk during the dance, which gave Penelope a few moments to catch her breath and gather her thoughts.

Perhaps she'd been a bit too harsh with Colin. She shouldn't have scolded him for asking her to dance, when the truth was, those dances were among her most cherished memories. Did it really matter if he'd only done it out of pity? It would have been worse if he'd never asked her at all.

She grimaced. Worse still, did this mean she had to apologize?

"Was something wrong with that éclair?" Colin inquired the next time they stepped toward each other.

A full ten seconds passed before they were close enough again for her to say, "I beg your pardon?"

"You look as if you've swallowed something vile," he said, loudly this time, for he'd clearly lost patience with waiting for the dance to allow them to speak.

Several people looked over, then stepped discreetly away, as if Penelope might actually be sick right there on the ballroom floor.

"Do you need to shout it to the entire world?" Penelope hissed.

"You know," he said thoughtfully, bending into an elegant bow as the music drew to a close, "that was the loudest whisper I've ever heard."

He was insufferable, but Penelope wasn't going to say so, because it would only make her sound like a character in a very bad romantic novel. She'd read one just the other day in which the heroine used the word (or one of its synonyms) on every other page.

"Thank you for the dance," she said, once they'd reached the perimeter of the room. She almost added, *You can now tell your mother that you've fulfilled your obligations,* but immediately regretted her impulse. Colin hadn't done anything to deserve such sarcasm. It wasn't his fault that men only danced with her when forced to by their mothers. He'd always at least smiled and laughed while doing his duty, which was more than she could say for the rest of the male population.

He nodded politely and murmured his own thanks. They were just about to part ways when they heard a loud female voice bark out, "Mr. Bridgerton!"

They both froze. It was a voice they both knew. It was a voice everyone knew.

"Save me," Colin groaned.

Penelope looked over her shoulder to see the infamous Lady Danbury pushing her way through the crowd, wincing when her ever-present cane landed on the foot of some hapless young lady. "Maybe she means a different Mr. Bridgerton?" Penelope suggested. "There are quite a few of you, after all, and it's possible—"

"I'll give you ten pounds if you don't leave my side," Colin blurted out.

Penelope choked on air. "Don't be silly, I—"

"Twenty."

"Done!" she said with a smile, not because she particularly needed the money but rather because it was strangely enjoyable to be extorting it from Colin. "Lady Danbury!" she called out, hurrying to the elderly lady's side. "How nice to see you."

"Nobody ever thinks it's nice to see me," Lady Danbury said sharply, "except maybe my nephew, and half the time I'm not even sure about him. But I thank you for lying all the same."

Colin said nothing, but she still turned in his direction and swatted his leg with her cane. "Good choice dancing with this one," she said. "I've always liked her. More brains than the rest of her family put together."

Penelope opened her mouth to defend at least her younger sister, when Lady Danbury barked out, "Ha!" after barely a second's pause, adding, "I noticed neither of you contradicted me."

"It is always a delight to see you, Lady Danbury," Colin said, giving her just the sort of smile he might have directed at an opera singer.

"Glib, this one is," Lady Danbury said to Penelope. "You'll have to watch out for him."

"It is rarely necessary that I do so," Penelope said, "as he is most often out of the country."

"See!" Lady Danbury crowed again. "I told you she was bright."

"You'll notice," Colin said smoothly, "that I did not contradict you."

The old lady smiled approvingly. "So you didn't. You're getting smart in your old age, Mr. Bridgerton."

"It has occasionally been remarked that I possessed a small modicum of intelligence in my youth, as well."

"Hmmph. The important word in that sentence being *small,* of course."

Colin looked at Penelope through narrowed eyes. She appeared to be choking on laughter.

"We women must look out for one another," Lady Danbury said to no one in particular, "since it is clear that no one else will do so."

Colin decided it was definitely time to go. "I think I see my mother."

"Escape is impossible," Lady Danbury crowed. "Don't bother to attempt it, and besides, I know for a fact you don't see your mother. She's attending to some brainless twit who tore the hem off her dress." She turned to Penelope, who was now exerting such effort to control her laughter that her eyes were glistening with unshed tears. "How much did he pay you not to leave him alone with me?"

Penelope quite simply exploded. "I beg your pardon," she gasped, clasping a hand over her horrified mouth.

"Oh, no, go right ahead," Colin said expansively. "You've been such a help already."

"You don't have to give me the twenty pounds," she said.

"I wasn't planning to."

"Only twenty pounds?" Lady Danbury asked. "Hmmph. I would have thought I'd be worth at least twenty-five."

Colin shrugged. "I'm a third son. Perpetually short of funds, I'm afraid."

"Ha! You're as plump in the pocket as at least three earls," Lady Danbury said. "Well, maybe not earls," she added, after a bit of thought. "But a few viscounts, and most barons, to be sure."

Colin smiled blandly. "Isn't it considered impolite to talk about money in mixed company?"

Lady Danbury let out a noise that was either a wheeze or a giggle—Colin wasn't sure which—then said, "It's always impolite to talk about money, mixed company or no, but when one is my age, one can do almost anything one pleases."

"I do wonder," Penelope mused, "what one *can't* do at your age."

Lady Danbury turned to her. "I beg your pardon?"

"You said that one could do *almost* anything one pleases."

Lady Danbury stared at her in disbelief, then cracked a smile. Colin realized he was smiling as well.

"I like her," Lady D said to him, pointing at Penelope as if she were some sort of statue for sale. "Did I tell you I like her?"

"I believe you did," he murmured.

Lady Danbury turned to Penelope and said, her face a mask of utter seriousness, "I do believe I couldn't get away with murder, but that might be all."

All at once, both Penelope and Colin burst out laughing.

"Eh?" Lady Danbury said. "What's so funny?"

"Nothing," Penelope gasped. As for Colin, he couldn't even manage that much.

"It's not nothing," Lady D persisted. "And I shall remain here and pester you all night until you tell me what it is. Trust me when I tell you that that is *not* your desired course of action."

Penelope wiped a tear from her eye. "I just got through

telling him," she said, motioning with her head toward Colin, "that he probably could get away with murder."

"Did you, now?" Lady Danbury mused, tapping her cane lightly against the floor the way someone else might scratch her chin while pondering a deep question. "Do you know, but I think you might be right. A more charming man I don't think London has ever seen."

Colin raised a brow. "Now, why don't I think you meant that as a compliment, Lady Danbury?"

"Of course it's a compliment, you dunderhead."

Colin turned to Penelope. "As opposed to *that,* which was clearly a compliment."

Lady Danbury beamed. "I declare," she said (or in all truth, declared), "this is the most fun I've had all season."

"Happy to oblige," Colin said with an easy smile.

"It's been an especially dull year, don't you think?" Lady Danbury asked Penelope.

Penelope nodded. "Last year was a bit tedious as well."

"But not as bad as this year," Lady D persisted.

"Don't ask me," Colin said affably. "I've been out of the country."

"Hmmph. I suppose you're going to say that your absence is the reason we've all been so bored."

"I would never dream of it," Colin said with a disarming smile. "But clearly, if the thought has crossed your mind, it must have some merit."

"Hmmph. Whatever the case, I'm bored."

Colin looked over at Penelope, who appeared to be holding herself very, very still—presumably to stave off laughter.

"Haywood!" Lady Danbury suddenly called out, waving over a middle-aged gentleman. "Wouldn't you agree with me?"

A vaguely panicked expression drifted across Lord Haywood's face, and then, when it became clear that he could not escape, he said, "I try to make a policy of *always* agreeing with you."

Lady Danbury turned to Penelope and said, "Is it my imagination, or are men getting more sensible?"

Penelope's only answer was a noncommittal shrug. Colin decided she was a wise girl, indeed.

Haywood cleared his throat, his blue eyes blinking fast and furious in his rather fleshy face. "Er, what, precisely, am I agreeing to?"

"That the season is boring," Penelope supplied helpfully.

"Ah, Miss Featherington," Haywood said in a blustery sort of voice. "Didn't see you there."

Colin stole just enough of a glance at Penelope to see her lips straighten into a small, frustrated smile. "Right here next to you," she muttered.

"So you are," Haywood said jovially, "and yes, the season is dreadfully boring."

"Did someone say the season is dull?"

Colin glanced to his right. Another man and two ladies had just joined the group and were avidly expressing their agreement.

"Tedious," one of them murmured. "Appallingly tedious."

"I have never attended a more banal round of parties," one of the ladies announced with an affected sigh.

"I shall have to inform my mother," Colin said tightly. He was among the most easygoing of men, but really, there were some insults he could not let pass.

"Oh, not this gathering," the woman hastened to add. "This ball is truly the only shining light in an otherwise dark and dismal string of gatherings. Why, I was just saying to—"

"Stop now," Lady Danbury ordered, "before you choke on your foot."

The lady quickly silenced herself.

"It's odd," Penelope murmured.

"Oh, Miss Featherington," said the lady who'd previously

been going on about dark and dismal gatherings. "Didn't see you there."

"What's odd?" Colin asked, before anyone else could tell Penelope how unremarkable they found her.

She gave him a small, grateful smile before explaining herself. "It's odd how the *ton* seems to entertain themselves by pointing out how unentertained they are."

"I beg your pardon?" Haywood said, looking confused.

Penelope shrugged. "I think the lot of you are having a jolly good time talking about how bored you are, that's all."

Her comment was met with silence. Lord Haywood continued to look confused, and one of the two ladies must have had a speck of dust in her eye, because she couldn't seem to do anything but blink.

Colin couldn't help but smile. He hadn't thought Penelope's statement was such a terribly complicated concept.

"The only interesting thing to do is read *Whistledown,*" said the nonblinking lady, as if Penelope had never even spoken.

The gentleman next to her murmured his assent.

And then Lady Danbury began to smile.

Colin grew alarmed. The old lady had a look in her eye. A frightening look.

"I have an idea," she said.

Someone gasped. Someone else groaned.

"A brilliant idea."

"Not that any of your ideas are anything but," Colin murmured in his most affable voice.

Lady Danbury shushed him with a wave of her hand. "How many great mysteries are there in life, really?"

No one answered, so Colin guessed, "Forty-two?"

She didn't even bother to scowl at him. "I am telling you all here and now. . . ."

Everyone leaned in. Even Colin. It was impossible not to indulge the drama of the moment.

"You are all my witnesses. . . ."

Colin thought he heard Penelope mutter, "Get *on* with it."

"One thousand pounds," Lady Danbury said.

The crowd surrounding her grew.

"One thousand pounds," she repeated, her voice growing in volume. Really, she would have been a natural on the stage. "One thousand pounds . . ."

It seemed the entire ballroom had hushed into reverent silence.

". . . to the person who unmasks Lady Whistledown!"

Chapter 3

This Author would be remiss if it was not mentioned that the most talked-about moment at last night's birthday ball at Bridgerton House was not the rousing toast to Lady Bridgerton (age not to be revealed) but rather Lady Danbury's impertinent offer of one thousand pounds to whomever unmasks . . .

Me.

Do your worst, ladies and gentlemen of the ton. You haven't a prayer of solving this mystery.

LADY WHISTLEDOWN'S SOCIETY PAPERS, 12 APRIL 1824

Precisely three minutes were required for news of Lady Danbury's outrageous dare to spread throughout the ballroom. Penelope knew this to be true because she happened to be facing a large (and, according to Kate Bridgerton, extremely precise) grandfather clock when Lady Danbury made her announcement. At the words, "One thousand pounds to the person who unmasks Lady Whistledown," the clock read forty-four minutes past ten. The long hand had advanced no farther than forty-seven when Nigel Berbrooke stumbled into the rapidly growing circle of people surrounding Lady Danbury and proclaimed her latest scheme "scrumbly good fun!"

And if Nigel had heard about it, that meant everyone had, because Penelope's brother-in-law was not known for his intelligence, his attention span, or his listening ability.

Nor, Penelope thought wryly, for his vocabulary. Scrumbly, indeed.

"And who do you think Lady Whistledown is?" Lady Danbury asked Nigel.

"No earthly idea," he admitted. "Ain't me, that's all I know!"

"I think we all know that," Lady D replied.

"Who do you think it is?" Penelope asked Colin.

He offered her a one-shouldered shrug. "I've been out of town too often to speculate."

"Don't be silly," Penelope said. "Your cumulative time in London certainly adds up to enough parties and routs to form a few theories."

But he just shook his head. "I really couldn't say."

Penelope stared at him for a moment longer than was necessary, or, in all honesty, socially acceptable. There was something odd in Colin's eyes. Something fleeting and elusive. The *ton* often thought him nothing more than a devil-may-care charmer, but he was far more intelligent than he let on, and she'd have bet her life that he had a few suspicions.

But for some reason, he wasn't willing to share them with her.

"Who do you think it is?" Colin asked, avoiding her question with one of his own. "You've been out in society just about as long as Lady Whistledown. Surely you must have thought about it."

Penelope looked about the ballroom, her eyes resting on this person and that, before finally returning to the small crowd around her. "I think it could very well be Lady Danbury," she replied. "Wouldn't that be a clever joke on everyone?"

Colin looked over at the elderly lady, who was having a

grand old time talking up her latest scheme. She was thumping her cane on the ground, chattering animatedly, and smiling like a cat with cream, fish, and an entire roast turkey. "It makes sense," he said thoughtfully, "in a rather perverse sort of way."

Penelope felt the corners of her mouth twist. "She's nothing if not perverse."

She watched Colin watching Lady D for another few seconds, then quietly said, "But you don't think it's her."

Colin slowly turned his head to face her, raising one brow in silent question.

"I can tell by the expression on your face," Penelope explained.

He grinned, that loose easy grin he so often used in public. "And here I thought I was inscrutable."

"Afraid not," she replied. "Not to me, anyway."

Colin sighed. "I fear it will never be my destiny to be a dark, brooding hero."

"You may well find yourself *some*one's hero," Penelope allowed. "There's time for you yet. But dark and brooding?" She smiled. "Not very likely."

"Too bad for me," he said jauntily, giving her another one of his well-known smiles—this one the lopsided, boyish one. "The dark, brooding types get all the women."

Penelope coughed discreetly, a bit surprised he'd be speaking of such things with her, not to mention the fact that Colin Bridgerton had never had trouble attracting women. He was grinning at her, awaiting a response, and she was trying to decide whether the correct reaction was polite maidenly outrage or a laugh and an I'm-such-a-good-sport sort of chuckle, when Eloise quite literally skidded to a halt in front of them.

"Did you hear the news?" Eloise asked breathlessly.

"Were you *running*?" Penelope returned. Truly a remarkable feat in such a crowded ballroom.

"Lady Danbury has offered one thousand pounds to whomever unmasks Lady Whistledown!"

"We know," Colin said in that vaguely superior tone exclusive to older brothers.

Eloise let out a disappointed sigh. "You do?"

Colin motioned to Lady Danbury, who was still a scant few yards away. "We were right here when it happened."

Eloise looked annoyed in the extreme, and Penelope knew exactly what she was thinking (and would most probably relate to her the following afternoon). It was one thing to miss an important moment. It was another entirely to discover that one's brother had seen the entire thing.

"Well, people are already talking about it," Eloise said. "Gushing, really. I haven't been witness to such excitement in years."

Colin turned to Penelope and murmured, "This is why I so often choose to leave the country."

Penelope tried not to smile.

"I know you're talking about me and I don't care," Eloise continued, barely pausing to take a breath. "I tell you, the *ton* has gone mad. Everyone—and I mean everyone—is speculating on her identity, although the shrewdest ones won't say a word. Don't want others to win on their hunch, don't you know."

"I think," Colin announced, "that I am not so in need of a thousand pounds that I care to worry about this."

"It's a lot of money," Penelope said thoughtfully.

He turned to her in disbelief. "Don't tell me you're going to join in this ridiculous game."

She cocked her head to the side, lifting her chin in what she hoped was an enigmatic—or if not enigmatic, at the very least slightly mysterious—manner. "I am not so well heeled that I can ignore the offer of one thousand pounds," she said.

"Perhaps if we work together . . ." Eloise suggested.

"God save me," was Colin's reply.

Eloise ignored him, saying to Penelope, "We could split the money."

Penelope opened her mouth to reply, but Lady Danbury's cane suddenly came into view, waving wildly through the air. Colin had to take a quick step to the side just to avoid getting his ear clipped off.

"Miss Featherington!" Lady D boomed. "You haven't told me who *you* suspect."

"No, Penelope," Colin said, a rather smirky smile on his face, "you haven't."

Penelope's first instinct was to mumble something under her breath and hope that Lady Danbury's age had left her hard enough of hearing that she would assume that any lack of understanding was the fault of her own ears and not Penelope's lips. But even without glancing to her side, she could feel Colin's presence, sense his quirky, cocky grin egging her on, and she found herself standing a little straighter, with her chin perched just a little higher than usual.

He made her more confident, more daring. He made her more . . . herself. Or at least the herself she wished she could be.

"Actually," Penelope said, looking Lady Danbury *almost* in the eye, "I think it's you."

A collective gasp echoed around them.

And for the first time in her life, Penelope Featherington found herself at the very center of attention.

Lady Danbury stared at her, her pale blue eyes shrewd and assessing. And then the most amazing thing happened. Her lips began to twitch at the corners. Then they widened until Penelope realized she was not just smiling, but positively grinning.

"I like you, Penelope Featherington," Lady Danbury said, tapping her right on the toe with her cane. "I wager half the ballroom is of the same notion, but no one else has the mettle to tell me so."

"I really don't, either," Penelope admitted, grunting slightly as Colin elbowed her in the ribs.

"Obviously," Lady Danbury said with a strange light in her eyes, "you do."

Penelope didn't know what to say to this. She looked at Colin, who was smiling at her encouragingly, then she looked back to Lady Danbury, who looked almost . . . maternal.

Which had to be the strangest thing of all. Penelope rather doubted that Lady Danbury had given maternal looks to her own children.

"Isn't it nice," the older lady said, leaning in so that only Penelope could hear her words, "to discover that we're not exactly what we thought we were?"

And then she walked away, leaving Penelope wondering if maybe she wasn't quite what she'd thought she was.

Maybe—just maybe—she was something a little bit more.

The next day was a Monday, which meant that Penelope took tea with the Bridgerton ladies at Number Five. She didn't know when, precisely, she'd fallen into that habit, but it had been so for close to a decade, and if she didn't show up on a Monday afternoon, she rather thought Lady Bridgerton would send someone over to fetch her.

Penelope rather enjoyed the Bridgerton custom of tea and biscuits in the afternoon. It wasn't a widespread ritual; indeed, Penelope knew of no one else who made a daily habit of it. But Lady Bridgerton insisted that she simply could not last from luncheon to supper, especially not when they were observing town hours and eating so late at night. And thus, every afternoon at four, she and any number of her children (and often a friend or two) met in the informal upstairs drawing room for a snack.

There was drizzle in the air, even though it was a fairly warm day, so Penelope took her black parasol with her for the short walk over to Number Five. It was a route she'd followed hundreds of times before, a few houses down to the corner of Mount and Davies Street, then along the edge of Berkeley Square to Bruton Street. But she was in an odd mood that day, a little bit lighthearted and maybe even a little bit childish, so she decided to cut across the northern corner of the Berkeley Square green for no other reason than she liked the squishy sound her boots made on the wet grass.

It was Lady Danbury's fault. It had to be. She'd been positively giddy since their encounter the night before.

"Not. What. I. Thought. I. Was," she sang to herself as she walked, adding a word every time the soles of her boots sank into the ground. "Something more. Something more."

She reached a particularly wet patch and moved like a skater on the grass, singing (softly, of course; she hadn't changed so much from the night before that she actually wanted someone to hear her singing in public), "Something moooore," as she slid forward.

Which was, of course (since it was fairly well established—in her own mind, at least—that she had the worst timing in the history of civilization), right when she heard a male voice call out her name.

She skidded to a halt and gave fervent thanks that she caught her balance at the very last moment instead of landing on her bottom on the wet and messy grass.

It was, of course, *him.*

"Colin!" she said in a slightly embarrassed voice, holding still as she waited for him to reach her side. "What a surprise."

He looked like he was trying not to smile. "Were you dancing?"

"Dancing?" she echoed.

"It looked like you were dancing."

"Oh. No." She swallowed guiltily, because even though she wasn't technically lying, it felt as if she were. "Of course not."

His eyes crinkled slightly at the corners. "Pity, then. I would have felt compelled to partner you, and I've never danced in Berkeley Square."

If he'd said the same to her just two days earlier, she would have laughed at his joke and let him be the witty and charming one. But she must have heard Lady Danbury's voice at the back of her head again, because she suddenly decided she didn't want to be the same old Penelope Featherington.

She decided to join in the fun.

She smiled a smile she didn't think she'd even known how to smile. It was wicked and she was mysterious, and she knew it wasn't all in her head because Colin's eyes widened markedly as she murmured, "That's a shame. It's rather enjoyable."

"Penelope Featherington," he drawled, "I thought you said you weren't dancing."

She shrugged. "I lied."

"If that's the case," he said, "then surely this must be my dance."

Penelope's insides suddenly felt very queer. This was why she shouldn't let whispers from Lady Danbury go to her head. She might manage daring and charm for a fleeting moment, but she had no idea how to follow through.

Unlike Colin, obviously, who was grinning devilishly as he held his arms out in perfect waltz position.

"Colin," she gasped, "we're in Berkeley Square!"

"I know. I just finished telling you I've never danced here, don't you recall?"

"But—"

Colin crossed his arms. "Tsk. Tsk. You can't issue a dare like that and then try to weasel out of it. Besides, dancing in Berkeley Square seems like the sort of thing a person ought to do at least once in his life, wouldn't you agree?"

"Anyone might see," she whispered urgently.

He shrugged, trying to hide the fact that he was rather entertained by her reaction. "I don't care. Do you?"

Her cheeks grew pink, then red, and it seemed to take her a great deal of effort to form the words, "People will think you are courting me."

He watched her closely, not understanding why she was disturbed. Who cared if people thought they were courting? The rumor would soon be proven false, and they'd have a good laugh at society's expense. It was on the tip of his tongue to say, *Hang society,* but he held silent. There was something lurking deep in the brown depths of her eyes, some emotion he couldn't even begin to identify.

An emotion he suspected he'd never even felt.

And he realized that the last thing he wanted to do was hurt Penelope Featherington. She was his sister's best friend, and moreover, she was, plain and simple, a very nice girl.

He frowned. He supposed he shouldn't be calling her a girl anymore. At eight-and-twenty she was no more a girl than he was still a boy at three-and-thirty.

Finally, with great care and what he hoped was a good dose of sensitivity, he asked, "Is there a reason why we should worry if people think we are courting?"

She closed her eyes, and for a moment Colin actually thought she might be in pain. When she opened them, her gaze was almost bittersweet. "It would be very funny, actually," she said. "At first."

He said nothing, just waited for her to continue.

"But eventually it would become apparent that we are not actually courting, and it would . . ." She stopped, swallowed, and Colin realized that she was not as composed on the inside as she hoped to appear.

"It would be assumed," she continued, "that you were the one to break things off, because—well, it just would be."

He didn't argue with her. He knew that her words were true.

She let out a sad-sounding exhale. "I don't want to subject myself to that. Even Lady Whistledown would probably write about it. How could she not? It would be far too juicy a piece of gossip for her to resist."

"I'm sorry, Penelope," Colin said. He wasn't sure what he was apologizing for, but it still seemed like the right thing to say.

She acknowledged him with a tiny nod. "I know I shouldn't care what other people say, but I do."

He found himself turning slightly away as he considered her words. Or maybe he was considering the tone of her voice. Or maybe both.

He'd always thought of himself as somewhat above society. Not really outside of it, precisely, since he certainly moved within it and usually enjoyed himself quite a bit. But he'd always assumed that his happiness did not depend upon the opinions of others.

But maybe he wasn't thinking about this the right way. It was easy to assume that you didn't care about the opinions of others when those opinions were consistently favorable. Would he be so quick to dismiss the rest of society if they treated him the way they treated Penelope?

She'd never been ostracized, never been made the subject of scandal. She just hadn't been . . . popular.

Oh, people were polite, and the Bridgertons had all befriended her, but most of Colin's memories of Penelope involved her standing at the perimeter of a ballroom, trying to look anywhere but at the dancing couples, clearly pretending that she really didn't want to dance. That was usually when he went over and asked her himself. She always looked grateful for the request, but also a little bit embarrassed, because they both knew he was doing it at least a little bit because he felt sorry for her.

Colin tried to put himself in her shoes. It wasn't easy. He'd always been popular; his friends had looked up to him at school and the women had flocked to his side when he'd entered society. And as much as he could say he didn't care what people thought, when it came right down to it . . .

He rather liked being liked.

Suddenly he didn't know what to say. Which was strange, because he *always* knew what to say. In fact, he was somewhat famous for always knowing what to say. It was, he reflected, probably one of the reasons he was so well liked.

But he sensed that Penelope's feelings depended on his next words, and at some point in the last ten minutes, her feelings had become very important to him.

"You're right," he finally said, deciding that it was always a good idea to tell someone she was correct. "It was very insensitive of me. Perhaps we should start anew?"

She blinked. "I beg your pardon?"

He waved his hand about, as if the motion could explain everything. "Make a fresh start."

She looked quite adorably confused, which confused *him,* since he'd never thought Penelope the least bit adorable.

"But we've known each other for twelve years," she said.

"Has it really been that long?" He searched his brain, but for the life of him, he couldn't recall the event of their first meeting. "Never mind that. I meant just for this afternoon, you ninny."

She smiled, clearly in spite of herself, and he knew that calling her a ninny had been the exact right thing to do, although in all truth he had no idea why.

"Here we go," he said slowly, drawing his words out with

a long flourish of his arm. "You are walking across Berkeley Square, and you spy me in the distance. I call out your name, and you reply by saying . . ."

Penelope caught her lower lip between her teeth, trying, for some unknown reason, to contain her smile. What magical star had Colin been born under, that he *always* knew what to say? He was the pied piper, leaving nothing but happy hearts and smiling faces in his wake. Penelope would have bet money—far more than the thousand pounds Lady Danbury had offered up—that she was not the only woman in London desperately in love with the third Bridgerton.

He dipped his head to the side and then righted it in a prompting sort of motion.

"I would reply . . ." Penelope said slowly. "I would reply . . ."

Colin waited two seconds, then said, "Really, any words will do."

Penelope had planned to fix a bright grin on her face, but she discovered that the smile on her lips was quite genuine. "Colin!" she said, trying to sound as if she'd just been surprised by his arrival. "What are you doing about?"

"Excellent reply," he said.

She shook her finger at him. "You're breaking out of character."

"Yes, yes, of course. Apologies." He paused, blinked twice, then said, "Here we are. How about this: Much the same as you, I imagine. Heading to Number Five for tea."

Penelope found herself falling into the rhythm of the conversation. "You sound as if you're just going for a visit. Don't you live there?"

He grimaced. "Hopefully just for the next week. A fortnight at most. I'm trying to find a new place to live. I had to give up the lease on my old set of rooms when I left for Cyprus, and I haven't found a suitable replacement yet. I had a bit of business down on Piccadilly and thought I'd walk back."

"In the rain?"

He shrugged. "It wasn't raining when I left earlier this morning. And even now it's just drizzle."

Just drizzle, Penelope thought. Drizzle that clung to his obscenely long eyelashes, framing eyes of such perfect green that more than one young lady had been moved to write (extremely bad) poetry about them. Even Penelope, levelheaded as she liked to think herself, had spent many a night in bed, staring at the ceiling and seeing nothing but those eyes.

Just drizzle, indeed.

"Penelope?"

She snapped to attention. "Right. Yes. I'm going to your mother's for tea as well. I do so every Monday. And often on other days, too," she admitted. "When there's, er, nothing interesting occurring at my house."

"No need to sound so guilty about it. My mother's a lovely woman. If she wants you over for tea, you should go."

Penelope had a bad habit of trying to hear between the lines of people's conversations, and she had a suspicion that Colin was really saying that he didn't blame her if she wanted to escape her own mother from time to time.

Which somehow, unaccountably, made her feel a little sad.

He rocked on his heels for a moment, then said, "Well, I shouldn't keep you out here in the rain."

She smiled, since they'd been standing outside for at least fifteen minutes. Still, if he wanted to continue with the ruse, she would do so as well. "I'm the one with the parasol," she pointed out.

His lips curved slightly. "So you are. But still, I wouldn't be much of a gentleman if I didn't steer you toward a more hospitable environment. Speaking of which . . ." He frowned, looking around.

"Speaking of what?"

"Of being a gentleman. I believe we're supposed to see to the welfare of ladies."

"And?"

He crossed his arms. "Shouldn't you have a maid with you?"

"I live just around the corner," she said, a little bit deflated that he didn't remember that. She and her sister were best friends with two of his sisters, after all. He'd even walked her home once or twice. "On Mount Street," she added, when his frown did not dissipate.

He squinted slightly, looking in the direction of Mount Street, although she had no idea what he hoped to accomplish by doing so.

"Oh, for heaven's sake, Colin. It's just near the corner of Davies Street. It can't be more than a five-minute walk to your mother's. Four, if I'm feeling exceptionally sprightly."

"I was just looking to see if there were any darkened or recessed spots." He turned back to face her. "Where a criminal might lurk."

"In *Mayfair*?"

"In Mayfair," he said grimly. "I really think you ought to have a maid accompany you when you journey to and fro. I should hate for something to happen to you."

She was oddly touched by his concern, even though she knew he would have extended equal thoughtfulness to just about every female of his acquaintance. That was simply the sort of man he was.

"I can assure you that I observe all of the usual proprieties when I am traveling longer distances," she said. "But truly, this is so close. Just a few blocks, really. Even my mother doesn't mind."

Colin's jaw suddenly looked quite stiff.

"Not to mention," Penelope added, "that I am eight-and-twenty."

"What has that to do with anything? I am three-and-thirty, if you care to know."

She knew that, of course, since she knew almost everything about him. "Colin," she said, a slightly annoyed whine creeping into her voice.

"Penelope," he replied, in exactly the same tone.

She let out a long exhale before saying, "I am quite firmly on the shelf, Colin. I needn't worry about all of the rules that plagued me when I was seventeen."

"I hardly think—"

One of Penelope's hands planted itself on her hip. "Ask your sister if you don't believe me."

He suddenly looked more serious than she had ever seen him. "I make it a point not to ask my sister on matters that relate to common sense."

"Colin!" Penelope exclaimed. "That's a terrible thing to say."

"I didn't say I don't love her. I didn't even say I don't like her. I adore Eloise, as you well know. However—"

"Anything that begins with *however* has got to be bad," Penelope muttered.

"Eloise," he said with uncharacteristic high-handedness, "should be married by now."

Now, *that* was really too much, especially in that tone of voice. "Some might say," Penelope returned with a self-righteous little tilt of her chin, "that you should be married by now, too."

"Oh, pl—"

"You are, as you so proudly informed me, three-and-thirty."

His expression was slightly amused, but with that pale tinge of irritation which told her he would not remain amused for long. "Penelope, don't even—"

"Ancient!" she chirped.

He swore under his breath, which surprised her, since she didn't think she'd ever heard him do so in the presence of a lady. She probably should have taken it as a warning, but she was too riled up. She supposed the old saying was true—courage spawned more courage.

Or maybe it was more that recklessness emboldened more recklessness, because she just looked at him archly and said, "Weren't both of your older brothers married by the age of thirty?"

To her surprise, Colin merely smiled and crossed his arms as he leaned one shoulder against the tree they were standing beneath. "My brothers and I are very different men."

It was, Penelope realized, a very telling statement, because so many members of the *ton,* including the fabled Lady Whistledown, made so much of the fact that the Bridgerton brothers looked so alike. Some had even gone so far as to call them interchangeable. Penelope hadn't thought any of them were bothered by this—in fact, she'd assumed they'd all felt flattered by the comparison, since they seemed to like each other so well. But maybe she was wrong.

Or maybe she'd never looked closely enough.

Which was rather strange, because she felt as if she'd spent half her life watching Colin Bridgerton.

One thing she did know, however, and should have remembered, was that if Colin had any sort of a temper, he had never chosen to let her see it. Surely she'd flattered herself when she thought that her little quip about his brothers marrying before they turned thirty might set him off.

No, his method of attack was a lazy smile, a well-timed joke. If Colin ever lost his temper . . .

Penelope shook her head slightly, unable even to fathom it. Colin would never lose his temper. At least not in front of her. He'd have to be really, truly—no, *profoundly*—upset to lose his temper. And that kind of fury could only be sparked by someone you really, truly, *profoundly* cared about.

Colin liked her well enough—maybe even better than he liked most people—but he didn't *care*. Not that way.

"Perhaps we should just agree to disagree," she finally said.

"On what?"

"Er . . ." She couldn't remember. "Er, on what a spinster may or may not do?"

He seemed amused by her hesitation. "That would probably require that I defer to my younger sister's judgment in some capacity, which would be, as I'm sure you can imagine, very difficult for me."

"But you don't mind deferring to *my* judgment?"

His smile was lazy and wicked. "Not if you promise not to tell another living soul."

He didn't mean it, of course. And she knew he knew she knew he didn't mean it. But that was his way. Humor and a smile could smooth any path. And blast him, it worked, because she heard herself sighing and felt herself smiling, and before she knew it she was saying, "Enough! Let us be on our way to your mother's."

Colin grinned. "Do you think she'll have biscuits?"

Penelope rolled her eyes. "I *know* she'll have biscuits."

"Good," he said, taking off at a lope and half dragging her with him. "I do love my family, but I really just go for the food."

Chapter 4

It is difficult to imagine that there is any news from the Bridgerton ball other than Lady Danbury's determination to discern the identity of This Author, but the following items should be duly noted:

Mr. Geoffrey Albansdale was seen dancing with Miss Felicity Featherington.

Miss Felicity Featherington was also seen dancing with Mr. Lucas Hotchkiss.

Mr. Lucas Hotchkiss was also seen dancing with Miss Hyacinth Bridgerton.

Miss Hyacinth Bridgerton was also seen dancing with Viscount Burwick.

Viscount Burwick was also seen dancing with Miss Jane Hotchkiss.

Miss Jane Hotchkiss was also seen dancing with Mr. Colin Bridgerton.

Mr. Colin Bridgerton was also seen dancing with Miss Penelope Featherington.

And to round out this incestuous little ring-around-the-rosy, Miss Penelope Featherington was seen speaking with Mr. Geoffrey Albansdale. (It would have been too perfect if she'd actually danced with him, don't you agree, Dear Reader?)

LADY WHISTLEDOWN'S SOCIETY PAPERS, 12 APRIL 1824

When Penelope and Colin entered the drawing room, Eloise and Hyacinth were already sipping tea, along with both of the Ladies Bridgerton. Violet, the dowager, was seated in front of a tea service, and Kate, her daughter-in-law and the wife of Anthony, the current viscount, was attempting, without much success, to control her two-year-old daughter Charlotte.

"Look who I bumped into in Berkeley Square," Colin said.

"Penelope," Lady Bridgerton said with a warm smile, "do sit down. The tea is still nice and hot, and Cook made her famous butter biscuits."

Colin made a beeline for the food, barely pausing to acknowledge his sisters.

Penelope followed Lady Bridgerton's wave to a nearby chair and took a seat.

"Biscuits are good," Hyacinth said, thrusting a plate in her direction.

"Hyacinth," Lady Bridgerton said in a vaguely disapproving voice, "do try to speak in complete sentences."

Hyacinth looked at her mother with a surprised expression. "Biscuits. Are. Good." She cocked her head to the side. "Noun. Verb. Adjective."

"Hyacinth."

Penelope could see that Lady Bridgerton was trying to look stern as she scolded her daughter, but she wasn't quite succeeding.

"Noun. Verb. Adjective," Colin said, wiping a crumb from his grinning face. "Sentence. Is. Correct."

"If you're barely literate," Kate retorted, reaching for a biscuit. "These *are* good," she said to Penelope, a sheepish smile crossing her face. "This one's my fourth."

"I love you, Colin," Hyacinth said, ignoring Kate completely.

"Of course you do," he murmured.

"I myself," Eloise said archly, "prefer to place articles before my nouns in my own writings."

Hyacinth snorted. "Your *writings*?" she echoed.

"I write many letters," Eloise said with a sniff. "And I keep a journal, which I assure you is a very beneficial habit."

"It does keep one disciplined," Penelope put in, taking her cup and saucer from Lady Bridgerton's outstretched hands.

"Do you keep a journal?" Kate asked, not really looking at her, since she had just jumped up from her chair to grasp her daughter before the two-year-old climbed on a side table.

"I'm afraid not," Penelope said with a shake of her head. "It requires far too much discipline for me."

"I don't think it is always necessary to put an article before a noun," Hyacinth persisted, completely unable, as always, to let her side of the argument go.

Unfortunately for the rest of the assemblage, Eloise was equally tenacious. "You may leave off the article if you are referring to your noun in a general sense," she said, pursing her lips in a rather supercilious manner, "but in this case, as you were referring to *specific* biscuits . . ."

Penelope wasn't positive, but she thought she heard Lady Bridgerton groan.

". . . then specifically," Eloise said with an arch of her brows, "you are incorrect."

Hyacinth turned to Penelope. "I am positive she did not use *specifically* correctly in that last sentence."

Penelope reached for another butter biscuit. "I refuse to enter the conversation."

"Coward," Colin murmured.

"No, just hungry." Penelope turned to Kate. "These *are* good."

Kate nodded her agreement. "I have heard rumors," she said to Penelope, "that your sister may become betrothed."

Penelope blinked in surprise. She hadn't thought that Felicity's connection to Mr. Albansdale was public knowledge. "Er, where have you heard rumors?"

"Eloise, of course," Kate said matter-of-factly. "She always knows everything."

"And what I don't know," Eloise said with an easy grin, "Hyacinth usually does. It's very convenient."

"Are you certain that neither one of you is Lady Whistledown?" Colin joked.

"Colin!" Lady Bridgerton exclaimed. "How could you even think such a thing?"

He shrugged. "They're certainly both smart enough to carry off such a feat."

Eloise and Hyacinth beamed.

Even Lady Bridgerton couldn't quite dismiss the compliment. "Yes, well," she hemmed, "Hyacinth is much too young, and Eloise . . ." She looked over at Eloise, who was watching her with a most amused expression. "Well, Eloise is not Lady Whistledown. I'm sure of it."

Eloise looked at Colin. "I'm not Lady Whistledown."

"That's too bad," he replied. "You'd be filthy rich by now, I imagine."

"You know," Penelope said thoughtfully, "that might be a good way to discern her identity."

Five pairs of eyes turned in her direction.

"She has to be someone who has more money than she ought to have," Penelope explained.

"A good point," Hyacinth said, "except that I haven't a clue how much money people ought to have."

"Neither do I, of course," Penelope replied. "But most of the time one has a *general* idea." At Hyacinth's blank stare, she added, "For example, if I suddenly went out and bought myself a diamond parure, that would be very suspect."

Kate nudged Penelope with her elbow. "Bought any diamond parures lately, eh? I could use a thousand pounds."

Penelope let her eyes roll up for a second before replying, because as the current Viscountess Bridgerton, Kate most certainly did not need a thousand pounds. "I can assure you," she said, "I don't own a single diamond. Not even a ring."

Kate let out an "euf" of mock disgruntlement. "Well, you're no help, then."

"It's not so much the money," Hyacinth announced. "It's the glory."

Lady Bridgerton coughed on her tea. "I'm sorry, Hyacinth," she said, "but *what* did you just say?"

"Think of the accolades one would receive for having finally caught Lady Whistledown," Hyacinth said. "It would be glorious."

"Are you saying," Colin asked, a deceptively bland expression on his face, "that you don't care about the money?"

"I would never say *that,*" Hyacinth said with a cheeky grin.

It occurred to Penelope that of all the Bridgertons, Hyacinth and Colin were the most alike. It was probably a good thing Colin was so often out of the country. If he and Hyacinth ever joined forces in earnest, they could probably take over the world.

"Hyacinth," Lady Bridgerton said firmly, "you are *not* to make the search for Lady Whistledown your life's work."

"But—"

"I'm not saying you cannot ponder the problem and ask a few questions," Lady Bridgerton hastened to add, holding up one hand to ward off further interruptions. "Good gracious, I would hope that after nearly forty years of motherhood I would know better than to try to stop you when you have your mind quite so set on something, nonsense as it may be."

Penelope brought her teacup to her mouth to cover her smile.

"It's just that you have been known to be rather"—Lady Bridgerton delicately cleared her throat—"single-minded at times . . ."

"Mother!"

Lady Bridgerton continued as if Hyacinth had never spoken. ". . . and I do not want you to forget that your primary focus at this time must be to look for a husband."

Hyacinth uttered the word "Mother" again, but this time it was more of a groan than a protest.

Penelope stole a glance at Eloise, who had her eyes fixed on the ceiling and was clearly trying not to break out in a grin. Eloise had endured years of relentless matchmaking at her mother's hands and did not mind in the least that she seemed to have given up and moved on to Hyacinth.

In truth, Penelope was surprised that Lady Bridgerton seemed to have finally accepted Eloise's unmarried state. She had never hidden the fact that her greatest aim in life was to see all eight of her children happily married. And she'd succeeded with four. First Daphne had married Simon and become the Duchess of Hastings. The following year Anthony had married Kate. There had been a bit of a lull after that, but both Benedict and Francesca had married within a year of each other, Benedict to Sophie, and Francesca to the Scottish Earl of Kilmartin.

Francesca, unfortunately, had been widowed only two years after her marriage. She now divided her time between her late husband's family in Scotland and her own in London. When in town, however, she insisted upon living at Kilmartin House instead of at Bridgerton House or Number Five. Penelope didn't blame her. If she were a widow, she'd want to enjoy all of her independence, too.

Hyacinth generally bore her mother's matchmaking with good humor since, as she had told Penelope, it wasn't as if she didn't want to get married eventually. Might as well let her mother do all the work and then she could choose a husband when the right one presented himself.

And it was with this good humor that she stood, kissed her mother on the cheek, and dutifully promised that her main focus in life was to look for a husband—all the while directing a cheeky, sneaky smile at her brother and sister. She was barely back in her seat when she said to the crowd at large, "So, do you think she'll be caught?"

"Are we still discussing that Whistledown woman?" Lady Bridgerton groaned.

"Have you not heard Eloise's theory, then?" Penelope asked.

All eyes turned to Penelope, then to Eloise.

"Er, what *is* my theory?" Eloise asked.

"It was just, oh, I don't know, maybe a week ago," Penelope said. "We were talking about Lady Whistledown, and I said that I didn't see how she could possibly go on forever, that eventually she would have to make a mistake. Then Eloise said she wasn't so sure, that it had been over ten years and if she were going to make a mistake, wouldn't she have already done so? Then I said, no, she was only human. Eventually she would have to slip up, because no one could go on forever, and—"

"Oh, I remember now!" Eloise cut in. "We were at your house, in your room. I had the most brilliant idea! I said to Penelope that I would wager that Lady Whistledown has already made a mistake, and it's just *we* were too stupid to have noticed it."

"Not very complimentary for us, I must say," Colin murmured.

"Well, I did intend *we* to mean all of society, not just us Bridgertons," Eloise demurred.

"So maybe," Hyacinth mused, "all I need to do to catch Lady Whistledown is peruse back issues of her column."

Lady Bridgerton's eyes filled with a mild panic. "Hyacinth Bridgerton, I don't like the look on your face."

Hyacinth smiled and shrugged. "I could have a great deal of fun with one thousand pounds."

"God help us all," was her mother's reply.

"Penelope," Colin said quite suddenly, "you never did finish telling us about Felicity. Is it true that she is to be engaged?"

Penelope gulped down the tea she'd been in the process of sipping. Colin had a way of looking at a person, his green eyes so focused and intent that you felt as if you must be the only two people in the universe. Unfortunately for Penelope, it also seemed to have a way of reducing her to a stammering imbecile. If they were in the midst of conversation, she could generally hold her own, but when he surprised her like that, turning his attention onto her just when she'd convinced herself she blended in perfectly with the wallpaper, she was completely and utterly lost.

"Er, yes, it is quite possible," she said. "Mr. Albansdale has been hinting at his intentions. But if he does decide to propose, I imagine he will travel to East Anglia to ask my uncle for her hand."

"Your uncle?" Kate asked.

"My uncle Geoffrey. He lives near Norwich. He's our closest male relative, although truth be told, we don't see him very often. But Mr. Albansdale is rather traditional. I don't think he would feel comfortable asking my mother."

"I hope he asks Felicity as well," Eloise said. "I've often thought it foolish that a man asks a woman's father for her hand before he asks her. The father doesn't have to live with him."

"This attitude," Colin said with an amused smile that was only partly hidden by his teacup, "may explain why you are as yet unmarried."

Lady Bridgerton gave her son a stern glare and said his name disapprovingly.

"Oh, no, Mother," Eloise said, "I don't mind. I'm perfectly comfortable as an old maid." She gave Colin a rather superior look. "I'd much rather be a spinster than be married to a bore. As," she added with a flourish, "would Penelope!"

Startled by Eloise's hand waving rather suddenly in her direction, Penelope straightened her spine and said, "Er, yes. Of course."

But Penelope had a feeling she wasn't quite as firm in her convictions as her friend. Unlike Eloise, she hadn't refused six offers of marriage. She hadn't refused any; she hadn't received even a one.

She'd told herself that she wouldn't have accepted in any case, since her heart belonged to Colin. But was that really the truth, or was she just trying to make herself feel better for having been such a resounding failure on the marriage mart?

If someone asked her to marry him tomorrow—someone perfectly kind and acceptable, whom she might never love but would in all probability like very well—would she say yes?

Probably.

And this made her melancholy, because admitting this to herself meant she'd really, truly given up hope on Colin. It meant she wasn't as true to her principles as she'd hoped she was. It meant she was willing to settle on a less-than-perfect husband in order to have a home and family of her own.

It wasn't anything that hundreds of women didn't do every year, but it was something that she'd never thought she'd do herself.

"You look very serious all of a sudden," Colin said to her.

Penelope jerked out of her musings. "Me? Oh. No, no. I just lost myself in my thoughts, that's all."

Colin acknowledged her statement with a brief nod before reaching for another biscuit. "Have we anything more substantial?" he asked, wrinkling his nose.

"If I'd known you were coming," his mother said in a dry voice, "I would have doubled the food."

He stood and walked to the bellpull. "I'll ring for more."

After giving it a yank, he turned back and asked, "Did you hear about Penelope's Lady Whistledown theory?"

"No, I haven't," Lady Bridgerton replied.

"It's very clever, actually," Colin said, stopping to ask a maid for sandwiches before finishing with, "She thinks it's Lady Danbury."

"Ooooh." Hyacinth was visibly impressed. "That's very cunning, Penelope."

Penelope nodded her head to the side in thanks.

"And just the sort of thing Lady Danbury would do," Hyacinth added.

"The column or the challenge?" Kate asked, catching hold of the sash on Charlotte's frock before the little girl could scramble out of reach.

"Both," Hyacinth said.

"And," Eloise put in, "Penelope told her so. Right to her face."

Hyacinth's mouth dropped open, and it was obvious to Penelope that she'd just gone up—way up—in Hyacinth's estimation.

"I should have liked to have seen that!" Lady Bridgerton said with a wide, proud smile. "Frankly, I'm surprised that didn't show up in this morning's *Whistledown*."

"I hardly think Lady Whistledown would comment upon individual people's theories as to her identity," Penelope said.

"Why not?" Hyacinth asked. "It would be an excellent way for her to set out a few red herrings. For example"—she held her hand out toward her sister in a most dramatic pose—"say I thought it was Eloise."

"It is not Eloise!" Lady Bridgerton protested.

"It's not me," Eloise said with a grin.

"But say I *thought* it was," Hyacinth said in an extremely beleaguered voice. "And that I said so publicly."

"Which you would never do," her mother said sternly.

"Which I would never do," Hyacinth parroted. "But just to be academic, let us pretend that I did. And say that Eloise really was Lady Whistledown. Which she's not," she hastened to add before her mother could interrupt again.

Lady Bridgerton held up her hands in silent defeat.

"What better way to fool the masses," Hyacinth continued, "than to make fun of me in her column?"

"Of course, if Lady Whistledown really *were* Eloise . . ." Penelope mused.

"She's not!" Lady Bridgerton burst out.

Penelope couldn't help but laugh. "But if she were . . ."

"You know," Eloise said, "now I *really* wish I were."

"What a joke you'd be having on us all," Penelope continued. "Of course, then on Wednesday you couldn't run a column making fun of Hyacinth for thinking you are Lady Whistledown, because then we'd all know it had to be you."

"Unless it was *you*." Kate laughed, looking at Penelope. "*That* would be a devious trick."

"Let me see if I have it straight," Eloise said with a laugh. "Penelope is Lady Whistledown, and she is going to run a column on Wednesday making fun of Hyacinth's theory that *I'm* Lady Whistledown just to trick you into thinking that I really *am* Lady Whistledown, because Hyacinth suggested that that would be a cunning ruse."

"I am utterly lost," Colin said to no one in particular.

"Unless *Colin* were really Lady Whistledown . . ." Hyacinth said with a devilish gleam in her eye.

"Stop!" Lady Bridgerton said. "I beg you."

By then everyone was laughing too hard for Hyacinth to continue, anyway.

"The possibilities are endless," Hyacinth said, wiping a tear from her eye.

"Perhaps we should all simply look to the left," Colin suggested as he sat back down. "Who knows, that person may very well be our infamous Lady Whistledown."

Everyone looked left, with the exception of Eloise, who looked right . . . right to Colin. "Were you trying to tell me something," she asked with an amused smile, "when you sat down to my right?"

"Not at all," he murmured, reaching for the biscuit plate and then stopping when he remembered it was empty.

But he didn't quite meet Eloise's eyes when he said so.

If anyone other than Penelope had noticed his evasiveness, they were unable to question him on it, because that was when the sandwiches arrived, and he was useless for conversation after that.

Chapter 5

It has come to This Author's attention that Lady Blackwood turned her ankle earlier this week whilst chasing down a delivery boy for This Humble Newssheet.

One thousand pounds is certainly a great deal of money, but Lady Blackwood is hardly in need of funds, and moreover, the situation is growing absurd. Surely Londoners have better things to do with their time than chase down poor, hapless delivery boys in a fruitless attempt to uncover the identity of This Author.

Or maybe not.

This Author has chronicled the activities of the ton *for over a decade now and has found no evidence that they do indeed have anything better to do with their time.*

LADY WHISTLEDOWN'S SOCIETY PAPERS, 14 APRIL 1824

Two days later Penelope found herself once again cutting across Berkeley Square, on her way to Number Five to see Eloise. This time, however, it was late morning, and it was sunny, and she did not bump into Colin along the way.

Penelope wasn't sure if that was a bad thing or not.

She and Eloise had made plans the week before to go shopping, but they'd decided to meet at Number Five so that they could head out together and forgo the accompaniment of their maids. It was a perfect sort of day, far more like June than April, and Penelope was looking forward to the short walk up to Oxford Street.

But when she arrived at Eloise's house, she was met with a puzzled expression on the butler's face.

"Miss Featherington," he said, blinking several times in rapid succession before locating a few more words. "I don't believe Miss Eloise is here at present."

Penelope's lips parted in surprise. "Where did she go? We made our plans over a week ago."

Wickham shook his head. "I do not know. But she departed with her mother and Miss Hyacinth two hours earlier."

"I see." Penelope frowned, trying to decide what to do. "May I wait, then? Perhaps she was merely delayed. It's not like Eloise to forget an appointment."

He nodded graciously and showed her upstairs to the informal drawing room, promising to bring a plate of refreshments and handing her the latest edition of *Whistledown* to read while she bided her time.

Penelope had already read it, of course; it was delivered quite early in the morning, and she made a habit of perusing the column at breakfast. With so little to occupy her mind, she wandered over to the window and peered out over the Mayfair streetscape. But there wasn't much new to see; it was the same buildings she'd seen a thousand times before, even the same people walking along the street.

Maybe it was because she was pondering the sameness of her life that she noticed the one object new to her vista: a bound book lying open on the table. Even from several feet away she could see that it was filled not with the printed word, but rather with neat handwritten lines.

She inched toward it and glanced down without actually touching the pages. It appeared to be a journal of sorts, and in the middle of the right-hand side there was a heading that was set apart from the rest of the text by a bit of space above and below:

22 February 1824
Troodos Mountains, Cyprus

One of her hands flew to her mouth. Colin had written this! He'd said just the other day that he'd visited Cyprus instead of Greece. She had no idea that he kept a journal.

She lifted a foot to take a step back, but her body didn't budge. She shouldn't read this, she told herself. This was Colin's private journal. She really ought to move away.

"Away," she muttered, looking down at her recalcitrant feet. "Away."

Her feet didn't move.

But maybe she wasn't quite so in the wrong. After all, was she really invading his privacy if she read only what she could see without turning a page? He *had* left it lying open on the table, for all the world to see.

But then again, Colin had every reason to think that no one would stumble across his journal if he dashed out for a few moments. Presumably, he was aware that his mother and sisters had departed for the morning. Most guests were shown to the formal drawing room on the ground floor; as far as Penelope knew, she and Felicity were the only non-Bridgertons who were taken straight up to the informal drawing room. And since Colin wasn't expecting her (or, more likely, hadn't thought of her one way or another), he wouldn't have thought there was any danger in leaving his journal behind while he ran an errand.

On the other hand, he *had* left it lying open.

Open, for heaven's sake! If there were any valuable secrets in that journal, surely Colin would have taken greater care to secret it when he left the room. He wasn't stupid, after all.

Penelope leaned forward.

Oh, bother. She couldn't read the writing from that distance. The heading had been legible since it was surrounded by so much white space, but the rest was a bit too close together to make out from far away.

Somehow she'd thought she wouldn't feel so guilty if she didn't have to step any closer to the book to read it. Never mind, of course, that she'd already crossed the room to get to where she was at that moment.

She tapped her finger against the side of her jaw, right near her ear. That was a good point. She had crossed the room some time ago, which surely meant that she'd already committed the biggest sin she was likely to that day. One little step was nothing compared to the length of the room.

She inched forward, decided that only counted as half a step, then inched forward again and looked down, beginning her reading right in the middle of a sentence.

in England. Here the sand ripples between tan and white, and the consistency is so fine that it slides over a bare foot like a whisper of silk. The water is a blue unimaginable in England, aquamarine with the glint of the sun, deep cobalt when the clouds take the sky. And it is warm—surprisingly, astoundingly warm, like a bath that was heated perhaps a half an hour earlier. The waves are gentle, and they lap up on the shore with a soft rush of foam, tickling the skin and turning the perfect sand into a squishy delight that slips and slides along the toes until another wave arrives to clean up the mess.

It is easy to see why this is said to be the birthplace of Aphrodite. With every step I almost expect to see her as in Botticelli's painting, rising from the ocean, perfectly balanced on a giant shell, her long titian hair streaming around her.

If ever a perfect woman was born, surely this would be the place. I am in paradise. And yet . . .

And yet with every warm breeze and cloudless sky I am reminded that this is not my home, that I was born to live my life elsewhere. This does not quell the desire—no, the compulsion!—to travel, to see, to meet. But it does feed a strange longing to touch a dew-dampened lawn, or feel a cool mist on one's face, or even to remember the joy of a perfect day after a week of rain.

The people here can't know that joy. Their days are always perfect. Can one appreciate perfection when it is a constant in one's life?

22 February 1824
Troodos Mountains, Cyprus

It is remarkable that I am cold. It is, of course, February, and as an Englishman I'm quite used to a February chill (as well as that of any month with an R in its name), but I am not in England. I am in Cyprus, in the heart of the Mediterranean, and just two days ago I was in Paphos, on the southwest coast of the island, where the sun is strong and the ocean salty and warm. Here, one can see the peak of Mount Olympus, still capped with snow so white one is temporarily blinded when the sun glints off of it.

The climb to this altitude was treacherous, with danger lurking around more than one corner. The road is rudimentary, and along the way we met

Penelope let out a soft grunt of protest when she realized that the page ended in the middle of a sentence. Who had he met? What had happened? *What danger?*

She stared down at the journal, absolutely *dying* to flip the page and see what happened next. But when she'd started reading, she had managed to justify it by telling herself she wasn't really invading Colin's privacy; he'd left the book open, after all. She was only looking at what he had left exposed.

Turning the page, however, was something else altogether.

She reached out, then yanked her hand back. This wasn't right. She couldn't read his journal. Well, not beyond what she'd already read.

On the other hand, it was clear that these were words worth reading. It was a crime for Colin to keep them for himself. Words should be celebrated, shared. They should be—

"Oh, for God's sake," she muttered to herself. She reached for the edge of the page.

"What are you doing?"

Penelope whirled around. "Colin!"

"Indeed," he snapped.

Penelope lurched back. She'd never heard him use such a tone. She hadn't even thought him capable of it.

He strode across the room, grabbed the journal, and snapped it shut. "What are you doing here?" he demanded.

"Waiting for Eloise," she managed to get out, her mouth suddenly quite dry.

"In the upstairs drawing room?"

"Wickham always takes me here. Your mother told him to treat me like family. I . . . uh . . . he . . . uh . . ." She realized that she was wringing her hands together and willed herself to stop. "It's the same with my sister Felicity. Because she and Hyacinth are such good friends. I—I'm sorry. I thought you knew."

He threw the leather-bound book carelessly onto a nearby chair and crossed his arms. "And do you make a habit of reading the personal letters of others?"

"No, of course not. But it was open and—" She gulped, recognizing how awful the excuse sounded the second the words left her lips. "It's a public room," she mumbled, somehow feeling like she had to finish her defense. "Maybe you should have taken it with you."

"Where I went," he ground out, still visibly furious with her, "one doesn't ordinarily take a book."

"It's not very big," she said, wondering why why *why* she was still talking when she was so clearly in the wrong.

"For the love of God," he exploded. "Do you *want* me to say the word *chamberpot* in your presence?"

Penelope felt her cheeks blush deep red. "I'd better go," she said. "Please tell Eloise—"

"*I'll* go," Colin practically snarled. "I'm moving out this afternoon, anyway. Might as well leave now, since you've so obviously taken over the house."

Penelope had never thought that words could cause physical pain, but right then she would have sworn that she'd taken a knife to the heart. She hadn't realized until that very moment just how much it meant to her that Lady Bridgerton had opened her home to her.

Or how much it would hurt to know that Colin resented her presence there.

"Why do you have to make it so difficult to apologize?" she burst out, dogging his heels as he crossed the room to gather the rest of his things.

"And why, pray tell, should I make it easy?" he returned. He didn't face her as he said it; he didn't even break his stride.

"Because it would be the nice thing to do," she ground out.

That got his attention. He whirled around, his eyes flashing so furiously that Penelope stumbled back a step. Colin was the nice one, the easygoing one. He didn't lose his temper.

Until now.

"Because it would be the nice thing to do?" he thundered. "Is that what you were thinking when you read my journal? That it would be a nice thing to read someone's private papers?"

"No, Colin, I—"

"There is nothing you can say—" he said, jabbing her in the shoulder with his index finger.

"Colin! You—"

He turned around to gather his belongings, rudely giving her his back while he spoke. "Not a thing that could justify your behavior."

"No, of course not, but—"

"OW!"

Penelope felt the blood drain from her face. Colin's yell was one of real pain. His name escaped her lips in a panicked whisper and she rushed to his side. "What's—Oh, my heavens!"

Blood was gushing from a wound on the palm of his hand.

Never terribly articulate in a crisis, Penelope managed to say, "Oh! Oh! The carpet!" before leaping forward with a piece of writing paper that had been lying on a nearby table and sliding it under his hand to catch the blood before it ruined the priceless carpet below.

"Ever the attentive nurse," Colin said in a shaky voice.

"Well, you're not going to die," she explained, "and the carpet—"

"It's all right," he assured her. "I was trying to make a joke."

Penelope looked up at his face. Tight white lines were etched in the skin around his mouth, and he looked very pale. "I think you'd better sit down," she said.

He nodded grimly and sagged into a chair.

Penelope's stomach did a rather seasickish sway. She'd never been terribly good with blood. "Maybe I'd better sit down, too," she mumbled, sinking onto the low table opposite him.

"Are you going to be all right?" he asked.

She nodded, swallowing against a tiny wave of nausea. "We need to find something to wrap this," she said, grimacing as she looked down at the ridiculous setup below. The paper wasn't absorbent, and the blood was rolling precariously along its surface, with Penelope desperately trying to keep it from dripping over the side.

"I have a handkerchief in my pocket," he said.

She carefully set the paper down and retrieved the handkerchief from his breast pocket, trying not to notice the warm beat of his heart as her fingers fumbled for the creamy white scrap of cloth. "Does it hurt?" she asked as she wrapped it around his hand. "No, don't answer that. Of course it hurts."

He managed a very wobbly smile. "It hurts."

She peered down at the gash, forcing herself to look at it closely even though the blood made her stomach turn. "I don't think you'll need stitches."

"Do you know much about wounds?"

She shook her head. "Nothing. But it doesn't look too bad. Except for . . . ah, all the blood."

"Feels worse than it looks," he joked.

Her eyes flew to his face in horror.

"Another joke," he reassured her. "Well, not really. It *does* feel worse than it looks, but I assure you it's bearable."

"I'm sorry," she said, increasing pressure on the wound to staunch the flow of blood. "This is all my fault."

"That I sliced open my hand?"

"If you hadn't been so angry . . ."

He just shook his head, closing his eyes briefly against the pain. "Don't be silly, Penelope. If I hadn't gotten angry with you, I would have gotten angry with someone else some other time."

"And you'd of course have a letter opener by your side when that happened," she murmured, looking up at him through her lashes as she bent over his hand.

When his eyes met hers, they were filled with humor and maybe just a touch of admiration.

And something else she'd never thought to see—vulnerability, hesitancy, and even insecurity. He didn't know how good his writing was, she realized with amazement. He had no idea, and he was actually embarrassed that she'd seen it.

"Colin," Penelope said, instinctively pressing harder on his wound as she leaned in, "I must tell you. You—"

She broke off when she heard the sharp, even clatter of footsteps coming down the hall. "That will be Wickham," she said, glancing toward the door. "He insisted upon bringing me a small meal. Can you keep the pressure on this for now?"

Colin nodded. "I don't want him to know I've hurt myself. He'll only tell Mother, and then I'll never hear the end of it."

"Well, here, then." She stood and tossed him his journal. "Pretend you're reading this."

Colin barely had time to open it and lay it across his injured hand before the butler entered with a large tray.

"Wickham!" Penelope said, jumping to her feet and turning to face him as if she hadn't already known he was coming. "As usual you've brought far more than I could possibly eat. Luckily, Mr. Bridgerton has been keeping me company. I'm certain that with his help, I'll be able to do justice to your meal."

Wickham nodded and removed the covers from the serving dishes. It was a cold repast—pieces of meat, cheese, and fruit, accompanied by a tall pitcher of lemonade.

Penelope smiled brightly. "I hope you didn't think I could eat all of this myself."

"Lady Bridgerton and her daughters are expected soon. I thought they might be hungry as well."

"Won't be any left after I'm through with it," Colin said with a jovial smile.

Wickham bowed slightly in his direction. "If I'd known you were here, Mr. Bridgerton, I would have trebled the portions. Would you like me to fix you a plate?"

"No, no," Colin said, waving his uninjured hand. "I'll get up just as soon as I . . . ah . . . finish reading this chapter."

The butler said, "Let me know if you require further assistance," and exited the room.

"Aaaaaahhh," Colin groaned, the moment he heard Wickham's steps disappear down the hall. "Damn—I mean, dash it—it hurts."

Penelope plucked a napkin off the tray. "Here, let's replace that handkerchief." She peeled it away from his skin, keeping her eyes on the cloth rather than the wound. For some reason that didn't seem to bother her stomach quite as much. "I'm afraid your handkerchief is ruined."

Colin just closed his eyes and shook his head. Penelope was smart enough to interpret the action to mean, *I don't care.* And she was sensible enough not to say anything further on the subject. Nothing worse than a female who chattered forever about nothing.

He'd always liked Penelope, but how was it he'd never realized how intelligent she was up till now? Oh, he supposed if someone had asked him, he would have said she was bright, but he'd certainly never taken the time to think about it.

It was becoming clear to him, however, that she was very intelligent, indeed. And he thought he remembered his sister once telling him that she was an avid reader.

And probably a discriminating one as well.

"I think the bleeding is slowing down," she was saying as she wrapped the fresh napkin around his hand. "In fact, I'm sure it is, if only because I don't feel quite so sick every time I look at the wound."

He wished that she hadn't read his journal, but now that she *had* . . .

"Ah, Penelope," he began, startled by the hesitancy in his own voice.

She looked up. "I'm sorry. Am I pressing too hard?"

For a moment Colin did nothing but blink. How was it possible he'd never noticed how big her eyes were? He'd known they were brown, of course, and . . . No, come to think of it, if he were to be honest with himself, he would have to admit that if asked earlier this morning, he'd not have been able to identify the color of her eyes.

But somehow he knew that he'd never forget again.

She eased up on the pressure. "Is this all right?"

He nodded. "Thank you. I would do it myself, but it's my right hand, and—"

"Say no more. It's the very least I can do, after . . . after . . ." Her eyes slid slightly to the side, and he knew she was about to apologize another time.

"Penelope," he began again.

"No, wait!" she cried out, her dark eyes flashing with . . . could it be passion? Certainly not the brand of passion with which he was most familiar. But there were other sorts, weren't there? Passion for learning. Passion for . . . literature?

"I must tell you this," she said urgently. "I know it was unforgivably intrusive of me to look at your journal. I was just . . . bored . . . and waiting . . . and I had nothing to do, and then I saw the book and I was curious."

He opened his mouth to interrupt her, to tell her that what was done was done, but the words were rushing from her mouth, and he found himself oddly compelled to listen.

"I should have stepped away the moment I realized what it was," she continued, "but as soon as I read one sentence I had to read another! Colin, it was wonderful! It was just like I was there. I could feel the water—I knew exactly the temperature. It was so clever of you to describe it the way you did. Everyone knows exactly what a bath feels like a half an hour after it has been filled."

For a moment Colin could do nothing but stare at her. He'd never seen Penelope quite so animated, and it was strange and . . . good, really, that all that excitement was over his journal.

"You—you liked it?" he finally asked.

"Liked it? Colin, I loved it! I—"

"Ow!"

In her excitement, she'd started squeezing his hand a bit too hard. "Oh, sorry," she said perfunctorily. "Colin, I really must know. What was the danger? I couldn't bear to be left hanging like that."

"It was nothing," he said modestly. "The page you read really wasn't a very exciting passage."

"No, it was mostly description," she agreed, "but the description was very compelling and evocative. I could see everything. But it wasn't—oh, dear, how do I explain this?"

Colin discovered that he was very impatient for her to figure out what she was trying to say.

"Sometimes," she finally continued, "when one reads a passage of description, it's rather . . . oh, I don't know . . . detached. Clinical, even. You brought the island to life. Other people might call the water warm, but you related it to something we all know and understand. It made me feel as if I were there, dipping my toe in right alongside you."

Colin smiled, ridiculously pleased by her praise.

"Oh! And I don't want to forget—there was another brilliant thing I wanted to mention."

Now he knew he must be grinning like an idiot. Brilliant brilliant brilliant. What a *good* word.

Penelope leaned in slightly as she said, "You also showed the reader how *you* relate to the scene and how it affects you. It becomes more than mere description because we see how you react to it."

Colin knew he was fishing for compliments, but he didn't much care as he asked, "What do you mean?"

"Well, if you look at—May I see the journal to refresh my memory?"

"Of course," he murmured, handing it to her. "Wait, let me find the correct page again."

Once he had done so, she scanned his lines until she found the section she was looking for. "Here we are. Look at this part about how you are reminded that England is your home."

"It's funny how travel can do that to a person."

"Do what to a person?" she asked, her eyes wide with interest.

"Make one appreciate home," he said softly.

Her eyes met his, and they were serious, inquisitive. "And yet you still like to go away."

He nodded. "I can't help it. It's like a disease."

She laughed, and it sounded unexpectedly musical. "Don't be ridiculous," she said. "A disease is harmful. It's clear that your travels feed your soul." She looked down to his hand, carefully peeling the napkin back to inspect his wound. "It's almost better," she said.

"Almost," he agreed. In truth, he suspected the bleeding had stopped altogether, but he was reluctant to let the conversation end. And he knew that the moment she was done caring for him, she would go.

He didn't think she wanted to go, but he somehow knew that she would. She'd think it was the proper thing to do, and she'd probably also think it was what he wanted.

Nothing, he was surprised to realize, could be further from the truth.

And nothing could have scared him more.

Chapter 6

Everyone has secrets.
Especially me.
LADY WHISTLEDOWN'S SOCIETY PAPERS, 14 APRIL 1824

"I wish I'd known you kept a journal," Penelope said, reapplying pressure to his palm.

"Why?"

"I'm not sure," she said with a shrug. "It's always interesting to find out that there is more to someone than meets the eye, don't you think?"

Colin didn't say anything for several moments, and then, quite suddenly, he blurted out, "You really liked it?"

She looked amused. He was horrified. Here he was, considered one of the most popular and sophisticated men of the *ton,* and he'd been reduced to a bashful schoolboy, hanging on Penelope Featherington's every word, just for a single scrap of praise.

Penelope Featherington, for God's sake.

Not that there was anything wrong with Penelope, of course, he hastened to remind himself. Just that she was . . . well . . . Penelope.

"Of course I liked it," she said with a soft smile. "I just finished telling you so."

"What was the first thing that struck you about it?" he asked, deciding that he might as well act like a complete fool, since he was already more than halfway there.

She smiled wickedly. "Actually, the first thing that struck me was that your penmanship was quite a bit neater than I would have guessed."

He frowned. "What does that mean?"

"I have difficulty seeing you bent over a desk, practicing your flicks," she replied, her lips tightening at the corners to suppress a smile.

If ever there were a time for righteous indignation, this was clearly it. "I'll have you know I spent many an hour in the nursery schoolroom, bent over a desk, as you so delicately put it."

"I'm sure," she murmured.

"Hmmmph."

She looked down, clearly trying not to smile.

"I'm quite good with my flicks," he added. It was just a game now, but somehow it was rather fun to play the part of the petulant schoolboy.

"Obviously," she replied. "I especially liked them on the H's. Very well done. Quite . . . flicky of you."

"Indeed."

She matched his straight face perfectly. "Indeed."

His gaze slid from hers, and for a moment he felt quite unaccountably shy. "I'm glad you liked the journal," he said.

"It was lovely," she said in a soft, faraway kind of voice. "Very lovely, and . . ." She looked away, blushing. "You're going to think I'm silly."

"Never," he promised.

"Well, I think one of the reasons I enjoyed it so much is that I could somehow feel that *you'd* enjoyed writing it."

Colin was silent for a long moment. It hadn't ever occurred to him that he enjoyed his writing; it was just something he *did.*

He did it because he couldn't imagine not doing it. How could he travel to foreign lands and not keep a record of what he saw, what he experienced, and perhaps most importantly, what he felt?

But when he thought back, he realized that he felt a strange rush of satisfaction whenever he wrote a phrase that was exactly right, a sentence that was particularly true. He distinctly remembered the moment he'd written the passage Penelope had read. He'd been sitting on the beach at dusk, the sun still warm on his skin, the sand somehow rough and smooth at the same time under his bare feet. It had been a heavenly moment—full of that warm, lazy feeling one can truly only experience in the dead of summer (or on the perfect beaches of the Mediterranean), and he'd been trying to think of the exact right way to describe the water.

He'd sat there for ages—surely a full half an hour—his pen poised above the paper of his journal, waiting for inspiration. And then suddenly he'd realized the temperature was precisely that of slightly old bathwater, and his face had broken into a wide, delighted smile.

Yes, he enjoyed writing. Funny how he'd never realized it before.

"It's good to have something in your life," Penelope said quietly. "Something satisfying—that will fill the hours with a sense of purpose." She crossed her hands in her lap and looked down, seemingly engrossed by her knuckles. "I've never understood the supposed joys of a lazy life."

Colin wanted to touch his fingers to her chin, to see her eyes when he asked her—*And what do you do to fill your hours with a sense of purpose?* But he didn't. It would be far too forward, and it would mean admitting to himself just how interested he was in her answer.

So he asked the question, and he kept his own hands still.

"Nothing, really," she replied, still examining her fingernails. Then, after a pause, she looked up quite suddenly, her chin rising so quickly it almost made him dizzy. "I like to read," she said. "I read quite a bit, actually. And I do a bit of embroidery now and then, but I'm not very good at it. I wish there were more, but, well . . ."

"What?" Colin prodded.

Penelope shook her head. "It's nothing. You should be grateful for your travels. I'm quite envious of you."

There was a long silence, not awkward, but strange nonetheless, and finally Colin said brusquely, "It's not enough."

The tone of his voice seemed so out of place in the conversation that Penelope could do nothing but stare. "What do you mean?" she finally asked.

He shrugged carelessly. "A man can't travel forever; to do so would take all the fun out of it."

She laughed, then looked at him and realized he was serious. "I'm sorry," she said. "I didn't mean to be rude."

"You weren't rude," he said, taking a swig of his lemonade. It sloshed on the table when he set the glass down; clearly, he was unused to using his left hand. "Two of the best parts of travel," he explained, wiping his mouth with one of the clean napkins, "are the leaving and the coming home, and besides, I'd miss my family too much were I to go off indefinitely."

Penelope had no reply—at least nothing that wouldn't sound like platitudes, so she just waited for him to continue.

For a moment he didn't say anything, then he scoffed and shut his journal with a resounding thud. "These don't count. They're just for me."

"They don't have to be," she said softly.

If he heard her, he made no indication. "It's all very well and good to keep a journal while you're traveling," he continued, "but once I'm home I still have nothing to do."

"I find that difficult to believe."

He didn't say anything, just reached for a piece of cheese off the tray. She watched him while he ate, and then, after he'd washed it down with more lemonade, his entire demeanor changed. He seemed more alert, more on edge as he asked, "Have you read *Whistledown* lately?"

Penelope blinked at the sudden change of subject. "Yes, of course, why? Doesn't everyone read it?"

He waved off her question. "Have you noticed how she describes me?"

"Er, it's almost always favorable, isn't it?"

His hand began to wave again—rather dismissively, in her opinion. "Yes, yes, that's not the point," he said in a distracted voice.

"You might think it more the point," Penelope replied testily, "if you'd ever been likened to an overripe citrus fruit."

He winced, and he opened and closed his mouth twice before finally saying, "If it makes you feel better, I didn't remember that she'd called you that until just now." He stopped, thought for a moment, then added, "In fact, I still don't remember it."

"It's all right," she said, putting on her best I'm-a-good-sport face. "I assure you, I'm quite beyond it. And I've always had a fondness for oranges and lemons."

He started to say something again, then stopped, then looked at her rather directly and said, "I hope what I'm about to say isn't abominably insensitive or insulting, given that when all is said and done, I've very little to complain about."

The implication being, Penelope realized, that perhaps *she* did.

"But I'm telling you," he continued, his eyes clear and earnest, "because I think maybe you'll understand."

It was a compliment. A strange, uncommon one, but a

compliment nonetheless. Penelope wanted nothing more than to lay her hand across his, but of course she could not, so she just nodded and said, "You can tell me anything, Colin."

"My brothers—" he began. "They're—" He stopped, staring rather blankly toward the window before finally turning back to her and saying, "They're very accomplished. Anthony is the viscount, and God knows I wouldn't want that responsibility, but he has a purpose. Our entire heritage is in his hands."

"More than that, I should think," Penelope said softly.

He looked at her, question in his eyes.

"I think your brother feels responsible for your entire family," she said. "I imagine it's a heavy burden."

Colin tried to keep his face impassive, but he'd never been an accomplished stoic, and he must have shown his dismay on his face, because Penelope practically rose from her seat as she rushed to add, "Not that I think he minds it! It's part of who he is."

"Exactly!" Colin exclaimed, as if he'd just discovered something that was actually important. As opposed to this . . . this . . . this inane discussion about his life. He had nothing to complain about. He *knew* he had nothing to complain about, and yet . . .

"Did you know Benedict paints?" he found himself asking.

"Of course," she replied. "Everyone knows he paints. He has a painting in the National Gallery. And I believe they are planning to hang another soon. Another landscape."

"Really?"

She nodded. "Eloise told me."

He slumped again. "Then it must be true. I can't believe no one mentioned it to me."

"You *have* been away," she reminded him.

"What I'm trying to say," he continued, "is that they both have a purpose to their lives. I have nothing."

"That can't be true," she said.

"I should think I would be in a position to know."

Penelope sat back, startled by the sharp tone of his voice.

"I know what people think of me," he began, and although Penelope had told herself that she was going to remain silent, to allow him to speak his mind fully, she couldn't help but interrupt.

"Everyone likes you," she rushed to say. "They adore you."

"I know," he groaned, looking anguished and sheepish at the same time. "But . . ." He raked a hand through his hair. "God, how to say this without sounding a complete ass?"

Penelope's eyes widened.

"I'm sick of being thought an empty-headed charmer," he finally blurted out.

"Don't be silly," she said, faster than immediately, if that were possible.

"Penelope—"

"No one thinks you're stupid," she said.

"How would—"

"Because I've been stuck here in London for more years than anyone should have to," she said sharply. "I may not be the most popular woman in town, but after ten years, I've heard more than my fair share of gossip and lies and foolish opinions, and I have never—not once—heard someone refer to you as stupid."

He stared at her for a moment, a bit startled by her passionate defense. "I didn't mean *stupid,* precisely," he said in a soft, and he hoped humble, voice. "More . . . without substance. Even Lady Whistledown refers to me as a charmer."

"What's wrong with that?"

"Nothing," he replied testily, "if she didn't do it every other day."

"She only *publishes* every other day."

"My point exactly," he shot back. "If she thought there was anything to me other than my so-called legendary charm, don't you think she would have said so by now?"

Penelope was quiet for a long moment, then she said, "Does it really matter what Lady Whistledown thinks?"

He slumped forward, smacking his hands against his knees, then yelping with pain when he (belatedly) remembered his injury. "You're missing the point," he said, wincing as he reapplied pressure to his palm. "I couldn't care less about Lady Whistledown. But whether we like it or not, she represents the rest of society."

"I would imagine that there are quite a few people who would take exception to that statement."

He raised one brow. "Including yourself?"

"Actually, I think Lady Whistledown is rather astute," she said, folding her hands primly in her lap.

"The woman called you an overripe melon!"

Two splotches of red burned in her cheeks. "An overripe citrus fruit," she ground out. "I assure you there is a very big difference."

Colin decided then and there that the female mind was a strange and incomprehensible organ—one which no man should even attempt to understand. There wasn't a woman alive who could go from point A to B without stopping at C, D, X, and 12 along the way.

"Penelope," he finally said, staring at her in disbelief, "the woman insulted you. How can you defend her?"

"She said nothing more than the truth," she replied, crossing her arms over her chest. "She's been rather kind, actually, since my mother started allowing me to pick out my own clothing."

Colin groaned. "Surely we were talking about something else at some point. Tell me we didn't *intend* to discuss your wardrobe."

Penelope's eyes narrowed. "I believe we were discussing your dissatisfaction with life as the most popular man in London."

Her voice rose on the last four words, and Colin realized he'd been scolded. Soundly.

Which he found extraordinarily irritating. "I don't know why I thought you'd understand," he bit off, hating the childish tinge in his voice but completely unable to edit it out.

"I'm sorry," she said, "but it's a little difficult for me to sit here and listen to you complain that your life is nothing."

"I didn't say that."

"You most certainly did!"

"I said I *have* nothing," he corrected, trying not to wince as he realized how stupid that sounded.

"You have more than anyone I know," she said, jabbing him in the shoulder. "But if you don't realize that, then maybe you are correct—your life is nothing."

"It's too hard to explain," he said in a petulant mutter.

"If you want a new direction for your life," she said, "then for heaven's sake, just pick something out and do it. The world is your oyster, Colin. You're young, wealthy, and you're a *man*." Penelope's voice turned bitter, resentful. "You can do anything you want."

He scowled, which didn't surprise her. When people were convinced they had problems, the last thing they wanted to hear was a simple, straightforward solution.

"It's not that simple," he said.

"It's exactly that simple." She stared at him for the longest moment, wondering, perhaps for the first time in her life, just who he was.

She'd thought she knew everything about him, but she hadn't known that he kept a journal.

She hadn't known that he possessed a temper.

She hadn't known that he felt dissatisfied with his life.

And she certainly hadn't known that he was petulant and spoiled enough to feel that dissatisfaction, when heaven knew he didn't deserve to. What right did he have to feel unhappy with his life? How dare he complain, especially to her?

She stood, smoothing out her skirts in an awkward, defensive gesture. "Next time you want to complain about the trials and tribulations of universal adoration, try being an on-the-shelf spinster for a day. See how that feels and then let me know what you want to complain about."

And then, while Colin was still sprawled on the sofa, gaping at her as if she were some bizarre creature with three heads, twelve fingers, and a tail, she swept out of the room.

It was, she thought as she descended the outer steps to Bruton Street, quite the most splendid exit of her existence.

It was really too bad, then, that the man she'd been leaving was the only one in whose company she'd ever wanted to remain.

Colin felt like hell all day.

His hand hurt like the devil, despite the brandy he'd sloshed both on his skin and into his mouth. The estate agent who'd handled the lease for the snug little terrace house he'd found in Bloomsbury had informed him that the previous tenant was having difficulties and Colin wouldn't be able to move in today as planned—would next week be acceptable?

And to top it off, he suspected that he might have done irreparable harm to his friendship with Penelope.

Which made him feel worst of all, since (A) he rather valued his friendship with Penelope and (B) he hadn't realized how much he valued his friendship with Penelope, which (C) made him feel slightly panicked.

Penelope was a constant in his life. His sister's friend—the one who was always at the fringes of the party; nearby, but not truly a part of things.

But the world seemed to be shifting. He'd only been back in England for a fortnight, but already Penelope had changed. Or maybe he'd changed. Or maybe she hadn't changed but the way he saw her had changed.

She mattered. He didn't know how else to put it.

And after ten years of her just being . . . *there,* it was rather bizarre for her to matter quite so much.

He didn't like that they'd parted ways that afternoon on such awkward terms. He couldn't remember feeling awkward with Penelope, ever—no, that wasn't true. There was that time . . . dear God, how many years ago was it? Six? Seven? His mother had been pestering him about getting married, which was nothing new, except this time she'd suggested Penelope as a potential bride, which *was* new, and Colin just hadn't been in the mood to deal with his mother's matchmaking in his usual manner, which was to tease her back.

And then she just hadn't stopped. She'd talked about Penelope all day and night, it seemed, until Colin finally fled the country. Nothing drastic—just a short jaunt to Wales. But really, what had his mother been thinking?

When he'd returned, his mother had wanted to speak with him, of course—except this time it had been because his sister Daphne was with child again and she had wanted to make a family announcement. But how was he to have known that? So he had not been looking forward to the visit, since he was sure it would involve a great deal of completely unveiled hints about marriage. Then he had run into his brothers, and they'd started tormenting him about the very same subject, as only brothers can do, and the next thing he knew, he announced, in a very loud voice, that he was not going to marry Penelope Featherington!

Except somehow Penelope had been standing right there in the doorway, her hand to her mouth, her eyes wide with pain and embarrassment and probably a dozen other unpleasant emotions that he'd been too ashamed to delve into.

It had been one of the most awful moments of his life. One, in fact, that he made an effort not to remember. He didn't think Penelope had ever fancied him—at least not any more than other ladies fancied him—but he'd embarrassed her. To single her out for such an announcement . . .

It had been unforgivable.

He'd apologized, of course, and she'd accepted, but he'd never quite forgiven himself.

And now he'd gone and insulted her again. Not in as direct a manner, of course, but he should have thought a bit longer and harder before complaining about his life.

Hell, it had sounded stupid, even to him. What did he have to complain about?

Nothing.

And yet there was still this nagging emptiness. A longing, really, for something he couldn't define. He was jealous of his brothers, for God's sake, for having found their passions, their legacies.

The only mark Colin had left on the world was in the pages of *Lady Whistledown's Society Papers.*

What a joke.

But all things were relative, weren't they? And compared to Penelope, he had little to complain about.

Which probably meant that he should have kept his thoughts to himself. He didn't like to think of her as an on-the-shelf spinster, but he supposed that was exactly what she was. And it wasn't a position of much reverence in British society.

In fact, it was a situation about which many people would complain. Bitterly.

Penelope had never once presented herself as anything less than a stoic—perhaps not content with her lot, but at least accepting of it.

And who knows? Maybe Penelope had hopes and dreams of a life beyond the one she shared with her mother and sister in their small home on Mount Street. Maybe she had plans and goals of her own but kept them to herself under a veil of dignity and good humor.

Maybe there was more to her than there seemed.

Maybe, he thought with a sigh, she deserved an apology.

He wasn't precisely certain what he needed to apologize for; he wasn't certain there *was* a precise thing that needed it.

But the situation needed *some*thing.

Aw, hell. Now he was going to have to attend the Smythe-Smith musicale this evening. It was a painful, discordant, annual event; just when one was sure that all the Smythe-Smith daughters had grown up, some new cousin rose to take her place, each more tone deaf than the last.

But that was where Penelope was going to be that evening, and that meant that was where Colin would have to be as well.

Chapter 7

Colin Bridgerton had quite the bevy of young ladies at his side at the Smythe-Smith musicale Wednesday night, all fawning over his injured hand.

This Author does not know how the injury was sustained—indeed, Mr. Bridgerton has been rather annoyingly tight-lipped about it. Speaking of annoyances, the man in question seemed rather irritated by all of the attention. Indeed, This Author overheard him tell his brother Anthony that he wished he'd left the (unrepeatable word) bandage at home.

Lady Whistledown's Society Papers, 16 April 1824

Why why *why* did she do this to herself?

Year after year the invitation arrived by messenger, and year after year Penelope swore she would never, as God was her witness, ever attend another Smythe-Smith musicale.

And yet year after year she found herself seated in the Smythe-Smith music room, desperately trying not to cringe (at least not visibly) as the latest generation of Smythe-Smith girls butchered poor Mr. Mozart in musical effigy.

It was painful. Horribly, awfully, hideously painful. Truly, there was no other way to describe it.

Even more perplexing was that Penelope always seemed to end up in the front row, or close to it, which was beyond excruciating. And not just on the ears. Every few years, there would be one Smythe-Smith girl who seemed aware that she was taking part in what could only be termed a crime against auditory law. While the other girls attacked their violins and pianofortes with oblivious vigor, this odd one out played with a pained expression on her face—an expression Penelope knew well.

It was the face one put on when one wanted to be anywhere but where one was. You could try to hide it, but it always came out in the corners of the mouth, which were held tight and taut. And the eyes, of course, which floated either above or below everyone else's line of vision.

Heaven knew Penelope's face had been cursed with that same expression many a time.

Maybe that was why she never quite managed to stay home on a Smythe-Smith night. Someone had to smile encouragingly and pretend to enjoy the music.

Besides, it wasn't as if she were forced to come and listen more than once per year, anyway.

Still, one couldn't help but think that there must be a fortune to be made in discreet earplugs.

The quartet of girls were warming up—a jumble of discordant notes and scales that only promised to worsen once they began to play in earnest. Penelope had taken a seat in the center of the second row, much to her sister Felicity's dismay.

"There are two perfectly good seats in the back corner," Felicity hissed in her ear.

"It's too late now," Penelope returned, settling down on the lightly cushioned chair.

"God help me," Felicity groaned.

Penelope picked up her program and began leafing through it. "If we don't sit here, someone else will," she said.

"Precisely my desire!"

Penelope leaned in so that only her sister could hear her murmured words. "We can be counted on to smile and be polite. Imagine if someone like Cressida Twombley sat here and snickered all the way through."

Felicity looked around. "I don't think Cressida Twombley would be caught dead here."

Penelope chose to ignore the statement. "The last thing they need is someone seated right in front who likes to make unkind remarks. Those poor girls would be mortified."

"They're going to be mortified anyway," Felicity grumbled.

"No, they won't," Penelope said. "At least not that one, that one, or that one," she said, pointing to the two on violins and the one at the piano. But that one"—she motioned discreetly to the girl sitting with a cello between her knees—"is already miserable. The least we can do is not to make it worse by allowing someone catty and cruel to sit here."

"She's only going to be eviscerated later this week by Lady Whistledown," Felicity muttered.

Penelope opened her mouth to say more, but at that exact moment she realized that the person who had just occupied the seat on her other side was Eloise.

"Eloise," Penelope said with obvious delight. "I thought you were planning to stay home."

Eloise grimaced, her skin taking on a decidedly green pallor. "I can't explain it, but I can't seem to stay away. It's rather like a carriage accident. You just can't *not* look."

"Or listen," Felicity said, "as the case may be."

Penelope smiled. She couldn't help it.

"Did I hear you talking about Lady Whistledown when I arrived?" Eloise asked.

"I told Penelope," Felicity said, leaning rather inelegantly across her sister to speak to Eloise, "that they're going to be destroyed by Lady W later this week."

"I don't know," Eloise said thoughtfully. "She doesn't pick on the Smythe-Smith girls every year. I'm not sure why."

"I know why," cackled a voice from behind.

Eloise, Penelope, and Felicity all twisted in their seats, then lurched backward as Lady Danbury's cane came perilously close to their faces.

"Lady Danbury," Penelope gulped, unable to resist the urge to touch her nose—if only to reassure herself that it was still there.

"I have that Lady Whistledown figured out," Lady Danbury said.

"You do?" Felicity asked.

"She's soft at heart," the old lady continued. "You see that one"—she poked her cane in the direction of the cellist, nearly piercing Eloise's ear in the process—"right over there?"

"Yes," Eloise said, rubbing her ear, "although I don't think I'm going to be able to hear her."

"Probably a blessing," Lady Danbury said before turning back to the subject at hand. "You can thank me later."

"You were saying something about the cellist?" Penelope said swiftly, before Eloise said something entirely inappropriate.

"Of course I was. Look at her," Lady Danbury said. "She's miserable. And well she should be. She's clearly the only one who has a clue as to how dreadful they are. The other three don't have the musical sense of a gnat."

Penelope gave her younger sister a rather smug glance.

"You mark my words," Lady Danbury said. "Lady Whistledown won't have a thing to say about this musicale. She won't want to hurt that one's feelings. The rest of them—"

Felicity, Penelope, and Eloise all ducked as the cane came swinging by.

"Bah. She couldn't care less for the rest of them."

"It's an interesting theory," Penelope said.

Lady Danbury sat back contentedly in her chair. "Yes, it is. Isn't it?"

Penelope nodded. "I think you're right."

"Hmmph. I usually am."

Still twisted in her seat, Penelope turned first to Felicity, then to Eloise, and said, "It's the same reason why I keep coming to these infernal musicales year after year."

"To see Lady Danbury?" Eloise asked, blinking with confusion.

"No. Because of girls like her." Penelope pointed at the cellist. "Because I know exactly how she feels."

"Don't be silly, Penelope," Felicity said. "You've never played piano in public, and even if you did, you're quite accomplished."

Penelope turned to her sister. "It's not about the music, Felicity."

Then the oddest thing happened to Lady Danbury. Her face changed. Completely, utterly, astoundingly changed. Her eyes grew misty, wistful. And her lips, which were usually slightly pinched and sarcastic at the corners, softened. "I was that girl, too, Miss Featherington," she said, so quietly that both Eloise and Felicity were forced to lean forward, Eloise with an, "I beg your pardon," and Felicity with a considerably less polite, "What?"

But Lady Danbury only had eyes for Penelope. "It's why I attend, year after year," the older lady said. "Just like you."

And for a moment Penelope felt the oddest sense of connection to the older woman. Which was mad, because they had nothing in common aside from gender—not age, not status, nothing. And yet it was almost as if the countess had somehow chosen her—for what purpose Penelope could never guess. But she seemed determined to light a fire under Penelope's well-ordered and often boring life.

And Penelope couldn't help but think that it was somehow working.

Isn't it nice to discover that we're not exactly what we thought we were?

Lady Danbury's words from the other night still echoed in Penelope's head. Almost like a litany.

Almost like a dare.

"Do you know what I think, Miss Featherington?" Lady Danbury asked, her tone deceptively mild.

"I couldn't possibly begin to guess," Penelope said with great honesty—and respect—in her voice.

"I think *you* could be Lady Whistledown."

Felicity and Eloise gasped.

Penelope's lips parted with surprise. No one had ever even thought to accuse her of such before. It was unbelievable . . . unthinkable . . . and . . .

Rather flattering, actually.

Penelope felt her mouth sliding into a sly smile, and she leaned forward, as if getting ready to impart news of great import.

Lady Danbury leaned forward.

Felicity and Eloise leaned forward.

"Do you know what *I* think, Lady Danbury?" Penelope asked, in a compellingly soft voice.

"Well," Lady D said, a wicked gleam in her eye, "I would tell you that I am breathless with anticipation, but you've already told me once before that you think that *I* am Lady Whistledown."

"Are you?"

Lady Danbury smiled archly. "Maybe I am."

Felicity and Eloise gasped again, louder this time.

Penelope's stomach lurched.

"Are you admitting it?" Eloise whispered.

"Of course I'm not admitting it," Lady Danbury barked, straightening her spine and thumping her cane against the floor with enough force to momentarily stop the four amateur musicians in their warm-up. "Even if it were true—and I'm not saying whether or not it is—would I be fool enough to admit it?"

"Then why did you say—"

"Because, you ninnyhead, I'm trying to make a point."

She then proceeded to fall silent until Penelope was forced to ask, "Which is?"

Lady Danbury gave them all an extremely exasperated look. "That *anyone* could be Lady Whistledown," she exclaimed, thumping her cane on the floor with renewed vigor. "Anyone at all."

"Well, except *me,*" Felicity put in. "I'm quite certain it's not me."

Lady Danbury didn't even honor Felicity with a glance. "Let me tell you something," she said.

"As if we could stop you," Penelope said, so sweetly that it came out like a compliment. And truth be told, it *was* a compliment. She admired Lady Danbury a great deal. She admired anyone who knew how to speak her mind in public.

Lady Danbury chuckled. "There's more to you than meets the eye, Penelope Featherington."

"It's true," Felicity said with a grin. "She can be rather cruel, for example. Nobody would believe it, but when we were young—"

Penelope elbowed her in the ribs.

"See?" Felicity said.

"What I was going to say," Lady Danbury continued, "was that the *ton* is going about my challenge all wrong."

"How do you suggest we go about it, then?" Eloise asked.

Lady Danbury waved her hand dismissively in Eloise's face. "I have to explain what people are doing wrong first," she said. "They keep looking toward the obvious people. People like your mother," she said, turning to Penelope and Felicity.

"Mother?" they both echoed.

"Oh, please," Lady Danbury scoffed. "A bigger busybody this town has never seen. She's exactly the sort of person everyone suspects."

Penelope had no idea what to say to that. Her mother *was* a notorious gossip, but it was difficult to imagine her as Lady Whistledown.

"Which is why," Lady Danbury continued, a shrewd look in her eye, "it can't be her."

"Well, *that,*" Penelope said with a touch of sarcasm, "and the fact that Felicity and I could tell you for certain that it's not her."

"Pish. If your mother were Lady Whistledown, she'd have figured out a way to keep it from you."

"My mother?" Felicity said doubtfully. "I don't think so."

"What I am trying to *say,*" Lady Danbury ground out, "prior to all of these infernal *interruptions*—"

Penelope thought she heard Eloise snort.

"—was that if Lady Whistledown were someone *obvious,* she'd have been found out by now, don't you think?"

Silence, until it became clear some response was required, then all three of them nodded with appropriate thoughtfulness and vigor.

"She must be someone that nobody suspects," Lady Danbury said. "She has to be."

Penelope found herself nodding again. Lady Danbury did make sense, in a strange sort of way.

"Which is why," the older lady continued triumphantly, "I am not a likely candidate!"

Penelope blinked, not quite following the logic. "I beg your pardon?"

"Oh, *please.*" Lady Danbury gave Penelope quite the most disdainful glance. "Do you think you're the first person to suspect me?"

Penelope just shook her head. "I still think it's you."

That earned her a measure of respect. Lady Danbury nodded approvingly as she said, "You're cheekier than you look."

Felicity leaned forward and said in a rather conspiratorial voice, "It's true."

Penelope swatted her sister's hand. "Felicity!"

"I think the musicale is starting," Eloise said.

"Heaven help us all," Lady Danbury announced. "I don't know why I—Mr. Bridgerton!"

Penelope had turned to face the small stage area, but she whipped back around to see Colin making his way along the row to the empty seat beside Lady Danbury, apologizing good-naturedly as he bumped into people's knees.

His apologies, of course, were accompanied by one of his lethal smiles, and no fewer than three ladies positively melted in their seats as a result.

Penelope frowned. It was disgusting.

"Penelope," Felicity whispered. "Did you just growl?"

"Colin," Eloise said. "I didn't know you were coming."

He shrugged, his face alight with a lopsided grin. "Changed my mind at the last moment. I've always been a great lover of music, after all."

"Which would explain your presence here," Eloise said in an exceptionally dry voice.

Colin acknowledged her statement with nothing more than an arch of his brow before turning to Penelope and saying, "Good evening, Miss Featherington." He nodded at Felicity with another, "Miss Featherington."

It took Penelope a moment to find her voice. They had parted most awkwardly that afternoon, and now here he was with a friendly smile. "Good evening, Mr. Bridgerton," she finally managed.

"Does anyone know what is on the program tonight?" he asked, looking terribly interested.

Penelope had to admire that. Colin had a way of looking at you as if nothing in the world could be more interesting than your next sentence. It was a talent, that. Especially now, when they all knew that he couldn't possibly care one way or another what the Smythe-Smith girls chose to play that evening.

"I believe it's Mozart," Felicity said. "They almost always choose Mozart."

"Lovely," Colin replied, leaning back in his chair as if he'd just finished an excellent meal. "I'm a great fan of Mr. Mozart."

"In that case," Lady Danbury cackled, elbowing him in the ribs, "you might want to make your escape while the possibility still exists."

"Don't be silly," he said. "I'm sure the girls will do their best."

"Oh, there's no question of them doing their best," Eloise said ominously.

"Shhh," Penelope said. "I think they're ready to begin."

Not, she admitted to herself, that she was especially eager to listen to the Smythe-Smith version of *Eine Kleine Nachtmusik*. But she felt profoundly ill-at-ease with Colin. She wasn't sure what to say to him—except that whatever it was she *should* say definitely shouldn't be said in front of Eloise, Felicity, and most of all Lady Danbury.

A butler came around and snuffed out a few candles to signal that the girls were ready to begin. Penelope braced herself, swallowed in such a way as to clog her inner ear canals (it didn't work), and then the torture began.

And went on . . . and on . . . and on.

Penelope wasn't certain what was more agonizing—the music or the knowledge that Colin was sitting right behind her. The back of her neck prickled with awareness, and she found herself fidgeting like mad, her fingers tapping relentlessly on the dark blue velvet of her skirts.

When the Smythe-Smith quartet was finally done, three of

the girls were beaming at the polite applause, and the fourth—the cellist—looked as if she wanted to crawl under a rock.

Penelope sighed. At least she, in all of her unsuccessful seasons, hadn't ever been forced to parade her deficiencies before all the *ton* like these girls had. She'd always been allowed to melt into the shadows, to hover quietly at the perimeter of the room, watching the other girls take their turns on the dance floor. Oh, her mother dragged her here and there, trying to place her in the path of some eligible gentleman or another, but that was nothing—nothing!—like what the Smythe-Smith girls were forced to endure.

Although, in all honesty, three out of the four seemed blissfully unaware of their musical ineptitude. Penelope just smiled and clapped. She certainly wasn't going to burst their collective bubble.

And if Lady Danbury's theory was correct, Lady Whistledown wasn't going to write a word about the musicale.

The applause petered out rather quickly, and soon everyone was milling about, making polite conversation with their neighbors and eyeing the sparsely laid refreshment table at the back of the room.

"Lemonade," Penelope murmured to herself. Perfect. She was dreadfully hot—really, what had she been thinking, wearing velvet on such a warm night?—and a cool beverage would be just the thing to make her feel better. Not to mention that Colin was trapped in conversation with Lady Danbury, so it was the ideal time to make her escape.

But as soon as Penelope had her glass in hand, she heard Colin's achingly familiar voice behind her, murmuring her name.

She turned around, and before she had any idea what she was doing, she said, "I'm sorry."

"You are?"

"Yes," she assured him. "At least I think I am."

His eyes crinkled slightly at the corners. "The conversation grows more intriguing by the second."

"Colin—"

He held out his arm. "Take a turn with me around the room, will you?"

"I don't think—"

He moved his arm closer to her—just by an inch or so, but the message was clear. "Please," he said.

She nodded and set her lemonade down. "Very well."

They walked in silence for almost a minute, then Colin said, "I would like to apologize to you."

"I was the one who stormed out of the room," Penelope pointed out.

He tilted his head slightly, and she could see an indulgent smile playing across his lips. "I'd hardly call it 'storming,' " he said.

Penelope frowned. She probably shouldn't have left in such a huff, but now that she had, she was oddly proud of it. It wasn't every day that a woman such as herself got to make such a dramatic exit.

"Well, I shouldn't have been so rude," she muttered, by now not really meaning it.

He arched a brow, then obviously decided not to pursue the matter. "I would like to apologize," he said, "for being such a whiny little brat."

Penelope actually tripped over her feet.

He helped her regain her balance, then said, "I am aware that I have many, many things in my life for which I should be grateful. For which I *am* grateful," he corrected, his mouth not quite smiling but certainly sheepish. "It was unforgivably rude to complain to you."

"No," she said, "I have spent all evening thinking about what you said, and while I . . ." She swallowed, then licked her lips, which had gone quite dry. She'd spent all day trying to think of the right words, and she'd thought that she'd found them, but now that he was here, at her side, she couldn't think of a deuced thing.

"Do you need another glass of lemonade?" Colin asked politely.

She shook her head. "You have every right to your feelings," she blurted out. "They may not be what I would feel, were I in your shoes, but you have every right to them. But—"

She broke off, and Colin found himself rather desperate to know what she'd planned to say. "But what, Penelope?" he urged.

"It's nothing."

"It's not nothing to me." His hand was on her arm, and so he squeezed slightly, to let her know that he meant what he said.

For the longest time, he didn't think she was actually going to respond, and then, just when he thought his face would crack from the smile he held so carefully on his lips—they were in public, after all, and it wouldn't do to invite comment and speculation by appearing urgent and disturbed—she sighed.

It was a lovely sound, strangely comforting, soft, and wise. And it made him want to look at her more closely, to see into her mind, to hear the rhythms of her soul.

"Colin," Penelope said quietly, "if you feel frustrated by your current situation, you should do something to change it. It's really that simple."

"That's what I do," he said with a careless shrug of his outside shoulder. "My mother accuses me of picking up and leaving the country completely on whim, but the truth is—"

"You do it when you're feeling frustrated," she finished for him.

He nodded. She understood him. He wasn't sure how it had happened, or even that it made any sense, but Penelope Featherington understood him.

"I think you should publish your journals," she said.

"I couldn't."

"Why not?"

He stopped in his tracks, letting go of her arm. He didn't really have an answer, other than the odd pounding in his heart. "Who would want to read them?" he finally asked.

"I would," she said frankly. "Eloise, Felicity . . ." she added, ticking off names on her fingers. "Your mother, Lady Whistledown, I'm sure," she added with a mischievous smile. "She does write about you rather a lot."

Her good humor was infectious, and Colin couldn't quite suppress his smile. "Penelope, it doesn't count if the only people who buy the book are the people I know."

"Why not?" Her lips twitched. "You know a lot of people. Why, if you only count Bridgertons—"

He grabbed her hand. He didn't know why, but he grabbed her hand. "Penelope, stop."

She just laughed. "I think Eloise told me that you have piles and piles of cousins as well, and—"

"Enough," he warned. But he was grinning as he said it.

Penelope stared down at her hand in his, then said, "Lots of people will want to read about your travels. Maybe at first it will only be because you're a well-known figure in London, but it won't take long before everyone realizes what a good writer you are. And then they'll be clamoring for more."

"I don't want to be a success because of the Bridgerton name," he said.

She dropped his hand and planted hers on her hips. "Are you even *listening* to me? I just told you that—"

"What are you two talking about?"

Eloise. Looking very, very curious.

"Nothing," they both muttered at the same time.

Eloise snorted. "Don't insult me. It's not nothing. Penelope looked as if she might start breathing fire at any moment."

"Your brother is just being obtuse," Penelope said.

"Well, that is nothing new," Eloise said.

"Wait a moment!" Colin exclaimed.

"But what," Eloise probed, ignoring him entirely, "is he being obtuse about?"

"It's a private matter," Colin ground out.

"Which makes it all the more interesting," Eloise said. She looked to Penelope expectantly.

"I'm sorry," Penelope said. "I really can't say."

"I can't believe it!" Eloise cried out. "You're not going to tell me."

"No," Penelope replied, feeling rather oddly satisfied with herself, "I'm not."

"I can't believe it," Eloise said again, turning to her brother. "I can't believe it."

His lips quirked into the barest of smiles. "Believe it."

"You're keeping secrets from me."

He raised his brows. "Did you think I told you everything?"

"Of course not." She scowled. "But I thought Penelope did."

"But this isn't my secret to tell," Penelope said. "It's Colin's."

"I think the planet has shifted on its axis," Eloise grumbled. "Or perhaps England has crashed into France. All I know is this is not the same world I inhabited just this morning."

Penelope couldn't help it. She giggled.

"And you're laughing at me!" Eloise added.

"No, I'm not," Penelope said, laughing. "Really, I'm not."

"Do you know what you need?" Colin asked.

"Me?" Eloise queried.

He nodded. "A husband."

"You're as bad as Mother!"

"I could be a lot worse if I really put my mind to it."

"Of that I have no doubt," Eloise shot back.

"Stop, stop!" Penelope said, truly laughing in earnest now.

They both looked at her expectantly, as if to say, *Now what?*

"I'm so glad I came tonight," Penelope said, the words tumbling unbidden from her lips. "I can't remember a nicer evening. Truly, I can't."

Several hours later, as Colin was lying in bed, staring up at the ceiling in the bedroom of his new flat in Bloomsbury, it occurred to him that he felt the exact same way.

Chapter 8

Colin Bridgerton and Penelope Featherington were seen in conversation at the Smythe-Smith musicale, although no one seems to know what exactly they were discussing. This Author would venture to guess that their conversation centered upon This Author's identity, since that was what everyone else seemed to be talking about before, after, and (rather rudely, in This Author's esteemed opinion) during the performance.

In other news, Honoria Smythe-Smith's violin was damaged when Lady Danbury accidentally knocked it off a table while waving her cane.

Lady Danbury insisted upon replacing the instrument, but then declared that as it is not her habit to buy anything but the best, Honoria will have a Ruggieri violin, imported from Cremona, Italy.

It is This Author's understanding that, when one factors in manufacture and shipping time, along with a lengthy waiting list, it takes six months for a Ruggieri violin to reach our shores.

LADY WHISTLEDOWN'S SOCIETY PAPERS, 16 APRIL 1824

There are moments in a woman's life when her heart flips in her chest, when the world suddenly seems uncommonly pink and perfect, when a symphony can be heard in the tinkle of a doorbell.

Penelope Featherington had just such a moment two days after the Smythe-Smith musicale.

All it took was a knock on her bedroom door, followed by her butler's voice, informing her:

"Mr. Colin Bridgerton is here to see you."

Penelope tumbled right off the bed.

Briarly, who had butlered for the Featherington family long enough so that he did not even so much as bat an eyelash at Penelope's clumsiness, murmured, "Shall I tell him you are not in?"

"No!" Penelope nearly shrieked, stumbling to her feet. "I mean, no," she added in a more reasonable voice. "But I will require ten minutes to prepare myself." She glanced in the mirror and winced at her disheveled appearance. "Fifteen."

"As you wish, Miss Penelope."

"Oh, and make certain to prepare a tray of food. Mr. Bridgerton is sure to be hungry. He's always hungry."

The butler nodded again.

Penelope stood stock-still as Briarly disappeared out the door, then, completely unable to contain herself, danced from foot to foot, emitting a strange squealing sort of noise—one that she was convinced—or at least hoped—had never before crossed her lips.

Then again, she couldn't remember the last time a gentleman had called upon her, much less the one with whom she'd been desperately in love for almost half of her life.

"Settle down," she said, spreading her fingers and pressing her flattened palms out in much the same motion she might make if she were trying to placate a small, unruly crowd. "You must remain calm. Calm," she repeated, as if that would actually do the trick. "Calm."

But inside, her heart was dancing.

She took a few deep breaths, walked over to her dressing table, and picked up her hairbrush. It would only take a few minutes to repin her hair; surely Colin wasn't going to flee if she kept him waiting for a short while. He'd expect her to take a bit of time to ready herself, wouldn't he?

But still, she found herself fixing her hair in record time, and by the time she stepped through the sitting room door, a mere five minutes had passed since the butler's announcement.

"That was quick," Colin said with a quirky grin. He'd been standing by the window, peering out at Mount Street.

"Oh, was it?" Penelope said, hoping that the heat she felt on her skin wasn't translating into a blush. A woman was supposed to keep a gentleman waiting, although not too long. Still, it made no sense to hold to such silly behavior with Colin, of all people. He would never be interested in her in a romantic fashion, and besides, they were friends.

Friends. It seemed like such an odd concept, and yet that was exactly what they were. They'd always been friendly acquaintances, but since his return from Cyprus, they'd become friends in truth.

It was magical.

Even if he never loved her—and she rather thought he never would—this was better than what they'd had before.

"To what do I owe the pleasure?" she asked, taking a seat on her mother's slightly faded yellow damask sofa.

Colin sat across from her in a rather uncomfortable straight-backed chair. He leaned forward, resting his hands on his knees, and Penelope knew instantly that something was wrong. It simply wasn't the pose a gentleman adopted for a regular social call. He looked too distraught, too intense.

"It's rather serious," he said, his face grim.

Penelope nearly rose to her feet. "Has something happened? Is someone ill?"

"No, no, nothing like that." He paused, let out a long breath, then raked his hand through his already mussed-up hair. "It's about Eloise."

"What is it?"

"I don't know how to say this. I—Do you have anything to eat?"

Penelope was ready to wring his neck. "For heaven's sake, Colin!"

"Sorry," he muttered. "I haven't eaten all day."

"A first, I'm sure," Penelope said impatiently. "I already told Briarly to fix a tray. Now, will you just tell me what is wrong, or do you plan to wait until I expire of impatience?"

"I think she's Lady Whistledown," he blurted out.

Penelope's mouth fell open. She wasn't sure what she'd expected him to say, but it wasn't this.

"Penelope, did you hear me?"

"Eloise?" she asked, even though she knew exactly who he was talking about.

He nodded.

"She can't be."

He stood and began to pace, too full of nervous energy to sit still. "Why not?"

"Because . . . because . . ." Because *why*? "Because there is no way she could have done that for ten years without my knowing."

His expression went from disturbed to disdainful in an instant. "I hardly think you're privy to everything that Eloise does."

"Of course not," Penelope replied, giving him a rather irritated look, "but I can tell you with absolute certainty that there is no way Eloise could keep a secret of that magnitude from me for over ten years. She's simply not capable of it."

"Penelope, she's the nosiest person I know."

"Well, that much is true," Penelope agreed. "Except for my mother, I suppose. But that's hardly enough to convict her."

Colin stopped his pacing and planted his hands on his hips. "She is always writing things down."

"Why would you think that?"

He held up his hand, rubbing his thumb briskly against his fingertips. "Inkstains. Constantly."

"Lots of people use pen and ink." Penelope motioned broadly at Colin. "You write in journals. I am certain you've had your share of ink on your fingers."

"Yes, but I don't *disappear* when I write in my journals."

Penelope felt her pulse quicken. "What do you mean?" she asked, her voice growing breathless.

"I mean that she locks herself in her room for hours on end, and it's after those periods that her fingers are covered with ink."

Penelope didn't say anything for an agonizingly long moment. Colin's "evidence" was damning, indeed, especially when combined with Eloise's well-known and well-documented penchant for nosiness.

But she wasn't Lady Whistledown. She couldn't be. Penelope would bet her life on it.

Finally Penelope just crossed her arms and, in a tone of voice that probably would have been more at home on an exceedingly stubborn six-year-old, said, "It's not her. It's not."

Colin sat back down, looking defeated. "I wish I could share your certainty."

"Colin, you need to—"

"Where the hell is the food?" he grumbled.

She should have been shocked, but somehow his lack of manners amused her. "I'm sure Briarly will be here shortly."

He sprawled into a chair. "I'm hungry."

"Yes," Penelope said, lips twitching, "I surmised as much."

He sighed, weary and worried. "If she's Lady Whistledown, it'll be a disaster. A pure, unmitigated disaster."

"It wouldn't be that bad," Penelope said carefully. "Not

that I think she's Lady Whistledown, because I don't! But truly, if she were, would it be so very dreadful? I rather like Lady Whistledown myself."

"Yes, Penelope," Colin said rather sharply, "it would be so very dreadful. She'd be ruined."

"I don't think she'd be *ruined*. . . ."

"Of course she'd be ruined. Do you have any idea how many people that woman has insulted over the years?"

"I didn't realize you hated Lady Whistledown so much," Penelope said.

"I don't hate her," Colin said impatiently. "It doesn't matter if I hate her. Everyone else hates her."

"I don't think that's true. They all buy her paper."

"Of course they buy her paper! Everyone buys her bloody paper."

"Colin!"

"Sorry," he muttered, but it didn't really sound like he meant it.

Penelope nodded her acceptance of his apology.

"Whoever that Lady Whistledown is," Colin said, shaking his finger at her with such vehemence that she actually lurched backward, "when she is unmasked, she will not be able to show her face in London."

Penelope delicately cleared her throat. "I didn't realize you cared so much about the opinions of society."

"I don't," he retorted. "Well, not much, at least. Anyone who tells you they don't care at all is a liar and a hypocrite."

Penelope rather thought he was correct, but she was surprised he'd admitted it. It seemed men always liked to pretend that they were wholly self-contained, completely unaffected by the whims and opinions of society.

Colin leaned forward, his green eyes burning with intensity. "This isn't about me, Penelope, it's about Eloise. And if she is cast out of society, she will be crushed." He sat back, but his entire body radiated tension. "Not to mention what it would do to my mother."

Penelope let out a long breath. "I really think you're getting upset over nothing," she said.

"I hope you're right," he replied, closing his eyes. He wasn't sure when he'd started to suspect that his sister might be Lady Whistledown. Probably after Lady Danbury had issued her now famous challenge. Unlike most of London, Colin had never been terribly interested in Lady Whistledown's true identity. The column was entertaining, and he certainly read it along with everyone else, but to his mind, Lady Whistledown was simply . . . Lady Whistledown, and that was all she needed to be.

But Lady Danbury's dare had started him thinking, and like the rest of the Bridgertons, once he got hold of an idea, he was fundamentally incapable of letting it go. Somehow it had occurred to him that Eloise had the perfect temperament and skills to write such a column, and then, before he could convince himself that he was crazy, he'd seen the ink spots on her fingers. Since then he'd gone nearly mad, unable to think about anything but the possibility that Eloise had a secret life.

He didn't know which irritated him more—that Eloise might be Lady Whistledown, or that she had managed to hide it from him for over a decade.

How galling, to be hoodwinked by one's sister. He liked to think himself smarter than that.

But he needed to focus on the present. Because if his suspicions were correct, how on earth were they going to deal with the scandal when she was discovered?

And she *would* be discovered. With all of London lusting after the thousand-pound prize, Lady Whistledown didn't stand a chance.

"Colin! Colin!"

He opened his eyes, wondering how long Penelope had been calling his name.

"I really think you should stop worrying about Eloise," she said. "There are hundreds and hundreds of people in London. Lady Whistledown could be any one of them. Heavens, with your eye for detail"—she waggled her fingers to remind him of Eloise's ink-stained fingertips—"*you* could be Lady Whistledown."

He shot her a rather condescending look. "Except for the small detail of my having been out of the country half the time."

Penelope chose to ignore his sarcasm. "You're certainly a good enough writer to carry it off."

Colin had intended to say something droll and slightly gruff, dismissing her rather weak arguments, but the truth was he was so secretly delighted about her "good writer" compliment that all he could do was sit there with a loopy smile on his face.

"Are you all right?" Penelope asked.

"Perfectly fine," he replied, snapping to attention and trying to adopt a more sober mien. "Why would you ask?"

"Because you suddenly looked quite ill. Dizzy, actually."

"I'm fine," he repeated, probably a little louder than was necessary. "I'm just thinking about the scandal."

She let out a beleaguered sigh, which irritated him, because he didn't see that she had any reason to feel so impatient with him. "What scandal?" she asked.

"The scandal that is going to erupt when she is discovered," he ground out.

"She's not Lady Whistledown!" she insisted.

Colin suddenly sat up straight, his eyes alight with a new idea. "Do you know," he said in a rather intense sort of voice, "but I don't think it matters if she is Lady Whistledown or not."

Penelope stared at him blankly for a full three seconds

before looking about the room, muttering, "Where's the food? I must be light-headed. Haven't you spent the last ten minutes positively going *mad* over the possibility that she is?"

As if on cue, Briarly entered the room with a heavily laden tray. Penelope and Colin watched in silence as the butler laid out the meal. "Would you like me to fix your plates?" he inquired.

"No, that's quite all right," Penelope said quickly. "We can manage for ourselves."

Briarly nodded and, as soon as he'd laid the flatware and filled the two glasses with lemonade, left the room.

"Listen to me," Colin said, jumping to his feet and moving the door so that it almost rested against the doorframe (but remained technically open, should anyone quibble about proprieties).

"Don't you want something to eat?" Penelope inquired, holding aloft a plate that she'd filled with various small snacks.

He snatched a piece of cheese, ate it in two rather indelicate bites, then continued, "Even if Eloise isn't Lady Whistledown—and mind you, I still think she is—it doesn't matter. Because if *I* suspect that she's Lady Whistledown, then surely someone else will as well."

"Your point being?"

Colin realized that his arms were reaching forward, and he stopped himself before he reached out to shake her shoulders. "It doesn't matter! Don't you see? If someone points his finger at her, she'll be ruined."

"But not," Penelope said, appearing to require a great deal of effort to unclench her teeth, "if she's not Lady Whistledown!"

"How could she prove it?" Colin returned, jumping to his feet. "Once a rumor is started, the damage is done. It develops a life of its own."

"Colin, you ceased to make sense five minutes ago."

"No, hear me out." He whirled to face her, and he was seized by a feeling of such intensity that he couldn't have ripped his eyes from hers if the house were falling down around them. "Suppose I told everyone that I had seduced you."

Penelope grew very, very still.

"You would be ruined forever," he continued, crouching down near the edge of the sofa so that they were more on the same level. "It wouldn't matter that we had never even kissed. *That,* my dear Penelope, is the power of the word."

She looked oddly frozen. And at the same time flushed. "I . . . I don't know what to say," she stammered.

And then the most bizarre thing happened. He realized that he didn't know what to say, either. Because he'd forgotten about rumors and the power of the word and all of that rot, and the only thing he could think of was the part about the kissing, and—

And—

And—

Good God in heaven, he wanted to kiss Penelope Featherington.

Penelope Featherington!

He might as well have said he wanted to kiss his sister.

Except—he stole a glance at her; she looked uncommonly fetching, and he wondered how he hadn't noticed that earlier that afternoon—she wasn't his sister.

She definitely wasn't his sister.

"Colin?" His name was a mere whisper on her lips, her eyes were quite adorably blinking and befuddled, and how was it he'd never noticed what an intriguing shade of brown they were? Almost gold near the pupil. He'd never seen anything like it, and yet it wasn't as if he hadn't seen her a hundred times before.

He stood—suddenly, drunkenly. Best if they weren't quite on the same latitude. Harder to see her eyes from up here.

She stood, too.

Damn it.

"Colin?" she asked, her voice barely audible. "Could I ask you a favor?"

Call it male intuition, call it insanity, but a very insistent voice inside of him was screaming that whatever she wanted *had* to be a very bad idea.

He was, however, an idiot.

He had to be, because he felt his lips part and then he heard a voice that sounded an awful lot like his own say, "Of course."

Her lips puckered, and for a moment he thought she was trying to kiss him, but then he realized that she was just bringing them together to form a word.

"Would—"

Just a word. Nothing but a word beginning with *W*. *W* always looked like a kiss.

"Would you kiss me?"

Chapter 9

Every week there seems to be one invitation that is coveted above all others, and this week's prize must surely go to the Countess of Macclesfield, who is hosting a grand ball on Monday night. Lady Macclesfield is not a frequent hostess here in London, but she is very popular, as is her husband, and it is expected that a great many bachelors plan to attend, including Mr. Colin Bridgerton (assuming he does not collapse from exhaustion after four days with the ten Bridgerton grandchildren), Viscount Burwick, and Mr. Michael Anstruther-Wetherby.

This Author anticipates that a great many young and unmarried ladies will choose to attend as well, following the publication of this column.

LADY WHISTLEDOWN'S SOCIETY PAPERS, 16 APRIL 1824

His life as he knew it was over.

"What?" he asked, aware that he was blinking rapidly.

Her face turned a deeper shade of crimson than he'd thought humanly possible, and she turned away. "Never mind," she mumbled. "Forget I said anything."

Colin thought that a *very* good idea.

But then, just when he'd thought that his world might resume its normal course (or at least that he'd be able to pretend it had), she whirled back around, her eyes alight with a passionate fire that astonished him.

"No, I'm not going to forget it," she cried out. "I've spent my life forgetting things, not saying them, never telling anyone what I really want."

Colin tried to say something, but it was clear to him that his throat had begun to close. Any minute now he'd be dead. He was sure of it.

"It won't mean a thing," she said. "I promise you, it won't mean anything, and I'd never expect anything from you because of it, but I could die tomorrow, and—"

"What?"

Her eyes looked huge, and meltingly dark, and pleading, and . . .

He could feel his resolve melting away.

"I'm eight-and-twenty," she said, her voice soft and sad. "I'm an old maid, and I've never been kissed."

"Gah . . . gah . . . gah . . ." He knew he knew how to speak; he was fairly certain he'd been perfectly articulate just minutes earlier. But now he didn't seem able to form a word.

And Penelope kept talking, her cheeks delightfully pink, and her lips moving so quickly that he couldn't help but wonder what they'd feel like on his skin. On his neck, on his shoulder, on his . . . other places.

"I'm going to be an old maid at nine-and-twenty," she said, "and I'll be an old maid at thirty. I could die tomorrow, and—"

"You're not going to die tomorrow!" he somehow managed to get out.

"But I could! I could, and it would kill me, because—"

"You'd already be dead," he said, thinking his voice sounded rather strange and disembodied.

"I don't want to die without ever having been kissed," she finally finished.

Colin could think of a hundred reasons why kissing Penelope Featherington was a very bad idea, the number one being that he actually *wanted* to kiss her.

He opened his mouth, hoping that a sound would emerge and that it might actually be intelligible speech, but there was nothing, just the sound of breath on his lips.

And then Penelope did the one thing that could break his resolve in an instant. She looked up at him, deeply into his eyes, and uttered one, simple word.

"Please."

He was lost. There was something heartbreaking in the way she was gazing at him, as if she might die if he didn't kiss her. Not from heartbreak, not from embarrassment—it was almost as if she needed him for nourishment, to feed her soul, to fill her heart.

And Colin couldn't remember anyone else ever needing him with such fervor.

It humbled him.

It made him want her with an intensity that nearly buckled his knees. He looked at her, and somehow he didn't see the woman he'd seen so many times before. She was different. She glowed. She was a siren, a goddess, and he wondered how on earth no one had ever noticed this before.

"Colin?" she whispered.

He took a step forward—barely a half a foot, but it was close enough so that when he touched her chin and tipped her face up, her lips were mere inches from his.

Their breath mingled, and the air grew hot and heavy. Penelope was trembling—he could feel that under his fingers—but he wasn't so sure that he wasn't trembling, too.

He assumed he'd say something flip and droll, like the devil-may-care fellow he was reputed to be. *Anything for you,* perhaps, or maybe, *Every woman deserves at least one kiss.* But as he closed the bare distance between them, he realized that there were no words that could capture the intensity of the moment.

No words for the passion. No words for the need.

No words for the sheer epiphany of the moment.

And so, on an otherwise unremarkable Friday afternoon, in the heart of Mayfair, in a quiet drawing room on Mount Street, Colin Bridgerton kissed Penelope Featherington.

And it was glorious.

His lips touched hers softly at first, not because he was trying to be gentle, although if he'd had the presence of mind to think about such things, it probably would have occurred to him that this was her first kiss, and it ought to be reverent and beautiful and all the things a girl dreams about as she's lying in bed at night.

But in all truth, none of that was on Colin's mind. In fact, he was thinking of quite little. His kiss was soft and gentle because he was still so surprised that he was kissing her. He'd known her for years, had never even thought about touching his lips to hers. And now he couldn't have let her go if the fires of hell were licking his toes. He could barely believe what he was doing—or that he wanted to do it so damned much.

It wasn't the sort of a kiss one initiates because one is overcome with passion or emotion or anger or desire. It was a slower thing, a learning experience—for Colin just as much as for Penelope.

And he was learning that everything he thought he'd known about kissing was rubbish.

Everything else had been mere lips and tongue and softly murmured but meaningless words.

This was a kiss.

There was something in the friction, the way he could hear and feel her breath at the same time. Something in the way she held perfectly still, and yet he could feel her heart pounding through her skin.

There was something in the fact that he knew it was *her.*

Colin moved his lips slightly to the left, until he was nipping the corner of her mouth, softly tickling the very spot where her lips joined. His tongue dipped and traced, learning the contours of her mouth, tasting the sweet-salty essence of her.

This was more than a kiss.

His hands, which had been lightly splayed against her back, grew rigid, more tense as they pressed into the fabric of her dress. He could feel the heat of her under his fingertips, seeping up through the muslin, swirling in the delicate muscles of her back.

He drew her to him, pulling her closer, closer, until their bodies were pressed together. He could feel her, the entire length of her, and it set him on fire. He was growing hard, and he wanted her—dear God, how he wanted her.

His mouth grew more insistent, and his tongue darted forward, nudging her until her lips parted. He swallowed her soft moan of acquiescence, then pushed forward to taste her. She was sweet and a little tart from the lemonade, and she was clearly as intoxicating as fine brandy, because Colin was starting to doubt his ability to remain on his feet.

He moved his hands along the length of her—slowly, so as not to frighten her. She was soft, curvy, and lush, just as he'd always thought a woman should be. Her hips flared, and her bottom was perfect, and her breasts . . . good God, her breasts felt good pressing against his chest. His palms itched to cup them, but he forced his hands to remain where they were (rather enjoyably on her derrière, so it really wasn't that much of a sacrifice.) Beside the fact that he really shouldn't be groping a gently bred lady's breasts in the middle of her drawing room, he had a rather painful suspicion that if he touched her in that way, he would lose himself completely.

"Penelope, Penelope," he murmured, wondering why her name tasted so good on his lips. He was ravenous for her, heady and drugged by passion, and he wanted desperately for her to feel the same way. She felt perfect in his arms, but thus far, she had made no reaction. Oh, she had swayed in his arms and opened her mouth to welcome his sweet invasion, but other than that, she had done nothing.

And yet, from the pant of her breath and the beat of her heart, he knew that she was aroused.

He pulled back, just a few inches so that he could touch her chin and tilt her face up toward his. Her eyelids fluttered open, revealing eyes that were dazed with passion, perfectly matching her lips, which were lightly parted, completely soft, and thoroughly swollen from his kisses.

She was beautiful. Utterly, completely, soul-stirringly beautiful. He didn't know how he hadn't noticed it all these years.

Was the world populated with blind men, or merely stupid ones?

"You can kiss me, too," he whispered, leaning his forehead lightly against hers.

She did nothing but blink.

"A kiss," he murmured, lowering his lips to hers again, although just for a fleeting moment, "is for two people."

Her hand stirred at his back. "What do I do?" she whispered.

"Whatever you want to do."

Slowly, tentatively, she lifted one of her hands to his face. Her fingers trailed lightly over his cheek, skimming along the line of his jaw until they fell away.

"Thank you," she whispered.

Thank you?

He went still.

It was *exactly* the wrong thing to say. He didn't want to be thanked for his kiss.

It made him feel guilty.

And shallow.

As if it had been something done out of pity. And the worst part was he knew that if all this had come to pass only a few months earlier, it *would* have been out of pity.

What the hell did that say about him?

"Don't thank me," he said gruffly, shoving himself backward until they were no longer touching.

"But—"

"I said *don't,*" he repeated harshly, turning away as if he couldn't bear the sight of her, when the truth was that he couldn't quite bear himself.

And the damnedest thing was—he wasn't sure why. This desperate, gnawing feeling—was it guilt? Because he shouldn't have kissed her? Because he shouldn't have liked it?

"Colin," she said, "don't be angry with yourself."

"I'm not," he snapped.

"I asked you to kiss me. I practically forced you—"

Now, there was a surefire way to make a man feel manly. "You didn't force me," he bit off.

"No, but—"

"For the love of God, Penelope, *enough*!"

She drew back, her eyes wide. "I'm sorry," she whispered.

He looked down at her hands. They were shaking. He closed his eyes in agony. Why why *why* was he being such an ass?

"Penelope . . ." he began.

"No, it's all right," she said, her words rushed. "You don't have to say anything."

"No, I should."

"I really wish you wouldn't."

And now she looked so quietly dignified. Which made him feel even worse. She was standing there, her hands clasped demurely in front of her, her eyes downward—not quite on the floor, but not on his face.

She thought he'd kissed her out of pity.

And he was a knave because a small part of him wanted her to think that. Because if she thought it, then maybe he could convince himself that it was true, that it was just pity, that it couldn't possibly be more.

"I should go," he said, the words quiet, and yet still too loud in the silent room.

She didn't try to stop him.

He motioned to the door. "I should go," he said again, even as his feet refused to move.

She nodded.

"I didn't—" he started to say, and then, horrified by the words that had nearly come out of his mouth, he actually did head toward the door.

But Penelope called out—of *course* she called out—"You didn't what?"

And he didn't know what to say, because what he'd started to say was, *I didn't kiss you out of pity.* If he wanted her to know that, if he wanted to convince himself of that, then that could only mean that he craved her good opinion, which could only mean—

"I have to go," he blurted out, desperate now, as if leaving the room might be the only way to keep his thoughts from traveling down such a dangerous road. He crossed the remaining distance to the door, waiting for her to say something, to call out his name.

But she didn't.

And he left.

And he'd never hated himself more.

Colin was in an exceedingly bad mood before the footman showed up at his front door with a summons from his mother. Afterward, he was beyond repair.

Bloody hell. She was going to start in on him again about getting married. Her summonses were *always* about getting married. And he really wasn't in the mood for it right now.

But she was his mother. And he loved her. And that meant he couldn't very well ignore her. So with considerable grumbling and a fair bit of cursing while he was at it, he yanked on his boots and coat, and headed out the door.

He was living in Bloomsbury, not the most fashionable section of town for a member of the aristocracy, although Bedford Square, where he had taken out a lease on a small but elegant terrace house, was certainly an upscale and respectable address.

Colin rather liked living in Bloomsbury, where his neighbors were doctors and lawyers and scholars and people who actually *did* things other than attend party after party. He wasn't ready to trade in his heritage for a life in trade—it was rather good to be a Bridgerton, after all—but there was something stimulating about watching professional men going about their daily business, the lawyers heading east to the Inns of the Court, the doctors northwest to Portland Place.

It would have been easy enough to drive his curricle across town; it had only been brought back to the mews an hour ago upon his return from the Featheringtons'. But Colin was feeling a bit in need of some fresh air, not to mention perverse enough to take the slowest means possible to Number Five.

If his mother intended to deliver another lecture on the virtues of marriage, followed by a lengthy dissertation on the attributes of each and every eligible miss in London, she could bloody well wait for him.

Colin closed his eyes and groaned. His mood must be worse than even he had thought if he was cursing in relation to his mother, whom he (and all the Bridgertons, really) held in the highest esteem and affection.

It was Penelope's fault.

No, it was Eloise's fault, he thought, grinding his teeth. Better to blame a sibling.

No—he slumped back into his desk chair, groaning—it was his fault. If he was in a bad mood, if he was ready to yank someone's head off with his bare hands, it was his fault and his fault alone.

He shouldn't have kissed Penelope. It didn't matter that

he'd *wanted* to kiss her, even though he hadn't even *realized* that he wanted to until right before she'd mentioned it. He still shouldn't have kissed her.

Although, when he really thought about it, he wasn't quite sure *why* he shouldn't have kissed her.

He stood, then trudged to the window and let his forehead rest against the pane. Bedford Square was quiet, with only a few men walking along the pavement. Laborers, they looked to be, probably working on the new museum being built just to the east. (It was why Colin had taken a house on the west side of the square; the construction could get very noisy.)

His gaze traveled north, to the statue of Charles James Fox. Now, there was a man with a purpose. Led the Whigs for years. He hadn't always been very well liked, if some of the older members of the *ton* were to be believed, but Colin was coming to think that perhaps being well liked was overrated. Heaven knew that no one was better liked than he was, and look at him now, frustrated and malcontent, grumpy and ready to lash out at anyone who crossed his path.

He sighed, planting one hand on the window frame and pushing himself back to an upright position. He'd better get going, especially if he was planning to walk all the way to Mayfair. Although, in truth, it really wasn't that far. Probably not more than thirty minutes if he kept his pace brisk (and he always did), less if the pavements weren't littered with slow people. It was longer than most members of the *ton* cared to be outside in London unless they were shopping or fashionably strolling in the park, but Colin felt the need to clear his head. And if the air in London wasn't particularly fresh, well, it would still have to do.

His luck that day being what it was, however, by the time he reached the intersection of Oxford and Regent Streets, the first splats of raindrops began to dance against his face. By the time he was turning off Hanover Square onto St. George

Street, it was pouring in earnest. And he was just close enough to Bruton Street that it would have been really ridiculous to have tried to hail a hackney to take him the rest of the way.

So he walked on.

After the first minute or so of annoyance, however, the rain began to feel oddly good. It was warm enough out that it didn't chill him to the bone, and the fat, wet sting of it almost felt like a penance.

And he felt like maybe that was what he deserved.

The door to his mother's house opened before Colin's foot had even found the top step; Wickham must have been waiting for him.

"Might I suggest a towel?" the butler intoned, handing him a large white cloth.

Colin took it, wondering how on earth Wickham had had time to get a towel. He couldn't have known that Colin would be fool enough to walk in the rain.

Not for the first time it occurred to Colin that butlers must be possessed of strange, mystical powers. Perhaps it was a job requirement.

Colin used the towel to dry his hair, causing great consternation to Wickham, who was terribly proper and surely expected Colin to retire to a private room for at least a half an hour to mend his appearance.

"Where's my mother?" Colin asked.

Wickham's lips tightened, and he looked pointedly down at Colin's feet, which were now creating small puddles. "She is in her office," he replied, "but she is speaking with your sister."

"Which sister?" Colin asked, keeping a sunny smile on his face, just to annoy Wickham, who had surely been trying to annoy him by omitting his sister's name.

As if you could simply say "your sister" to a Bridgerton and expect him to know who you were talking about.

"Francesca."

"Ah, yes. She's returning to Scotland soon, isn't she?"

"Tomorrow."

Colin handed the towel back to Wickham, who regarded it as he might a large insect. "I won't bother her, then. Just let her know I'm here when she's done with Francesca."

Wickham nodded. "Would you care to change your clothes, Mr. Bridgerton? I believe we have some of your brother Gregory's garments upstairs in his bedchamber."

Colin found himself smiling. Gregory was finishing up his final term at Cambridge. He was eleven years younger than Colin, and it was difficult to believe they could actually share clothing, but he supposed it was time to accept that his little brother had finally grown up.

"That's an excellent idea," Colin said. He gave his sodden sleeve a rueful glance. "I'll leave these here to be cleaned and fetch them later."

Wickham nodded again, murmured, "As you wish," and disappeared down the hall to parts unknown.

Colin took the steps two at a time up to the family quarters. As he sloshed down the hall, he heard the sound of a door opening. Turning around, he saw that it was Eloise.

Not the person he wanted to see. She immediately brought back all the memories of his afternoon with Penelope. Their conversation. The kiss.

Especially the kiss.

And even worse, the guilt he'd felt afterward.

The guilt he still felt.

"Colin," Eloise said brightly, "I didn't realize you—what did you do, *walk*?"

He shrugged. "I like the rain."

She eyed him curiously, her head cocking to the side as it always did when she was puzzling through something. "You're in a rather odd mood today."

"I'm soaking wet, Eloise."

"No need to snap at me about it," she said with a sniff. "I didn't force you to walk across town in the rain."

"It wasn't raining when I left," he felt rather compelled to say. There was something about a sibling that brought out the eight-year-old in a body.

"I'm sure the sky was gray," she returned.

Clearly, she had a bit of the eight-year-old in her as well.

"May we continue this discussion when I'm dry?" he asked, his voice deliberately impatient.

"Of course," she said expansively, all accommodation. "I'll wait for you right here."

Colin took his time while he changed into Gregory's clothes, taking more care with his cravat than he had in years. Finally, when he was convinced that Eloise must be grinding her teeth, he reentered the hall.

"I heard you went to see Penelope today," she said without preamble.

Wrong thing to say.

"Where did you hear that?" he asked carefully. He knew that his sister and Penelope were close, but surely Penelope wouldn't have told Eloise about *that*.

"Felicity told Hyacinth."

"And Hyacinth told you."

"Of course."

"Something," Colin muttered, "has got to be done about all the gossip in this town."

"I hardly think this counts as gossip, Colin," Eloise said. "It's not as if you're *interested* in Penelope."

If she had been talking about any other woman, Colin would have expected her to give him a sidelong glance, followed by a coy, *Are you?*

But this was Penelope, and even though Eloise was her very best friend, and thus her finest champion, even she couldn't imagine that a man of Colin's reputation and popularity would be interested in a woman of Penelope's reputation and (lack of) popularity.

Colin's mood shifted from bad to foul.

"Anyway," Eloise continued, completely oblivious to the thunderstorm that was brewing in her normally sunny and jovial brother, "Felicity told Hyacinth that Briarly told her that you'd visited. I was just wondering what it was about."

"It's none of your business," Colin said briskly, hoping she'd leave it at that, but not really believing she would. He took a step toward the stairwell, though, always optimistic.

"It's about my birthday, isn't it?" Eloise guessed, dashing in front of him with such suddenness that his toe crashed into her slipper. She winced, but Colin didn't feel particularly sympathetic.

"No, it's not about your birthday," he snapped. "Your birthday isn't even until—"

He stopped. Ah, hell.

"Until next week," he grumbled.

She smiled slyly. Then, as if her brain had just realized it had taken a wrong turn, her lips parted with dismay as she mentally backed up and headed in another direction. "So," she continued, moving slightly so that she better blocked his path, "if you didn't go over there to discuss my birthday—and there's nothing you could say now that would convince me you did—why *did* you go see Penelope?"

"Is nothing private in this world?"

"Not in *this* family."

Colin decided that his best bet was to adopt his usual sunny persona, even though he didn't feel the least bit charitable toward her at the moment, and so he slapped on the smoothest and easiest of his smiles, quirked his head to the side, and asked, "Do I hear Mother calling my name?"

"I didn't hear a thing," Eloise said pertly, "and what is wrong with you? You look very odd."

"I'm fine."

"You're not fine. You look as if you've been to the dentist."

His voice descended into a mutter. "It's always nice to receive compliments from family."

"If you can't trust your family to be honest with you," she volleyed, "who *can* you trust?"

He leaned fluidly back against the wall, crossing his arms. "I prefer flattery to honesty."

"No, you don't."

Dear God, he wanted to smack her. He hadn't done that since he was twelve. And he'd been horsewhipped for it. The only time he could recall his father laying a hand on him.

"What I want," Colin returned, arching one brow, "is an immediate cessation of this conversation."

"What you want," Eloise needled, "is for me to stop asking you why you went to see Penelope Featherington, but I think we both know *that* isn't likely to occur."

And that was when he knew it. Knew it deep in his bones, from his head to his toes, his heart to his mind that his sister was Lady Whistledown. All of the pieces fit. There was no one more stubborn and bullheaded, no one who could—or would—take the time to get to the bottom of every last piece of gossip and innuendo.

When Eloise wanted something, she didn't stop until she had it firmly in her grasp. It wasn't about money, or greed, or material goods. With her it was about knowledge. She liked knowing things, and she'd needle and needle and needle until you'd told her exactly what she wanted to hear.

It was a miracle no one had found her out sooner.

Out of nowhere he said, "I need to talk to you." He grabbed her arm and hauled her into the nearest room, which happened to be her own.

"Colin!" she shrieked, trying unsuccessfully to shake him off. "What are you doing?"

He slammed the door shut, let go of her, and crossed his arms, his stance wide, his expression menacing.

"Colin?" she repeated, her voice dubious.

"I know what you've been up to."

"What I've been—"

And then, damn her, she started laughing.

"Eloise!" he boomed. "I'm talking to you!"

"Clearly," she just barely managed to get out.

He held his ground, glaring at her.

She was looking away, nearly doubled over with laughter. Finally, she said, "What are you—"

But then she looked at him again and even though she'd tried to keep her mouth shut, she exploded again.

If she'd been drinking something, Colin thought without a trace of humor, it would have come out her nose. "What the hell is the matter with you?" he snapped.

That finally got her attention. He didn't know whether it was his tone of voice or maybe his use of profanity, but she sobered in an instant.

"My word," she said softly, "you're serious."

"Do I look like I'm joking?"

"No," Eloise said. "Although you did at first. I'm sorry, Colin, but it's just not like you to be glowering and yelling and all that. You looked rather like Anthony."

"You—"

"Actually," she said, giving him a look that was not nearly as wary as it should have been, "you looked more like yourself, trying to imitate Anthony."

He was going to kill her. Right here in her room, in his mother's house, he was going to commit sororicide.

"Colin?" she asked hesitantly, as if she'd just finally noticed that he had long since passed angry on his way to furious.

"Sit. Down." He jerked his head toward a chair. "Now."

"Are you all right?"

"SIT DOWN!" he roared.

And she did. With alacrity.

"I can't remember the last time you raised your voice," she whispered.

"I can't remember the last time I had cause to."

"What's wrong?"

He decided he might as well just come out and say it.

"Colin?"

"I know you're Lady Whistledown."

"Whaaaaat?"

"There's no use denying it. I've seen—"

Eloise jumped to her feet. "Except that it's not true!"

Suddenly he no longer felt quite so angry. Instead he felt tired, old. "Eloise, I've seen the proof."

"What proof?" she asked, her voice rising with disbelief. "How can there be proof of something that isn't true?"

He grabbed one of her hands. "Look at your fingers."

She did so. "What about them?"

"Inkstains."

Her mouth fell open. "From *that* you've deduced that I'm Lady Whistledown?"

"Why are they there, then?"

"You've never used a quill?"

"Eloise . . ." There was a great deal of warning in his voice.

"I don't have to tell you why I have inkstains on my fingers."

He said her name again.

"I don't," she protested. "I owe you no—oh, very well, fine." She crossed her arms mutinously. "I write letters."

He shot her an extremely disbelieving look.

"I do!" she protested. "Every day. Sometimes two in a day when Francesca is away. I'm quite a loyal correspondent. You should know. I've written enough letters with *your* name on the envelope, although I doubt half of them ever reached you."

"Letters?" he asked, his voice full of doubt . . . and derision. "For God's sake, Eloise, do you really think that will wash? Who the devil are you writing so many letters to?"

She blushed. Really, truly, deeply blushed. "It's none of your business."

He would have been intrigued by her reaction if he still weren't so sure that she was lying about being Lady Whistledown. "For God's sake, Eloise," he bit off, "who is going to believe that you're writing letters every day? I certainly don't."

She glared at him, her dark gray eyes flashing with fury. "I don't care what you think," she said in a very low voice. "No, that's not true. I am *furious* that you don't believe me."

"You're not giving me much to believe in," he said wearily.

She stood, walked over to him, and poked him in the chest. Hard. "You are my brother," she spat out. "You should believe me unquestioningly. Love me unconditionally. That's what it means to be family."

"Eloise," he said, her name coming out really as nothing more than a sigh.

"Don't try to make excuses now."

"I wasn't."

"That's even worse!" She stalked to the door. "You should be on your hands and knees, begging me for forgiveness."

He hadn't thought he had it in him to smile, but somehow that did it for him. "Now, that doesn't really seem in keeping with my character, does it?"

She opened her mouth to say something, but the sound that came out was not precisely English. All she managed was something along the lines of, "Ooooooooh," in an extremely irate voice, and then she stormed out, slamming the door behind her.

Colin slouched into a chair, wondering when she'd realize that she'd left him in her own bedchamber.

The irony was, he reflected, possibly the only bright spot in an otherwise miserable day.

Chapter 10

Dear Reader—

It is with a surprisingly sentimental heart that I write these words. After eleven years of chronicling the lives and times of the beau monde, This Author is putting down her pen.

Although Lady Danbury's challenge was surely the catalyst for the retirement, in truth the blame cannot be placed (entirely) upon that countess's shoulders. The column has grown wearisome of late, less fulfilling to write, and perhaps less entertaining to read. This Author needs a change. It is not so difficult to fathom. Eleven years is a long time.

And in truth, the recent renewal of interest in This Author's identity has grown disturbing. Friends are turning against friends, brothers against sisters, all in the futile attempt to solve an unsolvable secret. Furthermore, the sleuthing of the ton *has grown downright dangerous. Last week it was Lady Blackwood's twisted ankle, this week's injury apparently belongs to Hyacinth Bridgerton, who was slightly hurt at Saturday's soirée held at the London home of Lord and Lady Riverdale. (It has not escaped This Author's notice that Lord Riverdale is Lady Danbury's nephew.) Miss Hyacinth must have suspected someone in attendance, because she sustained her injuries while falling into the library after the door was opened while she had her ear pressed up to the wood.*

Listening at doors, chasing down delivery boys—and

these are only the tidbits that have reached This Author's ears! What has London Society come to? This Author assures you, Dear Reader, that she never once listened at a door in all eleven years of her career. All gossip in this column was come by fairly, with no tools or tricks other than keen eyes and ears.

I bid you au revoir, London! It has been a pleasure to serve you.

LADY WHISTLEDOWN'S SOCIETY PAPERS, 19 APRIL 1824

It was, not surprisingly, the talk of the Macclesfield ball.

"Lady Whistledown has retired!"

"Can you believe it?"

"What will I read with my breakfast?"

"How will I know what happened if I miss a party?"

"We'll never find out who she is now!"

"Lady Whistledown has retired!"

One woman fainted, nearly cracking her head against the side of a table as she slumped gracelessly to the floor. Apparently, she had not read that morning's column and thus heard the news for the first time right there at the Macclesfield ball. She was revived by smelling salts but then quickly swooned again.

"She's a faker," Hyacinth Bridgerton muttered to Felicity Featherington as they stood in a small group with the Dowager Lady Bridgerton and Penelope. Penelope was officially attending as Felicity's chaperone due to their mother's decision to remain home with an upset stomach.

"The first faint was real," Hyacinth explained. "Anyone could tell that by the clumsy way she fell. But this . . ." Her hand flicked toward the lady on the floor with a gesture of disgust. "No one swoons like a ballet dancer. Not even ballet dancers."

Penelope had overheard the entire conversation, as Hyacinth was directly to her left, and so she murmured, "Have you ever swooned?" all the while keeping her eyes on the unfortunate woman, who was now coming awake with a delicate fluttering of eyelashes as the smelling salts were once again wafted under her nose.

"Absolutely not!" Hyacinth replied, with no small measure of pride. "Swoons are for the tenderhearted and foolish," she added. "And if Lady Whistledown were still writing, mark my words, she would say the exact same thing in her next column."

"Alas, there are no words to mark anymore," Felicity answered with a sad sigh.

Lady Bridgerton agreed. "It's the end of an era," she said. "I feel quite bereft without her."

"Well, it's not as if we've had to go more than eighteen hours without her yet," Penelope felt compelled to point out. "We did receive a column this morning. What is there yet to feel bereft about?"

"It's the principle of it," Lady Bridgerton said with a sigh. "If this were an ordinary Monday, I would know that I'd receive a new report on Wednesday. But now . . ."

Felicity actually sniffled. "Now we're lost," she said.

Penelope turned to her sister in disbelief. "Surely you're being a little melodramatic."

Felicity's overblown shrug was worthy of the stage. "Am I? *Am I?*"

Hyacinth gave her a sympathetic pat on the back. "I don't think you are, Felicity. I feel precisely the same way."

"It's only a gossip column," Penelope said, looking around for any sign of sanity in her companions. Surely they realized that the world was not drawing to a close just because Lady Whistledown had decided to end her career.

"You're right, of course," said Lady Bridgerton, jutting her chin out and pursing her lips in a manner that was probably supposed to convey an air of practicality. "Thank you for being the voice of reason for our little party." But then she seemed to deflate slightly, and she said, "But I must admit, I'd grown rather used to having her around. Whoever she is."

Penelope decided it was well past time to change the topic. "Where is Eloise this evening?"

"Ill, I'm afraid. A headache," Lady Bridgerton said, small frowns of worry creasing her otherwise unlined face. "She hasn't been feeling the thing for almost a week now. I'm starting to grow concerned about her."

Penelope had been staring rather aimlessly at a sconce on the wall, but her attention was immediately brought back to Lady Bridgerton. "It's nothing serious, I hope?"

"It's nothing serious," Hyacinth answered, before her mother could even open her mouth. "Eloise never gets sick."

"Which is precisely why I'm worried," Lady Bridgerton said. "She hasn't been eating very well."

"That's not true," Hyacinth said. "Just this afternoon Wickham brought up a very heavy tray. Scones and eggs and I think I smelled gammon steak." She gave an arch look to no one in particular. "And when Eloise left the tray out in the hall it was completely empty."

Hyacinth Bridgerton, Penelope decided, had a surprisingly good eye for detail.

"She's been in a bad mood," Hyacinth continued, "since she quarreled with Colin."

"She quarreled with Colin?" Penelope asked, an awful feeling beginning to roil her stomach. "When?"

"Sometime last week," Hyacinth said.

WHEN? Penelope wanted to scream, but surely it would look odd if she demanded an exact day. Was it Friday? Was it?

Penelope would always remember that her first, and most probably only, kiss had occurred on a Friday.

She was strange that way. She always remembered the days of the week.

She'd met Colin on a Monday.

She'd kissed him on a Friday.

Twelve years later.

She sighed. It seemed fairly pathetic.

"Is something wrong, Penelope?" Lady Bridgerton asked.

Penelope looked at Eloise's mother. Her blue eyes were kind and filled with concern, and there was something about the way she tilted her head to the side that made Penelope want to cry.

She was getting far too emotional these days. Crying over the tilt of a head.

"I'm fine," she said, hoping that her smile looked true. "I'm just worried about Eloise."

Hyacinth snorted.

Penelope decided she needed to make her escape. All these Bridgertons—well, two of them, anyway—were making her think of Colin.

Which wasn't anything she hadn't been doing nearly every minute of the day for the past three days. But at least that had been in private where she could sigh and moan and grumble to her heart's content.

But this must have been her lucky night, because just then she heard Lady Danbury barking her name.

(What was her world coming to, that she considered herself lucky to be trapped in a corner with London's most acerbic tongue?)

But Lady Danbury would provide the perfect excuse to leave her current little quartet of ladies, and besides, she was coming to realize that in a very odd way, she rather liked Lady Danbury.

"Miss Featherington! Miss Featherington!"

Felicity instantly took a step away. "I think she means you," she whispered urgently.

"Of course she means me," Penelope said, with just a touch of hauteur. "I consider Lady Danbury a cherished friend."

Felicity's eyes bugged out. "You do?"

"Miss Featherington!" Lady Danbury said, thumping her cane an inch away from Penelope's foot as soon as she reached her side. "Not you," she said to Felicity, even though Felicity had done nothing more than smile politely as the countess had approached. "You," she said to Penelope.

"Er, good evening, Lady Danbury," Penelope said, which she considered an admirable number of words under the circumstances.

"I have been looking for you all evening," Lady D announced.

Penelope found that a trifle surprising. "You have?"

"Yes. I want to talk with you about that Whistledown woman's last column."

"Me?"

"Yes, you," Lady Danbury grumbled. "I'd be happy to talk with someone else if you could find me a body with more than half a brain."

Penelope choked on the beginnings of laughter as she motioned to her companions. "Er, I assure you that Lady Bridgerton—"

Lady Bridgerton was furiously shaking her head.

"She's too busy trying to get that oversized brood of hers married off," Lady Danbury announced. "Can't be expected to know how to conduct a decent conversation these days."

Penelope stole a frantic glance over at Lady Bridgerton to see if she was upset by the insult—after all, she had been trying to marry off her oversized brood for a decade now. But Lady Bridgerton didn't look the least bit upset. In fact, she appeared to be stifling laughter.

Stifling laughter and inching away, taking Hyacinth and Felicity with her.

Sneaky little traitors.

Ah, well, Penelope shouldn't complain. She'd wanted an escape from the Bridgertons, hadn't she? But she didn't particularly enjoy having Felicity and Hyacinth think they'd somehow pulled one over on her.

"They're gone now," Lady Danbury cackled, "and a good thing it is, too. Those two gels haven't an intelligent thing to say between them."

"Oh, now, that isn't true," Penelope felt compelled to protest. "Felicity and Hyacinth are both very bright."

"I never said they weren't smart," Lady D replied acidly, "just that they haven't an intelligent thing to say. But don't worry," she added, giving Penelope a reassuring—reassuring? whoever heard of Lady Danbury being reassuring?—pat on the arm. "It's not their fault that their conversation is useless. They'll grow out of it. People are like fine wines. If they start off good, they only get better with age."

Penelope had actually been glancing slightly to the right of Lady Danbury's face, peering over her shoulder at a man who she thought might be Colin (but wasn't), but this brought her attention right back to where the countess wanted it.

"Fine wines?" Penelope echoed.

"Hmmph. And here I thought you weren't listening."

"No, of course I was listening." Penelope felt her lips tugging into something that wasn't quite a smile. "I was just . . . distracted."

"Looking for that Bridgerton boy, no doubt."

Penelope gasped.

"Oh, don't look so shocked. It's written all over your face. I'm just surprised he hasn't noticed."

"I imagine he has," Penelope mumbled.

"Has he? Hmmph." Lady Danbury frowned, the corners of her mouth spilling into long vertical wrinkles on either side of her chin. "Doesn't speak well of him that he hasn't done anything about it."

Penelope's heart ached. There was something oddly sweet

about the old lady's faith in her, as if men like Colin fell in love with women like Penelope on a regular basis. Penelope had had to beg him to kiss her, for heaven's sake. And look how that had ended up. He'd left the house in a fit of temper and they hadn't spoken for three days.

"Well, don't worry over him," Lady Danbury said quite suddenly. "We'll find you someone else."

Penelope delicately cleared her throat. "Lady Danbury, have you made me your *project*?"

The old lady beamed, her smile a bright and glowing streak in her wrinkled face. "Of course! I'm surprised it has taken you so long to figure it out."

"But why?" Penelope asked, truly unable to fathom it.

Lady Danbury sighed. The sound wasn't sad—more wistful, really. "Would you mind if we sat down for a spell? These old bones aren't what they used to be."

"Of course," Penelope said quickly, feeling terrible that she'd never once considered Lady Danbury's age as they stood there in the stuffy ballroom. But the countess was so vibrant; it was difficult to imagine her ailing or weak.

"Here we are," Penelope said, taking her arm and leading her to a nearby chair. Once Lady Danbury was settled, Penelope took a seat beside her. "Are you more comfortable now? Would you like something to drink?"

Lady Danbury nodded gratefully, and Penelope signaled to a footman to bring them two glasses of lemonade, since she didn't want to leave the countess while she was looking so pale.

"I'm not as young as I used to be," Lady Danbury told her once the footman had hied off to the refreshment table.

"None of us are," Penelope replied. It could have been a flip comment, but it was spoken with wry warmth, and somehow Penelope thought that Lady Danbury would appreciate the sentiment.

She was right. Lady D chuckled and sent Penelope an appreciative glance before saying, "The older I get, the more I realize that most of the people in this world are fools."

"You're only just figuring that out now?" Penelope asked, not to mock, but rather because, given Lady Danbury's usual demeanor, it was difficult to believe that she hadn't reached that conclusion years ago.

Lady Danbury laughed heartily. "No, sometimes I think I knew that before I was born. What I'm realizing now is that it's time I did something about it."

"What do you mean?"

"I couldn't care less what happens to the fools of this world, but the people like you"—lacking a handkerchief, she dabbed at her eyes with her fingers—"well, I'd like to see you settled."

For several seconds, Penelope did nothing but stare at her. "Lady Danbury," she said carefully, "I very much appreciate the gesture . . . and the sentiment . . . but you must know that I am not your responsibility."

"Of course I know that," Lady Danbury scoffed. "Have no fear, I feel no responsibility to you. If I did, this wouldn't be half so much fun."

Penelope knew she sounded the veriest ninny, but all she could think to say was, "I don't understand."

Lady Danbury held silent while the footmen returned with their lemonade, then began speaking once she had taken several small sips. "I like you, Miss Featherington. I don't like a lot of people. It's as simple as that. And I want to see you happy."

"But I am happy," Penelope said, more out of reflex than anything else.

Lady Danbury raised one arrogant brow—an expression that she did to perfection. "Are you?" she murmured.

Was she? What did it mean, that she had to stop and think about the answer? She wasn't *un*happy, of that she was sure. She had wonderful friends, a true confidante in her younger sister Felicity, and if her mother and older sisters weren't women she'd have chosen as close friends—well, she still loved them. And she knew they loved her.

Hers wasn't such a bad lot. Her life lacked drama and excitement, but she was content.

But contentment wasn't the same thing as happiness, and she felt a sharp, stabbing pain in her chest as she realized that she could not answer Lady Danbury's softly worded question in the affirmative.

"I've raised my family," Lady Danbury said. "Four children, and they all married well. I even found a bride for my nephew, who, truth be told"—she leaned in and whispered the last three words, giving Penelope the impression that she was about to divulge a state secret—"I like better than my own children."

Penelope couldn't help but smile. Lady Danbury looked so furtive, so naughty. It was rather cute, actually.

"It may surprise you," Lady Danbury continued, "but by nature I'm a bit of a meddler."

Penelope kept her expression scrupulously even.

"I find myself at loose ends," Lady Danbury said, holding up her hands as if in surrender. "I'd like to see one last person happily settled before I go."

"Don't talk that way, Lady Danbury," Penelope said, impulsively reaching out and taking her hand. She gave it a little squeeze. "You'll outlive us all, I am certain."

"Pfffft, don't be silly." Lady Danbury's tone was dismissive, but she made no move to remove her hand from Penelope's grasp. "I'm not being depressive," she added. "I'm just realistic. I've passed seventy years of age, and I'm not going to tell you how many years ago that was. I haven't much time left in this world, and that doesn't bother me one bit."

Penelope hoped she would be able to face her own mortality with the same equanimity.

"But I like you, Miss Featherington. You remind me of myself. You're not afraid to speak your mind."

Penelope could only look at her in shock. She'd spent the last ten years of her life never quite saying what she wanted to say. With people she knew well she was open and honest and even sometimes a little funny, but among strangers her tongue was quite firmly tied.

She remembered a masquerade ball she'd once attended. She'd attended many masquerade balls, actually, but this one had been unique because she'd actually found a costume—nothing special, just a gown styled as if from the 1600s—in which she'd truly felt her identity was hidden. It had probably been the mask. It was overly large and covered almost all of her face.

She had felt transformed. Suddenly free of the burden of being Penelope Featherington, she felt a new personality coming to the fore. It wasn't as if she had been putting on false airs; rather, it was more like her true self—the one she didn't know how to show to anyone she didn't know well—had finally broken loose.

She'd laughed; she'd joked. She'd even flirted.

And she'd sworn that the following night, when the costumes were all put away and she was once again attired in her finest evening dress, she'd remember how to be herself.

But it hadn't happened. She'd arrived at the ball and she'd nodded and smiled politely and once again found herself standing near the perimeter of the room, quite literally a wallflower.

It seemed that being Penelope Featherington meant something. Her lot had been cast years ago, during that first awful season when her mother had insisted she make her debut even though Penelope had begged otherwise. The pudgy girl. The awkward girl. The one always dressed in colors that didn't suit her. It didn't matter that she'd slimmed and grown graceful and finally thrown out all of her yellow dresses. In this world—the world of London society and the *ton*—she would always be the same old Penelope Featherington.

It was her own fault just as much as anyone else's. A vicious circle, really. Every time Penelope stepped into a ballroom, and she saw all those people who had known her for so long, she felt herself folding up inside, turning into the shy, awkward girl of years gone past, rather than the self-assured woman she liked to think she'd become—at least in her heart.

"Miss Featherington?" came Lady Danbury's soft—and surprisingly gentle—voice. "Is something wrong?"

Penelope knew she took longer than she should have to reply, but somehow she needed a few seconds to find her voice. "I don't think I know how to speak my mind," she finally said, turning to look at Lady Danbury only as she uttered the final words of the sentence. "I never know what to say to people."

"You know what to say to *me*."

"You're different."

Lady Danbury threw her head back and laughed. "If ever there was an understatement . . . Oh, Penelope—I hope you don't mind if I call you by your given name—if you can speak your mind to me, you can speak it to anyone. Half the grown men in this room run cowering into corners the minute they see me coming."

"They just don't know you," Penelope said, patting her on the hand.

"And they don't know *you,* either," Lady Danbury quite pointedly replied.

"No," Penelope said, a touch of resignation in her voice, "they don't."

"I'd say that it was their loss, but that would be rather cavalier of me," Lady Danbury said. "Not to them, but to you, because as often as I call them all fools—and I do call them fools often, as I'm sure you know—some of them are actually rather decent people, and it's a crime they haven't gotten to know you. I—Hmmm . . . I wonder what is going on."

Penelope found herself unaccountably sitting up a little

straighter. She asked Lady Danbury, "What do you mean?" but it was clear that something was afoot. People were whispering and motioning to the small dais where the musicians were seated.

"You there!" Lady Danbury said, poking her cane into the hip of a nearby gentleman. "What is going on?"

"Cressida Twombley wants to make some sort of announcement," he said, then quickly stepped away, presumably to avoid any further conversation with Lady Danbury or her cane.

"I hate Cressida Twombley," Penelope muttered.

Lady Danbury choked on a bit of laughter. "And you say you don't know how to speak your mind. Don't keep me in suspense. Why do you detest her so?"

Penelope shrugged. "She's always behaved quite badly toward me."

Lady Danbury nodded knowingly. "All bullies have a favorite victim."

"It's not so bad now," Penelope said. "But back when we were both out—when she was still Cressida Cowper—she never could resist the chance to torment me. And people . . . well . . ." She shook her head. "Never mind."

"No, please," Lady Danbury said, "do go on."

Penelope sighed. "It's nothing, really. Just that I've noticed that people don't often rush to another's defense. Cressida was popular—at least with a certain set—and she was rather frightening to the other girls our age. No one dared go against her. Well, almost no one."

That got Lady Danbury's attention, and she smiled. "Who was your champion, Penelope?"

"Champions, actually," Penelope replied. "The Bridgertons always came to my aid. Anthony Bridgerton once gave her the cut direct and took me in to dinner, and"—her voice rose with remembered excitement—"he really shouldn't have done so. It was a formal dinner party, and he was supposed to escort in some marchioness, I think." She sighed, treasuring the memory. "It was lovely."

"He's a good man, that Anthony Bridgerton."

Penelope nodded. "His wife told me that that was the day she fell in love with him. When she saw him being my hero."

Lady Danbury smiled. "And has the younger Mr. Bridgerton ever rushed to your aid?"

"Colin, you mean?" Penelope didn't even wait for Lady Danbury's nod before adding, "Of course, although never with quite so much drama. But I must say, as nice as it is that the Bridgertons are so supportive. . . ."

"What is it, Penelope?" Lady Danbury asked.

Penelope sighed again. It seemed a night for sighs. "I just wish they didn't have to defend me so often. You'd think I could defend myself. Or at least comport myself in such a manner so that no defending was necessary."

Lady Danbury patted her hand. "I think you get on a great deal better than you think you do. And as for that Cressida Twombley . . ." Lady Danbury's face soured with distaste. "Well, she got her just desserts, if you ask me. Although," she added sharply, "people don't ask me as often as they should."

Penelope could not quite suppress a little snort of laughter.

"Look where she is now," Lady Danbury said sharply. "Widowed and without even a fortune to show for it. She married that old lecher Horace Twombley and it turned out he'd managed to fool everyone into thinking he had money. Now she has nothing but fading good looks."

Honesty compelled Penelope to say, "She is still quite attractive."

"Hmmph. If you like flashy women." Lady Danbury's eyes narrowed. "There is something far too obvious about that woman."

Penelope looked toward the dais, where Cressida was waiting, standing there with a surprising amount of patience while the ballroom quieted down. "I wonder what she is going to say."

"Nothing that could possibly interest me," Lady Danbury retorted. "I—Oh." She stopped, and her lips curved into the oddest of expressions, a little bit frown, a little bit smile.

"What is it?" Penelope asked. She craned her neck to try to see Lady Danbury's line of vision, but a rather portly gentleman was blocking her way.

"Your Mr. Bridgerton is approaching," Lady Danbury said, the smile edging out the frown. "And he looks quite determined."

Penelope immediately twisted her head around.

"For the love of God, girl, don't look!" Lady Danbury exclaimed, jamming her elbow into Penelope's upper arm. "He'll know you're interested."

"I don't think there's much of a chance he hasn't figured that out already," Penelope mumbled.

And then there he was, standing splendidly in front of her, looking like some handsome god, deigning to grace earth with his presence. "Lady Danbury," he said, executing a smooth and graceful bow. "Miss Featherington."

"Mr. Bridgerton," Lady Danbury said, "how nice to see you."

Colin looked to Penelope.

"Mr. Bridgerton," she murmured, not knowing what else to say. What *did* one say to a man one had recently kissed? Penelope certainly had no experience in that area. Not to mention the added complication of his storming out of the house once they were through.

"I'd hoped . . ." Colin began, then stopped and frowned, looking up toward the dais. "What is everyone looking at?"

"Cressida Twombley has some sort of announcement," Lady Danbury said.

Colin's face slid into a vaguely annoyed frown. "Can't

imagine what she has to say that I'd want to listen to," he muttered.

Penelope couldn't help but grin. Cressida Twombley was considered a leader in society, or at least she had been when she'd been young and unmarried, but the Bridgertons had never liked her, and somehow that had always made Penelope feel a little better.

Just then a trumpet blared, and the room fell silent as everyone turned their attention to the Earl of Macclesfield, who was standing on the dais next to Cressida, looking vaguely uncomfortable with all the attention.

Penelope smiled. She'd been told the earl had once been a terrible rake, but now he was a rather scholarly sort, devoted to his family. He was still handsome enough to be a rake, though. Almost as handsome as Colin.

But only almost. Penelope knew she was biased, but it was difficult to imagine any creature quite as magnetically good-looking as Colin when he was smiling.

"Good evening," the earl said loudly.

"Good evening to you!" came a drunken shout from the back of the room.

The earl gave a good-natured nod, a tolerant half-smile playing along his lips. "My, er, esteemed guest here"—he motioned to Cressida—"would like to make an announcement. So if you would all give your attention to the lady beside me, I give you Lady Twombley."

A low ripple of whispers spread across the room as Cressida stepped forward, nodding regally at the crowd. She waited for the room to fall into stark silence, and then she said, "Ladies and gentleman, thank you so much for taking time out of your festivities to lend me your attention."

"Hurry up with it!" someone shouted, probably the same person who had yelled good evening to the earl.

Cressida ignored the interruption. "I have come to the

conclusion that I can no longer continue the deception that has ruled my life for the last eleven years."

The ballroom was rocked with the low buzz of whispers. Everyone knew what she was going to say, and yet no one could believe it was actually true.

"Therefore," Cressida continued, her voice growing in volume, "I have decided to reveal my secret.

"Ladies and gentleman, *I am Lady Whistledown.*"

Chapter 11

Colin couldn't remember the last time he'd entered a ballroom with quite so much apprehension.

The last few days had not been among his best. He'd been in a bad mood, which had only been worsened by the fact that he was rather renowned for his good humor, which meant that everyone had felt compelled to comment on his foul disposition.

There was nothing worse for a bad mood than being subjected to constant queries of, "Why are you in such a bad mood?"

His family had stopped asking after he'd actually snarled—snarled!—at Hyacinth when she'd asked him to accompany her to the theater the following week.

Colin hadn't even been aware that he knew how to snarl.

He was going to have to apologize to Hyacinth, which was going to be a chore, since Hyacinth never accepted apologies gracefully—at least not those that came from fellow Bridgertons.

But Hyacinth was the least of his problems. Colin groaned. His sister wasn't the only person who deserved his apology.

And that was why his heart was beating with this strange, nervous, and completely unprecedented rapidity as he entered the Macclesfield ballroom. Penelope would be here. He knew she'd be here because she always attended the major balls, even if she was now most often doing so as her sister's chaperone.

There was something quite humbling in feeling nervous about seeing Penelope. Penelope was . . . Penelope. It was almost as if she'd always been there, smiling politely at the perimeter of a ballroom. And he'd taken her for granted, in a way. Some things didn't change, and Penelope was one of them.

Except she *had* changed.

Colin didn't know when it had happened, or even if anyone other than himself had noticed it, but Penelope Featherington was not the same woman he used to know.

Or maybe she was, and *he* had changed.

Which made him feel even worse, because if that was the case, then Penelope had been interesting and lovely and kissable years ago, and he hadn't the maturity to notice.

No, better to think that Penelope had changed. Colin had never been a great fan of self-flagellation.

Whatever the case, he needed to make his apology, and he needed to do it soon. He had to apologize for the kiss, because she was a lady and he was (most of the time, at least) a gentleman. And he had to apologize for behaving like a raving idiot afterward, because it was simply the right thing to do.

God only knew what Penelope thought he thought of her now.

It wasn't difficult to find her once he entered the ballroom. He didn't bother to look among the dancing couples (which angered him—why didn't the other men think to ask her to dance?). Rather, he focused his attention along the walls, and sure enough, there she was, seated on a long bench next to—oh, *God*—Lady Danbury.

Well, there was nothing else to do but walk right up. The way Penelope and the old busybody were clutching each other's hands, he couldn't expect Lady Danbury to disappear anytime soon.

When he reached the pair of ladies, he turned first to Lady Danbury and swept into an elegant bow. "Lady Danbury," he said, before turning his attention to Penelope. "Miss Featherington."

"Mr. Bridgerton," Lady Danbury said, with a surprising lack of sharpness in her voice, "how nice to see you."

He nodded, then looked to Penelope, wondering what she was thinking, and whether he'd be able to see it in her eyes.

But whatever she was thinking—or feeling—it was hidden under a rather thick layer of nervousness. Or maybe the nervousness was all she was feeling. He couldn't really blame her. The way he'd stormed out of her drawing room without an explanation . . . she had to feel confused. And it was his experience that confusion invariably led to apprehension.

"Mr. Bridgerton," she finally murmured, her entire bearing scrupulously polite.

He cleared his throat. How to extract her from Lady Danbury's clutches? He'd really rather not humble himself in front of the nosy old countess.

"I'd hoped . . ." he began, intending to say that he'd hoped to have a private word with Penelope. Lady Danbury would be ferociously curious, but there was really no other course of action, and it would probably do her good to be left in the dark for once.

But just as his lips were forming his query, he realized that something strange was afoot in the Macclesfield ballroom. People were whispering and pointing toward the small orchestra, whose members had recently laid their instruments down. Furthermore, neither Penelope nor Lady Danbury were paying him the least attention.

"What is everyone looking at?" Colin asked.

Lady Danbury didn't even bother looking back at him as she replied, "Cressida Twombley has some sort of announcement."

How annoying. He'd never liked Cressida. She'd been

mean and petty when she was Cressida Cowper, and she was meaner and pettier as Cressida Twombley. But she was beautiful, and she was intelligent, in a rather cruel sort of way, and so she was still considered a leader in certain society circles.

"Can't imagine what she has to say that I'd want to listen to," Colin muttered.

He spied Penelope trying to stifle a smile and flashed her an I-caught-you sort of look. But it was the sort of I-caught-you look that also said And-I-agree-completely.

"Good evening!" came the loud voice of the Earl of Macclesfield.

"Good evening to you!" replied some drunken fool in the back. Colin twisted to see who it was, but the crowd had grown too thick.

The earl spoke some more, then Cressida opened her mouth, at which point Colin ceased paying attention. Whatever Cressida had to say, it wasn't going to help him solve his main problem: figuring out exactly how he was going to apologize to Penelope. He'd tried rehearsing the words in his mind, but they never sounded quite right, and so he was hoping his famously glib tongue would lead him in the right direction when the time came. Surely she'd understand—

"Whistledown!"

Colin only caught the last word of Cressida's monologue, but there was no way he could have missed the massive collective indrawn breath that swept the ballroom.

Followed by the flurry of harsh, urgent whispers one generally only hears after someone is caught in a very embarrassing, very public compromising position.

"What?" he blurted out, turning to Penelope, who'd gone white as a sheet. "What did she say?"

But Penelope was speechless.

He looked to Lady Danbury, but the old lady had her hand over her mouth and looked as if she might possibly swoon.

Which was somewhat alarming, as Colin would have bet

large sums of money that Lady Danbury had never once swooned in all of her seventy-odd years.

"What?" he demanded again, hoping one of them would break free of her stupor.

"It can't be true," Lady Danbury finally whispered, her mouth slack even as she spoke the words. "I don't believe it."

"What?"

She pointed toward Cressida, her extended index finger quivering in the flickering candlelight. "That lady is not Lady Whistledown."

Colin's head snapped back and forth. To Cressida. To Lady Danbury. To Cressida. To Penelope. "*She's* Lady Whistledown?" he finally blurted out.

"So she says," Lady Danbury replied, doubt written all over her face.

Colin tended to agree with her. Cressida Twombley was the last person he'd have pegged as Lady Whistledown. She was smart; there was no denying that. But she wasn't clever, and she wasn't terribly witty unless she was poking fun at others. Lady Whistledown had a rather cutting sense of humor, but with the exception of her infamous comments on fashion, she never seemed to pick on the less popular members of society.

When all was said and done, Colin had to say that Lady Whistledown had rather good taste in people.

"I can't believe this," Lady Danbury said with a loud snort of disgust. "If I'd dreamed *this* would happen, I would never have made that beastly challenge."

"This is horrible," Penelope whispered.

Her voice was quavering, and it made Colin uneasy. "Are you all right?" he asked.

She shook her head. "No, I don't think I am. I feel rather ill, actually."

"Do you want to leave?"

Penelope shook her head again. "But I'll sit right here, if you don't mind."

"Of course," he said, keeping a concerned eye on her. She was still terribly pale.

"Oh, for the love of . . ." Lady Danbury blasphemed, which took Colin by surprise, but then she actually swore, which he thought might very well have tilted the planet on its axis.

"Lady Danbury?" he asked, gaping.

"She's coming this way," she muttered, jerking her head to the right. "I should have known I'd not escape."

Colin looked to his left. Cressida was trying to make her way through the crowd, presumably to confront Lady Danbury and collect her prize. She was, naturally, being accosted at every turn by fellow partygoers. She seemed to be reveling in the attention—no big surprise there; Cressida had always reveled in attention—but she also seemed rather determined to reach Lady Danbury's side.

"There's no way to avoid her, I'm afraid," Colin said to Lady Danbury.

"I know," she grumbled. "I've been trying to avoid her for years, and I've never succeeded. I thought I was so clever." She looked to Colin, shaking her head with disgust. "I thought it would be such fun to rout out Lady Whistledown."

"Er, well, it was fun," Colin said, not really meaning it.

Lady Danbury jabbed him in the leg with her cane. "It's not the least bit fun, you foolish boy. Now look what I have to do!" She waved the cane toward Cressida, who was drawing ever closer. "I never dreamed I'd have to deal with the likes of *her*."

"Lady Danbury," Cressida said, swishing to a stop in front of her. "How nice to see you."

Lady Danbury had never been known for her pleasantries, but even she outdid herself by skipping any pretense of a greeting before snapping, "I suppose you're here to try to collect your money."

Cressida cocked her head to the side in a very pretty, very practiced manner. "You did say you would give a thousand pounds to whomever unmasked Lady Whistledown." She shrugged, lifting her hands in the air and then twisting them gracefully until her palms were up in a gesture of false humility. "You never stipulated that I couldn't unmask myself."

Lady Danbury rose to her feet, narrowed her eyes, and said, "I don't believe it's you."

Colin liked to think that he was rather suave and unflappable, but even he gasped at that.

Cressida's blue eyes blazed with fury, but she quickly regained control of her emotions and said, "I would be shocked if you did not behave with a degree of skepticism, Lady Danbury. After all, it is not your way to be trusting and gentle."

Lady Danbury smiled. Well, perhaps not a smile, but her lips did move. "I shall take that as a compliment," she said, "and allow you to tell me that you meant it as such."

Colin watched the stalemate with interest—and with a growing sense of alarm—until Lady Danbury turned quite suddenly to Penelope, who had risen to her feet mere seconds after she had.

"What do you think, Miss Featherington?" Lady Danbury asked.

Penelope visibly started, her entire body jerking slightly as she stammered, "What . . . I . . . I beg your pardon?"

"What do you think?" Lady Danbury persisted. "Is Lady Twombley Lady Whistledown?"

"I—I'm sure I don't know."

"Oh, come, now, Miss Featherington." Lady Danbury planted her hands on her hips and looked at Penelope with an expression that bordered on exasperation. "Surely you have an opinion on the matter."

Colin felt himself stepping forward. Lady Danbury had no right to speak to Penelope in such a manner. And furthermore, he didn't like the expression on Penelope's face. She looked trapped, like a fox in a hunt, her eyes darting to him with a panic he'd never seen there before.

He'd seen Penelope uncomfortable, and he'd seen her pained, but he'd never seen her truly panicked. And then it occurred to him—she hated being the center of attention. She might poke fun at her status as a wallflower and a spinster, and she'd probably have liked a little more attention from society, but this kind of attention . . . with everyone staring at her and awaiting the merest word from her lips . . .

She was miserable.

"Miss Featherington," Colin said smoothly, moving to her side, "you look unwell. Would you like to leave?"

"Yes," she said, but then something strange happened.

She changed. He didn't know how else to describe it. She simply changed. Right there, in the Macclesfield ballroom, by his side, Penelope Featherington became someone else.

Her spine stiffened, and he could swear the heat from her body increased, and she said, "No. No, I have something to say."

Lady Danbury smiled.

Penelope looked straight at the old countess and said, "I don't think she's Lady Whistledown. I think she's lying."

Colin instinctively pulled Penelope a little closer to his side. Cressida looked as if she might go for her throat.

"I've always liked Lady Whistledown," Penelope said, her chin rising until her bearing was almost regal. She looked to Cressida, and their eyes caught as she added, "And it would break my heart if she turned out to be someone like Lady Twombley."

Colin took her hand and squeezed it. He couldn't help himself.

"Well said, Miss Featherington!" Lady Danbury exclaimed, clapping her hands together in delight. "That is exactly what I was thinking, but I couldn't find the words." She turned to Colin with a smile. "She's very clever, you know."

"I know," he replied, a strange, new pride brimming within him.

"Most people don't notice it," Lady Danbury said, twisting so that her words were directed to—and probably only heard by—Colin.

"I know," he murmured, "but I do." He had to smile at Lady Danbury's behavior, which he was certain was chosen in part to annoy the devil out of Cressida, who did *not* like to be ignored.

"I will not be insulted by that . . . by that *nothing*!" Cressida fumed. She turned to Penelope with a seething glare and hissed, "I demand an apology."

Penelope just nodded slowly and said, "That is your prerogative."

And then she said nothing more.

Colin had to physically wipe the smile from his face.

Cressida clearly wanted to say more (and perhaps commit an act of violence while she was at it), but she held back, presumably because it was obvious that Penelope was among friends. She had always been renowned for her poise, however, and thus Colin was not surprised when she composed herself, turned to Lady Danbury, and said, "What do you plan to do about the thousand pounds?"

Lady Danbury looked at her for the longest second Colin had ever endured, then she turned to *him*—dear God, the last thing he wanted to do was get involved in this disaster—and asked, "And what do you think, Mr. Bridgerton? Is our Lady Twombley telling the truth?"

Colin gave her a practiced smile. "You must be mad if you think I'm going to offer an opinion."

"You're a surprisingly wise man, Mr. Bridgerton," Lady Danbury said approvingly.

He nodded modestly, then ruined the effect by saying, "I pride myself on it." But what the hell—it wasn't every day a man was called wise by Lady Danbury.

Most of her adjectives, after all, were of the decidedly negative variety.

Cressida didn't even bother to bat her eyelashes at him; as Colin had already reflected, she wasn't stupid, just mean, and after a dozen years out in society, she had to know that he didn't much like her and certainly wasn't about to fall prey to her charms. Instead, she looked squarely at Lady Danbury and kept her voice evenly modulated as she asked, "What shall we do now, my lady?"

Lady Danbury's lips pursed together until she almost appeared mouthless, then she said, "I need proof."

Cressida blinked. "I beg your pardon?"

"Proof!" Lady Danbury's cane slammed against the floor with remarkable force. "Which letter of the word did you not understand? I'm not handing over a king's ransom without proof."

"One thousand pounds is hardly a king's ransom," Cressida said, her expression growing petulant.

Lady Danbury's eyes narrowed. "Then why are you so keen to get it?"

Cressida was silent for a moment, but there was a tightness in everything about her—her stance, her posture, the line of her jaw. Everyone knew that her husband had left her in bad financial straits, but this was the first time anyone had hinted as such to her face.

"Get me proof," Lady Danbury said, "and I'll give you the money."

"Are you saying," Cressida said (and even as he despised her, Colin was forced to admire her ability to keep her voice even), "that my word is not good enough?"

"That's precisely what I'm saying," Lady Danbury barked. "Good God, girl, you don't get to be my age without being allowed to insult anyone you please."

Colin thought he heard Penelope choking, but when he stole a glance at her, there she was at his side, avidly watching the exchange. Her brown eyes were huge and luminous in her face, and she'd regained most of the color she'd lost when Cressida had made her unexpected announcement. In fact, now Penelope looked positively intrigued by the goings-on.

"Fine," Cressida said, her voice low and deadly. "I will bring you proof in a fortnight's time."

"What sort of proof?" Colin asked, then mentally kicked himself. The last thing he wanted to do was embroil himself in this mess, but his curiosity had gotten the better of him.

Cressida turned to him, her face remarkably placid considering the insult she'd just been dealt by Lady Danbury—before countless witnesses. "You shall know it when I deliver it," she told him archly. And then she held out her arm, waiting for one of her minions to take it and lead her away.

Which was really quite amazing, because a young man (a besotted fool, from all appearances) materialized at her side as if she'd conjured him by the mere tilt of her arm. A moment later they were gone.

"Well," Lady Danbury said, after everyone had stood in reflective—or maybe stunned—silence for nearly a minute. "That was unpleasant."

"I've never liked her," Colin said, to no one in particular. A small crowd had gathered around them, so his words were heard by more than Penelope and Lady Danbury, but he didn't much care.

"Colin!"

He turned to see Hyacinth skidding through the crowd, dragging along Felicity Featherington as she barreled to his side.

"What did she say?" Hyacinth asked breathlessly. "We tried to get here sooner, but it's been such a crush."

"She said exactly what you would have expected her to say," he replied.

Hyacinth pulled a face. "Men are never good for gossip. I want exact words."

"It's very interesting," Penelope said suddenly.

Something about the thoughtful tone of her voice demanded attention, and in seconds the entire crowd had quieted.

"Speak up," Lady Danbury instructed. "We're all listening."

Colin expected such a demand to make Penelope uncomfortable, but whatever silent infusion of confidence she'd experienced a few minutes earlier was still with her, because she stood straight and proud as she said, "Why would someone reveal herself as Lady Whistledown?"

"For the money, of course," Hyacinth said.

Penelope shook her head. "Yes, but you'd think that Lady Whistledown would be quite wealthy by now. We've all been paying for her paper for years."

"By God, she's right!" Lady Danbury exclaimed.

"Perhaps Cressida merely sought attention," Colin suggested. It wasn't such an unbelievable hypothesis; Cressida had spent the bulk of her adult life trying to place herself at the center of attention.

"I'd thought of that," Penelope allowed, "but does she really want *this* sort of attention? Lady Whistledown has insulted quite a few people over the years."

"No one who means anything to me," Colin joked. Then, when it became obvious that his companions required an explanation, he added, "Haven't you all noticed that Lady Whistledown only insults the people who need insulting?"

Penelope cleared her throat delicately. "I have been referred to as an overripe citrus fruit."

He waved off her concern. "Except for the bits about fashion, of course."

Penelope must have decided not to pursue the matter any further, because all she did was give Colin a long, assessing stare before turning back to Lady Danbury and saying, "Lady Whistledown has no motive to reveal herself. Cressida obviously does."

Lady Danbury beamed, then all at once her face scrunched into a frown. "I suppose I'll have to give her the fortnight to come up with her 'proof.' Fair play and all that."

"I, for one, will be very interested to see what she comes up with," Hyacinth put in. She turned to Penelope and added, "I say, you're very clever, did you know that?"

Penelope blushed modestly, then she turned to her sister and said, "We must be going, Felicity."

"So soon?" Felicity asked, and to his horror, Colin realized that he'd mouthed the very same words.

"Mother wanted us home early," Penelope said.

Felicity looked truly perplexed. "She did?"

"She did," Penelope said emphatically. "And besides that, I am not feeling well."

Felicity nodded glumly. "I shall instruct a footman to see that our carriage is brought around."

"No, you stay," Penelope said, placing a hand on her sister's arm. "I will see to it."

"I will see to it," Colin announced. Really, what was the use of being a gentleman when ladies insisted upon doing things for themselves?

And then, before he even realized what he was doing, he'd facilitated Penelope's departure, and she left the scene without his ever having apologized to her.

He supposed he should have deemed the evening a failure for that reason alone, but in all truth, he couldn't quite bring himself to do so.

After all, he'd spent the better part of five minutes holding her hand.

Chapter 12

It wasn't until Colin woke up the following morning that he realized he still hadn't apologized to Penelope. Strictly speaking, it probably was no longer necessary that he do so; even though they'd barely spoken at the Macclesfield ball the night before, they seemed to have forged an unspoken truce. Still, Colin didn't think he'd feel comfortable in his own skin until he spoke the words, "I'm sorry."

It was the right thing to do.

He was a gentleman, after all.

And besides, he rather fancied seeing her that morning.

He'd gone to Number Five for breakfast with his family, but he wanted to head straight for home after seeing Penelope, so he hopped in his carriage for the trip to the Featherington home on Mount Street, even though the distance was short enough to make him feel utterly lazy for doing so.

He smiled contentedly and lay back against the squabs, watching the lovely springtime scene roll by his window. It was one of those perfect sorts of days when everything simply felt right. The sun was shining, he felt remarkably energized, he'd had an excellent morning meal . . .

Life really didn't get better than this.

And he was going over to see Penelope.

Colin chose not to analyze why he was so eager to see her;

that was the sort of thing an unmarried man of three-and-thirty didn't generally care to think about. Instead he simply enjoyed the day—the sun, the air, even the three neat town-houses he passed on Mount Street before spying Penelope's front door. There was nothing remotely different or original about any of them, but it was such a perfect morning that they seemed unusually charming butted up next to each other, tall and thin, and stately with their gray Portland stone.

It was a wonderful day, warm and serene, sunny and tranquil . . .

Except that just as he started to rise from his seat, a short flurry of movement across the street caught his eye.

Penelope.

She was standing on the corner of Mount and Penter streets—the far corner, the one that would be not be visible to anyone looking out a window in the Featherington home. And she was climbing into a hired hack.

Interesting.

Colin frowned, mentally smacking himself on the forehead. It wasn't *interesting*. What the hell was he thinking? It wasn't interesting at all. It might have been interesting, had she been, say, a *man*. Or it might have been interesting if the conveyance into which she'd just entered had been one from the Featherington mews and not some scruffy hired hack.

But no, this was Penelope, who was certainly not a man, and she was entering a carriage by herself, presumably heading to some completely unsuitable location, because if she were doing anything proper and normal, she'd be in a Featherington conveyance. Or better yet, with one of her sisters or a maid, or anyone, just not, damn it, by herself.

This wasn't interesting, it was idiotic.

"Fool woman," he muttered, hopping down from his carriage with every intention of dashing toward the hack, wrenching the door open, and dragging her out. But just as his right foot left the confines of his carriage, he was struck by the same madness that led him to wander the world.

Curiosity.

Several choice curses were grumbled under his breath, all of them self-directed. He couldn't help it. It was so unlike Penelope to be taking off by herself in a hired hack; he *had* to know where she was going.

And so, instead of forcibly shaking some sense into her, he directed his driver to follow the hack, and they rolled north toward the busy thoroughfare of Oxford Street, where, Colin reflected, surely Penelope intended to do a bit of shopping. There could be any number of reasons she wasn't using the Featherington carriage. Perhaps it was damaged, or one of their horses had taken ill, or Penelope was buying someone a gift and wanted to keep it a secret.

No, that wasn't right. Penelope would never embark on a shopping expedition by herself. She would take a maid, or one of her sisters, or even one of *his* sisters. To stroll along Oxford Street by herself was to invite gossip. A woman alone was practically an advertisement for the next *Whistledown* column.

Or used to be, he supposed. It was hard to get used to a life without *Whistledown*. He hadn't realized how accustomed he'd been to seeing it at his breakfast table whenever he was in town.

And speaking of Lady Whistledown, he was even more certain than ever that she was none other than his sister Eloise. He'd gone over to Number Five for breakfast with the express purpose of questioning her, only to be informed that she was still feeling poorly and would not be joining the family that morning.

It had not escaped Colin's notice, however, that a rather hefty tray of food had been sent up to Eloise's room. Whatever ailed his sister, it had not affected her appetite.

He hadn't made any mention of his suspicions at the

breakfast table; truly, he saw no reason to upset his mother, who would surely be horrified at the thought. It was difficult to believe, however, that Eloise—whose love of discussing scandal was eclipsed only by her thrill at discovering it—would miss the opportunity to gossip about Cressida Twombley's revelation of the night before.

Unless *Eloise* was Lady Whistledown, in which case she'd be up in her room, plotting her next step.

The pieces all fit. It would have been depressing if Colin hadn't felt so oddly thrilled at having found her out.

After they rolled along for a few minutes, he poked his head outside to make sure his driver had not lost sight of Penelope's carriage. There she was, right in front of him. Or at least he thought it was her. Most hired hacks looked the same, so he was going to have to trust and hope that he was following the right one. But as he looked out, he realized that they'd traveled much farther east than he would have anticipated. In fact, they were just now passing Soho Street, which meant they were nearly to Tottenham Court Road, which meant—

Dear God, was Penelope taking the carriage to his house? Bedford Square was practically right around the corner.

A delicious thrill shot up his spine, because he couldn't imagine what she was doing in this part of town if not to see him; who else would a woman like Penelope know in Bloomsbury? He couldn't imagine that her mother allowed her to associate with people who actually worked for a living, and Colin's neighbors, though certainly well enough born, were not of the aristocracy and rarely even of the gentry. And they all plodded off to work each day, doctoring and lawyering, or—

Colin frowned. Hard. They'd just rolled past Tottenham Court Road. What the devil was she doing this far east? He supposed her driver might not know his way around town very well and thought to take Bloomsbury Street up to Bedford Square, even though it was a bit out of the way, but—

He heard something very strange and realized it was the sound of his teeth grinding together. They'd just passed Bloomsbury Street and were presently veering right onto High Holborn.

Devil take it, they were nearly in the City. What in God's name was Penelope planning to do in the City? It was no place for a woman. Hell, he hardly ever went there himself. The world of the *ton* was farther west, in the hallowed buildings of St. James's and Mayfair. Not here in the City, with its narrow, twisting, medieval roads and rather dangerous proximity to the tenements of the East End.

Colin's jaw dropped progressively lower as they rolled on . . . and on . . . and on . . . until he realized they were turning down Shoe Lane. He craned his head out the window. He'd only been here once before, at the age of nine when his tutor had dragged him and Benedict off to show them where the Great Fire of London had started in 1666. Colin remembered feeling vaguely disappointed when he'd learned that the culprit was a mere baker who'd not dampened the ashes in his oven properly. A fire like that should have had arson or intrigue in its origin.

A fire like that was nothing compared to the feelings coming to a boil in his chest. Penelope had better have a *damned* good reason for coming out here by herself. She shouldn't be going *anywhere* unaccompanied, much less the City.

Then, just when Colin was convinced that Penelope was going to travel all the way to the Dover coast, the carriages crossed Fleet Street and ground to a halt. Colin held still, waiting to see what Penelope was up to even though every fiber of his being was screaming to leap out of the carriage and tackle her right there on the pavement.

Call it intuition, call it madness, but somehow he knew that if he accosted Penelope right away, he would never learn of her true purpose here near Fleet Street.

Once she was far enough away so that he could alight unnoticed, he jumped down from the carriage and followed her south toward some church that looked decidedly like a wedding cake.

"For God's sake," Colin muttered, completely unaware of blasphemy or puns, "now is not the time to find religion, Penelope."

She disappeared into the church, and his legs ate up the pavement after her, slowing only when he reached the front door. He didn't want to surprise her too quickly. Not before he found out what exactly she was doing there. His earlier words notwithstanding, he did not for one moment think that Penelope had suddenly developed a desire to extend her churchgoing habits to midweek visits.

He slipped quietly into the church, keeping his footsteps as soft as he could. Penelope was walking down the center aisle, her left hand tapping along each pew, almost as if she were . . .

Counting?

Colin frowned as she picked her pew, then scooted in until she was in the middle. She sat utterly still for a moment, then reached into her reticule and pulled out an envelope. Her head moved the teeniest bit to the left, then to the right, and Colin could easily picture her face, her dark eyes darting in either direction as she checked the room for other people. He was safe from her gaze at the back, so far in the shadows that he was practically pressed up against the wall. And besides, she seemed intent upon remaining still and quiet in her movements; she certainly hadn't moved her head far enough to see him behind her.

Bibles and prayer books were tucked in little pockets on the backs of the pews, and Colin watched as Penelope surreptitiously slid the envelope behind one. Then she stood and edged her way out toward the center aisle.

And that was when Colin made his move.

Stepping out of the shadows, he strode purposefully toward her, taking grim satisfaction in the horror on her face when she saw him.

"Col—Col—" she gasped.

"That would be Colin," he drawled, grasping her arm just above the elbow. His touch was light, but his grip was firm, and there was no way she could think that she might make an escape.

Smart girl that she was, she didn't even try.

But smart girl that she was, she did attempt a play at innocence.

"Colin!" she finally managed to get out. "What a . . . what a . . ."

"Surprise?"

She gulped. "Yes."

"I'm sure it is."

Her eyes darted to the door, to the nave, everywhere but to the pew where she'd hidden her envelope. "I've—I've never seen you here before."

"I've never been."

Penelope's mouth moved several times before her next words emerged. "It's quite appropriate, actually, that you'd be here, actually, because, actually . . . uh . . . do you know the story of St. Bride's?"

He raised one brow. "Is that where we are?"

Penelope was clearly trying for a smile, but the result was more of the openmouthed idiot sort of look. Normally this would have amused him, but he was still angry with her for taking off on her own, not giving a care to her safety and welfare.

But most of all, he was furious that she had a secret.

Not so much that she'd *kept* a secret. Secrets were meant to be kept, and he couldn't blame her for that. Irrational as it was, he absolutely could not tolerate the fact that she *had* a secret. She was Penelope. She was supposed to be an open book. He knew her. He'd always known her.

And now it seemed he'd never known her.

"Yes," she finally replied, her voice squeaking on the word. "It's one of Wren's churches, actually, you know, the ones he did after the Great Fire, they're all over the City, and actually it's my favorite. I do so love the steeple. Don't you think it looks like a wedding cake?"

She was babbling. It was never a good sign when someone babbled. It generally meant they were hiding something. It was already obvious that Penelope was making an attempt at concealment, but the uncharacteristic rapidity of her words told him that her secret was exceedingly large, indeed.

He stared at her for a very long time, drawn out over many seconds just to torture her, then finally asked, "Is that why you think it's appropriate that I'm here?"

Her face went blank.

"The wedding cake . . ." he prompted.

"Oh!" she squealed, her skin flushing a deep, guilty red. "No! Not at all! It's just that—What I meant to say was that this is the church for writers. And publishers. I think. About the publishers, that is."

She was flailing and she knew she was flailing. He could see it in her eyes, on her face, in the very way her hands twisted as she spoke. But she kept trying, kept attempting to keep up the pretense, and so he did nothing but give her a sardonic stare as she continued with, "But I'm sure about the writers." And then, with a flourish that might have been triumphant if she hadn't ruined it with a nervous swallow, "And you're a writer!"

"So you're saying this is my church?"

"Er . . ." Her eyes darted to her left. "Yes."

"Excellent."

She gulped. "It is?"

"Oh, yes," he said, with a smooth casualness to his words that was intended to terrify her.

Her eyes darted to her left again . . . toward the pew where she'd hidden her correspondence. She'd been so good until now, keeping her attention off of her incriminating evidence. He'd almost been proud of her for it.

"My church," he repeated. "What a lovely notion."

Her eyes grew round, scared. "I'm afraid I don't catch your meaning."

He tapped his finger to his jaw, then held out his hand in a thoughtful manner. "I believe I'm developing a taste for prayer."

"Prayer?" she echoed weakly. "You?"

"Oh, yes."

"I . . . well . . . I . . . I . . ."

"Yes?" he queried, beginning to enjoy this in a sick sort of way. He'd never been the angry, brooding type. Clearly, he hadn't known what he was missing. There was something rather pleasing in making her squirm. "Penelope?" he continued. "Did you have something to say?"

She swallowed. "No."

"Good." He smiled blandly. "Then I believe I require a few moments for myself."

"I'm sorry?"

He stepped to his right. "I'm in a church. I believe I want to pray."

She stepped to her left. "I beg your pardon?"

He cocked his head very slightly to the side in question. "I said that I want to pray. It wasn't a terribly complicated sentiment."

He could tell that she was straining hard not to rise to his bait. She was trying to smile, but her jaw was tense, and he'd wager that her teeth were going to grind themselves to powder within minutes.

"I didn't think you were a particularly religious person," she said.

"I'm not." He waited for her to react, then added, "I intend to pray for *you*."

She swallowed uncontrollably. "Me?" she squeaked.

"Because," he began, unable to prevent his voice from rising in volume, "by the time I'm done, prayer is the only thing that is going to save you!"

And with that he brushed her aside and strode to where she'd hidden the envelope.

"Colin!" she yelled, running frantically after him. "No!"

He yanked the envelope out from behind the prayer book but didn't yet look at it. "Do you want to tell me what this is?" he demanded. "Before I look myself, do you want to tell me?"

"No," she said, her voice breaking on the word.

His heart breaking at the expression in her eyes.

"Please," she begged him. "Please give it to me." And then, when he did nothing but stare at her with hard, angry eyes, she whispered, "It's mine. It's a secret."

"A secret worth your welfare?" he nearly roared. "Worth your life?"

"What are you talking about?"

"Do you have any idea how dangerous it is for a woman alone in the City? Alone anywhere?"

All she said was, "Colin, please." She reached for the envelope, still held out of her reach.

And suddenly he didn't know what he was doing. This wasn't him. This insane fury, this anger—it couldn't be his.

And yet it was.

But the troubling part was . . . it was Penelope who had made him thus. And what had she done? Traveled across London by herself? He was rather irritated at her for her lack of concern for her own safety, but that paled in comparison to the fury he felt at her keeping of secrets.

His anger was entirely unwarranted. He had no right to expect that Penelope share her secrets with him. They had no commitments to each other, nothing beyond a rather nice friendship and a single, albeit disturbingly moving, kiss. He certainly wouldn't have shared his journals with her if she hadn't stumbled upon them herself.

"Colin," she whispered. "Please . . . don't."

She'd seen his secret writings. Why shouldn't he see hers? Did she have a lover? Was all that nonsense about never having been kissed exactly that—nonsense?

Dear God, was this fire burning in his belly . . . *jealousy*?

"Colin," she said again, choking now. She placed her hand on his, trying to prevent him from opening the envelope. Not with strength, for she could never match him on that, just with her presence.

But there was no way . . . no way he could have stopped himself at that point. He would have died before surrendering that envelope to her unopened.

He tore it open.

Penelope let out a strangled cry and ran from the church.

Colin read the words.

And then he sank to the pew, bloodless, breathless.

"Oh, my God," he whispered. *"Oh, my God."*

By the time Penelope reached the outer steps to St. Bride's Church, she was hysterical. Or at least as hysterical as she'd ever been. Her breath was coming in short, sharp gasps, tears pricked her eyes, and her heart felt . . .

Well, her heart felt as if it wanted to throw up, if such a thing were possible.

How could he have done this? He'd followed her. *Followed her!* Why would Colin follow her? What would he have to gain? Why would he—

She suddenly looked around.

"Oh, damn!" she wailed, not caring if anyone heard her. The hack had left. She'd given specific instructions to the driver to wait for her, that she'd only be a minute, but he was nowhere in sight.

Another transgression she could lay at Colin's door. He'd delayed her inside the church, and now the hack had left, and she was stuck here on the steps of St. Bride's Church, in the middle of the City of London, so far from her home in Mayfair that she might as well have been in France. People were staring at her and any minute now she was sure to be accosted, because who had ever seen a gently bred lady alone in the City, much less one who was so clearly on the verge of a nervous attack?

Why why *why* had she been so foolish as to think that he was the perfect man? She'd spent half her life worshiping someone who wasn't even real. Because the Colin she knew—no, the Colin she'd *thought* she'd known—clearly didn't exist. And whoever this man was, she wasn't even sure she liked him. The man she'd loved so faithfully over the years never would have behaved like this. He wouldn't have followed her—Oh, very well, he would have, but only to assure himself of her safety. But he wouldn't have been so cruel, and he certainly wouldn't have opened her private correspondence.

She had read two pages of his journal, that was true, but they hadn't been in a sealed envelope!

She sank onto the steps and sat down, the stone cool even through the fabric of her dress. There was little she could do now besides sit here and wait for Colin. Only a fool would take off on foot by herself so far from home. She supposed she could hail a hack on Fleet Street, but what if they were all occupied, and besides, was there really any point in running from Colin? He knew where she lived, and unless she decided to run to the Orkney Islands, she wasn't likely to escape a confrontation.

She sighed. Colin would probably find her in the Orkneys, seasoned traveler that he was. And she didn't even want to *go* to the Orkneys.

She choked back a sob. Now she wasn't even making sense. Why was she fixated on the Orkney Islands?

And then there was Colin's voice behind her, clipped and so very cold. "Get up," was all he said.

She did, not because he'd ordered her to (or at least that was what she told herself), and not because she was afraid of him, but rather because she couldn't sit on the steps of St. Bride's forever, and even if she wanted nothing more than to hide herself from Colin for the next six months, at the moment he was her only safe means home.

He jerked his head toward the street. "Into the carriage."

She went, climbing up as she heard Colin give the driver her address and then instruct him to "take the long way."

Oh, God.

They'd been moving a good thirty seconds before he handed her the single sheet of paper that had been folded into the envelope she'd left in the church. "I believe this is yours," he said.

She gulped and looked down, not that she needed to. She already had the words memorized. She'd written and rewritten them so many times the previous night, she didn't think they'd ever escape her memory.

There is nothing I despise more than a gentleman who thinks it amusing to give a lady a condescending pat on the hand as he murmurs, "It is a woman's prerogative to change her mind." And indeed, because I feel one should always support one's words with one's actions, I endeavor to keep my opinions and decisions steadfast and true.

Which is why, Gentle Reader, when I wrote my column of 19 April, I truly intended it to be my last. However, events entirely beyond my control (or indeed beyond my approval) force me to put my pen to paper one last time.

Ladies and Gentleman, This Author is NOT Lady Cressida Twombley. She is nothing more than a scheming imposter, and it would break my heart to see my years of hard work attributed to one such as her.

LADY WHISTLEDOWN'S SOCIETY PAPERS, 21 APRIL 1824

Penelope refolded the paper with great precision, using the time to try to compose herself and figure out what on earth she was supposed to say at a moment like that. Finally, she attempted a smile, didn't quite meet his eyes, and joked, "Did you guess?"

He didn't say anything, so she was forced to look up. She immediately wished she hadn't. Colin looked completely unlike himself. The easy smile that always tugged at his lips, the good humor forever lurking in his eyes—they were all gone, replaced by harsh lines and cold, pure ice.

The man she knew, the man she'd loved for so very long—she didn't know who he was anymore.

"I'll take that as a no," she said shakily.

"Do you know what I am trying to do right now?" he asked, his voice startling and loud against the rhythmic clip-clop of the horses' hooves.

She opened her mouth to say no, but one look at his face told her he didn't desire an answer, so she held her tongue.

"I am trying to decide what, precisely, I am most angry with you about," he said. "Because there are so many things—so very *many* things—that I am finding it extraordinarily difficult to focus upon just one."

It was on the tip of Penelope's tongue to suggest something—her deception was a likely place to start—but on second thought, now seemed an excellent time to hold her counsel.

"First of all," he said, the terribly even tone of his voice suggesting that he was trying *very* hard to keep his temper in check (and this was, in and of itself, rather disturbing, as she hadn't been aware that Colin even possessed a temper), "I cannot believe you were stupid enough to venture into the City by yourself, and in a hired hack, no less!"

"I could hardly go by myself in one of our own carriages," Penelope blurted out before she remembered that she'd meant to remain silent.

His head moved about an inch to the left. She didn't know what that meant, but she couldn't imagine it was good, especially since it almost seemed as if his neck were tightening as it twisted. "I beg your pardon?" he asked, his voice still that awful blend of satin and steel.

Well, now she *had* to answer, didn't she? "Er, it's nothing," she said, hoping the evasion would reduce his attention on the rest of her reply. "Just that I'm not allowed to go out by myself."

"I am aware of that," he bit off. "There's a damned good reason for it, too."

"So if I wanted to go out by myself," she continued, choosing to ignore the second part of his reply, "I couldn't very well use one of our carriages. None of our drivers would agree to take me here."

"Your drivers," he snapped, "are clearly men of impeccable wisdom and sense."

Penelope said nothing.

"Do you have any idea what could have happened to you?" he demanded, his sharp mask of control beginning to crack.

"Er, very little, actually," she said, gulping on the sentence. "I've come here before, and—"

"What?" His hand closed over her upper arm with painful force. "What did you just say?"

Repeating it seemed almost dangerous to her health, so Penelope just stared at him, hoping that maybe she could break through the wild anger in his eyes and find the man she knew and loved so dearly.

"It's only when I need to leave an urgent message for my

publisher," she explained. "I send a coded message, then he knows to pick up my note here."

"And speaking of which," Colin said roughly, snatching the folded paper back from her hands, "what the *hell* is this?"

Penelope stared at him in confusion. "I would have thought it was obvious. I'm—"

"Yes, of course, you're bloody Lady Whistledown, and you've probably been laughing at me for weeks as I insisted it was Eloise." His face twisted as he spoke, nearly breaking her heart.

"No!" she cried out. "No, Colin, never. I would never laugh at you!"

But his face told her clearly that he did not believe her. There was humiliation in his emerald eyes, something she'd never seen there, something she'd never expected to see. He was a Bridgerton. He was popular, confident, self-possessed. Nothing could embarrass him. No one could humiliate him.

Except, apparently, her.

"I couldn't tell you," she whispered, desperately trying to make that awful look in his eyes go away. "Surely you knew I couldn't tell you."

He was silent for an agonizingly long moment, and then, as if she'd never spoken, never tried to explain herself, he lifted the incriminating sheet of paper into the air and shook it, completely disregarding her impassioned outcry. "This is stupidity," he said. "Have you lost your mind?"

"I don't know what you mean."

"You had a perfectly good escape, just waiting for you. Cressida Twombley was willing to take the blame for you."

And then suddenly his hands were on her shoulders, and he was holding her so tightly she could barely breathe.

"Why couldn't you just let it die, Penelope?" His voice was urgent, his eyes blazing. It was the most feeling she'd ever seen in him, and it broke her heart that it was directed toward her in anger. And in shame.

"I couldn't let her do it," she whispered. "I couldn't let her be me."

Chapter 13

"Why the hell not?"

Penelope could do nothing but stare for several seconds. "Because . . . because . . ." she flailed, wondering how she was supposed to explain this. Her heart was breaking, her most terrifying—and exhilarating—secret had been shattered, and he thought she had the presence of mind to *explain* herself?

"I realize she's quite possibly the biggest bitch . . ."

Penelope gasped.

". . . that England has produced in this generation at least, but for God's sake, Penelope"—he raked his hand through his hair, then fixed a hard stare on her face—"she was going to take the blame—"

"The credit," Penelope interrupted testily.

"The blame," he continued. "Do you have any idea what will happen to you if people find out who you really are?"

The corners of her lips tightened with impatience . . . and irritation at being so obviously condescended to. "I've had over a decade to ruminate the possibility."

His eyes narrowed. "Are you being sarcastic?"

"Not at all," she shot back. "Do you really think I haven't spent a good portion of the last ten years of my life contemplating what would happen if I were found out? I'd be a blind idiot if I hadn't."

He grabbed her by the shoulders, holding tight even as the carriage bumped over uneven cobbles. "You will be ruined, Penelope. Ruined! Do you understand what I am saying?"

"If I did not," she replied, "I assure you I would now, after your lengthy dissertations on the subject when you were accusing Eloise of being Lady Whistledown."

He scowled, obviously annoyed at having his errors thrown in his face. "People will stop talking to you," he continued. "They will cut you dead—"

"People never talked to me," she snapped. "Half the time they didn't even know I was there. How do you think I was able to keep up the ruse for so long in the first place? I was invisible, Colin. No one saw me, no one talked to me. I just stood and listened, *and no one noticed.*"

"That's not true." But his eyes slid from hers as he said it.

"Oh, it *is* true, and you know it. You only deny it," she said, jabbing him in the arm, "because you feel guilty."

"I do not!"

"Oh, *please,*" she scoffed. "Everything you do, you do out of guilt."

"Pen—"

"That involves me, at least," she corrected. Her breath was rushing through her throat, and her skin was pricking with heat, and for once, her soul was on fire. "Do you think I don't know how your family pities me? Do you think it escapes my notice that anytime you or your brothers happen to be at the same party as me, you ask me to dance?"

"We're polite," he ground out, "and we *like* you."

"*And* you feel sorry for me. You like Felicity but I don't see you dancing with her every time your paths cross."

He let go of her quite suddenly and crossed his arms. "Well, I don't like her as well as I do you."

She blinked, knocked rather neatly off her verbal stride. Trust him to go and *compliment* her in the middle of an argument. Nothing could have disarmed her more.

"And," he continued with a rather arch and superior lifting of his chin, "you have not addressed my original point."

"Which was?"

"That Lady Whistledown will ruin you!"

"For God's sake," she muttered, "you talk as if she were a separate person."

"Well, excuse me if I still have difficulty reconciling the woman in front of me with the harridan writing the column."

"Colin!"

"Insulted?" he mocked.

"Yes! I've worked very hard on that column." She clenched her fists around the thin fabric of her mint-green morning dress, oblivious to the wrinkled spirals she was creating. She had to do something with her hands or she'd quite possibly explode with the nervous energy and anger coursing through her veins. Her only other option seemed to be crossing her arms, and she refused to give in to such an obvious show of petulance. Besides, he was crossing his arms, and one of them needed to act older than six.

"I wouldn't dream of denigrating what you've done," he said condescendingly.

"Of course you would," she interrupted.

"No, I wouldn't."

"Then what do you think you're doing?"

"Being an adult!" he answered, his voice growing loud and impatient. "One of us has to be."

"Don't you dare speak to me of adult behavior!" she exploded. "You, who run at the very hint of responsibility."

"And what the hell does that mean?" he bit off.

"I thought it was rather obvious."

He drew back. "I can't believe you're speaking to me like this."

"You can't believe I'm doing it," she taunted, "or that I possess the nerve to do so?"

He just stared at her, obviously surprised by her question.

"There's more to me than you think, Colin," she said. And then, in a quieter tone of voice, she added, "There's more to me than *I* used to think."

He said nothing for several moments, and then, as if he just couldn't drag himself away from the topic, he asked, practically between his teeth, "What did you mean when you said I run from responsibility?"

She pursed her lips, then relaxed as she let out what she hoped would be a calming exhale. "Why do you think you travel so much?"

"Because I like it," he replied, his tone clipped.

"And because you're bored out of your mind here in England."

"And that makes me a child because . . . ?"

"Because you're not willing to grow up and do something adult that would keep you in one place."

"Like what?"

Her hands came up in an I-should-think-it-was-obvious sort of gesture. "Like get married."

"Is that a proposal?" he mocked, one corner of his mouth rising into a rather insolent smile.

She could feel her cheeks flushing deep and hot, but she forced herself to continue. "You know it's not, and don't try to change the subject by being deliberately cruel." She waited for him to say something, perhaps an apology. His silence was an insult, and so she let out a snort and said, "For heaven's sake, Colin, you're three-and-thirty."

"And you're eight-and-twenty," he pointed out, and not in a particularly kind tone of voice.

It felt like a punch in the belly, but she was too riled up to retreat into her familiar shell. "Unlike you," she said with low precision, "I don't have the luxury of asking someone. And unlike *you,*" she added, her intention now solely to induce the guilt she'd accused him of just minutes earlier, "I don't have a massive pool of prospective suitors, so I've never had the luxury of saying no."

His lips tightened. "And you think that your unveiling as Lady Whistledown is going to increase the number of your suitors?"

"Are you *trying* to be insulting?" she ground out.

"I'm trying to be realistic! Something which you seem to have completely lost sight of."

"I never said I was planning to unveil myself as Lady Whistledown."

He snatched the envelope with the final column in it back up off the cushioned bench. "Then what is this about?"

She grabbed it back, yanking the paper from the envelope. "I beg your pardon," she said, every syllable heavy with sarcasm. "I must have missed the sentence proclaiming my identity."

"You think this swan song of yours will do anything to dampen the frenzy of interest in Lady Whistledown's identity? Oh, excuse me"—he placed one insolent hand over his heart—"perhaps I should have said *your* identity. After all, I don't want to deny you your *credit*."

"Now you're just being ugly," she said, a little voice at the back of her brain wondering why she wasn't crying by now. This was Colin, and she'd loved him forever, and he was acting as if he hated her. Was there anything else in the world more worthy of tears?

Or maybe that wasn't it at all. Maybe all this sadness building up inside of her was for the death of a dream. Her dream of him. She'd built up the perfect image of him in her mind, and with every word he spat in her face, it was becoming more and more obvious that her dream was quite simply wrong.

"I'm making a point," he said, snatching the paper back from her hands. "Look at this. It might as well be an invitation for further investigation. You're mocking society, daring them to uncover you."

"That's not at all what I'm doing!"

"It may not be your intention, but it is certainly the end result."

He probably had something of a point there, but she was loath to give him credit for it. "It's a chance I'll have to take," she replied, crossing her arms and looking pointedly away from him. "I've gone eleven years without detection. I don't see why I'm in need of undue worry now."

His breath left him in a short punch of exasperation. "Do you have any concept of money? Any idea how many people would like Lady Danbury's thousand pounds?"

"I have more of a concept of money than you do," she replied, bristling at the insult. "And besides, Lady Danbury's reward doesn't make my secret any more vulnerable."

"It makes everyone else more determined, and that makes you more vulnerable. Not to mention," he added with a wry twist to his lips, "as my youngest sister pointed out, there is the glory."

"Hyacinth?" she asked.

He nodded grimly, setting the paper down on the bench beside him. "And if Hyacinth thinks the glory at having uncovered your identity is enviable, then you can be sure she's not the only one. It may very well be why Cressida is pursuing her stupid ruse."

"Cressida's doing it for the money," Penelope grumbled. "I'm sure of it."

"Fine. It doesn't matter why she's doing it. All that matters is that she is, and once you dispose of her with your idiocy"—he slammed his hand against the paper, causing Penelope to wince as a loud crinkle filled the air—"someone else will take her place."

"This is nothing I don't already know," she said, mostly because she couldn't bear to give him the last word.

"Then for the love of God, woman," he burst out, "let

Cressida get away with her scheme. She's the answer to your prayers."

Her eyes snapped up to his. "You don't know my prayers."

Something in her tone hit Colin squarely in the chest. She hadn't changed his mind, hadn't even budged it, but he couldn't seem to find the right words to fill the moment. He looked at her, then he looked out the window, his mind absently focusing on the dome of St. Paul's Cathedral.

"We really are taking the long way home," he murmured.

She didn't say anything. He didn't blame her. It had been a stupid non sequitur, words to fill the silence and nothing else.

"If you let Cressida—" he began.

"Stop," she implored him. "Please, don't say any more. I can't let her do it."

"Have you really thought about what you'd gain?"

She looked at him sharply. "Do you think I've been able to think of anything else these past few days?"

He tried another tactic. "Does it truly matter that people know you were Lady Whistledown? *You* know that you were clever and fooled us all. Can't that be enough?"

"You're not listening to me!" Her mouth remained frozen open, in an odd incredulous oval, as if she couldn't quite believe that he didn't understand what she was saying. "I don't need for people to know it was me. I just need for them to know it wasn't *her*."

"But clearly you don't mind if people think someone else is Lady Whistledown," he insisted. "After all, you've been accusing Lady Danbury for weeks."

"I had to accuse *some*one," she explained. "Lady Danbury asked me point-blank who I thought it was, and I couldn't very well say myself. Besides, it wouldn't be so very bad if people thought it was Lady Danbury. At least I like Lady Danbury."

"Penelope—"

"How would you feel if your journals were published with Nigel Berbrooke as the author?" she demanded.

"Nigel Berbrooke can barely string two sentences together," he said with a derisive snort. "I hardly think anyone would believe he could have written my journals." As an afterthought, he gave her a little nod as an apology, since Berbrooke was, after all, married to her sister.

"Try to imagine it," she ground out. "Or substitute whomever you think is similar to Cressida."

"Penelope," he sighed, "I'm not you. You can't compare the two. Besides, if I were to publish my journals, they would hardly ruin me in the eyes of society."

She deflated in her seat, sighing loudly, and he knew that his point had been well made. "Good," he announced, "then it is decided. We will tear this up—" He reached for the sheet of paper.

"No!" she cried out, practically leaping from her seat. "Don't!"

"But you just said—"

"I said nothing!" she shrilled. "All I did was sigh."

"Oh, for God's sake, Penelope," he said testily. "You clearly agreed with—"

She gaped at his audacity. "When did I give you leave to interpret my sighs?"

He looked at the incriminating paper, still held in his hands, and wondered what on earth he was meant to do with it at this moment.

"And *anyway,*" she continued, her eyes flashing with an anger and fire that made her almost beautiful, "it isn't as if I don't have every last word memorized. You can destroy that paper, but you can't destroy me."

"I'd like to," he muttered.

"*What* did you say?"

"Whistledown," he ground out. "I'd like to destroy Whistledown. You, I'm happy to leave as is."

"But I *am* Whistledown."

"God help us all."

And then something within her simply snapped. All her rage, all her frustration, every last negative feeling she'd kept bottled up inside over the years broke forth, all directed at Colin, who, of all the *ton,* was probably the least deserving of it.

"Why are you so angry with me?" she burst out. "What have I done that is so repellent? Been cleverer than you? Kept a secret? Had a good laugh at the expense of society?"

"Penelope, you—"

"No," she said forcefully. "You be quiet. It's my turn to speak."

His jaw went slack as he stared at her, shock and disbelief crowding in his eyes.

"I am proud of what I've done," she managed to say, her voice shaking with emotion. "I don't care what you say. I don't care what anyone says. No one can take that from me."

"I'm not trying—"

"I don't need for people to know the truth," she said, jumping on top of his ill-timed protest. "But I will be *damned* if I allow Cressida Twombley, the very person who . . . who . . ." Her entire body was trembling now, as memory after memory swept over her, all of them bad.

Cressida, renowned for her grace and carriage, tripping and spilling punch on Penelope's gown that first year—the only one her mother had allowed her to buy that wasn't yellow or orange.

Cressida, sweetly begging young bachelors to ask Penelope to dance, her requests made with such volume and fervor that Penelope could only be mortified by them.

Cressida, saying before a crowd how worried she was about Penelope's appearance. "It's just not *healthful* to weigh more than ten stone at our age," she'd cooed.

Penelope never knew whether Cressida had been able to hide her smirk following her barb. She'd fled the room, blinded by tears, unable to ignore the way her hips jiggled as she ran away.

Cressida had always known exactly where to stick her sword, and she'd known how to twist her bayonet. It didn't matter that Eloise remained Penelope's champion or that Lady Bridgerton always tried to bolster her confidence. Penelope had cried herself to sleep more times than she could remember, always due to some well-placed barb from Cressida Cowper Twombley.

She'd let Cressida get away with so much in the past, all because she hadn't the courage to stand up for herself. But she couldn't let Cressida have *this.* Not her secret life, not the one little corner of her soul that was strong and proud and completely without fear.

Penelope might not know how to defend herself, but by God, Lady Whistledown did.

"Penelope?" Colin asked cautiously.

She looked at him blankly, taking several seconds to remember that it was 1824, not 1814, and she was here in a carriage with Colin Bridgerton, not cowering in the corner of a ballroom, trying to escape Cressida Cowper.

"Are you all right?" he asked.

She nodded. Or at least she tried to.

He opened his mouth to say something, then paused, his lips remaining parted for several seconds. Finally, he just placed his hand on hers, saying, "We'll talk about this later?"

This time she did manage a short nod. And truly, she just wanted the entire awful afternoon to be over, but there was one thing she couldn't quite let go of yet.

"Cressida wasn't ruined," she said quietly.

He turned to her, a slight veil of confusion descending over his eyes. "I beg your pardon?"

Her voice rose slightly in volume. "Cressida said she was Lady Whistledown, and she wasn't ruined."

"That's because no one believed her," Colin replied. "And besides," he added without thinking, "she's . . . different."

She turned to him slowly. Very slowly, with steadfast eyes. "Different how?"

Something akin to panic began to pound in Colin's chest. He'd known he wasn't saying the right words even as they'd spilled from his lips. How could one little sentence, one little word be so very wrong?

She's different.

They both knew what he'd meant. Cressida was popular, Cressida was beautiful, Cressida could carry it all off with aplomb.

Penelope, on the other hand . . .

She was Penelope. Penelope Featherington. And she hadn't the clout nor the connections to save her from ruin. The Bridgertons could stand behind her and offer support, but even they wouldn't be able prevent her downfall. Any other scandal might have been manageable, but Lady Whistledown had, at one time or another, insulted almost every person of consequence in the British Isles. Once people were over their surprise, that was when the unkind remarks would begin.

Penelope wouldn't be praised for being clever or witty or daring.

She'd be called mean, and petty, and jealous.

Colin knew the *ton* well. He knew how his peers acted. The aristocracy was capable of individual greatness, but collectively they tended to sink to the lowest common denominator.

Which was very low, indeed.

"I see," Penelope said into the silence.

"No," he said quickly, "you don't. I—"

"No, Colin," she said, sounding almost painfully wise, "I do. I suppose I'd just always hoped *you* were different."

His eyes caught hers, and somehow his hands were on her shoulders, gripping her with such intensity that she couldn't possibly look away. He didn't say anything, letting his eyes ask his questions.

"I thought you believed in me," she said, "that you saw beyond the ugly duckling."

Her face was so familiar to him; he'd seen it a thousand times before, and yet until these past few weeks, he couldn't have said he truly knew it. Would he have remembered that she had a small birthmark near her left earlobe? Had he ever noticed the warm glow to her skin? Or that her brown eyes had flecks of gold in them, right near the pupil?

How had he danced with her so many times and never noticed that her mouth was full and wide and made for kissing?

She licked her lips when she was nervous. He'd seen her do that just the other day. Surely she'd done that at some point in the dozen years of their acquaintance, and yet it was only now that the mere sight of her tongue made his body clench with need.

"You're not ugly," he told her, his voice low and urgent.

Her eyes widened.

And he whispered, "You're beautiful."

"No," she said, the word barely more than a breath. "Don't say things you don't mean."

His fingers dug into her shoulders. "You're beautiful," he repeated. "I don't know how . . . I don't know when . . ." He touched her lips, feeling her hot breath on his fingertips. "But you are," he whispered.

He leaned forward and kissed her, slowly, reverently, no longer quite so surprised that this was happening, that he wanted her so badly. The shock was gone, replaced by a simple, primitive need to claim her, to brand her, to mark her as his.

His?

He pulled back and looked at her for a moment, his eyes searching her face.

Why not?

"What is it?" she whispered.

"You *are* beautiful," he said, shaking his head in confusion. "I don't know why nobody else sees it."

Something warm and lovely began to spread in Penelope's chest. She couldn't quite explain it; it was almost as if someone had heated her blood. It started in her heart and then slowly swept through her arms, her belly, down to the tips of her toes.

It made her light-headed. It made her content.

It made her whole.

She wasn't beautiful. She knew she wasn't beautiful, she knew she'd never be more than passably attractive, and that was only on her good days. But he thought she was beautiful, and when he looked at her . . .

She *felt* beautiful. And she'd never felt that way before.

He kissed her again, his lips hungrier this time, nibbling, caressing, waking her body, rousing her soul. Her belly had begun to tingle, and her skin felt hot and needy where his hands touched her through the thin green fabric of her dress.

And never once did she think, *This is wrong*. This kiss was everything she'd been brought up to fear and avoid, but she knew—body, mind, and soul—that nothing in her life had ever been so right. She had been born for this man, and she'd spent so many years trying to accept the fact that he had been born for someone else.

To be proven wrong was the most exquisite pleasure imaginable.

She wanted him, she wanted this, she wanted the way he made her feel.

She wanted to be beautiful, even if it was only in one man's eyes.

They were, she thought dreamily as he laid her down on the plush cushion of the carriage bench, the only eyes that mattered.

She loved him. She had always loved him. Even now,

when he was so angry with her that she barely recognized him, when he was so angry with her that she wasn't even sure she *liked* him, she loved him.

And she wanted to be his.

The first time he had kissed her, she had accepted his advances with a passive delight, but this time she was determined to be an active partner. She still couldn't quite believe that she was here, with him, and she certainly wasn't ready to let herself dream that he might ever be kissing her on a regular basis.

This might never happen again. She might never again feel the exquisite weight of him pressing against her, or the scandalous tickle of his tongue against hers.

She had one chance. One chance to make a memory that would have to last a lifetime. One chance to reach for bliss.

Tomorrow would be awful, knowing that he would find some other woman with whom to laugh and joke and even marry, but today . . .

Today was hers.

And by God, she was going to make this a kiss to remember.

She reached up and touched his hair. She was hesitant at first—just because she was determined to be an active, willing partner didn't mean she had a clue what she was doing. His lips were slowly easing all the reason and intelligence from her mind, but still, she couldn't quite help noticing that his hair felt exactly like Eloise's, which she had brushed countless times during their years of friendship. And heaven help her . . .

She giggled.

That got his attention, and he lifted his head, his lips touched by an amused smile. "I beg your pardon?" he queried.

She shook her head, trying to fight off her smile, knowing she was losing the battle.

"Oh, no, you must," he insisted. "I couldn't possibly continue without knowing the reason for the giggle."

She felt her cheeks burning, which struck her as ridiculously ill-timed. Here she was, completely misbehaving in the back of a carriage, and it was only *now* that she had the decency to blush?

"Tell me," he murmured, nibbling at her ear.

She shook her head.

His lips found the exact point where her pulse beat in her throat. "Tell me."

All she did—all she could do—was moan, arching her neck to give him greater access.

Her dress, which she hadn't even realized had been partially unbuttoned, slid down until her collarbone was exposed, and she watched with giddy fascination as his lips traced the line of it, until his entire face was nuzzled perilously close to her bosom.

"Will you tell me?" he whispered, grazing her skin with his teeth.

"Tell you what?" she gasped.

His lips were wicked, moving lower, then lower still. "Why you were laughing?"

For several seconds Penelope couldn't even remember what he was talking about.

His hand cupped her breast through her dress. "I'll torment you until you tell me," he threatened.

Penelope's answer was an arch of her back, settling her breast even more firmly in his grasp.

She liked his torment.

"I see," he murmured, simultaneously sliding her bodice down and moving his hand so that his palm grazed her nipple. "Then perhaps I'll"—his hand stilled, then lifted—"stop."

"No," she moaned.

"Then tell me."

She stared at her breast, mesmerized by the sight of it, bare and open to his gaze.

"Tell me," he whispered, blowing softly so that his breath brushed across her.

Something clenched inside Penelope, deep inside of her, in places that were never talked about.

"Colin, please," she begged.

He smiled, slow and lazy, satisfied and still somehow hungry. "Please what?" he asked.

"Touch me," she whispered.

His index finger slid along her shoulder. "Here?"

She shook her head frantically.

He trailed down the column of her neck. "Am I getting closer?" he murmured.

She nodded, her eyes never leaving her breast.

He found her nipple again, his fingers tracing slow, tantalizing spirals around it, then on it, and all the while she watched, her body growing tighter and tighter.

And all she could hear was her breath, hot and heavy from her lips.

Then—

"Colin!" His name flew from her mouth in a strangled gasp. Surely he couldn't—

His lips closed around her, and before she'd even felt more than the heat of him, she bucked off the bench in surprise, her hips pressing shamelessly against his, then settling back down as he ground against her, holding her immobile as he pleasured her.

"Oh, Colin, Colin," she gasped, her hands flying around to his back, pressing desperately into his muscles, wanting nothing other than to hold him and keep him and never let him go.

He yanked at his shirt, pulling it free from the waist of his breeches, and she followed his cue by slipping her hands under the fabric and running them along the hot skin of his back. She'd never touched a man this way; she'd never touched *anyone* like this, except maybe herself, and even then, it wasn't like she could easily reach her own back.

He groaned when she touched him, then tensed when her fingers skimmed along his skin. Her heart leaped. He liked this; he liked the way she was touching him. She hadn't the least clue what to do with herself, but he liked it just the same.

"You're perfect," he whispered against her skin, his lips blazing a trail back up to the underside of her chin. His mouth claimed hers again, this time with increased fervor, and his hands slid underneath to cup her derriere, squeezing and kneading and pressing her up against his arousal.

"My God, I want you," he gasped, grinding his hips down. "I want to strip you bare and sink into you and never let you go."

Penelope groaned with desire, unable to believe how much pleasure she could feel from mere words. He made her feel wicked, naughty, and oh-so-desirable.

And she never wanted it to end.

"Oh, Penelope," he was groaning, his lips and hands growing more frantic. "Oh, Penelope. Oh, Penelope, oh—" He lifted his head. Very abruptly.

"Oh, God."

"What is it?" she asked, trying to lift the back of her head from the cushion.

"We've stopped."

It took her a moment to recognize the import of this. If they'd stopped, that meant they'd most likely reached their destination, which was . . .

Her home.

"Oh, God!" She started yanking at the bodice of her gown with frantic motions. "Can't we just ask the driver to keep going?"

She'd already proven herself a complete wanton. There seemed little harm at this point in adding "shameless" to her list of behaviors.

He grabbed the bodice for her and hauled it into place. "What is the possibility your mother won't have noticed my carriage in front of your house yet?"

"Fairly good, actually," she said, "but Briarly will have done."

"Your butler will recognize my carriage?" he asked in disbelief.

She nodded. "You came the other day. He always remembers things like that."

His lips twisted in a grimly determined manner. "Very well, then," he said. "Make yourself presentable."

"I can race up to my room," Penelope said. "No one will see me."

"I doubt that," he said ominously, tucking in his shirt and smoothing his hair.

"No, I assure you—"

"And I assure you," he said, leaping on top of her words. "You will be seen." He licked his fingers, then ran them through his hair. "Do I look presentable?"

"Yes," she lied. In truth, he looked rather flushed, with swollen lips, and hair that didn't remotely adhere to a current style.

"Good." He hopped down from the carriage and held his hand out to her.

"You're coming in as well?" she asked.

He looked at her as if she'd suddenly gone daft. "Of course."

She didn't move, too perplexed by his actions to give her legs the orders to step down. There was certainly no reason he had to accompany her inside. Propriety didn't really demand it, and—

"For God's sake, Penelope," he said, grabbing her hand and yanking her down. "Are you going to marry me or not?"

Chapter 14

She hit the pavement.

Penelope was—in her opinion, at least—a bit more graceful than most people gave her credit for. She was a good dancer, could play the piano with her fingers arched perfectly, and could usually navigate a crowded room without bumping into an uncommon amount of people or furniture.

But when Colin made his rather matter-of-fact proposal, her foot—at the time halfway out of the carriage—found only air, her left hip found the curb, and her head found Colin's toes.

"Good God, Penelope," he exclaimed, crouching down. "Are you all right?"

"Just fine," she managed to get out, searching for the hole in the ground that must have just opened up, so that she could crawl into it and die.

"Are you certain?"

"It's nothing, really," she replied, holding her cheek, which she was certain now sported a perfect imprint of the top of Colin's boot. "Just a bit surprised, that is all."

"Why?"

"Why?" she echoed.

"Yes, why?"

She blinked. Once, twice, then again. "Er, well, it might have to do with your mentioning marriage."

He yanked her unceremoniously to her feet, nearly dislocating her shoulder in the process. "Well, what did you think I would say?"

She stared at him in disbelief. Was he mad? "Not *that,*" she finally replied.

"I'm not a complete boor," he muttered.

She brushed dust and pebbles off her sleeves. "I never said you were, I just—"

"I can assure you," he continued, now looking mortally offended, "that I do not behave as I did with a woman of your background without rendering a marriage proposal."

Penelope's mouth fell open, leaving her feeling rather like an owl.

"Don't you have a reply?" he demanded.

"I'm still trying to figure out what you said," she admitted.

He planted his hands on his hips and stared at her with a decided lack of indulgence.

"You must admit," she said, her chin dipping until she was regarding him rather dubiously through her lashes, "it did sound rather like you've, er—how did you say it—rendered marriage proposals before."

He scowled at her. "Of course I haven't. Now take my arm before it starts to rain."

She looked up at the clear blue sky.

"At the rate you're going," he said impatiently, "we'll be here for days."

"I . . . well . . ." She cleared her throat. "Surely you can forgive me my lack of composure in the face of such tremendous surprise."

"Now who's speaking in circles?" he muttered.

"I beg your pardon."

His hand tightened on her arm. "Let's just get going."

"Colin!" she nearly shrieked, tripping over her feet as she stumbled up the stairs. "Are you sure—"

"No time like the present," he said, almost jauntily. He

seemed quite pleased with himself, which puzzled her, because she would have bet her entire fortune—and as Lady Whistledown, she'd amassed quite a fortune—that he had not intended to ask her to marry him until the moment his carriage had ground to a halt in front her house.

Perhaps not even until the words had left his lips.

He turned to her. "Do I need to knock?"

"No, I—"

He knocked anyway, or rather banged, if one wanted to be particular about it.

"Briarly," Penelope said through an attempted smile as the butler opened the door to receive them.

"Miss Penelope," he murmured, one brow rising in surprise. He nodded at Colin. "Mr. Bridgerton."

"Is Mrs. Featherington at home?" Colin asked brusquely.

"Yes, but—"

"Excellent." Colin barged in, pulling Penelope along with him. "Where is she?"

"In the drawing room, but I should tell you—"

But Colin was already halfway down the hall, Penelope one step behind him. (Not that she could be anywhere else, seeing as how his hand was wrapped rather tightly around her upper arm.)

"Mr. Bridgerton!" the butler yelled out, sounding slightly panicked.

Penelope twisted, even as her feet continued to follow Colin. Briarly never panicked. About anything. If he didn't think she and Colin ought to enter the drawing room, he had to have a very good reason.

Maybe even—

Oh, *no*.

Penelope dug in her heels, skidding along the hardwood floor as Colin dragged her along by the arm. "Colin," she said, gulping on the first syllable. "Colin!"

"What?" he asked, not breaking his stride.

"I really think—Aaack!" Her skidding heels hit the edge of the runner carpet, sending her flying forward.

He caught her neatly and set her on her feet. "What is it?"

She glanced nervously at the door to the drawing room. It was slightly ajar, but maybe there was enough noise inside so that her mother hadn't yet heard them approaching.

"Penelope . . ." Colin prompted impatiently.

"Er . . ." There was still time to escape, wasn't there? She looked frantically about, not that she was likely to find a solution to her problems anywhere in the hall.

"Penelope," Colin said, now tapping his foot, "what the devil is the matter?"

She looked back to Briarly, who simply shrugged his shoulders. "This really might not be the best time to speak to my mother."

He raised one brow, looking rather like the butler had just seconds earlier. "You're not planning to refuse me, are you?"

"No, of course not," she said hastily, even though she hadn't truly accepted the fact that he even intended to offer for her.

"Then this is an excellent time," he stated, his tone inviting no further protest.

"But it's—"

"What?"

Tuesday, she thought miserably. And it was just past noon, which meant—

"Let's go," Colin said, striding forward, and before she could stop him, he pushed open the door.

Colin's first thought upon stepping into the drawing room was that the day, while certainly not proceeding in any manner he might have anticipated when he'd risen from bed that morning, was turning out to be a most excellent endeavor. Marriage to Penelope was an eminently sensible idea, and surprisingly appealing as well, if their recent encounter in the carriage was any indication.

His second thought was that he'd just entered his worst nightmare.

Because Penelope's mother was not alone in the drawing room. Every last Featherington, current and former, was there, along with assorted spouses and even a cat.

It was the most frightening assemblage of people Colin had ever witnessed. Penelope's family was . . . well . . . except for Felicity (whom he'd always held in some suspicion; how could one truly trust anyone who was such good friends with Hyacinth?), her family was . . . well . . .

He couldn't think of a good word for it. Certainly nothing complimentary (although he'd like to think he could have avoided an outright insult), and really, was there a word that effectively combined slightly dim, overly talkative, rather meddlesome, excruciatingly dull, and—and one couldn't forget this, not with Robert Huxley a recent addition to the clan—uncommonly loud.

So Colin just smiled. His great, big, friendly, slightly mischievous smile. It almost always worked, and today was no exception. The Featheringtons all smiled right back at him, and—thank God—said nothing.

At least not right away.

"Colin," Mrs. Featherington said with visible surprise. "How nice of you to bring Penelope home for our family meeting."

"Your family meeting?" he echoed. He looked to Penelope, who was standing next to him, looking rather ill.

"Every Tuesday," she said, smiling weakly. "Didn't I mention it?"

"No," he replied, even though it was obvious her question had been for the benefit of their audience. "No, you didn't mention it."

"Bridgerton!" bellowed Robert Huxley, who was married to Penelope's eldest sister Prudence.

"Huxley," Colin returned, taking a discreet step back. Best to protect his eardrums in case Penelope's brother-in-law decided to leave his post near the window.

Thankfully, Huxley stayed put, but Penelope's other brother-in-law, the well-meaning but vacant-minded Nigel Berbrooke, did cross the room, greeting Colin with a hearty slap on the back. "Wasn't expecting you," Berbrooke said jovially.

"No," Colin murmured, "I wouldn't think so."

"Just family, after all," Berbrooke said, "and you're not family. Not my family, at least."

"Not yet, anyway," Colin murmured, stealing a glance at Penelope. She was blushing.

Then he looked back at Mrs. Featherington, who looked as if she might faint from excitement. Colin groaned through his smile. He hadn't meant for her to hear his comment about possibly joining the family. For some reason he'd wanted to retain an element of surprise before he asked for Penelope's hand. If Portia Featherington knew his intentions ahead of time, she'd likely twist the whole thing around (in her mind, at least) so that she had somehow orchestrated the match herself.

And for some reason, Colin found that exceedingly distasteful.

"I hope I'm not intruding," he said to Mrs. Featherington.

"No, of course not," she said quickly. "We are delighted to have you here, at a *family* gathering." But she looked rather odd, not precisely undecided about his presence there, but certainly unsure of what her next move should be. She was chewing on her lower lip, and then she darted a furtive glance at Felicity, of all people.

Colin turned to Felicity. She was looking at Penelope, a

small secret smile fixed to her face. Penelope was glaring at her mother, her mouth twisted into an irritated grimace.

Colin's gaze went from Featherington to Featherington to Featherington. Something was clearly simmering under the surface here and if he weren't trying to figure out (A) how to avoid being trapped into conversation with Penelope's relations while (B) somehow managing to issue a proposal of marriage at the same time—well, he'd be rather curious as to what was causing all the secret, underhanded glances being tossed back and forth between the Featherington women.

Mrs. Featherington cast one last glance at Felicity, did a little gesture that Colin could have sworn meant, *Sit up straight,* then fixed her attention on Colin. "Won't you sit down?" she asked, smiling widely and patting the seat next to her on the sofa.

"Of course," he murmured, because there was really no getting out of it now. He still had to ask for Penelope's hand in marriage, and even if he didn't particularly want to do it in front of every last Featherington (and their two inane spouses), he was stuck here, at least until a polite opportunity to make his escape presented itself.

He turned and offered his arm to the woman he intended to make his bride. "Penelope?"

"Er, yes, of course," she stammered, placing her hand at the crook of his elbow.

"Oh, yes," Mrs. Featherington said, as if she'd completely forgotten about her daughter's presence. "Terribly sorry, Penelope. Didn't see you. Won't you please go and ask Cook to increase our order? We'll surely need more food with Mr. Bridgerton here."

"Of course," Penelope said, the corners of her lips quivering.

"Can't she ring for it?" Colin asked loudly.

"What?" Mrs. Featherington said distractedly. "Well, I

suppose she could, but it would take longer, and Penelope doesn't mind, do you?"

Penelope gave her head a little shake.

"I mind," Colin said.

Mrs. Featherington let out a little "Oh" of surprise, then said, "Very well. Penelope, er, why don't you sit right there?" She motioned to a chair that was not quite situated to be a part of the inner conversation circle.

Felicity, who was seated directly across from her mother, jumped up. "Penelope, please take my seat."

"No," Mrs. Featherington said firmly. "You have been feeling under the weather, Felicity. You need to sit."

Colin thought Felicity looked the picture of perfect health, but she sat back down.

"Penelope," Prudence said loudly, from over by the window. "I need to speak with you."

Penelope glanced helplessly from Colin to Prudence to Felicity to her mother.

Colin yanked her in closer. "I need to speak with her as well," he said smoothly.

"Right, well, I suppose there is room for both of you," Mrs. Featherington said, scooting over on the sofa.

Colin was caught between the good manners that had been drummed into his head since birth and the overwhelming urge to strangle the woman who would someday be his mother-in-law. He had no idea why she was treating Penelope like some sort of lesser-favored stepchild, but really, it had to stop.

"What brings you this way?" yelled Robert Huxley.

Colin touched his ears—he couldn't help himself—then said, "I was—"

"Oh, goodness," fluttered Mrs. Featherington, "we do not mean to interrogate our guest, do we?"

Colin hadn't really thought Huxley's question constituted an interrogation, but he didn't really want to insult Mrs. Featherington by saying so, so he merely nodded and said something completely meaningless like, "Yes, well, of course."

"Of course what?" asked Philippa.

Philippa was married to Nigel Berbrooke, and Colin had always thought it was a rather good match, indeed.

"I'm sorry?" he queried.

"You said, 'Of course,'" Philippa said. "Of course what?"

"I don't know," Colin said.

"Oh. Well, then, why did you—"

"Philippa," Mrs. Featherington said loudly, "perhaps you should fetch the food, since Penelope has forgotten to ring for it."

"Oh, I'm sorry," Penelope said quickly, starting to rise to her feet.

"Don't worry," Colin said through a smooth smile, grabbing hold of her hand and yanking her back down. "Your mother said Prudence could go."

"Philippa," Penelope said.

"What about Philippa?"

"She said Philippa could go, not Prudence."

He wondered what had happened to her brain, because somewhere between his carriage and this sofa, it had clearly disappeared. "Does it matter?" he asked.

"No, not really, but—"

"Felicity," Mrs. Featherington interrupted, "why don't you tell Mr. Bridgerton about your watercolors?"

For the life of him, Colin couldn't imagine a less interesting topic (except, maybe, for Philippa's watercolors), but he nonetheless turned to the youngest Featherington with a friendly smile and asked, "And how are your watercolors?"

But Felicity, bless her heart, gave him a rather friendly smile herself and said nothing but, "I imagine they're fine, thank you."

Mrs. Featherington looked as if she'd just swallowed a live eel, then exclaimed, "Felicity!"

"Yes?" Felicity said sweetly.

"You didn't tell him that you'd won an award." She turned to Colin. "Felicity's watercolors are very unique." She turned back to Felicity. "Do tell Mr. Bridgerton about your award."

"Oh, I don't imagine he is interested in that."

"Of course he is," Mrs. Featherington ground out.

Normally, Colin would have chimed in with, *Of course I am,* since he was, after all, an exceedingly affable fellow, but doing so would have validated Mrs. Featherington's statement and, perhaps more critically, ruined Felicity's good fun.

And Felicity appeared to be having a *lot* of fun. "Philippa," she said, "weren't you going to go after the food?"

"Oh, right," Philippa replied. "Forgot all about it. I do that a lot. Come along, Nigel. You can keep me company."

"Right-o!" Nigel beamed. And then he and Philippa left the room, giggling all the way.

Colin reaffirmed his conviction that the Berbrooke-Featherington match had been a good one, indeed.

"I think I shall go out to the garden," Prudence suddenly announced, taking hold of her husband's arm. "Penelope, why don't you come with me?"

Penelope opened her mouth a few seconds before she figured out what to say, leaving her looking a little bit like a confused fish (but in Colin's opinion a rather fetching fish, if such a thing were possible). Finally, her chin took on a resolute mien, and she said, "I don't think so, Prudence."

"Penelope!" Mrs. Featherington exclaimed.

"I need you to show me something," Prudence ground out.

"I really think I'm needed here," Penelope replied. "I can join you later this afternoon, if you like."

"I need you *now*."

Penelope looked to her sister in surprise, clearly not expecting quite so much resistance. "I'm sorry, Prudence," she reiterated. "I believe I'm needed here."

"Nonsense," Mrs. Featherington said breezily. "Felicity and I can keep Mr. Bridgerton company."

Felicity jumped to her feet. "Oh, no!" she exclaimed, her eyes round and innocent. "I forgot something."

"What," Mrs. Featherington asked between her teeth, "could you possibly have forgotten?"

"Uhh . . . my watercolors." She turned to Colin with a sweet, mischievous smile. "You did want to see them, didn't you?"

"Of course," he murmured, deciding he very much liked Penelope's younger sister. "Seeing as how they are so unique."

"One might say they are uniquely ordinary," Felicity said with an overly earnest nod.

"Penelope," Mrs. Featherington said, obviously trying to hide her annoyance, "would you be so kind as to fetch Felicity's watercolors?"

"Penelope doesn't know where they are," Felicity said quickly.

"Why don't you tell her?"

"For God's sake," Colin finally exploded, "let Felicity go. I need a private moment with you, anyway."

Silence reigned. It was the first time Colin Bridgerton had ever lost his temper in public. Beside him, Colin heard Penelope let out a little gasp, but when he glanced at her, she was hiding a tiny smile behind her hand.

And that made him feel ridiculously good.

"A private moment?" Mrs. Featherington echoed, her hand fluttering to her chest. She glanced over at Prudence and Robert, who were still standing by the window. They immediately left the room, although not without a fair bit of grumbling on Prudence's part.

"Penelope," Mrs. Featherington said, "perhaps you should accompany Felicity."

"Penelope will remain," Colin ground out.

"Penelope?" Mrs. Featherington asked doubtfully.

"Yes," he said slowly, in case she still didn't understand his meaning, "Penelope."

"But—"

Colin gave her such a glare that she actually drew back and folded her hands in her lap.

"I'm gone!" Felicity chirped, sailing out of the room. But before she closed the door behind her, Colin saw her give a quick wink to Penelope.

And Penelope smiled, love for her younger sister shining clearly in her eyes.

Colin relaxed. He hadn't realized just how tense Penelope's misery was making him. And she was definitely miserable. Good God, he couldn't wait to remove her from the bosom of her ridiculous family.

Mrs. Featherington's lips spread into a feeble attempt at a smile. She looked from Colin to Penelope and back again, and then finally said, "You desired a word?"

"Yes," he replied, eager to get this done with. "I would be honored if you would grant me your daughter's hand in marriage."

For a moment Mrs. Featherington made no reaction. Then her eyes grew round, her mouth grew round, her body—well, her body was already round—and she clapped her hands together, unable to say anything other than, "Oh! Oh!"

And then, "Felicity! Felicity!"

Felicity?

Portia Featherington jumped to her feet, ran to the door and actually screamed like a fishwife. "Felicity! Felicity!"

"Oh, Mother," Penelope moaned, closing her eyes.

"Why are you summoning Felicity?" Colin asked, rising to his feet.

Mrs. Featherington turned to him quizzically. "Don't you want to marry Felicity?"

Colin actually thought he might be sick. "No, for God's

sake, I don't want to marry Felicity," he snapped. "If I'd wanted to marry Felicity, I'd hardly have sent her upstairs for her bloody watercolors, would I?"

Mrs. Featherington swallowed uncomfortably. "Mr. Bridgerton," she said, wringing her hands together. "I don't understand."

He stared at her in horror, which then turned to disgust. "Penelope," he said, grabbing her hand and yanking her until she was pressed close to his side. "I want to marry Penelope."

"Penelope?" Mrs. Featherington echoed. "But—"

"But what?" he interrupted, his voice pure menace.

"But—but—"

"It's all right, Colin," Penelope said hastily. "I—"

"No, it is not all right," he exploded. "I've never given any indication I'm the least bit interested in Felicity."

Felicity appeared in the doorway, clapped her hand over her mouth, and quickly disappeared, wisely shutting the door behind her.

"Yes," Penelope said placatingly, shooting a quick look at her mother, "but Felicity is unmarried, and—"

"So are you," he pointed out.

"I know, but I'm old, and—"

"And Felicity is an *infant,*" he spat. "Good God, marrying her would be like marrying Hyacinth."

"Er, except for the incest," Penelope said.

He gave her an extremely unamused look.

"Right," she said, mostly to fill the silence. "It's just a terrible misunderstanding, isn't it?"

No one said anything. Penelope looked at Colin pleadingly. "Isn't it?"

"It certainly is," he muttered.

She turned to her mother. "Mama?"

"Penelope?" she murmured, and Penelope knew that her mother wasn't asking her a question; rather, she was still expressing her disbelief that Colin would want to marry her.

And oh, but it hurt so much. You'd think she'd be used to it by now.

"I would like to marry Mr. Bridgerton," Penelope said, trying to summon up as much quiet dignity as she could manage. "He asked me, and I said yes."

"Well, of course you would say yes," her mother retorted. "You'd have to be an idiot to say no."

"Mrs. Featherington," Colin said tightly, "I suggest you begin treating my future wife with a bit more respect."

"Colin, it's not necessary," Penelope said, placing her hand on his arm, but the truth was—her heart was soaring. He might not love her, but he cared about her. No man could defend a woman with such fierce protectiveness without caring for her a little.

"It *is* necessary," he returned. "For God's sake, Penelope, I arrived with you. I made it abundantly clear that I required your presence in the room, and I practically shoved Felicity out the door to fetch her watercolors. Why on earth would anyone think I wanted Felicity?"

Mrs. Featherington opened and closed her mouth several times before finally saying, "I love Penelope, of course, but—"

"But do you know her?" Colin shot back. "She's lovely and intelligent and has a fine sense of humor. Who wouldn't want to marry a woman like that?"

Penelope would have melted to the floor if she weren't already holding on to his hand. "Thank you," she whispered, not caring if her mother heard her, not even really caring if Colin heard her. Somehow she needed to say the words for herself.

Not what she thought she was.

Lady Danbury's face swam before her eyes, her expression warm and just a little bit cunning.

Something more. Maybe Penelope was something more, and maybe Colin was the only other person to realize that as well.

It made her love him all the more.

Her mother cleared her throat, then stepped forward and gave Penelope a hug. It was, at first, a hesitant embrace on both of their parts, but then Portia tightened her arms around her thirdborn daughter, and with a choked cry, Penelope found herself returning the hug in equal measure.

"I do love you, Penelope," Portia said, "and I am very pleased for you." She drew back and wiped a tear from her eye. "I shall be lonely without you, of course, since I'd assumed we would grow old together, but this is what's best for you, and that, I suppose, is what being a mother is all about."

Penelope let out a loud sniffle, then blindly reached for Colin's handkerchief, which he had already pulled from his pocket and was holding in front of her.

"You'll learn someday," Portia said, patting her on the arm. She turned to Colin and said, "We are delighted to welcome you to the family."

He nodded, not terribly warmly, but Penelope thought he made a rather nice effort considering how angry he'd been just moments earlier.

Penelope smiled and squeezed his hand, aware that she was about to embark upon the adventure of her life.

Chapter 15

"You know," Eloise said, three days after Colin and Penelope made their surprise announcement, "it's really a pity that Lady Whistledown has retired, because this would have been the coup of the decade."

"Certainly from Lady Whistledown's viewpoint," Penelope murmured, lifting her teacup to her lips and keeping her eyes trained on the wall clock in Lady Bridgerton's informal drawing room. Better not to look at Eloise directly. She had a way of noticing secrets in a person's eyes.

It was funny. Penelope had gone years without worrying that Eloise would discover the truth about Lady Whistledown. At least, not worrying overmuch. But now that Colin knew, it somehow felt as if her secret were floating about in the air, like particles of dust just waiting to form into a cloud of knowledge.

Maybe the Bridgertons were like dominoes. Once one found out, it was only a matter of time before they all fell.

"What do you mean?" Eloise asked, breaking into Penelope's nervous thoughts.

"If I recall correctly," Penelope said, very carefully, "she once wrote that she would have to retire if I ever married a Bridgerton."

Eloise's eyes bugged out. "She did?"

"Or something like that," Penelope said.

"You're joking," Eloise said, making a "pffft" sort of sound as she waved her hand dismissively. "She would never have been that cruel."

Penelope coughed, not really thinking that she could end the topic by faking a biscuit crumb in her throat, but trying nonetheless.

"No, really," Eloise persisted. "What did she say?"

"I don't recall, precisely."

"Try."

Penelope stalled by setting her cup down and reaching for another biscuit. They were alone for tea, which was odd. But Lady Bridgerton had dragged Colin off on some errand regarding the upcoming wedding—set for only a month hence!—and Hyacinth was off shopping with Felicity, who had, upon hearing Penelope's news, thrown her arms around her sister and shrieked her delight until Penelope's ears had gone numb.

As far as sisterly moments went, it had been something wonderful.

"Well," Penelope said, chewing on a bite of biscuit, "I believe she said that if I married a Bridgerton, it would be the end of the world as she knew it, and as she wouldn't be able to make heads or tails of such a world, she would have to retire immediately."

Eloise stared at her for a moment. "That's not a precise recollection?"

"One doesn't forget things like that," Penelope demurred.

"Hmmmph." Eloise's nose wrinkled with disdain. "Well, that was rather horrid of her, I must say. Now I doubly wish she were still writing, because she would have to eat an entire gaggle of crow."

"Do crows gather in gaggles?"

"I don't know," Eloise replied promptly, "but they should."

"You're a very good friend, Eloise," Penelope said quietly.

"Yes," Eloise said with an affected sigh, "I know. The very best."

Penelope smiled. Eloise's breezy reply made it clear that she wasn't in the mood for emotion or nostalgia. Which was fine. There was a time and a place for everything. Penelope had said what she wanted to say, and she knew that Eloise returned the sentiment, even if she preferred to joke and tease at that moment.

"I must confess, though," Eloise said, reaching for another biscuit, "you and Colin did surprise me."

"We surprised me as well," Penelope admitted wryly.

"Not that I'm not delighted," Eloise hastened to add. "There is no one I'd rather have as a sister. Well, aside from the ones I already have, of course. And if I'd ever dreamed the two of you were inclined in that direction, I'm sure I would have meddled horribly."

"I know," Penelope said, laughter forcing her lips up at the corners.

"Yes, well"—Eloise waved the comment away—"I'm not known for minding my own business."

"What's that on your fingers?" Penelope asked, leaning forward for a better look.

"What? That? Oh, nothing." But she settled her hands in her lap nonetheless.

"It's not nothing," Penelope said. "Let me see. It looks like ink."

"Well, of course it does. It *is* ink."

"Then why didn't you say so when I asked?"

"Because," Eloise said pertly, "it's none of your business."

Penelope drew back in shock at Eloise's sharp tone. "I'm terribly sorry," she said stiffly. "I had no idea it was such a sensitive subject."

"Oh, it's not," Eloise said quickly. "Don't be silly. It's just that I'm clumsy and I can't write without getting ink all over my fingers. I suppose I could wear gloves, but then *they'd* be stained, and I'd be forever replacing them, and I can assure you that I have no wish to spend my entire allowance—meager as it is—on gloves."

Penelope stared at her through her lengthy explanation, then asked, "What were you writing?"

"Nothing," Eloise said dismissively. "Just letters."

Penelope could tell from Eloise's brisk tone that she didn't particularly want to subject the topic to further exploration, but she was being so uncharacteristically evasive that Penelope couldn't resist asking, "To whom?"

"The letters?"

"Yes," Penelope replied, even though she thought that was rather obvious.

"Oh, no one."

"Well, unless they're a diary, they're not to *no one,*" Penelope said, impatience adding a short tinge to her voice.

Eloise gave her a vaguely affronted look. "You're rather nosy today."

"Only because you're being so evasive."

"They're just to Francesca," Eloise said with a little snort.

"Well, then, why didn't you say so?"

Eloise crossed her arms. "Perhaps I didn't appreciate your questioning me."

Penelope's mouth fell open. She couldn't remember the last time she and Eloise had had anything even remotely approaching a row. "Eloise," she said, her shock showing in her voice, "what is wrong?"

"Nothing is wrong."

"I know that's not true."

Eloise said nothing, just pursed her lips and glanced toward the window, a clear attempt to end the conversation.

"Are you angry with me?" Penelope persisted.

"Why would I be angry with you?"

"I don't know, but it's clear that you are."

Eloise let out a little sigh. "I'm not angry."

"Well, you're *some*thing."

"I'm just . . . I'm just . . ." She shook her head. "I don't know what I am. Restless, I suppose. Out of sorts."

Penelope was silent as she digested that, then said quietly, "Is there anything I can do?"

"No." Eloise smiled wryly. "If there were, you can be sure I'd have already asked it of you."

Penelope felt something that was almost a laugh rising within her. How like Eloise to make such a comment.

"I suppose it's . . ." Eloise began, her chin lifting in thought. "No, never mind."

"No," Penelope said, reaching out and taking her friend's hand. "Tell me."

Eloise pulled her hand free and looked away. "You'll think I'm silly."

"Maybe," Penelope said with a smile, "but you'll still be my very closest friend."

"Oh, Penelope, but I'm not," Eloise said sadly. "I'm not worthy of it."

"Eloise, don't talk such madness. I'd have gone right-out insane trying to navigate London and society and the *ton* without you."

Eloise smiled. "We did have fun, didn't we?"

"Well, yes, when I was with you," Penelope admitted. "The rest of the time I was bloody miserable."

"Penelope! I don't believe I've ever heard you curse before."

Penelope gave her a sheepish smile. "It slipped out. And besides, I couldn't possibly think of a better adjective to describe life for a wallflower among the *ton*."

Eloise let out an unexpected chuckle. "Now, that's a book I would like to read: *A Wallflower Among the Ton*."

"Not unless you're given to tragedies."

"Oh, come, now, it couldn't be a tragedy. It would have to be a romance. You're getting your happy ending, after all."

Penelope smiled. As strange as it was, she *was* getting her happy ending. Colin had been a lovely and attentive fiancé, at least for the three days that he'd been playing that role. And it couldn't have been particularly easy; they'd been subject to more speculation and scrutiny than Penelope could have imagined.

She wasn't surprised, though; when she (as Lady Whistledown) had written that the world would end as she knew it if a Featherington married a Bridgerton, she rather thought she'd been echoing a prevalent sentiment.

To say that the *ton* had been shocked by Penelope's engagement would have been an understatement, indeed.

But much as Penelope liked to anticipate and reflect upon her upcoming marriage, she was still a bit disturbed about Eloise's strange mood. "Eloise," she said seriously, "I want you to tell me what has you so upset."

Eloise sighed. "I'd hoped you'd forgotten about it."

"I've learned tenacity from the master," Penelope commented.

That made Eloise smile, but only for a moment. "I feel so disloyal," she said.

"What have you done?"

"Oh, nothing." She patted her heart. "It's all inside. I—" She stopped, looked to the side, her eyes settling on the fringed corner of the carpet, but Penelope suspected that she didn't see much of anything. At least nothing beyond what was rumbling about in her mind.

"I'm so happy for you," Eloise said, the words tumbling forth in odd bursts, punctuated by awkward pauses. "And I honestly think I can really, truly say that I'm not jealous. But at the same time . . ."

Penelope waited for Eloise to collect her thoughts. Or maybe she was collecting her courage.

"At the same time," she said, so softly that Penelope could barely hear her, "I suppose I always thought you'd be a spinster right along with me. I've chosen this life. I know that I have. I could have married."

"I know," Penelope said quietly.

"But I never did, because it never seemed right, and I didn't want to settle for anything less than what my brothers and sister have. And now Colin, too," she said, motioning toward Penelope.

Penelope didn't mention that Colin had never said he loved her. It didn't seem like the right time, or, frankly, the sort of thing she cared to share. Besides, even if he didn't love her, she still thought he cared about her, and that was enough.

"I would never have wanted you *not* to marry," Eloise explained, "I just never thought you would." She closed her eyes, looking quite agonized. "That came out all wrong. I've insulted you terribly."

"No, you haven't," Penelope said, meaning it. "I never thought I would marry, either."

Eloise nodded sadly. "And somehow, it made it all . . . all right. I was almost twenty-eight and unmarried, and you were already twenty-eight and unmarried, and we'd always have each other. But now you have Colin."

"I still have you, too. At least I hope I do."

"Of course you do," Eloise said fervently. "But it won't be the same. You must cleave unto your husband. Or at least that's what they all say," she added with a slightly mischievous spark in her eyes. "Colin will come first, and that is how it should be. And frankly," she added, her smile growing a bit sly, "I'd have to kill you if he didn't. He *is* my favorite brother, after all. It really wouldn't do for him to have a disloyal wife."

Penelope laughed out loud at that.

"Do you hate me?" Eloise asked.

Penelope shook her head. "No," she said softly. "If anything I love you all the more, because I know how difficult it must have been to be honest with me about this."

"I'm so glad you said that," Eloise said with a loud, dramatic sigh. "I was terrified you'd say that the only solution would be for me to find myself a husband as well."

The thought had crossed Penelope's mind, but she shook her head and said, "Of course not."

"Good. Because my mother has been saying it constantly."

Penelope smiled wryly. "I'd be surprised if she hadn't."

"Good afternoon, ladies!"

The two women looked up to see Colin entering the room. Penelope's heart did a little flip upon seeing him, and she found herself oddly out of breath. Her heart had been doing little flips for years whenever he walked into a room, but it was somehow different now, more intense.

Perhaps because she *knew*.

Knew what it was like to be with him, to be wanted by him.

To know that he would be her husband.

Her heart flipped again.

Colin let out a loud groan. "You ate all the food?"

"There was only one small plate of biscuits," Eloise said in their defense.

"That's not what I was led to believe," Colin grumbled.

Penelope and Eloise shared a glance, then both burst out laughing.

"What?" Colin demanded, leaning down to press a quick, dutiful kiss on Penelope's cheek.

"You sounded so sinister," Eloise explained. "It's just food."

"It's never just food," Colin said, plopping down in a chair.

Penelope was still wondering when her cheek would stop tingling.

"So," he said, taking a half-eaten biscuit off of Eloise's plate, "what were you two talking about?"

"Lady Whistledown," Eloise said promptly.

Penelope choked on her tea.

"Were you?" Colin said softly, but Penelope detected a definite edge in his voice.

"Yes," Eloise said. "I was telling Penelope that it is really too bad she's retired, since your engagement would have been quite the most newsworthy piece of gossip we've had all year."

"Interesting how that works out," Colin murmured.

"Mmmm," Eloise agreed, "and she surely would have devoted an entire column just to your engagement ball tomorrow night."

Penelope did not lower her teacup from her mouth.

"Do you want some more?" Eloise asked her.

Penelope nodded and handed her the cup, although she very much missed having it in front of her face as a shield. She knew that Eloise had blurted out Lady Whistledown's name because she did not want Colin to know that she had mixed feelings about his marriage, but still, Penelope fervently wished that Eloise had said anything else in reply to Colin's question.

"Why don't you ring for more food?" Eloise asked Colin.

"Already did so," he answered. "Wickham intercepted me in the hall and asked if I was hungry." He popped the last bite of Eloise's biscuit into his mouth. "Wise man, that Wickham."

"Where did you go today, Colin?" Penelope asked, eager to get the topic firmly off of Lady Whistledown.

He gave his head a beleaguered shake. "Devil if I know. Mother dragged me from shop to shop."

"Aren't you thirty-three years old?" Eloise inquired sweetly.

He answered her with a scowl.

"Just thought you'd be beyond the age of having Mother drag you about, that's all," she murmured.

"Mother will be dragging all of us about when we're doddering old fools, and you know it," he replied. "Besides, she's so delighted to see me married, I really can't bring myself to spoil her fun."

Penelope sighed. This had to be why she loved the man. Anyone who treated his mother so well would surely be an excellent husband.

"And how are your wedding preparations coming along?" Colin asked Penelope.

She hadn't meant to pull a face, but she did, anyway. "I have never been so exhausted in all my life," she admitted.

He reached over and grabbed a large crumb off of her plate. "We should elope."

"Oh, could we *really?*" Penelope asked, the words flying from her lips in an unsummoned rush.

He blinked. "Actually, I was joking, mostly, although it does seem a prime idea."

"I shall arrange for a ladder," Eloise said, clapping her hands together, "so that you might climb to her room and steal her away."

"There's a tree," Penelope said. "Colin will have no difficulty with it."

"Good God," he said, "you're not serious, are you?"

"No," she sighed. "But I could be. If you were."

"I can't be. Do you know what it would do to my mother?" He rolled his eyes. "Not to mention yours."

Penelope groaned. "I know."

"She'd hunt me down and kill me," Colin said.

"Mine or yours?"

"Both. They'd join forces." He craned his neck toward the door. "*Where* is the food?"

"You just got here, Colin," Eloise said. "Give them time."

"And here I thought Wickham a sorcerer," he grumbled, "able to conjure food with the snap of his hand."

"Here you are, sir!" came Wickham's voice as he sailed into the room with a large tray.

"See?" Colin said, raising his brows first at Eloise and then at Penelope. "I told you so."

"Why," Penelope asked, "do I sense that I will be hearing those words from your lips far too many times in my future?"

"Most likely because you will," Colin replied. "You'll soon learn"—he shot her an extremely cheeky grin—"that I am almost always right."

"Oh, *please,*" Eloise groaned.

"I may have to side with Eloise on this one," Penelope said.

"Against your husband?" He placed a hand on his heart (while the other one reached for a sandwich). "I'm wounded."

"You're not my husband yet."

Colin turned to Eloise. "The kitten has claws."

Eloise raised her brows. "You didn't realize that before you proposed?"

"Of course I did," he said, taking a bite of his sandwich. "I just didn't think she'd use them on me."

And then he looked at her with such a hot, masterful expression that Penelope's bones went straight to water.

"Well," Eloise announced, rising quite suddenly to her feet, "I think I shall allow you two soon-to-be-newlyweds a moment or two of privacy."

"How positively forward-thinking of you," Colin murmured.

Eloise looked to him with a peevish twist to her mouth. "Anything for you, dear brother. Or rather," she added, her expression growing arch, "anything for Penelope."

Colin stood and turned to his betrothed, "I seem to be slipping down the pecking order."

Penelope just smiled behind her teacup and said, "I am making it my policy never to get in the middle of a Bridgerton spat."

"Oh ho!" Eloise chortled. "You'll not be able to keep to that one, I'm afraid, Mrs. Soon-to-be-Bridgerton. Besides," she added with a wicked grin, "if you think this is a spat, I can't wait until you see us in full form."

"You mean I haven't?" Penelope asked.

Both Eloise and Colin shook their heads in a way that made her extremely fearful.

Oh, dear.

"Is there something I should know?" Penelope asked.

Colin grinned rather wolfishly. "It's too late now."

Penelope gave Eloise a helpless glance, but all she did was laugh as she left the room, closing the door firmly behind her.

"Now, *that* was nice of Eloise," Colin murmured.

"What?" Penelope asked innocently.

His eyes gleamed. "The door."

"The door? Oh!" she yelped. "The door."

Colin smiled, moving over to the sofa beside her. There was something rather delightful about Penelope on a rainy afternoon. He'd hardly seen her since they'd become engaged—wedding plans had a way of doing that to a couple—and yet she'd not been out of his thoughts, even as he slept.

Funny how that happened. He'd spent years not really ever thinking about her unless she was standing in front of his face, and now she had permeated his every last thought.

His every last desire.

How had this happened?

When had it happened?

And did it really matter? Maybe the only important thing was that he wanted her and she was—or at least she would be—his. Once he put his ring on her finger, the hows, whys, and whens would become irrelevant, provided that this madness he felt never went away.

He touched his finger to her chin, tipping her face up to the light. Her eyes shone with anticipation, and her lips—dear God, how was it possible that the men of London had never noticed how perfect they were?

He smiled. This was a permanent madness. And he couldn't have been more pleased.

Colin had never been opposed to marriage. He'd simply been opposed to a dull marriage. He wasn't picky; he just wanted passion and friendship and intellectual conversation and a good laugh every now and then. A wife from whom he wouldn't want to stray.

Amazingly, he seemed to have found that in Penelope.

All he needed to do now was make sure her Big Secret remained just that. A secret.

Because he didn't think he could bear the pain he'd see in her eyes if she were cast out of society.

"Colin?" she whispered, her breath quivering across her lips, making him *really* want to kiss her.

He leaned in. "Hmmm?"

"You were so quiet."

"Just thinking."

"About what?"

He gave her an indulgent smile. "You really have been spending too much time with my sister."

"What does that mean?" she asked, her lips twitching in such a way that he knew she'd never feel any compunction at poking fun at him. She would keep him on his toes, this woman.

"You seem," he said, "to have developed a certain penchant for persistence."

"Tenacity?"

"That, too."

"But that's a good thing."

Their lips were still mere inches apart, but the urge to continue the teasing conversation was too strong. "When you're persistently avowing your obedience for your husband," he murmured, "that's a good thing."

"Oh, really?"

His chin dipped into the barest hint of a nod. "And when you're tenaciously holding on to my shoulders when I'm kissing you, that's a good thing as well."

Her dark eyes widened so delightfully that he had to add, "Don't you think?"

And then she surprised him.

"Like this?" she asked, placing her hands on his shoulders. Her tone was daring, her eyes pure flirtation.

Lord, he loved that she surprised him.

"That's a start," he said. "You might have to"—he moved one of his hands to cover hers, pressing her fingers into his skin—"hold me a little more tenaciously."

"I see," she murmured. "So what you're saying is that I should never let go?"

He thought about that for a moment. "Yes," he answered, realizing that there was a deeper meaning in her words, whether she'd intended it or not. "That's exactly what I'm saying."

And then words were simply not enough. He brought his lips to hers, remaining gentle for barely a second before his hunger overtook him. He kissed her with a passion he hadn't even known he possessed. It wasn't about desire—or at least it wasn't *just* about desire.

It was about need.

It was about a strange sensation, hot and fierce inside of him, urging him to lay claim to her, to somehow brand her as his.

He wanted her desperately, and he had absolutely no idea how he could possibly make it through an entire month before the wedding.

"Colin?" Penelope gasped, just as he was easing her down onto her back on the sofa.

He was kissing her jaw, and then her neck, and his lips were far too busy for anything other than a low, "Mmm?"

"We're—Oh!"

He smiled, even as he nipped her earlobe gently with his teeth. If she could finish a sentence, then he clearly wasn't befuddling her as much as he ought.

"You were saying?" he murmured, then kissed her deeply on the mouth, just to torture her.

He lifted his lips off hers just long enough for her to say, "I just—" and then he kissed her again, reeling with pleasure when she groaned with desire.

"I'm sorry," he said, scooting his hands under the hem of her dress and then using them to do all sorts of wicked things to her calves, "you were saying?"

"I was?" she asked, her eyes glazed.

He moved his hands higher, until they were tickling the back of her knee. "You were saying *some*thing," he said, pressing his hips against her because he honestly thought he would burst into flame at that very moment if he did not. "I think," he whispered, sliding his hand over the soft skin of her thigh, "that you were going to say that you wanted me to touch you *here*."

She gasped, then groaned, then somehow managed to say, "I don't think that was what I was going to say."

He grinned against her neck. "Are you sure?"

She nodded.

"So then you want me to stop?"

She shook her head. Frantically.

He could take her now, he realized. He could make love to her right there on his mother's sofa and not only would she let him, she would enjoy herself in every way a woman should.

It wouldn't be a conquest, it wouldn't even be seduction.

It would be more than that. Maybe even . . .

Love.

Colin froze.

"Colin?" she whispered, opening her eyes.

Love?

It wasn't possible.

"Colin?"

Or maybe it was.

"Is something wrong?"

It wasn't that he feared love, or didn't believe in it. He just hadn't . . . expected it.

He'd always thought love would hit a man like a thunderbolt, that one day you'd be loitering about at some party, bored to tears, and then you'd see a woman, and you'd know instantly that your life would be changed forever. That was what had happened to his brother Benedict, and heaven knew that he and his wife Sophie were blissfully happy rusticating away in the country.

But this thing with Penelope . . . it had crept up on him. The change had been slow, almost lethargic, and if it was love, well . . .

If it was love, wouldn't he *know*?

He watched her closely, curiously, thinking that maybe he'd find his answer in her eyes, or the sweep of her hair, or the way the bodice of her gown hung slightly crookedly. Maybe if he watched her long enough, he'd know.

"Colin?" she whispered, starting to sound slightly anxious.

He kissed her again, this time with a fierce determination. If this was love, wouldn't it become obvious when they kissed?

But if his mind and body were working separately, then the kiss was clearly in league with his body, because while his mind's confusion remained just as blurry as ever, his body's need was brought into sharper focus.

Hell, now he was in pain. And he really couldn't do anything about it here in his mother's drawing room, even if Penelope would have been a willing participant.

He pulled back, letting his hand slip down her leg toward the edge of her skirt. "We can't do this here."

"I know," she said, sounding so sad that his hand stilled on her knee, and he almost lost his resolve to do the right thing and mind the dictates of propriety.

He thought hard and fast. It was possible that he could make love to her and no one would walk in on them. Heaven knew that in his current state, it would be an embarrassingly fast endeavor, anyway.

"When is the wedding?" he growled.

"A month."

"What would it take to change that to a fortnight?"

She thought about that for a moment. "Bribery or blackmail. Maybe both. Our mothers will not be easily swayed."

He groaned, letting his hips sink against hers for one delicious moment before heaving himself off. He couldn't take her now. She was going to be his wife. There would be plenty of time for midday tumbles on illicit sofas, but he owed it to her to use a bed for the first time, at least.

"Colin?" she asked, straightening her dress and smoothing her hair, even though there was no way she was going to make the latter look anything even approaching presentable without a mirror, hairbrush, and maybe even a maid. "Is something wrong?"

"I want you," he whispered.

She looked up at him, startled.

"I just wanted you to know that," he said. "I didn't want you to think I stopped because you didn't please me."

"Oh." She looked as if she wanted to say something; she looked almost absurdly happy at his words. "Thank you for saying that."

He took her hand and squeezed.

"Do I look a mess?" she asked.

He nodded. "But you're *my* mess," he whispered.

And he was very glad for that.

Chapter 16

As Colin liked to walk, and in fact frequently did so to clear his mind, it was no surprise that he spent much of the next day traversing Bloomsbury . . . and Fitzrovia . . . and Marylebone . . . and in fact several other London neighborhoods, until he looked up and realized that he was standing in the heart of Mayfair, in Grosvenor Square, to be precise, outside of Hastings House, town home of the Dukes of Hastings, the latest of whom happened to be married to his sister Daphne.

It had been a while since they'd had a conversation, anything above the usual family chitchat, that was. Of all his siblings, Daphne was the closest in age to him, and they'd always shared a rather special bond, even though they didn't see each other as much as they used to, what with Colin's frequent travels and Daphne's busy family life.

Hastings House was one of those enormous mansions that one could find scattered throughout Mayfair and St. James's. Large and square and constructed of elegant Portland stone, it was thoroughly imposing in its ducal splendor.

Which made it all the more amusing, Colin thought with a wry grin, that his sister was the current duchess. He couldn't imagine anyone less haughty or imposing. In fact, Daphne had had difficulty finding a husband when she'd been out on the marriage mart, precisely because she *was* so friendly and easy to be with. Gentlemen had tended to think of her as their friend and not as a prospective bride.

But all that had changed when she'd met Simon Bassett, Duke of Hastings, and now she was a respectable society matron with four children, aged ten, nine, eight, and seven. It still sometimes seemed odd to Colin that his sister was a mother, of all things, while he still lived the free and unfettered life of a bachelor. With only one year between them, he and Daphne had always passed through the various stages of life together. Even when she'd married, things hadn't seemed so very different; she and Simon attended the same parties he did and had many of the same interests and pursuits.

But then she'd started reproducing, and while Colin was always delighted to welcome a new niece or nephew into his life, each arrival had brought home the fact that Daphne had moved on in a way he had not.

But, he thought, smiling as Penelope's face drifted through his mind, he supposed all that would soon change.

Children. It was a rather nice thought, actually.

He hadn't consciously meant to visit Daphne, but now that he was here, he figured he might as well stop by and say hello, so he marched up the steps and gave the big brass knocker a sturdy clanking. Jeffries, the butler, opened the door almost immediately.

"Mr. Bridgerton," he said. "Your sister was not expecting you."

"No, I decided to surprise her. Is she at home?"

"I shall see," the butler said with a nod, even though they both knew that Daphne would never refuse to see a member of her family.

Colin waited in the drawing room while Jeffries informed Daphne of his presence, wandering idly about, feeling too restless to sit or even stand in one place. After a few minutes,

Daphne appeared in the doorway, looking slightly disheveled but happy as always.

And why shouldn't she be? Colin wondered. All she'd ever wanted in life was to be a wife and mother, and it seemed that reality had more than surpassed her dreams.

"Hello there, sister," he said with a sloppy smile as he crossed the room to give her a quick hug. "You've got . . ." He motioned to his shoulder.

She looked down at her own shoulder, then smiled sheepishly as she saw the large dark gray smudge on the pale pink fabric of her dress. "Charcoal," she explained ruefully. "I've been trying to teach Caroline to draw."

"You?" Colin asked doubtfully.

"I know, I know," she said. "She really couldn't have picked a worse tutor, but she only decided yesterday that she loves art, so I'm all she's got on such short notice."

"You should pack her off to see Benedict," Colin suggested. "I'm sure he'd be happy to give her a lesson or two."

"The thought had already crossed my mind, but I'm sure she'll have moved on to some other pursuit by the time I can make the arrangements." She motioned to a sofa. "Sit. You look rather like a caged cat over there, pacing as you are."

He sat, even though he felt uncommonly fidgety.

"And before you ask," Daphne said, "I already told Jeffries to see to food. Will sandwiches be enough?"

"Could you hear my stomach grumbling from across the room?"

"From across town, I'm afraid." She laughed. "Did you know that whenever it thunders, David says that it's your stomach?"

"Oh, good God," Colin muttered, but he was chuckling all the while. His nephew was a rather clever little fellow.

Daphne smiled broadly as she settled down against the

sofa cushions, folding her hands elegantly in her lap. "What brings you by, Colin? Not that you need a reason, of course. It's always lovely to see you."

He shrugged. "Just passing by."

"Did you visit Anthony and Kate?" she asked. Bridgerton House, where their eldest brother lived with his family, was just across the square from Hastings House. "Benedict and Sophie are already there with the children, helping to prepare for your engagement ball tonight."

He shook his head. "No, you're my chosen victim, I'm afraid."

She smiled again, but this time it was a softer expression, tempered by a fair dose of curiosity. "Is something wrong?"

"No, of course not," he said quickly. "Why would you ask that?"

"I don't know." She cocked her head to the side. "You seem odd, that's all."

"Just tired."

She nodded knowingly. "Wedding plans, I'm sure."

"Yes," he said, jumping on the excuse, although for the life of him, he wasn't even sure what it was he was trying to hide from her.

"Well, remember that whatever you're going through," she said with a peevish twist to her lips, "it's a thousand times worse for Penelope. It's always worse for women. Trust me."

"For weddings or for everything?" he asked mildly.

"Everything," she said promptly. "I know you men think you're actually in charge, but—"

"I wouldn't dream of thinking we're actually in charge," Colin said, and not entirely sarcastically.

Her face pinched into a peevish expression. "Women have far more to do than men. *Especially* with weddings. With all the fittings I'm sure Penelope has had for her wedding gown, she probably feels like a pincushion."

"I suggested eloping," Colin said conversationally, "and I think she rather hoped I was serious."

Daphne chuckled. "I'm so glad you're marrying her, Colin."

He nodded, not planning to say anything, and then somehow, he was saying her name. "Daff—"

"Yes?"

He opened his mouth, and then—"Never mind."

"Oh, no, you don't," she said. "Now you really have my curiosity piqued."

He drummed his fingers against the sofa. "Do you suppose the food might arrive soon?"

"Are you even hungry or are you merely trying to change the subject?"

"I'm always hungry."

She was silent for several seconds. "Colin," she finally asked, her voice soft and carefully gentle, "what were you going to say?"

He jumped to his feet, too restless to remain still, and began to pace. He stopped, turned to her, looked at her concerned face. "It's nothing," he started to say, except it wasn't nothing, and—

"How does one know?" he blurted out, not even aware that he hadn't completed his question until she replied, "How does one know what?"

He stopped in front of the window. It looked like it might rain. He'd have to borrow a carriage from Daphne unless he wanted to get soaked on the long walk home. Yet, he didn't know why he was even thinking about precipitation, because what he really wanted to know was—

"How does one know *what,* Colin?" Daphne repeated.

He turned around and just let the words break free. "How do you know if it's love?"

For a moment she just stared at him, her large brown eyes wide with surprise, her lips parted and utterly still.

"Forget I asked," he muttered.

"No!" she exclaimed, jumping to her feet. "I'm *glad* you asked. Very glad. I'm just . . . surprised, I must say."

He closed his eyes, thoroughly disgusted with himself. "I can't believe I just asked you that."

"No, Colin, don't be silly. It's really rather . . . sweet that you asked. And I can't even begin to tell you how flattered I am that you would come to me when—"

"Daphne . . ." he said warningly. She had a way of wandering off the topic, and he really wasn't in the right frame of mind to follow her errant thoughts.

Impulsively, she reached out and hugged him; then, her hands still on his shoulders, she said, "I don't know."

"I beg your pardon?"

She gave her head a little shake. "I don't know how you know it's love. I think it's different for everyone."

"How did you know?"

She chewed on her lower lip for several seconds before replying, "I don't know."

"What?"

She shrugged helplessly. "I don't remember. It's been so long. I just . . . *knew.*"

"So what you're saying," he said, leaning against the windowsill and crossing his arms, "is that if one doesn't know one's in love, then one probably isn't."

"Yes," she said firmly. "No! No, that's not what I mean at all."

"Then what do you mean?"

"I don't know," she said weakly.

He stared at her. "And how long have you been married?" he muttered.

"Colin, don't tease. I'm trying to be helpful."

"And I appreciate the attempt, but truly, Daphne, you—"

"I know, I know," she interrupted. "I'm useless. But listen to me. Do you like Penelope?" Then she gasped in horror. "We are talking about Penelope, aren't we?"

"Of course we are," he snapped.

She let out a relieved sigh. "Good, because if we weren't, then I can assure you I would have had no advice whatsoever."

"I'll go," he said abruptly.

"No, don't," she pleaded, placing her hand on his arm. "Stay, Colin, please."

He looked at her, sighing, feeling defeated. "I feel like an ass."

"Colin," she said, guiding him to the sofa and pushing him down until he sat, "listen to me. Love grows and changes every day. And it isn't like some thunderbolt from the sky, instantly transforming you into a different man. I know Benedict says it was that way for him, and that's just lovely, but you know, Benedict is *not* normal."

Colin very much wanted to take that bait, but he just couldn't summon the energy.

"It wasn't like that for me," Daphne said, "and I don't think it was like that for Simon, although truthfully, I don't think I've ever asked."

"You should."

She paused while her mouth was forming a word, leaving her looking like a surprised bird. "Why?"

He shrugged. "So you can tell me."

"What, do you think it's different for men?"

"Everything else is."

She grimaced. "I'm beginning to develop a fair dose of pity for Penelope."

"Oh, absolutely you should," he agreed. "I'll make a dreadful husband, to be sure."

"You will not," she said, batting his arm. "Why on earth would you say that? You would never be unfaithful to her."

"No," he agreed. He was quiet for a moment, and when he finally spoke again, his voice was soft. "But I might not love her the way she deserves."

"But you *might*." She threw up her hands in a gesture of

exasperation. "For heaven's sake, Colin, just the fact that you're sitting here asking your *sister* about love probably means you're more than halfway there."

"Do you think?"

"If I didn't *think* so," she said, "I wouldn't have *said* so." She sighed. "Stop thinking so hard, Colin. You'll find marriage a lot easier if you simply allow it to be."

He eyed her suspiciously. "When did you grow so philosophical?"

"When you came by to see me and forced the issue," she said promptly. "You're marrying the right person. Stop worrying so much."

"I'm not worrying," he said automatically, but of course he *was* worrying, so he didn't even bother to defend himself when Daphne shot him an extremely sarcastic look. But it wasn't as if he were worrying whether Penelope was the right woman. He was certain of that.

And he wasn't worried about whether his marriage would be a good one. He was certain of that, as well.

No, he was worrying about stupid things. About whether or not he loved her, not because it would be the end of the world if he did (or the end of the world if he didn't), but because he found it extremely unsettling not to know exactly what it was he was feeling.

"Colin?"

He looked over at his sister, who was regarding him with a rather bemused expression. He stood, intending to leave before he embarrassed himself beyond repair, then leaned down and kissed her cheek. "Thank you," he said.

She narrowed her eyes. "I can't tell if you're serious or are teasing me for being an utter lack of help."

"You *were* an utter lack of help," he said, "but it's an honest thank-you, nonetheless."

"Points for effort?"

"Something like that."

"Are you going over to Bridgerton House now?" she asked.

"Why, so I may embarrass myself with Anthony next?"

"Or Benedict," she said. "He's there, too."

The thing about large families was, there was never a lack of opportunity to make a fool of oneself with a sibling. "No," he said with a small, wry smile, "I think I'll walk home."

"Walk?" she echoed, gaping.

He squinted toward the window. "Do you think it might rain?"

"Take my carriage, Colin," she insisted, "and please wait for the sandwiches. There is sure to be a mountain of them, and if you leave before they arrive, I know I'll eat half, and then I'll hate myself for the rest of the day."

He nodded and sat back down, and was glad he did. He'd always been partial to smoked salmon. In fact, he took a plate with him in the carriage, staring out the window the whole way home at the pouring rain.

When the Bridgertons threw a party, they did it right.

And when the Bridgertons threw an engagement ball . . . well, had Lady Whistledown still been writing, it would have taken at least three columns to chronicle the event.

Even this engagement ball, thrown together at the last minute (due to the fact that neither Lady Bridgerton nor Mrs. Featherington were willing to allow their children the possibility of changing their minds during a long engagement), easily qualified as *the* party of the season.

Although part of that, Penelope thought wryly, had little to do with the party itself and everything to do with the continued speculation over why on earth Colin Bridgerton would choose a nobody like Penelope Featherington to be his wife. It hadn't even been this bad when Anthony Bridgerton had married Kate Sheffield, who, like Penelope, had never been considered a diamond of the first water. But at least Kate hadn't been *old.* Penelope couldn't even begin to count the number of times she'd heard the word *spinster* whispered behind her back during the past few days.

But while the gossip was a bit tedious, it didn't really bother her, because she was still floating along on the cloud of her own bliss. A woman couldn't spend her entire adult life in love with one man and then not be almost stupid with happiness after he asked her to marry him.

Even if she couldn't quite figure out how it had all happened.

It *had* happened. That was all that mattered.

And Colin was everything anyone could dream of in a fiancé. He stuck to her side like glue the entire evening, and Penelope didn't even think he was doing it to protect her from gossip. In all truth, he seemed rather oblivious to the talk.

It was almost as if . . . Penelope smiled dreamily. It was almost as if Colin were remaining by her side because he wanted to be there.

"Did you see Cressida Twombley?" Eloise whispered in her ear while Colin was off dancing with his mother. "She's green with envy."

"That's just her dress," Penelope said with an impressively straight face.

Eloise laughed. "Oh, I wish Lady Whistledown were writing. She would *skewer* her."

"I think Lady Whistledown is supposed to *be* her," Penelope said carefully.

"Oh, pish and tosh. I don't believe for one moment that Cressida is Lady Whistledown, and I can't believe that you do, either."

"Probably not," Penelope allowed. She knew that her secret would be better protected if she claimed to believe Cressida's story, but anyone who knew her would have found that so out of character that it would have been quite suspicious indeed.

"Cressida just wanted the money," Eloise continued disdainfully. "Or maybe the notoriety. Probably both."

Penelope watched her nemesis, holding court on the other side of the room. Her regular crowd of cronies milled about, but they were joined by new people, as well, most likely curious about the Whistledown gossip. "Well, she's succeeded with the notoriety, at least."

Eloise nodded her agreement. "I cannot even imagine why she was invited. There is certainly no love lost between the two of you, and none of us like her."

"Colin insisted upon it."

Eloise turned to her with gaping jaw. "Why?"

Penelope suspected that the main reason was Cressida's recent claim to be Lady Whistledown; most of the *ton* wasn't sure whether or not she was lying, but no one was willing to deny her an invitation to an event, just in case she really was telling the truth.

And Colin and Penelope shouldn't have had any reason to know for certain otherwise.

But Penelope couldn't reveal this to Eloise, so she told her the rest of the story, which was still the truth. "Your mother didn't want to cause any gossip by cutting her, and Colin also said . . ."

She blushed. It was really too sweet.

"What?" Eloise demanded.

Penelope couldn't speak without smiling. "He said he wanted Cressida to be forced to watch me in my triumph."

"Oh. My. Word." Eloise looked as if she might need to sit down. "My brother is in love."

Penelope's blush turned a furious red.

"He is," Eloise exclaimed. "He must be. Oh, you must tell me. Has he said so?"

There was something both wonderful and horrible in listening to Eloise gush. On the one hand, it was always lovely to share life's most perfect moments with one's best friend, and Eloise's joy and excitement were certainly contagious.

But on the other hand, they weren't necessarily warranted, because Colin didn't love her. Or at least he hadn't said so.

But he acted like he did! Penelope clung to that thought, trying to focus on that, rather than the fact that he'd never said the words.

Actions spoke louder than words, didn't they?

And his actions made her feel like a princess.

"Miss Featherington! Miss Featherington!"

Penelope looked to her left and beamed. That voice could belong to no one other than Lady Danbury.

"Miss Featherington," Lady D said, poking her cane through the crowd until she was standing right in front of Penelope and Eloise.

"Lady Danbury, how nice to see you."

"Heh heh heh." Lady Danbury's wrinkled face became almost young again from the force of her smile. "It's always nice to see me, regardless of what anyone else says. And *you,* you little devil. Look what you did."

"Isn't it the *best*?" Eloise asked.

Penelope looked to her closest friend. For all her mixed emotions, Eloise was truly, honestly, and forever would be thrilled for her. Suddenly it didn't matter that they were standing in the middle of a crowded ballroom, with everyone staring at her as if she were some sort of specimen on a biology plate. She turned and gave Eloise a fierce hug, whispering, "I do love you," in her ear.

"I know you do," Eloise whispered back.

Lady Danbury banged her cane—loudly—on the floor. "I'm still standing here, ladies!"

"Oh, sorry," Penelope said sheepishly.

"It's all right," Lady D said, with an uncharacteristic level of indulgence. "It's rather nice to see two girls who'd rather embrace than stab each other in the back, if you must know."

"Thank you for coming over to congratulate me," Penelope said.

"I wouldn't have missed this for the world," Lady Danbury said. "Heh heh heh. All these fools, trying to figure out what you did to get him to marry you, when all you really did was be yourself."

Penelope's lips parted, and tears pricked her eyes. "Why, Lady Danbury, that's just about the nicest—"

"No, no," Lady D interrupted loudly, "none of that. I haven't the time nor the inclination for sentiment."

But Penelope noticed that she'd pulled out her handkerchief and was discreetly dabbing her eyes.

"Ah, Lady Danbury," Colin said, returning to the group and sliding his arm possessively through Penelope's. "Good to see you."

"Mr. Bridgerton," she said in curt greeting. "Just came over to congratulate your bride."

"Ah, but I am surely the one who deserves the congratulations."

"Hmmmph. Truer words, and all that," Lady D said. "I think you might be right. She's more of a prize than anyone realizes."

"I realize," he said, his voice so low and deadly serious that Penelope thought she might faint from the thrill of it.

"And if you'll excuse us," Colin continued smoothly, "I must take my fiancée over to meet my brother—"

"I've met your brother," Penelope interrupted.

"Consider it tradition," he said. "We need to officially welcome you to the family."

"Oh." She felt rather warm inside at the thought of becoming a Bridgerton. "How lovely."

"As I was saying," Colin said, "Anthony would like to make a toast, and then I must lead Penelope in a waltz."

"Very romantic," Lady Danbury said approvingly.

"Yes, well, I am a romantic sort," Colin said airily.

Eloise let out a loud snort.

He turned to her with one arrogantly arched brow. "I am."

"For Penelope's sake," she retorted, "I certainly hope so."

"Are they always like this?" Lady Danbury asked Penelope.

"Most of the time."

Lady D nodded. "That's a good thing. My children rarely even speak to one another. Not out of any ill will, of course. They just have nothing in common. Sad, really."

Colin tightened his hand on Penelope's arm. "We really must be going."

"Of course," she murmured, but as she turned to walk toward Anthony, whom she could see across the room, standing near the small orchestra, she heard a loud and sudden commotion at the door.

"Attention! Attention!"

The blood drained from her face in under a second. "Oh, no," she heard herself whisper. This wasn't supposed to happen. Not tonight, anyway.

"Attention!"

Monday, her mind screamed. She'd told her printer Monday. At the Mottram ball.

"What is going on?" Lady Danbury demanded.

Ten young boys were racing into the room, nothing more than urchins, really, holding sheaves of paper, tossing them about like large rectangles of confetti.

"Lady Whistledown's final column!" they all yelled. "Read it now! Read the truth."

Chapter 17

Colin Bridgerton was famous for many things.

He was famous for his good looks, which was no surprise; all the Bridgerton men were famous for their good looks.

He was famous for his slightly crooked smile, which could melt a woman's heart across a crowded ballroom and had even once caused a young lady to faint dead away, or at least to swoon delicately, then hit her head on a table, which did produce the aforementioned dead faint.

He was famous for his mellow charm, his ability to set anyone at ease with a smooth grin and an amusing comment.

What he was *not* famous for, and in fact what many people would have sworn he did not even possess, was a temper.

And, in fact, due to his remarkable (and heretofore untapped) self-control, no one was going to get a glimpse of it that night, either, although his soon-to-be wife might wake up the next day with a *serious* bruise on her arm.

"Colin," she gasped, looking down at where he was gripping her.

But he couldn't let go. He knew he was hurting her, he knew it wasn't a terribly nice thing that he was hurting her, but he was so damned *furious* at that moment, and it was either squeeze her arm for all he was worth or lose his temper in front of five hundred of their nearest and dearest acquaintances.

All in all, he thought he was making the right choice.

He was going to kill her. As soon as he figured out some way to remove her from this godforsaken ballroom, he was absolutely going to kill her. They had agreed that Lady Whistledown was a thing of the past, that they were going to let matters lie. This was not supposed to happen. She was inviting disaster. Ruin.

"This is fabulous!" Eloise exclaimed, snatching a newssheet from the air. "Absolutely, positively smashing. I'll bet she came out of retirement to celebrate your engagement."

"Wouldn't that be nice?" Colin drawled.

Penelope said nothing, but she looked very, very pale.

"Oh, my heavens!"

Colin turned to his sister, whose mouth was hanging open as she read the column.

"Grab one of those for me, Bridgerton!" Lady Danbury ordered, swatting him in the leg with her cane. "Can't believe she's publishing on a Saturday. Must be a good one."

Colin leaned down and picked up two pieces of paper from the floor, handing one to Lady Danbury and looking down at the one in his hand, even though he was fairly certain he knew exactly what it would say.

He was right.

There is nothing I despise more than a gentleman who thinks it amusing to give a lady a condescending pat on the hand as he murmurs, "It is a woman's prerogative to change her mind." And indeed, because I feel one should always support one's words with one's actions, I endeavor to keep my opinions and decisions steadfast and true.

Which is why, Gentle Reader, when I wrote my column of 19 April, I truly intended it to be my last. However-

ever, events entirely beyond my control (or indeed my approval) force me to put my pen to paper one last time.

Ladies and Gentleman, This Author is NOT Lady Cressida Twombley. She is nothing more than a scheming imposter, and it would break my heart to see my years of hard work attributed to one such as her.

LADY WHISTLEDOWN'S SOCIETY PAPERS, 24 APRIL 1824

"This is the best thing I have ever seen," Eloise said in a gleeful whisper. "Maybe I am a bad person at heart, because I have never before felt such happiness at another person's downfall."

"Balderdash!" Lady Danbury said. "I *know* I am not a bad person, and I find this delightful."

Colin said nothing. He didn't trust his voice. He didn't trust himself.

"Where is Cressida?" Eloise asked, craning her neck. "Does anyone see her? I'll bet she's already fled. She must be mortified. I would be mortified if I were her."

"You would never be her," Lady Danbury said. "You're much too decent a person."

Penelope said nothing.

"Still," Eloise continued jovially, "one almost feels sorry for her."

"But only almost," Lady D said.

"Oh, for certain. Barely almost, truth be told."

Colin just stood there, grinding his teeth into powder.

"And I get to keep my thousand pounds!" cackled Lady Danbury.

"Penelope!" Eloise exclaimed, jostling her with her elbow. "You haven't said a word. Isn't this marvelous?"

Penelope nodded and said, "I can't believe it."

Colin's grip on her arm tightened.

"Your brother's coming," she whispered.

He looked to his right. Anthony was striding toward him, Violet and Kate hot on his heels.

"Well, this rather upstages us," Anthony said as he drew up alongside Colin. He nodded at the ladies present. "Eloise, Penelope, Lady Danbury."

"I don't think anyone is going to listen to Anthony's toast now," Violet said, glancing about the room. The buzz of activity was relentless. Errant newssheets still floated in the air, and all about them, people were slipping on the ones that had already landed on the floor. The hum of the whispers was constant and almost grating, and Colin felt like the top of his skull was going to blow off.

He had to get away. Now. Or at least as soon as possible.

His head was screaming and he felt too hot in his own skin. It was almost like passion, except this wasn't passion, it was fury, and it was outrage, and it was this awful, black feeling that he'd been betrayed by the one person who should have stood by him without question.

It was strange. He knew that Penelope was the one with the secret, the one with the most to lose. This was about her, not him; he knew that, intellectually, at least. But somehow that had ceased to matter. They were a team now, and she had acted without him.

She had no right to put herself in such a precarious position without consulting him first. He was her husband, or would be, and it was his God-given duty to protect her whether she desired it or not.

"Colin?" his mother was saying. "Are you well? You look a bit odd."

"Make the toast," he said, turning to Anthony. "Penelope isn't feeling well, and I need to take her home."

"You're not feeling well?" Eloise asked Penelope. "What's wrong? You didn't say anything."

To Penelope's credit, she managed a rather credible, "A bit of a headache, I'm afraid."

"Yes, yes, Anthony," Violet said, "do go ahead and make the toast now so that Colin and Penelope may have their dance. She really can't leave until you do."

Anthony nodded his agreement, then motioned for Colin and Penelope to follow him to the front of the ballroom. A trumpeter let out a loud squawk on his horn, signaling the partygoers to be quiet. They all obeyed, probably because they assumed the ensuing announcement would be about Lady Whistledown.

"Ladies and gentlemen," Anthony said loudly, accepting a flute of champagne from a footman. "I know that you are all intrigued by Lady Whistledown's recent intrusion into our party, but I must entreat you all to remember our purpose for gathering here tonight."

It should have been a perfect moment, Colin thought dispassionately. It was to have been Penelope's night of triumph, her night to shine, to show the world how beautiful and lovely and smart she really was.

It was his night to make his intentions well and truly public, to make sure that everyone knew that he had chosen her, and just as importantly, that she had chosen him.

And all he wanted to do was take her by the shoulders and shake her until he ran out of strength. She was jeopardizing everything. She was putting her very future at risk.

"As the head of the Bridgerton family," Anthony continued, "it gives me great joy whenever one of my siblings chooses a bride. Or groom," he added with a smile, nodding toward Daphne and Simon.

Colin looked down at Penelope. She was standing very straight and very still in her dress of ice-blue satin. She wasn't smiling, which must have looked odd to the hundreds of people staring at her. But maybe they would just think she was nervous. There were hundreds of people staring at her, after all. Anyone would be nervous.

Although if one was standing right next to her, as Colin

was, one could see the panic in her eyes, the rapid rise and fall of her chest as her breathing grew faster and more erratic.

She was scared.

Good. She should be scared. Scared of what could happen to her if her secret came out. Scared of what *would* happen to her once they had a chance to talk.

"Therefore," Anthony concluded, "it gives me great pleasure to lift my glass in a toast to my brother Colin, and his soon-to-be bride, Penelope Featherington. To Colin and Penelope!"

Colin looked down at his hand and realized that someone had placed a glass of champagne in it. He lifted his glass, started to raise it to his lips, then thought the better of it and touched it to Penelope's mouth instead. The crowd cheered wildly, and he watched as she took a sip, and then another and another, forced to keep drinking until he removed the glass, which he did not do until she was finished.

Then he realized that his childish display of power had left him without a drink, which he badly needed, so he plucked Penelope's glass from her hand and downed it in a single gulp.

The crowd cheered even harder.

He leaned down and whispered in her ear, "We're going to dance now. We're going to dance until the rest of the party joins us and we're no longer the center of attention. And then you and I will slip outside. And then we will talk."

Her chin moved in a barely perceptible nod.

He took her hand and led her onto the dance floor, placing his other hand at her waist as the orchestra began the first strains of a waltz.

"Colin," she whispered, "I didn't mean for this to happen."

He affixed a smile on his face. This was supposed to be his first official dance with his intended, after all. "Not now," he ordered.

"But—"

"In ten minutes, I will have a great deal to say to you, but for right now, we are simply going to dance."

"I just wanted to say—"

His hand tightened around hers in a gesture of unmistakable warning. She pursed her lips and looked at his face for the briefest of moments, then looked away.

"I should be smiling," she whispered, still not looking at him.

"Then smile."

"*You* should be smiling."

"You're right," he said. "I should."

But he didn't.

Penelope felt like frowning. She felt like crying, in all honesty, but somehow she managed to nudge her lips up at the corners. The entire world was watching her—her entire world, at least—and she knew they were examining her every move, cataloguing each expression that crossed her face.

Years she'd spent, feeling like she was invisible and hating it. And now she'd have given anything for a few brief moments of anonymity again.

No, not anything. She wouldn't have given up Colin. If having him meant that she would spend the rest of her life under close scrutiny from the *ton,* it would be worth it. And if having to endure his anger and disdain at a time like this was to be a part of marriage as well, then that would be worth it, too.

She'd known that he would be furious with her for publishing one last column. Her hands had been shaking as she'd rewritten the words, and she'd been terrified the entire time she'd been at St. Bride's Church (as well as the ride to and from), sure that he was going to jump out at her at any moment, calling off the wedding because he couldn't bear to be married to Lady Whistledown.

But she'd done it anyway.

She knew he thought she was making a mistake, but she simply could not allow Cressida Twombley to take the credit for her life's work. But was it so much to ask that Colin at least make the attempt to see it all from her point of view? It would have been hard enough allowing anyone to pretend to be Lady Whistledown, but Cressida was unbearable. Penelope had worked too hard and endured too much at Cressida's hands.

Plus, she knew that Colin would never jilt her once their engagement became public. That was part of the reason she'd specifically instructed her publisher to have the papers delivered on *Monday* to the Mottram ball. Well, that and the fact that it seemed terribly wrong to do it at her own engagement ball, especially when Colin was so opposed to the idea.

Damn Mr. Lacey! He'd surely done this to maximize circulation and exposure. He knew enough about society from reading Whistledown to know that a Bridgerton engagement ball would be the most coveted invitation of the season. Why this should matter, she didn't know, since increasing interest in *Whistledown* would not lead to more money in his pocket; *Whistledown* was well and truly through, and neither Penelope nor Mr. Lacey would receive another pound from its publication.

Unless . . .

Penelope frowned and sighed. Mr. Lacey must be hoping that she would change her mind.

Colin's hand tightened at her waist, and she looked back up. His eyes were on hers, startlingly green even in the candlelight. Or maybe it was just that she knew they were so green. She probably would have thought them emerald in the dark.

He nodded toward the other dancers on the floor, which was now crowded with revelers. "Time to make our escape," he said.

She returned his nod with one of her own. They had already told his family that she wasn't feeling well and wanted to go home, so no one would think overmuch of their departure. And if it wasn't quite *de rigeur* for them to be alone in his carriage, well, sometimes rules were stretched for affianced couples, especially on such romantic evenings.

A bubble of ridiculous, panicky laughter escaped her lips. The night was turning out to be the least romantic of her life.

Colin looked at her sharply, one arrogant brow raised in question.

"It's nothing," Penelope said.

He squeezed her hand, although not terribly affectionately. "I want to know," he said.

She shrugged fatalistically. She couldn't imagine what she could do or say to make the night any worse than it already was. "I was just thinking about how this evening was supposed to be romantic."

"It could have been," he said cruelly.

His hand slipped from its position at her waist, but he held on to her other hand, grasping her fingers lightly to weave her through the crowd until they stepped through the French doors out onto the terrace.

"Not here," Penelope whispered, glancing anxiously back toward the ballroom.

He didn't even dignify her comment with a reply, instead pulling her farther into the inky night, drifting around a corner until they were quite alone.

But they didn't stop there. With a quick glance to make sure that no one was about, Colin pushed open a small, unobtrusive side door.

"What's this?" Penelope asked.

His answer was a little shove at the small of her back, until she was fully inside the dark hallway.

"Up," he said, motioning to the steps.

Penelope didn't know whether to be scared or thrilled, but she climbed the stairs anyway, ever aware of Colin's hot presence, right at her back.

After they'd climbed several flights, Colin stepped ahead of her and pushed open a door, peeking out into the hall. It was empty, so he stepped out, pulling her along with him, dashing quietly through the hall (which Penelope now recognized as the family's private chambers) until they reached a room she had never before entered.

Colin's room. She'd always known where it was. Through all her years of coming here to visit with Eloise, she'd never once done more than trail her fingers along the heavy wood of the door. It had been years since he'd lived here at Number Five on a permanent basis, but his mother had insisted upon maintaining his room for him. One never knew when he might need it, she'd said, and she'd been proven right earlier that season when Colin had returned from Cyprus without a house under lease.

He pushed open the door and pulled her inside after him. But the room was dark, and she was stumbling, and when she stopped moving it was because his body was right there in front of hers.

He touched her arms to steady her, but then he didn't let go, just held her there in the dark. It wasn't an embrace, not really, but the length of her body was touching the length of his. She couldn't see anything, but she could feel him, and she could smell him, and she could hear his breathing, swirling through the night air, gently caressing her cheek.

It was agony.

It was ecstasy.

His hands slid slowly down her bare arms, torturing her every nerve, and then, abruptly, he stepped away.

Followed by—silence.

Penelope wasn't sure what she had expected. He would

yell at her, he would berate her, he would order her to explain herself.

But he was doing none of those things. He was just standing there in the dark, forcing the issue, forcing her to say something.

"Could you . . . could you light a candle?" she finally asked.

"You don't like the dark?" he drawled.

"Not now. Not like this."

"I see," he murmured. "So you're saying you might like it like this?" His fingers were suddenly on her skin, trailing along the edge of her bodice.

And then they were gone.

"Don't," she said, her voice shaking.

"Don't touch you?" His voice grew mocking, and Penelope was glad that she couldn't see his face. "But you're mine, aren't you?"

"Not yet," she warned him.

"Oh, but you are. You saw to that. It was rather clever timing, actually, waiting until our engagement ball to make your final announcement. You knew I didn't want you to publish that last column. I forbade it! We agreed—"

"We never agreed!"

He ignored her outburst. "You waited until—"

"We never agreed," Penelope cried out again, needing to make it clear that she had not broken her word. Whatever else she had done, she had not lied to him. Well, aside from keeping *Whistledown* a secret for nearly a dozen years, but he certainly hadn't been alone in that deception. "And yes," she admitted, because it didn't seem right to start lying now, "I knew you wouldn't jilt me. But I hoped—"

Her voice broke, and she was unable to finish.

"You hoped what?" Colin asked after an interminable silence.

"I hoped that you would forgive me," she whispered. "Or at least that you would understand. I always thought you were the sort of man who . . ."

"What sort of man?" he asked, this time after the barest hint of a pause.

"It's my fault, really," she said, sounding tired and sad. "I've put you on a pedestal. You've been so nice all these years. I suppose I thought you were incapable of anything else."

"What the hell have I done that hasn't been nice?" he demanded. "I've protected you, I've offered for you, I've—"

"You haven't tried to see this from my point of view," she interrupted.

"Because you're acting like an idiot!" he nearly roared.

There was silence after that, the kind of silence that grates at ears, gnaws at souls.

"I can't imagine what else there is to say," Penelope finally said.

Colin looked away. He didn't know why he did so; it wasn't as if he could see her in the dark, anyway. But there was something about the tone of her voice that made him uneasy. She sounded vulnerable, tired. Wishful and heartbroken. She made him want to understand her, or at least to try, even though he *knew* she had made a terrible mistake. Every little catch in her voice put a damper on his fury. He was still angry, but somehow he'd lost the will to display it.

"You are going to be found out, you know," he said, his voice low and controlled. "You have humiliated Cressida; she will be beyond furious, and she's not going to rest until she unearths the real Lady Whistledown."

Penelope moved away; he could hear her skirts rustling. "Cressida isn't bright enough to figure me out, and besides, I'm not going to write any more columns, so there will be no opportunity for me to slip up and reveal something." There was a beat of silence, and then she added, "You have my promise on that."

"It's too late," he said.

"It's not too late," she protested. "No one knows! No one knows but you, and you're so ashamed of me, I can't bear it."

"Oh, for the love of God, Penelope," he snapped, "I'm not ashamed of you."

"Would you *please* light a candle?" she wailed.

Colin crossed the room and fumbled in a drawer for a candle and the means with which to light it. "I'm not ashamed of you," he reiterated, "but I do think you're acting foolishly."

"You may be correct," she said, "but I have to do what I think is right."

"You're not thinking," he said dismissively, turning and looking at her face as he sparked a flame. "Forget, if you will—although I cannot—what will happen to your reputation if people find out who you really are. Forget that people will cut you, that they will talk about you behind your back."

"Those people aren't worth worrying about," she said, her back ramrod straight.

"Perhaps not," he agreed, crossing his arms and staring at her. Hard. "But it will hurt. You will not like it, Penelope. And *I* won't like it."

She swallowed convulsively. Good. Maybe he was getting through to her.

"But forget all of that," he continued. "You have spent the last decade insulting people. Offending them."

"I have said lots of very nice things as well," she protested, her dark eyes glistening with unshed tears.

"Of course you have, but those aren't the people you are going to have to worry about. I'm talking about the angry ones, the insulted ones." He strode forward and grabbed her by her upper arms. "Penelope," he said urgently, "there will be people who want to *hurt* you."

His words had been meant for her, but they turned around and pierced his own heart.

He tried to picture a life without Penelope. It was impossible.

Just weeks ago she'd been . . . He stopped, thought. What *had* she been? A friend? An acquaintance? Someone he saw and never really noticed?

And now she was his fiancée, soon to be his bride. And maybe . . . maybe she was something more than that. Something deeper. Something even more precious.

"What I want to know," he asked, deliberately forcing the conversation back on topic so his mind wouldn't wander down such dangerous roads, "is why you're not jumping on the perfect alibi if the point is to remain anonymous."

"Because remaining anonymous isn't the point!" she fairly yelled.

"You want to be found out?" he asked, gaping at her in the candlelight.

"No, of course not," she replied. "But this is my work. This is my life's work. This is all I have to show for my life, and if I can't take the credit for it, I'll be *damned* if someone else will."

Colin opened his mouth to offer a retort, but to his surprise, he had nothing to say. *Life's work.* Penelope had a life's work.

He did not.

She might not be able to put her name on her work, but when she was alone in her room, she could look at her back issues, and point to them, and say to herself, *This is it. This is what my life has been about.*

"Colin?" she whispered, clearly startled by his silence.

She was amazing. He didn't know how he hadn't realized it before, when he'd already known that she was smart and lovely and witty and resourceful. But all those adjectives, and a whole host more he hadn't yet thought of, did not add up to the true measure of her.

She was amazing.

And he was . . . Dear God above, he was jealous of her.

"I'll go," she said softly, turning and walking toward the door.

For a moment he didn't react. His mind was still frozen, reeling with revelations. But when he saw her hand on the doorknob, he knew he could not let her go. Not this night, not ever.

"No," he said hoarsely, closing the distance between them in three long strides. "No," he said again, "I want you to stay."

She looked up at him, her eyes two pools of confusion. "But you said—"

He cupped her face tenderly with his hands. "Forget what I said."

And that was when he realized that Daphne had been right. His love hadn't been a thunderbolt from the sky. It had started with a smile, a word, a teasing glance. Every second he had spent in her presence it had grown, until he'd reached this moment, and he suddenly *knew*.

He loved her.

He was still furious with her for publishing that last column, and he was bloody ashamed of himself that he was actually jealous of her for having found a life's work and purpose, but even with all that, he loved her.

And if he let her walk out the door right now, he would never forgive himself.

Maybe this, then, was the definition of love. When you wanted someone, needed her, adored her still, even when you were utterly furious and quite ready to tie her to the bed just to keep her from going out and making more trouble.

This was the night. This was the moment. He was brimming with emotion, and he had to tell her. He had to *show* her.

"Stay," he whispered, and he pulled her to him, roughly, hungrily, without apology or explanation.

"Stay," he said again, leading her to his bed.

And when she didn't say anything, he said it for a third time.

"Stay."

She nodded.

He took her into his arms.

This was Penelope, and this was love.

Chapter 18

The moment Penelope nodded—the moment before she nodded, really—she knew that she had agreed to more than a kiss. She wasn't sure what had made Colin change his mind, why he had been so angry one minute and then so loving and tender the next.

She wasn't sure, but the truth was—she didn't care.

One thing she knew—he wasn't doing this, kissing her so sweetly, to punish her. Some men might use desire as a weapon, temptation as revenge, but Colin wasn't one of them.

It just wasn't in him.

He was, for all his rakish and mischievous ways, for all his jokes and teasing and sly humor, a good and noble man. And he would be a good and noble husband.

She knew this as well as she knew herself.

And if he was kissing her passionately, lowering her to his bed, covering her body with his own, then it was because he wanted her, cared enough to overcome his anger.

Cared for her.

Penelope kissed him back with every ounce of her emotion, every last corner of her soul. She had years and years of love for this man, and what she lacked in technique, she made up in fervor. She clutched at his hair, writhed beneath him, unmindful of her own appearance.

They weren't in a carriage or his mother's drawing room this time. There was no fear of discovery, no need to make sure that she looked presentable in ten minutes.

This was the night she could show him everything she felt for him. She would answer his desire with her own, and silently make her vows of love and fidelity and devotion.

When the night was through, he would know that she loved him. She might not say the words—she might not even whisper them—but he would know.

Or maybe he already knew. It was funny; it had been so easy to hide her secret life as Lady Whistledown, but so unbelievably hard to keep her heart from her eyes every time she looked at him.

"When did I start needing you so much?" he whispered, raising his head very slightly from hers until the tips of their noses touched and she could see his eyes, dark and colorless in the dim candlelight, but so very green in her mind, focusing on hers. His breath was hot, and his gaze was hot, and he was making her feel hot in areas of her body she never even allowed herself to think about.

His fingers moved to the back of her gown, moving expertly along the buttons until she felt the fabric loosening, first around her breasts, then around her ribs, then around her waist.

And then it wasn't even there at all.

"My God," he said, his voice a mere shadow louder than breath, "you're so beautiful."

And for the first time in her life, Penelope truly believed that it might be true.

There was something very wicked and titillating about being so intimately bared before another human being, but she didn't feel shame. Colin was looking at her so warmly, touching her so reverently, that she could feel nothing but an overwhelming sense of destiny.

His fingers skimmed along the sensitive skin at the outside

edge of her breast, first teasing her with his fingernails, then stroking her more gently as his fingertips returned to their original position near her collarbone.

Something tightened within her. She didn't know if it was his touch or the way he was looking at her, but something was making her change.

She felt strange, odd.

Wonderful.

He was kneeling on the bed beside her, still fully clothed, gazing down at her with a sense of pride, of desire, of ownership. "I never dreamed you would look like this," he whispered, moving his hand until his palm was lightly grazing her nipple. "I never dreamed I would want you this way."

Penelope sucked in her breath as a spasm of sensation shot through her. But something in his words was unsettling, and he must have seen her reaction in her eyes, because he asked, "What is it? What is wrong?"

"Nothing," she started to say, then checked herself. Their marriage ought to be based on honesty, and she did neither of them a service by withholding her true feelings.

"What did you think I would look like?" she asked quietly.

He just stared at her, clearly confused by her question.

"You said you never dreamed I would look this way," she explained. "What did you think I would look like?"

"I don't know," he admitted. "Until the last few weeks, honestly I don't think I thought about it."

"And since then?" she persisted, not quite sure why she needed him to answer, just knowing that she did.

In one swift moment he straddled her, then leaned down until the fabric of his waistcoat scraped her belly and breasts, until his nose touched hers and his hot breath swarmed across her skin.

"Since then," he growled, "I've thought of this moment a thousand times, pictured a hundred different pairs of breasts, all lovely and desirable and full and begging for my attention, but nothing, and let me repeat this in case you didn't quite hear me the first time, *nothing* comes close to reality."

"Oh." It was really all she could think to say.

He shrugged off his jacket and waistcoat until he was clad only in his fine linen shirt and breeches, then did nothing but stare at her, a wicked, wicked smile lifting one corner of his lips as she squirmed beneath him, growing hot and hungry under his relentless gaze.

And then, just when she was certain that she couldn't take it for one more second, he reached out and covered her with both his hands, squeezing lightly as he tested the weight and shape of her. He moaned raggedly, then sucked in his breath as he adjusted his fingers so that her nipples popped up between them.

"I want to see you sitting up," he groaned, "so I can see them full and lovely and large. And then I want to crawl behind you and cup you." His lips found her ear and his voice dropped to a whisper. "And I want to do it in front of a mirror."

"Now?" she squeaked.

He seemed to consider that for a moment, then shook his head. "Later," he said, and then repeated it in a rather resolute tone. "Later."

Penelope opened her mouth to ask him something—she had no idea what—but before she could utter a word, he murmured, "First things first," and lowered his mouth to her breast, teasing her first with a soft rush of air, then closing his lips around her, chuckling softly as she yelped in surprise and bucked off the bed.

He continued this torture until she thought she might scream, then he moved to the other breast and repeated it all over again. But this time he'd freed up one of his hands, and it seemed to be everywhere—teasing, tempting, tickling. It was on her belly, then on her hip, then on her ankle, sliding up under her skirt.

"Colin," Penelope gasped, squirming beneath him as his fingers stroked the delicate skin behind her knee.

"Are you trying to get away or come closer?" he murmured, his lips never once leaving her breast.

"I don't know."

He lifted his head and smiled down at her wolfishly. "Good."

He climbed off of her and slowly removed the remainder of his clothing, first his fine linen shirt and then his boots and breeches. And all the while, he never once allowed his eyes to stray from hers. When he was done, he nudged her dress, already pooling about her waist, around her hips, his fingers pressing lightly against her soft bottom as he lifted her up to slide the fabric under her.

She was left before him in nothing but her sheer, whisper-soft stockings. He paused then, and smiled, too much of a man not to enjoy the view, then eased them from her legs, letting them flitter to the floor after he'd slid them over her toes.

She was shivering in the night air, and so he lay beside her, pressing his body to hers, infusing her with his warmth as he savored the silky softness of her skin.

He needed her. It was humbling how much he needed her.

He was hard, hot, and so desperately wracked with desire it was a wonder he could still see straight. And yet even as his body screamed for release, he was possessed of a strange calm, an unexpected sense of control. Somewhere along the way this had ceased to be about him. It was about her—no, it was about *them,* about this wondrous joining and miraculous love that he was only now beginning to appreciate.

He wanted her—God above, he wanted her—but he wanted her to tremble beneath him, to scream with desire, to thrash her head from side to side as he teased her toward completion.

He wanted her to love this, to love him, and to *know,* when they were lying in each other's arms, sweaty and spent, that she belonged to him.

Because he already knew that he belonged to her.

"Tell me if I do anything you don't like," he said, surprised by the way his voice was shaking over his words.

"You couldn't," she whispered, touching his cheek.

She didn't understand. It almost made him smile, probably *would* have made him smile if he weren't so concerned with making this, her first experience, a good one. But her whispered words—*you couldn't*—could mean only one thing—that she had no idea what it meant to make love with a man.

"Penelope," he said softly, covering her hand with his own, "I need to explain something to you. I could hurt you. I would never mean to, but I could, and—"

She shook her head. "You couldn't," she said again. "I know you. Sometimes I think I know you better than I know myself. And you would never do anything that would hurt me."

He gritted his teeth and tried not to groan. "Not on purpose," he said, the barest hint of exasperation tinging his voice, "but I could, and—"

"Let me be the judge," she said, taking his hand and bringing it to her mouth for a single, heartfelt kiss. "And as for the other . . ."

"What other?"

She smiled, and Colin had to blink, because he could swear she almost looked as if she were amused by him. "You told me to tell you if you did anything I didn't like," she said.

He watched her face closely, suddenly mesmerized by the way her lips were forming words.

"I promise you," she vowed, "I will like it all."

A strange bubble of joy began to rise within him. He didn't know what benevolent god had chosen to bestow her upon him, but he was thinking that he needed to be a bit more attentive next time he went to church.

"I will like it all," she said again, "because I'm with you."

He took her face in his hands, gazing down at her as if she were the most wondrous creature ever to walk the earth.

"I love you," she whispered. "I've loved you for years."

"I know," he said, surprising himself with his words. He had known, he supposed, but he'd thrust it from his mind because her love made him uncomfortable. It was hard to be loved by someone decent and good when you didn't return the emotion. He couldn't dismiss her, because he liked her and he'd not have been able to forgive himself if he'd trampled on her emotions. And he couldn't flirt with her, for much the same reasons.

And so he had told himself that what she felt wasn't really love. It had been easier to try to convince himself that she was merely infatuated with him, that she didn't understand what true love was (as if he did!), and that eventually she would find someone else and settle down into a happy and contented life.

Now that thought—that she might have married another—nearly left him paralyzed with fear.

They were side by side, and she was staring at him with her heart in her eyes, her entire face alive with happiness and contentment, as if she finally felt free now that she had spoken the words. And he realized that her expression held not one trace of expectation. She hadn't told him she loved him simply to hear his reply. She wasn't even waiting for his answer.

She had told him she loved him simply because she wanted to. Because that was what she felt.

"I love you, too," he whispered, pressing an intense kiss against her lips before moving away so that he could see her reaction.

Penelope gazed at him for a very long while before responding. Finally, with an odd, convulsive swallow, she said, "You don't have to say that just because I did."

"I know," he replied, smiling.

She just looked at him, her widening eyes the only movement on her face.

"And you know that, too," he said softly. "You said you know me better than you know yourself. And you know I would never say the words if I didn't mean them."

And as she lay there, naked in his bed, cradled in his embrace, Penelope realized that she *did* know. Colin didn't lie, not about anything important, and she couldn't imagine anything more important than the moment they were sharing.

He loved her. It wasn't anything she'd expected, nor anything she'd even allowed herself to hope for, and yet here it was, like a bright and shining miracle in her heart.

"Are you sure?" she whispered.

He nodded, his arms drawing her closer. "I realized it this evening. When I asked you to stay."

"How . . ." But she didn't finish the question. Because she wasn't even really sure what the question was. How did he know he loved her? How had it happened? How did it make him feel?

But somehow he must have known what she could not verbalize, because he answered, "I don't know. I don't know when, I don't know how, and to be honest, I don't care. But I know this much is true: I love you, and I hate myself for not seeing the real you all these years."

"Colin, don't," she pleaded. "No recriminations. No regrets. Not tonight."

But he just smiled, placing a single finger on her lips to silence her plea. "I don't think you changed," he said. "At least not very much. But then one day I realized I was seeing something different when I looked at you." He shrugged. "Maybe I changed. Maybe I grew up."

She placed her finger on his lips, quieting him in the same manner he'd done to her. "Maybe I grew up, too."

"I love you," he said, leaning forward to kiss her. And this time she couldn't reply, because his mouth remained on hers, hungry, demanding, and very, very seductive.

He seemed to know exactly what to do. Each flick of his tongue, each nibble of his teeth sent shivers to the very core of her being, and she gave herself over to the pure joy of the moment, to the white-hot flame of desire. His hands were everywhere, and she felt him everywhere, his fingers on her skin, his leg nudging its way between hers.

He was pulling her closer, rolling her on top of him as he slid onto his back. His hands were on her bottom, pulling her so tightly against him that the proof of his desire seared itself into her skin.

Penelope gasped at the astounding intimacy of it all, but her breath was caught by his lips, still kissing her with fierce tenderness.

And then she was on her back, and he was on top of her, and the weight of him was pressing her into the mattress, squeezing the air from her lungs. His mouth moved to her ear, then to her throat, and Penelope felt herself arching beneath him, as if she could somehow curve her body closer to his.

She didn't know what she was supposed to do, but she knew she had to move. Her mother had already conducted her "little talk," as she'd put it, and she'd told Penelope that she must lie still beneath her husband and allow him his pleasures.

But there was no way she could have remained motionless, no way she could have stopped her hips from pressing up against him, nor her legs from wrapping around his. And she didn't want to *allow* him his pleasures—she wanted to encourage them, to share them.

And she wanted them for herself as well. Whatever this was, building inside of her—this tension, this desire—it needed release, and Penelope couldn't imagine that that moment, that those feelings wouldn't be the most exquisite of her life.

"Tell me what to do," she said, urgency making her voice hoarse.

Colin spread her legs wide, running his hands along her sides until they reached her thighs and squeezed. "Let me do everything," he said, breathing hard.

She grabbed at his buttocks, pulling him closer. "No," she insisted. "Tell me."

He stopped moving for the barest of moments, looking at her in surprise. "Touch me," he said.

"Where?"

"Anywhere."

Her hands on his bottom relaxed slightly, and she smiled. "I *am* touching you."

"Move," he groaned. "Move them."

She let her fingers drift to his thighs, swirling gently as she felt the soft springiness of hair. "Like this?"

He nodded jerkily.

Her hands slid forward, until they were dangerously close to his member. "Like this?"

Abruptly, he covered one of her hands with his. "Not now," he said harshly.

She looked at him in confusion.

"You'll understand later," he grunted, spreading her legs even wider before sliding his hand between their bodies and touching her most intimate place.

"Colin!" she gasped.

He smiled devilishly. "Did you think I wouldn't touch you like this?" As if to illustrate his point, one of his fingers began to dance across her sensitive flesh, causing her to arch off the bed, her hips actually lifting them both before sagging back down as she shuddered with desire.

His lips found her ear. "There's much more," he whispered.

Penelope didn't dare ask what. This was already an awful lot more than her mother had mentioned.

He slid one finger inside her, causing her to gasp again (which caused him to laugh with delight), then began to stroke her slowly.

"Oh, my *God,*" Penelope moaned.

"You're almost ready for me," he said, his breath coming faster now. "So wet, but so tight."

"Colin, what are you—"

He slid another finger inside, effectively ending any chance she had for intelligent speech.

She felt stretched wide, and yet she loved it. She must be very wicked, a wanton at heart, because all she wanted was to spread her legs wider and wider until she was completely open to him. As far as she was concerned, he could do anything to her, touch her in any way he pleased.

Just as long as he didn't stop.

"I can't wait much longer," he gasped.

"Don't wait."

"I need you."

She reached up and grasped his face, forcing him to look at her. "I need you, too."

And then his fingers were gone. Penelope felt oddly hollow and empty, but only for a second, because then there was something else at her entrance, something hard and hot, and very, very demanding.

"This may hurt," Colin said, gritting his teeth as if he expected pain himself.

"I don't care."

He had to make this good for her. He had to. "I'll be gentle," he said, although his desire was now so fierce he had no idea how he could possibly keep such a promise.

"I want you," she said. "I want you and I need something and I don't know what."

He pushed forward, just an inch or so, but it felt like she was swallowing him whole.

She went silent beneath him, her only sound her breath running raggedly across her lips.

Another inch, another step closer to heaven. "Oh, Penelope," he moaned, using his arms to hold himself above her so as not to crush her with his weight. "Please tell me this feels good. *Please.*"

Because if she said otherwise, it was going to kill him to pull out.

She nodded, but said, "I need a moment."

He swallowed, forcing his breath through his nose in short bursts. It was the only way he could concentrate on holding back. She probably needed to stretch around him, to allow her muscles to relax. She'd never taken a man before, and she was so exquisitely tight.

All the same, he couldn't wait until they'd had a chance to do this enough so that he didn't have to hold back.

When he felt her relax slightly beneath him, he pushed forward a bit more, until he reached the undeniable proof of her innocence. "Oh, God," he groaned. "This is going to hurt. I can't help it, but I promise you, it's only this one time, and it won't hurt much."

"How do you know?" she asked him.

He closed his eyes in agony. Trust Penelope to question him. "Trust me," he said, weaseling out of the question.

And then he thrust forward, embedding himself to the hilt, sinking into her warmth until he knew he was home.

"Oh!" she gasped, her face showing her shock.

"Are you all right?"

She nodded. "I think so."

He moved slightly. "Is this all right?"

She nodded again, but her face looked surprised, maybe a little dazed.

Colin's hips began to move of their own volition, unable to remain still when he was so obviously near to a climax.

She was pure perfection around him, and when he realized that her gasps were of desire and not of pain, he finally let himself go and gave in to the overwhelming desire surging through his blood.

She was quickening beneath him, and he prayed that he could hold out until she climaxed. Her breath was fast and hot, and her fingers were pressing relentlessly into his shoulders, and her hips were squirming under him, whipping his need into a near-frenzy.

And then it came. A sound from her lips, sweeter than anything ever to touch his ears. She cried out his name as her entire body tensed in pleasure, and he thought—*Someday I will watch her. I will see her face when she reaches the height of pleasure.*

But not today. He was already coming, and his eyes were shut with the fierce ecstasy of it all. Her name was ripped from his lips as he thrust one last time, then slumped atop her, completely bereft of strength.

For a full minute there was silence, nothing but the rise and fall of their chests as they fought for breath, waited for the tremendous rush of their bodies to settle down into that tingly bliss one feels in the arms of one's beloved.

Or at least that was what Colin thought this must be. He had been with women before, but he had only just realized that he had never made love until he'd laid Penelope onto his bed and begun their intimate dance with a single kiss upon her lips.

This was like nothing he'd ever felt before.

This was love.

And he was going to hold on with both hands.

Chapter 19

It was not very difficult to get the wedding date pushed forward.

It occurred to Colin as he was returning to his home in Bloomsbury (after sneaking an extremely disheveled Penelope into her own house in Mayfair), that there might be a very good reason why they should be married sooner rather than later.

Of course, it was quite unlikely that she would become pregnant after only one encounter. And, he had to admit, even if she did become pregnant, the child would be an eight-month baby, which wasn't too terribly suspect in a world full of children born a mere six months or so following a wedding. Not to mention that first babies were usually late (Colin was uncle to enough nieces and nephews to know this to be true), which would make the baby an eight-and-a-half-month baby, which wasn't unusual at all.

So really, there was no urgent need to move up the wedding.

Except that he wanted to.

So he had a little "talk" with the mothers, in which he conveyed a great deal without actually saying anything explicit, and they hastily agreed to his plan to rush the wedding.

Especially since he *might* have *possibly* misled them to believe that his and Penelope's intimacies had occurred several weeks prior.

Ah, well, little white lies really weren't such a large transgression when they were told to serve the greater good.

And a hasty wedding, Colin reflected as he lay in bed each night, reliving his time with Penelope and fervently wishing she were there beside him, *definitely* served the greater good.

The mothers, who had become inseparable in recent days as they planned the wedding, initially protested the change, worrying about unsavory gossip (which in this case would have been entirely true), but Lady Whistledown came, somewhat indirectly, to their rescue.

The gossip surrounding Lady Whistledown and Cressida Twombley and whether the two were actually the same person raged like nothing London had heretofore seen or heard. In fact, the talk was so ubiquitous, so utterly impossible to escape, that no one paused to consider the fact that the date of the Bridgerton-Featherington wedding had been altered.

Which suited the Bridgertons and the Featheringtons just fine.

Except, perhaps, for Colin and Penelope, neither of whom were especially comfortable when talk turned to Lady Whistledown. Penelope was used to it by now, of course; nary a month had gone by in the past ten years when someone had not made idle speculation in her presence about the identity of Lady Whistledown. But Colin was still so upset and angry over her secret life that she'd grown uncomfortable herself. She'd tried to broach the subject with him a few times, but he'd become tight-lipped and told her (in a very un-Colin-like tone) that he didn't want to talk about it.

She could only deduce that he was ashamed of her. Or if not of her, precisely, then of her work as Lady Whistledown. Which was like a blow to her heart, because her writing was the one segment in her life that she could point to with a great sense of pride and accomplishment. She had *done* something. She had, even if she could not put her own name on her work, become a wild success. How many of her contemporaries, male or female, could claim the same?

She might be ready to leave Lady Whistledown behind and live her new life as Mrs. Colin Bridgerton, wife and mother, but that in no way meant that she was ashamed of what she had done.

If only Colin could take pride in her accomplishments as well.

Oh, she believed, with every fiber of her being, that he loved her. Colin would never lie about such a thing. He had enough clever words and teasing smiles to make a woman feel happy and content without actually uttering words of love he did not feel. But perhaps it was possible—indeed, after regarding Colin's behavior, she was now sure it was possible—that someone could love another person and still feel shame and displeasure with that person.

Penelope just hadn't expected it to hurt quite so much.

They were strolling through Mayfair one afternoon, just days before the wedding, when she attempted to broach the subject once again. Why, she didn't know, since she couldn't imagine that his attitude would have miraculously changed since the last time she'd mentioned it, but she couldn't seem to stop herself. Besides, she was hoping that their position out in public, where all the world could see them, would force Colin to keep a smile on his face and listen to what she had to say.

She gauged the distance to Number Five, where they were expected for tea. "I think," she said, estimating that she had five minutes of conversation before he could usher her inside and change the subject, "that we have unfinished business that must be discussed."

He raised a brow and looked at her with a curious but still very playful grin. She knew exactly what he was trying to do: use his charming and witty personality to steer the conversation where he wanted it. Any minute now, that grin would turn boyishly lopsided, and he would say something designed to change the topic without her realizing, something like—

"Rather serious for such a sunny day."

She pursed her lips. It wasn't precisely what she'd expected, but it certainly echoed the sentiment.

"Colin," she said, trying to remain patient, "I wish you wouldn't try to change the subject every time I bring up Lady Whistledown."

His voice grew even, controlled. "I don't believe I heard you mention her name, or I suppose I should say *your* name. And besides, all I did was compliment the fine weather."

Penelope wanted more than anything to plant her feet firmly on the pavement and yank him to a startling halt, but they were in public (her own fault, she supposed, for choosing such a place to initiate the conversation) and so she kept walking, her gait smooth and sedate, even as her fingers curled into tense little fists. "The other night, when my last column was published—you were furious with me," she continued.

He shrugged. "I'm over it."

"I don't think so."

He turned to her with a rather condescending expression. "And now you're telling me what I feel?"

Such a nasty shot could not go unreturned. "Isn't that what a wife is supposed to do?"

"You're not my wife yet."

Penelope counted to three—no, better make that ten—before replying. "I am sorry if what I did upset you, but I had no other choice."

"You had every choice in the world, but I am certainly not going to debate the issue right here on Bruton Street."

And they *were* on Bruton Street. Oh, *bother,* Penelope had completely misjudged how quickly they were walking. She only had another minute or so at the most before they ascended the front steps to Number Five.

"I can assure you," she said, "that you-know-who will never again emerge from retirement."

"I can hardly express my relief."

"I wish you wouldn't be so sarcastic."

He turned to face her with flashing eyes. His expression was so different from the mask of bland boredom that had been there just moments earlier that Penelope nearly backed up a step. "Be careful what you wish for, Penelope," he said. "The sarcasm is the only thing keeping my real feelings at bay, and believe me, you don't want *those* in full view."

"I think I do," she said, her voice quite small, because in truth she wasn't sure that she did.

"Not a day goes by when I'm not forced to stop and consider what on earth I am going to do to protect you should your secret get out. I love you, Penelope. God help me, but I do."

Penelope could have done without the plea for God's help, but the declaration of love was quite nice.

"In three days," he continued, "I will be your husband. I will take a solemn vow to protect you until death do us part. Do you understand what that means?"

"You'll save me from marauding minotaurs?" she tried to joke.

His expression told her he did not find that amusing.

"I wish you wouldn't be so angry," she muttered.

He turned to her with a disbelieving expression, as if he didn't think she had the right to mutter about anything. "If I'm angry, it's because I did not appreciate finding out about your last column at the same time as everyone else."

She nodded, catching her bottom lip between her teeth before saying, "I apologize for that. You certainly had the right to know ahead of time, but how could I have told you? You would have tried to stop me."

"Exactly."

They were now just a few houses away from Number Five. If Penelope wanted to ask him anything more, she would have to do it quickly. "Are you sure—" she began, then cut herself off, not certain if she wanted to finish the question.

"Am I sure of what?"

She gave her head a little shake. "It's nothing."

"It's obviously not nothing."

"I was just wondering . . ." She looked to the side, as if the sight of the London cityscape could somehow give her the necessary courage to continue. "I was just wondering . . ."

"Spit it out, Penelope."

It was unlike him to be so curt, and his tone prodded her into action. "I was wondering," she said, "if perhaps your unease with my, er . . ."

"Secret life?" he supplied in a drawl.

"If that is what you want to call it," she acceded. "It had occurred to me that perhaps your unease does not stem entirely from your desire to protect my reputation should I be found out."

"What, precisely," he asked in a clipped tone, "do you mean by that?"

She'd already voiced her question; there was nothing to do now but supply complete honesty. "I think you're ashamed of me."

He stared at her for three full seconds before answering, "I'm not ashamed of you. I told you once already I wasn't."

"What, then?"

Colin's steps faltered, and before he realized what his body was doing, he was standing still in front of Number Three, Bruton Street. His mother's home was only two houses away, and he was fairly certain they were expected for tea about five minutes ago, and . . .

And he couldn't quite get his feet to move.

"I'm not ashamed of you," he said again, mostly because he couldn't bring himself to tell her the truth—that he was jealous. Jealous of her achievements, jealous of her.

It was such a distasteful feeling, such an unpleasant emotion. It ate at him, creating a vague sense of shame every time someone mentioned Lady Whistledown, which, given the tenor of London's current gossip, was about ten times each day. And he wasn't quite certain what to do about it.

His sister Daphne had once commented that he always seemed to know what to say, how to set others at ease. He'd thought about that for several days after she'd said it, and he'd come to the conclusion that his ability to make others feel good about themselves must stem from his own sense of self.

He was a man who had always felt supremely comfortable in his own skin. He didn't know why he was so blessed—perhaps it was good parents, maybe simple luck. But now he felt awkward and uncomfortable and it was spilling into every corner of his life. He snapped at Penelope, he barely spoke at parties.

And it was all due to this detestable jealousy, and its attendant shame.

Or was it?

Would he be jealous of Penelope if he hadn't already sensed a lack in his own life?

It was an interesting psychological question. Or at least it would be if it were about anyone else but him.

"My mother will be expecting us," he said curtly, knowing that he was avoiding the issue, and hating himself for it, but quite unable to do anything else. "And your mother will be there as well, so we had better not be late."

"We're already late," she pointed out.

He took her arm and tugged her toward Number Five. "All the more reason not to dally."

"You're avoiding me," she said.

"How can I be avoiding you if you're right here on my arm?"

That made her scowl. "You're avoiding my question."

"We will discuss it later," he said, "when we are not standing in the middle of Bruton Street, with heaven knows whom staring at us through their windows."

And then, to demonstrate that he would brook no further protest, he placed his hand at her back and steered her none-too-gently up the steps to Number Five.

One week later, nothing had changed, except, Penelope reflected, her last name.

The wedding had been magical. It was a small affair, much to the dismay of London society. And the wedding night—well, that had been magical, too.

And, in fact, marriage was magical. Colin was a wonderful husband—teasing, gentle, attentive . . .

Except when the topic of Lady Whistledown arose.

Then he became . . . well, Penelope wasn't sure what he became, except that he was not himself. Gone was his easy grace, his glib tongue, everything wonderful that made him the man she'd loved for so very long.

In a way, it was almost funny. For so long, all of her dreams had revolved around marrying this man. And at some point those dreams had come to include her telling him about her secret life. How could they not? In Penelope's dreams, her marriage to Colin had been a perfect union, and that meant complete honesty.

In her dreams, she sat him down, shyly revealed her secret. He reacted first with disbelief, then with delight and pride. How remarkable she was, to have fooled all of London for so many years. How witty to have written such clever turns of phrase. He admired her for her resourcefulness, praised her for her success. In some of the dreams, he even suggested that he become her secret reporter.

It had seemed the sort of thing Colin would enjoy, just the sort of amusing, devious task that he would relish.

But that wasn't the way it had turned out.

He said he wasn't ashamed of her, and maybe he even thought that was true, but she couldn't quite bring herself to believe him. She'd seen his face when he swore that all he wanted was to protect her. But protectiveness was a fierce, burning feeling, and when Colin was talking about Lady Whistledown, his eyes were shuttered and flat.

She tried not to feel so disappointed. She tried to tell herself that she had no right to expect Colin to live up to her dreams, that her vision of him had been unfairly idealized, but . . .

But she still wanted him to be the man she'd dreamed of.

And she felt so guilty for every pang of disappointment. This was Colin! Colin, for heaven's sake. Colin, who was as close to perfect as any human being could ever hope to be. She had no right to find fault with him, and yet . . .

And yet she did.

She wanted him to be proud of her. She wanted it more than anything in the world, more even than she'd wanted *him* all those years when she'd watched him from afar.

But she cherished her marriage, and awkward moments aside, she cherished her husband. And so she stopped mentioning Lady Whistledown. She was tired of Colin's hooded expression. She didn't want to see the tight lines of displeasure around his mouth.

It wasn't as if she could avoid the topic forever; any trip out into society seemed to bring mention of her alter ego. But she didn't have to introduce the subject at home.

And so, as they sat at breakfast one morning, chatting amiably as they each perused that morning's newspaper, she searched for other topics.

"Do you think we shall take a honeymoon trip?" she asked, spreading a generous portion of raspberry jam on her muffin. She probably ought not to eat so much, but the jam was really quite tasty, and besides, she always ate a lot when she was anxious.

She frowned, first at the muffin and then at nothing in particular. She hadn't realized she was so anxious. She'd thought she'd been able to push the Lady Whistledown problem to the back of her mind.

"Perhaps later in the year," Colin replied, reaching for the jam once she was through with it. "Pass me the toast, would you?"

She did so, silently.

He glanced up, either at her or over at the plate of kippers—she couldn't be sure. "You look disappointed," he said.

She supposed she should be flattered that he'd looked up from his food. Or maybe he was looking at the kippers and she just got in the way. Probably the latter. It was difficult to compete with food for Colin's attention.

"Penelope?" he queried.

She blinked.

"You looked disappointed?" he reminded her.

"Oh. Yes, well, I am, I suppose." She gave him a faltering smile. "I've never been anywhere, and you've been everywhere, and I guess I thought you could take me someplace you especially liked. Greece, perhaps. Or maybe Italy. I've always wanted to see Italy."

"You would like it," he murmured distractedly, his attention more on his eggs than on her. "Venice especially, I think."

"Then why don't you take me?"

"I will," he said, spearing a pink piece of bacon and popping it into his mouth. "Just not now."

Penelope licked a bit of jam off her muffin and tried not to look too crestfallen.

"If you must know," Colin said with a sigh, "the reason I don't want to leave is . . ." He glanced at the open door, his lips pursing with annoyance. "Well, I can't say it here."

Penelope's eyes widened. "You mean . . ." She traced a large *W* on the tablecloth.

"Exactly."

She stared at him in surprise, a bit startled that he had brought up the subject, and even more so that he didn't seem terribly upset by it. "But why?" she finally asked.

"Should the secret come out," he said cryptically, just in case there were any servants about, which there usually were, "I should like to be in town to control the damage."

Penelope deflated in her chair. It was never pleasant to be referred to as damage. Which was what he had done. Well, indirectly, at least. She stared at her muffin, trying to decide if she was hungry. She wasn't, not really.

But she ate it, anyway.

Chapter 20

A few days later, Penelope returned from a shopping expedition with Eloise, Hyacinth, and Felicity to find her husband seated behind his desk in his study. He was reading something, uncharacteristically hunched as he pored over some unknown book or document.

"Colin?"

His head jerked up. He must not have heard her coming, which was surprising, since she hadn't made any effort to soften her steps. "Penelope," he said, rising to his feet as she entered the room, "how was your, er, whatever it was you did when you went out?"

"Shopping," she said with an amused smile. "I went shopping."

"Right. So you did." He rocked slightly from foot to foot. "Did you buy anything?"

"A bonnet," she replied, tempted to add *and three diamond rings,* just to see if he was listening.

"Good, good," he murmured, obviously eager to get back to whatever it was on his desk.

"What are you reading?" she asked.

"Nothing," he replied, almost reflexively, then he added, "Well, actually it's one of my journals."

His face took on a strange expression, a little sheepish, a

little defiant, almost as if he were embarrassed that he'd been caught, and at the same time daring her to ask more.

"May I look at it?" she asked, keeping her voice soft and, she hoped, unthreatening. It was strange to think that Colin was insecure about anything. Mention of his journals, however, seemed to bring out a vulnerability that was surprising . . . and touching.

Penelope had spent so much of her life regarding Colin as an invincible tower of happiness and good cheer. He was self-confident, handsome, well liked, and intelligent. How easy it must be to be a Bridgerton, she'd thought on more than one occasion.

There had been so many times—more than she could count—that she'd come home from tea with Eloise and her family, curled up on her bed, and wished that she'd been born a Bridgerton. Life was easy for them. They were smart and attractive and rich and everyone seemed to like them.

And you couldn't even hate them for living such splendid existences because they were so *nice.*

Well, now she was a Bridgerton, by marriage if not by birth, and it was true—life *was* better as a Bridgerton, although that had less to do with any great change in herself than it did because she was madly in love with her husband, and by some fabulous miracle, he actually returned the emotion.

But life wasn't perfect, not even for the Bridgertons.

Even Colin—the golden boy, the man with the easy smile and devilish humor—had raw spots of his own. He was haunted by unfulfilled dreams and secret insecurities. How unfair she had been when she'd pondered his life, not to allow him his weaknesses.

"I don't need to see it in its entirety," she reassured him. "Maybe just a short passage or two. Of your own choosing. Perhaps something you especially like."

He looked down at the open book, staring blankly, as if the

words were written in Chinese. "I wouldn't know what to pick out," he mumbled. "It's all the same, really."

"Of course it's not. I understand that more than anyone. I—" She suddenly looked about, realized the door was open, and quickly went to shut it. "I've written countless columns," she continued, "and I assure you, they are not all the same. Some I adored." She smiled nostalgically, remembering the rush of contentment and pride that washed over her whenever she'd written what she thought was an especially good installment. "It was lovely, do you know what I mean?"

He shook his head.

"That feeling you get," she tried to explain, "when you just *know* that the words you've chosen are exactly right. And you can only really appreciate it after you've sat there, slumped and dejected, staring at your blank sheet of paper, not having a clue what to say."

"I know *that,*" he said.

Penelope tried not to smile. "I know you know the first feeling. You're a splendid writer, Colin. I've read your work."

He looked up, alarmed.

"Just the bit you know about," she assured him. "I would never read your journals without your invitation." She blushed, remembering that that was exactly how she'd read the passage about his trip to Cyprus. "Well, not now, anyway," she added. "But it was *good,* Colin. Almost magical, and somewhere inside of you, you have to know that."

He just stared at her, looking like he simply didn't know what to say. It was an expression she'd seen on countless faces, but never on *his* face, and it was so very odd and strange. She wanted to cry, she wanted to throw her arms around him. Most of all, she was gripped by an intense need to restore a smile to his face.

"I know you must have had those days I described," she insisted. "The ones when you know you've written something good." She looked at him hopefully. "You know what I mean, don't you?"

He made no response.

"You do," she said. "I know you do. You can't be a writer and not know it."

"I'm not a writer," he said.

"Of course you are." She motioned to the journal. "The proof is right there." She stepped forward. "Colin, please. Please may I read a little bit more?"

For the first time, he looked undecided, which Penelope took as a small victory. "You've already read almost everything *I've* ever written," she cajoled. "It's really only fair to—"

She stopped when she saw his face. She didn't know how to describe it, but he looked shuttered, cut off, utterly unreachable.

"Colin?" she whispered.

"I'd rather keep this to myself," he said curtly. "If you don't mind."

"No, of course I don't mind," she said, but they both knew she was lying.

Colin stood so still and silent that she had no choice but to excuse herself, leaving him alone in the room, staring helplessly at the door.

He'd hurt her.

It didn't matter that he hadn't meant to. She'd reached out to him, and he'd been unable to take her hand.

And the worst part was that he knew she didn't understand. She thought he was ashamed of her. He'd told her that he wasn't, but since he'd not been able to bring himself to tell her the truth—that he was jealous—he couldn't imagine that she'd believed him.

Hell, he wouldn't have believed him, either. He'd clearly looked like he was lying, because in a way, he was lying. Or at least withholding a truth that made him uncomfortable.

But the minute she'd reminded him that he'd read everything she'd written, something had turned ugly and black inside of him.

He'd read everything she'd written because she'd *published* everything she'd written. Whereas his scribblings sat dull and lifeless in his journals, tucked away where no one would see them.

Did it matter what a man wrote if no one ever read it? Did words have meaning if they were never heard?

He had never considered publishing his journals until Penelope had suggested it several weeks earlier; now the thought consumed him day and night (when he wasn't consumed with Penelope, of course). But he was gripped by a powerful fear. What if no one wanted to publish his work? What if someone did publish it, but only because his was a rich and powerful family? Colin wanted, more than anything, to be his own man, to be known for his accomplishments, not for his name or position, or even his smile or charm.

And then there was the scariest prospect of all: What if his writing was published but no one liked it?

How could he face that? How would he exist as a failure?

Or was it worse to remain as he was now: a coward?

Later that evening, after Penelope had finally pulled herself out of her chair and drunk a restorative cup of tea and puttered aimlessly about the bedchamber and finally settled against her pillows with a book that she couldn't quite make herself read, Colin appeared.

He didn't say anything at first, just stood there and smiled at her, except it wasn't one of his usual smiles—the sort that light from within and compel their recipient to smile right back.

This was a small smile, a sheepish smile.

A smile of apology.

Penelope let her book rest, spine up, on her belly.

"May I?" Colin inquired, motioning to the empty spot beside her.

Penelope scooted over to the right. "Of course," she murmured, moving her book to the night table next to her.

"I've marked a few passages," he said, holding forward his journal as he perched on the side of the bed. "If you'd like to read them, to"—he cleared his throat—"offer an opinion, that would be—" He coughed again. "That would be acceptable."

Penelope looked at the journal in his hand, elegantly bound in crimson leather, then she looked up at him. His face was serious, and his eyes were somber, and although he was absolutely still—no twitching or fidgeting—she could tell he was nervous.

Nervous. Colin. It seemed the strangest thing imaginable.

"I'd be honored," she said softly, gently tugging the book from his fingers. She noticed that a few pages were marked with ribbons, and with careful fingers, she opened to one of the selected spots.

14 March 1819

The Highlands are oddly brown.

"That was when I visited Francesca in Scotland," he interrupted.

Penelope gave him a slightly indulgent smile, meant as a gentle scolding for his interruption.

"Sorry," he mumbled.

One would think, at least one from England would think, that the hills and dales would be a rich emerald green. Scotland resides, after all, on the same isle, and by all accounts suffers from the same rain that plagues England.

I am told that these strange beige hills are called tablelands, and they are bleak and brown and desolate. And yet they stir the soul.

"That was when I was rather high up in elevation," he explained. "When you're lower, or near the lochs, it's quite different."

Penelope turned to him and gave him a look.

"Sorry," he mumbled.

"Maybe you'd be more comfortable if you didn't read over my shoulder?" she suggested.

He blinked in surprise.

"I would think you've already read all this before." At his blank stare, she added, "So you don't need to read it now." She waited for a reaction and got none. "So you don't need to hover over my shoulder," she finally finished.

"Oh." He inched away. "Sorry."

Penelope eyed him dubiously. "Off the bed, Colin."

Looking much chastened, Colin pushed himself off the bed and flopped into a chair in the far corner of the room, crossing his arms and tapping his foot in a mad dance of impatience.

Tap tap tap. Tappity tap tap tap.

"Colin!"

He looked up in honest surprise. "What?"

"Stop tapping your foot!"

He looked down as if his foot were a foreign object. "Was I tapping it?"

"Yes."

"Oh." He pulled his arms in more tightly against his chest. "Sorry."

Penelope refocused her attention on the journal.

Tap tap.

Penelope jerked head up. "Colin!"

He planted his feet down firmly on the carpet. "I couldn't

help myself. Didn't even realize I was doing it." He uncrossed his arms, resting them on the upholstered side of the chair, but he didn't look relaxed; the fingers on both of his hands were tense and arched.

She stared at him for several moments, waiting to see if he was truly going to be able to hold still.

"I won't do it again," he assured her. "I promise."

She gave him one last assessing stare, then turned her attention back to the words in front of her.

As a people, the Scots despise the English, and many would say rightfully so. But individually, they are quite warm and friendly, eager to share a glass of whisky, a hot meal, or to offer a warm place to sleep. A group of Englishmen—or, in truth, any Englishman in any sort of uniform—will not find a warm welcome in a Scottish village. But should a lone Sassenach amble down their High Street—the local population will greet him with open arms and broad smiles.

Such was the case when I happened upon Inveraray, upon the banks of Loch Fyne. A neat, well-planned town that was designed by Robert Adam when the Duke of Argyll decided to move the entire village to accommodate his new castle, it sits on the edge of water, its whitewashed buildings in neat rows that meet at right angles (surely a strangely ordered existence for one such as I, brought up amid the crooked intersections of London).

I was partaking of my evening meal at the George Hotel, enjoying a fine whisky instead of the usual ale one might drink at a similar establishment in England, when I realized that I had no idea how to get to my next destination, nor any clue how long it would take to get there. I approached the proprietor (one Mr. Clark), ex-

plained my intention to visit Blair Castle, and then could do nothing but blink in wonder and confusion as the rest of the inn's occupants chimed in with advice. "Blair Castle?" Mr. Clark boomed. (He was a booming sort of man, not given to soft speech.) "Well, now, if ye're wanting to go to Blair Castle, ye'll certainly be wanting to head west toward Pitlochry and then north from there."

This was met by a chorus of approval—and an equally loud echo of disapproval.

"Och, no!" yelled another (whose name I later learned was MacBogel). "He'll be having to cross Loch Tay, and a greater recipe for disaster has never been tasted. Better to head north now, and then move west."

"Aye," chimed in a third, "but then he'll be having Ben Nevis in his way. Are you saying a mountain is a lesser obstacle than a puny loch?"

"Are you calling Loch Tay puny? I'll be telling you I was born on the shores of Loch Tay, and no one will be calling it puny in my presence." (I have no idea who said this, or indeed, almost everything forthwith, but it was all said with great feeling and conviction.)

"He doesn't need to go all the way to Ben Nevis. He can turn west at Glencoe."

"Oh, ho, ho, and a bottle of whisky. There isn't a decent road heading west from Glencoe. Are you trying to kill the poor lad?"

And so on and so forth. If the reader has noticed that I stopped writing who said what, it is because the din of voices was so overwhelming that it was impossible to tell anyone apart, and this continued for at least ten minutes until finally, old Angus Campbell, eighty years if he was a day, spoke, and out of respect, everyone quieted down.

"What he needs to do," Angus wheezed, "is travel

south to Kintyre, turn back north and cross the Firth of Lorne to Mull so that he can scoot out to Iona, sail up to Skye, cross over to the mainland to Ullapool, back down to Inverness, pay his respects at Culloden, and from there, he can proceed south to Blair Castle, stopping in Grampian if he chooses so he can see how a proper bottle of whisky is made."

Absolute silence met this pronouncement. Finally, one brave man pointed out, "But that'll take months."

"And who's saying it won't?" old Campbell said, with the barest trace of belligerence. "The Sassenach is here to see Scotland. Are you telling me he can say he's done that if all he's done is taken a straight line from here to Perthshire?"

I found myself smiling, and made my decision on the spot. I would follow his exact route, and when I returned to London, I would know in my heart that I knew Scotland.

Colin watched Penelope as she read. Every now and then she would smile, and his heart would leap, and then suddenly he realized that her smile had become permanent, and her lips were puckering as if she were suppressing a laugh.

Colin realized he was smiling, too.

He'd been so surprised by her reaction the first time she'd read his writing; her response had been so passionate, and yet she'd been so analytical and precise when she spoke to him about it. It all made sense now, of course. She was a writer, too, probably a better one than he, and of all the things she understood in this world, she understood words.

It was hard to believe it had taken him this long to ask for her advice. Fear, he supposed, had stopped him. Fear and worry and all those stupid emotions he'd pretended were beneath him.

Who would have guessed that one woman's opinion

would become so important to him? He'd worked on his journals for years, carefully recording his travels, trying to capture more than what he saw and did, trying to capture what he *felt*. And he'd never once showed them to anyone.

Until now.

There had been no one he'd wanted to show them to. No, that wasn't true. Deep down, he'd wanted to show them to a number of people, but the time had never seemed right, or he thought they would lie and say something was good when it wasn't, just to spare his feelings.

But Penelope was different. She was a writer. She was a damned good one, too. And if she said his journal entries were good, he could almost believe that it was true.

She pursed her lips slightly as she turned a page, then frowned as her fingers couldn't find purchase. After licking her middle finger, she caught hold of the errant page and began to read again.

And smiled again.

Colin let out a breath he didn't realize he'd been holding.

Finally, she laid the book down in her lap, leaving it open to the section she'd been reading. Looking up, she said, "I assume you wanted me to stop at the end of the entry?"

It wasn't quite what he'd expected her to say, and that befuddled him. "Er, if you want to," he stammered. "If you want to read more, that would be fine, I guess."

It was as if the sun had suddenly taken up residence in her smile. "Of *course* I want to read more," she gushed. "I can't wait to see what happened when you went to Kintyre and Mull and"—frowning, she checked the open book—"and Skye and Ullapool and Culloden and Grampian"—she glanced back down at the book again—"oh, yes, and Blair Castle, of course, if you ever made it. I assume you were planning to visit friends."

He nodded. "Murray," he said, referring to a school chum whose brother was the Duke of Atholl. "But I should tell you,

I didn't end up following the exact route prescribed by old Angus Campbell. For one thing, I didn't even find roads connecting half the places he mentioned."

"Maybe," she said, her eyes growing dreamy, "that is where we ought to go for our honeymoon trip."

"Scotland?" he asked, thoroughly surprised. "Don't you want to travel someplace warm and exotic?"

"To one who has never traveled more than one hundred miles from London," she said pertly, "Scotland *is* exotic."

"I can assure you," he said with a smile as he walked across the room and perched on the edge of the bed, "that Italy is *more* exotic. And more romantic."

She blushed, which delighted him. "Oh," she said, looking vaguely embarrassed. (He wondered how long he'd be able to embarrass her with talk of romance and love and all the splendid activities that went with them.)

"We'll go to Scotland another time," he assured her. "I usually find myself heading north every few years or so to visit Francesca, anyway."

"I was surprised that you asked for my opinion," Penelope said after a short silence.

"Who else would I ask?"

"I don't know," she replied, suddenly very interested in the way her fingers were plucking at the bedcovers. "Your brothers, I suppose."

He laid his hand on hers. "What do *they* know about writing?"

Her chin lifted and her eyes, clear, warm, and brown, met his. "I know you value their opinions."

"That is true," he acceded, "but I value yours more."

He watched her face closely, as emotions played across her features. "But you don't like my writing," she said, her voice hesitant and hopeful at the same time.

He moved his hand to the curve of her cheek, holding it there gently, making sure that she was looking at him as he spoke. "Nothing could be further from the truth," he said, a burning intensity firing his words. "I think you are a marvelous writer. You cut right into the essence of a person with a simplicity and wit that is matchless. For ten years, you have made people laugh. You've made them wince. You've made them *think,* Penelope. You have made people think. I don't know what could be a higher achievement.

"Not to mention," he continued, almost as if he couldn't quite stop now that he'd gotten started, "that you write about *society,* of all things. You write about society, and you make it fun and interesting and witty, when we all know that more often than not it's beyond dull."

For the longest time, Penelope couldn't say anything. She had been proud of her work for years, and had secretly smiled whenever she had heard someone reciting from one of her columns or laughing at one of her quips. But she'd had no one with whom to share her triumphs.

Being anonymous had been a lonely prospect.

But now she had Colin. And even though the world would never know that Lady Whistledown was actually plain, overlooked, spinster-until-the-last-possible-moment Penelope Featherington, *Colin* knew. And Penelope was coming to realize that even if that wasn't all that mattered, it was what mattered most.

But she still didn't understand his actions.

"Why, then," she asked him, her words slow and carefully measured, "do you grow so distant and cold every time I bring it up?"

When he spoke, his words were close to a mumble. "It's difficult to explain."

"I'm a good listener," she said softly.

His hand, which had been cradling her face so lovingly, dropped to his lap. And he said the one thing she never would have expected.

"I'm jealous." He shrugged helplessly. "I'm so sorry."

"I don't know what you mean," she said, not intending to whisper, but lacking the voice to do anything else.

"Look at yourself, Penelope." He took both of her hands in his and twisted so that they were facing one another. "You're a huge success."

"An anonymous success," she reminded him.

"But *you* know, and *I* know, and besides, that's not what I'm talking about." He let go of one of her hands, raking his fingers through his hair as he searched for words. "You have done something. You have a body of work."

"But you have—"

"What do I have, Penelope?" he interrupted, his voice growing agitated as he rose to his feet and began to pace. "What do I have?"

"Well, you have me," she said, but her words lacked force. She knew that wasn't what he meant.

He looked at her wearily. "I'm not talking about that, Penelope—"

"I know."

"—I need something I can point to," he said, right on top of her soft sentence. "I need a purpose. Anthony has one, and Benedict has one, but I'm at odds and ends."

"Colin, you're not. You're—"

"I'm tired of being thought of as nothing but an—" He stopped short.

"What, Colin?" she asked, a bit startled by the disgusted expression that suddenly crossed his face.

"Christ above," he swore, his voice low, the S hissing from his lips.

Her eyes widened. Colin was not one for frequent profanity.

"I can't believe it," he muttered, his head moving jerkily to the left, almost as if he was flinching.

"What?" she pleaded.

"I complained to you," he said incredulously. "I complained to you about Lady Whistledown."

She grimaced. "A lot of people have done that, Colin. I'm used to it."

"I can't believe it. I complained to you about how Lady Whistledown called me charming."

"She called me an overripe citrus fruit," Penelope said, attempting levity.

He stopped his pacing for just long enough to shoot her an annoyed look. "Were you laughing at me the whole time I was moaning about how the only way I would be remembered by future generations was in *Whistledown* columns?"

"No!" she exclaimed. "I would hope you know me better than that."

He shook his head in a disbelieving manner. "I can't believe I sat there, complaining to you that I had no accomplishments, when you had all of *Whistledown*."

She got off the bed and stood. It was impossible just to sit there while he was pacing like a caged tiger. "Colin, you couldn't have known."

"Still." He let out a disgusted exhale. "The irony would be beautiful, if it weren't directed at me."

Penelope parted her lips to speak, but she didn't know how to say everything that was in her heart. Colin had so many achievements, she couldn't even begin to count them all. They weren't something you could pick up, like an edition of *Lady Whistledown's Society Papers,* but they were just as special.

Perhaps even more so.

Penelope remembered all the moments he had made people smile, all the times he had walked past all of the popular girls at balls and asked a wallflower to dance. She thought of the strong, almost magical bond he shared with his siblings. If those weren't achievements, she didn't know what was.

But she knew that those weren't the sorts of milestones he

was talking about. She knew what he needed: a purpose, a calling.

Something to show the world that he was more than they thought he was.

"Publish your travel memoirs," she said.

"I'm not—"

"Publish them," she said again. "Take a chance and see if you soar."

His eyes met hers for a moment, then they slid back down to his journal, still clutched in her hands. "They need editing," he mumbled.

Penelope laughed, because she knew she had won. And he had won, too. He didn't know it yet, but he had.

"Everyone needs editing," she said, her smile broadening with each word. "Well, except me, I guess," she teased. "Or maybe I did need it," she added with a shrug. "We'll never know, because I had no one to edit me."

He looked up quite suddenly. "How did you do it?"

"How did I do what?"

His lips pursed impatiently. "You know what I mean. How did you do the column? There was more to it than the writing. You had to print and distribute. Someone had to have known who you were."

She let out a long breath. She'd held these secrets so long it felt strange to share them, even with her husband. "It's a long story," she told him. "Perhaps we should sit."

He led her back to the bed, and they both made themselves comfortable, propped up against the pillows, their legs stretched out before them.

"I was very young when it started," Penelope began. "Only seventeen. And it happened quite by accident."

He smiled. "How does something like that happen by accident?"

"I wrote it as a joke. I was so miserable that first season." She looked up at him earnestly. "I don't know if you recall, but I weighed over a stone more back then, and it's not as if I'm fashionably slender now."

"I think you're perfect," he said loyally.

Which was, Penelope thought, part of the reason she thought he was perfect as well.

"Anyway," she continued, "I wasn't terribly happy, and so I wrote a rather scathing report of the party I'd been to the night before. And then I did another, and another. I didn't sign them Lady Whistledown; I just wrote them for fun and hid them in my desk. Except one day, I forgot to hide them."

He leaned forward, utterly rapt. "What happened?"

"My family were all out, and I knew they'd be gone for some time, because that was when Mama still thought she could turn Prudence into a diamond of the first water, and their shopping trips took all day."

Colin rolled his hand through the air, signaling that she should get to the point.

"Anyway," Penelope continued, "I decided to work in the drawing room because my room was damp and musty because someone—well, I suppose it was me—left the window open during a rainstorm. But then I had to . . . well, you know."

"No," Colin said abruptly. "I don't know."

"Attend to my business," Penelope whispered, blushing.

"Oh. Right," he said dismissively, clearly not interested in that part of the story, either. "Go on."

"When I got back, my father's solicitor was there. And he was reading what I wrote. I was horrified!"

"What happened?"

"I couldn't even speak for the first minute. But then I realized he was laughing, and it wasn't because he thought I was foolish, it was because he thought I was good."

"Well, you *are* good."

"I know that now," she said with a wry smile, "but you have to remember, I was seventeen. And I'd said some pretty horrid things in there."

"About horrid people, I'm sure," he said.

"Well, yes, but still . . ." She closed her eyes as all the memories swam through her head. "They were popular people. Influential people. People who didn't like me very much. It didn't really matter that they were horrid if what I said got out. In fact, it would have been worse because they were horrid. I would have been ruined, and I would have ruined my entire family along with me."

"What happened then? I assume it was his idea to publish."

Penelope nodded. "Yes. He made all the arrangements with the printer, who in turn found the boys to deliver. And it was his idea to give it away for free for the first two weeks. He said we needed to addict the *ton*."

"I was out of the country when the column began," Colin said, "but I remember my mother and sisters telling me all about it."

"People grumbled when the newsboys demanded payment after two weeks for free," Penelope said. "But they all paid."

"A bright idea on the part of your solicitor," Colin murmured.

"Yes, he was quite savvy."

He picked up on her use of the past tense. "Was?"

She nodded sadly. "He passed on a few years ago. But he knew he was ill and so before he died he asked me if I wanted to continue. I suppose I could have stopped then, but I had nothing else in my life, and certainly no marriage prospects." She looked up quickly. "I don't mean to—That is to say—"

His lips curved into a self-deprecating smile. "You may scold me all you wish for not having proposed years ago."

Penelope returned his smile with one of her own. Was it any wonder she loved this man?

"But," he said rather firmly, "only if you finish the story."

"Right," she said, forcing her mind back to the matter at hand. "After Mr—" She looked up hesitantly. "I'm not certain I should say his name."

Colin knew she was torn between her love and trust for him, and her loyalty to a man who had, in all probability, been a father to her once her own had departed this earth. "It's all right," he said softly. "He's gone. His name doesn't matter."

She let out a soft breath. "Thank you," she said, chewing on her lower lip. "It's not that I don't trust you. I—"

"I know," he said reassuringly, squeezing her fingers with his. "If you want to tell me later, that's fine. And if you don't, that will be fine as well."

She nodded, her lips tight at the corners, in that strained expression people get when they are trying hard not to cry. "After he died, I worked directly with the publisher. We set up a system for delivery of the columns, and the payments continued the way they had always been made—into a discreet account in my name."

Colin sucked in his breath as he thought about how much money she must have made over the years. But how could she have spent it without incurring suspicion? "Did you make any withdrawals?" he asked.

She nodded. "After I'd been working about four years, my great-aunt passed away and left her estate to my mother. My father's solicitor wrote the will. She didn't have very much, so we took my money and pretended it was hers." Penelope's face brightened slightly as she shook her head in bewilderment. "My mother was surprised. She'd never dreamed Aunt Georgette had been so wealthy. She smiled for months. I've never seen anything like it."

"It was very kind of you," Colin said.

Penelope shrugged. "It was the only way I could actually use my money."

"But you gave it to your mother," he pointed out.

"She's my mother," she said, as if that ought to explain everything. "She supported me. It all trickled down."

He wanted to say more, but he didn't. Portia Featherington was Penelope's mother, and if Penelope wanted to love her, he wasn't going to stop her.

"Since then," Penelope said, "I haven't touched it. Well, not for myself. I've given some money to charities." Her face took on a wry expression. "Anonymously."

He didn't say anything for a moment, just took the time to think about everything she had done in the last decade, all on her own, all in secret. "If you want the money now," he finally said, "you should use it. No one will question your suddenly having more funds. You're a Bridgerton, after all." He shrugged modestly. "It's well known that Anthony settled ample livings upon all of his brothers."

"I wouldn't even know what to do with it all."

"Buy something new," he suggested. Didn't all women like to shop?

She looked at him with an odd, almost inscrutable expression. "I'm not sure you understand how much money I have," she said hedgingly. "I don't think I could spend it all."

"Put it aside for our children, then," he said. "I've been fortunate that my father and brother saw fit to provide for me, but not all younger sons are so lucky."

"And daughters," Penelope reminded him. "Our daughters should have money of their own. *Separate* from their dowries."

Colin had to smile. Such arrangements were rare, but trust Penelope to insist upon it. "Whatever you wish," he said fondly.

She smiled and sighed, settling back against the pillows. Her fingers idly danced across the skin on the back of his hand, but her eyes were far away, and he doubted she was even aware of her movements.

"I have a confession to make," she said, her voice quiet and even just a touch shy.

He looked at her doubtfully. "Bigger than *Whistledown*?"

"Different."

"What is it?"

She dragged her eyes off of the random spot on the wall she seemed to be focused upon and gave him her full attention. "I've been feeling a bit"—she chewed on her lip as she paused, searching for the right words—"impatient with you lately. No, that's not right," she said. "Disappointed, really."

An odd feeling began to prickle in his chest. "Disappointed how?" he asked carefully.

Her shoulders gave a little shrug. "You seemed so upset with me. About Whistledown."

"I already told you that was because—"

"No, please," she said, placing a gently restraining hand on his chest. "Please let me finish. I told you I thought it was because you were ashamed of me, and I tried to ignore it, but it hurt so much, really. I thought I knew who you were, and I couldn't believe that person would think himself so far above me that he would feel such shame at my achievements."

He stared at her silently, waiting for her to continue.

"But the funny thing is . . ." She turned to him with a wise smile. "The funny thing is that it wasn't because you were ashamed at all. It was all because you wanted something like that for your own. Something like *Whistledown*. It seems silly now, but I was so worried because you weren't the perfect man of my dreams."

"No one is perfect," he said quietly.

"I know." She leaned over and planted an impulsive kiss on his cheek. "You're the imperfect man of my heart, and that's even better. I'd always thought you infallible, that your life was charmed, that you had no worries or fears or unfulfilled dreams. But that wasn't really fair of me."

"I was never ashamed of you, Penelope," he whispered. "Never."

They sat in companionable silence for a few moments, and then Penelope said, "Do you remember when I asked you if we might take a belated honeymoon trip?"

He nodded.

"Why don't we use some of my Whistledown money for that?"

"*I* will pay for the honeymoon trip."

"Fine," she said with a lofty expression. "You may take it out of your quarterly allowance."

He stared at her in shock, then hooted with laughter. "You're going to give me pin money?" he asked, unable to control the grin that spread across his face.

"Pen money," she corrected. "So you can work on your journals."

"Pen money," he mused. "I like that."

She smiled and placed her hand on his. "I like you."

He squeezed her fingers. "I like you, too."

Penelope sighed as she settled her head on his shoulder. "Is life supposed to be this wonderful?"

"I think so," he murmured. "I really do."

Chapter 21

One week later, Penelope was sitting at the desk in her drawing room, reading Colin's journals and making notes on a separate piece of paper whenever she had a question or comment. He had asked her to help him edit his writing, a task she found thrilling.

She was, of course, overjoyed that he had entrusted this critical job to her. It meant he trusted her judgment, thought she was smart and clever, felt that she could take what he had written and make it even better.

But there was more to her happiness than that. She'd needed a project, something to do. In the first days after giving up *Whistledown,* she'd reveled in her newfound free time. It was like having a holiday for the first time in ten years. She'd read like mad—all those novels and books she'd purchased but never gotten around to reading. And she'd taken long walks, ridden her horse in the park, sat in the small courtyard behind her house on Mount Street, enjoying the fine spring weather and tipping her face up toward the sun for a minute or so at a time—long enough to bask in the warmth, but not so long as to turn her cheeks brown.

Then, of course, the wedding and its myriad details had consumed all of her time. So she really hadn't had much opportunity to realize what might be missing in her life.

When she had been doing the column, the actual writing of it hadn't taken too terribly long, but she always had to be on the alert, watching and listening. And when she wasn't writing the column she was thinking about writing the column or desperately trying to remember some clever turn of phrase until she could get home and jot it down.

It had been mentally engaging, and she hadn't realized how much she'd missed having her mind challenged until now, when she'd finally been given the opportunity again.

She was jotting down a question about Colin's description of a Tuscan villa on page 143 in volume two of his journals when the butler knocked discreetly on the open door to alert her to his presence.

Penelope smiled sheepishly. She tended to absorb herself entirely in her work, and Dunwoody had learned through trial and error that if he wanted to get her attention, he had to make some noise.

"A visitor to see you, Mrs. Bridgerton," he said.

Penelope looked up with a smile. It was probably one of her sisters, or maybe one of the Bridgerton siblings. "Really? Who is it?"

He stepped forward and handed her a card. Penelope looked down and gasped, first in shock, and then in misery. Engraved in classic, stately black on a creamy white background were two simple words: Lady Twombley.

Cressida Twombley? Why on earth would she come calling?

Penelope began to feel uneasy. Cressida would never call unless it was for some unpleasant purpose. Cressida never did anything unless it was for an unpleasant purpose.

"Would you like me to turn her away?" Dunwoody asked.

"No," Penelope said with a sigh. She wasn't a coward, and Cressida Twombley wasn't going to turn her into one. "I'll see her. Just give me a moment to put my papers away. But . . ."

Dunwoody stopped in his tracks and cocked his head slightly to the side, waiting for her to go on.

"Oh, never mind," Penelope muttered.

"Are you certain, Mrs. Bridgerton?"

"Yes. No." She groaned. She was dithering and it was one more transgression to add to Cressida's already long list of them—she was turning Penelope into a stammering fool. "What I mean is—if she's still here after ten minutes, would you devise some sort of emergency that requires my presence? My *immediate* presence?"

"I believe that can be arranged."

"Excellent, Dunwoody," Penelope said with a weak smile. It was, perhaps, the easy way out, but she didn't trust herself to be able to find the perfect point in the conversation to insist that Cressida leave, and the last thing she wanted was to be trapped in the drawing room with her all afternoon.

The butler nodded and left, and Penelope shuffled her papers into a neat stack, closing Colin's journal and setting it on top so that the breeze from the open window couldn't blow the papers off the desk. She stood and walked over to the sofa, sitting down in the center, hoping that she looked relaxed and composed.

As if a visit from Cressida Twombley could ever be called relaxing.

A moment later, Cressida arrived, stepping through the open doorway as Dunwoody intoned her name. As always, she looked beautiful, every golden hair on her head in its perfect place. Her skin was flawless, her eyes sparkled, her clothing was of the latest style, and her reticule matched her attire to perfection.

"Cressida," Penelope said, "how surprising to see you." *Surprising* being the most polite adjective she could come up with under the circumstances.

Cressida's lips curved into a mysterious, almost feline smile. "I'm sure it is," she murmured.

"Won't you sit down?" Penelope asked, mostly because she had to. She'd spent a lifetime being polite; it was difficult to stop now. She motioned to a nearby chair, the most uncomfortable one in the room.

Cressida sat on the edge of the chair, and if she found it less than pleasing, Penelope could not tell from her mien. Her posture was elegant, her smile never faltered, and she looked as cool and composed as anyone had a right to be.

"I'm sure you're wondering why I'm here," Cressida said.

There seemed little reason to deny it, so Penelope nodded.

And then, abruptly, Cressida asked, "How are you finding married life?"

Penelope blinked. "I beg your pardon?"

"It must be an amazing change of pace," Cressida said.

"Yes," Penelope said carefully, "but a welcome one."

"Mmmm, yes. You must have a dreadful amount of free time now. I'm sure you don't know what to do with yourself."

A prickling feeling began to spread along Penelope's skin. "I don't understand your meaning," she said.

"Don't you?"

When it became apparent that Cressida required an answer, Penelope replied, somewhat testily, "No, I don't."

Cressida was silent for a moment, but her cat-with-cream expression spoke volumes. She glanced about the room until her eyes fell on the writing desk where Penelope had so recently been sitting. "What are those papers?" she inquired.

Penelope's eyes flew to the papers on the desk, stacked neatly under Colin's journal. There was no way that Cressida could have known that they were anything special. Penelope had already been seated on the sofa when Cressida had entered the room. "I fail to see how my personal papers could be of your concern," she said.

"Oh, do not take offense," Cressida said with a little tinkle of laughter that Penelope found rather frightening. "I was merely making polite conversation. Inquiring about your interests."

"I see," Penelope said, trying to fill the ensuing silence.

"I'm very observant," Cressida said.

Penelope raised her brows in question.

"In fact, my keen powers of observation are quite well known among the very best circles of society."

"I must not be a link in those impressive circles, then," Penelope murmured.

Cressida, however, was far too involved in her own speech to acknowledge Penelope's. "It's why," she said in a thoughtful tone of voice, "I thought I might be able to convince the *ton* that I was really Lady Whistledown."

Penelope's heart thundered in her chest. "Then you admit that you're not?" she asked carefully.

"Oh, I think you know I'm not."

Penelope's throat began to close. Somehow—she'd never know how—she managed to keep her composure and say, "I beg your pardon?"

Cressida smiled, but she managed to take that happy expression and turn it into something sly and cruel. "When I came up with this ruse, I thought: *I can't lose*. Either I convince everyone I'm Lady Whistledown or they won't believe me and I look very cunning when I say that I was just pretending to be Lady Whistledown in order to ferret out the true culprit."

Penelope held very silent, very still.

"But it didn't quite play out the way I had planned. Lady Whistledown turned out to be far more devious and mean-spirited than I would have guessed." Cressida's eyes narrowed, then narrowed some more until her face, normally so lovely, took on a sinister air. "Her last little column turned me into a laughingstock."

Penelope said nothing, barely daring to breathe.

"And then . . ." Cressida continued, her voice dropping into lower registers. "And then you—*you!*—had the effrontery to insult me in front of the entire *ton*."

Penelope breathed a tiny sigh of relief. Maybe Cressida didn't know her secret. Maybe this was all about Penelope's public insult, when she'd accused Cressida of lying, and she'd said—dear God, what had she said? Something terribly cruel, she was sure, but certainly well deserved.

"I might have been able to tolerate the insult if it had come from someone else," Cressida continued. "But from someone such as you—well, that could not go unanswered."

"You should think twice before insulting me in my own home," Penelope said in a low voice. And then she added, even though she hated to hide behind her husband's name, "I am a Bridgerton now. I carry the weight of their protection."

Penelope's warning made no dent in the satisfied mask that molded Cressida's beautiful face. "I think you had better listen to what I have to say before you make threats."

Penelope knew she had to listen. It was better to know what Cressida knew than to close her eyes and pretend all was well. "Go on," she said, her voice deliberately curt.

"You made a critical mistake," Cressida said, pointing her index finger at Penelope and wagging it back and forth in short tick-tocky motions. "It didn't occur to you that I *never* forget an insult, did it?"

"What are you trying to say, Cressida?" Penelope had wanted her words to seem strong and forceful, but they came out as a whisper.

Cressida stood and walked slowly away from Penelope, her hips swaying slightly as she moved, the motion almost like a swagger. "Let me see if I can remember your exact words," she said, tapping one finger against her cheek. "Oh, no, no, don't remind me. I'm sure it will come to me. Oh, yes, I recall now." She turned around to face Penelope. "I believe you said you'd always liked Lady Whistledown. And then—and to give you credit, it was an evocative, memorable turn of phrase—you said that it would break your heart if she turned out to be someone like Lady Twombley." Cressida smiled. "Which would be me."

Penelope's mouth went dry. Her fingers shook. And her skin turned to ice.

Because while she hadn't remembered exactly what she'd said in her insult to Cressida, she did remember what she'd written in that last, final, column, the one which had been mistakenly distributed at her engagement ball. The one which—

The one which Cressida was now slapping down onto the table in front of her.

Ladies and Gentleman, This Author is NOT Lady Cressida Twombley. She is nothing more than a scheming imposter, and it would break my heart to see my years of hard work attributed to one such as her.

Penelope stared down at the words even though she knew each one by heart. "What do you mean?" she asked, even though she knew her attempt to pretend that she didn't know exactly what Cressida meant was futile.

"You're smarter than that, Penelope Featherington," Cressida said. "You know I know."

Penelope kept staring at the single, incriminating sheet of paper, unable to tear her eyes from those fateful words—

It would break my heart.

Break my heart.

Break my heart.

Break my—

"Nothing to say?" Cressida asked, and even though Penelope could not see her face, she felt her hard, supercilious smile.

"No one will believe you," Penelope whispered.

"I can barely believe it myself," Cressida said with a harsh laugh. "You, of all people. But apparently you had hidden depths and were a bit more clever than you let on. Clever enough," she added with noticeable emphasis, "to know that once I light the spark of this particular piece of gossip, the news will spread like wildfire."

Penelope's mind whirled in dizzying, unpleasant circles. Oh, God, what was she going to tell Colin? How would she tell him? She knew she had to, but where would she find the words?

"No one will believe it at first," Cressida continued. "You were right about that. But then they'll start to think, and slowly but surely, the pieces of the puzzle will fall into place. Someone will remember that they said something to you that ended up in a column. Or that you were at a particular house party. Or that they'd seen Eloise Bridgerton snooping about, and doesn't everyone know that the two of you tell each other everything?"

"What do you want?" Penelope asked, her voice low and haunted as she finally lifted her head to face her enemy.

"Ah, now, there's the question I've been waiting for." Cressida clasped her hands together behind her back and began to pace. "I've been giving the matter a great deal of thought. In fact, I put off coming here to see you for almost a full week until I could decide upon the matter."

Penelope swallowed, uncomfortable with the notion that Cressida had known her deepest secret for nearly a week, and she'd been blithely living her life, unaware that the sky was about to come crashing down.

"I knew from the outset, of course," Cressida said, "that I wanted money. But the question was—how much? Your husband is a Bridgerton, of course, and so he has ample funds, but then again, he's a younger son, and not as plump in the pocket as the viscount."

"How much, Cressida?" Penelope ground out. She knew

that Cressida was drawing this out just to torture her, and she held little hope that she would actually name a figure before she was good and ready.

"Then I realized," Cressida continued, ignoring Penelope's question (and proving her point), "that you must be quite wealthy, too. Unless you're an utter fool—and considering your success at hiding your little secret for so long, I've revised my initial opinion of you, so I don't think you are—you'd have to have made a fortune after writing the column for all those years. And from all outward appearances"—she gave a scornful glance to Penelope's afternoon dress—"you haven't been spending it. So I can only deduce that it is all sitting in a discreet little bank account somewhere, just waiting for a withdrawal."

"How much, Cressida?"

"Ten thousand pounds."

Penelope gasped. "You're mad!"

"No." Cressida smiled. "Just very, very clever."

"I don't have ten thousand pounds."

"I think you're lying."

"I can assure you I'm not!" And she wasn't. The last time Penelope had checked her account balance, she'd had £8246, although she supposed that with interest, it had grown by a few pounds since then. It was an enormous sum of money, to be sure, enough to keep any reasonable person happy for several lifetimes, but it wasn't ten thousand, and it wasn't anything she wished to hand over to Cressida Twombley.

Cressida smiled serenely. "I'm sure you'll figure out what to do. Between your savings and your husband's money, ten thousand pounds is a paltry sum."

"Ten thousand pounds is *never* a paltry sum."

"How long will you need to gather your funds?" Cressida asked, completely ignoring Penelope's outburst. "A day? Two days?"

"Two days?" Penelope echoed, gaping. "I couldn't do it in two weeks!"

"Aha, so then you *do* have the money."

"I don't!"

"One week," Cressida said, her voice turning sharp. "I want the money in one week."

"I won't give it to you," Penelope whispered, more for her own benefit than Cressida's.

"You will," Cressida replied confidently. "If you don't, I'll ruin you."

"Mrs. Bridgerton?"

Penelope looked up to see Dunwoody standing in the doorway.

"There is an urgent matter which requires your attention," he said. "Immediately."

"Just as well," Cressida said, walking toward the door. "I'm done here." She walked through the doorway, then turned around once she reached the hall, so that Penelope was forced to look at her, perfectly framed in the portal. "I'll hear from you soon?" she inquired, her voice mild and innocent, as if she were talking about nothing more weighty than an invitation to a party, or perhaps the agenda for a charity meeting.

Penelope gave her a little nod, just to be rid of her.

But it didn't matter. The front door may have thunked shut, and Cressida might be gone, but Penelope's troubles weren't going anywhere.

Chapter 22

Three hours later, Penelope was still in the drawing room, still sitting on the sofa, still staring into space, still trying to figure out how she was going to solve her problems.

Correction: problem, singular.

She had only one problem, but for the size of it, she might as well have had a thousand.

She wasn't an aggressive person, and she couldn't remember the last time she had a violent thought, but at that moment, she could have gladly wrung Cressida Twombley's neck.

She watched the door with a morose sense of fatalism, waiting for her husband to come home, knowing that each ticking second brought her closer to her moment of truth, when she would have to confess everything to him.

He wouldn't say, *I told you so*. He would never say such a thing.

But he would be thinking it.

It never occurred to her, not even for a minute, that she might keep this from him. Cressida's threats weren't the sort of thing one hid from one's husband, and besides, she was going to need his help.

She wasn't certain what she needed to do, but whatever it was, she didn't know how to do it alone.

But there was one thing she knew for sure—she didn't want to pay Cressida. There was no way Cressida would be satisfied with ten thousand pounds, not when she thought she could get more. If Penelope capitulated now, she'd be handing money over to Cressida for the rest of her life.

Which meant that in one week's time, Cressida Twombley would tell all the world that Penelope Featherington Bridgerton was the infamous Lady Whistledown.

Penelope reckoned she had two choices. She could lie, and call Cressida a fool, and hope that everyone believed her; or she could try to find some way to twist Cressida's revelation to her advantage.

But for the life of her, she didn't know how.

"Penelope?"

Colin's voice. She wanted to fling herself into his arms, and at the same time, she could barely bring herself to turn around.

"Penelope?" He sounded concerned now, his footsteps increasing in speed as he crossed the room. "Dunwoody said that Cressida was here."

He sat next to her and touched her cheek. She turned and saw his face, the corners of his eyes crinkled with worry, his lips, slightly parted as they murmured her name.

And that was when she finally allowed herself to cry.

Funny how she could hold herself together, keep it all inside until she saw him. But now that he was here, all she could do was bury her face in the warmth of his chest, snuggle closer as his arms wrapped around her.

As if somehow he could make all her problems go away by his presence alone.

"Penelope?" he asked, his voice soft and worried. "What happened? What's wrong?"

Penelope just shook her head, the motion having to suffice until she could think of the words, summon the courage, stop the tears.

"What did she do to you?"

"Oh, Colin," she said, somehow summoning the energy to pull herself far enough back so that she could see his face. "She knows."

His skin went white. "How?"

Penelope sniffled, wiping her nose with the back of her hand. "It's my fault," she whispered.

He handed her a handkerchief without ever taking his eyes off of her face. "It's not your fault," he said sharply.

Her lips slid into a sad smile. She knew that his harsh tone was meant for Cressida, but she deserved it as well. "No," she said, her voice laced with resignation, "it is. It happened exactly as you said it would. I wasn't paying attention to what I wrote. I slipped up."

"What did you do?" he asked.

She told him everything, starting with Cressida's entrance and ending with her demands for money. She confessed that her poor choice of words was going to be her ruin, but wasn't it ironic, because it really did feel like her heart was breaking.

But the whole time she spoke, she felt him slipping away. He was listening to her, but he wasn't there with her. His eyes took on a strange, faraway look, and yet they were narrowed, intense.

He was plotting something. She was sure of it.

It terrified her.

And thrilled her.

Whatever he was planning, whatever he was thinking, it was all for her. She hated that it had been her stupidity that had forced him into this dilemma, but she couldn't stem the tingle of excitement that swept across her skin as she watched him.

"Colin?" she asked hesitantly. She'd been done speaking for a full minute, and still he hadn't said anything.

"I'll take care of everything," he said. "I don't want you to worry about a thing."

"I assure you that that is impossible," she said with shaking voice.

"I take my wedding vows quite seriously," he replied, his tone almost frighteningly even. "I believe I promised to honor and keep you."

"Let me help you," she said impulsively. "Together we can solve this."

One corner of his mouth lifted into a hint of a smile. "Have you a solution?"

She shook her head. "No. I've been thinking all day, and I don't know . . . although . . ."

"Although what?" he asked, his brows rising.

Her lips parted, then pursed, then parted again as she said, "What if I enlisted the aid of Lady Danbury?"

"You're planning to ask her to pay off Cressida?"

"No," she said, even though the tone of his voice told her that his had not been a serious question. "I'm going to ask her to be me."

"I beg your pardon?"

"Everyone thinks she's Lady Whistledown, anyway," Penelope explained. "At least, quite a lot of people do. If she were to make an announcement—"

"Cressida would refute it instantly," Colin interrupted.

"Who would believe Cressida over Lady Danbury?" Penelope turned to him with wide, earnest eyes. "I wouldn't dare cross Lady Danbury in any matter. If she were to say she was Lady Whistledown, I'd probably believe her myself."

"What makes you think you can convince Lady Danbury to lie for you?"

"Well," Penelope replied, chewing on her lower lip, "she likes me."

"She likes you?" Colin echoed.

"She does, rather. I think she might like to help me, especially since she detests Cressida almost as much as I do."

"You think her fondness for you will lead her to lie to the entire *ton*?" he asked doubtfully.

She sagged in her seat. "It's worth asking."

He stood, his movements abrupt, and walked to the window. "Promise me you won't go to her."

"But—"

"Promise me."

"I promise," she said, "but—"

"No buts," he said. "If we need to, we'll contact Lady Danbury, but not until I have a chance to think of something else." He raked his hand through his hair. "There must be something else."

"We have a week," she said softly, but she didn't find her words reassuring, and it was difficult to imagine that Colin did, either.

He turned around, his about-face so precise he might have been in the military. "I'll be back," he said, heading for the door.

"But where are you going?" Penelope cried out, jumping to her feet.

"I have to think," he said, pausing with his hand on the doorknob.

"You can't think here with me?" she whispered.

His face softened, and he crossed back to her side. He murmured her name, tenderly taking her face in his hands. "I love you," he said, his voice low and fervent. "I love you with everything I am, everything I've been, and everything I hope to be."

"Colin . . ."

"I love you with my past, and I love you for my future." He bent forward and kissed her, once, softly, on the lips. "I love you for the children we'll have and for the years we'll have together. I love you for every one of my smiles, and even more, for every one of your smiles."

Penelope sagged against the back of a nearby chair.

"I love you," he repeated. "You know that, don't you?"

She nodded, closing her eyes as her cheeks rubbed against his hands.

"I have things to do," he said, "and I won't be able to concentrate if I'm thinking about you, worrying if you're crying, wondering if you're hurt."

"I'm fine," she whispered. "I'm fine now that I've told you."

"I will make this right," he vowed. "I just need you to trust me."

She opened her eyes. "With my life."

He smiled, and suddenly she knew that his words were true. Everything would be all right. Maybe not today and maybe not tomorrow, but soon. Tragedy couldn't coexist in a world with one of Colin's smiles.

"I don't think it will come to that," he said fondly, giving her cheek one affectionate stroke before returning his arms to his sides. He walked back to the door, turning the moment his hand touched the knob. "Don't forget about my sister's party tonight."

Penelope let out a short groan. "Do we have to? The last thing I want to do is go out in public."

"We have to," Colin said. "Daphne doesn't host balls very often, and she'd be crushed if we did not attend."

"I know," Penelope said with a sigh. "I know. I knew it even as I complained. I'm sorry."

He smiled wryly. "It's all right. You're entitled to a bit of a bad mood today."

"Yes," she said, trying to return the smile. "I am, aren't I?"

"I'll be back later," he promised.

"Where are you—" she started to ask, then caught herself. He obviously didn't want questions just then, even from her.

But to her surprise, he answered, "To see my brother."

"Anthony?"

"Yes."

She nodded encouragingly, murmuring, "Go. I will be fine." The Bridgertons had always found strength in other

Bridgertons. If Colin felt he needed his brother's counsel, then he should go without delay.

"Don't forget to prepare for Daphne's ball," he reminded her.

She gave him a halfhearted salute and watched as he left the room.

Then she moved to the window to watch him walk by, but he never appeared. He must have headed straight out the back to the mews. She sighed, allowing her bottom to rest against the windowsill for support. She hadn't realized just how much she'd wanted to catch one last glimpse of him.

She wished she knew what he was planning.

She wished she could be sure he even had a plan.

But at the same time, she felt oddly at ease. Colin would make this right. He'd said he would, and he never lied.

She knew that her idea to enlist the aid of Lady Danbury wasn't a perfect solution, but unless Colin came up with a better idea, what else could they do?

For now, she would try to push it all from her mind. She was so weary, and so very tired, and right now what she needed was to close her eyes and think of nothing but the green of her husband's eyes, the shining light of his smile.

Tomorrow.

Tomorrow she would help Colin solve their problems.

Today she would rest. She would take a nap and pray for sleep and try to figure out how she would face all of society this evening, knowing that Cressida would be there, watching and waiting for her to make a false move.

One would think that after nearly a dozen years of pretending she was nothing more than the wallflowerish Penelope Featherington, she'd be used to playing roles and hiding her true self.

But that was when her secret had been safe. Everything was different now.

Penelope curled up on the sofa and closed her eyes.

Everything was different now, but that didn't mean that it had to be worse, did it?

Everything would be fine. It would. It had to.

Didn't it?

Colin was starting to regret his decision to take a carriage over to his brother's house.

He'd wanted to walk—the vigorous use of his legs and feet and muscles seemed the only socially acceptable outlet for his fury. But he'd recognized that time was of the essence, and even with traffic, a carriage could convey him to Mayfair faster than could his own two feet.

But now the walls seemed too close and the air too thick, *and goddamn it,* was that an overturned milkwagon blocking the street?

Colin poked his head out the door, hanging out of the carriage even as they were still rolling to a halt. "God above," he muttered, taking in the scene. Broken glass littered the street, milk was flowing everywhere, and he couldn't tell who was screeching louder—the horses, which were still tangled in the reins, or the ladies on the pavement, whose dresses had been completely splattered with milk.

Colin jumped down from his carriage, intending to help clear the scene, but it quickly became apparent that Oxford Street would be a snarl for at least an hour, with or without his help. He checked to make sure that the milkwagon horses were being properly cared for, informed his driver that he would be continuing on foot, and took off walking.

He stared defiantly in the faces of each person he passed, perversely enjoying the way they averted their gaze when faced with his obvious hostility. He almost wished one of them would make a comment, just so he could have someone to lash out at. It didn't matter that the only person he really wanted to throttle was Cressida Twombley; by this point anyone would have made a fine target.

His anger was making him unbalanced, unreasonable. Unlike himself.

He still wasn't certain what had happened to him when Penelope had told him of Cressida's threats. This was more than anger, greater than fury. This was physical; it coursed through his veins, pulsed beneath his skin.

He wanted to hit someone.

He wanted to kick things, put his fist through a wall.

He'd been furious when Penelope had published her last column. In fact, he'd thought he couldn't possibly experience a greater anger.

He was wrong.

Or perhaps it was just that this was a different sort of anger. Someone was trying to hurt the one person he loved above all others.

How could he tolerate that? How could he allow it to happen?

The answer was simple. He couldn't.

He had to stop this. He had to *do* something.

After so many years of ambling through life, laughing at the antics of others, it was time to take action himself.

He looked up, somewhat surprised that he was already at Bridgerton House. Funny how it no longer seemed like home. He'd grown up here, but now it was so obviously his brother's house.

Home was in Bloomsbury. Home was with Penelope.

Home was anywhere with Penelope.

"Colin?"

He turned around. Anthony was on the pavement, obviously returning from an errand or appointment.

Anthony nodded toward the door. "Were you planning to knock?"

Colin looked blankly at his brother, just then realizing that he'd been standing perfectly still on the steps for God only knew how long.

"Colin?" Anthony asked again, his brow furrowing with concern.

"I need your help," Colin said. It was all he needed to say.

Penelope was already dressed for the ball when her maid brought in a note from Colin.

"Dunwoody got it from the messenger," the maid explained before bobbing a quick curtsy and leaving Penelope to read the note in privacy.

Penelope slid her gloved finger under the envelope flap and nudged it open, pulling out the single sheet of paper on which she saw the fine, neat handwriting that had become so familiar to her since she'd started editing Colin's journals.

I will make my own way over to the ball this evening. Please proceed to Number Five. Mother, Eloise, and Hyacinth are waiting to accompany you to Hastings House.

All my love,
Colin

For someone who wrote so well in his journals, he wasn't much of a correspondent, Penelope thought with a wry smile.

She stood, smoothing out the fine silk of her skirts. She'd chosen a dress of her favorite color—sage green—in hopes that it might lend her courage. Her mother had always said that when a woman looked good, she felt good, and she rather thought her mother was right. Heaven knows, she'd spent a good eight years of her life feeling rather *bad* in the dresses her mother had insisted looked good.

Her hair had been dressed in a loosely upswept fashion that flattered her face, and her maid had even combed something through the strands (Penelope was afraid to ask what) that seemed to bring out the red highlights.

Red hair wasn't very fashionable, of course, but Colin had

once said he liked the way the candlelight made her hair more colorful, so Penelope had decided that this was one case upon which she and fashion would have to disagree.

By the time she made her way downstairs, her carriage was waiting for her, and the driver had already been instructed to take her to Number Five.

Colin had clearly taken care of everything. Penelope wasn't sure why this surprised her; he wasn't the sort of man who forgot details. But he was preoccupied today. It seemed odd that he would have taken the time to send instructions to the staff about her delivery to his mother's house when she could have conveyed the order just as well herself.

He had to be planning something. But what? Was he going to intercept Cressida Twombley and have her shipped off to a penal colony?

No, too melodramatic.

Maybe he'd found a secret about her, and was planning to cross-blackmail her. Silence for silence.

Penelope nodded approvingly as her carriage rolled along Oxford Street. That had to be the answer. It was just like Colin to come up with something so diabolically fitting and clever. But what could he possibly have unearthed about Cressida in so short a time? In all her years as Lady Whistledown, she'd never heard even a whisper of anything truly scandalous attached to Cressida's name.

Cressida was mean, and Cressida was petty, but she'd never stepped outside the rules of society. The only truly daring thing she'd ever done was claim to be Lady Whistledown.

The carriage turned south into Mayfair, and a few minutes later, they came to a stop in front of Number Five. Eloise must have been watching at the window, because she virtually flew down the steps and would have crashed into the carriage had the driver not stepped down at that precise moment and blocked her path.

Eloise jumped from foot to foot as she waited for the driver to open the carriage door; in fact, she looked so impatient that Penelope was surprised she didn't brush past him and wrench the door open herself. Finally, ignoring the driver's offer of help, she climbed into the carriage, nearly tripping on her skirts and tumbling to the floor in the process. As soon as she'd righted herself, she looked both ways, her face pursed into an extremely furtive expression, and yanked the door shut, nearly taking off the driver's nose in the process.

"What," Eloise demanded, "is going on?"

Penelope just stared at her. "I could ask the same of you."

"You could? Why?"

"Because you nearly knocked over the carriage in your haste to climb inside!"

"Oh," Eloise sniffed dismissively. "You have only yourself to blame for that."

"Me?"

"Yes, you! I want to know what's going on. And I need to know tonight."

Penelope was quite certain that Colin would not have told his sister about Cressida's blackmail demands, not unless his plan was to have Eloise harangue Cressida to death. "I don't know what you mean," she said.

"You *have* to know what I mean!" Eloise insisted, glancing back up toward the house. The front door was opening. "Oh, bother. Mother and Hyacinth are coming already. *Tell* me!"

"Tell you *what*?"

"Why Colin sent us that abominably cryptic note instructing us to stick to you like *glue* all evening."

"He did?"

"Yes, and may I point out that he underlined the word *glue*?"

"And here I thought the emphasis was yours," Penelope said dryly.

Eloise scowled. "Penelope, this is not the time to poke fun at me."

"When *is* the time?"

"Penelope!"

"Sorry, I couldn't resist."

"Do you know what the note was about?"

Penelope shook her head. Which wasn't a complete lie, she told herself. She really didn't know what Colin had planned for this evening.

Just then the door opened, and Hyacinth bounded in. "Penelope!" she said with great enthusiasm. "*What* is going on?"

"She doesn't know," Eloise said.

Hyacinth shot her sister an annoyed look. "It figures you'd sneak out here early."

Violet poked her head in. "Are they quarreling?" she asked Penelope.

"Just a little," Penelope replied.

Violet sat next to Hyacinth across from Penelope and Eloise. "Very well, it's not as if I could stop them, anyway. But do tell, what did Colin mean when he instructed us to stick to you like glue?"

"I'm sure I don't know."

Violet's eyes narrowed, as if assessing Penelope's honesty. "He was quite emphatic. He underlined the word *glue,* you know."

"I know," Penelope replied, just as Eloise said, "I told her."

"He underlined it twice," Hyacinth added. "If his ink had been any darker, I'm sure I would have had to go out and slaughter a horse myself."

"Hyacinth!" Violet exclaimed.

Hyacinth just shrugged. "It's all very intriguing."

"Actually," Penelope said, eager to change the subject, or at least to twist it slightly, "what I'm wondering is, what will Colin wear?"

That got everyone's attention.

"He left home in his afternoon clothes," Penelope explained, "and didn't come back. I can't imagine your sister would accept anything less than full evening kit for her ball."

"He'll have borrowed something from Anthony," Eloise said dismissively. "They're precisely the same size. Same as Gregory, actually. Only Benedict is different."

"Two inches taller," Hyacinth said.

Penelope nodded, feigning interest as she glanced out the window. They'd just slowed down, the driver presumably trying to navigate through the crush of carriages that were choking Grosvenor Square.

"How many people are expected tonight?" Penelope asked.

"I believe five hundred were invited," Violet replied. "Daphne doesn't host parties very often, but what she lacks in frequency she makes up for in size."

"I'll say," Hyacinth muttered. "I hate crowds. I'm not going to be able to get a decent breath tonight."

"I'm lucky you were my last," Violet told her with weary affection. "I'd not have had the energy for any more after you, I'm sure."

"Pity I wasn't first, then," Hyacinth said with a cheeky smile. "Think of all the attention I could have had. Not to mention the fortune."

"You're already quite the heiress as it is," Violet said.

"And you always manage to find your way to the center of attention," Eloise teased.

Hyacinth just grinned.

"Did you know," Violet said, turning to Penelope, "that all of my children are going to be in attendance tonight? I can't remember the last time we were all together."

"What about your birthday party?" Eloise asked.

Violet shook her head. "Gregory wasn't able to get away from university."

"We're not expected to line up according to height and sing a festive tune, are we?" Hyacinth asked, only half joking. "I can see us now: The Singing Bridgertons. We'd make a fortune on the stage."

"You're in a punchy mood tonight," Penelope said to her.

Hyacinth shrugged. "Just getting myself ready for my upcoming transformation into glue. It seems to require a certain mental preparedness."

"A gluey frame of mind?" Penelope inquired mildly.

"Precisely."

"We must get her married off soon," Eloise said to her mother.

"You first," Hyacinth shot back.

"I'm working on it," Eloise said cryptically.

"What?" The word's volume was rather amplified by the fact that it exploded from three mouths at once.

"That's all I'm going to say," Eloise said, and in such a tone of voice that they all knew she meant it.

"I will get to the bottom of *this,*" Hyacinth assured her mother and Penelope.

"I'm sure you will," Violet replied.

Penelope turned to Eloise and said, "You don't stand a chance."

Eloise just lifted her chin in the air and looked out the window. "We're here," she announced.

The four ladies waited until the driver had opened the door, and then one by one they alighted.

"My goodness," Violet said approvingly, "Daphne has truly outdone herself."

It was difficult not to stop and look. All of Hastings House was ablaze with light. Every window had been adorned with candles, and outdoor sconces held torches, as did a fleet of footmen who were greeting the carriages.

"It's too bad Lady Whistledown isn't here," Hyacinth

said, her voice for once losing its cheeky edge. "She would have loved this."

"Maybe she *is* here," Eloise said. "In fact, she probably is."

"Did Daphne invite Cressida Twombley?" Violet asked.

"I'm sure she did," Eloise said. "*Not* that I think she's Lady Whistledown."

"I don't think anyone thinks that any longer," Violet replied as she lifted her foot onto the first step. "Come along, girls, our night awaits."

Hyacinth stepped forward to accompany her mother, while Eloise fell into line beside Penelope.

"There's magic in the air," Eloise said, looking around as if she'd never seen a London ball before. "Do you feel it?"

Penelope just looked at her, afraid that if she opened her mouth, she'd blurt out all of her secrets. Eloise was right. There was something strange and electric about the night, a crackling sort of energy—the kind one felt just before a thunderstorm.

"It almost feels like a turning point," Eloise mused, "as if one's life could change completely, all in one night."

"What are you saying, Eloise?" Penelope asked, alarmed by the look in her friend's eyes.

"Nothing," Eloise said with a shrug. But a mysterious smile remained upon her lips as she hooked her arm through Penelope's and murmured, "Let's be off. The night awaits."

Chapter 23

Penelope had been to Hastings House a number of times, both for formal parties and more casual visits, but never had she seen the stately old building look more lovely—or more magical—than it did that evening.

She and the Bridgerton ladies were among the first to arrive; Lady Bridgerton had always said that it was rude for family members even to consider fashionably late entrances. It was nice to be so early, though; Penelope was actually able to see the decorations without having to push through crushing crowds.

Daphne had decided not to use a theme for her ball, unlike the Egyptian ball last week and the Grecian one the week before. Rather, she had decorated the house with the same simple elegance with which she lived her everyday life. Hundreds of candles adorned the walls and tables, flickering in the night, reflecting off the enormous chandeliers that hung from the ceilings. The windows were swathed in a shimmery, silvery fabric, the sort of thing one might imagine a fairy to wear. Even the servants had changed their livery. Penelope knew that the Hastings servants usually wore blue and gold, but tonight their blue was adorned with silver.

It could almost make a woman feel like a princess in a fairy tale.

"I wonder how much this cost," Hyacinth said, eyes wide.

"Hyacinth!" Violet scolded, batting her daughter on the arm. "You know that it's impolite to ask about such things."

"I didn't ask," Hyacinth pointed out, "I wondered. And besides, it's only Daphne."

"Your sister is the Duchess of Hastings," Violet said, "and as such she has certain responsibilities to her station. You would do well to remember that fact."

"But wouldn't you agree," Hyacinth said, linking her arm around her mother's and giving her hand a little squeeze, "that it's more important simply to remember that she's my sister?"

"She has you there," Eloise said with a smile.

Violet sighed. "Hyacinth, I declare that you will be the death of me."

"No, I won't," Hyacinth replied. "Gregory will."

Penelope found herself stifling a laugh.

"I don't see Colin here yet," Eloise said, craning her neck.

"No?" Penelope scanned the room. "That's surprising."

"Did he tell you that he would be here before you arrived?"

"No," Penelope replied, "but for some reason I rather thought he would."

Violet patted her arm. "I'm sure he'll be here soon, Penelope. And then we'll all know what this big secret is that has him insisting we remain by your side. Not," she added hastily, her eyes widening with alarm, "that we view it as any sort of *chore*. You know we adore your company."

Penelope gave her a reassuring smile. "I know. The feeling is mutual."

There were only a few people ahead of them in the receiving line, so it wasn't very long before they were able to greet Daphne and her husband Simon.

"What," Daphne asked without preamble, just as soon as she was sure her other guests were out of earshot, "is going on with Colin?"

Since the question appeared to be directed mostly at her, Penelope felt compelled to say, "I don't know."

"Did he send you a note as well?" Eloise asked.

Daphne nodded. "Yes, we're to keep an eye on her, he said."

"It could be worse," Hyacinth said. "We're to stick to her like glue." She leaned forward. "He underlined *glue.*"

"And here I thought I wasn't a chore," Penelope quipped.

"Oh, you're not," Hyacinth said breezily, "but there's something rather enjoyable about the word *glue.* Slides off the tongue rather pleasingly, don't you think? Glue. Glooooooo."

"Is it me," Eloise asked, "or has she gone mad in the head?"

Hyacinth ignored her with a shrug. "Not to mention the drama of it. I feel as if I'm a part of some grand espionage plot."

"Espionage," Violet groaned. "Heaven help us all."

Daphne leaned forward with great drama. "Well, he told *us*—"

"It's not a competition, wife," Simon put in.

She shot him an annoyed look before turning back to her mother and sisters and saying, "He told us to make sure she stays away from Lady Danbury."

"Lady Danbury!" they all exclaimed.

Except for Penelope, who had a very good idea why Colin might want her to stay away from the elderly countess. He must have come up with something better than her plan to convince Lady Danbury to lie and tell everyone that *she* was Lady Whistledown.

It had to be the double-blackmail theory. What else could it be? He must have uncovered some horrible secret about Cressida.

Penelope was almost giddy with delight.

"I thought you were rather good friends with Lady Danbury," Violet said to her.

"I am," Penelope replied, trying to act perplexed.

"This is very curious," Hyacinth said, tapping her index finger against her cheek. "Very curious indeed."

"Eloise," Daphne suddenly put in, "you're very quiet tonight."

"Except for when she called me mad," Hyacinth pointed out.

"Hmmm?" Eloise had been staring off into space—or perhaps at something behind Daphne and Simon—and hadn't been paying attention. "Oh, well, nothing to say, I suppose."

"You?" Daphne asked doubtfully.

"Precisely what I was thinking," Hyacinth said.

Penelope agreed with Hyacinth, but she decided to keep that to herself. It wasn't like Eloise not to weigh in with an opinion, especially not on a night like this, which was growing more and more shrouded with mystery as each second passed.

"You all were saying everything so well," Eloise said. "What could I have possibly added to the conversation?"

Which struck Penelope as very odd. The sly sarcasm was in character, but Eloise *always* thought she had something to add to a conversation.

Eloise just shrugged.

"We should be moving along," Violet said. "We're beginning to hold up your other guests."

"I shall see you later," Daphne promised. "And—Oh!"

Everyone leaned in.

"You will probably want to know," she whispered, "that Lady Danbury is not here yet."

"Simplifies my job," Simon said, looking a bit weary of all the intrigue.

"Not mine," Hyacinth said. "I still have to stick to her—"

"—like glue," they all—including Penelope—finished for her.

"Well, I do," Hyacinth said.

"Speaking of glue," Eloise said as they stepped away from

Daphne and Simon, "Penelope, do you think you can make do with only two batches for a bit? I should like to step out for a moment."

"I will go with you," Hyacinth announced.

"You can't both go," Violet said. "I'm certain Colin didn't want Penelope left with only *me*."

"May I go when she's back, then?" Hyacinth grimaced. "It's not something I can avoid."

Violet turned to Eloise expectantly.

"What?" Eloise demanded.

"I was waiting for you to say the same thing."

"I'm far too dignified," Eloise sniffed.

"Oh, please," Hyacinth muttered.

Violet groaned. "Are you certain you wish us to remain by your side?" she asked Penelope.

"I didn't think I had a choice," Penelope replied, amused by the interchange.

"Go," Violet said to Eloise. "Just hurry back."

Eloise gave her mother a nod, and then, much to everyone's surprise, she reached forward and gave Penelope a quick hug.

"What was that for?" Penelope asked with an affectionate smile.

"No reason," Eloise replied, her returning grin rather like one of Colin's. "I just think this is going to be a special night for you."

"You do?" Penelope asked carefully, unsure of what Eloise might have figured out.

"Well, it's obvious *some*thing is afoot," Eloise said. "It's not like Colin to act with such secrecy. And I wanted to offer my support."

"You'll be back in just a few minutes," Penelope said. "Whatever is going to happen—if indeed anything is going to happen—you're not likely to miss it."

Eloise shrugged. "It was an impulse. An impulse born from a dozen years of friendship."

"Eloise Bridgerton, are you growing sentimental on me?"

"At this late date?" Eloise said with a look of mock outrage. "I think not."

"Eloise," Hyacinth interrupted, "will you *leave*? I can't wait all night."

And with a quick wave, Eloise was off.

For the next hour, they just milled about, mingling with the other guests, and moving—Penelope, Violet, and Hyacinth—as one giant being.

"Three heads and six legs have we," Penelope remarked as she walked toward the window, the two Bridgerton women bustling right alongside her.

"I beg your pardon?" Violet asked.

"Did you really want to look out the window," Hyacinth muttered, "or were you just testing us? And *where* is Eloise?"

"Mostly just testing you," Penelope admitted. "And I'm sure Eloise was detained by some other guest. You know as well as I that there are many people here from whom it is rather difficult to extract oneself from conversation."

"Hmmph," was Hyacinth's reply. "Someone needs to recheck her definition of *glue*."

"Hyacinth," Penelope said, "if you need to excuse yourself for a few minutes, please do go ahead. I shall be just fine." She turned to Violet. "You as well. If you need to leave, I promise I shall remain right here in the corner until you return."

Violet looked at her in horror. "And break our word to Colin?"

"Er, did you actually give him your word?" Penelope asked.

"No, but it was implied in his request, I'm sure. Oh, look!" she suddenly exclaimed. "There he is!"

Penelope tried to signal discreetly at her husband, but all her attempts at circumspection were drowned out by Hyacinth's vigorous wave and holler of, "Colin!"

Violet groaned.

"I know, I know," Hyacinth said unrepentantly, "I must be more ladylike."

"If you know it," Violet said, sounding every inch the mother she was, "then why don't you *do* it?"

"What would be the fun in that?"

"Good evening, ladies," Colin said, kissing his mother's hand before smoothly taking his place beside Penelope and sliding his arm around her waist.

"Well?" Hyacinth demanded.

Colin merely quirked a brow.

"Are you going to *tell* us?" she persisted.

"All in good time, dear sister."

"You're a wretched, wretched man," Hyacinth grumbled.

"I say," Colin murmured, looking about, "what happened to Eloise?"

"That's a very good question," Hyacinth muttered, just as Penelope said, "I'm sure she'll be back soon."

He nodded, not looking terribly interested. "Mother," he said, turning toward Violet, "how have you been?"

"You've been sending cryptic notes all over town," Violet demanded, "and you want to know how I've *been*?"

He smiled. "Yes."

Violet actually started wagging her finger at him, something she'd forbidden her own children from ever doing in public. "Oh, no, you don't, Colin Bridgerton. You are not going to get out of explaining yourself. I am your mother. Your mother!"

"I am aware of the relation," he murmured.

"You are not going to waltz in here and distract me with a clever phrase and a beguiling smile."

"You think my smile is beguiling?"

"Colin!"

"But," he acceded, "you did make an excellent point."

Violet blinked. "I did?"

"Yes. About the waltz." He cocked his head slightly to the side. "I believe I hear one beginning."

"I don't hear anything," Hyacinth said.

"Don't you? Pity." He grabbed Penelope's hand. "Come along, wife. I do believe this is our dance."

"But no one is dancing," Hyacinth ground out.

He flashed her a satisfied smile. "They will be."

And then, before anyone had a chance to comment, he'd yanked on Penelope's hand, and they were weaving through the crowds.

"Didn't you want to waltz?" Penelope asked breathlessly, right after they'd passed the small orchestra, the members of whom appeared to be taking an extended break.

"No, just to escape," he explained, slipping through a side door and pulling her along with him.

A few moments later they had ascended a narrow staircase and were secreted in some small parlor, their only light the flickering torches that blazed outside the window.

"Where are we?" Penelope asked, looking around.

Colin shrugged. "I don't know. It seemed as good a place as any."

"Are you going to tell me what is going on?"

"No, first I'm going to kiss you."

And before she had a chance to respond to that (not that she would have protested!) his lips found hers in a kiss that was hungry and urgent and tender all in one.

"Colin!" she gasped, in that split second when he took a breath.

"Not now," he murmured, kissing her again.

"But—" this was muffled, lost against his lips.

It was the sort of kiss that enveloped her, from her head to her toes, from the way his teeth nibbled her lips, to his hands, squeezing her bottom and sliding across her back. It was the sort of kiss that could easily have turned her knees to water and led her to swoon on the sofa and allow him to do anything to her, the more wicked the better, even though they were mere yards away from over five hundred members of the *ton,* except—

"Colin!" she exclaimed, somehow breaking her mouth free of his.

"Shush."

"Colin, you have to stop!"

He looked like a lost puppy. "Must I?"

"Yes, you must."

"I suppose you're going to say it's because of all the people just next door."

"No, although that's a very good reason to consider restraint."

"To consider and then reject, perhaps?" he asked hopefully.

"No! Colin—" She pulled herself from his arms and moved several feet away, lest his nearness tempt her into forgetting herself. "Colin, you need to tell me what is going on."

"Well," he said slowly, "I *was* kissing you. . . ."

"That's not what I meant, and you know it."

"Very well." He walked away, his footsteps echoing loudly in her ears. When he turned back around, his expression had turned deadly serious. "I have decided what to do about Cressida."

"You have? What? Tell me."

His face took on a slightly pained expression. "Actually, I think it might be best if I didn't tell you until the plan is under way."

She stared at him in disbelief. "You're not serious."

"Well . . ." He was looking longingly at the door, clearly hoping for an escape.

"Tell me," she insisted.

"Very well." He sighed, then sighed again.

"Colin!"

"I'm going to make an announcement," he said, as if that would explain everything.

At first she said nothing, thinking that maybe it would all become clear if she just waited a moment and thought about it. But that didn't work, and so she asked, her words slow and careful, "What sort of announcement?"

His face turned resolute. "I'm going to tell the truth."

She gasped. "About me?"

He nodded.

"But you can't!"

"Penelope, I think it's best."

Panic began to rise within her, and her lungs felt impossibly tight. "No, Colin, you can't! You can't do that! It's not your secret to reveal!"

"Do you want to pay Cressida for the rest of your life?"

"No, of course not, but I can ask Lady Danbury—"

"You're not going to ask Lady Danbury to lie on your behalf," he snapped. "That's beneath you and you know it."

Penelope gasped at his sharp tone. But deep down, she knew he was right.

"If you were so willing to allow someone else to usurp your identity," he said, "then you should have just allowed Cressida to do it."

"I couldn't," she whispered. "Not her."

"Fine. Then it's time we both stood up and faced the music."

"Colin," she whispered, "I'll be ruined."

He shrugged. "We'll move to the country."

She shook her head, desperately trying to find the right words.

He took her hands in his. "Does it really matter so much?" he said softly. "Penelope, I love you. As long as we're together, we'll be happy."

"It's not that," she said, trying to tug her hand from his so that she could wipe the tears from her eyes.

But he wouldn't let go. "What, then?" he asked.

"Colin, you'll be ruined, too," she whispered.

"I don't mind."

She stared at him in disbelief. He sounded so flip, so casual about something that would change his entire life, alter it in ways he couldn't possibly imagine.

"Penelope," he said, his voice so reasonable she could barely stand it, "it's the only solution. Either we tell the world, or Cressida does."

"We could pay her," she whispered.

"Is that what you really want to do?" he asked. "Give her all the money you've worked so hard to earn? You might as well have just let her tell the world she was Lady Whistledown."

"I can't let you do this," she said. "I don't think you understand what it means to be outside of society."

"And you do?" he countered.

"Better than you!"

"Penelope—"

"You're trying to act as if it doesn't matter, but I know you don't feel that way. You were so angry with me when I published that last column, all because you thought I shouldn't have risked the secret getting out."

"As it turns out," he remarked, "I was right."

"See?" she said urgently. "Do you see? You're still upset with me over that!"

Colin let out a long breath. The conversation was not moving in the direction he'd hoped. He certainly hadn't intended for her to throw his earlier insistence that she not tell anyone about her secret life back in his face. "If you hadn't published that last column," he said, "we wouldn't be in this position, that is true, but the point is now moot, don't you think?"

"Colin," she whispered. "If you tell the world I'm Lady

Whistledown, and they react the way we think they will, you'll never see your journals published."

His heart stood still.

Because that was when he finally understood her.

She had told him before that she loved him, and she had shown her love as well, in all the ways he'd taught her. But never before had it been so clear, so frank, so raw.

All this time she'd been begging him not to make the announcement—it had all been for him.

He swallowed against the lump that was forming in his throat, fought for words, fought even for breath.

She reached out and touched his hand, her eyes pleading, her cheeks still wet with tears. "I could never forgive myself," she said. "I don't want to destroy your dreams."

"They were never my dreams until I met you," he whispered.

"You don't want to publish your journals?" she asked, blinking in confusion. "You were just doing it for me?"

"No," he said, because she deserved nothing less than complete honesty. "I do want it. It *is* my dream. But it's a dream you gave me."

"That doesn't mean I can take it away."

"You're not."

"Yes, I—"

"No," he said forcefully, "you're not. And getting my work published . . . well, it doesn't hold a candle to my real dream, which is spending the rest of my life with you."

"You'll always have that," she said softly.

"I know." He smiled, and then it turned rather cocky. "So what do we have to lose?"

"Possibly more than we could ever guess."

"And possibly less," he reminded her. "Don't forget that I'm a Bridgerton. And you are now, too. We wield a bit of power in this town."

Her eyes widened. "What do you mean?"

He shrugged modestly. "Anthony is prepared to give you his full support."

"You told Anthony?" she gasped.

"I had to tell Anthony. He's the head of the family. And there are very few people on this earth who would dare to cross him."

"Oh." Penelope chewed on her lower lip, considering all this. And then, because she had to know: "What did he say?"

"He was surprised."

"I expected as much."

"And rather pleased."

Her face lit up. "Really?"

"And amused. He said he had to admire someone who could keep a secret like that for so many years. He said he couldn't wait to tell Kate."

She nodded. "I suppose you'll have to make an announcement now. The secret is out."

"Anthony will hold his counsel if I ask him to," Colin said. "That has nothing to do with why I want to tell the world the truth."

She looked at him expectantly, warily.

"The truth is," Colin said, tugging on her hand and pulling her close, "I'm rather proud of you."

She felt herself smiling, and it was so strange, because just a few moments earlier, she couldn't imagine ever smiling again.

He leaned down until his nose touched hers. "I want everyone to know how proud I am of you. By the time I'm through, there won't be a single person in London who doesn't recognize how clever you are."

"They may still hate me," she said.

"They may," he agreed, "but that will be their problem, not ours."

"Oh, Colin," she sighed. "I do love you. It's an excellent thing, really."

He grinned. "I know."

"No, I really do. I thought I loved you before, and I'm sure I did, but it's nothing like what I feel now."

"Good," he said, a rather possessive gleam appearing in his eyes, "that's the way I like it. Now come with me."

"Where?"

"Here," he said, pushing open a door.

To Penelope's amazement, she found herself on a small balcony, overlooking the entire ballroom. "Oh. Dear. God," she gulped, trying to yank him back into the darkened room behind them. No one had seen them yet; they could still make their escape.

"Tsk tsk," he scolded. "Bravery, my sweet."

"Couldn't you post something in the paper?" she whispered urgently. "Or just tell someone and allow the rumor to spread?"

"There's nothing like a grand gesture to get the point across."

She swallowed convulsively. As gestures went, this was going to be grand. "I'm not very good at being the center of attention," she said, trying to remember how to breathe in a normal rhythm.

He squeezed her hand. "Don't worry. I am." He looked out over the crowd until his eyes found those of their host, his brother-in-law, the Duke of Hastings. At Colin's nod, the duke began to move toward the orchestra.

"Simon knows?" Penelope gasped.

"I told him when I arrived," Colin murmured absently. "How do you think I knew how to find the room with the balcony?"

And then the most remarkable thing happened. A veritable fleet of footmen appeared as if from nowhere and began handing tall flutes of champagne to every guest.

"Here's ours," Colin said approvingly, picking up two glasses that were waiting in the corner. "Just as I asked."

Penelope took hers silently, still unable to comprehend all that was unfolding around her.

"It's probably a little flat by now," Colin said in a conspiratorial sort of whisper that she knew was meant to set her at ease. "But it's the best I could do under the circumstances."

As Penelope clutched Colin's hand in terror, she watched helplessly as Simon quieted the orchestra and directed the throng of partygoers to turn their attention to his brother and sister on the balcony.

His brother and sister, she thought in wonder. The Bridgertons really did inspire a bond. She never thought she'd see the day when a duke referred to her as his sister.

"Ladies and gentlemen," Colin announced, his strong, confident voice booming throughout the hall, "I would like to propose a toast to the most remarkable woman in the world."

A low murmur spread across the room, and Penelope stood frozen, watching everyone watching her.

"I am a newlywed," Colin continued, beguiling the partygoers with his lopsided smile, "and therefore you are all required to indulge me in my lovesick ways."

Friendly laughter rippled through the crowd.

"I know that many of you were surprised when I asked Penelope Featherington to be my wife. I was surprised myself."

A few unkind titters wafted through the air, but Penelope held herself perfectly still, completely proud. Colin would say the right thing. She knew he would. Colin always said the right thing.

"I wasn't surprised that I had fallen in love with her," he said pointedly, giving the crowd a look that dared them to comment, "but rather that it had taken so long.

"I've known her for so many years, you see," he continued, his voice softening, "and somehow I'd never taken the time to look inside, to see the beautiful, brilliant, witty woman she'd become."

Penelope could feel the tears trickling down her face, but she couldn't move. She could barely breathe. She had expected him to reveal her secret, and instead he was giving her this incredible gift, this spectacular declaration of love.

"Therefore," Colin said, "with all of you here as my witnesses, I would like to say—Penelope—" He turned to her, taking her free hand in his, and said:

"I love you. I adore you. I worship the ground you walk upon."

He turned back out to the crowd, lifted his glass, and said, "To my wife!"

"To your wife!" they all boomed, caught up in the magic of the moment.

Colin drank, and Penelope drank, even though she couldn't help but wonder when he was going to tell them all the real reason for this announcement.

"Put down your glass, dear," he murmured, plucking it from her fingers and setting it aside.

"But—"

"You interrupt far too much," he scolded, and then he swept her into a passionate kiss, right there on the balcony in front of the entire *ton*.

"Colin!" she gasped, once he gave her a chance to breathe.

He grinned wolfishly as their audience roared its approval.

"Oh, and one last thing!" he called to the crowd.

They were now stamping their feet, hanging on his every word.

"I'm leaving the party early. Right now, as a matter of fact." He shot a wicked, sideways grin at Penelope. "I'm sure you'll understand."

The men in the crowd hooted and hollered as Penelope turned beet red.

"But before I do, I have one last thing to say. One last little thing, in case you still don't believe me when I tell you that my wife is the wittiest, cleverest, most enchanting woman in all of London."

"Nooooo!" came a voice from the back, and Penelope knew it was Cressida.

But even Cressida was no match for the crowd, none of whom would let her pass, or even listen to her cries of distress.

"You might say that my wife has two maiden names," he said thoughtfully. "Of course you all knew her as Penelope Featherington, as did I. But what you didn't know, and what even I was not clever enough to figure out until she told me herself . . ."

He paused, waiting for silence to fall over the room.

". . . is that she is also the brilliant, the witty, the breathtakingly magnificent—Oh, you all know who I am talking about," he said, his arm sweeping out toward the crowd.

"I give you my wife!" he said, his love and pride flowing across the room. "Lady Whistledown!"

For a moment there was nothing but silence. It was almost as if no one even dared to breathe.

And then it came. Clap. Clap. Clap. Slow and methodical, but with such force and determination that everyone had to turn and look to see who had dared to break the shocked silence.

It was Lady Danbury.

She had shoved her cane into someone else's arms and was holding her arms high, clapping loud and proud, beaming with pride and delight.

And then someone else began to clap. Penelope jerked her head to the side to see who . . .

Anthony Bridgerton.

And then Simon Basset, the Duke of Hastings.

And then the Bridgerton women, and then the Featherington women, and then another and another and more and more until the entire room was cheering.

Penelope couldn't believe it.

Tomorrow they might remember to be angry with her, to feel irritated at having been fooled for so many years, but tonight . . .

Tonight all they could do was admire and cheer.

For a woman who had had to carry out all of her accomplishments in secret, it was everything she'd ever dreamed of.

Well, almost everything.

Everything she'd truly ever dreamed of was standing next to her, his arm around her waist. And when she looked up at him, at his beloved face, he was smiling down at her with such love and pride that her breath caught in her throat.

"Congratulations, Lady Whistledown," he murmured.

"I prefer Mrs. Bridgerton," she replied.

He grinned. "Excellent choice."

"Can we leave?" she whispered.

"Right now?"

She nodded.

"Oh, *yes,*" he said enthusiastically.

And no one saw them for several days.

Epilogue

Bedford Square, Bloomsbury
London, 1825

"It's here! It's here!"

Penelope looked up from the papers spread over her desk. Colin was standing in the doorway of her small office, jumping from foot to foot like a schoolboy.

"Your book!" she exclaimed, jumping to her feet as quickly as her rather ungainly body would allow. "Oh, Colin, let me see. Let me see. I can't wait!"

He couldn't contain his grin as he handed her his book.

"Ohhhh," she said reverently, holding the slim, leather-bound volume in her hands. "Oh, my." She held the book up to her face and inhaled deeply. "Don't you just love the smell of new books?"

"Look at this, look at this," he said impatiently, pointing to his name on the front cover.

Penelope beamed. "Look at that. And so elegant, too." She ran her finger over the words as she read, "*An Englishman in Italy,* by Colin Bridgerton."

He looked ready to burst with pride. "It looks good, doesn't it?"

"It looks better than good, it looks perfect! When will *An Englishman in Cyprus* be available?"

"The publisher says every six months. They want to release *An Englishman in Scotland* after that."

"Oh, Colin, I'm so proud of you."

He drew her into his arms, letting his chin rest on top of her head. "I couldn't have done it without you."

"Yes, you could," she replied loyally.

"Just be quiet and accept the praise."

"Very well," she said, grinning even though he couldn't see her face, "you couldn't. Clearly, you could never have been published without such a talented editor."

"You won't hear any disagreement from me," he said softly, kissing the top of her head before he let her go. "Sit down," he added. "You shouldn't be on your feet for so long."

"I'm fine," she assured him, but she sat down, anyway. Colin had been overly protective since the first moment she'd told him she was pregnant; now that she was only a month from her due date, he was insufferable.

"What are these papers?" he asked, glancing down at her scribblings.

"This? Oh, it's nothing." She started to gather them into piles. "Just a little project I was working on."

"Really?" He sat down across from her. "What is it?"

"It's . . . well . . . actually . . ."

"What is it, Penelope?" he asked, looking exceedingly amused by her stammers.

"I've been at loose ends since I finished editing your journals," she explained, "and I found I rather missed writing."

He was smiling as he leaned forward. "What are you working on?"

She blushed; she wasn't sure why. "A novel."

"A novel? Why, that's brilliant, Penelope!"

"You think so?"

"Of course I think so. What is it called?"

"Well, I've only written a few dozen pages," she said, "and there's much work to be done, but I think, if I don't decide to change it overmuch, that I will call it *The Wallflower*."

His eyes grew warm, almost misty. "Really?"

"It's a little bit autobiographical," she admitted.

"Just a little bit?" he returned.

"Just a little."

"But it has a happy ending?"

"Oh, yes," she said fervently. "It *has* to."

"It has to?"

She reached her hand across the table and rested it atop his. "Happy endings are all I can do," she whispered. "I wouldn't know how to write anything else."

The Duke And I

The irresistible Duke of Hastings has hatched a plan to keep himself free from the town's marriage-minded society mothers. He pretends to be engaged to the lovely Daphne Bridgerton. After all, it isn't as if the brooding rogue has any real plans to marry – though there is something about the alluring Miss Bridgerton that sets the Duke's heart beating a bit faster. And as for Daphne, surely the clever debutante will attract some very worthy suitors now that is seems a duke has declared her desirable.

But as Daphne waltzes across ballroom after ballroom with her 'fiancé', she soon forgets that their courtship is a complete sham. And now she has to do the impossible and keep herself from losing her heart and soul completely to the handsome hell-raiser who has sworn off marriage forever.

AVAILABLE FROM PIATKUS NOW!

A Night Like This

Gareth St Clair has a father who hates him and who is determined to ruin the St Clair estates. Gareth's sole heirloom is an old family diary, which may or may not contain the secrets of his past . . . and the key to his future. The problem is – it's written in Italian, of which Gareth speaks not a word.

All the town agreed: there was no one quite like Hyacinth Bridgerton. She's fiendishly smart, devilishly outspoken and – according to Gareth – probably best in small doses. But there's something about her – something charming and vexing – that grabs him and won't quite let go . . . And Hyacinth – or so she claims – speaks Italian . . .

AVAILABLE FROM PIATKUS NOW!

Everything and the Moon

When Robert Kemble stumbles across Victoria Lyndon in a hedgerow maze, he can't believe his eyes. The girl who'd torn him in two, who let him plan an elopement and then left him standing by the side of the road, was suddenly within arm's reach, and even though his fury still knew no bounds, she was impossible to resist.

Victoria's father had told her an earl would never marry a vicar's daughter, and he was right. Robert had promised her marriage, then danced off to London while she suffered the shame of a foiled elopement. But even though Victoria doesn't particularly enjoy her new life as a governess, when Robert offers her a job of a different sort – his mistress – she refuses, unable to sacrifice her honour, even for him.

But Robert won't take no for an answer, and he vows to make her his, through any means possible. Can these star-crossed lovers learn to trust again? And is love really sweeter the second time round?

AVAILABLE FROM PIATKUS NOW!